A white snake slid onto the table with a thump.

Kylar barely had time to register what it was before it struck at his face. He saw its mouth open, huge, fangs glittering. He was moving back, but too slowly.

Then the snake disappeared and Kylar was falling backward off the stool. He landed flat on his back but bounced up to his feet in an instant.

Blint was holding the snake behind the head. He had grabbed it out of the air while it was striking. "Do you know what this is, Kylar?"

"It's a white asp." It was one of the most deadly snakes in the world. Usually small like the one Blint held, they rarely grew longer than a man's forearm, but those bitten died within seconds.

"Actually, it's the price of failure."

Praise for the Night Angel Trilogy

"A compelling, epic tale of heroism, vengeance, and magic."
—The Greenman Review

"A book that I have wanted to read every chance I have gotten, it made me turn off television, it made me skip dessert, it even made me skip a shower once."
—BSCreview.com

"Overloaded with fun, *The Way of Shadows* is an absolute joy."
—BloodoftheMuse.com

"An impressive debut."
—SFFWorld.com

"A captivating page-turner that verges on the un-put-downable."
—TheBookBag.co.uk

D1236132

Books by Brent Weeks

Night Angel (omnibus)

THE NIGHT ANGEL TRILOGY

The Way of Shadows
Shadow's Edge
Beyond the Shadows

LIGHTBRINGER SERIES

The Black Prism
The Blinding Knife

NIGHT ANGEL

THE COMPLETE TRILOGY

Book 1: The Way of Shadows
Book 2: Shadow's Edge
Book 3: Beyond the Shadows

BRENT WEEKS

www.orbitbooks.net

Orbit
Hachette Book Group
237 Park Avenue, New York, NY 10017
www.HachetteBookGroup.com

First Compilation Edition: April 2012

Orbit is an imprint of Hachette Book Group, Inc.
The Orbit name and logo are trademarks of Little, Brown Book Group Limited.

The Hachette Speakers Bureau provides a wide range of authors for speaking events. To find out more, go to www.hachettespeakersbureau.com or call (866) 376-6591.

The publisher is not responsible for websites (or their content) that are not owned by the publisher.

The characters and events in this book are fictitious. Any similarity to real persons, living or dead, is coincidental and not intended by the author.

LCCN 2011943717

ISBN 978-0-316-20128-5

10 9 8 7 6 5 4 3 2 1

Printed in the United States of America

For Kristi,
Without your sacrifices, the life I'm living now
would still be just an unlikely dream.

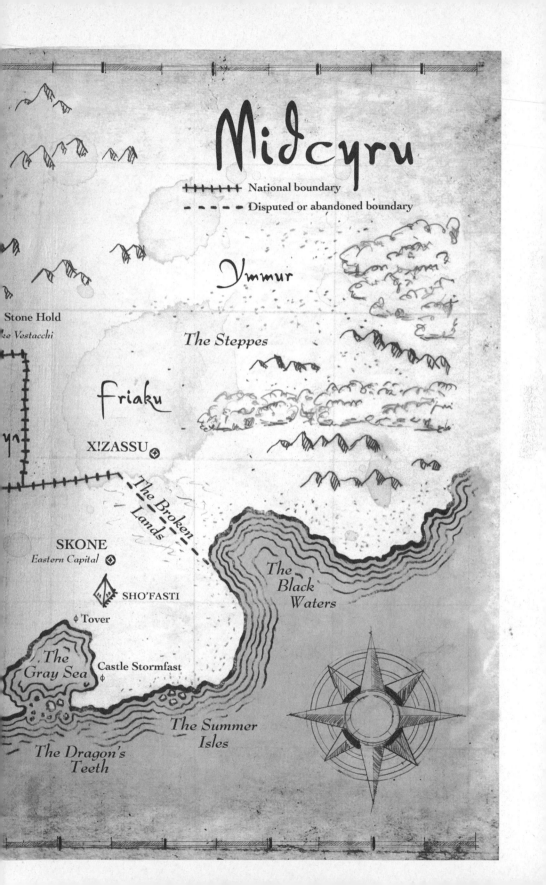

TABLE OF CONTENTS

BOOK 1

The Way of Shadows

For Kristi,
Confidante, companion, best friend, bride.
They're all for you.

ACKNOWLEDGMENTS

*I*t was all downhill after seventh grade. That was the year my English teacher, Nancy Helgath, somehow made me cool when she encouraged me to read Edgar Allan Poe to my classmates at lunch. They sat goggle-eyed as I read "The Pit and the Pendulum," "Berenice," and "The Raven." But I had eyes for only one: the tall, smart girl I had a crush on—and was terrified of—Kristi Barnes.

I soon started my first novel. I would go on to become an English teacher and a writer, and marry Kristi Barnes.

This book wouldn't have happened without my mother—for more than the obvious reason. I started reading late, and when I did, I hated it. This wasn't helped by a teacher who shouted "Choppy sentences!" at me for my inability to read aloud smoothly in the first grade. My mom took me out of school for a year to home school me (insert social awkwardness joke here), and her dedication and patience gave me a love for reading.

Thank you to my little sisters, Christa and Elisa, who begged for bedtime stories. An enthusiastic and forgiving audience is a must for a budding teenage storyteller. Any princesses in my books are their fault.

It's one thing to love reading; it's another to write. My high school English teacher, Jael Prezeau, is a teacher in a million. She inspired hundreds. She's the kind of woman who could chew you out, cheer you on, make you work harder than you've ever worked for a class, give you a B, and make you love it. She told me I couldn't break the grammar rules she taught me until I was published. It was a rule up with which I could not put. She tried.

In college, I briefly considered politics. Horror. A few people turned me from disaster. One was an industrial spy I met in Oxford. On reading a story I'd written, he said, "I wish I could do what you do." Huh? Then my best friend Nate Davis became the editor of our college literary journal and held a contest for the best short story. Wonder of wonders, I won the cash prize, and realized I'd earned slightly better than minimum wage. I was hooked. (It was better than I would do again for a long, long time.) I started a new novel, and whenever I tried to do my homework, I could count on Jon Low to come knocking on my door. "Hey, Weeks, you got another chapter for me yet?" It was irritating and flattering at once. I had no idea I was being prepared for having an editor.

I must thank the Iowa Writers Program for rejecting me. Though I still sometimes wear all black and drink lattes, they helped me decide to write the kind of books I like rather than the books I ought to like.

My debt to my wife, Kristi, cannot be overstated. Her faith kept me going. Her sacrifices awe me. Her wisdom has rescued me from many a story dead end. To get published, you have to defy overwhelming odds; to marry a woman like Kristi, you have to knock them out.

My agent Don Maass has an understanding of story that I've not seen rivaled. Don, you've been a reality check, a wise teacher, and an encourager. You make me a better writer.

Huge thanks to the amazing editorial team at Orbit. Devi, thanks for your many insights, your enthusiasm, and your guidance ushering me through an unfamiliar process. Tim, thanks for taking a chance on me. Jennifer, you were my first contact at Orbit, and I have to tell you, the fact that I'd e-mail you a question and get an answer the same morning was a big deal. Of course, then you started sending me paperwork—and then I knew I wasn't dreaming. Alex, thanks for your brilliant Web page design, the beautiful billboards, full page scratch-and-sniff ads in the *New York Times,* and those nifty little cardboard display stands at Borders. They're fab. Lauren, thank you for taking my ones and zeros and making something real. Hilary, copyeditor extraordinaire, a special thanks for two words: bollock dagger. They made the novel.

I also want to thank all the other people at Orbit and Hachette who do the real work while we artists sit in cafés wearing black, drinking lattes. I'd mention you by name, but I don't know your names. However, I do appreciate what you do to take my words and make something out of them. So, layout people, art people (by the way, Wow!), office go-fers, accountants, lawyers, and the mail guy, thanks.

Crazy dreamers need a lot of encouragers. Kevin, your being proud of me is about the best thing a little brother can get. Dad, one of my first memories is of sharing my worry with you about the space shuttle poking holes in the atmosphere and letting out all of Earth's air. Rather than rushing to correct me, you listened—and still do. Jacob Klein, your encouragement and friendship over the years have been invaluable. You were there at the very beginning (4 A.M. in Niedfeldt, I think). To the Cabin Guys at Hillsdale College (Jon "Missing Link" Low, Nate "My Head Looks Like PK's Butt" Davis, AJ "My Girlfriend Will Clean It Up" Siegmann, Jason "I Love Butter" Siegmann, Ryan "Mystery Puker" Downey, Peter "GQ" Koller, Charles "Sand Vest" Robison, Matt "No Special Sauce" Schramm), I couldn't have shared a slum house with better wangs. Dennis Foley, you were the first professional writer who gave me time and guidance. You said you'd tell me if I should give up and get a real job—and that I shouldn't. Cody Lee, thanks for the unbridled enthusiasm; it still makes me smile. Shaun and Diane McNay, Mark and Liv Pothoff, Scott and Kariann Box, Scott and Kerry Rueck, Todd and Lisel Williams, Chris Giesch, Blane Hansen, Brian Rapp, Dana Piersall, Jeff and Sandee Newville, Keith and Jen Johnson—thanks for believing in us and helping make the years of work and waiting not just tolerable, but fun.

Thanks to everyone over the years who, on finding out I was a writer, didn't ask, "Oh, are you published?"

Last, thanks to you, curious reader who reads acknowledgments. You do realize the only people who usually read acknowledgments are looking for their own name, right? If you're quirky enough to read acknowledgments without knowing the author, you and I are going to get along fine. Picking up a book by an author you've never read is a leap of faith. Here's my offer: you give me a couple of pages, and I'll give you a helluva ride.

1

*A*zoth squatted in the alley, cold mud squishing through his bare toes. He stared at the narrow space beneath the wall, trying to get his nerve up. The sun wouldn't come up for hours, and the tavern was empty. Most taverns in the city had dirt floors, but this part of the Warrens had been built over marshland, and not even drunks wanted to drink standing ankle-deep in mud, so the tavern had been raised a few inches on stilts and floored with stout bamboo poles.

Coins sometimes dropped through the gaps in the bamboo, and the crawlspace was too small for most people to go after them. The guild's bigs were too big and the littles were too scared to squeeze into the suffocating darkness shared with spiders and cockroaches and rats and the wicked half-wild tomcat the owner kept. Worst was the pressure of the bamboo against your back, flattening you every time a patron walked overhead. It had been Azoth's favorite spot for a year, but he wasn't as small as he used to be. Last time, he got stuck and spent hours panicking until it rained and the ground softened beneath him enough that he could dig himself out.

It was muddy now, and there would be no patrons, and Azoth had seen the tomcat leave. It should be fine. Besides, Rat was collecting guild dues tomorrow, and Azoth didn't have four coppers. He didn't even have one, so there wasn't much choice. Rat wasn't understanding, and he didn't know his own strength. Littles had died from his beatings.

Pushing aside mounds of mud, Azoth lay on his stomach. The dank earth soaked his thin, filthy tunic instantly. He'd have to work fast. He was skinny, and if he caught a chill, the odds of getting better weren't good.

Scooting through the darkness, he began searching for the telltale metallic gleam. A couple of lamps were still burning in the tavern, so light filtered through the gaps, illuminating the mud and standing water in strange rectangles. Heavy marsh mist climbed the shafts of light only to fall over and over again. Spider webs draped across Azoth's face and broke, and he felt a tingle on the back of his neck.

He froze. No, it was his imagination. He exhaled slowly. Something glimmered and he grabbed his first copper. He slithered to the unfinished pine beam he had gotten stuck under last time and shoveled mud away until water filled the depression. The gap was still so narrow that he had to turn his head sideways to squeeze underneath it. Holding his breath and pushing his face into the slimy water, he began the slow crawl.

His head and shoulders made it through, but then a stub of a branch caught the back of his tunic, tearing the cloth and jabbing his back. He almost cried out and was instantly glad he hadn't. Through a wide space between bamboo poles, Azoth saw a man seated at the bar, still drinking. In the Warrens, you had to judge people quickly. Even if you had quick hands like Azoth did, when you stole every day, you were bound to get caught eventually. All merchants hit the guild rats who stole from them. If they wanted to have any goods left to sell, they had to. The trick was picking the ones who'd smack you so you didn't try their booth next time; there were others who'd beat you so badly you never had a next time. Azoth thought he saw something kind and sad and lonely in this lanky figure. He was perhaps thirty, with a scraggly blond beard and a huge sword on his hip.

"How could you abandon me?" the man whispered so quietly Azoth could barely distinguish the words. He held a flagon in his left hand and cradled something Azoth couldn't see in his right. "After all the years I've served you, how could you abandon me now? Is it because of Vonda?"

There was an itch on Azoth's calf. He ignored it. It was just his imagination again. He reached behind his back to free his tunic. He needed to find his coins and get out of here.

Something heavy dropped onto the floor above Azoth and slammed his face into the water, driving the breath from his lungs. He gasped and nearly inhaled water.

"Why Durzo Blint, you never fail to surprise," the weight above Azoth said. Nothing was visible of the man through the gaps except a drawn dagger. He must have dropped from the rafters. "Hey, I'm all for calling a bluff, but you should have seen Vonda when she figured out you weren't going to save her. Made me damn near bawl my eyes out."

The lanky man turned. His voice was slow, broken. "I killed six men tonight. Are you sure you want to make it seven?"

Azoth slowly caught up with what they'd been saying. The lanky man was the wetboy Durzo Blint. A wetboy was like an assassin—in the way a tiger is like a kitten. Among wetboys, Durzo Blint was indisputably the best. Or, as the head of Azoth's guild said, at least the disputes didn't last long. *And I thought Durzo Blint looked kind?*

The itch on Azoth's calf itched again. It wasn't his imagination. There was something crawling up the inside of his trousers. It felt big, but not as big as a cockroach. Azoth's fear identified the weight: a white wolf spider. Its poison liquefied flesh in a slowly spreading circle. If it bit, even with a healer the best an adult could hope for was to lose a limb. A guild rat wouldn't be so lucky.

"Blint, you'll be lucky if you don't cut your head off after all you've been drinking. Just in the time I've been watching, you've had—"

"Eight flagons. And I had four before that."

Azoth didn't move. If he jerked his legs together to kill the spider, the water would splash and the men would know he was there. Even if Durzo Blint had looked kind, that was an awful big sword, and Azoth knew better than to trust grown-ups.

"You're bluffing," the man said, but there was fear in his voice.

"I don't bluff," Durzo Blint said. "Why don't you invite your friends in?"

The spider crawled up to Azoth's inner thigh. Trembling, he pulled his tunic up in back and stretched the waist of his trousers, making a gap and praying the spider would crawl for it.

Above him, the assassin reached two fingers up to his lips and whistled. Azoth didn't see Durzo move, but the whistle ended in a gurgle and a moment later, the assassin's body tumbled to the floor. There were yells as the front and back doors burst open. The boards flexed and jumped. Concentrating on not jostling the spider, Azoth didn't move, even when another dropping body pushed his face briefly under water.

The spider crawled across Azoth's butt and then onto his thumb. Slowly, Azoth drew his hand around so he could see it. His fears were right. It was a white wolf spider, its legs as long as Azoth's thumb. He flung it away convulsively and rubbed his fingers, making sure he hadn't been bitten.

He reached for the splintered branch holding his tunic and broke it off. The sound was magnified in the sudden silence above. Azoth couldn't see anyone through the gaps. A few feet away, something was dripping from the boards into a puddle. It was too dark to see what it was, but it didn't take much imagination to guess.

The silence was eerie. If any of the men walked across the floor, groaning boards and flexing bamboo would have announced it. The entire fight had lasted maybe twenty seconds, and Azoth was sure no one had left the tavern. Had they all killed each other?

He was chilled, and not just from the water. Death was no stranger in the Warrens, but Azoth had never seen so many people die so fast and so easily.

Even taking extra care to look out for the spider, in a few minutes, Azoth had gathered six coppers. If he were braver, he would have looted the bodies in the tavern, but Azoth couldn't believe Durzo Blint was dead. Maybe he was a demon, like the other guild rats said. Maybe he was standing outside, waiting to kill Azoth for spying on him.

Chest tight with fear, Azoth turned and scooted toward his hole. Six coppers was good. Dues were only four, so he could buy bread tomorrow to share with Jarl and Doll Girl.

He was a foot from the opening when something bright flashed in front of his nose. It was so close, it took a moment to come into focus. It was Durzo Blint's huge sword, and it was stuck through the floor all the way into the mud, barring Azoth's escape.

Just above Azoth on the other side of the floor, Durzo Blint whispered, "Never speak of this. Understand? I've done worse than kill children."

The sword disappeared, and Azoth scrambled out into the night. He didn't stop running for miles.

Four coppers! Four! This isn't four." Rat's face was so rage-red his pimples only showed as a scattering of white dots. He grabbed Jarl's threadbare tunic and lifted him off the ground. Azoth ducked his head. He couldn't watch.

"This is four!" Rat shouted, spit flying. As his hand slapped across Jarl's face, Azoth realized it was a performance. Not the beating—Rat was definitely hitting Jarl—but he was hitting him with an open hand. It was louder that way. Rat wasn't even paying attention to Jarl. He was watching the rest of the guild, enjoying their fear.

"Who's next?" Rat asked, dropping Jarl. Azoth stepped forward quickly so Rat wouldn't kick his friend. At sixteen, Rat was already as big as a man and he had fat, which made him unique among the slaveborn.

Azoth held out his four coppers.

"Eight, puke," Rat said, taking the four from Azoth's hand.

"Eight?"

"You gotta pay for Doll Girl, too."

Azoth looked around for help. Some of the bigs shifted and looked at each other, but no one said a word. "She's too young," Azoth said. "Littles don't pay dues till they're eight."

Attention shifted to Doll Girl, who was sitting in the dirty alley. She noticed the looks and withered, shrinking into herself. Doll Girl was tiny, with huge eyes, but beneath the grime, her features were as fine and perfect as her namesake's.

"I say she's eight unless she says different." Rat leered. "Say it, Doll Girl, say it or I'll beat up your boyfriend." Doll Girl's big eyes got bigger and Rat laughed. Azoth didn't protest, didn't point out that Doll Girl was mute. Rat knew. Everyone knew. But Rat was the Fist. He only answered to Ja'laliel, and Ja'laliel wasn't here.

Rat pulled Azoth close and lowered his voice. "Why don't you join my pretty boys, Azo? You'll never pay dues again."

Azoth tried to speak, but his throat was so tight that he only squeaked. Rat laughed again and everyone joined him, some enjoying Azoth's humiliation, some just hoping to put Rat in a good mood before their turn came. Black hatred stabbed through him. Azoth hated Rat, hated the guild, hated himself.

He cleared his throat to try again. Rat caught his eye and smirked. Rat was big, but he wasn't stupid. He knew how far he was pushing Azoth. He knew Azoth would crumple, afraid, just like everyone else.

Azoth spat a wad of phlegm onto Rat's face. "Go bugger yourself, Ratty Fatty."

There was an eternity of stunned silence. A golden moment of victory. Azoth thought he could hear jaws dropping. Sanity was just starting to reassert itself when Rat's fist caught him on the ear. Black spots blotted out the world as he hit the ground. He blinked up at Rat, whose black hair glowed like a halo as it blocked the noon sun, and knew he was going to die.

"Rat! Rat, I need you."

Azoth rolled over and saw Ja'laliel emerging from the guild's building. His pale skin was beaded with sweat though the day wasn't hot. He coughed unhealthily. "Rat! I said now."

Rat wiped his face, and seeing his rage cool so suddenly was almost more frightening than seeing its sudden heat. His face cleared, and he smiled at Azoth. Just smiled.

* * *

"Hey-ho, Jay-Oh," Azoth said.

"Hey-ho, Azo," Jarl said, coming to join Azoth and Doll Girl. "You know, you're about as smart as a box of hair. They'll be calling him Ratty Fatty behind his back for years."

"He wanted me to be one of his girls," Azoth said.

They were propped against a wall several blocks away, sharing the stale loaf Azoth had bought. The smells of baking, though less intense this late in the day, covered at least some of the smells of sewage, rotting garbage piled on the banks of the river, and the rancid bite of the urine and brains of the tanneries.

If Ceuran architecture was all bamboo and rice fiber walls and screens, Cenarian architecture was rougher, heavier, lacking the studied simplicity of Ceuran design. If Alitaeran architecture was all granite and pine, Cenarian architecture was less formidable, lacking the deliberate durability of Alitaeran structures. If Osseini architecture was airy spires and soaring arches, Cenarian architecture only soared above one story in a few nobles' manses on the east side. Cenarian buildings were everything squat and dank and cheap and low, especially in the Warrens. A material that cost twice as much was never used, even if it lasted four times as long. Cenarians didn't think long term because they didn't live long term. Their buildings frequently incorporated bamboo and rice fiber, both of which grew nearby, and pine and granite, which were not too far away, but there was no Cenarian style. The country had been conquered too many times over the centuries to pride itself on anything but survival. In the Warrens, there wasn't even pride.

Azoth absently ripped the loaf into thirds, then scowled. He'd made two about the same size, and one third smaller. He put one of the bigger pieces on his leg and handed the other big piece to Doll Girl, who followed him like a shadow. He was about to hand the small piece to Jarl when he saw Doll Girl's face pucker in disapproval.

Azoth sighed and took the small piece for himself. Jarl didn't even notice. "Better one of his girls than dead," Jarl said.

"I won't end up like Bim."

"Azo, once Ja'laliel buys review, Rat'll be our guild head. You're eleven. Five years till you get review. You'll never make it. Rat'll make Bim look lucky compared to you."

"So what do I do, Jarl?" Ordinarily, this was Azoth's favorite time. He was with the two people he didn't have to be afraid of, and he was silencing the insistent voice of hunger. Now, the bread tasted like dust. He stared into the market, not even seeing the fishmonger beating her husband.

Jarl smiled, his teeth brilliant against his black Ladeshian skin. "If I tell you a secret can you keep it quiet?"

Azoth looked from side to side and leaned in. The loud crunching of bread and smacking of lips beside him stopped him. "Well, *I* can. I'm not so sure about Doll Girl."

They both turned toward where she sat, gnawing on the heel of the loaf. The combination of the crumbs stuck to her face and her scowl of outrage made them howl with laughter.

Azoth rubbed her blonde head and, when she kept scowling, pulled her close. She fought against him, but when he let his arm drop, she didn't scoot away. She looked at Jarl expectantly.

Jarl lifted his tunic and removed a rag he'd had tied around his body as a sash. "I won't be like the others, Azo. I'm not just going to let life happen to me. I'm gonna get out." He opened the sash. Tucked within its folds were a dozen coppers, four silvers, and impossibly, two gold gunders.

"Four years. Four years I've been saving." He dropped two more coppers into the sash.

"You mean all the times Rat's slapped you around for not making your dues, you've had this?"

Jarl smiled and, slowly, Azoth understood. The beatings were a small price to pay for hope. After a while, most guild rats withered and let life beat them. They became animals. Or they went crazy like Azoth had today and got themselves killed.

Looking at that treasure, part of Azoth wanted to strike Jarl, grab the sash, and run. With that money, he could get out, get clothes to replace his rags, and pay apprentice fees somewhere, anywhere. Maybe even with Durzo Blint, as he'd told Jarl and Doll Girl so many times.

Then he saw Doll Girl. He knew how she'd look at him if he stole that sash full of life. "If any of us make it out of the Warrens, it'll be you, Jarl. You deserve it. You have a plan?"

"Always," Jarl said. He looked up, his brown eyes bright. "I want you to take it, Azo. As soon as we find out where Durzo Blint lives, we're going get you out. All right?"

Azoth looked at the pile of coins. Four years. Dozens of beatings. Not only did he not know if he would give that much for Jarl, but he'd also thought of stealing it from him. He couldn't hold back hot tears. He was so ashamed. He was so afraid. Afraid of Rat. Afraid of Durzo Blint. Always afraid. But if he got out, he could help Jarl. And Blint would teach him to kill.

Azoth looked up at Jarl, not daring to look at Doll Girl for fear of what might be in her big brown eyes. "I'll take it."

He knew who he'd kill first.

3

*D*urzo Blint pulled himself on top of the small estate's wall and watched the guard pass. *The perfect guard,* Durzo thought: a bit slow, lacking imagination, and dutiful. He took his thirty-nine steps, stopped at the corner, planted his halberd, scratched his stomach under his gambeson, checked in all directions, then walked on.

Thirty-five. Thirty-six. Durzo slipped out of the man's shadow and eased himself over the edge of the walkway. He held on by his fingertips.

Now. He dropped and hit the grass just as the guard thumped the butt of his halberd on the wood walkway. He doubted the guard would have heard him anyway, but paranoia begat perfection in the wetboy's trade. The yard was small, and the house not much bigger. It was built on the Ceuran design, with translucent rice paper walls. Bald cypress and white cedar formed the doors and arches and cheaper local pine had been used for the frame and the floors. It was spartan like all Ceuran houses, and that fit General Agon's military background and his ascetic personality. More than that, it fit his budget. Despite the general's many successes, King Davin had not rewarded him well—which was part of why the wetboy had come.

Durzo found an unlocked window on the second floor. The general's wife was asleep in the bed: they weren't so Ceuran as to sleep on woven mats. They were, however, poor enough that the mattress was stuffed with straw rather than feathers. The general's wife was a plain woman, snoring gently and sprawled more in the middle than to one side of the bed. The covers on the side she was facing had been disturbed.

The wetboy slid into the room, using his Talent to soften the sound of his footsteps on the hardwood floor.

Curious. A quick glance confirmed that the general hadn't just come for a nocturnal conjugal visit. They actually shared the room. Perhaps he was even poorer than people thought.

Durzo's brow furrowed under his mask. It was a detail he didn't need to know. He drew the short poisoner's knife and walked toward the bed. She'd never feel a thing.

He stopped. The woman was turned *toward* the disturbed covers. She'd been sleeping close to her husband before he got up. Not on the far side of the bed, the way a woman merely doing her marital duties would.

It was a love match. After her murder, Aleine Gunder had planned to offer the general a quick remarriage to a rich noblewoman. But this general, who'd married a lowborn woman for love, would react quite differently to his wife's murder than a man who'd married for ambition.

The idiot. The prince was so consumed with ambition that he thought everyone else was, too. The wetboy sheathed the knife and stepped into the hall. He still had to know where the general stood. Immediately.

"Dammit, man! King Davin's dying. I'd be surprised if he's got a week left."

Whoever had spoken was mostly right. The wetboy had given the king his final dose of poison tonight. By dawn, he would be dead, leaving a throne in contention between one man who was strong and just, and another who was weak and corrupt. The underworld Sa'kagé was not disinterested in the outcome.

The voice had come from the receiving room downstairs. The wetboy hurried to the end of the hall. The house was so small that the receiving room doubled as the study. He had a perfect view of the two men.

General Brant Agon had a graying beard, close-trimmed hair that he didn't comb, and a jerky way of moving, keeping his eyes on everything. He was thin and sinewy, his legs slightly bowed from a life in the saddle.

The man across from him was Duke Regnus Gyre. The wing-backed chair creaked as he shifted his weight. He was a huge man, both tall and wide, and little of his bulk was fat. He folded ringed fingers on his belly.

By the Night Angels. I could kill them both and end the Nine's worries right now.

"Are we deceiving ourselves, Brant?" Duke Gyre asked.

The general didn't answer immediately. "My lord—"

"No, Brant. I need your opinion as a friend, not as a vassal." Durzo crept closer. He drew the throwing knives slowly, careful with the poisoned edges.

"If we do nothing," the general said, "Aleine Gunder will become king. He is a weak, foul, and faithless man. The Sa'kagé already owns the Warrens; the king's patrols won't even leave the main roads, and you know all the reasons that's only bound to get worse. The Death Games entrenched the Sa'kagé. Aleine doesn't have the will or the inclination to oppose the Sa'kagé now, while we can still root them out. So are we deceiving ourselves in thinking that you'd be a better king? Not at all. And the throne is yours by rights."

Blint almost smiled. The underworld's lords, the Sa'kagé Nine, agreed with every word—which was why Blint was making sure Regnus Gyre didn't become king.

"And tactically? We could do it?"

"With minimal bloodshed. Duke Wesseros is out of the country. My own regiment is in the city. The men believe in you, my lord. We need a strong king. A good king. We need you, Regnus."

Duke Gyre looked at his hands. "And Aleine's family? They'll be part of the 'minimal bloodshed'?"

The general's voice was quiet. "You want the truth? Yes. Even if we don't order it, one of our men will kill them to protect you, even if it meant hanging. They believe in you that much."

Duke Gyre breathed. "So the question is, does the good of many in the future outweigh the murder of a few now?"

How long has it been since I had such qualms? Durzo barely stifled an overpowering urge to throw the daggers.

The suddenness of his rage shook him. *What was that about?*

It was Regnus. The man reminded him of another king he'd once served. A king worthy of it.

"That's for you to answer, my lord," General Agon said. "But, if I may, is the question really so philosophical?"

"What do you mean?"

"You still love Nalia, don't you?" Nalia was Aleine Gunder's wife.

Regnus looked stricken. "I was betrothed to her for ten years, Brant. We were each other's first lovers."

"My lord, I'm sorry," the general said. "It's not my—"

"No, Brant. I never speak of it. As I decide whether to be a man or a king, let me." He breathed deeply. "It's been fifteen years since Nalia's father broke our betrothal and married her to that dog Aleine. I should be over it. I am, except when I have to see her with her children and have to imagine her sharing a bed with Aleine Gunder. The only joy my marriage has given me is my son Logan, and I can scarce believe her own has been better."

"My lord, given the involuntary nature of both of your weddings, could you not divorce Catrinna and marry—"

"No." Regnus shook his head. "If the queen's children live, they will always be a threat to my son, whether I exile them or adopt them. Nalia's eldest boy is fourteen—too old to forget that he was destined for a throne."

"The right is on your side, my lord, and who knows but that answers unforeseen may arise to these problems once you sit on the throne?"

Regnus nodded unhappily, obviously knowing he held hundreds or thousands of lives in his hands, not knowing he held his own as well. *If he plots rebellion, I'll kill him now, I swear by the Night Angels. I serve only the Sa'kagé now. And myself. Always myself.*

"May generations unborn forgive me," Regnus Gyre said, tears gleaming in his eyes. "But I will not commit murder for what may be, Brant. I cannot. I will swear fealty."

The wetboy slid the daggers back into their sheaths, ignoring the twin feelings of relief and despair he felt.

It's that damned woman. She's ruined me. She's ruined everything.

Blint saw the ambush from fifty paces away, and walked right into its teeth. The sun was still an hour from rising and the only people on the twisting streets of the Warrens were merchants who'd fallen asleep where they shouldn't have and were hurrying home to their wives.

The guild—Black Dragon from the guild glyphs he'd passed—was hiding around a narrow choke point in the alley where guild rats could spring up to clog both ends of the street and also attack from the low rooftops.

He had affected a bad right knee and pulled his cloak tight around his shoulders, the hood pulled low over his face. As he limped into the trap, one of the older children, a *big* as they called them, jumped into the alley ahead of him and whistled, brandishing a rusty saber. Guild rats surrounded the wetboy.

"Clever," Durzo said. "You keep a lookout before dawn when most of the other guilds are sleeping, and you're able to jump a few bags who've been out all night whoring. They don't want to explain any bruises from fighting to their wives, so they hand over their coins. Not bad. Whose idea was that?"

"Azoth's," a big said, pointing past the wetboy.

"Shut up, Roth!" the guild head said.

The wetboy looked at the small boy on the rooftop. He was holding a rock aloft, his pale blue eyes intent, ready. He looked familiar. "Oh, now you've given him away," Durzo said.

"You shut up, too!" the guild head said, shaking the saber at him. "Hand over your purse or we'll kill you."

"Ja'laliel," a black guild rat said, "he called them 'bags.' A merchant wouldn't know we call 'em that. He's Sa'kagé."

"Shut up, Jarl! We need this." Ja'laliel coughed and spat blood. "Just give us your—"

"I don't have the time for this. Move," Durzo said.

"Hand it—"

The wetboy darted forward, his left hand twisting Ja'laliel's sword hand, snatching the saber, and his body spinning in. His right elbow cracked against the guild head's temple, but he pulled the blow so it wouldn't kill.

The fight was over by the time the guild rats flinched.

"I said I don't have time for this," Durzo said. He threw back his hood.

He knew he was nothing special to look at. He was lanky and sharp-featured, with dark blond hair and a wispy blond beard over lightly pock-marked cheeks. But he might have had three heads from the way the children shrank back.

"Durzo Blint," Roth murmured.

Rocks rattled to the ground.

"Durzo Blint," the name passed through the guild rats in waves. He saw fear and awe in their eyes. They'd just tried to mug a legend.

He smirked. "Sharpen this. Only an amateur lets his blade rust." He threw the saber into a gutter clotted with sewage. Then he walked through the mob. They scattered as if he might kill them all.

Azoth watched him stride into the early morning mists, disappearing like so many other hopes into the sinkhole of the Warrens. Durzo Blint was every-thing Azoth wasn't. He was powerful, dangerous, confident, fearless. He was like a god. He'd looked at the whole guild arrayed against him—even the bigs like Roth and Ja'laliel and Rat—and he'd been amused. Amused! *Someday,* Azoth swore. He didn't quite dare even think the whole thought, lest Blint sense his presumption, but his whole body yearned for it. *Someday.*

When Blint was far enough away not to notice, Azoth followed.

The bashers guarding the Nine's subterranean chamber eyed Durzo sourly. They were twins and two of the biggest men in the Sa'kagé. Each had a lightning bolt tattooed down his forehead.

"Weapons?" one said.

"Lefty," Durzo said in greeting, removing his sword, three daggers, the darts strapped to his wrist, and a number of small glass balls from his other arm.

"I'm Lefty," the other one said, patting down Blint vigorously.

"You mind?" Durzo asked. "We both know if I wanted to kill anyone in there I could, with or without weapons."

Lefty flushed. "Why don't I ram this pretty sword—"

"What Lefty means is, why don't you pretend not to be a threat, and we'll pretend we're the reason," Bernerd said. "It's just a formality, Blint. Like asking someone how they are when you don't care."

"I don't ask."

"I was sorry to hear about Vonda," Bernerd said. Durzo stopped cold, a lance twisting through his guts. "Really," the big man said. He held the door open. Glanced at his brother.

Part of Durzo knew he should say something cutting or threatening or funny, but his tongue was leaden.

"Um, Master Blint?" Bernerd said. Recovering, Durzo stepped into the Nine's meeting room without raising his eyes.

It was a place to inspire fear. Carved from black fireglass, a platform dominated the room. Nine chairs sat on the platform. A tenth chair sat above them like a throne. There was only bare floor facing the chairs. Those the Nine interviewed would stand.

The chamber was a tight rectangle, but it was deep. The ceiling was so high it disappeared in the darkness. It gave those questioned the feeling of being interrogated in hell. That the chairs, walls, and even the floor were carved with little gargoyles, dragons, and people, all screaming, did nothing to cool the effect.

But Durzo walked in with an easy familiarity. The night held no terrors for him. The shadows welcomed his eyes, hid nothing from him. *At least that much is left me.*

The Nine had their cowls on, except for Momma K, though most knew there was no hiding their identities from Durzo. Above them, the Shinga, Pon Dradin, sat in his throne. He was as still and silent as usual.

"Ith the wife dead?" Corbin Fishill asked. He was a fashionable, handsome man with a reputation for cruelty, especially toward those children in the guilds he managed. The laughter his lisp might have provoked somehow dried up under the ever-present malice on his face.

"Things aren't as you expected," Durzo said. He gave his report briefly. The king would soon die, and the men whom the Sa'kagé had feared would try to succeed him would not press their claim. That left the throne to Aleine Gunder, who was too weak to dare interfere with the Sa'kagé.

"I would suggest," Durzo said, "that we make the prince promote General Agon to lord general. Agon would keep the prince from consolidating his power, and if Khalidor makes any move—"

The tiny former slave master interrupted, "While we acknowledge your…complaint against Khalidor, Master Blint, we aren't to squander our political capital on some general."

"We don't have to," Momma K said. The Mistress of Pleasures was still beautiful, though it had been years since she was the city's most celebrated courtesan. "We can get what we want by pretending someone else asked for it." Everyone stopped and listened. "The prince was willing to buy off the general with a political marriage. So we tell him that Agon's price is a political appointment instead. The general won't ever know, and the prince isn't likely to ask about it."

"And that gives us leverage to reopen the slavery issue," the slave master said.

"I'll be damned if we turn slavers again," another said. He was a big man gone to fat, with heavy jowls, small eyes, and scarred fists befitting the master of the Sa'kagé's bashers.

"That converthation can wait. Blint doethn't need to be here for that," Corbin Fishill said. He turned his heavy-lidded eyes to Blint. "You didn't kill tonight." He let the statement hang, unadorned.

Durzo looked at him, refusing to take the provocation.

"Can you thtill do it?"

Words were useless with a man like Corbin Fishill. He spoke the language of meat. Durzo walked to him. Corbin didn't flinch, didn't turn aside as Durzo came toward the platform, though several of the Nine were clearly nervous. Under Fishill's velvet trousers, Blint could see his muscles bunch.

Corbin kicked at Durzo's face, but Durzo had already moved. He slammed a needle deep into Corbin's calf and stepped back.

A bell rang and a moment later, Bernerd and Lefty burst into the room. Blint crossed his arms and made no move to defend himself.

Blint was tall, but his mass was all lean muscle and sinew. Lefty charged like a warhorse. Durzo merely extended both hands, unclenched, but when Lefty crashed into him, the impossible happened. Instead of crushing the smaller man, Lefty's sprint ended instantly.

His face stopped first, his nose popping against Durzo's open hand. The rest of him continued forward. His body lifted parallel to the ground, then crashed to the stone floor.

"Thtop!" Corbin Fishill shouted.

Bernerd skidded to a halt in front of Durzo and then knelt by his brother. Lefty was moaning, his bleeding nose filling the mouth of a rat carved into the rock floor.

Corbin pulled the needle out of his calf with a grimace. "What ith thith, Blint?"

"You want to know if I can still kill?" Durzo put a small vial in front of the basher. "If that needle was poisoned, this is the antidote. But if the needle wasn't poisoned, the antidote will kill you. Drink it or don't."

"Drink it, Corbin," Pon Dradin said. It was the first time the Shinga had spoken since Blint entered. "You know, Blint, you'd be a better wetboy if you didn't know you were the best. You are—but you still take your orders from me. The next time you touch one of my Nine, there will be consequences. Now get the hell out."

The tunnel felt wrong. Azoth had been in other tunnels before, and if he wasn't exactly comfortable with moving through the cloying dark by touch, he could still do it. This tunnel had started out like any other: rough cut, winding, and of course dark. But as it plunged deeper into the earth, the walls got straighter, the floor smoother. This tunnel was important.

But that was different, not wrong. What was wrong was one step in front of Azoth. He squatted on his heels, resting, thinking. He didn't sit. You only sat when you knew there was nothing you'd have to run away from.

He couldn't smell anything different, though the air was as heavy and thick as gruel down here. If he squinted, he thought could see something, but he was pretty sure that was just from squeezing his eyes. He extended his hand again. Was the air cooler just there?

Then he was sure he felt the air shift. Sudden fear arced through Azoth. Blint had passed through here twenty minutes ago. He hadn't carried a torch. Azoth hadn't thought about it then. Now he remembered the stories.

A little puff of sour air lapped at his cheek. Azoth almost ran, but he didn't know which way was safe to run. He had no way to defend himself. The Fist kept all the weapons. Another puff touched his other cheek. *It smells. Like garlic?*

"There are secrets in this world, kid," a voice said. "Secrets like magical alarms and the identities of the Nine. If you take another step, you'll find one of those secrets. Then two nice bashers with orders to kill intruders will find you."

"Master Blint?" Azoth searched the darkness.

"Next time you follow a man, don't be so furtive. It makes you conspicuous."

Whatever that meant, it didn't sound good. "Master Blint?"

23

He heard laughter up the tunnel, moving away.

Azoth jumped to his feet, feeling his hope slip away with the fading laughter. He ran up the tunnel in the dark. "Wait!"

There was no response. Azoth ran faster. A stone grabbed his foot and he fell roughly, skinning his knees and hands on the stone floor. "Master Blint, wait! I need to apprentice with you. Master Blint, please!"

The voice spoke just over him, though when he looked, Azoth could see nothing. "I don't take apprentices. Go home, kid."

"But I'm different! I'll do anything. I've got money!"

But there was no response. Blint was gone.

The silence ached, throbbed in time with the cuts on Azoth's knees and palms. But there was no help for it. He wanted to cry, but crying was for babies.

Azoth walked back to Black Dragon territory as the sky lightened. Parts of the Warrens were shaking off their drunken slumber. Bakers were up, and smiths' apprentices were starting forge fires, but the guild rats, the whores, the bashers, and the sneak thieves had gone to sleep, and the cutpurses, cons, sharps, and rest of those who worked the daylight were still asleep.

Usually, the smells of the Warrens were comfortable. There was the permeating smell of the cattle yards over the more immediate smells of human waste glooping through wide gutters in every street to further foul the Plith River, the rotting vegetation from the shallows and backwaters of the slow river, the less sour smell of the ocean when a lucky breeze blew, the stench of the sleeping never-washed beggars who might attack a guild rat for no reason other than their rage at the world. For the first time to Azoth, rather than home, the smells denoted filth. Rejection and despair were the vapors rising from every moldering ruin and shit pile in the Warrens.

The abandoned mill here, once used for hulling rice, wasn't just an empty building the guild could sleep in. It was a sign. Mills on the west shore would be looted by those so desperate they'd break past whatever bashers the mill owners hired. It was all garbage and rejection, and Azoth was part of it.

When he got to the guild home, Azoth nodded to the lookout and slipped inside with no attempt at stealth. The guild was used to children getting up to piss in the night, so no one would think he'd been out. If he tried to sneak in, he'd just draw attention to himself.

Maybe that was what furtive meant.

Lying down in his usual spot next to the window, he slipped between Doll Girl and Jarl. It got cold here, but the floor was flat and there weren't many splinters. He nudged his friend. "Jay-Oh, you know what furtive means?"

But Jarl rolled away, grunting. Azoth poked him again, but Jarl wouldn't move. *Long night, I guess.*

Like all the guild rats, Azoth, Jarl, and Doll Girl slept close to each other for warmth. Usually Doll Girl got the middle because she was small and got cold so easy, but tonight Jarl and Doll Girl weren't lying close to each other.

Doll Girl scooted close and wrapped her arms around him, squeezing tightly, and Azoth was glad for her warmth. A worry gnawed at the back of his mind like a rat, but he was too tired. He slept.

The nightmare started when Azoth woke.

"Good morning," Rat said. "How's my favorite little guttershite?" The glee on Rat's face told Azoth that something was seriously wrong. Roth and Harelip stood on either side of Rat, almost bursting with excitement.

Doll Girl was gone. Jarl was gone. Ja'laliel was nowhere to be seen. Blinking against the sunlight streaming through the guild home's torn roof, Azoth stood and tried to orient himself. The rest of the guild was gone, either working, scavenging, or just deciding that now would be a good time to be outside. So they'd seen Rat come in.

Roth stood by the back door, and Harelip stood behind Rat in case Azoth ran for the front door or a window.

"Where were you last night?" Rat asked.

"I had to piss."

"Long piss. You missed the fun." When Rat spoke like that, totally flat, no affect in his voice, Azoth felt a fear too deep to shiver out. Azoth knew violence. He'd seen sailors murdered, had seen prostitutes with fresh scars, had a friend die from a vendor's beating. Cruelty walked the Warrens holding hands with poverty and rage. But the dead look in Rat's eyes marked him as more of a freak than Harelip. Harelip had been born without part of his lip. Rat had been born without a conscience.

"What did you do?" Azoth asked.

"Roth?" Rat lifted his chin at the big.

Roth opened the door, said, "Good boy," as if speaking to a dog, and

Brent Weeks

grabbed something. He hauled it inside, and Azoth saw that it was Jarl. Jarl's lips were swollen, both eyes black and so big he could barely see through the slits. He was missing teeth and he had crusted blood on his face from where his hair had been pulled so hard his scalp bled.

He was wearing a dress.

Azoth felt hot and cold tingles on his skin, a rush of blood to his face. He couldn't show Rat weakness. He couldn't move. He turned so he wouldn't throw up.

Behind him, Jarl let out a little whimper. "Azo, please. Azo, don't turn away from me. I didn't want—"

Rat struck him across the face. Jarl fell to the ground and didn't move.

"Jarl's mine now," Rat said. "He thinks he'll fight every night, and he will. For a while." Rat smiled. "But I'll break him. Time's on my side."

"I'll kill you. I swear it," Azoth said.

"Oh, are you Master Blint's apprentice now?" Rat smiled as Azoth shot Jarl a look, feeling betrayed. Jarl turned his face to the floor, his shoulders shaking as he cried silently. "Jarl told us all about it, sometime between Roth and Davi, I think. But I'm confused. If Master Blint apprenticed you, why are you here, Azo? You come back to kill me?"

Jarl's tears stilled and he turned, grasping at straws.

There was nothing to say. "He wouldn't take me," Azoth admitted. Jarl slumped.

"Everyone knows he doesn't take apprentices, stupid," Rat said. "So here's the deal, Azo. I don't know what you've done for him, but Ja'laliel's ordered me not to touch you, and I won't. But sooner or later, this'll be my guild."

"Sooner, I think," Roth said. He wiggled his eyebrows at Azoth.

"I have big plans for Black Dragon, Azo, and I won't let you get in my way," Rat said.

"What do you want from me?" Azoth's voice came out thin and reedy.

"I want you to be a hero. I want everyone who doesn't dare stand up to me themselves to look at you and start to hope. And then I will destroy everything you've done. I will destroy everything you love. I will destroy you so completely that no one will ever defy me again. So do your best, do your worst, do nothing at all. I win no matter what. I always do."

Azoth didn't pay dues the next day. He hoped Rat would hit him. Just once, and he'd be off the pedestal, he'd just be another guild rat. But Rat didn't hit him. He'd raged and swore, his eyes smiling, and told Azoth to bring double next time.

Of course, he brought nothing. He merely extended an empty hand, as if already beaten. It didn't matter. Rat raged, accused him of defying him,

26

and didn't lay a hand on him. And so it was, every dues day. Gradually, Azoth went back to work and started accumulating coppers to put in Jarl's pack. The days were awful: Rat didn't let Jarl speak to Azoth, and after a while, Azoth didn't think Jarl even wanted to speak to him. The Jarl he knew disappeared by slow degrees. It didn't even help when they stopped making him wear the dress.

The nights were worse. Rat took Jarl every night while the rest of the guild pretended not to hear. Azoth and Doll Girl huddled together and in the quiet punctuated by low weeping afterward, Azoth lay on his back for long hours, plotting elaborate revenge that he knew he'd never carry out.

He became reckless, cursing Rat to his face, questioning every order the boy gave and championing anyone Rat beat. Rat swore back, but always with that little smile in his eyes. The littles and the losers in the guild started deferring to Azoth and looking at him with worshipful eyes.

Azoth could feel the guild reaching a critical mass the day two bigs brought him lunch and sat with him on the porch. It was a revelation. He'd never believed that any of the bigs would follow him. Why would they? He was nothing. And then he saw his mistake. He'd never made plans for what to do when bigs joined him. Across the yard, Ja'laliel sat, miserable, coughing blood and looking hopeless.

I'm so stupid. Rat had been waiting for this. He'd arranged for Azoth to be a hero. He'd even told him. This wasn't going to be a coup. It was going to be a purge.

"Father, please, don't go." Logan Gyre held his father's destrier, ignoring the predawn chill and holding back tears.

"No, leave it," Duke Gyre told Wendel North, his steward, who was directing servants with chests full of the duke's clothing. "But I want a thousand wool cloaks sent within a week. Use our funds and don't ask for repayment. I don't want to give the king an excuse to say no." He clasped gauntleted hands behind his back. "I don't know what shape the garrison's stables are in, but I'd like to have word from Havermere of how many horses they can send before winter."

"Already done, milord."

On every side, servants were coming and going, loading the wagons that would travel north with provisions and supplies. A hundred Gyre knights made their own last-minute preparations, checking their saddles, horses, and weapons. Servants who would be leaving their families said hurried goodbyes.

Duke Gyre turned to Logan, and just seeing his father in his mail brought tears of pride and fear to Logan's eyes.

"Son, you're twelve years old."

"I can fight. Even Master Vorden admits that I handle a sword almost as well as the soldiers."

"Logan, it isn't because I don't believe in your abilities that I'm making you stay. It's because I do. The fact is, your mother needs you here more than I need you in the mountains."

"But I want to go with you."

"And I don't want to leave at all. It doesn't have anything to do with what we want."

"Jasin said Niner is trying to embarrass you. He said it's an insult for a duke to be given such a small command." He didn't mention the other things Jasin had said. Logan didn't consider himself quick-tempered, but in the three months since King Davin had died and Aleine Gunder had assumed the title Aleine IX—known condescendingly as Niner—Logan had been in half a dozen fights.

"And what do you think, son?"

"I don't think you're afraid of anyone."

"So Jasin said I was afraid, did he? Is that where you got the bruises on your knuckles?"

Logan grinned suddenly. He was as tall as his father, and if he didn't have Regnus Gyre's bulk yet, their guards master Ren Vorden said it was only a matter of time. When Logan fought other boys, he didn't lose.

"Son, make no mistake. Commanding the garrison at Screaming Winds is a slight, but it's better than exile or death. If I stay, the king will give me one or the other eventually. Each summer, you'll come train with my men, but I need you here, too. For half the year you'll be my eyes and ears in Cenaria. Your mother—" he broke off and looked past Logan.

"Thinks your father is a fool," Catrinna Gyre said, coming up behind them suddenly. She had been born to another ducal family, the Graesins, and she had their green eyes, petite features, and temper. Despite the early hour, she was dressed in a beautiful green silk dress edged with ermine, her hair brushed glossy. "Regnus, if you get on that horse, I never want to see you come back."

"Catrinna, we aren't having this discussion again."

"That jackal will hurl you against my family, you know that. Destroy you, destroy them—he wins no matter what."

"*This* is your family, Catrinna. And I've made my decision." Duke

Gyre's voice carried with a whip crack of command, an edge that made Logan want to shrink and not be noticed.

"Which of your harlots are you taking with you?"

"I'm not taking any of the maidservants, Catrinna, though some of them will be hard to replace. I'm leaving them here out of respect for your—"

"How stupid do you think I am? You'll just find sluts there."

"Catrinna. Go inside. Now!"

She obeyed and Duke Gyre watched her go. He spoke without turning toward Logan. "Your mother . . . there are things I'll share with you when you're older. For now, I expect you to honor her, but you will be Lord Gyre while I'm gone."

Logan's eyes went wide.

His father clapped him on the shoulder. "That doesn't mean you get to skip your lessons. Wendel will teach you everything you need to know. I swear the man understands more about running our lands than I do. I'm only a four-day ride away. You have a fine mind, son, and that's why you have to stay. This city is a vipers' nest. There are those who would destroy us. Your mother has seen hints of that, and it's been part of her troubles. I'm gambling with you, Logan. I wish I didn't have to, but you're the only piece I have left to play. Surprise them. Be smarter, better, braver, and faster than anyone expects. It's not a fair burden for me to put on you, but I must. I'm counting on you. House Gyre is counting on you. All our retainers and vassals are counting on you, and maybe even the kingdom itself."

Duke Gyre swung up onto his huge white destrier. "I love you, son. But don't let me down."

The darkness was as close and cold as the dead's embrace. Azoth squatted against the alley wall, hoping the night wind covered the sound of thunder in his heart. The fifth big who'd joined him had stolen a shiv from Rat's weapons cache, and Azoth clutched the thin metal so tightly his hand hurt.

There was still no motion in the alley. Azoth stuck the blade in the dirt of the alley and put his hands in his armpits to keep them warm. Nothing might happen for hours. It didn't matter. He was running out of chances. He'd wasted too much time as it was.

Rat wasn't stupid. He was cruel, but he had plans. Azoth didn't. He'd been flailing in his fear for three months. Flailing when he could have been planning. The Fist had declared his intentions. That made it easy enough. Azoth knew some of what he was planning; all he had to do was piece together how. Now, as he thought, he could feel himself slipping into Rat's skin all too easily, thinking Rat's thoughts.

A purge isn't good enough. A purge will give me safety for a couple of years. Other guild heads have killed to keep their power. Killing doesn't make me different. Azoth worked on the idea. Rat didn't have small ambitions. Rat had bottled up his hatred for three months. Why would he be willing to not even hit Azoth for three months?

Destruction. That's what it came down to. Rat would destroy him in spectacular fashion. He would sate his own cruelty and advance his power. He would do something so awful that Azoth would become a story the guilds would tell. He might not even kill him, just leave him maimed in some horrific way so that everyone who met Azoth would fear Rat more.

There was a shuffling sound in the alley and Azoth tensed. Slowly, so slowly, he pulled out the shiv. The alley was tight, the buildings sagging so close a grown man could touch both walls at the same time. Azoth had chosen it for that reason. He wouldn't let his quarry slip past him. But now the walls seemed malevolent, stretching hungry fingers toward each other, closing out the stars, grabbing for him. Wind muttered over the roofs, telling tales of murder.

Azoth heard the shuffle again and relaxed. A scarred old rat emerged from under a pile of moldering boards and sniffed. Azoth held still as the rat waddled forward. It sniffed at Azoth's bare feet, nudged them with a wet nose, and sensing no danger, moved forward to feed.

Just as the rat moved to bite, Azoth buried the shiv behind its ear and into the ground beneath. It jerked but didn't squeak. He withdrew the thin iron, satisfied with his stealth. He checked the alley again. Still nothing.

So where am I weak? What would I do to destroy me if I were Rat?

Something tickled his neck and he brushed it away. *Curse the bugs.*

Bugs? It's freezing out here. His hand came down from his neck warm and sticky.

Azoth turned and lashed out, but the shiv went spinning from his hand as something struck his wrist.

Durzo Blint squatted on his heels not a foot away. He didn't speak. He just stared, his eyes colder than the night.

There was a long pause as they stared at each other, neither saying a word. "You saw the rat," Azoth said.

An eyebrow lifted.

"You cut me where I cut it. You were showing me that you're as much better than me as I am better than the rat."

A hint of a smile. "A strange little guild rat you are. So smart, so stupid."

Azoth looked at the shiv—now magically in Durzo's hand—and felt ashamed. He *was* stupid. What had he been thinking? He was going to threaten a wetboy? But he said, "I'm going to apprentice with you."

Blint's open hand cracked across his face and sent him sprawling into the wall. His face scraped against rock and he landed heavily.

When he rolled over, Blint was standing over him. "Give me one good reason why I shouldn't kill you," Blint said.

Doll Girl. She wasn't only the answer to Blint's question, she was Azoth's weakness. She was where Rat would strike. A wave of nausea swept over Azoth. First Jarl and now Doll Girl.

"You should," Azoth said.

Blint raised an eyebrow again.

"You're the best wetboy in the city, but you're not the only one. And if you won't apprentice me and you don't kill me, I'll train under Hu Gibbet or Scarred Wrable. I'll spend my life training just for the moment I have my chance at you. I'll wait until you think I've forgotten today. I'll wait until you think it was just a dumb guild rat's threat. After I'm a master, you'll jump at shadows for a while. But after you jump a dozen times and I'm not there, you won't jump just once, and that's when I'll be there. I don't care if you kill me at the same time. I'll trade my life for yours."

Durzo's eyes barely had to shift to go from dangerously amused to simply dangerous. But Azoth didn't even see them through the tears brimming in his own eyes. He only saw the vacant look that had come into Jarl's eyes and imagined seeing it in Doll Girl's. He imagined her screams if Rat came and took her every night. She'd scream wordlessly for the first few weeks, maybe fight—bite and scratch for a while—and then she wouldn't scream anymore, wouldn't fight at all. There would just be grunting and the sounds of flesh and Rat's pleasure. Just like Jarl.

"Is your life so empty, boy?"

It will be if you say no. "I want to be like you."

"No one wants to be like me." Blint drew a huge black sword and touched the edge to Azoth's throat. In that moment, Azoth didn't care if the blade drank his life's blood. Death would be kinder than watching Doll Girl disappear before his eyes.

"You like hurting people?" Blint asked.

"No, sir."

"Ever killed anyone?"

"No."

"Then why are you wasting my time?"

What was wrong with him? Did he really mean that? He couldn't. "I heard you don't like it. That you don't have to like it to be good," Azoth said.

"Who told you that?"

"Momma K. She said that's the difference between you and some of the others."

Blint frowned. He pulled a clove of garlic from a pouch and popped it into his mouth. He sheathed his sword, chewing.

"All right, kid. You want to get rich?" Azoth nodded. "You're quick. But can you tell what your marks are thinking and remember fifty things at once? Do you have good hands?" Nod. Nod. Nod.

"Be a gambler." Durzo laughed.

Azoth didn't. He looked at his feet. "I don't want to be afraid anymore."

"Ja'laliel beats you?"

"Ja'laliel's nothing."

"Then who is?" Blint asked.

"Our Fist. Rat." Why was it so hard to say his name?

"He beats you?"

"Unless you'll...unless you'll do things with him." It sounded weak, and Blint didn't say anything, so Azoth said, "I won't let anyone beat me again. Not ever."

Blint kept looking past Azoth, giving him time to blink away his tears. The full moon bathed the city in golden light. "The old whore can be beautiful," he said. "Despite everything."

Azoth followed Blint's gaze, but there was no one else in sight. Silver mist rose from the warm manure of the cattle yards and coiled around old broken aqueducts. In the darkness, Azoth couldn't see the Bleeding Man freshly scrawled over his own guild's Black Dragon, but he knew it was there. His guild had been losing territory steadily since Ja'laliel got sick.

"Sir?" Azoth said.

"This city's got no culture but street culture. The buildings are brick on one street, daub and wattle the next, and bamboo one over. Titles Alitaeran, clothes Callaean, music all Sethi harps and Lodricari lyres—the damn rice

32

paddies themselves stolen from Ceura. But as long as you don't touch her or look too close, sometimes she's beautiful."

Azoth thought he understood. You had to be careful what you touched and where you walked in the Warrens. Pools of vomit and other bodily fluids were splattered in the streets, and the dung-fueled fires and fatty steam from the constantly boiling tallow vats covered everything with a greasy, sooty sheen. But he had no reply. He wasn't even sure Blint was talking to him.

"You're close, boy. But I never take apprentices, and I won't take you." Blint paused, and idly spun the shiv from finger to finger. "Not unless you do something you can't."

Hope burst into life in Azoth's breast for the first time in months. "I'll do anything," he said.

"You'd have to do it alone. No one else could know. You'd have to figure out how, when, and where. All by yourself."

"What do I have to do?" Azoth asked. He could feel the Night Angels curling their fingers around his stomach. How did he know what Blint was going to say next?

Blint picked up the dead rat and threw it to Azoth. "Just this. Kill your Rat and bring me proof. You've got a week."

Solon Tofusin led the nag up Sidlin Way between the gaudy, close-packed manses of the great families of Cenaria. Many of the houses were less than a decade old. Others were older but had been recently remodeled. The buildings along this one street were qualitatively different from all the rest of Cenarian architecture. These had been made by those hoping their money could purchase culture. All were ostentatious, trying to rival their neighbors by their exotic design, whether in builders' fantasies of Ladeshian spires or Friaki pleasure domes or in more accurately articulated Alitaeran mansions or perfect scale imitations of famous Ceuran summer palaces. There was even what he thought he recognized from a painting as a bulbous Ymmuri temple, complete with prayer flags. Slave money, he thought.

It wasn't slavery that appalled him. On his island, slavery was common. But not like it had been here. These manses had been built on pit fighters and baby farms. It had been out of his way, but he'd walked through the Warrens to see what the silent half of his new home city was like. The squalor there made the wealth here obscene.

He was tired. Though not tall, he was thick. Thick through the stomach and, mercifully, still thicker through the chest and shoulders. The nag was a good horse, but she was no warhorse, and he had to walk her as often as he rode.

The large estates loomed ahead, differentiated from the others not so much by the size of the buildings as by the amount of land within the walls. Where the manses were packed side by side, the estates sprawled. Guards presided over gates of ironwood rather than intricate grillwork—gates built long ago for defense, not decoration.

The gate of the first estate bore the Jadwin trout inlaid with gold leaf. Through the sally port, he saw a lavish garden filled with statues, some marble, some covered with beaten gold. *No wonder they have a dozen guards.* All the guards were professional and a few furlongs short of handsome, which gave credence to the rumors about the duchess, and he was more than happy to pass the Jadwin estate. He was a handsome man with olive skin, black eyes, and hair still black as a night untouched by the gray shadows of dawn. Sharing a house with a voracious duchess whose husband left on frequent and lengthy embassies was trouble he didn't need.

Not that I'll find less where I'm going. Dorian, my friend, I hope this was genius. He didn't want to consider the other possibility.

"I am Solon Tofusin. I'm here to see Lord Gyre," Solon said as he arrived in front of the Gyre estate's gate.

"The duke?" the guard asked. He pushed his helm back and scraped a hand across his forehead.

The man's a simpleton. "Yes, Duke Gyre." He spoke slowly and with more emphasis than was necessary, but he was tired.

"That's a crying shame," the guard said.

Solon waited, but the man didn't elaborate. *Not a simpleton, an ass.* "Is Lord Gyre gone?"

"Nawp."

So that's what this is about. The red hair should have tipped me off. Solon said, "I know that after millennia of being raided, the smarter Ceurans moved inland, leaving your ancestors on the coast, and I realize that when Sethi pirates raided your village they carried off all the presentable women—again leaving your ancestors—so through no fault of your own, you're both stupid and ugly. But might you attempt to explain how Lord Gyre is both gone and not gone? You can use small words."

Perversely, the man looked pleased. "No marks on your skin, no rings through your face, you don't even talk like a fish. And you're fat for a fish, too. Let me guess, they offered you to the sea but the sea gods wouldn't take you and when you washed up on the beach you were nursed by a troll who mistook you for one of her own."

"She was blind," Solon said, and when the man laughed, he decided he liked him.

"Duke Gyre left this morning. He won't be back," the guard said.

"He won't be back? You mean ever?"

"Not my place to talk about it. But no, not ever, unless I miss my guess. He's gone to command the garrison at Screaming Winds."

"But you said Lord Gyre isn't gone," Solon said.

"The duke named his son the Gyre until he returns."

"Which will be never."

"You're quick for a fish. His son Logan is the Gyre."

Not good. For the life of him, Solon couldn't remember if Dorian had said Duke Gyre or Lord Gyre. Solon hadn't even considered that there might be two heads of House Gyre. If the prophecy was about Duke Gyre, he needed to get riding, now. But if it were about his son, Solon would be leaving his charge at the time he needed him most.

"May I speak with Lord Gyre?"

"Can you use that steel?" the guard asked. "If you can't, I'd suggest you hide it."

"Excuse me?"

"Don't say I didn't warn you. Come with me." The guard called to another atop the wall, who came to hold the gate while the Ceuran led Solon into the estate. A stable boy took the nag, and Solon kept his sword.

He couldn't help but be impressed. The Gyre estate had a permanence about it, the deliberate gravitas of an old family. Acanthus was planted inside the walls and out, growing from red soil Solon knew must have been brought in especially for the purpose. The thistly plants hadn't just been chosen to keep beggars or thieves from the walls, they also had long associations with Alitaeran nobility. The manse itself was similarly daunting, all heavy stone and broad arches and thick doors that could withstand a siege engine. The only compromise strength had made with beauty were the climbing blood roses that framed each door and every ground floor window. Against the backdrop of black stone and iron-barred windows, their perfect red hue was striking.

Solon didn't pay attention to the ringing of steel until the guard walked past the entry to the manse and around to the back of the building. Here, with a view across the Plith to Castle Cenaria, several guards were watching as two men bundled in practice armor pummeled each other. The smaller man was retreating, going back in circles as the larger man's blows thudded on his shield. The smaller man stumbled, and his opponent bull-rushed, leveling him with a shield like a ram. The man raised his sword, but the next blow sent it flying and the next rang his helmet like a bell.

Logan Gyre tore off his helmet and laughed, helping the guard to his feet. Solon's heart sank. This was Lord Gyre? He was a child in a giant's body, baby fat still on his face. He couldn't have been more than fourteen, probably younger. Solon could imagine Dorian laughing. Dorian knew he didn't like children.

The Ceuran guard stepped forward and spoke quietly to Lord Gyre.

"Hello," the boy lord said, turning to Solon. "Marcus tells me you fancy yourself quite a swordsman. Are you?"

Solon looked at the Ceuran, who gave him a self-satisfied smile. *His name is Marcus?* Even the names in this country were a mess. With little regard for people's origins, Alitaeran names like Marcus or Lucienne mixed freely with Lodricari names like Rodo or Daydra, Ceuran names like Hideo or Shizumi, and normal Cenarian names like Aleine or Felene. About the only names most people wouldn't name their children were the slaves names common in the Warrens, like Scar or Harelip. "I can hold my own, Lord Gyre. But it is words I wish to exchange with you, not blows." *If I go now, my old mare and I can make it to the garrison in six, maybe seven days.*

"We will speak then—after we spar. Marcus, get him some practice armor." The men looked pleased, and Solon saw that they loved this young lord like he was their own son. And laughed too easily and spoiled him. He was suddenly the Gyre, and the men were still entranced by the novelty of the idea.

"I don't need it," Solon said.

The chuckling stopped and the men looked at him.

"You want to spar without armor?" Logan asked.

"I don't want to spar at all, but if it is your will, I shall consent—but I won't fight with a practice blade." The men hooted at the prospect of seeing this short Sethi fight their giant, unarmored. Only Marcus and one or two others looked troubled. With the thick armor Logan wore, there was little danger that he would be seriously injured, even with a sharp sword. But the danger was there. In his eyes, Solon saw that Logan knew it too. He was

36

suddenly doubting if he should have been quite so brash with someone who he knew nothing about, someone who might well wish him harm. Logan was looking again at Solon's stocky build.

"Milord," Marcus said, "maybe it would be best if—"

"Agreed," Logan said to Solon. He pulled his helmet on and locked the visor. He unlimbered his sword and said, "Ready when you are."

Before Logan could react, Solon jabbed his fingers through the boy's visor and grabbed the nosepiece. He yanked Logan forward and twisted. The boy slammed into the ground with a grunt. Solon drew a knife from Logan's belt and held it to the boy's eye, his knee resting on the side of Logan's helmet, holding it in place.

"Do you yield?" Solon asked.

The boy's breaths were labored. "I yield."

Solon released him and stood, brushing the dust from the leg of his breeches. He didn't offer to help Lord Gyre stand.

The men were quiet. Several had drawn swords, but none moved forward. It was obvious that if Solon had meant to kill Logan, he would have already done it. No doubt they were thinking about what Duke Gyre would have done to them if such a thing had happened.

"You're a fool boy, Lord Gyre," Solon said. "A buffoon performing for men you may one day have to ask to die for you." *He said Duke Gyre, surely Dorian said* Duke *Gyre. But he sent me here. Surely he would have sent me to the garrison directly if he meant the duke. The prophecy wasn't about me. Dorian couldn't have known that I would be held up, that I would get to the city this late. Could he?*

Logan removed his helmet, and he was red-faced, but he didn't let his embarrassment flare into anger. He said, "I, I deserved that. And I deserved the manhandling you just gave me. Or worse. I'm sorry. It is a poor host who assaults his guests."

"You know they've been losing on purpose, don't you?"

Logan looked stricken. He glanced at the man he'd been fighting as Solon arrived, then stared at his own feet. Then, as if it took an effort of will, he raised his eyes to Solon's. "I see that you speak true. Though it shames me to learn it, I thank you." And now his men looked ashamed. They'd been letting him win because they loved him, and now they had shamed their lord. The men weren't just pained, they were in misery.

How does this boy command such loyalty? Is it just loyalty to his father? As he watched Logan look at each of the men in turn—staring until each met his gaze and then looked away—Solon doubted that. Logan let the pained silence sit and grow.

"In six months' time," Logan said, addressing the men, "I will serve at my father's garrison. I will not sit safely in the castle. I will fight, and so will many of you. But since you seem to think sparring is entertainment, very well. You will entertain yourselves by sparring until midnight. All of you. Tomorrow, we will start training. And I expect all of you to be here an hour before dawn. Understood?"

"Yes, sir!"

Logan turned to Solon. "Sorry about that, Master Tofusin. About all of it. Please call me Logan. You'll stay for dinner, of course, but can I also have the servants prepare a room for you?"

"Yes," Solon said. "I think I'd like that."

Every time Vürdmeister Neph Dada met with Rat, it was in a different place. Rooms in inns, cellars of boat shops, bakeries, east side parks, and dead-end alleys in the Warrens. Ever since Neph had figured out that Rat was afraid of the dark, he'd made sure they always met at night.

Tonight, Neph watched Rat and his bodyguards enter the tiny old over-full graveyard. It wasn't as dark as Neph would have hoped; taverns and game halls and whorehouses huddled not thirty paces away. Rat didn't dismiss his bodyguards immediately. Like most parts of the Warrens, the graveyard was less than a foot above the waterline. The Rabbits, as the natives of the Warrens were called, buried their dead directly in the mud. If they had the money, they erected sarcophagi above ground, but ignorant immigrants had buried their dead in coffins after some riot or another years ago, and the ground had swollen above those graves as the coffins fought to float to the surface. Several had broken open, their contents devoured by feral dogs.

Rat and his bodyguards looked sick with fright. "Go on," Rat finally said to his bigs, nonchalantly picking up a skull and tossing it at one of them. The boy stepped back quickly and the skull, weak with age or disease, shattered on a stone.

"Hello, child," Neph rasped into Rat's ear. Rat flinched and Neph smiled his gap-toothed smile, his long, sparse white hair falling in a greasy trickle to his shoulders. Neph stood so close the boy took a step back.

"What do you want? Why am I here?" Rat asked.

"Ah, petulance and philosophy all bound up in one." Neph shuffled closer. He'd grown up in Lodricar, east of Khalidor. The Lodricari thought men who distanced themselves so much that you couldn't even smell their breath were hiding something. Merchants in Cenaria who dealt with the Lodricari complained bitterly about it, but stood close eagerly enough when Lodricari coins were at stake. But Neph didn't stand close for cultural reasons. He hadn't lived in Lodricar for half a century. He stood close because he liked to see Rat's discomfort.

"Ha!" Neph said, exhaling a gust of rotten air over Rat's face.

"What?" Rat said, trying not to edge back.

"I haven't given up on you yet, you great stupid boy. Sometimes you manage to learn despite yourself. But that's not what I'm here for. Not what you're here for, either. It's time to move. Your enemies are arrayed against you but not yet organized."

"How do you know that?"

"I know more than you think, Ratty Fatty." Neph laughed again, and spittle flew onto Rat's face. Rat almost struck him then, Neph could tell. Rat had become a guild Fist for a reason. But of course he'd never hit Neph. The old man knew he looked frail, but a Vürdmeister had other defenses.

"Do you know how many boys your father has whelped?" Neph asked.

Rat looked around the graveyard as if Neph hadn't already checked for anyone eavesdropping. The boy was hopelessly stupid. Stupid, but capable of cunning, and utterly ruthless. Besides, Neph didn't have many choices. When he'd come to Cenaria, he'd been placed in charge of four boys. The most promising one had eaten some bad meat in the first year and died before Neph had even known he was sick. This week, the second had been killed in territory fight between guilds. That left Neph with only two. "His Holiness has fathered one hundred and thirty-two boys the last time I counted. Most of those lacked Talent and were culled. You are one of forty-three who are his seed. I've told you this before. What I haven't told you is that each of you is given a task, a test to prove your usefulness to your father. If you pass, you may one day become Godking yourself. Can you guess what your task is?"

Rat's beady eyes glittered with visions of opulent splendor.

Neph slapped him. "Your task, boy."

Rat rubbed his cheek, trembling with rage. "Become Shinga," he said quietly.

Well, the boy aimed higher than Neph would have guessed. Good. "His Holiness has declared that Cenaria will fall, as will all the southlands. The Sa'kagé is the only real power in Cenaria, so, yes, you will become Shinga. Then you will give your father Cenaria and everything in it—or, more likely, you will fail and die and one of your brothers will do this."

"There are others in the city?" Rat asked.

"Your father is a god, but his tools are men, and thus fail. His Holiness plans accordingly. Now my little failure-in-waiting, what is your brilliant plan to deal with Azoth?"

Rage roared high in Rat's eyes once more, but he controlled it. One word from Neph, and Rat would be one more corpse floating in the Plith by morning, and they both knew it. In truth, Neph was testing him. Cruelty was Rat's greatest asset—Neph had seen Rat's bloodthirstiness cow older boys who might have killed him—but it was worthless if he couldn't control it.

Rat said, "I'll kill Azoth. I'll make him bleed like—"

"What you can't do is kill him. If you do, he will be forgotten; another will take his place. He must live broken, where all the world can see him."

"I'll beat him in front of everyone. I'll break his hands and—"

"What happens if his *lizards* rush to defend him?"

"They, they wouldn't. They're too afraid."

"Unlike other boys I know," Neph said, "Azoth isn't stupid. He knew what it meant when those bigs came to him. He may have even been planning for this all along. The first thing he'll expect is that you'll get scared and try to beat him. So he'll have a plan for it."

Neph watched the realization settle on Rat that he might actually lose control of the guild. If he lost the guild, he'd lose his life.

"But you have a plan," Rat said. "A way I can destroy him, don't you?"

"And I might even share it," Neph said.

It was coming. Azoth could feel it as he lay on the floor, surrounded by his lizards, his guild. *His.* Fifteen littles and five bigs. Half the littles in Black Dragon and a quarter of the bigs were his now. They slept peacefully around him, probably even Badger, who was supposed to only be feigning sleep.

Azoth hadn't slept for four days. The night he'd come home from talking to Blint and every night since, he'd lain awake, plotting, doubting, feverish with excitement about a life without Rat. And the rising light of day had melted his plans with the fog. He'd called those who stood with him his lizards as a joke—they certainly weren't dragons—but the children had taken the name proudly, deaf to the despair in the label.

During the days, he'd acted, given orders, formed his pathetic lizards into a force, done anything to keep his mind off killing Rat. How long would Rat wait? The time for a purge was now. Everyone was waiting to see what Rat would do. Everyone was still sure that he would do something. If he didn't, though, and soon, his faithful would start to doubt him, and he'd lose the guild in an instant.

Azoth had even given orders for three of the littles he trusted most to guard Doll Girl at all times. Then he'd doubted himself. It wasn't a good use of the strength he had. He needed those littles bringing him information: listening to the others in the guild, searching the other guilds to see if any of the neighboring guilds would like the lizards to join them. Besides, what could three littles do against all of Rat's bigs? Children who were eight, ten, and eleven respectively weren't going to stop Rat's fifteen- and sixteen-year-olds. He'd ended up assigning two of the bigs who had joined him first to watch over her, and had kept her close during every waking hour.

He was slipping, though. The nights without sleep were catching up with him. His mind was a muddle. It was only a matter of time until he made a stupid mistake. And all of it was because he didn't have the guts to kill Rat.

He could do it tonight. It would be easy, really. Rat had gone out before midnight with two bigs, but when they got back, he'd fall asleep instantly. The bastard never had trouble sleeping. Azoth had the shiv. He even had a real knife that one of the bigs had stolen. All he had to do was walk up to Rat and stick it in him. Anywhere in the stomach would work. Even if Rat's dragons were loyal enough to take him to a healer, they'd certainly take all of his money. What healer was going to work for free on a guild rat? All Azoth had to do was wait until five minutes after Rat got back, then get up to piss. On his way back in, he'd kill him.

It was the only way Doll Girl would ever be safe.

He knew what becoming a wetboy would mean. Everything would change. Wetboys were knives in the dark. Azoth would learn how to fight, how to kill. He wouldn't just learn how, he'd do it. Blint would expect him to kill. That niggled at him like a stare from Doll Girl that wouldn't really count unless he met her eyes. But he didn't think much about the specifics of murdering. He held onto that image of Durzo Blint, laughing at the entire guild. Durzo Blint, laughing at Rat and his little army. Durzo Blint, fearless. Durzo Blint, who Azoth could *be*.

Blint would take him away. Azoth wouldn't lead Black Dragon. He wouldn't even lead his lizards. But he didn't want to. He didn't want the littles looking at him like he was their father, the bigs who towered over him looking at him like he knew what he was doing, like he would keep them all safe. He couldn't even keep himself safe. This was all a fraud. He was a fraud. He'd been set up, and they didn't even see it

The unmistakable sound of the front door being moved aside heralded Rat's return. Azoth was so scared he would have wept if he hadn't told Badger to stay awake. He couldn't weep in front of his bigs. He was sure Rat would come over to him, have the bigs lift him up, and take him away to some horrific punishment that would make Jarl's look easy. But true to form, Rat pushed into his harem, lay down, and was asleep in seconds.

A wetboy wouldn't cry. Azoth tried to slow his breathing, tried to listen to see if Rat's bodyguards were asleep, too.

Wetboys weren't afraid. They were killers. Other people were afraid of them. Everyone in the Sa'kagé was afraid of them.

If I lie here and try to sleep again, I might sleep here with nothing happening for another night or another week, but Rat will get me. He'll destroy everything. Azoth had seen the look in his eyes. He believed Rat would destroy him, and he didn't believe that it would be a week before he did. *It's either that or I kill him first.* In his mind, Azoth saw himself as a hero, like something out of a bard's tale: giving Jarl his money back, giving Ja'laliel enough to buy review, everyone in the guild loving him for killing Rat, and Doll Girl speaking for the first time, approval glowing in her eyes, telling how brave he was.

It was stupid, and he couldn't afford stupidity.

He had to piss. Azoth got up angrily and walked out the back door. Rat's bodyguards didn't even shift in their sleep as he walked past them.

The night air was cold and rank. Azoth had been spending most of the collection money to feed his lizards. Today, he'd bought fish. The ever-hungry littles had gotten into the entrails and eaten them and gotten sick. His urine arcing into the alley, he thought that he should have had someone watching out for that. It was just something else he'd missed.

He heard a scuffing sound from inside and turned, lacing his breeches up. Looking into the darkness, though, he saw nothing. He was losing it, jumping at sounds when there were three score guild rats pressed together in the house, sleeping, moaning on empty bellies, and rolling into their neighbors.

Suddenly, he smiled and touched the shiv. There might be a hundred things he didn't know and a thousand more he couldn't control, but he knew what he needed to do now.

Rat had to die; it was that simple. What happened to Azoth after he did it didn't even matter. Whether they thanked him or killed him, he had to kill Rat. He had to kill him before Rat got to Doll Girl. He had to kill him now.

And with that, the decision was made. Azoth held the shiv up along his wrist and stepped inside. Rat would be sleeping wedged in with his harem. It would only be two steps out of Azoth's way. Azoth would pretend to stumble in case the bigs were watching, and then plunge the shiv into Rat's stomach. He would stab him over and over until Rat was dead or he was.

Azoth was within four steps of his attack when he came in sight of his own sleeping space.

Badger was lying on his back in the darkness, a thin line drawn across his neck, black on white skin. His eyes were open, but he wasn't moving.

Doll Girl's space was empty. She was gone, and so was Rat.

9

*H*e lay in the darkness, too stunned to weep. Even in his sudden blind shock, Azoth knew that Rat's bigs couldn't be asleep. This was what they had been waiting for. Azoth had left for the barest minute, and they had taken Doll Girl. It wouldn't even do him any good to wake the whole guild. In the darkness and confusion, he'd never know just which of Rat's bigs was gone. And what would he do even if he knew? Even if he knew who was gone, he wouldn't know where they'd gone. Even if he knew where they'd gone, what would he do?

He lay in the darkness, stumbling over thoughts, staring at the sagging ceiling. He'd heard them. Damn him forever. He'd heard the sound and didn't even go look.

He lay in the darkness, finished. The watch changed. The sun rose. The guild rats stirred, and he stared at the sagging ceiling, waiting for it to collapse on him like everything else. He couldn't have moved if he wanted to.

He lay in the light. Children were shrieking, littles pulling at him, shouting something. Something about Badger. Questions. It was all words. Words were wind. Someone shook him, but he was far away.

It wasn't until long after that that he woke. There was only one sound that could have brought him out of his trance: Rat, laughing.

Tingles shot across his skin and he sat upright. He still had the shiv. There was dried blood on the floor, but Azoth barely saw it. He stood and started walking toward the door.

That terrible laugh rang out again, and Azoth ran.

The moment he stepped through the door, out of the corner of his eye he saw the shadow of the doorframe elongate and snap forward. It was as fast as a trapdoor spider he'd once seen, and just as effective. He slammed into the shadow like he'd run into a wall. His head rang as he was pulled back into the deep shadows between the guild building and the ruin next to it.

"So eager for death, little one?"

Azoth couldn't shake his head, couldn't shake loose. The shadow had a hand like iron over his face. Slowly, he realized it was Master Blint.

"Five days, kid. Five days you had to kill him." He was whispering in Azoth's ear, the faintest hint of garlic and onions laced through his breath. In front of them, Rat was talking with the guild, laughing and making them laugh with him. Some of Azoth's lizards were there, laughing too, hoping to escape Rat's notice.

So it begins already. Whatever Azoth had accomplished was already coming apart. The rest of the lizards were gone. Doubtless they'd come crawling back later to see what had happened. Azoth couldn't even be mad at them for it. In the Warrens, you did what you had to to survive. It wasn't their failure; it was his. Blint was right: the bigs on either side of Rat were ready. Rat himself was ready. If Azoth had charged out there, he would have died. Or worse. All the time he'd had to plan, and he'd done nothing. He would have deserved that death.

"Calm now, kid?" Blint asked. "Good. Because I'm going to show you what your hesitation cost."

Solon was ushered in to dinner by an old man with a stooped back and a smartly pressed uniform adorned with gold braid and the Gyre's soaring white falcon on a field sable, which over the centuries had become barely recognizable as the gyrfalcon it was. A northern falcon. And not Khalidoran or even Lodricari, gyrfalcons were only found in the Freeze. *So the Gyres are hardly more native to Cenaria than I am.*

Dinner was set in the great hall, a strange choice to Solon's mind. It wasn't that the great hall wasn't impressive—it was too much so. It must have been almost as large as Castle Cenaria's own great hall, adorned with tapestries, banners, shields of long-dead enemies, enormous canvasses, statuary in marble and gold leaf, and a ceiling mural depicting a scene from the Alkestia. In the midst of such grandeur, the table was dwarfed to insignificance, though it was fifteen paces long.

"Lord Solon Tofusin, of House Tofusin, Windseekers of Royal House Bra'aden of the Island Empire of Seth," the old man announced. Solon was pleased that the man had either known or dug up the appropriate titles, even if Seth was scarcely an empire these days. Solon walked forward to greet Lady Gyre.

She was an attractive woman, stately, with the dark green eyes and the dusky skin and delicate bones of House Graesin. Though she had an admirable figure, she dressed modestly by Cenarian standards: the neckline high, the hemline coming down almost to her slim ankles, the gray gown fitted but not tight.

"Blessings, my Lady," Solon said, giving the traditional Sethi open-palmed bow, "may the sun smile upon you and all storms find you in port." It was a little much, but so was having three people dine in a hall large enough to have its own weather.

She hmmphed, not even bothering to speak to him. They sat and servants brought out the first course, a mandarin duck soup with fennel. "My son warned me of what you were, but you speak quite well, nor have you seen fit to put metal through your face. And you're wearing clothes. I'm quite pleased." Evidently the good duchess had heard about her son's luck with sparring Solon and didn't appreciate having her son humbled.

"Is it true, then?" Logan asked. He was at one end of the table, his mother at the other, and Solon unfortunately in the middle. "Do the Sethi really go naked on their ships?"

"Logan," Catrinna Gyre said sharply.

"No. If I may, Lady Gyre, that's a common misperception. Our island splits the hottest current in the Great Sea, so it's quite warm there even in the winter. In the summer, it's nearly intolerable. So though we don't wear as much clothing or as heavy clothing as people do here, we aren't without our own standards of modesty."

"Modesty? You call women who run about on boats half-naked modest?" Lady Gyre asked. Logan looked enrapt by the idea.

"Not all of them are modest, of course. But to us, breasts are about as erotic as necks. It might be pleasant to kiss them, but there's no reason to—"

"You go too far!" Lady Gyre said.

"On the other hand, a woman who shows her ankles is obviously hoping not to go below decks alone. Indeed, Lady Gyre," he lifted an eyebrow and pretended to look at her ankles, though they were too far away and on the other side of table legs. "Sethi women would think you quite brazen."

45

Catrinna Gyre's face went ashen.

Before she could say anything, though, Logan laughed. "Ankles? Ankles? That's so...dumb!" He wolf-whistled. "Nice ankles, mother." He laughed again.

A servant arrived with the second course, but Solon didn't even see him set it down. *Why do I do this?* It wouldn't be the first time his sharp tongue had cut his own throat.

"I see that your lack of respect isn't confined to striking Lord Gyre," the duchess said.

Now he's Lord Gyre. So, the men weren't stupid; they weren't babying Logan; she'd probably ordered them not to hit Logan in practice.

"Mother, he was never disrespectful to me. And he didn't mean to disrespect you, either." Logan looked from his mother to Solon, and found stony gazes on each. "Did you, Lord Tofusin?"

"Milady," Solon said, "my father once told me that there are no lords on the practice field because there are no lords on the battlefield."

"Nonsense," she said. "A true lord is always a lord. In Cenaria we understand this."

"Mother, he means that enemy swords cut nobles as surely as they cut peasants."

Lady Gyre ignored her son and said, "What is it that you want from us, Master Tofusin?"

It was a rude thing to ask a guest, and not least for addressing him as a commoner. Solon had been counting on the Gyres' courtesy to give him long enough to figure out that very thing. He had thought that he could watch and wait, dine with the Gyres at every meal, and be afforded a fortnight or two before he announced any intention of his plans. He thought he might like the boy, but this woman, gods! He might be better off with the Jadwin seductress.

"Mother, don't you think you're being a little—"

She didn't even look at her son; she just raised her palm toward him and stared at Solon, unblinking.

So that's how it is.

Logan wasn't just her son. For all that he was only a boy, Logan was Catrinna Gyre's lord. In that contemptuous gesture, Solon read the family's history. She raised her hand, and her son was still young enough, still inexperienced enough, that he went silent like a good son rather than punished her like a good lord. In that contempt and the contempt she'd greeted him with, Solon saw why Duke Gyre had named his son Lord Gyre in his own absence. The duke couldn't trust his own wife to rule.

"I'm waiting," Lady Gyre said. The chill in her voice made his decision.

Solon didn't like children, but he loathed tyrants. *Damn you, Dorian.* "I've come to be Lord Gyre's adviser," he said, smiling warmly.

"Ha! Absolutely not."

"Mother," Logan said, a touch of steel entering his voice.

"No. Never," she said. "In fact, Master Tofusin, I'd like you to leave."

"Mother."

"Immediately," she said.

Solon didn't move, merely held his knife and two-pronged fork—he was glad he remembered how the Cenarians used the things—over his plate, willing himself not to move.

"When are you going to let Lord Gyre act like Lord Gyre?" he asked her.

"When he's ready. When he's older. And I will not be questioned by some Sethi savage who—"

"Is that what the duke commanded you when he named his son lord in his absence? Let Logan be lord once he's ready? My father once told me that delayed obedience is really disobedience."

"Guards!" she called.

"Dammit, mother! Stop it!" Logan stood so abruptly his chair clattered to the ground behind him.

The guards were halfway to Solon's chair. They suddenly looked caught, conspicuous. They looked at each other and slowed, vainly tried to approach quietly, their chain mail jingling with every step.

"Logan, we'll speak about this later," Catrinna Gyre said. "Tallan, Bran, escort this man out. Now."

"I am the Gyre! Don't touch him," Logan shouted.

The guards stopped. Catrinna's eyes flashed fury. "How dare you question my authority. You second-guess your mother in front of a stranger? You're an embarrassment, Logan Gyre. You shame your family. Your father made a terrible mistake in trusting you."

Solon felt sick, and Logan looked worse. He was shaken, suddenly wavering, about to fold. *The snake. She destroys what she should protect. She shatters her own son's confidence.*

Logan looked at Tallan and Bran. The men looked wretched to be so visibly witnessing Logan's humiliation. Logan shrank, seemed to deflate.

I have to do something.

"My Lord Gyre," Solon said, standing and drawing all eyes. "I'm terribly sorry. I don't wish to impose on your hospitality. The last thing I would wish to be is an occasion for strife in your family, and indeed, I forgot myself and spoke too frankly to your mother. I am not always attuned to . . . tempering the truth for Cenarian sensibilities. Lady Gyre, I apologize for any offense you or your lord may have taken. Lord Gyre, I apologize if you felt I treated you lightly and will of course take my leave, if you will grant it." A little twist on the *if you will grant it.*

Logan stood straighter. "I will not."

"My lord?" Solon painted puzzlement on his face.

"I've found too much tempering and not enough truth in this house, Lord Tofusin," Logan said. "You've done nothing to offend me. I'd like you to stay. And I'm sure my mother will do all she can to make you feel welcome."

"Logan Gyre, you will not—" Catrinna Gyre said.

"Men!" Logan said to the guards loudly to cut her off. "Lady Gyre is tired and overwrought. Escort her to her chambers. I'd appreciate it if one of you would watch her door this night in case she requires anything. We will all dine in the usual room in the morning."

Solon loved it. Logan had just confined his mother to her chambers and put a guard on the door to keep her there until morning, all without giving her an avenue for complaint. *This boy will be formidable.*

Will be? He already is. And I've just chained myself to him. It wasn't a comfortable thought. He hadn't even decided to stay. Actually, half an hour ago, he'd decided not to decide for a few weeks. Now he was Logan's.

Did you know this would happen, Dorian? Dorian didn't believe in coincidences. But Solon had never had his friend's faith. Now, faith or no faith, he was committed. It made his neck feel tight, like wearing a slave collar two sizes too small.

The rest of an excellent meal passed in silence. Solon begged his lord's leave and went looking for the nearest inn that served Sethi wine.

10

*H*er face was destroyed. Azoth had once seen a man kicked square in the face by a horse. He'd died wheezing on broken teeth and blood. Doll Girl's face was worse.

Azoth looked away, but Durzo grabbed a handful of his hair and turned him back. "Look, damn you, look. This is what you've done, boy. This is what hesitation costs. When I say kill, you kill. Not tomorrow, not five days later. You kill that second. No hesitation. No doubts. No second thoughts. Obedience. Do you understand the word? I know better than you do. You know nothing. You are nothing. This is what you are. You are weakness. You are filth. You are the blood bubbling out of that little girl's nose."

Sobs burst from Azoth's throat. He thrashed and tried to turn away, but Durzo's grip was steel. "No! Look! This is what you've done. This is your fault! Your failure! Your deader did this. A deader shouldn't do anything. A deader is dead. Not five days from now—a deader is dead as soon as you take the contract. Do you understand?"

Azoth threw up, and still Durzo held his hair, turning him so his vomit didn't splatter on Doll Girl. When he was done, Durzo turned him around and let go. But Azoth turned away, not even wiping the puke from his lips. He looked at Doll Girl. She couldn't last long. Every breath was labored. Blood welled, dribbled, dripped, slid onto the sheets, onto the floor.

He stared until her face disappeared, until he was only seeing red angles and curves where once that doll-pretty face had been. The red angles went white-hot and branded his memory, searing him. He held perfectly still so the scars on his mind would give a perfect image of what he'd done, would perfectly match the lacerations on her face.

Durzo didn't say a word. It didn't matter. He didn't matter. Azoth didn't matter. All that mattered was the bloody little girl lying on bloody sheets. He felt something inside collapsing, something squeezing the breath out of his body. Part of him was glad; part of him cheered as he felt himself being crushed, compacted into insignificance, into oblivion. This was what he deserved.

But then it stopped. He blinked and noticed there were no tears in his eyes. He *wouldn't* be crushed. Something in him refused to be crushed. He turned to Durzo.

"If you save her, I'm yours. Forever."

"You don't understand, boy. You've already failed. Besides, she's dying. There's nothing you can do. She's worthless now. A girl on the street is worth exactly what she can get for whoring. Saving her life is no kindness. She won't thank you for it."

"I'll find you when he's dead," Azoth said.

"You've already failed."

"You gave me a week. It's only been five days."

Durzo shook his head. "By the Night Angels. So be it. But if you come without proof, I'll end you."

Azoth didn't answer. He was already walking away.

*   *   *

She wasn't dying fast, but she was certainly dying. Durzo couldn't help but have a certain detached professional rage. It had been sloppy, cruel work. With the horrible wounds on her face, it was obvious that she had been intended to live and live with hideous scars that would forever shame her. But instead, she was dying, wheezing out her life through a broken bloody nose.

There was nothing he could do for her, either. That was quickly evident. He'd killed both of the bigs who had been guarding her after the butchery, but he suspected that neither of them had been the cutter. They had both seemed a little too horrified at the evil they were part of. Some part of Durzo that still had a shred of decency demanded he go kill the twist who had done this immediately, but he'd tended to the little girl first.

She was lying on a low cot in one of the smaller safe houses he owned in the Warrens. He cleaned her up as well as he could. He knew a lot about preserving life: he'd learned that as he learned about killing. It was just a matter of approaching the line between life and death from the opposite side. So it was quickly apparent that her wounds were beyond his skills. She'd been kicked, and she was bleeding inside. That would kill her even if the blood she was losing from her face didn't.

"Life is empty," he told her still form. "Life is worthless, meaningless. Life is pain and suffering. I'm sparing you if I let you die. You'll be ugly now. They'll laugh at you. Stare at you. Point at you. Shudder. You'll overhear their questions. You'll know their self-serving pity. You'll be a curiosity, a horror. Your life is worth nothing now."

He had no choice. He had to let her die. It was only kind. Not just, perhaps, but kind. *Not just*. The thought ate at him, and her ugliness and blood, her wheezing, ate at him.

Maybe he needed to save her. For the boy. Maybe she would be just the goad to move him. Momma K said Azoth might be too kind. Maybe from this Azoth would learn to act first, act fast, kill anyone who threatened him. The boy had already waited too long. It was a risk either way. The boy had sworn himself to Durzo if he saved her, but what would having this cripple around do to a boy? She'd be a living reminder of failure.

Durzo couldn't allow Azoth to destroy himself over a girl. He wouldn't allow it.

The wheezing decided him. He wouldn't kill her himself, and he wasn't such a coward that he'd run away and let her die alone. Fine. He'd do what he could to save her. If she died, it wasn't his fault. If she lived, he'd deal with Azoth.

But who the hell could save her?

*   *   *

Solon stared at the dregs of his sixth glass of, to be charitable, lousy Sethi red. Any honest vintner on the island would have been ashamed to serve such dreck at their least favorite nephew's coming of age. And dregs? The glass must have been at least half dregs. Someone needed to tell the innkeeper this wine wasn't meant to be aged. It was supposed to be served within a year. At the outside. Kaede wouldn't have tolerated it.

So he told the innkeeper. And realized from the look on the man's face that he'd already told him. At least twice.

Well, to hell with it. He was paying good money for bad wine, and he kept hoping after a few glasses he might not notice just how bad it was. He was wrong. Every glass just made him a little more irritable about the poor quality. Why would someone ship a bad wine all the way across the Great Sea? Did they actually make a profit on it?

As he put down another silver, he realized it was because of homesick fools like himself that they made a profit on it. The thought made him sick. Or maybe that was the wine. Someday he'd have to convince Lord Gyre to invest in Sethi wines.

He slumped further in his chair and waved for another glass, ignoring the few other patrons and the bored innkeeper. This was really an inexcusable exercise in self-pity, the likes of which he would have whipped out of Logan Gyre if he saw him indulging in something so juvenile. But he'd traveled so far, and for what? He remembered Dorian's smile, that mischievous little grin the girls never stopped cooing over.

"A kingdom rests in your hands, Solon."

"What do I care about Cenaria? It's half a world away!"

"I didn't say the kingdom was Cenaria, did I?" That damn grin again. Then it faded. "Solon, you know I wouldn't ask this if there were any other way—"

"You don't see everything. There's got to be another way. At least tell me what I'm supposed to do. Dorian, you know what I'd be leaving. You know what this will cost me."

"I do," Dorian said, his aristocratic features showing the pain a great lord might feel when sending men to their deaths to accomplish some necessary goal. "He needs you, Solon—"

Solon's memories were abruptly cut short with the jab of a dagger into his spine. He sat bolt upright, sloshing the dregs of his seventh glass onto the table.

"That's enough, friend," a low voice said into his ear. "I know what you are, and I need you to come with me."

"Or else?" Solon asked, dizzy. Who could know that he was here?

"Yes. Or else." Amused.

"Or else what? You're going to kill me in front of five witnesses?" Solon asked. He rarely drank more than two glasses of wine at any time. He was too impaired for this. Who the hell was this man?

"And you're supposed to be smart," the man said. "If I know what you are and still threaten you, do you think I lack the will to kill you?"

He had Solon there. "And what's to stop me—"

The dagger jabbed his spine again. "Enough talk. You've been poisoned. You do what I say and I'll give you the antidote. Does that answer the rest of your questions?"

"Actually—"

"You'll know you're really poisoned because any time now your neck and armpits will start itching."

"Uh-huh. Ariamu root?" Solon asked, trying to think. Was he bluffing? Why would he bluff?

"Plus a few other things. Last warning."

His shoulder started itching. Damn. He could have taken care of ariamu root by itself, but this . . . "What do you want?"

"Head outside. Don't turn, don't say anything."

Solon walked to the door, almost trembling. The man had said "what you are" not "who you are." That might have referred to being Sethi, but his other comment obviously didn't. The Sethi might be famous or infamous for many things, but rightly or wrongly, intelligence wasn't one of them.

He'd barely touched the street when he felt the dagger jab his spine again. A hand drew his sword from the scabbard. "That won't be necessary," Solon said. Was that his imagination, or was his neck itching? "Show me what you want."

The poisoner led him around the building where two horses were waiting. Together they rode south and then across the Vanden Bridge. They were swallowed by the Warrens, and though Solon didn't think the man had been taking turns solely to get him lost, he soon was. Damn wine.

Finally, they stopped in front of one tiny shack among many. He dismounted unsteadily and followed the man inside. The poisoner wore dark clothes and a voluminous gray-black cloak with its hood up. All Solon could see was that he was tall, obviously athletic, and probably thin. The man nodded toward the door, and Solon stepped inside.

The smell of blood hit him instantly. A little girl was lying on a low bed, barely breathing, barely bleeding, her face a gory mess. Solon turned. "She's dying. There's nothing I can do."

"I did what I could," the man said. "Now you do what you do. I've left all the tools you may need."

"Whatever you think I am, you're wrong. I'm no healer!"

"She dies, you die." Solon felt the weight of the man's eyes on him. Then the poisoner turned and left.

Solon looked at the closed door and felt despair rising like twin waves of darkness coming from each side. Then he shook himself. Enough. So he was tired, still drunk, poisoned, itchy, and never had been much good at healing to begin with. Dorian had said that someone here needed him, hadn't he? So surely Solon couldn't die yet.

Unless, of course, just making Logan stand up to his mother was all that Solon had been needed for.

Well. That's the problem with prophecy, isn't it? You never know. Solon knelt by the little girl and began working.

Momma K crossed her legs in the absently provocative way that only a veteran courtesan could. Some people fidgeted habitually. Momma K seduced habitually. With a figure most of her girls could only envy, she could pass for thirty, but Momma K was unashamed of her age. She'd thrown a huge party for her own fortieth birthday. Few of those who'd told her she outshone her own courtesans had been lying, for Gwinvere Kirena had been the courtesan of an age. Durzo knew of a dozen duels that had been fought over her, and at least as many lords had proposed to her, but Gwinvere Kirena would be chained to no man. She knew too well all the men she knew.

"He really does have you nervous, this Azoth. Doesn't he?" Momma K said.

"No."

"Liar." Momma K smiled, all full red lips and perfect teeth.

"What gave me away?" Durzo asked, not really interested. He *was* nervous, though. Things had spun suddenly out of control.

"You were staring at my breasts. You only look at me like I'm a woman when you're too distracted to keep your guard up." She smiled again. "Don't worry—I think it's sweet."

"Don't you ever stop?"

"You're a simpler man than you like to think, Durzo Blint. You really only have three refuges when the world overwhelms you. Do you want me to tell you what they are, my big, strong wetboy?"

"Is this the kind of thing you talk about with clients?" It was a cheap shot. Moreover, it was the kind of comment a whore would have been hit with enough times that she was well armored against it now.

She didn't even blink. "No," she said. "But there was a rather pathetically endowed baron who liked to have me pretend I was his nursemaid and when he was naughty, I'd—"

"Spare me." It was a loss to have her stop, but she'd have gone on for ten minutes, and not skipped a single detail.

"Then what do you want, Durzo? Now you're staring at your hands again."

He *was* staring at his hands. Gwinvere could be more trouble than she was worth, but her advice was always good. She was the most perceptive person he knew and smarter than he was by a long shot. "I want to know what to do, Gwinvere." After a long moment of silence, he looked up from his hands.

"About the boy?" she asked.

"I don't think he has it in him."

When Azoth came around the corner, Rat was sitting on the back porch of the ruin the guild called home. Azoth's heart seized at the sight of the ugly boy. Rat was alone, waiting for him. He was spinning a short sword on its point. Spots of rust interplayed with the winking of the waning moon on bright steel as it spun.

In this unguarded moment, Rat's face seemed as mutable as that spinning steel, one moment the monster Azoth had always known, the next moment an overgrown, scared child. Azoth shuffled forward, more confused and frightened by that glimpse of humanity than soothed. He'd seen too much.

He came forward through the stench of the alley that the whole guild used as their toilet. He didn't even care to watch where he put his feet. He was hollow.

When he looked up, Roth was standing, that familiar cruel grin on his lips, the rusty sword pointing at Azoth's throat.

"That's far enough," Rat said.

Azoth flinched. "Rat," he said, and swallowed.

"No closer," Rat said. "You've got a shiv. Give it to me."

Azoth was on the verge of tears. He took the shiv from his belt and held it out, handle first. "Please," he said. "I don't want to die. I'm sorry. I'll do whatever you want. Just don't hurt me."

Rat took the shiv.

"I'll give him that he's smart," Durzo said. "But it takes more than intelligence. You've seen him here with all the other guild rats. Does he have that...?" He snapped his fingers, unable to find the word.

"Most of them I only see in the winter. They sleep on the streets the rest of the year. I give them a roof, Durzo, not a home."

"But you've seen him."

"I've seen him." She would never forget him.

"Gwinvere, is he cunning?"

Rat tucked the shiv in his belt and patted Azoth down. He found no other weapons. His fear dissolved and left only exultation. "Don't hurt you?" he asked. He backhanded Azoth.

It was almost ridiculous. Azoth practically flew from the force of the blow. He sprawled in the dirt and got up slowly, his hands and knees bleeding. *He's so small!*

How did I ever fear this? Azoth's eyes bled fear. He was crying, making little whimpers in the darkness. Rat said, "I'm going to have to hurt you, Azoth. You've made me. I didn't want it to be this way. I wanted you with me."

It was all too easy. Azoth had come back to the guild already destroyed. Rat didn't like it. He wanted to do something to seal Azoth's humiliation.

He stepped forward and grabbed Azoth's hair. He pulled him up to his knees, enjoying the little cries of pain the boy gave.

He owed what would come next to Neph. Rat didn't particularly like boys more than girls. He didn't see much difference. But Rat never would have thought of this as a weapon if Neph hadn't told him how much it broke a person's spirit to be forced.

It had become one of Rat's favorites. Anyone could make a girl scared, but the boys in the guild feared him more than they had ever feared anyone. They looked at Bim or Weese or Pod or Jarl and they melted. And the more he had done it, the more it stirred him. Just looking at Azoth now, on his knees, eyes round with fear, made Rat's loins stir. There was nothing like watching the fire of defiance roar high and then, quickly or over many nights, die, flare up again, and die forever.

"A wetboy has to lose himself," Durzo said. "No, abandon himself. To be a perfect killer, he has to wear the perfect skin for each kill. Gwinvere, you understand, don't you?"

She recrossed her long legs. "Understanding is what sets courtesans apart from whores. I get under the skin of every man to walk through my doors. If I know a man, I know how to please him. I know how to manipulate him so that he'll try to buy my love and become competitive with the others trying to do the same thing, but not become jealous of them."

"A wetboy has to know his deaders like that," Durzo said.

"And you don't think Azoth can do that?"

"Oh no. I think he can," Durzo said. "But after you know a man or a woman like that—after you wear their skin and walk a few miles in it, you can't help but love them—"

"But it's not real love," Gwinvere said quietly.

"—and when you love them, that's the moment a wetboy has to kill."

"And that's what Azoth can't do."

"He's too soft."

"Even now, even after what happened to his little friend?"

"Even now."

"You were right," Azoth said through his tears. He looked up at Rat standing over him, moonlight throwing his shadow over Azoth. "I knew what you wanted, and I wanted it, too. I just...I just couldn't. But I'm ready now."

Rat looked down at him, a faint light of suspicion blooming in his eyes.

"I found a special place for us..." Azoth stopped. "But it doesn't matter, we can do it here. We should do it here." Rat's eyes were hard, but unreadable. Azoth stood slowly, holding on to Rat's hips. "Let's just do it here. Let the whole guild hear us. Let everyone know."

His whole body was shaking and there was no way to hide it. Revulsion was arcing through him like lightning, but he kept his face hopeful, pretended his trembling was pure naive uncertainty. *I can't. I can't. Let him kill me. Anything but...* If he thought, if he considered anything for another second, he was lost.

Azoth reached a trembling hand up to Rat's cheek, and stood, then stood on tiptoe and kissed him.

"No," Rat said, slapping him. "We do this my way."

"To ply this trade, a man has to value nothing, has to sacrifice..." Durzo trailed off.

"Everything?" Gwinvere asked. "Like you've done so well? My sister might have words about that."

"Vonda's dead because I didn't," Durzo said. He wouldn't meet Gwinvere's gaze. Out the window, night was just beginning to lose its hold on the city.

Looking at Durzo there, his hard, pockmarked face glowing yellow sorrow in the lamplight, Gwinvere softened. "So you fell in love, Durzo. Not even wetboys are immune. Love is a madness."

"Love is failure. I lost everything because I failed."

"And what do you do if Azoth fails?" Gwinvere asked.

"I let him die. Or I kill him."

"You need him," she said gently. "You told me yourself that he'll call a ka'kari to you."

Before Durzo could say anything, there was a knock at the door.

"Come," Momma K said.

One of Gwinvere's maids, obviously a former courtesan herself, now too old for the brothels, poked her head in the door. "There's a boy to see you, milady. His name is Azoth."

"Show him in," Gwinvere said.

Durzo looked at her. "What the hell is he doing here?"

"I don't know." Gwinvere was amused. "I suppose that if he's the kind of boy you can mold into a wetboy, he can't be without certain resources."

"Damn, I left him not three hours ago," Durzo said.

"So?"

"So I told him I'd kill him if I saw him without proof. You know I can't make idle threats." Durzo sighed. "You might have been right, but it's out of my hands."

"He's not here for you, Durzo. He's here to see me. So why don't you do your little shadow thing and disappear?"

"My little shadow thing?"

"Now, Durzo."

The door opened and a bleeding, wretched boy was shown in. But even beat up as he was, Gwinvere would have picked him out from a thousand guild rats. This guild rat had fire in his eyes. He stood straight even though his face was abraded, his mouth and nose dribbling blood. He looked at her unabashedly, but was either young enough or smart enough that he looked at her eyes rather than at her cleavage.

"You see more than most, don't you," Momma K said. It wasn't a question.

He didn't even nod. He was too young to be mocking her tendency to state questions, so there was something else in that flat stare he was giving her.

Of course. "And you've seen something terrible, haven't you?"

Azoth just looked at her with big eyes, trembling. He was a picture of the naked innocence that died every day in the Warrens. It stirred something in her that she'd thought long dead. Without so much as a word, she knew she could offer the boy a mother's arms, a mother's embrace, a safe place. She could give a refuge, even to this child of the Warrens, who'd probably never been held in his life. A soft look, a touch on his cheek, and a word, and he would collapse into her arms and cry.

And what will Durzo do? Vonda had barely been dead three months. He'd lost more than lover when she'd died, and Gwinvere didn't know if he'd ever recover. *Will he understand that Azoth's tears don't make him weak?*

To be honest with herself, Gwinvere knew that holding Azoth wouldn't be just for Azoth. She couldn't remember the last time she'd held someone who hadn't paid for the privilege.

And what will Durzo do if he sees real love now? Will it make him be human, or will he tell himself Azoth is too weak and kill him rather than admit that he needs him?

It all took her just a second to read the boy and weigh her options. There was too much at stake. She couldn't do it.

"So, Azoth," she asked, folding her arms under her breasts, "who'd you kill?"

The blood drained from Azoth's face. He blinked as fear suddenly cleared his eyes of the tears that were threatening.

"First kill, too," Momma K said. "Good."

"I don't know what you're talking about," Azoth said, too quickly.

"I know what a killer looks like." Her voice was sharp. "So who did you kill?"

"I need to talk to Durzo Blint. Please. Where is he?"

"Right here," Blint said, behind Azoth. Azoth flinched. "And since you've found me," Blint continued, "someone better be dead."

"He..." Azoth looked at Momma K, obviously wondering if he could speak in front of her. "He is."

"Where's the body?" Blint demanded.

"It's, it's in the river."

"So there's no proof. How convenient."

"Here's your proof," Azoth shouted, suddenly furious. He threw what he was holding at Durzo. Durzo snatched it out of the air.

"You call this proof?" Durzo asked. He opened his hand and Momma K saw he held a bloody ear. "I call it an ear. Ever known a man to die from losing an ear, Gwin?"

Momma K said, "Don't you put me in the middle of this, Durzo Blint."

"I can show you the body," Azoth said.

"You said it's in the river."

"It is."

Durzo hesitated.

"Damn you, Durzo. Go," Momma K said. "You owe him that much."

The sun sat fully above the horizon when they arrived at the boat repair shop. Durzo went inside alone and came out ten minutes later, rolling down a wet sleeve. He didn't look down at Azoth as he asked, "Son, he was naked. Did he..."

"I got the noose around his foot before, before he could...I killed him before." In cold and distant tones, Azoth told him everything. The night was fading like a bad dream, and what he remembered doing, he couldn't believe he had done. It must have been someone else. As he told his story, Blint looked at him in a way no one ever had before. It might have been pity. Azoth didn't know. He'd never seen pity before.

"Did Doll Girl make it?" Azoth asked.

Durzo put his hands on Azoth's shoulders and looked into his eyes. "I don't know. She looked bad. I got the best person I could find to try to save her. Kid," Blint looked away, blinking. "I'm going to give you one more chance."

"Another test?" Azoth's shoulders slumped. His voice was flat, deflated. He couldn't even spare the energy for outrage. "You can't. I did everything you said."

"No more tests. I'm giving you one more chance to reconsider. You've done everything I asked. But this isn't the life you want. You want off the street? I'll give you a bag of silver and apprentice you to a fletcher or an herbalist on the east side. But if you come with me, you trade everything for it. Once you do this work, you'll never be the same. You will be alone. You will be different. Always.

"And that's not the worst of it. I'm not trying to scare you. Well, maybe I am. But I'm not exaggerating. I'm not lying to you. The worst of it, kid, is this: Relationships are ropes. Love is a noose. If you come with me, you must forswear love. Do you know what that means?"

Azoth shook his head.

"It means you can bang as many women as you want, but you can never love one. I won't allow you to ruin yourself *over a girl*," Durzo's voice filled with violence. His hands were claws on Azoth's shoulders, his eyes predator's eyes. "Do you understand?"

"What about Doll Girl?" Azoth asked. He must have been tired. He knew mentioning her was a mistake before he finished the question.

"You're ten, eleven years old? You think you love her?"

"No." *Too late.*

"I'll let you know if she lives, but if you come with me, Azoth, you will never talk to her again. You understand? You apprentice to my fletcher or the herbalist, you can see her as much as you want. Please, kid. Take it. This might be your last chance for happiness."

Happiness? I just don't want to be afraid anymore. Blint wasn't afraid. People were afraid of him. They whispered his name in awe.

"You follow me now," Blint said, "and by the Night Angels, you *belong* to me. Once we start, you become a wetboy or you die. The Sa'kagé can't afford to do it any other way. Or you stay, and I'll find you in a few days and take you to your new master."

Blint stood and brushed his still-damp hands as if washing them of the matter. He turned abruptly and strode into the shadows of an alley.

Stepping out from the niche he'd been standing in, Azoth looked down the street toward the guild home, a hundred paces away. Maybe he didn't need to go with Blint now. He'd killed Rat. Maybe he could go back and everything would be all right.

Go back to what? I'm still too little to be the guild head. Ja'laliel's still dying. Jarl and Doll Girl were still both maimed. There would be no hero's welcome for Azoth. Roth or some other big would take over the guild, and Azoth would be afraid again, as if nothing had ever happened.

But he promised me an apprenticeship! Yes, he'd promised, but everyone knew you didn't trust adults.

Blint was still confusing. It didn't sound right how he talked about Doll Girl, but just now Azoth had seen something in the wetboy. There was something in him that cared. There was something in the legendary killer that wanted the best for Azoth.

Azoth didn't believe that Doll Girl was worthless just because she wasn't pretty anymore. He didn't know if he could kill again. He didn't know what

Blint would do to him or why. But whatever that something was that he had seen in the wetboy, it was far more precious to Azoth than all his doubts.

Down the street, Jarl stepped out of the guild home. He saw Azoth, and even from that distance, Azoth saw him smile, white teeth brilliant against his Ladeshian skin. From the blood on the back porch and Rat's absence, they must have guessed that he was dead. Jarl waved and started hurrying toward Azoth in the dazzling sunlight.

Azoth turned his back on his best friend and stepped into the shadows' embrace.

12

"Welcome home," Master Blint's voice was tinged with sarcasm, but Azoth didn't hear it. The word *home* held magic. He'd never had a home.

Durzo Blint's house crouched deep in the Warrens underneath the ruins of an old temple. Azoth stared in open wonder. From the outside, it looked like there was nothing here, but Blint had several rooms—none of them small.

"You'll learn to fight here," Blint said, locking, unlocking, and relocking each of three bolts on the door. The room was wide and deep, and crammed with equipment: various targets, pads filled with straw, and every kind of practice weapon, beams suspended above the ground, strange tripods with wood appendages, cables, ropes, hooks, and ladders.

"And you'll learn to use those." Blint pointed to the weapons lining the walls, each neatly outlined in white paint. There were weapons of every size and shape from single-edged daggers to enormous cleavers. Blades straight or curving, one- or two-edged, one- or two-handed, with different colors and patterns of steel. Swords with hooks, notches, and barbs. Then there were maces, flails, axes, war hammers, clubs, staves, pole arms, sickles, spears, slings, darts, garrotes, short bows, longbows, crossbows.

The next room was just as amazing. Disguises and equipment lined the walls, each painstakingly outlined. But here there were also tables covered with books and vials. The books bristled with bookmarks. The jars covered a huge table and were filled with seeds, flowers, leaves, mushrooms, liquids, and powders.

"These are the base ingredients for most of the poisons in the world. As soon as Momma K teaches you how to read, you'll read and memorize most of what's in these books. The poisoner's art *is* an art. You will master it.

"Yes, sir."

"In a couple of years, when your Talent quickens, I'll teach you to use magic."

"Magic?" Azoth was feeling more exhausted by the second.

"You think I accepted you because of your looks? Magic is essential to what we do. No Talent, no wetboy."

Azoth started to totter, but before he could collapse, Master Blint grabbed him by the back of his ragged tunic and guided him to the next room. There was only one pallet and Blint didn't set him on it, but guided him instead to a spot by a small fireplace.

"First kills are hard," Blint said. He seemed to be speaking from far away. "Some time this week, you'll probably cry. Do it when I'm gone."

"I won't cry," Azoth vowed.

"Sure. Now sleep."

"Life is empty. When we take a life, we aren't taking anything of value. Wetboys are killers. That's all we do. That's all we are. There are no poets in the bitter business," Blint said.

He must have left while Azoth slept, because Azoth now held a sword small enough for an eleven-year-old in his fist, feeling awkward.

"Now attack me," Blint said.

"What?"

The side of Blint's sword smashed into Azoth's head.

"I order. You obey. No hesitations. Got it?"

"Yes, sir." Azoth climbed to his feet and picked up the sword. He rubbed his head.

"Attack," Blint said.

Azoth did, wildly. Blint deflected his blows or stepped to one side so that Azoth fell over from the force of his own swings. All the while, Blint spoke.

"You aren't making art, you're making corpses. Dead is dead." He parried quickly and Azoth's blade went skittering across the floor. "Grab that." Blint walked after Azoth and engaged him again. "Don't play with your kills. Don't go for the one-thrust beautiful finish. Cut someone twenty times and let them collapse from blood loss—then finish them. Don't make it beautiful. You aren't making art, you're making corpses."

And so the lessons continued, physical action with a continuously running monologue, each lesson summarized, demonstrated, and summarized again.

In the study: "Never taste death. Every vial, every jar in here is death. If you're working with death, you'll get powders, pastes, and salves on your hands. Never lick the death on your fingers. Never touch death to your eyes. You'll wash your hands with this liquor and then this water, always into this basin which is used for nothing else and will only be emptied where I show you. Never taste death."

On the street: "Embrace the shadows.... Breathe the silence.... Be ordinary, be invisible.... Mark the man.... Know every out...."

When he made mistakes, Blint didn't yell. If Azoth didn't block correctly, he was merely drawing his wage when the wood practice sword crashed into his shin. If he couldn't recite the lessons of the day and expand on any that Blint asked about, he got cuffed for every one he forgot.

It was all even-handed. It was all fair, but Azoth never relaxed. If he failed too much, just as dispassionately as Master Blint cuffed Azoth, he might kill him. All it would take would be for Blint to not pull one blow short. Azoth wouldn't even know he'd failed until he found himself dying.

More than once he wanted to quit. But there was no quitting. More than once, he wanted to kill Blint. But trying would mean death. More than once, he wanted to cry. But he'd vowed he wouldn't—and he didn't.

"Momma K, who's Vonda?" Azoth asked. After his reading lessons, she took a cup of ootai before they started on politics, history, and court etiquette. After he trained with Blint all morning, he studied with her through the afternoon. He was exhausted and sore all the time, but he slept through the whole of every night and woke warm, not shivering. The gnawing voice and debilitating weakness of hunger was only a memory.

He never complained. If he did, they might make him go back.

Momma K didn't answer immediately. "That is a very delicate question."

"Does that mean you won't tell me?"

"It means I don't want to. But I will because you may need to know, and the man who should tell you won't." She closed her eyes for a moment, and when she continued, her voice was flat. "Vonda was Durzo's lover. Durzo had a treasure and Khalidor's Godking wanted it. You remember what I taught you about Khalidor?"

Azoth nodded.

Momma K opened her eyes and lifted her eyebrows.

He grimaced, then recited. "Khalidor is our northern neighbor. They've always said Cenaria and most of Midcyru is theirs, but they can't take it because Logan's dad is at Screaming Winds."

"The pass at Screaming Winds is highly defensible," Momma K suggested. "And the prize?" When Azoth looked at her blankly, she said, "Khalidor could go around the mountains the long way, but they don't because…"

"Because we're not really worth it, and the Sa'kagé runs everything."

"Cenaria is corrupt, the treasury is empty, the Ceurans raid us from the south—and the Lae'knaught holds our eastern lands, and they hate Khalidorans even more than they hate most mages. So yes, we're not worth taking."

"Isn't that what I said?"

"You were right, but not for all the right reasons," she said. She sipped her ootai again, and Azoth thought she'd forgotten his original question, or that she hoped he had. Then she said, "To get Durzo's treasure, the Godking kidnapped Vonda and proposed a trade: the treasure for Vonda's life. Durzo decided that his treasure was more important, so he let her die. But something happened, and Durzo lost his treasure too. So Vonda died for no reason whatsoever."

"You're mad at him," Azoth said.

Momma K's voice had no inflection whatever, and her eyes were dead. "It was a great treasure, Azoth. If I were Durzo, I might've done the same, except for one thing…." She looked away. "Vonda was my little sister."

Solon caught the edge of the halberd with his long sword and heaved it aside, then stepped in and kicked one of Logan's men in the stomach. A few years ago, that kick would have reached his helmet. He supposed he should be thankful that he could beat the Gyre's guards at all, but that was what came of having as his best friends a prophet and a second-echelon blade master. *Feir would have words about how fat I've let myself get. And slow.*

"My lord," Wendel North said, approaching the fighting men.

Logan stepped away from a match he was losing and Solon followed him. The steward gave Solon a flat stare, but didn't protest his presence. "Milord, your mother has just returned."

"Oh? Where was she, Wendel, uh, I mean, Master North?" Logan asked. With the men, he did better, but acting the lord to a man who had probably been in charge of spanking him a few weeks ago was beyond Logan right now. Solon didn't allow himself to grin, though. Let Lady Gyre undermine Logan's authority. He would have no part of that.

"She spoke with the queen."

"Why?"

"She put forth a petition for guardianship."

"What?" Solon asked.

"She is asking the crown to appoint her to be duchess until the duke returns, or until my lord reaches the age of majority—which in this country, Master Tofusin, is twenty-one."

"But we have my father's letters appointing me," Logan said. "The king can't interfere with a house's appointments unless they're guilty of treason."

Wendel North pushed his glasses up his nose nervously. "That's not altogether true, milord."

Solon looked back at the guards, who were beginning to quit sparring and drift closer. "Back to it, dogs!" They jumped to obey.

"The king may appoint a guardian to an underage lord if the previous lord of that house hasn't left the necessary provisions," Wendel said. "It comes down to this: your father left two copies of the letter appointing you lord in his absence. He gave one to your mother, and the other to me. As soon as I heard where Lady Catrinna went, I checked my copy, which I kept under lock and key. It's gone. Forgive me, Lord Gyre," The steward flushed. "I swear I had no part in this. I thought I had the only key."

"What did the queen say?" Solon asked.

Wendel blinked. As Solon had guessed, Wendel knew, but he hadn't wanted to let Solon know how extensive his network of eyes-and-ears was. After a moment, the steward said, "The matter might have been handled fairly easily, but the king doesn't let the queen make any decisions without him. He interrupted them while they were speaking. He said that he would take the matter under advisement. I'm sorry. I don't know what that means."

"I'm afraid I do," Solon said.

"What?" Logan asked.

"Who's your family's solicitor?"

"I asked you first," Logan said.

"Boy!"

"Count Rimbold Drake," Logan said, sulking a little.

"It means we need to speak with Count Drake. Now."

*   *   *

65

"Do I have to wear the shoes?" Azoth asked. He didn't like shoes. You couldn't feel the ground to know how slick it was, and they pinched.

"Nah, we'll go see Count Drake with you wearing a nobleman's tunic and barefoot," Durzo said.

"Really?"

"No."

For all the times Azoth had envied the merchants' and lords' sons at the markets, he'd never thought of how uncomfortable their clothes were. But Durzo was his master now, and he was already impatient with how long it was taking Azoth to get ready, so Azoth kept his mouth shut. He hadn't been Durzo's apprentice for long, and he still worried the wetboy would throw him out.

They walked across Vanden Bridge to the east side. To Azoth, it was a revelation. He'd never even tried to cross Vanden Bridge and hadn't believed the guild rats who claimed to have made it past the guards. On the east side of the river, there were no ruins, no empty buildings at all. There were no beggars on the streets. It smelled different, foreign, alien. Azoth couldn't smell the manure of the cattle yards at all. Even the gutters were different. There was only one every third street, and none in the major streets. People didn't just throw their slops and sewage out the windows and let them accumulate until they gradually flowed away. Here, they carried them to the third street and dumped them there to flow down stone channels in the cobblestone streets so that even those streets were safe to walk in. Most alarming, though, was that the people smelled wrong. Men didn't smell of sweat and their labors. When a woman passed, she smelled only lightly of perfume rather than overpoweringly of it with the stale odors of sweat and sex laced underneath. When Azoth asked Blint about it, the wetboy just said, "You're going to be a lot of work, aren't you?"

They passed a wide building that was billowing steam. Glistening, perfectly coifed men and women were emerging. Azoth didn't even ask. "It's a bath house," Blint said. "Another Ceuran import. The only difference is that here the men and women bathe separately, except in Momma K's, of course."

The owner of the Tipsy Tart greeted Blint as Master Tulii. He answered her with an accent and an effete attitude and ordered his carriage brought around.

Once they were under way, Azoth asked, "Where are we going? Who's Count Drake?"

"He's an old friend, a noble who has to work for a living. He's a solicitor." When Azoth looked puzzled, Master Blint said, "A solicitor is a man who does worse things within the law than most crooks do outside it. But he's a good man. He's going to help me make you useful."

"Master?" Azoth asked. "How's Doll Girl?"

"She's not your problem anymore. You're not to ask about her again." A minute passed as the streets rolled by. Durzo finally said, "She's in bad shape, but she'll live."

He said nothing more until they were shown into the count's tiny estate.

Count Drake was a kindly looking man of perhaps forty. He had a pince nez tucked in a pocket of his vest and he limped as he closed the door behind them and took a seat behind a desk piled high with stacks of papers.

"I never thought you'd take an apprentice, Durzo. In fact, I seem to remember you swearing it—and swearing at great length," the count said.

"And I still believe every word I said," Durzo said gruffly.

"Ah, you're either being terrifically subtle or making no sense at all, my friend." Count Drake smiled, though, and Azoth could tell it was a real smile, without malice or calculation.

Despite himself, Durzo smiled, too. "They've been missing you, Rimbold."

"Really? I wasn't aware of anyone shooting at me for some time." Durzo laughed, and Azoth almost fell out of his chair. He hadn't thought the wetboy was capable of laughter.

"I need your help," Durzo said.

"All I have is yours, Durzo."

"I want to make this boy new."

"What are you thinking?" Count Drake asked, looking at Azoth quizzically.

"A noble of some sort, relatively poor. The kind who gets invited to social events but doesn't attract attention."

"Hmm," Count Drake said. "The third son of a baron, then. He'll be upper nobility, but nobody important. Or wait. An eastern baron. My second cousins live two days' ride beyond Havermere, and most of their lands have been seized by the Lae'knaught, so if you want an ironclad identity, we could make him a Stern."

"That will do."

"First name?" Count Drake asked Azoth.

"Azoth," Azoth said.

"Not your real name, son," the count said. "Your new name."

"Kylar," Durzo said.

The count produced a piece of blank paper and put on the pince nez. "How do you want to spell that? K-Y-L-E-R? K-I-L-E-R?"

Durzo spelled it and the solicitor wrote it down. Count Drake grinned. "Old Jaeran punning?"

"You know me," Durzo said.

"No, Durzo, I don't think anyone does. Still, kind of ominous, don't you think?"

"It fits the life."

For about the hundredth time, Azoth felt like he was not simply a child but an outsider. It seemed everywhere there were secrets that he couldn't know, mysteries he couldn't penetrate. Now it wasn't just muted conversations with Momma K about something called a ka'kari, or Sa'kagé politics, or court intrigues, or magic, or creatures from the Freeze that were imaginary but Durzo insisted did exist, or others that he insisted didn't, or references to gods and angels that Blint wouldn't explain to him even when he did ask. Now it was his own name. Azoth was about to demand an explanation, but they were already moving on to other things.

The count said, "How soon do you need this and how solid does it have to be?"

"Solid. Sooner is better."

"I thought so," the count said. "I'll make it good enough that unless the real Sterns come here, no one will ever know. Of course, you're still left with a rather significant problem. You have to train him to be a noble."

"Oh no I don't."

"Of course you..." the count trailed off. He clicked his tongue. "I see." He adjusted his pince nez and looked at Azoth. "When shall I take him?"

"In a few months, if he lives that long. There are things I need to teach him first." Durzo looked out the window. "Who's that?"

"Ah," Count Drake said. "That's the young Lord Logan Gyre. A young man who will make a fine duke one day."

"No, the Sethi."

"I don't know. Haven't seen him before. Looks like an adviser."

Durzo cursed. He grabbed Azoth's hand and practically dragged him out the door.

"Are you ready to obey?" Durzo demanded.

Azoth nodded quickly.

"See that boy?"

"You call that a boy?" Azoth asked. The young man the count had called Logan Gyre wore a green cloak with black piping, fine black leather boots polished to a high sheen, a cotton tunic, and a sword. He was twenty paces from the door and was being shown in by a porter. His face looked young, but his frame made him look years older than Azoth. He was huge, already taller than Azoth would probably ever be and thicker and wider than any-one he knew, and he didn't look fat. Where Azoth felt awkward and clumsy in his clothes, Logan looked comfortable, confident, handsome, lordly. Just looking at him made Azoth feel shabby.

"Start a fight with him. Distract the Sethi until I can get out."

"Logan!" a girl cried out from upstairs.

"Serah!" Logan called, looking up.

Azoth looked at Master Blint, but he was gone. There was no time to say anything. It didn't matter whether he understood or not. There were mys-teries he wasn't allowed to understand yet. He could only act or wait, obey or disobey.

The porter opened the door and Azoth stepped back around the corner, out of sight. As Logan stepped inside and looked up the stairs, a smile curving his lips, Azoth stepped around the corner.

They collided and Azoth landed on his back. Logan almost tripped over him as Azoth rolled to the side and caught Logan's foot in the stomach.

"Oof!"

Logan caught himself on the banister. "I'm so sorry—"

"You fat ape!" Azoth staggered to his feet, holding his stomach. "You clumsy guttershite—" he cut off as he realized all the curses he knew would mark him as coming from the Warrens.

"I didn't—" Logan said.

"What's going on?" the girl asked from the top of the stairs. Logan looked up, a guilty look flashing across his face.

Azoth punched him in the nose. Logan's head rocked back.

"Logan!" the Sethi man shouted.

But Logan's mild expression was gone. His face was a mask, intense, but not furious. He grabbed Azoth's cloak and lifted him off the ground.

Azoth panicked; he threw punches blindly, screaming, his fists grazing Logan's cheeks and chin.

"Logan!"

"Stop it!" Logan shouted in Azoth's face. "Stop it!" Azoth went crazy, and Logan's intensity flashed into fury. He shifted his hands and held Azoth off the ground with one, then buried his other fist in Azoth's stom-ach once, twice. The wind rushed from Azoth's lungs. Then a fist the size of a sledge flattened his nose, blinding him with instant tears and pain.

Then, amid distant shouting, he felt himself being spun in a tight circle and—briefly—flying.

Azoth's head slapped against hardwood and the world flashed bright.

14

$\mathcal{L}$ogan had insisted on going upstairs to help the countess take care of young Kylar Stern. He was mortified, and apparently not solely because he'd lost his temper in front of Count Drake's pretty daughter. For Solon, it had been an instructive ten seconds.

Count Drake and Solon were left alone. The count led him to his office. "Why don't you sit down?" the count said, taking his own seat behind his desk. "Where are you from, Master Tofusin?"

It was either courtesy or bait. Solon chuckled. "That's the first time I've been asked that question." He gestured to himself as if to say, *Just look at my skin*.

The count said, "I don't see any clan rings, or any scars where they've been removed."

"Well, not all Sethi wear the rings."

"I was under the distinct impression that they did," Count Drake said.

"What is this? What are you after?"

"I'm curious about who you really are, Master Tofusin. Logan Gyre is not only a fine young man whom I regard almost as a son, he's also suddenly the lord of one of the most powerful houses in the land. I've never seen you or heard of you, and suddenly you're his adviser? That strikes me as peculiar. I don't care that you're Sethi—if you are—but I've spent some time on Hokkai and Tawgathu, and the only Sethi who don't pierce their cheeks are the exiles stripped of clan and family. But if you are an exile, you should have scars from your rings being torn out, and you have none."

"Your knowledge of our culture is admirable, but incomplete. I am of House Tofusin, Windseekers of the Royal House. My father's appointment was to Sho'cendi."

"An ambassador to the red mages?"

"Yes. Sho'cendi accepts students from all over the world. As I had no magical talent, I received my education among the merchants and nobles, who are not as tolerant. Not having the rings made life a little easier. There's more to it than that, but I don't think the rest of my story is any of your business."

"Fair enough."

"What took you to Seth?" Solon asked.

"Slavery," the count said. "Before I became fully part of the movement that finally ended slavery here seven years ago, I thought a more moderate path might work. I went to Hokkai to see if I could learn ways to make slaves' lives better."

From the small size of his house—which was very small for a noble, even one as low as a count—Solon knew that Count Drake hadn't been one of the slavers who felt guilty about his newfound wealth. He must have been a real crusader all along.

"It's totally different in Seth," Solon said. "The Year of Joy changes everything."

"Yes, I advanced the idea here, even got the law passed, but the Sa'kagé immediately suborned it. Instead of every slave being freed on the seventh year, slaves were to be freed seven years from the beginning of their indenture. The Sa'kagé claimed it was simpler, that it would be ridiculous to buy a slave in the sixth year and own them for only a month or a week. Of course, in practice, the Sa'kagé's people kept the records, so where in your country, the seventh year is full of celebration as every slave is freed, here the years passed and slaves were never freed. Slaves became slaves for life. They were beaten, scourged, given to the Death Games, their children sent to the baby farms."

"I've heard those became truly awful," Solon said.

"The Sa'kagé set them up, saying that they would be places where the children of prostitutes might be redeemed. Slaves, true, but redeemed. It sounded good, but it gave us places like the House of Mercy. Sorry, I shouldn't go on. It was a dark time. Is that boy ever coming down?"

"Maybe we should get started," Solon said. "I don't think this will wait, and from the way Logan was looking at your daughter, they might be talking a while."

The count chuckled. "Are you testing me now?"

"Does Duke Gyre know?"

"Yes. He and I are friends. Regnus is loath to demand control of Logan's flirtations, given the circumstances of his own marriage."

"I'm not familiar with those. Can you enlighten me?" Solon asked.

"It's not my place. Anyway, Logan and Serah will grow out of it. What appears to be the problem?"

"Catrinna Gyre."

"Careful," the count said.

"Did the duke give you letters that declared his son Lord Gyre in his absence?"

"He spoke of it, but he had to leave quickly. He said his steward would bring them."

"Lady Gyre has stolen the letters and destroyed them. Then she went to the queen."

"She went to whom?" The count was astonished.

"Is that unusual?"

"They have no love for each other. What happened?" Count Drake asked.

"Lady Gyre asked to be made Logan's guardian. The king overheard them. He came in and said he would take it under advisement. What does that mean?"

Count Drake removed his pince nez and rubbed the bridge of his nose. "It means that if he acts quickly, he can appoint a guardian for Logan."

"Will Catrinna Gyre do such a poor job?" Solon asked.

Count Drake sighed. "Legally, the king can put anyone in Logan's place that he wants so long as they're related to him, which means almost anyone in the nobility. And once he's got a guardian in place, even Regnus won't be able to rescind the appointment. Catrinna has just delivered House Gyre to the king."

"But you're Duke Gyre's solicitor—and he told you his wishes. Doesn't that carry any weight?" Solon asked.

"If the king were interested in the truth, yes. As is, to save the Gyres, we'd need the Gyre family parchment, the duke's Great Seal, and a reckless willingness to forge a state document. The king holds court in half an hour. I'd guess this will be the first item on the agenda. There's just no time."

Solon cleared his throat and produced a roll of heavy parchment and a large seal.

Count Drake grinned and snatched the parchment. "I think I suddenly like you, Master Tofusin."

"Wendel North helped me with the wording," Solon said. "I thought I'd leave the signature and the seal to you."

Count Drake rummaged through his desk, found a letter from the duke, and laid it on top of the writ of guardianship. With quick, sure strokes, he forged the duke's signature flawlessly. Count Drake looked up guiltily and said, "Let's just call it an artifact of a misspent youth."

Solon dribbled sealing wax on the parchment. "Then here's to misspent youth."

"Next time you'll move," Blint said as Azoth groaned his way back into consciousness.

"I don't think I'll ever move again. My head feels like someone threw it against a wall."

Blint laughed, the second time Azoth had heard him do that recently. He was sitting on the edge of Azoth's bed. "You did well. They thought you were embarrassed because you got knocked down in front of Drake's daughter, so they decided it was all harmless kid stuff. The young lord Gyre was mortified that he hit you—apparently he's a real big friendly giant, never loses his temper. The fact you're about a quarter his size and Serah was furious with him also helps. They were all quite impressed."

"Impressed? That's stupid."

"In their world fighting has rules, so fighting means risking embarrassment and pain and at worst risking your looks if you get a broken nose or an unfortunate scar. It doesn't mean dying or killing. In their world, you can fight a man and then become his friend. In fact, you're going to play it so Logan does become your friend, because with a man like him, you can only come out of this as a great friend or a terrible enemy. Do you understand that, *Kylar?* We'll work together on your new identity soon."

"Yes, sir. Sir, why didn't you want Master Tofusin to see you? That's why you made me fight Logan, isn't it? To be a distraction?"

"Solon Tofusin is a magus. Most magi—that's male mages—can't tell if you're Talented just by looking at you. On the other hand, most magae—female mages—can. There are disguises against their sight that I'll teach you later, but I didn't have the time to do it and I didn't feel like going upstairs and jumping out a window."

Azoth was confused. "But he doesn't act like a mage."

"And how would you know?" Durzo asked.

"Uh..." Azoth didn't think saying, "He isn't like the mages in stories" was going to please Durzo.

"The truth is," Durzo said, "Solon hasn't told Logan or anyone else that he's a mage, and you won't tell anyone either. When you know a man's secrets, you have power over him. A man's secret is his weakness. Every man has a weakness, no matter..." Master Blint's voice dropped to nothing, his eyes suddenly distant, lifeless. He stood and left without a word.

Azoth closed his eyes, confused. He wondered about his new master. He wondered about the guild. He wondered if Ja'laliel had bought review. He wondered how Jarl was doing. Most of all, he wondered about Doll Girl.

"Hey-ho, Azo."

"Hey-ho, Jay-Oh," Azoth said. Even as he gave the words the same stress he always had, Azoth felt part of himself die. This was supposed to be one of his last outings as Azoth. Soon, he would have to become Kylar. He would walk differently, talk differently. He wouldn't ever visit his old neighborhoods in the Warrens. But now he saw that Azoth's world was already dying, that he would never connect with Jarl again. It had nothing to do with the lies Kylar would tell, and everything to do with Rat. It was different now. It always would be.

Azoth and Jarl looked at each other for a long moment in the common room of Momma K's house. It was almost midnight, and the guild rats would soon be shooed out of the house. They were welcome in the common room all day, but they were allowed to sleep here only in the winter, and then only if they obeyed her rules: no fighting, no stealing, no going anywhere but the kitchen and the common room, and no bothering the adults who visited. Any guild rat who broke the rules got his entire guild banned from Momma K's for the winter. Usually, it was a death sentence for the offender, because it meant the whole guild would have to sleep in the sewers to stay warm, and they would kill him for that.

Still, the place was always crowded. There was a fireplace and a floor covered with soft rugs good for sleeping on. Those rugs had once been clean, but were now stained from their filthy bodies. Despite the damage, Momma K never got mad at them—and every few months, new rugs showed up. There were durable chairs the guild rats were allowed to sit on, toys, dolls, and piles of games they could play. Sometimes Momma K even brought them treats. Here they gambled and bragged and gossiped freely with anyone who was here, even children outside their own guild. It was the only place the guild rats were allowed to resemble children. It was the only safe place they knew.

Coming back, it looked different. What had seemed so recently the very lap of luxury now was just a plain room, with plain furnishings and simple toys because the guild rats would ruin anything better. They would stain everything and break anything delicate, not from malice but from ignorance. The place was the same; it was Azoth who had changed. Azoth—or Kylar, whichever he was—marveled at the stench of the guild rats. Didn't they smell themselves? Weren't they ashamed, or was it just him, ashamed to see what he had been?

As he always did after his reading lesson with Momma K, Azoth had looked for Jarl. But now that they were face to face, neither could find anything to say.

"I need your help," Azoth said finally. There was no way to cover what he wanted. He wasn't here to visit a friend. He was here to do a job.

"My help?"

"I need to know what's happened to Doll Girl. Where is she? And I need to know what's happening with the guilds."

"I guess you wouldn't know."

"No." Guilds weren't part of his life now. Nothing was like it used to be.

"Your master hit you?" Jarl asked, looking at Azoth's black eyes.

"I got this in a fight. He does hit me, but not like—" Azoth cut off.

"Not like Rat?"

"How is he?" Azoth said, trying to cover.

"Why don't you tell me? You're the one who killed him."

Azoth opened his mouth, but seeing two littles in Momma K's front room, stopped.

"Blint made you kill Rat to see if you could do it, didn't he?" Jarl asked, his voice low.

"No. Are you crazy?" In his head, he could hear the echoes of Master Blint's voice from their training: "Word gets out. Word always gets out."

Hurt filled Jarl's eyes, and he said nothing for a long time. "I shouldn't push, Azoth. I'm sorry. I should just thank you. Rat...he messed me up bad. I'm so confused all the time. I hated him, but sometimes.... When Rat disappeared and I saw you walking away with Blint..." Jarl blinked rapidly and stared away. "Sometimes I hate you. You left me with no one. But that's not right. You didn't do anything wrong. Just Rat...and me."

Azoth didn't know what to say.

Jarl blinked furiously again. "Shut up, Jarl. Shut up." He dashed the tears from his eyes with fists. "What do you need?"

There was something Azoth should say, he knew it. Some assurance he should give, but he didn't know what it was. Jarl had been his friend—was his friend, wasn't he?—but he'd changed. Azoth had changed. He was supposed to be Kylar now, but instead, he was just a fraud straddling two worlds and trying to hold on as they tore apart. Whatever the cataclysm named Rat had left Azoth holding onto, one thing was certain. A chasm had opened between him and Jarl, and Azoth was afraid to even approach it, didn't understand what it was, didn't know anything except that it made him feel dirty and scared. Jarl was letting him put the walls back up by asking his simple question—a simple question that could be answered simply, a problem that they could actually resolve.

"Doll Girl," Azoth said. He felt relieved to back away from his once-friend and guilty that he felt relieved.

"Oh," Jarl said. "You know she got...?"

"Is she all right now?"

"She's alive. But I don't know if she's going to make it. They make fun of her. Without you around, she isn't like she used to be. I've been sharing my food with her, but the guild's falling apart. Things are too bad. We don't have enough food."

The guild, not our guild. Azoth kept his face blank, refused to show how much that hurt. It shouldn't have hurt. He was the one who'd wanted out, he was the one who left, but it still made him feel empty.

You will be alone. You will be different. Always.

"Ja'laliel's almost dead; turns out Rat stole his review money. And now they lost the waterfront to Burning Man, and others are closing in."

"They?"

Jarl's face twisted. "If you've got to know, they threw me out of Black Dragon. Threw us all out. Didn't want buggers and Rat-lovers, they said."

"You don't have a guild?" Azoth asked. It was a disaster. Guild rats without a guild were fair game for anyone. That Jarl had stayed alive since being expelled was surprising, that he'd had food to share with Doll Girl was amazing, and that he was willing to was humbling.

"Some of us have banded together for a little while. They call us the Buggers. I'm going to try to join Two Fist on the north side. Rumor is they might get the market on Durdun soon," Jarl said.

That was Jarl. Always had a plan.

"They're willing to take Doll Girl, too?"

He was answered with guilty silence.

"I asked. I did, Azoth. They just won't do it. If you—" Jarl's mouth opened to say more, then closed.

"I'm not going to make you ask, Jarl. I've been looking for you to give it back." Azoth lifted his tunic and unwrapped the sash full of coins. He handed it to Jarl.

"Azoth, this—this is twice as heavy as it was."

"I'll take care of Doll Girl. Give me a couple weeks. Can you take care of her for that long?"

Jarl's eyes were filling with tears, and Azoth was afraid his would too. They called each other Jarl and Azoth now, not Jay-Oh and Azo.

Azoth said, "I'm going to tell Momma K how smart you are and see if she has work for you. You know, if things don't work out with Two Fist."

"You'd do that for me?"

"Sure, Jay-Oh."

"Azo?" Jarl said.

"Yeah?"

Jarl hesitated, swallowed. "I just wish..."

"Me too, Jarl. Me too."

The price of disobedience is death. The words kept running through his head every day as Azoth planned his disobedience.

Azoth's training was brutally hard, but it wasn't brutal. In the guilds, a Fist might beat you to make a point and make a mistake that left you permanently maimed. Master Blint never made mistakes. Azoth hurt exactly as much as Blint wanted him to. Usually, that was a lot.

But so what? Azoth had two meals a day. He could eat as much as he wanted, and Blint worked the soreness out of his muscles every day as they trained.

At first everything was curses and beatings. Azoth couldn't do anything right. But curses were just air, and beatings were just momentary pain. Blint would never maim Azoth, and if he chose to kill him, there was nothing Azoth could do to stop him anyway.

It was the closest thing to safety he'd ever known.

Within weeks, he realized he liked the training. The sparring, the blunted practice weapons, the obstacle courses, even the herb lore. Learning reading with Momma K was hard. *But so what?* Two hours of frustration a day was nothing. Azoth's life was good.

Within a month, he realized that he was Talented. It wasn't obvious, and if he hadn't been so keyed in to Master Blint's every mood and reaction, he would never have noticed, but now and then, he'd see a faint look of surprise as he mastered some new skill more quickly than Master Blint had expected.

It made him work all the harder, hoping to see that look not once a week, but once a day. For her part, Momma K made him decipher squiggles for longer than he could imagine. She had a way of smiling and saying just the right thing that it pulled him along through the hours. Words were power, she said. Words were another sword for the man who wielded them well. And he would need them if the world was to believe that he was Kylar Stern, so Momma K worked with him on his alternate identity, quizzing him with likely questions other nobles would ask, helping him come up with harmless stories about growing up in eastern Cenaria, and teaching him the rudiments of etiquette. She told him Count Drake would teach him the rest once he went to live with the Drakes. When Azoth walked in the Drakes' door, she said, he would be Kylar forever after. Blint would train him in a safe house on the east side. Momma K would meet with him in one of her homes on the east side. Only when he started accompanying Blint on jobs would he return to the Warrens.

Azoth worked hard for her and without complaint except for one time when he got disgusted at his own stupidity and threw a book across the room. He worked in the hell of Momma K's displeasure for a week until he brought her some flowers he'd stolen and she forgave him.

He'd given Jarl plenty of money to take care of Doll Girl, but Jarl wouldn't be able to just give her the money; someone would steal it. The worst part of it was that she was alone. Mute and with a horribly beaten face, she wouldn't be making any friends, either.

The price of disobedience is death, Master Blint had said. And he'd forbidden him to see Doll Girl again. Ever.

Momma K told Azoth that Master Blint would eventually come to like him and trust him, but that when he said things like that, for now Azoth should take it as law. That made Azoth hopeful—until she clarified: street law, which was immutable and omnipotent; not the pathetic king's law. It was a shame, because Azoth had to see Doll Girl one last time.

When he did get his chance, it was through no guile of his own. Master Blint had a job, so he simply left Azoth to his own devices. He left a list of chores, too, but Azoth knew that if he hurried, he could finish all the chores and still have several hours before he was supposed to meet with Momma K for his reading lesson.

He threw himself into his work with a fury. He dusted the weapons room, climbing up on a ladder to reach the higher rows of weapons and the equipment out of his reach. He checked and cleaned the wood practice weapons. He oiled and cleaned the weapons Master Blint had used recently. He worked a different kind of oil into the leather targets and dummies that Master Blint made him attack by the hour. He checked the seams on the ones Master Blint himself had kicked, and finding several burst, sewed them shut again. He wasn't very good with a needle, but Master Blint tolerated less than perfect work here—if nowhere else. He swept the floor, and as always, didn't throw the dirt out into the street, but collected it in a small bin. Master Blint didn't want him to leave the safe house. Not ever, unless he was under direct orders.

He found himself cleaning one of Blint's daggers a second time. It was a long thin blade with tiny gold filigree. Through chance or age, the gold was thin in the grooves that had been etched for it, so blood had collected in every narrow groove of the filigree—Blint had used this blade recently, and he must have been in a hurry when he sheathed it. So Azoth found himself using the point of another fine dagger to pick out the blood.

He should have soaked the blade in water and then scrubbed it vigorously, but this was his last chore. It was still three hours until he was supposed to be at Momma K's. If he had to work on chores until then, it wouldn't be his fault that he didn't leave.

"What happens if you do nothing?" Blint had asked him. "Nothing. There's a price and a terrible freedom to that, boy. Remember it." Master Blint had been speaking of making your move on a deader when things looked risky, but Azoth could feel the burden of those words now.

If I do something, what's the worst that could happen? Master Blint kills me. That was pretty bad. The odds of it were low, though. Unlike other wetboys who might spend their whole lives in the Warrens, Master Blint only took jobs from people who could afford his prices. That usually meant nobles. That always meant east side. So he'd be on the opposite side of the city from Azoth.

The real worst case if I do nothing? Doll Girl dies.

He put down the dagger with a grimace.

Finding Doll Girl was easier said than done. The Black Dragon guild had ceased to exist. It was just gone. Kylar went to their old territory and found that it had been swallowed by Red Hand, Burning Man, and Rusty Knife. The old Black Dragons scrawled on buildings and aqueducts were already fading. He wore a pair of daggers, but he didn't have to use them. Once, he was stopped by some Burning Men, but one of the bigs used to be one of his lizards. The boy spoke a few words to the others who were about to try to rob Azoth, and they eased away. The lizard never said a word to him.

He crisscrossed their old territory half a dozen times, but he never found Doll Girl. Once, he thought he saw Corbin Fishill, someone he'd always known was important, and who he now knew—Master Blint had told him—was one of the Nine. But all the guild rats he saw kept their distance.

Time was running out when Azoth finally thought of the old bakery. Doll Girl was there, alone. She had her back to him, and for a moment, he paused, afraid to get her attention. Then she turned.

Rat's sadism was evident. A month hadn't been long enough for her wounds to heal. It had only been long enough to show both what her face must have looked like for the last weeks, and what it would look like for the rest of her life. Rat had beaten her first, just beat her into submission or unconsciousness. Then he'd taken a knife to her face.

One deep cut looped from the corner of her left eye to the corner of her mouth. It had been stitched with dozens of tiny stitches, but the resulting scar would tug the corner of Doll Girl's mouth up into an unnatural grin forever. Her other cheek bore a broad X-shaped cut, which was matched again by a smaller X across her lips in front. Eating, smiling, frowning— moving her mouth at all must have been excruciating. One of her eyes was still swollen, and Azoth wasn't sure if she'd ever be able to see out of it again. The rest of the wounds looked like they would fade. A scab on her forehead, the barest yellow around her other eye as the black faded, and a nose that must have been reset because Azoth was sure Rat had broken it.

All in all, her face was, and was supposed to be, a testament to cruelty. Rat wanted anyone who ever looked at Doll Girl to know that she hadn't just had an accident. He wanted everyone to know that this had been done deliberately. For a moment, Azoth wished Rat's death had been even more horrible.

Then time seemed to start again. He was staring at Doll Girl, staring at his friend's face with open horror. Her eyes, that had been so full of surprise and sudden hope, brimmed full with tears. She covered herself and turned away, crying silently, her thin shoulders shaking.

He sat next to her. "I came as soon as I could. I've got a master now and I had to disobey him just to be here, but I couldn't leave you here. Things have been bad, huh?" She started sobbing.

He could just imagine the names they must have called her. Sometimes he wanted to kill everyone in the Warrens. How could they make fun of Doll Girl? How could they hurt her? It was a miracle she was still alive. A miracle, and Jarl. Jarl must have risked his life a dozen times.

Azoth scooted over and pulled her close. She turned and clung to him as if her tears would wash her away. He held her and cried.

Time passed. Azoth felt like he'd been squeezed dry. He wasn't sure how long he'd held her, but he knew it had been too long. "I have good news," he told her.

She looked up at him with those big brown eyes.

"Come with me," he said.

Doll Girl followed him out of the Warrens, over the Vanden Bridge, and to Count Drake's. Her eyes widened as they headed toward the count's house, and further when the old porter opened the door for Azoth and showed them in.

Count Drake was in his office. He rose and ushered them in, somehow not even registering surprise at how awful Doll Girl's face looked. He was a better person than Azoth.

"Has Azoth told you why you're here, young lady?" the count asked. The

name was a deliberate choice, Azoth saw. Doll Girl was part of Azoth's life—
she wouldn't be part of Kylar's. She wasn't going to know his new name.

Doll Girl shook her head shyly, clinging to Azoth.

"We've found a family for you, Doll Girl," Count Drake said. "They
want you to come and be their daughter. They're going to take care of you.
You'll never have to sleep on the streets again. They serve in a house here
on the east side. If you don't want to, you never have to go back to the Warrens ever again."

Of course, it had all been a little more involved than that. Count Drake
had known the family for some time. They had taken in other slaveborn
orphans over the years, but couldn't afford to feed another. So Azoth had
sworn that he would provide for her out of his wages, which were already
generous, and which Master Blint had told him would increase as he
became more useful. Count Drake hadn't been enamored of keeping any
secret from Master Blint, but after Azoth had explained what had happened, he'd been willing to help.

Doll Girl clung to Azoth, either not understanding or not believing what
the count had just said.

Count Drake stood. "Well, I'm sure you have some things you probably
wish to tell her, and I need to get the coach in order, so if you'll excuse
me?" He left them alone, and Doll Girl looked at Azoth with accusing eyes.

"You never were dumb," he said.

She squeezed his hand, hard.

"My master ordered me not to see you. Today is the last time we ever get
to see each other." She tugged on his hand, face pugnacious. "Yes, ever," he
said. "I don't want it to be this way, but he'll kill me if he finds out I defied
him even this much. I'm sorry. Please don't be mad at me."

She was crying again and there was nothing he could do.

"I have to go now. He might be back any time. I'm sorry." He tore his
eyes from her and stepped toward the door.

"Don't leave me."

The voice sent a lance of ice down his spine. He turned, incredulous. It
was a little girl voice, exactly like you'd expect if you didn't know Doll Girl
was a mute.

"Please?" Doll Girl said. It was a pretty voice, incongruous coming out
of a beaten mask of a face Rat had left her.

Azoth's eyes filled with tears again, and he ran out the door—

Straight into someone tall and lean and as hard as if he'd been cut out of
solid rock. Azoth fell on his butt and stared up in horror.

Master Blint's face was purple with fury. "You dare?" he shouted. "After all I've done for you, you defy me? I just killed one of the Nine and what do you do? You walk around the killing ground for two hours, so everyone knows Blint's apprentice was there. You may have cost me everything!"

He swept Azoth off the ground as if he were a kitten and hit him. Azoth's tunic tore in Blint's hand as he fell back from the force of the blow. But Blint came forward, and this time his closed fist crashed against Azoth's jaw.

Azoth's face rebounded off the count's floor and he barely saw Doll Girl flying at Master Blint as the huge black sword cleared its sheath.

"Don't hurt her!" Azoth shouted. Insanely, he threw himself at Blint and grabbed Retribution's blade, but Blint was a force of nature. He didn't even slow as he scooped Doll Girl up and deposited her in the hall. He locked the door, unlocked it, and relocked it in rapid succession. He turned back to Azoth, but whatever he was about to say died. The great black sword was still locked in Azoth's hands, cutting to the bone. Except that now it wasn't black. The blade was glowing blue.

Incandescent blue fire surrounded Azoth's hand, burning cold into his cut fingers, spreading down the blade—

"No, not that! It's mine!" Blint cried. He flung the sword aside as if it were an adder, away from both of them. If there had been fury in his eyes before, now it turned to absolute unreasoning rage. Azoth didn't even see the first blow. He didn't even know how he'd reached the floor again. Something wet and sticky was blocking out his vision.

Then the world faded into repeated heavy blows and exploding light and pain and the sharp garlicky breath of Master Blint and distant shouting and banging on a door that seemed further and further away.

16

*D*urzo gazed into the frothy brown ale as if it held answers. It didn't, and he had a choice to make. The usual forced gaiety of the brothel swirled around him, but nobody male or female bothered him. Perhaps it was Retribution unsheathed on the table in front of him. Perhaps it was merely the look on his face.

Don't hurt her! Azoth had yelled. As if Durzo would murder some seven-year-old girl. What kind of a monster did the boy think he was? Then he remembered beating the shit out of the boy, artlessly pounding that yielding child flesh, beating him unconscious before Count Drake broke the door down and grabbed him. He'd almost killed Count Drake for that, he'd been so wild. The count had fixed such a look on Durzo—damn Count Drake and his damn holy eyes.

That incandescent blue. Damn it. Damn all magic. In that flash of blue on Retribution, he'd seen his hope die. The hope had been dying since Vonda died, but that blue was a door slamming shut forever. It meant Azoth was worthy as Durzo was not, as if all of Durzo's years of service were worth nothing. The boy was taking from him all that made him special. What did that leave for Durzo Blint?

Ashes. Ashes, and blood, and nothing more.

Suddenly the sword Retribution before him seemed a mockery. *Retribution? Giving people what they deserve? If I really did that, I'd shove that damn blade down my own throat.*

The last time he'd been so close to madness had been when Vonda died, four months and six days ago. Sighing, he swirled the ale around in the glass, but he didn't drink. Time enough for that later. Later, after he made his decision, he'd need a drink. He'd need twelve, no matter what he decided.

He'd drunk a lot with Vonda. It pissed her sister off. Of course, the whole relationship had pissed Momma K off. She'd forbidden Durzo to see her innocent little sister. She'd forbidden Vonda to see the wetboy. Momma K, so smart in other matters, had probably done more to get their relationship going than anything. Surrounded by easy flesh, whether he paid for it or not, Gwinvere's little sister was suddenly intriguing. He wanted to know if the virginal bit was an act.

It was. He'd been disappointed but had hidden it. It was hypocrisy, anyway, and she'd had plenty of other mysteries. Vonda didn't always treat him well, but at least she didn't fear him. He didn't think she understood him enough to fear him. She seemed to just glide along on the surface of life while others had to plunge into the sewer water. Durzo hadn't understood her, and it had entranced him.

After their affair started, he might have kept it secret. He could have; he knew Gwinvere's schedule well enough that they could have kept things going for years. Even with Gwinvere's insight, Durzo knew how to be inscrutable. But it hadn't happened. Vonda had told her. Probably announced it immediately, if Durzo knew Vonda. It might have been a little callous, but Vonda didn't know what she was doing.

"End this now, Durzo Blint," Gwinvere had told him, quite calmly.

"She'll destroy you. I love my sister, but she will be your ruin." It had all been words. Words to get Gwinvere's way, as always. With all her power, it infuriated her that she couldn't run the lives of those she really wanted to.

She'd been right, of course. Maybe not in the way she had meant it, but she'd been right. Gwinvere always had understood him better than anyone else, and he'd understood her. They were mirrors to each other. Gwinvere Kirena would have been perfect for him—if he could love what he saw in the mirror.

Why am I thinking about this? It's all old shit. It's all finished. There was a choice to be made: did he raise the boy and hope, or did he kill him now?

Hope. Right. Hope is the lies we tell ourselves about the future. He'd hoped before. Dared to dream about a different life, but when it came time—

"You look pensive, Gaelan Starfire," a Ladeshian bard said, seating himself across from Durzo without waiting to be asked.

"I'm deciding who to kill. Call me that again and you jump to the front of the list, Aristarchos."

The bard smiled with the confidence of a man who knows he has perfect white teeth that only set off a handsome face. By the Night Angels.

"We've been awfully curious about what's been happening for the last few months."

"You and the Society can go to hell," Durzo said.

"I think you like the attention, *Durzo Blint*. If you wanted us dead, we'd be dead. Or are you really bound by this code of retribution? It's of considerable debate in the society."

"Still fighting over the same questions, huh? Don't you all have anything better to do? Talk talk talk. Why don't you do something productive for once?"

"We're trying, Durzo. In fact, that's why I'm here. I want to help you."

"How kind."

"You've lost it, haven't you?" Aristarchos asked. "Have you lost it, or has it abandoned you? Do the stones really choose their own masters?"

Durzo noticed he was spinning the knife from finger to finger again. It wasn't to intimidate the Ladeshian—who laudably enough didn't even glance at it—it just kept his hands busy. It was nothing. He stopped it. "Here's why I've never been friends with any of you, Aristarchos: I don't know if your little circle has ever been interested in me, or if it's only interested in my power. Once, I was almost convinced to share some of my mysteries, but I realized that what I share with one of you, I share with all of you. So tell me, why would I give my enemies such power?"

"Is that what we've come to?" Aristarchos asked. "Enemies? Why then do you not wipe us from the face of the earth? You're uniquely suited to such a task."

"I don't kill without cause. Fear isn't enough to motivate me. It may be beyond your comprehension, but I can hold power without using it."

Aristarchos stroked his chin. "Then you are a better man than many have feared. I see now why you were chosen in the first place." Aristarchos stood. "Know this, Durzo Blint. I am far from home and have not the means I might wish, but if you call on me, I will give you what help I can. And knowing that you have deemed the cause just will be enough explanation for me. Good day."

The man walked out of the brothel, smiling and winking at the whores who seemed disappointed to lose his business. He wore his charm like a mask, Durzo saw.

The masks change, but the masquers remain the same, don't they? Durzo had lived with the bilge waste of humanity for so long, he saw filth in every heart. He knew the filth was there; he was right about that. Filth and darkness were even in Rimbold Drake's heart. But Drake didn't act from that darkness, did he? No. That masquer—if only that one—had changed.

Fear isn't enough to motivate me, he'd said—while planning to murder a child. *What kind of a monster am I?*

He was caught now. Truly and desperately caught. He'd just killed Corbin Fishill. The man's death had been sanctioned by the Shinga and the rest of the Nine. Corbin had been managing the guilds as if he were in Khalidor, setting guild against guild, encouraging open war between them and doing absolutely nothing to regulate brutality within the guilds. Khalidorans did such things in the belief that the best would naturally rise. But the Sa'kagé wanted members, not monsters.

Worse, they now had some indication that Corbin actually had been working for Khalidor. That was inexcusable. Not taking the work, but taking it without reporting it to the rest of the Nine. Loyalties had to be to the Sa'kagé first.

The kill had been sanctioned, and it had been just. That didn't mean that Corbin's friends would accept it. Durzo had killed members of the Nine before, but he always took extra care to conceal whose work it was. Now Azoth had tromped around his killing grounds for hours, a little before the job was done and a lot after. Enough people knew or guessed Durzo had taken Azoth as his apprentice that they couldn't fail to link the two. It was sloppy wet work, they'd say. Maybe Durzo Blint is slipping.

Being the best made him a target. The appearance of weakness gave every second-rate wetboy hope that they could move up. Azoth couldn't have known, of course. Still didn't know so many things. But in that flash of blue light from Retribution's blade, Durzo had seen his own death. If he let the boy live, Durzo would die. Sooner or later.

And there it was. The divine economy. For someone to live, someone had to die.

Durzo Blint made his decision, and started drinking.

"Master Blint hasn't come to see me."

"No," Momma K said.

"It's been four days. You said he wasn't mad anymore," Azoth said, making fists with his hands. He thought he had cut them, but they were fine. Lots of other places on his body hurt, so he hadn't just imagined being beaten, but his hands were fine.

"Three days. And he's not mad. Drink this."

"No. I don't want any more of that stuff. It makes me feel worse." He regretted the words as soon as he said them. Momma K's eyebrows went up and her eyes went cold. Even huddled in warm blankets in a spare bedroom here in her house, when her eyes turned frosty, nothing could make you feel warm.

"Child, let me tell you a story. Have you ever heard of the Snake of Haran?" Azoth shook his head.

"The snake has seven heads, but each time you cut one head off, two more grow in its place."

"Really? There's really such a thing?"

"No. In Haran they call it the Snake of Ladesh. It's imaginary."

"Then why did you tell me about it?" Azoth asked.

"Are you being deliberately obtuse?" When he didn't answer, she said, "If you'll let me finish, you'll see the story is an analogy. Analogies are lies grown-ups tell."

"Why?" Being stuck in bed was making Azoth petulant.

"Why does anyone tell lies? Because they're useful. Now drink your medicine and then shut your mouth," Momma K said.

Azoth knew he was pushing it, so he didn't ask any more. He drank the thick mint-and-anise-flavored brew.

"Right now the Sa'kagé has its own Snake of Haran, Azoth...*Kylar*. Do you know Corbin Fishill?"

Azoth nodded. Corbin was the handsome, impressive young man who had sometimes come and talked to Ja'laliel.

"Corbin was one of the Nine. He ran the children's guilds."

"Was?" Azoth almost squeaked. He wasn't supposed to know Corbin was even important, much less how important.

"Durzo killed him three days ago. When the baby farms were shut down, the Sa'kagé was given a chance to literally raise its own army. But Corbin was allowing or encouraging guild war that was wiping out the slaveborn. And he was a spy. The Sa'kagé thought he was a Ceuran spy, but now they think he was taking money from Khalidor. The Khalidorans paid him in Ceuran gold, probably in case he was found, and also so he wouldn't start spending the money immediately and bring attention to himself.

"Now that Corbin is dead, his things have been searched, and unfortunately, there hasn't been any clear answer. If he was Khalidoran, he was far more dangerous than we had thought, and the Sa'kagé should have brought him in and had him tortured until they knew for sure, but at the time, they thought it was more important to set a graphic example of what happens to those who mismanage Sa'kagé endeavors. The problem now is bigger.

"We don't think Corbin was in place long enough to cultivate any loyalty to Khalidor among the guilds—street rats don't care much where their meals come from—but the fact Khalidor would work on taking over the guilds tells us that they are thinking long term."

"How do you know he wasn't just the easiest person they could get in the Sa'kagé?"

Momma K smiled. "We don't. Khalidor is putting down some rebellions right now, and it's not going well for them. But the Godking has earned a reputation as a man who plans for victory, and my guess is that he thinks it may be years before he's ready to march south, but he wants Cenaria to fall at the slightest blow when he does. If he controls the Sa'kagé, taking the city will be easy. Our problem is that if he was able to get a man as highly placed as Corbin, then there may be dozens of others. The other heads of the snake may show up at any time. Anyone we trust may be working for Khalidor."

"Why's that your problem?" Azoth asked.

"It's my problem because I'm one of the Nine, too, Kylar. I'm the Mistress of Pleasures."

Azoth's mouth formed a little O. Always before, the Sa'kagé had been something dangerous, huge, and distant. He supposed it fit—everyone knew Momma K had been a whore and that she was wealthy—but he'd never even thought of it. Being the Mistress of Pleasures meant that Momma K controlled all of the prostitution in Cenaria. Everyone who plied the pleasure trade ultimately answered to her.

She smiled. "Aside from my girls' more...strenuous duties, they also keep their ears open. You'd be amazed at how talkative men can be in front of what they think is just a dumb whore. I'm in charge of the Sa'kagé's spies. I need to know what Khalidor is doing. If I don't know, the Sa'kagé doesn't know, and if we don't know, the country may fall. Believe me, we do not want Garoth Ursuul as our king."

"Why are you telling me all this?" Azoth said. "I'm nobody."

"Azoth was nobody. You are about to become Kylar Stern," she said, "And I think you're smarter than Durzo gives you credit for. I'm telling you because we need you on our side. Azoth was stupid to go wandering the other day, and it may cost you or Durzo your lives. But if you had known what was happening, you wouldn't have gone there. You did the wrong thing, but Durzo shouldn't have beaten you for showing initiative. In fact, I'm sure he's sorry for beating you, though he'll never apologize. It isn't in the man to admit he's wrong. We need you to be more than an apprentice, Kylar. We need you to be an ally. Are you ready for that?"

Azoth—Kylar—nodded slowly. "What do you want me to do?"

Kylar tried to gawk at the right things as he was ushered through the Gyre estate. Azoth, Momma K had told him, would gawk at anything big or gold. Baronet Kylar Stern would gawk only at things that were both—and the art. Logan had invited him to visit to make amends for hitting him, and Kylar's first job for the Sa'kagé was to make sure they became friends.

The porter escorted him to another, better-dressed man—Kylar almost greeted him as Duke Gyre before realizing he must be the Gyre's chamberlain. The chamberlain took him through a vast entry hall with dual stairs that climbed three stories flanking an enormous marble statue of two men, twins, facing each other in battle, each seeing the same opening in the other's defense, each lunging. It was one of the most famous statues in the world, Momma K had told Kylar: The Grasq Twins' Doom. In history, Momma K said, the Grasq twins had been heavily armored and during a long battle each had lost the thin tabards that at the time were all men wore over plate mail and all that identified them if they were separated from their standard bearers. They had indeed killed each other, though each had avoided the other in earlier battles. Here, the men were naked except for a shield and sword. Because of the shields' placement, each was seeing his twin's face for the first time even as he struck the death blow.

The chamberlain took Kylar up the stairs and down one long wing of the estate. The hallway was wider than most of the alleys in the Warrens. Both sides were crowded with marble busts and paintings of men speaking, men fighting, men seizing women, families moving, women mourning, the aftermath of battles, and horrible monsters boiling out of gaps in the ground. Every picture was framed with heavy gold leaf. Most were big. Walking behind the chamberlain, Kylar could gawk as much as he wanted, and he did. Then they stopped at a huge door. The chamberlain rapped on it with the staff he carried and opened the door to a library with dozens of shelves in orderly rows and the walls lined with books and scrolls to a height of two stories.

"My lord, Baronet Kylar Stern."

Logan Gyre rose from a table with an open scroll laid across it. "Kylar! I was just finishing—I borrowed this scroll from—oh, never mind. Welcome!"

"Thank you for inviting me, Duke Gyre; your estate is beautiful. The statue of the Grasq twins is breathtaking." He was reciting it the way Momma K had taught him, but now he meant it.

"Please, Logan. You're most kind. You really like it?" Logan asked.

The "you're most kind" gave him away. Logan was trying as hard to be an adult as Kylar was. Kylar was nervous because he was a fraud, but "Duke" Logan felt like a fraud, too. The title was too big and too new for him to feign comfort convincingly. So Kylar answered honestly, "Actually, I think it's amazing. I just wish they weren't naked."

Logan burst out laughing. "I know! Most the time I don't notice it anymore, but every once in a while I come in the door and—there's two huge naked men in my house. Because of my new duties I'm meeting all of my father's retainers and friends, again. Really it's a chance for ladies to introduce their daughters and hope I fall madly in love. I was greeting a lady and her daughter, I won't name names, but they are beautiful women and very prim, very modest. So I'm pretty tall, right? and they both have to really look up to look me in the eye, and as I'm talking and I'm in the middle of a story and the mom is tittering and the daughter looks utterly captivated, and I start to wonder if I've got something in my hair or on my ear or something, because they both keep glancing just a bit to the side."

"Oh no," Kylar said, laughing.

"I glance over my shoulder, and there's ... well, there, three times life size, is marble...genitalia. And there's this moment where they realize that I've noticed that they've been looking over my shoulder the whole time, and I realize this is the first time that the daughter has ever seen a naked man—and I totally forget what story I was telling them."

They laughed together, Kylar desperately thankful that Logan had given enough context so he could figure out what "genitalia" meant. Did all nobles talk like this? What if next time Logan gave the punch line without the context? Logan pointed to a portrait on the library wall of a square-jawed bald man dressed in an unfamiliar style. "I have him to thank for that. My great-great-great grandfather, the art lover."

Kylar smirked, but he felt he'd been slapped. Logan knew things about his great-great-great grandfather. Kylar didn't even know who his father was. There was a silence, and Kylar knew it was his turn to fill it. "I, uh, heard that the Grasq twins actually led like six battles against each other."

"You know their story?" Logan asked. "Not many people our age do."

Belatedly, Kylar realized the risk of posing as a story lover to this man who loved books—and could actually read them. "I really like old stories," Kylar said. "But my parents don't really have any use for me 'wasting my time filling my head with stories.'"

"You really do like stories? Aleine always starts pretending to snore when I talk about history." *Aleine? Oh, Aleine Gunder, Prince Aleine Gunder X.* Logan's world really was different. "Look at this," he beckoned Kylar to the table. "Here, read this part."

Be happy to, if I could read. Kylar's heart seized up. His disguise was still so fragile. "You're making me feel like my tutors," he said, waving it off. "I don't want to read for an hour while you're twiddling your thumbs. Why don't you tell me the good parts?"

"I feel like I'm doing all the talking," Logan said, suddenly awkward. "It's kind of rude."

Kylar shrugged. "I don't think you're being rude. Is it a new story, or what?"

Logan's eyes lit up and Kylar knew he was safe. "No, it's the end of the Alkestia Cycle, right before the Seven Kingdoms fall. My father's having me study the great leaders of the past. In this case, Jorsin Alkestes, of course. When they were under siege at Black Barrow, his right hand man, Ezra the Mad—well, it wasn't Black Barrow yet, and Ezra didn't go hide out in Ezra's Wood for another fifty years or something—anyway, Ezra's maybe the best magus ever, behind Emperor Jorsin Alkestes himself. They're under siege at what's now Black Barrow and Ezra starts making the most amazing stuff: the war hammers of Oren Razin; fire and lightning traps even un-Talented soldiers can use; Curoch, the sword of power; Iures, the staff of law; and then these six magic artifacts, *ka'kari*. They each look like a glowing ball, but the Six Champions can squeeze one and it melts and covers their whole bodies like a second skin and gives them power over their element. Arikus Daadrul gets this skin of silver liquid metal that makes him impervious to blades. Corvaer Blackwell becomes Corvacr the Red, the master of fire. Trace Arvagulania goes from grossly ugly to the most beautiful woman of the era. Oren Razin gets earth, weighs a thousand pounds and turns his skin to stone. Irenaea Blochwei gets the power of everything green and growing. Shrad Marden gets water and can suck the very liquid from a man's blood.

"The thing that has always made me curious is that Jorsin Alkestes was a great leader. He brought together so many Talented people, and lots of them were difficult and egotistical, and he put them in harness together, and they *worked*. But at the end, he insults one of his best friends, Acaelus Thorne, and gives a ka'kari to Shrad Marden instead, whom he doesn't even like. Do you know Acaelus Thorne?"

"I've heard the name," Kylar offered. That much was true. Sometimes the guild rats would huddle around a window to one of the taverns when a bard visited, but they could only hear bits and pieces of the stories.

"Acaelus was this amazing fighter but a noble fool. No subtlety. He hated lies, politics, and magic, but put a sword in his hand, and he'd go charging an enemy force solo if he had to. He was so crazy and so good that his men would follow him anywhere. But he was all about honor, and seeing lesser men honored before him was a huge insult. It was that insult that led Acaelus to betray Jorsin. How could Jorsin have missed it? He had to have known he was insulting him."

"What do you think?" Kylar asked.

Logan scrubbed a hand through his hair. "It's probably something boring, like that there was a war going on, and everyone was exhausted and starving and not thinking clearly and Jorsin just made a mistake."

"So what does that teach you about being a leader?" Kylar asked.

Logan looked perplexed. "Eat your vegetables and get enough sleep?"

"How about 'be nice to your inferiors, or they might kick your ass'?" Kylar suggested.

"Are you asking me to spar, Baronet Stern?"

"Your exalted dukeliness, it will be my pleasure to take you down."

$\mathcal{K}$ylar stepped into the safe house, flushed from his victory. He'd got three touches to Logan's two. Logan fought better, but as Momma K had told Kylar, he'd also grown a foot in the last year and hadn't adjusted to his new height yet. "Not only did I just make Logan Gyre my friend," Kylar said, "I also beat him in sparring."

Durzo didn't even look up from the calcinator. He turned the flame up higher beneath the copper dish. "Good. Now never spar with him again. Hand me that."

Hurt, Kylar took a flask from under the whirling tubes of the alembic and gave it to him. Durzo poured the thick blue mixture onto the calcinator. For the moment, it sat there, still. Small bubbles began forming and within moments the mixture was boiling rapidly.

"Why not?" Kylar asked.

"Get the slops, boy." Kylar grabbed the pig's slop bowl and brought it to the table.

"We fight differently from what any of this city's sword masters teach. If you spar with Logan, you will adopt his by-the-book style and become a worthless fighter, or you'll give away that you're being taught something utterly different, or both."

Kylar scowled at the calcinator. His master was right, of course, and even if he weren't, his word was law. The blue mixture was now a dark blue powder. Durzo lifted the copper plate from the flames with a thick wool pad and scraped the powder into the slop bowl. He grabbed another copper plate and poured more of the blue mixture into it and put it above the flames, setting the first aside to cool with a heavy mitt. "Master, do you know why Jorsin Alkestes would insult his best friend by not giving him a ka'kari?"

"Maybe he asked too many questions."

"Logan said Acaelus Thorne was the most honorable of Jorsin's friends, but he betrayed Jorsin and that led to the fall of the Seven Kingdoms," Kylar said.

"Most people aren't strong enough for our creed, Kylar, so they believe comforting illusions, like the gods, or Justice, or the basic goodness of man. Those illusions fail in war. It breaks men. That's probably what happened to Acaelus."

"Are you sure?" Kylar asked. Logan's reading of it had been so different.

"Sure?" Blint asked, scornfully. "I'm not sure about what the nobles here did seven years ago when they ended slavery. How would anyone be sure about what happened hundreds of years ago far away? Take that to the pig." Kylar picked up the slops and took them to the pig they'd recently acquired for Master Blint's experiments.

As he was returning, he saw Blint staring at him as if about to say something. Then there was a small whoosh as flame leaped from the copper plate behind Master Blint. Before Kylar could flinch, Blint whirled around. A phantom hand stretched out from his hands and grabbed the metal plate directly from the fire and set it down on the table. Then the hand was gone. It happened so fast, Kylar wasn't sure he hadn't imagined it.

The plate was smoking and what should have been blue powder was now a black crust. A black crust that Kylar had no doubt he would soon be scraping off until the copper shone.

Blint swore. "See, you get caught up in the past and you become useless to the present. Come on, let's see if that stinking pig's still alive. Then we need to do something with your hair."

The pig wasn't still alive, and after the amount of poison it had ingested, it wasn't safe to eat, so Kylar spent half the day cutting it into pieces and burying it. After that, Master Blint made him strip to the waist and rubbed a pungent paste through his hair. It burned his scalp and Blint made him keep it in for an hour. But when he finally rinsed the hair clean, Blint showed him his own reflection in the glass and he barely recognized himself. His hair was white blond.

"Just be thankful you're young, or I would have had to smear it on your eyebrows, too," Blint said. "Now get dressed. The Azoth clothes. The Azoth persona."

"I get to go with you? On a job?"

"Get dressed."

"I understand why 'Apparent Consumption' is nine hundred gunders. I'm sure you have to do multiple poisonings to mimic the disease," the noble said. "But fifteen hundred for apparent self-murder? Ridiculous. Stab your man and put the knife in his hand."

"How about we start again," Master Blint said quietly. "You speak as if

I'm the best wetboy in the city, and I'll speak as if there's a chance this side of hell that I'll take the job."

The tension sat thick in the upstairs room of the inn. Lord General Brant Agon wasn't pleased, but he took a breath, ran a hand through his gray hair, and said, "Why does faking a suicide cost fifteen hundred gold?"

"A properly staged suicide takes months," Master Blint said. "Depending upon the deader's history. If I'm after a known melancholic, that can be shortened to six weeks. If he's tried to suicide before, it can be as little as a week. I gain access in one way or another and administer special concoctions."

Azoth was trying to pay attention, but there was something about being back in his old clothes that made the illusions of the last weeks come crashing down. Kylar was gone—and not because Azoth was following orders and pretending to be Azoth. Kylar had been a mask of confidence. It had fooled Logan, and it had fooled Azoth for a little while, but the mask had fallen away. He was Azoth. He was weak. He didn't understand what he was doing here, or why, and he was scared.

Blint continued, not so much as glancing at him, "The deader becomes depressed, withdrawn, suspicious. Symptoms gradually worsen. Then maybe a favorite pet dies. The target is already peevish and paranoid, and soon he lashes out at his friends. The friends who visit—at least those who take refreshment—grow irritable while they are with the deader. They quarrel. They stop visiting. Sometimes the target writes the note himself. Sometimes he even commits the suicide himself, though I monitor that closely to make sure he chooses an appropriate method for the effect desired. When given proper time, no one suspects anything but self-murder. The family itself will often hush up the details, and scatter what little evidence there is."

"By the High King's beard, is such a thing possible?" the lord general asked.

"Possible? Yes. Difficult? Very. It takes a considerable number of carefully mixed poisons—do you know that everyone reacts differently to poisons?—and a huge amount of my time. If a forged note is required, the target's correspondence and journals are analyzed so that not only the handwriting, but also the writing style and even certain choices of wording are identical." Durzo smiled wolfishly. "Assassination is an art, milord, and I am the city's most accomplished artist."

"How many men have you killed?" the lord general asked.

"Suffice it to say I'm never idle."

The man fiddled with his beard and continued looking through the handbill Master Blint had given him, obviously unsettled. "May I ask about others, Master Blint?" he said, suddenly respectful.

"I prefer that you only inquire about those deaths you're seriously considering," Master Blint said.

"Why is that?"

"I value secrets very highly, as I must. So I don't like to discuss my methodology. And, to be honest, knowing too much tends to frighten those who employ me. I had a client some time ago who was very proud of his defenses. He asked me how I'd fulfill a contract on him. He irritated me, so I told him.

"Afterward, he tried to hire another wetboy to kill me. He was turned down by every professional in Cenaria. He ended up hiring an amateur."

"You give yourself the status of a legend," the lord general said, his thin face pinching.

Of course Durzo Blint was a legend! Who would hire him if they didn't know that? At the same time, hearing Master Blint speak of his trade to a noble—to someone like Count Drake—was eerie. It was like Azoth's two worlds were being pressed uncomfortably close to each other, and he could feel the noble's awe in himself.

In the guild, Durzo Blint had been a legend because he had power, because people were afraid of him, and he never had to be afraid of anyone. That was what had drawn Azoth to him. But this noble was awed for different reasons. To him, Durzo Blint was a creature of the night. He was a man who could come violate those things he held dear. He undermined all of what the lord general had thought safe. The man didn't look afraid; he looked disgusted.

"I'm not suggesting that I terrify every wetboy in the city." Master Blint smiled. "The fact is that we professionals are, if not a close group, at least a small one. We're colleagues, some of us even friends. The second wetboy he went to was Scarred Wrable—"

"I've heard of him," Brant Agon said. "Apparently the second best assassin in the city."

"Wetboy," Blint corrected. "And a friend of mine. He told me what this client was doing. After that—well, if a military metaphor works better for you—it would be like trying a small raid on a city that was expecting it instead of an unsuspecting city. In the second case it might work, in the first it's suicide."

"I see," the lord general said. He paused for a moment, apparently surprised Master Blint knew who he was, then suddenly grinned, "And you're a tactician, too."

"How so?"

"You haven't had many contracts taken out on you since you started telling that story, have you?"

Master Blint smiled broadly. These were two men, Azoth saw, who understood each other. "Not a one. After all, diplomacy is an extension of warfare," Blint said.

"We usually say that warfare is an extension of diplomacy," Brant Agon said. "But I think I agree with you. I once found myself outnumbered and forced to hold a position against the Lae'knaught for two days to wait for reinforcements. I had some captives, so I put them in a vulnerable position and told their guards we would receive reinforcements at dawn. During the fighting, the prisoners were allowed to get free and promptly told their superiors the news. The Lae'knaught army was so disheartened that they held back until we *had* been reinforced. That diplomacy saved our lives. Which brings us back to the matter at hand," the lord general said. "I need some diplomacy that's not on this list of yours. I'm afraid I've not been completely forthright with you, Master Blint," the lord general said. "I'm here for the king."

Master Blint's face went suddenly devoid of emotion.

"I understand that by telling you that, we might lose the man who provided me with your name. But the king deems this to be worth risking the lives of both a contact and one of his ministers—namely, myself."

"You haven't done anything foolish like surround the building with soldiers, have you?" Master Blint asked.

"Nothing of the kind. I'm here alone."

"Then you've made one wise choice today."

"More than one. We've chosen you, Master Blint. And I've chosen to be honest with you, which I hope you appreciate.

"As you know, the king's wealthy, but not politically or militarily strong. That's a bitter pill, but it's not news. Our kings haven't been strong for a hundred years. Aleine Gunder wishes to change that. But in addition to internal struggles of which you no doubt know more than I'd care to learn, the king has recently learned of some rather devious plots to steal vast sums of money not only from the treasury, but—in a multitude of schemes—also from almost every nobleman in the country. The idea being, we think, that Cenaria becomes so impoverished that we'll be unable to maintain an army."

"Sounds like a lot of money to steal without anybody noticing," Master Blint said.

"The Chancellor of the Exchequer has noticed—he's the one arranging it. But no one else has noticed, yet. The schemes are little short of brilliant. The plot won't even ripen for six or ten years. Men are being placed in key positions and as yet have done nothing wrong. There's more, much more, but you don't need to know it."

"What do I need to know?" Blint asked, his eyes heavy-lidded.

"I've made a study of you, Master Blint," the lord general said. "Though information about you is difficult to find. Everyone knows that the Sa'kagé holds an enormous amount of power here. People outside the country know it. Khalidor knows it.

"The king needs you for more than a dozen jobs, spanning years. Some will involve simple assassination, some will involve information planting, and some will not involve killing at all, but simply being seen. Godking Ursuul must believe the Sa'kagé and its assets have an alliance with us."

"You want me to become a government agent."

"Not...exactly."

"And I suppose you'd give me a pardon for all I've done?" Master Blint asked.

"I've been authorized to offer that."

Master Blint stood, laughing. "No, Lord General. Good day."

"I'm afraid I can't take no for an answer. The king has forbidden it."

"I do hope you're not planning on threatening my life," Master Blint said.

"First," the lord general said, looking at Azoth for the first time, "we'll kill the boy."

19

Master Blint shrugged. "So?"

"And we'll kill your lover. I believe her name's Vonda?"

"You can kill the bitch. But that might give you some trouble, considering she's four months dead."

The lord general didn't even pause. "And we'll kill this 'Momma' Kirena who seems to be your only friend. Then we'll come after you. I don't want it to be this way, but this is what the king offers."

"You're making two mistakes," Master Blint said. "First, you're assuming that I value other people's lives more than my own. How can you know what I do and believe such a thing? Second, you're assuming that I value my own life."

"Please understand. I'm under orders. Personally, I'd rather have nothing to do with you," the lord general said. "I think it's beneath the dignity of a king to hire criminals. I think it's immoral and foolish for him to put money in your purse rather than chains on your wrists. I find you abhorrent. A wreck of a human being barely resembling what once must have been a man. But the king has decided we need a sellsword like you. I'm a soldier. I've been sent to get you, and I won't fail."

"And you're making a tactical blunder," Master Blint said. "The king might kill my apprentice, my friend, and even me, but at the least, he will have lost his lord general. A poor trade."

"I don't think he would find my death to be such a very great loss," the lord general said.

"Ah, figured that out, have you?" Blint asked. "This may be the first time you've seen me, Brant Agon, but it isn't the first time I've seen you."

The lord general looked puzzled. "So you've seen me. So have half the people in the city."

"Does your wife still crowd your side of the bed? Sweet, isn't it? Does she still wear that drab nightgown with the daisies embroidered on the hem? You really love her, don't you?"

Lord General Agon froze.

"You call me abhorrent?" Durzo asked. "You owe me your life!"

"What?"

"Didn't you ever wonder why you got a promotion instead of a knife in the back?"

From his eyes, even Azoth could tell that the lord general had.

"I was in your house the night King Davin died, when you and Regnus Gyre met. I was to kill your wife as a warning to you. Later, the prince would offer you a better marriage to a young noblewoman who would be able to give you sons. And I was authorized to kill both you and Regnus if you were plotting treason. I spared you—and I don't get paid unless I leave corpses. I don't expect your gratitude, lord general, but I demand your respect!"

Lord General Agon's face went gray. "You...you told Aleine that my price was the promotion. He thought he bought me off with a promotion rather than a wife." Azoth could see him mentally reviewing comments he must have heard over the last four months, and getting sicker and sicker. "Why?"

"You're the illustrious general, the old war hero. You tell me." Durzo sneered.

"Putting me in charge of the army divided the Sa'kagé's enemies. It kept the king from putting someone he could trust in charge of the military. You bastards have got people everywhere, don't you?"

"Me? I'm just a sellsword. I'm just a wreck of a human being."

The general's face was still gray, but his back never bent an inch. "You've...you've given me much to think about, Master Blint. Though I still believe the murders you've committed merit hanging, I dishonored you and myself with my hasty words. I apologize. My apology, however, has no effect on the king's determination that you serve him. I—"

"Get out," Master Blint said. "Get out. If you reconsider your threats, I'll be here for a few minutes."

The general rose, and watching Master Blint carefully, walked to the door. He opened it, and kept his eyes on Master Blint until he closed the door behind himself. Azoth heard his steps echo down the hall.

Master Blint stared at the door and scooted back from the table. Instead of relaxing now that the general was gone, he tensed. Everything about him spoke of potential action. He looked like a mongoose waiting for a serpent to strike.

"Step away from the door, Azoth," he said. "Stand by the window."

There was no hesitation. Azoth had learned that lesson. He didn't have to understand; he just had to obey.

He heard a crash on the stairs and loud cursing. Azoth stood by the window and looked at Master Blint, but the man's pockmarked face betrayed nothing.

Moments later, the door banged open. The lord general lurched in, sword drawn. "What have you done?" he roared. His knees bowed and he leaned heavily against the doorframe to keep from falling.

Master Blint didn't say anything.

The general blinked and tried to straighten, but a spasm passed through his body as his stomach cramped. It passed, and he said, "How?"

"I put a contact poison on the door latch," Master Blint said. "It seeps right through the skin."

"But if we'd reached a deal . . ." the lord general said.

"I'd have opened the door for you. If you'd worn gloves, I had other plans. Now I want you to listen very closely. The king is an incompetent, treacherous, foul-mouthed child, so I'm going to make this very clear. I'm a first-rate wetboy. He's a second-rate king. I won't work for him. If you want, you can hire me yourself: I'll kill the king, but I won't kill for him. And there's no way you or he can pressure me.

"I know he won't believe that, because Aleine Gunder is the kind of man who believes he can get whatever he wants. So here's why he's going to believe." Master Blint stood. "First, I'm going to leave a message for him tonight in the castle. Second, you're going to investigate what happened to Count Yosar Glin. He was the client who betrayed me. Third, there's what has already happened to you. And fourth—do sit, Agon, and put away the sword. It's insulting."

Lord General Agon crashed into a chair. The long sword fell from his fingers. He didn't appear to have the strength to pick it up. Regardless, his eyes were still clear, and he was hearing every word Master Blint said.

"Lord General, I don't care who he kills. I know you have this inn surrounded, that there are crossbowmen covering the windows of this room. They don't matter. More important, the king's threats don't matter. I will be no man's lapdog. I serve who I will, when I will, and I will never serve Aleine Gunder. Azoth, come here."

Azoth went to his master, wondering why Blint had used his name. He stood in front of Master Blint, who rested his hands on Azoth's shoulders and turned him to face General Agon.

"Azoth here is my best apprentice. He's agile. He's smart. He learns things after being told once. He works tirelessly. Azoth, tell the general what you've learned about life."

Without hesitation, Azoth said, "Life is empty. Life is meaningless. When we take a life, we aren't taking anything of value. Wetboys are killers. That's all we do. That's all we are. There are no poets in the bitter business."

"Lord General," Blint said, "are you with me?"

"I'm with you," the general said, fire raging in his eyes.

Master Blint's voice was ice. "Then know this: I'd kill my own apprentice before I'd let you use him against me."

The general jerked sharply in his chair as if shocked. He was staring at Azoth. Azoth followed his gaze to his own chest.

Several inches of bloodied steel were protruding from him. Azoth saw them and felt an uncomfortable pushing, spreading sensation from his back all the way through his center. It seemed cool, then warm, then painful. He blinked his eyes slowly and looked back to the general, whose eyes were full of horror. Azoth looked at the steel.

He recognized that blade. He'd cleaned it that day he went looking for Doll Girl. He hoped Master Blint would at least wipe it down before he brought it back for Azoth to clean. It had filigree on the blade that held blood if you let it dry there. Azoth had had to use the point of a stiletto to pick it out. It took hours.

Then Azoth was drawn to the location of the dagger. At that angle on a child's chest, it would have clipped the fat vessel above the heart. If so, the deader would go down as soon as the dagger was drawn out. There would be a lot of blood. The deader would die within seconds.

Azoth's body jerked as the dagger disappeared. He was vaguely aware of his knees folding. He slumped over sideways and felt something warm spilling over his chest.

The wood planks of the floor jostled him unmercifully as he sprawled over them. He lay facing up. Master Blint was holding a bloody dagger in his hand and saying something.

Did Master Blint just stab me? Azoth couldn't believe it. What had he done? He thought Master Blint had been pleased with him. It must have been Doll Girl. He must have still been mad about it. It had seemed things were going so well. There was white-gold light everywhere. And he was warm. So warm.

"Your Majesty, please!"

King Aleine Gunder IX threw himself down into his throne. "Brant, it's one man. One!" He swore a stream of curses. "You'd have me send my family to the country for fear of one man?"

"Your Majesty," Lord General Brant Agon said, "the definition of 'man' might not cover Durzo Blint. I understand the implications—"

"Indeed! Do you know the talk it will cause if I send my family away on a moment's notice?" The king cursed again, unconsciously. "I know what they say about me. I know! I'll not give them this to drool on, Brant."

"Your Majesty, this assassin is not given to idle threats. For the sake of all that's holy, he murdered his own apprentice just to make a point!"

"A sham. Come on, general. You were drugged. You didn't know what was going on."

"My body was afflicted, not my mind. I know what I saw."

The king sniffed, then curled his lip as he caught the faint odor of brimstone in the air. "Dammit! Can't those idiots make anything work?"

One of the ducts that carried hot air from the Vos Island Crack just north of the castle had broken again. *He doesn't appreciate how much the engineers save us every year by heating the entire castle with pipes embedded in the very stones. He doesn't care that the turbines spinning in the wind rising from the Crack give him the power of two hundred windmills. That he smells brimstone once a fortnight infuriates him.* Agon wondered what god Cenaria had offended to deserve such a king.

He should have pushed Regnus Gyre. He should have spelled it out to him more clearly. He should have lied to him about what would happen to Nalia's children by Aleine. He could have served Regnus proudly. Proudly and honorably.

"Maybe you saw him kill a boy," the king said. "Who cares?" *You should. Regnus would have.* "It was obviously some street rat he picked up for the purpose of impressing you."

"With all due respect, sire, you're mistaken. I've dealt with formidable men. I faced Dorgan Dunwal in single combat. I fought Underlord Graeblan's Lae'knaught lancers. I—"

"Yes, yes. A thousand goddam battles from my goddam father's time. Very impressive," the king said. "But you never learned anything about ruling, did you?"

General Agon stiffened. "Not like you have, Your Majesty."

"Well, if you had, *general,* you'd know that you can't damage your own reputation." He cursed long and unfluently again. "Flee my own castle in the night!"

There was no working with him. The man shamed Agon and should have shamed himself. Yet Agon was sworn to him, and he'd decided long ago that an oath measured the man who gave it. It was like his marriage; he wouldn't take back his vows simply because his wife couldn't give him children.

But did vows hold when your own king had plotted to take your life? And not in honorable battle, but with an assassin's blade in the night?

That had been before Agon had sworn his allegiance to the man, however. Now that he had sworn, it didn't matter that—had he known then what he knew now—he would have chosen to die rather than serve Aleine Gunder IX.

"Your Majesty, may I at least have permission to hold an exercise tonight for my guards and include your mage? The Captain is in the habit of doing such things unannounced to keep the men at the ready." *Though I wonder why I preserve your empty head.*

"Oh, to hell with you, general. You and your goddam paranoia. Fine. Do as you please."

General Agon turned to leave the throne room. The king's predecessor, Davin, had been empty-headed too. But he'd known it, and he'd deferred to his counselors.

Aleine X, this king's son, was only fourteen years old, but he showed promise. He seemed to have gotten some of his mother's intelligence, at least. *If X were old enough to take power, maybe I'd provoke this assassin. Dear God, maybe I'd hire him.* General Agon shook his head. That was treason, and it had no place in a general's mind.

*   *   *

Fergund Sa'fasti had been appointed to serve in Cenaria more for his political acuity than his Talent. The truth was, he'd barely earned his blue robe. But his talents if not his Talent had served him well in Cenaria. The king was both stupid and foolish, but he could be worked with, if one didn't mind petulance and showers of curses.

But tonight Fergund was wandering the castle as if he were a guard. He'd appealed to the king, but Aleine IX—they called him Niner, short for "the nine-year-old" and not "the ninth," only when drinking with friends— had cursed him and ordered him to do whatever the lord general said.

As far as Fergund was concerned, Lord General Agon was a relic. It was too bad that he hadn't been able to adapt to Niner. The old man had things to offer. Then again, the fewer counselors the king had, the more important Fergund became.

Disgusted with his night's assignment—what was he looking for, anyway?—Fergund continued his lonely circuit of the castle yard. He'd considered asking for an escort, but mages were supposed to be more deadly than any hundred men. If that wasn't exactly true in his case, it didn't do him any good to advertise the fact.

The castle yard was an irregular diamond three hundred paces wide and almost four hundred long. It was bordered on the northwest and southeast by the river as the Plith—split for half a mile by Vos Island—came rushing back together south of the castle.

The yard was animated with the sounds of men, horses, and dogs settling down for the night. It was early enough that men were still up gambling in the barracks, and the sounds of a lyre and good-natured cursing floated a short way into the dense fog.

Fergund pulled his cloak tighter around his shoulders. The sliver of moon wasn't doing much to penetrate the cold fog pouring off the rivers and through the gates. The wet air kissed Fergund's neck and he regretted his recent haircut. The king had mocked his long hair, but Fergund's lover had adored it.

And, now that his hair was short, the king mocked him for that.

The fog billowed strangely at the iron gate and Fergund froze. He embraced the power—*embrace?* he'd always thought it felt more like a wrestling match—and peered through the fog. Once he held it, the power calmed him. He could see nothing threatening, and his hearing and sight were sharper.

Breathing deeply, Fergund made himself continue past the gate. He didn't know if it was his imagination, but it felt like the fog pressed against the whole wall of the castle like an invading army and poured in through the breach of the iron gate. Fog pooled almost to his shoulders, and the torches mounted over the heads of the two guards did little to cut the mist.

Nodding to them, Fergund turned and started walking back to the castle. He felt a weight between his shoulder blades as of eyes boring into him and repressed the urge to look over his shoulder. But as he walked toward the stables, the feeling only grew. The air felt heavy, so thick it was like walking through soup. The fog seemed to curl around him in his passing and lick at the back of his bare neck, taunting him.

With the rising of the fog, the moon and stars totally disappeared. The world was enveloped in cloud.

Fergund stumbled as he passed by the corner of the stables. He threw a hand out to steady himself against the wood, but felt something yielding for a moment before it disappeared. Something like he'd touched a man standing there.

Staggering back in fear, Fergund clawed for the embrace. He could see nothing. There was no one there. Finally his Talent came to him. He caught a brief flicker of movement into the stables—but it might have been his imagination.

Had he smelled garlic? Surely that could only be his imagination. But why would he imagine such a thing? He hesitated for a long moment. But he was a weak mage, not a weak man. He readied a fireball and drew his knife. He came wide around the corner, straining every sense magical and mundane.

He jumped through the door and looked around frantically. Nothing. The horses were in their stalls, their odors mingling with the heavy fog. He could hear only the stamping of hooves and the even breathing of sleeping animals. Fergund probed the darkness for any sign of movement, but saw nothing.

The longer he looked, the more foolish he felt. Part of him thought he should go deeper into the stables, and part of him wanted to leave now. No one would know that he'd left. He could go to the other side of the castle and wander there. On the other hand, if he single-handedly caught an intruder, the king would doubtless reward him well. If Niner was good for anything, it was rewarding his friends.

Slowly, Fergund drew the fire he'd prepared into visible form. It flickered a little and then held, burning in his palm. A horse in the first stall snorted, suddenly shying back, and Fergund moved to shush the beast. But with fire in one hand and a gleaming knife in the other, the horse was hardly calmed.

It whinnied loudly and stomped on the ground, waking its neighbors.

"Shh!" Fergund said. "Relax, it's only me."

But an unfamiliar man with magefire was too much for the animals. They started neighing loudly. The stallion in the second stall started kicking.

"Wooja stop skearin' 'orses?" a loud voice said behind him. Fergund was so startled he dropped his knife and lost the fire in his hand. He wheeled around. It was just the stable master, a squat, bearded man from the isle of Planga. Dorg Gamet came in behind Fergund, holding a lantern. He gave Fergund a look of pure disdain while the mage picked his knife gingerly out of a pile of horse droppings.

Dorg moved down the row quickly, and at his touch and his voice, the horses calmed instantly. Fergund watched, feeling awkward. Finally Dorg came back past him.

"I was just patrol—"

"Use a lantern, ya lut," Dorg said. He stuck his lantern into Fergund's hand. He walked away, saying to himself, "Skearin' ma damn 'orses with wytchfire."

"It's magefire. There's a difference!" Fergund said to his back.

Dorg stormed out of the stables, and Fergund had barely turned around when he heard a thump.

Fergund ran outside. Dorg was lying on the ground, unconscious. Before he could shout anything, Fergund felt something hot in his neck. He reached a hand up and felt someone take the lantern gently out of his other hand. His muscles went rigid.

The light went out.

21

*W*hat the hell have you done?" Momma K asked, looking up as Durzo crashed through the door.

"Good work," Durzo said. "And with time left for a night out." He grinned sloppily. He reeked of alcohol and garlic.

"I don't care about your binges. What have you done to Azoth?" She looked at the still form lying on the bed in her home's guest room.

"Nothin'," Durzo said, grinning foolishly. "Check. Ain't nothin' wrong with him."

"What do you mean? He's unconscious! I came back here and the servants were all in a flutter because you'd appeared here with—they said it was a corpse. I came up and Azoth was here. I can't wake him. He's dead to the world."

For some reason, that set Durzo off. He started laughing.

Momma K slapped him, hard.

"Tell me what you've done. Have you poisoned him?"

That brought Durzo back. He shook his head, trying to clear it. "He's dead. Has to be dead."

"Whatever do you mean?"

"Gwinvere gorgeous," Durzo said. "I can't say. Someone threatened me. Someone who can do what they said. Said they'd come after Azo first, then you—and they knew about Vonda!"

Momma K drew back. Who had the power to threaten Durzo? Who or what could scare Durzo Blint?

Durzo sank onto a chair and put his face in his hands. "They have to think he's dead. 'Specially after tonight."

"You faked killing Azoth?"

Durzo nodded. "To show I didn't care. To show they couldn't push me."

But you do, Momma K thought, and they can. She knew Durzo was thinking it, too. The wetboy had never been as invincible as he seemed. And when his control cracked, it burst wide open. The best Momma K could do was make sure that Durzo went to one of her brothels and have someone keep an eye on him. He might be there for two or three days straight, but she could make sure he was safe. Relatively.

"I'll take care of the boy," Momma K heard herself saying. "Do you have any idea what to do with him once he wakes up?"

"He'll stay with the Drakes like we were planning. He's dead to this world."

"What did you use?"

Durzo looked at her, confused.

"What poison—never mind, just tell me, how long will he be unconscious?"

"I dunno."

Momma K's eyes narrowed. She wanted to slap him again. The man was insane. Even for a poisoner as gifted as Durzo, it was too easy to mis-judge with a child. A child wasn't simply a scaled-down adult. Durzo could have killed him. Durzo might have killed him. Azoth might never recover. Or he might wake and be an idiot, or not have the function of his limbs.

"You knew he might die," she said.

"Sometimes you have to gamble." Durzo patted his pockets, looking for garlic.

"You're starting to love that boy, and it scares the hell out of you. Part of you wants him dead, doesn't it, Durzo?"

"If I have to listen to your chitchat, can't you at least give me a drink?"

"Tell me."

"Life's empty. Love is failure. Better he dies now than gets us both killed later." With that, Blint seemed to deflate. Momma K knew he would say no more.

"How long will you be whoring?" she asked.

"I dunno," Blint said, barely stirring.

"Damn you! Longer or shorter than usual?"

"Longer," Durzo said after a minute. "Definitely longer."

The stream of curses preceded the king into the throne room by a good ten seconds. Lord General Agon could hear servants scurrying out of the way, see the guards at the entrances of the throne room shifting uncomfortably, and note that whatever staff members didn't absolutely need to be there were fleeing.

King Aleine IX barged in. "Brant! You pile of—" the lord general mentally erased the long list of repulsive things he resembled and refocused his attention when Niner got to the point. "What happened last night?"

"Your Majesty," the lord general said, "we don't know."

Another stream of curses, some of them more creative than usual, but Niner wasn't terribly creative, and no one dared to swear in his presence, so his arsenal was limited to variations on the word *shit*.

"What we do know is this," Brant Agon said. "Someone broke into the castle. I suppose we can assume it was the man we've spoken about." No need for listening spies to learn everything.

"Durzo Blint," the king said, nodding.

The lord general sighed. "Yes, Your Majesty. He apparently rendered unconscious one guard in the castle itself, and Fergund Sa'fasti, and your stable master in the stables."

More curses, then "What do you mean, 'rendered unconscious'?" The king paced back and forth.

"They didn't have any marks on them, and they couldn't remember anything, though the guard had a small puncture wound on his neck, as if from a needle."

The king cursed more and then cursed the abashed mage. As usual, Agon found himself getting more bored than offended. The king's curses didn't mean anything except "Look at me, I'm a spoiled child." Niner finally stumbled across another point: "There was nothing else?"

"We haven't found anything yet, sire. None of the guards outside your rooms, your wife's, your daughters', or your son's reported seeing anything unusual."

"It isn't fair," the king said, stomping over to his throne. "What have I done to deserve this?" he threw himself down in his throne—and squealed.

He practically flew out of the throne. He clutched Lord General Agon. "Oh gods! I'm feeling faint. I'm dying! Damn you all! I'm dying! Guards! Help! Guards!" The king's voice pitched higher and higher and he started crying as the guards blew whistles and rang bells and the throne room roared to life.

General Agon plucked the king's hands free and put the weak-kneed man in the arms of his sycophant, Fergund Sa'fasti, who didn't know enough to hold on. The king collapsed to the ground and wept like a child. General Agon ignored him and strode to the throne.

In a moment, he saw what he was looking for: a fat, long needle, pointing up from a well-worn cushion on the throne. He tried to pull it out with his fingers, but the needle stuck. It was supported so that it wouldn't just fold over if the king sat on it wrong.

General Agon drew his knife and slit the cushion open. He pulled out the needle, ignoring the bells, ignoring the guards pouring into the room, surrounding the king and herding everyone else into a side room where they could be held and questioned.

Lord General Agon pulled out the needle. A note tied to it said, "I could have been poisoned."

"Move aside!" a little man from the back was calling out, pushing soldiers out of his way. It was the king's physician.

"Let him through," the lord general ordered. The soldiers moved back from the king, who was whimpering on the floor.

Brant motioned to the physician, showed him the note, and whispered, "The king will need some poppy wine, maybe a lot. But he isn't poisoned."

"Thank you," the man said. Behind him, the king had pulled down his pants and was arching his neck trying to see the wound on his buttock. "But believe me, I know how to deal with him."

The general suppressed a smile. "Escort the king to his apartments," he told the guards. "Set a watch on the door, with two captains inside the room. The rest of you return to your duties."

"Brant!" the king yelled as the guards picked him up. "Brant! I want him dead! Dammit, I want him dead!"

Brant Agon didn't move until the throne room was empty once more.

The king wanted to wage war against a shadow, a shadow with no corporeal parts except the steel of its blades. That was what it would be to assassinate a wetboy. Or worse. How many men would die before the king's pride was salved?

"Milord?" a woman asked tentatively. It was one of the housekeepers. She had a wrapped bundle in her hands. "I was...chosen to report for the housekeepers, sir. But with the king gone and all...Could I...?"

The general looked at her closely. She was an old woman, obviously afraid for her life. He bet she was "chosen" by having pulled a short straw. "What is it?"

"Us housekeepers found these. Someone left them in each of the royal bedchambers, sir."

The housekeeper handed him the bundle. Six black daggers were inside it.

"Where?" Brant asked, choking the word out.

"Under—under the royal family's pillows, sir."

Little feet pattered into Azoth's consciousness. It was a strange sound to hear when you were dead, but Azoth couldn't sort it out any other way. Bare little feet on stone. He must be outside, because the sound didn't reverberate against any walls. He tried to open his eyes and failed. Maybe this is what it was to be dead. Maybe you never left your body. Maybe you laid inside your corpse and had to just *feel* as you slowly decomposed. He hoped dogs didn't get to him. Or wolves. He'd had terrifying dreams of a wolf grinning at him, yellow eyes ablaze. If he were stuck in his dead body, what would happen if they started tearing pieces of him off? Would he find oblivion like he'd finally fallen asleep or would he just split into pieces of consciousness, and slowly dissipate into the soil after passing through the bellies of a dozen beasts?

Something touched his face and his eyes leapt open. He heard the startled gasp before his eyes could focus on who had made it. It was a little girl, maybe five years old, her eyes so wide they covered half of her face.

"Never seen a corpse?" he asked.

"Father! Father!" she shrieked with all the surprising volume small children can muster.

He groaned as the sound jammed knives in his head and he fell back on the pillows. *Pillows?* So he wasn't dead. That was probably supposed to be a good thing.

When he woke again, time must have passed, because the room was light and airy. Wide windows had been thrown open, and cherrywood furnishings and marble flooring gleamed in the sunlight. Azoth recognized the molded ceiling; he'd stared at it before. He was in Count Drake's guest room.

"Back from the dead, are you?" Count Drake asked. He was smiling. Seeing the look on Azoth's face, he added, "Here, now, sorry. Don't think about that. Don't think at all. Eat."

He set a plate full of steaming eggs and ham in front of Azoth, along with a glass of well-watered wine. The food spoke directly with Azoth's stomach, completely bypassing higher cognitive functions. It was several minutes later when he realized the plate and the glass were both empty.

"Better," the count said. He sat on the edge of the bed and absently polished his pince nez. "Do you know who I am and where you are? Good. Do you remember who you are?"

Azoth nodded slowly. *Kylar.*

"I've been given some messages for you, but if you're not feeling well enough…"

"No, please," Kylar said.

"Master *Tulii* says that your work now is to get ready for your new life, and to get well. To wit, 'Keep your arse in bed. I expect you to be ready when I come get you.'"

Kylar laughed. That was Master Blint all right. "When is he coming, then?"

A troubled look passed over the count's face. "Not for a while. But you don't need to worry about that. You'll be living here now. Permanently. You'll continue your lessons with your master, of course, but we'll be doing all we can to get the look of the street off of you. Your master said to tell you that you aren't going to be well as soon as you expect. There's something else I want to tell you, though. About your little friend."

"You mean…?"

"She's doing well, Kylar."

"She is?"

"Her new family has named her Elene. She has good clothes, three meals a day. They're good people. They'll love her. She'll have a real life now. But if you're to be of any use to her, you need to get well."

Kylar felt as if he were floating. The sunlight streaming through the windows seemed brighter, sharper. An arrangement of orange roses and lavender glowed on the sill. He felt good in a way he hadn't since before Rat had become Black Dragon's Fist.

"They even took her to a mage and she said she'll be fine, but she couldn't do anything for the scars."

Someone had just outlined all his happiness with tar.

"I'm sorry, son," Count Drake said. "But you've done the best you can, and I promise you, she'll have a better life than she ever could have on the street."

Kylar barely heard him. He stared out the window, away from the count. "I can't pay you yet. Not until I start getting my wages again from Master... my master."

"There's no rush. Pay me when you can. Oh, and one last thing your master asked me to pass along. He said, 'Learn from these people those things that will make you strong, forget the rest. Listen much, speak little, get well, and enjoy this. It may be the only happy time of your life.'"

Kylar was bedridden for weeks. He tried to sleep as much as the Drakes told him to, but he had far too much time. He'd never had time before; he didn't like it. When he'd been on the street, every moment had been spent worrying about his next meal, or worrying about Rat or any of the older boys or girls terrorizing him. With Master Blint, he'd been kept so busy training that he didn't have time to think.

Sitting in bed all day and all night, he had nothing but time. Training was impossible. Reading was possible, but still excruciating. For a while, Azoth spent his time becoming Kylar. With the guidelines Master Blint had given him, and the facts that anyone checking would find, he had made up more stories about his family, the area he was from, and the adventures he'd had, keeping them harmless, the way people liked to think eleven-year-olds' lives were.

He soon mastered that, though, and most of the time thought of himself as Kylar. He was getting to know Count Drake's daughters, too. Ilena was the pretty five-year-old he'd scared half to death when he first woke; Mags was a gangly eight, and Serah an alternately awkward and aloof twelve. They provided some diversion, but the countess kept them from "bothering" Kylar so he could "get his rest."

The count and countess were fascinating, but Count Drake was working most of the time and the countess had definite ideas about eleven-year-old boys—which didn't coincide at all with what Kylar knew about eleven-year-old boys. He could never decide if she knew what he was and pretended not to so she could reform him, or if Count Drake had kept her in the dark.

She was willowy, fair-skinned, and blue-eyed, an earthly vision of the heavenly beings the Drakes believed in. Like the count, she had beliefs about serving Kylar herself, as if to prove that she didn't think herself above it. But it wasn't a false humility: when Kylar had gotten terribly ill the first week and vomited all over the floor, she'd come in and held him until he was done shaking, and then she'd rolled up her sleeves and cleaned up the vomit herself. He'd been too sick to even be properly horrified until long afterward.

He couldn't count the times she came in to stuff him with food or check on how he was feeling or to read him stupid kid books. The books were full of valiant heroes who killed evil wytches. Children never had to dig through heaps of garbage and vomit outside an inn looking for scraps of edible food. Older boys never tried to bugger them. They never abandoned their friends. The princesses they saved never had their faces battered beyond recognition. No one was ever so badly scarred that a mage couldn't fix it.

Kylar hated the stories, but he knew the countess only wanted the best for him, so he nodded and smiled and cheered when the heroes won—as they did every time.

No wonder all the little nobles want to lead armies. If it were like the books their mothers read, it would be fun. It would be fun if you felt satisfied when the bad guy died rather than wanting to puke because you saw raw cartilage and gushing blood where you cut off an ear. Blood wafting in a million beautiful swirls with water as he bled to death, held under the water by the rope you'd tied around his ankle.

The countess always interpreted his shaking and nausea after she was done with the stories as a need for more rest, so after raising memories to haunt Kylar's room, she'd leave him with their angry ghosts.

Every night Kylar became Azoth. Every night Azoth turned from the repair bay and saw Rat walking toward him, naked, hairy, massive, eyes glowing with lust. Every night Azoth watched Rat splashing into the water, straining against the weight tied to his ankle. Every night he watched Rat carve Doll Girl's face.

The nightmares woke him, and he lay in bed fighting the memories. Azoth had been weak, but Azoth was no more. Kylar was strong. Kylar had acted. Kylar would be like Master Blint. He would never be afraid. It was better now. It was better to lie in a bed having nightmares than it was to listen to Jarl getting buggered, weeping.

Sleeping again only moved him from one nightmare to another. Day brought little relief, and only slowly did the memories fade. Every morning, he told himself that he'd done what he had to, that he'd had to kill Rat, that he'd had to abandon Doll Girl, that he'd had to leave Jarl, that it was best that he never see them again, that he couldn't have known what would happen to Doll Girl. He told himself that life was empty, that he wasn't taking away anything of value when he took a life.

He wouldn't have made it without Logan Gyre's visits. Every other day, Logan would come to see him, inevitably with Serah Drake. At first, Kylar thought he came because he still felt guilty, but that soon passed. They enjoyed each other's company, and they became fast friends. Logan was strange: he was as smart as Jarl, and he'd read hundreds of books. Kylar didn't think he would survive for a week in the Warrens, but at the same time, he spoke about court politics as if it were all so easy. He knew the names, histories, friends, and enemies of scores of courtiers, and knew the major life events and important motivations of every highly ranked noble in the kingdom. Half the time, Kylar didn't know if he didn't understand what Logan was talking about because it was all part of the courtly life he'd never known, or just because Logan liked to use big words. A *sesquipedalian,* he called himself. Whatever that meant.

Nonetheless, the friendship worked, and Serah Drake helped it work by happening to stop by often so she could be with Logan. She filled in the gaps. Kylar couldn't count the times he sat silent because he hadn't understood some reference Logan had made. The silence would begin to stretch, but before Logan could ever ask him why he didn't understand, Serah would get uncomfortable and launch into something else entirely. The chatter might have driven Kylar mad if he hadn't been so thankful for it. Anyway, maybe this was how noble girls were.

Kylar was sitting in bed one morning after having spent another night cowering under the covers. He'd dreamed that he had been the one beating Doll Girl, that it had been *his* feet kicking her, and exultation writhed in *his* eyes as her beauty melted in the heat of his fury.

Count Drake came in. His fingers were ink-stained and he looked tired. He pulled a chair close to the bed.

"We think the danger's passed," he said.

"Excuse me?" Kylar said.

"I'm sorry we've had to keep you in the dark, Kylar, but we had to make sure you didn't do anything rash. In the past few weeks, there have been a number of attempts on your master's life. And consequently, there are now four fewer wetboys in the city. After three attempts, your master let the king know that if there were any more attempts, the king would die next."

"Master Blint killed the king?" Kylar asked.

"Shhh! Don't say that name. Not even here," Count Drake said. "One of the Nine, Dabin Vosha, the man in charge of the Sa'kagé's smuggling, heard about your master's threat to the king. He decided it would be a good time to make his own play for power and sent a wetboy after Durzo, thinking Durzo would either be killed or would kill the king in retaliation. Durzo found out and killed both the wetboy and Vosha."

"You mean all this has been happening while I've been lying in bed."

"There was no way you could help," Count Drake said.

"But what did Dabin Vosha have against Master—my master?" Kylar had never even heard the name.

"I don't know. Maybe nothing. That's the way the Sa'kagé works, Kylar. There are plots within plots, and most of them go nowhere. Most of them take one step and then die, like this one. If you worry about what everyone is trying to do, you become a spectator and not a player.

"Anyway, the king's learned of the last attempt on your master's life and has become very frightened. Usually, this would be good news, but he's rather clumsily consolidating his power. Logan is going to have to spend a while out of the city."

"He was just starting to be my friend," Kylar said.

"Believe me, son, a man like Logan Gyre will be your friend for life."

23

Someone slapped Kylar. Not gently.

"Wake up, boy."

Kylar clawed his way out of a nightmare and saw the face of Master Blint, a foot away, about to slap him again. "Master—" he stopped. "Master Tulii?"

"Good to see you remember me, Kylar," Master Blint said.

Master Blint got up and shut the door. "I don't have much time. Are you well yet? Don't lie to please me."

"I'm still a little weak, sir, but I'm getting better." Kylar's heart was pounding. He'd been desperate to see Master Blint for weeks, but now that he was here, Kylar was inexplicably angry.

"You'll probably feel terrible for a few more weeks. Either the kinder-peril and avorida paste interacted in a way I didn't expect, or it might have something to do with your Talent."

"What's that mean? The Talent?" Kylar asked. His words were sharper than he'd intended, but Blint didn't seem to notice.

"Well, if it was that." Master Blint shrugged. "Sometimes a body doesn't react well to magic at first."

"I mean, what does it mean? Will I be able to—"

"Fly? Become invisible? Scale walls? Throw fire? Walk as a god among mortals?" Blint smirked. "Doubtful."

"I was going to ask if I'll be able to move as fast as you do." Again, that edge came into his voice.

"I don't know yet, Kylar. You'll be able to move faster than most men without the Talent, but there aren't many who are as gifted as I am."

"What will I be able to do, then?"

"You're weak, Kylar. We'll talk about this later."

"I don't have anything to do! I can't even get out of bed. No one tells me anything."

"Fine. It means everything and nothing," Master Blint said. "In Waeddryn or Alitaera, they'd call you a mage and six different schools would fight over where and what you should study and what color robes you should wear. In Lodricar or Khalidor, they'd call you a meister and you'd grow the vir on your arms like tattoos and worship your king as a god while you plotted how to stab his royal back. In Ymmur, you'd be a stalker, an honored and honor-able hunter of animals and sometimes men. In Friaku, you'd be *gorathi,* a Furied warrior invincible in your clan and one day a king versed in the arts of subjugation and slavery. In the west, well, you'd be in the ocean." He grinned.

Kylar didn't.

"The mages guess—they'd say *hypothesize* to make it more respect-able—that different countries produce different Talents and that's why men with pale skin and blue eyes become wytches while swarthy men are warrior *gorathi.* They say that's why the only mages they get from Gandu are Healers. They see men with yellow skin who can heal and proclaim that yellow skin means healing. But they're wrong. Our world is divided, but the Talent is one. Every people recognizes some form of magic—except for the Lae'knaught who hate magic and simultaneously don't believe in it, but that's a different subject—but every people has its own expectations about magic. Gandu once produced some of the most destructive archmagi the world has known. They saw horrors you couldn't imagine, and because of that, they turned away from magic as weaponry. The only magic they value is healing magic. So as centuries have passed, they've added greatly to their knowledge of healing magics, and lost most others. A Gandian who is greatly Talented with fire is a shame to himself and his family."

"So we'd never hear about him," Kylar said.

"Right. There's an intersection between what the people around you know well enough to teach, what you're naturally good at, and what it is possible for you to learn. So the Talent both is what it is and it is what it has to be. Like your mind."

Kylar just looked at him.

"Take it this way: some people can add long lists of numbers in their heads, right? And some can speak a dozen languages. To do that, they have to be smart, right?"

"Right."

"But just because you can learn to add lists of numbers doesn't mean you will. But a woman who handles account books and has a gift for numbers can. Or a diplomat might have a gift for languages, but if he never learns another language, he'll still only know one."

Kylar nodded.

"The woman with a head for numbers could probably learn another language if she worked hard enough, but she'll never be fluent in a dozen, and the man will never be able to add columns of numbers mentally. Do you see where this is going?"

Kylar thought, and Master Blint waited. "We know that I'm Talented but not how or how much, so you can't tell what I'll be able to do."

"Right," Master Blint said. "From having me teach you, you'll definitely learn some things. You need to hide? Your Talent will bend some light away. You need to walk quietly? It will muffle your steps. But like any talent, it has limits. If you walk in the noonday sun, you'll be seen. If you step on dry leaves, you'll be heard. You're Talented; you're not a god. You might have the smoothest tongue in the world, but if you swear at the king, you'll meet the headsman."

"If I know twelve languages, and you speak to me in a thirteenth, I won't know what you're saying."

"Sometimes you do listen," Master Blint said. "I have to go now. Count Drake will take care of you. He's a good man, Kylar. Too good. You can trust him with your life; just don't get him started on your soul. And think of yourself as Kylar always. Azoth is dead."

"Dead?" That released all the memories and fear and anger that had been building up in Kylar like pressing the trigger plate of a crossbow. Just like that his mask fell away, and he was Azoth once more.

Azoth grabbed Master Blint's arm. "I—I really d—"

"No! No you didn't. Does this look like hell?" Blint gestured. "Ha. And they wouldn't let me visit heaven."

But Azoth could remember looking down at a knife sticking out of his chest—it had seemed so real. *How could such a thing be?*

"I couldn't work for them," Master Blint said. "I'd be a bloody sword to them. They wouldn't be able to clean me, and they wouldn't be able to sheathe me. They'd have killed me eventually. It's easier to keep your eye on your enemies than on your friends."

"So you've been killing wetboys?" Azoth asked, trying to get a hold of himself. For weeks, he'd been keeping himself from thinking about that afternoon, but now he couldn't hold it back. He remembered the look in the lord general's eyes, the utter shock. He remembered following those eyes to his own chest....

"Nobody good would take the job on me. Men like Wrable and Gibbet and Severing get paid too well doing regular jobs to risk their lives taking on a real wetboy. Now remember, you're a Stern. You're proud of that, even if you are poor. The Sterns are barons, so they're upper nobility, but at the lowest level—"

"I know," Azoth said, cutting him off. "I know."

Was it just his imagination, or had Master Blint just looked guilty? The wetboy fished in a pocket and popped a garlic clove in his mouth. If it were anyone else, Azoth would have sworn he was trying to distract him, rushing to get out of the room before Azoth could pin him down. *Why was I so eager to please a man who was willing to murder me?*

I thought he cared. In the weeks that he'd been here in bed, Kylar had been alone. He'd left everything of his old life. He'd had real friends in Jarl and Doll Girl. They had cared about him. Now he was pretending to be friends with Logan Gyre—and even he had left. Not even Momma K came to visit.

It almost physically hurt when the count and countess came in at the same time. They so obviously loved each other; they were safe and happy and real together. Even Logan and Serah sometimes traded looks that made it obvious they liked each other. Those looks, that love, filled Kylar with a yearning so deep he thought his chest was going to cave in. It wasn't just hunger; a guild rat knew hunger like he knew the sewers where he huddled for warmth in the winter. Hunger wasn't comfortable, but it was familiar and it was nothing to fear. This was a thirst, like his whole body was parched, drying up, about to crumple. He was dying of thirst on the shores of the world's biggest lake.

None of it was for him. To him, that lake was an ocean. It was salt sea that if he drank would make him thirstier and thirstier until he went mad and died. Love was death for a wetboy. Madness and weakness and vulnerability and death, not just for the wetboy himself, but also for anyone he loved. Everything about Azoth's life was dead. He'd sworn that he would never love, but he'd never seen anything like what the count and countess shared when he'd promised that. It would be tolerable if anyone cared about him at all.

In the time he'd been with Master Blint, he'd started to think that the wetboy liked him, cared about him. He'd believed that sometimes Master Blint was even proud of him. Even though everything about the gray-haired lord general was foreign to Azoth, there was something right in the outrage and disbelief that had been in his eyes when Master Blint stabbed Azoth. He shouldn't have done it.

Azoth burst into tears. "How could you do it? What's wrong with you? It wasn't right."

Blint was caught off-guard for a moment, then he was suddenly furious. He grabbed Azoth's tunic and shook him. "Damn you! Use your head! If you aren't smarter than this, I *should* have killed you. Did he believe me when I said I didn't care if they killed you?"

Azoth looked away, admitting it. "You planned it all along."

"Of course I did! Why do you think we bleached your hair? It was the only way to save you. Azoth had to die so Kylar could live. Otherwise they had a hold. Any attachment you make in this life will be used against you. That's why we're strong. That's why four wetboys couldn't kill me. Because I have no attachments. That's why you can't fall in love. It makes you weak. As soon as you find something you can't walk away from, you're trapped, doomed. If anyone thinks I give the hair on a rat's arse what happens to you, you become a target. For everyone."

How does he do it? How is he so strong?

"Now look. Look at my damn hands!" Blint held them up. Both were empty. He made a fist and smacked it down on one arm. A bloody dagger sprouted from the opposite side. He jerked his hand away and the knife pulled back through his flesh. Then it frayed apart like smoke and disappeared.

"I have a small Talent with illusions, Kylar. I did a better job with yours because I had to sell it. But all I did was hit you in the back with a knockout needle, then hold the illusion until it took effect."

"But I felt it," Kylar said. He was regaining his balance. The tears were gone. He was thinking of himself as Kylar again.

"Sure you felt it. You felt me hit you and you saw a dagger coming out of your chest. At the same time your body was trying to fight off a dozen minor poisons. You made what sense of it you could. It was a gamble. That illusion used up almost all the power I can use in a day. If Agon's men had stormed the place, we would have been finished. The poisons I used wreaked havoc with your body. They could have killed you. Again, a gamble I had to make."

Master Blint does care what happens to me. It hit him like lightning. Master Blint had risked using up his power to save Azoth. Even if it were just the affection a master might have for a talented apprentice, Blint's approval washed over Azoth—*Kylar!*—as if the wetboy had given him a hug.

No adult had ever cared what happened to him. The only other person who'd ever risked anything for him was Jarl, and Jarl was part of another life.

The truth was, Azoth hated Azoth. Azoth was a coward, passive, weak, afraid, disloyal. Azoth had hesitated. Master Blint didn't know it, but the poisons on the needle *had* killed Azoth. He was Kylar now, and Kylar would be everything Azoth hadn't dared to be.

In that moment, Azoth became Kylar and Kylar became Blint's. If he had ever obeyed his master half-heartedly before, or out of fear, if he had ever fantasized about one day coming back and killing him for how hard the training was, it all dried up and blew away now. Master Blint was being hard on Kylar because life was hard. Life was hard, but Blint was harder, stronger, tougher than anything the Warrens could throw at him. He forbade love because love would destroy Kylar. Master Blint knew better than Kylar did. He was strong and he would make Kylar strong. He was fierce and Kylar would be fierce. But it was all for Kylar. It was all to protect him, to make him the best wetboy he could be.

So it wasn't love. So what? It was something. Maybe nobles got to live on the shores of that lake and drink at their pleasure. That life hadn't been decreed for a guild rat. Kylar's life was a desert life. But there is life in the desert, and a small oasis had Kylar's name on it. There was no room for Azoth. The oasis was too small and Azoth was too thirsty. But Kylar could do it. Kylar would do it. He'd make Master Blint proud.

"Good," Master Blint said. Of course, he couldn't see what Kylar was thinking, but Kylar knew the eagerness in his eyes was unmistakable. "Now, boy, are you ready to become a sword in the shadows?"

24

"*G*et up, boy. It's time to kill."

Kylar was awake instantly. He was fourteen years old, and the training had sunk in enough that he went through his survival checklist instantly. For each question, there was only a terse answer. Each sensation got only the briefest moment of his attention. *What woke you?* Voice. *What do you see?* Darkness, dust, afternoon light, shack. *What do you smell?* Blint, sewage, the Plith. *What do you feel?* Warm blanket, fresh straw, my bed, no warning tingles. *Can you move?* Yes. *Where are you?* Safe house. *Is there danger?* The last question, of course, was the culmination. He could move, his weapons were in their sheaths, all was well.

That wasn't guaranteed, not even here, in this dingy safe house in the shadow of one of the few sections of the ancient aqueduct that was still standing. More than once, Durzo had tied a sword to the ceiling over Kylar's bed, and the damn thing was nearly invisible when you had to look at it point first. Durzo had woken Kylar, and when he didn't recognize the danger within three seconds, Durzo had cut the rope. Fortunately, he'd capped the point that first time, and the second time. The third time, he didn't.

Another time, Durzo had had Scarred Wrable—only Durzo called him Ben—wake Kylar. Scarred Wrable had even worn Durzo's clothes and mimicked his voice perfectly—that was part of Scarred Wrable's Talent. That time, Kylar hadn't been caught. Even a garlicky meal didn't give a man the same smell as chewing the cloves straight.

Decoding Durzo's words came last. Time to kill.

"You think I'm ready?" Kylar asked, his heart pounding.

"You were ready a year ago. I just needed the right job for your first solo."

"What is it?" *I was ready a year ago?* Blint's compliments came like that, when they came at all. And usually, even a grudging compliment would be followed by some criticism.

"It's at the castle, and it's got to be finished today. Your deader is twenty-six years old, no military training, shouldn't be armed. But he's well-liked, a busy little bee. Very busy. An *assassin* would incur...ancillary fatalities." He said *assassin* with a sneer, as would any wetboy. "But it doesn't matter for the contract. The deader just has to die. Just finish the job."

Kylar's heart pounded. So this was how it was going to be. This wasn't a simple test. It wasn't, Can Kylar kill solo? It was, Can Kylar do what a wetboy does? Can Kylar decide a suitable entry strategy (to the castle itself, no less), can he kill solo, can he do it without killing innocents, can he get out after the hit? Oh, and can he use his Talent, the true measure of what separates a wetboy from a common assassin.

How the hell does Blint come up with these things? The man had a brilliance for ferreting out and exploiting Kylar's weaknesses, especially his biggest weakness of all: Kylar hadn't been able to use the Talent. Not yet. Not even once. It should have quickened by now, Blint said. He was forever pushing Kylar in new ways, hoping that some new extreme of stress, of need, might bring it out of him. Nothing had worked yet.

Durzo had wondered aloud if he should just kill Kylar. Instead, he'd decided that as long as Kylar could do everything a wetboy could do, Durzo would keep training him. He promised that it would ultimately fail. It was impossible. A wetboy wasn't a wetboy without the Talent.

"Who took out the contract?" Kylar asked.

"The Shinga."

"You're trusting me with that?"

"You're going in this afternoon. If you fuck it up, I go in tonight, and I bring the Shinga two heads." Kylar didn't have to ask who the other head would belong to.

"What did the deader do?"

"You don't need to know."

"Does it matter?"

A knife appeared in Durzo's hand, but his eyes weren't violent. He was thinking. He flipped the knife from finger to finger. Finger, finger, finger, stop. Finger, finger, finger, roll. Kylar had seen a bard do that once with a coin, but only Durzo used a knife.

"No," Durzo said. "It doesn't. Name's Devon Corgi and let's just say that when most people try to turn away from the darkness, they want to take a few bags packed with goodies with them. It slows them down. They never make it. I've only known one man in all my life who was willing to pay the full price of leaving the Sa'kagé."

"Who was it?"

"Boy, in two hours, you've got a date with a deader. You've got better questions to ask."

*   *   *

"Devon Corgi?" The guard furrowed his brow. "Nah, don't know him. Hey, Gamble, you know a Devon Corgi?" he asked another guard walking through the castle's enormous west gate.

It was almost too easy. Kylar had long ago stolen the tunic and bag that was the uniform of the city's most widely used courier service. People who didn't have their own servants employed boys—east side boys, never guild rats—to take their messages. Whenever guards had looked like they might ask questions, Kylar walked up to them and asked for directions.

Don't they know? Can't they see? These men were guards, they were supposed to be protecting Devon Corgi and everyone else in here, and they were going to direct a killer right to him? How could they be so dumb? It was an uneasy feeling of power. It was gratifying that all the hours with Blint were definitely doing something. Kylar was becoming dangerous. And yet—how could they not see what he was?

"Sure, he's the one came in all this week with his eye twitchin', jumping at shadows. I think he's up in the north tower. If you want me to take your message, I could. I'm on duty in ten minutes, it's the first stop on my rounds."

"No thanks. I'm hoping for a good tip. Which way is it?"

As the guard gave Kylar directions, he tried to formulate his plan. The kill itself shouldn't be hard. A kid could get much closer than a grown-up before he roused suspicion, and then it would be too late. The hard part was finding the man. Devon didn't just have an office somewhere. He moved around. That added all sorts of risk, especially because Kylar needed to get the kill done today. The north tower sounded good. Isolated. The guard coming sounded bad. Kylar had just talked to the man, and told him who he was looking for.

With the makeup Blint had used on him, Kylar looked totally different and younger by years. But it was best to let every death be a mystery. *A wetboy leaves corpses, not evidence.* So Kylar would find Corgi and hide until the guard came and left, then he'd kill him.

In and out, no problem, even without the Talent.

The castle was awe-inspiring. Though Blint always spoke of it with scorn, it was the most magnificent building Kylar had ever seen. It was the same black granite as the old aqueducts in the Warrens, quarried in the mountains on the Ceuran border. The entire quarrying industry was owned by the Sa'kagé, so now only the wealthy could afford to build with stone. It was one of the reasons most of the aqueduct pillars were gone now. The non-Sa'kagé poor in the Warrens scavenged the rock for their own use, or their own black–black market sale (bilking the Sa'kagé entailed distinct dangers) to the middle class.

The castle had been built four hundred years ago, when for the thirty years of King Abinazae's rule Cenaria was a major power. He had barely finished the castle when he decided to push further east and take the Chantry, and several thousand magae had ended his ambitions permanently. The castle had first been constructed on the motte-and-bailey design at least a hundred years earlier. Surrounded by the natural moat of the Plith River, Vos Island had been built up into a larger hill, on top of which sat the fortress. What was now the north side of the Warrens had been the original bailey. The Warrens were on a narrow peninsula that dropped off sharply into the sea except for the last half mile, which flattened out before the shoreline. The design was so defensible that neither the wood fortress nor the wood-walled Warrens had ever been taken. But the city had expanded along with King Abinazae's pride, so Castle Cenaria had been built of stone and the city jumped to the east shore of the Plith. The aqueducts, however, were a mystery. They had been there long before King Abinazae and seemed to serve no purpose, as the Plith was freshwater—if not terribly clean.

Leaving the diamond-shaped castle yard, Kylar walked up stone stairs that had been climbed by so many feet over the centuries that the middle of each step dipped several inches lower than the sides. The guards ignored him, and he assumed the attitude of a servant. It was one of his most frequent guises. Blint liked to say that a good disguise cloaked a wetboy better than the shadows. Kylar could walk right past almost anyone he knew with the exception of Count Drake. Not much escaped him.

Soon he passed through most of the buzz of activity that filled the inner yard and the great hall. He went past the lines of people waiting for an audience in the throne room, past the open double doors of the gardens, and made his way to the north tower. The halls were busy everywhere until he stepped into the north tower's antechamber.

Devon Corgi wasn't there. For the first time taking pains to be silent, Kylar opened the door that led to the stairs and climbed them quietly. The stairway was blank. Nothing decorative, no niches, no statues, no ornamental curtains or anything that would afford Kylar a place to hide.

He made his way to the top of the tower. It was, it seemed, just a large bedchamber, currently not being used. A young man balancing a large ledger book was going through the drawers of a bureau, apparently taking an inventory of the neatly folded sheets for the enormous featherbed and the alternate curtains for the large shuttered window. Kylar waited. Devon was turned sideways to the door, and without the Talent to shadow Kylar's approach, there was a good chance the man would see him enter.

The waiting was always the worst. Keyed up with no place to go, Kylar began to entertain fantasies that the guard was going to come up the stairs at any minute. Seeing him here, this late, he'd search him. Searching him, he'd find the slit in Kylar's trousers. Finding that hand-sized slit, he'd find the long knife strapped to Kylar's inner thigh. But there was nothing for it, Kylar waited just out of sight, listening, willing his ears to hear even the scritch of the quill on the ledger.

Finally, he checked and saw Devon disappearing into the closet on the far side of the nearly circular chamber. Kylar crept into the chamber and looked for places to hide. His feet made no sound, not even the sound of leather scuffing against stone. Master Blint had taught Kylar how to boil the sap of the rubber tree to make a shoe sole that was soft and silent. It was expensive to import, and only a little quieter than properly worked leather, but to Master Blint, even the smallest margin mattered. It was why he was the best.

There were no good places to hide. A *great* place to hide was one where Kylar would be able to see the entire room, keep his weapons at ready, and be able to move quickly either to strike or to escape. A *good* place to hide gave a decent view and the ability to strike or escape with only a little difficulty. This room had no dark corners. It was practically a circle. There were rice paper screens, but they'd been folded and were leaning against the wall. Pitifully, the only place to hide was under the bed. If Kylar were a wetboy, perhaps he could have vaulted up a wall and dangled off the chains of the chandelier, but that wasn't an option.

Under the bed? Master Blint will never let me live this down.

But there was no other option. Kylar dropped flat onto his toes and fingertips crawled under the bed. It was good he was still slight, because there wasn't much space. He was uncomfortably in place when he heard someone coming up the stairs.

The guard. Finally. Now take a quick look and get the hell out.

He'd chosen the side of the bed with a view of the closet, and that meant that he didn't have a view of the stairs, but from the sound of the footsteps, he became certain that it wasn't a guard. Devon stepped out of the closet holding a chest, and guilt flashed across his face.

"You can't be here, Bev," he said.

"You're leaving," the unseen woman said. It was an accusation.

"No," he said. His eye started twitching.

"You stole from them, and now you're stealing from the king, and for some reason I'm surprised you'd lie to me. You asshole." Kylar heard her turn, and then Devon was stepping close to the bed, putting the chest down on it, his legs just inches away from Kylar.

"Bev, I'm sorry." He was moving toward the door, and Kylar was stricken with panic. What if Devon went after her, and she went down the steps?

Kylar would have to kill both of them on the stairs, knowing that the guard would be coming along any minute. "Bev, please—"

"Go to hell!" she said, and slammed the door.

Wish granted. It was the blackest kind of humor, Durzo's kind of humor. He liked to say that the irony of overheard conversations was one of the best perks of the bitter business, though he said that the wisdom of last words was highly overrated. *Wish granted?* Kylar didn't like that he'd even thought that. Everything this man had planned was about to end, and Kylar was smirking about it.

Devon swore to himself, but he didn't follow the woman. "Where's that guard anyway? He was supposed to be here by now."

This was what it was like, Durzo had told Kylar. You come in at the end of a drama—whether it's just started or has been going on for years, your arrival signals the end—and you rarely get to know what the story was about. Who was Bev to Devon? His lover? His partner in crime? Just a friend? His sister?

Kylar didn't know. He'd never know.

There was jingling on the stairs, muffled behind the door. Devon picked up his ledger. The door opened.

"'Lo, Dev," the guard said.

"Oh, hello, Gamble." Devon sounded nervous.

"That courier find you?"

"Courier?"

"Little shite musta got lost. Everything fine up here?"

"Sure, just fine."

"See ya round."

Devon waited until the guard had been gone thirty seconds, and then he stepped close to the bed and started stuffing his pockets. Kylar couldn't see with what.

Here it is. The guard would be far enough away now that even if Devon managed to cry out, he wouldn't be heard. Devon stepped away from the bed toward the bureau and Kylar crawled out from beneath the bed like a bug. He stood and drew the knife. Devon was mere paces away. Kylar's heart was pounding. He thought he could hear the rush of blood in his ears.

Kylar did everything right. Low ready stance, advancing quietly but quickly, balanced so that if at any moment the deader reacted, Kylar wouldn't be caught flat-footed. He brought the knife up to eye level, preparing to grab Devon and give him what Durzo called the red grin—a slash across the jugular and deep through the windpipe.

Then he imagined Doll Girl giving him the look she'd given him when he took the biggest piece of bread for himself. *What are you doing, Azoth? You know this is wrong.*

He recovered late, and it was as if his training abandoned him. Kylar was inches away from Devon, and Devon still hadn't heard him, but the very nearness panicked Kylar. He stabbed for Devon's neck and must have made some sound, because Devon was turning. The knife bit into the back of Devon's neck, hit spine, and bounced out. Because of his convulsively tight grip that Durzo would have beaten Kylar for, the knife bounced right out of his hand, too.

Devon turned and yelped. It seemed he was more surprised by Kylar's sudden appearance than by the sting in his neck. He stepped back at the same time Kylar did. He put a hand to his neck, looked at his fingers and saw the blood. Then they both looked down to the knife.

Devon didn't go for it. Kylar scooped up the knife and as he stood, Devon dropped to his knees.

"Please," he said. "Please don't."

It seemed incredible. The man's eyes were big with fear—looking at little Kylar, whose disguise made him look even smaller and younger. There was nothing frightening about him, was there? But Devon looked like a man who's seen his judgment come. His face was white, eyes round, pitiful, helpless.

"Please," he said again.

Kylar slashed his throat in a fury. Why didn't he protect himself? Why didn't he even try? He was bigger than Kylar. He had a chance. Why must he act like a sheep? A big stupid human lamb, too dumb to even move. The cut was through the windpipe, but barely clipped one jugular. It was deep enough to kill, but not fast. Kylar grabbed Devon's hair and slashed again, twice, slightly up, so the blood shot down rather than up. Not a drop got on Kylar. He'd done it just like Durzo had taught.

There was a sound on the stairs. "Devon, I'm sorry," Bev said before she even got into the room. "I just had to come back. I didn't mean—" She stepped into the room and saw Kylar.

She saw his face, she saw the dagger in his hand, she saw him holding the dying Devon by his hair. She was a plain young woman wearing a white serving dress. Wide hips, wide-spaced eyes, mouth open in a little O and beautiful raven hair.

Finish the job.

The training took hold. Kylar was across the room in an instant. He yanked the woman forward, swept a foot in, pivoted, and she flipped over onto the ground. He was as inexorable as Durzo Blint. The woman was beneath him, face down on the carpet that covered this section of floor. The next move was to slide the knife between her ribs. She'd hardly feel it. He wouldn't have to see her face.

He hesitated. It was his life against hers. She'd seen him. His disguise was good only as long as no one knew there was a fourteen-year-old murderer about. She'd seen his face. She had intruded on a deader. She was just collateral damage. An ancillary fatality, Blint said. A wetboy would do what needed to be done. It was less professional but sometimes unavoidable. It doesn't matter, Blint had said. Just finish the job.

Blint only allowed him to live so long as he proved he could do everything a wetboy did, even without the Talent.

Yet here she was, face down, Kylar straddling her on the floor, the point of his dagger pricking her neck, his left hand twisting her hair, trying not to imagine the red blood blooming on her white servant's dress. She'd done nothing.

Life is empty. Life is meaningless. When we take a life, we aren't taking anything of value. I believe it. I believe it.

There had to be another way. Could he tell her to run? To tell no one? To leave the country and never come back? Would she do it? No, of course not. She'd run to the nearest guard. As soon as she was in the presence of some burly castle guard, any fear Kylar might inspire in her would look as small and weak as a guild rat with a knife.

"I told him what would happen if he stole from the Sa'kagé," she said, her voice oddly calm. "That bastard. With everything else he took from me, he didn't even have the decency to die alone. I was coming to apologize, and now you're going to kill me, aren't you?"

"Yes," Kylar said, but he was lying. He had moved the knife to the correct place on her back, but it refused to move.

Out of the corner of his eye, he saw a shadow shift on the stairs. He didn't move, didn't acknowledge that he'd seen it, but he felt a chill. It was the middle of the afternoon; there were no torches burning now, no candles. That shadow could only be Master Blint. He'd followed Kylar. He'd watched everything. The job was for the Shinga, and it wouldn't be botched.

Kylar slid the knife between her ribs, pulled it sideways, felt the shudder and the sigh of the woman dying beneath him.

He stood and pulled the knife from her flesh, his mind suddenly detached, pulling away from him as it had the day in the boat shop with Rat. He wiped the red blade on her white dress, sheathed it along his thigh, and checked himself in the room's mirror for blood, just like he'd been taught.

It was all the sorrow in the world to him that he was clean. There wasn't any blood on his hands.

When he turned, Blint stood in the open doorway, arms folded. Kylar just looked at him, still hovering somewhere behind his own body, glad for the numbness.

"Not great," Durzo said, "but acceptable. The Shinga will be pleased." He pursed his lips, seeing the distance in Kylar's eyes. "Life is meaningless," Durzo said, rolling a garlic clove between his fingers. "Life is empty. When we take a life, we take nothing of value."

Kylar stared at him blankly.

"Repeat it, damn you!" Durzo's hand moved and a knife blurred through the air, thunking into the bureau behind Kylar.

He didn't even flinch. He repeated the words mechanically, fingers atingle, feeling again and again that easy slip of meat parting around the knife. Was it so easy? Was it so simple? You just pushed, and death came? Nothing spiritual about it. Nothing happened. No one was whisked to Count Drake's heaven or hell. They just stopped. They stopped talking, stopped breathing, stopped moving, finally stopped twitching. Stopped.

"That pain you feel," Master Blint said almost gently, "is the pain of abandoning a delusion. The delusion is meaning, Kylar. There is no higher purpose. There are no gods. No arbiters of right and wrong. I don't ask you to like reality. I only ask you to be strong enough to face it. There is nothing beyond this. There is only the perfection we attain by becoming weapons, as strong and merciless as a sword. There is no essential good in living. Life is nothing in itself. It's a place marker that proves who's winning, and we are the winners. We are always the winners. There is nothing but the winning. Even winning means nothing. We win because it's an insult to lose. The ends don't justify the means. The means don't justify the ends. There is no one to justify to. There is no justification. There is no justice. Do you know how many people I've killed?"

Kylar shook his head.

"Me neither. I used to. I remembered the name of every person I killed outside of battle. Then it was too many. I just remembered the number. Then I remembered only the innocents. Then I forgot even that. Do you know what punishments I've endured for my crimes, my *sins*? None. I am proof of the absurdity of men's most treasured abstractions. A just universe wouldn't tolerate my existence."

He took Kylar's hands. "On your knees," he said. Kylar knelt at the edge of a pool of the blood seeping from the woman's body.

"This is your baptism," Master Blint said, putting both of Kylar's hands in the blood. It was warm. "This is your new religion. If you must worship, worship as the other wetboys do. Worship Nysos, god of blood, semen, and wine. At least those have power. Nysos is a lie like all the gods, but at least he won't make you weak. Today, you've become an assassin. Now get out, and don't wash your hands. And one more thing: when you've got to kill an innocent, don't let them talk."

Kylar staggered through the streets like a drunk. Something was wrong with him. He should feel something, but instead, there was only emptiness. It was like the blood on his hands had burst from some soul wound.

The blood was drying now, getting sticky, the bright red fading to brown everywhere but inside his clenched fists. He hid his hands, hid the blood, hid himself, and his mind—less numb than his heart—knew that there was a point in this, too. He would be a wetboy, and he would always be hiding. Kylar himself was a mask, an identity assumed for convenience. That mask and every other would fit because before his training was done, every distinguishing feature of the Azoth who had been would be obliterated. Every mask would fit, every mask would fool every inspector, because there would be nothing underneath those masks.

Kylar couldn't wear his courier disguise into the Warrens—couriers never went to the Warrens—so he headed to an east side safe house on a block crowded with the tiny homes of artisans and those servants not housed at their lords' estates. He rounded a corner and ran straight into a girl. She would have gone sprawling if he hadn't grabbed her arms to catch her.

"Sorry," he said. His eyes took in the simple servant's white dress, hair bound back, and a basket full of fresh herbs. Last, he saw the gory red smears he'd just left on each of her sleeves. Before he could disappear, start running down the street before she saw how he'd stained her, the arcs and crosses of scars on her face clicked into place like the pieces of a puzzle.

They were white now, scars now, where he had branded them into his mind as deep, red, inflamed cuts, burst tissue, dribbling blood, the rough scrape and muted gurgle of blood being swallowed, blood bursting in little bubbles around a destroyed nose. He only had time to see unmistakable scars and unmistakable big brown eyes.

Doll Girl looked down demurely, not recognizing this murderer as her Azoth. The downward glance showed her the gore on her sleeves, and she looked up, horror etched every feature not already etched with scars.

"My God," she said, "you're bleeding. Are you all right?"

He was already running, sprinting heedlessly through the market. But no matter how fast he ran, he couldn't outrun the concern and the horror in those beautiful eyes. Those big brown eyes followed him. Somehow, he knew they always would.

25

You ready to be a champion?" Master Blint asked.

"What are you talking about?" Kylar asked. They'd finished the morning's sparring and he'd done better than usual. He didn't even think he'd be sore tomorrow. He was sixteen years old now, and it seemed like the training was finally starting to pay off. Of course, he still hadn't won a single fight with Master Blint, but he was starting to have hope. On the other hand, Blint had been in a foul mood all week.

"The king's tourney," Master Blint said.

Kylar grabbed a rag and mopped his face. This safe house was small and it got stiflingly hot. King Aleine Gunder IX had convinced the Blademasters to certify a tourney in Cenaria. Of course, they might watch and decide that not even the winner was good enough to be a Blademaster, but on the other hand, they might decide that three or four contestants were. Even a first echelon Blademaster could find great work at any royal court in Midcyru. But, typically, Blint had sneered about the whole affair. Kylar said, "You said the king's tourney was for the desperate, the rich, and the foolish."

"Mm-hmm," Blint said.

"But you want me to fight anyway," Kylar said. He guessed that made him "desperate." Most children's Talent quickened by their early teens. His still hadn't, and Blint was losing his patience.

"The king's holding the tourney so he can hire the winners to be bodyguards. He wants to make sure he isn't hiring any wetboys, so this tourney has a special rule: no one Talented allowed. There will be a maja at the tourney to check all the contestants, a Chantry-trained healer. She's also there to ward the swords so the contestants don't kill each other and to heal anyone who gets hurt. The Nine have decided to flex their muscle. They want one of their own to win, to remind everyone who's who in this city. So it's a situation that fits you like a peg leg fits a cripple. Not that that's a coincidence. This tourney wouldn't even be happening if they hadn't suggested it. The Nine knows all about you and your little problem."

"What?" Kylar was incredulous. He hadn't even known they knew who he was. What if he lost?

"Hu Gibbet showed off his apprentice Viridiana to the Nine this week. A girl, Kylar. I watched her fight. She's Talented, of course. She'd take you, no problem."

Kylar felt a wave of shame. Hu Gibbet was a murderer of the vilest sort. Hu loved murder, loved cruelty for its own sake. Hu never failed, but he also always killed more than just the target. Blint despised him. Kylar was making his master look second-best to a butcher.

"Wait," Kylar said. "Isn't the tourney today?"

It was noon when Kylar arrived at the stadium on the north side of the Warrens. It had only been used for horse races for the last twelve years. Before that, it had been the home of the Death Games. As Kylar approached, he could hear the crowds within. The stadium could hold fifteen thousand people, and it sounded full.

He walked in a cocky glide. It was meant not only to suggest an arrogant young swordsman, but also to disguise his own natural stride. Count Drake wouldn't attend an event that he saw as reminiscent of the Death Games, but Logan Gyre might, as would any number of the young nobles Kylar had to interact with on a fairly regular basis. Usually, Kylar felt no anxiety when he was disguised. First, he was good enough with disguises now that he didn't feel much danger. Second, anxiety drew attention like a lodestone. But now his stomach was in an uproar because his disguise was no disguise at all.

Master Blint had given him the clothes without comment. They were wetboy grays as fine as anything Master Blint owned himself. These were the mottled gray and black that made a better camouflage in darkness than pure black did, the mottling breaking up the human shape. They were fitted perfectly, thin and tight on his limbs, but not impeding his movement. He suspected that the slender cut had another purpose: the Nine wanted him to look as young as possible. *We sent an un-Talented child as our champion. He thrashed you. What happens when we send a wetboy?*

His clothes were completed with a black silk—silk!—cloak, a black silk mask that left only holes for his eyes, a slit for his mouth, and a shock of his dark hair uncovered. He'd rubbed a paste into his hair to make it look utterly black and pulled it into short, disheveled points. In place of his black weapons harness, Blint had given him one of gold, with gold sheaths for each of his daggers, throwing knives, and sword. They stood out starkly against the drab wetboy grays. Blint had rolled his eyes as he gave it to Kylar. "If you've got to go for melodrama, you might as well do it right," he said.

Like this is my *fault?*

Few people lingered on the streets, but when Kylar strode to the side entrance of stadium, spectators and vendors gawked at him. He walked inside and found the fighters' chamber. There were over two hundred men and a couple dozen women inside. They ranged from huge bashers Kylar recognized to mercenaries and soldiers to indolent young noblemen to peasants from the Warrens who had no business holding a sword. The desperate, the rich, and the foolish indeed.

He was noticed immediately and a silence spread through the men joking too loudly, soldiers stretching, and women checking and double-checking their blades.

"Is that everyone?" a bookish woman asked, coming in from a side room. She almost bumped into the huge man who was walking in with her as he stopped abruptly. Kylar's breath caught. It was Logan. Logan wasn't going to watch—he was going to compete. Then the maja saw Kylar. She covered her surprise better than most. "I—I see. Well, young man, come with me."

Acutely aware of maintaining his cocky glide, Kylar walked right past Logan and the others. It was oddly satisfying to hear whispers erupt behind him.

The examination room had once been used to treat injured slave fighters. It had the feel of a room that had seen a lot of death. There were even gutters around at the base of each wall so blood could be washed away easily. "I'm Sister Drissa Nile," the woman said. "And though Blademasters learn to use all edged weapons, for this tourney you can only use your sword. I'm going to have to ask you to remove your other weapons."

Kylar gave her his best Durzo Blint stare.

She cleared her throat. "I suppose I could bind them magically to their sheaths. You won't be able to draw them for perhaps six hours, when the weaves dissipate."

Kylar nodded acquiescence. As she muttered under her breath, wrapping weaves around each of his sheaths, he studied the brackets that had been posted on the wall. He found Logan quickly, then actually looked for a few moments for his own name. *Like the Nine entered me under my real name.* "What am I listed as?" Kylar asked.

She paused and pointed. "I'm going to go out on a limb and guess that's you." The name was listed as "Kage." Drissa muttered, and an accent appeared out of nowhere over the E. "Kagé, the Shadow. If the Sa'kagé didn't send you, young man, you'd better find yourself a fast horse."

No pressure. Kylar was just glad to see that he was in the opposite bracket from Logan. His friend had grown into his height. Logan Gyre was no longer clumsy; he had a huge reach, and he was strong, but training for an hour every other day wasn't the same as training for hours every day under Master Blint's tutelage. Logan was a good fighter, but there was no way he'd make it to the top of his own bracket, which meant Kylar wouldn't have to face him.

Kylar drew his sword and Sister Nile warded it. He tested the edge and it was not just flat but blunted in a small circle around each edge, which showed she knew what she was doing. Even a practice sword could cut if you sliced someone hard enough. At the same time, the weaves didn't appear to add any weight to the blade, or to change how it traveled through the air. "Nice," Kylar said. He was trying to be as laconic as Durzo so he didn't give away his voice. Most of Kylar's voice disguises still made him sound like a child trying to sound like a man. It was more embarrassing than effective.

"The rules of the tourney are the first swordsman to touch his opponent three times wins. I've bonded a ward to each fighter's body that makes opponents' swords react. The first time you touch your opponent, your sword will glow yellow. Second, orange. Third, red. Now, the last thing," she said. "Making sure you have no Talcnt. I'll have to touch you for this."

"I thought you could See."

"I can, but I've heard rumors of people being able to disguise their Talent, and I won't break my oath to make sure this fight is fair, not even here, not even for the Sa'kagé." Drissa put her hand on his hand. She mumbled to herself the whole time. As Blint had explained it, women needed to speak to use their Talent, but apparently it didn't need to be comprehensible.

She stopped abruptly and looked him in the eye. She chewed her lip and then put her hand back on his. "That's no disguise," she said. "I've never seen...Do they know? They must, I suppose, or they wouldn't have sent him, but..."

"What are you talking about?" Kylar asked.

Sister Nile stepped back reluctantly, as if she didn't appreciate having to deal with a human being when she had something far more interesting on her hands. "You're broken," she said.

"Go to hell."

She blinked. "I'm sorry, I meant...People colloquially speak about 'having the Talent' as if it's simple. But it's not simple. There are three things that must all work together for a man or woman to become a mage. First, there's your *glore vyrden,* roughly your life-magic. It's magic gleaned perhaps from your living processes, like we get energy from food, or maybe it's from your soul—we don't know, but it's internal. Half of all people have a glore vyrden. Maybe everyone, just in most it's too small to detect. Second, some people have a conduit or a process that translates that power into magic or into action. It's usually very thin. Sometimes it's blocked. But say a man's brother has a loaded hay wagon fall on him—in that extremity, the man might tap his glore vyrden for the only time in his life and be able to lift the wagon. On the other hand, men who have a glore vyrden and a wide-open conduit tend to be athletes or soldiers. They sometimes perform far better than the men around them, but then, like all others, it takes them time to recuperate. The amount of magic they can use is small and quickly exhausted. If you told them they were using magic, they wouldn't believe you. For a man to be a mage, he needs a third component as well: he must be able to absorb magic from sunlight or fire so that he can refill his glore vyrden again and again. Most of us absorb light through the eyes, but some do it through the skin. That is why, we think, Friaku's gorathi go into battle naked, not to intimidate their foes, but to give themselves access to as much magic as possible."

"So what's that got to do with me?" Kylar asked.

"Young man, you can absorb magic, either through your eyes like a magus, or through your skin. Your skin is practically glowing with it. I'd guess you would have a natural bent toward body magics. And your glore vyrden? I've never seen one like it. You could use magic for half the night and not empty it. It's perfect for a wetboy. But..." She grimaced. "I'm sorry. Your conduit."

"What, it's blocked? Is it bad?" He already knew it was blocked. Blint had been trying to break the block for years. That also made sense of why Blint had made him lie out in the sun, or sit uncomfortably close to forge fires—he'd been trying to force an overflow of magic, so that Kylar couldn't help but use it.

"You have no conduit."

"Will you fix it? Money's no object," Kylar said, his chest tight.

"It's not a matter of drilling a hole. It's more like making new lungs. This is not something any healer in the Chantry has even seen, much less tried to fix, and with a Talent of your Talent's magnitude, my guess is that the attempt would be lethal to you and the healer both. Do you know any magi who would risk their life for you?"

Kylar shook his head.

"Then I'm sorry."

"Could the Gandians help me? They have the best healers, don't they?"

"I'm going to choose not to take offense at that, though most Sisters would. I've heard wild stories from the men's green school. Not that I believe it, but I heard of a magus who saved a dying woman's unborn child by putting it in her sister's womb. Even if that's true, that's dealing with pregnancy, and we healers work with difficult pregnancies all the time. What you've got we never see. People come to us because they're sick. They bring their children to the Chantry or one of the men's schools because they've set a barn on fire, or healed a playmate, or thrown a chair at someone's head using only their minds. People like you don't come to us; they just feel frustrated by life, like they're supposed to be something more than they are, but they can never break through."

"Thanks," Kylar said.

"Sorry."

"So that's it. There's nothing for me?"

"I'm sure the ancients could have helped you. Maybe there's some forgotten old manuscript in a Gandian library that could help. Or maybe there's someone at the Chantry who is studying Talent disorders and I simply don't know about it. I don't know. You could try. But if I were you, I wouldn't throw my life away looking for something you're never going to find. Make your peace with it."

This time, Kylar didn't have to try. The Durzo Blint glare came to his eyes no problem.

26

$\mathcal{K}$ylar walked onto the sands of the stadium ready to hurt someone. The stands were full to overflowing. Kylar had never seen so many people. Vendors walked the aisles hawking rice, fish, and skins of ale. Noblemen and women had servants fanning them in the rising heat, and the king sat in a throne, drinking and laughing with his retinue. Kylar thought he even spied a sour-faced Lord General Agon to one side. The crowd buzzed at the sight of Kagé.

Then the gate opened opposite him and a big peasant stepped in. There was a smattering of disinterested cheering. No one really cared who won, they were just happy that another fight was about to start. A horn blew and the big peasant drew a big rusty bastard sword. Kylar drew his own blade and waited. The peasant charged Kylar and lifted his blade for an overhead chop.

Kylar jumped in, jabbed his blade hard into the man's stomach, then as the peasant tripped past, Kylar slashed his kidney and hamstring. His sword glowed yellow-orange-red.

Everyone seemed taken off guard except for the Blademasters, sitting in a special section in their red and iron-gray cloaks. They pealed a bell immediately.

There were a few cheers and a few boos, but most of the audience seemed more startled than anything. Kylar sheathed his sword and walked back into the fighters' chamber as the peasant dusted himself off, cursing.

He waited alone, sitting still, not talking to anyone. Just before his next turn, a huge basher with a tattoo of a lightning bolt on his forehead sat next to him. Kylar thought his name was Bernerd. Maybe it was Lefty—no, Lefty was the twin with the broken nose.

"You've got Nine fans out there who'd love it if you'd make a bit of a show next time," the big basher said, then he moved on.

Kylar's second opponent was Ymmuri. The horse lords didn't often come to the city, so the audience was excited. He was a small man, covered with layers of brown horsehide, even his face masked behind leather. He too had kept the knives at his belt, big forward-curving gurkas. His blade was a scimitar, excellent for slashing from horseback, but not as good for a swordfight. Further, the Ymmuri was drunk.

As ordered, Kylar played with him, dodging heavy slashes at the last moment, mixing in spin kicks and acrobatics, basically violating everything Durzo had taught him. Against a competent opponent, Durzo said, you never aim a kick higher than your opponent's knee. It's simply too slow. And you don't leave your feet. Jumping commits you to a trajectory you can't change. The only time to use a flying kick was what the Ceurans had developed it for: to unseat cavalry when you yourself were on foot and had no other option. This time when Kylar won, the crowd roared.

As Kylar came in from his fight, he saw Logan going out. Logan's opponent was either Bernerd or Lefty. Kylar hoped the twin wouldn't be too hard on him. A few minutes later, though, Logan came in, flushed and triumphant. Bernerd (or Lefty) must have gotten overconfident.

Kylar's third fight was against a local sword master who made his living tutoring young noblemen. The man looked at Kylar as if he were the vilest snake in Midcyru, but he was overeager on his ripostes. After scoring a single touch on Kylar, he lost and stormed off.

It was only when Logan won his third fight against another sword master that Kylar smelled a rat. Then Kylar won his fourth fight against a veteran soldier—oddly enough, a low-ranking one and not from a good family, but against whom Kylar should have had a tough match. The soldier wasn't a good pretender. Kylar almost didn't attack the openings the man left; they were so blatant that Kylar was sure they were traps.

Then he understood. The peasant had been real. The Ymmuri had been drugged. The sword master had been intimidated. The soldier had been bought. It was a single-elimination tourney, so now there were only sixteen men left. Kylar recognized four of them as Sa'kagé, which meant there were probably another four Sa'kagé he didn't recognize. The Nine had stacked the brackets. It infuriated him. But he sailed through his last fights as if they mattered, doing jumping spin kicks, arm bars, leg sweeps, elaborate disarming combos, and everything else ridiculous he could think of.

He'd thought that the Nine believed in him, that they were giving a real chance, do or die. But this was just another scam. There were great fighters here, but they'd been bought off. No doubt the bookies were making money hand over fist as Kylar rose through one bracket and none other than Logan Gyre rose through the other. Logan, tall, handsome Logan, the scion of a leading family, was hugely popular. So Logan's first fights had been staged to be very close so the Sa'kagé could depress the odds against him. Then Logan had sailed through the more recent rounds. Great fighters took their dives at unlikely times, padding the Sa'kagé coffers further.

In most cases, it was done convincingly. When a semi-competent swordsman was trying to stab you, it didn't take much pretence to miss a block. But Kylar could tell, and he could tell that the Blademasters could tell. They looked furious, and Kylar imagined it would be a long time before they could be convinced to hold a tourney in Cenaria again. The process must be so obviously corrupt to them that Kylar doubted they would grant him Blademaster status even if he earned it twice over.

Just as obvious was that the king couldn't tell, at least not until one of the Blademasters went over and talked to him. Aleine jumped to his feet and it took his counselors some time before they could calm him enough to make him sit. So the Nine had made their point with the king, but there was still money to be made, and if Kylar guessed correctly, the Nine wanted to make their point with the whole city.

Kylar was disgusted as he walked out onto the sand to face Logan. It was the last fight. This was for the championship. There was no good way out. He had half a mind to toss his sword at Logan's feet and surrender—but the king would think that the Sa'kagé was declaring its support for Logan. Then it would only be so long before he hired a wetboy to go visit the Gyre estate—or a simple assassin, if the Sa'kagé wouldn't take the job. Nor could Kylar let him win after a close fight. Now that the king knew the Sa'kagé had stacked the whole event, he would think they were trying to make Logan look good. So what was Kylar supposed to do? Humiliate his best friend?

The earlier elation had faded completely from Logan's face. He was dressed in fine, light chain mail with black links in the shape of a gyrfalcon on front and back, and the crowd roared as the two came together, but neither of the young men paid the crowd any attention.

"I'm not good enough to make it this far. You've set me up," Logan said. "I've been trying to decide what to do about it. I was thinking of throwing my sword down and capitulating to spoil it for you. But you're Sa'kagé, and I'm a Gyre. I'll never surrender to darkness and corruption. So what's it going to be? Do you have another blade hidden that isn't warded? Are you going to kill me publicly, just to remind Cenaria whose boot is on her throat?"

"I'm just a sword," Kylar said, his voice as gruff as Blint's.

Logan scoffed. "A sword? You can't excuse what you are so easily. You're a man who's betrayed every part of his better nature, who at every junction has decided to walk deeper into the darkness, and for what? Money." Logan spat. "Kill me if that's what you've been paid for, Shadow, because I tell you this: I will do my best to kill you."

Money? What did Logan know about money? He'd had money every day of his life. One of his worn-out gloves could be sold to feed a guild rat for months. Kylar felt hot rage wash through his blood. Logan didn't know anything—and yet he couldn't be more right.

Kylar leapt forward at the exact moment the horn blew, not that he cared whether he was following the rules. Logan began to draw his sword, but Kylar didn't bother. He launched himself forward with a lunging kick at Logan's sword hand.

The kick connected before Logan had the sword halfway out of the sheath. It smacked the hilt from his fingers and twisted him to the side. Kylar ran into Logan, twined a foot around the bigger man's legs, and carried them both to the ground.

Kylar landed on top of him and heard the breath whoosh from Logan's lungs. He grabbed each of Logan's arms and yanked them up behind his back, trapping them in one hand. He grabbed a fistful of Logan's hair with the other hand and slammed his face into the sand as hard as he could, again and again, but the sand was too yielding to knock him out.

Standing, Kylar drew his sword. The sounds of Logan moaning and his own heavy breathing seemed to be the only sounds in all the world. The stadium was silent. There wasn't even any wind. It was hot, so damned hot. Kylar slashed viciously across Logan's left kidney and then his right. The sword was warded, so it didn't cut of course, but it was still like getting smacked with a cudgel.

Logan cried out in pain. He sounded suddenly so young. Despite his huge body, Logan was barely eighteen, but the sound embarrassed Kylar. It was weakness. It was humiliating, infuriating. Kylar looked around the stadium. Somewhere, the Nine were here watching, each dressed as an ordinary man, pretending to share his neighbors' horror. Pretending to be friends with men they despised, men they would betray for nothing more than money.

There was a noise behind Kylar, and he saw Logan had fought to his hands and knees. He was struggling to stand. His face was bleeding from a hundred tiny cuts from the sand, and his eyes were unfocused.

Kylar lofted his glowing orange sword to the crowd. Then he spun and smashed the flat of the blade into the back of Logan's head. His friend crumpled, unconscious, and the crowd gasped.

Humiliating Logan had been the only way to save him, but humiliation served in such a dishonorable manner would not draw attention to Logan's defeat, but instead to the Sa'kagé. They were vile, and shameless, and omnipotent, and today Kylar was their avatar. He tossed the red sword down and raised his hands to the crowd once more, this time in dual one-fingered salutes. *To hell with all of you. To hell with me.*

Then he ran.

27

The Modaini Smoking Club's windows were Plangan plate glass cut into wedges and fanciful zoomorphic shapes. If you looked at the shapes in the glass, you could ignore the outside world completely, which was the point. If you looked at the shapes, you wouldn't notice the bars on the other side of the window. Kylar stood at that window, staring through those bars at a girl down in the Sidlin Market.

She was bargaining with a vendor for produce. Doll Girl—Elene—was growing up, perhaps fifteen years old now that Kylar was eighteen. She was beautiful—at least from this safe distance. From here he could see her body, supple curves clad in a simple serving dress, her hair pulled back and shining gold in the sun, and the flash of an easy smile. Though he couldn't make out her scars from this distance, through the colored glass, her white dress was blood red. The leaded zoomorphic whorls reminded him of the whorls of her scars.

"She'll destroy you," Momma K said behind him. "She's part of a different world from any you'll ever know."

"I know," he said quietly, barely glancing over his shoulder. Momma K had come into the room with a new girl, an east side girl, young and pretty. Momma K was combing the girl's blonde hair out. The Modaini Smoking Club was very different from most of the brothels in the city. The courtesans here were trained in the arts of conversation and music as much as the arts of the bedchamber. There was no scandalous dress, no nudity, no groping in the public areas, and no commoners allowed.

Momma K had found out about Kylar's excursions long ago, of course. You couldn't keep anything secret from Momma K. She'd argued with him about it, and still made her comments whenever she happened to be here, but once she'd found out that he wouldn't stop coming, she'd made him swear that he come into the smoking club and watch from inside. If he was going to be stupid, she said, he might as well be safe. If he went outside, sooner or later he'd bump into the girl and talk to her and bed her and fall in love with her and get himself killed for his defiance.

"Don't be shy," Momma K said to the girl. "You're soon going to be doing a lot more while a man's in the room than changing your clothes."

Kylar didn't turn as he heard the sounds of clothes being shed. Just what he needed. He was depressed already.

"I know it's scary your first time, Daydra," Momma K said gently. "It's a hard business. Isn't that right, Kylar?"

"It had better be. It doesn't do much when it's soft."

Daydra giggled, more from her nerves than Kylar's cleverness, no doubt. He didn't turn from the barred window. He was soaking his eyes in Elene. What would her clear brown eyes say as she looked at the girl behind him, preparing for her first client?

"You're going to feel guilty at first, Daydra," Momma K said. "Expect it. Ignore it. You're not a slut, you're not a liar. You're an entertainer. Men don't buy a fine Sethi wine because they're thirsty. They buy it because it makes them feel good and buying it makes them feel good about themselves. That's why they come here, too. Men will always pay for their vices, whether it's wine or lifting your skirt—"

"Or murder," Kylar said, touching the full coin purse and the dagger at his belt.

He could almost feel a chill in the air, but Momma K ignored him and continued on. "The secret is to decide what you won't sell. Never sell your heart. Some girls won't kiss. Some won't be kept by one man. Some won't perform certain services. I did it all, but I kept my heart."

"Did you?" Kylar said. "Really?" He turned, and his heart jumped into his throat. Through Momma K's art, Daydra now looked identical to Elene. Similar build, similar glorious curves, the same gleaming gold hair, the same simple servant's dress, similar to everything but that she was on this side of the bars, close enough to touch, and Elene was out there. Daydra had an uncertain smile, like she couldn't believe how he was talking to Momma K.

Momma K was furious. She swept across the room and grabbed Kylar's ear like he was a naughty little boy. She hauled him out of the room by his ear onto the second-story landing. It was full of overstuffed chairs and fine rugs, with a bodyguard sitting in one corner and doors leading to four different courtesans' rooms. Stairs led down to a parlor lined with suggestive but not explicit paintings and leather-bound books. Momma K finally released his ear and closed the door behind her quietly.

"Damn you, Kylar. Daydra is terrified already. What the hell are you doing?"

"Telling an ugly truth." He shrugged. "Telling lies. Whatever."

"If I wanted truth I'd look in the goddam mirror. This life isn't about truth, it's about making the best of what you've got. This is about that girl, isn't it? That madness. You saved her, Kylar. Now let her go. She owes you everything."

"She owes me her scars."

"You're a damned fool. Have you ever looked at what's happened to all the other girls in your guild? Not even ten years out, they're drunks and riot weed smokers, cutpurses and cripples, beggars and cheap whores, fifteen-year-old mothers with starving children, or unable to bear children at all because they've used tansy tea so many times. I promise you Elene's not the only girl from your guild with scars given to her by some twist. But she is the only one with a hope and a future. You gave her that, Kylar."

"I should have—"

"The only thing you could have done better was murder that boy earlier—before he did anything to you. If you'd been the kind of child capable of murder, you wouldn't have been the kind of boy who cared what happened to some little girl. The truth is that even if they were your fault, Elene's scars are a small price for the life you've given her."

Kylar turned away. The landing had a window overlooking the market, too. It was simple glass, clear, neither cut nor colored like the glass in the courtesan's room. It too was barred, though with simple straight iron, the bars' edges as sharp as one of Blint's knives. Elene had come closer and he could see her scars, but then she smiled and her scars seemed to disappear.

How often did girls in the Warrens smile like that? Kylar found himself smiling in response. He felt lighter than he could ever remember. He turned and smiled at Momma K. "I wouldn't have expected to find absolution from you."

She didn't smile back. "It's not absolution, it's reality. And I'm the perfect person to give you that. Besides, you carry guilt as badly as Durzo."

"Durzo? Durzo never feels guilty about anything," Kylar said.

A flicker of disgust passed over her face. She turned to look at Elene. "End this farce, Kylar."

"What are you talking about?"

"Durzo told you the rules: you can fuck but you can never love. He doesn't see what you're doing, but I do. You believe you love Elene, so you won't fuck at all. Why don't you get this out of your system?" Her voice got gentle. "Kylar. You can't have that girl out there. Why don't you take what you can have?"

"What are you talking about?"

"Go in to Daydra. She'll thank you for it. It's on the house. If you're worried because you're inexperienced, she's a virgin, too." *"Too"? Gods, did Momma K have to know everything?*

"No," Kylar said. "No thanks, I'm not interested."

"Kylar, what are you waiting for? Some glorious soul union with that girl out there? It's just fucking, and that's all you get. That's the deal, Kylar, and you knew it when you started. We all make our deals. I did, Durzo did, and you did too."

Giving up, Momma K gestured to one of her bashers downstairs to let a client through.

A hairy-knuckled slob wheezed his way up the stairs. Though richly dressed, he was fat and ugly and foul smelling and grinning broadly with black teeth. He paused on the landing, licking his lips, a slack-jawed picture of lust. He nodded to Momma K, winked conspiratorially at Kylar, and went into the virgin courtesan's room.

"Maybe they were bad deals," Kylar said.

"It doesn't matter. There's no going back."

*F*eir Cousat knocked on a door high inside the great pyramid of Sho'cendi. Two knocks, pause, two, pause, one. When he and Dorian and Solon had been students at the magi's school of fire, they hadn't rated such prestigious rooms. But he and Dorian hadn't been given the rooms now so much to thank them for their historic services as to keep an eye on them.

The door cracked open, and Dorian's eye appeared on the other side. Feir always thought it was funny: Dorian was a prophet. He could foretell the fall of a kingdom or the winner of a horserace—a lucrative trick when Feir could convince him to do it—but he couldn't tell who was at his own door. He said that prophesying concerning himself involved spiraling uncomfortably close to madness.

Dorian ushered Feir inside and barred the door behind him. Feir felt himself passing through an improbably high number of wards. He looked at them. A ward against eavesdropping he'd expected. A ward against entry was unusual to maintain when you were in the room yourself. But the truly strange one was a ward to keep magic in. Feir fingered the threads of the weave, shaking his head in astonishment. Dorian was the kind of magus born once a generation. After studying at Hoth'salar, the Healers' School on Gandu, and mastering all they had to teach him by the time he was six-teen, Dorian had come to the school of fire and mastered fire magics while not even pretending to be interested in them. He'd only stayed because he'd become friends with Feir and Solon. Solon's talents were almost solely in Fire, but he was the strongest of the three. Feir wasn't sure why the two had become friends with him. Maybe because he wasn't threatened by their excellence. They were so obviously the kind of men who'd been touched by the gods that Feir didn't even think to be jealous for a long time. Maybe it helped that he'd been born a peasant. It probably also helped that whenever he was struggling with his studies and started to be jealous, one or the other of his friends would suggest sparring with him.

Feir looked fat, but he could move and he trained daily with the Blade-masters, who kept their central training facility mere minutes from Sho'cendi.

For Solon or Dorian to volunteer to spar with him was to volunteer for bruises. Dorian could heal bruises later, but they still hurt.

Dorian had half-packed saddlebags open on the bed.

Feir sighed. "You know the Assembly's forbidden you to leave. They don't care about Cenaria. Honestly, if Solon weren't there, I wouldn't either. We could send him a message to leave." The school's leaders hadn't phrased it that way, of course. They were more worried about delivering the continent of Midcyru's only—perhaps the world's only—prophet into the God-king's hands.

"You don't even know the best part yet," Dorian said, grinning like they were children.

Feir felt the blood draining from his face. The wards to keep magic in the room suddenly made sense. "You aren't planning to steal it."

"I could make the argument that it's ours. The three of us were the ones who tracked it, found it, and brought it back. They stole it from us first, Feir."

"You agreed it would be safer here. We let them take it from us."

"So I'm taking it back," Dorian said, shrugging.

"So it's you against all the world again."

"It's me *for* all the world, Feir. Will you come with me?"

"Come with you? Is this the madness?" When Dorian's gift for prophecy had surfaced, one of the first things he'd tried was to tell his own future. He'd learned that no matter what he did, he would go mad one day. Delving into his own future would only hasten that day's arrival. "I thought you said you had still had a decade or so."

"Not so long, now," Dorian said. He shrugged like it didn't matter, as if it didn't break his heart, exactly the way he'd shrugged when he'd asked Solon to go to Cenaria, knowing it would cost Solon Kaede's love. "Before you answer, Feir, know this: if you come with me, you will regret it many times, and you will never again walk the halls of Sho'cendi."

"You make such a convincing plea," Feir said, rolling his eyes.

"You will also save my life at least twice, own a forge, be known throughout the world as the greatest living weaponsmith, have a small part in saving the world, and die satisfied, if not nearly so old as you or I hoped."

"Oh, that's better," Feir said sarcastically, but his stomach was doing flips. Dorian rarely told what he knew, but when he did, he never lied. "Just a small part in saving the world?"

"Feir, your purpose in life isn't your happiness. We're part of a much bigger story. Everyone is. If your part is unsung, does that make it worthless? Our purpose on this trip isn't to save Solon. It's to see a boy. We will face many dangers to get there. Death is a very real possibility. And do you know what that boy needs from us? Three words. Maybe two if the name counts as only one. Do you want to know what they are?"

"Sure."

" 'Ask Momma K.' "

"That's it? What's it mean?" Feir asked.

"I have no idea."

Sometimes a seer could be a pain in the ass. "You ask for a lot from me," Feir said.

Dorian nodded.

"I'll regret it if I say yes?"

"Many times. But not in the end."

"It might be easier if you told me less."

"Believe me," Dorian said, "I wish I didn't have such a clear view of what lies before you down each possible choice here. If I told you less, you would hate me for holding back. If I told you more, you might not have the heart to carry on."

"Enough!" Gods, was it going to be that bad?

Feir looked at his hands. He'd have a forge. He'd be known throughout the world for his work. It had been one of his dreams. Maybe he could even marry, have sons. He thought of asking Dorian, but didn't dare. He sighed and rubbed his temples.

Dorian broke into a big smile. "Good! Now help me figure out how we're going to get Curoch out of here."

Feir was sure he had misunderstood. Then he felt the blood draining from his face. There were wards on the door to keep magic *in*. "When you say 'here' you mean 'here, in the school.' Like I still have a chance to convince you *not* to try to steal the most guarded artifact in Midcyru. Right?"

Dorian threw back the covers on the bed. There was a plain sheathed sword on it. It looked entirely normal, except that the sheath was made entirely of lead, and it covered the sword entirely, even the hilt, damping the magic. But this wasn't just a magic sword. It was more like The Magic Sword. This was Curoch, Emperor Jorsin Alkestes' sword. The Sword of Power. Most magi weren't even strong enough to use it. If Feir (or most others) tried, it would kill him in a second. Dorian had said even Solon couldn't use it safely. But after Jorsin Alkestes' death, there had been quite a few magi who had been able to—and they'd destroyed more than one civilization. "At first, I thought I was going to have to prophesy my own future to get it, but instead, I prophesied the guards'. Everything worked perfect except one guard came down a hallway that he only had maybe a one in a thousand chance of taking. I had to knock him out. The good news is, he's going to be nursed back to health by a lovely girl whom he'll later marry."

"You're telling me there's some guard unconscious upstairs right now, just waiting to be found? While we're talking? Why are you even doing this?"

"Because he needs it."

"He? You're stealing Curoch for 'ask Momma K' boy?" Feir asked.

"Oh no, well, not directly. The boy who needs to hold Curoch—the one the whole world needs to hold Curoch—isn't even born yet. But this is our only chance to take it."

"Gods, you're serious," Feir said.

"Stop pretending this changes anything. You've already decided. We're going to Cenaria."

Sometimes a seer could be a pain in the ass? Try always.

29

*W*hat is your problem!" Master Blint screamed.

"I don't—" Kylar said.

"Again!" Blint roared.

Kylar stopped the practice knife with an X block, crossing his wrists in front of him. He tried to grab Durzo's hand and twist, but the wetboy slipped aside.

They ranged around the practice building of Blint's newest safe house, vaulting off walls, maneuvering each other into beams, attempting to use every uneven edge of the floor against each other. But the match was even.

The nine years Kylar had spent under Blint's tutelage had seen him harden and grow. He was maybe twenty now. He was still not as tall as Blint and never would be, but his body was lean and taut, and his eyes were the same light blue. As he sweated and fought, every muscle in his arms, chest, and stomach was distinct and moving precisely to its task, but he couldn't make himself really engage.

Durzo Blint saw it, and it infuriated him. Swearing long and eloquently, Master Blint compared his attitude unfavorably with a lackadaisical prostitute's, his face with unlikely and unhealthy body parts, and his intelligence with several species of farm animals. When he attacked again, Kylar could see him mentally ratcheting up the level.

One of the many dangerous things about Master Blint was that even when he was furious, it never showed in his fighting. His fury would only be allowed expression after you were lying on the ground, usually bleeding.

He moved Kylar across the open room slowly, hand clenched in fist or extending in knife hand, the practice knife glittering in quick arcs and jabs. For a fraction of a second, he overextended a stab and Kylar managed to slip around it and hit Master Blint's wrist.

But Master Blint held onto the knife, and as he drew it back, the dull blade caught Kylar's thumb.

"That impatience cost you a thumb, boy."

With his chest heaving, Kylar stopped, but he didn't take his eyes off of Master Blint. They'd already practiced with swords of several kinds, with knives of varying lengths. Sometimes they fought with the same weapon, and sometimes they'd mismatch—Master Blint taking a double-edged broadsword against a Gandian blade, or Kylar taking a stiletto against a gurka. "Anyone else would have lost the knife," Kylar said.

"You're not fighting anyone else."

"I wouldn't fight you if you were armed and I wasn't."

Master Blint drew back the knife and threw it past Kylar's ear. Kylar didn't flinch. It wasn't that he didn't still wonder sometimes if Master Blint was going to kill him. It was that he knew he couldn't stop him.

When Blint attacked again, it was full speed. Kick met stop kick, punches were diverted, jabs dodged, blows absorbed against arms, legs, and hips. There were no tricks, nothing showy. Just speed.

In the midst of the flashing limbs, as usual, Kylar realized that Master Blint would win. The man was simply better than Kylar. It was usually about now that Kylar would try something desperate. Master Blint would be waiting for it.

Kylar unleashed a storm of blows, fast and light as a mountain breeze. None of them alone would hurt Master Blint even if they connected, but any would cause him to miss the next. Kylar fought faster and faster, each blow being brushed aside or only connecting with flesh tensed for the impact.

One low spear hand got through, jabbing Master Blint's abdomen. As he hunched over involuntarily, Kylar went for the full strike on Blint's chin—then stopped. Blint lashed up fast enough that he would have blocked the strike, but with no contact where he'd expected it, he brought the block too far and couldn't bring his hand back before Kylar lashed his still-cocked fist at his nose.

But Kylar's strike didn't catch Master Blint. It was brushed aside by an unseen force like an invisible hand. Stumbling, Kylar tried to recover and block Durzo's kick, but it blew through his hands with superhuman force. Kylar smashed into the beam behind him so hard that he heard it crack. He dropped to the ground.

"Your turn," Blint said. "If you can't touch me, I'll have a special punishment for you."

"Special punishment"? Beautiful.

Hunched on the ground with both arms throbbing, Kylar didn't answer. He stood, but when he turned, in Blint's place stood Logan. But the sneer on Logan's face was all Durzo Blint. It was an illusion, an illusion seven feet tall, matching Blint's moves precisely. Kylar kicked viciously at his knee—but his foot went right through the figure, shattering the illusion and touching nothing at all. Blint stood two feet behind it. As Kylar staggered off balance, Blint raised a hand. With a whoosh, a phantom fist shot from his hand and knocked Kylar off his feet.

Kylar bounced back to his feet in time to see Blint leap. The ceiling was twelve feet high, but Blint's entire back hit it—and stuck to it. He started crawling, and then disappeared as shadows writhed over him and merged with the greater darkness of the ceiling. First Kylar could hear Blint moving to a spot above him, then the sound cut off abruptly. Blint's Talent was covering even the scuffing sound of brushing against wood.

Moving constantly, Kylar searched the ceiling for any shadow out of place.

"Scarred Wrable can even throw his voice, or any other sound," Blint said, from the far corner of the ceiling. "I wonder if you could."

Kylar saw, or thought he saw, the shadow moving back toward him. He flung a throwing knife at the shadow—and it burst apart, leaving his knife quivering in the wood. It was another illusion. Kylar turned slowly, trying to hear the slightest sound out of place over the pounding of his heart.

The slight brush of cloth hitting the floor behind him made him spin and lash out. But there was nothing there except Blint's tunic in a pile on the floor. A thump announced Blint himself landing behind Kylar. Kylar spun once more, but something caught his left hand, then his right.

Master Blint stood bare-chested, a dead look in his eyes, his real hands at his sides. Kylar's wrists were held in the air by magic. Slowly, his arms were pulled apart until he was spread-eagled, then further. Kylar held his silence for as long as he could, then screamed as he felt his joints on the verge of dislocating.

The bonds dropped and Kylar crumpled, defeated.

Durzo shook his head in disappointment—and Kylar attacked. His kick slowed as it approached Durzo's knee as if it were sinking into a spring, then bounced back, spinning him hard and throwing him in a tangle to the floor.

"Do you see what just happened?" Durzo asked.

"You kicked my ass again," Kylar said.

"Before that."

"I almost hit you," Kylar said.

"You fooled me and you would have destroyed me, but I used my Talent and you still refuse to use yours. Why?"

Because I'm broken. Since meeting Drissa Nile four years ago, Kylar had thought a hundred times about telling Durzo Blint what she'd told him: he didn't have a conduit, and it couldn't be fixed. But the rules had always been clear. Kylar became a wetboy, or he died. And as Blint had just proved again, Kylar wouldn't be a wetboy without the Talent. Telling Blint the truth had always seemed like a quick way to die. Kylar had tried everything to get his Talent to work or to learn about anything that might help, but had found nothing.

Blint breathed deeply. When he spoke again, his voice was calm. "It's time for some truth, Kylar. You're a good fighter. Deficient still with pole arms and clubs and crossbows and—" He was starting to lecture but noticed it. "Regardless, you're as good at hand-to-hand fighting and with those Ceuran hand-and-a-half swords you like as any fighter I've seen. Today you would've had me. You won't win next time, but you'll start winning. Your body knows what to do, and your mind has got it mostly figured out, too. In the next few years, your body will get a bit faster, a bit stronger, and you'll get cleverer by half. But your weapons training is finished, Kylar. The rest is practice."

"And?" Kylar asked.

"Follow me. I've got something that may help you."

Kylar followed Blint to his workroom. This one was smaller than the one Azoth had first seen in Blint's old safe house, but at least this house had doors between the animals' pens and the work area. It smelled much better. It was also familiar now. The books lining the shelves were like old friends. He and Blint had even added dozens of recipes to them. In the past nine years, he had come to appreciate Blint's mastery of poisons.

Every wetboy used poisons, of course. Hemlock, and blood flower, and mandrake root, and ariamu were all local and fairly deadly. But Blint knew hundreds of poisons. There were entire pages of his books crossed out, notes scrawled in Durzo's tight angular hand, "Fool. Dilutes the poison." Other entries were amended, from how long it took for the poison to take effect to what the best methods for delivery were, to how to keep the plants alive in foreign climes.

Master Blint picked up a box. "Sit."

Kylar sat at the high table, propping an elbow on the wood and holding his chin. Blint upended the box in front of him.

A white snake slid onto the table with a thump. Kylar barely had time to register what it was before it struck at his face. He saw its mouth open, huge, fangs glittering. He was moving back, but too slowly.

Then the snake disappeared and Kylar was falling backward off the stool. He landed flat on his back but bounced up to his feet in an instant.

Blint was holding the snake behind the head. He had grabbed it out of the air while it was striking. "Do you know what this is, Kylar?"

"It's a white asp." It was one of the most deadly snakes in the world. They were small, rarely growing longer than a man's forearm, but those they bit died within seconds.

"No, it's the price of failure. Kylar, you fight as well as any non-Talented man I've ever seen. But you're no wetboy. You've mastered the poisons; you know the techniques of killing. Your reaction speed is peerless; your instincts are good. You hide well, disguise well, fight well. But doing those things *well* is shit, it's nothing. An *assassin* does those things well. That's why assassins have targets. Wetboys have deaders. Why do we call them deaders? Because when we take a contract, the rest of their short lives is a formality. You have the Talent, Kylar, but you aren't using it. Won't use it. You've seen a little of what I have to teach you, but I can't teach it to you until you tap your Talent."

"I know. I know," Kylar said, refusing to meet his master's gaze.

"The truth is, Kylar, I didn't need an apprentice when you came along. Never did. But I heard a rumor that an ancient artifact was hidden in Cenaria: the silver ka'kari. They say Ezra the Mad himself made it. It's a small silver ball, but when you bond it, it makes you impervious to any blade and it extends your life indefinitely. You can still be killed any way that doesn't involve metal, but immortality, Kylar! And then you came along. Do you know what you are? Did that maja Drissa Nile tell you?"

Durzo knew about Drissa Nile? "She said I was broken."

"The ka'kari were made for people 'broken' like you are. There's supposed to be an attraction between people who are vastly Talented but don't have a conduit and the ka'kari. You were supposed to call it, Kylar. You don't know how to bond it, so you'd call it, hand it over, and I'd be immortal."

"And I'd still be broken," Kylar said bitterly.

"Once I had it, we could have Drissa study it. She's a great healer. Even if it took her a few years, it would have been fine. But we're running out of time," Durzo said. "Do you know why I can't just let you be an *assassin*?" Even now he sneered.

Kylar had wondered a hundred times, of course, but he'd always figured it was because Blint's pride wouldn't let him have a failed apprentice.

"Our Talent allows us to swear a magically binding oath of service to the Shinga. It keeps the Shinga safe, and it keeps us above suspicion. It's a weak compulsion, but to break it a wetboy would have to submit himself to a mage or a meister, and all the mages in this city work for the Sa'kagé and only an idiot would submit to a meister. You've become a skilled assassin, Kylar, and it's making the Shinga nervous. He doesn't like being nervous."

"Why would I ever do anything against the Shinga? It would be signing my own death warrant."

"That's not the point. Shingas who aren't paranoid don't live long."

"How could you never tell me all this?" Kylar demanded. "All the times you've beaten me for not using my Talent—it's like beating a blind man because he can't read!"

"Your desperation to use your Talent is what calls the ka'kari. I was helping you. And I'm going to help you some more." He gestured to the snake in his hand. "This is motivation. It's also the kindest poison I know." Master Blint held Kylar with his eyes. "Getting that ka'kari has always been your final test, boy. Get it. Or else."

The air took on a chill. There it was. Kylar's last warning.

Master Blint put away the snake, collected a few of his weapons, grabbed the bag he already had packed, and picked Retribution off its pegs on the wall. He checked the big black blade, then slid it back into its scabbard. "I'm going to be gone for a while," he said.

"I'm not coming with you?"

"You'd get in the way."

Get in the way? The casual way Blint said it hurt almost as much as the fact that it was true.

30

I don't like it," Solon said.

Regnus Gyre stared into the winds that blew his silver hair almost straight back. The Twins were quiet today, so there was only the sound of the wind rushing over the wall. He listened to the wind as if it were trying to tell him something.

"After ten years, a summons," Solon said. "Why would the king do such a thing on the eve of your son's majority?"

"What's the best reason to gather all your enemies in one place?" Regnus asked, barely raising his voice enough to be heard over the wind. It was still cold even in late spring. Screaming Winds was never warm. The north wind cut through wool, made a mock of the beards and long hair the men grew to hold some extra iota of heat in.

"To smash them," Solon said.

"Better to smash them before they can gather," Regnus said. "The king knows that I'll do everything in my power to be home for my son's ascendance. That means traveling fast. That means a small escort."

"Clever of him not to command a small escort," Solon said. "I'd have put such subtlety beyond him."

"He's had ten years to think about this, my friend, and the help of his weasel." His weasel was Fergund Sa'fasti, a magus who was not exactly Sho'cendi's finest moralist. Fergund also knew Solon by sight and would gladly tell the world Solon was a magus if he thought it would cause mischief. Fergund was why Solon had been staying with Regnus year-round as Logan took more responsibilities at court.

It was, he was beginning to think, a serious mistake.

"So you think they'll attack us on the way?" Solon asked.

Regnus nodded into the wind.

"I don't suppose I'll be able to convince you not to go?" Solon asked.

Regnus smiled, and Solon couldn't help but love the man. For all that it had crippled his house and destroyed any ambitions Regnus might have had for the throne, taking command of Screaming Winds had given Regnus life.

There was fire in Regnus Gyre, something fierce and proud like a warrior king of old. His command had clear authority, and the power of his presence made him father, king, and brother to his men. In the simple fight against evil, he excelled, even reveled. The highlanders of Khalidor, some of whom had never bowed the knee to any man, were warriors. They lived for war, thought it a disgrace to die in bed, believed the only immortality was immortality through deeds of arms sung by their minstrels.

They called Regnus the *Rurstahk Slaagen,* the Devil of the Walls, and in the last ten years, their young men had smashed themselves against those walls, tried to climb them, tried to sneak past them, tried to bribe their way through them, climbed over the Twins and tried to descend on Screaming

Winds from behind. Every time, Regnus had crushed them. Frequently, he did it without losing a man.

Screaming Winds was made of three walls at the three narrowest points in the only pass between Cenaria and Khalidor. Between the walls were killing fields sown thick by Regnus's engineers with caltrops, pits, snares, and deadfalls of rock from the surrounding mountains. Twice clans had made it past the first wall. The traps had reaped such a harvest of death that none had survived to tell what they found beyond it.

"It could be genuine, I suppose," Solon said. "Logan says he has become close friends with the prince. Maybe this is the prince's influence at work."

"I don't think much of the prince," Regnus said.

"But he thinks a lot of Logan. We can hope that the prince takes after his mother. This may even be her work."

Regnus said nothing. He wouldn't say Nalia's name, not even now.

"Hope for the best, plan for the worst?" Solon asked. "Ten of our best men, extra horses for all of us, and go down the coast road instead of the main road?"

"No," Regnus said. "If they've set one ambush, they'll have set two. We might as well make them play their gambit on open ground."

"Yessir." Solon only wished he knew who the other players were.

"You still write letters to that Kaede woman?"

Solon nodded, but his body went rigid. His chest felt hollow. Of course the commander would know. A letter sent every week, and never a one received.

"Well, if you don't get a letter after this one, at least you'll know it's not because yours are boring." Regnus clapped a hand on Solon's shoulder.

Solon couldn't help but smile ruefully. He didn't know how Regnus did it, but somehow in his company it was as easy to face heartbreak as it was to face death.

Momma K sat on the balcony of an estate that had no business being where it was. Against all tradition and sanity, Roth Grimson's opulent estate had been built in the middle of the Warrens.

She didn't like Roth and never had, but she met few people in her work that she did like. The fact was, she had to deal with Roth because she couldn't afford to ignore him. He was one of the Sa'kagé's rising stars. Not only was he intelligent, but everything he touched seemed to turn to gold. After the guild wars, he had emerged as the guild head of the Red Bashers, and had promptly taken over half of the Warrens.

Of course, the Sa'kagé had stepped in, only beginning with Durzo's assassination of Corbin Fishill, but it had taken years to get things truly settled. There had been, of course, curiosity among the Nine at how Roth had managed his guild so well that they'd claimed so much territory. And Roth obviously hadn't liked her questions, but he'd accepted them. A word from her and he'd never be on the Nine. Another word, and he'd be dead. He was smart enough to know that.

Roth was in his late twenties. A tall, formidable young man who carried himself like a prince among dogs. Close-set blue eyes, dark hair, a penchant for fine clothing: today he wore a gray tunic decorated with the Plangan knotwork that was just coming into fashion, matching breeches, and high boots worked in silver. He wore his black hair lightly oiled, a wavy lock sometimes drooping into his eyes.

"If you ever tire of working for our Master of Coin, you'd do well in one of my brothels. The men would adore you." She threw that out just to see how he'd take it.

He laughed. "I'll keep that in mind."

With a wave, he signaled the servants to bring their breakfast. Their little table graced the edge of the balcony, and they sat beside each other. Apparently, Roth wanted her to admire his estate. Probably he was hoping she'd ask him why he'd built here.

She didn't want to give him the satisfaction. Besides, she'd already looked into it. The reasons were good enough, she knew. He had some waterfront, which would allow him to do some smuggling, though the dock was too small for high profitability and royal attention. He'd also been able to purchase the land for a pittance, though he'd had to hire so many bashers during the construction he'd lost the savings. When the poor had been displaced, both the honest and the thieves among them had been eager to steal whatever they could from the fool who would build a manse on their side of the river. The bashers had probably beaten hundreds. Momma K knew that they had killed at least half a dozen. It was death to be found on Grimson's grounds without permission.

The walls were high, lined with crushed glass and metal spikes that stood as pointed shadows in the dawn light. Bashers manned those walls, men who were both efficient and enjoyed their work. None of the locals tried to intrude anymore. The amateurs had either already tried and paid the price or knew of others who had. The professionals knew they could cross Vanden Bridge and find easier pickings.

His gardens were beautiful, if given to flowers and plants that kept low to the ground so that his archers didn't have their killing angles obscured.

The splashes of vermilion, green, yellow, and orange of his gardens were a stark contrast against the grays and dingy browns of the Warrens.

The servants brought the first course, halved blood oranges with a caramelized sugar crust. Roth opened with a comment on the weather. Not a particularly inspired choice, but Momma K didn't expect more.

He moved on to commenting on his gardens as the servants brought hot sweetbread. He had the newly rich's irritating propensity for revealing how much things had cost. He should have known that she would be able to tell from the quality of the service and the meal exactly how much he was spending on this estate of his. When would he get to the point?

"So there's going to be an opening on the Nine," Roth said. Abruptly done. He should have divulged an amusing anecdote from his work and used that to lead here. Momma K was starting to doubt this one.

"Yes," she said. She let it sit. She wasn't going to make this easy. The sun was just rising above the horizon and the sky was turning a glorious orange. It was going to be a scorching day; even at this hour she barely needed the shawl around her shoulders.

"I've been working with Phineas Seratsin for six years. I know the job better than anyone."

"You've been working *for* the Trematir, not with him."

His eyes flashed, but he said nothing. A dangerous temper, then. Master Grimson didn't like to be corrected.

"I think your spies must not be smart enough to have seen the amount of work I do versus what that old man does."

She lifted an eyebrow. "Spies?"

"Everyone knows you have spies everywhere."

"Well. Everyone knows. It must be so, then."

"Oh, I see," Roth said. "It's one of those things everyone knows but I'm not supposed to mention because it's rude."

"There are people within this organization with whom it is dangerous to be rude, boy. If you're asking for my vote, you'd do well to make a friend of me."

He motioned to the servants, who took their plates and replaced them with cuts of spiced meats and a lightly broiled egg dish with cheese.

"I'm not asking," he said quietly.

Momma K finished her eggs and began on the braised meat. Delightful. The man must have brought a chef from Gandu. She ate and looked at the lightening sky, the sun rising slowly over the great iron gate to Grimson's estate. If he took that comment back, she'd let him live.

"I don't know how you have such influence on the Nine, but I know I need your vote, and I will have it," Roth said. "I will take your vote, or I will take your niece."

The meat that a moment ago had seemed so delightfully spiced, that seemed to melt in Momma K's mouth, suddenly tasted like a mouthful of sand.

"Pretty girl, isn't she? Adorable little braids. It's so sad about her mother dying, but wonderful that she had a rich aunt to find her a place to live, and in the castle itself, no less! Still, a rich old whore ought to have done better than have her niece raised by a serving woman."

She was frozen. *How did he find out?*

The ledgers. Her ledgers were done all in code, but Phineas Seratsin was the Sa'kagé's Master of Coin. He had access to more financial records than the next five people in the kingdom combined. Roth must have followed the records and found payments made to a serving woman in the castle. She was a frightened woman. A single threat from Roth and she'd have folded.

Roth stood, his plate already empty. "No, do sit. Finish your breakfast."

She did, mechanically, using the time to think. Could she spirit the girl away? She couldn't use Durzo for this, but he wasn't the only wetboy she knew.

"I am a cruel man, Gwinvere. Taking a life is . . ." Roth shivered with remembered ecstasy. "Better. Better than any of the pleasures you sell. But I control my appetites. And that's what makes us human rather than slaves, isn't it?"

He was pulling on a thick leather glove. The portcullis of his gate was rising as he spoke. Outside, Momma K saw dozens of ragged peasants gathered. Obviously, this was a daily ritual.

Below, four servants were carrying a table laden with food into the garden. They set it down and walked back inside.

"These wretches are slaves to their appetites. Slaves, not men."

The starving peasants behind pushed forward and those in front were pushed inside. They looked at the spiked portcullis above them and then at Roth and Momma K. But their eyes were mostly on the food. They looked like animals, hunger driving them wild.

A young woman made a break for it. She sprinted forward. After she had only taken a few steps, others followed her. There were old men and young, women, children, the only thing they seemed to have in common was desperation.

But Momma K couldn't see the reason for their frenzy. They reached the

156

food and tore into it, stuffing pockets full of sausages, stuffing their mouths full of delicacies so rich they'd probably be sick later.

A servant handed an arbalest to Roth. It was already drawn and loaded.

"What are you doing?" Momma K asked.

The peasants saw him and scattered.

"I kill by a very simple pattern," Roth said, lifting the weapon. He pressed the trigger plate and a young man dropped with a bolt in his spine.

Roth set the point of the arbalest down, but instead of cranking the winch to draw back the string, he grabbed the string with his glove and drew it back by hand. For the barest moment, black tattoo-like markings rose up as if from beneath the surface of his skin and writhed with power. It was impossible.

He shot again and the young woman who had been the first to run for the table fell gracelessly.

"I feed my little herd every day. The first week of the month, I kill on the first day. The second week, the second day." He paused as the arbalest drew level again. He shot and another woman dropped as a bolt blew through her head. "And so on. But I never kill more than four."

Most of the peasants were gone now, except for one old man moving at a crawl toward the gate that was still thirty paces distant. The bolt clipped the old man's knee. He fell with a scream and started crawling.

"The slaves never figure it out. They're ruled by their bellies, not their brains." Roth waited until the old man reached the gate, missed a shot, then tried again, killing him. "See that one?"

Momma K saw a peasant come in through the portcullis. All the others had scattered.

"He's my favorite," Roth said. "He figured out the pattern." The man walked inside, unafraid, nodded to Roth, and then went to the table and started to eat without haste.

"Of course, he could tell the others and save a few lives. But then I might change the pattern, and he'd lose his edge. He's a survivor, Gwinvere. Survivors are willing to make sacrifices." Roth handed the arbalest and the glove to a servant and regarded Momma K. "So, the question is, are you a survivor?"

"I've survived more than you'll ever know. You have your vote." She'd kill him later. There was no showing weakness now. No matter how she felt. He was an animal, and he would sense her fear.

"Oh, I want more than a vote. I want Durzo Blint. I want the silver ka'kari. I want . . . much more. And I'll get it, with your help." He smiled. "How'd you like the braised peasant?"

She shook her head, distracted, looking blankly at her empty plate. Then she froze. In the garden, servants were collecting the bodies and bringing them inside.

"You did say 'pheasant,'" she said.

Roth just smiled.

31

*W*ell, if you don't look like the south end of a northbound horse," Logan said as he intercepted Kylar in the middle of the Drake's yard.

"Thanks," Kylar said. He stepped past Logan, but his friend didn't move. "What do you want, Logan?"

"Hmm?" Logan asked. He was a picture of innocence, at least, if a picture of innocence could be so tall. Nor was he able to get by with the big-oaf routine. For one thing, Logan was far too intelligent for anyone to take a dumb act seriously. For another, he was too damn handsome. If there were a model of perfect masculinity in the realm, it was Logan. He was like a heroic statue made flesh. Six months a year with his father had lined his big frame with muscle and given him a hard edge that had more than just the young women of Cenaria swooning. Perfect teeth, perfect hair, and of course, ridiculous amounts of money that would be his when he reached twenty-one—in three days—filled out the picture. He drew almost as much attention as his friend Prince Aleine—and even more from the girls who weren't interested in being bedded and then dropped the next day. His saving grace was that he had absolutely no idea how attractive he was or how much people admired and envied him. It was why Kylar had nicknamed him Ogre.

"Logan, unless you were just standing in the yard, you came out here when you saw me come in the gate, which means you were waiting for me. Now you're standing there rather than walking with me, which means you don't want anyone to overhear what you're about to say. Serah *isn't* in her regular place two steps behind you, which means she's with your mother shopping for dresses or something."

"Embroidery," Logan admitted.

"So what is it?" Kylar asked.

Logan shifted from one foot to the other. "I hate it when you do that.

You could've let me get to it in my own time. I was going to—hey, where do you think you're going?"

Kylar kept walking. "You're stalling."

"All right. Just stop. I was just thinking that sometime we ought to pull out the old fisticuffs," Logan said.

Fisticuffs. And people expected that someone so big to be dumb.

"You'd beat me black and blue," Kylar said, smiling the lie. If they fought, Logan would ask questions. He'd wonder. It was unlikely, but he might even guess that it hadn't truly been nine years since they'd last fought.

"You don't think I'd win, do you?" Logan asked. Ever since Logan had been humiliated in the fight at the stadium, he'd gotten serious about training. He put in hours every day with the best non-Sa'kagé sword masters in the city.

"Every time we've fought you slaughtered me. I'm—"

"Every—? Once! And that was ten years ago!"

"Nine."

"Regardless," Logan said.

"If you caught me with one of those anvils you pass off as your fists, I'd never get up," Kylar said. That was true enough.

"I'd be careful."

"I'm no match for an ogre." Something was wrong. Logan asked him to fight about once a year, but never so strenuously. Logan's honor wouldn't allow him to push a friend who'd made a decision clear, even if he didn't understand why. "What's this about, Logan? Why do you want to fight?"

Lord Gyre looked down and scratched his head. "Serah's asked why we don't spar with each other. She thinks it would be a good match. Not that she wants to see us get hurt, but..." Logan trailed off awkwardly.

But you can't help but want to show off a little, Kylar thought. He said, "Speaking of good matches, when are you going to march to the headsman's block and finally marry her?"

Ogre breathed a big sigh. All of his sighs were big, but this was a proportionally big sigh. It took a while. He grabbed a stable boy's stool and sat on it, oblivious of his fine cloak dragging in the dirt.

"Actually, I spoke with Count Drake about that a couple days ago."

"You did?" Kylar asked. "And?"

"He approves—"

"Congratulations! When'll it be, you big about-to-be-un-bachelored bastard?"

Ogre stared at nothing. "But he's worried."

"Are you joking?"

Logan shook his head.

"But he's known you since you were born. Your families are best friends. She's marrying up in terms of title. Way up. You've got great prospects and you two have been practically betrothed for years. What can he possibly be worried about?"

Logan fixed his eyes on Kylar's. "He said you'd know. Is she in love with you?"

Oof. "No," Kylar said after too long a pause.

Logan noticed. "Is she?"

Kylar hesitated. "I think she doesn't know who she loves herself." It was a lie of omission. Logan was on the wrong track. Serah didn't love Kylar, and he didn't even like her.

"I've loved her for my whole life, Kylar."

Kylar didn't have anything to say.

"Kylar?" Ogre stared at him intently.

"Yes?"

"Do you love her?"

"No." Kylar felt sick and furious, but his face showed nothing. He'd told Serah she had to confess to Logan, demanded it. She'd promised she would.

Logan looked at him, but his face didn't clear the way Kylar expected it to.

"Sir," a voice said behind Kylar. Kylar hadn't even heard the porter approaching.

"Yes?" he asked the old man.

"A messenger just came with this for you."

Kylar opened the unsealed message to avoid looking at Logan. It read: "You must see me. Tonight at the tenth hour. Blue Boar. —Jarl"

A chill shot through Kylar. *Jarl*. He hadn't heard from Jarl since he'd left the streets. Jarl was supposed to think he was dead. That meant Jarl was either seeking him because he needed Kylar Stern or because he knew that Kylar was Azoth. Kylar couldn't imagine any reason that Jarl would need to see Kylar Stern.

If Jarl knew who he was, who else knew, too?

Master Blint was already gone. Kylar would have to see him. He'd have to take care of this on his own.

"I have to go," he said. He turned and strode toward the gate.

"Kylar!" Logan said.

Kylar turned. "Do you trust me?" he asked.

Logan raised his hands helplessly. "Yes."

"Then trust me."

*   *   *

The Blue Boar was one of Momma K's nicest brothels. It was off Sidlin Way on the east side, not far from the Tomoi Bridge. It had a reputation for having some of the best wines in the city, a fact not a few merchants mentioned when their wives asked awkward questions. "A friend told me she saw you go into the Blue Boar today." "Yes, of course, dear. Business meeting. Wonderful wine selection."

It was Kylar's first visit. The brothel had three stories. The first, where food and wine were served, resembled a nice inn. A sign denoted the second floor as the "lounge" and the third as "guest rooms."

"Hello, my lord," a breathy voice said next to Kylar as he stood awkwardly just inside the entrance.

He turned and felt his cheeks growing hot. The woman stood very close to him, close enough that the spicy scent of her perfume wafted over him. Her voice was pitched low and inviting, too, like they shared secrets or soon could. But that was nothing compared with what she was wearing. He had no idea if it would be called a dress, for though it covered her from neck to ankles, it was made entirely of white lace, it wasn't a tight pattern, and she wasn't wearing anything underneath it.

"Excuse me?" he said, pulling his gaze back up to her eyes, and blushing even deeper.

"Is there any way I can help you? Would you like me to bring you a glass of Sethi red and explain our range of services?" She seemed amused at his difficulties.

"No thank you, milady," he said.

"Perhaps you'd prefer to come to the lounge and speak with me more . . . privately," she said, running a finger along his jawline.

"Actually, I'd, um, prefer not to. Thank you all the same."

She arched an eyebrow at him as if he had suggested something devilish. "Normally I like a man to warm me up a little, but if you want to go straight to my room, I'd be—"

"No!" Kylar said, then realized he'd raised his voice and people were turning to look at him. "I mean, no thank you. I'm here to see Jarl."

"Oh, you're one of those," she said, her voice abruptly normal. The switch was total, jarring. Kylar noticed for the first time that she wasn't even his age. She couldn't be more than seventeen. Involuntarily, he thought of Mags. "Jarl's in the office. That way," she said.

Now that she'd abandoned seducing him, Kylar saw her differently. She looked hard, brittle. As he walked away, he heard her say, "Seems the good-looking ones always hoe the other row."

He didn't know what she meant, but he kept walking, worried she was laughing at him. He was halfway through the tables on his way to the office when he looked back. She was plying her trade with an older merchant, whispering something in his ear. The man beamed.

Kylar knocked on the door of the office.

The door opened. "Come in, quickly," Jarl said.

Kylar stepped inside, his mind a whirl. Jarl—for it was undoubtedly his old friend—had grown into a handsome man. He was impeccably dressed in the newest fashion, his tunic indigo silk, his pants tight fawnskin adorned with a belt of worked silver. Jarl's dark hair had been woven into a multitude of small long braids, each oiled and drawn back. He had an appraising look in his eyes.

There was a slight sound of cloth on cloth from the corner. Someone moving toward Kylar from behind his field of vision. Kylar kicked instinctively.

His foot caught the bodyguard in the chest. Though the guard was a big man, Kylar could feel ribs cracking. The man flew backward into the wall. He slid down and lay on the floor, unmoving.

Scanning the rest of the room in an instant, Kylar saw no other threats. Jarl had his hands spread to show he had no weapons.

"He wasn't going to attack you. He was just making sure you didn't have weapons. I swear it." Jarl looked at the man on the floor. "By the High King's balls, you've killed him."

Scowling, Kylar looked at the man, sprawled unconscious in the corner. He knelt by him and put fingers against the man's neck. Nothing. He ran his hands across the man's chest to feel if one of the broken ribs might have penetrated his heart. Then he slammed his fist down the man's chest. And again.

"What the hell are you—" Jarl cut off as the man's chest suddenly rose.

The bodyguard coughed and moaned. Kylar knew that every breath would be agony for the man. But he'd live.

"Get someone to take care of him," Kylar said. "His ribs are broken."

Eyes wide, Jarl went into the main room and came back a few moments later with two more bodyguards. Like the first, they were big and brawny, and looked like they might be able to use the short swords at their sides. They merely glared at Kylar and picked up the big man between them.

They carried him out of the room and Jarl closed the door behind them. "You've learned a thing or two, haven't you?" Jarl said. "I wasn't testing you. He insisted on being here. I didn't think . . . never mind."

After a moment of staring at his friend, Kylar said, "You look well."

"Don't you mean, 'How in the nine hells did you find me, Jarl?' " Jarl laughed.

"How in the nine hells did you find me, Jarl?"

Jarl smiled. "I never lost you. I never believed you were dead."

"No?"

"You never could get anything past me, Azoth."

"Don't say that name. That boy's dead."

"Is he?" Jarl asked. "That's a shame."

Silence sat in the room as the men looked at each other. Kylar didn't know what to do. Jarl had been his friend, Azoth's friend anyway. But was he Kylar's friend? That he knew who Kylar was, maybe had known for years, told Kylar that he wasn't an enemy. At least not yet. Part of Kylar wanted to believe that Jarl just wanted to see him, wanted a chance to say goodbye that they'd never been afforded on the street. But he'd spent too many years with Master Blint to take such a naive view. If Jarl had called him in now, it was because Jarl wanted something.

"We've both come a long way, haven't we?" Jarl asked.

"Is that what you brought me here to talk about?"

"A long way," Jarl said, disappointed. "Part of me was hoping you hadn't changed as much as I have, Kylar. I've been wanting to see you for years. Ever since you left, really. I wanted to apologize."

"Apologize?"

"I didn't mean to let her die, Kylar. I just couldn't get away much. I tried, but even sometimes when I did get away I couldn't find her. She had to move around a lot. But then she just disappeared. I never even found out what happened. I'm so sorry." Tears gleamed in Jarl's eyes and he looked away, his jaw clenched tight.

He thinks Elene is dead. He blames himself. He's been living with that guilt for all these years. Kylar opened his mouth to tell him that she was alive, that she was doing well from all the reports he got, that sometimes he watched her from afar on the days she went out shopping, but no sound came. Two can keep a secret, Blint used to say, if one of them is dead. Kylar didn't know Jarl now. He was managing one of Momma K's brothels, so Jarl certainly reported to her, but maybe he reported to others as well.

It was too dangerous. Kylar couldn't tell him. *Relationships are ropes that bind. Love is a noose.* The only thing that kept Kylar safe was that no one knew there was a noose with his name on it. Even he didn't know where Elene was. She was safe somewhere on the east side. Maybe married by now. She would be seventeen, after all. Maybe even happy. She looked happy, but he didn't even sneak close. Master Blint was right. The only thing keeping Elene safe was Kylar's distance.

Jarl's guilt wasn't enough to outweigh Elene's safety. Nothing was. *Dammit, Master Blint, how do you live like this? How can you be so strong, so hard?*

"I never held it against you," Kylar said. It was pathetic. He knew it wouldn't help, but there was nothing more he could offer.

Jarl blinked and when he met Kylar's eyes, his dark eyes were dry. "If that were all, I never would have asked you to come. Durzo Blint has enemies, and so do you."

"That's not exactly news," Kylar said. No matter that he and Blint never spoke about the jobs they did, and that anyone who knew of their work first-hand was dead. Word got out. Word always gets out. Another wetboy would attribute a job to them. A client would brag about who he'd hired. They had enemies they'd wronged, and more enemies who only thought that Durzo had wronged them. It was one of the costs of being the best. The families of deaders never attributed a successful hit to a second-rate wetboy.

"Do you remember Roth?"

"One of Rat's bigs?" Kylar asked.

"Yes. Apparently, he's smarter than we ever realized. After Rat died... well, everyone left like the guild was burning down. The other guilds moved in and took our territory. Everyone had to scramble to survive. Roth didn't make any friends when he was Rat's right hand. He nearly got killed half a dozen times. Apparently he always blamed you."

"Me?"

"For killing Rat. If you hadn't killed him, no one would have dared come after Roth. He never believed you were dead, either, but he hasn't been in a position to find out who you became. That's changing."

Kylar's chest was tight. "Does he know I'm alive?"

"No, but he'll sit with the Nine within the year, maybe sooner. There's a spot open right now that he's trying for. From a position of that kind of power, he'll find you. I haven't even met him, but the stories I hear... He's a real twist. Cruel. Vengeful. He frightens me, Kylar. He frightens me like no one since you know who."

"So that's why you invited me here? So you could tell me that Roth is coming after me?" Kylar asked.

"Yes, but there's more to it," Jarl said. "There's going to be a war."

"War? Hold on. What's your part, Jarl? How do you know all this?"

Jarl paused. "You've spent the last ten years under Master Blint's tutelage. I've spent the last ten years under Momma K's. And just as you've learned more than fighting, I've learned more than…fornicating. This city's secrets flow through its bedchambers." That was Momma K speaking, sure enough.

"But why are you helping me? A lot's changed since we were guild rats stealing bread."

Jarl shrugged, looked away again. "You're my only friend."

"Sure, when we were children—"

"Not 'you were.' You are. You're the only friend I've ever had, Kylar."

Trying to beat back his sudden guilt—how long had it been since he'd thought of Jarl?—Kylar said, "What about everyone here? The people you work with?"

"Coworkers, employees, and clients. I've even got something like a lover. But no friends."

"You've got a lover and she's not your friend?"

"Her name's Stephan. She's a fifty-three-year-old cloth merchant with a wife and eight children. He gives me protection and beautiful clothes, and I give him sex."

"Oh." Suddenly the whore's muttering about hoeing the other row made a lot more sense. "Are you happy here, Jarl?"

"Happy? What the hell kind of question is that? Happy doesn't have anything to do with it."

"I'm sorry."

Jarl laughed bitterly. "Where'd you get your innocence back, Kylar? You said Azoth was dead."

"What are you talking about?"

"Are you going to leave now that you know I'm a bugger?"

"No," Kylar said. "You're my friend."

"And you're mine. But if I hadn't seen you nearly kill Gerk just now, I'd wonder if you really were a wetboy. How do you kill people and keep your soul intact, *Kylar?*" He gave the name a little twist.

"How do you keep your soul intact and whore?"

"I don't."

"Me neither," Kylar said.

Jarl went quiet. He studied Kylar intently. "What happened that day?"

Kylar knew what Jarl was asking. A tremor passed through him. "Durzo told me if I wanted to be his apprentice, I had to kill Rat. After what he did to Doll Girl…I did it."

"Easy as that, huh?"

Kylar debated lying, but if anyone deserved the truth, it was Jarl. He'd suffered more at Rat's hands than anyone. After holding back about Doll Girl, he couldn't do it again.

Kylar told him the whole story, like he hadn't told anyone since Master Blint.

The description of the gore and how pathetic Rat had been didn't move Jarl. His face remained passive. "He deserved it. He deserved it and then some," Jarl said. "I only wish I'd had the nerve to do it. I wish I could have watched." He dismissed it with an effeminate wave of his hand. "I've got a client coming, so listen," Jarl said. "Khalidor is going to invade. Different parts of the Sa'kagé have been mobilized, but they're mostly smoke screens. Probably only the Nine know what's really happening, maybe only the Shinga. I can't even tell which side we're going to take.

"The thing is, we can't afford for Cenaria to lose this war. I don't know if the Nine realize that. The Ursuuls have put forward claims on Cenaria for generations, but several months ago Godking Ursuul demanded a tribute of some special gem and free passage, claiming to be more interested in taking war to Modai than here. King Gunder told him where he could go—and it wasn't across the king's highways.

"A source told me the Godking vowed to make us an example. He's got more than fifty wytches, maybe many more. I don't think King Gunder can field ten mages to stand against them."

"But the Sa'kagé will survive," Kylar said. Not that he gave a damn about them. He was thinking about the Drakes and Logan. The Khalidorans would kill them.

"The Sa'kagé will survive, Kylar, but if all the businesses are burned down, there's no money to extort. If all the merchants are broke, they can't gamble or go whoring. Some wars we could profit from. This one will ruin us."

"So why tell me?"

"Durzo's in the middle of it."

"Of course he is," Kylar said. "Probably half the nobles in the army's chain of command are trying to off their superiors so they can take their places. But Master Blint wouldn't take a job that would seriously endanger the city. Not if things are as bad as you say."

Jarl shook his head. "I think he's working for the king."

"Master Blint would never work for the king," Kylar said.

"He would if they had his daughter."

"His what?"

32

$\mathcal{L}$ord General Agon stood in the middle of the brushed white gravel of the castle's statue garden and tried not to look as uneasy as he felt. *Damn fine place to meet an assassin.*

Ordinarily, he would think it was fine place to meet an assassin. Though Blint had ordered him not to bring soldiers, if he had been of a mind to do so, there were any number of places for them to hide. Of course, that this meeting was happening within the castle grounds should also have made Agon feel better. It might have, if Blint hadn't been the one who suggested it.

The night wind blew a cloud across the moon and Agon strained to hear the slight crunch of gravel that would herald Blint's arrival. He had no doubt that Blint could make it into the castle. His memory was as sharp as the daggers that they'd once found under the royal pillows. Still, he had his orders.

He looked at the statues around him. They were heroes, every one of them, and he wondered what he was doing in their company. Usually this garden was a haven. He would walk on the serene white and black rock and stare at these marble heroes, wondering how they might act if they were in his shoes. Tonight, their shadows loomed and lingered. Of course it was his imagination, but he still remembered that Blint had been in his bedroom ten years ago, ready to do murder. Nothing was safe with a man like that.

There was the slightest crunch of gravel under one of the statues. Agon turned and without thinking gripped his sword.

"Don't bother," Durzo Blint said.

Agon whipped back around. Durzo was standing not two feet away. Agon stepped back.

"The noisy one was one of yours. Not me." Blint smiled wolfishly. "But wait, didn't I tell you not to bring men?"

"I didn't," Agon said.

"Mm-hmm."

"You're late," Agon said. He had his equilibrium back now. It was unsettling dealing with a man who didn't value life. He believed that Blint really didn't, now. There was a rationale behind it, too. The only way he himself could deal with Blint was to realize that he could be killed but that that wasn't important; his life or death wasn't why he had summoned Blint; his life or death wasn't vital to what they would talk about. Still, a part of him asked, how can wetboys live like this?

"Just making sure I knew where all your soldiers were hidden," Blint said. He was wearing a killing outfit, Agon realized queasily. A tunic of mottled dark gray cotton, thin but cut for easy movement, pants of the same material, a harness with a score of throwing weapons, some of which the general didn't even recognize. What he did recognize was that the points of some of those weapons bore more than steel. Poison.

Is he bluffing? Agon hadn't brought soldiers. Even if his life wasn't vital to this discussion, he wasn't going to throw it away. "I keep my word, even to a Sa'kagé thug," he said.

"The funny thing is, I believe you, Lord General. You're many things, but I don't think you're either dishonorable or stupid enough to betray me. Are you sure you don't want me to kill the king? You have the army. If you're smart and lucky, you might be king yourself."

"No," Agon said. "I keep my vows." *If only those words didn't burn as I spoke them.*

"I'd give you a discount." Blint laughed.

"Are you ready to hear the job?" Agon asked.

"It seems we've had this conversation before," Blint said. "My answer remains the same. I only showed up because I miss your smiling face, Lord General. And to show that your—let's be honest—rather pathetic defenses still can't keep me out should you choose to try to make my life difficult."

"You haven't even heard what the job is. The king respects your talents now. He will pay better than anyone has ever paid you. He wishes you—"

"To protect his life. I know. Hu Gibbet took a contract on him." Durzo ignored the stricken look on Agon's face. "Sorry. I won't take the job. I'd never take a job for that foul sack of wind. Let's be honest. Aleine Gunder, who ridiculously fashions himself 'the Ninth' as if he had any connection to the previous eight kings who bore the name Aleine, is a waste of skin."

Someone burst out from under the tall statue of Duke Gunder behind Agon. Agon's heart sank as he recognized the man's gait.

Aleine Gunder IX threw back his hood. "Guards! Guards!"

Archers and crossbowmen sprang up from every balcony, bush, and shadow in sight. Others came running from the perimeter of the garden.

"My liege. What a surprise," Blint said, sweeping into a perfect court bow. "Who would have expected to find you hiding in your father's shadow?"

"You shitting...shitting!...shit!" the king yelled. "What are you doing?" he yelled at the guards. "Surround him!" The guards surrounded Durzo,

Agon, and the king in a tight circle. They looked nervous to have the king standing so close to a wetboy, but none of them dared invoke the king's ire by forcibly separating them.

"Your Majesty," Agon said, stepping in front of the king before the man tried to hit Durzo Blint. Tried to hit Durzo Blint!

"You will work for me, assassin," the king said.

"No. I've said it before, but maybe you need to hear it yourself. I'm willing to kill you, but I won't kill for you."

The guards were less than pleased by this, of course, but Agon held up a hand. With the guards pressed so close, the archers were useless. *Brilliant, Your Majesty.* If it came to bloodshed, both he and the king would die, and he'd give even odds that Blint wouldn't.

"Fine, then," the king said.

"Fine, then." Blint smiled joylessly.

The king smiled back. "We'll kill your daughter."

"My what?"

The king's smile grew. "Look into it." He laughed.

A dangerous second stretched out and Agon wondered if he was about to be holding a dead king in his arms. Then there was a blur of motion. Even though he was looking right at him, Durzo Blint moved faster than his eye could follow. He flipped up over the circle of soldiers, caught a statue and changed his trajectory.

A moment later, there was a scuttling sound up the side of the castle wall, akin to a cat's claws scraping as it climbed a tree.

Startled, one of the soldiers discharged his crossbow—mercifully, it was pointed into the air. Agon shot a look at the man.

The man swallowed. "Sorry, sir."

The king walked inside, and it was only two minutes later that Agon realized how close Durzo had brought him to speaking treason in front of the king.

Kylar felt the air stir as someone opened the front door of the safe house. He lifted his eyes from the book in front of him and reached for the short sword unsheathed on the table.

He had a perfect view of the door from his chair, of course. Master Blint wouldn't set up his workroom any other way. But he would have known it was Master Blint just by the sound: click-CLICK-click. Click-CLICK-click. Click-CLICK-click. Master Blint always locked, unlocked, and then relocked every lock. It was just another of his superstitions.

He didn't ask his master about the job. Blint never liked to talk about a job right after it. The Night Angels didn't like it, he said. Kylar interpreted that, *Let my memories fade.*

The vial of white asp venom was sitting on the table with the rest of Blint's collection, but to distract himself as much as Blint, Kylar said, "I don't think it'll work. I've been looking over your books. They haven't got anything about this."

"They'll write a new book," Blint said. He started putting the poisoned blades in special cases, and wiping off the ones bearing poison that spoiled over time.

"I know animals can eat some poisons and it doesn't make them sick. And I know their meat will make you sick if you eat it. Our experiments have proved that. But then your deader's just sick. That's fine as far as it goes, but this dual poison thing—I don't get it."

Blint hung up his weapons harness. "Your deader eats the pork, he feels nothing. Maybe a little tipsy. He eats the quail, he gets dizzy. He eats both, he gets dead. It's called *potentiation*. The poisons work together to reach their fullest potential."

"But you've still got to get an entire pig and a flock of quail past the food tester."

"Big places use multiple tasters. By the time they suspect anything, the deader's dead," Blint said.

"But then you poison everyone in the room. You can't control—"

"I control everything!" Blint shouted. He threw a knife down and walked out, slamming the door so hard it set every weapon on the wall jingling.

Elene stared at the blank page and dipped the drying quill back into the ink pot. Further down the table in the Drakes' dining room, Mags and Ilena Drake were playing a game of tiles. Mags, the older sister, was concentrating intently, but Ilena kept glancing at Elene.

"Why," Elene said, "do I always get crushes on unattainable men?" Elene Cromwyll had been friends with Mags and Ilena Drake for years. The gap between a servant and a count's daughters should have precluded friendship, but the Drakes counted all as equal before the One God. As they'd grown older, the girls had become more aware of how odd their friendship was, so it had become more private, but no less real.

"That groundskeeper Jaen was attainable," Ilena said, moving a tile. Mags scowled at the move and then at her fifteen-year-old sister.

"That lasted two hours," Elene said. "Until he opened his fat mouth."

"You must have had a crush on Pol at some point," Mags said.

"Not really. He just loved me so much I thought I should love him back," Elene said.

"At least Pol was real," Ilena said.

"Ilena, don't be a brat," Mags said.

"You're just mad because you're losing again."

"I am not!" Mags said.

"I'll win in three moves."

"You will?" Mags looked at the tiles. "You little snot. I, at least, am so glad you turned Pol down, Elene," Mags said. "But it does leave you without an escort to our party."

Elene had abandoned the quill and buried her face in her hands. She sighed. "Do you have any idea what I wrote to him last year?" She stared at the blank paper in front of her.

"I didn't know Pol could read," Ilena said.

"Not Pol. My benefactor."

"Whatever you wrote, he didn't stop sending money, did he?" Ilena asked, ignoring her sister's murderous glance. Ilena Drake was only fifteen, but most of the time, she seemed in pretty good control of Mags, if not her oldest sister Serah.

"He's never stopped. Not even when I told him that we had more than enough money. But it's not about the money, Lena," Elene said. "Last year I told him that I was in love with him." She couldn't quite bear to confess that she'd smudged the ink with her own tears. "I told him I was going to call him Kylar, because Kylar's nice and I never found out my benefactor's name."

"And now you do like Kylar . . . who you've also never talked to."

"I'm totally hopeless. Why do I let you talk to me about boys?" Elene asked.

"Ilena can't help but talk about Kylar," Mags said with the air of a big sister about to pull rank. "Because she has a crush on him herself."

"I do not!" Ilena shrieked.

"Then why'd you say so in your journal?" Mags said. Mags's voice lilted, mimicking Ilena's, " 'Why won't Kylar talk more to me?' 'Kylar talked to me today at breakfast. He said I'm sweet. Is that good or does he still just see me as a little girl?' It's gross, Ilena. He's practically our brother."

"You wytch!" Ilena yelled. She leaped over the table and attacked Mags. Mags screamed, and Elene watched, frozen between horror and laughter.

The girls were screaming, Ilena pulling Mags's hair and Mags starting to fight back. Elene got to her feet, figuring she'd better stop them before someone got hurt.

The door crashed open, almost blowing off its hinges, and Kylar stood there, sword in hand. The entire atmosphere of the room changed in the blink of an eye. Kylar exuded a palpable aura of danger and power. He was primal masculinity. It washed over Elene like a wave that threatened to yank her from her feet and pull her out to sea. She could hardly breathe.

Kylar flowed into the room in a low stance, the naked sword held in both hands. His eyes took in everything at once, flicked to every exit, to the windows, the shadows, even to the corners of the ceiling. The girls on the floor stopped, a handful of Mags's hair still clenched in Ilena's hand, guilt written all over their faces.

His pale, pale blue eyes seemed so familiar. Was it just Elene's fantasies that put that flicker of recognition in them? Those eyes touched hers and she felt a tingle all the way up her spine. He was looking at her—her, not her scars. Men always looked at her scars. Kylar was seeing *Elene*. She wanted to speak, but there were no words.

His mouth parted as if he, too, was on the edge of words, but then he turned white as a sheet. His sword flashed back into a sheath and he turned. "Ladies, your pardon," he said, ducking his head. Then he was gone.

"Good God," Mags said. "Did you see that?"

"It was scary," Ilena said, "and..."

"Intoxicating," Elene said. Her face felt hot. She turned away as the girls stood. She sat and picked up the quill. As if she could write now.

"Elene, what's going on?" Mags asked.

"When he saw my face, he looked like death warmed over," Elene said. *Why?* He'd barely even looked at her scars. That was what scared away most of the boys.

"He'll come around. You're an angel. Give him a chance. We'll ask him to the party for you and everything," Ilena said.

"No. No, I forbid it. He's a baronet, Lena."

"A poor baronet whose lands have been taken by the Lae'knaught."

"He's just another unattainable man. I'll get over it."

"He doesn't have to be unattainable. If he joins the faith...In the eyes of the God, all men are created equal."

"Oh, Lena, don't dangle that in front of me. I'm a serving girl. A scarred serving girl. It doesn't matter what the God sees."

"It doesn't matter what the God sees?" Mags asked gently.

"You know what I mean."

"Logan might marry Serah, and that's as big a gap as there is between a poor baronet and you."

"A noble marrying a lower noble is frowned on, but a noble marrying a commoner?"

"We're not saying you should marry him. Just let us ask him to the party."

"No," Elene said. "I forbid it."

"Elene—"

"That's final." Elene looked at the girls until each grudgingly gave their assent. "But," she said, "you could tell me a little more about him."

"Kylar," Count Drake called out as Kylar tried to sneak past his office to get up the stairs. "Would you come in for a moment?"

There was nothing for it but to obey, of course. Kylar cursed inwardly. Today was turning into a long day. He'd been hoping to get a few hours of sleep before doing his predawn chores for Master Blint. He had a good idea what this was about, so when he stepped into the count's office, he had to try not to feel like a boy about to have his father explain sex to him.

The count hadn't been touched by the years. He would look forty if he lived to be a hundred. His desk was in the same place, his clothes were the same cut and color, and when he was warming up to a difficult conversation he still rubbed the bridge of his nose where his pince nez sat.

"Have you made love to my daughter?" the count asked.

Kylar's chin dropped. So much for warming up. The count watched him expressionlessly.

"I haven't laid a hand on her, sir."

"I wasn't asking about your hands."

Kylar goggled. This was the man who talked about the God as often as most farmers talked about the weather?

"No, don't worry, son. I believe you. Though I suspect it hasn't been for any lack of effort on Serah's part."

The blood rushing to Kylar's entire face was answer enough.

"Is she in love with you, Kylar?"

He shook his head, almost relieved to be asked a question he could answer. "I think Serah wants what she thinks she can't have, sir."

"Does that include making love to numerous young men, none of whom is Logan?"

Kylar spluttered, "I hardly think it's right or honorable for me to—"

The count raised a hand, pained. "Which is not the answer you would have given if you thought the charge was false. You'd have said absolutely not, and then that you didn't think it was right or honorable for me to ask. And you'd have been right." He rubbed the bridge of his nose and blinked. "I'm sorry, Kylar. That wasn't fair of me. Sometimes I still use the wits the God gave me in dishonorable ways. I'm trying to do what's right, whether or not that measures up with what men call honorable. There's a gap between those, you know?"

Kylar shrugged, but no answer was required.

"I'm not interested in condemning my baby girl, Kylar," the count said, "I've done far worse in my life than she'll ever dream of. But more than her happiness is at stake. Is Logan aware of her . . . indiscretions?"

"I asked her to tell him, but I don't believe she has, sir."

"You know that Logan has asked for my permission to marry Serah?"

"Yes, sir."

"Should I give him my blessing?"

"You couldn't hope to gain a better son."

"For my family, it would be wonderful. Is it right for Logan?"

Kylar hesitated. "I think he loves her," he said finally.

"He wants to know within two days," the count said. "When he turns twenty-one he takes possession of the Gyre household and becomes one of the richest and most powerful men in the realm, even given how the king has interfered with his house in the last decade. Sixth in the line of succession. First behind the royals. People will say he's marrying beneath himself. They'll say she isn't worthy of him." The count looked away. "I don't usually give a damn what they think, Kylar, because they think it for all the wrong reasons. This time, I'm afraid they'll be right."

Kylar couldn't say anything.

"I've prayed for years that my daughters would find the right men to be their husbands. And I've prayed that Logan would marry the right woman. Why doesn't this feel like the answer?" He shook his head again and squeezed the bridge of his nose. "Forgive me, I've asked you a dozen questions you can't possibly answer, and haven't asked the one you can."

"What's that, sir?"

"Do you love Serah?"

"No, sir."

"And that girl? The one you've been sending money to for almost a decade?"

Kylar flushed. "I've sworn not to love, sir."

"But do you?"

Kylar walked out the door.

As Kylar stepped into the hall, the count said, "You know, I pray for you, too, Kylar."

33

The whorehouse had closed hours ago. Upstairs, the girls slept on fouled sheets amid the brothel smells of stale alcohol, stale sweat, old sex, wood smoke, and cheap perfume. The doors were locked. All but two of the plain copper lamps downstairs had been extinguished. Momma K didn't allow her brothels to waste money.

There were only two people downstairs, both of them at the bar. Around the man's seat were the remains of a dozen smashed glasses.

He finished the thirteenth beer, lifted the glass, and threw it onto the floor. It shattered.

Momma K poured Durzo another beer from the tap, not even blinking. She didn't say a word. Durzo would speak when he was ready. Still, she wondered why he'd chosen this brothel. It was a hole. She sent her attractive girls elsewhere. Other brothels she'd bought had been worth fixing, but this one huddled deep in the Warrens, far from main roads in the maze of shacks and hovels. This was where she'd lost her maidenhead. She'd been paid ten silvers, and had counted herself lucky.

It wasn't high on her list of places to visit.

"I should kill you," Durzo said finally. They were the first words he'd spoken in six hours. He finished his beer and shoved it along the bar. It slid several feet, fell over, rolled off the bar, and cracked.

"Oh, so you do have the power of speech?" Momma K said. She grabbed another glass and opened the tap.

"Do I have a daughter too?"

Momma K froze. She closed the tap too late and beer spilled all over.

"Vonda made me swear not to tell you. She was too scared to tell you and then when she died. . . . You can hate Vonda for what she did, Durzo, but she did it because she loved you."

Durzo gave her a look of such disbelief and disgust that Gwinvere wanted to hit his ugly face.

"What do you know about love, you whore?"

She had thought that no one could hurt her with words. She'd heard every whore comment in the book, and had added a few besides. But something in how Durzo said it, something about that comment—coming from him!—struck her to the core. She couldn't move. She couldn't even breathe.

Finally, she said, "I know if I'd had the chance for love that you had, I would have quit whoring. I would have done anything to hold onto that. I was *born* into this chamber pot of a life; you're the one who chose it."

"What's my daughter's name?"

"So that's it? You bring me here to remind me how many times I got fucked in this stinking hole? I remember. I remember! I whored so my baby sister wouldn't have to. And then you came along. You fucked me five times a week and told Vonda you loved her. Got her pregnant. Left. I could have told her that much was a given. That part of the story's so predictable it's not even worth repeating, is it? But you weren't just any john. No, you got her kidnapped too. And then what? Did you go after her? No, you showed exactly how much you loved her. Called their bluff, didn't you? You always were willing to gamble with other people's lives, weren't you, Durzo? You coward."

Durzo's glass exploded against the keg behind her. He was trembling violently. He pointed a finger in her face. "You! You don't have any right. You would have given it all up for love? Horseshit. Where's the man in your life now, Gwin? You don't whore anymore, so there's nothing for a man to be jealous of, right? But there's still no man, is there? Do you want to know why you're the perfect whore? For the same reason there's no man. Because you don't have the capacity for love. You're all cunt. You suck everyone dry and make them pay you for the pleasure. So don't give me that bleeding heart, I-did-it-to-save-my-sister horseshit. It's always been power for you. Oh sure, there are women who whore for money or for fame or because they don't have any other options. But then there are *whores*. You might not fuck anymore, Gwin, but you will *always* be a whore. Now. What. Is. Her. Name?" He bit off each word like moldy bread.

"Uly," Gwinvere said quietly. "Ulyssandra. She lives with a nurse in the castle."

She looked at the beer she was holding in her hand. She didn't even remember filling it. *Was this what Durzo reduced her to? A submissive little....* She didn't even know. She felt like she'd been eviscerated, that if she looked down, she'd see ropes of her own intestines coiled around her feet.

It took all of her strength to spit in the beer and set it on the counter with even a shadow of nonchalance.

"Well, it's tough to be a victim of circumstance," Durzo said. His voice had that killing edge on it.

"You aren't.... You wouldn't kill your own child." Not even Durzo could do that, could he?

"I won't have to," Durzo said. "They'll kill her for me."

He picked up the beer, smiled at Gwinvere over the spit, and drank. He finished half the beer at a gulp and said, "I'm leaving. It smells like old whore in here." He poured the rest of his beer onto the floor and set the glass carefully on the bar.

Kylar woke two hours before dawn and briefly wondered if death would be too high a price to pay for a full night's sleep. The correct answer, however, was unavoidable, so after a few minutes, he dragged himself out of bed. He dressed quietly in the dark, reaching into his third drawer where his wetboy grays were folded as always and reaching into his ash jar to smear his features black.

In the past nine years, he'd learned to compensate for not having the Talent. When Blint was in an optimistic mood, which was increasingly rare, he praised Kylar for it. He said that too many wetboys relied on their Talent for everything and that he kept his mundane talents honed for unpredictable situations. In the bitter business, unpredictable situations were the norm. Besides, Blint said, if there's almost no noise of a footstep to cover in the first place, you don't have to use as much of your Talent to muffle it.

Sometimes Kylar's adaptability showed itself in more spectacular ways, but mostly it was in these little things, like putting his grays in the same dresser, the same way every time he washed them. At least, he hoped it was his adaptability and not Blint's mania for organization infecting him. Seriously, what was it with the man's locking locks three times and spinning knives and the garlic and the Night Angel this and Night Angel that?

The window opened silently and Kylar crept across the roof. Years of practice taught him where he could walk and where he had to crawl to be unheard by those below. He slipped over the edge of the house, dropped onto the flagstones in the courtyard, and vaulted off a rock to grab the edge of the wall. He raised himself to peek over the edge, saw no one, pulled himself over the wall, and then moved stealthily up the street.

He probably could have just walked; sneaking wasn't really necessary once he got out of sight of the Drake's home and until he got within sight of the herbiary, but it was a bad habit to get into. *A job is a job, it isn't done till it's done.* Another of Blint's pearls, there. Thanks.

Tonight, it wasn't just Blint's ingrained discipline that kept him creeping from shadows to shadow, making the two-mile walk to the herbiary take almost an hour. Tonight, Jarl's words kept going through his head. "You have enemies. You have enemies."

Maybe it was time he moved out of the Drakes' house. For their safety. He was twenty years old, and though of course he didn't have the income of a noble, Blint was more than generous with his wages. In fact, Blint didn't really care about money. He didn't spend much on himself, aside from the infrequent binges on alcohol and rent girls. He did buy the best equipment and ingredients for poisons, but what he bought he kept forever. With what he made for each kill and the frequency with which he took jobs, Blint had to be wealthy. Probably obscenely wealthy. Not that Kylar cared. He'd adopted much of Blint's attitude. He gave Count Drake a portion of his wages for Elene and still had plenty left over. He kept some in coins and jewels and split the rest between investments Momma K and Logan made for him. It meant nothing to him because money couldn't buy him any-thing. His cover as a poor country noble and his real work as a journeyman wetboy kept him from living a lifestyle that would attract attention. So even if he had wanted to spend his money, he couldn't afford to.

He could move out, though. Rent a small home further south on the east side, at the edges of one of the less fashionable neighborhoods. Blint had told him that if you bought the cheapest house in a neighborhood, no mat-ter how expensive the neighborhood, you were invisible. Even if your neighbors noticed you, they'd take pains not to notice you.

Then Kylar was at the shop. The Sa'kagé had long had an arrangement with herbalists in the city. The herbalists made sure they kept certain plants on hand that weren't strictly legal, and the Sa'kagé made sure that the herb-alists' shops were never burglarized. The crown knew about it but was powerless to stop it.

Goodman Aalyep's Herbiary was frequented by rich merchants and the nobility, so he had refused to keep illicit herbs openly in his shop, fearing that such defiance in the very face of authority might not be ignored. He'd been able to refuse the Sa'kagé, but no one refused Master Blint. Goodman Aalyep supplied Durzo with the rarest herbs. In return, Master Blint made sure no one else in the Sa'kagé so much as went near his shop.

It fell to Kylar to gather the necessaries and drop off the money, which he was doing tonight. The benefit to running these errands wasn't only that he learned the trade, or that he established relationships with the people who would supply him in the future, it was also that he could build his own collection. An elaborate collection like Master Blint's took years and thou-sands or even tens of thousands of gunders to build.

The bad part was losing sleep. It didn't do for a young noble to sleep until noon unless he'd been out carousing with his friends. So even though he wouldn't get home until almost dawn, Kylar would have to wake with the sun.

He grumbled silently, remembering a time when sneaking through the streets of Cenaria at night had been fun.

The back door of the shop, as always, was locked. Goodman Aalyep kept good locks on his doors, too. Though he'd never met him—they only wrote notes—Kylar felt he knew Goodman Aalyep, and the man was a strange one. With Durzo Blint's protection in the Sa'kagé, the man could have safely left his doors wide open. No one in the city would dare steal from him.

But as Blint said, a man's greatest treasures are his illusions. For all the man claimed to hate teaching, he seemed to have an aphorism for every occasion. Kylar selected the proper pick and anchor from the kit on the inside of his belt, and he knelt in front of the door and started working. He sighed. It was a new lock, and from Master Procl's, the best locksmith in the city. New locks, even if they weren't high quality, always tended to be tighter, and if losing an anchor wasn't the end of the world, it was still irritating to break one.

Kylar raked the pick over the pins. Four pins, two of them a little loose. That meant it was the work of one of Procl's journeymen and not the master himself. In ten seconds, he turned the anchor, bending it, and the door opened. Kylar cursed silently—he'd have to get another new anchor—then tucked his tools away. Someday, he was going to have to commission a set of mistarille picks and anchors like Master Blint had. Or at least one anchor. Mistarille would flex but never break, but it was more expensive by weight than diamonds.

Goodman Aalyep's claim that his business was an herbiary wasn't an idle boast. It had three rooms: the large comfortable shop with labeled glass jars for the display of herbs, a tiny office, and the herbiary in which Kylar stood. The little room was humid, and the wet, fecund odors were almost overwhelming.

Checking on the progress of some fungi, Kylar was pleased. Several lethal mushrooms would be ready within a week. Mushrooms were one kind of plant Goodman Aalyep could grow with impunity in his shop— lethal varieties were indistinguishable from edible mushrooms to anyone except trained herbalists and, of course, trained poisoners.

Treading carefully so he didn't step on any of the boards that creaked, Kylar moved through the rest of the herbiary, judging the plants with a practiced eye. Kylar lifted the third plant box in the second row and saw six bundles carefully packed in individual lambskin pouches. He lifted them out and checked that each was what he had ordered. Four bundles for Master Blint, and two for himself. Kylar put the herbs in the pack secured flush against his back under his cloak, and put the purse with Aalyep's money into the little space. He set the planter back in position.

Then something felt wrong. In the blink of an eye Kylar drew two short swords.

But he didn't move a step. The feeling of wrongness continued, not something wrong of itself, but just something here and now and close. There was no sound. There was no attack, just a slight pressure, as of the softest possible touch of a finger.

Kylar focused on the sensation even as his eyes scanned the shop and his ears strained to hear the slightest sound. It was like a touch, but it was pressing past him, toward—

The lock on the back door clicked home. He was trapped.

Restraining an impulse to run to the door and fling it open, Kylar stayed utterly still. No one was in the room with him. Of that he was certain. But he thought—yes, he could hear someone breathing in the shop.

Then he realized that it was more than one person. One was breathing quickly, shallowly, excited. The other was breathing lightly but slowly. Not tense, not excited. That scared Kylar.

Who could ambush a wetboy and not even be nervous?

Afraid of losing all initiative, Kylar moved slowly toward the wall that separated the herbiary from the shop. If he was right, one of the men was standing just on the other side of it. Sheathing a short sword—to be silent he had to do it so slowly that it was painful—Kylar then drew out the Ceuran hand-and-a-half sword he carried in a back scabbard.

He brought the tip of the blade close to the wall and waited for the slightest sound.

There was nothing. Now he couldn't even hear the excited man breathing. That meant the excited one must be on the other side of this wall, while the calm man was further.

Kylar waited. He trembled with anticipation. One of the men on the other side of the entry was a wytch. Were they with the Khalidorans Jarl had warned him about? Kylar pushed the thought out of his head. He could worry about that later. Whoever they were, they had trapped him. Whether they thought he was Master Blint or just a common thief didn't matter.

But which one was the wytch? The nervous one? He wouldn't have thought so, but the feeling that had pressed past him and had locked the door had seemed to come from that side.

A board creaked. "Feir! Back!" the man further away from Kylar shouted. Kylar rammed his sword through the finger-thick pine.

He yanked the sword back as he charged through the entry. He burst through the curtain and launched himself off the doorpost and over the sales counter, toward the man he'd tried to stab.

The man was on the ground, rolling over as Kylar took a slice at his head. He was huge. Bigger even than Logan, but proportioned like a tree trunk, thick everywhere, with no definable waist or neck. For all that, even on his back, he was bringing up a sword to block Kylar's blow.

He would have blocked it, too, if Kylar's sword had been whole. But half of Kylar's Ceuran blade was lying on the ground by the man, sheared off with magic a moment after he had rammed it through the wall.

Finding no sword where he expected it, the big man's parry went wide as Kylar attacked from his knees. Without the full weight of the blade, Kylar brought his half-sword down faster than the big man could react and stabbed for his stomach.

Then Kylar felt as if his head were inside the soundbow of a temple bell. There was a concussion, pitched low but focused, as if a cornerstone had fallen two stories and landed an inch from Kylar's head.

The force blew him sideways through one shelf of herb jars and into a second, sending them crashing down underneath him.

Then there was nothing but the light flashing in front of Kylar's eyes. His sword was gone. He blinked, vision slowly returning. He was face down on the floor with a shattered shelf, lying amid the remnants of broken jars and scattered herbs.

He heard a grunt from the big man, and then footsteps. Kylar kept still, not having to fake much to appear incapacitated. A few inches from his nose, he was slowly able to make out some of the plants. Pronwi seed, Ubdal bud, Yarrow root. This shelf should have—and there it was, near his hand, delicate Tuntun seed, ground to powder. If you breathed it, it would make your lungs hemorrhage.

The footsteps came closer and Kylar lurched, spinning to one side and flinging Tuntun powder in an arc. He came to his feet and drew a pair of long knives.

"Enough, Shadowstrider."

Air congealed around Kylar like a jelly. He tried to dive away, but the jelly became as hard as rock.

The two men regarded Kylar through the cloud of Tuntun seed hanging frozen in the air.

The blond mountain folded meat-slab arms across his chest. "Don't tell me you expected this, Dorian," he growled at the other man.

His friend grinned.

"Not much to look at, is he?" the Mountain asked.

The smaller man, Dorian, wore a short black beard under intense blue eyes, had a sharp nose and straight white teeth. He reached forward and took some of the floating Tuntun powder between two fingers. Black hair lightly oiled, blue eyes, pale skin. Definitely Khalidoran. He was the wytch. "Don't be a sore loser, Feir. Things would gone badly for you if I hadn't broken his sword."

Feir scowled. "I think I could hold my own."

"Actually, if I hadn't intervened, right now he'd be wondering how he was going to move such a large corpse. And that was without his Talent."

That got an unhappy grunt. The smaller man waved a hand and the Tuntun powder fell to the ground in a tidy pile. He looked at Kylar and the bonds holding him shifted, forcing him to stand upright, with his hands down at his sides, though still holding the knives. "Is that more comfortable?" he asked, but didn't seem to expect a reply. He touched Kylar's hand with a single finger and stared into him as if his eyes were cutting him open. He frowned. "Look at this," he said to Feir.

Feir accepted the hand Dorian put on his shoulder and stared at Kylar the same way. Kylar stood there, not knowing what to say or do, his mind filled with questions that he wasn't sure he should give voice to.

After a long moment, Feir said, "Where's his conduit? It almost seems shaped, like there's a niche for..." He exhaled sharply. "By the Light, he ought to be..."

"Terrifying. Yes," Dorian said. "He's a born ka'karifer. But that's not what worries me. Look at this." Kylar felt something twist in him. He felt as if he were being turned inside out.

Whatever he was seeing, it scared Feir. His face was still, but Kylar could almost feel the sudden tension in his muscles, the slight tang of fear in the air.

"There's something here that resists me," Eyes said. "The stream's winning. The Shadowcloaked makes it worse."

"Let it go," Feir said. "Stay with me."

Kylar felt whatever had been pulling him open drop away, though his body was still bound in place. Dorian rocked back on his heels, and Feir grabbed his shoulders in meaty hands and held him up.

"What'd you call me? Who are you?" Kylar demanded.

Dorian smirked, regaining his balance as if by the force of good humor alone. "You ask who *we* are, Wearer of Names? It's Kylar now, isn't it? Old Jaeran punning. I like that. Was that your sense of humor, or Blint's?" At the startled look on Kylar's face, he said, "Blint's apparently."

Dorian looked through Kylar again, as if there were a list inside him that he was reading. "The Nameless. Marati. Cwellar. Spex. Kylar. Even Kagé, not terribly original, that."

"What?" Kylar asked. This was ridiculous. Who were these men?

"Sa'kagé means Lords of the Shadow," Dorian said. "Thus Kagé means 'Shadow,' but I don't suppose that one's your fault. In any case, you ought to be more curious. Did it never occur to you to wonder why your peers had common names like Jarl, or Bim, or slave names like Doll Girl or Rat, and you were burdened with Azoth?"

Kylar went cold. He'd heard that wytches could read minds, but he'd never believed it. And those names. That wasn't a random list. "You're wytches. Both of you."

Feir and Dorian looked at each other.

"Half right," Dorian said.

"A little less than half, really," Feir said.

"But I was a wytch," Dorian said. "Or, more properly, a meister. If you ever have the misfortune of meeting one, you may not want to use a slur."

"What are you?" Kylar asked.

"Friends," Dorian said. "We've made a long journey to help you. Well, not only to help you, but to help you and—"

"And we've come at great personal cost and greater risk," Feir interrupted, looking at Dorian sharply.

"We hope you have no doubt that we could kill you. That if we wished you harm, we could have already done it," Dorian said.

"There are more types of harm than just killing. A wetboy knows that," Kylar said.

Dorian smiled, but Feir still looked wary. Kylar felt the bonds release him. That unnerved him. They'd seen how fast he could move and yet they released him, armed.

"Allow me to introduce us," Dorian said. "This is Feir Cousat, one day to be the most renowned swordsmith in all Midcyru. He is Vy'sana and a Blademaster of the Second Echelon."

Great. "And you?" Kylar asked.

"You won't believe me." Dorian was enjoying this.

"Try me."

"I am Sa'seuran and Hoth'salar, and once a Vürdmeister of the twelfth *shu'ra*."

"Impressive." Kylar had no idea what those were.

"What should be important to you is that I'm a prophet. My name is Dorian," Dorian said with a native Khalidoran accent. "Dorian Ursuul."

"You were right," Feir said. "He doesn't believe you."

Aside from carelessness, the only things that could kill wetboys were other wetboys, mages, and wytches. In Blint's estimation, wytches were the worst. He hadn't neglected Kylar's education. "Let me see your arms," Kylar said.

"Ah, so you know about the vir," Dorian said. "How much do you know about them?" Dorian bared his arms to the elbows. There were no marks on them.

"I know that all wytches have them, that they grow in proportion to the wytch's power and their intricacy shows the wytch's level of mastery," Kylar said.

"Don't do it, Dorian," Feir said. "I'm not going to lose you over this. Let's tell him the words and get the hell out of here."

Dorian ignored him. "Only men and women who are Talented can use the vir. It's easier to manipulate than the Talent and more powerful. It's also terribly addictive and, if one dare speak in moral absolutes—which I do—it's evil," Dorian said, his eyes bright, holding Kylar. "Unlike the Talent, which can be good or bad like any talent, it is in itself evil, and it corrupts those who use it. It has proven useful to my family to have all meisters marked, so they are. My ancestors never saw any reasons to be marked ourselves unless we so chose. The Ursuuls can make their vir disappear at will, so long as they aren't using it."

"Blint must have skipped that lesson," Kylar said.

"A pity it is, too. We're the most dangerous Vürdmeisters you could possibly imagine."

"Dorian, just tell him the words. Let's—"

"Feir!" Dorian said. "Silence. You know what to do."

The big man obeyed, glowering at Kylar.

"Kylar," Dorian said. "You're asking a drunkard who's quit drinking to take just one glass of wine. I'll live in misery for weeks for this. Feir will have to watch me constantly to see that I don't slip away to that madness. But you're worth it."

Feir's mouth tightened, but he didn't say a word.

Dorian held his arms out and a shimmer passed over them. As Kylar stared at them, it looked as if veins deep in the man's arms were wriggling, struggling to get to the surface of his skin. Then, rapidly, they rose all together. Dorian's arms turned black like a million fresh tattoos were being inked over each other. Layer knotted on layer, each distinct, interlocking with those below and above, darker over lighter with darker still coming in above. It was beautiful and terrible. The vir swelled with power and moved, not just with Dorian's arms, but independently. It seemed that they wanted to burst free of the confines of his skin. The darkness of the vir spread to the room, and Kylar was sure it wasn't his imagination: the vir were sucking the light from the room.

Dorian's eyes dilated until the cool blue irises were tiny rims. A fierce joy rose in his face and he looked ten years younger. The vir started to swell, crackling audibly.

Feir picked up Dorian like most men might pick up a doll and shook him violently. He shook and didn't stop shaking. It would have been comical if Kylar weren't too scared to move. Feir just shook and shook until the room was no longer dark with power. Then he set Dorian down in a chair.

The man groaned and abruptly looked frail and older once more. He spoke without raising his head. "I'm glad you're convinced, Shadowstrider."

It had convinced him, but Dorian couldn't know that. "How do I know it wasn't an illusion?" Kylar asked.

"Illusions don't suck light. Illusions—" Feir said.

"He's just being stubborn, Feir. He believes." Dorian glanced at Kylar and quickly looked away. He groaned. "Ah, I can't even look at you now. All your futures...." He squeezed his eyes shut.

"What do you want from me?" Kylar asked.

"I can see the future, Nameless One, but I am only human, so I pray that I can be wrong. I pray that I am wrong. By everything I've seen, if you don't kill Durzo Blint tomorrow, Khalidor will take Cenaria. If you don't kill him by the day after that, everyone you love will die. Your Sa'kagé count, the Shinga, your friends old and new, all of them. If you do the right thing once, it will cost you a year of guilt. If you do the right thing twice, it will cost you your life."

"So that's what this is? All this is just a setup so I'll betray Master Blint? Did your masters think I would buy it?" Kylar said. "Oh, you learned a lot about me, must have cost a fortune to buy all that information."

Dorian held up a weary hand. "I don't ask you to believe it all now. It's too much all at once. I'm sorry for that. You think now that we're Khalidorans and we want you to betray Blint so that he can't stop us. Maybe this will convince you that you're wrong: What I beg of you above all else is that you kill my brother. Don't let him get the ka'kari."

Kylar felt as if he'd just been stung. "The what?"

"Feir," Dorian said. "Say the words we came to say."

"Ask Momma K," Feir said.

He shook his head. "Wait! What? Ask her about the ka'kari?"

"Ask Momma K," Feir said.

"What about your brother, who is he?"

"If I tell you now, you'll lose when you fight him." Dorian shook his head, but still didn't look at Kylar. "Damn this power. What good is it if I can't tell you in a way you'll understand? Kylar, if time is a river, most people live submerged. Some rise to the surface and can guess what's going to happen next, or can understand the past. I'm different. When I don't concentrate, I detach from the flow of time. My consciousness floats above the river. I see a thousand thousand paths. Ask me where a leaf will fall, and I couldn't tell you. There are too many possibilities. There's so much noise, like I'm trying to follow a drop of rain from the clouds to a lake, then over a waterfall and pick it out in the river two leagues downstream. If I can touch someone or chant rhymes, it gives me focus. Sometimes." Dorian seemed to be looking through the wall, lost in reverie.

"Sometimes," he said, "sometimes when I transcend the river, I start to see a pattern. Then it isn't like water, it's a fabric made up of every insignificant decision of every peasant as much as it is of great decisions by kings. As I begin to comprehend the vastness and intricacy of that skein, my mind starts to pull apart." He blinked, and he turned his eyes to Kylar. He squinted, as if even looking at him caused him pain.

"Sometimes it's merely images, totally unbidden. I can see the anguish on the young man's face who will watch me die, but I don't know who he is or when that will be or why he'll care. I know that tomorrow, a square vase will give you hope. I see a little girl crying over your body. She's trying to pull you away but you're too heavy. Away from what? I don't know."

Kylar felt a chill. "A girl? When?" Was it Ilena Drake?

"I can't tell. Wait." Dorian blinked and his face went rigid. "Go, go now. Ask Momma K!"

Feir threw open the front door. Kylar stared from one mage to the other, stunned at the abruptness of his dismissal.

"Go," Feir said. "Go!"

Kylar ran into the night.

For a long moment, Feir stared after him. He spat. Still staring into the depths of the night, he said, "What didn't you tell him?"

Dorian let out a shaky breath. "He's going to die. No matter what."

"How does that fit?"

"I don't know. Maybe he's not what we hoped."

35

$\mathcal{K}$ylar ran, but Doubt ran faster. The sky was lightening in the east, and the city was showing its first signs of life. The odds of running into a patrol were small, especially because Kylar knew better than to run on the roads past the rich shops that somehow saw patrols more frequently than roads with poor shops, but if he did run into guards, what would he say? *I was just out for a morning walk with dark gray clothes, illegal plants, a small arsenal, and my face smudged with ash.* Right.

He slowed to a walk. Momma K's wasn't far now, anyway. What was he doing? Obeying a madman and a giant? He could almost see the vir rising from Dorian's arms, and it turned his stomach. Maybe not a madman. But what was their piece? The only people Kylar knew who did things just because they should were the Drakes, and he figured that they were the exception to the rule. In the Sa'kagé, in the court, in the real world, people did what was best for themselves.

Feir and Dorian hadn't denied that they had other motives for coming to Cenaria, but they certainly acted like he was the most important thing. They'd acted like they really believed he would change the course of the kingdom! It was madness. But he had believed them.

If they were just liars, wouldn't they try to tell him how great things would be if he killed Blint? Or were they just that much cleverer than most liars? It seemed that by what Dorian had said that Kylar was going to lose everything no matter what he did. What kind of fortune-teller told you that?

Still, Kylar found himself jogging again, and then running, startling a laundress filling her buckets with water. He stopped at Momma K's door and suddenly felt uneasy again. Momma K stayed up late and woke early every day, but if there was one time of the day that he could be sure she'd be in bed, it was right now. It was the only time of day that the door would be locked. *Dammit, would you just make a decision?*

Kylar rapped on the door quietly, berating himself for being a coward, yet deciding all the same that he would leave if no one answered it.

The door opened almost immediately. Momma K's maid looked almost as surprised as Kylar was. She was an old woman, wearing a shift, with a shawl around her shoulders. "Well, good morning, my lord. If you aren't a sight. I couldn't sleep, I just kept on thinking that we'd run out of flour for some reason, though I checked it just last night, for some reason I couldn't get it out of my mind that it was all gone. I was just walking past the door to check it when you knocked—oh by the twelve nipples of Arixula, I'm chattering like a daft old ninny."

Kylar opened his mouth, but a word wouldn't fit in the cracks of the ex-prostitute's rambling, edgewise or any other way.

" 'Time for a swift blow to the head, and a heave into the river, mistress,' I tell her, and she just laughs at me. I do wish I were young, if only so I could see the look on your face like I used to get. Once these old sacks would make men stand up and take notice. You'd walk right into a wall because you couldn't take your eyes off. It used to be that the sight of me in my night clothes—of course, I didn't wear old lady's rags like this, neither, but if I wore the kind of stuff I used to, I'm afraid I'd scare the children. It does make me miss the—"

"Is Momma K awake?"

"What? Oh, actually, I think so. She hasn't been sleeping well, poor girl. Maybe a visit will do her good. Though I think it was a visit from that Durzo that's got her knickers in such a bunch. It's hard at her age, going from what she's been to being like me. Almost fifty years old she is. It reminds me—"

Kylar edged past her and walked up the stairs. He wasn't even sure the old woman noticed.

He knocked and waited. No response. A sliver of light peeked through the crack along the sill, though, so he opened the door.

Momma K sat with her back to him. Two candles burned almost to nubs provided the only illumination in the room. She barely stirred when Kylar came in. Finally, she turned slowly toward him. Her eyes were swollen and red as if she'd been up all night crying. *Crying? Momma K?*

"Momma K? Momma K, you look like hell."

"You always did know just the thing to say to the ladies."

Kylar stepped into the room and closed the door. It was then he noticed the mirrors. Momma K's bedside mirror where she put on makeup, her hand mirror, even her full-length mirror, every one of them was smashed. Shards twinkled feebly from the floor in the candlelight.

"Momma K? What's going on here?"

"Don't call me that. Don't ever call me that again."

"What's going on?"

"Lies, Kylar," she said, looking down at her lap, her face half concealed in the shadows. "Beautiful lies. Lies I've worn so long I don't remember what's beneath them."

She turned. In a line down the middle of her face, she'd wiped off all her makeup. The left half of her face was free of cosmetics for the first time Kylar had ever seen. It made her look old and haggard. Fine wrinkles danced across the once delicate—now merely small and hard—planes of Gwinvere Kirena's face. Dark circles under her eyes gave her a ghostly vulnerability. The effect of half of her face being perfectly presented and the other stripped was ludicrous, ugly, almost comic.

Kylar covered his shock too slowly, not that he could ever hide much from her, but Momma K seemed satisfied to be wounded.

"I'll assume you're not here just to stare at the sideshow freak, so what do you want, Kylar?"

"You're not a sideshow—"

"Answer the question. I know what a man with a mission looks like. You're here for my help. What do you need?"

"Momma K, dammit, quit—"

"No, damn you!" Momma K's voice cracked like a whip. Then her mismatched eyes softened and looked beyond Kylar. "It's too late. I chose this. Damn him, but he was right. I chose this life, Kylar. I've chosen every step. It's no good switching whores in the middle of a tumble. You're here about Durzo, aren't you."

Kylar knuckled his forehead, put off track. He could read the look in her face, though. It said, "Discussion over." Kylar surrendered. Was he here about Durzo? Well, it was as good of a place to start as any.

"He said he's going to kill me if I don't find the silver ka'kari. I don't really even know what it is."

She took a deep breath. "I've been trying to get him to tell you for years," she said. "Six ka'kari were made for Jorsin Alkestes' six champions. The people who used the ka'kari weren't mages, but the ka'kari gave them magelike powers. Not like the feeble mages of today, either, the mages of seven centuries ago. You are what they were. You're a ka'karifer. You were born with a hole in your Talent that only a ka'kari can bridge."

Momma K and Durzo had known all of this, and they hadn't thought to tell him? "Oh, well, thanks. Can you direct me to the nearest magical artifact store? Perhaps one with a discount for wetboys?" Kylar asked. "Even if there were such things, they've either been collected by the mages or they're at the bottom of the ocean or something."

"Or something."

"Are you saying you know where the silver is?"

"Consider this," Momma K said "You're a king. You manage to get a ka'kari, but you can't use it. Maybe you don't have anyone you trust who can. What do you do? You keep it for a rainy day, or for your heirs. Maybe you never write down what it is because you know that people will go through your things when you die and steal your most valuable possession, so you plan to tell your son someday before he takes the throne. In some way or another, though, as kings so often do, you get yourself killed before you can have that talk. What happens to the ka'kari?"

"The son gets it."

"Right, and doesn't know what it is. Maybe even knows it's important, that it's magical, but like you said, if he ever tells the mages, they'll take it from him or from his heirs sooner or later. So he keeps it, and he keeps it secret. After enough generations pass, it becomes just another jewel in the royal treasury. By the time seven hundred years go by, it's switched hands dozens of times, but no one has a clue what it is. Until one day, Khalidor's God-king demands a tribute that includes one particular jewel, and a remarkably stupid king gives the very same jewel to his mistress."

"You mean—" Kylar said.

"I just found out today that Niner gave Lady Jadwin the silver ka'kari, the Globe of Edges. It looks like a small, oddly metallic jewel, like a diamond with a silver tint to it. It also happens to be one of Queen Nalia's favorite jewels. She thinks it's lost, and she's furious, so tomorrow night, someone the king trusts—I don't know who—will be sent to get it back. The Jadwins are having a party that night. So tomorrow, the ka'kari will be exposed. No royal guards, no mages, no magically warded treasury. Lady Jadwin will either be carrying it or it will be in her room. Kylar, you need to understand what's at stake. The ka'kari supposedly choose their own masters, but the Khalidorans believe they can magically force a bond. If the Godking succeeds... imagine the havoc a Godking would wreak if he could live forever."

It made prickles go up the back of Kylar's scalp. "You really mean this, don't you? Have you told Durzo?"

"Durzo and I ... I'm not too inclined to help Durzo just now. But there's more, Kylar. I'm not the only one who knows this." Anguish twisted her features and she looked away.

"What do you mean?"

"Khalidor has hired someone to get it. That's how my spies found out in the first place. Supposedly the job is a smash-and-dash."

"Supposedly?"

"They've hired Hu Gibbet."

"Nobody would hire Hu for a smash-and-dash. The man's a butcher."

"I know," Momma K said.

"Then who's his deader?"

"Take your pick. Half the nobles in the realm will be there. Your friend Logan has accepted his invitation, perhaps even the prince will be there. Those two do seem to be inseparable; for all that they are night and day to each other."

"Momma, who's your spy? Can you get me an invitation?"

She smiled mysteriously. "My spy can't help you, but I know someone who can. In fact, despite my best efforts, you know her too."

Kylar had walked up to men in broad daylight within paces of the city guard to kill them. He'd crawled under tables while a cat clawed him as guards searched the room for intruders. He'd had to break into a vat of wine and hide inside it as a noble's wine taster had picked out an appropriate bottle for dinner. He'd waited a yard from a fully stoked oven after he'd poisoned a stew while a cook debated with himself on what spice he'd added too much of to make it taste so strange.

But he'd never been this nervous.

He stared at the door, a narrow servants' entrance, in dismay. He was a beggar today, come to beg a crust. His hair was lank and greasy, smeared with ash and tallow. His skin was tough and brown, hands gnarled and arthritic. To get to that door, he had to make it through the guards at the estate's tall gate.

"Oy, old man," a stumpy guard with a halberd said. "Whatcha be wanting?"

"I heard my little girl is here. Miss Cromwyll. I hoped she might find me a crust, is all."

That woke up the other guard, who had only given Kylar a cursory glance. "What'd you say? You're related to Miss Cromwyll?" The protective air around the man, who must have been nearly forty, was palpable.

"No, no, she's not mine," Kylar protested, scraping a laugh across his lungs. "Just an old friend."

The guards looked at each other. "You gwyna go find 'er and bring 'er out here at this time of day with the goin's on tonight?" Stumpy asked.

The other shook his head, and with a grumble, started patting Kylar down gingerly. "Swear I'll get lice off of one of Miss Cromwyll's strays one of these days."

"Ah know it, but she's worth it, inn't she?"

"You're not so magnamorous when you're the one patting the beggars, Birt."

"Ah, stuff it."

"Go on. Kitchen's that way," the older guard told Kylar. "Birt, I'm lenient with ya, but if you tell me to stuff it one more time, I'll show you the business end o' my boot—"

Kylar shuffled to the kitchen favoring a stiff knee. The guards, for all their talk, were professionals. They held their weapons like they knew what to do with them, and though they hadn't seen through his disguise, they hadn't neglected their duty to search him. Such discipline boded ill for him.

Though he took his time walking and memorizing the layout of the estate grounds, the walk wasn't nearly long enough. The Jadwins had been dukes for five generations, and the manse was one of the most beautiful in the city. The Jadwin estate overlooked the Plith River, and directly faced Cenaria Castle. Just north of the estate was East Kingsbridge, which was ostensibly for military use, but it was rumored to be used more often for the king's nocturnal liaisons. If Lady Jadwin really was the king's mistress, the Jadwin estate was perfectly placed for easy access. The king also kept the duke running all over Midcyru on diplomatic missions that everyone but the duke knew were pure pretense.

The manse itself was set on a small central hill that allowed it to look over the river, despite twelve-foot spiked walls that bordered the entire property.

With a trembling hand he masked as a palsy, Kylar knocked at the servants' entrance.

"Yes?" The door opened and a young woman wiping her hands on an apron looked at Kylar expectantly.

She was a beautiful woman, maybe seventeen, with an hourglass figure that even through a servant's woolens obviously would have been the envy of any of Momma K's rent girls. The scars were still there, an X on her cheek, an X across her full lips, and a loop from the corner of her mouth to the outside of her eye. The scar gave her a permanent little grin, but the kindness of her mouth eased the cruelty of the scar.

Kylar remembered how her eye had looked, swollen grossly. He'd been afraid she would never see out of it. But her eyes, both of them, were clear and bright brown, sparkling with goodness and happiness. Doll Girl's nose had been broken to mush, and Elene's wasn't completely straight, but it didn't look bad. And she had all her teeth—of course, he realized, she'd been young enough that she'd only lost small teeth in the beating.

"Come in, grandfather," she said quietly. "I'll find you something to eat." She offered her arm, and didn't seem offended by his staring. She took him to a small side room with a narrow table for the servants who needed to be within earshot of the kitchen. Calmly, she told a woman ten years older than she was that she needed her to take over while Elene took care of her guest. From her tone and the older woman's reaction, Kylar could see that Elene was adored here, and that she took care of beggars all the time.

"How are you, grandfather? Can I get a salve for your hands? I know it's painful on these chilly mornings."

What had he done to deserve this? He'd come as the most foul sort of beggar, and she showered him with kindness. He had nothing to give her, yet she treated him like a human being. This was the woman who had almost died because of his arrogance and stupidity, his failure. The only ugliness in her life was because of Kylar.

He'd thought he'd set aside his guilt two years ago when Momma K had told him the simple truth that he'd saved Elene from worse than scars. But looking at those scars up close threatened to throw him right back to that hell.

She put a crust covered with fresh hot gravy down on the table, and started to cut it into smaller pieces. "Would you like to sit here? We'll just make this a little easier to chew, yes?" she said, speaking loudly the way people who work with old people learn to. She smiled and the scars tugged at her full lips.

No. He'd put her here, with these people who adored her, where she could afford to share a crust. Elene had made her own choices to become who she was, but he had made those choices possible. If there was one good thing he'd done, it was this. He closed his eyes and breathed deeply. When he opened his eyes and looked at her without guilt darkening his vision, she was stunning. Elene's hair was lustrous gold, aside from the scars her skin was flawless, eyes large and bright, cheekbones high, lips full, teeth white, neck slender, figure entrancing. She was leaning forward to cut the crust for him, her bodice gapping in front—

Kylar tore his eyes away, trying to slow his pulse. She noticed his sharp move and looked at him. He met her eyes. Her look was quizzical, open. He was going to ask this woman to betray her employer?

A tangled snarl of emotions that he'd kept shoved into some dark corner closet of his soul surged and burst through the doors. Kylar choked on a sob. He blinked his eyes hard. *Get a hold of yourself.*

Elene put her arm around him, heedless of his filthy clothing and stench. She didn't say anything, didn't ask anything, just touched him. Tingles shot through him, and his emotions surged again.

"Do you know who I am?" Kylar asked. He didn't use the beggar voice.

Elene Cromwyll looked at him strangely, uncomprehending. He wanted to stay hunched, to hide from those gentle eyes, but he couldn't. He straightened his back and stood up, and stretched his fingers.

"Kylar?" she asked. "It is you! What are you doing here? Did Mags and Ilena send you? Oh my God, what did they tell you?" Her cheeks flushed and her eyes lit with hope and embarrassment. It wasn't fair that a woman could be so beautiful. Did she know what she was doing to him?

Her face was the face of a girl surprised by a boy in the best way. Oh, gods. She thought he was here to ask her to Mags's party. Elene's expectations were about to meet reality like a toddler charging the Alitaeran cavalry.

"Forget Kylar," he said, though it pained him. "Look at me and tell me who you see."

"An old man?" she said. "It's a very good costume, but it isn't a costume party." She flushed again as if she were presuming too much.

"Look at me, Doll Girl." His voice was strangled.

She stopped, transfixed, peering into his eyes. She touched his face. Her eyes went wide. "Azoth," she whispered. She put a hand on the table to steady herself. "Azoth!" She flung herself at him so fast, he almost tried to block her attack. Then she was squeezing him. He stood stock still, his mind refusing to understand for a long moment: she was hugging him.

He couldn't make himself move, couldn't think; he simply felt. The smooth skin of her cheek brushed his scruffy, unshaven one. Her hair filled his nostrils with the clean scent of youth and promise. She hugged him fiercely, the notes of strong hard arms joining with supple firm stomach and back joining with the pure feminine softness of her chest pressed against his making a chord of perfect acceptance.

Tentatively, he lifted his hands from his sides and touched her back. He tasted salt on his lips. A tear, his tear. His chest convulsed uncontrollably, and suddenly he was sobbing. He grabbed her, and she squeezed him harder still. He felt her crying, staccato breaths shaking her slender frame. And for a moment, the world was reduced to a single hug, reunion, joy, acceptance.

"Azoth, I heard you were dead," Elene said, all too soon.

You will always be alone. Kylar froze up. If tears could stop halfway down a cheek, his would have.

He released Elene deliberately, stepped back. Her eyes were red, but still shining as she dabbed her tears away with a handkerchief. A sudden desire to sweep her into his arms and kiss her crashed over him in a wave. He blinked, held himself still until reality could reassert itself. He opened his mouth, couldn't say a thing, couldn't ruin it. He tried again, ready to lay out his lies, couldn't. *Relationships are ropes. Love is a noose. Durzo told me. He gave me a chance. I could have been a fletcher, an herbalist. I chose this.*

"I was ordered never to see you. By my master." His tongue was leaden. "Durzo Blint."

He could tell even Elene had heard of Durzo Blint. Her eyes tightened in confusion. He could see her working through it: if Durzo was his master, that meant...He saw a quick little disbelieving smile, as if she were about to say, "But wetboys are monsters, and you're not a monster." But then the smile faded. Why else would her Azoth never contact her? How else would a guild rat disappear so completely?

Her eyes grew distant. "When I was hurt, I remember you arguing with someone, demanding that he save me. I thought it was a dream. That was Durzo Blint, wasn't it?"

"Yes."

"And you...now you're what he is?" Elene asked.

"Close enough." Actually, *I'm not even a full-fledged horror, I'm just an assassin, a hack.*

"You apprenticed with him so he would save me?" she asked, her voice barely above a whisper. "You became what you are because of me?"

"Yes. No. I don't know. He gave me a chance to leave after I killed Rat, but I didn't want to be afraid anymore, and Durzo was never afraid, and even as an apprentice, he paid me so well that I could—" he stopped.

Her eyes narrowed as she puzzled it out. "That you could support me," she finished. She put her hands over her mouth.

He nodded. *Your beautiful life is built on blood money.* What was he doing? He should be lying to her, the truth could only destroy. "I'm sorry. I shouldn't have told you. I—"

"You're sorry?!" Elene interrupted him. He knew what the next words out of her mouth would be: *You're a failure. Look at what you've done to me.* "What are you talking about?" she asked. "You've given me everything! You fed me on the streets when I was too young to find food for myself. You saved me from Rat. You saved me when your master was going to let me die. You put me with a good family who loved me."

"But—aren't you mad at me?"

She was taken aback. "Why would I be mad at you?"

"If I hadn't been so arrogant, that bastard wouldn't have come after you. I humiliated him! I should have been watching. I should have protected you better."

"You were eleven years old!" Elene said.

"Every scar on your face is my fault. Gods, look at you! You would have been the most beautiful woman in the city! Instead, you're here, giving crusts to beggars."

"Instead of where?" she asked quietly. "Do you know any girls who've been prostitutes since they were children? I do. I've seen what you saved me from. And I'm grateful for it every day. I'm grateful for these scars!"

"But your face!" Kylar was on the edge of tears again.

"If this is the worst ugliness in my life, Azoth, I think I'm pretty lucky." She smiled, and despite the scars, the room lit up. She was breathtaking.

"You're beautiful," he said.

She actually blushed. The Drake sisters were the only girls Kylar knew who blushed, and Serah didn't blush anymore. "Thank you," she said, and touched his arm. At her touch, shivers went through him.

He looked into her eyes, and then he blushed, too. He'd never been so mortified in his life. *Blushing!* That only made it worse. She laughed, not a laugh at him in his discomfort, but a laugh of such innocent joy it pained him. Her laugh, like her voice, was low, and it brushed over him like a cool wind on a hot day.

Then her laughter passed and a look of profound sorrow stole over her face. "I'm so sorry, Azoth—Kylar. I'm sorry for what you've had to pay to put me here. I don't even know what to think. Sometimes it seems the God's hand doesn't reach very far into the Warrens. I'm sorry." She looked at him for a long time and another tear tracked down her cheek. She ignored it, just absorbing him. "Are you a bad man, Kylar?"

He hesitated. Then said, "Yes."

"I don't believe you," she said. "A bad man would have lied."

"Maybe I'm an honest villain." He turned away.

"I think you're still the boy who shared his bread with his friends when he was starving."

"I always took the biggest piece," he whispered.

"Then we remember differently," Elene said. She heaved a deep breath and brushed her tears away. "Are you . . . are you here for work?"

It was a shot in the solar plexus. "There's a wetboy coming to kill someone at the party tonight and steal something. I need an invitation to get in."

"What are you going to do?" she asked.

In truth, Kylar had barely thought about it. "I'm going to kill him," he said. And it was the truth. Hu Gibbet was the kind of twist who started killing beggars when he had to go too long between jobs. He needed murder like a drunkard needs wine. If Kylar came and stole the silver ka'kari first, Hu Gibbet would come after him. Hu was a full wetboy, and reputed to be as strong of a fighter as Durzo. Kylar's only chance to kill him would be to catch him off-guard. Tonight.

Elene still didn't look at him. "If you're a wetboy, you've got other ways to get in. You must know forgers. Kylar Stern must have contacts. Maybe an invitation from me would be the easiest way in, but that's not why you came. You came here to case the place, didn't you?"

His silence was answer enough.

"All these years," Elene said, turning her back, "I thought Azoth was dead. And maybe he is. Maybe I helped kill him. I'm sorry, Kylar. I'd give my life to help you. But I can't give you what's not mine to give. My loyalty, my honor, belongs to the God. I can't betray my lady's trust. I'm afraid I'm going to have to ask you to leave."

It was a gentler banishment than he deserved, but banishment all the same. Kylar hunched and curled his fingers into arthritic claws and left. He turned once he reached the gate, but Elene wasn't even watching him go.

37

Like all good ambushes, this one came at a time and place where they least expected it. Solon and Regnus and his men had made it down the mountains, over the central plains, and had come within two miles of Cenaria's sprawling northern edge.

Duke Gyre and his men were between two wide rice paddies on the raised road when they came upon a man leading a cart horse. Several peasants were working in the paddies, but they were dressed simply, trouser legs rolled up to their knees, obviously devoid of armor or weapons. The carter pulled his old horse to the side, looking at the men in armor intently.

Solon should have noticed it earlier, of course. Peasants didn't wear long sleeves in the paddies. But it wasn't until he was within twenty paces of the carter that he saw it. The Vürdmeister dropped the horse's reins and brought his wrists together, green fire roaring down his vir and filling each hand. He clapped his wrists together and wytchfire spurted forward.

The wytchfire hit the guard to Solon's left and went right through him. The magic was designed to melt off in layers like an icicle as it punched through each man. It was the size of a man's head as it went through the first man, then the size of a man's fist as it hit the second, then the size of a man's thumb as it hit the third. In an instant, all three were dead, flames roaring off their flesh, burning on the blood that spilled out of the men as if it were oil.

A second later, wytchfire hit the guards from each side as a Vürdmeister on either side of the road hurled death into their midst. Another three men dropped.

That left Solon, Duke Gyre, and two guards. It was a tribute to the men's discipline that they did anything at all, but Solon knew they were doomed. One guard rode right. Duke Gyre and the other guard rode left, leaving Solon to take care of the Vürdmeister on the road.

Solon didn't move. The Vürdmeister had set their ambush so they'd have ample time to get off two or three balls of wytchfire. Twelve swordsmen were no match for three wytches.

There was no time to weigh the consequences. Not even time to draw the sunlight streaming onto the paddies into magic. Solon drew directly on his *glore vyrden* and threw three tiny sparks through the air. They flew as fast as arrows and somehow avoided hitting the duke or his guards. Both Vürdmeister were gathering green fire again as the sparks, each hardly as big as a fingertip, touched their skin.

They weren't even close to lethal. Solon didn't have enough magic to face even one Vürdmeister alone, much less all of them together. But the sparks shocked them. A small shock, but enough to tense their muscles for a second and totally break their concentration. Before they could gather their wits, three swords descended with all the force of three galloping horses and three battle-hardened arms, and the two wytches to either side of the road died.

Solon threw the spark at the wytch on the road last, and the man blocked it. Indeed, it wasn't so much blocking as merely snuffing. The spark flew toward him and then died as if it were a fiery twig being dropped in the ocean. His counterattack was a gush of fire that roared toward Solon with the sound and rage of a dragon's breath.

There was no blocking it. Solon flung himself from the saddle and threw another spark as he fell to the ground and rolled off the road.

The wytch didn't even bother to quench the spark as it flew a good ten feet wide of him. He turned, bridling almost fifty feet of fire as if it were a living thing and turning it in his hands to follow Solon.

The spark hit the cart horse's flank. The old beast was already terrified by the blood, the sounds, and the flash of unnatural fire. It jerked against the cart and then reared and lashed out with its hooves.

The Vürdmeister never even heard the horse's whinny beneath the roar of the flames. One second, he was reining the stream of fire down the bank of the road onto Solon, and the next, a hoof caught him in the back. He dropped on all fours, not knowing anything but that something was terribly wrong. He gasped and turned to see the horse regain its balance. Then horse and cart ran right over the man, crushing him into the road.

Solon pulled himself out of the water and mud of the rice paddy as the cart horse ran as it must not have run in ten years. His own horse was dead, of course, its skull a smoking ruin and the smell of burnt hair and cooked meat mingling over its half-ruined corpse.

The wytchfire was barely smoldering on the bodies of the dead guards now. Even as he watched, it guttered out. Wytchfire spread horribly fast, but only lasted about ten seconds.

Ten seconds? Has it only been that long?

The sound of hooves brought Solon back into reality. He looked up at Duke Gyre, whose face was still and hard.

"You're a mage," the duke said.

"Yes, my lord," Solon said heavily. The lines were written now, by Solon's silence. The duke had no choice. Confronted with such a surprise, a more clever man would have pretended to have known Solon was a mage all along. Then he could have decided what to do with him later. Duke Gyre was too straightforward for that. It was his strength and his weakness.

"And you've been reporting on me to other mages."

"Only, only to friends, my lord." It was weak, and it made him sound weak to say it, Solon knew, but he couldn't imagine that it could all disappear like this. Surely his friendship with Regnus, surely ten years of service were worth more than this.

"No, Solon," Duke Gyre said. "Loyal vassals don't spy on their lords. You've saved my life this day, but you've been betraying me for years. How could you?"

"It wasn't—"

"For my life, I give you yours. Begone. Take one of the horses and go. If I ever see your face again, I'll kill you."

"Stay with him," Dorian had said. "His life depends on it. A kingdom depends on it. 'By your word—or silence—a brother king lies dead.' " But he'd never said how long Solon had to serve his Lord Gyre, had he? Solon bowed low in front of his friend and took a bridle from Gurden, who looked too stunned for emotion. Solon mounted and turned his back on Lord Gyre.

Did I save Cenaria today, or doom it?

38

Kylar's afternoon had been frantic. He'd had to get Logan to get someone else to get him an invitation, and then when he'd tried to find Durzo, the wetboy was gone, leaving a typically terse note: "On a job." Durzo didn't often give Kylar a lot of detail on his jobs, but lately Kylar felt that he was being more and more excluded, as if Durzo were trying to create space between them so that it would be easier to kill Kylar when the time came.

Durzo's absence had meant that Kylar didn't have to confess to talking with Elene, botching it, and probably tightening security at the Jadwin estate all at once, so it wasn't altogether a bad thing. Now, because he'd told Logan he was coming to the party, he had to come without a disguise, but because he'd told Elene he was coming, if she saw him, she'd report him immediately.

That was why he'd come in a carriage, even though it would seem odd for a young noble alone not to ride. The carriage stopped at the gate and he handed his invitation to Birt. The man didn't recognize him, of course. He just looked over the invitation carefully and waved him in. Kylar was glad to see the man. If he was still guarding the door, it meant that the Jadwins didn't have enough guards to replace all the ones who'd worked earlier in the day and still guard the party. Maybe they hadn't believed Elene. After all, how would a serving girl know about the plots of wetboys?

Kylar took one step out of his carriage and froze. The carriage directly in front of his was open and a whip-thin man was stepping out of it. It was Hu Gibbet, all in chocolate leather and silks like a lord, long blond hair combed and gleaming, smiling with the disdain of a man superior to those around him. Kylar ducked back into his carriage. So it was true. He counted to ten and then, afraid that his driver would wonder what he was doing and maybe call attention to him, he stepped out of the carriage himself. He saw

Hu disappearing inside. Kylar followed, producing the invitation again for the guards in front of the monstrous white oak door.

"So have you gotten the old goat's permission?" Prince Aleine asked.

Logan looked at his friend on the other side of the long table heaped high with every delicacy the Jadwins thought would impress their guests. The table was near one of the walls of the vast great hall of white marble and white oak. Against the monochrome background, the nobles were a riot of color. Several of the realm's most influential hecatonarchs, priests of the hundred gods, mingled in their myriad-colored robes. A band of minstrels in flamboyant cloaks and makeup fought for attention with lords and ladies high and low. Terah Graesin had shown up to the last big party two weeks ago in a scandalously low-cut red gown with a soaring hem. Terah was eighth in line for the throne, after the prince, the Gunder daughters, Logan, and her father Duke Graesin, and she adored the attention her position gave her. Her daring had touched off a new fashion, so this week all the gowns were either red or dared to expose more leg or breast or both than most prostitutes did. This was fine for Terah Graesin, who was somehow able to look glamorous instead of cheap. Most women weren't so fortunate.

"I spoke with the count this morn—" Logan said when he was suddenly silenced as breasts went past. No, not just breasts. The breasts. They were perfect. Not precipitously exposed, but perfectly shaped, these floated past him, held in a gossamer embrace of fabric rejoicing to cling to such nubile curves. Logan didn't even see the woman's face. Then, as she walked past, the sweet curves of swaying hips and a flash of lean, muscular calves.

"And?" the prince asked. He looked at Logan expectantly, holding a plate with little samples of every delicacy on the table. "What'd he say?"

Logan face flamed. Too much time in the wilds. Except that that wasn't really true. His eyes seemed unattached to his mind at all, controlled directly from elsewhere. He moved further down the line, trying to remember what he'd been saying, his plate still empty as he rejected a few delicacies fricasseed, flambéed, or frosted. "He said—ah, my favorite!" Logan started heaping strawberries on his plate, grabbed a bowl, and filled it with chocolate fondue.

"Somehow I'm sure whatever Count Drake said, it wasn't 'ah, my favorite,'" Prince Aleine said, arching an eyebrow. "If he said no, you don't have to be embarrassed. Everyone knows Count Drake is a little off. Their family mixes with commoners."

"He said yes."

"Like I said," the prince said. "He's a little off." He smiled and Logan laughed. "When are you going to propose?"

"Tomorrow. It'll be my birthday. Then no one can stop me."

"Does Serah know?" the prince asked.

"She suspects that I might do it soon, but she thinks that I need some time to consolidate my household and speak with my parents about it first."

"Good."

"What do you mean?" Logan asked.

They had reached the end of the long table. The prince stepped close to him. "I wanted to give you a birthday present myself. I know you've got feelings for Serah and I respect that, but Logan, you're a duke's son. Tomorrow you'll become one of the most powerful men in the realm, behind only the other dukes and my family. My father would love for you to marry Serah, and we both know why. If you marry her, you'll set your family back from the throne for two generations."

"Your Highness," Logan said, awkward.

"No, it's true. My father fears you, Logan. You are admired, respected, even held in awe here. That you've been gone half of every year hasn't alienated you like my father hoped. Instead, it's made you romantic. The hero off fighting for us on the borders, keeping the Khalidorans at bay. The king fears you, but I don't, Logan. His spies look at you and they can't believe that you are what you appear to be: a scholar, a fighter, and a loyal friend of the prince. They're schemers, so they see schemes. I see a friend. There are those who would destroy your family, Logan, by any means, and they won't tell me what they're planning—but I won't allow it. In fact, I'll do all I can to stop it." He looked down, grabbed a bit of fried plantain off a plate. "I'm here tonight to do a favor for my father. In return, he promised to give me whatever I ask. *Whatever* I ask."

"That's some favor," Logan said.

The prince waved a hand. "King Stupid gave my mother's favorite jewel to his mistress. I'm here to get it back. It doesn't matter. You know my sister?"

"Of course." Jenine was here somewhere. She was usually described as "sunny": very pretty, and very fifteen.

"She's smitten with you, Logan. She's been in love with you for two years. Talks about you all the time."

"You're joking. I've barely exchanged two words with her."

"So what," the prince said. "She's a great kid. She's pretty, only getting prettier, and she has my mother's intelligence—I know how important that is to you, my vituperative friend."

"I'm not vituperative," Logan said.

"See? I don't even know if you are or not. I just grabbed the biggest word I know. But Jeni would."

"What are you saying, Your Highness?"

"Jenine's your birthday present, Logan. If you want her. Marry her. Just give me the word."

Logan was stunned. "That's, that's quite the birthday present."

"Your family will be restored. Our children will grow up together. One of your grandchildren could share the throne with one of mine. You've been the best friend a man could ask for, Logan, and friends are something most princes don't get. I want to do well by you. You'll be happy, I promise it. Jenine is turning into an amazing woman. As I think you've noticed." The prince nodded.

Logan saw her then, looking at him across the room, and he realized he'd already seen her tonight. Or at least her breasts.

His face flamed. He tried to summon words, but they abandoned him. Jenine stood there across the room, with the elegance of a woman far older, at least until one of her friends said something to her and she started giggling.

The prince laughed. "Say yes, and you can do all the things you were imagining a minute ago. Legitimately."

"I, I…" Logan's jaw worked. "I'm in love with Serah, Your Highness. Thank you for your offer, but—"

"Logan! Do everyone a favor. Say yes. Your parents will be overjoyed. Your family will be saved. Jenine will be ecstatic."

"You didn't tell her, did you?"

"Of course not. But think about it. Serah's great. But let's be honest, she's kind of pretty, but she's not as smart as you like, and you know what the rumors say about her getting around—"

"She's the opposite of a loose woman, Aleine. She hasn't even more than kissed *me*."

"But the rumors—"

"The rumors are because people hate her father. I love her. I'm going to marry her."

"Excuse me," a young blonde said. She slid between them and brushed past the prince to reach for a sweet roll. She was a scandal in red. The friction between her chest and the prince's nearly pulled her breasts free of her dress, which had something more like a navel-line than a neckline. The prince noticed, Logan saw. But then, he usually did. And so did Logan.

"I'm Viridiana," the girl said, catching the prince's eyes as they came back up. "I'm so sorry, excuse me." Not that it was an apology. Not that it was an accident.

Viridiana slipped back into the crowd, her dancer's body carrying the prince's eyes and his thoughts away from Logan. "Well, uh, think about it. Let's talk tomorrow, before you ask," the prince said, watching Viridiana head out to the back porch. She looked over her shoulder, and seeing him looking, smiled.

The prince looked down at his plate, piled high with a little bit of each delicacy on the table. Then he looked at Logan's, piled high with just one thing. "This, my friend," the prince said, "is the difference between us. If you'll excuse me, I've seen a dish I simply must sample."

Logan sighed. His eyes fell on Jenine again, who was still looking at him. It looked like her friends were urging her to go talk to him.

Damnation. Where's Serah?

There were guards on every stair. This wasn't good news. Kylar had made his way surreptitiously through the party, trying to look so ordinary that no one gave him a second glance, but it wasn't easy. Especially doing it while keeping an eye out for Hu Gibbet, who most likely was doing the same thing. If Hu saw him, Kylar would lose the only advantage he had.

He made his way onto the back porch. Normally, he would have avoided it, because it was liberally strewn with couples. If one thing was guaranteed to make you feel lonely, it was seeing other people kissing passionately in an alcove in the moonlight.

Now, though, Kylar was looking for a way to the second floor. A balcony hung just above the porch, and if he could figure out a route, he could climb to it quickly enough that no one would even notice. Of course, once he was upstairs, he'd still have to find the ka'kari, but he bet it was in the duchess's room. People liked to keep their favorite jewels close.

The wall had no trellises. Maybe he could jump off the rail and vault off the wall high enough to grab the edge of the balcony, a good fifteen feet above. He could probably do it, but he'd have to get it on the first try. If he fell, no one would be able to ignore the noise he made when he crashed through the rose bushes below.

Still, it's better than standing here. Kylar breathed deeply.

"Kylar?" It was a woman's voice. "Kylar, hello. What are you doing here?"

Kylar turned guiltily. "Serah! Hello." She looked like she'd spent all day getting ready for the night. Her dress was modestly cut, but classic, beautiful, and obviously far more expensive than anything Count Drake could afford. "Wow, Serah. That dress . . ."

She smiled and glowed, but only for a moment. "Logan's mother gave it to me."

He turned and grabbed the rail. Across the river, behind high walls, the castle towers gleamed in the moonlight, as near and unreachable as Serah herself.

She came and stood beside him. She said, "You know Logan is going to—"

"I know."

She put her hand on his. He turned and they looked into each other's eyes. "I'm so confused, Kylar. I want to say yes to him. I think I love him. But I also—"

He swept her into his arms roughly, throwing an arm around her back and a hand behind her neck. He pulled her to him and kissed her. For a moment, she gasped. And then she was kissing him back.

In the distance, as if all the way across the river, somewhere in the castle, he heard a door slam. But it was so far away, surely it didn't matter. Then he felt Serah stiffen in his arms and pull back.

A hand clapped on Kylar's shoulder, not gently.

"What the hell are you doing!" Logan shouted, spinning Kylar around.

Heads popped out of nooks and the porch went still. Kylar saw the prince's head among them.

"Something I should have done a long time ago," Kylar said. "You mind?"

"Oh shit," the prince said. He started trying to disentangle himself from the young blonde who was wrapped around him in an alcove.

Kylar turned away from Logan as if to kiss Serah again, but Logan hauled him back around. Kylar's fist came first and caught Logan on the jaw. The big man stumbled back and blinked his eyes.

Serah shrank away, horrified, but she was already forgotten. Logan came forward, his hands up like a proper boxer. Kylar dropped into an unarmed fighting stance, Wind Through Aspens.

Logan came in and fought as Kylar knew he would: honorably. His punches came in above the belt. Textbook jabs and hooks. He was fast, far faster than he appeared, but fighting in such a rule-bound style, he might as well have been a cripple. Kylar wove in among his punches, brushing them aside, falling back slowly.

A crowd gathered in moments. Someone shouted that there was a fight and people started pouring outside.

The guards, admirably enough, were the first ones out. They moved forward to stop them.

"No," the prince said. "Let them fight."

The guards stopped. Kylar was so surprised he didn't dodge and the next punch knocked the wind out of him. He staggered back as Logan came in, his weight on his toes, crowding Kylar back against the railing.

Kylar gasped a few breaths, blocking his friend's punches with difficulty. As his wind returned, rage swept over him. He blocked a punch up, ducked beneath it, and rained four quick punches on Logan's ribs, sliding away from the railing.

Logan turned and swept a gale through the air with a huge roundhouse, stepping forward at the same time. Kylar dropped beneath the blow and flicked a foot into Logan's pelvis. Instead of taking a step, Logan found that his foot wasn't where he'd told it to be. He fell. Then Kylar's fist caught him across the face and he crashed to the ground.

"Don't get up," Kylar said.

There was a stunned silence from the crowd, followed by murmurs. They'd never seen anything like what Kylar was doing, but however effective it was, it wasn't noble to kick a man while boxing. Kylar didn't care. He had to finish this immediately.

Logan got up on his hands and knees, then on his knees, obviously about to stand. Gods, it was just like in the arena. Logan didn't know when to stay down. Kylar kicked him in the side of the head and he went down hard.

Serah rushed forward to Logan's side. "Well, Serah, you always wanted us to spar. Looks like I win." Kylar smiled triumphantly at her. The murmurs started immediately, all of them disapproving.

Serah slapped him with a crack that rattled his teeth. "You aren't half the man Logan is." She knelt by Logan, and Kylar could see that he'd suddenly ceased to be part of her world.

He straightened his tunic and cloak and pushed through the crowd. The first rows stepped back for him, as if even touching him would bring them shame, but as he pushed his way inside, people were still pushing outside, desperate to see the fight that they didn't know was already finished. Within a few feet of the door, he became just another noble in the crowd. He followed a wall to the servants' staircase, which was now unguarded, and went upstairs.

Well, that hadn't exactly been a roaring success. It had cost him his reputation and had quite possibly revealed his presence to Hu Gibbet. But it had gotten him up the stairs, and for now, that was all that mattered. He could worry about the consequences tomorrow. The rest of the job would be easier. It had to be, right?

Hu Gibbet had been tempted to head up the stairs as soon as the guards abandoned them to go break up some fool nobles' fight. The unguarded stairs were a temptation, but he was confident of his skills. Besides, his plan would still work, and it would give him information he couldn't get if he walked upstairs now.

Lady Jadwin was standing near the doors to the porch, either distraught or pretending to be. It was one of those little mysteries of life that the king had chosen her as his mistress. Surely there were more attractive women who would sleep with a king, even this king. Lady Jadwin was living proof of the hazards of inbreeding. She was a tall woman with a horse's face, large enough and old enough that she certainly didn't belong in the dress she was wearing tonight, and known to be sexually voracious by everyone in the kingdom—except her husband.

He figured that the distress was an act. Lady Jadwin was a passionate woman, but generally unflappable. This would probably be her excuse to go upstairs.

There. She spoke briefly to one of her guards, then went back to apologizing to the guests streaming back in from outside, most of them disappointed at having missed the fun.

The guard, having the subtlety of most guards, walked directly to the guard just now resuming his post at the servants' stair. He leaned close and whispered an order. The man nodded. Meanwhile, the duchess waited until the prince came through the door. She spoke a few words to him, then began feigning more distress as he disengaged himself from a young blonde hanging on his arm.

After a few more seconds, the duchess excused herself, told her husband that she wasn't feeling well, turned down what must have been an offer to send someone with her, and went up the grand stair by herself. Doubtless, she'd told him she just needed to lie down for a little while. "Enjoy the party, dear," she'd said, or something.

The prince was more circumspect, but not difficult to follow. He made his way to the sweet meats, chatted with a few ladies politely, excused himself and walked to the washroom, which was just down the hall from the servants' stair. He emerged from the dark hallway a minute later, looked quickly to see that no one was looking at him, and walked past the guard, who pretended not to see him.

Hu followed hard on the prince's heels, wrapping himself in shadows. The guard was so busy not seeing the prince, the wetboy probably could have slipped past him even without them.

The servants' stair opened on the grand hallway by the duke's chambers. The floors were the same white marble, with the middle of the hall covered by a red carpet for its entire length, all the way from this wing to the opposite one, where the duchess's chambers were. The lights were dimmed as a visual redirection for the guests who might have been at past parties where both floors were open to guests.

Kylar had no idea how long he had to get the Globe of Edges, but he was sure faster was better. It occurred to him that he wasn't the only person who might have seized the opportunity of the stairs being unguarded. Hu Gibbet might already be upstairs.

The only advantage Kylar had—he hoped—was that Hu probably wasn't coming just for a smash-and-dash. He was probably coming to kill someone. If that had been Kylar's goal, the simplest way would be to wait until the duchess gave the ka'kari to the king's agent, whoever it was, and then kill both of them. That way, Hu would get to satisfy his bloodlust and he would kill the two people who knew for sure what had happened. The king wouldn't know if the jewel had been stolen or not, and would have no way to ask without publicly acknowledging that Lady Jadwin was his mistress.

If that guess was right, Kylar had until Lady Jadwin came upstairs to get the Globe of Edges. It might be another hour, or it might be two minutes.

Halfway down the hallway, a guard was walking toward him. Kylar stepped backward into the corner, where the shadows were deeper. But then the guard turned and walked down the grand staircase. It was Kylar's chance. He walked forward quickly, with no attempt at stealth. His chest tightened as he stepped past the one area of the hallway that was well-lit. The landing at the top of the stairs was bathed in light, but with six steps, eyes locked straight forward, he made it across.

The corridor was lined with disturbing sculptures and excellent paintings. Unless Kylar missed his guess, the duke was something of an artist. The brilliant and diverse paintings were obviously selected by a man with a keen eye and a deep purse. Though similarly striking, the sculptures were unmistakably the product of one vision.

Pained figures appeared to be tearing themselves from the rock. One stumbling woman looked over her shoulder with terror writ in every feature. A man raged at the cloud of black marble that enveloped his hands. A nude woman lay back erotically into the cloud devouring her, rapture on her face.

Even in the hurry Kylar was in, the sculpture stopped him in his tracks. It was beautiful. Devastating. It mixed sensuality with something unsettling that Kylar couldn't identify. And it was unmistakably Elene.

So that's how it is. Kylar felt as if something were tearing the lining of his stomach. It felt empty, raw. *Of course she sleeps with him. He's a duke; she's a servant, and it's hard to say no. Even if she wanted to. Maybe she didn't. It happens all the time.*

He looked at the statue closely, giving a cursory glance to the supple limbs, narrow waist, and high breasts—and found what he was looking for. Though he'd given her a perfect nose, with the lightest of scratches, the duke had hinted at the scars on her face. So the man didn't just see them as imperfections. He was interested in the mysteries beneath.

This isn't the time for art appreciation, damn you. With a lump in his throat, Kylar jogged down the hall on the balls of his feet. He grabbed the pouch from his back and had his picks out by the time he reached the door. No light or sound came from the room, so he picked the lock quickly. It had only three pins, so it opened in three seconds. Kylar stepped inside and locked the door after himself. If Hu came to the door, he'd have three seconds' warning before the wetboy came.

Kylar drew the bollock dagger he'd strapped to the small of his back. The blade was a foot long, and he'd prefer something ten times its size if he had to fight Hu, but it was the best he'd been able to smuggle in.

He cased the room quickly. Most people, aware of the number of difficulties already present in a thief's life, were kind enough to use the same few hiding places. Kylar checked the mattress, behind the paintings, even the floor under the bureau and several of the chairs for trapdoors. Nothing. He checked the writing desk's drawers for false bottoms. Still nothing.

Most people who kept items of great value wanted to be able to check on them without much hassle, so Kylar didn't even go into the enormous closet. Unless Duchess Jadwin was comfortable handing her most prized possession to a servant, the Globe would be somewhere easily reached.

It didn't help that the duchess seemed to be quite the collector. There were knickknacks everywhere. And flowers, probably brought in for the duke's homecoming, sprouted from every flat surface in the room, obscuring Kylar's view.

So the duke bought his wife some flowers. And, from the musky smell in the air and the rumpled covers on the bed, apparently had been welcomed home enthusiastically.

Then one of the vases caught Kylar's eye. It was ornately carven jade, but more important, it had a square base. Kylar picked it up from the writing desk. Roses, spray roses, stargazer lilies, and snapserpents splayed every which way. Ignoring the flowers, he took it to the mantel and pushed aside a hardwood jewel box.

There was an indentation in the stone of the mantelpiece. A square indentation. Kylar felt a surge of hope.

The prophet was right.

The base fit the indentation and Kylar turned it; there was a muffled click. Kylar pulled all the knickknacks off the mantel and put them on the ground. On hidden hinges the entire mantelpiece opened up.

Ignoring the documents and gold bullion, Kylar grabbed the jewelry box. It was large, large enough to hold the Globe of Edges. Kylar opened it.

Empty.

Gritting his teeth, Kylar replaced the case and closed the mantel. So there was his lesson in prophecy. "A square vase will give you hope," Dorian had said. He hadn't said that it would turn out to be a false hope. *Damn!* Kylar paused long enough to fit a knockout needle into a small trap, just in case Hu came in here instead of following the duchess.

Replacing the knickknacks and putting the vase back on the desk, Kylar tried to think. Where could it be? Everything that could have gone wrong tonight had. The only point of light was that he hadn't seen Elene.

Elene! The leaden feeling in his stomach told Kylar that he knew exactly where the ka'kari was.

40

The prince felt hands grab him as soon as he stepped out of the staircase. An instant later, Lady Jadwin was pressing hot lips against his mouth. She pressed him back as he retreated until he bumped into the door of the duke's chambers.

He tried to hold her back, but she just reached past him and pulled the latch. He almost fell as the door opened behind him. She closed the door behind herself and locked it.

"My lady," he said. "Stop. Please."

"Oh yes, I'll stop," she said. "When it pleases me. Or should I say, after *you* please me?"

"I told you, we're finished. If my father finds out—"

"Oh, bugger your father. He's as much of a bumbler out of bed as he is in it. He'll never know."

"Your husband is just downstairs—anyway, it doesn't matter, Trudana. You know what I'm here for."

"If your father wants his globe back, he can come get it himself," she said. She put her hand on the front of his breeches.

"You know he couldn't come see you here," the prince said. "It'd be a slap in my mother's face."

"He gave it to me. It was a present."

"It's magic. My father thought it was just a stone, but Khalidor demanded it. Why would they do that if it weren't—no!" he slapped her hand away as she tugged open the laces.

"I know you like it," the duchess said.

"I do like it. But we're finished. It was a mistake, and it will never happen again. Besides, Logan is waiting for me downstairs. I told him what I was doing." The lie came out easily. Anything to get away from this woman. The worst of it was how much he had enjoyed her. The woman might be ugly, but she was more skilled than almost any of the women he'd bedded. Still, waking up and seeing her the first thing in the morning was more than he wanted to think about ever again.

"Logan's your friend," she said. "He'll understand."

"He's a great friend," the prince said. "But he sees things in black and white. Do you know how uncomfortable he was with me leaving him downstairs while I came upstairs with my father's mistress? I need you to get the gem. Now." Sometimes, he could just thank the gods that Logan was a known prig.

"Fine," she said peevishly.

"Where is it? Your husband could come in any second."

"My husband just came home today."

"So?"

"So whatever else he is, the pig's faithful, so he's practically burning with passion whenever he gets back from a diplomatic assignment. He's recuperating downstairs. The poor dear, I think I exhausted him." She laughed, and it was a harsh, callous sound. "I kept imagining it was you—" With what she must have imagined was a seductive look, she shrugged her shoulders and the front of her dress fell open. She rubbed up against his body and tugged at the laces of his breeches again.

"Trudana, please. Please keep that on. Where is it?" He didn't even look at her body, and he could tell it infuriated her.

"As I was saying," she said finally, "I knew you'd be here tonight, so I gave the globe to my maid. She's just two doors down. Are you satisfied?" She hitched up her dress and walked to her dresser. She looked at herself in the mirror.

The prince turned without saying anything. He'd thought this was going to be easy, that he was going to make his father owe him a huge favor for doing practically nothing. Now he saw that Trudana Jadwin was going to be a lifelong enemy. Never again, he promised himself. I will never sleep with a married woman again.

He didn't even pay any attention to the sound of a drawer sliding open. He didn't even want to look at Trudana. He wasn't even going to stay long enough to lace up his breeches. One second more was one second too many.

His hand was on the latch when he heard the rapid shuffle of her feet. Then something hot lanced into his back. It felt like a wasp sting. Then Trudana's body crushed into him, and he felt the stinger sink deeper. His head smacked against the door in front of him, and he felt the sting again.

It wasn't a sting. It was too deep. He gasped as roaring filled his ears. There was something wrong with one of his lungs. He wasn't breathing right. The stabbing continued and the roaring receded. The world took on a startling clarity.

He was being stabbed to death. By a woman. It was embarrassing, really. He was the prince. He was one of the top swordsmen in the realm, and this fat-assed old woman with saggy, uneven breasts was killing him.

She was breathing, practically gasping in his ear, the same way that she had when they made love. And she was speaking, crying as if every stab were somehow hurting her. The self-pitying bitch. "I'm sorry, oh, oh, I'm sorry. You don't know what he's like. I have to I have to I have to."

The stabbing continued, and it irritated him. He was already dying, his lungs filling with blood. Coughing, he tried to clear them, which succeeded in spraying blood on the door, but his lungs were mincemeat and blood just rushed back into the gaps.

He slumped, hit his knees in front of the door, and she finally stopped. His vision was going dark, and his face slumped forward into the door.

The last thing he saw, through the keyhole, was an eye on the opposite side of the keyhole, emotionlessly watching him die.

He found the door with no problem. It was locked, but he picked it in seconds. *Let her be asleep. Please.*

Easing open the door of the cramped room, Kylar found himself staring at an oversized meat cleaver. It was being held by Elene. She was very much awake.

In the darkness, Elene obviously didn't recognize him. She looked torn between screaming and hacking at him. Her eyes locked on the sword in his hand. She decided to do both.

Slapping her hand with the flat of his bollock dagger, Kylar launched the knife out of her grip. He dodged a grasping hand and got behind her in a moment, clapping a hand over her mouth.

"It's me. It's me!" he said as he had to twist this way and that to dodge flying elbows. He couldn't hold a hand over her mouth and pin both arms and stop the kicks she was aiming at his groin. "Be quiet or your mistress dies!"

As she seemed to regain her sanity, Kylar finally let Elene go. "I knew it!" she said, furiously but quietly. "I knew I couldn't trust you. I knew it was just going to be you."

"I meant your mistress will die because your noise will bring the wetboy here."

Silence, then, "Oh."

"Yes." In the dim moonlit room, he couldn't be sure, but Kylar thought he saw her blushing.

"You could have knocked," she said.

"Sorry. Old habit."

Suddenly awkward, she picked up the cleaver off the bed and put it under her pillow. Looking down at her nightgown, which was disappointingly chaste, she seemed embarrassed. She grabbed a robe and turned her back while she pulled it on.

"Relax," Kylar said as she turned back to face him. "It's a little late for modesty. I saw your statue. You look good naked." Why had he twisted that last bit to make her sound like a whore? Even if she was sleeping with the duke, what choice did she have? She was a servant in the man's house. It wasn't fair, but Kylar still felt betrayed.

Elene folded as if he'd hit her in the stomach.

"I begged her not to display it," Elene said. "But she was so proud of it. She said I should be proud too."

"She?"

"The duchess," Elene said.

"The duchess?" Kylar repeated stupidly. *Not the duke. Not the duke?*

He felt at once vastly relieved and more confused than ever. Why should he feel relieved?

"Did you think I'd model naked for the duke?" she asked. "What do you think, that I'm his mistress?" Her eyes widened as she saw the expression on his face.

"Well..." Kylar felt like he'd unjustly accused her, then felt mad that she was making him feel embarrassed for drawing a perfectly good conclusion, then felt mad that he was wasting time talking to a girl when a wetboy was probably waiting out in the hall. *This is madness.* "It happens," he said defensively.

Why am I doing this?

For the same reason I've watched her from afar. Because I'm intoxicated by her.

"Not with me," Elene said.

"You mean you're a..." he was trying to sound snide, but he trailed off. Why was he trying to sound snide?

"A virgin? Yes," she said, unembarrassed. "Are you?"

Kylar clenched his jaw. "I—look, there's a killer here."

Elene seemed about to comment about Kylar avoiding her question, then her look darkened as the joy leached out of it. "Two," she said quietly.

"What?"

"Two killers."

She meant him. Kylar nodded, again feeling a lump in his throat, and suddenly he was ashamed of what he was. "Yes, two. I saw Hu coming in, Elene. Is the Globe safe?"

He was watching her eyes. As expected, they darted to where she'd hidden it: the bottom of her closet.

"Yes," she said. "It's..." her voice died. "You're going to steal it."

"I'm sorry," Kylar said.

"And now you know where I hid it. You set me up."

She was naive, but she wasn't stupid. "Yes."

Anger built in her brown eyes. "Is there even an assassin, or was it all a lie?"

"There is one. I give you my word," Kylar said, looking away.

"For all that's worth."

Ouch. "I am sorry, Elene, but I have to."

"Why?"

"It's hard to explain," he said.

"I spent all day being embarrassed about everything I'd ever written to you. I spent all day feeling terrible how much you'd given for me. I didn't even tell the guards you were coming because I thought—I thought … You're a real piece of work, *Kylar*," she said. "I guess Azoth really did die."

Not like this. Not like this.

"I really do have to take it," he said.

"I can't let you do that," she said.

"Elene, if you stay here, they'll think you helped me. If Hu doesn't kill you, the Jadwins might. They could throw you in the Maw. Elene, come with me. I couldn't live with myself if they did that."

"You'll manage. Just take a new name. Throw money at whatever makes you feel guilty."

"They'll kill you!"

"I won't repay good with evil."

He was running out of time. He had to get out of here.

Kylar exhaled. So everything was going to go the worst possible way tonight. "Then I'm sorry for this," he said, "but it's to save you."

"What is?" she asked.

Kylar punched her, twice. Once in the mouth, hard enough to draw blood. And once in her beautiful, piercing eyes, hard enough that they would blacken and swell shut, so they wouldn't see what he did. As she staggered backward, he spun her around and clamped her in a chokehold. She flailed vainly against his grip, doubtless thinking he was killing her. But he merely held her and jabbed a needle in her neck. In seconds, she was unconscious.

She'll never forgive me for this. I'll never forgive me for this. Kylar laid her on the floor and pulled out a knife. He cut his hand and dripped blood onto Elene's face to make it look like she'd been beaten. It was gross, and the contrast of her beauty with the ugliness of what he was doing made him uncharacteristically squeamish, but it had to be done. She had to look like a victim. Looking at her there, unconscious, was like eating his own little slice of the bitter business. The bitterness of the business was the truth of the business. Even here, when he hadn't killed, when he didn't have to bathe in the all-permeating odors of death, Kylar had closed the eyes that saw the truth of him, blackened the eyes of light that illuminated the darkness in him, had bloodied and blinded the eyes that pierced him. *Who says there are no poets in the bitter business?*

Finished, Kylar arranged Elene's limbs in a suitably graceless pattern.

The silver ka'kari was tucked in a slipper in the bottom of the closet. Kylar held it up to examine it in the moonlight. It was a plain, metallic sphere, utterly featureless. In truth, it was a little disappointing. Despite the metallic sheen, it was translucent, which was novel. Kylar had never seen anything like that, but he'd been hoping the ka'karı would do something spectacular.

He tucked the ball into a pouch and moved to the door. So far, so good. Well, actually, so far tonight had been pretty much an unmitigated disaster. But getting out should be relatively easy. If he couldn't sneak past the guard at the bottom of the servants' stairs, he could walk right up to the man and pretend that he'd been looking for the toilet and had needed to go so badly that he'd gone for the first available one. The guard would give him a warning that the upstairs was off limits, Kylar would say they should have guards at the bottom of the steps if they didn't want anyone to go up them, the guard would be chagrined, and Kylar would go home. Not foolproof, but then, tonight Kylar would have distrusted anything that was foolproof.

Looking through the keyhole, he watched the hallway and listened closely for thirty seconds. There was nothing out there.

The moment he cracked the door, someone kicked the other side with more than mortal strength. The door blew into him, hitting his face first, then his shoulder. It launched him back into the room.

He almost kept his feet, but as he flew back, he tripped over Elene's unconscious body and went down hard. He slid across the stone floor until his head collided with the wall.

Barely holding onto consciousness, black spots exploding in front of his eyes, Kylar must have drawn the pair of daggers on pure instinct because his hands protested in pain as the daggers were knocked out of them.

"Boy?"

Kylar had to blink several times before he could see again. When his vision cleared, the first thing he saw was the knifepoint an inch from his eye. He followed that up the gray-clad arm and hooded body.

Woozy, Kylar wondered why he wasn't dead. But even before Hu pulled back his hood, Kylar knew.

Momma K had betrayed them. She'd sent him to kill the wrong man.

"Master Blint?" he asked.

41

*W*hat are you doing!" Master Blint backhanded Kylar soundly. He stood, furious, the illusory features of Hu Gibbet melting away like smoke.

Kylar staggered to his feet, his head still spinning and his ears ringing. "I had to—you were gone—"

"Gone planning this!" Blint whispered hoarsely. "Gone planning this! Never mind now. We've got three minutes until the guard's next round." He nudged Elene's limp form with a toe.

"That one's still alive," Durzo Blint said. "Kill her. Then go find the ka'kari while I fix the deader. We'll discuss your punishment later."

I'm too late. "You killed the duchess?" Kylar asked, rubbing his shoulder where the door had hit him when Durzo burst in.

"The deader was the prince. Someone else got there first." Boots were clomping up the steps. Durzo unsheathed Retribution and checked the hallway.

Gods, the prince? Kylar looked at the unconscious girl. Her innocence was irrelevant. Even if he didn't kill her, they'd think she helped steal the ka'kari and kill the prince.

"Kylar!"

Kylar looked up, dazed. It was all like a bad dream. It couldn't be happening. "I already..." He held out the pouch limply.

Scowling, Durzo snatched it away from him and turned it over. The Globe of Edges fell into his hand. "Damn. Just what I thought," he said.

"What?" Kylar asked.

But Durzo wasn't in any mood to answer questions. "Did the girl see your face?"

Kylar's silence was enough.

"Take care of it. Kylar, that's not a request. It's an order. Kill her."

Thick white scars crisscrossed what had once been a beautiful face. Her eyes were swelling, blackening—and that was as much Kylar's fault as the ten-year-old scars were.

"Love is a noose," Blint had told him when he began his apprenticeship a decade ago.

"No," Kylar said.

Durzo looked back. "What did you say?" Black blood dribbled down Retribution, pooling on the floor.

There was still time to stop. Time to obey, and live. But if he let Elene die, Kylar would be lost in shadow forever.

"I won't kill her. And I won't let you. I'm sorry, master."

"Do you have any idea what that means?" Durzo snapped. "Who is this girl that she's worth being hunted for the rest of your short—" he stopped. "She's Doll Girl."

"Yes, master. I'm sorry."

"By the Night Angels! I don't want apologies! I want obedien—" Durzo held up a finger for silence. The footfalls were close now. Durzo threw open the door and blurred into the hall, inhumanly fast, Retribution flashing silver in the low light.

The guard fell in two thumps. It was Stumpy, the older guard who'd frisked Kylar so gingerly when he'd cased the estate this morning.

The hall lantern behind Durzo swaddled darkness's favorite child in shadow, casting his form over Kylar and making his face invisible. Silhouetted, black blood dripped from the tip of Retribution. Drip, drip. Durzo's voice strained like bending steel. "Kylar, this is your last chance."

"Yes," Kylar said, his bollock dagger hissing against its scabbard as he turned to face the man who'd raised him, who'd been more than a father to him. "It is."

There was the sound of something metallic rolling across marble. It came toward Kylar. He raised a hand and felt the ka'kari slap into his outstretched palm.

He turned his hand over and saw the ka'kari burning a brilliant, incandescent blue. It was stuck to his palm. As he looked, runes began burning on the surface of the globe. They shifted, changed, as if trying to speak to him. Blue light bathed his face and he could see through the ka'kari. It was sucking blood from the cut on his palm. He looked up and saw dismay on Master Blint's face.

"No! No, it's mine!" Blint yelled.

The ka'kari pooled like black oil in an instant.

Blue light exploded like a supernova. Then the pain came. The cold in Kylar's hand became pressure. It felt like his hand was splitting apart. Staring at the now uniformly burning puddle in his hand with horror, Kylar saw that it was shrinking. It was pushing itself *into* his hand. Kylar felt the ka'kari enter his blood. Every vein bulged and contorted, freezing as the ka'kari passed through him.

He didn't know how long it lasted. He sweated and shivered and sweated coldly. Gradually the cold faded from his limbs. More gradually still, warmth replaced it. Perhaps seconds, perhaps half an hour later, Kylar found himself on the floor.

Oddly, he felt good. Even face down on stone, he felt good. Complete. Like a gap had been bridged, a hole had been filled. *I'm a ka'karifer. I was born for this.*

Then he remembered. He looked up. From the look of frozen horror on Durzo's face, it all must have taken only seconds. Kylar jumped to his feet, feeling stronger, healthier, more full of energy than he could ever remember.

The look on Durzo's face wasn't anger. It was grief. Bereavement.

Kylar slowly turned his hand over. The skin was still cut on his palm, but it wasn't bleeding anymore. The ka'kari had seemed to push into—

No. It couldn't have.

From every pore in his hand, black poured out like sweat. It congealed. In a moment, the ka'kari rested in his palm.

A strange glee filled Kylar. Fear followed. He wasn't sure the glee was all his own. It was as if the ka'kari were happy to have found him. He looked back to Durzo, feeling stupid, so far out of his depth he didn't know how to act.

It was then he realized how clearly he could see Durzo's face. The man still stood in the hallway, the lantern behind him. A moment before—before the ka'kari—his face had been all but invisible. Kylar could still see the shadows falling on the floor where Durzo blocked the light, but he could see *through* them. It was like looking through glass. You could tell the glass was there, but it didn't impede your vision. Kylar glanced around Elene's little room and saw that the same applied to everything he looked at. The darkness welcomed his eyes now. His eyes were sharper, clearer—he could see further, could see the castle across the river as if it were high noon.

"I have to have the ka'kari," Durzo said. "If he doesn't get it, he'll kill my daughter. Night Angels have mercy, Kylar, what have you done?"

"I didn't! I didn't do anything!" Kylar said. He held the ka'kari out. "Take it. You can have it. Get your daughter back."

Durzo took it from him. He stared into Kylar's eyes, his voice sorrowful, "You bonded it. It bonds for life, Kylar. Your Talent will work now, whether you're holding it or not, but its other powers won't work for anyone else until you're dead."

There was sound of feet running up the steps. Someone must have heard Durzo's yell. Kylar had to go now. The import of Durzo's words was barely beginning to register.

Durzo turned to face whoever was coming up the steps, and the prophet's words echoed in Kylar's ears: "If you don't kill Durzo Blint tomorrow, Khalidor will take Cenaria. If you don't kill him by the day after that, everyone you love will die. If you do the right thing once, it will cost you years of guilt. If you do the right thing twice, it will cost you your life."

The bollock dagger was in his hand. Durzo's back was turned. Kylar could end it now. Not even Durzo's reflexes could stop him when Kylar was this close. It would mean stopping an invasion, saving everyone he loved— surely that meant he held Elene's life in his hands right now. Logan's. Maybe the Drakes'. Maybe the whole invasion hinged on this. Maybe hundreds or thousands of lives were balanced now on the point of his dagger. A quick, painless cut, and Durzo would die. Hadn't he said that life was empty, worthless, meaningless, cheap? He wouldn't be losing anything of value when he lost his life, he'd sworn that.

Durzo had said it, and more, but Kylar had never really believed him. Momma K had already stabbed Durzo in the back with her lies; Kylar couldn't do it with his hands.

The moment took on a startling clarity. It froze like a diamond and rotated before his eyes, every facet gleaming, futures shearing off and sparkling. Kylar looked from Elene on his right hand to Durzo on his left, from Durzo to Elene, Elene to Durzo. There was his choice, and their futures. He could kill Elene, the woman he loved, or he could kill Durzo, who had raised him as his son. In every facet, this truth glared pitilessly: If one lived, the other must die.

"No," Kylar said. "Master, do it. Kill me."

Durzo looked at him as if he couldn't believe his ears.

"She's only seen me. She won't be a threat to anyone if I'm dead. You can take the ka'kari and save your daughter."

Blint's eyes filled with a look Kylar had never seen before. The hard, jagged cast of his master's face seemed to ease and it made him seem a different man, not old and tired and worn, but younger, a man more like Kylar than Kylar had ever imagined Blint could look. Durzo blinked as bottomless wells of grief threatened to spill over in tears. He shook his head. "Just go, son."

Kylar wanted to go. He wanted to run away, but he was right. It was the only way. He stood there, frozen, but not with indecision. He was just praying that Durzo would act before he lost his courage. *What am I saying? I don't want to die. I want to live. I want to take Elene out of here. I want to—*

The door to the duke's chambers opened and the blood-spattered duchess stumbled out, screaming, "Assassin! Assassin! He's killed the prince!"

Durzo acted instantly. He slammed into Kylar, driving them both into Elene's room. It took all of Kylar's presence of mind to not trample Elene, but Durzo was still moving. He had a hold of Kylar's cloak and was swinging him with the surprising speed and force of his Talent. Kylar exploded through the window and out into the night.

By the grace of the God, or His cruelty, or sheer dumb luck, or Durzo's preternatural skills, Kylar landed squarely in the center of a hedge. He crashed through it, rolling out of control, and popped out onto the ground. It was ridiculous; nothing was broken, nothing was sprained, he didn't even get scratched. He looked up and saw guests craning their heads on the balcony where so recently he'd kissed Serah, but they were on the other side of lamps and couldn't make him out.

Then the screaming from inside was taken up by others, women's voices and men's. Orders were being shouted and armed men were running, clanking and ringing in their chain mail. Kylar looked up at the second story with his heart in his throat. He didn't know whether to curse or laugh. The decision was out of his hands for now. He was alive, and it felt good.

There was nothing else to do. Kylar jogged to the estate's garden gate, broke the lock, and disappeared into the night.

42

The Godking Garoth Ursuul was awake before the functionary knocked on his bedchamber door. No one could approach this room without waking him. It meant less sleep than he might like, but he was an old man now; he didn't need much sleep. Besides, it kept the slaves on their toes.

The room wasn't what one might expect of a Godking. It was open, light and airy, filled with beautiful Plangan stained glass and ivory mirrors and Sethi lace on the bed and dire bear rugs from the Freeze on the floors and freshly cut flowers on the desk and the mantel, all chosen and arranged by a slave with aesthetic sensibilities. Garoth cared for none of it but the paintings. Portraits of his wives lined the walls. His wives had come from almost every nation in Midcyru, and with few exceptions, all were beautiful. Petite or willowy, buxom or boyish, pale or dark, the images all pleased Garoth Ursuul. He was a connoisseur of feminine beauty, and he spared no expense in indulging this vice. It was, after all, a service to his family and the world that he breed the best sons possible. That was where the unattractive women came in. He'd experimented with kidnapping women from royal families in hopes that they might produce more acceptable sons. Two of his current nine aethelings had been born of such women, so Garoth supposed that nobles might produce acceptable sons at a slightly better rate than the rabble, but it was ever so much more tedious to breed with an ugly woman.

Partly for his sons' sake and partly for his own amusement, he'd even indulged in making some of the women love him. It had been surprisingly easy; he hadn't had to lie as much as he'd expected. Women were so willing to do that to themselves. He'd heard that love made the sex better, but he wasn't impressed. With magic, he could make a woman's body respond to him however he pleased, and there was a joy in watching a woman try to hold her fury and hatred while his magic pleased her in ways she'd never felt before. Unfortunately, such pleasures did have their price: those wives had to be watched closely; he'd lost two to suicide.

The functionary's hand banged on the door and Garoth gestured it open. The functionary came in on his knees, scooting forward, crossing his arms on his chest. "My god, my majestic king—"

Garoth sat up. "Out with it. You have a message from the Jadwin slut."

"She reports that she has killed the prince, but has lost possession of the ka'kari. So sorry, Your Holiness."

"Doubtless it's another counterfeit," Garoth said, addressing himself, not the functionary. "Have the ships arrived for the Modaini invasion?"

Cenaria he could deal with whenever he pleased, but a straight march south would tie up his armies for weeks or months. That damned Duke Gyre had turned the defenses at Screaming Winds into a serious obstacle. He could take it, of course. He could probably defeat any army in the world now except the Alitaerans', but a Godking didn't waste men or meisters on frontal assaults. Not when he had other options.

Besides, what conqueror would really want a hive like Cenaria, anyway? He'd almost do better to exterminate everyone there and send his own subjects to colonize the city.

Garoth Ursuul's interest wasn't in temporal power. The bid for Cenaria was just an amusement. He had far more reliable intelligence that the red ka'kari was in Modai. Once there, he would have Cenaria surrounded. He could probably take the country without even fighting for it. Then, Ceura, and a strike right into the mages' heart, Sho'cendi. He wouldn't have to face Alitaera until he was sure of victory.

"Two ships are still passing through Cenarian waters."

"Good, then—"

"Your Holiness—" the man squeaked as he realized whom he had just interrupted.

"Hopper?"

"Yes, Your Holiness?" Hopper's voice was barely a whisper.

"Don't ever interrupt me again."

Hopper nodded, wide-eyed.

"Now what did you have to say?"

"Lady Jadwin claims to have seen someone bond the ka'kari in the hallway outside her room. Her description was...accurate."

"By Khali's blood." Garoth breathed. A ka'kari, after all this time. A ka'kari someone had bonded. That almost made it easier. A ka'kari alone was small enough it could be hidden or lost anywhere, but a ka'kari that was bonded would be kept close by whomever bonded it.

"Reroute those ships. And order Roth to go ahead with the assassinations. The Gyres, the Shinga, all of them. Tell Roth he's got twenty-four hours."

Something was terribly wrong. Regnus Gyre knew that as soon as he reached the gates of his home. No guards were standing outside. Even with how many of his servants and guards the king had managed to have fired or driven off in the last decade, that was disturbing. The lamps were still burning inside the manse, which was odd, an hour past midnight.

"Should I call out, my lord?" Gurden Fray, his guard, asked.

"No." Regnus dismounted and looked through his saddlebags until he found the key. He opened the gate and drew his sword.

On either side of the gate, out of the lamplight, was a body. Each had his throat cut.

"No," Regnus said. "No." He started running for the manse.

He burst through the front door and saw red everywhere. At first his mind refused to accept it. In every room, he found the dead. All looked like they had been caught unawares. Nothing was broken. There were no signs of violent conflict at all, except the bodies. Not even the guards had fought. Almost everyone had had his throat slashed. Then the bodies had been turned so they would bleed as much as possible. Here, old Dunnel was seated upside down in a chair. There Marianne, who had been Logan's wet nurse, was laid down the stairs with her head on the bottom step. It was as if Death himself had strolled through the house, and no one had even tried to stop him. Everywhere, Regnus saw trusted servants, friends, dead.

He found himself running up the stairs, past the statue of the Grasq

Twins, toward Catrinna's room. In the hall, he saw the first signs of a struggle. An errant sword had smashed a display case. A portrait of his grandfather had a chunk of frame missing. The guards here had died fighting, the killing wounds on their chests or faces. But the winner was clear, because each body had had its throat cut, and its legs propped up on the walls. The puddles from a dozen men met, coating the floor as if it were a lake of blood.

Gurden knelt, his fingers touching a friend's neck. "They're still warm," he said.

Regnus kicked open the door of his room. It banged noisily; if it had been closed and locked earlier in the night, it wasn't now.

Four men and two women were there, stripped, lying face down in an open circle. Above them, naked, hanging upside down from one foot tied to the chandelier high above while the other leg flopped grotesquely, was Catrinna. Cut into the backs of the corpses, one word to each, were the words: LOVE AND KISSES, HU GIBBET. The knife standing straight out of his steward Wendel North's back served as the period.

Regnus ran. He ran from room to room, checking the dead, calling out their names, turning them over to look at their faces. He became dimly aware of Gurden shaking him.

"Sir! Sir! He's not here. Logan's not here. We have to leave. Come with me."

He let Gurden drag him outside, and the smell of air without blood in it was sweet. Someone was repeating over and over, "Oh my God. Oh my God. Oh my God." It was him. He was babbling. Gurden paid no attention to him, just pulled him along, stumbling.

They got to the front door just as six of the king's elite lancers rode up to it with lances leveled.

"Hold!" their lieutenant called. His men fanned out around Regnus and Gurden. "Hold! Are you Regnus Gyre?"

Something about the bared steel and the sound of his own name wakened him. "Yes," he said, looking at his bloody clothes. Then, stronger, "Yes, I am he."

"Lord Gyre, I've been ordered to arrest you. I'm sorry, sir." He was young, this lieutenant. His eyes were wide, as if he couldn't believe whom he was arresting.

"Arrest me?" His mind was slowly coming back under his power, like a horse that had taken the bit in its teeth and galloped its own way, and was now willing to submit once more.

"Yes, my lord. For the murder of Catrinna Gyre."

A wave of cold washed through Regnus. He could brace, or he could break. He clenched his jaw, and the tears that sprang from his eyes seemed oddly out of place with the command in his voice. "When did you get your orders, son?"

"An hour ago, sir," the lieutenant said, then looked peeved that he'd so automatically obeyed a man he was supposed to be arresting.

"She hasn't been dead fifteen minutes. So tell me, what does that say about your orders?"

The lieutenant's face blanched. A moment later, the lances were wavering. "Our captain said you'd been seen killing—doing it, sir. An hour ago he said that." The lieutenant looked at Gurden. "Is it true?"

"Go see for yourself," Gurden said.

The lieutenant went inside, leaving the men nervously guarding them. Some of the men peeked through the windows and quickly looked away. Regnus felt impatient, as though, if he were given time, he might think again, might detach from his mind. Tears were running down his cheeks again, and he didn't know why. He had to think. He could find out the captain's name, but the man was also just obeying orders. Whether from the Sa'kagé, or the king.

Several minutes later, the lieutenant emerged. He had vomit in his beard and was shaking violently. "You may go, Lord Gyre. And I'm sorry....Let him go."

The men withdrew and Regnus mounted, but he didn't leave. "Will you serve the men who massacred my whole family?" Regnus asked. "I intend to find my son, and I intend to find who—" His voice betrayed him, and he had to clear his throat. "Come with me, and I swear you will serve with honor." His voice cracked on the last word, and he knew he could say no more.

The lieutenant nodded. "We're with you, sir." The men nodded, and Regnus had his first squad. "My lord," the lieutenant said. "I, I cut her down, sir. I couldn't leave her like that."

Regnus couldn't speak. He sawed at his reins viciously and galloped for the gates. *Why didn't I do that? She was my wife. What kind of man am I?*

Lord General Agon was one of the few nobles who hadn't been at the Jadwins' party last night. He hadn't been invited. Not that he felt left out.

The sun was just creeping over the horizon, and the situation didn't look any better in the light of day. Usually, of course, the city guard would handle a murder. But usually the victims of murder weren't heirs to the throne. Agon needed to oversee this one personally.

"Why don't you tell me what really happened, milady," Agon said. No matter what he did here, he was going to be the loser.

Lady Jadwin sniffled. She was genuinely distraught. Agon was sure of that. What he wasn't sure of was whether it was because she had been caught, or because she was sorry the prince was dead. "I have told you," she said. "A wetboy—"

"A what?"

She stopped.

"How do you know what a wetboy is, Trudana?"

She shook her head. "Why are you trying to confuse me? I'm telling you, an assassin was here, standing in this hallway. Do you think I beheaded my own guard? Do you think I'm strong enough for that? Why won't you listen to Elene? She'll tell you."

Blast. He had thought about that. Not only did he doubt that Lady Jadwin was strong enough to behead a man, but she had no weapon to do it with. And if she'd just murdered the prince without saying a word, why would she cry out and draw people upstairs before she had a chance to clean the blood off her hands and face?

"Explain this," he said. He lifted the red dress she'd worn the night before. His men had discovered it wadded up in the closet. It was still damp with hardening blood. A lot of blood.

"After—after the assassin stabbed the prince, he fell, and I—I caught him. And he died in my arms. I tried to go get help, but the assassin was still in the hall. I was terrified. I panicked. I couldn't stand to have his blood all over me."

"What were the two of you doing alone in the bedchamber?"

The duchess stared at him as if her eyes were hot coals. "How dare you!"

"How dare you, Trudana?" Agon said. "How dare you cheat on your husband not just with the king but also with the king's son? What kind of perverse pleasure did you take out of that? Did you like making the prince betray his father?"

She tried to slap him, but he moved.

"You can't slap everyone in the kingdom, Trudana. We found the bloody knife in your room. Your servants vouch that it's yours. I'd say the odds are that you're going to be beheaded. Unless, that is, the king decides you deserve a common traitor's death on the wheel."

At those words, Trudana Jadwin paled and turned green, but she didn't say another word. Agon gestured angrily, and his men took her away.

"That was unworthy of you," a woman said.

Agon turned and saw Elene Cromwyll, the Jadwins' maidservant who'd been found beaten up and unconscious in her room. She was curvaceous, pretty except for the scars and bruises on her face. But Lady Jadwin fancied herself an artist, so she liked to surround herself with pretty things.

"Yes," Agon said. "I suppose it was. But seeing what she's done . . . what a waste."

"My mistress has made many poor choices," Elene said. "She's hurt many people, destroyed marriages, but she isn't a murderer, Lord General. My lord, I know what happened here last night."

"Really? So you're the one." His voice was more cutting than he intended. He was still trying to put the pieces together himself. How had that guard, Stumpy, who now resembled his nickname more than ever, been killed? Why would the duchess kill the prince silently and change her clothes but not finish washing her hands and face before screaming for help?

Surely, if she'd been cold-blooded enough to murder the prince, maybe in a cold rage as he left her, and been self-possessed enough to start hiding the evidence, she would have done a better job of it before calling people to her.

But then, some of the guests had claimed it was a man's voice they had heard yell upstairs. The guard? Had he stumbled upon the murder, yelled wordlessly, and then been beheaded? Beheading someone wasn't easy. Agon knew that. Even if you cut between the vertebrae, it took substantial strength. Agon had examined Stumpy, and the blade had cut *through* the vertebra.

He turned his eyes back to Elene. "Sorry," he said. "This has been a difficult night. Any way you can help would be welcome."

She looked up, and there were tears in her eyes. "I know who killed the prince. He's a wetboy masquerading as a lord. I knew what he was, and I knew that he was coming, but I didn't think he'd hurt anybody. His name is Kylar. Kylar Stern."

"What?" Agon said.

"It's true. I swear it."

"Look, young lady, your loyalty to your mistress is admirable, but you don't need to do this. If you hold to that story, you'll go to jail. At the least. If you're found to be an accomplice, or even an unwitting accessory to the murder of the prince, you may be hanged. Are you sure you want to do that, just to save Trudana Jadwin?"

"It isn't for her." Tears coursed down her cheeks.

"Then it's for this Kylar Stern? He was the young man who had the fight with Logan Gyre? You must hate him fiercely."

She just looked away. In the rising sunlight, the tears on her cheeks glowed like jewels. "No, sir. Not at all."

"Lord General," a soldier said quietly from the doorway. He looked shaken. "I just came from the Gyre estate, sir. It's chaos there. There are hundreds of people going through the house, wailing, sir. They're dead, sir."

"Get a hold of yourself. What do you mean dead? You mean murdered?"

"More like butchered, sir."

"Who's been murdered, soldier?"

"Sir. All of them."

43

The king fidgeted in his throne. It was a vast piece of ivory and horn inlaid with gold tracery, and it made him look a boy. The audience chamber was empty today except for the regular guards, several guards hidden in the room's secret exits, and Durzo Blint. The emptiness made the chamber seem cavernous. Banners and tapestries adorned the walls, but did nothing to stave off the perpetual chill of such a large stone room. Seven pairs of pillars held the high ceiling and two sets of seven steps each led to the throne.

Durzo stood quietly, waiting for the king to initiate the conversation. He already had a battle plan, if it came to that. It was second nature to him. The meister standing by the king would have to die first, then the two guards flanking the throne, then the king himself. With his Talent, he could probably jump from the throne up to the passage above it, currently obscured by a banner. He'd kill the archer within, and from there he'd be uncatchable.

Like all battle plans, it would last only until the first move, but it was always useful to have a general plan, especially when you had no idea what your enemies knew. Durzo felt himself reaching into his garlic pouch, but he forced his hand to be still. Now was no time to show nerves. It was harder to stop his hand than he would have guessed, something about the bite of garlic was comforting when he was stressed.

"You let my boy die," the king said, rising. "They killed my boy last night and you did nothing!"

"I'm not a bodyguard."

The king grabbed a spear from the guard standing beside him and threw it. Durzo was surprised at how good a throw it was. Had he stood still, the spear would have caught him in the sternum.

But of course he didn't stand still. He swayed to the side, not even moving his feet, with careless—and he hoped infuriating—ease.

The spear bounced off the floor and then hissed as wood and steel slid across stone. There was a rattle of armor and the whisper of arrows being drawn back all around the room, but the guards didn't attack.

"You're not shit unless I say so!" the king said. He strode forward, coming down his double flight of seven steps to stand in front of Durzo. Tactically, a poor move. He was now blocking at least three of the archers' shots. "You're...you're shit! You shitting, shitting shit!"

"Your Majesty," Durzo said gravely. "A man of your stature's cursing vocabulary ought to extend beyond a tedious reiteration of the excreta that fills the void between his ears."

The king looked momentarily confused. The guards looked at each other, aghast. The king saw the look, and realized from their expressions that he'd been insulted. He backhanded Durzo, and Durzo let the blow fall. Any quick motion now, and a nervous archer might loose his arrow.

The king wore rings on all of his fingers, and two of them carved furrows in Durzo's cheek.

Durzo clenched his jaw to quell the rising black fury. He breathed once, twice. He said, "The only reason you're alive right now isn't that I'm not willing to trade my life for yours, Aleine. I'd hate to be killed by amateurs. But know this: if you ever lay a hand on me again, you'll be dead less than a second later. Your Majesty."

King Aleine Gunder IX lifted his hand, seriously contemplating becoming the late King Aleine Gunder IX. He lowered his hand, but a triumphant gleam filled his eyes. "I won't have you killed yet, Durzo. I won't have you killed because I have something better than death for you. You see, I know about you, Durzo Blint. I know. You have a secret, and I know it."

"Forgive my quaking."

"You have an apprentice. A young man styling himself as a noble. Kyle something or other. A young man staying with those holier-than-thou Drakes, quite a student of the sword, isn't he, Master Tulii?"

A chill shot down Durzo's spine. *Night Angels have mercy.* They knew. It was bad. Worse than bad. If they knew Kylar was his apprentice, it couldn't be long before they pinned the prince's death on him. Especially with the spectacle Kylar had made of himself by fighting with Logan Gyre. If Durzo's apprentice had been involved with killing the prince, the king would assume he had done it with Durzo's approval, if not under his orders.

Roth would not be pleased.

The garlic crunched in his mouth, giving a soothing jolt to his senses. He took a breath and willed himself to relax. *How had they done it?*

Master Tulii. Dammit. Anything can go wrong, and something will. Durzo hadn't been betrayed. There was no grand scheme. That name meant that one of the king's spies had been watching the Drakes. Probably just routine spying on a formerly powerful man. The spy had seen Durzo enter and had recognized him. Probably the spy had been one of the guards the king had tried to awe him with in the statue garden. It didn't matter.

"Oh, I wish Brant were here right now to see that look on your face, Durzo Blint. In fact, where is Brant?" the king asked a chamberlain.

"Sire, he's in the castle now, on his way here to report. He went to the Gyre estate after investigating . . . matters at the Jadwin estate."

Durzo's throat tightened. Agon would have put the pieces together about Kylar. If he came in while Durzo was still here, Durzo would die.

The king shrugged. "His loss." At the word, grief and fury rippled through the little king, and he seemed abruptly a different man. "You let them kill my boy, you shit, so I'm going to kill yours. His death will come from the last hand he'd expect, and it will be arriving—oh!—any moment now."

"I heard you had a little tussle with Logan last night," Count Drake said.

Kylar blinked through bleary eyes and went from dead tired to wide-awake in the space of a second. He'd only slept for a few hours, and he'd had the nightmare again. Every death he saw made him dream of Rat's.

They were seated at the breakfast table and Kylar had a forkful of egg poised in front of his mouth. He stuffed it in to give himself a little time. "Mit wuv nuffin," he said.

This was a disaster. If Count Drake knew about the fight, he might know about the prince's death. Kylar had thought that he'd have time to pack his things and leave this morning before the Drakes got word. That he needed to leave was undeniable. He just thought he'd have a little more time.

"Serah was quite upset," the count said. "She took Logan to her aunt's house near the Jadwins' to have his wounds tended. She just got back a few minutes ago."

"Oh." Kylar chewed more eggs mechanically. If Serah had left right after the fight, she and Count Drake didn't know about the prince yet. Apparently Kylar's perfect streak of bad luck was breaking. But now that he knew that matters of life and death weren't threatening him, he realized that

Serah coming home and telling Count Drake what had happened last night would have other implications.

"I gave Logan my permission to propose to her yesterday. You knew that, didn't you?"

That would be the count's gentle way of saying *why the hell did you kiss my Serah and beat up my future son-in-law and your best friend after you told me you had no feelings for her?*

"Um..." Out of the corner of his eye, Kylar saw someone pass the window quickly, and a moment later, the old porter toddled after, looking upset.

The front door banged open. A moment later, the door to the dining room slammed open with such force that the dishes on the table rattled.

"Milord," the porter protested.

Logan stormed into the room, red-eyed but regal. He held a claymore the size of Alitaera in his hand.

Kylar jumped to his feet, sending his chair crashing into the wall. He was pinned in a corner. Count Drake was rising, shouting something, but he was too slow. Nothing could stop Logan now.

Logan hefted the claymore. Kylar hefted a butter knife.

"I'm engaged!" Logan shouted. He swept Kylar into a massive hug.

By the time Logan released him, Kylar's heart had started beating again. Count Drake collapsed into his chair in relief.

"You big bastard!" Kylar said. "Congratulations! I told you it would work, didn't I?"

"Work?" Count Drake asked, recovering his voice.

Logan plowed forward, ignoring the count. "Well, you didn't have to hit me so hard."

"I had to convince her," Kylar said.

"You nearly widowed her! I haven't been beaten so badly since that fight in the arena."

"Excuse me," the count said. "Work? Convince her?"

They stopped and looked at the count guiltily. "Well," Logan said, "Kylar said Serah really did love me and she only needed to be reminded, and..." he trailed off.

"Kylar, are you telling me your fight was staged? You made a fool of yourself in public, deceived my daughter, and traded her affections like a cheap trinket?"

"That's not exactly..." He couldn't match the count's stare. "Yes, sir."

"And you dragged Logan into this? Logan, who ought to know better?" the count asked.

"Yes, sir," Kylar said. At least Logan was looking as pained as he felt.

The count looked from one of them to the other, then broke into a grin. "God bless you!" he said, sweeping Kylar into a hug.

After he released Kylar, Count Drake turned. There were tears in his eyes as he gripped Logan's forearms, "And God bless you. Son."

Lord General Agon stormed into the castle, flanked by his bodyguards. The day had already been long, and the sun had only been up three hours.

Seeing the look on his face, the men guarding doors in the castle made sure he didn't have to wait for them to open. Servants quickly disappeared out of the halls.

Walking into the audience chamber, he passed a cloaked man coming out who seemed vaguely familiar, but the man had his hood up and his face was invisible. One of the king's spies, no doubt. Agon didn't have time for him.

None of the news was good. The Gyres were the foremost family in the realm. To have their murder come on the same night the prince was killed was too much to bear. Agon had liked the prince, but the Gyres had been his friends. And what he'd seen at their estate, he wouldn't wish on his worst enemy. The pieces weren't fitting.

This had all the marks of a move, a big move, a play for the throne. But why this way? Killing the prince shook everything, of course, but killing the Gyres' servants and Lady Gyre did nothing politically. Did it? As of today, his birthday, Logan Gyre became the Gyre in his father's absence. If you wanted to wipe out a family, you started with the heirs, not everyone else, and unless the news was still en route, both Gyre heirs were still alive.

The prince's death wasn't only a terrible blow to the Gunder line, it was an enormous scandal. The king's affairs had been ignored, but finding the prince dead after apparently having had relations with the king's mistress would shed all sorts of unflattering light on the entire Gunder line. The assassination, if it were such, wasn't just a tragedy. It was a horror and an embarrassment.

The lord general wondered whether the horror or the embarrassment would be foremost on the king's mind. What would the queen do?

He approached the throne and climbed the stairs. The usual men were there, talking with the king. Agon trusted none of them.

"Out," he roared. "All of you, out!"

"Excuse me," Fergund Sa'fasti said. "But as the king's chief—"

"OUT!" Agon bellowed in his face.

The mage shrank and joined the men streaming out of the room. Agon motioned to his bodyguards to step outside, too.

The king didn't even look up. At length, he said, "I'm ruined, Brant. What will history say about me?"

That you were weak, ineffectual, selfish, and immoral. "Sire, we have more pressing matters."

"Everyone's talking about it, Brant. My son—she murdered my boy—" the king started weeping.

So the man is capable of thinking of others. If only he'd show his humanity more often.

"Your Highness, the duchess didn't kill your son."

"What?" the king looked up at Agon through bleary eyes.

"Sire, it was a wetboy."

"I don't care who actually did it, Brant! Trudana was behind it. Trudana and Logan Gyre."

"Logan Gyre? What are you talking about?"

"You think you're the only person I have working on this, Brant? My spies have already told me. Logan was behind it all. That bitch Trudana just cooperated. I've already sent men to arrest him."

Agon reeled. It couldn't be. In fact, he was sure it wasn't. "Why would Logan do such a thing?" he asked. "Logan was one of your son's best friends. He's isn't ambitious in the least. By the gods, he just got engaged to Serah Drake. A count's daughter!"

"It didn't have anything to do with power or ambition, Brant. It was jealousy. Logan felt that my son had totally humiliated him over some trivial matter. You know how boys get. It's just like the Gyres to covet our every success. Besides, I have witnesses who heard Logan threaten him."

It was all rattling together, the pieces spinning and falling into place. Kylar Stern, the false noble, the wetboy, was a close friend of Logan's. In a fit of rage, Logan hired Kylar to kill the prince. It all fit—except that it was Logan. Agon knew him, and he didn't believe it.

"Which wetboy did they hire, Brant?" the king asked.

"It was Kylar Stern," Agon said.

The king snorted. "Huh. The gods must be with me for once."

"Sire?"

"I just hired Hu Gibbet's apprentice to go kill him, a girl wetboy, if you can believe it. Kylar is Blint's apprentice. Or was. He's probably dead by now."

Kylar is Blint's apprentice? The picture that had been slowly spinning together burst apart. The king had hired Blint! Blint's apprentice wouldn't have killed his employer's son. Would he?

The name Hu Gibbet had been carved into the bodies at the Gyre estate. Of course, only a fool would carve his own name onto such a massacre. But from his hours at the estate, Agon was sure that all the murders had been the work of a single man. He could think of no one who could kill so many people except a wetboy, and the style certainly fit what he had heard of Hu Gibbet. He couldn't imagine Durzo Blint mutilating bodies. Blint would consider it unprofessional.

Hu Gibbet would only sign his name if he thought the authorities would never have a chance to come after him. The king said the prince's murder didn't have anything to do with power, but this was Cenaria. Everything had to do with power.

If Durzo Blint's apprentice really had killed the prince, why would he have left a witness? Blint's apprentice would be as professional as Blint himself. A witness was a loose end that was easy to tie up.

It was all about power.

Agon scowled. "Has there been any word from our garrison at Screaming Winds?"

"No."

"So the Khalidoran army is at least four days away. What are you planning to do about the festival tonight?"

"I'm not going to celebrate Midsummer's on the day after my son's death."

The lord general had a sinking feeling. "My king, I think perhaps you should."

"I will not host a party for my boy's murderers." The king's eyes flashed, and he looked less like a petulant child and more like a king than Agon had ever seen. "I have to do something!" the king said. "Everyone will think..." He went on, but Agon ignored him.

Everyone will think. That was the key. *What will everyone think?*

The prince was dead, killed in a shameful way either by the king's mistress or by a wetboy. The beloved Gyres were dead or imprisoned. Agon suspected now that an assassin had probably made his way into Screaming Winds and killed Regnus as well. It wouldn't make sense to leave him alive. Not when someone was going to such pains to set plans in motion.

Everyone will think that the king ordered his own son killed in a jealous rage, and that to get back at his unfaithful mistress he framed her.

With the right rumors, everyone's bewilderment over why the Gyres had been murdered could be turned, too. People would connect all the murders, but how?

The Gyres were next in line for the throne after the Gunders, though the family had never challenged the king. The king, weak and jealous, could be portrayed as paranoid all too easily. And the Gyres were far more respected than the Gunders. Lord Gyre's faithful service would be seen as being rewarded with treachery and murder.

Logan—the new Lord Gyre—had been seized by the king, and the king's natural inclination would be to keep him in prison. But Logan was known to be absolutely moral, without ambitions. For the gods' sakes, he was betrothed to a lowly Drake!

So if the king were to die, who would succeed him?

The vastly popular Logan Gyre would be in prison, where he could easily be killed. The king's son was dead. His eldest daughter was fifteen, the others even younger, too young to hold the throne in a nation at war. His wife Nalia might try to take the throne, but the king had feared her and marginalized her as much as he could, and she seemed content to stay out of politics. The Jadwins were finished after their part in the scandal. That left the kingdom's two other duchies. Either Duke Graesin or Duke Wesseros, the queen's father, could make a grab for power. But the queen's brother, Havrin, was out of the country, so he seemed an unlikely usurper. Duke Graesin was feeble. Any of a dozen lesser families might try for the throne.

But no one could hold it. It would be a civil war in which the four main parties were equally matched. Civil war of a kind far worse than the civil war that Regnus had feared ten years ago when he allowed Aleine to take the throne.

Where did that leave the other players he'd been worried about so much recently? Where did the Sa'kagé and Khalidor fit? If the price were right, Khalidor could buy the Sa'kagé's help.

And then all the pieces snapped together for him at once.

Lord General Agon swore loudly. He cursed so rarely that the king stopped in midsentence. Aleine looked at Agon's face, and whatever he read there made him afraid.

"What is it? What is it, Brant?"

All these years, he and the king had been so focused on Khalidor that they'd never thought of a threat coming from within. Khalidor was taking out the entire line of succession, and manipulating the king into helping. Once all the heirs who were both legitimate and powerful were eliminated, Khalidor would kill the king. They would act quickly, before he could establish a new line of succession, before he could consolidate power or mend the relationships he was about break. Then they could watch the chaos, and march when they pleased.

"Your Highness, you must listen. This is the prelude to a coup. We may only have days. If it starts, all our preparations against Khalidor will be useless. And you'll be the first to die."

The king's face was painted with fear. "I'm listening," he said.

After congratulating Logan a few more times, Kylar had excused himself to let the young duke speak with his father-in-law-to-be. Serah was in the back of the house getting changed, and they had agreed that she probably shouldn't see Logan and Kylar being friendly until after the wedding.

"I'll understand if I'm not invited," Kylar had said. "But if you ever do tell her, I'll expect an apology. Congratulations."

He climbed up the stairs to his room, pitched his tunic in a corner, and stared into the looking glass. "And congratulations to you. Your master is going to kill you and all the women in your life hate you."

Next to the mirror, he noticed a bundle of letters bound together with a ribbon. He picked it up. Scrawled on a scrap of paper in Blint's hand was a note: "Since you've crossed the line, I guess there's no reason to hide these from you anymore."

What? Kylar untied the ribbon and read the first letter. It had been written by a child, all big letters and disconnected thoughts: "Thank you so ~~mutch~~. much. I love it here. You are great. It is my birthday today. I love you. -Elene" An adult had written below that. "Sorry, Count Drake, she overheard us talking about her lord benefactor. She's been wanting to write this letter since we started teaching her how to write. She wouldn't let go of the idea once she got aholt of it. Tell us if we shouldn't let her write no more. -Humbly Yours, Gare Cromwyll."

Kylar was spellbound. There was a letter for each year, each getting longer, the handwriting better. He felt like he was watching Elene grow up before his eyes. She, too, had changed her name, but there was no denial in her of what she had been, no divorce from her previous weakness and vulnerability.

When she was fifteen, she wrote, "Pol asked if I get mad because my face got cut up. He said it's not fair. I said it's not fair that I got out of the Warrens while so many others never did. Look at everything I've got! And it's all because of you...."

Kylar had to flip through the letters, just skimming them. He was living on borrowed time. Sooner or later word would arrive about the prince's death. And damn! the girl could write a lot. He flipped to the last letter. It was dated just a few days ago.

"You don't know what you've done for me. I've told you about all the ways your money has saved my family, especially when my adoptive father died, but you've done more than that. Just knowing that somewhere out there, there's a young lord who cares about me (me! a slaveborn girl with a scarred face!) has made all the difference. You've made me feel special. Pol proposed to me last week." Kylar had a sudden impulse to find this Pol and kick his ass. "I would have said yes, even though I hate his temper and...other things, too. The point is, just that you're out there caring about me makes me believe that I'm worth more than a lousy marriage to the first man who will propose to a scarred girl. It gives me faith that the God has something better for me." *Oh, she's a God person. Great.* So that was how she knew the Drakes. "Thank you. And sorry about my last letter, I'm totally mortified by what I wrote. Please ignore everything I said."

Huh? Kylar turned back to the last letter and couldn't help grinning. Elene had been deep in the throes of full-blown sixteen-year-old–girl romanticism. "I think I'm in love with you. In fact, I'm sure of it. Last year when I went to Count Drake's to drop off my letter—mother *finally* lets me do a few things by myself—I think I saw you. Maybe it wasn't you. But it could have been you. There's this boy there, a young lord like you. He's so handsome and they totally love him. I mean, you can just tell how much everyone thinks of him, even Count Drake. I mean, I know he's not really you because he's not rich like you are. Because his family is poor, he lives with the Drakes..." Kylar's breath caught. Elene had seen him. She had seen him a year ago and she thought he was handsome. She thought he was handsome? "...but what does money matter when you have love?"

There were...*no*...yes, there were tear splotches on the page.

Well, Kylar had grown up around three girls. It didn't totally surprise him. He just wondered when Elene had started crying. "So since you're the strong silent type, and you never write back to my letters, I've decided I'm going to call you Kylar. ~~I suppose you might be fat and ugly and have a big nose and...~~ I am SO sorry. I should start over, but mother says I already use too much paper as it is. I'm sorry. I am a total brat. But can't you write back to me even once? Have Count Drake give it to me next year when I drop off my letter? Pol says I'm not infatuated with a man, I'm infatuated with a bag of money." Elene didn't know anything about him, but hey, she'd been barely sixteen, and Kylar still wanted to kick Pol's ass. "But I'm not. And it's not infatuation. I love you, Kylar."

A chill washed through him at those words. How he wanted to hear those words! How he wanted to hear them from *her*. And here they were. Here they were in knots and knots of his duplicity. She said those words to him, not thinking he was lie, not knowing Count Drake gave her letters to Durzo, not knowing Kylar really was her young benefactor, not knowing Kylar was really Azoth, not knowing Kylar was a killer, not knowing that for that one time she'd seen him that he had seen her hundreds of times: twice every week, whenever he could make it, in the market off Sidlin Way. He'd watched her grow up in that market, told himself a thousand times that next week he wouldn't go and try to catch a glimpse of her, and always succumbed. He'd watched from afar and come to have his own infatuation, hadn't he? He'd told himself that she was just forbidden fruit, that that was all that appealed to him about her. He'd told himself he just wanted to see that she was well. When that didn't work, he told himself that it would pass.

He was twenty years old now, and he was still waiting for it to pass. His sudden hope—she'd been infatuated with him!—hit reality like Gandian porcelain hitting the floor. The delicate tracery of thin possibilities smashed. Now the stricken look on her face yesterday made more sense. The revelations that could have been so poignant for her—I am Kylar and Azoth and your young lord and I love you, too!—had hit her like a sledge hammer instead. I am Kylar and Azoth and your young lord...and a murderer. Help me. Give me your trust so I can betray it.

There wasn't time for self-pity, and Kylar had already indulged in too much of it. He'd left behind a witness who knew he was a wetboy and who knew he was Kylar Stern, and who believed him guilty of stealing the Globe of Edges, if not worse. So he'd quite possibly thrown away an identity he'd spent ten years building for a little ball that he hadn't even kept.

The buckets of hot water that the maid usually put in his room in the morning were empty. For some reason, that set him off. He felt his eyes getting hot, and tears threatening. It was so ridiculous, he almost laughed. Those empty buckets were the smallest inconvenience, but it was like the gods or Drake's One God wanted to crush him. Everything that could go wrong had.

Master Blint was going to kill him. The woman he was trading his life to save hated him. Even Serah Drake, who had been unsure about whether she loved him or Logan just last night now hated him. The worst part of it was that it was all his fault. Everything that had gone wrong had gone wrong because of decisions he had made.

Well, at least the empty buckets weren't his fault. Kylar grabbed the buckets and walked down the hall. He ran into the maid coming up the stairs with two buckets full of steaming water.

"Hello," he said. He didn't recognize her, but she was prettier than most of the girls Mistress Bronwyn hired.

"Hello I'm so sorry I'm late it's my first day and I don't know where to find everything I'm really sorry," she said. She squeezed past him and Kylar couldn't help but notice her large breasts gliding across his bare chest. She disappeared into his room and he followed.

"I can take those if you—"

"You aren't mad, are you?" she asked. "Please don't tell Count Drake or Mistress Bronwyn that I was late I don't think she likes me and if I mess up on my first day I'm sure she'll throw me out and I need this job ever so bad sir." She had set down the buckets, and she was wringing her hands.

"Whoa," Kylar said. "Relax. I'm not mad. I'm Kylar." He extended a hand and a smile.

She seemed to warm instantly. She smiled and took his hand. Her eyes flicked briefly over his bare chest and stomach. Briefly, but appreciatively. "Hello. I'm Viridiana."

The porter showed a handsome Ladeshian man into the den. Logan had stepped out to grab something to eat from the kitchen, so Count Drake was alone. "Sir," the porter said, "he insisted that he must deliver a message in person."

"Very well. Thank you," Count Drake said.

The Ladeshian had such presence that it seemed odd for him to be acting as a messenger. He looked rather like a courtier or a bard. He was holding something in his hand that took all Count Drake's attention away from the man. It was an arrow; its entire length, including steel head and feathers, had been painted a glossy red the color of fresh blood.

As soon as the porter stepped out, the man said, "Good morning, my lord. I wish our meeting could be under different circumstances, but I'm afraid my message is quite important. This comes from Durzo Blint. He said, 'If he's still alive, give this to the boy and tell him to meet me for dinner at the Tipsy Tart.'" The man bowed and presented the red arrow to the count.

From the doorway, Logan laughed. "'If he's still alive'? I guess one of Kylar's friends saw me coming here this morning, huh?"

Count Drake chuckled. "I'm sure you scared *everyone* who saw you." He turned to the messenger. "I'll give it to him, thank you."

"My lord," the Ladeshian said, turning to Logan. "We mourn your loss." He bowed again and walked out.

Logan shook his head. "Was that a bachelor joke?"

"I don't know. I visited Ladesh once, and I never did understand their humor. Maybe I should take this upstairs."

"Here I thought we were about to have the big father-son dialectic about marital intimacies."

Count Drake smiled. "You put it so primly."

"Serah's pretty prim," Logan said.

"Believe me, there's nothing prim about marital intimacies, Logan." Count Drake looked at the arrow in his hand and put it aside. "Well, the first thing you have to understand about lovemaking is . . ."

Viridiana rubbed her shoulder and said, "It's so nice to see someone nice I thought this place was going to be awful to work at after how mean Mistress Bronwyn was you don't mind do you?"

"No, not at all," Kylar said, not really sure what he was not minding, but sure that he wasn't supposed to.

As if it were the most natural thing in the world, Viridiana untied the laces of her bodice, which Kylar had already noticed was unusually tight. "Oh, that's better," she said, drawing a deep breath. She closed and locked the door and then walked over to the buckets, peeling off her bodice and dropping it.

"Um," Kylar said. Then Viridiana bent over to pick up the water buckets again.

She must have had six feet of cleavage, because Kylar was totally lost in it. His mouth opened, but no words came out. It was with an unseemly amount of effort that he pulled his eyes up. Viridiana was watching him, and even as his face got hot, he saw that she was anything but displeased. With a deft twist, she released her tightly bound hair, and it cascaded around her face in long curls. "Are you ready for your bath, my lord?"

"No! I mean—I mean—"

"You want to bathe *after*," she said, walking forward. She reached behind her back and started opening buttons.

After? Kylar stepped back, but his resistance was crumbling. *Why not? What the hell have I been waiting for? For Elene?* Viridiana filled his vision, full lips, gorgeous hair that he could practically feel already in his fingertips, on his chest. Those breasts. Those hips. And she wanted him. It would be sex, just sex, not lovemaking. Not some grand expression of romance and commitment. Just passion. Simpler. More like Momma K's version of things. Less like Count Drake's version. But damn. Her body was more persuasive than a room full of scholars.

His calves hit his bed and he almost fell. "I, I don't really feel very comf—"

Her hand came up to his chest, and then she slammed it into him. He was falling back as her other hand came up from behind her dress in a glimmering metallic arc.

By the time his back hit the bed, she was straddling him, her knees pinning his arms to his sides, one hand grabbing his hair, the other pressing the knife to his neck.

"Comfortable?" she asked, finishing his sentence. She wasn't kidding with the knife; it was pressed against the side of his neck just at the point where a little pressure would break the skin, and it was poised over an artery. As his lungs filled with gasps of air, he had to try not to move his neck.

"Ah, shit," he said. "You're Hu Gibbet's apprentice, Vi. Viridiana, Vi, how'd I miss it?"

She smiled joylessly. "Who're you working for? The prince was my deader."

"Seriously. How embarrassing. To be taken in by another wetboy. Hmm. Or are you a wetgirl?"

"Not the way you're hoping." She ground her hips against him and he blushed.

She pinched his cheek. "You aren't too ugly, you know. It'll be a shame to kill you."

"The shame's all mine, I assure you."

"Don't feel bad," she said. "Part of my Talent is a glamour. It's to your credit you weren't actually drooling."

"You mean those are an illus—"

"Move your hands and die," she said. "The body's real, thanks."

"I should say thank you, but this knife at my throat is muting my appreciation some."

"If you're trying to charm your way out of this, you need practice. Who're you working for?"

"You're working for the king," Kylar said. "Aren't you?"

"Backbone," she said. "I like that."

"Wetting myself would be awfully messy for both of us," Kylar said. She chuckled and he smiled as charmingly as he could. "Was that better?"

"Better. I'll give you one for effort. I took this job from the king. He was a little peeved that you killed his son. So I take his money, but I take my orders from Roth. Last chance now," she pressed the knife a little further into his skin and he had to lean his head as far to the side as he could to keep it from cutting him.

"Maybe you can appreciate my dilemma," Kylar said, straining his neck.

"If I don't answer, you'll kill me painfully but it will take a while. If I do answer, you'll kill me quickly but soon."

"Or you can try to string this out for as long as you can and hope some-one saves you. You're smart. I suppose you'd have to be. We've all been curious why Blint would choose an apprentice without the Talent. I guess smart wins it."

"You all? You've been taking bets on me? Wait, they say I don't have the Talent?"

"Like they say, there are no secrets worth knowing in the Sa'kagé," Vi said. "So you aren't going to tell me who you were working for, are you? Probably just another one sent by Roth. When he wants a job done, he makes sure it gets done. There's even a rumor he got Lady Jadwin to do it, but I know a wetboy's work when I see it."

"You're kind of chatty, aren't you?" Kylar said.

If he had a hand free, he would have slapped himself. *Note: when attempting to buy time, do not criticize the prolixity of your captor.*

Her beautiful face turned ugly for half a second, and Kylar saw the Hu Gibbet in her. Then she smiled, but Hu didn't leave her eyes. "In the next life," she said. "Work on that charm."

The next feeling would be the glide of a knife, the flesh of his neck part-ing, warmth. Kylar's muscles bunched with need and desperation.

There was a knock on the door. "Kylar?" the count said. Vi flinched and turned her head.

Kylar threw his head to the side and bucked, trying to throw her off. Or that's what he told his body to do. Instead, he felt energy pouring through him like lightning on a leash. A brief euphoria, power swelling through him, well-being as if he'd been sick his entire life and now felt health for the first time. It was the Talent that Durzo had always said he had, and now it was his.

Vi flew into the air, but she held onto Kylar's hair and one of her legs got tangled with one of his. So instead of flying off him, she flew up and then crashed back down on top him. She tried to slash him, but both of his hands were up now, and he caught both of her arms and rolled.

They fell off the bed and he landed on her. She grunted and raised a knee between his legs. It was like the sun exploding in his pants. He groaned and it was all he could do not to let go of her hands as she rolled on top of him.

"Kylar?" the count shouted through the door. "Do you have a lady in there?"

I wouldn't call her a lady. Kylar's stones hurt so bad, he could barely move, much less fight. "Help!"

"You're pathetic," she said.

He could only grunt.

She launched herself off of him. He struggled to his feet as the door burst open, but he was too slow. She was already throwing her knife at Count Drake.

The count threw himself to the side, and the knife sailed past him harmlessly. Instantly, he had a throwing knife in his own hand, but he hesitated. Vi saw his hand raised and leaped for the window.

Kylar grabbed the knife from the count's hand and threw it as Vi disappeared through the window. He thought he saw it sink into her shoulder. He grabbed the sword that was secreted under his bed, but when he looked out the window, she was gone.

The count looked shaken. He was holding a red arrow in his other hand. "I hesitated," he said. From anyone else, it would have been a concession of defeat, but Count Drake sounded victorious. "After all these years, I wondered, but it's true. I really have changed. Thank you, God."

Kylar looked at him strangely. "What are you talking about?"

"Kylar, we have to talk."

I'll be dead in a day or two, so please pay attention, Jarl," Momma K said.

Jarl hesitated for a moment, and then sipped the ootai she'd poured him.

Damn, but the boy can be cold. But then, that was why she was having this talk with him, rather than with anyone else. "Tomorrow or the next day, Kylar or Durzo will come here and kill me," she said. "Because I sent Kylar to kill a man he thought was Hu Gibbet, but actually was Durzo, disguised as Hu. Whichever one lived through their fight now knows that I lied, and that I betrayed them both. I know that you were once friends with Kylar, Jarl—"

"I still am."

"Fine. I wasn't going to ask you to avenge me. I'm ready for justice. Life from here is just a series of disappointments anyway." *Was that pity in the boy's eyes? She thought it was, but she didn't care. He'd understand if he lived to be this old.*

"What can I do to help you, Momma K?"

"I don't want you to help me. Things are happening fast, Jarl. Maybe too fast. Roth's making a play at becoming Shinga. I suspect we'll be hearing the sad news that Pon Dradin is dead any time now."

"You're not going to warn him? You're just going to let Roth kill him?"

"Two reasons, Jarl. Knowing either of them could cost you your life. Are you ready to be a player on this stage?"

He scowled, actually thought about it, and then nodded.

"First, I'm going to let Pon Dradin die because I've been compromised. Roth blackmailed me into betraying Durzo and Kylar. I won't share how. I've been humiliated enough. All that matters is that Roth owns me. I can't oppose him in any way that he might detect or suspect or it will cost me something I value more than my life. So I'm going to die. I want you to replace me."

"You want me to take your seat on the Nine?"

She smiled into her *ootai*. "I was never just the Mistress of Pleasures, Jarl. I've been the Shinga for nineteen years." She had some satisfaction in the way her unflappable protégé's eyes widened. He sank back in his chair.

"Gods," he said. "That explains a few things."

She laughed, and for what felt like the first time in years, she really felt like laughing. If exposing your throat always felt like this, she thought she understood for the first time why Durzo had loved the danger in his work. It made you appreciate being alive, standing this close to death.

"Tell me how it works," he said.

It was what she would have said in his place. She would have accepted what the Shinga had said about her death and immediately started looking for how it would affect her, rather than expressing any sorrow that the Shinga would be dead. Or perhaps, in Jarl's place, she would have given some moue of sorrow that her mistress would die, but it would have been a lie. Jarl gave no such pretense, and maybe she could respect him for that. He'd learned her lessons well. But it still hurt.

"I'm sorry," he said. He sounded like he really meant it. Maybe he did. Or maybe he was just sorry that she was sinking into such softness that at the approach of her death she who had taught him how to manipulate his own pities and loves should want him to do that toward her. She couldn't tell. Jarl was what she had made him to be. It was worse than looking in a mirror.

"Everyone in the Sa'kagé knows who their boss is. The smarter ones know who their representative on the Nine is. Of course, the Shinga's identity is an open secret, which means not a secret at all. Put that together, and if you pool a few thieves and whores, you can figure out the entire power structure of the Sa'kagé. That's been fine for the last fourteen years, because things have been so stable."

"Was that stability because of your leadership, or just luck?" Jarl asked.

"My leadership," she said honestly. "I had the last king killed and put Aleine on the throne, so we haven't had pressure from above, and I've handled all the pressures from within. But the normal state of any Sa'kagé is upheaval, Jarl. Thieves and murderers and cutpurses and whores don't tend to stay united. Assassinations are common. During your life it's been far more peaceful than ever before.

"The first five years I was Shinga, we lost eight 'Shingas.' Six were assassinations from outside. Two I had to have killed myself because they tried to take my power. Only two seats on the Nine remained unchanged. For the last fourteen years, Pon Dradin has been able to indulge his vices freely so long as he attended the meetings and kept his mouth shut and didn't step out of line. I never expected him to last so long."

"So only the Nine know who's really the Shinga?"

"And the wetboys, but they take a magically binding oath of service. The system does have its drawbacks. Pon is nearly as rich as I am just from kickbacks and bribes, and every new member of the Nine finds out that he's been sucking the wrong tocs for however long it took to climb the ranks. It irritates some of them mightily, but it also keeps some people off the Nine who don't belong there. Best of all, it's kept me alive and in power."

"What does Roth mean to this?"

"Roth has just joined the Nine. He isn't in on the secret. That's why Pon will die sometime today or tomorrow. Roth thinks killing him will make him Shinga. But that actually exposes the greatest flaw in all my secrecy: if only eight people know who the real Shinga is, Roth only has to convince those eight that he is the Shinga now."

"If the rest of the Nine are so afraid of him, how do I take his power?" Jarl asked.

Momma K smiled. "Exactly that. You take it. I won't leave you defenseless, of course." She reached into her desk and pulled out a small book. "My spies. I hope I don't need to tell you that the longer it is before you burn this book, the less your life is worth."

He took the book. "I'll memorize it immediately."

She leaned back in her chair. "He's in a strong position, Jarl. People are terrified of him."

"So that's everything?" Jarl asked.

"You'll forgive me if I don't tell you where all my riches are stored. An old woman has to protect herself, just in case I live through this. Besides, if I die, you'll have plenty of time to find it all."

"Can I ask your advice?" he asked. She nodded. "I followed the men you asked about," Jarl said.

Momma K nodded. She didn't prod Jarl with questions. They'd worked together for long enough that she knew he would tell her everything.

"They were definitely wytches. They attempted an ambush on Regnus Gyre with a small retinue north of the city. Most of his men were wiped out, and all of them would have been except that he had a mage with him."

Momma K raised an eyebrow.

"I was viewing them from a distance, but Regnus and the mage quarreled afterward and rode separate directions. My guess was that Lord Gyre didn't know his man was a mage."

"This mage defeated three wytches?"

"Everything spectacular came from the wytches, but when the smoke cleared—and I mean that literally—he was the only one standing. The man fought with his wits. He stalled two of the wytches until Lord Gyre's soldiers could cut them down. He made a horse trample the third. I don't understand magic, so maybe there was more I didn't see, but that was what it looked like."

"Go on."

"Lord Gyre had only one man left after he and the mage quarreled. They took a circuitous route through the city and arrived at his manse after midnight. You've heard what was there?"

"Twenty-eight dead. Hu Gibbet was given free rein."

"Roth's orders?" Jarl asked.

She nodded. "Unfortunately, the wetboys' oath does have a number of loop holes."

"It was horrific. Anyway, Lord Gyre persuaded the men who came to arrest him to join him instead, and they are now hiding at a cousin's house, trying to quietly gather as much support as they can. The mage is Sethi, first name Solon. I couldn't find anything else yet. As of half an hour ago, he was staying at the White Crane."

"You never disappoint, Jarl."

He was about to ask a question when there was a knock on the door. A maid came in and handed a slip of paper to Momma K. She handed it to Jarl. "The cipher's in the front of your book."

In a minute, he had it decoded. "Pon Dradin's dead." Jarl looked up at her. "What do I do now?"

"That, my apprentice," she said. "Is your problem."

"Kylar, I want to talk about your future."

This should be brief.

Count Drake pulled his pince nez from his vest pocket and didn't put them on. He just waved them as he spoke. "I've got a proposal for you, Kylar. I've been thinking about this a lot, and Kylar, you're not cut out to be a wetboy. No, listen to me, I want to give you a way out, son. Kylar, I want you to marry Ilena."

"Sir?"

"I know it seems abrupt, but I want you to think about it."

"Sir, she's only fifteen."

"Oh, I don't mean now. What I propose is that, well, Kylar, that you get betrothed. Ilena's been infatuated with you for years, and I propose that we give it a couple of years to see if anything comes of it, while you're . . . well, while you're learning my business."

"I'm not sure I understand, sir. In fact, I'm sure I don't understand."

The count slapped his pince nez against his hand. "Kylar, I want you to—I want to give you the chance to leave the life you're in. Learn my business and take it over for yourself someday. I've spoken with the queen, and with her permission, I've found out that we could transfer my title to you. You'd be a count, Kylar. It's nothing special, I know, but it would make you legitimate. You could be what you've been pretending all these years."

Kylar's mouth dropped open. "Transfer your title? What do you mean, *transfer* it?"

"Oh, Kylar, the title hasn't done me any good anyway. Bah! I don't have any sons to pass it on to anyway. You need it and I don't. Anyway, I want to do this, even if the whole betrothal with Ilena doesn't appeal to you. This would give you time, Kylar. Time to figure out what you want to do with your life. It cuts you free. Free of *them*."

Free. Out of the Sa'kagé. It was the most noble gesture Kylar had ever heard of—and after last night, it was too late.

Kylar looked at the floor and nodded. "It won't work, sir. I'm sorry. Believe me, I'm . . . You've been more than kind to me, far kinder than I deserve. But I don't think that"—he nodded toward the picnic Logan and Serah were sharing—"is for me."

"I know you're planning on leaving, Kylar."

That was the count. Right to it. "Yessir," Kylar said.

"Soon?"

"I meant to be gone already."

"Then maybe the God led me to speak with you now. Durzo told you not to listen to my preaching, I suppose?" Count Drake was looking out the window, but his voice was aggrieved.

"He said if I believed you, it'd get me killed."

"A fair enough statement, I suppose," Count Drake said. He turned and faced Kylar. "He used to work for me, you know."

"Excuse me? Durzo?"

That brought a small smile.

"Before he was a wetboy?" Kylar could hardly imagine that there had been a time before Durzo Blint was a wetboy, though he supposed there must have been.

The count shook his head. "No. He used to kill people for me. That's how we know each other. That's how he knew he could trust me with you. Durzo doesn't have much of a social life outside his work, you know."

"You? You ordered kills?"

"Not so loud. My wife knows, but there's no need to frighten the maids. I've tried to not preach at you with words, but rather let my life stand testimony to what I know, Kylar. But maybe I've erred in that. A saint once said, 'Preach at all times. When necessary, use words.' Can I take a minute of your time?"

Some part of him wanted to say no. Not only was it awkward to hear someone you respect try to sell you something that you knew you weren't going to buy, but Kylar was living on borrowed time. It seemed that at any minute news would arrive accusing Kylar of last night's theft, and this whole pretty picture would pop like a bubble. Logan would know him for what he was. Serah would have another chance to berate him. The count would get that disappointed look on his face that cut to the bone. Kylar knew the count would be disappointed in him, would never really know how much good Kylar had done last night and at what cost to himself. The count would be disappointed regardless of what Kylar did now, but Kylar didn't have to see it.

"Of course," he said. It was the right answer. This man had raised Kylar, had allowed him to live a life impossible for a guild rat. Kylar owed it to him.

"My father inherited a large fortune from his father, enough that he mingled with Gordin Graesin, Brand Wesseros, and Darvin Makell—I guess you wouldn't know about the Makells, they were wiped out in the Eight Years' War. Anyway, he tried to impress these sons of dukes by throwing money around. Lavish parties, gambling, renting out entire brothels. It didn't help that his own father died while he was still young. Of course, our family was soon in poverty. My father took his own life. So at the age of nineteen, I took control of a house on the brink of ruin. I had a good head for business, but I saw it as beneath me. Like many who have no reason for pride, that very lack of reason for it made me the prouder.

"But certain realities have a way of making themselves felt, and debt is one of them. Not surprisingly, one of my father's debtors had a way that I could make 'easy money.' I started working for the Sa'kagé. The man who recruited me was the Trematir. If he'd been better at his job, he would have only gotten me deeper and deeper in the Sa'kagé's debt, but I soon found out that I understood men and money and the ways they work together better than he did. Strangely enough, I had fewer qualms.

"I put my money into whatever made money. Specialty brothels to cater to any appetite, no matter how depraved. I started gambling dens and brought in experts from around the world to help me better separate my patrons from their money. I funded spice expeditions and bribed guards not to investigate the cargo. When one of my businesses was threatened, I had bashers take care of the problem. The first time they went too far and accidentally killed a man, I was shocked, but he wasn't someone I liked, and it was for my family, and I didn't have to see it, so that made it palatable. When I clashed with the Trematir, it was an easy decision to hire Durzo. I was naive enough that I didn't realize he went to the Shinga immediately to get permission first. They gave it to him, and I became the Sa'kagé Master of Coin."

Kylar was hearing every word, but he couldn't believe it. This couldn't be the Count Drake he had grown up with. Rimbold Drake had been on the Nine?

"I traveled a lot, setting up businesses in other countries with fairly good success, and it was then I had my horrible revelation. Of course, I didn't see the horror in it at the time. I could only see my own brilliance. In four years, I had paid off my family's debts, but now, I saw a way to make real money. I sold the Sa'kagé on the idea. It took us ten years, but we got our people in place and we legalized slavery. It was introduced in a limited form, of course. For convicts and the utterly destitute. People who couldn't care for themselves, we said. Our brothels filled with slave girls whom we no longer had to pay to work. We started the Death Games—another of my bright ideas—and they became a sensation, an obsession. We built the arena, charged the admission, monopolized the food and wine sold, ran the gambling, sometimes stacked the odds. We made money faster than we'd ever imagined possible. I hired Durzo so often that we became friends. Even he wouldn't take all the jobs I offered. He always had his own code. He'd take jobs on the people who were trying to take my business for themselves, but if I wanted someone dead who was just trying to stop me, I had to hire Anders Gurka or Scarred Wrable or Jonus Severing or Hu Gibbet.

"You have to understand with all this, I never considered myself a bad person. I didn't like the Death Games. I never watched, never went in the holds of the slave galleys where men lived and died chained to their oars, never visited the baby farms that sometimes became child brothels, never visited the scenes of Blint's work. I just said words, and money poured in like rain. The funny thing was, I wasn't even ambitious. I was richer than anyone in the kingdom with the exception of some upper nobility, the Shinga, and the king, and I was comfortable with that. I just couldn't stand incompetence. Otherwise, I'm sure the Shinga would have killed me. But she didn't have to, because I wasn't a threat, and Durzo told her that." The count shook his head. "I'm rambling, sorry, but I don't get to tell these stories anymore." He sighed.

"My mistake came when I fell in love with the wrong woman. For some reason, I was attracted to Ulana. Not just attracted, obsessed, and it took me a long time to figure out why. I even avoided her, it was so painful to be in her presence. But I finally figured out that it was because she was so unlike me. You see, Kylar, she was pure. And strangely, she seemed to love me, too. Of course she had no idea what I really was. I did none of my business under my own name, and few of the nobles had any idea of the kind of wealth that was becoming mine. The deeper I sank into the darkness, the more I loved her, and the more my shame grew. How can one love the light and live in darkness?"

The question lanced through Kylar. He felt ashamed.

"She started working on the slavery issue, Kylar, and she decided that she was going to visit the baby farms and the slave galleys and the fighting pits. I couldn't very well let her go alone, so for the first time, I saw my handiwork." The count's eyes grew distant. "Oh Kylar, how she moved among those wretches. In all the stench of human waste and despair and evil, she was a fresh cool breeze, a breath of hope. She was light in the dark places I'd made. I saw a champion pit fighter, a man who'd killed fifty men, weep at her touch.

"I was a man tearing in half. I decided to get out, but like most moral cowards, I didn't want to pay the full price. So I traveled to Seth, where slavery is so different. I came back and in secret helped pass a law that would free the slaves every seven years. The Sa'kagé allowed it to pass but tacked on a provision that made it effectively void. Then one day Ulana, who was then my fiancée, came to my estate, weeping. Her father and mother had been badly hurt in a carriage accident. She thought her mother was dying, and she needed me. At the same time, the Nine were meeting in my parlor because King Davin was on the verge of outlawing slavery again and that, of course, would cost us millions. Do you know whom I sent away, Kylar?"

"You sent away the Nine?" Kylar was aghast. Such an insult would mean death.

"I sent Ulana away."

"Damn. Um, sorry."

"No, that's how I felt. Damned. That's where the God found me, Kylar. I couldn't do it anymore. I was dead inside. I thought it would be the death of me to cut my ties to the Sa'kagé, especially when I realized that it wouldn't be enough to hand over my empire intact to someone who could continue it. Instead, I had to use all my cunning to hand it over to men who would tear it to pieces.

"So that's what I did. I used the money I had made to fund those who would rebuild the good I had destroyed and destroy the obscenities I had built. When I was done, I was penniless, my family was bankrupt, and I had dozens of powerful enemies. I went to Ulana, told her everything, and broke our engagement."

"What did she do?" Kylar asked.

"It broke her heart to learn what I'd been, Kylar, and to learn that she'd known so little of me when she thought she knew everything. It took time, but she forgave me. I couldn't believe that. But she really did. It took me longer to forgive myself, but a year later, after slavery was outlawed once more—in part because of my own efforts against it—we were married. I've had to work hard for the last twenty years. I've often been held back by my old reputation, and sometimes by my new one. You know how most of the nobles look on those of us who actually work. But my money is clean. And the God has been good. My family has enough. My children are a joy to me. Logan has proposed to Serah, and she's said yes. I get to have Logan as a son. How haven't I been blessed? Anyway, I should have told you this long ago. Maybe you already knew some of it through the Sa'kagé."

"No, sir. I had no idea," Kylar said.

"Son, I hope you see now that I do understand. I know what lies the Sa'kagé tells, and I know what it can cost to get out. The God was gracious to me. He didn't make me pay all that I owed, but maybe I had to be willing to pay the full price. That's how repentance is different from regret. I had been sorry about how slavery turned out, but I wasn't willing to take responsibility for it. Once I was, the God could work in me."

"But sir, how are you still alive? I mean, you didn't just leave, you destroyed a business that earned them millions!"

Count Drake smiled. "God, Kylar. The God and Durzo. Durzo likes me. He thinks I'm a fool, but he likes me. He's protected me. He's not a man to cross lightly."

Thanks for the reminder.

"The point is, Kylar, if you want to turn away from what you do, you can. You might miss your work. I imagine that you're excellent, and there is a joy in excellence. You can't pay for all you've done. But you aren't beyond redemption. There's always a way out. And if you're willing to make the sacrifice, the God will give you the chance to save something priceless. But I'm here to tell you, miracles do happen. Like this one," he pointed out the window and shook his head, incredulous. "My daughter, marrying a man as good as Logan. May the God be with them."

Kylar was blinking through tears, so he almost missed the count leaning forward further, looking toward the front gate. His eyes cleared as soon as he saw the soldiers push past the old porter. Kylar was on his feet in a moment, but the soldiers didn't come to the front door. They stopped when they reached Logan and Serah, and the count opened the window to hear the captain as he unrolled a scroll.

"Duke Logan Gyre, you are hereby under arrest for high treason in the murder of Prince Aleine Gunder."

46

Count Drake was out the door in an instant. Kylar hesitated at the very place he'd run into Logan ten years ago and started their friendship with a fistfight. He shouldn't go out. There was no time to think how much the guards knew, but if they thought Logan had been involved in the prince's death, who knew what else they thought? The king must be totally paranoid. Whatever was happening, it was never a good idea to bring yourself to the guards' attention.

But seeing the bewilderment on Logan's face dug into Kylar. He was just standing there as the smaller men disarmed him. He looked like a dog you'd kicked for no reason, eyes wide. Cursing himself for his stupidity, Kylar followed Count Drake.

"I demand an explanation," Count Drake said. Despite his limp, he somehow moved with authority. All eyes turned to him.

"We're, we're making an arrest, sir. I'm afraid that's all I can tell you," the captain said. He was a thick little man with yellow skin and almond eyes, but it seemed to take all of his determination just to stand before the count and not be blown away.

"You're attempting to arrest a duke, and you don't have the authority to do that, Captain Arturian. By the third amendment to the common law in the eighth year of the reign of King Hurol II, the arrest of dukes of the realm must be justified by habeas corpus, two witnesses, and a motive. Incarceration requires two of those three."

Captain Arturian swallowed and seemed to be holding his spine straight only by an act of will. "We, um, habeas corpus is holding the corpse? So I have to bring two witnesses or provide motive before you'll let me arrest the duke?"

"If you have the corpse," Count Drake said.

The man nodded. "We, uh, we do, sir. The prince's body was found last night at the Jadwin estate, and the motive is a matter of...uh. It doesn't bear speaking, sir."

"If you attempt to arrest Duke Gyre at my home outside the provisions of the law, as a noble of the land, I have the right and the obligation to protect him with the force of arms."

"We'd slaughter you!" one of the guards said, laughing.

"And if you did, you'd touch off civil war. Is that what you want?" Count Drake asked. The man who'd spoken fell silent, and Vin Arturian went gray. "Either produce a motive that would lead a man of known moral excellence like Duke Gyre to kill one of his best friends, or begone."

"Milord," Captain Arturian said, his eyes downcast. "Forgive me. The motive was jealousy."

For some reason, Kylar's eyes moved to Serah. She still looked stricken by the news, but as the captain grew more awkward, she seemed to shrink into herself, as if she knew what he was going to say next.

"Duke Gyre found out that the prince was having...sexual relations with your daughter."

"That's ludicrous!" Logan said. "That's the most ridiculous thing I've ever heard. For godsake, she hasn't even made love with me! Her fiancé! Aleine gets around, but he would never—"

Logan looked at Serah and never finished the sentence. "Serah, you...you didn't. Tell me you didn't." It was as if his soul had been stripped naked and all the darts in the world sank into it at once.

Serah keened, a sound of such woe it tore the heart, but none of the men moved. She ran away, back into the house, but they stood transfixed in Logan's pain.

Logan turned to the count. "You knew?"

Rimbold Drake shook his head. "I didn't know who, but she said she'd told you. That all was forgiven."

Logan looked at Kylar.

"The same," Kylar said quietly.

Logan took it like another dart. He struggled for breath. "Captain," he said, "I'll go with you."

The soldier who'd spoken before moved forward at the captain's signal and started putting the manacles on Logan's hands. "Damn, boy," he said quietly, obviously only for Logan's ears, but in the stillness of the yard his words were clearly audible. "You got fucked without even getting fucked first."

It was only the second time Kylar had seen Logan lose his temper, but the last time, he'd been a boy and he hadn't been nearly as powerful as he was now. Maybe a wetboy would have noticed the muscles tensing in Logan's shoulders and arm. Maybe a wetboy would have had the reflexes to dodge, but the guard didn't stand a chance. Logan ripped his hand away before the second manacle clicked shut and hit the guard in the face. Kylar didn't think he'd ever seen anyone hit so hard. Master Blint, with his Talent-strengthened muscles, could probably hit that hard, but he wouldn't have the mass behind the blow that Logan did.

The guard flew backward. Literally. His feet left the ground and he knocked over the two men behind him.

Kylar's Ceuran blade was in his hand before the guards hit the ground, but before he could wade into battle, he felt the count's fingers dig into his arms.

"No!" the count said.

Guards piled onto Logan, who roared.

"No," the count said. "It is better..." his face was as pained as Logan's, torn between sorrow and conviction. "It is better to suffer evil than to do evil. You will not kill innocent men in my house."

Logan didn't put up a fight. The men took him down to the ground, put the manacles on him behind his back, put a second set on his legs, and finally stood him up.

"Did the count say your name is Kylar? Kylar Stern?" Captain Arturian asked.

Kylar nodded.

"The crown charges you with treason, membership in the Sa'kagé, accepting payment for murder, and the murder of Prince Aleine Gunder. We have a witness, corpse, and motive, Count Drake. Men, arrest him."

The captain might have been sympathetic, but he wasn't a fool. Kylar had been so caught up in what was happening to Logan that he hadn't noticed the men circle behind him. At the captain's word, he felt two men take hold of his arms.

He swung his arms forward, only hoping to throw the men off balance so he could fall backward between them. But once again his Talent was there like a coiled viper, and he was suddenly stronger than he'd ever been. The men flew forward and crunched together, meeting along the blade of Kylar's sword. If he'd turned the blade, he could have gutted either of them, even through their boiled leather gambesons. Instead, he sheathed the sword—how had he done it that fast?—he was still falling backward from throwing the guards harder than he intended, and the sword was already sheathed.

Turning his fall into a back handspring was child's play. Kylar turned and ran toward a wall on one side of the count's small garden. He jumped to grab the lip of the twelve-foot-high wall, and found the wall approaching instead at the level of his knees. It sent him over the wall in a vicious spin, and only by rolling into a ball and some significant luck was he able to land on the other side without killing himself.

He stood and let the Talent go. There were cries coming from within the walls, but they'd never catch him. Kylar was a wetboy now in truth. He wondered what Blint would say. Kylar had achieved his lifelong dream, and he couldn't have been more miserable.

"How was it?" Agon asked Captain Arturian, as they walked through the halls of the castle toward the Maw.

"It was...awful. Absolutely awful, sir. I'd say it ranks with the worst things I've ever done."

"Regrets, captain? They say he killed one of your men."

"If I may be blunt, he rid me of a fool that I couldn't kick out because the man's sister is a baroness. The idiot had it coming. I know it's not my place to say, lord general, but you didn't see Logan's face. He's not guilty. I'd swear it."

"I know. I know, and I'm going to do everything I can to save him." They passed the guards who held the underground gate that separated the tunnels beneath the castle from those of the Maw. The nobles' cells were on the first level. They were small, but in relative terms, luxurious. Agon had Elene placed in one of these cells, though her status didn't afford it. He couldn't bear to have her put any lower, and if the king asked, he'd say that he wanted her kept close for further questioning.

Agon stopped outside Logan's cell. "Vin," he said. "Does he know about his family yet?"

The squat man shook his head. "I'd already lost one man, sir. I didn't know what he would do if we told him."

"Fair enough. Thank you." It wasn't the dismissal Agon would have given to one of his subordinates, but though the lord general's rank was the

second only to the king's, the captain of the king's guards wasn't technically under Agon's command. Fortunately, though they weren't friends, they
were on good enough terms that Captain Arturian took the cue and excused
himself.

It wasn't going to be fun to tell a man who'd been jailed for a murder he
didn't commit that his family had been slaughtered, but it was Agon's duty.
He always did his duty.

Before he unlocked the door, Agon knocked as if he were coming for a
visit. As if they were anywhere else besides the Maw. There was no response.

He opened the door. The nobles' cells were ten feet square, all rock polished smooth to prevent suicides. Each had a bare rock bench that served as
a bed, and fresh straw was brought in every week. It was luxury only compared to the rest of the Maw, and even with fresh straw, nothing could erase
the rotten-egg stench or the ripe tang of massed humanity in an enclosed
space that wafted up from the rest of the cells. Logan looked oblivious. He
looked like hell. Tears streamed down his bruised face. He looked up when
Agon came in, but his eyes took a long time to focus. He looked lost, his big
shoulders slouched, big hands open on his lap, hair askew. He wasn't alone.
The queen was seated beside him, holding one of those limply open hands
as one would hold a child's.

Bless the woman. She'd come to tell him herself.

King Aleine IX had totally missed with Nalia Wesseros. Nalia could
have been one of his greatest allies. *What a queen she would have made
for Regnus Gyre.* Instead, she'd accepted being pushed to the fringes of
Aleine's Cenaria, even welcomed it, and had done everything she could to
mother her four—now three—children. Agon had long suspected that the
children were all that kept her alive.

"My queen. My lord," Agon said.

"Pardon me if I don't rise," Logan said.

"None necessary."

"They say that my father is dead, too. Or they say that he did it. That the
king sent men to arrest him for killing my mother. What happened?"
Logan asked.

"As far as I know, your father is alive. He arrived with only one or two
men. He was attacked outside the city. Someone was trying to wipe out all
the Gyres but you. Men were sent to arrest him, but not on the king's orders.
I haven't found out who did give the orders. Not yet. Those men either fled
the city, or they joined your father. I don't know which."

"Lord General, I didn't kill Aleine," Logan said. "He was my friend.
Even if he did . . . what they say he did."

"We know. We—the queen and I—don't think you did it."

"He talked to me last night, you know? He knew I was going to propose to Serah. He tried to persuade me not to. He reminded me of the rumors about Serah getting around. He had this crazy idea that I marry Jenine. I thought it was strange, but that he was being magnanimous. It wasn't magnanimity. It was guilt. Damn him!"

Logan looked at the queen. "I'm sorry. I shouldn't talk this way, but I'm so, so angry—and I feel so guilty for it at the same time! I would have forgiven them, Your Majesty. I would have. Gods! Why didn't they just tell me?"

They cried silently together and the queen just squeezed Logan's hand.

After a minute, Logan looked up at Agon. "They say Kylar did it. At Count Drake's, I saw him move. He was fast. Too fast. But are you sure?"

Gods. The boy had just been betrayed by his fiancée and the prince. Now he wanted to know if he'd been betrayed by his best friend as well. Agon didn't know if he would survive it—and he needed him to survive it—but Logan deserved the truth. It wasn't in Agon to give him less. "I'm sure Kylar was upstairs when Aleine died. I'm sure he's a wetboy. I doubt his real name is Kylar or that he's a Stern, but I won't know that for two weeks. We've sent a rider to their estates but it's a week's ride each way. I can't put everything together in any other way, son, and I've been trying."

"Your being here is a kindness," Logan said. His back straightened. "And I don't want to take that away from you, but I'm guessing that you want something from me or you wouldn't both have come here. Not now. Not so soon."

The queen and the lord general looked at each other. Something passed between them, and the general said, "You're right, Logan. The truth is, the kingdom's in peril. I wish that we could be sensitive to your grief. You know that your father is one of my dearest friends and what happened to your house is more than a tragedy. It's a monstrosity.

"But we have to ask you to put your feelings aside, for a time. We don't know how bad the threat is, but I believe that it's dire. When the king decided to get rid of your father one way or another ten years ago, it was I who suggested Screaming Winds. I knew that your father would make the garrison there a real stronghold, and I believed that Khalidor would invade sooner or later. Perhaps because he did such an excellent job, that invasion hasn't come. Most people want to believe that it won't come, because they know that if the might of Khalidor marches, we don't stand a chance.

"I believe that the prince, your mother, and your servants were the first casualties in a war. A new kind of war that uses assassins instead of armies to gain its will. We can stop armies, we've been preparing for that. Assassins are a different story."

"Begging the queen's pardon," Logan said, "why should I care if the king's head rolls? He's been no friend to the Gyres."

"A fair question," the queen said.

"On a personal level," Agon said, "you should care because if the king dies, you'll either stay in prison forever or you'll be killed. On a national level, if the king dies, there will be civil war. Troops will be called back to the respective houses to which they are loyal, and Khalidor's armies will pour over our borders. Even united, our country couldn't stand against Khalidor's might. Our only strategy has been to make it so costly to take us that the price would be too high. With our armies scattered, we'd be defenseless."

"So you think an assassination attempt is coming?" Logan asked.

"Within days. But Khalidor's plans rest on certain assumptions, Logan. So far, they've been valid assumptions. They knew that you would be arrested. No doubt they've already planted rumors to stir up the people against the king, suggesting that everything that's happened has been his fault or his plan. We have to do something beyond anything Khalidor has considered."

"And what's that?"

The queen said, "Khalidor has hired Hu Gibbet, perhaps the best wetboy in the city. If he wants to kill Aleine, he probably can. The best way to save the king's life is if the taking of it won't gain Khalidor anything. Maybe it's the only way. We have to assure the line of succession. In a time of peace or if she were older, Jenine might take the throne, or I might, but now.... That simply wouldn't be possible. Some of the houses would refuse to follow a woman into war."

"Well, what are you supposed to do? Have another son?"

Agon looked queasy. "Sort of."

The queen said, "We need someone who's popular enough to win the people's trust back to the throne, and whose claim to the crown would be beyond dispute."

Logan looked at him and sudden understanding washed over him. Emotions warred on his face. "You don't know what you're asking."

"Yes, I do," the queen said quietly. "Logan, has your father ever spoken of me?"

"Only in terms of highest praise, Your Majesty."

"Your father and I were betrothed, Logan. For ten years, we knew we were going to marry. We fell in love. We named the children we would someday have. The king was dying without heirs, and our marriage was to have secured the throne for House Gyre. Then my father betrayed Regnus and broke his word to your grandfather by marrying me in secret to Aleine

Gunder. There were only enough witnesses present to ensure the legality of the marriage. I wasn't even allowed to send a message to your father beforehand. The king lived for another fourteen years, long enough for me to have children, long enough for your father to marry and have you, long enough for your father to take control of House Gyre. Long enough for House Gunder to fabricate some ridiculous history that supposedly gave Aleine the right to be called Aleine IX, as if he were a legitimate king. When King Davin died, your father could have gone to war to take the throne. He could have won it, but he didn't, for my sake and the sake of my children.

"I was sold into a marriage I despised, Logan, to a man I never loved, and for whom I could never make love grow in my breast. I know what it is to be sold for politics. I even know my literal price in the lands and titles my family secured after the king's death." There was iron in her as she spoke, clearly, calmly, every inch the queen. "I still love your father, Logan. We've barely spoken in twenty-five years. He had to marry a Graesin after I married a Gunder, just to keep the House Gyre from becoming isolated and wiped out like the Makells were. He accepted a marriage that I've heard had little love in it. So if you think it pleases me to do to you what was done to me, you couldn't be more mistaken."

Logan's father had never spoken of such things, but his mother—it was suddenly so clear—his mother had been reminding Regnus of it for years. Her sidelong comments. Her constant suspicions that Regnus had other lovers, though Logan knew he hadn't. His father's angry remark once that there was only one woman she had any right to envy.

"I have hope that your marriage will not be the agony mine has been," Queen Gunder said.

Logan put his face in his hands. "Your Majesty, words can't express the...fury I feel toward Serah. But I gave her father my word that I would marry her."

"The king can legally dissolve such bonds for the good of the realm," Agon said.

"The king can't dissolve my honor!" Logan said. "I swore! And dammit! I still love Serah. I *still* love her. It's all playacting, isn't it? What's the plan, that the king adopt me? That I be his heir until you bear him another son?"

"This *playacting* gets us through a crisis, son," Agon said. "And it keeps your family from being destroyed. You have to stay alive if you want that to happen. It also happens to save you from disgrace and prison, even if we're wrong about the plot."

"Logan," the queen said, her voice again quiet. "It isn't playacting, but we've convinced the king that it is. He is a despicable man, and if it's up to him, he will never let Regnus's son take the throne."

"Your Majesty," Agon interrupted. "Logan doesn't need to—"

"No, Brant. A person ought to know what they're being asked to give." She looked him in the eye, and after a moment, he looked down. She turned to Logan. "My hope has been my children, Logan, and I lay Aleine's death at my husband's feet. If he'd not gotten involved with that Jadwin whore..." She blinked her eyes, refusing to let tears fall. "I have given the king all the sons he will have from me. I will not share his bed again. Ever. He will be told that if he seeks to force me to his bed or replace me as queen, we have retained the services of a wetboy to make sure he finds an early grave. The fact is, Logan, if you say yes, you will one day be king."

He said nothing.

"Most men would leap at the chance for such power," Agon said. "Of course, most men make terrible kings. We know you wouldn't ask for this, but you aren't only the right man for it; you're the only man for it."

"Logan was the name Regnus and I had decided on for our first son," the queen said. "I know what I'm asking, Logan. And I'm asking."

The game wasn't going well. The pieces were spread out before Dorian like armies. Except that they weren't like armies; they were armies, though in this game, few of the soldiers wore uniforms. Even those who did moved with reluctance. The Fool King shamed the Commander. The Reluctant King was kneeling somewhere at this moment. The Mage in Secret's secret had split him from the King Who Might Have Been. The Shadow that Walks and the Courtesan couldn't decide which side they were on. The Rent Boy was moving fast, but too slow, too slow. The Prince of Rats had marshaled his vermin, and they would rise from the Warrens, a tide of human filth. Even the Rogue Prince and the Blacksmith might play a part, if....

Blast! It was hard enough, just envisioning the pieces as they were. From there, he could often focus on one piece and see the choices it faced: the Commander as a drunk king shouted in his face, the Shadow that Walks as he faced the Apprentice in a honeymoon chamber. But just as he was fixing the pieces in space, setting their relative positions, he'd start seeing one or more at a different time. Seeing where the Blacksmith would be in seventeen years, stooped over a forge, urging his son back to work, didn't do him any good in figuring out how to keep Feir alive until that day.

He went back to work. Now where was the Kidnapped?

Sometimes he felt as if he were but a breath of wind over the field of battle. He could see everything, but the most he could hope to do was blow one or two killing arrows off course. Where is that Mage in Secret? Ah.

"Open the door, quick," Dorian said.

Feir looked up from the little table where he was seated, dragging a whetstone across the face of his sword. They were in a little house they'd rented off Sidlin where Dorian said they would be left alone. Feir rose and opened the door.

A man was just disappearing past it, walking determinedly down the street. His hair and gait were familiar. He must have seen something out of the corner of his eye— —of course, the blond mountain that was Feir was hard to miss—because he turned on his heel, his hand dropping to his sword.

"Feir?"

Feir looked almost as surprised as Solon was, so Dorian said, "Both of you, inside."

They came in, Feir giving a customary grumble about how Dorian never told him anything, and Dorian just smiling. *So much to see, so much to know.* It was easy to miss things right under your nose.

"Dorian!" Solon said. He embraced his old friend. "I ought to wring your neck. Do you know how much trouble your little 'Lord Gyre' bit cost me?"

Dorian laughed. He knew. "Oh, my friend," he said, holding onto Solon's arms. "You did well."

"You look well, too," Feir said. "You were fat when you left. Look at you now. A decade of military service has done you right."

Solon smiled, but the smile faded fast. "Dorian, seriously, I have to know. Did you mean that I needed to come serve Logan, or did you mean Regnus? I thought you'd said Lord Gyre and not Duke Gyre, but when I got here, there were two Lords Gyre. Did I do the right thing?"

"Yes, yes. They both needed you, and you saved both of them several times. Some you know, some you don't." Perhaps the most important thing Solon had done was something he would never appreciate: he had encouraged Logan's friendship with Kylar. "But I won't lie to you. Keeping your secret was something I didn't foresee. I thought you would have shared it years ago. Down most paths I see now, Regnus Gyre will lose his life."

"I'm a coward," Solon said.

"Pah," Feir said. "You're many things, Solon, but you're not a coward."

Dorian kept silent, and let his eyes speak empathy. He knew differently. Solon's silence had been cowardice. Dozens of times he'd tried to speak, but he could never summon the courage to risk his friendship with Regnus Gyre. The worst of it was that Regnus would have understood and laughed about it, if he'd heard it from Solon's own lips. But discovering deceit in a friend felt like betrayal to a man who'd had his fiancée sold out from under him to another man.

"Your powers have grown," Solon said.

"Yes, he's truly insufferable now," Feir said.

"I'm surprised the brothers at Sho'cendi let you come here," Solon said.

Dorian and Feir looked at each other.

"You left without permission?" Solon asked.

Silence.

"You left against their direct orders?"

"Worse," Dorian said.

Feir barked a laugh that told Solon he'd been put into another plan of Dorian's that he couldn't believe.

"What did you do?" Solon asked.

"It belonged to us, really. We're the ones who found it again. They didn't have any right," Dorian said.

"You didn't."

Dorian shrugged.

"Where is it?" Solon asked. From the bland looks on their faces, he knew. "You brought it here?!"

Feir walked to the little bed and threw back the blankets. Curoch lay sheathed on the bed. The scabbard was white leather, inlaid with gold Hyrillic script and capped with gold.

"That's not the original scabbard, surely."

"It's work like this that makes me want to never be a sword smith," Feir said. "The scabbard is the original. Woven thick with magic as fine as Gandian silk, and I think all that's just to preserve the leather. It won't stay dirty, won't take a mark. The gold inlay is real, too. Pure gold. Hardened to where it would stand against iron or even steel. If I could figure out that technique alone, my heirs would be rich to the twelfth generation."

"We've barely dared unsheathe the sword, and of course we haven't tried to use it," Dorian said.

"I should hope not," Solon said. "Dorian, why would you bring it here? Have you seen something?"

He shook his head. "Artifacts of such power skew my vision. They themselves and the lusts they invoke are so intense that it fogs my sight."

Suddenly, he was drifting again, but drifting was too gentle a word for it. His vision latched onto Solon and images streamed past him. Impossible visions. Solon against incredible odds. Solon as a white-haired old man, except not old, but—blast, the image disappeared before he could understand it. Solon Solon Solon. Solon dying. Solon killing. Solon on a storm-tossed ship. Solon saving Regnus from a wetboy. Solon killing the king. Solon dooming Cenaria. Solon propelling Dorian into Khalidor. A beautiful woman in a chamber of a hundred portraits of beautiful women. Jenine. Dorian's heart lurched. Garoth Ursuul.

"Dorian? Dorian?" the voice was distant, but Dorian grabbed onto the sound and pulled himself back to it.

He shook himself, gasping as if emerging from a cold lake.

"It's getting worse as you get stronger, isn't it?" Solon asked.

"He trades his mind for the visions," Feir said. "He won't listen to me."

"My sanity isn't necessary for the work I must do," Dorian said simply. "My visions are." The dice were in his hand, not just two dice, a whole handful of dice, each with a dozen faces. *How many twelves can I throw?* He would be throwing blind; he could see that Solon already was thinking he should leave, that no matter how good it was to see his old friends, he had to try to save Regnus Gyre. But Dorian had a feeling. That was the damnable thing. Sometimes it was as logical as a sesch game. Sometimes it was just an itch.

"Anyway, where were we?" he asked, playing the oblivious seer. "Feir doesn't have enough Talent to use Curoch. If he tried, he'd either burn or explode. No offense, friend, you have finer control than either of us. I could use it, but only safely as a meister; my mage powers probably aren't strong enough. Of course using it with the vir would be a total disaster. I don't even know what I'd do. Of us, Solon, you're the only mage in the room, or the country for that matter, who could hope to even hold it without dying, though it would be a near thing. You'd die if you tried to use more than a fraction of its power. Hmm." He gazed into space as if he were suddenly caught by another vision. The line was set.

"Surely you didn't bring it all this way for nothing," Solon said.

Set and sprung.

"No. We had to get it away from the brothers. It was our only chance. If we'd waited until after we returned, they would have known they couldn't trust us. It would have been kept far from us."

"Dorian, you still believe in that one God of yours, don't you?" Solon asked.

"I think he sometimes confuses himself with Him," Feir said. It was uncharacteristically bitter and it struck Dorian deeply. It hurt because it was deserved. He was doing it right now.

"Feir's right," Dorian said. "Solon, I was setting you up to take the sword. I shouldn't treat you that way. You deserve better and I'm sorry."

"Damn," Solon said. "You knew I was thinking of taking it?"

Dorian nodded. "I don't know if it's the right thing or not. I didn't know you'd walk in our door until a second before you did. With Curoch, everything gets twisted. If you use it, Khalidor may well take it from us. That would be a disaster far greater than losing your friend Regnus, or even losing this entire country."

"The risk is unacceptable," Feir said.

"What good does it do anyone if we don't use it?" Solon said.

"It keeps it out of the hands of the Vürdmeisters!" Feir said. "That's good enough. There's only a handful of mages in the world who could hold Curoch without dying, and you know it. We also know that there are dozens of Vürdmeisters who could. With Curoch in their hands, what could stop them?"

"I have a feeling about this," Dorian said. "Maybe the God is nudging me. I just think it's right. I feel like it's connected to the Guardian of Light."

"I thought you'd given up on those old prophecies," Solon said.

"If you take Curoch, the Guardian will be born in our lifetimes." Even as Dorian said it, he knew it was true. "I've been living so long saying I had faith, but it isn't really faith when you just do what you see, is it? I think the God wants us to take this crazy risk. I think he'll bring good out of it."

Feir threw up his hands. "Dorian, the God is always your out. You run into a wall rationally and you say the God is speaking to you. It's ridiculous. If this one God of yours created everything like you say, he also gave us reason, right? Why the hell would he make us do something so irrational?"

"I'm right."

"Dorian," Solon said. "Can I really use it?"

"If you use it, everyone in fifty miles will know it. Maybe even the ungifted. You run all the normal risks of drawing too much power, but your upper limit is higher than its lowest threshold. Things are happening too fast for me to see much, but I'm going to tell you this, Solon. The invasion force was headed for Modai." *Until Kylar didn't kill Durzo Blint.* "So they were prepared for a different kind of war. The boats arrive tonight. They have sixty meisters."

"Sixty! That's more than some of our schools," Feir said.

"There are at least three Vürdmeisters capable of calling forth pit wyrms."

"If I see any little men with wings, I'll run," Solon said.

"You're mad," Feir said. "Dorian, we need to leave. This kingdom's doomed. They'll capture Curoch; they'll capture you, and then what hope will the rest of the world have? We need to pick a battle we can win."

"Unless the God is with us, we won't win any battles, Feir."

"Don't give me that God bullshit! I won't let Solon take Curoch, and I'm taking you back to Sho'cendi. Your madness is taking you."

"Too late," Solon said. He scooped up the sword from the bed.

"We both know I can take that away from you," Feir said.

"In a swordfight, sure," Solon agreed. "But if you try to take it, I'll just draw power through it and stop you. Like Dorian said, every meister within fifty miles will know we have an artifact here, and they'll all come looking for it."

"You wouldn't," Feir said.

Solon's face took on an intensity Dorian hadn't seen since he'd left *Sho'fasti* wearing his first blue robes. Now, as then, the slab of a man looked more like a soldier than like one of the foremost mages of the day. "I will do it," Solon said. "I've given ten years of my life for this backwater, and they've been good years. It's been damn good to stand for something rather than just watch from the side and criticize everyone who's actually doing something. You should try it. You used to, you know? What happened to the Feir Cousat who went and took this sword in the first place? I'm going to do something here. Don't spoil my chance to make it be useful. Come on, Feir, if we *can* fight Khalidor, how could we *not*?"

"Once you make your mind up, you're about as easy to move as Dorian," Feir said.

"Thank you," Solon said.

"I didn't mean it as a compliment."

48

The man who had ordered soldiers to arrest Regnus hadn't been much use. They'd captured him coming out of an inn after lunch. His interrogation had been short if not kind. He'd given them his commanding officer's name, one Thaddeus Blat.

Thaddeus Blat was currently being entertained upstairs in a brothel called the Winking Wench. Regnus and his men were waiting downstairs, seated at various tables, and not doing a good job of remaining inconspicuous.

It all made Regnus nervous. He didn't know this man, but soldiers tended to visit brothels in the middle of the afternoon only when they knew something big was going to happen. Something from which they might not return. He also didn't like being out in public. Years ago, he wouldn't have been able to go anywhere without people recognizing his face. He had been presumed to be the next king, after all. But that had been years ago. Few people looked at him twice now. He was a big, threatening man in the Warrens. Apparently, that outweighed the fact that he was a rich nobleman in the Warrens.

Finally the man came downstairs. He was swarthy, with a single thick black eyebrow and a face etched with a permanent glower. Regnus stood after the man walked past and followed him to the stable. They'd already paid the stable boy to abandon his post, and by the time Regnus got there, Thaddeus Blat was bleeding from his nose and the corner of his mouth, disarmed, held by four soldiers, and cursing.

"That's not what I want to hear coming out of your mouth, Lieutenant," Regnus said. He gestured and the men kicked the back of Blat's knees so he dropped in front of the trough. Regnus grabbed a handful of hair and pressed his head under water.

"Tie his hands. This may take a few minutes," Regnus said.

Blat came up gasping and flailing, but the soldiers bound his hands in short order. Thaddeus Blat spat toward Regnus, missed, and cursed him.

"Slow learner," Regnus said, and heaved. The man went under and this time Regnus waited until he stopped flailing. "When they stop fighting," he said to his men, "it means they understand for the first time that they might actually die unless they really concentrate. I think he'll be a little more polite this time."

He pulled Blat up, his dark hair plastered to his forehead down to his single brow, and Blat saved his air for breathing for a long moment. "Who are you?" he asked.

"I'm Duke Regnus Gyre, and you're going to tell me everything you know about my people's death."

The man cursed him again.

"Turn him a little," Regnus said. They did, and he drove his fist into the man's solar plexus, driving the wind from his lungs. Thaddeus Blat only had time to suck in half a breath before he went under.

Regnus held him below the water until bubbles burst on the surface, then he dragged Thaddeus up, but only for a moment. Then he pushed him back down again. He repeated the process four times. When he pulled Blat up the fifth time, he released his head.

"I'm running out of time, Thaddeus Blat, and I've got nothing to lose by killing you. I've already killed my wife and all my servants, remember? So if I have to put your face under that water one more time, I'm going to hold it there until you're dead."

Real fear was painted across the lieutenant's face in dripping watercolors. "They don't tell me anything—no, wait! I swear it. I don't get my new orders until tonight. But this one goes all the way to the top. To the top of the Kin, you know?"

"The Sa'kagé?"

"Yeah."

"Not good enough. Sorry."

They plunged his head back under the water and he thrashed like a demon, but on his knees, with his hands tied, there was nothing he could do. "You set a limit, and then you break it," Regnus said. "Most people can hold out if they've been given a limit. They tell themselves, 'I can hold out that long.' Let him up."

The man spluttered as he came up, spitting out inhaled water and wheezing. "You think of anything else?" Regnus asked, but he didn't give Thaddeus time to respond.

He dunked the man again. "Sir," one of the soldiers said, looking a little queasy. "If you don't mind my asking, how do you know all this?"

Regnus grinned. "I got captured by the Lae'knaught during a border raid when I was young. But we don't have the time to use everything I learned from them. Up."

"Wait!" Thaddeus Blat cried out. "I overheard them saying that Hu Gibbet's next deader was the queen. Her and her daughters. That's all I know. Gods, that's all I know. He's going to kill them tonight in the queen's chambers after the banquet. Please don't kill me. I swear that's all I know."

They had promised Kaldrosa Wyn a man-o'-war and put her on a sea cow instead. The Sethi pirate hadn't been able to say no to the money. *Damn the mother who whelped me, why didn't I say no?* Looking over the port side, she barked an order and men scurried to adjust the sails to catch another cupful of wind. *Sails? Bedsheets, more like.* The sails were too small. The ship and its sister were too fat and ungainly to outrun a rowboat piloted by a one-handed monkey. In short, the Cenarian warships would be on them in minutes, and there wasn't a damn thing Kaldrosa Wyn could do about it.

"If you're going to do something, now might be a good time," she told the circle of wytches sitting on the barge's deck.

"Wench," the leader of the wytches said, "no one tells a meister his work. Understood?" The man's eyes didn't rise from her bare breasts until the last word.

"Then to hell with ya," Kaldrosa said. She spat over the side, not betraying the queasiness that rose in her at the touch of that wytch's eyes. The bastards had been staring at her breasts for the entire trip. Normally around foreigners, she'd have covered herself, but she liked making the Khalidorans uncomfortable. Wytches were another matter.

Kaldrosa reefed the sails and had the men below decks start rowing, but even that was hopeless. Khalidoran craftsmanship. They'd even designed the oars poorly. They were too short. Even with the hundreds of men she was carrying, she couldn't translate their strength into speed because not enough men could man the oars at once, nor was there room below for full sweep. She cursed her greed and the wytches—quietly.

In minutes, the three Cenarian warships were on them. It was a shame. In all the ocean, Cenaria couldn't have had more than a dozen ships in her navy, and Kaldrosa had found the three best ships of it. In her *Sparrowhawk* or any Sethi ship with a Sethi crew, she'd be safe.

The wytches finally stood as the first Cenarian ship drew within a hundred paces. They were going to ram her sea cow at an angle and sheer off the oars. Eighty paces. Seventy. Fifty. Thirty.

The wytches had their hands twined. They were chanting and it seemed darker on deck than it had been a moment before, but nothing was happening. The sailors and soldiers on the Cenarian ship were shouting to each other and at her, getting ready for the collision and the battle to follow.

"Damn you," she yelled, "do something!"

Out of the corner of her eye, she thought she saw something immense pass by, under the ship. She turned to brace for the impact, but instead only got a face full of water. There was a tremendous crack, and when her vision cleared, she saw pieces of the Cenarian ship flying through the air. But not many pieces. Not enough to account for an entire ship.

Then she saw the rest of the ship through the shallow blue waters. Somehow, it had been sucked down in an instant. The flying pieces were merely what had broken off the decks and the sails as the water broke over the ship.

The sea went black, as if a thick cloud had passed in front of the sun, but it undulated. It took Kaldrosa a moment to realize that something enormous was passing beneath her ship. Something absolutely immense. She saw the wytches chanting, more than their hands intertwined now. It seemed as if the black tattoos that all of them wore had torn free of their hands and were holding each other, pulsing with power. The wytches were sweating as if under tremendous strain.

Water swelled as if an immense arrow were passing just under the surface of the sea—and then stopped as it reached the second Cenarian warship. The men on its deck, fifty paces away, were shouting, shooting arrows into the water, brandishing swords, the captain trying to turn the ship.

For five seconds nothing happened, then two gray massive somethings slapped against the Cenarian ship's deck. They were too big for Kaldrosa to even guess what they could be for a moment—each one covered nearly a quarter of the ship's hull. Then the ship bounced ten paces out of the sea, straight up, and Kaldrosa saw that they were fingers of a massive gray hand. Then the hand went down and the entire ship disappeared under the waves, bursting apart as the water closed over it, throwing splinters in a wave.

Then the black shape was moving again. It was too big to be real. And this time, the men on the last Cenarian ship were screaming. Kaldrosa heard orders being shouted, but there was too much chaos. The ship drifted, even though it had closed the distance with her sea cow while the other ships had been being destroyed, and was now almost touching it.

The sea swelled again, but this time there was no pause. The leviathan swam beneath the Cenarian ship at incredible speed, rising high enough in the water that spines from its back rose thirty feet in the air.

The spines cut the ship in half and two flicks of a gray tail smashed each half into the ocean. The Khalidoran soldiers who'd crowded the deck—Kaldrosa hadn't even noticed them emerging—cheered.

She was about to begin ordering them back to their places when the cheering suddenly stopped. The soldiers were pointing. She followed their gaze and saw that swell rising again, this time pointed straight for them. The wytches were sweating freely, open panic on their faces.

"No!" a young wytch shouted. "That won't work. Like *this*."

Something rippled out from the wytches toward the leviathan. It met the oncoming beast, and nothing happened. The soldiers cried out in horror.

Then the huge shape turned and went out to sea.

The soldiers cheered and the wytches collapsed on the deck. But something wasn't finished. Kaldrosa saw that immediately. Even as she ordered the oars pulled and the sails raised once more, she kept an eye on the wytches.

The leader was speaking to the young man who—if Kaldrosa guessed correctly—had taken control and saved all of their lives. The young man shook his head, staring at the deck.

"Obedience unto death," she heard him say.

The leader spoke again, too low for Kaldrosa to make out, and the other eleven wytches gathered around the two men. They laid their hands on the young man who'd saved them all, and Kaldrosa saw his tattoos rise from below his skin. They swelled and swelled until his arms were black, and then they burst—not outward, away from the wytch's body, but in, as if they were veins that had been overfilled and now leaked through the rest of his body. The ruptured tattoos bled beneath the young man's skin and he collapsed to the deck, twitching violently. In moments, his entire body was black. He thrashed and choked, and in moments he was dead.

Everyone else on the ship was studiously ignoring the wytches. Kaldrosa found herself the only one watching the exchange. The leader of the wytches said a word, and the other wytches tossed the corpse overboard. Then he turned and watched her with too-blue eyes.

Never again, Kaldrosa swore to herself. *Never again.*

"Do you know the secret of effective blackmail, Durzo?" Roth asked. He was seated at a fine oak table incongruously placed in a typical Warrens hovel. Durzo stood before him like a chastened courtier standing before the king. Roth's chair was even raised. The presumption.

"Yes," Durzo said. He wasn't in any mood for games.

"Refresh me," Roth said, looking up from the reports he'd been reading. He was not amused.

Durzo cursed himself and cursed fate. He'd done everything to avert this, paid every price of misery, and yet it had come. "Use your hold to get a better hold."

"You've made that difficult for me, Durzo. You've convinced everyone that you don't give a damn about anything."

"Thank you." Durzo didn't smile. It wasn't in him to play the abased servant.

"The problem is, I'm more clever than you are."

"Cleverer."

Roth's close-set eyes narrowed at Blint's blithe monotone. Roth was a lean young man with an angular face obscured by an oiled black goatee and long hair. He disliked making words for their own sake. He disliked people. He stuck out an open hand. Waited.

Durzo tossed him the bit of pretty silver glass.

Roth looked at it briefly and threw it back, unamused. "Don't toy with me, assassin. I know there was a real one there. We have two spies who saw someone bond it."

"Then they should have told you someone got there first."

"Really?"

Roth was mimicking Momma K's tendency to state questions. He probably thought it made him seem authoritative. Roth was out of his league if he thought mimicking Momma K would be enough to hold power. Part of Durzo wanted to tell Roth that Momma K was the Shinga. Roth obviously didn't know, and Momma K had betrayed Durzo, but Durzo had no taste for using rats to do a man's work. If he killed Gwinvere, he'd do it with his own hands. *If? I'm going soft. When. She betrayed me. She must die.*

"Really," Durzo answered, with no intonation.

"Then I think it's time for you to meet another of my *cards*." There was no signal that Durzo could see, but an old man stepped into the hovel instantly. The creature was short and bent still further by more years than a mortal frame should endure. He had piercing blue eyes and a fringe of silver hair combed over a bald dome of head.

The man gave a toothless grin. "I am Vürdmeister Neph Dada, counselor and seer to His Majesty."

Not just any wytch. A Vürdmeister. Durzo Blint felt old. "How exalted. I thought you called your dog kings His Holiness," Durzo said.

"His Majesty," Neph Dada said, "Roth Ursuul, ninth aetheling of the Godking." He bowed to Roth.

By the Night Angels. He wasn't kidding.

Neph Dada grabbed Durzo's chin with a frail hand and pulled it down toward himself until Durzo looked into his eyes. "He knows who took the Globe of Edges," Neph said.

There was no denying it. Not with a Vürdmeister here. Vürdmeisters were supposed to be able to read minds. It wasn't true, but it was close enough. Most of them couldn't do it, Durzo knew. Even those who could didn't actually read minds. The way Durzo had heard it explained, longer ago than he liked to remember, was that they could see hints of images that their subject had seen. The best Vürdmeisters could intuit a lot of truth from a few images, though. It was almost the same thing at this point. *How can I take advantage of the differences between what I've seen and what I know?*

"It was my apprentice," Durzo said.

Roth Ursuul—*by the Night Angels, Ursuul?*—raised an eyebrow.

"He doesn't know what it is," Durzo said. "I don't know who sent him. He never does jobs without telling me."

"Perhaps you should not be so sure of this?" Neph said.

"I'll get the ka'kari for you. I just need some time."

"Ka'kari?" Roth asked.

Roth had never used the word. It was a stupid mistake. Totally uncharac-teristic. Durzo was falling apart.

"The Globe of Edges," Durzo said.

"I've given you a chance to be honest with me, Durzo. So what I'm going to do is your own fault." Roth motioned to one of the guards at the entrance to the hovel. "The girl."

Several moments later, a little girl was carried in. She was drugged, whether chemically or magically, and the guard had some trouble carrying her limp body. She was maybe eleven years old, skinny and dirty, but not the skinny and dirty of a street rat—healthy skinny, healthy dirty. Her black hair was long and curly, and her face had the same angelic-demonic cast that her mother's had had. She would be even prettier than Vonda, some day. She took her height from Durzo, but thank the gods, everything else from her mother. Uly was a damn fine-looking kid. It was the first time Durzo had seen his daughter.

It made him ache somewhere that was already sore.

"You've already chosen not to cooperate enthusiastically, Durzo," Roth said. "So usually, I'd make an example of you. We both know I can't do that. I need you too much, at least for the next few days. So maybe I should, say, cut off her hand as a warning, and let the little girl know that it's because you won't stop it. That you are choosing to hurt her. Perhaps some-thing like that would help gain your cooperation?"

Durzo was frozen, just looking at his daughter. *His daughter! How had he put her in the hands of this man?* She had been the king's leverage, and Roth had taken her right out from under the man's nose.

"How about this?" Roth said. "We'll cut off a hand or you cut off a finger."

There was a way out. Even now, there was a way. One of his knives was poisoned. He'd put the asp poison it. For Kylar. It would be painless, espe-cially for such a small person. She'd be dead in seconds. Maybe Roth would be surprised enough that Durzo could get away. Maybe.

He could kill his daughter and probably be killed himself, and Kylar would live. Or this Roth Ursuul would demand he kill Kylar and get the ka'kari. That would have been easy enough to fake, if Roth didn't have a Vürdmeister.

Could he kill his own daughter? He'd be letting them kill Kylar if he didn't.

"She didn't do anything," Durzo said.

"Spare me," Roth said. "You've got too much blood on your hands to cry about the suffering of innocents."

"Hurting her isn't necessary."

Roth smiled. "You know, from anyone else, I'd laugh. Do you remember what happened the last time you called an Ursuul's bluff?" Durzo couldn't keep his expression blank; grief flashed through him. "Who'd have thought," Roth said. "My father takes the mother and I take the daughter. Have you learned your lesson, Durzo Blint? I think you have. My father will be pleased that I'm closing the circle. He tried to blackmail you for a false ka'kari and failed. I'll blackmail you for a true ka'kari and succeed." Neph's eyes flashed when Roth said that. It was clear he didn't appreciate the prince's presumption, but Durzo was still reeling. He couldn't see any way to take advantage of that tiny split between the men.

"Here's how blackmail is going to work for you, Durzo Blint: if I think you're resisting me, your daughter will die. And there are other, shall we say *indignities*, that she will suffer first. Let your imagination work on what those might be—I know I'll let mine. She'll be a husk by the time we're finished. I will spend months eking out every drop of suffering from her mind and body before we kill her, and I enjoy such work. I am one of Khali's most dedicated disciples. Do you understand me, Blint? Am I being clear?"

"Perfectly." His jaw was tense. He couldn't kill her. By the Night Angels. He just couldn't do it. He'd think of something. He always had before. There was some way out of this. He would find it, and he would kill both of these men.

Roth smiled. "Now tell me everything about this apprentice of yours. And I mean everything."

49

Kylar stepped out of the shadows of the Blue Boar's office and grabbed Jarl around the throat with his arm, putting a hand over his mouth.

"Mmm mmmph!" Jarl protested against Kylar's hand.

"Quiet, it's me," Kylar whispered in his ear. Wary of Jarl shouting, he released his friend slowly.

Jarl rubbed his throat. "Damn, Kylar. Take it easy. How did you get in here?"

"I need your help."

"I'll say. I was just going to come looking for you."

"What?"

"Look in the top drawer. You can read it as fast as I could tell you," Jarl said.

Kylar opened the drawer and read the note. Roth was Roth Ursuul, a Khalidoran prince. He'd just been elected Shinga. Kylar was a suspect in the prince's murder. The king's men were looking for him. Kylar tossed the note aside.

"I need your help, just one more time, Jarl."

"Are you telling me you knew all that?"

"It doesn't change anything. I need your help."

"Is this going to get me killed?"

"I need to know where Momma K is hiding."

Jarl's eyes narrowed. "Do I need to ask why?"

"I'm going to kill her."

"After all she's done for you? You—"

"She betrayed me, Jarl, and you know it. She manipulated me into trying to kill Durzo Blint. She's so good, I thought it was my own idea."

"Maybe you should get her story before you kill her. Maybe murder shouldn't be your first resort against the people who've helped you," Jarl said.

"She convinced me that to save a friend, I had to kill Hu Gibbet, except that it wasn't Hu. It was Durzo. She betrayed us. She made me ruin a friend and take away everything he loves."

"I'm sorry, but I can't help you."

"I'm not asking," Kylar said.

"Are you going to beat it out of me?" Jarl asked.

"I'll do what I have to."

"She's hiding out," Jarl said, unafraid. "She had a terrible fight with Blint not long ago. I don't know what it was about. But she's helped me, and I won't betray her."

"You know she'd give you up in a second, Jarl."

"I know," Jarl said. "I might sell my body, Kylar, but I do what I can to keep the rest of me. I've only got a few shreds of dignity left. If you take those, you won't just be killing Momma K."

"It's one thing to say you'll keep a secret to the death. It's quite another to go through with it," Kylar said. "I've never tortured anyone, Jarl, but I know how."

"If you were going to torture me, you'd already have started, my friend."

They stared at each other until Kylar looked away, defeated.

"If you need help with anything else, I'll do it, Kylar. I hope you know that."

"I do." Kylar sighed. "Just be ready, Jarl. Things are going to happen faster than anyone expects."

There was a knock at the door.

"Yes?" Jarl asked.

A bodyguard poked his bald head in. "D—Durzo Blint to see you, sir." He looked terrified.

Kylar tried to draw on his Talent to cloak himself in shadows the way he had done when he came into the Blue Boar.

Nothing happened. *Oh, shit.* He practically dived behind Jarl's desk.

"Sir?" the bodyguard asked Jarl, not seeing Kylar through the crack of the door he had opened.

"Uh, show him in," Jarl said.

The door closed and soon opened once more. Kylar didn't dare to look. If he exposed enough of his face to be able to see Durzo, Durzo would see him.

"I won't waste your time or mine," Kylar heard Durzo say. Steps whisked softly across the floor and the desk groaned as someone sat on it. "I know you're Kylar's friend," Durzo said, only inches above Kylar.

Jarl made a sound of acknowledgment.

"I want you to get a message to him as soon as possible. I already sent him the message, but I need to make sure he gets it. Tell him I must speak with him. I'll be at the Tipsy Tart. I'll be there for the next two hours. Tell him it's *arutayro*."

"Spell that," Jarl said, moving to his desk and grabbing a quill from the inkpot.

Durzo spelled it, and then Jarl made a strangled sound of protest as Durzo must have grabbed him.

"Get it to him fast, rent boy. It's important. I'll hold you responsible if he doesn't get it." The desk protested again as Durzo got off it and walked out.

After the door closed, Kylar crawled out from under the desk.

Jarl's eyes widened. "You were under the desk?"

"Can't always be fancy."

Jarl shook his head. "You're unbelievable." As he wadded up the paper that had his note on it, he said, "What does *arutayro* mean?"

"Bloodless. It means we don't kill each other while we're meeting."

"And you trust him? After you tried to kill him last night?"

"Blint will kill me, but he'll do it professionally. He thinks I deserve that much. Mind if I use your window? I have a lot to do before I see him."

"Help yourself."

Kylar threw open the window, then turned to his friend. "I'm sorry. I had to try. I have to kill her and you were the fastest way to find her."

"Sorry I couldn't help."

Crawling out the window, Kylar moved out of Jarl's line of sight, then tried to draw the shadows again. This time it worked easily. *Perfect.* He couldn't even tell what he had done differently from what he did in the office.

By the Night Angels. Kylar figured that learning to control his Talent would have been hard enough if he had Durzo to explain it to him. Figuring it out on his own would be well-nigh impossible.

He moved back to the window. After a minute, Jarl checked the window, then walked to his desk and scrawled a quick note. He summoned a boy to his office and handed him the note.

Kylar circled around the building, and followed the boy after he came out a side door. He'd known Jarl wouldn't tell him—and he hoped his friend never figured out that Kylar had used him anyway.

The messenger boys were of uneven quality. Some of them made their passes so well that Kylar could barely follow them. Others simply held the letter out to the next boy.

It took a half hour for them to get to a small house on the east side. Kylar recognized the guard who took the message from the last boy. He was a Ymmuri with almond-shaped eyes and straight black hair. Kylar had seen the man at Momma K's house before. It was good enough. Momma K was here. Kylar would deal with her later.

He headed to the Tipsy Tart.

Durzo Blint was seated against a wall, with a wrapped bundle on the table. Kylar joined him, removed the sash from his waist, and set each of his weapons in it: the dagger and wakizashi that had been tucked into the sash, the Ceuran hand-and-a-half sword across his back, two daggers from his sleeves, throwing knives and darts from his waistband, and a tanto from one boot.

"That all?" Blint asked sardonically.

Kylar rolled up the sash and set it beside Blint's, which was just as large. "Looks like we'll both be working soon."

Blint nodded and set down mug of a foul Ladeshian stout exactly in the center of a board so that it didn't cross any of the cracks.

"You wanted to speak with me?" Kylar said, wondering why Blint was drinking. Blint never drank when he had to work.

"They have my daughter. They made threats. Credible threats. This Roth is a real twist."

"They'll kill her if you don't give them the ka'kari," Kylar guessed.

Blint only drank in response.

"So you have to kill me," Kylar said.

Blint stared him in the eye. It was a yes.

"Is it just the job, or did I fail?" Kylar asked, butterflies roaring in his stomach.

"Fail?" Blint looked up from the stout, snorted. "A lot of wetboys go through what we call the Crucible. Sometimes it's designed deliberately for journeymen wetboys who have some serious problem—anything that hinders a gifted apprentice from becoming a gifted wetboy. Sometimes, it happens to a wetboy after he's a master. It's one of the reasons there are so few old wetboys.

"My Crucible was Vonda, Gwinvere's little sister. We thought we were in love. We thought certain realities didn't apply to us. I became a wetboy with an obvious weakness and Garoth Ursuul kidnapped her. He was looking for a ka'kari, as he still is. So was I."

"I don't know what-all it does. I can't even use my Talent all the time. Can I use the ka'kari when I don't even have it in my possession?"

"Stop interrupting. This story has a point, and you should know better than to expect me to give you a tutorial on the very day I'm going to have to kill you," Durzo said. "Suffice it to say that the power of a ka'kari is vast. I'd been working for years to get one. Garoth Ursuul had been doing the same. He thought a ka'kari would give him an edge over the princes and the Vürdmeisters so he could become Godking. So he took Vonda and told me where he was holding her, and told me that if I went for the ka'kari, he'd kill her."

"You've never done well with threats," Kylar said.

"I think I've *always* done well with them," Durzo said. "The thing was, there was going to be a limited time to get the ka'kari. The man who'd allegedly bonded the ka'kari was on his death bed, so the time to get it would be immediately after he died. Naturally, Garoth had Vonda held way outside of town. I knew that the Sa'kagé was going to poison the man that night. I guessed that Garoth knew it too. I couldn't be two places at once, so I had to make a choice.

"I knew Garoth Ursuul. He's a master of traps. He's smarter than I am. More devious. So I guessed that if I went for Vonda, either the traps or meisters of his would kill me. I knew of one trap he'd used before that would use my entrance as a trap's trigger that would kill her. That was like him, turning my attempt to save Vonda into the very thing that killed her. Getting the ka'kari would just make a sweet deal sweeter for him. That was my Crucible, Kylar. Would I fling myself into a trap in an attempt to be a hero, or would I use my mind, give up Vonda for lost, and get the ka'kari?"

"You chose the ka'kari."

"It was a fake." Durzo studied the tabletop, and his voice shook. "Afterward, I sprinted, stole a horse, ran it to death, but it was half an hour after dawn when I got to the house where Vonda was. She was dead. I checked all the windows, but couldn't find any sign of traps. I'll never know if it's because he had someone remove them, or if they were purely magical, or if they were never trapped at all. The bastard. He did it on purpose." Blint took a long pull from his stout. "I'm a wetboy, and love is a noose. The only way to redeem my choice was to become the best wetboy ever."

Kylar felt a lump in his throat.

"That's why we can't have love, Kylar. That's why I did everything I could to keep you out of it. I made one mistake, let myself be weak one time, and now after all these years, it's come back to haunt me. You're not going to die because you failed, Kylar. You'll die because I did. That's the way things work. Others always pay for my failures. I failed, Kylar, because I thought you only go through the Crucible once. I was wrong. Life is the crucible."

From what Kylar could see, Durzo's choice had never stopped haunting him. The man was a shell. He was a legendary wetboy, but he'd sacrificed everything to that god. Kylar had always wanted to be Durzo, had always held his skills in awe. Durzo was the best, but where was the man beneath the legend?

"So my Crucible was Elene." Kylar chuckled on the hollowness inside him. "There's no way you'll fight with me, against them?"

"And let Roth torture and kill my daughter? Here's my choices, kid: You die or my daughter dies." Durzo pulled a gold gunder from a pouch. "Crowns Roth wins, castles I lose."

He flipped the coin. It bounced on the table and, impossibly, landed on edge.

"There's always another choice," Kylar said, slowly releasing his Talent. *Damn, it actually worked.*

Blint centered and re-centered his empty mug on the table. "I worked for almost fifteen years to get the Globe of Edges, Kylar. I didn't know where it was. I didn't know if it was bonded to someone. I didn't know what kind of magical defenses protected it. I knew people like you were supposed to call the ka'kari, and that your need for it would make the call stronger. That's why I took you on jobs in every corner of the city. How could I have known King Gunder had it and thought it was just jewelry? No one talked about it because no one knew it was special. No one cared. And I thought maybe I was wrong, that you just had a block. That if I pushed you enough, you'd use your Talent. After working for fifteen years, you think it'd be easy to just hand it over? You think it's easy to give away fifteen years of your life?"

"But you were going to." Kylar was amazed.

"Hell no. Once I had it, I'd never have given it away," Durzo said. But Kylar didn't believe him. Blint had been planning to give him the ka'kari all along—until Roth.

"Master, work with me. Together we can take Roth."

Durzo was silent for a few moments. "You know, I used to be like you, kid. For a long time. You should have known me back then. You would've liked me. We might have been friends."

I do like you, master. I'd like to be your friend, Kylar said, but only in his mind. Somehow those words wouldn't force their way past his lips. Maybe it didn't matter. Durzo wouldn't believe him anyway.

"Roth's a Khalidoran prince, kid. He's got a Vürdmeister. Soon he'll have more wytches than all the southlands have mages and an army to boot. He owns the Sa'kagé. There's no hope. There's no way to oppose him now. The Night Angels themselves wouldn't try it."

Kylar threw up his hands, fed up with Blint's fatalism and his superstitions. "Here I thought they were invincible."

"They're immortal. It's not the same thing." Blint popped a garlic clove. "You can take what you need from my place. I wouldn't want you to die just because I've got better gear."

"I won't fight you, master."

"You'll fight. You'll die. And I'll miss you."

"Master Blint?" he said, remembering something Dorian had said. "What does my name mean?"

" 'Kylar'? You know the word *cleave?*"

"To cut, right?" Kylar asked. "Like a meat cleaver."

"Yes, but it has another meaning, too. In old wedding ceremonies, a husband and wife were commanded to cleave together."

"Like cleavage?"

Blint smirked, but the dark cloud over him didn't shift. "Right. *Cleave* means both 'to come together' and 'to split apart.' Two opposite meanings. Your name's like that. It means one who kills and one who is killed."

"I don't understand," Kylar said.

"You will. May the Night Angels watch over you, kid. Remember, they have three faces."

"What?"

"Vengeance, Justice, and Mercy. They always know which to show. And remember the difference between vengeance and revenge. Now get out of here."

Kylar stood and stashed his weapons expertly. His hip brushed the table as he stood and the balanced coin wobbled and fell before he could reach out with his Talent again and stop it. He ignored it, refused to see it as an omen. "Master Blint," he said, looking his master in the eye and bowing, "*kariamu lodoc*. Thank you. For everything."

"Thank you?" Master Blint snorted. He picked up the coin. It was castles. *Castles I lose.* "Thank you? You always were the damnedest kid."

*K*ylar had an hour before Durzo came after him. He knew that because he'd watched Durzo drink a full mug of stout, and Durzo Blint wouldn't work when he had alcohol in him.

It was the perfect time to go to Master Blint's safe house. He might get lucky and be able to figure out how Master Blint intended to kill him from what tools were missing.

To be careful, he used the back alleys to get to the safe house. In short order, Kylar disarmed the trap on the lock, then searched for the second trap. If he'd been fully visible, he would have felt exposed, but his Talent obeyed him this time and covered him with shadows. He still had no idea how well he was concealed, but in the heavily shadowed and rarely traveled street, he felt comfortable taking his time. The second trap was embedded in the doorframe opposite the latch. Kylar shook his head. And Blint said he was no good at traps. Setting a trap which used the release of pressure from the bolt itself for a trigger was no easy feat.

Having disarmed that trap, Kylar started picking the lock. Blint had always told him that setting more than two traps on a door was a waste of time. You should get someone with the first trap, but if it was set so poorly that it made them overconfident, you might get them with a perfectly placed second trap. After that, only an idiot wouldn't check the door over so carefully that they'd find anything you could hide.

Kylar didn't have to fumble with the rake. He'd practiced on this door for years, so he pressed the tumbler in place almost instantly. Then he felt something wrong. He threw his fingers apart and dropped the rake just as the spring released. A black needle darted out between his spread fingers, grazing his knuckle and almost breaking the skin.

"Whew." The black compound on the needle was henbane and kinderperil. It wouldn't have been fatal, but it would make a person ill for days, and he wouldn't have had time to get far before the poison did its work on him. It was a nasty bit of business—and its presence meant that Master Blint was still testing him. *"Only an idiot wouldn't check the door over carefully after two traps." Gods.*

Kylar stepped inside carefully. This safe house wasn't as spacious as the one where he'd spent his first months with Master Blint, and with the animals in it, it had been terribly noisy, smelly, and dirty.

Now the animals were gone. Kylar scowled. A cursory examination told him they'd been here this morning.

Moving further in, Kylar saw a letter sitting on Durzo's desk. He drew a knife in each hand and opened the letter without touching it. He doubted Durzo would use a contact poison in the paper, but he hadn't thought the wetboy would put a third trap on the door, either.

"Kylar," it read in Durzo's tight, controlled script:

"Relax. Killing you with contact poison would be terribly unsatisfying. I'm glad the third trap didn't get you, but if you had used what you thought you knew about me instead of checking, you'd have deserved it.

"I'll miss you. You're the closest to family I'll ever have. I'm sorry I brought you into this life. Momma K and I did everything we could to make you a wetboy. I suppose it's to your credit that we failed. You mean more to me than I ever thought another person could."

Kylar blinked back tears. There was no way he could kill the man who'd written this. Durzo Blint was more than his master; he was his father.

"Tonight it ends," the letter continued. "If you want to save your friend, you'd better find me. —A Thorne"

A thorn? Well, Blint was certainly prickly enough to call himself a thorn, but he was also usually a good speller. And what did he mean about saving my friend? Did Durzo know where Elene was? Why was he threatening her? Or was he talking about Jarl? The blood drained from Kylar's face.

The animals were gone. Everything else Blint owned was still here, so he wasn't moving.

The animals would look fine to a cook, and the taste tester who tried the foods wouldn't be affected for hours—long enough for the foods to be served at a dinner.

Blint only drank after he finished a job.

The animals were gone. All of them. There weren't many places that could take all of them.

"Oh shit." Blint was poisoning the nobles at the Midsummer's banquet. Elene wouldn't be there, of course. Neither would Jarl. Blint must have known something he didn't. It must mean that Logan would be there.

Roth was attempting his coup. Tonight.

Kylar felt dizzy. He threw a hand down on the table to steady himself and set the glass vials and beakers to clinking against each other. His eyes raised to one he'd stared at for years. The asp poison was there. It was low. Blint had really meant the threats. For a while after talking with him at the arutayro, after seeing the letter, Kylar might have thought Blint wouldn't kill him. But he would. It was all professional for Blint. He'd crossed a line years ago when he let Vonda die, and there was no going back.

It was classic Durzo Blint. He was giving Kylar a chance now, giving him enough information so that he would show up, enough motivation so he'd fight, but when it came to the fight, Blint would do everything in his power to win. He always had.

Kylar's body knew what to do even though his mind was far away. He threaded cotton through the tiny holes on a tiny poisoner's knife and dripped asp venom on it.

Logan didn't like rabbit, so Kylar prepared the antidotes for the poisons they'd fed the pheasants and starlings and hoped that Logan didn't touch the pork. Alone, it wouldn't be fatal, but there was no antidote for it. If Logan got really sick, there was no way Kylar could carry him.

He scoured his body without soap so as to have as little scent as possible. He strapped knives to his bare forearms and a tanto to one calf. Pulled on his trousers and tunic, both tight, mottled black, made of Gandian cotton. Buckled his weapons harness. Checked the belt for his poisons and grappling hooks. Slid home the poisoner's knife in its special sheath. Slapped home daggers and his Ceuran hand-and-a-half sword.

Then he saw Retribution. Blint had left the big black sword on the wall. He'd left his favorite sword for Kylar. Doubtless, he'd make some quip about either taking it off his body, or if things went the other way, not needing it anymore.

He really means it. This is really to the death. Kylar lifted the sword reverently and strapped it to his back. It was heavier than he was used to using, but with his Talent, it would be perfect.

Finally ready, he walked to the door, then stopped. He put his head against the wood and just breathed, breathed. How had it come to this?

Tonight, either he or Master Blint would die. Kylar didn't even know what he was going to do when he got to the castle. But if he didn't do something, Logan would die.

51

*D*urzo crept along the rafters supporting the roof of Castle Cenaria's Great Hall, cloaked in shadows. His work had a lot of variety. He'd always liked that. But he'd never wanted to be a maid.

Yet somehow, he found himself pushing a damp rag over wood, scooping up dust meticulously, scooting forward slowly as he cleared each inch. Strangely enough, hovering fifty feet over the floor of the hall, the rafters hadn't been dusted recently. And Durzo hated being dirty.

Still, no matter how careful he was, he couldn't help but dislodge little clumps of dust from time to time—clumps that would puff out like clouds heavy with snow and drift downward, marking his otherwise invisible progress.

The nobles below, mercifully, weren't exactly staring at the ceiling. The festivities were in full swing. The events of the night before had brought out everyone. Voices drifted up to the rafters in a dull roar as men and women celebrated Midsummer's Eve and gossiped about what the king could possibly be doing. Obviously, the biggest morsel was what Logan was doing at the high table. Everyone knew he'd been arrested, and they couldn't keep their eyes off him. Why was he here?

For his part, Logan was sitting like a man doomed—which was exactly what Durzo suspected he was. Knowing Aleine, the king had summoned Logan so he could publicly humiliate him in front of all the peers of the realm. Maybe he'd announce Logan's death sentence. Maybe he'd have it carried out at the table.

Durzo moved again and dislodged a large clump of decades-old dust. He watched, helpless, as it spiraled down toward one of the side tables. Part of the clump broke apart in the air, but part of it hit the arm of a gesticulating noblewoman.

She brushed her arm and continued her story without a pause.

Brushing more dust and still moving slowly, Durzo gritted his teeth. He was slipping. Of course, he always told himself he was slipping. It kept him sharp. Maybe this time, though, he really was. Too much was happening. It was all too personal.

Durzo reached a joint where several beams came together to support the roof. There was no way to stay on top of the rafter and get past. He would have to go around or under. Whoever had designed these rafters hadn't had convenient skulking in mind.

Setting climbing hooks around each of his wrists, Durzo wedged his fingers where two beams came together at an angle. It was painful, but a wetboy learned to ignore pain. He swung out over space, letting his feet release the beam. He wondered what the fat noblewoman below him would think if her dinner were suddenly crushed by a falling shadow. He held his entire weight by his fingertips and used his weight to wedge his fingers deeper into the painful crack, then released his right hand and swung to grab the other side of the joint, past the solid surface where all the beams came together.

He had only his long reach to thank for making it. He got three fingertips into the crack on the far side of the beam. As he shifted his weight, the dust in the crack was just enough to slide his fingertips off.

Blint rolled his wrist forward as his fingers slipped. He dropped three inches, and then the wrist hook caught in the crack his fingers had just left. The hook held. Blint released his left hand and his body swung again—now he'd fall directly on the woman, instead of on her food. He pulled against the iron hook biting into his wrist and was able to reach high enough to grab with his fingers. He swung again, pulled out the hook, and grabbed the edge of the beam with his other hand.

He hung there, fingertips holding his entire weight from the same side of the beam, and the grip slick with an inch of dust. Had he thought he liked his work?

But with practiced grace, he swung sideways and caught the edge with a foot. Deftly, he wriggled back up onto the beam, ignoring the dust he pushed off the beam as he did so. Some risks you can't help.

And some you can. I haven't exactly minimized my risks, have I? Durzo tried not to think about it, but scooting along the beam acting like a cleaning lady didn't take his full attention. He'd given Kylar all the hints he needed to interrupt what Roth had planned here. And he'd given him motive to make sure he came here rather than leaving town. *It's bad luck, old boy.* But what was bad luck to him now? He was going to lose no matter what.

At the head table, the king stood. His face was flushed and he wobbled. He raised his glass. "My friends, my subjects, today is Midsummer's Eve. We have much to celebrate and much to mourn. I—words have abandoned me in light of what's happened in the last day. Our kingdom has endured the grievous loss of Catrinna Gyre and her entire household at the hands of her murderous husband, and the loss of our beloved prince." The king choked out the words and his emotion was so obvious that not a few eyes brimmed with equal tears. The prince had been young and dashing if unwise, and the Gyres had been respected for decades personally and for generations familially.

"Today we gather to celebrate Midsummer's Eve. Some might wonder why we celebrate in the shadow of such dark deeds. I'll tell you why. We wish to celebrate the lives of our loved ones, not yet mourn their deaths." On the king's left hand, Lord General Agon was nodding his head with grim approval. Durzo wondered how much of this speech was Agon's. Most of it, he suspected.

The king drank from his glass, forgetting that he was in the middle of a toast. The nobles throughout the room looked confused. Should they drink, or was the king not finished? Half chose each, but the king continued, gaining volume. "I'll tell you why we're here. We're here because *the bastards who murdered my boy aren't going to stop me.* They aren't going to get me. They aren't going to stop me from doing whatever the hell I please!"

Lord General Agon looked alarmed. Aleine IX had slipped into the first person singular from the royal plural. He must have had more to drink than was apparent.

"And I'll tell you what is our sovereign pleasure. There are schemers, plotters—traitors!—here tonight. Yes! And I swear to you traitors, you will die!" The king had gone purple with rage. "I know you're here. I know what you're doing! But it's fucking not going to fucking work!"

Well, look who learned a new word.

"No, sit down, Brant!" the king shouted as the lord general stood.

The nobles were stricken silent.

"Some of you have betrayed us to Khalidor. You've murdered our prince! You've killed my boy! Logan Gyre, stand!"

Serah Drake was sitting near the back according to her rank, but even from above, Durzo could see the terror on her face. She thought the king was going to have Logan executed publicly, and she wasn't alone.

Logan Gyre stood, shaken. He was handsome, and from what Durzo knew, formidable, and popular with both the assembled nobles and the small folk of the city.

"Logan," the king shouted, "You've been charged with my son's death. And yet here you are tonight, celebrating! Did you kill my boy?"

Several nobles cried out in alarm, shouting that Logan would never be involved in such a thing. The king's soldiers looked scared. They looked to Captain Arturian for guidance. He nodded and two guards stepped up beside Logan.

Well, Durzo thought, finally coming directly over the head table where the king and Logan were seated, if threats don't make Kylar want to kill me, this will. The innocent always lose.

"Let him speak!" the king roared. He let off a stream of curses, and the crowd quieted. The tension hung thick over them.

Logan spoke loudly and clearly. "Your Majesty, your son was my friend. I deny all charges."

The king was silent for a long moment. Then he said, "I believe you, Duke Gyre." He turned to the nobles. "Lord Gyre has been found blameless in our sight. Logan Gyre, will you serve your country at all costs?"

Durzo paused, as stunned as the nobles were.

"I will," Logan spoke clearly, but there was obvious tension in his face. His eyes had locked on Serah Drake's.

What the hell is going on? This had the feel of something scripted.

"Then Lord Gyre, we pronounce you Crown Prince of Cenaria, and we announce your marriage of this afternoon to our own daughter, Jenine. Logan Gyre, you shall be our heir until such time as an heir is born to our royal house. Do you accept this duty and this honor?"

"I do."

The apprehension in the Great Hall had turned to disbelief, then awe.

Jenine Gunder moved to stand beside Logan, looking as awkward as a fifteen-year-old can. Durzo heard a little cry from Serah Drake. Her hands flew up to her mouth. Then she fled. But nobody besides Logan and Durzo noticed, because even as she ran for the exit, a cheer broke out, rapidly spreading to every throat.

The king tossed off his wine, and the nobles joined his toast, saluting Logan. "Prince Gyre! Prince Gyre! Logan Gyre!"

The king sat, but the cheering continued. All eyes were on Logan and Jenine. The king looked irritated. That the nobles were chanting "Prince Gyre" instead of the traditional "Prince Logan" might have been simply because it was easier to chant, but it also drove home that Logan wasn't a Gunder—and everyone was happy about it.

Logan graciously if somewhat woodenly accepted the applause, nodding to his friends, then he blushed as his new wife took his hand. Her face glowed with embarrassment at her own boldness and adoration for her husband. The nobles loved it. But as the approval roared to a crescendo, the king looked more and more vexed.

And still, the cheering continued. The servants were cheering. The guards were cheering. It was as if the nobles felt a black cloud lifting from their futures. Not a few were saying, *"What a king Logan Gyre will make!"* Hurrahs rang out.

Aleine Gunder was turning purple again, but no one was paying him the slightest attention.

"Prince Gyre! Prince Gyre!"

"Long live Prince Gyre! Hurrah!"

The king jumped to his feet, apoplectic. "Now go! Go consummate this marriage," he shouted at Logan, who wasn't five paces away. Lord General Agon stood, but the king shoved him away roughly.

Logan looked at Aleine, shocked. The nobles quieted.

"Are you deaf?" the king shouted. "Go fuck my daughter!"

The princess turned white. So did Logan. Then she flushed red, mortified. She looked like she wanted to sink through the floor. At the same time, barely controlled rage washed over Logan's face in a crimson wave. The honor guards on either side of him looked stunned. Durzo wondered if the king had gone mad.

The nobles didn't make a sound. No one even breathed.

"Out! Get out! Go fuck. GO FUCK!" the king yelled.

Trembling, livid, Logan looked away and led his wife from the hall. The nervous guards followed.

"And the rest of you," the king said, "Tomorrow we mourn my son, and I swear that I'll find out who killed my boy if I have to string up the lot of you!"

The king sat abruptly and started weeping like a child. Durzo had frozen in place for the entire exchange. The nobles looked baffled, horrified. They slowly sat, staring at the king in silence.

Durzo's mind was racing. Roth hadn't foreseen this. Couldn't have. But Durzo was sure that Roth was in the castle, maybe in this very hall. A guard with one of the minor nobles was their signal man. If he took off his helmet, the coup was off.

It gave him a moment to digest what had just happened—not the king's madness, but Logan's marriage. It was a brilliant bit of intrigue. Now if the king were killed, instead of four houses having equal claims while Logan Gyre rotted in the Maw, Logan Gyre would clearly be the king. With his reputation and the endorsement of the Gunders, he would get quicker obedience from the noble houses than even King Gunder had.

It was a brilliant move, but it was too late. Roth had men throughout the castle. He probably couldn't afford to try again later. If the coup had been planned for tomorrow, Logan's marriage might have changed everything.

As it was, Logan and Jenine would just be added to the list of those who had to die.

As Durzo waited, it appeared that Roth agreed. A servant approached the signal guard and spoke with him. The man nodded and kept his hands off his helmet. The coup was on.

Whatever Roth would have to fix, it would involve killing Prince Logan Gyre now—who would be conveniently tucked away in the north tower where he'd be easy to find. Roth would probably want to assign that job to Durzo, but Durzo had no intention of giving the Khalidoran the chance. He would do what he had promised, but he wouldn't kill Kylar's friend.

During the first course, the nobles had already eaten the rabbits Durzo had prepared. He'd been feeding those rabbits hemlock for a year. The amount in a portion was a small enough dose that nothing would happen to the diners unless they'd also eaten the starling appetizers. In less than a half hour, the nobles would feel ill. Hemlock poisoning started peacefully enough. Already, the nobles' legs should be losing feeling. If anything, they might notice that their legs felt heavy. Soon, the feeling would spread up. Then they'd start vomiting. Anyone unlucky enough to have eaten seconds would begin convulsing.

The timing now was tricky. Poisoning wasn't an exact science, and someone might notice something amiss at any time. Durzo needed to act before that happened.

He secured one end of his rope to the beam. It was black silk—ridiculously expensive, but the slenderest and least visible rope Durzo owned. Fixing the harness he'd designed specifically for this mission, Durzo wrapped the rope through it and slid off the beam.

Steadying his swaying against the beam, Durzo looked down at his target. The king was directly below him. Durzo tucked in his knees and folded over. The harness bit into his shoulders, and he let out slack, slipping down toward the floor, head first.

Now timing was everything. In one hand, Durzo held the rope. By adjusting its position and tension against the harness, he could dive quickly toward the floor or stop easily. When he moved, he would need to move quickly: he was shrouded in shadows so that he was barely visible, but he couldn't shroud the rope.

In a room this cavernous, a rope swaying above the king as if holding weight would be noticed. The king's guards were good. Vin Arturian made sure of that.

With his other hand, Durzo pulled out two tiny pellets. Both were compounds from various mushrooms. Durzo had been able to make the pellets tiny, but they didn't dissolve quickly and for this job he couldn't use a powder.

The nobles were still silent. The king was barely crying now, but he noticed the nobles looking at him.

"What are you staring at?" he shouted. He cursed them roundly. "This is my daughter's wedding feast! Drink, damn you! Talk!" The king drained his wine again.

The nobles pretended to be talking, and soon that pretense became a furor of speculation. Durzo imagined that they were wondering if the king had lost his mind. He wondered the same himself.

He wondered what they'd think after the king drank his next goblet of wine.

A servant came and filled the king's goblet. The king's cupbearer sipped the wine first and swished it around his mouth. Then he gave it to the king who set it down on the table with a thump.

"Your Majesty," Lord General Agon said at the king's left hand. "May I have a word with you?"

The king turned and Durzo pushed the rope forward. He dropped like a bolt. Ten feet above the table, he pulled the rope back and jerked to a stop. Ten feet was still a long way to drop something so light, but he'd been practicing. But as he tightened the rope, it twisted, and suddenly, he was spinning. Not fast, but spinning.

It didn't matter. There was no time to try again.

The first pellet splashed solidly in the center of the king's goblet. The second hit the edge and tinged off. The pellet rolled several inches across the table by the king's plate.

Durzo coolly drew another pellet and dropped it in.

The king picked up the goblet and was about to drink when Lord General Agon said, "Your Majesty, perhaps you've had enough to drink." He reached a hand to take the goblet from the king.

Durzo didn't waste time seeing what the king would do. He drew a short tube from his back and looked beyond Agon to the king's mage, Fergund Sa'fasti. He saw the man, but the rope spun him away before he could shoot the blow dart.

He was trying for a leg shot. His hope was that the hemlock would have deadened the mage's legs enough that he wouldn't even notice the sting. But on the next rotation, he didn't have a clear shot because the king and the lord general were gesticulating wildly.

Damn robes! The mage's robes left barely six inches of his calf visible. Durzo came around again and abandoned the calf shot. The mage had shifted his feet and Durzo only had one of the darts—whatever they were baited with, it was a Khalidoran secret that was supposed to disable the mage's magical abilities.

Durzo puffed on the blowgun. The dart stuck into the mage's thigh.

He saw a brief flash of irritation on the man's face. The mage reached down toward his thigh—and was jostled by the Sa'kagé servant. "Sorry, sir. More wine?" the man asked the mage, snatching the dart. He was good. With hands like that, he must be one of the best cutpurses in the city. But of course, Roth would only use the best.

"Mine's full, you idiot," the mage said. "You're supposed to serve the wine, not drink it."

Durzo flipped over and scrambled up the rope, not an easy feat with silk. He rested when he got onto the beam. He had no idea if the king had drunk the wine or not. But his part was done. The only thing to do now was wait.

Drink yourself blind, then," Agon said. He didn't care if the king heard him. He didn't care if the king killed him.

Just when I thought I could deal with this bastard. He disgraces his own daughter and shames a man who's given everything he loves to serve the throne.

Agon had been able to steer the king through the marriage of Logan Gyre and Jenine Gunder, but the king had hated the idea. He was jealous of Logan's looks and intelligence, jealous of how much people approved of his choice, and angry that Jenine had been excited to marry Logan rather than resigned to it.

But if Agon had done one valuable thing in his ten years of serving this hell-spawned brat, it had been convincing the king to appoint Logan crown prince.

Not that Logan would ever forgive him, but it was for the good of the realm. Sometimes duty required a man to do things he would do almost anything to avoid. It had been duty that had compelled Agon to serve

Aleine IX, and only duty. Like Agon, Logan wasn't a man who would shirk his duty, but also like Agon, that didn't mean he had to like it.

Logan would probably hate Agon for it for the rest of his life, but Cenaria would get a good king. With Logan's intelligence, popularity, and integrity, the country might even become something more than a den of thieves and murderers. Agon was willing to pay the price, but it didn't sit well with him. He'd seen himself in Logan's eyes—realizing he was pledged to a destiny he would never have chosen. He'd seen the look on Serah Drake's face. Logan would live with the guilt of that betrayal for the rest of his life. The sight had seared him. Agon had barely been able to touch his food tonight.

The king tossed back the rest of his wine. The nobles were still buzzing. It wasn't the pleasant hum of conversation usual at Midsummer's Eve. Their tones were hushed, their glances furtive. Everyone offered an opinion on what the king was doing, why he would appoint an heir and then insult him in the same breath.

It was madness.

Slowly, the king emerged from his tears and silence. He stared around the Great Hall with hate-filled eyes. His lips moved, but Agon had to lean close to hear what he was saying. He wasn't surprised to hear the king muttering curses, one after another, droning on and on, mindless in his rage.

Then the king burst out laughing. The hall quieted once more, and the king laughed louder. He pointed at one of the nobles, an unassuming count named Burz. Everyone followed the king's finger and stared at Count Burz.

The count stiffened and reddened, but the king said nothing. His attention wandered and he stared cursing to himself again. For long moments, nobles continued staring at Count Burz, then looked at the king.

Then Chancellor Stiglor, who was seated at the head table, stood up with a cry and shouted, "There's something in the food!" The chancellor tottered and collapsed back into the chair, his eyes rolling up in his head.

Next to him, a man the king had always hated, Lord Ruel, suddenly slumped forward. His face smacked into his plate and he lay still.

The king laughed. Agon turned to him. The king wasn't even looking at Lord Ruel, but the timing couldn't have been worse.

Someone cried, "We're poisoned!"

"The king has poisoned us!"

Agon turned to see who had shouted, but he couldn't tell. Had a servant said it? Surely no servant would dare.

Another voice took up the shout, "The king! The king's poisoned us!"

Laughing, the king jumped to his feet and stumbled drunkenly. He shouted obscenities as the Great Hall erupted in chaos. Chairs squeaked as lords and ladies stood. Some of them wobbled and fell. An old lord started retching onto his plate. A young lady collapsed, vomiting.

Agon was on his feet, shouting orders to the soldiers.

The side door by the head table burst open and a man in Gyre livery pushed in, holding his hands up to show he was unarmed. His livery was torn and bloody. A gash bled beside his eyes, streaming blood down his face.

Gyre livery? None of Logan's servants were here tonight.

"Treachery!" the servant shouted. "Help! Soldiers are trying to murder Prince Logan! The king's soldiers are trying to murder Prince Logan! We're outnumbered. Please help!"

Agon turned to the king's guards, drawing his sword. "There has to be some mistake. You, you, and you, come with me." He turned to the bleeding messenger, "Can you take us to the—"

"No!" the king bellowed, his laughter instantly turning to rage.

"But sire, we have to protect—"

"You will not take my men. They will stay here! You will stay here! And you, Brant! You're mine. Mine! Mine!"

To Agon, it seemed he saw the king for the first time. He'd seen Aleine IX as a foul, wicked child for so long that he'd forgotten what a foul, wicked child with a crown could do.

Agon looked to the king's guards. Disgust was written on their faces. He could tell they ached to go defend Logan, their prince, but duty forbade them from disobeying their king.

Logan, their prince.

Suddenly, it became so simple. Duty and desire became one for the first time in years. "Captain Arturian," Agon barked in his command voice, so that every royal guard heard him. "Captain! What's your duty if the king dies?"

The squat man blinked. "Sir! My duty would be to protect the new king. The prince."

"Long live the king," Agon said.

The king was staring at him, confused. His eyes widened as Agon's sword swung back.

Aleine was halfway through a curse when Agon's sword struck his head off.

King Aleine Gunder IX's corpse hit the table and knocked over chairs before coming to rest on the floor.

Before any of the guards could attack him, Agon raised his sword over his head with both hands.

"I'll answer for this, I swear. Kill me if you must, but now your duty is to the prince. Save him!"

For a second, none of them moved. The rest of the panic in the hall seemed far away. The ladies screaming, men shouting, servants armed only with meat knives trying to defend their retching lords, shouts of "Treachery!" and "Murder!" ringing in the air.

Then Captain Arturian shouted, "The king is dead; long live the king! To the prince! To King Gyre!"

Together, Agon, the king's guards, and a dozen knife-wielding nobles ran from the Great Hall.

Before Kylar got within sight of West Kingsbridge, he slowed to a walk. He willed himself to be a shadow, and looked at himself. He looked like a raggedly cut piece of darkness. That was good; Durzo had told him that the ragged edges obscured the humanness of his figure and made a wetboy harder to recognize. Kylar thought that his Talent would also be muffling his steps—he wanted it to—but he had no idea if it was. He couldn't afford to find out the hard way.

He rounded the corner and saw the guards. West Kingsbridge was controlled with a large gate like the castle's own gates. Hand-thick oak reinforced with iron, twenty feet high and spiked along the top, with a smaller gate inset. The big, mailed guards looked nervous. One was fidgeting, awkwardly turning his whole head to look to the sides. The other was more calm, pointedly staring every direction except down to the river. Kylar came closer. He recognized the men despite their helmets, and not only because the twins had matching lightning bolt tattoos on their faces. They were bashers, and good ones: Lefty—he was the one with the crooked nose—and Bernerd.

Kylar looked where Bernerd wasn't looking. In the darkness, an unwieldy barge squatted on the river like a beached sea cow. Its doors were open, but no one held any lights. But darkness no longer affected Kylar's eyes. If he'd had more time, he would have marveled about that—as night fell, if anything his vision improved as the shadows became more uniform.

Through the open doors of the barge, he saw rank upon rank of soldiers. Each wore Cenarian livery, but with a red kerchief tied around one arm. Common soldiers with kerchiefs on their left, officers with them on their right.

The soldiers weren't Cenarian. Under their helmets, secreted in the shadows of the night, Kylar saw the stark, cold features of northmen: hair as black as a raven's wing and eyes as blue as frozen lakes. They were big, raw-boned men, weathered and hardened from exposure to the elements and battle. So they weren't just Khalidorans. They were Khalidoran high-landers, the Godking's fiercest, most elite troops. All of them.

In daylight, that would be obvious to any Cenarian in the castle. But at night, it would take time for the Cenarian soldiers to realize that they were being attacked by a foreign enemy. The Cenarian soldiers would figure out that the armbands were what the Khalidorans were using to identify each other, but it would take time. Each new group that encountered the Khalidorans would have to learn it for themselves.

Kylar saw another barge pulling up the river, only a hundred paces away. Khalidoran highlanders tended to be broader and deeper of chest than most Khalidorans, and while a few free tribes still held out in the mountains, those who had been absorbed into the empire had become its most feared fighters.

Four or five hundred highlanders. Kylar couldn't tell, but he guessed that the other barge was full of the elite soldiers too. If so, Khalidor meant to take the castle tonight. The rest of the country would crumple like a body deprived of its head.

Several wytches were talking as they climbed the switchbacks from the water up to the bridge. They were scanning the sky over the castle, apparently looking for some sign.

Indecision held Kylar frozen. He had either to get inside to save Logan—surely Roth would have either Hu or Durzo kill all the dukes, especially after all of Logan's fighting on the Khalidoran border. Just as surely, the murder would happen shortly, if it hadn't already. Kylar could go inside and try to stop the hit, or could try to oppose the Khalidorans out here.

By myself? Madness.

But just watching the barge pull closer to the bridge made him furious. He knew he should feel no loyalty to Cenaria, but he was loyal to Logan and Count Drake. If this army got into the castle, it would be a massacre.

So he needed to fight inside and outside. Great.

Kylar looked at the Sa'kagé impostors manning the bridge. Bashers wouldn't know or care about the bridge's defenses, much less have the discipline to dismantle them. All they had done was turn the crank that lifted the massive iron river gate.

Then, in the sky above the castle, Kylar saw a long arc of blue-green flame. He started walking.

The wytches looked pleased. They conferred with an officer, who started barking orders. One of the Khalidorans raised a torch and waved it twice. Lefty and Bernerd took torches of their own, walked to either side of the bridge, and waved twice.

All clear. Right.

Kylar drew Retribution. As it hissed out of the scabbard, the bashers turned. Lefty blinked and leaned forward. With the torches in their hands blotting out their night vision, all they saw was a thin strip of dark metal bobbing and floating through the air. Then it moved with terrible speed.

In a moment, both men were dead. Kylar replaced the torch he'd plucked from Bernerd's hand and checked the men on the barges. They had already formed up and were walking, single-file, up the narrow switchbacks that led to the bridge.

Grabbing the keys off Bernerd's body, Kylar opened the gate and slipped through the inset door. The crank and the release for the river gate were there. The gate itself was simply a massive, counterweighted portcullis that could drop into the water. In this case, onto a ship.

Kylar threw the release. The river gate dropped two feet—and didn't crunch. It *clanged*. Kylar looked over the side of the bridge. The river gate had slammed down onto magical stops that glowed and sparked in the darkness. Wytches were on the deck of the first barge, shouting.

He ran into the guard station. There was a fire pit with a cauldron full of stew, cooking paraphernalia, a helmet, several cloaks, chests for the men's personal belongings, and a set of knucklebones on the low table. There was a closet full of old broad carpets stuffed in fat buckets.

Kylar rushed out of the guard station. Surely the king wouldn't have left his military bridge with only that defense. The pilings of the bridge were wood sheathed in iron—impervious to fire. The sheathed wood still got wet, but couldn't breathe and release the water it absorbed, so every beam rotted within years and had to be replaced.

Why would the king be so particular about fire?

And then Kylar saw why. Along either side of the bridge were long wooden beams set on pivots. On the end of each beam was a huge clay globe as wide as Kylar was tall. At least part of the clay was molded over iron because a mooring rope was tied to an iron loop at the top of the globe. Several small handles also protruded from the sides.

Pulling on one handle, Kylar found a bracket. As he slid it out, a wash of oil fumes swept over his face.

It took him several precious seconds of staring at the entire contraption to understand. The arms would swing out over the side of the bridge, holding the globes full of oil, then drop them onto any boat passing underneath—and hopefully set it on fire in spectacular fashion.

He rushed back to the gate and grabbed the torches the guards had been carrying. He closed and locked the gate quickly. The advance party of Khalidorans were almost to the bridge.

What am I doing?

The first barge was just starting under the bridge. There was no time. Kylar kicked a safety latch holding the beam in place and pushed on it. It didn't move. He stumbled and almost tripped over taut ropes at his feet, cursed, and flung himself against the beam again. Hadn't the damned soldiers ever greased this thing?

Finally it occurred to him to use his Talent. He felt power flowing through him—he could lift a wagon on his back. He pressed against the beam and could feel himself shimmering, the ragged black covering and uncovering his skin as he redirected his Talent.

If I'm lucky, they won't even know I'm here until it's too late.

A ball of crackling green wytchfire flew over the globe, missing it by a yard. Yells sounded from below. Whether the wytches saw Kylar or just his torches, they weren't pleased.

Kylar pushed against the beam, but with nothing to brace his feet against, he just slid across the planks. The beam barely moved.

A ball of wytchfire caromed off the globe and ricocheted up into the sky. Kylar ignored it. Something white was blooming above the deck of the barge—now directly under him. A small creature took shape in front of a red-haired wytch and started flying up like a hummingbird. The wytch chanted, his vir-marks thick with power, directing the creature.

Kylar heaved and the ropes at his feet tripped him hard.

The homunculus took shape as it zoomed toward Kylar. It was small, barely a foot tall, and pasty pale. It wore the likeness of the red-haired wytch like ill-fitting clothes. It landed on the globe gently and then rammed steely claws into the iron as if it were butter. It turned to Kylar and hissed, baring its fangs.

Kylar scuttled back and almost fell off the edge of the bridge.

A concussion thudded below. The air in front of the red-haired wytch rippled like a pond absorbing the shock of a thrown rock. Something was moving as if it were just under the surface of the air. Something huge. Reality itself seemed to be stretching—

And tearing. Kylar saw hell and rushing skin as reality itself ripped under the pressure of the wyrm's passage.

It was coming for him.

Twenty feet from him, reality frayed and tore. Kylar had one glimpse of a gigantic, lamprey-like circular mouth. It seemed to throw its mouth inside out in a spiny cone. Then the narrowest ring of teeth hit the homunculus and the teeth snapped in the opposite direction, tearing into the pasty creature. Each successive circle of teeth pulled and snapped onto everything surrounding the homunculus with hideous strength, the cone inverting, sucking everything in.

The last, widest row of teeth snapped closed on the widest part of the iron globe and the pit wyrm whipped back into its hole as suddenly as it had emerged. The air rippled again and then faded as if nothing had happened.

The homunculus was gone. So was three quarters of the globe, clay crunched and iron sheered off as if it were lard. Oil dribbled onto the water beside the barge. The soldiers cheered. The first barge had passed the bridge, and the second barge was just emerging.

Feeling weak, Kylar scooted back and almost fell on ropes again. He cursed loudly. Then his eyes followed the ropes. They were connected to a pulley system—attached to the beam.

"I'm an *idiot!*" Grabbing a rope, Kylar pulled it hand over hand as fast as he could. The arm supporting the second globe swung out over the side of the bridge smoothly and easily. Kylar heard a yell, and two green missiles flew past.

Next to the pulley, there was another rope. Thin. Probably important.

Kylar yanked it and the beam holding the clay globe suddenly dropped. The globe dropped with it. For a moment, Kylar was afraid that he'd just dropped his only weapon straight into the water, but the mooring rope swung the globe like a pendulum a foot above the river. The globe slammed into the second barge at the waterline.

There was no explosion. The side of the boulder that struck the barge was iron beneath a patina of fired clay. It burst through the side of the barge as if the hull were birchbark and blasted through crowded ranks of highlanders.

The rest of the globe was clay. It disintegrated. The oil that filled the globe splashed violently over men and their gear, soaking the wood decks.

Kylar looked at the barge from above. A nice hole gaped at the waterline and the men inside were screaming, but he'd hoped for something more impress—

BOOM!

The barge exploded. Flames leaped out of the hole the globe had made and tore it to three times its original size. Fire burst from the portholes. The doubled and redoubled screams of men were swallowed in the sudden roar of flames.

Men who'd been standing on the deck of the ship were thrown off their feet, and not a few of them into the water. Their armor dragged them hopelessly under the gentle waves.

As quickly as it had sprung up, the gush of fire disappeared. Smoke continued to roll out of the portholes, and men were streaming up onto the deck. The barge listed heavily. An officer, bleeding from a gash on his head, was bellowing orders, but to no avail. Soldiers leapt from the deck to swim for the shore that looked so close—and dropped like rocks. The water wasn't deep, but with heavy armor, it was deep enough.

Having paused for several moments to turn from feeding on oil to feeding on wood, the fire advanced again like an insatiable beast. Fire roared up out of every deck on the ship, and even as the barge drifted forward, Kylar saw that it wasn't going to make it to shore. A few men had the sense to tear off their armor before they leaped overboard, and others were clinging to bridge pilings, but at least two hundred highlanders would never fight on Cenarian soil.

The gate behind Kylar shook as something struck it. He cursed himself. He shouldn't have stayed, shouldn't have watched while he could have been running.

No Cenarian soldiers had come running during his battle, and weren't coming even now, two minutes after the first signal. However bad this was, whatever was happening at the castle must be worse.

The gate blew apart and wytches aglow with power strode through its smoking remains.

Kylar ran for the castle.

53

*W*ith Neph Dada and a dozen soldiers in Cenarian livery trailing behind him, Roth sprinted across the catwalk. He reached a small room, turned right, and pounded up a narrow set of stairs.

It was a dizzying maze of corridors, walkways, and service stairs, but it would get Roth and his men to the north tower twice as fast as any other route. Time was of the essence. So many plans that Roth had planted, watered, and coaxed into bloom over the past years were bearing fruit tonight. Like a greedy child, he wanted to taste every one and let the bloody juices spill down his chin.

The queen and her two younger daughters were dying right now, Roth realized with regret. It was too bad. Too bad he wouldn't get to see it. He hoped nobody would move the bodies before he could come inspect them. He'd given orders, but though he trusted Hu Gibbet to carry them out meticulously, this was a war. There was no telling what would happen.

There was no help for it, though. There was no way he would have missed watching the king die.

How exquisite that was! If Roth hadn't been dodging around corners, he'd have burst out laughing.

He'd planned to have a bolt cranked in his crossbow and pointed at the king's forehead all night. He'd planned to be the one to kill the king himself, but Captain Arturian's security had been too tight. Roth had been able to get into the Great Hall, but he hadn't been able to bring a weapon. It had been a small disaster. If Durzo Blint hadn't come through for him, the entire plot would have failed. Father would have killed him.

But it didn't fail. Durzo had come through for him, and what a virtuoso performance it had been. The poisoning of the guests had been brilliant. Roth had been in the kitchens as the food tasters had tried every dish, and not a one had even been ill. The delivery of the king's poison had been a marvel of athleticism. The concoction itself had worked even better than Blint had promised. Roth would find more work for that man. With Durzo as his tool, Roth would dispense such exquisite agonies as he'd never before imagined. Herbs! He'd never even thought of their potential. Durzo would be just the one to guide him in all their uses. Who would have imagined that herbs given to the king would push Agon over the edge?

He had positively giggled when the lord general had relieved the fool king of his head. It had been better than doing it himself. He'd never had the particular thrill of watching a man commit what he himself must have seen as treason. There was something very fine about seeing a man damn himself.

Roth and his men had tarried in the Great Hall just long enough to see that the lord general and his men had taken the bait and were on their way, and then they had run.

If he had planned this right—and Roth planned everything right—he'd taste even finer fruits than Agon's betrayal tonight. Father would be so pleased.

Six hundred of the Godking's elite highlanders were to arrive at the castle within the next half hour. A thousand more would arrive at dawn. The king had told Roth that he wanted to lose less than half of those by the time he arrived with an occupying army the next day.

Roth thought he would lose less than a quarter. Perhaps far less. He'd pass his *uurdthan* brilliantly. The Godking would appoint Roth King of

Cenaria, and take the title of High King for himself. In time, he'd pass the entire empire to Roth.

Pushing future glories from his mind, Roth came to a stop in the last narrow corridor as his men caught up. The door before him would open on unseen hinges into the stairway at the bottom of the north tower. Roth motioned to his men.

They slammed the hidden door open and burst into the hall, swords flashing. The two honor guards posted at the base of the tower didn't stand a chance. They barely had time to register surprise before they were dead.

"We hold this door. Agon doesn't go upstairs," Roth said. "The prince and princess are next." He checked his crossbow.

Logan sat on the edge of the bed, waiting. He closed his eyes and rubbed his temples. He was, for the moment, alone in the bedchamber at the top of the north tower. Jenine Gunder—no, Jenine *Gyre*—had left him to get ready.

To get ready.

Logan felt ill. He'd fantasized about lovemaking, of course, but he'd done his best to confine his desires to one woman—and that woman wasn't Jenine.

When Serah had accepted his proposal, he'd thought his fantasies were going to come true. They'd been planning their wedding just this morning.

Now this.

He heard the soft scuff of bare feet on rug and looked up. Jenine's hair was down, curling luxuriantly halfway down her back. She wore a silky, translucent white gown and an anxious smile. She was breathtaking. Every hint her evening gown had given last night—gods! was that only last night?—was fulfilled, every sensuous promise exceeded. Logan's eyes drank in her curves, her hips sweeping to a narrow waist, waist swelling to those perfect breasts, curve yielding to curve with the sweetness that inspired art. He feasted on the gold of her skin in the candlelight, the darker circles of her nipples showing faintly through her gown, the flutter of her pulse at her throat, the bashfulness in her stance. He wanted her. He wanted to take her. Lust roared through him, dimming the rest of the room, swallowing all the world except the beauty before him and his thoughts of what he was about to do.

He looked away. Ashamed. A lump swelled in his throat and cut off his breath.

"Am I so ugly?" she asked.

He looked up and saw her arms crossed over her breasts, instant tears in her eyes. Pained, he looked away again.

"No. No, my lady. Please, come here."

She didn't move. It wasn't enough.

Logan met her eyes. "Please. You're so pretty, so, so beautiful you bewilder me. You make me ache. Come sit with me. Please."

Jenine sat next to him on the bed, close, but not touching him. Logan had known little about her before today. Even his father had considered her too rich a match for him. He only knew that she was well-liked, "sunny," "settling down," and not yet sixteen. Logan could understand "sunny." She'd practically glowed at dinner—until her father had spoken. The bastard. Logan understood now a little of how his father must have felt, seeing the woman he loved married to that.

The term "settling down" had been applied to Jenine's brother, too. For the prince, it had meant that people thought he was finally leaving off his more obvious wenching and starting to assume some of the responsibilities of ruling. But Logan imagined that for Jenine, "settling down" probably meant she didn't play tag in the castle anymore.

She was so different from Serah—and she was his wife.

"I'm—I was engaged to another woman this morning. A woman I loved for years...I still love her, Jenine. Can I call you that?"

"You may call me whatever pleases you, my lord husband." Her voice was chilly. He'd hurt her. She was hurt, and for all the wrong reasons. Damn, she was young. But then, he hadn't been the only one who'd been handed a lot of surprises in the last day.

"Have you ever been in love, Jenine?"

She considered his question with more gravity than he would have expected from a fifteen-year-old. "I've...liked boys."

"It's not the same," Logan snapped. He regretted his tone instantly.

"Are you going to cheat on me?" She shot right back. "With her?"

It hit Logan between the eyes. This couldn't be easy for Jenine, either. How must she feel, liking him, marrying him, knowing he was in love with someone else? Logan put his face in his hands. "I swore our wedding vows because the king asked me to, because the nation needed it. But I swore those vows, Jenine. I will be faithful to you. I will do my duty."

"And your duty to produce an heir?" she asked.

The chill hadn't thawed at all. He should have known better, but he answered. "Yes."

She flopped on the bed, pulled her gown up roughly, and spread her legs. "Your duty awaits, my lord," she said, turning her face away, staring at the wall.

"Jenine—look at me!" He covered her nakedness and—thank the

gods—looked only at her face as he spoke, though even now her body cried out to him. It made him feel like an animal. "Jenine, I will be as good a husband as I can. But I can't give you my heart. Not yet. I look at you and, and I feel wrong for wanting to make love to you. But you're my wife! Dammit, it would be easier if you weren't so—so damn beautiful! If I could just look at you without wanting to—to do what we're supposed to do tonight. Do you understand?"

She obviously didn't, but she sat back up and folded her legs under her. Abruptly she was a girl again, blushing for what she'd just done, but her eyes intent.

Logan threw his hands up. "I don't blame you. I don't understand it myself. It's all so twisted up. Nothing makes sense since Aleine—"

"Please, don't talk about my brother tonight. Please?"

"I've lost everything. Everything's . . . everything's wrong." How could he be so selfish? He'd lost a friend, but she'd lost her big brother. She must be aching, too. "I'm sorry," he said.

"No. I'm sorry," Jenine said, her eyes teary but her gaze steady. "I've known for my whole life that I'd be married to whomever the country needed me to marry. I've tried not to even have crushes because I knew that my father might tell me any day that he needed me. I've been trying *not* to like you for two years. I know you think I'm a silly girl, but do you know who some of my potential husbands were? A Ceuran prince who likes boys, another who's sixty, an Alitaeran who's six, a Lodricari who doesn't speak our language and already has two wives, Khalidorans who treat their women as chattel, and a Modaini who's been twice widowed under suspicious circumstances.

"Then there was you. Everyone likes you. A good king would have made the match to heal the split between our families, but my father hates you. So I had to watch you, hear stories about you from my brother and from all the other girls, hear that you're brave, you're honorable, you're loyal, you're smart. My brother told me that you were the only man he knew who wouldn't be intimidated by my mind. Do you know what it's like to have to use small words and pretend not to understand things so you don't get a *bad reputation?*"

Logan wasn't sure he understood. Surely women never had to pretend not to be stupid. Did they?

"When I found out I was marrying you," Jenine said, "it felt like all my little-girl dreams were coming true. Even with my father behaving like— and Serah—and Aleine . . ." She took a deep breath. "I'm sorry, my lord husband. You've been honest with me. I know you didn't ask for this. I'm sorry you had to lose her so I could have you. I know you've had a lot of bad surprises recently." Her chin raised and she spoke like a princess. "But I'm going to do all I can to be a good surprise, my lord. I'm going to strive to be worthy of your love."

By the gods, what a woman! Logan had looked at Jenine last night and seen breasts. He had seen her giggling with her friends and seen a child. He was a fool. Jenine Gunder—Jenine Gyre—was a princess born to be a queen. Her poise, her deliberate self-sacrifice, her *strength* awed him. He had hoped his wife might grow to become a good match for him. Now, he hoped that he might grow to become a match for this woman.

"And I'll do all I can to make our love grow, Jenine," Logan said. "I just—"

She put a finger on his lips. "Will you call me Jeni?"

"Jeni?" Logan touched the soft smooth skin of her cheek, and let his eyes roam over her body. *I'm allowed to do this. I can do this. I should do this.* "Jeni? May I kiss you?"

She abruptly became an uncertain girl again, until their lips met. Then, even with all her hesitations, uncertainty, and naïveté, to Logan she was all that was warm and soft and beautiful and loving in the world. She was all that was woman, and she was altogether lovely. His arms circled her and he pulled her close.

Some minutes later, Logan pulled away from her on the bed, turning his head toward the door.

"Don't stop," she said.

Hob-nailed boots pounded up the stairs outside the door. Lots of boots.

Not even pausing to pull on his clothes in the darkness, Logan rolled off Jenine and caught up his sword.

54

Regnus Gyre ducked back into a hallway as Brant Agon ran past with a dozen royal guards, and inexplicably, a few fat nobles.

"Long live the king! To the prince!" one of them yelled.

To the prince? The rumors must have been wrong then. Regnus had heard that Aleine Gunder had been murdered last night.

Had the lord general been alone, Regnus would have called out to his old friend, but not with Vin Arturian there. Vin was duty-bound to arrest Regnus, and he would, even if he didn't like it.

There was shouting in the distance, toward the center of the castle, but Regnus couldn't make out any words. Having so much happening that he didn't understand made him anxious, but he could do nothing about whatever was happening elsewhere in the castle. He only had six men, none of them in armor. It had been hard enough to smuggle themselves in as servants and still bring swords. All he could hope to do was find Nalia and get her out of here.

The queen's chambers were on the second floor of the castle in the northeast quarter. Regnus and his men had been walking through the castle nonchalantly, in two groups of three, trying not to attract the servants' attention, but now he gestured sharply. His men gathered around him, and he started jogging.

They got to the queen's chamber without running into a single servant or guard. It was unbelievably good luck. Against even a pair of royal guards, who would be armed and armored, Regnus and his unarmored men might all have died.

Regnus pounded on the great door, and then opened it. A lady-in-waiting who'd been about to open the door fell back in surprise.

"You!" she said. "Milady, run! Murderer!"

Nalia Gunder was seated in a rocking chair, embroidery obviously untouched in her lap. She stood immediately, but waved the servant off. "Don't be a fool. Begone." Her two younger daughters, Alayna and Elise, both looked like they had been crying. They stood uncertainly, neither old enough to recognize Duke Gyre.

"What are you doing here?" Queen Nalia asked. "How did you get here?"

"Your life's in danger. The man who attacked my estate last night has been hired to kill you tonight. Please, Nal—please, my queen." He looked away.

"My lord," she said. It was how a queen might greet a favored vassal. It was also how a lady might address her husband. In those two words, Regnus heard her say, "I've never loved anyone but you." "My lord," she said again. "Regnus, I'll go wherever you lead, but we can't go without them. If I'm in danger, they are too."

"Your girls can come along."

"I mean Logan and Jenine. They wed this afternoon."

Long live the king! To the prince! The nobles' brief cries suddenly made sense. They'd abbreviated it: The king is dead; long live the king. They meant long live the new king. The prince. Logan.

King Gunder was dead. Logan was the new king.

A better man would have had other thoughts first, Regnus knew—a better husband would have had other thoughts first—but his first thought was that Nalia's husband was dead. The hateful little man who'd caused so much misery was gone; his own wife was gone, too. He and Nalia were both suddenly, miraculously freed from twenty-two years of bondage. Twenty-two years, and what he'd thought was a life sentence had suddenly been commuted.

He'd consigned himself to the satisfactions of a proud father and an able commander, never believing that he'd have anything but marital agony to come home to. Now, happiness wasn't just a dim possibility, it was here, one step away, beaming at him, eyes full of love. What a difference it would be to come home to Nalia, to share her home, her conversation, her life, her bed.

If she would have him, he could marry Nalia. He would marry her.

The other implications came to him more slowly. Logan was the new king? The genealogists would have nightmares if Regnus and Nalia had children. He didn't care.

He laughed aloud, his heart was so light. Then he stopped. Agon, the guards, and the nobles had been running to his son, armed with dinner knives.

Logan was in danger. Those men had been running to save him. Logan was in danger, and Regnus had turned aside.

There wasn't time to explain everything, to tell Nalia that she was free, that Aleine was dead. Regnus had to act. He had no idea how much time they had left.

"They're in trouble! Follow me!" Regnus shouted, lifting his sword. "We—" something hot lanced through his back and then was gone.

Regnus turned and rubbed his chest, irritated. He saw something black flit into the shadows as blood suddenly bloomed from one of his men's throats. As if they were marionettes whose strings had been cut, his men fell one after another in rapid succession, dead. Regnus's hand came away from his chest sticky.

He looked down. Blood was spreading on the front of his tunic over his heart. He looked up at Nalia. The shadow was behind her, holding her. One black hand held her chin up, the other held the long thin short sword that had killed Regnus, but Nalia's eyes were fixed on him and wide with horror.

"Nalia," he said. He dropped to his knees. His vision was going white. He tried to keep his eyes open, but then he realized his eyes *were* open, and it didn't matter any more.

*   *   *

Lord General Agon and his ragtag band of nobles and royal guards were not making good time. Through the centuries, the castle had undergone several expansions, and no simplifications. Twice the general's men had been stopped by a locked door, argued the relative merits of hacking it down or going around, and decided to go another way.

Now they ran down the last hallway to the north tower—the royal guards sprinting, Agon running, and several of the nobles wheezing their way down the long hall. The nobles had long since given up their earlier enthusiastic cries of "to the prince" and "long live King Gyre!" They were saving their breath now.

Agon entered the tower's antechamber to the sound of men cursing and beating at the door to the stairs.

One of the royal guards, Colonel Gher, was standing at the entrance to the antechamber. "Hurry, my lords," he urged the last two paunchy nobles.

Scanning the room, Lord Agon let the younger, more athletic men attack the thick door to the stairs. The room wasn't large, barely twenty feet square, sparsely furnished, with ceilings so high they were lost in the darkness, and just two doors: one to the stairs and one to the hall. There was no going around this door.

Something wasn't right. That the door was locked meant that the guards posted here had either been killed or subverted.

Lord General Agon looked over his shoulder to where Colonel Gher was ushering the last nobles into the room. Agon pushed past Logan's cousin, the fat lord lo-Gyre, and started to shout a warning, but before he could get a word out, Colonel Gher's mailed fist caught him in the chin.

Falling backward, Agon could only watch from the floor as Colonel Gher slammed the doors and threw the bolt.

One of the royal guards threw his shoulder into the door an instant later, but it held, and a moment later, Agon heard the door being barred.

"Trapped," Lord Urwer said helpfully.

For a moment, everyone in the room stopped. As the Lord General stood with the assistance of one of the royal guards, he could see the implications hitting the men.

If they'd just been betrayed by one of their own, then the attempt on the prince's life wasn't isolated or poorly planned. Everything in the last few days had been orchestrated—from Prince Aleine's death to their own arrival at this dead end. Their odds of surviving weren't good.

"What do we do, sir?" one of the guards asked.

"Get through that door," Lord Agon said, pointing to the door guarding the stairs. It was probably too late. They would probably find enemy soldiers and dead royals up those stairs. But Agon had long ago learned not to waste time on the battlefield lamenting what you should have done, what you should have seen. Recriminations could come later, if there was a later.

The guards had renewed their assault on the door when the twang-hiss of a crossbow bolt rang out.

A royal guard went down, his mailed chest pierced as easily as if he'd been wearing silk. Agon cursed and stared around the room for murder holes in the walls. He could see none.

The men looked around wildly, trying to guard against an enemy that attacked from nowhere.

Twang-hiss. Another guard stumbled into his comrades and fell dead.

Agon and the men looked up into the darkness. A low-hanging chandelier destroyed their chances of seeing beyond it. A low laugh echoed out of the gloom it hid.

Guards and nobles alike scrambled for whatever cover they could find, but there was precious little to be had.

One soldier rolled behind a thickly stuffed wing-backed chair. A noble tore a portrait of Sir Robin from a wall and held it before himself like a shield.

"The door!" Agon barked, though his heart was clouding with despair. There was no way out. The man or men shooting them not only had numbers and traitors in the castle, they also knew the castle's secrets. The paranoid King Hurlak had honeycombed his expansion of the castle with secret rooms and spy holes. Because he knew where they were, this assassin had merely to sit in place and murder them all. There was no way to stop him.

Twang-hiss. The soldier sitting behind the great chair stiffened as the bolt tore through the chair's back and penetrated his. The assassin was letting them know the hopelessness of their plight.

"The door!" Agon shouted.

With the kind of courage many commanders would demand but few would get, the rest of the guards jumped up and began hacking at the door. They knew that some of them would die doing it, but they also knew it was their only way out, their only hope for life.

Twang-hiss. Another royal guard crumpled in the middle of a swing at the door. Lord Ungert, weakly holding the portrait before himself, wailed like a little girl.

Twang-hiss. A soldier seemed to leap sideways as a bolt punched through his ear hole and threw him bloodily into the doorframe.

A rent appeared in the door. One of the remaining three royal guards gave a shout of triumph.

An arrow flew in through the gash in the door and buried itself in his shoulder. The man spun around once before a bolt from above clove his spine.

Both of the last two guards snapped. One dropped his sword and fell to his knees. "Please," he begged. "Please no. Please no. Please..."

The last was Captain Arturian. He attacked the door like a man possessed. He was a strong man, and the door shuddered and rocked under his blows, the gap widening, stretching to reach the latch.

He dodged as two arrows sped through the hole and past his head, then attacked once more. Another arrow streaked past Vin Arturian, and Agon saw his head whip back. His cheek had been grazed, cut in a neat line, his ear sliced in half.

Screaming, Captain Arturian threw his sword through the hole like a spear. He grabbed the latch and tore it out of the door, jerking as an arrow went into his arm and out the other side. Ignoring it, he seized the door and heaved, tearing it from the frame.

Five Khalidoran archers wearing Cenarian livery stood on the stairs with arrows drawn. Six swordsmen and a wytch stood behind them. Another archer lay at their feet, the guard's sword sprouting from his stomach. The five archers released their arrows simultaneously.

Riddled with arrows, Captain Vin Arturian dropped backward. His body landed next to the guard on his knees, who shrieked.

Twang-hiss. The shriek ended in a gurgle and the young man fell, drowning in his own blood.

Then came one of those eerily normal moments in the chaos of battle that Lord Agon had seen before but could never get used to.

One of the archers handed his bow off, stepped into the room, and grabbed the door. "Excuse me," he said to the captain he'd just helped kill. His voice wasn't sarcastic, simply polite. He pulled the door out of the captain's death-clenched fingers, stepped back into the stairwell and propped the door in place as Lord Agon and the nobles watched him.

In that no-time before reality came crushing back into place, Lord Agon looked at the nobles. They looked at him. These were the men who'd been willing to put their own lives at stake to rescue the prince. Brave men, if some of them fools, he thought as he looked at Lord Ungert shielding himself with a painting. These were the men he'd led to death.

The trap was clever. The "Gyre servant" who'd announced the attack on Logan had doubtless been one of the usurper's men. The ploy not only split the royal guard, taking most of them away from the Great Hall, it also neatly separated the wheat from the chaff. The lords who had come with Agon weren't even exactly the men he himself would have expected to defend Prince Logan, but they were all men who had shown their loyalties in the only way that mattered—with their actions.

By killing these men, the Khalidor would eliminate the very men most likely to oppose them. Brilliant.

Under the sound of the dying soldier's gurgling and rasping breath, Agon heard another sound. His ears identified it immediately. It was a crossbow's windlass being cranked.

Click-click-clack. Click-click-clack.

"So you know whom to curse as you die," a voice, darkly amused, said from his hideout above them. "I'm Prince Roth Ursuul."

"Ursuul!" Lord Braeton cursed.

"Oh, it's an honor then," Lord lo-Gyre said.

The bolt caught lo-Gyre through his fat stomach and struck with such force that it tore out of his back, taking a good part of his viscera with it. He sat roughly against a wall.

Several of the lords damned Ursuul as he had invited. Some went to comfort Lord lo-Gyre, wheezing and shaking on the floor. Lord General Agon remained standing. Death would find him on his feet.

Click-click-clack. Click-click-clack.

"I want to thank you, Lord General," Roth said. "You have served me well. First you killed the king for me—a nice bit of treason, that—and then despite that, you were able to lead these men to my trap. You will be rewarded well."

"What?" old Lord Braeton asked, looking at Brant with alarm. "Say it's not true, Brant."

The next bolt went through Lord Braeton's heart.

"It's a lie," Lord Agon said, but Lord Braeton was dead.

Click-click-clack. Click-click-clack.

Lord Ungert looked at Agon, terrified. The canvas shook in his hands. "Please, tell him to stop," he begged Agon as he saw that he was the last noble standing. "I didn't even want to follow you. My wife made me."

A small hole appeared in Sir Robin's painted shield and Lord Ungert staggered backward. For a long moment, he stood against the wall, grimacing, canvas still in hand. He looked disgusted, as if the canvas should have stopped the crossbow bolt. Then he fell on the painting, breaking the frame to splinters.

Click-click-clack. Click-click-clack.

"Bastard," Lord lo-Gyre said between thin gasps, staring at Lord General Agon. "You bastard."

The next bolt hit Lord lo-Gyre between the eyes.

Lord General Agon raised his sword defiantly.

Roth laughed. "I wasn't lying, Lord General. You'll have your reward."

"I'm not afraid," Lord General Agon said.

Click-click-clack. Click-click-clack. The bolt hit Agon's knee and he felt bones shatter. He stumbled to the chair and fell. Moments later, another bolt tore through his elbow. It felt like it had torn his arm off. He barely held himself sitting on the floor, clutching the arm of the chair like a man drowning.

"My wetboy told me I could trust you to run blindly into this trap. After all, you were stupid enough to trust him," Roth said.

"Blint!"

"Yes. But he didn't tell me you'd betray your king! That was delicious. And marrying Lord Gyre into the royal family? Friend of yours, isn't he? You cost Logan his life with that. I know you're not afraid to die, Lord General," Roth said. "The reward I give you is your life. Go live with your shame. Go on, now. Crawl away, little bug."

"I'll spend the rest of my sorry life hunting you down." Agon said between gritted teeth.

"No, you won't. You're a whipped dog, Brant. You could have stopped me. Instead, you helped me every step of the way. My men and I are going upstairs now. The prince and princess will die because you didn't stop me. So why would I kill you? I couldn't have done this without you."

Roth left the lord general there, gasping on the floor. Shattered.

55

Sergeant Bamran Gamble drew the Alitaeran longbow with the broad muscles of his back. It didn't matter if you were as strong as an ox; you couldn't draw an Alitaeran longbow with your arms. This bow was thick yew, seven feet long unstrung, and it could punch through armor at two hundred paces. He'd heard of men hitting a four-foot target at over five hundred paces, but thank the God, he didn't need to do that.

He stood on the roof of the guardhouse in the castle yard. They'd been barricaded in by a traitor, but the coward had either not had the stomach or not had the torch to set fire to the guardhouse with them inside it. Gamble's men had knocked a hole in the roof and lifted him out.

The wytch's first bolt had flown high past the sergeant's head before he'd even strung his bow. The wytch was the only meister in the yard, stationed to keep an eye on things, evidently. From Gamble's perch, he could see that more troops were streaming over the East Kingsbridge even now, but he had eyes only for the wytch. It was a woman, her hair red, skin pale. She was breathing heavily, as if the last bolt had taken something out of her, but she was already pulling herself together, chanting, the black vir on her arms straining.

If he missed, he wouldn't get a second shot. The wytch would aim this shot low, and it would set fire to the thatch roof of the guardhouse. More than forty of Sergeant Gamble's men would die.

His back flexed and the broadhead slid back. Three fingers slid toward his face; the gut string touched his lips. There was no aiming. It was purely instinctive. A ball of fire ignited between the wytch's palms. The broadhead jumped right through the flame, and the power that would have carried the arrow through armor had no trouble piercing ethereal flame or a young woman's sternum. She was blasted off her feet as if tied to a horse at full gallop. The arrow pinned her body to the great door behind her.

Sergeant Gamble wasn't conscious of having drawn another arrow. If he'd had a choice, he would have chosen to get off the roof and let his men out, but suddenly, battle was singing in his veins. After seventeen years as a soldier, he was fighting for the first time.

The arrow touched his lips and leapt away. This one hit another wytch leading a file of highlanders across the bridge. It was a brilliant shot, one of the best shots of Gamble's entire life. It flew between three rows of running soldiers and hit a wytch in the armpit as she pumped her arms while running. It blew her sideways off the edge of the bridge. She tumbled, limp, into the waters of the Plith.

The highlanders didn't even slow. That was when Sergeant Gamble knew they were in trouble. Two archers and a wytch peeled off from the group and began looking for him, but all the other men proceeded across the bridge. As the archers drew their arrows, the wytch touched each and fire attached to each arrowhead.

Gamble slid down the roof and dropped into the yard as two burning arrows sank into the thatch. The fire spread unnaturally fast. By the time he unbarred the door, there was already smoke pouring out of the inside of the barracks.

"What do we do, sir?" one of the men asked as they crowded around him.

"They can't take us all at once, so they're trying to separate us. I'd guess there's two, maybe three hundred of them. We gotta get to the lower barracks." There would be two hundred men there. That would be even odds, at least, not that Sergeant Gamble thought even numbers would even anything, not against Khalidoran highlanders and wytches.

"To hell with that," a young guard said. "I'm not dying for Niner. We still got East Kingsbridge. I'm outta here."

"You head for that bridge, Jules, and it's the last thing you'll do," Sergeant Gamble said. "This is what they pay us for. Anything less than our duty is betrayal, just like Conyer locking us in the barracks to die."

"They don't pay us shit."

"We knew what they paid when we signed up."

"You do what you gotta do, sir." Jules sheathed his sword and turned confidently. He started jogging for the bridge.

Every man of his thirty-nine was looking at Sergeant Gamble.

He drew, whispered a prayer for two souls as the string touched his lips, and sent an arrow through the back of Jules's neck. *I'm turning into a regular war hero, aren't I? Skilled at killing women and my own men.*

"We're going to fight," he said. "Any questions?"

Kylar sprinted through the servants' quarters unseen. Still no soldiers had come running. Things had to be bad somewhere for the soldiers not to have organized any resistance.

Abruptly, he was on a fight. At least one detachment of highlanders must have come in another way, because twenty of them were busy slaughtering twice as many Cenarian soldiers.

The Cenarians were on the verge of breaking, even as their sergeant was bellowing orders at them. The sight of the man's face stopped Kylar. He knew that sergeant. It was Gamble, the guard who'd come into the north tower the day of Kylar's first kill.

Kylar joined the fray and killed Khalidorans as easily as a scythe cuts wheat. It was simple labor. There was no joy in killing men who could barely see him.

At first, no one noticed him. He was a smear of darkness deep in the bowels of a castle constructed of dark stone and lit with flickering torches. Then he saved Gamble's life, beheading one Khalidoran and eviscerating another as they cornered the officer.

Kylar didn't even slow. He was a whirlwind. He was the first face of the Night Angels; he was vengeance. Killing was no longer an activity, it was a state of being. Kylar became killing. If every drop of guilty blood he spilled might blot out a drop of innocent blood, he would be clean tonight.

The feeling of mail parting, of leather parting, of flesh parting along the icy judgment that was Retribution was the best feeling in the world. Kylar was lost in a madness, a kind of bizarre meditation, spinning, thrusting, lunging, cleaving, piercing, battering, smashing, ruining faces, snuffing futures. It passed all too quickly. For in what couldn't have been more than half a minute, every last Khalidoran was dead. None was even dying. The killing wrath was nothing if not thorough.

The effect on the Cenarians was monumental. These sheep-in-guards'- armor stood, gaping, at the ragged darkness that was Kylar. Their weapons weren't even raised. They didn't stand in ready positions. They just marveled at Death's avatar among them.

"The Night Angel fights for you," he said. He'd already paused too long. Logan could be dying right now. He ran deeper into the castle.

All the doors were closed, and the halls were eerily quiet. He could only assume that the servants were huddled in their rooms or already fleeing.

The pounding of many footsteps keeping time brought him up short. Kylar sank into a shadowed doorway near a corner. He might be safe from the eyes of men, but there were things more dangerous than men in the castle tonight.

"There must be a good two hundred of their soldiers trapped downstairs," one of the officers was saying to a man whose narrow build gave him away as a wytch even though he wore armor and a sword. "It'll hold for maybe fifteen minutes, meister."

"And the nobles in the garden?" the wytch demanded.

His answer was lost in the tramp of the highlanders' feet as they wound past Kylar and into the distance.

So the nobles were trapped in the garden. Kylar had never been to the garden before—indeed had avoided the castle as much as possible—but he'd seen paintings of the garden, and if the artists hadn't taken too much license, Kylar supposed he could find it. He guessed that was as good of a place as any to look for Logan and Durzo.

As he wound deeper into the castle toward the garden, dead men began to clutter the halls, their blood slickening the floors. Kylar didn't even slow as he ran past. The dead were mostly nobles' guards.

Poor bastards. Kylar didn't have much sympathy for men who took up the profession of arms and then didn't train themselves, but these men had been massacred. Well over forty guards were dead and dying, kicking and frothing in pain. Kylar only saw eight highlanders dead.

Following the blood and the corpses led Kylar to double doors of walnut, barred from the outside. He lifted the bar and eased the door open.

"What in the hell?" a gruff voice with a Khalidoran accent said.

Retreating from the crack to stand behind yet another picture of Niner standing in a heroic pose, Kylar saw several highlanders guarding a room full of nobles. There were men, women, and even a few children in the group. They were disheveled and frightened. Some were crying. Some were throwing up, poisoned.

Footsteps tapped across the floor from beyond Kylar's line of sight, and the highlanders he could see readied their weapons. The point of a halberd hooked the corner of the door and pulled it open, revealing a squat Khalidoran officer as thick as he was tall.

The officer pulled the other door open with the halberd, then he beckoned and two men jumped into the hall, back to back, swords raised. They looked right at the statue, right at Kylar, who'd pressed himself against the statue's back, putting his arms behind its arms, his legs behind its legs.

"Nothing, sir," one said.

Inside the garden, which wasn't nearly as grand as it looked in the paintings, were ten guards and forty or fifty nobles—none of them armed. Mercifully, the highlanders had no wytches with them. Kylar assumed wytches were too valuable to be wasted guarding prisoners.

The nobles included some of the highest in the land. Kylar recognized more than a few of the king's ministers. That they were all here meant that Roth believed he would take over the castle quickly, and he wanted to be able to personally decide whom to kill and whom to add to his own government.

The men and women looked dazed. They didn't seem to believe what had happened to them. It was beyond their comprehension that their world could turn so completely upside down so quickly. Many were obviously ill. Some were torn and bloodied, but others were absolutely untouched. Some ladies whose hair was still perfectly coifed wept while others bearing gashes and torn skirts seemed poised and calm.

Behind Kylar a soldier said, "Bleeding mercy, Cap! It didn't just unbar itself!"

"We're here to guard this room, and we stay here."

"But we don't know what's out there . . . sir."

"We stay," the squat captain said in a voice that brooked no argument.

Kylar almost felt bad for the young highlander. The young man's instincts were right. One day he'd have been a good officer.

But that didn't stop Kylar from dropping the shadows a pace away from him.

He told himself he wasn't becoming visible to be fair. He'd need his strength later.

The young Khalidoran's sword had barely cleared its scabbard when Kylar disemboweled him. Then he danced past the man, throwing a knife with his left hand, parting hardened leather armor and ribs with an upward cut, and guiding a sword hand past his side and the sword into another soldier's body in a smooth motion. Kylar jerked his head forward into a highlander's face and spun with the man quickly. The man's back absorbed the captain's halberd with a meaty crunch.

Kylar dropped under a slash and stabbed up into a highlander's groin with his wakizashi. On his back, he knocked the man backward with a kick, and used the force of the kick to spring to his feet.

Six men were dead or down. Four remained. The first was impetuous. He charged with a yell, something about Kylar killing his brother. A parry and riposte, and brother joined brother. The last three moved forward together.

A quick cut deprived one of sword and sword hand, and the next crossed swords with Kylar five times before he didn't dodge back far enough and fell eyeless from the slash across his face. Kylar jumped over the sweeping halberd and turned to face the officer. He reversed his grip on his sword and stabbed behind him, impaling the one-armed soldier.

The officer dropped the halberd and drew a rapier. Kylar smiled at the extremes of the man's weapon choices and then looked over the officer's shoulder. The man started to turn, frowned, and didn't look back.

A pretty noblewoman smashed the back of his head in with a planter. Flowers and soil flew everywhere, but the planter itself didn't so much as crack.

"Thank you for saving us," she panted, "but damn you for looking at me. You could have gotten me killed." She was one of the women whose hair and makeup hadn't been the least disturbed by whatever violence had brought her here. She looked completely unruffled by having just crushed a man's skull. She merely brushed dirt from her dress and checked to see if she'd dragged it through any blood. Kylar was surprised that she hadn't spilled out of her low-cut dress when she'd run. He recognized her.

"He didn't look back, did he?" Kylar asked Terah Graesin, glad for the black silk kerchief over his face. He'd worn the mask out of habit, but if he hadn't, some of these nobles would have recognized him.

"Well, I never—"

There was a knock on the door, and she and everyone else froze. Three knocks, two knocks, three, two. A voice called out, "New orders, Cap! His Majesty says to kill 'em all. We need your soldiers to help quell resisters in the courtyard."

"You need to leave immediately," Kylar said loudly enough that all the nobles could hear him. "There's at least two hundred more highlanders coming over West Kingsbridge. They're probably the ones fighting in the courtyard right now. If you want to live, collect whatever weapons you can and free the soldiers who are trapped downstairs. Others are already heading there. With them, you can make it out of the castle. You can start a resistance. You've already lost the castle; you've lost the city. If you don't move fast, you'll lose your lives."

The news hit the nobles crowding around Kylar like cold water. Some of them shrank even more, but a few of them seemed to find their backbones as he spoke.

"We'll fight, sir," Terah Graesin said. "But some of us have been poisoned—"

"I know those poisons. If you've lived this long, you've taken a small enough dose that you'll recover within a half hour. Where's Logan Gyre?"

"Excuse me, I'm Terah Graesin, now Queen Graesin. If you—"

Kylar's eyes narrowed. "Where's. Logan. Gyre?"

"Dead. He's dead. The king's dead. The queen's dead. The princesses are dead, all of them."

The world rocked. Kylar felt as if he'd been clubbed in the stomach. "Are you sure? Did you see it?"

"We were with the king in the Great Hall when he died, and I found the queen and her younger daughters in their chambers before I got caught. They were...it was awful." She shook her head. "I didn't see Logan and Jenine, but they must have been the first to die. After the king announced their marriage, they'd not left the Great Hall ten minutes before the coup started. The lord general took men to try to save them, but he was too late. These men were just bragging about how they slaughtered the royal guards."

"Where?"

"I don't know, but it's too—"

"Does anyone know where Logan went?" Kylar shouted.

He saw from the looks on their faces that some of them knew, but they weren't going to tell him because they were afraid he would leave them. The cowards. He heard a moan further back in the garden and he pushed through the standing nobles to see a pasty pale man sweating on his back. His mouth was crusted with froth and there was a puddle of vomit near his head. He looked so bad that Kylar almost didn't recognize him. It was Count Drake.

Kylar knelt by the count and grabbed leaves from his herb pouch and began stuffing them in the count's mouth.

"You have an antidote?" one of the sick but standing nobles asked. "Give it to me."

"Give it to me!" another demanded. They began pushing forward. Kylar whipped Retribution out and put the point on a noble's throat.

"If any of you touch me or him, I'll kill you. I swear."

"He's only a count!" a fat, quivering noblewoman said. "He's poor! I'll give you anything!"

The hard, vengeful part of Kylar wanted to withhold the antidote just to repay their meanness, their pettiness. Instead, he grabbed the bag of antidote and tossed it to Terah Graesin. "Give it to those who need it most. It won't save anyone who's already unconscious, and anyone still standing doesn't need it."

Her mouth opened at being so frankly commanded, but she obeyed.

Time was slipping through Kylar's fingers. He was here. He was in the castle, but he had no idea where in the castle he needed to be. He looked down at the count, wondering if he was too late to save him.

The count stirred. His eyes opened, slowly focused. He was going to make it. "North tower," he said.

"That's where Logan went?"

The count nodded and then lay back, exhausted.

"It's too late for them," Terah Graesin said. "Fight with us. I'll give you lands, titles, a pardon—"

But heedless of the nobles' gasps, Kylar wrapped himself in shadows and ran.

Roth's men pounded up the stairs and kicked open the door to the bedchamber. Roth and Neph Dada followed as the eleven men pressed into the room amid grunts and cries. Even though the double doors were wide enough for three abreast, with four ranks of men in front of him, Roth couldn't see what was happening, except to know that it wasn't good. There was the sound of flesh hitting flesh, the sound of a sword cutting through mail, the sound of a skull bursting like a melon.

Beside him, Neph Dada had extended his vir-marked arms. He muttered and a quarter of the vir wriggled. An eerily silent concussion blew men in every direction. Even Roth's men were blasted off their feet.

The three directly in front of him hurtled backward, but as Roth braced for the impact, they smacked against an invisible barrier Neph had erected to protect him.

Neph spoke again and the room filled with light. Roth stepped inside with Neph as everyone recovered.

Logan tried to jump to his feet, too, but his limbs were anchored to the floor as if by a great weight. He was naked and furious. Roth sheathed his sword as eight of his men collected their scattered weapons. Six men lay on the floor, all bleeding from deep wounds. Three of them were dead, three would be soon. Apparently Logan Gyre was no slouch with a sword.

On the bed, wearing a hiked-up translucent nightgown, lay the princess. She was thrashing, terrified, but she couldn't cover herself. Neph had immobilized her, too.

Roth sat down on the bed next to the girl and let his eyes roam over her nubile body. He licked a finger, put it at the base of her neck, and traced it down her body.

"I hope I'm not interrupting anything," he said.

Jenine Gunder's eyes flashed. She was blushing from his casual perusal, but she was furious, too.

Roth put a finger to her lips and shushed her before she could say anything. "I just came to congratulate you on your recent nuptials, my dove," he said. "How is everything? Are you satisfied with the wealth of your husband's endowments?" he asked.

He looked over at the naked Logan and scowled. "Well, I suppose you are. And my dear Duke Gyre—stand him up," Roth ordered. "Or should I say Prince Gyre? Don't lose heart. I've seen her mother naked, and in time she'll—"

Logan lunged forward, but his bonds held. One of the men hit him across the face.

Roth continued as if there had been no interruption. He clucked his tongue. "In time. There's the rub. In time, the princess might grow into these rather admirable breasts and hips." He smiled at her and pinched a cheek. Roth stood, and Neph's magic lifted Jenine from the bed to stand, trembling, next to her husband.

"But you don't have time. I hope you've enjoyed your marriage. And Logan, friend, I hope you've not been wasting your time with foreplay— because your marriage is over."

The moment drew out. There was nothing Roth loved so much as watching bewilderment turn to dread turn to despair.

"Who are you?" Logan asked, his eyes betraying no fear.

"I'm Roth. I'm the man who ordered your brother's death, Jenine."

Ignoring Logan, Roth watched the words break over the girl like a wave. But he didn't stop, didn't let her voice a denial.

"I'm Roth, the Shinga of the Sa'kagé. I'm the man who ordered your father's death, Jenine. Not ten minutes ago, I watched his head roll off the high table.

"I'm Prince Roth Ursuul of Khalidor. I'm the man who ordered your sisters' and your mother's deaths, Jenine. If you listen, you might hear their cries." He put a finger to his ear and an attentive look on his face, mocking.

"You two are all that's left between me and Cenaria's crown, Jenine. And I'm going to take that crown. I'm afraid I'm going to have to kill you. Do you want to choose which of you dies first?"

With each revelation, he watched her eyes, fed hungrily on her dying hope, gorged himself on her ripening despair. Roth drew a knife and turned her so she faced Logan.

Logan cried out wordlessly, but Neph had gagged him. He bucked and strained against the bonds, his muscles taut, swelling huge, but escaping Neph's magic was impossible. He could sooner tear stars from the heavens.

"My lord," a soldier called from the hall. "One of the barges has been destroyed. The meisters need you to help quell the resistance."

Watching the hope bloom in the young girl's eyes gave Roth a shiver of excitement. "Resistance," he said. "Maybe they'll save you! But wait, your hero is already here. Logan, are you just going to stand there? Aren't you going to save her?"

The muscles in Logan's arms and legs bulged and the magical bonds shifted and thinned until Neph spoke again and they redoubled. The prince couldn't move.

"I guess not," Roth said, turning back to Jenine. "But you're the princess! Surely the royal guards will come. Why, I bet even now the lord general is leading men here to rescue you!" He brushed his hair back over a mangled ear. "But I killed Agon and all the royal guards. There are no more heroes. No one can save you, Jenine."

Roth stepped behind Jenine and trailed his free hand up her slender stomach. He ripped her nightgown open, tore it off, and cupped a breast in his hand. As a tear rolled from her eye, he bent and kissed her neck like a lover. His eyes locked on Logan's, mocking.

Then, where he'd kissed her, he cut her throat.

Roth gave her a shove, and Jenine stumbled into Logan's arms, the right side of her neck a fountain of blood. Neph loosed Logan's bonds enough that he could hold the girl, but not enough to reach up to try to stop the bleeding.

Logan's eyes were wells of horror and pity. A sound like beatific music to Roth's ears, the sound of a soul at its utmost limit of suffering, escaped Logan's lips. He held the small, gasping girl to his chest. Roth devoured his horror, trying to lock this memory into his mind, knowing he would need this on the long dark nights.

But then Logan pulled back, turned so Roth couldn't see his face, and looked into Jenine's face.

"I'm here, Jeni," Logan said, holding the girl's eyes with his own. "I'm not going to leave you." The gentleness in his voice infuriated Roth. It was as if Roth didn't matter anymore. With his soothing voice, Logan was pulling Jenine and himself out of this world of darkness, walling them off somewhere Roth couldn't go.

As Jenine stared into Logan's eyes, Roth could see her relax—not into death, but from despair. "You really would have loved me, wouldn't you?" she said.

Roth knew he should have cut deeper, should have slashed her windpipe and not just that single artery. He struck Logan across the face, but his blow might have been the buzzing of a gnat for all it did. The big man didn't even lose eye contact with the princess.

"Jeni. Jeni," he said quietly. "I already love you. I'll be with you soon."

"You're dying!" Roth shouted, not a pace away, but he might have been a summer breeze. Jenine's knees trembled and Logan pulled her back into his embrace, closing his eyes and whispering in her ear as her life bled out against his chest.

"My lord, they need you now," the messenger said, more urgently.

Logan didn't even look at Roth as Jenine shuddered against his chest. He just kept whispering assurances. She sucked in three more labored breaths, and then sighed her life out in Logan's arms, her eyes fluttering closed. Neph released the bonds holding her slowly and she crumpled to the floor.

"No! No!" Roth yelled. She wasn't even *afraid*. He'd done everything right and she wasn't even afraid to die. Who wasn't afraid to die? It wasn't right. It wasn't fair.

He slapped Logan. Once and again. And again. And again. "You won't die so easy, Logan Gyre," Roth snarled. He turned to his men. The muscle in his jaw twitched. "Take him to the Maw and give him to the sodomites."

"My lord!" the messenger said, rushing into the room again. "You must—"

Roth grabbed a handful of the messenger's hair. He stabbed at the man's face in a fury, wildly, again and again. He flung the man sideways and tried to cut his throat, but caught him above the ear instead. The knife turned and a fat strip of hairy scalp came off in Roth's hand. The man wailed until Roth grabbed him again and cut his throat.

Meanwhile, Neph had opened the hidden door out of the chamber. He lifted the princess's body with magic and floated it before him.

"Neph, what are you doing?"

"The Godking wishes to have the heads of all the royal family displayed. Whatever you're planning, I'd advise you to hurry."

He didn't address Roth by his title. Everything was going wrong and Father would be here soon. Roth turned, panting, the gory strip of hair and flesh in his fist. He trembled with rage and the men holding Logan went as white as paste. "Bring me his head when they're finished. But before you give him to the sodomites, cut his cock off and bring me his sack for a purse. I want him to bleed to death as they fuck him."

56

The antechamber at the base of the north tower stank overwhelmingly of blood and feces released in death, the bitter tang of urine threaded through the stench. Kylar gagged as he opened the barred door.

A quick glance told the story. The men had been trapped in the room, ambushed by a crossbowman. Kylar scowled. A crossbowman? In a room this small?

Then he saw the narrow platform by the ceiling, plainly visible in the shadows that now welcomed Kylar's eyes. From the way the bodies were scattered, it had just been the one man, shooting the royal guards and nobles like fish in a barrel.

So this was what happened to the men who'd come to save their prince. From the streaks of blood going out the door, it looked like only one man had survived to drag himself away.

Sickened, Kylar ran up the stairs. He found six dead Khalidorans at the entryway. The rest of the story was clear enough. Caught in bed with his wife—Logan's clothes were scattered around the room—Logan had sprung up and fought. He'd killed six fully armed Khalidorans, but from the burn marks on the floor, he'd been hurt or disabled with magic.

Then, from the wide, sticky puddle of blood, it was obvious that Roth had either killed Logan slowly so that he bled copiously, or had killed both him and his wife. Neither body was in the room. The Khalidorans would want Logan's body along with the rest of the royal family's bodies so the whole kingdom could see they were dead, the line of succession wiped out.

A torn nightgown lay on the floor. The princess, young and beautiful as she was, was probably in a room somewhere being raped until she died of it.

Kylar tried to interpret it another way. His mind analyzed the scene, trying to ward off the shock of despair. Was it possible the princess had been killed and Logan was alive?

But soldiers wouldn't keep Logan alive and kill a princess whom they could rape. Logan was a warrior, a renowned swordsman, and the heir to the throne. The assassinations of the rest of the royal family had been carried out brutally but precisely, carefully. If the Khalidorans were going to make an exception and spare one life for any length of time, it wouldn't be Logan's.

Grief hit Kylar like a physical blow. Logan was dead. His best friend was dead. Dead, and the blame could only be placed on Kylar.

He could have stopped it. Kylar could have killed Durzo last night. Durzo's back had been there, a target he couldn't miss. Dorian had told him. Told him!

What pain hadn't he inflicted on Logan? He'd allowed the murder of Logan's friend Aleine, concealed the truth about Serah's and Aleine's affair, got him sent to prison for murder, and forced him to break his engagement. Now Logan had been forced to marry a girl he didn't know and had been murdered, his wife of less than an hour raped and killed.

Sinking to the floor, Kylar wept. "Logan, I'm sorry. I'm sorry. It's all my fault." He reached a hand to steady himself, and found it in the puddle of blood. He looked at his bloody, bloody hand. Bloody as it had been bloodied in this very chamber, five years ago when he'd finished his first solo kill. Bloody as it had been bloody continually since he murdered his first innocent. This was where murder had brought him. It had brought him full circle, his murder of one innocent leading inexorably to the murder of more. In the last five years, he'd done exactly what he'd intended to do: he'd become more and more like Durzo Blint. He'd become a killer. He slept uneasily, so he slept light, so he was ever more dangerous. He was always on edge, and the blood that first covered his hands in this very room had never been washed clean. It had only been added to. It was no mistake that Logan's blood was on his hands now, no coincidence.

The Drakes liked to talk about a divine economy: the God turning weeping into laughter, sorrow into joy. A wetboy was the merchant prince of the satanic economy. Murder begat murder, and as Durzo had said, others always paid the price.

Must others always pay for my failures? Is there no other way? The blood on his hands said no, no. *This is reality; it's hard, uncomfortable, hateful, but it's true.*

"I'm breaking my own rules," a blur of shadows said.

Kylar didn't look up. He didn't care if he died. But the man said no more. After a long moment, Kylar asked bitterly, " 'Don't play fair. A kill is a kill'?"

Durzo stepped out of the shadows. "Kylar, I have one last rule to teach you."

"And what's that, master?"

"You're almost a wetboy now, Kylar. And now that you've learned to win almost any fight, there's one more rule: Never fight when you can't win."

"Fine," Kylar said. "You win."

Durzo stood there a long moment. "Come, apprentice. Here is your Crucible."

"Is that all your life is?" Kylar asked, finally looking up. "Tests and challenges?"

"My life? That's all *life* is."

"That's not good enough," Kylar said. "These people shouldn't be dying. Khalidor shouldn't be winning. It's not right."

"I never said it's right. My world isn't cut into black and white, right and wrong, Kylar. Yours shouldn't be either. Our world only has better and worse, shadows lighter and darker. Cenaria couldn't win against Khalidor no matter what happened tonight. This way, a few nobles die rather than tens of thousands of peasants. It's better this way."

"Better? My best friend's dead and they're probably raping his wife! How can you stand by and do nothing? How can you help them?"

"Because life's empty," Durzo said.

"Bullshit! If you believed that, you'd have died a long time ago!"

"I did die a long time ago. All the good passes by and all the evil passes by, and we can't do a damn thing to change anything or anybody, Kylar. Least of all ourselves. This war will come and go, there will be a victor, and people will die for nothing. But we'll be alive. Like always. At least, I will."

"It's not right!"

"What do you want? Justice? Justice is a fairy tale. A myth with soft fur and reassuring strength."

"A myth you believed in, once upon a time," Kylar said, gesturing to the word JUSTICE etched into Retribution's blade.

"I used to believe a lot of things. That doesn't make them true," Durzo said.

"Who's better off? Logan or us? Logan could sleep at night. I hate myself. I dream of murder and wake in cold sweat. You drink yourself oblivious and blow your money on whores."

"Logan's dead," Durzo said. "Maybe he'll wear a crown in the next life, but that doesn't do him much good now, does it?"

Kylar looked at Durzo strangely. "And you're the one who says life is empty, meaningless. That we don't take anything of value when we take a life. Look how you hold on to yours. You fucking hypocrite."

"Every man worth a damn is a hypocrite." Durzo reached into a breast pocket and pulled out a folded scrap of paper. "If you kill me, this is for you. It explains things. Consider it your inheritance. If I kill you...well, when I die, I'll take a break on my way to the lowest plane of hell and stop to talk."

Durzo tucked the paper in a breast pocket and drew a huge sword with a long red ribbon dangling from its hilt. It was a longer, heavier blade than Retribution, but with his Talent, Durzo could wield it with a single hand.

"Don't do this," Kylar said. "I don't want to fight you."

The wetboy closed on him. Kylar stood still, making no move to defend himself. "Did you already give him the Globe of Edges?" Kylar asked.

The wetboy stopped. He reached into a pouch and pulled out the silvery globe. "This?" he said. "This is nothing. Another fake." He hurled the globe through at the window. Glass broke as it punched through the window and sailed out into darkness.

"What have you done?" Kylar asked.

"By the Night Angels!" Durzo said. "You bonded my ka'kari. You stole it from me. You still don't understand?"

It was like he was speaking another language. *Bonded?* Kylar thought he'd bonded the ka'kari—must have, because his Talent worked now. And Durzo said it was glass?

"Unbelievable," Durzo said, shaking his head. "Draw your sword and fight, boy."

"It's my sword now, is it?" Kylar asked.

"Not for long. You aren't worthy to succeed me." Durzo raised his blade.

"I don't want to fight you," Kylar said, refusing to draw the blade. "I won't fight you."

Durzo struck. At the last second, Kylar drew Retribution and blocked. Talent-strengthened blow met Talent-strengthened blow. The blades shivered from the impact.

"I knew it was in you," Durzo said. He smiled fiercely.

Any delusion Kylar might have had that Durzo would take it easy on him because he hadn't had time to learn to use his Talent dissolved instantly. Durzo launched into a blistering attack so fast it should have been impossible.

Kylar staggered backward, blocking some blows and jumping back to avoid more. Durzo used every weapon in his arsenal. His sword blurred through combinations, whipping the hilt ribbon into a scintillant red stream. The ribbon's purpose was to pull an opponent's eyes from the point of danger. Anyone who let his attention wander would find a steel reminder in his ribs.

But it wasn't just the sword that confused Kylar. Durzo would follow a cut at Kylar's head with a kick at his knee then a spinning backhand with his free hand at his face. Combinations followed and flowed into each other in a raging river of deadly motion.

Blocking and dodging, Kylar retreated back and back. Durzo didn't give him time to think, but Kylar was aware of the room. It took up the entire top floor of the tower, so it formed a large circle flattened at one end for the entrance and at the other for a closet.

The very familiarity of fighting against Durzo slowly calmed him. Of course, he'd always lost, but things would be different this time. They had to be.

The surge of power flowed through his arms with a rush of tingles that made him feel like every hair on his body was standing on end. He parried a thrust and Durzo's blade was slapped aside as if it weighed a quarter of what it did. Blint recovered in a blink, but he stopped advancing.

Kylar was standing a yard from the wall with a cherry-wood bureau next to him. Blint's sword flicked toward his eyes, but it was a feint. Blint's real attack was a kick at Kylar's leading knee. Kylar dropped backward toward the wall and lashed out with a foot, halting Blint's foot as it came forward. Expecting his sword to meet resistance, Blint slashed too hard. His heavy blade slashed deeply into the bureau.

The stone wall slapped against Kylar's back as he stumbled and levered himself upright again. But instead of trying to drag his sword out of the bureau, Durzo reached over his shoulders and grabbed twin hook swords. Each bore a crescent-shaped blade over the knuckles, but was otherwise a normal sword with a hooked point for catching an enemy's sword.

"I hate those," Kylar said.

"I know."

Kylar attacked, still trying to adjust to the Talent's effect on his fighting. So far as he could tell, it could make his muscles move more quickly and more powerfully, but there was a limit to how fast even two Talented fighters could fight. The Talent didn't help you make decisions faster, so it wasn't a simple matter of accelerating regular fighting. Kylar had to be more careful—and he still had no idea if the Talent would defend his body itself. If Blint got through Kylar's defenses with a Talent-aided kick, would it crush his ribs like twigs, or were they strengthened as well?

The only way to find out was no way to find out.

Blint let Kylar come forward, using the hook swords defensively. Then, as they neared the bed, he started using the hooks. As Kylar struck, Durzo turned his blade down to the hook and wrenched Retribution aside. He followed with an overhand slash with the other sword.

Leaping backward, Kylar found himself being driven toward one of the tower's broad windows. Durzo strode in and caught a slow slash, but instead of sweeping it aside, he caught it with his other hook, trapping Kylar's blade.

As Kylar lunged forward, Blint guided the blade past his head and wrenched it free. Retribution clattered on the floor behind Kylar. Blint kicked him in the chest, his foot barely slowed by the arms Kylar brought up as he drew daggers.

Kylar slammed into the window and felt glass break, wood splinter, and the latch burst. He had the sickening sensation of launching into space.

Clawing for something, anything, Kylar turned, twisting with the desperate grace of a falling cat. Abandoned to gravity, his daggers spun away, glittering in the moonlight.

Kylar punched his fingers through a delicate windowpane. His hand clamped on wood and jagged glass as his momentum swung the window open.

His face met the tower wall with a crunch. Glass glided through the flesh of his fingers then ground against bone as his hand slipped. Held.

Blinking, he dangled by one hand. Blood coursed down his arm. Blood coursed down his face. He hung two hundred feet over the basalt of the castle's foundation and the broad expanse of the river. Steam escaped from the single volcanic vent that opened on Vos Island and obscured a barge pulled up to the shore. The steam shone in the moonlight, and far below, by the ship, Kylar saw men talking. Even from this height, he could hear the ringing of steel, and catch glimpses of Khalidoran invaders overwhelming foot soldiers in the castle courtyard.

Then Sergeant Gamble emerged from the front gate. He was leading the nobles and more than two hundred Cenarian soldiers. They were trying to escape the castle, just as Kylar had told them, but even as they pushed toward the east gate, the Khalidorans were reinforced by more than a hundred highlanders coming from the opposite side of the castle.

In seconds, the courtyard had become the frontline of the battle and the war for Cenaria. The castle and the city were lost. If the nobles were slaughtered, so was all of Cenaria. If the nobles could press through the massed highlanders and get across East Kingsbridge, they could begin a resistance.

It was the dimmest sort of hope, but hope had never come in the blinding bright variety in Cenaria.

Something popped and Kylar dropped four inches. He scrambled up the window frame as the next hinge tore out of the sill. The last hinge protested and popped out.

Kylar hurled himself at the storm shutter tied back against the tower wall. His fingers raked over slats. Caught. Three slats broke and then finally arrested his fall.

The window sailed peacefully below him, turning end over end in the whistling wind. It hit the rocks just paces short of the river—exactly where Kylar would land if he fell. The window exploded into splinters and slivers of glass.

Kylar looked up. The shutter's hinges were straining, slowly pulling out of the rock.

Perfect.

Durzo Blint stood in the carnage and saw none of it. Bodies were strewn about the bedchamber. Freshly cut lilies bloomed next to the royal bed— white lilies flecked red with blood.

A delicate, once-white nightgown lay soaking in a wide pool of crimson near his feet. The floor mosaic was scorched in a black circle. The acrid tang of wytchfire smothered the hint of perfume in the air.

But Durzo saw only the open window in front of him. His pockmarked face looked stricken. Wind howled through the window, sending the curtains fluttering and his gray hair into his eyes.

His fingers flipped a blade end over end in his right hand. Finger to finger to finger, stop. Finger to finger to finger, spin. He noticed what he was doing and jammed the dagger into a sheath. His face set and he pulled his mottled gray and black cloak around his shoulders, covering a belt full of darts, daggers, and numerous tools and pouches.

It wasn't supposed to end like this. It wasn't supposed to be so empty. He turned his back to the window, then stopped. His head cocked to the side as he heard something over the screaming wind.

Kylar willed himself to release the shutter with his bloody right hand. His hand found empty sheaths for daggers that matched the empty scabbard on his back. Grunting, he contorted himself to draw a tanto from his calf. His fingers were deadened, lacerated, weak. The tanto almost slipped out of them.

The ropes tying the shutter against the wall parted easily. Rusty hinges creaked loudly. Kylar stiffened, but there was no help for the noise. He took two quick breaths, then launched off the tower wall with both feet. He swung back toward the open window and heaved his body up with the force of his Talent as if he swinging on a giant swing.

The shutter tore away from the tower in his hands, and he barely made it high enough not to slam into the wall, instead sliding into the bedchamber along the floor.

His body swept Durzo's feet out from under him and the wetboy fell on top of Kylar, one of his hook swords going flying out the window. The shutter was between them, trapping Durzo's hands in an awkward position. Kylar slapped the shutter into Durzo's face.

"I don't—" Kylar slammed the shutter into Durzo's face with all of his strength and Talent. The man flew off him.

Kylar rolled aside and jumped to his feet.

But Blint was already up. He kicked a footstool at Kylar. Kylar blocked it with a foot, but it caught him off-balance and tripped him. He landed face-first on a decorative rug.

Running forward like lightning, Blint raised the hook sword. Instead of trying to stand or roll aside, Kylar grabbed the rug and yanked.

Durzo lurched forward faster than he expected and cut only air as his knees collided with Kylar's shoulder. He flipped over headfirst.

Durzo's heavy curved sword was still lodged in the bureau next to the window, but Retribution was closer. Kylar grabbed it and turned.

"—want to—"

The wetboy lunged to grab the hook sword off the ground.

"—fight you!" Kylar jumped on the hook sword.

Durzo pulled up with all the strength of his Talent. For an instant, it seemed the iron core of the blade would hold. Then the sword snapped an inch from the hilt.

"You might not want to, son, but there's something in you that refuses to die," Durzo said. He threw the broken blade aside, but didn't draw any other weapon.

"Master, don't make me fight you," Kylar said, pointing the blade at Durzo's throat.

"You made your choice when you disobeyed me."

"Why'd you do it?"

"I wouldn't have apprenticed you, but I thought you were something you're not. May the Night Angels forgive me."

"I don't mean me!" Kylar's hands shook on the sword. "Why'd you make me betray my best friend?"

"Because you broke the rules. Because life's empty. Because I broke the rules too." Durzo shrugged. "It catches up."

"That's not good enough!"

Durzo tented his hands and pursed his lips. "Logan died screaming, you know. Pathetic."

Kylar lashed out. The sword streaked for Durzo's neck. But Durzo didn't flinch. The blade slapped into his palm and stopped as if it didn't even have an edge.

But Durzo's hands were still tented in front of him. The hand holding Kylar's sword was made of pure magic.

It flung Retribution out of Kylar's grip. Other hands bloomed in the air, striking at him. Kylar blocked and stumbled back as Durzo walked forward calmly, surging with Talent.

There was nothing Kylar could do. He blocked faster and faster, but the hands came faster still. Dimly, a few hands of his own Talent bloomed in front of him and blocked some of the attacks, but it wasn't enough. Durzo drove him back and back.

Finally, hands latched onto each of Kylar's limbs and pinned him to the wall. He couldn't move an inch.

"Ah, kid," Durzo said. "If I could have taught you to use your Talent, you'd have been something really special."

Durzo drew a throwing dagger. Spun it in his fingers. Brought it up. He paused as if to say something, then shook his head.

"I'm sorry, Kylar."

"Don't be. Life's empty, right?"

Durzo sighed. He was staring at Retribution, gleaming blackly at Kylar's feet, as close as the moonlight and as far away as the moon. The look on his scarred face was anguish, regret.

Following his gaze, Kylar stared at the black sword that Durzo had carried for so many years, and remembered—

Scowling, Durzo had snatched the pouch away from him and turned it over. The Globe of Edges fell into his hand. "Damn. Just what I thought," he said, his voice harsh in the quiet of the Jadwin hallway.

"What?" Kylar asked.

It was a fake, another fake ka'kari.

But Durzo wasn't in any mood to answer questions. "Did the girl see your face?"

Kylar's silence was enough.

"Take care of it. Kylar, that's not a request. It's an order. Kill her."

"No," Kylar said.

"What did you say?" Durzo asked, incredulous. Black blood was dribbling down Retribution, pooling on the floor.

"I won't kill her. And I won't let you."

"Who is this girl that she's worth being hunted for the rest of your short—" he stopped. "She's Doll Girl."

"Yes, master. I'm sorry."

"By the Night Angels! I don't want apologies! I want obedien—" Durzo held up a finger for silence. The footfalls were close now. Durzo blurred into the hall, inhumanly fast, his sword flashing silver in the low light.

His sword flashed *silver?* Retribution's blade is black.

There was the sound of something metallic rolling across marble toward Kylar. He raised a hand and felt the ka'kari slap into his outstretched palm.

"No! No, it's mine!" Blint yelled.

The ka'kari pooled like black oil in an instant.

What had Durzo just said? The silver was another fake. You stole *my* ka'kari. Not a silver ka'kari at all. A black ka'kari. The ka'kari Durzo had been carrying for years, hidden covering the blade of Retribution.

The ka'kari choose their own masters. For some reason, the black ka'kari had chosen Kylar. Maybe had chosen him years ago, the day Durzo had beaten him for seeing Doll Girl again. That day, when a blue glow had surrounded the black blade. When Durzo had shouted, "No, not that! It's mine!" as incandescent blue fire had burned into Kylar's fingers. Durzo had thrown it away from Kylar so Kylar couldn't complete the bond, because once Kylar completed the bond, Kylar wouldn't call the silver ka'kari for Durzo. Now they knew he hadn't called it because it had been a fake. There had never been any ka'kari in the city except Durzo's black.

And Durzo had known from that very day that if he let Kylar live, the black ka'kari was lost to him forever. Durzo had even left it for him tonight so that Kylar would have a chance.

But now it was too late.

Durzo looked like there was more he wanted to say to Kylar, some way he wanted to vent his anguish. But he'd never been a man of words.

Instead, mere paces away, he hurled the knife at Kylar's face.

Time didn't slow.

The world didn't contract to the point of the spinning knife.

But despair flash-boiled in the heat of an insane hope in Kylar's heart. He didn't even notice his hand come up, didn't know how it had broken free, couldn't say how the ka'kari had gone from the blade on the floor into his hand. It was just there.

In that unslowed fraction of a second, black goo flipped from his fingertips and splattered across the knife spinning toward his chest like spit against pavement.

When Kylar looked again, the knife was just *gone*.

Ting.

Kylar looked down to see what had made the sound. The ka'kari was rolling across the floor coming toward him. It wobbled as it rolled and when it climbed up his boot and dissolved into his skin, Kylar felt a rush of power.

With a mental shrug, Kylar burst through the phantasmal hands holding him to the wall. Settling smoothly on his feet, he extended a hand toward his old master and released the power arcing through him.

Durzo was hurled away as if all the force of a hurricane had been unleashed in his face. He tumbled end over end, sliding and rolling across the room until he slapped against the wall.

With the Talent, Kylar caught up Retribution and brought it to his hand.

"Don't fight when you can't win," Kylar said. "And don't fight when you don't want to win. Right?"

Durzo struggled to his feet and stood, weaponless. He took a ready position and smirked. "Sometimes you have to fight."

"Not this time," Kylar said. He raised the sword and came forward at a run. Durzo didn't move; he just looked Kylar in the eye, ready. At the last second, Kylar dodged to the side and dove through the window into the moonlit air whipping the north tower.

One of those men on the boat had been Roth.

57

*L*ogan had no intention of letting *anyone* use his sack for a coin purse, much less Roth Ursuul. In fact, he intended to kill the bastard. He wasn't worried that he was unarmed and still naked—Roth had supposed it would strip him of his dignity—rage gave him power. All the cruelty and depravity and horror Logan had seen in the last day had transformed him. He would be a man again, later. Now he was hard, crystal-clear frozen rage. Logan figured that even with his hands bound he could kill both guards.

With the fury that was arcing through his body, he didn't think there was much of anything that could stop him.

Except magic. Roth had known it, too, and he'd sent his wytch, Neph Dada, to escort Logan to the dungeon. Neph had obviously memorized the layout of the castle, because he threaded through servants' hallways and back staircases and cellars effortlessly.

The city of Cenaria had only one gaol, connected to the castle by a single tunnel—now overrun with Khalidoran highlanders—and separated from the rest of the city by the two forks of the Plith River. Prisoners were taken to the gaol by barge. Few left. The felons who came here might as well have been devoured by the earth herself.

Or, the sliver of Logan that wasn't rage thought as a peculiar smell assaulted his senses, maybe it was called The Maw for different reasons. Fumes were constantly escaping from the north side of Vos Island and filling the air of the prison with the smell of brimstone before finally finding the open air.

Neph Dada paused before an iron gate while one of the men guarding Logan fumbled for a key. Neph glared at the man and waved a hand in front of the lock, the tendrils of black on his arm not quite moving in time with his arm. The lock clicked.

The guard produced the correct key and smiled weakly.

"I've other matters to attend to," Neph said. "Can you handle him by yourselves from here?"

"Yes, sir," the guard said, looking at Logan nervously.

Logan's heart smiled. Fighting two armed men while naked wasn't exactly good odds, but with Neph's magical bonds holding his arms motionless and giving his legs barely enough space to shuffle, there was *nothing* he could do.

"Good. The bonds will hold for ten minutes," Neph said.

"Plenty of time, sir," the guard said.

With a snort, Neph left them. The big-nosed guard locked the iron gate, giving Logan time to adjust to the dim room. To the right and left were heavy doors with iron-barred windows.

"In case you're wondering," Nose said. "These are the nicest suites in the place. Real sweet places. For nobles. Not for you, though." He chuckled.

Logan looked at the man flatly.

"Ramp up there goes to the surface. Not for you, either."

The weasel-faced guard looked at Nose, "You always taunt dead men?"

"Always," Nose said, stuffing a finger up his nose. "What?" he said as Weasel looked at him. "I was scratching."

"Shut up," Weasel said. "We down on three?"

"Yeah, all the way to the Howlers. Let's make it quick." Nose tapped on the fourth door as he passed it. "I'll be right back for ya, sweetheart!"

There was a little cry from the cell, but the woman inside didn't look up.

"That bitch makes me hot," Nose said. "You seen her?"

Weasel shook his head, so Nose continued, "Got more scars on her face than a highlander's got fleas, but who needs to look at her face, huh?"

"The prince will rip your throat out if you touch her," Weasel said.

"Ah, how's he gonna know?"

"He's coming down tonight. Wants to free our Sa'kagé boys and check on that wench and some little kid they dragged in," Weasel said.

"Tonight? Hell, she won't take me five minutes," Nose said. He laughed.

They wended their way through two levels of manmade tunnels, the smells of massed humanity thickening and mingling with potent brimstone, sewage, and other smells Logan couldn't identify. He tested his bonds periodically, but there was no change. He was barely mobile. Nonetheless, he kept his eyes open for his chance. Simple escape wouldn't be good enough. He had to kill both guards, get the keys, and remember the way out.

The Howlers were on the third floor, but as they came into the natural caves, merely widened with tools, Logan heard no howling.

"We don't want to go no further," Nose said, pausing in front of a double-banded iron door. "These bastards here will do all we need. I'm not gonna even try to get him out of the Hole. I don't go near those animals."

"The Hole?" Logan asked.

Nose leered, but seemed eager to terrify him. "Hell's Asshole. For the rapists, killers, and twists so bad that hangin's too good for 'em. They drop 'em in there and let 'em devour each other. They hafta get their water off the rocks, and the guards never throw in enough bread. Sometimes they piss on it first."

"So who's going to...you know?" Weasel asked, drawing his blade awkwardly. "Those bonds won't hold forever."

"Who's going to what?" Nose asked.

"You know. Cut 'em off."

Logan tested the bonds, but they were still strong. His arms were locked at his sides, his torso held ramrod straight, and his feet could only move a few inches at a time—and the guards knew it. *Oh gods*. He was running out of time.

"I'll do it," Nose said with a snarl. He grabbed a catchpole and draped the noose over Logan's neck, then handed the pole to Weasel. "You hold him. We can't take any chances. Gimme that."

Weasel handed his knife to Nose. It was just an ordinary knife, but Logan's eyes fixed on it. Fear began to mix with rage, and he felt that ice thawing. Melting. *They're going to do it. Gods, no.* He thrashed, thrashed his arms and legs like an animal. But no matter how he shook or twisted or turned, he barely moved an inch

Nose laughed, and Weasel just tightened the rope on his throat until Logan was turning purple. He didn't care. *Let them kill me now. Oh, gods!* Nose said, "It's too bad you haven't worked with me longer."

"Why's that?" Weasel asked, nervously holding the catchpole with both hands.

Nose rammed the knife into Weasel's eye. The man stood up on his tiptoes and twitched violently, then fell.

"Because I would have tried to cut you in, instead of cutting you off," Nose said. He laughed to himself and cut the noose off Logan's neck. Logan stared at him, stunned to silence, his rage and fear slow to fade.

Nose didn't pay him any attention. "When you can move, put these on. Sorry they didn't send someone more your size," Nose said, stripping the clothes off Weasel's corpse.

"Who the hell are you?" Logan asked.

"Don't matter," Nose said, throwing Weasel's breeches at Logan. "What matters is who I work for." He lowered his voice so the prisoners wouldn't overhear him. "I work for Jarl. A friend of a friend of yours."

"Who?"

"Jarl said to say he's the friend of a friend." Nose cut away Weasel's underclothes with the knife. "I'm just telling you what I was told to—"

"What the hell are you doing?" Logan interrupted.

"Cutting his sack off."

"Oh, shit!" Logan shut his eyes, and would have turned away if the magical bonds had allowed it.

Nose ignored him and cut. "Damn! Well, it ain't pretty, but it'll do. Good for us his hair's the same color as yourn, eh?" He stood and shook a piece of flesh at Logan. "Look, pretty boy, this wasn't my idea. But if Roth finds this sack after you and I are conveniently 'killed during the uprising,' we might both stay alive. Understand?"

"No."

"Too bad. We don't have time. That shite I was talking about on our way down here was true. There's a woman and a little girl up in the first set of cells. Jarl wants us to get 'em out. He wants to know why Roth wants 'em. Looks like those bonds are weakening. Grab a leg."

Logan found he could move his arms if he pushed hard enough, and his feet were almost loose. He grabbed one of Weasel's feet—avoiding looking at his crotch—and started dragging him with Nose.

"So you said all that just so I'd know it?" Logan asked.

Nose scowled at the long iron bars set over a dark gap in the floor. The Hole was deep enough that in the meager torchlight Logan couldn't see the bottom of it. Nose grabbed a key and unlocked a small grate at the near side of the bars. Snuffling noises and grunts that Logan would barely call human drifted up from the Hole.

"And to see if he knew anything I didn't before I killed him," Nose said. "Help me dump him in. Don't worry, it's plenty deep and the sides are sheer."

Logan moved forward reluctantly to help. He still couldn't move enough to squat to grab the grate, so Nose dragged it open and Logan shoved Weasel into the Hole.

Demonic cries of glee pierced the air and a fight promptly broke out below.

Shivering, Logan stepped away from the Hole. "What's the plan now?"

"The plan?" Nose looked down into the darkness and shook his head. "We get the hell out. If Roth wins tonight, he'll be hot to find you. Jarl will have several men report seeing your body. Someone else will have seen me dead and will finally admit to having looted my body. He'll show your 'coin purse' to Roth."

"That's pretty thin," Logan said. "Will you shut that damn grate?"

"There's hundreds of men dying upstairs. Trying to find out what happened to any one of them will be impossible. Roth knows that. Anyway, it's the best we can do and keep your head on your shoulders at the same time. Jarl will have to decide if the 'coin purse' bit is too much."

Nose stared back into the Hole, where the unmistakable sounds of feeding could be heard. He turned to Logan and smirked. "Kinda makes ya wonder, don't it?"

Logan shook his head, sickened. He looked back at Nose in time to see a thin lasso sail out of the Hole. It dropped neatly over Nose's shoulders.

In a blink, Logan saw that the rope was braided of sinews and he had an inane thought: *What animal down here is big enough that they could make a rope of its sinews?*

Nose's eyes filled with terror, then the lasso jerked tight and yanked him off his feet. He smacked full-length across the open grate and spread his arms and legs to keep from falling in. But raising his arms brought the noose off his shoulders and around his neck. A wild cackle sounded from the Hole. Logan staggered forward, moving faster than he had for half an hour, but he was too slow.

Nose's eyes bulged as pressure mounted on the rope around his neck.

There must have been five men pulling it. His arms weakened as he blinked at Logan, eyes bulging grotesquely.

Then his arms folded and he slid into the Hole.

Logan tried to grab for the man. Instead, he stumbled, tripped against the last vestiges of his bonds and found himself rolling toward the Hole himself.

He gripped the bars and found himself staring down. He could vaguely make out the forms of men in a knot, limbs rising and falling, screeching and tearing at each other and Nose, who was flailing and screaming.

For a full minute, Logan was stuck there, unable to move his arms and legs far enough to push himself away. Nose gradually stopped shrieking and the dark forms retreated from each other to feed.

Then one of the men saw Logan and shouted.

Logan flung himself to the side as hard as he could. He felt the weakened magic strain and snap. He flopped on his back on the jagged stones, then sat and flipped the grate closed.

The key had fallen out of Nose's hand when the rope had jerked him from his feet, but Logan was shaking too badly to lock the grate. Unsteadily, he got to his feet and walked up the hall.

Logan pulled on Weasel's clothes, stretching them over his taller, more muscular body. He was lucky that the man's clothing had been baggy or it wouldn't have fit him at all. After pulling on boots that pinched his feet terribly, Logan stood.

He tried to find the strength to go back and lock the grate. If he never saw a prison again, he knew he would still have nightmares of this day for the rest of his life. The last thing he wanted was to go back down the long hallway to the Hole.

But he couldn't let animals like that have even the slimmest chance of escape.

He walked down the long hall carefully, slowly, even though he knew he should hurry. Several paces from the grate, he stopped. It was undisturbed, but he could still hear the sounds of men tearing meat. He wanted to vomit.

The sound of approaching voices came to Logan from above. The long rock halls carried their words.

"Hey, you!" a voice with a Khalidoran accent demanded.

One of the men in the last set of cells before the Hole answered, but Logan couldn't distinguish his words.

"Did a couple of soldiers and a prisoner come this way?"

Logan froze as the prisoner murmured something.

"See?" the voice said. "They didn't come this way. And believe me, you don't want to go down to the Hole."

Logan silently blessed the prisoner who'd lied probably more out of the habit of lying to authorities than to save him.

"And you think a prisoner is going to tell you the truth?" a man with a cultured Khalidoran accent asked. "The prince demanded confirmation that Logan Gyre is dead. All your men are cooperating and searching the rest of this dungeon. Are you trying to hinder us?"

"No, sir!"

An unnatural, unflickering red light illuminated the long hallway.

A wytch! Oh shit, where can I go?

In the feeble torchlight, Logan examined the hallway again. But there were no niches, no crawl spaces. It was a dead end.

Have I been spared from death so many times just for this?

Logan considered a mad rush at the men. With only a knife, it would be tight, but if he could kill the wytch first he might have a chance.

"This is a place of power; I feel dizzy with it," a different voice said.

"Indeed," the first wytch answered, "I've not felt so much evil in one space since—well, since I last met with our liege."

For some reason, they found that humorous. Logan's heart broke as he heard at least six men laughing.

Six men. Maybe five wytches. At least two. Even if it were two wytches and four soldiers, Logan was lost. And the red light was growing brighter; they were only steps away.

With dread, Logan looked down at the grate. It was the only way. Count Drake had told him that life was precious, that suicide was a coward's way out, a sin against the God by flinging his gift back in his holy face.

What was it Kylar had told him once? They had been propositioned by black-black market prostitutes, girls who operated outside of the Sa'kagé's control and protection. The girls, neither more than twelve, had offered themselves specifically for degrading practices Logan hadn't even heard of. Kylar had just said, "You'd be surprised at what you'd do to stay alive."

You'd be surprised at what you'd do to stay alive.

Logan opened the grate and slipped inside. He hung on the iron bars by one hand while he locked it. Then he tucked the key back into a pocket, drew his knife, and dropped into hell.

*I*t wasn't until Kylar was flying through the air that he realized just exactly how far down it was to the river. He had no excuse, really. He'd been dangling out of this very window, looking at this very view, not five minutes ago. Except now the view was enlarging. Rapidly. He was going to clear the rocks. That was good. He was also going to hit the river at incredible speed, face first. Maybe a trained diver could have taken such a plunge without harm, but Kylar wasn't a diver.

The river filled all his vision and he flung his hands out. A thin wedge of Talent wrapped around him.

Then he plunged into the river. His outstretched hands did nothing, but the wedge of Talent protected him and drove him under the river's skin like a splinter.

The wedge collapsed an instant after he hit and the water slapped him as brutally as if a giant had clapped his hands together over the whole of Kylar's body.

He was dreaming again, if it was called a dream when.... *When what?* The thought dribbled through Kylar's fingers and he lost it.

It was the dream he dreamt whenever he'd seen death for the last ten years. Like always, for a brief moment, he knew it was a dream. He knew it was a dream, but by the time he realized what dream it was, he couldn't pull away. It swelled around him, and he was eleven again.

The boat repair shop is dark, abandoned, cold in the silver moonlight. Azoth is terrified beyond terror even though he planned this. Now he turns and Rat is behind him, naked.

Azoth edges toward the hole where boats once were lifted from the filthy waters of the Plith, edges toward rope and the rock tied to it and the noose he knotted on the end.

"Kiss me again," Rat says, and he's right in front of Azoth, hands grabbing at him lustfully. "Kiss me again."

Where's the noose? *He'd put it here, hadn't he? He sees the rock that was supposed to drag Rat to a watery death but where's the—Rat pulls him close and his breath is hot on Azoth's face, and his hands are pulling at Azoth's clothes—*

Kylar hit the bottom of the river with a bump. His eyes flicked open and he saw Retribution inches away from his face. In the shock of hitting the water, it had been torn from his grasp. He was lucky he hadn't cut himself to pieces with it. He was lucky that the silver blade had plunged straight to the bottom with him.

Suddenly aware of the burning in his lungs, Kylar grabbed Retribution and pulled for the surface.

How long have I been down here? It couldn't have been more than a moment, or he would have drifted away and drowned. Seconds later, Kylar was surprised to find himself breathing air again and uninjured, at least from the fall. His nose and fingers were still bleeding, though, briefly staining the waters around him. The current jostled him up against a rock and he pulled himself up.

He'd washed up on the rocks on the Vos Island side under East Kingsbridge, directly across the river from the Jadwin estate. The bank of the river where he stood was also the foundation of the castle wall, so to go upstream, he had to half climb and half swim. It took him ten exhausting minutes to get to a point where he could climb out of the water again.

The docks where he'd seen Roth were at the northern tip of the island. To get there, he'd have to either continue through the water and the boulders along the river, or he'd have to go through the squat, stinking building that covered the Vos Island Crack.

Kylar didn't think he could make it over the rocks for another ten or twenty minutes. Even if Roth were still there when he arrived, Kylar was too weak to go that way. His nose had finally stopped bleeding, and he'd wrapped his hand so it wasn't bleeding too badly, but if he tried to swim, it would bleed again. His hand throbbed and his whole body felt weak from the blood he'd lost.

If it were any other night, Kylar would have left. He was in no shape to attempt an assassination. But logic didn't mean much. Not tonight. Not after what Roth had done.

The building on the Vos Island Crack was built of stone in a square, thirty paces on a side and only a single story above ground. It was supposed to be a marvel of engineering, but Kylar knew little about it. He supposed nobles weren't impressed by a marvel that smelled like rotten eggs.

It was stupidity to go on. Kylar was so exhausted he could barely even think of using his Talent. It took a certain kind of strength of its own to do that. He propped himself against the heavy door, gathering his strength. He was still holding Retribution. Looking down at the blade, he stared at the word etched into the blade. JUSTICE. Except it didn't say "justice" now. He blinked.

MERCY, it said in the same silver script, exactly where it used to say JUSTICE in black. On the hilt, perpendicular to that, now also silver where it had been ka'kari-black, it said VENGEANCE.

The ka'kari was gone. Kylar was so tired-stupid that for a moment he despaired. Then he remembered where it had gone. *It went into my skin?* Just how tired was he? Surely that must have been his imagination. A hallucination.

He turned his hand over and black sweat suddenly poured from his palm like oil, fluid for an instant, then suddenly congealing into a warm metal sphere. It was midnight black now, utterly featureless. A black ka'kari. Logan's stories had mentioned only six: white, green, brown, silver, red, and blue. Emperor Jorsin Alkestes and his archmagus Ezra had given them to six champions, slighting one of Jorsin's best friends, who then betrayed him. After the war, the six ka'kari had been objects of great lust, and those who carried them died quickly.

Kylar tried to remember the name of the betrayer. It was Acaelus Thorne. Jorsin hadn't slighted him after all. By pretending to slight him, Jorsin had given his best friend a way to escape—and keep an artifact out of enemy hands. Because no one had known of the black's existence, Acaelus hadn't been hunted. Acaelus had survived.

Durzo had signed his letter "A Thorne."

"Oh, gods," Kylar breathed. He couldn't think about it now, couldn't stop or he wouldn't be able to start moving again. "Help me," Kylar said to the ka'kari. "Please. Serve me." He squeezed the ka'kari and it dissolved, rushing along his skin, up over his clothes, over his face, over his eyes. He flinched, but he could still see perfectly—still see through the dark as if it were natural. He looked down at his hands, his black sword, and saw them shimmer with magic and disappear. They weren't just cloaked in shadows, as wetboys cloaked themselves. They disappeared. Kylar wasn't a shadow like before. He was invisible.

There was no time to marvel; he had work to do. It had been ten minutes or more since he'd seen Roth on the dock. If Roth was going to die tonight, Kylar needed to move. He picked the lock and stepped inside.

The inside of the building was stiflingly hot. Wooden catwalks surrounded a mammoth central chimney fifteen paces in diameter. It was made of broad sheets of metal riveted together and supported by an external wood frame. The chimney descended at least four stories into the ground to meet the natural crack in the earth's crust.

Looking into the shadowed depths of the Crack, Kylar understood why people called this a marvel. The men who worked here not only harnessed the power of the hot air that blew out of the earth itself, they also kept the Plith River from spilling into the earth.

If that happened, the river would boil; the fish would die; the fishermen would be wiped out; and Cenaria would lose its major source of food.

Even now, oblivious to the chaos not a quarter of a mile away, men were working: servicing ropes, checking pulleys, greasing gears, replacing sections of sheet metal.

Kylar crossed a long catwalk, took a few turns, and found himself at a crossroads where he could go to a door below ground level or go up to a maintenance door by the outlet of the chimney on the north side of the building—where Roth would be.

He went down. The door was set beside double doors used for bringing in huge pieces of equipment. Kylar eased it open a crack.

A young wytch was standing outside, her hair pulled back and vir-marked arms folded. She was looking up a long stone ramp. Someone was talking to her, but Kylar couldn't see the other person. Beyond her were a dozen others, dressed similarly.

Kylar eased the door shut. He went back to the other branch of the catwalk and opened the door set into the horizontal section of the chimney.

Bent sideways, the chimney was more like a steam tunnel here. It was fifteen paces across until it pinched down to four paces at the last fan. The floor was sheet metal reinforced underneath so the workers could stand inside it as they worked on either the massive fan set just before the chimney turned straight down, or the much smaller last fan before the hot air escaped into the Cenarian night. The northern fan spun slowly enough that Kylar should be able to see Roth through it.

He stepped inside carefully, testing the floor to see if it would squeak as he put his weight on it. It didn't. But even before Kylar closed the door behind himself, he had a vaguely uneasy feeling.

Cooled from its long journey up the metal chimney, sulfuric smoke poured sluggishly through the tunnel into the night air outside. Heavy smoke filled the bottom third of the tunnel, curling and rolling. The only light came from the moon outside but was filtered through the spinning fan. Between the dense smoke and the dancing shadows, Kylar's vision was no better than any other man's.

There's someone here.

59

*D*urzo's heart had just leapt out that goddam window. He walked to the window and watched until he saw Kylar surface.

Amazing. *In all my years, I never tried anything so dumb, and here he does it on his first day—and it works.* Kylar clambered onto shore and began working his way north. Durzo knew where he was headed. The stubborn fool. He'd always had that streak, from the time he'd refused to accept that he'd failed in Rat's murder and had gone and killed the twist in the next three hours.

Kylar did what he thought was right, and to hell with the consequences, to hell with what anyone thought, even Durzo. He reminded Durzo of Jorsin Alkestes. Kylar had chosen his loyalty to Durzo, had clung to it despite Durzo. He'd put faith in Durzo Blint as Jorsin had put faith in him. Kylar was just a damned kid, but he'd also put his faith in a much worse man than Acaelus Thorne.

The pain resonated along every string in Durzo Blint's life. He'd been a thousand kinds of fraud in his years, so everyone who had believed in him during his deceptions could be written off, but Jorsin had known him. Kylar had known him. Not for the first time in seven centuries, existence ached. All the world was salt and Durzo Blint was an open wound. *Where did I go wrong?*

He moved, because like every man Acaelus Thorne had been, Durzo Blint was a man of action. His Talent puddled around his hands and feet— funny that it still worked like that, despite losing the ka'kari—and he stepped out of the window. He didn't fall.

The magic around his feet gripped the stone and he pitched forward, catching himself with his hands so that he hung face down on the castle wall like an insect. Kylar hadn't learned all of Durzo's tricks. Hell, he hadn't even seen all of Durzo's tricks.

He knew where Kylar was headed, and he knew how to get there faster than Kylar could, so he was in no hurry. The clash of arms in the courtyard attracted his attention. He cloaked himself in shadows and crawled down to the courtyard.

The battle was deadlocked. Two hundred Cenarian guardsmen and the forty or more useless nobles with them couldn't budge the hundred Khalidorans who were blocking the gate to East Kingsbridge. The Khalidorans had half a dozen meisters with them, but this late in the battle, they weren't doing much except psychologically. They'd used pretty much as much magic as they were able to.

With eyes long honed in battle and the arts of assassination, Durzo picked out the cornerstones of the battle. Sometimes that was simple. Officers were usually important. Meisters always were, but sometimes there were simple soldiers in the lines who were strength for the men around them. If you killed the cornerstones, the whole battle would shift. On the Khalidoran side, the cornerstones were two officers and three of the meisters and one giant of a highlander. On the Cenarian side, there were only two: a sergeant with an Alitaeran longbow and Terah Graesin.

The sergeant was a simple soldier, probably in his first battle despite his age, and Durzo knew the look on his face. He was a man who had joined the military to find his measure and had finally found it in battle. He had passed his own Crucible, and approved of himself. It was a potent thing, that approval, and every man around the sergeant felt it.

Terah Graesin, of course, would have stood out in any crowd. She was all tits and haughtiness, a vision in a torn cerulean gown. She believed no harm would dare step into her presence. She believed everyone around her would obey her, and the men felt that, too.

"Sergeant Gamble," a familiar voice said, just below Durzo. The sergeant loosed another arrow, killing a meister, but not one of the important ones.

Count Drake emerged from the front gate and grabbed the sergeant. "Another hundred highlanders on their way," Count Drake said, his voice almost swallowed by the clash of arms and the press of men back and forth in the courtyard.

The sight of the count packed the wound Kylar had opened with more salt. Durzo had thought the count was staying home, but here he was, still ill from Durzo's poison, about to die with all the rest.

"Dammit!" Sergeant Gamble cursed.

Durzo turned away from them. The Cenarians would be slaughtered. It was out of his hands. He had his own date with judgment.

"Night Angel," the sergeant yelled. "If you fight with us still, fight now! Night Angel! Come!"

Durzo froze. He could only guess Kylar had already intervened in the castle somehow. *Very well, Kylar. I'll do this for you, and the count, and for Jorsin, and for all the fools who believe that even a killer may accomplish some good.*

"Give me your bow," Durzo said. It was a hard, menacing voice, pitched with Talent to carry. Sergeant Gamble's head whipped around and he and Count Drake looked at the shadow over the gate. The sergeant threw him his bow and a fresh quiver of arrows.

Durzo caught the bow in his hand and the quiver with his Talent. As he drew one arrow, he pulled another from the quiver with his Talent. He squatted against the vertical face of the wall and in an instant locked his deaders into his mind's eye.

The giant highlander went down first, an arrow catching him between the eyes. Then the meisters, every last one of them, then the officers, then a wedge of the highlanders directly in front of the bridge. Durzo emptied the quiver of twenty arrows in less than ten seconds. It was, Durzo thought, some damn fine shooting. Of course, Gaelan Starfire had been quite a hand with the longbow.

Durzo tossed the bow back to Sergeant Gamble, who didn't seem to comprehend yet what had happened. Count Drake was a different matter. He didn't even look at the courtyard as the Cenarian line surged forward into the gap. He wasn't surprised at the sudden hesitation in the Khalidoran ranks that within seconds would turn into a rout. He was looking toward Durzo.

Sergeant Gamble uttered an awed curse, but Count Drake's mouth opened to bestow a blessing. Durzo couldn't take it. He was already gone.

No more blessings. No more mercy. No more salt. No more light in my dark corners. Let this end. Please.

60

Fear flashed through Kylar. He dropped into the smoke. A thunk and a metal whine resounded above him. He rolled and saw one knife sticking out of the door and one sticking through the sheet metal of the chimney.

"So you figured out that it will make you invisible, huh?" Durzo Blint said from somewhere in the darkness near the huge fan at the south end of the tunnel.

"Dammit, Blint! I told you I don't want to fight," Kylar said, then moved away from where he'd been standing when he spoke.

He scanned the darkness. Even if Durzo weren't fully invisible, in the smoke and flickering interplay of light and shadow he might as well be.

"That was quite a dive, boy. You trying to become a legend yourself?" Durzo asked, but his voice oddly strangled, mournful. Kylar stumbled. Durzo was now by the smaller fan at the north end of the tunnel. He must have passed within a pace of Kylar to get there.

"Who are you?" Kylar asked. "You're Acaelus Thorne, aren't you?" Kylar almost forgot to move.

A knife sailed a hand's breadth from Kylar's stomach and pinged off the wall.

"Acaelus was a fool. He played the Devil and now I draw the Devil's due." Durzo's voice was raw, husky. He'd been weeping.

"Master Blint," Kylar said, adding the honorific for the first time since before he'd taken the ka'kari. "Why don't you join me? Help me kill Roth. He's outside, isn't he?"

"Outside with a boatload of meisters and Vürdmeisters," Durzo said. "It's over, Kylar. Khalidor will hold the castle within an hour. More highlanders arrive at dawn, and an army of Khalidoran regulars is already marching for the city. Anyone who could have led an army against them is dead or fled."

There was a distant gong, reverberating up the raw throat of the chimney. Warm air started blowing up from the depths.

Kylar felt sickened. His work had been for nothing. A few soldiers killed, a few nobles saved—it hadn't changed anything.

He padded over to the small north fan, which was now turning faster. Through its blades, he could see Roth conferring with the wytches.

Durzo was right. There were dozens of wytches. Some were getting back into their boat, but at least a score were accompanying Roth, who also had a bodyguard of a dozen gigantic highlanders.

"Roth killed my best friend," Kylar said. "I'm going to kill him. Tonight."

"Then you'll have to go through me."

"I won't fight you."

"You've always wondered if you'd be able to beat me when it came down to it," Durzo said. "I know you have. And you have your Talent and the ka'kari now. As a boy, you swore you wouldn't let anyone beat you. Not ever again. You said you wanted to be a killer. Have I made you one or not?"

"Damn you! I won't fight you! Who's Acaelus?" Kylar shouted.

Durzo's voice rose, chanting over the sound of fans and hot wind:

"The hand of the wicked shall rise against him,
But it shall not prevail.
Their blades shall be devoured
The swords of the unrighteous shall pierce him
But he shall not fall
He shall leap from the roofs of the world
and smite princes..."

Blint trailed off. "I never made it," he said quietly.

"What are you talking about? What is that? Is that a prophecy?"

"That isn't me, just like the Guardian of Light wasn't Jorsin. It's you, Kylar. You are the spirit of retribution, the Night Angel. You are the vengeance I deserve."

Vengeance stems from a love of justice and a desire to redress wrongs. But revenge is damning. Three faces has the Night Angel, the avatar of Retribution: Vengeance, Justice, Mercy.

"But I don't have anything to avenge. I owe you my life," Kylar said.

Durzo's face grew somber. "Yes, this life of blood. I served that goddam ka'kari for almost seven hundred years, Kylar. I served a dead king and a people who weren't worthy of him. I lived in the shadows and I became like the shadow-dwellers. I gave all I was for some dream of hope that I never understood in the first place. What happens when you strip away all the masks a man wears and you find not a face beneath them but nothing at all? I failed the ka'kari once. *Once* I failed in seven hundred years of service, and it abandoned me.

"I didn't age a day, Kylar, not a day, for seven hundred years. Then came Gwinvere, and Vonda. I loved her, Kylar."

"I know," Kylar said gently. "I'm sorry about Vonda."

Durzo shook his head. "No. I didn't love Vonda. I just wanted—I wanted Gwinvere to know how it felt to have someone you love sharing other people's beds. I fucked them both and I paid Gwinvere, but it was Vonda I made a whore. That was why I wanted the silver ka'kari at first—to give it to Gwinvere, so she wouldn't die as everyone I've loved has died. But King Davin's rock was a fake, so I left it for Garoth Ursuul's men to find. The only way to save Vonda would have been to give them my ka'kari. I balanced her life against my power and my eternal life. I didn't love her, so the price was too high. I let her die.

"That was the day the ka'kari stopped serving me. I began to age. The ka'kari became nothing more than black paint on a sword that mocked me with the word JUSTICE. Justice was that I get old, lose my edge, die. You were my only hope, Kylar. I knew you were a ka'karifer. You would call the ka'kari to you. There were rumors that there was another in the kingdom. The black ka'kari had rejected me, but maybe the silver would not. A slim hope, but a hope for another chance, for redemption, for life. But you only called my ka'kari. You began to bond it that day I beat you, the day you risked your life to save that girl. I was insane. You were taking from me the only thing I had left. Reputation gone, honor gone, excellence fading, friends dead, the woman I loved hating me, and then you took my hope." He looked away. "I wanted to end you. But I couldn't." He threw a garlic clove in his mouth. "I knew that first kill wasn't in you. Not even that twist Rat. I knew you couldn't kill someone for what he *might* do."

"What?" Kylar's skin prickled.

"The streets would have devoured you. I had to save you. Even if I knew it would come to this."

"What are you saying?" Kylar asked. *No. God, please no. Don't let it fit.*

"Rat didn't mutilate Doll Girl," Durzo said. "I did."

The smoke half-filled the tunnel now. The huge fan turned slowly and the smaller fan was spinning as fast as Kylar's heart was beating. The moonlight was chopped into pieces and scattered wantonly through the roiling smoke.

Kylar couldn't move. Couldn't breathe. Couldn't even protest. It was a lie. It had to be a lie. He knew Rat. He'd seen his eyes. He'd seen the evil there.

But he'd never seen Durzo's evil, had he? Kylar had seen his master kill innocents, yet he'd never let himself see the evil there.

The big fan spun quickly now. Its whup-whup-whup chopped time into pieces, marked its passage as if time had significance.

"No." Kylar could barely force the word through the stranglehold of truth tightening his throat. Blint would do it. *Life is empty. Life is empty. A street girl is worth exactly what she can get for whoring.*

"No!" Kylar shouted.

"It ends now, Kylar." Durzo shimmered and disappeared, the darkness embracing him. Kylar felt rage, stark, hot rage rush through him.

Under the sounds of the protesting fans and the hot wind, Kylar barely heard the footsteps. He wheeled and dived.

The smoke swirled as the shadowy wetboy ran past him.

He heard a sword clearing a scabbard and he drew Retribution. A shadow appeared, too close, too fast. They clashed and Kylar's sword went flying. He dove backward.

Kylar came to his feet slowly, silently, straining his senses, crouching low in the smoke. The rage overcame his fatigue, and he channeled it, forced it to bring clarity.

He looked for any advantage, but there was little to be found. He could stand close to the huge southern fan and it would protect his back, but Blint could easily knock him into the spinning blades. They weren't so sharp or turning so fast that they'd sever a limb, but they'd certainly stun him. In a fight against Durzo, that would mean death.

Handholds were set into the walls and ceiling of the tunnel at intervals so the workers could replace sections. But where Kylar stood, the handholds were at least ten feet over his head.

A brief jolt of his Talent coursed through him as he leapt. He found a rung in his grip. As his right hand flexed, he almost fell. He'd forgotten that the window had slashed his hand open.

Kylar swung and looped his feet behind another rung to stabilize himself. His right hand was too weak to hold his weight, so he drew the tanto with that hand. The gong sounded again as Kylar looked at the tanto. It was straight, eight inches long, and had an angled point for punching through armor. With his hand as weak as it was, he couldn't slash with this knife.

He sheathed the tanto, popped the catch on a special sheath, and drew out a short curving knife only half the size of the tanto. Four tiny holes up the spine of the blade were stuffed with cotton. The sheath was wet. Kylar didn't know if the white asp poison had been washed off by the river or not. But he had no choice.

The wind slowed and then stopped abruptly. The great fans still spun, rattling on their greased axles.

Kylar held still and waited. The smoke was gradually drifting lower again, no longer filling the entire tunnel. The next time Durzo moved through the smoke, Kylar would be able to see the disturbance even if he couldn't see the wetboy himself.

The fans rattled down to a bare whisper and soon Kylar could hear no other sound but the pounding of his pulse in his own ears. He was straining now, not just to see or hear the wetboy, but merely to hold himself in place—and hold himself there silently.

If Durzo heard him, Kylar was totally exposed. With his feet locked behind the rung, he wouldn't be able to move quickly. And he made a huge target.

His only advantage would be surprise. But Durzo had taught him that that was the most important advantage of all.

A minute passed.

The fans went completely silent. Even the low mutter of voices from outside was gone. The smoke, cooling once more, settled back into its cradle along the bottom of the tunnel.

Agonizingly slowly, Kylar turned his head, careful that not even his collar rustled. Surely with the smoke this low, drifting slowly as it did to the north, he should be able to see something, some eddy, some curl out of place.

He breathed the way he moved: slowly, carefully. His nose, bloodied earlier against the tower wall, allowed air to pass only through one nostril. His left arm was burning; his legs ached, but still he made no move, no sound.

Dread grew in his heart as he hung there. How could he fight Durzo? How many men had his master killed? How many times had Durzo beaten him in every test, every challenge? How could Kylar fight now, injured and weak as he was? Durzo could wait on the bottom of the tunnel forever. He'd probably placed himself by the smaller north fan. With the light at his back, he'd see as soon as Kylar dropped and be on him in a second.

Who was Kylar to kill a legend?

He tried to still the racing of his heart. His throat was tight. The hot emotions that had fueled him throughout the night cooled. He was cold. Empty. Durzo was right, justice had no place in this world. Logan was dead. Elene had been beaten, and the men who had done all the evil Kylar could imagine were winning. They always had. They always would.

He couldn't hold on much longer. Durzo would hear the sound of his heart, thudding as it was against his chest. He forced himself to breathe slowly.

Patience! Patience.

He drew a slow breath again and paused. There was the slightest tang on the air.

Garlic! Both master and apprentice had had the same thought. Durzo was hanging exactly as Kylar was, mirror-image, inches away, poised watching the smoke for the slightest eddy.

Kylar jerked his head up and lashed out with the little knife. He must have made a sound, because the smear of darkness that had been just one rung above him was moving too.

His knife cut cloth and he blocked an attack with his other hand as they both dropped off the ceiling.

Kylar hit the floor heavily, splashing in the puddle gathered in the tunnel's bottom and hitting the metal so hard that he felt a sting in his neck. He rolled and jumped to his feet. He heard the ring of a sword clearing its scabbard.

Durzo winked back into visibility. Kylar let himself become visible too. He was too tired to maintain invisibility for another second. He felt like a wrung-out rag. He stared at three feet of steel in Blint's hand and the four inches in his own.

"So it comes to this," Durzo said. "I don't suppose you have any more tricks like that one up in the tower?"

"I don't even know how that happened," Kylar said. "I've got nothing left."

"Good thing I didn't let you go after Roth then, isn't it?" Durzo said, that infuriating little smirk on his lips.

Kylar didn't have it in him to get angry. He was a shell. "I don't see how it matters," he said. "But I'd rather my blood was on his head than yours."

He sheathed the dagger.

"You used the asp venom, didn't you?" Durzo said. He laughed. "Of course you did." Durzo saluted Kylar and sheathed his sword.

Then he sagged and had to grab onto a rung on the wall to keep from falling. "I always wondered how it really felt," Durzo said. He reached up to the gash in his tunic. Kylar had thought he'd only cut cloth, but Durzo's chest bled from a shallow cut.

"Master!" Kylar rushed to him and kept him from falling as he swooned again.

Blint chuckled, his face was a cadaverous white. "I haven't worried about dying in a long time. It's not so bad." He winced. "It's not so good either. Kylar, promise me something."

"Anything."

"Take care of my little girl. Save her. Momma K will know where they've got her."

"I can't," Kylar said. "I would, but I can't."

He turned his head and pulled Durzo's dart out of his neck. At first, he'd thought the twinge in his neck was from hitting the ground, but as soon as he moved, he knew better. It was a poisoned dart. Kylar was dying, too.

Durzo laughed. "Lucky throw," he said. "Get me out of this tunnel. I'll have to smell brimstone soon enough."

Kylar pulled the two of them out of the door of the tunnel. He helped Durzo sit on the walkway and then sat across from him. Kylar was exhausted.

Maybe the poison on the dart was king snake venom with hemlock, then.

"You really love that Elene girl, don't you?"

"I do," Kylar said. "I really do." Oddly, that was his only regret. He should have been a different man, a better man.

"I should be dead by now," Durzo said.

"The knife got wet." Was that touch of dizziness the poison?

Durzo tried to laugh, but eyes filled with sorrow instead. "Jorsin told me, 'Six ka'kari for six angels of light, but one ka'kari stands watch in the night.' The black has chosen you, Kylar. You are the Night Angel now. Give these petty, ungrateful people better than they deserve. Give them hope. This is your master's piece: Kill Roth. For this city. For my daughter. For me." His fingers dug painfully into Kylar's arm. "I'm sorry, son. Sorry for all of it. Someday, maybe you can forgive...." his eyes dipped drowsily and he fought to open them, to stay focused.

Durzo wasn't making sense. He knew Kylar was dying. It must have been the poison. "I do forgive you," Kylar said. "May our deaths not be on each other's heads."

Durzo's eyes lit suddenly and he seemed to rally against the poison in his veins. He smiled. "I didn't poison...the dart....The letter..." Durzo died in mid-breath, a slight tremor passing through his body, his eyes still fixed on Kylar.

Kylar closed Durzo's eyes. A hollow enormity swallowed his stomach. A cry was stuck somewhere inside him, lost in the dark emptiness in his throat. Kylar stood woodenly, not taking enough care. The corpse slid from his lap, its head smacking roughly on the iron walkway. Its limbs were loose, graceless, lying in an uncomfortable position. Unmoving. Just like any corpse. In life, every man was unique. In death, every man was meat. Durzo was like any deader.

Numb, Kylar reached into the corpse's breast pocket and pulled out the letter Durzo had said was his inheritance. It was just under where Kylar had cut the wetboy's chest.

The letter was soaked with blood. Whatever words had been scrawled on the paper were illegible. Whatever Durzo had meant to excuse, whatever he had meant to explain, whatever gift he had meant to give Kylar with his last words had died with him. Kylar was alone.

Kylar dropped to his knees, all his strength gone. He took the dead wetboy in his arms and wept. He stayed there for a long time.

61

*D*awn found Kylar stumbling through the streets to one of his safe houses. Before he'd finally left, he'd erected a cairn over Durzo's body on the northern tip of Vos Island. At that hour, no one had been in sight. Kylar had stolen a rowboat from the dock and let the current carry him to the Warrens, too exhausted to paddle.

He'd docked at the shop where he'd killed Rat. It was still dark and inconspicuous, perfect for his kind of work. He wondered if Rat was still anchored in the muck, his unquiet spirit staring up at Kylar's little boat with the hatred and evil that had once lived in his adolescent heart.

It was a morning for lonely meditations. Kylar disabled the traps on his door automatically and stumbled inside. Blint had been right. It would have been suicide to go after Roth last night. Kylar had been so exhausted he'd thought it was poison working on him. He probably wouldn't have made it through a single meister.

It might be worth it to trade life for life to rid the earth of Roth Ursuul, but Kylar wasn't going to die for nothing. He locked the door, then stopped and turned back. He locked each of the three locks three times. Lock, unlock, lock. *For you, master.*

He took the pitcher of water and filled the basin with water and took the soap and began cleaning the blood from his hands. The face in the mirror was cold, calm as he washed the last vestiges of his master's life away. Blood marred the handle of the pitcher, just a little. Just a small, dark smear from the blood on his hands.

Kylar snatched the pitcher up and hurled it through the mirror. Both pitcher and mirror shattered, spraying glass and porcelain and water against the wall, into the room, onto his clothes, onto his face. He dropped to his knees and wept.

Finally, he slept. When he woke, he felt better than he had any right to. He washed himself and felt refreshed. As he scraped off his stubble, he caught himself grinning in one of the shards of the mirror. *Blint didn't mean to kill me at all, but he couldn't resist putting a dart in me just to show that he could. The old bastard. Kylar laughed. The* really *old bastard.*

It was gallows humor, but he needed whatever he could find.

He got dressed and armed, thinking mournfully of the gear he'd lost last night. Daggers, poisons, grappling hooks, throwing knives, tanto, poisoner's knife—he'd lost all of his favorites except for Retribution. *Mourning my gear, but not Logan or Durzo or Elene.* It was so ridiculous that Kylar laughed again.

He was, he decided, a little off. Maybe it was natural. He'd never lost anyone he really cared about before. Now he'd lost three in one night.

The streets were crowded in the late afternoon when Kylar finally emerged from his safe house. Rumors were flying about what had happened at the castle in the night. An army had appeared from thin air. An army had boiled up out of the Vos Island Crack. An army of mages from the south had come. No, they were wytches from the north. Highlanders had killed everyone in the castle. Khalidor was going to raze the entire city.

Few of the rumormongers seemed worried. Kylar saw a few people with their belongings loaded onto carts or wagons and heading out of the city, but there weren't many. No one else seemed to believe that anything bad could happen to them.

Momma K's hideout was still being guarded by the sinewy Cewan pretending to fix the fence. Kylar didn't bother becoming invisible. He approached the man unhurriedly, leaned over to ask directions and put a hand on the man's concealed short sword. The man tried to draw too late and found the sword locked in Kylar's grip. Kylar broke the man's sternum with an open-handed strike, leaving him gasping, his mouth working like a fish's.

Kylar took the keys from the man's belt and opened the door. He locked it after himself and embraced the shadows.

Invisible, he found Momma K in the study looking over reports from her brothels. He read them silently over her shoulder. She was trying to piece together what had happened at the castle.

The needle sank into the sagging flesh at the back of her arm. She cried out and clawed at it. She pulled the needle out then turned her chair slowly, looking ancient.

"Hello, Kylar," she said. "I expected you yesterday."

He appeared in the other chair, a lounging young Death. "How'd you know it was me?"

"Durzo would have used a poison that would leave me in agony."

"It's a tincture of ariamu root and jacinth spoor," Kylar said. "The agony's coming."

"A slow poison. So you decided to give me time. What for, Kylar? To apologize? To cry? To beg?"

"To think. To remember. To regret."

"So this is retribution. There's a new young killer on the streets doling out what old whores deserve."

"Yes, and you deserve to lose the very thing that made you betray Durzo."

"And what's that, oh wise one?" She smiled a serpent's smile.

"Control." Kylar's tone was flat, apathetic. "And don't reach for the bell rope. I've got a hand crossbow, but it's not accurate. I might hit your hand rather than the rope."

"Control, is that what you call it," Momma K said, her back ramrod straight, not making it a question. "Do you know that rapes aren't spread out evenly, even among working girls? Some girls get raped again and again. Others never do. The ones who get raped are the victims. The rapist bastards can somehow tell. It's not 'control,' Kylar. It's dignity. Do you know how much dignity a fourteen-year-old has when her pimp won't protect her?

"When I was fourteen, I was taken to a noble's house and enjoyed for fifteen hours by him and his ten closest friends. I had to make a choice after that, Kylar, and I chose dignity. So if you think giving me a poison that makes me shit myself to death is going to make me beg, you're sadly mistaken."

Kylar was unmoved. "Why did you betray us?"

Momma K's defiance slowly faded as Kylar sat there with a wetboy's patience. She didn't answer him for a minute, five minutes. He sat with all the patience of Death. By now, he knew, she had to be feeling queasy.

"I loved Durzo," she said.

Kylar blinked. "You what?"

"I've slept with hundreds of married men in my life, Kylar, so I never saw the most flattering portrait of marriage. But if he'd asked me, I would have married Durzo Blint. Durzo is—was, I suppose you killed him? Yes, I thought so. Durzo was a good man in his way. An honest man." Her lips twitched. "I couldn't handle honesty. He told me too many unlovely truths about myself, and that hard, dark thing that lives in me couldn't bear the light."

She laughed. It was a bitter, ugly sound. "Besides, he never stopped loving Vonda, a woman utterly unworthy of him."

Kylar shook his head. "So you thought you'd kill him? What if he'd killed me?"

"He loved you like a son. Once you bonded the ka'kari, he told me. A life for a life, he said. The divine economy, he called it. He knew then that he'd die for you, Kylar. Oh, he fought it sometimes, but Durzo was never as unprincipled as he wanted to believe. Besides, he changed when Vonda died.

"I warned him, Kylar. She was a lovely, careless girl. The kind of woman born without a heart, so she couldn't imagine breaking anyone else's. Durzo was exciting for her. He was nothing more than her rebellion, but she died before he ever saw through her, so she was always perfect in his sight. She was forever a saint, and I was always spit-in beer."

"He didn't love her," Kylar said.

"Oh, I knew that. But Durzo didn't. For every other way that he was unique, Durzo thought excitement plus fucking is the same thing as love, just like every other man." She suddenly hunched over in pain as her stomach spasmed.

Kylar shook his head. "He told me he was trying to make you jealous, make you feel how he felt when you were with other men. When she died, he thought you could never forgive him. Gwinvere, he loved you."

She snorted in disbelief. "Why would he say such a thing? No, Kylar. Durzo was going to let his daughter die."

"That's why you betrayed him?"

"I couldn't let her die, Kylar. Don't you understand? Uly is Durzo's daughter, but she's not my niece."

"Then who's her m—...No."

"I couldn't keep her. I knew that. I always hated taking tansy tea, but that time, I couldn't do it. I sat with the cup growing cold in my hands, telling myself something like this would happen—and still I couldn't drink. A Shinga with a daughter, what more perfect target could there be? Everyone would know my weakness. Worse, everyone would see me as just another woman. I could never hold my power if that happened. So I left the city, had her in secret, and hid her away. But how could he let Uly die, even thinking she was Vonda's? How could he? Roth threatened him, but Durzo called his bluff. You don't know Roth. He would have done it. The only way I could save Uly was for Durzo to die first. If Durzo was dead, Roth wouldn't have to carry out his threat. I had to choose between the man I've loved for fifteen years and my daughter, Kylar. So I chose my daughter. Durzo wanted to die anyway, and now I do too. You can't take anything from me that I won't gladly give."

"He didn't call their bluff."

Momma K couldn't seem to grasp it. "Uh-uh," she said, shaking her head. He could see the edifice of suppositions she'd built crash down brick by brick. A Durzo who let himself be blackmailed was a Durzo who cared for a daughter he'd never seen. A Durzo who could do that was a Durzo who could love. She'd hardened her heart against him because she thought he didn't care, and couldn't.

So for fifteen years she'd been hiding her love for a man who had been hiding his love for her. That meant she'd betrayed the man who loved her. In pitting Kylar against Durzo, she'd killed the man who loved her. "Uh-uh. Uh-uh. No."

"His dying wish was that I save her. He said you'd know where she is."

"Oh gods." The words barely squeezed out, a strangled sound. Another spasm passed through her and she seemed to welcome the pain. She wanted to die.

"I'll save her, Momma K. But you need to tell me where she is."

"She's in the Maw. In the nobles' cells with Elene."

"With Elene?" Kylar stood bolt upright. "I have to go back." He got to the door, then turned and drew Retribution. Momma K looked at him hollowly, still absorbing his words.

"I used to wonder why Durzo called this 'Retribution' and not 'Justice,'" Kylar said. He drew the ka'kari off the sword and exposed the word MERCY on the steel beneath it. "Or, if this is what was under JUSTICE, why not call it MERCY? But now I know. You've shown me, Momma K. Sometimes people shouldn't get what they deserve. If there isn't more in the world than justice, it's all for nothing."

He reached into his pouch and pulled out a tiny vial of the antidote. He set it on Momma K's desk. "That's mercy. But you'll have to decide if you want to accept it. You've got half an hour." He opened the door. "I hope you'll take it, Momma K," Kylar said. "I'd miss you."

"Kylar," she called out as he reached the door. "Did he really—did he really say he loved me?"

Her mouth was set, her face tight, her eyes hard, but tears rolled down her cheeks. It was the only time he'd ever see her cry. He nodded gently and left her then, her back bent, sunk on the cushions of her chair, cheeks wet, her eyes fixed grimly on the bottle of life.

62

Kylar hurried to the castle. Even going as fast as he could, he might be too late. The effects of the coup were being felt throughout the city. The Sa'kagé's bashers had been among the first to figure out the most practical consequence of a coup: with no one to report to, and no one to pay them, the city guards didn't work. No guards, no law. The corrupt guards who had worked for the Sa'kagé for years were the first to start looting. After that, the looting spread like plague. Khalidoran highlanders and meisters were stationed on Vanden Bridge and on the east bank of the Plith to keep the looting confined to the Warrens. Apparently, Khalidor's invasion leaders wanted the city intact, or at least they wanted to do the more profitable looting themselves.

Kylar killed two men about to murder a woman, but otherwise didn't pay any attention to the looters. He cloaked himself and snuck across the river, dodging meisters who should have been more attentive.

When he got to the east side, he stole a horse. He was thinking about the Night Angels. Blint had talked about them over the years, but Kylar had never paid any attention to him. He'd always thought them just another superstition, some last vestige of old, dead gods.

Then Kylar thought about how Elene would take it even if he did rescue her. The thought made him ill. She was in gaol because of him. She thought he'd killed the prince. She hated him. He tried to plan how he was going to kill Roth—a man who would be guarded by meisters, Khalidoran high-landers, and maybe the odd Sa'kagé basher. That didn't make Kylar feel any better. The more he thought, the worse he felt.

He didn't even know if meisters could see him when he was cloaked, but the only way he could test that had serious drawbacks. He had, however, finally used his head and taken a look at himself in a mirror to see if the ka'kari was as effective as he thought. He'd been amazed. Wetboys bragged about being ghosts, about being invisible, but that was all it was: braggado-cio. No one was invisible.

The only other wetboy Kylar had seen go stealthing looked like a big blob of an indeterminate something. Blint had looked like a six foot smear of mottled darkness—good enough for all practical purposes when the light was poor. And when Blint held still, he dwindled to a shadow of a shadow.

But Kylar was *invisible*. All wetboys became more visible when they moved. When Kylar moved, there wasn't so much as a distortion in the air.

It almost irritated him that he'd spent so much time learning to sneak without his Talent. It seemed like wasted effort. Then he thought of having to sneak past the wytches. Maybe the effort wasn't wasted after all.

He rode up Sidlin Way to Horak Road, then veered around the Jadwin estate, leaving his horse and cloaking himself with the ka'kari. The sun was setting as he scouted East Kingsbridge.

As he'd expected, the security was daunting. A score of Khalidoran regulars were stationed in front of the gate. Two meisters paced among them. Two more talked together on the other side of the gate. At least four boats patrolled Vos Island, going around it in measured circles.

It was a good thing Kylar wasn't planning on getting into the castle. It was a good thing he'd come with a small arsenal. Dodging from rock to rock, tree to shrub, Kylar moved to the bridge. He unlimbered the heavy crossbow from his pack. He hated crossbows. They were unwieldy, slow, and could be shot by any idiot who could point.

Kylar fitted the special bolt in place, checked the silk spool and braced his body against the side of the bridge. What was it that Blint used to tell him? That he should practice more with weapons he didn't like?

Scowling, Kylar aimed. Thanks to the iron sheathing on the bridge pilings, his target was tiny. He'd have to hit the last piling above the iron sheathing where the wood was exposed, a target four inches wide from forty paces away, with a slight breeze. This crossbow's accuracy at that range was within two inches. So he had two inches to spare.

If he erred, he had to make sure he erred right. Up or down and the bolt would hit iron—and the sound would wake the dead. Left and the bolt would fly past the bridge and hit the rocks of the castle, and probably rebound to splash in the river.

Kylar hated crossbows.

He waited until the boat was almost directly underneath the bridge. If he made the shot—*when* he made it—he'd take advantage of the boatmen having just left the brilliance of the dying sun and coming into the shadow of the castle. Their vision wouldn't be good. He exhaled half a breath and pulled smoothly, riding the release point until the catch gave.

The bolt sped from the crossbow, the spool whizzing faintly—and the bolt sailed four inches to the right of the last piling.

Kylar grabbed the still-unreeling rope as it went taut. The bolt jerked to a stop not three feet from the castle wall.

The bolt started falling and Kylar pulled it in hand over hand as fast as he could. The rope draped over one of the crossbeams to the right of the piling he'd aimed for. It swung back toward the piling. Kylar dragged in rope as fast as he could, but the bolt pinged off the iron sheathing.

The hooks on the bolt caught and Kylar drew the rope taut, flush against the underside of the bridge.

A meister stepped to the edge of the bridge, holding onto the railing nervously. He looked down and saw the boat passing under the bridge. "Hey!" he called. "Watch it!"

A lightly armed boatman looked up, squinting in the gloom. "Right, you piece of—" He swallowed his words as he realized he was speaking to a meister.

The meister disappeared and the boatman starting haranguing his rowers. Both boatman and wytch thought the other had made the sound.

Without pausing to consider how lucky he was, Kylar secured his end of the line and hid the crossbow. The next boat was still a good distance away. Kylar threw a leg over the line, approached the precipice that sloped off to the river, and slipped out into space.

For a long time, he thought he was going to die as the silk rope drooped toward the river. *It's come free!* But he held on, and the rope finally accepted his weight. He climbed across the chasm almost upside down, pulling himself with his hands, his legs crossed over the rope. The droop of the rope meant that after he crossed the halfway point he was climbing sideways and up.

Instead of fighting it, Kylar just pulled himself as far as the second-to-last piling. He looked at the iron sheathing. It was pitted with age and exposure. It was also vertical. Not exactly the best climbing surface.

There was no good choice. Kylar had to get off the rope before the next boat came. He was invisible, but the drooping rope wasn't.

He flung himself from the rope to the piling—and fell. He slapped all of his limbs around the iron sheathing, but its diameter was so great that his arms couldn't reach around it. The uneven iron surface didn't provide enough friction to stop his descent, but it was enough to tear at the skin on the insides of his arms and his inner thighs.

He hit the water slowly enough that the splash was quiet. He clambered back up to the surface and held himself against the piling as the next boat passed.

With the number of weapons he was wearing, he couldn't swim, but when he pushed himself off the piling, he sank close enough to shore that he was able to walk along the river bottom and pull himself out of the water before he drowned. Barely.

He moved north, along the same route he'd followed the night before. Kylar was glad Blint was dead. The wetboy would never have let him live this down. Between the missed shot and the undoubtedly embarrassing cuts he'd have on his inner thighs, Blint would have had gibes for a decade. Kylar could hear it now: "Remember that time you tried to hump the bridge?"

Kylar found a perch inside the boathouse and cleaned his weapons. He'd have to assume that all of his poisons had washed away—for the second day in a row. He wrung out his clothes, but didn't dare take the time to let them dry fully. Now that he was here, he wanted to get in and get out, fast. He looked around the boathouse. It wasn't guarded. Evidently the Khalidorans thought their patrols were enough.

Two men guarded the long ramp down that led to the Maw. They were tense, obviously uncomfortable with their assignment. Kylar didn't blame them. Between the stink, the periodic cries, and the occasional rumblings in the earth, he wouldn't have been comfortable either.

Retribution slashed left and right and the men died. He pulled their bodies into the brush and took the keys to the door.

The entrance to the Maw was designed to terrify the men and women incarcerated there. On opening the gate, Kylar saw that the ramp down did indeed look like a tongue leading down a gigantic throat. Hooked teeth were carved out of the black volcanic glass around him, and torches were set behind red glass to look like two flickering, demonic eyes.

Nice. Kylar ignored everything except for the sounds of men. He glided down the tongue and turned down a hall toward the nobles' cells. From Durzo's friends he'd gained a rough idea of the layout of the place, but he'd certainly never had any wish to visit.

He found the cell he was looking for, checked the door for traps, and spent a moment waiting in the hallway, just listening. It was insane—he was afraid to open the door. He was more afraid to face Elene and Uly than he was to sneak past wytches and fight the Sa'kagé.

Gods! He was here to save Elene, and he was scared what she would say. Ridiculous. Or maybe what she wouldn't say, just how she'd look at him. He'd given everything for her! But she didn't know that. All she could know was that she'd done nothing and now she was in jail.

Well, it wasn't going to get any better by waiting.

Kylar picked the lock, released the ka'kari's cloaking, and pulled down his black mask.

The ten-by-ten cell was occupied by a pallet and a pretty little urchin sitting on Elene's lap. Kylar hardly noticed the little girl. His eyes were glued on Elene. She stared back at him, stunned. Her face was a mask—more literally than Kylar would have liked, since both of her eyes were blackened from when he'd hit her. She looked like a scarred raccoon.

If it wasn't his fault and it were someone else, Kylar would have chuckled.

"Father!" the little girl cried out. She squirmed out of Elene's lap. Still staring at Kylar, Elene barely noticed her go. Uly threw her arms around Kylar and hugged. "Mother said you'd come! She swore you'd save us. Is she with you?"

Tearing his gaze away from Elene, whose eyes had suddenly narrowed, Kylar tried to pry the little girl loose. "Uh, you must be Uly," he said.

Mother? Did she mean Momma K? Or her nurse? He'd straighten out this "father" business later. What was he going to say? *"Sorry, your mother's probably dead and I'm the one who killed her but I changed my mind about it and gave her the antidote so it's not my fault if she is dead, and I killed your father last night, too. I'm his friend. Sorry."*

He bent down so she could look him in the eye. "Your mother isn't with me, Uly. But I am here to save you. Can you be very very quiet?"

"Quiet as a mouse," she said. The kid was fearless. Either she had no sense, or Elene had done a helluva job calming her fears.

"Hello, Elene," he said, standing.

"Hello, whatever your name is."

"His name's Durzo, but we can call him Zoey," Uly said. Kylar winked at her, glad for the interruption. Even if children were generally intolerable, she'd averted a conversation he wasn't interested in having—especially not now, not here.

Elene glanced at Uly then back to him, her eyes asking, *Is she yours?* Kylar shook his head. "You coming?" he asked.

She scowled. He took it for a yes.

"Follow me," he told Uly. "Quiet as a mouse, right?" Best to get moving, and fast. Messy emotional issues could wait until later, or never.

They followed as he walked, visible and nervous, to the ramp. Elene walked holding Uly's hand and stopped as Kylar went ahead. When they got to the carvings of teeth, Elene pulled Uly close and began speaking to her in soothing tones.

Kylar walked up the ramp and eased the door open a crack.

361

The door shook as three arrows smacked into the wood.

"Shit!" Kylar said.

It had been too easy. Kylar should have known. He'd been counting on the chaos to throw everyone off. Locking the door again, Kylar snapped the key off in the lock. *Let the bastards break it down.*

"Back up the tunnel!" he said, pulling Elene into a jog. "You won't see me, but I'll be here. I'll protect you. Just listen for my voice," he said as the black ooze of the ka'kari bubbled out of his pores.

If Elene were startled to have him disappear before her eyes, she hid it well. She jogged, pulling Uly along. "Do I need to run?" she asked the empty air.

"Just walk fast," Kylar said.

The gate that led underground to the castle was unguarded. Thank the gods for that. Maybe the chaos of taking over an entire country would help him. Maybe a patrol outside had just stumbled across the bodies.

Kylar locked the gate and broke off the other key. They climbed a staircase slowly and emerged in a service hallway in the castle proper.

From the hallway, they quickly came upon an intersection. Down one hall, off-duty Khalidoran soldiers were slouching against a wall and sharing a joke. Kylar stopped Elene and walked toward them, then heard one of them call something to someone inside the open room behind them.

If he killed them, whoever was in that room would sound an alarm. He could make it, but Elene and Uly wouldn't. He went back to Elene.

"Go when I say," he said. "Now."

Elene threw her shawl over her head and struggled across the hallway, her back bent and her face down, one foot turned in and dragging along the floor. She looked like an old crone. And she blocked most of Uly from view.

It took her longer to get across the opening, but when one of the soldiers saw her, he didn't even say anything to the others.

"Nice trick," Kylar said, catching up with her as she resumed her normal fast stride.

"Where I grew up, stupid girls don't stay virgins," Elene said.

"You grew up on the east side," Kylar said. "It's not exactly like the Warrens over there."

"You think it's safer to work around oversexed nobles?"

"Where are we going?" Uly asked.

"Shh," Kylar said as they approached another intersection. The hallway they had been following led to the kitchens. From the raucous voices there, though, that wasn't the way to take Elene and Uly. The door to the right was locked, and the hall left was clear.

Kylar pulled out his picks, risking the possibility of someone stepping out of the kitchens. He didn't like the idea of following the path of least resistance.

The lock came open quickly, but something heavy had been wedged against the door on the other side. Probably a servant had done his best to block it during the coup.

"Where are we going?" Uly asked again.

Kylar had known her cuteness would grate on him; he'd just hoped it would take longer than this. He let Elene hush her this time.

With his Talent, he could kick through the door and whatever was blocking it—but the noise would bring whoever was in the kitchens, and Kylar felt a sense of urgency. He didn't want to leave the girls here while he scouted.

"Left," he whispered.

This corridor twisted and rose up several flights of steps. Kylar heard the jingling of mail and the slap of feet in hobnailed boots behind them.

"Hurry!" he said. The men behind them were moving at a slow jog, so they weren't chasing escaped prisoners but just responding to orders. Kylar dropped back to the staircase and caught a brief glimpse of at least twenty men.

He ran to catch up with Elene and Uly. They were passing doors, and heedless of who might hear, Kylar started testing the latches. Every one was locked.

"Why are we going to the throne room?" Uly asked.

Kylar stopped. Elene stared at Uly, looking as surprised as he felt. "What?" he asked.

"Why are we going—"

"How do you know where we're going?" Kylar asked.

"I live here. Mother's a maid. Our room's just—"

"Uly, do you know a way out? A way that doesn't go to the throne room? Quick!"

"I'm not supposed to come up here," she said. "I get in trouble."

"Dammit!" Kylar said. "Do you know a way out or not?!"

She shook her head, frightened. *That would have just been too easy, wouldn't it?*

"Great with children, aren't you?" Elene said. She touched Uly's cheek and squatted on her heels to look her in the face. "Have you come up here, Uly?" Elene asked gently. "We won't be angry if you have, I promise."

But Uly was too frightened to say anything.

The footsteps were getting closer.

"Move!" Kylar said, grabbing Elene's hand to get her running, making her drag the brat.

He didn't like this. It was too tidy. Too convenient that there was only one path.

One path. That's it! There's never just one path in this castle. Kylar scanned the walls and ceilings as he ran. He didn't even try the doors that they passed. They turned another corner. Kylar skittered to a stop.

He shimmered back into visibility. "Elene, do you see that third panel?" He pointed up.

"No," she said. "But what do I need to do?"

"Push on it. I'll lift you. There are secret corridors throughout the castle. Find your way out. Maybe Uly can help you."

She nodded and Kylar squatted against the wall. Elene hitched up her skirts and stepped on his thigh. She scowled as she realized that climbing up on him would drape her skirts over his head, but she didn't hesitate to step up to his shoulders and finally into his hands. She walked her hands up the wall for balance. Then Kylar stood and extended his hands, lifting her high into the air.

Elene pushed the panel open and slipped inside a crawl space. She had turned around by the time Kylar picked up Uly.

"Can you catch?" he asked.

"I'd better," she said. The footsteps were almost on top of them.

Kylar tossed Uly up in the air easily. *Damn but the Talent is useful.*

Elene caught her and started to slip until her own shoulders were sticking out over space. Then she must have braced herself against something inside the crawl space, because she stopped. She grunted, and with Uly wiggling to help, was able to pull the girl up with her.

"*Oh,* I've been here," Uly said.

Kylar took out a dagger and tossed it up to Elene.

She caught it. "What am I supposed to do with this?"

"Aside from the obvious?" he asked.

"Thanks. Now come on. There's room. Hurry."

Kylar didn't move. *Dorian said, 'If you do the right thing twice, it will cost you your life.' Blint said, 'There are things more valuable than life.' The count said, 'You can't pay for all you've done. But you aren't beyond redemption. There's always a way out. And if you're willing to make the sacrifice, the God will give you the chance to save something priceless.'*

He looked at Elene. *Something priceless indeed.* He smiled at her. She looked at him like he was crazy.

"Kylar, hurry!"

"It's a trap, Elene. If they lose me here, they'll search the hidden passages. I can't protect you in the crawl-spaces, they're too cramped. Get out of the castle. Go to Jarl at the Blue Boar, he'll help you."

"They'll kill you, Kylar. If it's a trap you can't—"

"I did look," he interrupted. He smirked. "And you've got great legs."

He winked—and disappeared.

Vürdmeister Neph Dada damned Roth Ursuul for the hundredth time of the day. Serving an aetheling of the Godking was supposed to be an honor. Like all the Godking's honors, this one came with strings attached. If an aetheling failed his *uurdthan,* his Vürdmeister was punished with him. And obedience was required. Total obedience, except in things that might displease the Godking.

Which was why Neph was cursing. He wasn't precisely disobeying Roth, but he was undoing something the prince had begun. Something, in fact, that Roth believed he had accomplished. Something that it was taking all of Neph's abilities to stop. Mercifully, Roth had been too busy securing the castle and the city to ask where his Vürdmeister was. Besides, he had sixty meisters to command now, three of them Vürdmeisters almost as powerful as Neph. If Roth had sent men after him, the small servant's room Neph had commandeered was isolated enough that they had never been able to find him.

His work—his petty deceit, and rebellion, and gamble for the Godking's favor—lay stretched out on the bed. She was a beautiful girl—not that the Godking needed another beautiful girl—but she had spirit. Fiery, intelligent, and best of all a widowed, virgin bride, and a princess. Jenine Gyre was a prize indeed. A prize to crown the Godking's harem. A prize Neph had snatched from the very jaws of Death.

Every Vürdmeister as old as he was knew volumes about preserving life, of course. It was in their own self-interest as they grew old. *But I am a genius. A genius.*

His plan had crystallized as Roth had ranted, meaningless words exploding from the boy like diarrhea. As usual. His cut had been fortunate. Just one side of the neck, not so deep that it cut the windpipe. Neph let her bleed until she was losing strength, then tickled a little tendril of magic against her diaphragm to push the air from her lungs, two more to close her eyes, a fourth to seal the wound on her neck, some quick movement to take attention away from her body so no one would notice that she was still breathing, and the girl had been his.

He'd killed seven serving girls looking for the right kind of blood for her. *Sloppy work.* He should have done better, but it had been enough. He'd decided to leave the scar. It gave the princess a certain something. And as a finishing touch, he'd found a girl in the city who looked like the princess and had her head mounted over the east gate with the rest of the royal family's. If you got the right color of hair and styled it correctly, all you had to do was beat the face enough, and it could look like anyone's head. Still, he thought, he'd done brilliant work, even if it had been exhausting.

Tomorrow morning, the Godking would arrive and he'd dispense either favor or punishment to Roth Ursuul. Either way, Neph would prosper.

Something made him pause before he went out the door. Something felt odd outside. He walked to his window, threw open the wooden shutters—no glass for the servants' rooms—and stared through the hole into the ghastly Cenarian statue garden.

The meisters had set up their camp there, figuring it to be a center of power. Vürdmeister Goroel had always enjoyed thumbing his nose at the conquered countries' gods and dead kings. It was pure playacting not to take rooms in the castle, but when the meisters went to war, Goroel liked to show the Godking that they were roughing it. *Insufferable.*

A man climbed up onto one of the statues. Neph couldn't see his features clearly, but he certainly wasn't Khalidoran. *Sethi? What's a Sethi man with a sword doing climbing a statue in the middle of a war?* A giant of a blacksmith with blond hair stood below him, looking around anxiously. Neph shook his head. Vürdmeister Goroel wouldn't take such an insult lightly.

"Wytches of the Godking!" the man shouted, his voice booming, amplified a dozen times over with magic. *A mage?* "Wytches of the false Godking, hear me! Come to me! This day, on this rock, you will be shattered! Come and let your arrogance find its reward!"

Had he not spoken heresy, the wytches might have let Vürdmeister Goroel deal with him, but heresy would be stopped. Must be stopped. Instantly. Fully thirty meisters drew on their vir.

Neph's magical senses exploded. He lurched against the wall and collapsed. It felt like a thousand demons were screaming in unison into each of his ears. Magic like a bonfire—like a second sun—exploded through the castle. Neph felt his vir tingling, burning as magic washed toward him. He hadn't been holding his vir, and that was surely the only thing that saved him. The power pouring through the castle was more magic than he'd ever imagined. More magic than the Godking himself could wield.

Specks of magic leapt up to meet it. The meisters, Neph could tell. The meisters who hadn't already been holding their vir grabbed it. They might as well have been flies trying to extinguish a bonfire with the wind from their wings. The magic sought them out, wrapped around them, burned them to pillars of ash. He could feel the tendrils of their power snapping, bursting apart one by one.

The conflagration was in the courtyard, in that odd Cenarian statue garden. Should Neph stay here and live? Did he dare go face that fire? What would this titan of a mage do if Neph dared to confront him? What would the Godking do to him if he didn't?

An odd, detached thought came to Kylar as he opened the last door and walked toward the throne room. *That's why those guards outside the Maw were nervous—they were bait. Now I am, too.*

His next thought was of Durzo's creed: Life is empty. It was a creed Durzo himself had betrayed, an empty creed. It neither saved life nor made it better. For a wetboy, it made life safer because it obliterated his conscience. Or tried to. Durzo had tried to live that creed and had found himself too noble for it.

Kylar wondered what had brought him to this. He was ready to die. Was it pride, that he thought he could defy any odds? Was it duty to Durzo, that he thought he had to pay back the debt of his life by saving Uly? Was it revenge, that he hated Roth so much that he would die to kill him? Was it love?

Love? I'm a fool. He felt something for Elene, it was true. Something intense and intoxicating and unreasonable. Maybe it was love, but what did he love, Elene or an image of her, glimpsed from afar, pieced together with the glue of assumption?

Maybe it was just some last vestige of romanticism that had brought him here, some sludge left over from the stories of princes and heroes Ulana Drake had read to him. Maybe he'd spent too long with people who believed in false virtues like valor and self-sacrifice that Durzo had tried to teach him to despise. Maybe he'd been infected.

But why he was here didn't really matter. This was the right thing to do. He was worthless. If his empty life could ransom Elene's life, then he would have accomplished something good. It would be the only thing he had ever done that he could be proud of. And if he gave Uly a chance too, so much the better.

He'd have his own chance, too: his chance at Roth. Kylar had gone into other fights feeling confident, but this was different. As he stepped into the short hall to the throne room, Kylar felt at peace.

A high-pitched whine cut the air. The men who'd been standing in the room looking to the door adjusted their grips on their weapons.

A magical alarm to tell them I've arrived, then.

There were highlanders, of course. He'd expected that. But he hadn't expected thirty. And there were wytches. He'd expected that, too. But not five.

The doors at the dead end where he'd lifted Elene and Uly banged open and another ten highlanders poured in behind him.

Taking a few quick steps, Kylar leapt into the throne room at the level of the floor, hoping to make it past the first attacks. The room was huge, the ivory and horn throne set above the seats of the assembly by two broad sets of seven steps separated by a flat landing. Roth sat in the throne, flanked by two wytches. The others stood on the landing. The highlanders were spread around the perimeter of the room.

The leap took him past the whirring swords of two highlanders who were cutting blindly at the air in front of the door, hoping to get lucky and hit the invisible wetboy.

Drawing Retribution from its back scabbard, Kylar rolled to his feet.

A swarm of tiny hands appeared in the air as the wytches chanted. The hands were looking for him, plucking at him. They seethed over the ground leaping and clawing at each other as they groped for him.

He jumped away, cutting at the hands, but his sword passed through them harmlessly; there was nothing for him to cut.

They swarmed over him and the hands thickened, strengthened as two of the wytches chanted in time with each other. Then, as the hands pulled him upright, Kylar felt something else seize him. He felt like a baby caught in giant's fingers.

It tore at him and he felt the ka'kari's cloaking strip open. He let it go. It wouldn't do him much good to be partly invisible if he couldn't move.

Well, that was glorious. In all the history of stupid men intentionally springing traps set for them, that was probably the lamest result ever.

Kylar had hoped—hell, expected—that he'd at least take a few guards with him. Maybe a wytch. Two would have been nice. Durzo would be shaking his head in disgust.

"I knew you'd come, Blint," Roth crowed from the throne. He hopped to his feet and waved to the wytches. Kylar was lifted off his feet and shot forward, carried magically up the stairs and deposited on the landing below the throne.

Blint? Gods. I sprang a trap that wasn't even set for me.

The magic fingers tore away Kylar's mask. "Kylar?" Roth said, astonished. He burst out laughing.

"My prince, beware," a red-haired wytch at Roth's right said. "He has the ka'kari."

Roth slapped his hands together and laughed again, as if unable to believe his luck. "And just in time! Oh, Kylar, if I were another man, I'd almost let you live."

The witty riposte dried on Kylar's tongue as he saw into Roth's eyes. If most of his deaders had a cupful of darkness in their souls, Roth had a river, boundless and bleak, a roaring, devouring darkness with a voice like thunder. Here was a man who hated all that was lovely.

"Captain," Roth said, "where are the girl and the scarred wench?"

One of the men who'd entered after Kylar said, "We've lost them, Your Majesty."

"I'm disappointed, Captain," Roth said, but his voice was jubilant. "Unlose them."

"Yes, Your Highness," the soldier said. He grabbed his ten highlanders and headed back into the hall.

Roth turned back to Kylar. "Now," he said. "Dessert. Kylar, do you know how long I've been looking for you?"

Kylar blinked and tore himself away, somehow shut his senses off to the evil in the man before him. He forced nonchalance into his voice. "Since I'm the man who's going to kill you, I'd guess—oh, since you first looked in a mirror and realized just how damn ugly you are."

Roth clapped his hands. "How droll. You know, Kylar, I feel like you've been in my shadow for years, opposing everything I've done. Stealing my ka'kari really irritated me."

"Well, I aim to vex," Kylar said. He wasn't really listening. Opposing him for years? Roth really was crazy. Kylar didn't even know him. But let the man rant as long as he wanted. Kylar surreptitiously flexed against the bonds of magic.

They were like steel. This was not going well. Kylar didn't have a plan. He didn't even have the beginning of a plan. He didn't think that there was a plan that might have worked even if he'd been smart enough to think of it. The Khalidoran soldiers had encircled him, the wytches were watching him like vultures, their vir wiggling faintly, and Roth looked altogether far too pleased with himself.

"And vex you do. You seem to turn up at the most inopportune moments."

"Just like that rash you picked up from the rent boys, huh?"

"Oh, *personality*. Excellent. I haven't had a really satisfying kill since yesterday."

"If you fell on your sword, we'd all be satisfied."

"You had your chance to kill me, Kylar." Roth shrugged. "You failed. But I didn't know you were a wetboy. I only got your real name yesterday, and killing you had to wait while I gained a kingdom for my father."

"I won't hold it against you." *I had my chance?*

"So gracious in defeat. Did Durzo teach you that?"

Kylar had no response. It was probably stupid at this point to feel irked that he seemed to have lost a point in the battle of wits, but then if Kylar had been smarter, he wouldn't have been here in the first place.

"I must say," Roth said. "I've not been impressed with this generation of wetboys. Hu's apprentice was as much of a disappointment as you are. I mean, *really*. Durzo would have at least killed one of my men before we caught him, don't you think? I'm afraid you're a poor shadow of your master, Kylar. By the way, where is he? It's not like him to have an inferior do a job that concerns him."

"I killed him last night. For working for you."

The prince clapped his hands with glee and giggled. "I think that's the most lovely thing I've ever heard. He betrayed me by saving you, and you betrayed him for working for me. Oh, Kylar," Roth came down the steps to stand in front of him. "If I could trust you damn wetboys, I'd hire you in a heartbeat. But you're too dangerous. And, of course, you've bonded my ka'kari."

Roth's wytch shifted, obviously nervous to have Roth standing so close to Kylar.

The wytch must know something I don't, Kylar thought. He couldn't move a muscle. He was totally helpless.

Wait. That's it. That's exactly *why he's nervous. He thinks the ka'kari's a threat. And if he thinks it is, maybe it is.*

Roth drew a beautiful long sword from a hip scabbard. "I'm disappointed with you."

"Why's that?" Kylar asked, racking his brain to think of how he might use the ka'kari. What did he know about it? It enabled his Talent. It made him see through shadows. It made him invisible. It came out of his skin, and hid him more perfectly than any wetboy could hide.

But how?

"I'd hoped this would be fun," Roth said. "I was going to tell you how hard you made my life. But you're like Blint. You don't even care if you live or die." Roth raised the sword.

"Sure I do," Kylar said, showing fear. "How hard have I made your life?"

"Sorry, I'm not going to give you the satisfaction."

Oh, come on! "Not for me," Kylar said. "You know your father's meisters and soldiers are going to report everything they've seen and heard to him. Why not give them the whole story?" It was clumsy, but with his life on the line, it was harder to think quickly than he would have imagined.

Roth paused, thinking.

It was useless. The ka'kari just did what it did. It had eaten a knife last night, for the God's sake! There was no telling by what logic it operated— if any. It was just magic.

Absorbs. Eats. That's *what it does!* He'd felt a huge jolt of power after it had absorbed the knife. *The Devourer.* Blint had called it the Devourer. He was close, maybe.

"Sorry," Roth said. "I don't perform for anyone. Not even you. This is just between us, Azoth." Roth handed his sword to the wytch to his left and smoothed his long hair back over his ears—

Except he didn't have ears. The left ear looked like it had been melted off. The right ear had been cut off.

Azoth had been pushed to his knees in the middle of the boat shop. It had been hard to get Rat to come into the dark shop, but he'd done it. Now Rat's foot was squarely in the middle of the noose Azoth had laid on the floor, but Azoth couldn't move. He couldn't draw a full breath. Rat was inches away, terrifying in his nakedness, giving an order. He clouted Azoth. Azoth tasted blood. He found himself moving. He grabbed the noose and snugged the knot tight against Rat's ankle. Rat shouted and raised his knee sharply into Azoth's face.

He landed on the big rock and scraped his back, falling between the rock and the hole in the floor where boats had once been lowered into the river's foul waters. He scrambled and braced his thin arms against the rock, and lifted his eyes, expecting the older boy to be already to be on him.

Rat looked at Azoth, at the hole, at the rock, at the rope, at his ankle. Azoth would never forget the look in Rat's eyes. It was terror. Then Rat lunged, and Azoth shoved the rock into the hole.

The rope went tight and Rat was pulled to the side in midlunge. He scrambled, grabbing for Azoth, missing. His fingers raked the rotting wood floor as he slid and disappeared into the hole. There was a splash.

But moments later, Azoth heard crying. He walked to the edge of the hole.

Rat was holding on by his fingertips, begging. It was impossible. Then Azoth saw that his rock had landed on one of the lattice-like support beams that held the shop up over the river. It was balanced precariously, but as long as Rat held tension on the rope, it wouldn't drag him into the depths.

Azoth walked to Rat's pile of clothing and found his dagger. Rat was pleading, tears coursing down his pimply cheeks, but Azoth heard only the roar of blood in his ears. He squatted by Rat, careful but fearless. Even now, Rat's arms were shaking from holding his weight; he was too fat to hold himself for long, too fat to let go with one hand and grab Azoth.

With a quick motion, Azoth grabbed his ear and sliced it off. Rat screamed and let go.

His body hit the rock, dislodged it. The last thing Azoth saw was his terrified face as he was pulled under the water, then even that was obscured by his hands churning, reaching for something, anything—finding nothing.

Azoth waited and waited, and then staggered away.

The pimples were gone. He'd grown a beard to cover the few pits they'd left. The build was right, though he'd lost weight since he left the Warrens, but that jaggedly cut ear, and his eyes—*gods! how didn't I notice those dead eyes?*—the eyes were the same.

"Rat," Kylar breathed. His plan burst into a thousand shards. His heart stopped. He felt like a child again, waiting in line for Rat to beat him, too cowardly to do anything but weep.

"I'm dead, right? Funny, that's what they told me about you." Roth shook his head, but his voice was low. This was just for him. "Neph burned off my other ear to punish me for what you did. You cost me three years, Azoth. Three years before I became a guild head again. I held my breath for—gods it seemed like forever. Forever working at the knot you tied on my ankle, bleeding my life out into that filthy water until Neph finally pulled me out. He watched the whole thing, said he was debating letting me die. Neph had to kill one of my bigs—you remember Roth, don't you?—and put him in my place before your master came. I had to move to some shitty guild on the opposite side of the Warrens and start all over. You almost made me fail my father." He was shaking with rage. He exposed his melted ear again. "This was the *least* of my punishments. And then you conveniently 'died.' I never believed it, Azoth. I knew you were out there, just waiting for me. Believe me, if I had time, I would torture you for years,

I would push you to the end of human endurance and beyond. I'd heal you just to make you hurt again." He closed his eyes and lowered his voice once more. "But I don't have that luxury. If I leave you alive, my father might come up with other plans for you. He might do something else with the ka'kari. I paid for that ka'kari, and I intend to bond it immediately." He smiled grimly. "Any last words?"

Kylar had lost his focus, gotten distracted. Fear and horror had made his mind wander from the puzzle, when nothing should have been as important. Durzo had taught him better. Fear was to be acknowledged, then ignored. Where had he been? Devourer? Magic? "Shit," he said, not realizing he spoke aloud.

Roth arched an eyebrow. "Hmm. Boring, but accurate enough." His grip turn on his sword, and his shoulder rolled back. The blade was coming up. The man was going to cut his head off. Everything in Kylar cried out for help.

A boom sounded somewhere below the range of human hearing, but Kylar felt it wallop his stomach like a thunder crack. His vision went blue-white with magic. He could see the magic streaming through the air as fast as an arrow, a wall of magic.

The castle itself rocked and everyone fell. Everywhere he looked, Kylar saw the same stunned looks. Roth was sprawled on the stairs, his sword still in hand, mouth wide.

Kylar suddenly felt one of the magic bonds holding him snap. He looked toward the others and saw that the magic—it looked like a storm of blue-white rain falling sideways, flying invisibly through walls and people—was spattering against the bonds, collecting around them. The bonds were as black as the wytches' vir, and the blue magic hissed and spat wherever it touched the black.

Then the blue magic latched on to the wytches' magic and roared up the black tendrils like wildfire climbing a hill to the wytches holding them.

Shrieks burst from three of the wytches and the bonds holding Kylar disappeared as three living blue torches lit the room. But Kylar's eyes were drawn to himself. The ka'kari was covering him like a black skin, and everywhere the blue magic pelted him, the magic danced like a puddle in the rain, then disappeared—and the ka'kari swelled more powerful.

The Devourer ate magic, too.

Then the magical shockwave was gone.

There was the briefest silence, then Roth screamed at the wytches who hadn't been using the vir—the two wytches in the room still alive, "Get him!" Roth plucked his sword from the stairs and swung it at Kylar's face.

Incredibly, the wytches obeyed instantly. Bonds leapt into place around Kylar's arms and legs. Everywhere the bonds touched Kylar, in response to his will, the ka'kari swelled, twisted through them, shifted, sucked, and devoured them.

Kylar threw himself back against the bonds even before they were completely dissolved. He burst through them with all the strength of his Talent as Roth's sword slashed the air inches from his throat.

He tore through the shriveling bonds and flew back clumsily, his feet tearing free last, tripping him. He twisted in the air and threw a knife with his off hand.

A soldier grunted and hit the floor.

Kylar landed below the second flight of steps, flat on his back. The impact knocked the wind out of him, but even as he slid across the floor his sword was moving. Highlanders stood to the left and right of him and his sword flashed twice, cutting through boots and ankles on either side of him.

Three highlanders had fallen, but others were already attacking. Kylar flipped his feet over his head and stood, gasping but ready to fight.

64

Solon tried to climb down from the statue. King Logan Verdroekan had been one of the earliest kings of Cenaria, perhaps mythic, and Solon couldn't remember what he'd done, for all that it must have been heroic to have Regnus Gyre name his son after him. And he must have been special to get a statue of such size, holding his sword aloft in defiance. Solon had chosen it not for its metaphoric significance but simply because he wanted every meister in the garden to see him. Every meister that had used vir within five hundred paces in the few seconds he'd been able to hold Curoch was dead.

Curoch lay on the stones beneath him. Feir was snatching it up and wrapping it in a blanket. He was shouting at Solon, but Solon couldn't make out the words. He still felt as if he were on fire. Every vein in his body was tingling so fiercely it was hard to even feel Verdroeken's stone sword under his fingers. Solon had perched on the dead king's shoulders and held onto the stone sword for balance, holding Curoch aloft the same way when he'd released the magic. He shifted his grip, his legs shaking, and suddenly fell.

Feir didn't quite catch him, but he at least broke his fall.

"I can't walk," Solon said. His brain was burning, his vision flaring every color in the rainbow, his scalp felt afire. "It was amazing, Feir. Such a tiny piece of what it can do..."

Feir grabbed him and threw him over his shoulders as a lesser man might lift a child. He said something, but Solon couldn't quite make it out. He said it again.

"Oh, I got about fifty of them. Maybe ten left," Solon said. "One on the east bridge." He was trying to remember what Dorian had told him. Something urgent. Something he hadn't let Feir hear.

Don't let Feir die. He's more important than the sword.

"I'm going to have to set you down," Feir said. "Don't worry. I'm not leaving you."

In outrageous hues of green and blue, Khalidoran soldiers were swarming in front of the east gate. Solon couldn't even remember leaving the garden. He laughed at what he saw. Feir was using Curoch as a *sword*.

Watching Feir with a sword was more than amazing; it was a privilege. Feir had always been a natural, deceptively quick, unbelievably strong, his movements as precise as a dancer's. In hues of green and blue and red, Feir demolished the soldiers. There was no extended swordplay. At most, each soldier had time to swing his own weapon once, miss or have it parried, and then die.

Feir cursed, but when Solon tried to follow his gaze, the riot of colors was too intense. The big man lifted him, threw him over a shoulder again, and started running. Solon saw the wood of the bridge beneath Feir's feet.

"Hold on tight," Feir said.

Not a moment too soon, Solon latched onto Feir's belt on either side of the man's broad back. Feir dodged to the side and his great shoulders rolled. With his feet sticking out in front of Feir and his head merely bobbing along behind him, all Solon saw was a brief flash of Curoch. Feir spun— the right way so Solon wasn't flung off—and Curoch came up again, then he was running full speed once more. Solon saw three bodies behind them, lying on the bridge. The man had killed three men while holding Solon over his shoulder. Astounding.

Feir said, "Dorian told me our hope is in the water, but not to jump. Look for a rope!"

Solon lifted his head, as if he would be much help in finding a rope while bouncing on Feir's back. He didn't see a rope, but he did see a meister behind them, conjuring a ball of wytchfire. He tried to yell, but couldn't draw breath.

"Damn you, Dorian!" Feir was shouting. "What goddam rope?"

"Down!" Solon said.

With the reflexes of the sword master he was, Feir dropped instantly. Wytchfire crackled over their heads and burst against a dozen Khalidoran soldiers holding the far gate in front of them. Solon went sprawling and was almost brained by one of the great fire pots that guarded the bridge.

The old wytch behind them—from the thickness of his vir Solon guessed he was a Vürdmeister—was drawing magic once more. Feir grabbed Solon's collar and threw him behind the fire pot. The move put Solon in a safe place, but exposed Feir. This time it wasn't wytchfire, but something else Solon had never seen. An angry red beam didn't so much fly as streak through the air toward Feir. He threw up a magical shield and ducked.

The shield barely deflected the beam—again into a soldier running to join the fray—but the force of the magic blew Feir's shield apart and flung him to the other side like a rag doll. Curoch spun from his grasp.

Drawing on strength he didn't know he had, Solon grabbed Feir and pulled him into the shadow of the fire pot with him.

Two more meisters were running to join the Vürdmeister and soldiers were behind them. The gate at the far end of the bridge opened and soldiers were pouring through.

Feir sat up and looked out at Curoch, twenty feet away, exposed. "I can use it," he said. "I can save it."

"No!" Solon said. "You'll die."

The soldiers and the meisters had paused, regrouping, advancing slowly now, cautious and orderly.

"I don't matter, Solon. We can't let them have it."

"You wouldn't even live long enough to use it, Feir. Not even if you were willing to trade your life for one second of power."

"It's right there!"

"And so is this," Solon said, motioning to the edge of the bridge.

Feir looked. "You've got to be joking."

Over the edge, a black silk rope had been tied to the underside of either end of the bridge. It only extended out below them when the wind blew. Feir was looking not at the rope but at the fall.

"Hey, it's prophecy, right? It has to work," Solon said. If only the world would stop flashing yellow.

"It never works out exactly like Dorian says!"

"If he told you that you were going to do this, would you have come?"

"Hell no. And don't you nod knowingly to me. I get enough of that from Dorian." Feir looked at the approaching soldiers and meisters. "Right. You first."

He's going to go after Curoch. The heroic idiot.

"I can't," Solon said. "I'm not strong enough to grab the rope. I'll die if I go alone."

Feir stood. "Just let me try—" he reached out with his Talent and grabbed the sword. Instantly, hands of vir crackled visibly over his magic and started climbing toward him. Solon slashed the magic loose with his own.

Spots exploded in front of Solon's eyes. "Oh, don't do that. Don't do that, please. Oh."

"Let me ride pony-back, Feir." Solon didn't have time to explain. The meisters were close.

"I'm crazy, and you're fat," Feir said. But he picked up Solon and put him on his back.

"Magically too. I've got a plan. And I am not fat."

For all that he second-guessed plans when they were all safe, Feir knew to obey in battle. He opened himself quickly, and Solon dipped into Feir's Talent. He lashed himself onto Feir's back with magical bonds. Then he quickly readied five thin weaves. It still hurt, but not nearly as much as using his own Talent.

"Now," he said. "Jump."

Feir leaped over the side of the bridge. The rope was in the perfect place—not because of the wind or the power of prophecy, but because Solon pulled it there with magic. As Feir grabbed the rope, Solon activated the other weaves.

Holes were torn in the sides of each of the fire pots and air inside them suddenly compressed, jetting the oil in the pots out onto the bridge. The last weave dropped a little spark in middle of the oil.

There was a satisfying whoosh. The river suddenly lit orange and white and heat washed over the falling mages.

Then things were happening too rapidly to follow. Feir had caught the rope with both hands and a leg. He immediately flipped upside down. The sudden change in direction caught Solon's arm across Feir's shoulder and snapped it. If it weren't for the magical bonds holding him, he would have dropped like a stone. The rope, anchored on both sides of the bridge, first stretched, bowing down toward the middle. Because Feir and Solon hadn't made it to the middle of the bridge, that meant they zipped headfirst for fifteen paces. Then the rope tore loose at the castle end.

Solon was watching light explode over them, distantly aware that they were swinging with terrific speed toward the river. The bridge was engulfed in flames leaping merrily into the night. Or maybe that was pain exploding in his head. Then they slapped into something cold and hard.

He took a breath. It was bad timing. The cold hard stuff had become cold wet stuff. They were under water. He coughed as Feir came to the surface, and Solon thought dimly that the man was either a hell of a swimmer or something was dragging them out.

Feir was on his knees in the shallows, holding up his hands. From his perch on the man's back, Solon saw that Feir's hands had been torn to bloody pieces by the rope. He could see bone.

"Ah, you're better off than I thought you'd be," Dorian's voice was saying as his magic hauled them out of the river. "Stop lollygagging, you two. We need to get going if we're going to make it to Khalidor in time."

"Lollygagging?" Solon asked, glad to find that he had strength to be outraged.

"Khalidor?" Feir said.

"Well, that is where my bride is waiting. I can't wait to find out who she is. I think Curoch is going to find its way there, too."

Feir cursed, but Solon—broken arm, purple vision, and all—just laughed.

65

As they came within the arc of his sword or the reach of his lashing feet or striking fists, men went down like grain in a summer storm. To Kylar, who had always been gifted at fighting, battle suddenly made sense. The chaos unfolded into beautifully intricate, interlocking, and logical patterns.

Just by looking at a man's face, he could judge instantly: parry left, hesitate, lunge, clear. A man died and fell far enough away that he didn't impede Kylar's movements. Next, sweep right, roll in, bear fist to nose. Spin, hamstring, throat. Parry, riposte. Stab.

Parsed to the individual percussion of each chamber of his heart, battle had a rhythm, a music. Not a sound was out of place. The tenor of ringing steel layered over a bass of the fists and feet hammering flesh—soft to hard,

hard to soft—and the baritone of men's curses, punctuated by the staccato percussion of rending mail.

With his Talent singing, Kylar was a virtuoso. He fought in a fine frenzy, a dancer possessed. Time never slowed, but he found his body reacting to sights he didn't consciously see—turning, dodging under blows his mind never registered, striking with the awesome speed and grace of that angel of death, the Night Angel.

The highlanders sought to overwhelm him by force of numbers. Their blades caught the air within an inch of Kylar's ear, within half an inch of his stomach, a quarter of an inch from his thigh. He rode the front of each beat, cut the margins closer and closer, until the bodies he was killing were being pushed forward instead of falling back, and pressing in closer on him.

He sheathed Retribution and grabbed the hand holding a blade aimed at his belly and yanked a skinny highlander across the circle to stab his fellow. Reaching around his own back with a knife, he diverted a sword thrust while his other knife found an eye socket.

Two spears came for him and he dropped to the floor, yanking both forward. As each impaled a body, he swung up, destroying another highlander's face with a kick.

But the situation was hopeless. Within a cage of tangled weapons and thrashing, dying men, he'd be trapped in moments.

Light as a cat, he sprang to the back of a man dying on his knees and vaulted off the shoulder of one of the impaled spear bearers.

As he flipped sideways through the air, a ball of green wytchfire the size of his fist streaked through the air at him. It caught his cloak and broke into pieces. He landed on his feet and ducked under a sword cut. His cloak burst into green flame. Kylar tore the cloak off as he dove between two spears.

Holding one edge of the cloak, he came to his feet and wrapped the cloak around another of his attackers. The green flame raced for the man's skin, and there burned a fierce blue as he screamed.

Another ball of wytchfire sizzled through the air and Kylar dove behind one of the pillars supporting the high ceiling.

There were two beats of rest. Kylar had killed or disabled more than half the Khalidorans, but now the others played to their strengths. Point, counterpoint.

"To the captain! Keep a meister in view!" Roth shouted. Men streamed to the captain to form a wedge between Kylar and Roth, who had retreated to the throne to watch.

But Kylar wasn't wasting his time as he stood in the protection of the pillar. He knew that if he wanted a chance at Roth, he had to kill the wytches. Both of them were eyeing the spaces between the pillars where he would have to run.

He pooled the ka'kari in his hand, and keeping the feel of those fingers of magic in his mind, willed it to dribble down the length of his sword. Seeming to sense his urgency, the ka'kari coated the steel instantly. Both ka'kari and steel shimmered out of visibility.

Kylar dodged out from the pillar and the fingers were on him instantly. He cut in a quick circle and felt them shrivel and die out of existence. Grabbing the edge of one of the long tapestries that covered the walls of the throne room, Kylar moved toward the pillar, but not before wytchfire leaped from a wytch's fingers.

If he'd had time to think about it, Kylar wouldn't have tried to block with his sword—it was insanity to try to block magic—but it was his ingrained response. The flat of his blade hit the green globe of fire. Instead of bursting, the fire whooshed *into* the blade.

Kylar dodged around a pillar with the tapestry in one hand and a sword now visible because of the green flame crackling through it. With all the strength of his Talent, he leaped.

He soared into the air in the middle of the throne room, and then as the tapestry met a pillar, it abruptly changed his trajectory and launched him up the steps.

The other wytch must have thrown wytchfire that Kylar hadn't seen, because the tapestry gave way and tore a moment before Kylar was going to release it. He hit the landing between the flights of stairs with eight feet of burning tapestry in his hands. He hurled it toward the highlanders and slashed at the wytch chanting not two steps away.

The top of the wytch's head opened, exposing his brain. The man spun, but his lips completed his incantation. The thick black tendrils that had been squirming under the skin of his arms fattened grotesquely like rippling muscles and tore free of the wytch's arms, bursting through his skin.

Power roared from the dying wytch and he staggered, trying to find Kylar. Kylar jumped behind him. He kicked the wytch so hard that the man lifted off the ground and crashed into the highlanders.

The flailing black tendrils ripped into the men, sucking them in like greedy hands and chewing through them with a sound like logs in a sawmill.

Even as the black tendrils were tearing through the soldiers, Kylar felt more than saw the white light forming behind him. He turned in time to see the homunculus streaking through the air. It dodged under his desperate slash and stabbed tiny claws into his chest.

He was already jumping to the side when he felt the concussion and saw the air ripple. Reality bubbled in a line toward him. The rippling air curved, following him as he ran. Then the air tore open. He vaulted all the way to the wall and nearly caught another ball of wytchfire with his face.

The pit wyrm lunged forward into reality, barely missing him. It thrashed, furious, tearing the hole open wider and hooking fiery claws around two of the pillars, mere feet away. Kylar ripped the homunculus from his chest and slapped it onto a soldier's face.

As the pit wyrm lunged again, Kylar leapt straight up. Its lampreylike mouth shot out, latched onto the screaming man, and sucked him back into the pit. By the time Kylar landed, both pit wyrm and soldier were gone.

Kylar turned and jumped for the top of the stairs, but he was too slow. Even as he left the ground, he saw a blur of light streaking toward him. There was no time to draw a throwing knife. Kylar hurled his sword at the last wytch.

The bolt of magic blasted his left shoulder. As the momentum of his leap carried him up and forward, the blast made him flip end over end backward. He crunched into the marble floor at the foot of the throne and felt his left knee shatter.

For a long moment, his eyes refused to focus. He blinked and blinked and finally cleared the blood away. He saw Retribution buried to the hilt through a wytch ten paces away, its blade black with his ka'kari.

He realized that he was viewing the dead wytch through a pair of legs. His eyes followed the legs up to Roth's face.

"Stand up," Roth said. He plunged his long sword through Kylar's lower back.

Kylar gagged as Roth twisted the blade in his kidney. Then the hot metal lifted away. Something pulled Kylar to his feet.

The pain was like a cloud making everything fuzzy and indistinct. Confused, Kylar stared at the dead wytches. *Who picked me up?*

"All the aethelings of Godking Ursuul are wytchborn," Roth said. "Didn't you know?"

Kylar stared at Roth dumbly. Roth was Talented? The invisible hands released him and he folded as he put weight on his destroyed left leg. The marble floor jarred him once more.

"Get up!" Roth said. He stabbed Kylar's groin and cursed him. Kylar dropped his head onto the marble as Roth's screaming became inarticulate.

The sound of Roth's voice faded to a murmur next to the roaring voice of pain.

The pain flashed in another bar through his stomach as Roth stabbed him again. Then he must have picked Kylar up again, because Kylar felt his head lolling to one side. If he'd felt pain before, now it became agony.

Every part of his body was being scoured with fire, dipped in alcohol, packed with salt. His eyelids were lined with crushed glass. His optic nerves were being chewed by little teeth. And after his eyes, every tissue, sinew, muscle, and organ marinated in misery in its turn. He was screaming.

But his mind cleared.

Kylar blinked. He was standing before Roth, and he was aware. Aware and dismayed. He must have landed on his left knee when he'd crashed to the marble, because it was demolished. He was bleeding inside—his intestines leaking slow death into his viscera, stomach acids scorching his intestines, a kidney pouring black blood. His left shoulder looked like it had kissed a giant's hammer.

"You won't die easy," Roth said. "I won't allow it. Not after what you've done. Look what you've done! My father will be furious."

There it was. He was dying. Kylar could perch unsteadily on his one good leg, but he had no weapons. His sword and the ka'kari were ten paces away—they might as well have been across the ocean. No weapons, and Roth was—even now—careful not to come within range of his hands. Kylar didn't have so much as a belt knife.

"Are you ready to die?" Roth said, his eyes glowing malevolence.

Kylar was staring at his right hand. Of all the beaten, sliced, and smashed places on his body, his fingers were healthy, perfect, healed. Wasn't that the hand he'd cut on the window last night? "I'm ready," he said, surprising himself.

"Any regrets?" Roth asked.

Kylar looked into Roth, and understood him. Kylar had always had enough darkness in his soul to understand evil men. Roth was trying to wring anguish from him. Roth wanted to kill him while he thought of all the things he hadn't done. Roth reaped despair. "Dying well is easy," Kylar said, "it only takes a moment of courage. It's living well that I couldn't do. What's death compared to that?"

"You're about to find out," Roth spat.

Kylar smirked, and then smiled as rage washed over Roth.

"Killing Logan was more fun," Roth said. He rammed his sword into Kylar's chest.

Logan! The thought cut through Kylar more cruelly than the sword in

Roth's hand. Kylar had lived by the sword. Dying by it was neither unexpected nor unjust. But Logan had never even wanted to hurt anyone. Roth killing Logan wasn't right. It wasn't fair. It wasn't just.

Kylar stared at the steel stabbed through his chest. He took Roth's hand in his own and pulled, pulled himself up the sword, impaling himself to the hilt. Roth's eyes widened.

"I am the Night Angel," Kylar said, gasping on the steel through his lung. "This is justice. This is for Logan."

There was a ting and the sound of metal rolling on marble. The ka'kari leaped for Kylar's hand—

And was caught squarely by Roth. Triumph lit his eyes. He laughed.

But Kylar grabbed Roth's shoulders and stared him in the eye. "I am the Night Angel," Kylar repeated. "This is justice. This is for Logan." Kylar lifted his right hand.

Roth looked confused. Then he looked at his left hand. The ka'kari was turning to liquid and gliding through his fingers. His hands scrambled as they'd scrambled across the wood floor of the boat shop, and found nothing. The ka'kari slapped into Kylar's palm and formed an enormous punch dagger on his fist.

Kylar slammed his fist into Roth's chest.

Roth looked down, his disbelief turning to horror as Kylar drew the dagger out, his horror turning to fear as his heart pumped blood directly into his lungs.

Roth shrieked a shrill denial of his own mortality.

Kylar released the prince and tried to step away, but his limbs refused to obey him. His knee buckled and he crashed to the ground with the Khalidoran prince.

Roth and Kylar lay eye to eye on the marble at the foot of the throne, staring at each other, dying. Each trembled as uncontrollable twitches ran through his limbs. Each breathed terrible, labored breaths in time with the other. Roth's eyes brimmed with fear, panic so intense it paralyzed. He seemed to no longer see Kylar lying inches away. His gaze grew more distant and filled with soul-deep terror.

Kylar was content. This Night Angel had apportioned death—and death was his portion. It wasn't nice, but it was just. This sentence was deserved. Watching Roth's eyes finally glaze in restless death, Kylar wished there were something more beautiful to find in death than justice. But he didn't have the strength to turn away from this life, this death, this terrible justice.

Then someone turned him over. A woman. She came into focus slowly.

It was Elene. She pulled Kylar into her lap, stroked his hair. She was crying. Kylar couldn't see her scars. He reached a hand up, touched her face. She was angelic.

Then he saw his hand. It was perfect, whole, and amazingly, unbloodied. For the first time in his life, his hands were clean. *Clean!*

Death came. Kylar yielded.

Terah Graesin had just paid a fortune to one of the prettiest men she'd ever seen. Jarl said he spoke for the Shinga, but he carried himself with such assurance, she wondered if he might not be the Shinga himself. She hadn't liked handing over so much money to the Sa'kagé, but she hadn't had any choice. The Godking's army would arrive with the dawn, and she'd already spent too long in the city.

The coup had not gone according to the Godking's plan. The Khalidorans controlled the bridges, the castle, and the city's gates, but some of them had only skeleton crews. That would change when the rest of the army arrived, and Terah Graesin and her nobles needed to be gone when that happened. If she hadn't paid half her fortune to Jarl, she would have had to leave behind all of it. A queen made the hard decisions, and with everyone else dead, a queen was what she was, now.

It was midnight. The wagons were packed. The men were waiting. It was time.

Terah stood outside her family's mansion. Like the other ducal families' homes, theirs was old, a veritable fortress. A looted fortress now. A looted fortress smelling of the barrels and barrels of oil they had poured in every room, over the precious heirlooms too heavy to carry, and into the grooves they'd cut in every centuries-old beam. It was time. Jarl's wetboys were supposed to slaughter the Khalidorans holding the city's east gate at midnight. All the other nobles were huddled outside their own houses. From her elevated front porch, she could see some of them up and down Horak Street, waiting to see if she'd really do it.

She locked the mansion in her mind. After she returned, she would rebuild this for her family, twice as splendid as before.

Terah Graesin walked to the street and took the torch from Sergeant Gamble. The archers gathered around her. She personally lit every arrow. At her nod, they loosed them.

The mansion went up in flame. Fire poured from the windows and reached for the heavens. Queen Terah Graesin didn't look. She mounted her horse and led her column, her pathetic army of three hundred soldiers and twice as many servants and shopkeepers into the street toward the east gate.

Across the east side, the great houses lit up one by one. They were the funeral pyres of fortunes. Not only were the nobles losing everything, but so too were all those who depended on them for their employment. But the fires of destruction were also beacons of hope. You may have won, Cenaria was saying, but your victory is no triumph. You can force me from my home, but you will not live in it. I will leave you nothing but scorched earth.

In response to those great fires, across the city, smaller fires rose, too. Shopkeepers set fire to their shops. Blacksmiths stoked their furnaces so hot they would crack. Bakers destroyed their ovens. Millers sank their millstones in the Plith. Warehouse owners set fire to their storehouses. Livestock owners slaughtered their herds. Captains confined to the Plith by wytches' magic scuttled their own ships.

Thousands joined the exodus. The trickle of nobles and their servants became a flood. The flood became a host, an army marching out of the city—marching in defeat, but marching. Some drove wagons, some rode, some walked barefoot with empty hands and empty bellies. Some cursed; some prayed; some stared over their shoulders with haunted eyes; some wept. Some left brothers and sisters and parents and children, but every one of Cenaria's orphaned sons and daughters carried a small, dim hope in their hearts.

I shall return, it vowed. *I shall return.*

Neph stood as far to one side as he could among the meisters, generals, and soldiers waiting to greet Godking Garoth Ursuul as he rode across West Kingsbridge with his retinue. The Godking wore a great ermine cloak that accentuated the paleness of his northern skin. His chest was bare aside from the heavy gold chains of his office. He was robust, thick-bodied but muscular, vigorous for his age. The Godking pulled his stallion to a halt before the courtyard gate. Six heads on pikes greeted him. A seventh pike stood empty.

"Commander Gher."

"Yes, my liege—uh, my god, Your Holiness, sire." The former royal guard cleared his throat. Things were not good. Though Roth's and Neph's plans had seemed to go without a problem, somehow the Godking's armies had sustained far heavier losses than they'd planned. A boatload of highlanders dead. Many of the nobles who ought to be dead escaped. Great swathes of the city aflame. The heart of Cenaria's industry and economy reduced to ashes.

There was no resistance yet, but with so many nobles still alive, it would come. The meisters that were supposed to have been a devastating spearhead into the heart of Modai were now dead. More than fifty meisters dead, at a stroke, without any explanation except rumors of some mage with more Talent than anyone since Ezra the Mad and Jorsin Alkestes. The Ceuran invasion ended before it began. The Godking's son murdered just as he completed his uurdthan.

The Sa'kagé would have to be brought to heel, fires literal and figurative would have to be put out. Someone would have to answer for it. Neph Dada was trying to figure out how to make sure it wasn't him.

"Why is there an empty pike on my bridge?" the God-king asked. "Anyone?"

Commander Hurin Gher shifted in his saddle, stupidly looking at the empty pike. "We haven't found prince's—I mean, the pretender's—um, Logan Gyre's body yet, sire. We, we do know that he's dead. We have three reports confirming his death, but in all the fighting.... We're, we're working on it."

"Indeed." Godking Ursuul didn't look at Hurin Gher. He was studying the faces of the royal family above him. "And this *Shadow* that killed my son? He's dead, too?"

Neph felt a chill at the quiet menace in the Godking's query. When the Khalidorans had first gone into the throne room, they thought some elite unit must have wiped out all the Khalidorans in the room, but Neph had been able to revive a man who'd had his feet cut off. He swore he'd seen most of the fight before he passed out. It was one man. A shadow. The Night Angel, he called him. The story was already getting out among the men.

A man who walked unseen, who could kill thirty highlanders and five meisters and one of the Godking's own aethelings. A man impervious to steel and to magic. It was nonsense, of course. With all the blood they'd found, the man must be dead. But without a body....

"Someone dragged his body away, sir. We followed the blood trail through the hidden passages. It was a lot of blood, sire. If it really was just one man, he's dead."

"It seems we have a lot of dead people without bodies, Commander. Find them. In the meantime, put up another head. Preferably one that looks like Logan Gyre's."

It wasn't fair. Ferl Khalius had been among the first highlanders on Cenarian soil. He'd been one of the few to get off the burning, sinking barge, and that only because he'd had the wits to throw off his armor before jumping in, so he didn't drown like so many others had. He'd joined another unit and fought barehanded until he could arm himself from the highlanders who died in the first assault on the courtyard. He'd personally killed six Cenarian soldiers and two nobles, six nobles if you counted children, which he didn't.

And what had he been given to recognize his heroism, his cunning? The shit duty. Certain units were being given looting privileges—the good units on the west side, what the barbarians called the Warrens, and the best units looting the remains of the east side with the officers. Ferl's unit was all dead, so he got assigned with clearing the rubble on the east bridge.

It wasn't only dirty—it was dangerous. The wytches had extinguished the fire, but many of the planks were weak, some of them cracking or breaking if you stood on them. The pilings were fine: sheathed in iron, they were impervious to the fire, but you couldn't stand on the pilings, so a fat lot of good that did.

The worst part of the job was the bodies. Some of them were like seared steak, crusted black on the outside, but cracked and oozing inside. And the stench of burnt flesh and burnt hair! He was picking through the bodies, taking whatever looked promising and dumping the bodies over the side of the bridge. Some of the units would be glad to have their dead back for proper burial, but Ferl wasn't going to carry the damned stinking things across this bridge. To the abyss with them.

Then he saw a sword. It must have been under one of the bodies when the fire had started, because it was untouched. There wasn't even smoke damage on the hilt. It was a beautiful blade, the hilt carved with dragons. It was the kind of sword that befitted the leader of a warband. Or a warlord. With such a sword, Ferl's clan would hold him in awe. Awe he deserved. He was supposed to bring anything unusual he found to one of the Vürdmeisters. *Sure, after how well they've treated me.*

Looking at the other men working on the bridge and seeing that none were watching, he drew his sword, set it aside, and slid his prize into its sheath. Not a perfect fit, but good enough for the moment. The hilt was a problem, what with those dragons, but he'd wrap leather bindings around it soon enough. He was good with his hands. Give him a few hours, and this sword would look like any other.

The sword brightened his outlook considerably. It wasn't really enough to repay his valor, but it was a start.

The meister walked down the last corridor to what the Southron barbarians called Hell's Asshole. The nauseating-intoxicating wash of torment engulfed her. She missed a step and stumbled against the wall. The soldier accompanying her turned. He looked scared.

"It's nothing," she said. She walked to the grate covering the hole. A few words and red light burned in front of her.

The creatures in the Hole squinted and shrank back. She spoke again and the light descended into the Hole. She examined each prisoner. Ten men, one woman, and one simpleton with filed teeth. None of them could be the usurper.

She turned, slightly dizzy, and walked out, trying not to flee.

A minute later, a big man rolled out from an overhang carved in the stone.

The woman looked at him and shook her head. "You're a fool. Nothing they could do to you would be as bad as staying here. Look at you. You're soft. The Hole will break you, Thirteen."

Logan stared at her flatly, a grimy woman with gaping holes in her dress, short a few teeth. The look on her face was the only thing approaching human kindness that was to be found in this hole. "Though all the detritus of humanity pass through this hole and all the fires of perdition rise from it, I will not be broken," Logan said.

"He use a lotta big words, don't he?" the big man named Fin said. He smiled a smile full of bloody gums, one of the first symptoms of scurvy, and wrapped his sinew rope back around his body. "Lotta meat on that big fucker. We'll eat real good."

Scurvy meant food deficiencies. Food deficiencies meant Fin had lived long enough to get sick from food deficiencies. Fin was a survivor. Logan turned his eyes to him and pulled out his knife—literally his only edge against these animals. "Let me make this real simple," he said, having to stifle the impulse to say "really" instead of "real." "You will not break me. The hole will not break me. I will not break. I. Will. Not. Be. Broken."

"What's your name, love?" the woman asked.

Logan found himself grinning. Something fierce and primal was rising inside him. Something inside him said, where others have failed, have faltered, have fallen, I will be triumphant; I am different; I am cut of a new cloth; I will rise. "Call me King," he said, and he smiled a fuck-you through the angst and the sorrow, and he was potent.

That was it. That was survival. That was the secret. That was the living flame hidden in the ashes of his burned-out heart. If only he could hold it.

EPILOGUE

Elene knocked on the door of the cooper's shop, her hair covered, back bent, and foot twisted sideways in the dust. The Khalidoran army had arrived yesterday and King Garoth Ursuul was rewarding his troops for their valor by allowing selected soldiers to take what they desired. It wasn't a good day to be a pretty woman on the streets of Cenaria.

It had taken her two harrowing days to find this place. The cooper unbolted the door and signaled her in, gesturing to the back of the shop. Jarl was at a table covered with papers, fat sacks of money at his feet. "I've found your way out," he said. "A Khalidoran caravan master has agreed to take you. You'll have to lie in a compartment used to smuggle barush tea and worse things until you get outside the gates, but it's big enough to hold you and the girl. You leave at nightfall."

"You can trust this smuggler?" Elene asked.

"I can't trust anyone," Jarl said, exhausted. "He's Khalidoran and you're beautiful. But because he's Khalidoran, he has the best chance of getting through the gates. And he's worked with us for twenty years. I've made it in his best interest to take you safely."

"You must have paid him a fortune," Elene said.

"Only half of one," Jarl said, the shadow of a smile coming to his lips. "The other half he gets when you send me word that you've made it safely."

"Thank you."

"It's the least I could do for Kylar." Jarl looked down, ashamed. "It's also the most I can do."

Elene hugged him. "It's more than enough. Thank you."

"The girl's downstairs. She won't leave his bo—she won't leave him."

*   *   *

He recognized this place. The white-gold warmth suffused him, his flesh gloried in the light. He moved through the tunnel with sure and easy steps. Eagerness without hurry.

Gentle fingers closed his eyes.

A child shrieked. Regrets. Sorrow. Darkness. Cold.

He blinked away the nightmare. Breathed. Let the white-gold light hold him again.

"Grab his arm, Uly. Help me."

Cold stones slid under his back. Discomfort. Pain. Hopelessness.

Then even the cold and the jostling faded.

He walked forward unsteadily in the tunnel. Broke into a jog. This was where he belonged now. Here, without pain.

A tear splashed on his face. A woman spoke, but he couldn't make out the words.

He stumbled and fell. He lay there, terrified, but the nightmare didn't come back. He got up to his knees, stood. At the next step he smacked up against...nothing.

He put his hands out and felt the invisible barrier. It was as cool as iron and as smooth as glass. Beyond it, the warmth increased, the white-gold light beckoned him. Were those people up ahead?

Something was pulling him aside, away. He felt twisted, and slowly a chamber came into focus—not the chamber, for the chamber itself remained indistinct, it seemed full of people intensely curious to see him, but he couldn't make them out. All that was truly in focus was a man seated before him on a low throne, and two doors. The door at his right hand was of beaten gold. Light leaked around every edge, the same warm white-gold light Kylar had just been in. The door to his left hand was plain wood with a simple iron latch. The man's face was dominated by lambent, lupine yellow eyes. He wasn't tall, but he exuded authority, potency.

"What is this place?" Kylar asked.

A toothy smile. "Neither heaven nor hell. This, if you will, is the Antechamber of the Mystery. This is my realm."

"Who are you?"

"It pleased Acaelus to call me The Wolf."

"Acaelus? You mean Durzo?" Kylar asked.

"Before you, there is a choice. You may proceed through one door or the other. Choose the gold, and I will release you back to where you just were, and you will have my apology for interrupting your journey."

"My journey?"

"Your journey to heaven or hell or oblivion or reincarnation or whatever it is that death holds."

"Do you know?" Kylar asked.

"This is the Antechamber of the Mystery, Azoth. You will find no answers here, just choices." The Wolf grinned, and it was a joyless grin, a predatory grin. "Through the wood door, you will go back to your life, your body, your time—or nearly so. It will take a few days for your body to heal. You will be the Night Angel in truth, as Acaelus was before you. Your body will be immune to the scourge of time as Acaelus' was—something that perhaps one must become old to appreciate. You will also heal at a rate beyond that of mortal men. What you call your Talent will grow. You can still be killed; the difference is, you will come back. You will be a living legend."

It sounded wonderful. Too good, even. *I'd be like Acaelus Thorne. I'd be like Durzo.* The latter thought gave him pause. The burden of immortality—however it worked—or the power of it or sheer press of so much time was what had turned Acaclus Thorne, the prince, the hero, into Durzo Blint, the hopeless, bitter murderer. He remembered his snide remark to Durzo:

"Here I thought the Night Angels were invincible."

"They're immortal. It's not the same."

"Why would you do this for me?" Kylar asked.

"Perhaps I don't do anything at all. Perhaps it is the ka'kari's work."

"What's the price?"

"Ah, Durzo has taught you well, hasn't he?" The Wolf looked almost mournful. "The truth is, I don't know. I can only tell you what I have heard from those more enlightened than I. They believed that coming back from death as you would was such a violation of the natural order of things that this unnatural life cost the afterlife. That for his seven centuries of life, Acaelus traded all eternity. But they might be wrong. It might have no influence on eternity whatsoever—or there may be no eternity to influence. I'm the wrong . . . man . . . to ask, for I have chosen this life myself."

Kylar walked toward the golden door. It was so beautiful there. He'd had such peace. What fool would trade the eternal peace and happiness in that gold light for the blood and gore and dishonor and despair and duplicity of the life he'd led?

As he stepped closer to it, the door changed. The gold melted, puddled to the ground in an instant and a raging inferno leapt up, eager to devour Kylar. Then it was gone, and the gold door was back. Kylar shot a look at the Wolf.

"Eternity," the Wolf said, "might not be a pleasant place for you."

"You did that?"

"A simple illusion. But if you sat in judgment of Kylar Stern, would you give him eternal paradise?"

"You're not exactly disinterested in my choice, are you?"

"You've become a player, Night Angel. No one is disinterested in your choice."

How long Kylar stood there, he didn't know. All he knew was that if he made the wrong choice, he might have a very very long time to regret it. The mathematical formulae were no help; they were full of infinities and zeroes, with no way of knowing on which side of the equation they landed. There was no hedged bet when you might be throwing away eternity in paradise or avoiding eternity in hell or taking an eternal existence on earth with all its flaws, weighed against merciful oblivion. Kylar didn't have Count Drake's faith in a loving God or Durzo's faith that there was no such God. He knew that he had done a lot of evil, by anyone's definition. He knew that he had done some good. He'd given his life for Elene.

Elene. She filled his mind and his heart so utterly that it ached. If he chose life, even if she accepted him, she would grow old and die in the smallest fraction of his life. The odds were that she never would accept him, never could.

All the ifs and maybes rose and fell in great towers of foundationless suppositions, but Elene remained. Kylar loved her. He had always loved her.

Elene was the risk he would take every time.

He made his choice and ran toward the plain door. He screamed—

—and jerked upright.

Elene screamed. Uly screamed.

Taking huge, gasping breaths, Kylar ripped open his blood-encrusted tunic.

His chest was smooth, the skin perfect. He touched his demolished shoulder. It was whole, as healthy as the fingers of his right hand. There wasn't a scar on his body.

He sat there blinking, not even glancing at Uly or Elene, who were frozen, staring at him.

"I'm alive. I'm alive?"

"Yes, Kylar," Momma K said, coming into the room. Her calm was surreal.

Kylar sat stupidly for a moment. It had all been real. He said, "Unbelievable. Kylar: one who kills and is killed. Durzo knew all along."

Uly, seeming to take her cue from the calm Kylar and Momma K were showing, seemed to be fine with Kylar sitting up and talking when he'd been dead a moment before. Elene was not doing as well. She stood up abruptly and walked out the door.

"Elene, wait," Kylar said. "Wait, just tell me one thing." She stopped and looked at him, confused, terrified and hopeful at the same time, her eyes full of tears. "Who was it who gave you those scars? It wasn't Durzo, was it? It was Rat, right?"

"You come back from the dead to ask me that? Of course it was Rat!" She fled.

"Wait! Elene, I'm sorry!" He tried to move, but it seemed he'd used up all his strength to sit up. She was gone. "Wait, what the hell am I sorry about?"

Uly looked at Kylar accusingly. "You aren't going to let her go, are you?"

Kylar held onto the edge of the bed like a lifeline. He looked at Uly, and raised a hand helplessly—and had to quickly put it down to keep from falling over. "How can I stop her?"

Uly stomped her foot and stormed out of the room.

Momma K was laughing, but it was a different laughter than he'd heard from her before, deeper, fuller, truly happy, as if with the same act of will that had made her choose life, she'd set aside her cynicism. "I know what you're thinking, Kylar. Durzo lied to you when he told you he'd hurt Elene. Of course he did. It was the only way he could save you. You had to kill him to succeed him. The ka'kari couldn't complete the bond until its former master died."

They sat there in silence, Kylar thinking of how Durzo's death cast his life in a completely different light. It was disconcerting to think how wrong he'd been about his master, thinking him so hateful—actually believing Durzo was capable of mutilating Doll Girl—but Kylar liked the picture that was emerging. Durzo Blint, the legend, had been Acaelus Thorne, the hero. Kylar wondered how many other heroes' names his master had worn. He felt a stabbing pain, an emptiness in his stomach, a surge toward tears that he suppressed. "I'm going to miss him," he said, his throat tight.

Momma K's eyes mirrored his. "Me too. But it's going to be all right. I don't know why, but I really believe that."

Kylar nodded. "So you decided to live," he said, blinking tears away. He didn't want to break down in front of Momma K.

"And so did you." She arched an eyebrow at him, somehow holding both grief and happiness and amusement in her eyes all at once. "She loves you, Kylar. Whether she realizes it or not. She dragged you out of the castle by herself. She refused to leave you. Jarl's men found her. It was only when they got you here that Uly saw your wounds were healing."

"She's furious with me," Kylar said.

"Furious the way a woman in love gets. I know."

"Have you told Uly who her mother is?" Kylar asked.

"No, and I never will. I won't raise her into this."

"She needs a family."

"I was hoping you and Elene would be interested in the job."

Night came to the east shore of the Plith River in a smothering cloud. The city had been burning all day and the night winds wafted the smell over the entire city. Fires reflected in the Plith, and low-hanging clouds held the ashy air like a pillow against the face of the city.

A wagon clattered down a street, its driver hunched, face muffled against the malodorous air. He overtook a crippled woman with a bent back and a foot turned sideways.

"Want up?" his scratchy voice asked.

The woman turned expectantly. Her face too was muffled, but her eyes were young, though both eyes had been blackened.

Her Khalidoran driver was supposed to be dark-haired and fat. This man was white-haired, lean as a rail, stooped and almost lost in his clothes. She shook her head and turned away.

"Please, Elene?" Kylar asked with his own voice.

She flinched. "I should be scared of you, shouldn't I?"

"I'd never hurt you," he said.

Eyebrows above the eyes he'd blackened lifted incredulously.

"Well, not *really* hurt you."

"What are you doing?" she asked, looking around. There was no one else out on the streets.

"I'd like to take you away from here," Kylar said, brushing back his bleached hair and smiling through his makeup. "You and Uly both. We can go anywhere. I'm going to pick her up next."

"Why me, Kylar?"

He was dumbfounded. "It's always been you. I l—"

"Don't you say you love me," she said. "How could you love this?" She jerked the scarf down and pointed at her scars. "How could you love a freak?"

He shook his head. "I don't love your scars, Elene. I hate them—"

"And you'll never see past that."

"I'm not finished," he said. "Elene, I've watched over you since we were children. For a long time, you're right, I couldn't see past your scars. I'm not going to give you some crap that they're beautiful. Your scars are ugly, but you aren't, Elene. The woman I see when I look at you is amazing. She's smart, she's got a quick tongue, and she's got such a heart that it makes me believe that people can be good despite all I've seen to the contrary for my whole life."

His words were sinking into her, he could tell. *Oh, Momma K, tell me I learned something about words from you. Tell me I learned something despite myself.*

Elene's hands waved like little birds. "How can you say that? You don't know me!"

"Aren't you still Doll Girl?"

Her hands came down, the little birds fluttering to rest. "Yes," she said. "But I don't think you're still Azoth."

"No," he admitted. "I'm not. I don't know who I am. Right now, I only know I'm not my master and I won't live like he did."

Hope seemed to leach out of her. "Kylar," she said, and he saw that the name was a deliberate choice, "I will always be grateful to you. But we would be a disaster. You would destroy me."

"What are you talking about?"

"Momma K said your master intercepted all my letters."

"Yes, but I've had a busy afternoon catching up," Kylar said.

She smiled sadly. "And you still don't understand?"

Do girls ever make sense? He shook his head.

"When we were children, you were the one who protected me, who looked out for me. You were the one who put me with a real family. I wanted to be with you forever. Then when I was growing up, you were my benefactor who made me special. You were my secret young lord whom I loved so desperately and so foolishly. You were my Kylar, my poor nobleman that the Drake girls told me stories about. Then you were the one who came to save me in gaol."

He paused and paused. "You say that like it's a bad thing."

"Oh, Kylar. What happens to that silly girl when it turns out I'm not good enough for the man I've loved for my whole life?"

"*You* not good enough?"

"It's a fairy tale, Kylar. I don't deserve it. Something will happen. You'll find somebody prettier or you'll get tired of me, and then you'll leave me, and I'll never recover, because the only kind of love I have to offer is stupid and blind and so deep and powerful that I feel like I'm cracking just to hold it in. I can't just swoon and fall into bed with you, because you'll hop right out and get on with your life, and I never will."

"I'm not asking you to make love with me."

"So I'm too ugly for—"

He couldn't say a damn thing right. "Enough!" he roared, emotion filling his voice so suddenly that it shocked her into silence. "I think you're the
most beautiful woman I've ever seen, Elene. And the purest. And the best.
But I'm not asking you to fuck!"

Consternation played over her features, but she obviously didn't like
being yelled at.

"Elene," he said quietly. "I'm sorry I yelled. I'm sorry I hit you—even if
it was to save you. I've thought I was dying twice in the last few days—
maybe I did die, I don't know. What I do know is that when I thought I was
dying, you were my regret. No! Not your scars," he said as she touched her
face. "I regretted that I hadn't turned myself into the kind of man that you
could be with. That it wouldn't be *just* for me to be with you, even if you
wanted me. Our lives started in the same shit hole, Elene, but somehow
you've turned into you, and I've turned into this. I don't like what I've done.
I don't like who I've become. You don't deserve a fairy tale? I don't deserve
another chance, but I'm asking you for one. You're afraid that love is too
risky? I've seen what happens when you don't risk it. Momma K and my
master loved each other, but they were too afraid to risk it and that destroyed
them. We risk everything either way.

"I'm willing to risk it to see the world through your eyes, Elene. I want
to know you. I want to be worthy of you. I want to look in the mirror and
like who I see. I don't know what's next, but I know I want to face it with
you. Elene, I'm not asking you to fuck. But maybe some day, I'll earn the
right to ask you for something more permanent." He turned, and facing her
was harder than facing thirty highlanders. He extended his hand. "Please,
Elene. Will you come with me?"

She scowled fiercely at him, then looked away. Her eyes were shiny with
tears, but it could have been from all the ash in the air. She blinked quickly
before looking back up at him. She searched his face for a long moment.
He met her big brown eyes. He had turned away from them so many times,
afraid she would see what he really was. He had turned away, afraid that
she couldn't bear the sight of his filth. Now he met that gaze. He opened
himself to it. He didn't hide his darkness. He didn't hide his love. He let her
gaze go all the way through him.

To his wonder, her eyes filled with something softer than justice, something warmer than mercy.

"I'm so scared, Kylar."

"Me too," he said.

She took his hand.

BOOK 2

Shadow's Edge

For Kristi, for never doubting—not even when I did
&
For Kevin, because it's a big brother's job to
make a little brother tough. What you taught me, I've needed.
(But I never have been right since that dirt clod incident.)

1

*W*e've got a contract for you," Momma K said. As always, she sat like a queen, her back straight, sumptuous dress perfect, hair immaculately coifed if gray at the roots. This morning she had dark circles under her eyes. Kylar guessed that none of the Sa'kagé's surviving leaders had slept much since the Khalidoran invasion.

"Good morning to you, too," Kylar said, settling into the wing-backed chair in the study. Momma K didn't turn to face him, looking instead out her window. Last night's rain had quenched most of the fires in the city, but many still smoked, bathing the city in a crimson dawn. The waters of the Plith River that divided rich eastern Cenaria from the Warrens looked as red as blood. Kylar wasn't sure that was all because of the smoke-obscured sun, either. In the week since the coup, the Khalidoran invaders had massacred thousands.

Momma K said, "There's a wrinkle. The deader knows it's coming."

"How's he know?" The Sa'kagé wasn't usually so sloppy.

"We told him."

Kylar rubbed his temples. The Sa'kagé would only tell someone so that if the attempt failed, the Sa'kagé wouldn't be committed. That meant the deader could only be one man: Cenaria's conqueror, Khalidor's Godking, Garoth Ursuul.

"I just came to get my money," Kylar said. "All of Durzo's—my safe houses burned down. I only need enough to bribe the gate guards." He'd been giving her a cut of his wages to invest since he was a child. She should have plenty for a few bribes.

Momma K flipped silently through sheets of rice paper on her desk and handed one to Kylar. At first, he was stunned by the numbers. He was involved in the illegal importation of riot weed and half a dozen other addictive plants, owned a race horse, had a stake in a brewery and several other businesses, part of a loan shark's portfolio, and owned partial cargos of items like silks and gems that were legitimate except for the fact the Sa'kagé paid 20 percent in bribes rather than 50 percent in tariffs. The sheer amount of information on the page was mind-boggling. He didn't know what half of it meant.

"I own a house?" Kylar asked.

"Owned," Momma K said. "This column denotes merchandise lost in the fires or looting." There were checks next to all but a silk expedition and one for riot weed. Almost everything he had owned was lost. "Neither expedition will return for months, if at all. If the Godking keeps seizing civilian vessels, they won't come back at all. Of course, if he were dead—"

He could see where this was going. "This says my share is still worth ten to fifteen thousand. I'll sell it to you for a thousand. That's all I need."

She ignored him. "They need a third wetboy to make sure it works. Fifty thousand gunders for one kill, Kylar. With that much, you can take Elene and Uly anywhere. You'll have done the world a good turn, and you'll never have to work again. It's just one last job."

He wavered only for a moment. "There's always one last job. I'm finished."

"This is because of Elene, isn't it?" Momma K asked.

"Momma K, do you think a man can change?"

She looked at him with a profound sadness. "No. And he'll end up hating anyone who asks him to."

Kylar got up and walked out the door. In the hallway, he ran into Jarl. Jarl was grinning like he used to when they were growing up on the streets and he was up to no good. Jarl was wearing what must be the new fashion, a long tunic with exaggerated shoulders paired with slim trousers tucked into high boots. It looked vaguely Khalidoran. His hair was worked into elaborate microbraids capped with gold beads that set off his black skin.

"I've got the perfect job for you," Jarl said, his voice lowered, but unrepentant about eavesdropping.

"No killing?" Kylar asked.

"Not exactly."

"Your Holiness, the cowards stand ready to redeem themselves," Vürdmeister Neph Dada announced, his voice carrying over the crowd. He was an old man, veiny, liver-spotted, stooped, stinking of death held at bay with magic, his breath rattling from the exertion of climbing up the platform in

Cenaria Castle's great yard. Twelve knotted cords hung over the shoulders of his black robes for the twelve shu'ras he'd mastered. Neph knelt with difficulty and offered a handful of straw to the Godking.

Godking Garoth Ursuul stood on the platform inspecting his troops. Front and center were nearly two hundred Graavar highlanders, tall, barrel-chested, blue-eyed savages who wore their black hair short and their mustaches long. On either side stood the other elite highland tribes that had captured the castle. Beyond them waited the rest of the regular army that had marched into Cenaria since the liberation.

Mists rose from the Plith River on either side of the castle and slid under the rusty teeth of the iron portcullises to chill the crowd. The Graavar had been broken into fifteen groups of thirteen each, and they alone had no weapons, armor, or tunics. They stood in their trousers, pale faces fixed, but sweating instead of shivering in the cool autumn morning.

There was never commotion when the Godking inspected his troops, but today the silence ached despite the thousands gathered to watch. Garoth had gathered every soldier possible and allowed the Cenarian servants and nobles and smallfolk to watch as well. Meisters in their black-and-red half-cloaks stood shoulder to shoulder with robed Vürdmeisters, soldiers, crofters, coopers, nobles, field hands, maids, sailors, and Cenarian spies.

The Godking wore a broad white cloak edged with ermine thrown back to make his broad shoulders look huge. Beneath that was a sleeveless white tunic over wide white trousers. All the white made his pallid Khalidoran skin look ghostly, and drew sharp attention to the vir playing across his skin. Black tendrils of power rose to the surface of his arms. Great knots rose and fell, knots edged with thorns that moved not just back and forth but up and down in waves, pressing out from his skin. Claws raked his skin from beneath. Nor were his vir confined to his arms. They rose to frame his face. They rose to his bald scalp and pierced the skin, forming a thorny, quivering black crown. Blood trickled down the sides of his face.

For many Cenarians, it was their first glimpse of the Godking. Their jaws hung slack. They shivered as his gaze passed over them. It was exactly as he intended.

Finally, Garoth selected one of the pieces of straw from Neph Dada and broke it in half. He threw away one half and took twelve full-length pieces. "Thus shall Khali speak," he said, his voice robust with power.

He signaled the Graavar to climb the platform. During the liberation, they had been ordered to hold this yard to contain the Cenarian nobles for slaughter. Instead, the highlanders had been routed, and Terah Graesin and her nobles had escaped. That was unacceptable, inexplicable, uncharacteristic for the fierce Graavar. Garoth didn't understand what made men fight one day and flee the next.

What he did understand was shame. For the past week, the Graavar had been mucking stables, emptying chamber pots, and scrubbing floors. They had not been allowed to sleep, instead spending the nights polishing their betters' armor and weapons. Today, they would expiate their guilt, and for the next year, they would be eager to prove their heroism. As he approached the first group with Neph at his side, Garoth calmed the vir from his hands. When the men drew their straws, they must think it not the working of magic or the Godking's pleasure that spared one and condemned another. Rather, it was simple fate, the inexorable consequence of their own cowardice.

Garoth held up his hands, and together, all the Khalidorans prayed: *"Khali vas, Khalivos ras en me, Khali mevirtu rapt, recu virtum defite."*

As the words faded, the first soldier approached. He was barely sixteen, the least fringe of a mustache on his lip. He looked on the verge of collapse as his eyes flitted from the Godking's icy face to the straws. His naked chest shone with sweat in the rising morning light, his muscles twitching. He drew a straw. It was long.

Half of the tension whooshed out of his body, but only half. The young man next to him, who looked so alike he must have been his older brother, licked his lips and grabbed a straw. It was short.

Queasy relief washed over the rest of the squad, and the thousands watching who couldn't possibly see the short straw knew that it had been drawn from their reactions. The man who'd drawn the short straw looked at his little brother. The younger man looked away. The condemned man turned disbelieving eyes on the Godking and handed him the short straw.

Garoth stepped back. "Khali has spoken," he announced. There was a collective intake of breath, and he nodded to the squad.

They closed on the young man, every one of them—even his brother—and began beating him.

It would have been faster if Garoth had let the squad wear gauntlets or use the butts of spears or the flat of blades, but he thought it was better this way. When the blood began flowing and spraying off flesh as it was pummeled, it shouldn't get on the squad's clothing. It should get on their skin. Let them feel the warmth of the young man's blood as he died. Let them know the cost of cowardice. Khalidorans did not flee.

The squad attacked with gusto. The circle closed and screams rose. There was something intimate about naked meat slapping naked meat. The young man disappeared and all that could be seen was elbows rising and disappearing with every punch and feet being drawn back for new kicks. And moments later, blood. With the short straw, the young man had become their weakness. It was Khali's decree. He was no longer brother or friend, he was all they had done wrong.

In two minutes, the young man was dead.

The squad reformed, blood-spattered and blowing hard from exertion and emotion. They didn't look at the corpse at their feet. Garoth regarded each in turn, meeting the eyes of every one, and lingering on the brother. Standing over the corpse, Garoth extended a hand. The vir poked out of his wrist and extended, clawlike, ragged, and gripped the corpse's head. Then the claws convulsed and the head popped with a wet sound that left dozens of Cenarians retching.

"Your sacrifice is accepted. Thus are you cleansed," he announced, and saluted them.

They returned his salute proudly and took their places back in the formation in the courtyard as the body was dragged away.

He motioned the next squad. The next fourteen iterations would be nothing but more of the same. Though tension still arced through every squad—even the squads who'd finished would lose friends and family in other squads—Garoth lost interest. "Neph, tell me what you've learned about this man, this *Night Angel* who killed my son."

Cenaria Castle wasn't high on Kylar's list of places to visit. He was disguised as a tanner, a temporary dye staining his hands and arms to the elbow, a spattered woolen tradesman's tunic, and a number of drops of a special perfume his dead master Durzo Blint had developed. He reeked only slightly less than a real tanner would. Durzo had always preferred disguises of tanners, pig farmers, beggars, and other types that respectable people did their best not to see because they couldn't help but smell them. The perfume was applied only to the outer garments so if need arose, they could be shed. Some of the stench would still cling, but every disguise had drawbacks. The art was matching the drawbacks to the job.

East Kingsbridge had burned during the coup, and though the meisters had repaired most of its length, it was still closed, so Kylar crossed West Kingsbridge. The Khalidoran guards barely glanced at him as he passed them. It seemed everyone's attention—even the meisters'—was riveted to a platform in the center of the castle yard and a group of highlanders standing bare-chested in the cold. Kylar ignored the squad on the platform as he scanned for threats. He still wasn't sure if meisters could see his Talent, though he suspected they couldn't as long as he wasn't using it. Their abilities seemed much more tied to smell than magi's—which was the main reason he'd come as a tanner. If a meister came close, Kylar could only hope that mundane smells interfered with magical ones.

Four guards stood on each side of the gate, six on each segment of the diamond-shaped castle wall, and perhaps a thousand in formation in the yard, in addition to the two hundred or so Graavar highlanders. In the crowd of several thousand, fifty meisters were placed at regular intervals. In the center of it all, on the temporary platform, were a number of Cenarian nobles, mutilated corpses, and Godking Garoth Ursuul himself, speaking with a Vürdmeister. It was ridiculous, but even with the number of soldiers and meisters here, this was probably the best chance a wetboy would have to kill the man.

But Kylar wasn't here to kill. He was here to study a man for the strangest job he'd ever accepted. He scanned the crowd for the man Jarl had told him about and found him quickly. Baron Kirof had been a vassal of the Gyres. With his lord dead and his lands close to the city, he'd been one of the first Cenarian nobles to bend the knee to Garoth Ursuul. He was a fat man with a red beard cut in the angular lowland Khalidoran style, a large crooked nose, weak chin, and great bushy eyebrows.

Kylar moved closer. Baron Kirof was sweating, wiping his palms on his tunic, speaking nervously to the Khalidoran nobles he stood with. Kylar was easing around a tall, stinking blacksmith when the man suddenly threw an elbow into Kylar's solar plexus.

The blow knocked the wind from Kylar, and even as he hunched over, the ka'kari pooled in his hand and formed a punch dagger.

"You want a better look, you get here early, like the rest of us did," the blacksmith said. He folded his arms, pushing up his sleeves to show off massive biceps.

With effort, Kylar willed the ka'kari back into his skin and apologized, eyes downcast. The blacksmith sneered and went back to watching the fun.

Kylar settled for a decent view of Baron Kirof. The Godking had worked his way through half of the squads, and Sa'kagé bookies were already taking bets on which number out of each group of thirteen would die. The Khalidoran soldiers noticed. Kylar wondered how many Cenarians would die for the bookies' callousness when the Khalidoran soldiers went roaming the city tonight, in grief for their dead and fury at how the Sa'kagé fouled everything it touched.

I've got to get out of this damned city.

*   *   *

The next squad had made it through ten men without one drawing the short straw. It was almost worth paying attention as the men got more and more desperate as each of their neighbors was spared and their own chances became grimmer. The eleventh man, fortyish and all sinew and gristle, pulled the short straw. He chewed on the end of his mustache as he handed the straw back to the Godking, but otherwise didn't betray any emotion.

Neph glanced to where Duchess Jadwin and her husband were seated on the platform. "I examined the throne room, and I felt something I've never encountered before. The entire castle smells of the magic that killed so many of our meisters. But some spots in the throne room simply...don't. It's like there was a fire in the house, but you walk into one room and it doesn't smell like smoke."

Blood was flying now, and Garoth was reasonably certain that the man must be dead, but the squad continued beating, beating, beating.

"That doesn't match what we know of the silver ka'kari," Garoth said.

"No, Your Holiness. I think there's a seventh ka'kari, a secret ka'kari. I think it negates magic, and I think this Night Angel has it."

Garoth thought about that as the ranks reformed, leaving a corpse before them. The man's face had been utterly destroyed. It was impressive work. The squad had either worked hard to prove their commitment or they hadn't liked the poor bastard. Garoth nodded, pleased. He extended the vir claw again and crushed the corpse's head. "Your sacrifice is accepted. Thus are you cleansed."

Two of his bodyguards moved the corpse to the side of the platform. They were stacked there in their gore so that even though the Cenarians couldn't see each man's death, they would see the aftermath.

When the next squad began, Garoth said, "A ka'kari hidden for seven hundred years? What mastery does it bestow? Hiding? What does that do for me?"

"Your Holiness, with such a ka'kari, you or your agent could walk into the heart of the Chantry and take every treasure they have. Unseen. It's possible your agent could enter Ezra's Wood itself and take seven centuries' worth of artifacts for you. There would then be no more need for armies or subtlety. At one stroke, you could take all Midcyru by the throat."

My agent. No doubt Neph would bravely volunteer to undertake the perilous task. Still, the mere thought of such a ka'kari occupied Garoth through the deaths of another teenager, two men in their prime, and a seasoned campaigner wearing one of the highest awards for merit that the Godking bestowed. That man alone had something akin to treason in his eyes.

"Look into it," Garoth said. He wondered if Khali knew of this seventh ka'kari. He wondered if Dorian knew of it. Dorian his first acknowledged son, Dorian who would have been his heir, Dorian the prophet, Dorian the Betrayer. Dorian had been here, Garoth was sure of it. Only Dorian could have brought Curoch, Jorsin Alkestes' mighty sword. Some magus had appeared with it for a single moment and obliterated fifty meisters and three Vürdmeisters, then disappeared. Neph was obviously waiting for Garoth to ask about it, but Garoth had given up on finding Curoch. Dorian was no fool. He wouldn't have brought Curoch so close if he thought he might lose it. How do you outmaneuver a man who can see the future?

The Godking squinted as he crushed another head. Every time he did that, he got blood on his own snow-white clothing. It was deliberate—but irritating all the same, and there was nothing dignified about having blood squirt in your eye. "Your sacrifice is accepted," he told the men. "Thus are you cleansed." He stood at the front of the platform as the squad took its place back on the parade ground. For the entire review, he hadn't turned to face the Cenarians who were sitting on the platform behind him. Now he did.

The vir flared to life as he turned. Black tendrils crawled up his face, swarmed over his arms, through his legs, and even out from his pupils. He allowed them a moment to suck in light, so that the Godking appeared to be an unnatural splotch of darkness in the rising morning light. Then he put an end to that. He wanted the nobles to see him.

There wasn't an eye that wasn't huge. It wasn't solely the vir or Garoth's inherent majesty that stunned them. It was the corpses stacked like cordwood to each side and behind him, framing him like a picture. It was the blood-and-brain-spattered white clothing he wore. He was awesome in his power, and terrible in his majesty. Perhaps, if she survived, he'd have Duchess Trudana Jadwin paint the scene.

The Godking regarded the nobles and the nobles on the platform regarded the Godking. He wondered if any of them had yet counted their own number: thirteen.

He extended his handful of straw toward his nobles. "Come," he told them. "Khali will cleanse you." This time, he had no intention of letting fate decide who would die.

Commander Gher looked at the Godking. "Your Holiness, there must be some—" he stopped. Godkings didn't make mistakes. Gher's face drained of color. He drew a long straw. It was several moments before it occurred to him not to appear too relieved.

Most of the rest were lesser nobles—the men and women who'd made the late King Aleine Gunder IX's government work. They had all been so easily subverted. Extortion could be so simple. But it gained Garoth nothing to kill these peons, even if they had failed him.

That brought him to a sweating Trudana Jadwin. She was the twelfth in the line, and her husband was last.

Garoth paused. He let them look at each other. They knew, everyone who was watching knew that one or the other of them would die, and it all depended on Trudana's draw. The duke was swallowing compulsively. Garoth said, "Out of all the nobles here, you, Duke Jadwin, are the only one who was never in my employ. So obviously you didn't fail me. Your wife, on the other hand, did."

"What?" the duke asked. He looked at Trudana.

"Didn't you know she was cheating on you with the prince? She murdered him on my orders," Garoth said.

There was something beautiful about standing in the middle of what should be an intensely private moment. The duke's fear-pale face went gray. He had clearly been even less perceptive than most cuckolds. Garoth could see realization pounding the poor man. Every dim suspicion he'd ever brushed aside, every poor excuse he'd ever heard was hammering him.

Intriguingly, Trudana Jadwin looked stricken. Her expression wasn't the self-righteousness Garoth expected. He'd thought she'd point the finger, tell her husband why it was his fault. Instead, her eyes spoke pure culpability. Garoth could only guess that the duke had been a decent husband and she knew it. She had cheated because she had wanted to, and now two decades of lies were collapsing.

"Trudana," the Godking said before either could speak, "you have served well, but you could have served better. So here is your reward and your punishment." He extended the straws toward her. "The short straw is on your left."

She looked into Garoth's vir-darkened eyes and at the straws and then into her husband's eyes. It was an immortal moment. Garoth knew that the plaintive look in the duke's eyes would haunt Trudana Jadwin for as long she lived. The Godking had no doubt what she would choose, but obviously Trudana thought herself capable of self-sacrifice.

Steeling herself, she reached for the short straw, then stopped. She looked at her husband, looked away, and pulled the long straw for herself.

The duke howled. It was lovely. The sound pierced every Cenarian heart in the courtyard. It seemed pitched perfectly to carry the Godking's message: this could be you.

As the nobles—including Trudana—surrounded the duke with death in their hearts, every one of them feeling damned for their participation but participating all the same, the duke turned to his wife. "I love you, Trudana," he said. "I've always loved you." Then he pulled his cloak up over his face and disappeared in the thudding of flesh.

The Godking could only smile.

As Trudana Jadwin hesitated over her choice, Kylar thought that if he had taken Momma K's job, now would be the perfect moment to strike. Every eye was on the platform.

Kylar had turned toward Baron Kirof, studying what shock and horror looked like on his face, when he noticed that only five guards stood on the wall beyond the baron. He recounted quickly: six, but one of them held a bow and a handful of arrows in his bow hand.

A harsh crack sounded from the center of the yard, and Kylar caught a glimpse of the back section of the temporary platform splitting off and falling. Something flashing scintillating colors flew up into the air. As everyone else turned toward it, Kylar turned away. The sparkle bomb exploded with a small concussion and an enormous flash of white light. As hundreds of civilians and soldiers alike cried out, blinded, Kylar saw the sixth soldier on the wall draw an arrow. It was Jonus Severing, a wetboy with fifty kills to his name. A gold-tipped arrow streaked toward the Godking.

The Godking's hands were clasped over his eyes, but shields like bubbles were already blooming around him. The arrow hit the outermost shield, stuck, and burst into flame as the shield popped. Another arrow was already on the way, and it passed through the fraying outer shield and hit one closer in. The next popped and the next as Jonus Severing shot with amazing speed. He was using his Talent to hold his spare arrows in midair so that as soon as he released a shot, the next arrow was already coming to his fingertips. The shields were breaking faster than the Godking could reform them.

People were screaming, blinded. The fifty meisters around the yard were throwing shields up around themselves, knocking anyone nearby off their feet.

The wetboy who'd been hiding beneath the platform jumped onto the platform on the Godking's blind side. He hesitated as one last wavering shield bloomed inches from the Godking's skin, and Kylar saw that he wasn't a wetboy at all. It was a child of perhaps fourteen, Jonus Severing's apprentice. The boy was so focused on the Godking, he didn't keep low, didn't keep moving. Kylar heard the snap of a bowstring nearby and saw the boy go down even as the Godking's last shield popped.

People were charging toward the gates, trampling their neighbors. Several of the meisters, still blinded and panicked, were flinging green missiles indiscriminately into the crowd and the soldiers around them. One of the Godking's bodyguards tried to tackle the Godking to get him out of danger. Dazed, the Godking misinterpreted the move and a hammer of vir blasted the huge highlander through the nobles on the platform.

Kylar turned to find who'd killed the wetboy's apprentice. Not ten paces away stood Hu Gibbet, the butcher who had slaughtered Logan Gyre's entire family, the best wetboy in the city now that Durzo Blint was dead.

Jonus Severing was already fleeing, not sparing a moment of anguish for his dead apprentice. Hu released a second arrow and Kylar saw it streak into Jonus Severing's back. The wetboy pitched forward off the wall and out of view, but Kylar had no doubt he was dead.

Hu Gibbet had betrayed the Sa'kagé, and now he'd saved the Godking. The ka'kari was in Kylar's hand before he was even aware of it. *What, I wouldn't kill the architect of Cenaria's destruction, but now I'm going to kill a bodyguard?* Of course, calling Hu Gibbet a bodyguard was like calling a bear a furry animal, but the point remained. Kylar pulled the ka'kari back into his skin.

Ducking so Hu wouldn't see his face, Kylar joined the streams of panicked Cenarians flooding out the castle gate.

2

The Jadwin estate had survived the fires that had reduced so much of the city to rubble. Kylar came to the heavily guarded front gate and the guards opened the sally port for him wordlessly. Kylar had only stopped to strip out of his tanner's disguise and scrub his body with alcohol to rid himself of the scent, and he was certain that he'd arrived before the duchess, but word of the duke's death had flown faster. The guards had black strips of cloth tied around their arms. "Is it true?" one of them asked.

Kylar nodded and made his way to the hut behind the manse where the Cromwylls lived. Elene had been the last orphan the Cromwylls took in, and all her siblings had moved on to other trades or to serve other houses. Only her foster mother still served the Jadwins. Since the coup, Kylar, Elene, and Uly had stayed here. With Kylar's safe houses burned or inaccessible, it was the only choice. Kylar was thought to be dead, so he didn't want to stay in any of the Sa'kagé safe houses where he might be recognized. In any case, every safe house was full to breaking. No one wanted to be out on the streets with the roving bands of Khalidorans.

No one was in the hut, so Kylar went to the manse's kitchen. Eleven-year-old Uly was standing on a stool, leaning over a tub of soapy water, scrubbing pans. Kylar swept in and picked her up under one arm, spun her around as she squealed, and set her back down on the stool. He gave her a fierce look. "You been keeping Elene out of trouble like I told you?" he asked the little girl.

Uly sighed. "I've been trying, but I think this one's hopeless."

Kylar laughed, and she laughed too. Uly had been raised by servants in Cenaria Castle, believing for her own protection that she was an orphan. The truth was that she was the daughter of Momma K and Durzo Blint. Durzo had only found out about her in the last days of his life, and Kylar had promised him that he would look after the girl. After the initial awkwardness of explaining that he wasn't her father, things had gone better than Kylar could have expected.

"Hopeless? I'll show you hopeless," a voice said. Elene carried a huge cauldron with the grime of yesterday's stew baked onto the sides and set it down next to Uly's stack of dishes.

Uly groaned and Elene chuckled evilly. Kylar marveled at how she'd changed in a mere week, or perhaps the change was in how he saw her. Elene still had the thick scars Rat had given her as a child: an X across her full lips, one on her cheek, and a crescent looping from her eyebrow to the corner of her mouth. But Kylar barely noticed them. Now, he saw radiant skin, eyes bright with intelligence and happiness, her grin lopsided not because of a scar but from planned mischief. And how a woman could look so good in modest servant's woolens and an apron was one of the great mysteries of the universe.

Elene grabbed an apron from a hook and looked at Kylar with a predatory gleam in her eye. "Oh, no. Not me," Kylar said.

She looped the apron over his head and pulled him close slowly and seductively. She was staring at his lips and he couldn't help but stare at hers as she wet them with her tongue. "I think," she said, her voice low, her hands gliding across his sides, "that..."

Uly coughed loudly, but neither of them acknowledged her.

Elene pulled him against her, her hands on the small of his back, her mouth tilting up, her sweet scent filling his nostrils. "...that's much better." She yanked the apron knot tight behind his back and released him abruptly, stepping back out of range. "Now you can help me. Do you want to cut the potatoes or the onions?" She and Uly laughed at the outrage on his face.

Kylar leapt forward and Elene tried to dodge, but he used his Talent to grab her. He'd been practicing in the last week, and though so far he could only extend his reach a pace or so behind his own arms, this time it was enough. He pulled Elene in and kissed her. She barely pretended to put up a fight before kissing him back with equal fervor. For a moment, the world contracted to the softness of Elene's lips and the feel of her body tight against his.

Somewhere, Uly started retching loudly. Kylar reached out and swatted the dishwater toward the source of his irritation. The retching was abruptly replaced with a yelp. Elene disentangled herself and covered her mouth, trying not to laugh.

Kylar had managed to drench Uly's face completely. She raised her hand and swatted water back at him, and he let it hit him. He rubbed her wet hair in the way he knew she didn't like, and said, "All right, squirt, I deserved that. Truce now. Where are those potatoes?"

They settled smoothly into the easy routine of kitchen work. Elene asked him what he'd seen and learned, and though he checked constantly for eavesdroppers, he told her everything about studying the baron and help-lessly watching the assassination attempt. Such sharing was, perhaps, the most boring thing a couple could do, but Kylar had been denied the boring luxuries of everyday love for his whole life. To share, simply to speak the truth to a person who cared, was unfathomably precious. A wetboy, Durzo had taught Kylar, must be able to walk away from everything at a moment's notice. A wetboy is always alone.

So this moment, this simple communion, was why Kylar was finished with the way of shadows. He'd spent more than half his life training tire-lessly to become the perfect killer. He didn't want to kill anymore.

"They needed a third man for the job," Kylar said. "To be a lookout and backup knife man. We could have done it. Their timing was so good. One second different and they would have pulled it off with only the two of them. If I'd been there, Hu Gibbet and the Godking both would be dead. We'd have fifty thousand gunders." He paused at a black thought. " 'Gunders.' Guess they won't be calling them that anymore, now that all the Gunders are dead." He sighed.

"You want to know if you did the right thing," Elene said.

"Yes."

"Kylar, there are always going to be people so bad that we think they deserve to die. In the castle when Roth was...hurting you, I was this close to trying to kill him myself. If it had been only a little longer...I don't know. What I do know is what you've told me about what killing has done to your soul. No matter what good it seems to do for the world, it destroys you. I can't watch that, Kylar. I won't. I care about you too much."

It was the one precondition Elene had for leaving the city with Kylar: that he give up killing and violence. He was still so confused. He didn't know if Elene's way was right, but he'd seen enough to know that Durzo's and Momma K's wasn't. "You really believe that violence begets violence? That fewer innocent people will die in the end if I give up killing?"

"I really do," Elene said.

"All right," Kylar said. "Then there's a job I need to do tonight. We should be able to leave in the morning."

*H*ell's Asshole was no place for a king. Appropriately, the Hole was the lowest extremity of the gaol Cenarians called the Maw. The entrance to the Maw was a demonic visage carved from jagged black fireglass. Prisoners were marched straight into its open mouth, down a ramp often made slick by fear-loosened bladders. In the Hole itself, the stone carver's art had been eschewed for the sheer visceral fears evoked by tight spaces, the dark, heights, the eerie howling of the wind rising from the depths, and the knowledge that every prisoner with whom you shared the Hole had been deemed unworthy of a clean death. The Hole was unrelentingly hot and reeked of brimstone and human waste in its three forms: their shit, their dead, and their unwashed flesh. There was only a single torch, far overhead, on the other side of the grate that separated the human animals from the rest of the prisoners in the Maw.

Eleven men and one woman shared the Hole with Logan Gyre. They hated him for his knife and for his powerful body and for his cultured accent. Somehow, even in this nightmare menagerie of freaks and twists, he was different, isolated.

Logan sat with his back to the wall. There was only one wall because the Hole was a circle. In the middle was a hole five paces wide that opened into a chasm. The chasm's sides were perfectly vertical, perfectly sheer fireglass. There was no guessing how deep it was. When the prisoners kicked their waste into the hole, they heard no sound. The only thing that escaped the Hole was the deep stench of a sulphuric hell and the intermittent wailing made by the wind or the ghosts or the tortured souls of the dead or whatever it was that made that sanity-breaking sound.

At first, Logan had wondered why his fellows would defecate against the wall and only later—if ever—kick the feces down the hole. The first time he had to go, he knew: you'd have to be insane to squat near the Hole. You couldn't do anything down here that made you vulnerable. When one inmate had to move past another, he shuffled quickly and suspiciously, snarling and hissing and cursing in such strings that the words lost meaning. Pushing another inmate into the Hole was the easiest way to kill.

What made it worse was that the shelf of rock that circled the Hole was only three paces wide and the ground slanted down toward the Hole. That shelf was all the world to the Holers. It was the thin, slippery slope to death. Logan hadn't slept in the seven days since the coup. He blinked his eyes. Seven days. He was starting to get weak. Even Fin, who got most of the last meat, hadn't eaten in four days.

"You're bad luck, Thirteen," Fin said, glaring at him over the chasm. "They ain't fed us since you got here." Fin was the only one who called him Thirteen. The rest had accepted the name he'd given himself in a moment of madness: King.

"You mean since you *ate* the last guard?" Logan asked. "You think that might have something to do with it?"

That got chuckles from everyone except Gnasher the simpleton, who just smiled blankly through teeth filed to sharp points. Fin said nothing, just kept chewing and stretching the rope in his hands. The man already wore an entire coil of rope that was so thick it almost obscured a frame as sinewy as the ropes themselves. Fin was the most feared of the inmates. Logan wouldn't call him the leader because that would have implied that the inmates had a social order. The men were like beasts: shaggy, their skin so dirty he couldn't guess what color they had been before their imprisonment, eyes wild, ears alert to the slightest sound. Everyone slept light. They'd *eaten* two men the day he'd arrived.

Arrived? I jumped in. I could have had a nice clean death. Now I'm here forever, or at least until they eat me. Gods, they'll eat me!

He was distracted from his rising horror and despair by motion on the other side of the Hole. It was Lilly. She alone didn't cling to the wall. She was heedless of the hole, fearless. A man reached out and grabbed her dress. "Not now, Jake," she told the one-eyed man.

Jake held on for a moment more, but when she lifted an eyebrow at him, he dropped his hand and cursed. Lilly sat down next to Logan. She was a plain woman, her age indeterminate. She could have been fifty, but Logan guessed she was closer to twenty: she still had most of her teeth.

She didn't speak for a long time. Then, when the interest in why she had moved had subsided, she scratched at her crotch absently and said, "What you gonna do?" Her voice was young.

"I'm going to get out, and I'm going to take back my country," he said.

"You hold onto that King shit," she said. "Make 'em think you're crazy. I see you looking round like a little boy lost. You're living with animals. You want to keep living, you be a monster. You want to hold onto something, you bury it deep. Then do what you gotta." She patted his knee and went over to Jake.

In moments, Jake was rutting on top of her. The animals didn't care. They didn't even watch.

The madness was taking him. Dorian stayed in the saddle only from instinct. The external world seemed distant, unimportant, buried under mist while the visions were near, vital, vibrant. The game was on and the pieces were moving, and Dorian's vision was expanding as it never had before. The Night Angel would flee to Caernarvon and his powers were growing, but he wasn't using them.

What are you doing, boy? Dorian grabbed onto that life and followed it backward. He'd spoken with Kylar once, and had prophesied his death. Now he knew why he hadn't also foreseen that this Night Angel would die and wouldn't die. Durzo had confused him. Dorian had seen Durzo's life intersecting with other lives. He had seen but he hadn't understood.

He was tempted to try to follow Durzo's lives back to the first life, when Durzo had received the ka'kari that Kylar now bore. He was tempted to see if he could find Ezra the Mad's life—surely such a life would burn so brilliantly he couldn't miss it. Maybe there he could follow Ezra, learn what Ezra knew, learn how he had learned it. Ezra had made the ka'kari seven centuries ago, and the ka'kari had made Kylar immortal. It was only three steps to one of the most respected and reviled magi of history. Three steps! To find someone so famous who had been dead so long. It was tempting, but it would take time. Maybe months. But oh, the things he could learn!

The things I could learn about the past while the present falls apart. Focus, Dorian. Focus.

Clambering back onto Kylar's life, Dorian followed it from his youth in the Warrens, his friendship with Elene and Jarl, Jarl's rape, Elene's maiming, Kylar's first kill at eleven, Durzo's apprenticeship, Momma K's instruction, Count Drake's softening influence, Kylar's friendship with Logan, meeting again with Elene, stealing the ka'kari, the coup at the castle, killing his master, and finding Roth Ursuul—*my little brother*, Dorian thought—*and as much of a monster as I once was.*

Focus, Dorian. He thought he heard something, a yell, some motion in the mundane world, but he wouldn't let himself be distracted again. He was just starting to get somewhere. There! He watched as Kylar poisoned Momma K for justice, and gave her the antidote for mercy.

He could know what choices a man made, but without knowing why, Dorian wouldn't be able to guess which way Kylar would turn in the future. Kylar had already taken less obvious routes, impossible routes. Given the choice of taking his lover's life or his mentor's, he'd chosen to give his own. The bull had offered each of its horns, and Kylar had vaulted over the bull's head. That was the Kylar that mattered. In that moment, Dorian saw Kylar's naked soul. *Now I have you, Kylar. Now I know you.*

There was a sudden pain in Dorian's arm, but now that he had a firm grip on Kylar, he wasn't letting go. Kylar ached to synthesize the cruel realities of the street with the pious impulses Count Drake had somehow infected him with. Infected? The word came from Kylar. So, like Durzo, he sometimes saw mercy as weakness.

You are going to be damnably difficult, aren't you? Dorian laughed as he watched Kylar dealing with Caernarvon's incompetent Sa'kagé, as Kylar picks herbs, as he pays taxes, as he will fight with Elene, as he tried to be a normal human being. But he isn't doing well, the pressure is building. Kylar takes out his wetboy grays, goes out on the roofs—*funny, he does that regardless of the choices he makes up to this point*—and then one night, there's a knock on the door and Jarl shows up to stretch Kylar on another crux between the woman he loves and the life he hates and the friend he loves and the life he ought to hate and one duty and another duty and honor and betrayal. Kylar is Shadow in Twilight, a growing colossus with one foot planted in the day and another in the night, but a shadow is an ephemeral beast and twilight must either darken into night or lighten into day. Kylar opens the door for Jarl, futures crashing—

"Dammit, Dorian!" Feir is slapping him. Dorian was suddenly aware that Feir must be about to do it several times, because his jaw had throbbed on both sides. Something will be seriously wrong with his left arm. He looks, confusions crashing in his head—trying to find the right speed of time.

There was an arrow sticking out of his arm. A black-bated Khalidoran highlander's arrow. Poisoned.

Feir slapped him again.

"Stop! Stop!" Dorian said, waving his hands around. It made his left arm blossom into pain. He groaned and squeezed his eyes shut, but he was back. This is sanity. "What's happened?" he asked.

"Raiders," Feir said.

"A bunch of idiots trying to take something home to brag about," Solon said. Something, of course, would have been Solon's, Feir's, and Dorian's ears. One of the four corpses already wore two ears dangling from a necklace. They looked fresh.

"They're all dead?" Dorian asked. It was time to do something about that arrow.

Solon nodded unhappily and Dorian read the story of the brief battle around their camp. The attack had come as Feir and Dorian were setting up camp. The sun was dipping into a notch in the Faltier Mountains and the raiding party had come from the mountain, thinking the sun would blind them. Two archers tried to cover their friends' approach, but the shot was steeply downhill and their first arrows had missed.

After that, the outcome had been a foregone conclusion. Solon was no mean hand with a sword, and Feir—mountainous, monstrously strong and quick Feir—was a second-echelon Blade Master. Solon had let Feir handle the swordsmen. He'd been too late to save Dorian taking an arrow, but he had killed both archers with magic. The whole thing had probably taken less than two minutes.

"The pity is, they're from the Churaq clan," Solon said, nudging one of the black-tattooed youths. "They'd have happily killed the Hraagl clan bastards guarding the Khalidoran baggage train we're following."

"I thought Screaming Winds was impregnable," Feir said. "How'd the raiders get on this side of the border?"

Solon shook his head. It drew Dorian's attention to his hair, which was a flat black except at the roots. Since Solon had killed fifty meisters by using Curoch—and nearly killed himself from the sheer amount of magic he'd used to do it—his hair was growing in white. Not old man salt-and-pepper white, but a snow-white that struck a sharp contrast against a face that showed a man in his prime, handsome, with olive Sethi skin, and features chiseled from a military life. Solon had complained at first that his vision was either all in wild colors or black and white from using Curoch, but that seemed to have cleared. "Impregnable, yes," Solon said. "Impassable for an army, yes. But this late in the summer, these young men can climb the mountains. Lots of them die on the climb, or storms come up out of nowhere and wash them off the rock, but if they're lucky and strong, nothing stops them. You ready with that arrow yet, Dorian?"

Though all three men were magi, there was no question of them helping him, not with this. Dorian was a Hoth'salar, a Brother of Healing; his hopes to cure his own growing madness had driven him to the healers' highest ranks.

Water suddenly soaked Dorian's arm around the arrowhead.

"What was that?" Feir asked, looking green.

"All the moisture from the blood that's already poisoned. It should all stick to the arrow when you pull it out," Dorian said.

"Me?" Feir asked, the squeamish look on his face totally at odds with his huge frame.

"You're ridiculous," Solon said. He reached over and ripped out the arrow. Dorian gasped and Feir had to catch him. Solon stared at the arrow. The barbs had been bent down flat so they wouldn't tear flesh on their way out, but the shaft was covered in a black shell of blood and the poison coaxed into a crystalline structure. It had swelled the shaft to three times its original width.

Even as Dorian was heaving breaths in and out, flows of magic began dancing in the air like tiny fireflies, like a hundred spiders spinning glowing webs, tapestries of light. This was the part that impressed the other men. Theoretically, any magus could heal himself, but for some reason, it not only tended not to work well but was also intensely painful to heal more than the smallest wound. It was as if the patient had to feel every pain and discomfort and irritation and itching that a wound would have inflicted in the entire time it was healing. When a magus healed someone else, he could numb the patient. When he healed himself, numbing anything could lead to mistakes and death. Female mages, magae, on the other hand, had no such problems. They routinely healed themselves.

"You're incredible," Solon said. "How do you do that?"

"It's just focus," Dorian said. "I've had lots of practice." He smiled and shook himself as if casting off his weariness, and suddenly his face was animated and he was totally present with them in a way that was becoming rare.

Solon looked bereaved. Dorian's madness was irreversible. It would grow until he was a babbling idiot who slept outside or in barns. He would come to be totally disregarded and have only one or two moments of lucidity each year. Sometimes, those moments would come when no one was around for him to tell what he had learned.

"Stop it," Dorian told Solon. "I've just had a revelation." He said it with a little smirk to let them know it really had been a revelation. "We're going the wrong way. At least you are," Dorian said, pointing to Feir. "You need to follow Curoch south to Ceura."

"What do you mean?" Feir asked. "I thought we *were* following the sword. Anyway, my place is with you."

"Solon, you and I have to go north to Screaming Winds," Dorian said.

"Wait," Feir said.

But Dorian's eyes had glazed again. He was gone.

"Lovely," Feir said. "Just lovely. I swear he does that on purpose."

*I*t was past midnight when Jarl joined them in the Cromwylls' little hut. He was more than an hour late. Elene's foster mother was asleep in the bedroom they all shared, so Kylar and Elene and Uly were all sitting in the front room. Uly had fallen asleep against Kylar, but she jerked upright instantly, terrified, as Jarl came in.

What am I dragging this little girl into? Kylar thought. But he just squeezed her, and when she got her bearings, she calmed down, embarrassed.

"Sorry," Jarl said. "The palies are . . . punishing the Warrens for the assassination attempt. I wanted to get back to check on some things, but they've sealed the bridges. No bribe's enough today." Kylar could tell Jarl was avoiding details because Uly was in the room, but considering how bad things were in the Warrens before the assassination attempt, Kylar could barely imagine how they must be tonight.

Kylar wondered how much worse it would have been if the Godking had actually been killed. Violence begets violence indeed. "Does this mean the job's canceled?" he asked, so Elene and Uly wouldn't ask more about the Warrens.

"It's on," Jarl said. He handed a purse to Elene. It looked suspiciously light. "I took the liberty of bribing the gate guards in advance. The price has already gone up, and I guarantee tomorrow it will go up again. You have the list of times when the guards we bribed are working this week?" Jarl opened a pack and took out a cream-colored tunic, trousers, and high black boots.

"Memorized," Kylar said.

"Look," Elene said, "I know Kylar's used to doing jobs where he doesn't know why he's doing what he's doing, but I need to understand this. Why is someone paying five hundred gunders for Kylar to pretend to die? That's a fortune!"

"Not to a Khalidoran duke. Here's the best I've been able to put it together," Jarl said. "The dukes in Khalidor aren't the same as our dukes because the nobility in Khalidor is always inferior to the meisters. But the meisters still need people to manage the peasants and so forth, so Duke Vargun is rich, but he's had to fight for every scrap of power he has. He came to Cenaria hoping to advance himself, but the position he thought he would get—leading Cenaria's royal guard—was given to Lieutenant Hurin Gher, now Commander Gher."

"To pay him off for leading Cenaria's nobles into an ambush during the coup, the traitor," Kylar said.

"Exactly. Commander Gher goes to the docks one morning a week with a few of his most trusted men to pick up Sa'kagé bribe money and pretend to be patrolling. This morning he's going to see his rival, Duke Vargun, commit the murder of a minor Cenarian noble, Baron Kirof. Commander Gher will happily arrest the duke. In a few days or weeks, the 'dead' Baron Kirof will show up. Commander Gher will be disgraced for arresting a duke for no reason, and most likely, Duke Vargun will take his job. A number of things could go wrong, which is why Kylar's only getting five hundred gunders."

"It sounds awfully complicated," Elene said.

"Trust me," Jarl replied, "when it comes to Khalidoran politics, this is simple."

"How's the Sa'kagé going to turn this to their advantage?" Kylar asked.

Jarl grinned. "We tried to get hold of Baron Kirof, but apparently the duke isn't too stupid. Kirof's already gone."

"The Sa'kagé would have kidnapped Baron Kirof? Why?" Elene asked.

Kylar said, "If the Sa'kagé grabbed Kirof, they could blackmail Commander Gher. Commander Gher would know the moment Kirof showed up, he'd be doomed, so the Sa'kagé would have owned him."

"You know," Elene said, "sometimes I try to imagine what this city would be like without the Sa'kagé, and I can't. I want to get out of here, Kylar. Can I come with you tonight?"

"There's not enough space for an adult," Jarl answered for him. "Anyway, they'll be back by dawn. Uly? Kylar? You ready?"

Kylar nodded, and, grim-faced, Uly copied him.

Two hours later, they were at the docks ready to split up. Uly would hide beneath the dock in a raft camouflaged to look like a clump of driftwood. When Kylar fell in the water, she would extend a pole for him to grab so that he could surface out of sight. There would barely be room enough in the little raft for Uly to crouch and Kylar's head to emerge. After he emerged, the "driftwood" would eventually drift downstream a few hundred paces to another dock where they would emerge.

"What if it all goes wrong? I mean, really wrong?" Uly asked. The night's cold had left Uly's cheeks red. It made her look even younger.

"Then tell Elene I'm sorry." Kylar brushed the front of his cream-colored tunic. His hands were trembling.

"Kylar, I'm scared."

"Uly," he said, looking into her big brown eyes, "I wanted to tell you...I mean I wish..." He looked away. "Uh, I wish you wouldn't call me by my real name when we're on a job." He patted her head. She hated that. "How do I look?"

"Just like Baron Kirof...if I squint real hard." That was for the head pat, he knew.

"Have I ever told you you're a pain in the ass?" he asked her.

She just grinned.

In a few hours, the docks would be swarming with longshoremen and sailors, preparing their cargoes for the rising sun. For the moment, though, it was quiet except for the lapping of waves. The dock's private night watch had been paid off, but the bigger fear was of the groups of Khalidoran soldiers who might wander by, looking for blood. Mercifully, it seemed most of them were in the Warrens tonight.

"Well then, see you on the other side," he said, smirking. It was the wrong thing to say. Uly's eyes filled with tears. "Go on," he said, more gently. "I'll be fine." She went, and when she was safely out of sight, his face began shimmering. Kylar's lean young face put on a second chin, a red beard sprouted in the Khalidoran fashion, his nose grew crooked, and his eyebrows became great, wide brushes. *Now* he was Baron Kirof.

He pulled out a hand mirror and checked himself. He scowled. The illusory nose shrank a little. He opened his mouth, smiled, scowled, and winked, seeing how the face moved. It wasn't good, but it would have to do. Uly would have helped him get the face right, but the less she knew about his little talents, the better. He started down the dock.

"Dear gods," Duke Tenser Vargun said as he approached. "Is that you?" The duke was sweaty and pasty pale even in the light of the torches on the end of the dock.

"Duke Vargun, I got your message," Kylar said loudly, extending his hand and clasping the duke's wrist. He lowered his voice. "You'll be fine. Just do everything like we planned."

"Baron Kirof, thank you," the duke said, a bit dramatically. He lowered his voice again. "So you're the player."

"Yes. Let's try not to put me out of work."

"I've never killed anyone before."

"Let's make sure tonight isn't your first," Kylar said. He looked at the jeweled dagger tucked into the duke's belt. It was an heirloom in the duke's family, and its inexplicable loss would be part of the evidence that the duke really had killed Baron Kirof. "If you do this, you'll be going to prison, and not a nice one. We can call it off." Kylar waved his hands around as he talked the way the real Baron Kirof did when he was nervous.

"No, no." The duke sounded like he was trying to convince himself. "Have you ever done this before?"

"Set up someone by pretending to be someone else? Sure. Pretended to get killed? Not so much."

"Don't worry," the duke said. "I—" Tenser's eyes flicked past Kylar and his voice went tight with fear. "They're here."

Kylar jerked away from the duke as if startled. "Is that a threat?" he barked. It was only a fair imitation of the baron's voice, but blood covers a multitude of acting sins.

The duke grabbed his arm. "You'll do as I tell you!"

"Or what? The Godking will hear about this." They definitely had the guards' attention now.

"You'll say nothing!"

Kylar shook his arm free. "You aren't smart enough to take the throne, Duke Vargun. You're a coward, and..." He dropped his voice. "One stab. The blood bladder is right over my heart. I'll do everything else." He contorted Baron Kirof's face into a sneer and turned away.

The duke grabbed Kylar's arm and yanked him back. With a savage motion, Vargun rammed the dagger—not into the sheep's bladder of blood, but into Kylar's stomach. He stabbed once, twice, then again and again.

Staggering backward, Kylar looked down. His cream-colored silk tunic was dripping red-black blood. Tenser's hands were gory and flecks of red dotted the blue of his cloak.

"What are you doing?" Kylar choked out, barely hearing the whistle blowing at the far end of the dock. He swayed, grabbing at the end of the railing to hold himself up.

Sweating profusely, his black hair hanging in lank ropes, Tenser ignored him. Every trace of the hesitant, bumbling noble he'd been only a minute before had disappeared. He grabbed a fistful of Kylar's hair. For him, it was a lucky grab. An inch forward, and he would have destroyed the illusory face Kylar wore.

As footsteps began pounding down the dock, Duke Vargun let Kylar drop to his knees. Through eyes dimming with pain, Kylar saw Commander Gher charging down the dock with his sword drawn and two guards at his heels. Duke Vargun dragged the dagger across Kylar's throat, sending blood spurting. Then, with as much emotion as a woodcutter burying his ax in a stump for the next time he's going to split wood, Duke Vargun jammed his dagger into Kylar's shoulder.

"Stop! Stop now or die!" Commander Gher roared.

Duke Vargun propped a calfskin boot on Kylar's shoulder and smiled. With a shove, he propelled Kylar off the dock and into the river.

The water was so cold Kylar went numb—or maybe that was from the blood loss. He'd inhaled before he hit the water, but one lung wasn't cooperating. In moments air bubbled out of his mouth, and—disconcertingly—his throat.

Then there was agony as he breathed the thick, dirty water of the Plith. He thrashed weakly, but only for a moment. Then the calm descended. His aching body was only a distant pulse. Something jabbed his body and he tried to grab for it instinctively. He was supposed to grab. There was something he was supposed to remember about a catchpole.

But if his hand even moved, he couldn't tell. The world didn't go black, didn't fade into darkness. His vision went white, his brain starving as blood poured from his neck. Something jabbed him again. He wished it would go away. The water was warm, a perfect peaceful cloud.

Duke Tenser Vargun tore his eyes away from the hungry river and lifted his hands. He turned slowly and said, "I'm unarmed. I surrender." He smiled as if he couldn't help it. "And a good evening to you, *Commander.*"

Will this Godking flay me or fuck me?

Vi Sovari sat in the receiving chamber outside Cenaria Castle's throne room, straining to overhear the Godking while she toyed with the guard who couldn't help but stare at her. Anything she could learn about why she'd been summoned might save her life. Her master, Hu Gibbet, had just brought in Duke Tenser Vargun—one of the Khalidoran nobles who had come in to help assimilate Cenaria into the Khalidoran Empire. Apparently, the duke had murdered some Cenarian noble.

It had to pose an interesting problem for the king who styled himself a god. Tenser Vargun was a trusted vassal, but letting him off would have serious ramifications. The Cenarian nobles who'd bent the knee to serve Garoth and been allowed to keep at least portions of their lands might find their spines and rebel. The Cenarian nobles who were in hiding would have new evidence of Khalidoran brutality to rally more people to their banners.

But why is Master Gibbet here? Hu had exuded that air of clever self-satisfaction that Vi knew all too well.

She crossed her legs to recapture the guard's attention. In fighting terms, the terms Hu Gibbet had taught Vi, it was a feint. The motion of her legs got his attention, turning her head to the side gave him safety, and leaning forward gave him a view. She didn't dare invoke a glamour this close to the Godking, but that was fine. Cleavage had its own magic.

She wore a fitted cerulean dress, so light it was faintly translucent. She had made her intentions clear to Master Piccun, so the tailor kept the dress simple—hardly any embroidery, just a little in the old Khalidoran runic style around the hem and wrists, an inscription from an ancient erotic poem. No lace, no frills, just clean lines and curves. Master Piccun was an inveterate letch, and this was the only dress he'd declared fit for the Godking. "The man has dozens of wives," the tailor sniffed. "Let those cows speak with silk. You will sing the sweet tones of flesh."

If the guard was like most men, he would stare for two to four seconds, double-check that no one was noticing him stare, and then stare again. The trick was—*Now.*

Vi flicked her eyes up suddenly and caught the guard just as he was starting to stare again. She pinned him to the wall with her eyes. Guilt flashed across his features and before he could cover it with boldness or glance away, she stood and walked toward him.

He was Khalidoran, of course, so she adjusted accordingly. Khalidorans' sense of personal space didn't extend as far as Cenarians'. Pricking the bubble of his personal space, with all the attendant connotations, meant stepping so close that he could smell not just her perfume but her breath. She stepped in and held him with her eyes for one more second, until he was about to speak.

"Excuse me," she said, still looking him in the eye, her expression intense. "May I sit here?"

"I wasn't staring—I mean—"

She sat in his chair, a foot from the door, her shoulders forward, face turned up, angelic. She wore her blonde hair up so the elaborately woven plaits didn't obscure the view.

It was too tempting. The guard's eyes shifted the fraction of an inch from her eyes to her cleavage and then leapt back to her face. "Please?" she said with a little smile that told him yes, she'd seen and no, she didn't mind.

He cleared his throat. "I, uh, don't think that would be a problem," he said.

Vi instantly forgot him and listened.

"...can't go directly to the Hole, that would defeat the purpose," a tenor voice said. That would be Duke Vargun. But he sounded confident.

What? How can he sound confident?

Vi heard her master reply, but couldn't tell what he said. Then the God-king spoke, but she caught nothing but "—common cells until the trial. . . . Then the Hole . . ."

"Yes, Your Holiness," Duke Vargun said.

Vi's head spun. Whatever they were planning, the Khalidoran duke had nothing in his voice that suggested a prisoner begging for clemency. He sounded like an obedient vassal, accomplishing some high purpose with a reward waiting at the end of it.

She didn't have any time to try to put it together before the doors opened and her master led Duke Vargun out. Contradicting what she'd just heard, the duke looked beaten, both physically and mentally, his clothes disheveled and dirty, and his eyes stuck to the floor.

Hu Gibbet turned to her as they walked past. The wetboy had such delicate features that he couldn't be called handsome. With fine blond hair that reached his shoulders, large eyes, and a sculpted figure, he was still beautiful even in his mid-thirties. He smiled his serpent's smile at Vi and said, "The Godking will see you now."

Vi felt a chill, but she just stood and walked into the throne room. From this room, the late king Gunder had hired her to kill Kylar Stern. As she was apprenticed to Hu Gibbet, Kylar was apprenticed to the city's other great wetboy, Durzo Blint, who was more respected, equally feared, and less reviled than her own master. Killing Kylar was to have been Vi's master's piece, the last kill of her apprenticeship. It would have meant freedom, freedom from Hu.

She'd botched it, and later that very day in this very room, someone they called the Night Angel had killed thirty Khalidorans, five wytches, and the Godking's own son. Vi thought she might be the only person who suspected that Kylar *was* the Night Angel. *Nysos! Kylar stepped into legend the same day I had him under my knife. I could have aborted a legend.*

There was no sign of the battle now. The throne room had been cleaned of blood and fire and magic, and stood pristine. On each side, seven columns supported the arched ceiling, and thick Khalidoran tapestries draped the walls to fight the autumnal chill. The Godking sat on the throne, surrounded by guards, Vürdmeisters in their black-and-red robes, advisers, and servants.

Vi had expected her summons, but she had no idea of the reason for it. Did the Godking know Kylar was the Night Angel? Was she to be punished for letting the Godking's son die? Did the man with dozens of wives want to fuck another pretty girl? Or was he just curious to see the city's only female wetboy?

"You think you're clever, Viridiana Sovari?" the Godking asked. Garoth Ursuul was younger than she had expected, maybe fifty, and still vigorous. He was thick through the arms and body, bald as an egg, and his eyes fell on her like a millstone.

"Pardon me, Your Holiness," she started to make it a question, then changed her mind. "Yes. And it's Vi."

He beckoned her forward, and she climbed the fourteen steps to stand directly in front of his throne. He looked her up and down, not surreptitiously as men so often did, nor hot and boldly. Garoth Ursuul looked at her as if she were a pile of grain and he was trying to guess her weight.

"Take off your dress," he said.

The inflection of his voice gave her nothing to work with. It might have been a comment on the weather. Did he want her to seduce him? She didn't care if Garoth Ursuul banged her, but she planned to be lousy if he did. Becoming the Godking's lover was too dangerous. She'd been warming one monster's bed since puberty, and she didn't fancy trading up. Still, god or king or monster, Garoth Ursuul was one you didn't cross.

So Vi obeyed instantly. In two seconds, Master Piccun's dress slid to the floor. Vi hadn't worn undergarments, and she had worn perfume between her knees. It was the most punctilious obedience. He couldn't fault her for it, but at the same time, she knew sudden nudity wasn't nearly as enticing as slow disrobing or the tease of lace undergarments. Let Ursuul think her an ineffectual tease, let him think her a slut, let him think whatever he wanted, as long as he did it from a distance. Besides, she wouldn't give any man the satisfaction of seeing her back down. Vi felt the stares of every courtier, adviser, Vürdmeister, servant, and guard in the room. She didn't care. Her nudity was her armor. It blinded the drooling fools. They couldn't see anything else while they saw her body.

Garoth Ursuul looked her up and down again, his eyes not shifting in the least. "You wouldn't be any fun," the Godking said. "You're already a whore."

For some reason, from this terrible man, those words sank in with barbs. She stood naked before him, and he'd completely lost interest. It was what she'd wanted, but it still hurt.

"All women are whores," she said. "Whether they sell their bodies or their smiles and their charm or their childbearing years and submission to a man. The world makes a woman a whore, but a woman makes her terms. Your Holiness."

He seemed amused at her sudden fire, but his amusement passed. "Did you think I wouldn't see what you did with my guard? Did you think you could eavesdrop on *me?*"

"Of course I did," Vi said, but now her flippancy was a farce. *He saw me? Through the wall?* She knew she had to hold on to her bravado or she might dissolve right into the floor. With the Godking, if you wanted to win, you had to play as if you despised life. But she'd heard about gamblers who'd lost.

The Godking chuckled, and his courtiers followed his lead. "Of course you did," he said. "I like you, *moulina.* I won't kill you today. Not many women would get in a pissing match with a king, much less a god."

"I'm not like any woman you've ever met," Vi said before she could stop herself.

His smile withered. "You give yourself too much credit. For that, I will break you. But not today. Your Sa'kagé is giving us trouble. Go to your little underworld friends and find out who the real Shinga is. Not a figurehead. Find out, and kill him."

Vi felt naked for the first time. Her armor wavered. God or man, Garoth

Ursuul had titanic confidence. He told her he would break her, and then exhibited not the slightest concern that she would disobey him. It wasn't a bluff. It wasn't arrogance. It was a simple exercise of the prerogatives of vast power. The courtiers eyed her now like the dogs under a king's table eyed a fine scrap of meat that might fall to the floor. Vi wondered if the Godking would give her to one of them—or all of them.

"Do you know," the Godking said, "that you're wytchborn? As you southrons say, Talented. So here's your incentive. If you kill this Shinga, we'll call it your master's piece, and not only will you be a master wetboy, but I'll train you myself. I'll give you power far beyond anything Hu Gibbet could even imagine. Power over him, if you wish. But if you fail me—well." He smiled a thin-lipped smile. "Don't fail. Now begone."

She went, her heart thumping. Success meant betraying her world. Betraying the Cenarian Sa'kagé, the most feared underworld in Midcyru! It meant killing their leader for a reward she wasn't sure she wanted. Train to become a wytch with the Godking himself? Even as he spoke, she imagined his words were webs, binding her tighter and tighter to him. It was almost tangible, a spell draping over her like a net, daring her to struggle. She felt sick. Obedience was the only possibility. However bad success was, failure wasn't an option. She'd heard the stories.

"Vi!" the Godking called. She stopped, halfway to the door, feeling a shiver at that horror using her name. But the Godking was smiling. Now his eyes touched her naked body the way a man's eyes might. Something flashed like a shadow toward her and she snatched the wad of cloth out of the air on reflex. "Take your dress," he said.

6

I feel like I've been breathing sawdust for a week," Kylar said.

"River water. Five minutes," Uly answered. Terse. Snotty.

Kylar struggled to open his eyes, but when he did, he still saw nothing. "So you did pull me out. Where are we, Uly?"

"Take a whiff." She was acting tough, which meant he'd really scared the hell out of her. *Is this what little girls do?*

He got half a breath in before coughing on the stench. They were in Momma K's boathouse on the Plith.

"Nothing like warm sewage on a cool night, huh?" Uly said.

Kylar rolled over. "I thought that was your breath."

"Which smells as good as you look," she said.

"You ought to be respectful."

"You ought to be dead. Go to sleep."

"Do you think domineering is cute?"

"You need to sleep. I don't know what dumb earrings have to do with it."

Kylar laughed. It hurt.

"See?" Uly said.

"Did you get the dagger?"

"What dagger?"

Kylar grabbed her by the front of her tunic.

"Oh, the one I had to use a prybar to get out of your shoulder?" she asked. No wonder his shoulder hurt. He'd never seen Uly quite so snotty and glib. If he didn't watch it, she'd burst into tears. It was one thing to feel like an ass. It was another to feel like a helpless ass.

"How long have I been...out?"

"A day and a night."

He cursed quietly. It was the second time Uly had seen him murdered, his body mutilated. If she had an ironclad conviction that Kylar was coming back, he was glad. He had promised her that he would, but he'd never known. All he knew was that he'd come back once. The Wolf, the strange yellow-eyed man he'd met in the place between life and death, hadn't made any guarantees. Indeed, this time Kylar hadn't met him at all. Kylar had been hoping to ask him a few questions, like how many lives he got. What if it had only been two?

"And Elene?" he asked.

"She went to get the wagon. The guards Jarl bribed are only on duty for another hour."

Elene had gone alone to get the wagon? Kylar was so tired. He could tell Uly was right on the verge of tears again. What kind of a man put a little girl through this? He wasn't much of a substitute father, but he used to think that he was better than nothing.

"You should sleep," she said, doing her best to be gruff again.

"Make sure..." He was so sore he couldn't complete the thought, much less the sentence.

"I'll take care of you, don't worry," Uly said.

"Uly?"

"Yes?"

"You did good work. Great work. I owe you. Thanks. I'm sorry." Kylar could almost feel the air around the girl go all warm and gooey. He groaned. He wanted to say something witty and mean like Durzo would have, but before he could find the words, he was asleep.

When Kaldrosa Wyn joined the queue behind the Lightskirt Tavern at noon, there were already two hundred women standing behind the brothel. Two hours later, when the line started moving, it was three times that. The women were as diverse a group as could be found in the Warrens, from guild rats as young as ten who knew that Momma K wouldn't hire them but were so desperate they came anyway to women who had lived on the rich east side just a month ago but had lost their homes in the fires and then been herded into the Warrens. Some of those were weeping. Others just wore vacant expressions, clutching shawls tight around them. And some were long-time Rabbits, laughing and joking with their friends.

Working for Momma K was the safest gig a rent girl could get. They traded stories how the Mistress of Pleasures dealt with their new Khalidoran clientele. They claimed that when the twists hurt you, they had to pay you enough silvers to cover the bruise. Another claimed it was enough crowns to cover it, but no one believed her.

When Duchess Terah Graesin—the old duke her father had been killed in the coup—led the resistance out of the city, her followers had all put their shops and homes to the torch. The fires, of course, didn't stop after devouring the properties of those who left. Thousands who'd stayed had been made homeless. It was even worse in the Warrens, where the poor were packed like cattle. Countless hundreds had died. The fires had burned for days.

The Khalidorans wanted the east side to get productive as quickly as possible. Those who were homeless were seen as an encumbrance, so soldiers forced them into the Warrens. The dispossessed nobles and artisans had become desperate, but desperation changed nothing. Being forced into the Warrens was a death sentence.

For the past month, the Godking had allowed his soldiers to do whatever they wished in the Warrens. The men would descend in packs to sate whatever lusts motivated them. Chanting that godsdamned prayer to Khali, they raped, they killed, they stole the Rabbits' meager possessions merely to throw them in the river and laugh. It seemed it couldn't get worse, but after the assassination attempt, it had.

The Khalidorans had moved through the Warrens in an organized fashion, block by twisting block. They made mothers choose which of their children would live and put the others to the sword. Women were raped in front of their families. Wytches played sick games blasting off body parts. When anyone offered resistance, they rounded up and publicly executed dozens.

There were rumors of safe hideouts deeper in the Warrens, underground, but only people well-connected in the Sa'kagé could get into those. Everyone had places to hide, but the soldiers came every night and sometimes during the day. It was only a matter of time before they caught you. Beauty had become a curse. Many of the women who had lovers or husbands or even protective brothers had lost them. Resistance meant death.

So women came to Momma K's brothels because they were the only safe places in the Warrens. If you were going to get raped, many figured, you might as well get paid for it. Apparently the brothels still did good business, too. Some Khalidorans didn't like the risks of going into the Warrens. Others just liked being assured of bedding a clean and beautiful woman.

Already though, the brothels didn't have many openings—and no one wanted to speculate why they had any at all.

Kaldrosa had held off as long as she could. It wasn't supposed to be like this. That Vürdmeister, Neph Dada, had recruited her specifically because she was a former Sethi pirate who'd been marooned in the Warrens years ago. She hadn't sailed in ten years—and had never been a captain, despite what she told the Vürdmeister. But she was Sethi, and she had promised she could navigate a Khalidoran ship through the Smugglers' Archipelago up the Plith River to the castle. In return, she would get to keep the ship.

It had sounded like a fine price for an unsavory bit of work. Kaldrosa Wyn had no loyalty to Cenaria, but working for the Khalidorans was enough to make anyone's skin crawl.

Maybe they even would have kept their part of the deal—giving her that sea cow of a barge that wasn't worth the nails holding it together. Maybe she could have cobbled together a crew to join her, too—except that some bastard had sunk her ship during the invasion.

She'd been able to swim to shore, which was more than she could say for the two hundred armored clansmen she'd been ferrying, who were now feeding fish. Four rapes and two times of Tomman being beaten half to death later, here she was.

"Name?" the girl at the door asked, holding a quill and paper. She had to be eighteen, a good decade younger than Kaldrosa, and she was stunning: hair perfect, teeth perfect, long legs, tiny waist, full lips, and a musky-sweet scent that made Kaldrosa aware of how foul she herself must smell. She despaired.

"Kaldrosa Wyn."

"Occupation or special talents?"

"I was a pirate."

The girl perked up. "Sethi?"

Kaldrosa nodded, and the girl sent her upstairs. In another half an hour, Kaldrosa Wyn stepped into one of the small bedrooms.

The woman here was young and beautiful, too. Blonde, petite but curvy, with big eyes and amazing clothes.

"I'm Daydra. You ever worked the sheets?"

"I assume you don't mean sails."

Daydra chuckled, and even that was pretty. "A real pirate, huh?"

Kaldrosa touched her clan rings, four small hoops in a crescent framing her left cheekbone. "Tetsu clan off Hokkai Island." She gestured to the captain's chain she wore—which she put on herself as soon as she got the job for Khalidor. She opted for the finest silver herringbone chain she could afford. It looped from her left earlobe to the lowest of her clan rings. It was a merchant captain's chain, a merchant captain of humble birth. Military captains and the bolder pirate captains wore chains looped from earlobe to earlobe behind their heads so there was less chance they'd get ripped off in battle. "A pirate captain," she said, "but never caught. If you're caught, you're either hanged or they rip out your rings and exile you. There's some disagreement about which is worse."

"Why'd you quit?"

"I tangled with a royal Sethi pirate hunter a few hours before a storm. We gave almost as good as we got, but the storm drove us onto the rocks of the Smugglers' Archipelago. Since then, I've just done whatever." Kaldrosa didn't mention that "whatever" included getting married and working for Khalidor.

"Show me your tits."

Kaldrosa untied her laces and wriggled out of her top.

"I'll be damned," Daydra said. "Very good. I think you'll do fine."

"But you're all so beautiful," Kaldrosa said. Stupid as it was to protest, she couldn't believe her luck was turning.

Daydra smiled. "Beautiful we've got. Every one of Momma K's girls has to be pretty, and you are. What you've got is exotic. Look at you. Clan rings. Olive skin. Even your tits are tanned!"

Kaldrosa was suddenly thankful that she'd been so stubborn on her ship that she'd gone topless to make the Khalidoran soldiers stare. It had given her a fierce sunburn, but her skin had darkened and the color hadn't faded yet.

"I don't know how you've managed a tan," Daydra said, "but you'll have to keep it up, and talk like a pirate. If you want to work for Momma K, you're going to be the Sethi pirate girl. You have a husband or a lover?"

Kaldrosa hesitated. "Husband," she admitted. "The last beating nearly killed him."

"If you do this, you'll never get him back. A man can forgive a woman who leaves whoring for him, but he'll never forgive one who goes whoring for him."

"It's worth it," Kaldrosa said. "To save his life, it's worth it."

"One more thing. 'Cause sooner or later you'll ask. We don't know why the palies do it. Every country's got twists who like hurting rent girls, but this is different. Some will take their pleasure first and only hurt you afterward, like they're embarrassed. Some won't hurt you at all, but they'll brag afterward that they did and pay Momma K's fines without complaining. But they'll always say those same words. You've heard them?"

Kaldrosa nodded. "*Khali vas,* something or other?"

"It's Old Khalidoran, a spell or a prayer or something. Don't think about it. Don't make excuses for them. They're animals. We'll protect you as well as we can and the money's good, but you'll have to face them every day. Can you do that?"

Words stuck in Kaldrosa's throat, so she nodded again.

"Then go to Master Piccun and tell him you want three pirate girl costumes. Make him finish taking your measurements before he bangs you."

Kaldrosa's eyebrows shot up.

"Unless you have a problem with that."

"You don't think we'll have any trouble, do you?" Elene asked. They were lying down in the wagon, spending one last night under the stars after three weeks on the road. Tomorrow they would enter Caernarvon and their new life.

"I left all my troubles in Cenaria. Well, except for the two that tagged along with me," Kylar said.

"Hey!" Uly said. Despite being as scary-smart as her real mother, Momma K, she was still eleven and easily baited.

"Tagged along?" Elene asked, propping herself up on an elbow. "As I recall, this is my wagon." That much was true. Jarl had given them the wagon, and Momma K had loaded it with herbs Kylar could use to start an herbiary. Perhaps in a nod to Elene's sensibilities, most of them were even legal. "If anyone tagged along, it was you."

"Me?" Kylar asked.

"You were making such a pathetic spectacle that I was embarrassed for you. I just wanted to stop your begging."

"Well, here I thought you were a helpless—" Kylar said.

"And now you know better," Elene said, self-satisfied, settling back into her blankets.

"Ain't that the truth. You've got so many defenses, a man would be lucky to get lucky with you once in a thousand years," Kylar said with a sigh.

Elene gasped and sat up. "Kylar Thaddeus Stern!"

Kylar giggled. "Thaddeus? That's a good one. I knew a Thaddeus once."

"So did I. He was a blind idiot."

"Really?" Kylar said, his eyes dancing. "The one I knew was famous for his gigantic—"

"Kylar!" Elene interrupted, motioning toward Uly.

"His gigantic what?" Uly asked.

"Now you did it," Elene said. "His gigantic what, Kylar?"

"Feet. And you know what they say about big feet." He winked lasciviously at Elene.

"What?" Uly asked.

"Big shoes," Kylar said. He settled back down in his own blankets, as smug as Elene had been moments before.

"I don't get it," Uly said. "What's it mean, Elene?"

Kylar chuckled evilly.

"I'll tell you when you're older," Elene said.

"I don't want to know when I'm older. I want to know now," Uly said.

Elene didn't answer her. Instead, she punched Kylar in the arm. He grunted.

"Are you going to wrestle now?" Uly asked. She had climbed out of her blankets and was sitting between them. "Because you always end up kissing. It's gross." She scrunched up her face and made wet kissing noises.

"Our little contraceptive," Kylar said. Much as he loved Uly, Kylar was convinced that she was the only reason that after three wonderful weeks on the trail with the woman he loved, he was still a virgin.

"Will you do that again?" Elene asked Uly, laughing and wisely heading off the what's-a-contraceptive question.

Uly scrunched her face and made the kissing sounds again, and soon the three of them dissolved in laughter that devolved into a tickle fight.

Afterwards, sides aching from laughing so hard, Kylar listened to the sounds of the girls breathing. Elene had a gift for falling asleep as soon as her head touched a pillow, and Uly wasn't far behind. Tonight, Kylar's wakefulness was no curse. He felt his very skin was glowing with love. Elene rolled over and nuzzled on his chest. He inhaled the fresh scent of her hair. He couldn't remember having felt so good, so accepted, in his entire life. She would drool on him, he knew, but it didn't matter. Drool was somehow cute when Elene did it.

No wonder Uly got disgusted. He *was* pathetic. But for the first time in his life, Kylar felt like a good man. He'd always been good at things, good at lock picking, climbing, hiding, fighting, poisoning, disguising himself, and killing. But he'd never felt *good* until Elene. When she looked at him, the Kylar he saw reflected in her eyes wasn't repulsive. He wasn't a murderer; he was the substitute father who had tickle fights with an eleven-year-old; he was the love who told Elene she was beautiful and made her believe it for the first time in her life; he was a man with something to give.

That was the man Elene saw when she looked at him. She believed so many good things about him that Kylar alternated between believing it himself and thinking she was absolutely crazy. But being persuaded felt great.

Tomorrow, they'd reach Caernarvon, and for a time, they would stay with Elene's Aunt Mea. With her help—she was a midwife who knew herbs—Kylar would set up a little herbiary. Then he would overcome Elene's fading objections to fornication, and the way of shadows would be behind him forever.

8

After maybe twelve days, maybe fifteen, maybe it only felt like so many, Logan finally surrendered to sleep. In his dream, he heard voices. They were whispering, but in the stone environs of the Hole, every whisper carried.

"He's got a knife."

"If we all take him, it doesn't matter. Look how much meat there is on him!"

"Quiet," someone said. Logan knew he should move, should check the knife, should wake up, but he was so tired. He couldn't stay awake forever. It was too hard.

He thought he heard a woman's voice, screaming through a hand covering her mouth. There was a slap and the scream stopped. Then there was another slap and another and another.

"Easy, Fin. You kill Lilly, we'll fuckin' gut you. She's the only slit we got."

Fin cursed Sniffles, then said, "You scream again, bitch, and I'll rip out your hair and your fingernails. You don't need those to fuck. Got it?"

Then the voice faded, and the heat faded, and the howling faded, and the stink faded, and Logan was truly dreaming. He was dreaming of his wedding night. He was married to a girl he barely knew, but as he talked in their bedchamber, as nervous as the beautiful fifteen year-old girl across from him, he felt sudden hope blossom in his heart. This girl was a woman he could love, and inexplicably, she was his. Jenine would be his wife and one day, his queen, and he knew he could love her.

Jenine's dead. Stop this.

He saw in her big eyes that she could love him, too, that their marriage bed would not be a place of duty, but one of joy. Her cheeks colored as he stared at her as his wife. His eyes claimed her—not arrogantly, but confidently, gently, accepting her and rejoicing in her beauty—and when he pulled her close, she folded into him. Her lips were hot.

Then, it seemed like only a second later, they were still kissing, still taking off each other's clothes, and feet were pounding up the stairs toward their room. Logan was pulling back from her and the door burst open and Khalidoran soldiers poured into the room—

Logan's eyes snapped open and his fists flew as bodies landed on top of him.

As far as fights went, it was pathetic. Logan hadn't eaten in two weeks, so he was as weak as a puppy. But the other inmates, aside from the meat they'd gorged on a few weeks ago, had been subsisting on bread and water for months or years. They were gaunt, hollow shadows of the men they had once been, so the fight proceeded slowly and clumsily.

Logan heaved one man off and punched another across the jaw, but two more were there instantly, their flesh made slick and muddy by their filth and their sweat. Fin landed on Logan's hip while Jake tore at Logan's face with long nails. Shaking another man off, Logan fought his way to his feet and flung Jake off.

The man fell into the Hole and disappeared.

Just like that, the fight was over.

"What'd you do that for?" Sniffles asked. "We could have used that meat. You fucker, you threw away meat."

For a moment, their fury crested and Logan thought they would attack him again. He reached to his hip to pull out the knife. It was gone.

On the other side of the Hole, Fin looked at him. He picked his bloody, scurvied gums with the point of the knife. Time was on his side, now.

Logan had thought the Holers had no society, but he'd been wrong. There were camps down here, too. The Holers were split into the animals and the monsters, the weak and the strong. Fin led the animals, who ranked mostly according to their crimes: murderers then rapists then slavers then pedophiles. The monsters were Yimbo, a big-boned red-haired Ceuran whose tongue had been cut out; Tatts, a pale Lodricari covered in tattoos who could speak but never did; and Gnasher, a misshapen simpleton with massive shoulders and a twisted spine and teeth filed to sharp points. The monsters survived only through the others' fear of them, and their willingness to fight.

Now, as they all starved, the tenuous society was breaking down. Logan had no friends, no knife, no place. Among the animals, he was now a wolf without a pack. Among the monsters, he was a dog without his steel tooth.

He had tried to see the inmates as men. Men debased and humiliated and reviled and evil, but men. He tried to see in them something good, some image within them of the gods or the God who had made them. But in the shadows of the Hole, he saw only animals and monsters.

Logan went and sat by Gnasher. The man gave him a simpleton's smile made horrible by his filed teeth.

Then there was a sound that made everyone freeze. Footsteps resounded through the corridor above the Asshole. Logan slipped into the one narrow overhang that would hide him from view as a torch-illumined face appeared over them. "I'll be," the guard said. He was black-haired, pale, and hulking, with a smashed nose, plainly Khalidoran.

The guard opened the grate but kept a close eye on the inmates fifteen feet below him. Fin didn't even unlimber his ropes.

"Figured a few of you would have died by now," the guard said. "Thought you'd be real hungry." He reached into a sack and pulled out a large loaf of bread. Every inmate looked at him with such longing that he laughed. "Well, then, here you go." The guard tossed them the loaf, but it sailed into the Hole.

The prisoners cried out, thinking it was a mistake. The guard produced another loaf and tossed it into the Hole too. The prisoners crowded around the Hole, even Fin and Lilly. The next loaf bounced off of Sniffles's fingertips and he almost fell in after it.

The guard laughed. He locked the grate and walked away, whistling a cheery tune. Several of the inmates wept.

He didn't come back. The days passed in agony. Logan had never known such debilitating weakness.

Four nights later—if the term wasn't meaningless, Logan thought of it as night because most of the Hole's inhabitants were asleep and the howling winds shrieked loudest at what the Holers called noon—Fin cut one of his pedophiles' throats. In moments, everyone was awake and fighting over the body. When Sniffles started beating on Gnasher to try to get the man to let go of some bloody scrap Logan preferred not to identify, Gnasher dropped the scrap and attacked him. Sniffles tried to fight him off, but Gnasher handled him like he was a child. Yanking Sniffles's arms out of the way, Gnasher sank his filed teeth into the man's neck.

In the ensuing fight over the body, an entire leg was thrown clear and landed next to Logan. When Scab came after it, Logan snatched it up. To his own horror, he stared Scab down until the man turned and left.

Logan took the leg back to the wall and wept, because no matter how hard he looked at it, he saw only meat.

9

Compared to Cenaria, Caernarvon was paradise. There were no Warrens here, no stark division of have and have-not, no occupying army, no stench of ash and death, no vacant stares of despair. The capital of Waeddryn had flourished under an unbroken line of twenty-two queens.

Twenty-two queens. The thought was strange to Kylar, until he realized that Momma K had ruled the Sa'kagé and the streets of Cenaria for more than twenty years.

"State your business," the gate guard said, eyeing their wagon. The people here were taller than Cenarians, and Kylar had never seen so many with blue eyes or with such bright hair—every color from almost white to fiery red.

"I buy and sell medicinal herbs. We've come here to start an apothecary," Kylar said.

"Where from?"

"Cenaria."

The guard looked pensive. "Heard things are real bad there. If you're setting up shop on the south side, be careful. There's some tough neighborhoods down..." he trailed off as he caught sight of the scars on Elene's face.

Faster than he would have thought possible, Kylar was furious. Elene's scars were all that marred otherwise perfect beauty. A brilliant smile, deep brown eyes that defied the boring plainness of the word brown, eyes that only a poet could adequately describe and only a legion of bards adequately praise, skin that begged to be touched and curves that demanded it. *With all that, how can he only see scars?* But saying anything would only cause a scene. The guard blinked. "Uh, go on," he said.

"Thanks." Kylar wasn't worried about Caernarvon's Sa'kagé. They were strictly small time: mugging, picking pockets, street prostitution, and gambling on the dog fights and bull baiting. Some brothels and gambling dens actually stayed in business without being affiliated with them. Kylar's childhood street gang was more organized than the crime here.

They drove through the city, gawking at the people and the sights like bumpkins. Caernarvon sat at the confluence of the Wy, the Red, and the Blackberry rivers, and its streets were bursting with commerce and the multiplicity of people who flowed with the money. They passed olive-skinned, strong-featured Sethi wearing short loose trousers and white tunics, red-haired Ceurans with their two swords and their odd fashion of braiding multicolored locks of hair into their own, a few Ladeshians, and even an almond-eyed Ymmuri. They made a game of it, surreptitiously pointing and trying to guess who was from where.

"How about him?" Uly asked, pointing at a nondescript man in plain woolens. Kylar scowled.

"Yes, let's hear it, hotshot," Elene said, wearing an impish grin. "And don't point, Uly." The man had no distinguishing characteristics. No tattoos, standard tunic and trousers for Caernarvon, brown hair cut short, no Modaini patrician nose, nothing distinctive; even his fairly tan skin that could have come from half a dozen countries. "Ah," Kylar said. "Alitaeran."

"Prove it," Elene said.

"Only Alitaerans look that smug."

"I don't believe it."

"Ask him," Kylar said.

Elene shook her head, sinking back, suddenly shy.

"Hey, master!" Uly shouted as their wagon rolled past him. "Where ya from?"

"Uly!" Elene said, mortified.

The man turned and drew himself to his full height. "I hail from Alitaera, by the grace of the God the greatest nation in all Midcyru."

"The gods, you mean," the Waeddryner he was bargaining with said.

"No, unlike you Waeddryner dogs, Alitaerans say what they mean," the merchant said, and in a moment they were arguing about religion and politics and Uly was forgotten.

"I am pretty amazing," Kylar said.

Elene groaned. "You're probably Alitaeran yourself."

Kylar laughed, but that "probably" soured in his mouth. *Probably,* because he was a guild rat, an orphan, maybe slaveborn. Like that Alitaeran, he couldn't even guess where his parents had been from. He couldn't guess why they'd abandoned him. Were they dead? Alive? Important somehow, like every orphan dreams? While Jarl had been busy saving pennies to get out of the guild, Kylar had been dreaming of why his noble parents might have been forced to abandon him. It was useless, foolish, and he thought he'd given it up long ago.

The closest thing he'd had to a father was Durzo—and Kylar had become what all men curse: a patricide. Now here he was, a loose string, tied to nothing before or behind.

No, that wasn't true. He had Elene and Uly. And he had the freedom to love. That freedom cost something, but it was worth the price.

"Are you all right?" Elene asked him, her brown eyes concerned.

"No," Kylar said. "As long as we're together, I'm great."

In a few minutes, they had left the northern markets and were getting deeper into the shipping district. Even here almost all the buildings were stone—a big change from Cenaria, where stone was so expensive that most of the houses were wood and rice paper. Local punks lounged in the stoops of houses and warehouses and mills, sullenly watching them go past with the universal expression of adolescents with something to prove.

"Are you sure this is the right road?" Kylar asked.

Elene winced. "No?"

Kylar kept the wagon moving, but it didn't matter. Six of the teens stood and followed a black-toothed man with a mop of greasy black hair toward them. The youths reached under steps or beneath piles of trash to find weapons. They were street weapons, clubs and knives and a length of heavy chain. The man leading them stood in front of the wagon and grabbed the near horse's bridle.

"Well, honey," Kylar said, "time to meet our friendly neighborhood Sa'kagé."

"Kylar, remember what you promised," Elene said, taking his arm.

"You don't really expect me to…" He let the question die as he saw the look in her eyes.

"Afternoon," their leader said, slapping a club into his palm. He smiled broadly, showing off two black front teeth.

"Honey," Kylar said, ignoring him. "This is different. You have to see that."

"Other people get through this sort of thing without anybody dying."

"Nobody will die if we do this my way," Kylar said.

The black-toothed man cleared his throat. Dirt looked permanently tattooed into his visage and two protruding, crooked, and blackened front teeth dominated his face. "Excuse me, lovers. I don't mean to interrupt—"

"You can wait," Kylar said in a tone that brooked no argument. He turned back to Elene. "Honey."

"Either do what you promised or do what you've always done," Elene said.

"That's not permission."

"No. It's not."

"Excuse me," the man said again. "This—"

"Let me guess," Kylar said, mimicking the man's swagger and accent. "This here's a toll road, and we need to pay a toll."

"Uh. That's right," the man allowed.

"How'd I guess?"

"I was gonna ask that—hey, you shut your mouth. I'm Tom Gray and this here—"

"Is your road. Sure. How much?" Kylar asked.

Tom Gray scowled. "Thirteen silvers," he said.

Kylar counted the seven men aloud. "Wait, doesn't that screw your bashers? They get one silver each and you get six?" Kylar asked. Tom Gray blanched. The boys looked at him angrily. Kylar was right, of course. Small-time thugs. "I'll give you seven," Kylar said.

He pulled out his small coin purse and started tossing silvers to each of the young men. "You get that much with no effort. Why risk a fight? That's as much as Tom was going to give you anyway."

"Hold on," Tom said. "If he gave us that much that easy he's got to have more. Let's take him."

But the young men weren't buying it. They shrugged, shook their heads, and shuffled back to their stoops.

"What are you doing?" Tom demanded. "Hey!"

Kylar flicked the reins and the horses started forward. Tom had to jump aside to avoid being crushed. He twisted his ankle as he landed. Kylar pulled his front lips back to make himself look as buck-toothed as Tom and raised his hands helplessly. The young men and Uly laughed.

They spent the night at an inn, and Aunt Mea found them early in the morning and guided them through a tangle of alleys to her house. She was in her forties, looked a decade older, and had been widowed for almost twenty years, since soon after her son, Braen, was born. Her husband had been a successful rug merchant, so her house was large, and she assured Kylar and Elene that they could stay as long as they liked. Aunt Mea was a midwife and healer with plain features, twinkling eyes, and shoulders like a longshoreman.

"So," Aunt Mea said, after a breakfast of eggs and ham, "how long have you two been married?"

"About a year," Kylar said. He figured that if he initiated the lies, Elene might be able to keep them going. Elene was a terrible liar. He looked at her, and sure enough, she was blushing.

Aunt Mea took it to be embarrassment and laughed. "Well, I did figure you were a little young to be this young lady's natural mother. How'd you find your new mother and father, Uly?"

Kylar sat back, stifling the urge to supply the answer himself. If he answered for everyone, not only would he look like an ass, he'd look suspicious. Sometimes you just had to let the bones roll where they may.

"The war," Uly said. She swallowed, looked down at her plate, and said nothing more. It wasn't even a lie, and the emotion on Uly's face was plainly real. Uly's nurse had been killed in the fighting. Uly still cried about it sometimes.

"She was at the castle during the coup," Elene said.

Aunt Mea set down her knife and spoon—they didn't use forks in Caernarvon, much to Kylar's irritation. "I tell you what, Uly. We're going to take good care of you. You'll be safe and you'll even have your own room."

"And toys?" Uly asked.

Something about the open, hopeful expression on Uly's face made Kylar ache. Little girls should be playing with dolls—why hadn't he ever given Uly a doll?—not fishing bodies out of rivers.

Aunt Mea laughed. "And toys," she said.

"Aunt Mea," Elene said. "We're already putting you out enough. We have money for toys, and Uly can stay with us. You've already—"

"I won't hear of it," Aunt Mea said. "Besides, you two are still newlyweds. You need all the privacy you can get, although heaven knows, Gavin and I managed to plow the row quite a few times when we shared a one-room shack with his parents." Elene blushed crimson, but Aunt Mea kept talking. "But I'd guess an eleven-year-old isn't quite as good about ignoring noises in the night. Am I right?"

Now Kylar blushed. Aunt Mea looked at him, and then looked at Uly, who looked puzzled.

"Are you telling me you haven't since you left Cenaria?" Aunt Mea said. "Surely you'd slip away sometimes in the morning when Uly was still asleep? No? That trip has to be what, three weeks? That's an eternity for you youngsters. Well. This afternoon, Uly and I will go for a good long walk. The bed in your room creaks some, but if you worry too much about that sort of thing, Uly will never have a little brother, eh?"

"Please," Kylar begged, shaking his head. Elene was mortified.

"Hmmph," Aunt Mea said, looking at Elene. "Well. If you're finished with your breakfast, why don't we go meet my son?"

Braen Smith worked in a shop attached to the house. He had his mother's broad, plain features and wide shoulders. As they approached, he threw a barrel hoop he was shaping onto a stack of similar ones and removed his gloves. "Morning," he said.

His eyes immediately went to Elene. A quick glance at her scarred face and then a too-appreciative weighing of her assets. It wasn't the quick up-and-down that men instinctively gave every woman. Kylar wouldn't have minded that. But this wasn't a look. It was a linger, and right to Elene's face. Or rather, right to her breasts.

"Niceta meetcha," Braen said, sticking his hand out to Kylar. He looked at Kylar, weighing, evaluating. Predictably enough, he tried to crush Kylar's hand.

A trickle of Talent took care of that. Without a whisper of tension in his face or his forearm, Kylar clamped down on the monstrous paw in his grip and took it right to the edge of breaking. A little more and every bone in the man's hand would shatter. After a moment, he backed off and merely matched the man, rough hand to rough hand, muscle to muscle, and eye to eye—-even if he did have to look up and Braen outweighed him by a third. The panic cleared from Braen's eyes and Kylar could see him wondering if he'd imagined the initial force of Kylar's grip.

"Kylar," Elene muttered through clenched teeth as if he were making a spectacle of himself. But Kylar didn't break eye contact. There was something being settled here, and if it was primal and barbaric and petty and stupid, it was still important.

Elene didn't like being ignored. "I suppose next you'll compare the size of your—" she broke off, embarrassed.

"Good idea," Kylar said as the man finally released his hand. "What do you say, Braen?" Kylar loosened his belt.

Mercifully, Braen laughed. The rest of them followed, but Kylar still didn't like him. Braen still didn't like him, either. Kylar could tell.

"Well, niceta meetcha," Braen said again. "I got a big order to finish." He bobbed his head and picked up a hammer, flexing his pained fingers surreptiously.

For the rest of the morning and afternoon, Aunt Mea showed them around Caernarvon. Though it was larger than Cenaria, the city didn't have the chaotic feel of Kylar's home. Most streets were paved and wide enough for two wagons and numerous pedestrians to pass at the same time. Vendors who set up shop infringing on that space were so quickly punished that few tried it. Sudden crushes pushed the crowds together whenever two wagons did pass, but there were accepted standards here and had been long enough that the wagons all traveled in six-inch-deep ruts in the paving stones. Even the sewers in the streets passed through pipes, with grates at intervals for the collection of new sewage. It made the city almost not smell like a city.

Castle Caernarvon dominated the north side. It was sometimes called the Blue Giant for its bluish granite. The blue walls were seamless, as flat and smooth as glass except for the numerous arrow slits and murder holes at the gates. Two hundred years ago, Aunt Mea said, eighteen men had held the castle for six days against five thousand.

Around the castle, of course, were the great houses. The city got dirtier and more crowded the closer it came to the docks. As in most places, the rich and noble liked to live away from everyone else and everyone else liked to live as close to the rich as they could. Here though, that was one line that was not regulated—unlike Cenaria's poor, who were legally bound to the west side of the Plith. Those who made the money to move could do so here. The possibility for advancement seemed to energize the entire city.

Caernarvon was the gold and glittering fools' gold of hope. Its vice was greed. In his own imagination, every merchant here was the emperor of the next trading empire. Cenaria was the smothering, stinking blanket of despair. Its vice was envy. No one built empires there. They just wanted a piece of someone else's.

"You're awfully quiet," Elene said.

"It's different here," Kylar said. "Even before Khalidor came, Cenaria was sick. This is better. I think we can make a home here."

Gods, he was about to become one of those merchants he'd been despising. Not that he had great ambitions. Being an herbalist and apothecary was really the only thing he could do besides kill. It wasn't anything he would ever dream about. What would he dream? About opening a second shop? Dominating the city's herb trade? He'd once held a country's future in his hands—he could have changed everything with one betrayal, killing a man he'd ended up killing anyway.

If I had, Logan would be alive...

As Aunt Mea led them home, he tried to force his mind into a merchant rut. He had a small amount of gold hidden in the wagon, and a fortune in herbs. Had they been robbed on the way here, the bandits wouldn't even have known what to steal.

"Well, the house is just down this street," Aunt Mea said. "Braen's out buying supplies. Uly and I are going to a little sweetmeats shop to give you two some time to get reacquainted." She winked at Kylar while Elene blushed, but then Aunt Mea's face darkened. "What's that?" she asked.

Kylar looked toward the house. Wisps of smoke were rising and thickening rapidly.

He joined the crowd running toward Aunt Mea's house—in the city, a fire was such a threat that everyone grabbed buckets and ran to help—but by the time he got there, the barn was entirely consumed with flame. It was too late to save anything. The crowds threw water on the nearby buildings while Kylar held Elene and Uly mutely.

The barn was a total loss. Their two horses and Aunt Mea's old nag were left as smoking, stinking mounds of meat. There was almost nothing left of the wagon. The arsonist had found the hidden chest with its gold. The fortune in herbs had gone up in smoke.

The only thing left was a long, thin box bound to the wagon's bent axle.

The lock was intact. Kylar opened it and there were his wetboy grays and his sword Retribution, untouched, not even smelling of smoke, mocking his impotence.

$\mathcal{B}$ad news, Your Holiness," Neph Dada said as he came into the Godking's bedchamber. A young Cenarian noblewoman named Magdalyn Drake was tied to the bed and whimpering into her gag, but both she and the Godking were still dressed.

Garoth was sitting on the bed beside her. He caressed a knife up her bare calf. "Oh, what is it?"

"One of your spies in the Chantry, Jessie al'Gwaydin, is dead. She was last seen in the village of Torras Bend."

"The Dark Hunter killed her?"

"I assume so. Our man said that Jessie was planning to study the creature," Neph said.

"So she went into the wood and never came back."

"Yes, Your Holiness," Neph said. He rubbed his stooped back as if in pain. It wasn't only to remind the Godking of his age, but also of the burdens Neph bore in serving.

With a savage motion, the Godking stabbed the mattress so high between Magdalyn's legs that Neph thought he'd stabbed the girl. She squealed through the gag and bucked, trying to get away. Heedless, Garoth cut toward her feet, shearing her dress to the hem and sending feathers into the air.

Abruptly, he was calm once more. He left the knife sticking out of the mattress, folded the cut dress back and put his hand gently on the girl's naked thigh. She trembled uncontrollably.

"It is *so* hard to get spies in the Chantry. Why do they insist on throwing their lives away, Neph?"

"For the same reason they join us in the first place, Your Holiness: ambition."

Garoth looked at the Vürdmeister wearily. "That was a rhetorical question."

"I have some good news as well," Neph said. He straightened a little, forgetting his back. "We've captured a Ladeshian bard named Aristarchos. I think you'll want to interrogate him personally."

"Why?"

"Because I Viewed him, and what he's seen is remarkable."

Garoth narrowed his eyes. "Out with it."

"He believes he has seen the bearer of a ka'kari. A black ka'kari."

"Stop looking at me!" Stephan said. He was a fat cloth merchant, some former lover with a grudge who swore that he could tell Vi who the Shinga was. Either the Shinga was a woman, or Stephan had little preference which field he plowed, because this had been his price.

Vi lay under him. She moved with the dexterity of an athlete and the skill of a courtesan trained by Momma K herself, but her eyes were utterly dispassionate. She wasn't moaning, wasn't making faces. She wouldn't pretend pleasure and it was giving Stephan problems. Like most men, he was three-quarters talk and one-quarter cock. A little less than a quarter, at the moment.

He pulled back and cursed his limpness. He was sweaty and he stank under the smell of his fine oils. Vi couldn't help but give him a condescending smile. "I thought you were gonna give it to me good," she said.

His face flushed, and she wondered why she was sabotaging him. He was no more or less than any man, and she still needed to learn what he had to tell her. Taunting him was only going to make this take longer.

"Let your hair down," he said.

"Forget my hair." Nysos, couldn't they leave one damned thing alone? She rolled over and shimmied her hips, reaching out with her Talent to grab him. Then she did things to help him forget.

When she was fifteen and Master Gibbet had taken her to Momma K, the courtesan had watched the wetboy bang her, then said, "Child, you fuck like you don't even feel it. Do you?"

There was no lying to Momma K, so Vi had admitted it. Her sex was totally numb. "Well," Momma K had said, "you'll never be the best, but it's nothing we can't overcome. The oldest magic is sex magic. With your tits and all the Talent you've got, I can still make you into something special." So Vi used her skills now, cursing the effete asshole in a whisper—the words didn't have to match her intent, but like all Talented women, she had to speak to use her powers.

Stephan moaned like a dumb animal and in moments he was finished.

While he was still in a stupor, as a little fuck-you, she wiped herself clean on his fine cloak and sat cross-legged on the bed in the armor of her nudity.

"Tell me, fat man," she said, looking at his pale rolls with such distaste that he covered himself in shame. He turned away.

"By all the gods, do you have to—"

"Tell me."

Stephan covered his eyes. "He used to get runners. They knew to come to my house. I sometimes overheard bits and pieces, but he was always so careful. He burned the few letters he got, always went outside to talk with the runners. But the night of the invas—the liberation—he got a runner, and he wrote a note here." Stephan grabbed a robe and pulled it around himself before walking over to his desk. He pulled out a sheet of Ceuran rice paper and handed it to her. It was blank.

"Hold it up to the light," he said.

Vi held the paper up in front of a lantern and could see faint impressions on it. "Save Logan Gyre," it read, in a neat, tiny script, "and the girl and the scarred woman if you can. I will reward you beyond your wildest dreams." Instead of a name, it was signed with two symbols: a heavy-lidded eye circumscribing a star, drawn without lifting pen from paper, and beside it a nine-pointed star. The first was the glyph of the Sa'kagé; the second the symbol of the Shinga. The two together meant every resource the Sa'kagé had was at the recipient's disposal.

"He left after that," Stephan said. "And never came back. I told him I loved him and he won't even see me."

"His name, fat man. Tell me his name."

"Jarl," he said. "Gods forgive me, the Shinga is Jarl."

In one of her poorest safe houses, all darkness and rats and roaches like everywhere in the Warrens, Jarl and Momma K were meeting with a dead man. He smiled as he pulled himself into the room. His right leg was bound with splints so he couldn't bend his knee, and his right arm was in a sling. Blood had seeped through the bandages around his elbow. He had a crutch, but instead of tucking it under his arm, he had to hold it in his right hand. The injury to his elbow kept him from using the crutch on the side his knee demanded, so he more hopped than limped. He had short-cropped gray hair, was muscular in a stringy-tough-old-man way, and though his face was drawn and gray, he smiled.

"Gwinvere," he said. "It's good to see that the years have respected you at least."

She smiled, and rather than commenting on his appearance—he looked like he'd been sleeping in gutters, his fine garments were soiled, and he stank—she said, "It's good to see you've not lost your silver tongue."

Brant Agon hopped to a chair and sat. "Reports of my demise and all that."

"Brant, this is Jarl, the new Shinga. Jarl, this is Baronet Brant Agon, formerly Lord General of Cenaria."

"What can I do for you, Lord General?" Jarl asked.

"You're too kind. I come here as little more than what you see: I look like a beggar, and I've come to beg. But I am more than a beggar. I've fought on every border this country has. I've fought in duels. I've led squads of two men, and I've led campaigns with five thousand. You're facing a fight. Khalidor has scattered our armies, but the power in Cenaria is the Sa'kagé, and the Godking knows it. He'll destroy you unless you destroy him first. You need warriors, and I am one. Wetboys have their place, but they can't do everything—as you saw a few weeks ago, they might only make things worse. I, on the other hand, can make your men more efficient, more disciplined, and better at killing. Just give me a place and put me in charge of men."

Jarl rocked back in his chair and tented his fingers. He stared at Brant Agon for a long time. Momma K schooled herself to silence. She'd been Shinga for so long, it was hard to risk letting Jarl make missteps, but she'd made her decision. Let Jarl take the life and the power and the gray hairs. She would help until he didn't need her help anymore.

"Why are you here, Lord Agon?" Jarl asked. "Why me? Terah Graesin has an army. If you'd had your way, the Sa'kagé would have been wiped out years ago."

Momma K said, "We heard you were killed in an ambush."

"Roth Ursuul spared me," Brant said bitterly. "As a reward for my stupidity. It was my idea that Logan Gyre marry Jenine Gunder. I thought that if the king's line were assured, it would prevent a coup. Instead, it just got Logan and Jenine killed, too."

"Khalidor would never have let them live," Momma K said. "In fact, it's a mercy for Jenine. She could've been taken for Ursuul's entertainment, and the stories I've heard—"

"Anyway," Agon interrupted, unwilling to hear any absolution. "I crawled away. When I got home, my wife had been taken. I don't know if she's dead or if she's one of the 'entertainments.'"

"Oh, Brant, I'm so sorry," Momma K said.

He continued without looking at her, his face rigid. "I decided to live and make myself useful, Shinga. The noble houses want to fight a regular war. Duchess Graesin will try to wink and flatter her way to a throne. They don't have the will to win. I do, and I think you do too. I want to win. Failing that, I want to kill as many Khalidorans as I can."

"Are you proposing to serve me or be my partner?" Jarl asked.

"I don't give a rat's ass," Brant said. He paused. "And I know a lot more about rats' asses now than I ever thought I would."

"And what happens if we win?" Jarl asked. "You go back to trying to eliminate us?"

"If we win, you'll probably decide I'm too dangerous and have me killed." Brant smiled thinly. "At the moment, that doesn't bother me much."

"So I see." Jarl ran his hands over his dark microbraids, thinking. "I'll have no divided loyalty, Brant. You'll serve me, and only me. Do you have a problem with that?"

"Everyone I've sworn anything to is dead," Brant said. He shrugged. "Except maybe my wife. But I have some questions. If you're the new Shinga, who's the old one? Is he still alive? How many fronts is this war going to have?"

Jarl was silent.

"I'm the old Shinga," Momma K said. "I'm retiring, and not because Jarl is forcing me to. I've been grooming him for this for years, but now events have forced our hand. The Warrens are our center of power, Brant, and they're dying. Starvation is already a problem, but pestilence comes next. The Godking doesn't care what happens here. He hasn't set up any power structure at all. If we want to survive—and by we, I mean the Sa'kagé, but I also mean Cenaria and every wretched soul in the Warrens—things have to change. We can still get wagons and boats in; the soldiers check the cargoes for weapons, and they demand bribes, but we can survive that. What we can't survive is what happens once every wagon that comes in loaded with food gets plundered. People are starving and there are no guards to stop the theft, and if one wagon is plundered, every wagon thereafter will be. If that happens, the merchants will stop sending anything in. Then everyone will die. We aren't there yet, but we're close."

"So what are you going to do?" Brant asked.

"We're going to set up a quiet government. Everyone knows me," Momma K said. "I can hire bashers to guard wagons; I can adjudicate disputes; I can direct the building of shelters."

"That makes you a target," Brant said.

"I'm a target no matter what," Momma K said. "We've lost some of the wetboys, and I don't mean they're dead. The wetboys swear a magically binding oath of obedience to the Shinga. The Godking has broken that bonding. I've learned that Hu Gibbet told the Godking who I was. Garoth doesn't believe a woman could be the Shinga, so now he's searching for the real one. But he might change his mind any day, whether I act publicly or whether I stay in the shadows. I can't control that, so I might as well do what needs to be done."

Momma K was as calm as any veteran warrior going into battle. She could tell that Brant Agon was astounded.

"Tell me my part," Brant said.

Jarl said, "You take your pick of my men and make them wytch hunters. After that, I want you to make defenses we can use if the army comes to the Warrens in force. The Khalidorans have wytches, soldiers, and some of our best people on their side. The only reason I'm still alive is that they don't know who I am. But welcome aboard."

"My pleasure." Brant Agon bowed awkwardly because of his injuries and followed a big bodyguard out the door.

When he was gone, Jarl turned to Momma K. "You didn't tell me you knew each other."

"I don't think I do know this Brant Agon," she said.

"Answer the question."

A slight smile touched her lips, amused and a little proud that Jarl was taking command. "Thirty years ago Brant fell in love with me. I was naive. I thought I loved him, too, and I ruined him."

"Did you love him?" Jarl asked, rather than ask what happened. The question was proof to Momma K that she'd chosen the right man to succeed her. Jarl could find cracks. But it was one thing to admire his ability, and another to experience it.

She smiled a smile that didn't reach her eyes. It wouldn't fool Jarl for a second, but after all these years, the mask was pure reflex. "I don't know. I don't remember. What does it matter?"

12

"Gaelan Starfire is said to have thrown the blue ka'kari into the sea, creating the Tlaxini Maelstrom," Neph said. "If so, it may well be there still, but I have no idea how we would recover it. The white has been lost for six centuries. We once believed it to be at the Chantry, but your grandmother disproved that. The green was taken to Ladesh by Hrothan Steelbender and lost. I verified that Hrothan arrived in Ladesh some two hundred and twenty years ago, but could find nothing more. The silver was lost during the Hundred Years' War, and could be anywhere from Alitaera to Ceura, unless Garric Shadowbane somehow destroyed it. The red was cast into the heart of Ashwind Mountain—what is now Mount Tenji in Ceura—by Ferric Fireheart. The brown is rumored to be at the Makers' school in Ossein, but I doubt it."

"Why?" Garoth Ursuul asked.

"I don't think they could resist using it. With the mastery of earth, those petty Makers would become a hundred times more skilled in a heartbeat. Something they Made would appear sooner or later, and it would be clear that someone was Making at the level they did of old. That hasn't happened. Either the men of that school are less ambitious than I believe possible, or it isn't there. The other rumor was that it was bound into Caernarvon's Blue Giant—the castle. I take that to be nothing more than a semieducated boast. It's not a particularly clever place to hide a ka'kari."

"But we have a solid lead on the red?"

"When Vürdmeister Quintus passed through Ceura, he said that the explosions of Mount Tenji are at least partly magical. The problem with that, and with the blue, is that—even if we could get at it—there's some doubt about whether even a ka'kari would be intact after having been exposed to so much elemental power for so long."

"You don't give me much, Neph."

"It's not exactly collecting seashells." His voice sounded greasy. He hated that.

"A deep insight." Garoth sighed. "And the black?"

"Not so much as a whisper. Not even in the oldest books. If what I Viewed was real, and the Ladeshian isn't simply delusional, it's the best kept secret I've ever heard of."

"That is the point of a secret, isn't it?" Garoth asked.

"Huh?"

"Fetch our Ladeshian songbird. I'll be needing some Dust."

Elene wanted him to sell the sword. For the past ten nights, they'd played their parts as if they were wooden puppets. Except that once in a while even puppets got to play different roles.

"You don't even look at it, Kylar. It just stays in that chest under the bed."

Her dark eyebrows pushed together, forming the little worry wrinkles that he was getting to know so well.

He sat on the bed, rubbing his temples. He was so tired of this. So tired of everything. Did she really expect him to answer? Of course she did. It was all words and wasted air. Why did women always believe that talking about a problem would fix it? Some issues were corpses. Hot air made them fester and rot and spread their disease to everything else. Better to bury it and move on.

Like Durzo. Worm food.

"It was my master's sword. He gave it to me," Kylar said, only a little late for his cue.

"Your master gave you a lot of things, beatings not least among them. He was an evil man."

That one stirred some rage. "You don't know anything about Durzo Blint. He was a great man. He died to give me a chance—"

"Fine, fine! Let's talk about what I do know," Elene said. She was on the verge of tears again, damn her. She was just as frustrated as he was. What made it worse was that she wasn't trying to manipulate him with those tears. "We're destitute. We lost everything, and we made Aunt Mea and Braen lose a lot, too. We have the means to make it right, and they deserve it. It's our fault those hoodlums torched the barn."

"You mean my fault," Kylar said. He could hear Uly crying in her room. She could hear them shouting through the wall.

If he'd dealt with Tom Gray his way, the man would have been too frightened come within five blocks of Aunt Mea's. Kylar knew the music of the streets. He spoke the language of meat, played the subtle chords of intimidation, sang fear into the hearts of men. He knew and loved that music. But the notes of the songs Durzo taught weren't syllogisms. There was no thesis, counterpointed with antithesis, harmonized into synthesis. It wasn't that kind of music. The music of logic was too patrician for the streets, too subtle, the nuances all wrong.

The wetboy's leitmotif, whenever he played, was suffering, because everyone understands pain. It was brutal—but not without nuances. Without betraying his Talent, Kylar could have dealt with all six street toughs and Tom Gray. The young men would have left with bruises and astonishment. Tom, Kylar would have hurt. How much would have been Tom's choice. But even if she had had let him, could he have shown Elene that? What if she had seen his joy?

He looked at her face and she was so beautiful he found himself blinking back tears.

What the hell was that about?

Kylar said, "Why don't we skip all the horseshit where I say the sword is priceless and you say that means we'd have enough to start our shop and I say I just can't do it but I can't explain why so you say that I really do want to be a wetboy and you're just holding me back—and then you start crying. So why don't you just start crying, and then I'll hold you, and then we'll kiss for an hour, and then you'll stop me from going further, and then you'll fall asleep easily while I lie awake with my balls aching? Can we hop right to the kissing part? Because the only part of our whole fucking lives that I enjoy is when I think you're enjoying yourself as much as I am and I think maybe tonight we'll finally fuck. What do you say?"

Elene just took it. He could see her eyes welling, but she didn't cry.

"I say I love you, Kylar," Elene said quietly. Her face calmed and the worry wrinkle disappeared. "I believe in you, and I'm with you, no matter what. I love you. Do you hear me? I love you. I can't understand why you won't sell the sword..." she breathed. "But I can accept it. All right? I won't bring it up again."

So now he was really the bastard. He was sitting on a fortune instead of using it to support his wife and his daughter and pay back people who'd suffered for him. But she was going to accept him. How noble. The worst of it was he knew—dammit, he knew because he could always see through her—that she wasn't grabbing the moral high ground to be a bitch. She was trying to do the right thing. It just made the contrast between them that much more pronounced.

She doesn't know me. She thinks she knows me, but she doesn't. She accepted me thinking Kylar was just an older, slightly dirtied version of Azoth. I'm not dirty, I am filth. I kill people because I like it.

"Come to bed, honey," Elene said. She was undressing, and swell of her breasts through her shift and the curves of her hips and her long legs roused the same fire in him it always did. Her skin glowed in the candlelight and his eyes fixed on the point of one nipple as she blew out the candle. He was already in his undergarments, and he wanted her. He wanted her so fiercely it shook him.

He lay down, but he didn't touch her. The ka'kari had cursed him with perfect vision despite any darkness. Cursed, because he could still see her. He could see the pain on her face. His lust was a chain and he felt a slave to it and it disgusted him, so when she turned toward him and touched him, he didn't move. He rolled onto his back and stared at the ceiling.

Looks like I skipped everything to the balls aching part.

I shouldn't be here. What am I doing? Happiness isn't for murderers. I

*can't change. I'm worthless. I'm nothing. An herbalist without herbs, a
father who's not a father, a husband who's not a husband, a killer who
doesn't kill.*

*That sword is me. That's why I can't get rid of it. It's what I am. A
sheathed sword worth a fortune sitting in the bottom of a trunk. Worse
than useless. A waste.*

He sat up in the bed, then stood. He reached underneath the bed and
pulled out the narrow chest.

Elene sat up as he started pulling on his wetboy grays. "Honey?" she
said.

He dressed in moments—Blint had made him practice even this—strapping knives to his arms and legs, securing a set of picks to a wrist and a
folding grapnel to the small of his back, adjusting the gray folds of cloth so
they'd dampen all sound, strapping Retribution to his back, and pulling on
a black silk mask.

"Honey," Elene said, her voice tight. "What are you doing?"

He didn't go out the door and walk down the stairs. No, not tonight.
Instead, he opened the window. The air smelled good. Free. He sucked a
great breath deep into his lungs and held it as if he could trap that freedom
within him. At the irony of the thought, he let it out all at once and looked
at her.

"Just what I always do, love," Kylar said. "I'm fucking it up." With a
surge of his Talent, he leapt out into the night.

Ferl Khalius had been given the shit duty again. After his unit had been
slaughtered during the invasion, he'd been picked for every bad assignment: throwing bodies off that rickety half-burnt bridge; helping the cooks
move supplies into the castle; helping the meisters build the Godking's new
wall around the city; double and triple guard duties—and never a choice
assignment like on the Vanden Bridge where the guards took a week's pay
home in bribes every shift just for letting a few crooks across. Now this.

He looked at his prisoner with disgust. The man was fat, with the soft
hands of a southron noble, though he wore his red beard in the Khalidoran
fashion. His nose was crooked and his eyebrows looked like brushes. He
stared at Ferl with obvious anxiety.

Ferl wasn't supposed to talk to him. Ferl wasn't supposed to know who
he was. But from the first, he'd had a bad feeling about this, ever since a
captain had told him the Vürdmeisters wanted to see him. They'd requested
him by name. He was to report immediately.

That was something no Khalidoran wanted to hear. Ferl thought it was about his little souvenir, the dragon-hilted sword he'd taken from the bridge. But that hadn't been why they'd wanted him, though he'd nearly wet himself when he saw he was speaking with the Lodricari Vürdmeister Neph Dada himself. No Vürdmeister was normal, but Neph was spooky even for a Vürdmeister. Ferl had stared at the twelve knotted cords representing the shu'ras Neph had mastered for the entire time Neph spoke. It was too scary to look at his face.

Neph had given Ferl and Ferl alone this assignment. He was forbidden to speak about it with other soldiers, forbidden to even associate with them for the duration of the assignment. He and the noble were confined to some tradesman's house on the east side. Meisters had hastily made part of the house a prison. *Meisters* had done the work. There was only one reason for that: this was so important it had to be done instantly and without anyone's knowledge. Then they'd left him with enough food for several months and forbidden him to leave.

That left everything feeling wrong. Ferl Khalius hadn't become second—now first—in his warband by being stupid. He'd spoken with the noble and learned his name was Baron Kirof. The baron claimed not to know why he had been imprisoned. He protested his innocence and loyalty to Khalidor—and the fact he wasted his breath telling a mere soldier told Ferl that Baron Kirof wasn't very bright.

Disobeying his orders, Ferl snuck away and found out that Baron Kirof had supposedly been murdered. The good Khalidoran duke, Tenser Vargun, was now rotting in the Maw for having killed a Cenarian noble who wasn't dead.

That's when Ferl knew he was screwed. His imagination couldn't paint any picture in which things turned out well for Ferl Khalius. Why would you assign a man without a unit to this? Because you could kill him and no one would notice. When the time came, Baron Kirof would be released or killed—the only reason to keep him alive when he was supposed to be dead had to be so they could produce him at some point. But Ferl? Ferl would just be evidence that the Vürdmeisters were lying.

I should have gone back to Khalidor. He'd been offered a job tending the oxen of the baggage train. He'd almost taken it. If he had, he might be on his way back to his clan by now. But everyone who escorted the treasure to Khalidor was thoroughly searched before they were released, and that would mean losing his precious sword. So he'd stayed, sure he could pick up a small fortune while they sacked the city. Right.

"I should kill you," Ferl said. "I should kill you just to spite them."

The fat man turned a paler shade. He could tell that Ferl meant it.

"Tell me, fatty," Ferl said. "If the Vürdmeisters told you that you could live if you lied about who kidnapped you, would you do it?"

"What kind of stupid question is that?" Baron Kirof asked.

So they'd known Kirof would play along. "You're a brave man, aren't you, fatty?"

"What?" Baron Kirof asked. "I can't understand your accent. Why do you keep calling me forty?"

"Fatty. Fatty!"

"I'm not forty. I'm thirty-six."

Ferl's hand darted through the bars and he grabbed a handful of the baron's blubber and squeezed it as hard as he could. Baron Kirof's eyes widened and he squealed and tried to pull away, but Ferl held him against the bars by his fat. "Fatty! Fatty!" he said. He grabbed the baron's cheek and squeezed it with his other hand. The man flailed, trying to knock Ferl's hands away, but he was too weak. He wailed. "Fatty!" Ferl yelled in his face. Then he released him.

The baron dropped back in his cell onto his bed and rubbed his cheek and his love handle, his eyes misty with tears. "Fatty?" he asked, wounded.

Ferl was lucky he didn't have a spear on hand. "Get your fat ass moving," he said. "We're leaving."

Just moving, leaping from roof to roof, flying over the world below, filled Kylar's heart with joy. Cenaria's buildings had been a mix of Ceuran-style rice fiber and bamboo houses with steep clay-shingled roofs and red brick and wood homes with thatch. It was rarely possible to move from roof to roof. Here, hundreds of miles from the nearest rice paddy and without the threat of snow, all the roofs were flat and solid clay, supported with good wood. For a man of Kylar's talents, they made a highway in the air.

Kylar reveled in it. He reveled in the strength of his muscles, reveled in the way the night air tasted and the secret power of moving through the night as a shadow. Everything was right. Nothing fit like his wetboy grays.

Designed by Cenaria's best tailor, Master Piccun, they moved with him. The mottled colors broke up his silhouette and would have made even a man without Talent difficult to see.

He paused at the edge of a building, rolling his neck, and limbering up his back as he scooted back. The gap to the warehouse roof was a good twenty feet wide. He blew out a breath, and ran. His steps made scritching noises as he sprinted toward the edge. He leapt and his legs kept pumping as if he were running on air as he flew over the alley. He cleared the warehouse roof easily, landing six feet in.

He hurtled straight at a wall where the part of the roof rose to a smaller third story. It was too high for him to jump and grab the edge. Instead, he ran up the wall as far as he could and then vaulted off it. He reached for the roof beams that extended out of the building, but he missed. His fingers were half a foot below the bottom of the beam.

Phantom hands whooshed out from his hands, extending his reach, and pulled the beam into his grasp. Kylar flipped up and landed on the top of the three-inch-wide beam. He wobbled for a moment, then steadied himself and stepped onto the roof.

He pumped his arm and whooped. It had only taken him three tries. Not bad. Not bad at all. Next time he'd try it while invisible. He was beginning to understand what his master had told him once about how much he would have to learn once he could use his Talent. Just shifting from using his Talent to leap to using it to extend the phantom hands was almost more than he could manage. Doing that while invisible and running full speed—well, he had nothing but time to train, did he?

For what? Time to train for what?

The thought soured the night air blowing in off the rivers. The freedom he'd felt blew away like fog. He was training for nothing. He was training because he couldn't stand to lie next to Elene with his thoughts and emotions and lust warring in him. He alternated between wanting to tear her clothes off and take her roughly and wanting to shake her and scream at her. He feared the intensity of those emotions, feared how they overlapped. That wasn't making love. That he even thought of it made him sick.

He leapt across another huge gap and a couple strolling arm in arm and he heard their surprised questions to each other—did something just fly over us?—he laughed aloud, and all his thoughts dissolved in the poppy liquor of action, movement, freedom.

As he slid past a small gang waiting to ambush whatever drunk might stumble down their alley, Kylar was fully alive. He didn't even need his powers. He was just there, every sense attuned, every fiber of his being poised to act—if one of the hoodlums discovered him, he'd have to use his powers, flee, attack, jump, duck, hide— something. As he slid past a hood holding a knife in one hand and a wineskin in the other, he could smell the man. Kylar had to regulate his breathing in time with the hood's so he wouldn't be heard, had to test every footstep, had to watch the changing light as the moon slid in and out of the clouds, had to watch the faces of all four young men as they joked and talked and passed a pipe of riot weed around.

"Hey, shut up!" the man nearest Kylar said. "We'll never get anyone if you idiots keep talking."

The men quieted. The hood's eyes passed straight over Kylar. Kylar had to keep himself from gasping aloud—there was something in the man's eyes. Something dark. It itched at something in the back of Kylar's mind.

Down the alley, a man stumbled out of an inn. He braced himself against a wall and then turned to walk toward the ambush.

What am I doing? Kylar realized that he didn't even have a plan. *I'm mad. I have to get out of here.* He hadn't broken his word to Elene. Not yet. After all, he'd never promised not to go out at night. He'd sworn not to kill.

He had to go. Now. If they started beating the drunk, he didn't know what he'd do. Or maybe he knew exactly what he'd do, and he couldn't do that.

The ka'kari oozed out of his pores like a sheen of iridescent black oil. It covered his skin and his clothes in an instant—covered him, shimmered for the briefest instant, and disappeared.

One of the hoodlums on the other side of the alley frowned and opened his mouth, but changed his mind and shook his head, sure that he'd imagined whatever-it-was he thought he saw.

Kylar leapt five feet in the air and grabbed the edge of the roof. He pulled himself up and started running away. When he heard a shout—and was that the thud of a cudgel hitting flesh?—he didn't stop. He didn't look.

He was only four blocks away, still fleeing, heading toward Aunt Mea's house when he saw a girl being followed by three more hoodlums.

What the hell was she doing out this late? Anyone in this part of town had to know how stupid it was for a girl—a pretty golden-haired girl, of course—to travel alone.

It was none of his business. Golden Hair looked over her shoulder and Kylar could see her tear-streaked face. Wonderful. Some stupid emotional girl being emotional and stupid.

He stopped. *Dammit. You can't save the world, Kylar. You're not really the Night Angel. You're only a shadow and shadows can't touch anything.*

Now he swore again, loudly. In the street below, all four characters in the little melodrama looked up to the rooftop, but of course they didn't see him. They didn't see him drop into the street and start following them.

If they caught her, he'd have to kill them. He'd have to hurt them to get them off her, and then what was he going to do? Beat them up as an invisible man? Let them spread those stories? Someone would connect him to the Night Angel, sooner or later, and then everything would go to hell. No, if they caught her, and he had to break his promise to Elene, then he'd go all the way. So there was only one thing to do: make sure they didn't catch her.

Golden Hair did the first sensible thing she'd done all night—she started running. The hoodlums split up and started after her. Kylar drew Retribution off his back, but in its scabbard. He ran behind one of the running hoodlums, timed the man's steps, and with the sheathed sword he knocked one foot behind the other in the middle of the man's stride. The hoodlum went down hard, and his partner barely had time to look over his shoulder before he too encountered the ground in a far more intimate fashion than he would have liked.

Both men cursed, but they weren't too bright. They jumped up and started running after the girl again, once more closing ground rapidly. This time, Kylar tripped one into the other one. The men went down in a tangle of limbs and began cursing and hitting each other. By the time they got up, the girl was gone.

Kylar lost sight of the girl and the last hoodlum. He leapt up to a roof and sprinted after the girl. As he ran, he dropped his invisibility so he could use all of his Talent for speed. After flying across several more rooftops, he caught sight of Golden Hair again. She was a block away from the only house in a dim alley that had a lantern burning in the window. Doubtless it was her home.

Then Kylar saw the last hoodlum, coming down an intersecting alley Golden Hair would have to pass. The man caught sight of her and sank back into the shadows.

There was no time. Kylar was still more than a block behind them. He sprinted to the edge of a building and leapt unseen over Golden Hair, drawing Retribution before he landed in the little alley, right in front of the hoodlum.

The man had drawn a knife and in an instant Kylar saw from the pools of darkness in his eyes a deep, unreasoning hatred spawned from some perceived slight. The man had murdered before, and he planned to murder Golden Hair tonight. Kylar didn't know how he knew, but he knew. And seeing that darkness that demanded death, it came to him that he'd seen it before. He'd seen it in Prince Ursuul's eyes. Only afterward had he decided he must have been imagining things.

There was a moment of stunned silence as hoodlum and Night Angel stared at each other.

"Mother? Father?" the girl called out as she passed the alley.

The hoodlum attacked and Retribution darted out, punching through the hoodlum's solar plexus, driving the air from his lungs and pinning him to the wall.

Around the corner, a door was flung open and Golden Hair was ushered inside in a storm of blubbered apologies and forgiveness and tears. Kylar gathered that she'd fought with her parents about something none of them remembered and had stormed off.

The hoodlum twitched. He was straining to breathe, but he couldn't because Retribution had crushed his ribs and pushed them hard against his diaphragm. His legs were completely limp. Kylar must have at least partially cut his spine, because the only thing keeping him standing was the sword pinning him to the wall.

The man was already dead, he just hadn't figured it out yet.

Damn me, what have I done? Kylar pulled Retribution back and the hoodlum fell. Dispassionately, Kylar stabbed the sword into his heart. He was committed now. He couldn't leave the body here. It was unprofessional, and its discovery would certainly wreck the tenuous happiness he could hear through the open windows. There was a little blood on the wall, so Kylar blotted it up with the hoodlum's cloak, and then scrubbed dirt over it.

Inside, it was all joy and reconciliation. Mother served a kettle of ootai and clucked about how worried they had been. The girl was telling her story of how she'd been followed and run away and been so terrified and somehow the men kept falling.

Kylar felt a surge of pride, followed by disgust at how sweetly domestic it was.

But that was a lie. He wasn't disgusted. He was moved. Moved and profoundly lonely. He was left outside, in the streets with the dead, alone. He kicked dirt over the blood on the ground, and stuffed rags into the corpse's wounds.

"Praise the God," mother said. "Your father and I have been praying for you the whole time."

That's me, Kylar thought as he hefted the body over his shoulder, *the answer to everyone's prayers. Except Elene's.*

*   *   *

"Why would anyone destroy a ka'kari, Neph?" The Godking was pacing in one of his state rooms.

"The southrons are frequently illogical, Your Holiness."

"But surely these heroes who supposedly destroyed the ka'kari—Garric Shadowbane, Gaelan Starfire, Ferric Fireheart—surely they must have been wytchborn. Not trained as meisters, of course, but Talented. Such warriors could have bonded the ka'kari themselves. And they didn't? We're saying that at least three warriors chose to destroy artifacts that could have made them ten times more powerful than they already were? Great men are not so selfless."

"Your Holiness," Neph said, "you're attempting to duplicate the thought processes of a people who embrace the virtues of weakness. These are people who tout compassion over justice, mercy over strength. Theirs is a diseased philosophy, a species of madness. Of course they do the inexplicable. Look at how eagerly Terah Graesin rushes to her doom."

The Godking waved that away. "Terah Graesin is a fool, but not all southrons are. If they were, my forefathers would have overrun them centuries ago."

"Surely they would have," Neph Dada said, "if not for the incursions from the Freeze."

Garoth dismissed that. The average meister had always been stronger than the average mage, often had more companions in his craft, and he and his fellows weren't split into bickering schools spread halfway across Midcyru. The Khalidoran armies were as good as most and better than many. Despite those advantages, the Godkings' ambitions had been foiled time and again.

"I feel...opposed," Garoth said.

"Opposed, Your Holiness?" Neph asked. He coughed and wheezed.

"Maybe these southrons really believe what they claim to about mercy and protecting the weak, though our experience here tells me they don't. But the call of power is not easily ignored, Neph. Perhaps one saint of their faiths might destroy a ka'kari that he could use. But how could all six ka'kari disappear and stay hidden for so long? You're talking generations of saints—each new guardian as virtuous as the one before. It doesn't make sense. One of them would fail."

"The ka'kari *have* surfaced from time to time."

"Yes, but ever more rarely as the centuries have passed. The last time was fifty years ago," Garoth said. "Someone has been trying to destroy or at least hide the ka'kari. That's the only thing that makes sense."

"So *someone* out there has been squirreling away ka'kari for seven centuries?" Neph asked, deadpan.

"Of course not some*one*," Garoth said. "But some...group. I find a small conspiracy much easier to swallow than a conspiracy of every southron saint who ever lived." He paused, following the idea. "Think about their very names—Shadowbane, Fireheart, Starfire?—those aren't surnames. They're assumed names. If I'm right, it may be that Garric Shadowbane, Ferric Fireheart, and Gaelan Starfire were the champions of this group, their avatars, as it were."

"And their avatar today...?" Neph asked.

Garoth smiled. "Now has a name. This morning, my Ladeshian bard sang. The man who walked these halls with a ka'kari, who killed my son, was either the legendary Durzo Blint or his apprentice Kylar Stern. Durzo Blint is dead. So if Kylar Stern is this avatar..." Garoth stopped dead. "It would explain why those heroes were willing to destroy a ka'kari. Because they couldn't use another. Because they'd already bonded one. They were the bearers of the black ka'kari."

"Your Holiness, is it not possible that rather than destroy those ka'kari they kept them?"

Garoth considered it. "It's possible. And Kylar might not be allied with them at all."

"In which case they might be trying to add the black to their collection," Neph said.

"We can't know that. We can't know anything until we get Kylar Stern. My songbird will make the perfect assassin. In the meantime, Neph, contact every meister and agent we have in the southlands and tell them to keep an eye out. I don't care if it costs me this entire kingdom, get me Kylar Stern. Alive, dead, whichever, just bring me that damned ka'kari."

14

The first weeks in Hell's Asshole had been the darkest, before Logan had become a monster. He'd made his bargains with the devil and with his own body. He'd eaten the meat that came to him that awful day, and when Fin had killed Scab, Logan had eaten flesh again. Logan had to kill Long Tom for that meat, and that killing had made him a monster. Being a monster made him safe. But he wasn't content to be safe. He wasn't content to merely survive. Logan lived with the feral, primal side of himself, but he wouldn't let that be all he was.

He shared his meat. He'd given some to Lilly, not for sex as the other Holers did, but for decency. She'd given him the advice that kept him human. He also shared with the other monsters: Tatts and Yimbo and Gnasher. He kept the choicest parts for himself—at least the choicest parts he could bear to eat. Arms and legs were one thing, but eating a man's heart, his brains, his eyes, cracking his bones to suck the marrow, that Logan wouldn't do. It was a thin line, and one he knew he would cross if things got much worse, but for now, he'd sunk deep enough, so he shared for squeamishness and he shared for nobility.

It was his first step to reclaiming his humanity. Fin would kill him the first chance he had. The monsters didn't care, so it was still possible to get them on his side. It wouldn't be loyalty, but anything might make all the difference.

Gnasher was a different story. Logan stayed close to Gnasher. He figured that the simpleton was the least likely to betray him, although he'd learned early on why Gnasher had been given his name. Every night, Gnasher ground his teeth. It was so loud that Logan was surprised the man had molars left.

The third week in, Logan woke to the sudden silence of Gnasher's teeth and listened in the darkness. Gnasher was listening, and his ears must have been better than Logan's, because a moment later, Logan heard footsteps.

Two Khalidoran guards appeared above their grate and looked down with distaste. The first was the one they hated. He opened the grate as he always did, and tossed their bread down the hole as he always did. It didn't matter that they knew he was going to do it, the monsters and the animals alike, even Logan, got up and stood around the Hole, hoping to get lucky with a bad throw. It only happened once or twice, but that was enough to keep their hope alive.

"Watch this," the guard said. He tore open the last loaf and pissed all over it, soaking it in urine. Then he tossed it in.

Logan, being the tallest, got most of it. He devoured it instantly, ignoring the stench, ignoring the warm wetness dripping down his chin, ignoring the debasement.

The Khalidoran roared with laughter. The second guard laughed uncertainly.

The next day the second guard came back, alone. He had bread, and it was clean, and he threw it to them, one loaf for each prisoner. With a thick accent and not looking any of them in the eye, he promised that he would bring bread every time he had a shift that he didn't share with Gorkhy.

That gave them all strength and hope and a name for the man they hated above all others.

Slowly, society returned. That first night, everyone had been so overwhelmed just to have bread that they hadn't even tried to steal loaves from each other. As they gained strength, they did fight. Within a few days, the mute Yimbo tangled with Fin and got killed. Logan watched, hoping for an opportunity to get Fin, but the fight was over too quickly. Fin's knife was too much of an advantage.

When the bread came, Logan made sure he got more than most—not only for the status, but to stay strong. He'd already lost every ounce of fat he'd ever had, and now he was losing his muscle. He was all sinews and lean hard muscles, but he was still big and he needed his strength. Still, he shared what he could with Lilly and Gnasher and Tatts.

More than two months in he made a breakthrough. He'd been feeling nervous, getting more and more on edge about Fin, with his damn sinew ropes that kept getting longer. Logan slept and woke to the sound of the demons that he now sometimes imagined made the howling noise—it wasn't wind, he was sure of that. It was either demons or the spirits of all the poor bastards who'd been thrown into the Hole over the centuries. His head throbbed in time with the howling. His jaw ached. He'd been grinding his teeth all night.

Then he found his humanity.

"Gnash," he said. "Gnasher, come here."

The big man looked at him blankly.

Logan scooted over and very slowly put his hands on Gnasher's jaw. He was afraid that Gnasher might snap at him—and if Gnasher bit him, down here an infection and death were more likely than not—but he reached up anyway. Gnasher looked puzzled, but he let Logan slowly massage his jaw. In moments, the look on the simple man's face changed. The tension in his face that Logan had assumed was part of his deformity relaxed.

When Logan stopped, the man roared and grabbed Logan. Logan thought that he was going to die, but Gnasher just hugged him. When Gnasher released him, Logan knew he had a friend for life, no matter in this Hole life was nasty, brutish, and short. He would have wept—but he had no capacity for tears.

* * *

She had to kill Jarl.

Vi stood outside of Hu Gibbet's safe house and leaned her head against the doorframe. She needed to go inside, face Hu, get ready, and go kill Jarl. As simple as that, and her apprenticeship would be done and she'd never have to face Hu again. The Godking had even promised she could kill Hu if she wanted.

During the year Vi had spent learning the trade at Momma K's, Jarl had been her only friend. He had gone out of his way to help, especially in her first weeks when she'd been such a disaster. Because of his handsome, exotic Ladeshian features, quick tongue, intelligence, and warmth, everyone had liked Jarl, and not just the men and women who lined up for his services. (Lined up only figuratively, of course. Momma K would never tolerate anything so crass as a queue in the Blue Boar.) But Vi had always felt a kind of special bond between them.

Vi stopped thinking. She had a job to do. She checked the door again for traps. There were none. Hu got careless when he had company. She opened the door slowly, standing to one side and holding her open hands in the gap. Sometimes when Hu was blasted on mushrooms, he attacked first and didn't ask questions. When no attack came, Vi walked in.

Hu sat bare-chested in the corner of the cluttered front room in a rocking chair, but the chair was still and his eyes were closed. He wasn't asleep, though. Vi was intimately attuned to her master's every nuance; she knew how he breathed when he really slept. He held crochet hooks in his hands and a tiny, nearly completed white wool cap. A baby's bonnet this time, the sick fuck.

Pretending to believe he was asleep, Vi glanced in the bedroom. Two women were lying in the bed. Vi ignored them and started gathering her gear.

Finding Jarl would be no problem. She had only to put out word that she wanted to meet with him, and he'd welcome her. His guards would make sure she had no weapons, but after a time alone with him, they'd relax or Jarl would dismiss the guards and she could kill him with her bare hands. The problem was how not to kill Jarl.

She wasn't going to do it. Fuck the Godking. But the only way the Godking would excuse her disobedience in this was if she could do something else that pleased him even more.

Vi unlocked a wide cabinet and slid a drawer out. It held her collection of wigs, the best money could buy. Vi had become an expert at taking care of them, styling them, putting them on, and affixing them firmly enough for the rigors of her trade at a moment's notice. There was something comforting about the tug on her scalp of a firm ponytail, sometimes drawn so tight under her wig that it gave her a headache. At Momma K's, Vi had been introduced to a Talented courtesan who told Vi she could teach her to change the color or style of her own hair with the Talent, but Vi wasn't interested. She might share her body, or Hu might take her body, but her hair was her own, and it was precious to her. She didn't even like men to touch the wigs, but she could tolerate it. When she whored, she wore a wig for the slight margin of disguise it gave her—flaming redheads weren't that common outside Ceura. When she was working as a wetboy, she wore her hair in that same tight ponytail. It was sensible, controlled, and efficient, just like her. The only time her hair hung loose was in the few minutes before bedtime, and then only when she was alone and safe.

After selecting a fine, straight chin-length black wig and a long, wavy brunette, Vi grabbed the creams she needed to dye her eyebrows and makeup to darken her complexion, then packed her weapons.

She was tying her saddlebags closed when a hand grabbed her breast and squeezed viciously. Vi gasped, flinching in pain and surprise, and hating herself a moment afterward. Hu chuckled low in her ear, pressing his body against her back. "Hello, gorgeous, where've you been?" he asked, trailing his hands down to her hips.

"Working. Remember?" she said, turning with difficulty. When he let her turn, she knew he was still blasted.

He wrapped himself around her, and the revulsion and hatred warred for one moment with the familiar passivity before losing. She let him push her head to one side so he could nuzzle her neck. He kissed her gently, then stopped. "You're not wearing that perfume I like," he said, still mellow, but with a note of surprise in his voice that she could be so stupid. Vi knew him well enough to know he was a hairsbreadth from violence.

"I've been working. For the Godking." Vi didn't let the smallest iota of fear sneak into her voice. Showing fear to Hu was like throwing bloody meat to a pack of wild dogs.

"Oooh," Hu said, abruptly mellow once more. His eyes were widely dilated. "I've been having a little party. Celebrating." He waved toward the bedroom. "I got a countess and a...damn, can't remember, but the other one's a wildcat. You wanna join us?"

"What are you celebrating?" Vi asked.

"Durzo!" Hu said. He released Vi abruptly and danced in a little circle, grabbing another mushroom off a table and popping it in his mouth, and trying to grab one more, but missing. "Durzo Blint is dead!" He laughed.

Vi scooped up the mushroom he'd missed. "Really? I heard that rumor, but you're sure?" Hu had always hated Durzo Blint. The two were mentioned in the same breath as the city's best wetboys, but usually Durzo's name came first. Hu had killed men for saying that, but he'd never gone after Durzo. If he'd thought he could kill Durzo, she knew, he would have.

"Momma K was friends with him, and she didn't believe he was dead, so she took some men to where he was buried—and sure enough! Dead dead dead." Hu laughed again. He grabbed the mushroom from Vi, then stopped dancing. "Unlike his apprentice, the job you fucked up." He took a flask of poppy spirits and drank. "I was going to go kill him, you know, just to piss off Blint's ghost. A hundred crowns I wasted in bribes, and turns out he left the city. Whoa," he rocked on his feet. "That one was potent. Help me sit down."

Vi's chest tightened. That was her answer. Kylar Stern was the Night Angel. He'd killed the Godking's son. Killing Kylar was the only thing that might please the Godking enough for him to forgive for not killing Jarl. She grabbed Hu's arm and guided him to his chair, making sure he avoided the razor-lined baby bonnet. "Where is he, master? Where did he go?"

"You know, you don't come around enough. After all I've done for you, you bitch." His face turned ugly and he pulled her roughly into his lap. The minutes before Hu passed out were dangerous: he might fumble weakly as a drunk, and then use the crushing strength of his Talent to compensate and hurt or kill her accidentally. So she fell into his arms, quiescent, making herself numb. Hu was distracted by her body. He tried to caress her, but fumbled his hand across the folds of her tunic instead.

"Where is Blint's apprentice, master?" Vi asked. "Where did he go?"

"He moved to Caernarvon, gave up the way of shadows. Who's the best now, huh?"

"You're the best," Vi said, easing off his lap. "You've always been the best."

"Viridiana," Hu said. She froze. He never called her by her full name. She turned warily, wondering if the mushrooms had been harmless, the poppy wine just water. It wouldn't be the first time he'd pretended intoxication to test her loyalty. But Hu's eyes were half-lidded, his figure totally relaxed in his chair. "I love you," Hu said. "These bitches got nothing..." his words trailed off and his breath took on the cadence of sleep.

Vi suddenly wanted to bathe. She grabbed her saddlebags and her sword. Then stopped.

Hu was unconscious. She was sure of it. She could draw her blade and bury it in his heart in less than a second. He deserved it a hundred times over. He deserved a hundred times worse. She took the hilt in her hand and drew the blade slowly, silently. She turned and looked at her master, thinking of a thousand humiliations he'd inflicted on her. A thousand defilements until he'd broken her. It was hard to breathe.

Vi turned on her heel, sheathed the sword, and flung the saddlebags over her shoulder. She got as far as the door, then paused. She walked back to the bedroom. The women were awake now, one blasted with a glassy-eyed stare, the other one buck-toothed and busty.

"Hu gets bored," Vi said. "I give you a coin flip chance of living through every day you spend with him. If you want to leave, he's asleep now."

"You're just jealous," the buck-toothed one said. "You just want him for yourself."

"Your funeral," Vi said, and left.

15

*I*s the Sa'kagé at war, or not?" Brant asked.

Jarl shifted in his seat. Momma K said nothing. She was letting him lead, if he could.

The safe house had taken on the appearance of a war room, that was sure. Brant had brought maps. He was gathering data on Khalidoran troop strength, noting where each unit was stationed, where food and supplies were distributed, and constructing a chart of the Khalidoran military hierarchy, cross-referenced with where the Sa'kagé had informants, along with ratings of the informants' reliability and access.

"That's a more difficult question to answer than—" Jarl said.

"No," Brant said. "It's not."

"I feel that we're in a kind of war—"

"You feel? Are you a leader or a poet, sissy boy?"

"Sissy boy?" Jarl demanded. "What's that mean?"

Momma K stood up.

"Sit down," both men said.

They looked at each other, scowling. Momma K sniffed, and sat. After a moment, Jarl said, "I'm waiting for an answer."

"Do you have a dick or do you just suck them?" Brant asked.

"Are you hoping to get lucky?" Jarl asked.

"Wrong answer," Brant said, shaking his head. "A good leader is never snide—"

Jarl punched him in the face. The general collapsed. Jarl stood over him, and drew a sword. "That's how I lead, Brant. My enemies underestimate me, and I hit them when they aren't expecting it. I listen to you, but you serve me. The next time you make a dick comment, I'll have yours fed to you." His face was cool. He brought the sword up between Brant's legs. "That's not an idle threat."

Brant found his crutch, stood with Jarl's help and brushed off his new clothes. "Well, we've just had a teachable moment. I'm touched. I think I'll write a poem. Your answer is ...?"

The poem comment almost set Jarl off. He was about to say something when he saw Momma K's mouth twitch. It was a joke. *So this is military humor.* Jarl shook his head. This was going to be a challenge.

Good gods, the man was a bulldog. "We're at war," Jarl said, not liking the feeling of giving in.

"How good is your grip on the Sa'kagé?" Brant asked. "Because I've got serious problems here. Or rather, you do."

"Not great," Jarl said. "The Khalidorans have had a galvanizing influence, but revenue is way down, and command is breaking down: people not reporting to superiors, that sort of thing. A lot of people think the occupation is bound to get easier now. They want business as usual."

"Sounds smart of them. What's your master plan to oppose them?"

Jarl frowned. There was no master plan, and Brant made that seem incredibly stupid. "We—I—had planned to see what they did. I wanted to learn more about them and then oppose them however I needed to."

"Does it strike you as a good idea to let your enemy launch fully formed stratagems on you and then be forced to react from a position of weakness?" Brant asked.

"That's more a rhetorical bludgeon than a question, general," Jarl said.

"Thank you," the general said. Momma K suppressed a smile.

"What do you propose?" Jarl asked.

"Gwinvere ruled the Sa'kagé in total secrecy, with puppet Shingas, right?"

Jarl nodded.

"So who's been the puppet Shinga since Khalidor invaded?"

Jarl winced. "I, uh, haven't exactly installed one."

"Not exactly?" Brant arched a bushy gray eyebrow.

"Brant," Momma K said. "A little gentler."

Brant adjusted his arm in its sling, wincing. "Look at it from the street,

Jarl. For more than a month, they've had no leader. Not just a bad leader. None, Gwinvere's little government has been helping everyone and so far it's going well, but your Sa'kagé thugs—sorry, *people*—have been in the same boat as everyone else. So why keep paying dues? Gwinvere was able to be a shadow Shinga, because there was never a threat like this. This is a war. You need an army. Armies need a leader. You need to be that leader, and you can't do that from the shadows."

"If I announce who I am, they'll kill me."

"They'll try," Brant said. "And they'll succeed unless you can collect a core of competent people who are absolutely loyal to you. People willing to kill and to die for you."

"These aren't soldiers from good families who've been brought up on loyalty and duty and courage," Jarl said. "We're talking about thieves and prostitutes and pickpockets, people who only think about themselves and their own survival."

"And that's what they'll say," Momma K said so quietly Jarl barely heard her, "unless you see what they may be, and make them see it."

"When I was a general, my best soldiers came from the Warrens," Brant said. "They became the best because they had everything to gain."

"So what exactly do you propose?" Jarl asked.

"I propose you work yourself out of a job," Brant said. "Give your crooks a dream of a better life, a better way for their children, and a chance to see themselves as heroes, and you'll have yourself an army."

He paused to let it sink in, and soon Jarl's heart was pounding, his mind racing. It was audacious. It was big. It was a chance to use power for more than just keeping power. He could see the outlines of a plan starting to fit together. His mind was already tapping what people he would place in which positions. Fragments of speeches were glomming together. Oh, it was seductive. Brant wasn't just telling Jarl to give the crooks a dream; Brant was giving Jarl a dream. He could be a different type of Shinga. He could be noble. Revered. If he were successful, he could probably even become legitimate, be given real titles by whichever noble family he put back in power. Gods, it was seductive!

But it meant revealing himself. Committing himself. Right now, he was a secret. Everyone thought he was just a retired rent boy. Less than a dozen people knew he was the Shinga. If he wanted to, he could just stop communicating with them. If he didn't try, he couldn't fail.

"Jarl," Momma K said, her voice gentle. "Just because it's a dream doesn't mean it's a lie."

He looked from one to the other of them, wondering how deeply they read him. Momma K probably read him to the core. It was scary. He should have suspected something just by her silence, but he couldn't be angry with her. She'd had more patience with him than he deserved.

Work myself out of a job. Elene had said she couldn't imagine Cenaria without the Sa'kagé polluting everything, but Jarl could. It would be a city where birth on the west side didn't mean hopelessness, exploitation, time in the guilds, poverty, and death. He'd been lucky to get a job working for Momma K. The Warrens offered almost no honest jobs, certainly not for orphans. The Sa'kagé was fed directly from a self-renewing underclass of whores and thieves who abandoned their children as they themselves had been abandoned before. But it could be different, couldn't it?

Just because it's a dream doesn't mean it's a lie. They were suggesting he inject hope into the Warrens. "Fine," Jarl said. "On one condition, Brant: if they kill me—whichever they it happens to be—I want you to write a poem for my funeral."

"Agreed," the general said, grinning, "and I'll make it real emotional."

16

$\mathcal{K}$ylar sat on the bed in the darkness looking at Elene's sleeping form. She was the kind of girl who just couldn't stay up late, no matter how she tried. The sight of her filled him with such tenderness and wretchedness he could hardly bear it. Since she'd promised not to ask him to sell Retribution, she'd been true to her word. No surprise there, but she hadn't even hinted.

He loved her. He wasn't good enough for her.

He'd always believed that you became like those you spent your time with. Maybe that was part of it. He loved all the things about her that he wasn't. Openness, purity, compassion. She was smiles and sunshine, and he belonged to the night. He wanted to be a good man, ached for it, but maybe some people were just born better than others.

After that first night, he'd sworn to himself that he wouldn't kill again. He would go out and train, but he wouldn't kill. So he trained for nothing and honed abilities he'd sworn not to use. Training was a pale imitation of battle, but he would be satisfied with it.

His resolution held for six days, then he was down at the docks and found a pirate savagely beating a cabin boy Kylar had only intended to separate them, but the pirate's eyes demanded death. Retribution delivered it. On the seventh night, he'd been practicing simply hiding outside a midtown tavern, trying to avoid places that were likely to bring him across pimps or thieves or rapists or murderers. A man had passed by who ran a circle of child pickpockets—a tyrant who kept the children in line through sheer brutality. Retribution found the man's heart before Kylar could stop himself On the eighth night, he'd been in the nobles' district, hoping to find less violence there, when he heard a nobleman beating his mistress. The Night Angel came in invisibly and broke both the man's arms.

Kylar held Retribution in his lap, looking at Elene. Every day, he promised himself he wouldn't kill, not ever again, and he hadn't killed for six nights. But part of him knew that was because he'd been lucky. The worst part of it was that he didn't feel guilty for the murders. He'd felt awful every time he'd killed for Durzo. These kills did nothing. He felt guilty only for lying.

Maybe he was becoming a Hu Gibbet. Maybe he needed killing now. Maybe he was becoming a monster.

Each day he worked with Aunt Mea. Durzo had rarely praised Kylar, so he'd never realized how much he had learned from the old wetboy, but as Kylar spent hours with Aunt Mea, cataloguing her herbs, repackaging some of them so they would keep longer, throwing out those that had lost their potency, labeling the rest with dates and notes on their origins, he began to see how much he did know. He was nowhere near Durzo's level of proficiency, but the man had had a few centuries on him.

He had to be careful, though. Aunt Mea used many herbs medicinally that he had used for poison. She had once set aside the roots of a silverleaf, saying they were too dangerous and that she could only use the leaves. Without thinking, he'd drawn up a chart of the lethal doses of the plant's leaves, roots, and seeds by their various preparations, whether in a tincture, a powder, a paste, or a tea, cross-referenced by body weight, sex, and age of the—he almost wrote of the "deader," and only changed it to "patient" at the last second. When he looked up, Aunt Mea was staring at him.

"I've never seen such a detailed chart," she said. "This is . . . very impressive, Kylar."

He tried to be more careful after that, but they consistently ran into the same problems. Over his career, Durzo had experimented thousands of times with all kinds of herbs. When he'd had a deader that he could kill without a deadline, he'd tried five or six different herbs. Kylar was beginning to appreciate that Durzo had probably known more about herbs than anyone alive—though he had usually been hired to kill healthy people, so sometimes what Kylar knew was useless.

One day, a man came to Aunt Mea's shop desperate for help. His master was dying and four other physickers had been unable to help him. Aunt Mea sometimes did more than midwifing so the servant had come to her as a last resort. But Aunt Mea had been gone. Kylar had felt too awkward to go to the sick man's house, but after quizzing the servant, he'd made a potion. He heard later that the man recovered. It was strangely warming. He'd saved a life, just like that.

Still, he felt guilty living on Aunt Mea's charity. He'd spent several weeks putting her shop in order, because despite her gift for working with people, her organization skills were abominable. But he hadn't done anything valuable for her. He wasn't making her any money. Elene had gotten a job as a maid, but the pay was barely enough to cover their food. Braen was getting more and more surly, muttering about freeloaders, and Kylar couldn't blame him.

Kylar brushed his fingertips over Retribution. Every time he strapped the blade on, he acted as judge and executioner. The blade had become the emblem of his oath-breaking.

Not tonight. Kylar put it back in its box and, gathering his Talent, leapt out the window. He crossed the roofs to find Golden Hair's house and put everything else out of his mind. He had to worry all day long; he wasn't going to ruin his nights too.

The whole family was there, asleep in their little one-room shack. Kylar turned to go but something stopped him. The girl and her father were asleep. The mother's lips were moving. At first, Kylar thought she was dreaming, but then her eyes opened and she got out of bed.

She didn't light any candles. She briefly looked out the narrow window, where Kylar stood invisible. She looked afraid, so much so that he double-checked his invisibility. But her eyes weren't fixed on him. He looked behind himself, but there was nobody in the street. Golden Hair's mother shivered and knelt by the bed.

Praying! Sonuvabitch. Kylar was at once embarrassed and angry to witness something so personal. He wasn't sure why. He cursed silently and turned to go.

Three armed men were coming down the street. Kylar recognized two of them as the guys who'd chased Golden Hair the other night.

"She's a wytch, I'm telling you," one of the thugs said to the man Kylar didn't recognize.

"It's true, Shinga, I swear," the other said.

You're joking. Caernarvon's Shinga himself was checking out some thugs' story about a wytch? A wytch! As if a wytch would have tripped the men rather than killing them.

Kylar heard something and looked back inside. The woman had woken her husband and both were praying now. It was odd, because from their bed, there was no way they could have seen the Sa'kagé thugs. Maybe the woman had some Talent.

Praying for protection. Kylar sneered, and the small mean part of him wanted to leave. Let their God solve his own problems. Kylar got as far as turning his back, but he couldn't do it.

"Barush," one of the thugs whispered to the Shinga. "What do we do?"

The Shinga slapped the man.

"Sorry! Sorry!" the man whined. "I mean, Shinga Sniggle, what do we do?"

"We kill them."

Good gods. It was stunning. The Sa'kagé here was such a bad parody of a Sa'kagé that Kylar wanted to laugh. Except it wasn't funny. The Shinga *slapped* men to get their respect? In Cenaria, when Pon Dradin had looked at men with less than full approval, they wilted. And he hadn't even been the real Shinga.

Kylar almost left from sheer disgust. The ineptitude!

Still, one didn't need much to kill. A wetboy knew that.

Oh, it made a lovely quandary, didn't it? Here he was, maybe one of the most skilled killers in the world. He could kill all three men before they could make a sound. And yet he couldn't even hurt them. In front of him were the dregs of the underworld, and they would kill while he couldn't. Lovely.

They were only twenty paces away. "What if . . . what if she uses wytchery again, Shinga?" Of course they didn't bother to formulate their plan before they got to the target. That would be a bit professional.

Barush Sniggle snorted, approaching the door. "I ain't afraid of that shit."

As Kylar saw the man's eyes, his hand went to his back—but Retribution was gone. His momentary surprise was enough to break him free of the killing impulse. He'd sworn. Damn him, he'd sworn. There had to be another way. Tonight, there would be another way.

So Kylar materialized in front of the Shinga. Or rather, parts of him did. He let some light shine through the ka'kari that covered him so that he appeared with a smoky translucence. The curve of an oily-iridescent black bicep shimmered in and out of visibility, then the curve of broad shoulders, the V of his torso, the lines of his chest muscles—all of them exaggerated so they seemed larger than they were. They faded in and out of sight like a ghost.

Barush Sniggle froze, and then Kylar topped it with his masterstroke. The ka'kari became solid over his eyes, making them gleam like metallic black jewels in midair. Then the rest of his face appeared, covered in a mask of black shimmering metal molded to his skin. It was menacing. It was more than menacing. It was the very face of Judgment, of Retribution made flesh, and at what Kylar saw within the Shinga's eyes—hatred-envygreedmurder betrayal—the mask became fierce. Kylar had to dig his fingernails into his palms to keep from ending him.

The Shinga dropped his cudgel, nerveless. Kylar wasn't surprised; he knew what the man was seeing—because, well, because he'd practiced it in the mirror.

"This family," Kylar said in a voice as silky soft as a stalking cat, "is under my protection."

He brought his left hand up and flexed it. With a hiss, the ka'kari slid out into a long, smoking punch dagger. Low blue fire sprang up in his eyes. It was totally gratuitous—it spoiled his night vision, not to mention feeling unpleasant, but the effect was worth it.

The Shinga shook, petrified, his mouth slack, and Kylar saw a stain spreading on the man's trousers and a puddle collecting around his feet.

"Run," Kylar said, showing a glimpse of blue fire in his mouth. *I'm not going to taste anything for a week.*

The thugs broke and ran, dropping their weapons, but Kylar felt no satisfaction. Just when he thought he couldn't paint himself any further into a corner, he'd done so brilliantly. What had Durzo Blint told him more than a decade ago? "A threat's a promise, boy. On the street, you can lie about everything except your threats. An empty threat is surrender."

Feeling sick, Kylar looked into the house. The woman and her husband were still kneeling by their bed, holding hands. They hadn't seen or heard anything. As Kylar looked in, though, the woman squeezed her husband's hand.

"We're going to be all right," she finally said aloud. "I can tell. I feel better now."

I'm glad one of us does.

"Not that long ago, you in this room were wives, mothers, a potter, a brewer, a seamstress, a ship captain, a glass blower, an importer, a moneychanger," Jarl said.

This was Jarl's sixth time preaching and it hadn't gotten easier. As he looked around at the rent girls and bashers of the Craven Dragon gathered before their shift, he saw awkwardness. They were whores now—and not by choice. Most didn't like to acknowledge that they had ever been anything else. It was too hard.

"Not that long ago," Jarl said. "I was a bender."

That lifted eyebrows, though Jarl bet they already knew he'd been a rent boy. He'd chosen the slur on purpose, to show it had no power over him. Even among whores, rent boys were second-class. They might be adored by the girls, but the clientele treated male prostitutes like dirt. A whore—though a whore—was still a woman, but a bender was something less than a man. That the new Shinga used to be one wasn't the kind of thing one would expect him to admit, much less announce.

"Not that long ago, the Sa'kagé was primarily smuggling riot weed and tobacco and whiskey," he said.

Together, Jarl and Momma K had set up a lot of new brothels since the invasion. Most of them barely broke even, but that wasn't the point. They'd done it to protect as many women and men as they could. The Craven Dragon, however, was one of the lucrative ones because it catered to the exotic. There was a girl named Daydra who could have been Elene Cromwyll's twin, without the scars. Virginal was her gig. Her suitemate, Kaldrosa Wyn, played a Sethi pirate. There were silk-clad Ladeshians and heavily kohled Modainis and bell-wearing Ymmuri dancing girls.

"Now," Jarl said, and paused, "you're whores, I'm the Shinga, and the Sa'kagé still smuggles the same damned things. Like nothing's changed. But I'll tell you something: I've changed. I got out. I'm different. I took my second chance and did something with it, and you can, too." It was the only part of the sermon Jarl thought might be a lie.

He'd asked Momma K about it. "Why don't people argue about whether the earth is flat?" she asked.

Jarl shrugged. "It's general knowledge."

"Exactly," she said. "The things that evoke passion are the things we can't know for certain."

"Ah, like the gods," Jarl said.

"It doesn't matter whether you're sure everything you say is true. It matters that you passionately want to believe they're true—because then you'll be compelling. And in the end, what matters is not whether the girls believe your arguments. What matters is that they believe in you."

It was the kind of thing the old Momma K would have said. Jarl was vaguely disappointed. She had seemed different after the coup, after Kylar had poisoned her and given her the antidote. Perhaps the pressure of looking in the face of unrelenting evil was destroying her hope. But her pragmatism had the ring of truth, so Jarl preached on.

Jarl hadn't banged since he'd become Shinga. He hadn't slept with a man since he left Stephan's house the night of the invasion, but he hadn't slept with a woman, either. He'd survived all his life by doing what he had to, always building his web of friends and influence, always looking to the future when he wouldn't have to whore.

That future had arrived so suddenly he didn't know what to do with it. Freedom lay useless in his hands. He didn't know how to feel. It reminded him of Harani iron bulls. He'd never seen one, of course, but it was said they captured the young calves and bound them to a stake with thick chains. By the time the iron bulls were full grown—more than fifteen feet high at their mighty shoulders—they could snap the chains, but they didn't. Their handlers staked them out with thin rope. The iron bulls were so sure they couldn't get free, they never tried.

Jarl had been chained to sex and pleasing his clientele for so long that now he felt sexless. He'd never had a choice before. Most of his clients were men, but there had been women too, from the entire range of levels of attractiveness. Now that he had a choice, he couldn't make it. He couldn't have said with any certainty whether he would have preferred men or women if the life of a rent boy hadn't been forced on him.

The girls at the brothels treated him differently now. They looked at him differently. They flirted.

It was terrifying. Flirtation carried demands. There were appropriate and inappropriate responses to learn and he didn't know the rules of sex outside a brothel. His regulars had always spoken of it as being unsatisfying—but then their experiences couldn't exactly be representative or everyone would be regulars at a brothel, wouldn't they?

He was losing his focus. He couldn't think about this now. Hope had to be sold as a whole package.

"Of all the women in the Warrens," Jarl said, "you're the luckiest. You were lucky enough to become whores here." He shook his head. "Lucky enough to become whores. Six months ago, most of you would have crossed the street rather than pass a whore. Now you are whores, and I'm the Shinga, and the Sa'kagé is still doing the same damn things.

"King Ursuul thinks you're finished. He plans to let the winter kill off most everyone in the Warrens. He figures that by the time the food riots get going, everyone will be so weak his soldiers will have no trouble with us. He figures that the Sa'kagé is too passive and too greedy to stop him. He plans to split us apart by offering us scraps off his table to destroy each other. The funny thing is," Jarl said, "he's right. We've learned that in the spring he's bringing down another army and a few thousand colonists, all of them men. He plans to kill everyone in the Warrens except you. Again, you'll be the lucky ones. You'll be married off to whichever Khalidoran buys you.

"Now maybe the Khalidorans will change and they'll stop with the beatings and the bedroom humiliations once you're their wives. Ursuul expects that you are such cowards you'll hold onto that diseased hope. He expects that sick hope to paralyze you until it's too late, until your men are dead, your friends are scattered, and the Sa'kagé's strength is broken. In a year, you'll start bearing sons for your new Khalidoran husbands and have the joy of watching them turn into monsters who treat their wives as their fathers treat you. It'll be normal. You'll bear daughters who will think it's normal to be kicked and spit on and forced to—well, you know all the things they'll be forced to do. Your daughters won't resist. They'll look to your cowardice and believe that such is a woman's lot. It'll be normal. That's what the king expects will happen, and he's been right about everything so far."

Jarl had them now. He could see the horror in their eyes. Most rent girls thought only of today. They weren't stupid. They knew they couldn't work the sheets forever, but because they didn't see any good options for the future, they decided not to think about the future at all. It was too crushing.

These women were in survival mode. Raising the specter of bearing their own daughters into the same life forced them to think beyond themselves, beyond today. And Jarl hadn't been lying. These women would be the best off. If he could sell the women who had the most to lose, half the battle would be won.

"Things have changed in the last few months for each of us, for each of you and for me. Now I say it's time for things to change for all of us together. I say it's time for the Sa'kagé to change. We've been at war and we've been losing. Do you know why? Because we haven't been fighting. The Khalidorans want us to quietly die? Fuck 'em. We'll fight in ways they've never seen. The Khalidorans are going to starve us? Fuck 'em. If we can smuggle riot weed, we can smuggle grain. They want to kill your men? We'll hide 'em. They want to conduct raids? We'll know where they're going before they do. They want to gamble? We'll cheat. They want to drink? We'll piss in their beer."

"What can we do?" one of the girls asked. It was a planted question.

He smiled. "Right now? I want you to dream. I want you to think—not about going back to what we had before Khalidor came—I want you to dream of something better. I want you to dream of a day when being born in the Warrens doesn't guarantee dying in the Warrens. I want you to dream of getting a second chance and what could happen for this city and this country if everyone got a second chance. Dream of raising your children in a city where they don't have to be afraid all the time. A city without corrupt judges or Sa'kagé extortion. A city with a dozen bridges over the Plith, and not a guard on one of them. A city where things are different—because of us.

"I know you're scared right now. Your shift starts in a few minutes, and you have to go face those fuckers again. I know. It's fine to be frightened, but I'm telling you, be brave inside. The time is coming when you will be needed. If the nobles want to win this war and take this country back, they're going to need us, and our help is going to come at a price. Our price is a city that's different, and you and I get to decide how. You and I have that power. So for now, we can go on with things as usual, or we can dream and get ready. Out of everyone in the Warrens, you ladies have the most to lose." He walked over to the pirate girl Kaldrosa Wyn and touched her cheek beneath one blackened eye.

"But tell me, is this what you gave up your husband for? A crown for a black eye, one more when they hurt you so bad you can't work the next day? Is this what you deserve?"

Tears leaked from Kaldrosa's eyes.

"I say hell no. You came here because it was the best you could do. You get a crown for a black eye because it's the best Momma K could negotiate. As your Shinga, I'm here to tell you that the best isn't good enough. We've been thinking too small. We've been trying to survive, and I for one am sick of surviving. The next time I hear a scream of pain, I want it to come from a Khalidoran throat."

"Hell yes," one of the girls whispered.

He could see passion burning in their eyes now. Gods, they looked fierce!

Jarl raised a hand. "For now, just watch, just wait. Be ready. Be brave. Because when our chance to roll the bones comes, we're gonna cheat and we're gonna roll three sixes."

"Honey," Elene said, shaking Kylar gently. "Honey, get up."

"Ass," he said.

"What?"

"AAASSSS."

Elene laughed. "You do look like someone sat on you," she said, hugging him. She sniffed and grimaced. "And you do stink..."

"Ass," he said, wounded.

"Honey. We've got to go shopping today, remember?"

He grabbed a pillow and pulled it over his head. Elene leaned over to grab the pillow, but Kylar wouldn't let go of it. So she sang the good morning song. It consisted of the words *good* and *morning,* repeated thirty-seven times. It was one of Kylar's favorites. "GOOD morn-ing, good MORN-ing, good morning, GOOD morning..."

"ASS assing, ass ASSing, ass assing," Kylar harmonized into the pillow.

She pulled on the pillow and Kylar grabbed her and flipped her onto the bed next to him. He was so strong and so quick there was no resisting. He pulled the pillow away, rolled on top of her, and kissed her.

"Uhn uhn!" she said. Oh, his lips felt good.

"What?" he asked thirty seconds later.

"Morning mouth," she said, grimacing. It was a lie, of course. With the way his lips felt, she wouldn't have cared if he did have bad breath. But he didn't. His breath never smelled. Not just never smelled bad; he could chew mint leaves or moldy cheese and his breath wouldn't smell at all. It was the same with the rest of his body. Put perfume on him, and it just disappeared. Probably something to do with the ka'kari, he'd guessed.

So now he smiled his mock-predatory smile. "I'll show you morning mouth," he said. He pushed through her flailing hands and kissed her neck, and then lower on her neck, and then he was pulling down the neckline of her dressing gown and her hands weren't flailing anymore and his lips—

"Ah! Shopping!" she rolled out of his arms. He let her go.

Kylar flopped back on the bed and she pretended to straighten her dress while she admired the muscles of his bare torso. Aunt Mea had taken Uly out for the day. The house was empty. Kylar was so cute when his hair was squashed from sleep, and he was gorgeous, and his lips were the most amazing things in the world. Not to mention his hands. She wanted to feel his skin against hers. She wanted to put her hands on his chest. And vice versa.

Sometimes in the morning they cuddled while he was barely conscious, and it had become her favorite time of day. Once or twice her shift had ridden up during the night and she had found herself spooned against him, skin to skin. Well, maybe her shift didn't ride up all by itself, and she wouldn't have dared it if she didn't know he'd been out for hours the night before and wouldn't possibly wake up.

It made her warm just thinking about it. Why not? part of her asked. So there were the religious reasons. Can an ox and a wolf be yoked together? She didn't even know if Kylar believed in the God. He always got uncomfortable when she talked about it. Her foster mother had told her to make her decisions before she got her heart involved, but that was water under the bridge and down the river and around the bend. Uly needed her. Kylar needed her, and she had never been needed like that before. Kylar made her feel beautiful and good. He made her feel like a lady. He made her feel like a princess. He loved her.

He practically was her husband. They said they were married, they lived together, slept in the same bed, acted as father and mother to Uly. Probably the only reason she hadn't already made love with Kylar was that by the time he actually touched her most nights, she was so tired she could barely move. If he tried in the morning what he did at night, she'd have surrendered her maidenhead in about five seconds. She could almost feel his breath in her ear. She imagined doing some of the things Aunt Mea had talked about so blithely—things that had set her face burning, but sounded ever so wonderful. She was feeling so brazen that she even knew which one she'd try first.

Didn't the scriptures say "let your yes be yes and your no be no"? She'd said she was Kylar's wife. He'd said he was her husband. She'd take him past the ringery Aunt Mea had told her about and they could formalize things in the Waeddryner way later. Afterward.

Kylar sat up in bed and she leaned close behind him, her hands moving to the ties of her dressing gown. She opened it.

"Gods," Kylar said, giving her a quick peck on the cheek without turning around far enough to see the rest of her, "I've got to piss like a warhorse."

He stood and started pulling on clothes. For a moment, Elene was frozen. Her dressing gown hung open, her body exposed.

"What are we shopping for?" Kylar asked, pulling his tunic over his head.

She had barely laced up her dress when his head poked out of his tunic.

"Well?" he asked.

"What?" She felt like someone had just dumped cold water over her head.

"Oh, Uly's birthday, right? We getting her a doll or something?"

"Yes, that's it," she said. What had she been thinking?

Tenser performed his job capably enough, Vürdmeister Neph Dada thought. At one point, he even managed to cough up blood. For the time being, his performance would be remembered as cold-blooded defiance. Once he was exonerated, it would be reinterpreted as brave defiance.

The man Tenser was alleged to have murdered, the Cenarian Baron Kirof, had never been found. But on the troth of the Cenarian captain of the guard who said he'd seen Tenser do the deed, Tenser was quickly found guilty. The announcement of his punishment from the Godking's own mouth had garnered gasps. The Cenarian nobility had expected a fine, perhaps imprisonment with credit for time already served, maybe deportation to Khalidor. That he would be thrown into the Hole was viewed as worse than a death penalty. Of course, that was the point.

Tenser couldn't very well infiltrate the Sa'kagé if he were dead or deported. By doing time in the worst gaol in the country, he would earn unrivalled credibility with the Sa'kagé. When Baron Kirof was produced—alive—Tenser would be exonerated and he would again have all the access of a Khalidoran duke—but, more important, he would pretend to hold an abiding hatred for the Godking for his false imprisonment. Duke Tenser Vargun would offer the Sa'kagé whatever they wanted. And then he would destroy them from within.

The Godking, as always, had more than one plan. By punishing a Khalidoran duke so severely, he showed that he was a just ruler. The Cenarians who were wavering would have one more excuse to submit. They would go back to their lives and the noose would only tighten on the rebels as their friends abandoned them.

At the same time, the news of Tenser's imprisonment would overshadow anything else, so today he was releasing dozens of criminals from the Maw and incarcerating hundreds of suspected rebels. With the shocking news about Tenser, people would barely notice.

After the sentence was announced, Neph escorted Tenser and the guards to the Hole.

Tenser looked at him suspiciously. A lot of Khalidorans didn't think much of their long-vanquished Lodricari neighbors, but with Tenser, the antipathy seemed both general and personal. "What do you want?"

"Just to share some news that might be helpful," Neph said. He couldn't hide his pleasure. "Baron Kirof has disappeared. Someone kidnapped him, apparently."

The blood drained from Tenser's face. If the baron was lost, he would never leave the Hole.

"We'll find him," Neph said. "Of course, if we find him dead..." Neph chuckled. If Kirof was dead, Vargun was useless. If useless, a failure. If a failure, dead. With magic, Neph opened the iron gate that separated the castle's tunnels from the Maw's. "My lord? Your cell awaits."

Jarl rubbed his temples. They'd been interviewing prisoners released from the Maw all day. The prisoners had only learned of the coup after the fact, when wytches appeared, searching for something. The wytches left empty-handed, so it didn't seem important.

What was important was that a former brothel manager called Whitey had been awake when two guards had led a prisoner toward the Hole. He'd been awake and he'd stayed awake. He swore that neither the two guards nor their prisoner, a big blond naked man, had left.

Furthermore, Whitey recognized one of the guards, a foul man who'd been on Jarl's payroll, whom Jarl had sent to the castle with a very specific task. The wytches coming after them had gone as far as the Maw, but there had been no sounds of fighting, no indications that they had seen anyone. It was impossible, and Whitey couldn't make any sense of it.

Jarl dismissed Whitey. "Is it possible?" he asked Momma K.

"What do you think," she said, stating the question.

"What are you talking about?" Brant Agon asked.

"It proves he was alive later than we thought," Jarl said.

"And we know that the head they put up wasn't his," Momma K said. "That's suggestive."

"Gods," Jarl said.

"What?" Brant asked. "What?"

"Logan Gyre," Jarl said.

"What? He was killed in the north tower," Brant said.

"What would you do if you had just killed a guard deep in the Maw and were changing into his clothes when you saw six wytches were coming your way? There's only one way out, and that way was blocked by the wytches," Jarl said.

Brant was thunderstruck. "You're not saying Logan jumped into the Hole," Brant said. He'd been down to the Hole once.

"I'm saying Logan Gyre might still be alive," Jarl said.

"Hold on," Momma K said. She got up and started looking through a stack of papers. "If I recall correctly...ah, here. Remind me that we need to give this girl a bonus. She has a regular who likes to brag. 'Gorkhy throws their bread down the Hole and watches them try to grab it without falling in. He says at least three of the prisoners have been...'" Momma K cleared her throat, but when she continued her voice was level. "'Three of the prisoners have been eaten by the others in the time Gorkhy's been starving them.' She describes 'a giant of a man almost seven feet tall. Several times he's been able to reach bread that Gorkhy tried to throw down the Hole. Gorkhy has special hatred for the man, the one they call King.'" Momma K looked up. "This report is only three days old."

Quietly, Brant said, "No one like that has been thrown in the Hole in the last ten years."

All three of them sat back.

"If this Gorkhy tells his superiors about a giant of a man named King..." Momma K said.

"Logan will die that day," Jarl said.

"We have to save him," Brant said.

Jarl and Momma K shared a look.

"We need to think where this fits in with our strategy," Momma K said.

"You're not thinking of leaving him there," Brant said.

Momma K examined her blood-red nails.

"Because that isn't an option," Brant said. "He's the only man we could possibly rally the country behind. Jarl, if you really want to do what you've said, this is your chance. If you rescue Logan, he'll give you lands and titles and a pardon. So don't tell me that you're even thinking of leaving our king in that hell."

"Are you done?" Momma K asked. He said nothing, but his jaw tensed. "We are thinking of it. We're thinking of it because we think of everything. That's why we win. I'm even thinking how we could save him if we want to. Have you started thinking about that yet, or are you still blustering about how noble and good you'll be?"

"Dammit, I'm still blustering," he said, but a smile escaped. Momma K shook her head and smiled despite herself.

"How are your men coming, Brant?" Jarl asked.

"I'll make good soldiers of them, given a decade or two."

"How many do you have?" Jarl asked.

"No, no," Momma K said.

"A hundred," Agon said. "Maybe thirty would be of some use in a fight. Ten might be formidable. A few great archers. One who might make a third-rate wetboy. All of them undisciplined. They don't trust each other yet. They fight as individuals."

"We haven't even talked through this yet," Momma K said.

Jarl said, "Consider it talked through. We're doing it."

Momma K opened her mouth. Jarl held her gaze until she looked down. "As you will, Shinga," she said.

"I'll assume that our source wouldn't be able to get Gorkhy to help us?"

Momma K looked at the paper, but she wasn't even reading it. "Not for this."

As Brant and Momma K debated different ways of getting into the Maw, Jarl was thinking. He'd announced himself two weeks ago, and he was preaching to an eager audience. The people of the Warrens—the Rabbits, as they were derisively called for their numbers, their fears, and their maze of alleys—wanted hope. His message was water for parched tongues. Rebellion sounded great to people who had nothing to lose. But in speaking, he'd necessarily spoken to the Godking's spies.

He'd already avoided one assassination attempt. There were bound to be more. Unless Jarl got some wetboys to protect him, they'd get him sooner or later.

"I'm going to Caernarvon," Jarl said.

"You're running away?" Brant asked.

"If I travel light, I can be back in a month."

"Granted, but what does that give you?"

"Another month of life?" Jarl said with a smile.

Momma K said, "You think he'll come back?"

Brant looked confused.

"For Logan? In a heartbeat," Jarl said.

"If anyone can get Logan out, he can," Momma K said.

"Who?" Brant asked.

"And once Hu Gibbet and the other wetboys hear he's protecting you, I wouldn't be surprised if they back off," Momma K said.

"Who? Who?"

"Since Durzo Blint died, probably the best wetboy in the city," Jarl said.

"Except he's not in the city anymore," Momma K said.

"Fine, the best in the business."

"Except he's not in the business anymore."

"That's about to change," Jarl said.

"Will you take anyone?" Momma K said.

"You're just trying to spite me, aren't you?" Brant asked.

"No," Jarl said, ignoring him and answering Momma K. "It'll be less conspicuous to smuggle one out." Jarl turned to Brant, "Brant, I have a task for you while I'm gone."

"You're talking about Kylar Stern, aren't you?"

Jarl smiled. "Yes. Are you an honest man, General?"

The general sighed. "Everywhere except on the battlefield."

Jarl clapped him on the shoulder. "Then I want you to figure out how Logan Gyre's army is going to destroy the Godking's."

"Logan doesn't have an army," Brant said.

"That's Momma K's problem," Jarl said.

"Pardon me?" she asked.

"Terah Graesin does. I want you to figure out how it's going to become Logan's."

"What?" Momma K asked.

"Now if you'll excuse me," Jarl said, "I've got a date in Caernarvon."

18

"*D*id I die and not notice?" Kylar asked. He was moving through the death fog again, the familiar moving-without-moving feeling against his skin. A cloaked figure stood beyond the edge of the fog, as ethereal as the fog itself, and Kylar was sure it was the Wolf, but he hadn't died. Had he? Had someone killed him in his sleep? He'd just lain down—

"What is this? A dream?" Kylar asked.

The cloaked man turned, and Kylar's tension melted. It wasn't the Wolf. It was Dorian Ursuul.

"A dream?" Dorian asked. He squinted at Kylar through the fog. "I suppose so, if a peculiar variety thereof." He smiled. He was a handsome man, if intense. His black hair was disheveled, his blue eyes intelligent, his features balanced. "Why is it, my shadow-striding friend, that we don't fear dreams? We lose consciousness, lose control, things happen with no apparent logic and abiding by no apparent rules. Friends appear and morph into strangers. Environments shift abruptly, and we rarely question it. We don't fear dreams, but we do fear madness, and death terrifies us."

"What the hell is going on?" Kylar asked.

Dorian smirked. He looked Kylar up and down. "Amazing. You look exactly the same, but you're totally different, aren't you?"

Gods, had it only been a couple of months since he'd met Dorian?

"You've become formidable, Kylar. You have gravitas now. You're a force to be reckoned with, but your mind hasn't caught up with your power, has it? Reforming your identity is taking you time. That's understandable. Not many people have to kill a father figure and become an immortal on the same day."

"Get to the point." Dorian always knew too much. It was unnerving.

"This is a dream, as you said. And yes, I did summon you. It's a nice bit of magic I just discovered. I hope I remember it when I wake. If I wake. I'm not sure I'm asleep. I'm in one of my little reveries. I have been for a long time now. My body's at Screaming Winds. Khali is coming. The garrison will fall. I'll survive, but worse days are to come for me. I've been watching my own future, Kylar, something very dangerous to do. I've found a few things that have made me lose heart and stop looking. So while I've been marshaling my courage, I've been following you. I saw that you needed someone you could be honest with. Count Drake or Durzo would have been better, but they clearly can't be here, so here I am. Even killers need friends."

"I'm not a killer anymore. I've given that up."

"In my visions," Dorian said as if Kylar hadn't spoken, "I see myself coming to a place where my happiness is one lie away. I will look into the eyes of the woman I love who also loves me and know that whether I lie or tell the truth, she'll be devastated. In this, we are brothers, Kylar. The God gives simpler problems to lesser men. I'm here because you need me."

Kylar's pique unraveled. He looked into the fog. The entire place seemed a fit metaphor for his life—stuck in twilight with nothing definite, nothing solid, no simple path.

"I'm trying to change," Kylar said, "but I'm not making it. I thought I could just break with my past and move and be done with it. I walk into a room and I case it. I look for exits, see how high the ceilings are, check potential threats, how good the traction on the floor is. If a man stares at me from an alley, I figure out how I'll kill him—and it feels good. I feel in control."

"Until?" Dorian asked.

Kylar hesitated. "Until I remember. I have to make myself think that my instincts are wrong. And then I hate what I've become."

"And what have you become?" Dorian asked.

"A murderer."

"You're a liar and killer, but you're no murderer, Kylar."

"Well, thanks."

"What's the Night Angel, Kylar?"

"I don't know. Durzo never told me."

"Horseshit. Why don't you trust yourself? Why don't you ask Elene to trust you? Why don't you trust her with the truth?"

"She'd never understand."

"How do you know?"

What if she did? What if, once she knew him all the way down to the depths, then she rejected him? What would that do to him?

"You two are so young you don't know your asses from your elbows," Dorian said. "But *you* are starting to figure yourself out. Elene's accepted a tiny box as her faith, and you're way outside of what she knows about the God. She's got the arrogance of youth that tells her that what she knows about the God is all there is to know about Him. She loves you, so she wants you to stay in that box with her. And that box is too small for you. You can't understand a God who's all mercy and no justice. That cute, fuzzy God wouldn't last two minutes in the Warrens, would he? Well, I hate to tell you this, but Elene's eighteen. All she knows about the God isn't all that much.

"Kylar, I don't think the God finds you abhorrent. The horror is having profound power in one hand and a strong moral sense in the other and absolutely no foundation to stand on. For the last couple of months, you've tried to accept Elene's moral conclusions while rejecting her premises. And you say she's not logical? Where do you stand, Shadow in Twilight?

"You've got choices to make, but here's another hard truth: you *can't* be whatever you want to be. The list of things you'll never be is a long one— even if you do live forever. Do you want to know what's at the top? Mild-mannered herbalist. You're as meek as a wolf, Kylar—and that's what Elene loves about you and it's what she fears about you. You can't keep telling her it's all right, that this disguise is who you really are. It's not. Why don't you trust Elene enough to ask her to love the man you really are?"

"Because I hate him!" Kylar roared. "Because he loves killing! Because she doesn't understand evil and he does. Because he never feels so alive as when I'm bathed in blood. Because he is a virtuoso with the sword and I love what he can do. Because he is the Night Angel and the angel is in the night and the night is in me! Because he is the Shadow That Walks. Because he believes some people cannot be saved, only stopped. Because when he kills an evil man, I feel not just the pleasure of mastery, I feel the whole world's pleasure at the retribution—an evil man is an affront and I erase the blot. I balance the imbalance. He loves that—and Elene would have to lose the innocence I love about her for her to understand that man."

"This man," Dorian said, poking Kylar's chest, "and this one—" he poked Kylar's forehead—"are on their way to madness. Take it from one who knows."

"I can change," Kylar said, but his voice was hopeless.

"A wolf might become a wolfhound, son, but it will never be a lap dog."

"We are at war," Speaker Istariel Wyant said. Her voice was nasal, the accent High Alitaeran. She liked making pronouncements.

Ariel had wedged her bulk into a too-small chair in the Speaker's office, high within the Alabaster Seraph. She was puffing from the climb up the stairs. *One meal a day until I can manage the climb without wheezing. One.*

Sometimes Ariel hated flesh, hated being chained to something so weak and needy. It took such care, such slavish devotion, and wanted such pampering. It was a perpetual distraction from things more important, like what the Speaker wanted of her.

Istariel Wyant was a tall, imperious woman with a patrician nose and brows plucked down to thin lines. She had knobby joints that made her look lanky rather than willowy, and despite her pinched middle-aged face, she had the most beautiful long blonde hair of any woman Ariel knew. Istariel adored her hair. Not a few of the Sisters whispered that she must have rediscovered some lost weave to make it so thick and glossy. It wasn't true, of course, Istariel's mother had had the same hair. It was one reason their father had married her after Ariel's mother died. Besides, Istariel wasn't that Talented.

"This war is not just over what it means to be a maja, but what it means to be a woman."

Seeing the undisguisedly ironical look on Ariel's face, Istariel changed tack. "How have you been, sister?"

Of course, every full maja was addressed as "Sister," but Istariel warmed the word. Used for Ariel, "sister" hearkened back to the supposedly halcyon days of their youth together, some fifty years ago. Istariel definitely wanted something.

"Fine," Ariel said.

Istariel tried again, valiantly. "And how are your studies progressing?"

"The last two years of my life have probably been a complete waste," Ariel said.

"Still the same old Ariel." Istariel tried to say it lightly, as if amused, but she didn't quite put in the effort to make it convincing. She probably thought that because Ariel didn't use any finely nuanced social snubs, she wasn't aware of them.

When they had been younger and Ariel had cared more about what her aristocratic little sister thought of her, it had been a bitter irony for her. Ariel had always fallen squarely in Istariel's blind spot. The near-genius with which Istariel instantly understood the men and women around her had never extended to Ariel, with whom she spent so much time. When Istariel looked at her, she saw Ariel's broad peasant face and thick peasant limbs, her lack of social graces and lack of concern for the important things—privilege, power, and position—and she saw a peasant. Istariel thought she understood Ariel, so she stopped thinking about her at all. Now she even allowed her eyes to flick down.

"Yes, I've gotten fat," Ariel said.

Istariel blushed. *How she must hate how I can still make her feel like a child.* "Well," Istariel said, "I, I suppose you have put on a little ..."

"And how are you, Speaker?" Ariel asked. Why was it she could master the eighty-four variations of the Symbeline weave with perfect timing, structure, and intonation, but not make conversation? Surely small talk should be reducible to perhaps a few hundred typical questions, delineated into conversation trees according to the conversant's responses, how well one knew the conversant, what the current events were, and one's position relative to the conversant.

Timing of the questions and the length of one's responses would have to be studied as well, but many weaves required exact timing, too, and Ariel's rhythm was perfect. One might have to take into account the physical setting: one would speak differently in the Speaker's office than in a tavern. Topics of study could include how to deal with distractions, appropriate degrees of eye contact or physical touch, taking into account cultural variations, and of course the differences in speaking with men and women, subdivided by whether one were oneself a man or a woman. Ariel supposed she might have to include children in the study as well, and it would be important to include how to speak with those toward whom you had varying degrees of friendship or interest, romantic or otherwise. Or should it? Should one make small talk differently with a woman whom you thought you might like to befriend than with a woman you had no interest in? Were there socially appropriate ways to curtail dull conversations?

That made Ariel smile. In her book, curtailing dull conversations would be a huge plus.

Still, the project as a whole had little to do with magic. Perhaps nothing. Indeed, she decided that the study, while worthy, would be a poor use of her own gifts.

"But you're really not listening, are you?" Istariel said.

Ariel realized that her sister had been speaking for some time. It had all been meaningless, but Ariel had forgotten to pretend to be paying attention. "Sorry," she said.

Istariel waved it away, and Ariel realized that Istariel was almost relieved that Ariel was back to acting the way she expected—Ariel, the distracted, oblivious genius, big brain and bigger Talent and nothing else. It allowed Istariel to feel superior. "I got you thinking, didn't I?" Istariel asked.

Ariel nodded.

"About what?"

She shook her head, but Istariel cocked an eyebrow at her. It was an I'm-the-Speaker look. Ariel grimaced.

"I was thinking about how bad I am at small talk, and wondering why," Ariel said.

Istariel grinned—they might have been teenagers again. "And formulating a course of study on it?"

She frowned deeply. "I decided I'm the wrong person for the task."

Istariel laughed out loud. It was irritating. Istariel was a snorter. "What were you saying?" Ariel asked. She tried to look interested. Istariel, though pompous and a snorter, was the Speaker.

"Oh, Ariel, you don't care, and you're not very good at pretending you do."

"No, I don't. But you do, so I can listen politely."

Istariel shook her head as though she couldn't believe Ariel, but she settled down and—mercifully—stopped snorting. "Forget it. The war I was talking about? Some of the younger sisters want to form a new order."

"Another bunch who want to disavow the Alitaeran Accord and become war magae?" What a waste. They spent their time trying to change the rules rather than ignoring them and making them moot.

"Nothing so simple. These ladies propose to call themselves the Chattel."

"Oh my."

Tyros were not allowed to marry, but many Sisters eventually decided to. Of those, most went back to wherever they had come from or where their husbands lived. Some stayed on at the Chantry, but few rose to high levels. Often, that was simply a matter of choice; the women decided that with children, husbands, and homes, they'd rather be with their families full time.

Sometimes, though, ambitious Sisters wanted it all. They wanted to be married to the Chantry and to a man. Those never rose as high as they believed they deserved, because after a certain level, the other Sisters wanted leaders for whom the Chantry was their whole family. The women who sacrificed family for the Seraph saw it as their right to be promoted beyond those who worked half-jobs, no matter how brilliantly. The attitude even extended to married Sisters who didn't have children, because Sisters assumed that they would eventually throw away everything worthwhile to tend a man and his brats, like any peasant woman. The Sisters quietly called them chattel, voluntary housekeepers and broodmares to men, and they said the chattel wasted the Chantry's time and money and—worst— their own talents.

Usually, the comments went unchallenged because the vast majority of the Sisters at the Chantry were single. Either they were instructors or they were students. It was considered rude to call a married Sister a chattel to her face, but it happened.

If the married Sisters formed an order—and Ariel couldn't see how they could be denied—they would have tremendous power. Their numbers included more than half of all the Sisters. If they became a bloc, things would change radically.

"It's a ploy, of course," the Speaker said. "Most of the . . . married Sisters aren't militant enough to rally behind such a name. It's just a shot over the bow to let us know they're serious."

"What do they want?" Ariel asked.

Istariel's eye twitched, and she rubbed it. "Many things, but one of the primary demands is that we start a new school of magic here. A school that breaks with our traditions."

"How much of a break?"

"A men's school, Ariel."

That was more than a break from tradition. It was a seismic upheaval.

"We believe some of them have married magi already."

"What do you want me to do?" Ariel asked immediately.

"About this?" Istariel said. "Nothing. Heavens no. Forgive me, sister, but you're the last person to help with this. It requires a lighter touch. I have something else for you. The leader of the married sisters is Eris Buel. I can't oppose her directly. I need someone ambitious, respected, and young to carry our standard."

Which of course excluded Ariel. "You describe perhaps a third of our sisters, or would, if you added unscrupulous."

Istariel's eyes went hot and then cold. Ariel knew she had overstepped the bounds, but Istariel wouldn't do anything about it. She needed her. Besides, Ariel had said it not so much because it was true as for the quarter of a second when Istariel would either look guilty or not.

She had.

"Ari, not even you may speak that way to me."

"What do you want?" Ariel asked.

"I want you to bring Jessie al'Gwaydin back to the Chantry."

Ariel thought about it. Jessie al'Gwaydin would be an ideal rock to crush Eris Buel against. She was everything the Chantry loved: well-spoken, good-looking, intelligent, nobly born, and willing to pay her dues to climb to the top. She wasn't terribly Talented, but she might be a good leader one day, if she had some sense knocked into her.

"She's studying the Dark Hunter in Torras Bend," Istariel said. "I know it's dangerous, but I gave her sufficient warning that I'm sure she won't do anything precipitous." Istariel chuckled. "In fact, I threatened to send you after her if she wasn't good. I'm sure it will please her enormously to see you."

"And if she's dead?" Ariel asked.

Istariel's grin faded. "Find me someone the Chattel can't ignore. Someone who will do what needs to be done."

There was a terrible latitude in that ambiguity. But latitude could be used both ways, and the fact was, Ariel would rather be included. *Oh, sister, you play with a terrible fire. Why would you use me for this?* "Done," Ariel said.

Istariel signaled that she was dismissed, and Ariel walked to the door. "Oh," Istariel said, as if it had slipped her mind, "whomever you bring, make sure she's married."

Kylar was outside the shop closing up when he sensed he was being watched. He curved his fingers unconsciously to check the knives strapped to his forearms, but there were no knives there. He closed the big shutters over the counter where they displayed their wares and fitted the lock on it, feeling suddenly vulnerable.

It wasn't being weaponless that made him feel vulnerable. A wetboy was a weapon. He felt vulnerable because of his oath. No killing, no violence. What did that leave him with?

Whoever it was, they were standing in the shadows of the alley beside the shop. Kylar had no doubt they were waiting for him to walk to the front door, which was only steps away from the alley. With his Talent, he could get into the door and lock it—and give away his abilities. Or he could run away—and leave Uly unprotected.

Seriously. Before there had been a woman in his life, things had been so simple.

Kylar walked toward the door. The man was disheveled and wearing rags, with the bloodshot eyes and missing teeth of a riot weed addict. The knives the Ladeshian held seemed serviceable enough, though. He leapt out of the alley. Kylar expected the man to demand money, but he didn't.

Instead, he attacked instantly, screaming insanity. It sounded like he was saying, "Don't kill me! Don't kill me!" Kylar simply moved and the addict went sprawling. Kylar leaned against the wall, puzzled. The man picked himself up and charged. Kylar waited. Waited. Then he moved abruptly. The addict smashed into the wall.

After kicking away the bleeding man's daggers, Kylar rolled him over with a foot.

"Don't kill me yet," the man said, spluttering through the blood streaming from his nose. "Please, immortal. Don't kill me yet."

"I brought you a present," Gwinvere said.

Agon looked up from the paper he was writing. It was a list of the strengths and weaknesses of their tactical situation in the Warrens. So far, it was a depressing list. He got up from the table and followed Gwinvere into the next room of her house, trying not to think about how good she smelled. It made his heart ache.

Her dining room table was covered with a cloth that had ten lumps beneath it.

"Aren't you going to open it?" Gwinvere asked.

Agon raised an eyebrow at her; she laughed. He pulled the cover cloth off and gasped.

On the table were ten unstrung short bows. They were adorned with simple, almost crude scrimshaw of men and animals, mostly horses.

"Gwinvere, you shouldn't have."

"That's what my accountants tell me."

He picked one up and tried to bend it.

"Careful," she said. "The man who...procured these bows said you need to warm them by a fire for half an hour before you string them. Otherwise they'll break."

"They really are Ymmuri bows," Agon said. "I've never even seen one before." The bows were one of the marvels of the world. No one but the Ymmuri knew the secret of their construction, though Agon could plainly see that somehow they used not only wood but also horn and glue from melted horse hooves. They could punch an arrow through heavy armor at two hundred paces, a feat only Alitaeran longbows could match. And these bows were short enough to be used from horseback. Agon had heard stories of the lightly armored horse lords riding circles around heavily armored companies, outside the range of traditional archers, shooting the entire company to pieces. Every time lancers charged, the light Ymmuri on their little ponies fled, shooting arrows the whole way. No one had yet figured out how to counter such an attack. Thank the gods no one had ever united the Ymmuri, or they would overrun all of Midcyru.

The bows would be perfect for Agon's wytch hunters. He caressed the one in his hand.

"You know the way to a man's heart, Gwinvere," he said, delighted as a child with a new toy.

She smiled and for a golden moment he smiled too. Gwinvere was beautiful, so smart, so capable, so formidable, and now as she looked in his eyes, somehow fragile, rocked by the death of Durzo, the man she'd loved for fifteen years. Gwinvere was deep and mysterious, and though he'd thought himself too old to be stirred by such things, he was stirred by her beauty. Her smell—gods, was that the same perfume she'd worn all those years ago? It shook him to his core. But there, at his core, he saw his wife. Whether she was dead or alive, he might never know. He could never mourn, never move on, never give up hope without giving up on her and somehow betraying her.

His smile dropped a notch, and Gwinvere saw it. She touched his arm. "I'm glad you like them." She walked to the door, then turned. "Just tell your men that each of those bows cost more than they'll make in their lives." And she smiled. It was a smile to give them a ramp back up to levity. A smile that told him she saw, she knew, and though she didn't reciprocate his interest, she wouldn't use it against him.

Agon barked a laugh, accepting her lead. "I'll take it out of their hides."

More shocking than the mugger's words was his face. He was the same man whom Kylar had sworn he'd seen briefly from Count Drake's window the day Vi tried to kill him.

Kylar dosed the man with poppy wine, and took him to a home for the treatment of addicts. Addicts from wealthy families, of course. The treatment itself was simple: mostly, time. The attendants administered teas and other herbs of doubtful usefulness, restrained the addict, cleaned up the diarrhea and vomit, and waited. The walls were thick, the cells separate and private. Kylar had no trouble with the guards, who took one look, saw an addict, and let them in.

"Please restrain me," the Ladeshian said as they entered a tiny cell. There was a writing desk, a chair, a basin and pitcher, and a bed, but the walls were blank brick. It was deliberately spartan. The fewer things in the room, the less likely a suicide attempt would be successful.

"I don't think you'll get out of control for a few hours at the least," Kylar said.

"Don't be so sure."

So Kylar bound him to the bed with the thick leather straps and the man looked relieved. He smiled his gap-toothed addict's smile. It turned Kylar's stomach. Hadn't this man once had a brilliant smile?

"Who are you?" Kylar asked. "And what is it you think you know about me?"

"I know that you have a ka'kari, Kylar Stern. I knew Durzo Blint and I know you were his apprentice and I know this is your second incarnation. You used to be called Azoth."

Kylar's stomach flipped. "Who are you?"

The man smiled again, a huge smile, as if he had gotten so used to smiling to show his perfect white teeth that he hadn't yet adjusted to his addict's grin. Oddly, now that he was bound, he seemed arrogant. "I am Aristarchos ban Ebron, shalakroi of Benyurien in the Silk province of Ladesh."

"Is shalakroi the Ladeshian name for a riot weed addict?"

The hauteur fell from the man's face like a load of bricks. "No. I'm sorry. And I'm sorry for the attempt on your life. I wasn't in control of myself."

"I could tell."

"I don't think you understand," Aristarchos said.

"I've seen addicts before."

"I'm not just an addict, Kylar." He smiled a wry, lopsided smile that showed more of his rotten teeth. "Same thing every addict would say, huh? I tried to get out of Cenaria when the city fell, but my Ladeshian skin betrayed me. The Khalidorans stopped me and interrogated me about the silk trade. They hate the silk monopoly as much as the rest of you Midcyri. That interrogation would have been fine, but a Vürdmeister named Neph Dada saw me. He has the Viewing. I don't know what he saw, but they began torturing me." His eyes grew distant. "That was bad. What was worse was that they force-fed me some seeds after every time. They took the pain away. They made everything better. I didn't even recognize what they were. The Khalidorans didn't let me sleep. They'd just torture me, feed me seeds, torture me. They didn't even ask questions until he came."

"He?" Kylar felt sick to his stomach.

"I...fear to speak his name," Aristarchos said, ashamed of his fear and yet frightened to silence nonetheless. He began drumming his fingers.

"The Godking?"

He nodded. "The cycle just kept going until they didn't have to force the seeds on me anymore. I begged for them. The second time he came, he used magic on me....He's fascinated with compulsion. Magical, chemical, and blends of the two, he said. I was just another experiment. After a while, I...I gave them your name, Kylar. He laid a compulsion on me to kill you. I had a box with my seeds in it that would only open once I obeyed." A tremor passed through him. "You see? I tried riot weed to get me by. I tried poppy wine. Nothing works. I thought if I could get here fast enough, I could warn you. I did hold some things back. They don't know you come back from death. They don't know about the Society or your incarnations."

It was all going too fast for Kylar. The implications were exploding in a hundred different directions. "What society?" Kylar said.

Aristarchos looked incredulous, his fingers even stopped their drumming. "Durzo never told you?"

"Not a word."

" 'The Society of the Second Dawn ' "

"Never heard of it."

" 'The Society of the Second Dawn is devoted to the study of reputed immortals, the delineations of their abilities, and the confinement of said powers to those who would not abuse them.' We're a secret society, spread over all the world. It's how I was able to find you. We were founded centuries ago. Back then we thought there were dozens of immortals. Over the years, we concluded that there were at most seven, and maybe just one. The man you knew as Durzo Blint was also Ferric Fireheart, Vin Craysin, Tal Drakkan, Yric the Black, Hrothan Steelbender, Zak Eurthkin, Rebus Nimble, Qos Delanoesh, X!rutic Ur, Mir Graggor, Pips McClawski, Garric Shadowbane, Dav Slinker, and probably a dozen others we don't know."

"That's half the stories of Midcryu."

Aristarchos was starting to shiver and sweat, but he continued in a level voice, "He successfully masqueraded as a native of at least a dozen different cultures, probably twice that. He spoke more languages than I've even heard of—at least thirty, not counting dialects—and all of them so fluently natives couldn't detect an accent. There were times when he would disappear for twenty or even fifty years—we don't know if he lived in solitude or married and settled down in remote regions. But he appeared in every major conflict for six centuries, and not always on the side you would expect. Two hundred years ago, as Hrothan Steelbender, he fought with the Alitaeran expansion campaigns for the first thirty years of the Hundred Years' War, and then 'died' and fought with the Ceurans against them as the sword-saint Oturo Kenji."

Now it was Kylar who was shivering. He remembered when his guild had tried to mug Durzo. When they saw who he was, they shrank back from the legendary wetboy. Legendary wetboy! How little they knew. How little Kylar had known. He felt an unreasoning stab of resentment.

How could Durzo not tell him? He'd been like a son to the man. He'd been closer to him than anyone—and he hadn't told Kylar anything. Kylar had only seen a bitter, superstitious shell of a man, and thought himself somehow superior to him.

Kylar hadn't known Durzo Blint at all. And now the hero out of legends—dozens of legends—was dead. Dead at Kylar's hands. Kylar had destroyed something without knowing its worth. He hadn't known the man he'd called his master and now he never would. It felt like a hole in his stomach. He felt numb and distant and angry and near tears all at once. Durzo was dead, and Kylar missed him more than he could have imagined.

The beads of sweat were sticking out on Aristarchos's face now. He had wadded the bed sheets in his fists. "If you have any questions you need to ask me about his incarnations or yours or anything at all, please ask quickly. I'm not...feeling well."

"Why do you keep saying incarnations like I'm some kind of god?" It wasn't a great question, but the real questions were so big that Kylar didn't even know how to ask them.

"You are worshipped in a few remote areas where your master wasn't very careful about showing the full extent of his powers."

"What?!"

"The Society says incarnations because 'lives' is too confusing, and we aren't sure if you have as many lives as you want, or a finite number, or just one life that never ends. None of us have ever actually seen you die. 'Incarnations' has its critics, too, but that's mainly among the Modaini separatists who believe in reincarnation. Let me tell you, your existence really throws them for a theological loop." Aristarchos's legs were twitching, almost convulsing. "I'm sorry," he said, "there's so much I wish I could tell you. So much I wish I could ask."

Suddenly, among all the big questions about Durzo, about Kylar's powers, about the Godking and what he knew or thought he knew, Kylar just saw a man sweating on a bed, a man who'd lost his teeth and his good looks for Kylar, a man who'd been tortured and made an addict, who'd been compelled to try to kill Kylar and had fought against it with everything he had. He'd done all that for a man he didn't even know.

So Kylar didn't ask about the Society, or magic, or what Aristarchos could do for him. That could come later, if they both lived until later. "Aristarchos," he said, "what is a shalakroi?"

The man was taken off guard. "I—it's a little below a Midcyri duke, but it's not an inherited position. I scored better than ten thousand other students on the Civil Service examinations. Only a hundred scored higher in all Ladesh. I ruled an area roughly the size of Cenaria."

"The city?"

Aristarchos smiled through his sweat and clenched muscles. "The country."

"It's an honor to meet you, Aristarchos ban Ebron, shalakroi of Benyurien."

"The honor is mine, Kylar ban Durzo. Please, will you kill me?"

Kylar turned his back on the man.

Pride and hope whooshed out of Aristarchos with his breath. He slumped in the bed, suddenly small. "This is no kindness, my lord." He convulsed again, and strained against the leather bonds. His veins bulged on his forehead and his emaciated arms "Please!" he said as the convulsion passed. "Please, if you won't kill me, will you give me my box? Just one seed? Please?"

Kylar left. He took the box and burned it. Aside from a poisoned-needle trap, it was empty.

20

Your Holiness, our assassin is dead," Neph Dada said as he stepped onto the Godking's balcony. "I apologize to report this failure, though I do wish to point out that I recommended—"

"He didn't fail," Garoth Ursuul said, not turning from his view of the city.

Neph opened his mouth, remembered to whom he was speaking, and closed it. He hunched a little lower.

"I gave him a task he could thwart so that he might accomplish the one I desired," the Godking said. Still staring over the city, he massaged his temples. "He found Kylar Stern. Our ka'karifer is in Caernarvon."

He picked a note from his pocket. "Transmit this message to our agent there to give to Vi Sovari. She should be arriving any day."

Neph blinked convulsively. He'd thought he knew everything the Godking was doing. He'd thought that his own mastery of the vir was within a hairsbreadth of the Godking's, and now, blithely, the man had given him this. It set Neph's ambitions back months. Months! How he hated the man. Garoth could track exact locations magically? Neph had never heard of such a thing. What did it mean? Did Garoth know about the camp at Black Barrow? Neph's meisters had been abducting villagers for his experiments, but it was so far away, Neph had been so careful. No, it couldn't be that.

But the Godking was giving him notice. He was telling Neph that he had his eye on him, that he had his eye on everything, that he would always know more than he told even Neph, that his powers would always be beyond what Neph expected. As the Godking's warnings went, it was gentle.

"Is there something else?" the Godking asked.

"No, Your Holiness," Neph said. He managed to keep his voice perfectly calm.

"Then begone."

Despite all the reasons he had to be grumpy, when Elene was in a good mood, it was hard not to be happy. After a quick breakfast and a cup of ootai to stave off weariness, Kylar found himself wandering the streets with her, hand in hand. She was wearing a cream-colored dress with a brown taffeta bodice the color of her eyes. It looked fabulous in its simplicity. Of course, Kylar had never seen Elene wear anything that he thought looked less than great, but when she was happy she was twice as beautiful as usual.

"This is cute, isn't it?" he asked, picking up a doll from a merchant's table. Why was Elene happy? He couldn't remember having done anything good.

Ever since he'd started going out at night, he'd expected to have The Talk. Instead, one night she'd grabbed his hand—he'd almost jumped out of his skin, so much for being the imperturbable wetboy—and she said, "Kylar, I love you, and I trust you."

She hadn't said anything since then. He sure hadn't. What was he supposed to say? "Um, actually, I have killed some people, but it was an accident every time, and they were all bad"?

"I don't think we can really afford much," Elene said. "I just wanted to spend the day with you." She smiled. Maybe it was just a mood swing. Mood swings had to have an up side, right?

"Oh," he said. He only felt a little awkward holding hands with her. At first, he'd felt like everyone was staring at them. Now, though, he saw that only a few people looked at them twice, and of those, most seemed to be approving.

"Aha!" a round little man bellowed at them. "Perfect. Perfect. Absolutely lovely. Marvelous, you are. Yes, yes, come right in."

Kylar was so startled he barely stopped himself from a quickly rearranging the man's face. Elene laughed and poked the tense muscles of Kylar's arm. "Come on, brawny," she said. "This is shopping. It's fun."

"Fun?" he asked as she pulled him into the little well-lit shop.

The fat little man quickly handed them off to a pretty girl of maybe seventeen who smiled brightly at them. She was petite, with a slender figure, dazzling blue eyes, and a large mouth that made her smile huge. It was Golden Hair. Kylar goggled as his daylight and shadow worlds crossed.

"Hello," Golden Hair said. She glanced down at the wedding bands on their hands. "I'm Capricia. Have you ever been to a ringcry before?"

After Kylar didn't say anything for a long moment, Elene gently dug an elbow into his ribs. "No," she said.

Kylar blinked. Elene was shaking her head at him, obviously thinking he was ogling Capricia, but she didn't look mad, just bemused. He shook his head, *No, it's not like that.*

She cocked an eyebrow at him. *Right.*

"Well, let's start at the beginning then," Capricia said, pulling out a wide drawer lined with black velvet and putting it on a counter. It was filled with tiny, paired rings of gold and silver and bronze, some decorated with rubies or garnets or amethyst or diamonds or opals, some plain, some textured. "You've seen people wearing these all over the city, right?"

Elene nodded. Kylar looked at her blankly. He looked at Capricia. She wasn't wearing one, not that he could see. Were they toe-rings? He stood on his tiptoes to see over the counter to see Capricia's feet.

Capricia caught him looking and laughed. She had the kind of laugh that made you want to join in, even when she was laughing at you. "No, no," she said. "I don't wear one! I'm not married. Why are you looking at my feet?"

Elene slapped her forehead. "Men!"

"Oh," Kylar said. "They're earrings!"

Capricia laughed again.

"What?" he asked. "Women wear matching earrings where we come from. These are all different sizes."

The girls laughed louder and it dawned on him. The earrings weren't for women; they were for couples. One for the man; one for the woman. "Oh," he said.

That would explain all the men he'd seen wearing earrings. He scowled. He could have said which men were concealing weapons in their clothing and known their likely degrees of proficiency with them; what did he care about what they wore in their ears?

"Wow. Look at those," Elene said, pointing a pair of silvery-gold sparkling rings that looked suspiciously expensive. "Aren't they beautiful?" She turned to Capricia. "Will you tell us all about the rings? We're, ahem, a little unfamiliar with the tradition." Conspicuously, they didn't look at Kylar.

"Here in Waeddryn, when a man wishes to marry a woman, he buys a set of rings and gives them to her. Of course, there is a public ceremony, but the wedding itself is performed in private. You two are married already, right?"

"Right," Kylar said. "We're just new to the city."

"Well, if you're looking to get married in the Waeddryner way, but maybe don't have the money or the inclination for a big ceremony, it's very simple. You don't have to worry about the ceremony at all. The marriage is recognized as long as you've been nailed."

"Nailed?" Kylar asked, his eyes widening.

Capricia flushed. "I mean, as long as you've affixed the seal of your love, or been ringed. But, well, most people just call it getting nailed."

"I'm guessing that's not part of the usual pitch," Kylar said.

"Kylar," Elene said, elbowing him as Capricia flushed again. "Can we see the wedding knives?" she asked sweetly.

Capricia pulled out another drawer lined with black velvet. It was full of ornate daggers with tiny tips.

Kylar recoiled.

Capricia and Elene giggled. "It gets scarier," Capricia said. She smiled her huge smile. "Generally right before...ah, right before the marriage is consummated," she was trying to sound professional, but her ears were bright pink. "Sorry, I've never actually had to explain this. I—Master Bourary usually—never mind. When a man and woman marry, the woman has to give up a lot of her freedom."

"The woman does?" Kylar asked. The look Elene gave him this time was less amused. He swallowed his laughter.

"So the nailing—the ringing or affixing of the seal—"

"Just call it nailing," Kylar said.

"I slipped up, I'm really supposed to call it—" she saw the look on Kylar's face "—right. When the bride and groom retire to their bedchamber, the man gives the rings and the wedding knife to the bride. The man must submit to her. Often, she will..." Capricia blinked and her ears went pink again. She cleared her throat. "Often, she will entice the groom for some time. Then she pierces her own left ear wherever she desires and places her ring there. Then she sits astride her husband on the marriage bed and pierces his left ear."

Kylar's mouth dropped open.

"It's not that bad. It just depends on where your wife decides to—" Capricia looked up as Master Bourary walked into the shop, "affix the seal. Through the ear lobe isn't that bad, but some women will pierce, well, like Master Bourary's wife."

Kylar looked at the round, grinning little man. He wore a glittering gold earring sparkling with rubies. It was through the top of his ear. "Hurt like hell," Master Bourary said. "They call it breaking the maidenhead."

A little moue of pain escaped Kylar's lips. "What?"

Elene was blushing, but her eyes were dancing. For a second he could swear that she was imagining nailing him.

"Well, it's only fair, isn't it?" Master Bourary said. "If a woman has to deal with pain and blood on her wedding night, why shouldn't a man? I tell you what, it makes you gentler. Especially if she twists your ear to remind you!" He guffawed. "That's what you get after twenty generations of queens." He laughed ruefully, but he didn't seem displeased by it.

These people, Kylar realized, were totally mad.

"But that's not the magical part," Capricia said, realizing Kylar was fast losing interest. "When the wife places the ring on her husband's ear, she has to focus all of her love and devotion and desire to be married on the ring, and only then will it seal. If the woman doesn't truly want to be married, it won't even seal."

"But once sealed," Master Bourary said, "neither heaven nor hell can open the ring again. Look," he said. He reached over and slipped the wedding ring off of Kylar's left hand. "Barely a difference in the tan under your ring, huh? Haven't been hitched long?"

"You could make some good ring mail with that trick," Kylar said, trying to circumvent the pitch.

"Oh, honey, stop it, I'm swooning," Elene said, tugging at the bodice of her dress as if she were getting overheated. "You're so romantic."

"Well, actually," Master Bourary said, "the first practitioners of our art were armorers. But look," he said, turning his attention to Elene, obviously seeing her as a more friendly target for his pitch. "With this ring, he can slip it off, it could fall off by itself, who knows? He goes to a tavern and bumps into some tart, and how's she to know that she's poaching on another woman's land? Not that you would ever do that, of course, sir. But with our rings, a married man is always known to be married. Really it's a protection even for women who would flirt with a man without realizing he was married.

"And . . . if a man or woman wants a divorce—well, you've got to rip that damn ring right out of your ear. Cuts down on divorces, I promise you. But affixing the seal isn't done out of fear, to keep a man or a woman from cuckolding their spouse. It's deeper than that. When a man and woman are sealed, they activate an ancient magic in these rings, a magic that grows as their love grows. It's a magic that helps you feel what your spouse is feeling, a magic that deepens your love and understanding for each other, that helps you communicate more clearly, that—"

"And let me guess," Kylar said. "The more expensive rings have more magic."

Elene's elbow was anything but gentle this time. "Kylar," she said through her teeth.

Master Bourary blinked. "Let me assure you, young master, every ring I make is imbued with magic, even the simplest and cheapest copper band of mine won't break. But yes, I absolutely do spend more time and energy on the gold and mistarille rings. Not only because the people who buy those rings pay more, but also because those materials hold a spell far better than copper or bronze or silver ever could."

"Right," Kylar said. "Well, thanks for your time." He pulled Elene out of the store.

She was not pleased. She stopped in the street. "Kylar, you are a complete ass."

"Honey, didn't you hear what he just said? Some armorer a long time ago had a Talent that would seal metal rings together. Good talent for an armorer, he can bang out ring mail in days rather than months. Then he gets smart and figures that he can make a lot more money by selling each ring for hundreds of gold than for selling a full set of ring mail for maybe fifty. And lo and behold, an industry's born. It's all horseshit. All that 'growing to understand each other better' stuff? That's what happens to everyone who gets married. And oh, the gold ones have more magic ... how obvious is that? Did you see how many of their rings were gold? They probably get nine tenths of the poor idiots in this city to save up for a gold ring they can't afford because what woman is going to be happy if she gets a copper ring that 'barely holds the spell'?"

"I would," she said quietly.

It took the wind out of him.

She covered her face. "I thought if you ever wanted to get married for real, that, you know. It would be a way we could make it official. If we ever wanted to. I mean, I know we're not ready for that. I'm not suggesting that we do that right away or anything."

Why am I always the asshole?

Because she's too good for you.

"So you knew what that place was?" he asked, more gently, although he was still pissed off, though he couldn't have said whether it was at her or at himself.

"Aunt Mea told me about it."

"Is that why you've been nibbling on my ears at night?"

"Kylar!" she said.

"Is it?"

"Aunt Mea said it works wonders." Elene couldn't meet his gaze; she was totally mortified.

"Well maybe for these twists!"

"Kylar!" Elene raised her eyebrows, as if to say, *We are in the middle of a crowded market, would you shut up?*

He looked around. He'd never seen so many earrings in his life. How hadn't he noticed it before? And he was right, almost every one of them was gold and everyone wore their hair in ways that left their ears exposed.

"I've seen that girl before," Kylar said.

"Capricia?"

"I was out the other night and some hoodlums were coming to hurt her. Before, I would have killed them. Instead, I scared them."

She looked uncertain why he was telling her this now. "Well, that's great. You see? Violence doesn't solve—"

"Honey, one of them was the Shinga. I made a vengeful man *wet* himself in front of his subordinates. Violence was the only solution. That girl's in deeper trouble now than before I helped her." He swore under his breath. "Why'd you even take me in there? We don't even have enough to buy Uly a birthday present. How would we afford those?"

"I'm sorry, all right?" Elene said. "I just wanted to see what it was like."

"It's the sword, isn't it? You still want me to sell the sword."

"Quit it! I haven't said anything about the sword. I'm sorry. I thought you might be interested. I'm not asking you to buy me anything." She wasn't looking at him now, and she certainly wasn't holding his hand. Well, that was better than tears. Wasn't it?

He walked beside her for a while as she pretended to browse through the open air shops, picking up produce, examining cloth, looking at dolls they couldn't afford.

"So," he said finally. "Since we're already fighting..."

She turned and looked up at him, not laughing. "I don't want to talk about sex, Kylar."

He raised his hands in mock surrender. Still trying to be funny. Still failing.

"Kylar, do you remember how it feels to kill?"

He didn't have to think back that far. It was triumphant, the terrible pleasure of mastery, followed by desolation, a sick hollowness in his chest, knowing that even a hardened criminal might have changed and now would never have that chance. Did she understand part of him loved it?

"Honey, we all only have so much time and so many gifts. You have more gifts than most, and I know you want to do good. I know you're passionate about that, and I love that about you. But look what happens when you try to save the world with a sword. Your master tried, and look what a bitter, sad old man he became. I don't want to see that happen to you. I know that after the wealth you had and the things you did that being an apothecary seems like a small ambition. It's not small, Kylar. It's huge. You can do so much more good for the world by being a good father, and a good husband, and a healer, than you ever could by being a killer. Do you think it's a mistake the God has given you an ability to heal? That's the divine economy. He is willing to cover over what we've destroyed with new and beautiful things.

"Like us. Who'd have imagined that you and I could get safely off the streets and find each other again? Who would have imagined we could adopt Uly? She's got a chance now—after being born to an assassin and a madam. Only the God could do that, Kylar. I know you don't believe in him yet, but his hand is at work here. He's given us this chance, and I want to hold onto it. Stay with me. Leave that life. You weren't happy there. Why would you want to go back?"

"I don't," he said. But it was only half true. Elene came into his arms, but even as he held her, he knew he was false.

21

In the early afternoon heat, Kylar paused outside a shop in the nobles' district. He stepped into an alley and thirty seconds later thought that he was wearing a fair facsimile of Baron Kirof's face. He wished he'd thought to change into a nicer tunic. Of course, after the fire, he only had one other tunic, and it was worse than this one. It was probably possible to wear illusory clothes like his illusory face, but that was too much for Kylar to juggle—he imagined trying to make an illusory robe flap realistically as he moved and quickly decided his own clothes would do. He tucked the box under his arm and headed inside.

Grand Master Haylin's shop was a huge, squat square. The inside was well-lit and more richly appointed than any smithy Kylar had ever seen. Row on row of armor lined the walls, and rack on rack of weapons sat before them. It was clean, too, and hardly smoky—Grand Master Haylin must have figured out a clever flue system, because the sales area and the work area weren't separated. Kylar saw one of the under-armorers helping a noble pick out the ore that would become his sword. Another noble watched as apprentices hammered on steel that would become his cuirass. The customers were funneled through the work area, confined to special blue rugs so they didn't get in the way of the apprentices and journeymen. It was a good gimmick, and doubtless worth its weight in gold. Though whether the nobles were paying for great weapons and armor or just an experience, Kylar wasn't sure.

The racks of weapons and armor here by the door were nothing special, doubtless the work of the under-armorers and journeymen. But that wasn't what he was looking for. Kylar looked to the back and finally saw the man himself.

Grand Master Haylin was mostly bald, with a fringe of gray hair around a knobby pate. He was lean and stooped and appeared to be near-sighted, though of course he had the muscular shoulders and arms of a much younger man. His leather apron was pitted and stained from work, and he was guiding an apprentice's hand, showing the boy the correct angle to strike the metal. Kylar headed toward him.

"Excuse me? Hello, my lord, how may I help you?" a smiling young man said, intercepting him. He was a little too smiley.

"I need to speak with the Grand Master," Kylar said, the sinking feeling in his stomach telling him that Haylin was going to prove to be much farther away than just across the shop.

"I'm afraid he's working, but I'd be happy to help you with whatever you require." Smiley's brief glance down at Kylar's clothes told him he didn't expect this to be important. Just what Kylar needed: some bureaucratic *lut*.

Kylar looked over Smiley's shoulder and gaped. It was an expression he'd never tried with Baron Kirof's face, but it must have been acceptable, because Smiley turned to see what was wrong.

Kylar went invisible. He felt like a bad child when Smiley turned around and saw no one there.

"What the...?" Smiley said. He rubbed his eyes. "Hey," he said to a coworker behind the counter, "did you just see me talking to a fat red-bearded guy?"

The man behind the counter shook his head. "You seein' things again, Wood?"

Smiley shook his head and walked back toward the counter, cursing under his breath.

Kylar walked through the shop, invisible. Dodging scurrying apprentices, he came to stand by Grand Master Haylin's elbow. The man was inspecting a dozen of his under-armorer's swords that were laid out on a table for his approval.

"The third one wasn't properly fired," Kylar said, appearing behind the smith. "There's a weakness right just above the hilt. And the next one's poorly tempered."

Grand Master Haylin turned and looked at Kylar's feet—two paces outside the blue carpet, then he looked at the weak sword. He tossed it into an empty red crate. "Werner," Haylin said to a young man who was swearing at an apprentice. "That's the third reject this month. One more and you're done."

Werner blanched. He immediately left off cursing the apprentice.

"As for this," Grand Master Haylin said to Kylar, gesturing to the poorly tempered sword. "You know what happens when you scatter diamonds in front of chickens?"

"Tough poultry?"

"Valuable gizzards. It's a waste, son. This is for an army order. For two hundred fifty queens for a hundred swords, some peasant sword swinger can spend more time with a whetstone. You know your swords, but I'm a busy man. What do you want?"

"Five minutes. Privately. It'll be worth your time."

The Grand Master raised an eyebrow but acquiesced. He led Kylar up the stairs to a special room. As they passed Smiley, the young man said, "You can't—you can't—"

Grand Master Haylin cocked an eyebrow at the young man. Smiley's greasy smile withered. "Don't mind that," Haylin said. "That's my fifth son. Bit of a throw-off, huh?"

Kylar didn't know what that meant, but he nodded. "I'd toss him in the reject crate."

Haylin laughed. "Wish I could do the same with his mother. My third wife is the answer to all the first two's prayers."

The special room was obviously used as infrequently as possible. A fine walnut table with several chairs occupied the center, but most of the room was given to display cases. Fine swords and expensive suits of armor filled the room like an elite guard. Kylar looked at them closely. Several were the Grand Master's work: master pieces to demonstrate what he was capable of, but others were old, in a variety of styles and periods of armament, show pieces. Perfect.

"You're down to three minutes," Haylin said, squinting at Kylar.

"I'm a man of special talents," Kylar said, sitting across from the man.

The Grand Master arched an eyebrow again. He did have terrifically expressive eyebrows.

Kylar ran his fingers through his red hair and changed it to dirty blond. He passed his hand over his face and his nose grew sharper, longer. He scrubbed his face as if washing it, and the beard disappeared to reveal lightly pockmarked cheeks and sharp eyes. Of course, it was all show. He didn't have to touch his face—but this man seemed to appreciate demonstrations.

Grand Master Haylin's face went dead white and his jaw dropped. He blinked rapidly and his voice came out as a croak. He cleared his throat. "Master Starfire? Gaelan Starfire?"

"You know me?" Kylar asked, stunned. Gaelan Starfire was the hero of a dozen bard's tales. But the face Kylar was wearing was Durzo Blint's.

"I was—I was just a boy when you came to my grandfather's shop. You said—you said you might come back long after we'd given up on you. Oh, sir! My grandfather said it might be in my father's time or mine, but we never believed him."

Disoriented, Kylar tried to think. Durzo was Gaelan Starfire? Kylar knew that Durzo hadn't been known by the same name for seven hundred years, of course. But *Gaelan Starfire?* That name hadn't even been mentioned among all the others that Aristarchos had claimed for his master.

It sent a pang of grief through Kylar. He hadn't known, and some smith in Caernarvon had. How little he knew the man who'd raised him, the man who'd died for him. Durzo had turned bitter by the time Kylar had known him. Who had he been when he'd been Gaelan Starfire, fifty years ago? Kylar suspected that he could have been friends with that man.

"We've kept it secret, I swear," Grand Master Haylin said. Kylar was still disoriented. This man, who was old enough to be his grandfather, who was at the height of his fame, was treating Kylar like—like he was an immortal, nearly a god. "What can I do for you, my lord?"

"I don't, I don't..." Kylar said. "Please, don't treat me differently because of your grandfather. I just wanted you to take me seriously; I didn't think you'd remember that. I didn't even remember you. You've changed quite a bit." He smirked to seal the lie.

"And you haven't changed at all," Haylin said, stunned. "Um, all right," he said, his eyebrows waggling up and down in quick succession as he tried to pull himself together. "Um. Well. What are you looking for?"

"I'm looking to sell a sword." Kylar drew Retribution off his back and laid it on the table.

Haylin picked up the big sword appreciatively in his thick, callused hands, then immediately set it down. He stared at the hilt, blinking. He ran his fingers over it, his eyes wide. "You never drop this sword, do you?" he said.

Kylar shrugged. Of course he didn't.

Still looking like he wasn't sure he was awake, the Grand Master spit on his palm and grabbed the sword again.

"What'd you—"

A drop of moisture wicked off the hilt onto the table. Grand Master Haylin released the sword and opened his palm. It was completely dry. He gave a little cry, but he couldn't take his eyes off the sword. He leaned closer and closer until his nose was almost against it. He turned the blade to look at it on edge.

"By the gods," he said. "It's true."

"What?" Kylar said.

"The coal matrices. They're perfect. I'd bet my right arm every last one has four links, don't they? The blade's a perfect diamond, my lord. So thin you can barely see it, but unbreakable. Most diamonds can be sheared with another diamond, because they're never perfect, but if there are no flaws anywhere—this blade is indestructible, and not just the blade, the hilt, too. But my lord, if this is . . . I thought your sword was black."

Kylar touched the blade and let the ka'kari whoosh out of his skin to cover it. The word MERCY inscribed in the blade was covered with JUSTICE in ka'kari black.

Grand Master Haylin looked pained. "Oh my lord. . . . My grandfather told us. . . . I never understood. I feel blind, yet I'm almost happy for my blindness."

"What are you talking about?"

"I don't have the Talent, Lord Starfire. I can't begin to see how amazing this blade is. My grandfather could, and he said it haunted him all his days. He knew what Talent had gone into this blade, he could see it, but he could never equal it. He said it made the work of his own hands look cheap and tawdry—and he was famous for his work. But I never thought to see Retribution with my own eyes. My lord, you can't sell this."

"Well, it doesn't come in black," Kylar said lightly, sucking the ka'kari back into his hand. "If that knocks a bit off the price."

"My lord, you don't understand. Even if I could give you what this is worth—even if I could somehow fix a price on it—I could never—it's worth more than I'll make in my whole life. Even if I could buy it, I could never sell it; it's too valuable. Maybe one or two collectors in the world have the wealth and the appreciation to buy such a sword. Even then, my lord, this isn't a sword that belongs on display, it belongs in the hand of a hero. It belongs in your hand. Look, a hilt that won't slip from your hand even if it's bloody or wet. The moisture slides right off. It's not just brilliant, it's practical. That's not a showpiece. It's art. It's killing art. Like you." He threw his hands up and slumped in his chair, as if exhausted just by the sight of Retribution. "Though my grandfather did say the inscription was in Hyrillic—oh my."

The MERCY on the blade shifted before their eyes, into a language Kylar couldn't read. He was stunned. It had never done that before.

A snake wriggled in his stomach and strangled his guts, a snake of losing something whose value he couldn't even calculate. It was the same feeling he felt as he thought of his dead master, a man whose worth he had barely known.

"Nonetheless," he said, his throat tight. "I must sell it." If he kept it, he would kill again. He had no doubt of it. In his hand, it was pitiless justice. He had to sell it, if he was to stay true to Elene. As long as he held onto the sword, he held onto his old life.

"My lord, do you need money? I'll give you whatever you want."

The small, mean part of Kylar considered it. Surely this man could spare more than enough money for what Kylar needed. "No, I, I need to sell it. It's . . . it has to do with a woman."

"You're selling an artifact worth a kingdom so you can be with a woman? You're immortal! Even the longest marriage will end in a tiny fraction of your life!"

Kylar grimaced. "That's right."

"You're not just selling this sword, are you? You're giving it up. You're giving up the way of the sword."

Looking at the tabletop, Kylar nodded.

"She must be some woman."

"She is," Kylar said. "What can you give me for it?"

"It depends on how soon you need it."

Kylar didn't know if he could keep his courage up. He knew what he was about to say would probably cost him thousands, but losing Elene would cost more. He'd never really cared about being rich anyway. "Just whatever you can get me before I leave."

"Before you leave the city?"

"Before I leave the shop." Kylar swallowed, but that damn lump wouldn't disappear.

The Grand Master opened his mouth to protest, but he could see Kylar's mind was made up. "Thirty-one thousand queens," he said. "Maybe a few hundred more, depending on what sales we've done today. Six thousand in gold, the rest in promissory notes redeemable at most money changers, though for that sum, you'd have to hit half the money changers in the city. You'll have to go to the Blue Giant directly if you want to change it all."

Kylar goggled at the sum. It would be enough buy a house, repay Aunt Mea, start a shop with a huge inventory, buy an entire wardrobe for Elene, and still put some away, in addition to buying a pair of the finest wedding rings money could buy. And the man was protesting it wasn't nearly enough?

~A good price for your birthright, huh?~

The thought almost took the wind out of Kylar. He stood abruptly. "Done," he said. He walked to the door and grabbed it.

"Um...my lord," Grand Master Haylin said. He gestured to his own face.

"Oh." Kylar concentrated and his features fattened and his hair reddened again.

Within five minutes, a still-stunned Smiley had helped load a chest of sovereigns—worth twenty queens each—and watched as his father put a thick wad of promissory notes on top of that. It totaled 31,400 queens. The chest wasn't large, but it weighed as much as two large men. The Grand Master called for a horse, but Kylar asked if they would put two broad leather straps on it instead. Journeymen and apprentices stopped to watch, but Kylar didn't care. Smirking, Haylin attached them himself.

"My lord," Haylin said, finishing with the straps. "If you ever want it back, it's here."

"Perhaps. In your grandsons' time."

Grandmaster Haylin smiled broadly.

Kylar knew he shouldn't have said it so loudly. He shouldn't have waved off the horse. He didn't care. Somehow, it just felt so good to be speaking with a man who knew something of what he was and wasn't afraid or disgusted—even if the man did think he was his master. But then, Kylar was probably more like Gaelan Starfire than Durzo Blint had been anyway. It felt so good to be known and accepted, he didn't care that he was being reckless.

With a surge of his Talent, Kylar hoisted the chest onto his back. Open gasps filled the smithy. The truth was, it was almost too heavy to carry even with the Talent. Kylar nodded to Grand Master Haylin and walked out.

"Who the hell was that?" Kylar heard Smiley ask.

"Someday, when you're ready, I might tell you," the Grand Master said.

22

*H*ello," Kylar said to Capricia when he returned to the ringery.

"Hello," she said, surprised. She was alone, closing up the shop.

"The ass is back." He grimaced. "Sorry about...before."

"What?" she said. "No, you were fine. I understand that it all seems strange if you're not from here. Men never like it—though the women have to pierce their ears, too, and they never complain." She shrugged.

"Right, well..." Kylar said, then he realized he had nothing to say. What was it about jewelry that made him feel inadequate? "Right," he finished lamely.

"Honestly," she said, "most men barely notice the pain. I mean, their brides make sure they're distracted. Technically, you consummate the marriage only after the nailing, but most cases, it's pretty much only technically."

Kylar coughed. He'd been thinking about that. "Uh, do you remember which ones she was pointing to?" Kylar asked.

"Of course," Capricia said. She laughed. "I'm afraid they're the ones that really hold the spells." Her eyes twinkled and he blushed.

"I have the misfortune of having a wife with excellent taste."

"It reflects well on her other choices," Capricia said, smiling her big smile at him. Whatever the fallout with the Shinga was going to be, Kylar was glad he'd saved her. She pulled out the drawer and set it in front of him. As she set it down, she scowled and grabbed a pair of rings out of the drawer. "Just a second," she said, and knelt behind the counter, tucking them away, then she stood back up. "I think it was one of these," she said, pointing to several along the top row of woven gold and mistarille entwined.

"How much are these?" he asked.

"Twenty-four hundred, twenty-eight hundred, and thirty-two hundred."

He whistled in spite of himself.

"We do have similar styles in white and yellow gold that are more affordable," Capricia said. "The mistarille makes them pretty ridiculous."

Jorsin Alkestes' sword had been mistarille with a core of hardened gold, Durzo said. It took a special forge to melt mistarille because it wouldn't melt until it was three times hotter than steel. Once it attained its working heat, it retained it for hours, unlike other metals that had to be reheated over and over. Smiths found it a pure joy and a pure terror to work with, because after that first heating and the first hours they had to work with, it wouldn't melt again. They only got one chance to get it right. Only a smith with substantial Talent could attempt any large-scale work with mistarille.

"Does anyone wear pure mistarille rings?" he asked as he scanned the rings. He could have sworn Elene's eyes had lit up when she saw one of these sets. Which one was it?

She shook her head. "Even if you could afford it, you wouldn't want it, Master Bourary says. He says that some of the simpler spells actually hold better in gold. Even the oldest rings combine the two metals. He has a pair that his great-great-great-something grandfather made that look like pure mistarille, but they contain a core of yellow gold and diamond. It's pretty amazing. He lined the mistarille with tiny holes so you can see the gold and diamonds sparkling through it if the light is right."

Kylar was almost starting to believe the talk about spells. Either Master Bourary was the real thing, or he'd been very careful to learn how to speak about magic from people who were.

It still felt like madness, to be looking at rings that cost two or three thousand gold. He should have asked Grand Master Haylin about the rings this afternoon. The Grand Master would have known if they were legitimate. But Kylar's heart was light. He'd already sold his birthright. He was committed. Now it was just a matter of finding the perfect ring to please the woman he loved, the woman who was saving him from becoming the bitter wreck Durzo Blint had become.

Really, the magic in the rings didn't matter. What mattered was letting Elene know what she was worth to him.

"There was one set, I swear it was in this box," Kylar told Capricia. "What were those ones you put away?"

"Those were just a display set—well, not actually a display set. The queen got furious with a gem merchant who wouldn't sell her some jewels a decade ago and she outlawed display sets. So it's not technically a display set, but it's not really for sale. We have other drawers; it might have been in one of those."

"Just show me the ones I asked about," Kylar said. He was suddenly skeptical. Was this a sales ploy? He'd seen it done before—a pretty girl tells a guy, "Here, this is very nice," as she sets aside something ridiculously expensive and pulls out something cheap, and the man instantly says, "What about those?" to prove his manhood.

But Capricia didn't come across like that. She seemed genuine. She pulled out the rings and set them in front of him. Just looking at them, Kylar could see the size of his shop's inventory shrinking.

"Those are the ones," he said. The design was seductively simple and elegant, a bare half-twist of silvery metal that somehow sparkled gold in the light when he picked up the larger one.

Capricia gasped and raised a hand as if he were going to break it. He gazed into one of the shop's mirrors and held up the earring by his left earlobe. It looked kind of effete, but then, apparently none of the thousands of men he'd seen around the city worried about looking effete.

"Hmm," he said. He moved the earring up higher on his ear. That looked a little more masculine. "What's the most painful place a woman can nail a guy?"

"Right about," she leaned forward and pointed, but he couldn't see it in the mirror. He moved and her finger touched his ear. "Oh!" she said. "I'm so sorry. I didn't mean to touch—"

"What?" he said. Then he remembered. "Oh, no, it's my fault. Seriously, where I come from, ears are no big deal. Did you say right here? So it goes over the top?" He checked the mirror. Yes, definitely more masculine, and it would hurt like hell. For some reason, that made him feel better.

He picked up the smaller earring and—being careful not to touch her— held it up to Capricia's ear. It was beautiful.

"I'll take them," he said.

"I'm really sorry," she said. "We don't have anything exactly like that for sale, but Master Bourary could make something that looks almost identical."

"You said there were no display items," Kylar said.

"Not technically. After the queen proclaimed the law—well, everything's for sale. They just put ridiculous prices on what they don't want to sell."

"And these are one of those?" Kylar asked. Now the house was getting smaller.

"These are actually the rings I was telling you about earlier. The ones Master Bourary's great-great-great grandfather made, mistarille over gold with diamonds?" She smiled weakly. "I'm sorry. I'm not trying to embarrass you. They weren't even supposed to be in this case."

"How ridiculous a price are we talking?" Kylar asked.

"Ridiculous," she said.

"How ridiculous?"

"Totally ridiculous." She winced.

Kylar sighed. "Just tell me."

"Thirty-one thousand four hundred queens. Sorry."

It hit Kylar in the stomach. It was a coincidence, of course, but...Elene would call it the divine economy. He'd sold Retribution for exactly what it would cost to marry her.

With nothing left over? *Elene, if this is your God's economy, you serve a niggardly God. I don't even have enough left to buy a wedding knife.*

"On the bright side," Capricia said, forcing a chuckle, "we'd throw in a wedding knife free."

A block of ice dropped into Kylar's stomach.

"I'm sorry," she said, mistaking the stricken expression on his face. "We do have some lovely—"

"You get paid a commission on your sales?" he asked.

"One-tenth of anything over a thousand in sales a day," she said.

"So, if you sold these, what would you do with—what?—more than three thousand queens?"

"I don't know—why are you—"

"What would you do?"

She shrugged and started to answer, stopped, and finally said, "I'd move my family. We live in a pretty rough neighborhood and we keep having trouble with—oh, what does it matter? Believe me, I've dreamed about it ever since I started working here. I thought about selling those rings and how it would change everything for us. I used to pray about it every day, but my mother says we're safe enough. Anyway, the God doesn't answer greedy prayers like that."

Kylar's heart went cold. They'd move away from that vengeful, arrogant little Shinga. Kylar wouldn't have to commit murder to keep them safe.

"No," Kylar said, pocketing the mistarille earrings and grabbing a wedding knife. "He answers them like this." He heaved the chest onto the counter and opened it. Capricia gaped. Her hands shook as she unfolded note after note. She looked up at Kylar, tears filling her eyes.

"Tell your parents your guardian angel said to move. Not next week. Not tomorrow. Tonight. When I saved you, I embarrassed the Shinga. He's sworn revenge."

Her eyes stayed huge, but she nodded imperceptibly. Her hand popped up like an automaton's. "Gift box?" she asked in a strangled voice. "Free."

He took the jewelry box from her hand and walked out the door, locking it behind him. He tucked the earrings in the decorative box, and dropped it all in a pocket, suddenly as poor as a pauper. He'd sold his birthright. He'd given away one of the last things he had to remember Durzo by. He'd traded a magical sword for two metal circles. And now he didn't have a copper to his name. Thirty-one thousand four hundred queens and he didn't even have enough left over to buy Uly a birthday present.

We're finished, God. From now on, you answer your own fucking prayers.

23

Are you and Elene going to be all right?" Uly asked. They were working together that evening, Uly fetching ingredients while Kylar brewed a draught that reduced fevers.

"Of course we are. Why?"

"Aunt Mea says it's fine you fight so much. She says that if I'm scared I just have to listen and if I hear the bed creaking after you fight, I'll know things will be all right. She says that means that you've made up. But I never hear the bed creaking."

Blood rushed to Kylar's cheeks. "I, well, I think . . . You know, that's a question you should ask Elene."

"She said to ask you, and she got all embarrassed too."

"I'm not embarrassed!" Kylar said. "Hand me the mayberry."

"Aunt Mea says it's wrong to lie. I've seen horses mating at the castle, but Aunt Mea says it's not scary like that."

"No," Kylar said quietly, mashing the mayberry with a pestle, "it's scary in its own way."

"What?" Uly asked.

"Uly, you are way too young for us to have this conversation. Yarrow root."

"Aunt Mea said you might say that. She said she'd talk to me about it if you were too embarrassed. She just made me promise to ask you first." Uly handed him the knotted brown root.

"Aunt Mea," Kylar said, "thinks about sex too much."

"Ahem," a voice said behind Kylar. He flinched.

"I'm going out to check on Mistress Vatsen," Aunt Mea said. "Do you need anything?"

"Um, uh, no," he said. Surely she couldn't have that bland look on her face if she'd heard what he just said.

"Kylar, are you all right?" she asked. She touched his hot cheek. "You look strangely flushed." She rummaged through the newly organized shelves—it seemed to take her longer than when they had been a mess—and tucked a few things in her basket. When she walked past Kylar, who was bent over the potion as if it took all of his concentration, she pinched his butt.

He practically hit the ceiling, though he strangled back a shout. Uly looked at him quizzically.

"You're right," Aunt Mea said at the door. "But don't you get any ideas. I'm too old for you."

Kylar flushed brighter and she laughed. He could hear her continuing to laugh heartily even as she walked down the street.

"Crazy old coot," he said. "Noranton seed."

Uly handed him the vial of flat, purplish seeds, and screwed her mouth into a tight line. "Kylar, if things don't work out with Elene, will you marry me?"

He dropped the entire vial into the mixture.

"WHAT?"

"I asked Elene how old you were and she said twenty. And Aunt Mea said her husband was nine years older than her and that's even further apart than you and me. And I love you and you love me and you and Elene fight all the time but you and me never fight..."

Kylar was confused at first. He and Elene hadn't fought for more than a week. Then he realized that Uly had been spending her nights over at one of her new friend's houses—probably because Kylar and Elene's fighting had upset her so much. Now Uly had an eager, scared look on her face that told him how he answered her could break her heart. Specifically, the first thought that popped into his head—I don't love you like that—was not going to be a good choice.

How did I get into this? I've got to be the first father in Midcyru to ever have to explain sex to his daughter while still a virgin myself.

What was he supposed to say? "I'm not actually married to Elene yet, so when we fight we can't make up the way I'd like. In fact, if we could make up the way I'd like, we probably wouldn't fight in the first place"? Kylar couldn't wait until he actually married Elene. All their conflicts about sex would finally be behind them. What a relief!

In the meantime, Uly was staring at him, waiting, big eyes wide, uncertain. Oh no, that looked like a lip quiver.

The opening door saved him. A well-dressed man stepped inside, a house crest embroidered in the chest of his tunic. He was tall and spare, but his face was pinched, making him look like a rodent.

"Is this Aunt Mea's?" he asked.

"Yes, it is," Kylar said. "But I'm afraid Aunt Mea just stepped out for a while."

"Oh that's fine," the man said. "You're her assistant, Kyle?"

"Kylar."

"Ah, yes. You're younger than I expected. I've come here for your help."

"Mine?"

"You're the man who saved Lord Aevan, aren't you? He's been telling everyone who will listen that you did with one potion what a dozen physickers couldn't with months of treatment. I am the head steward of High Lord Garazul. My lord has gout."

Kylar rubbed his jaw. He stared at the bottles lining the walls.

"I can return later if you wish," the steward said.

"No, it won't take a minute," Kylar said. He started grabbing bottles and giving orders to Uly. She was the perfect helper, quick and silent. He soon had four bowls mixing simultaneously, two over heat, two cold. In another two minutes, he was done. The steward looked utterly fascinated by the whole process. It made Kylar think that Grand Master Haylin was onto something in showing off the creation process. He knew in that moment that if he ever had a big shop, he'd set it up in exactly the same way—give people a show along with their potions. It was an oddly satisfying little dream.

"Here's what you need to do," Kylar said. "Give him two spoonfuls of this every four hours. I'm guessing your master is fat, hardly ever gets out? Loves his drink?"

The steward said, "He's got a little extra... well, yes, fat as a leviathan, in fact. Drinks like one, too."

"That potion will take care of the pain in his feet and joints. It will help the gout a little, but as long as he's fat and drinks a lot of wine, he'll never get better. He'll need to buy this same potion every time his gout flares up for the rest of his life. You tell him if he wants the gout gone, he needs to stop drinking. If he won't, which I'm betting will be the case, start putting two drops of this—" Kylar handed the man the second vial, "in every glass of his wine. It will give him a terrific headache. Make sure you do it every time he takes wine. While you're at it, you can give him this each morning and night for his bad stomach. And feed him less. Give a little of this last one with each meal, it should help him feel full sooner."

"How'd you know he had a bad stomach?"

Kylar smiled mysteriously. "And take him off everything else the physickers have ordered, especially the bloodletting and the leeches. He should be a new man in six weeks, if you make him lose weight."

"How much?" the steward asked.

"Depends on how fat he is," Kylar said.

The steward laughed. "No, how much do I owe you?"

Kylar thought about it. He did some math of what the ingredients had cost and doubled it. He told the steward.

The mousy man looked at him, astonished. "A bit of advice, young man. You should get a shop on the north side, because if this works, there's a lot of noble business that's going to be coming your way. And another thing: if this even helps a little, you should charge twice that. If it actually does what you said, you should charge ten times that—otherwise the nobles won't believe it's real."

Kylar smiled, warmed just to hear someone speak to him as if he knew what he was doing—which he did. "Well then, you owe me ten times what I said before."

The steward laughed. "If Lord Garazul gets better, I'll do better than that. Here's all I've got on me in the meantime." He tossed Kylar two new silver coins. "Good day, young master."

Watching the man go, Kylar was surprised how good it felt. Maybe it was better to heal than to kill. Or maybe it was just good to feel appreciated. How had Durzo done it? He'd been a dozen different heroes over the ages—maybe scores of different heroes. Hadn't he ever wanted to just announce himself? Tell everyone who he was, and have them show the proper awe? *Here I am, adore me.*

But Durzo had never come across like that. Kylar had grown up with him and had never had a clue that his master was the Night Angel, much less any of the other identities he'd had. Why not? Durzo had seemed arrogant in certain parts of his life. He'd certainly shown a huge disdain for most wetboys and most of the Sa'kagé, but he'd never equated himself with the great heroes of history.

The pang of loss cut Kylar again. Gods, Durzo had been dead three months—and despite the passage of time, it wasn't getting any better.

Kylar felt the little box in his pocket. *He died so I could have Elene.* Kylar tried to push Durzo from his mind with that thought. *Let's just get through Uly's birthday, and then I can ask Elene to marry me. Then Uly can hear more creaking than she's ever imagined.*

"Kylar," Uly said, jerking him out of his reverie. "Are you going to answer my question?"

Ah, shit. "Uly," he said gently. "I know you don't feel like it, and you're certainly as smart as someone a lot older, but you're still a..." He furrowed his brow, knowing the next part wasn't going to go over well. "You're still a child." It was true, dammit.

"No I'm not."

"Yes, you are."

"I just had my first moon blood this week. Aunt Mea says that means I'm a woman now. It really hurt and it scared me at first. My stomach got real sore and my back and then—"

"Ah!" Kylar waved his hands, trying to make her stop.

"What? Aunt Mea said it was nothing to be embarrassed about."

"Aunt Mea's not your father!"

"Who is?" Uly asked, quick as a whip.

Kylar said nothing.

"And who's my mother? You know, don't you? My nurses always treated me different from the other children. The last one always got scared whenever I got hurt. When I got a cut on my face once, she was so afraid it would be a scar that she didn't sleep for weeks. Sometimes a lady would watch us play in the gardens, but she always wore a cloak and hood. Was she my mother?"

Mute, Kylar nodded. It was exactly what Momma K would have done. She had doubtless stayed away for Uly's safety as much as she could bear, but every once in a while, the defenses would have broken down.

"She's important?" Uly asked. Every orphan's wish. Kylar knew.

Kylar nodded again.

"Why'd she leave me?"

Kylar blew out a breath. "You deserve the answer to that, Uly, but I can't tell you. It's one of the secrets I know that don't belong to me. I promise I'll tell you when I can."

"Are you going to leave me? If we got married, I could go with you."

If anyone thought children couldn't suffer pain as deeply as adults, Kylar wished they could see Uly's eyes now. For all he loved her, he'd been treating her as a child rather than as a human being. Uly's brief life was a history of abandonment: her father, her mother, one nurse after another. She just wanted something solid in her life.

Kylar hugged her. "I won't abandon you," he swore. "Not ever. Not. Ever."

24

*V*i rode into Caernarvon as the sun set. In her weeks on the trail, she'd decided her strategy. Surely Kylar would be known to the Sa'kagé here. If he was at all like Hu Gibbet, he wouldn't like to go long without killing. If he had taken any jobs, the Shinga would know him. Such a skilled wetboy wouldn't pass without notice.

On the other hand, if Kylar hadn't taken any work, chances were still good that the Sa'kagé's eyes and ears would know he had come to Caernarvon. Vi had heard precious little praise for Caernarvon's Sa'kagé, and if Kylar were truly committed to hiding himself, Vi would never find him, but it had been three months. Criminals always went back to their crimes, even if they had plenty of money, if only because they didn't know what else to do with themselves. What was a wetboy without killing?

The shops were all closed. The decent families were home for the night, and the inns and brothels were just starting to roar as Vi passed deeper into the southern section of the city. She was wearing white fawn-skin riding pants and a loose men's tunic of cotton. Her red hair was pulled back in a simple tight ponytail. In Cenaria, the rainy season was starting, but here the summer lingered on and Vi believed in being comfortable as she traveled, fashion be damned. She only worried about fashion when she needed something from it. Still, after two hard weeks in the saddle, she wouldn't mind a bath.

She rode down the fourth bad street in a row, wondering why she hadn't been mugged yet. She'd concealed all her weapons to make herself look totally vulnerable. What was wrong with these people?

Twenty minutes later, someone finally stepped out of the shadows.

"Nice night we're having, innit?" the man said. He was scruffy, dirty, inebriated. Perfect. He held a cudgel in one hand and a wineskin in the other.

"Are you robbing me?" Vi asked.

Half a dozen teenagers came out of the shadows and surrounded her.

"Well, I—" the man grinned, displaying two black front teeth. "This here's a toll road and you're going to have—"

"If you're not robbing me, get the hell out of my way. Or are you a complete idiot?"

The smile disappeared. "Well, I am," he said, finally. "Robbing you, that is. Tom Gray don't get outta no bitch's way." Then he almost brained himself as he tried to drink from his cudgel instead of the wineskin. The boys laughed, but one of them took her black mare's reins.

"I need to see the Shinga," she said. "Can you take me to him, or do I need to find someone else to mug me?"

"You're not going anywhere until you give me thirteen—"

One of the boys coughed.

"—er, fourteen silvers." His eyes traced over her breasts, and he added, "And maybe a little somethin' somethin' besides."

"How about you take me to the Shinga, and I'll leave your pathetic manhood intact?" Vi said.

Tom's face darkened. He threw the wineskin to one of the boys and stepped toward Vi, raising his cudgel. He grabbed her sleeve and yanked her out of the saddle.

Using the momentum of his pull, Vi flipped off the saddle and kicked him in the face, landing lightly on her feet as Tom Gray went sprawling.

"Can any of the rest of you take me to the Shinga?" she asked, ignoring Tom.

They all looked confused at how Tom had ended up on the other side of the street with a bloody nose, but after a moment, a scrawny young man with a big nose said, "Shinga Sniggle don't let us just come up to him any old time. But Tom's friends with him."

"Sniggle?" Vi asked, smirking. "That's not really his name, is it?"

Tom picked himself up off the ground. He roared and charged Vi.

Not even looking at him, she waited until he was two steps away and poked her foot into his hip in mid-stride. When his foot didn't come forward to take the next step as he'd expected, he went skidding across the cobblestones at Vi's feet. She didn't break eye contact with the boy.

"I, uh, yes, Barush Sniggle," the boy said, looking at Tom. He didn't seem to find anything comical about it. "Who are you?" he asked.

She contorted her fingers into the thieves' sign.

"That's a little different than ours," the young man said. "Where you from?"

"Cenaria," she said.

All of them took a step back. "No shit?" he said. "Cenarian Sa'kagé?"

"Now you," Vi said, grabbing Tom Gray by his greasy hair. "Are you going to take me to the Shinga? Or do I have to break something?"

He swore at her.

She broke his nose.

He sputtered blood and swore again.

"Slow learner, huh?" She hit him in his broken nose, and then grabbed his head. Jamming her fingers deep into the pain points behind his ears, she lifted him to his feet. He screamed with surprising vigor. It was unfortunate she'd broken his nose first, because he sprayed blood all over her. Vi didn't mind, though. Nysos was the god of the potent liquids: blood, wine, and semen. It had been weeks since she'd given him an offering. Perhaps this would appease him until she found Kylar.

She held her fingers deep in those pain points, letting Tom Gray scream, letting him spray blood over her shirt and face. The boys cowered back, about to break and run.

"Enough!" a voice called from the darkness.

Vi released Tom and he fell.

A short, squat figure walked forward. "I am the Shinga," he said.

"Barush Sniggle?" she asked. Shinga Barush Sniggle had a potbelly, small eyes under lank blond hair, and a cruel mouth. He walked with a swagger despite his small size. Perhaps the hulking bodyguard by his side helped with that.

"What do you want, wench?" the Shinga demanded.

"I'm hunting. My deader's name is Lord Kylar Stern. He's about my height, light blue eyes, dark hair, athletic, about twenty years old."

"A deader?" Sniggle asked. "Like you're a wetboy? A wet girl?"

"Wasn't Kylar the name of that guy who busted Tom's chops a couple weeks ago?" the big-nosed young man asked one of the other teenagers.

"Sounds like him," another young man said. "Think he's still staying with Aunt Mea. But he ain't no lord."

"Shut up," Barush Sniggle said. "You don't say another damn word, you got me? Tom, get your ass off the ground and bring that bitch here."

Amazing. Kylar had made it so simple. He thought he was far enough away, was confident that everyone thought he was dead. She had all she needed now. It would be a simple matter to find him, and it would be an easy matter to kill him, too. She tingled with excitement. She still had a two-inch scar on her shoulder from him, despite having let one of those foul wytches heal her.

"I think I might just have to take you back to my place," Barush Sniggle said. "We'll find out how much of a wet girl you are."

"Never heard that one before," she said. The bodyguard had one of her arms, and a triumphant Tom Gray had the other.

"She's one hot bitch, ain't she?" Tom Gray said, grabbing a breast.

She ignored him. "Don't make me do something you'll regret," she told the Shinga.

"Can I have her after you're done?" Tom asked. He squeezed her breast again and then he petted her hair.

"DON'T TOUCH MY HAIR!" she yelled.

Both the bodyguard and Tom flinched at her sudden fury. Barush Sniggle forced a laugh a moment later.

"You little guttershite, you sewer froth, you touch my hair and I swear I'll rip you apart," Vi said, trembling.

He swore at her and ripped out the leather thong that bound her hair back. Her hair fell loose around her shoulders for the first time in years. She stood exposed, naked, and the men were laughing.

She went out of her mind. She was swearing, the Talent arching through her so powerfully it hurt. Her arms blasted through the men's hold on them and her fists cracked Tom Gray's and the bodyguard's ribs simultaneously. Before Tom could double up, she grabbed his hair in one hand. She stabbed fingers at the corners of his eyes, deep into the sockets, and tore his eyes out. She spun and men were screaming and running and in her confusion and fury she didn't even know which one to chase.

Vi didn't know how much time passed while she vented her shame and fury on the two men.

When she came to herself, her hair covered with a blood-soaked rag, she was sitting on a stoop. The Shinga and the boys had fled. There was no one on the street except for her imperturbable horse, standing still until she called it as she trained it, and two man-shaped lumps lying in the street.

Walking unsteadily toward the horse, she passed right by what had been Tom Gray and the bodyguard. The corpses were a ruin. She'd—Nysos—she'd never even drawn a weapon, and she'd done this. Her stomach lurched and she vomited in the street.

It's just a simple job. The Godking will forgive me for not killing Jarl. I'll be a master. I'll never have to serve Hu Gibbet in the bed or anywhere else, not ever again. I kill Kylar, and then I'm free. It's close, Vi. So close. You can make it.

Sister Jessie al'Gwaydin was dead. Ariel was sure of it. The villagers hadn't seen her for two months and her horse was still in the innkeeper's stable. It wasn't like Jessie, but taking risks was. Stupid girl.

Sister Ariel knelt as she entered the oak grove, not to pray, but to extend her senses. This grove was as far toward the Iaosian Forest as the locals were willing to go. The villagers of Torras Bend prided themselves on their practicality. They saw nothing superstitious or foolish about giving the Hunter the same wide berth their ancestors had. The tales they had told her weren't wild-eyed ravings. Indeed, they were believable because of their lack of detail.

Those who entered the forest didn't leave. Simple as that.

So the villagers fished in the meandering Red River and collected wood right up to the edge of the grove, but there they stopped. The effect was jarring. Centuries-old oaks abutted directly on bare fields. In some places, younger oaks had been cut down, but once the trees reached a certain age, the villagers wouldn't touch them. The oak grove had been slowly expanding for centuries.

She felt nothing here, nothing beyond the cool of a forest, smelled nothing except clean damp air. When she rose and walked slowly through the low undergrowth, she kept her senses attuned, pausing frequently, stopping when she imagined she felt the slightest trembling in the air. It made for slow progress, but Ariel Wyant Sa'fastae was noted for her patience, even among the Sisters. Besides, it was recklessness that had gotten Jessie al'Gwaydin killed. Probably.

Though it was only a mile wide, it took her a long time to traverse the oak grove. Each afternoon, after marking her progress, she returned to the inn and slept and took her only meal of the day—the weight was coming off, blast it, if slowly. Each night she returned to the forest, on the chance that whatever magics had been placed on the forest were affected by the time of day.

On the third day, Ariel came within sight of the forest itself, and the line between the oak grove and the forest proper was stark—obviously magical. Still, she didn't hurry her progress. Instead, she moved even more slowly, more carefully. On the fifth day, her patience paid off.

Ariel was thirty paces from the line between oakgrove and forest when she felt the ward. She stopped so abruptly she almost fell down. She sat, heedless of the dirt, and crossed her legs. The next hour she spent simply touching the ward, trying to get a feel for its texture and strength, without using magic of her own.

Then she began to chant softly. Though she worked long into the night checking and double-checking and triple-checking that she was right and that she hadn't missed anything, the weaves were simple. One simply registered whether a human had crossed the boundary. The second, slightly more complicated, marked the intruder. It was a weak weave that clung to

clothing or skin and dissipated after only a few hours. Cleverly, Ezra—
Ariel was making an assumption, but she thought it was good one—had
put the weave so low to the earth that it might mark the intruder's shoes, so
low that it would be covered by the undergrowth.

The real cunning of it, though, was the placement. How many magi had
seen the obvious line thirty paces beyond this and walked right through the
trap before they raised their defenses?

It would be easy to circumvent the trap now that she saw it, but Sister
Ariel didn't. Instead, she wrote her findings in her journal, and returned to
Torras Bend. If she'd made any mistakes, she would die before she got back
to the inn. It made for a tense walk. Her soul soared at the thought of dismantling Ezra's ancient magic, but she didn't give in to the temptations of
arrogance.

The Speaker's letters were getting shriller, demanding that Ariel find
Jessie, that Ariel do something to help her avert the rising crisis with the
Chattel. Ariel kept her eyes open, hoping to find a woman who might serve
her sister's purposes, but the villagers of Torras Bend were careful to send
away every child who showed the least Talent. Ariel wouldn't find what
Istariel needed here.

So she ignored the letters. There was a time and a place for haste. It
wasn't here and it wasn't now.

25

"Viridiana Sovari?"

Hearing her name made Vi skid to a stop in the crowded market. A dirty
little man bobbed his head nervously. He extended a note toward her, but
she didn't take it. He was being careful not to stand close to her and he
wasn't ogling her, so she guessed that he had an inkling of what she was.
He smiled obsequiously, shot a look at her breasts, then stared stubbornly
at his feet.

"Who are you?" she asked.

"No one important, miss. Just a servant of our...mutual master," he
said, eyeing the crowd around them. Her heart turned to ice. No. It couldn't

be. He extended the note again, and as soon as she took it, he disappeared into the crowd.

"*Moulina,*" the note read. "We are curious indeed how you knew Jarl was going to Caernarvon, but that you did know tells us that you are indeed the best. We also desire that you deal with Kylar Stern. We prefer him alive. If this is not possible, we require his body and all belongings, no matter how trivial. Bring them immediately."

Vi closed the note. It was impossible that the Godking knew where she was. Impossible that a note from him had beat her here. Impossible that Jarl could be here—Jarl, whose identity was supposed to be secret. Jarl, whom she'd been fleeing! Impossible to do what the Godking asked. But the greatest impossibility was the only impossibility now: it was impossible to escape. Vi was the Godking's slave. There was no way out.

Somehow Kylar had been roped into making the dinner for Uly's birthday. Aunt Mea had said no man should be intimidated by a kitchen, and Elene had said that compared to the potions he made, a dinner and dessert should be easy, and Uly just giggled as they put him in a frilly lace apron and dabbed his nose with flour.

So Kylar found himself with his sleeves rolled up, trying to figure out arcane cooking terms like blanching and roux and proofing. From Uly's giggles, he suspected they'd stuck him with the hardest recipe they could find, but he played along.

"What do I do after the jelly, uh, weeps?" he asked.

Uly and Elene giggled. Kylar struck a pose with the spatula, and they laughed out loud.

The door to the smithy opened and Braen walked in, dirty and smelly. He gave Kylar a flat look that made him lower the spatula, deflated, but he refused to wipe the flour from his nose. Braen turned his eyes to Elene and looked her up and down.

"When's dinner?" he asked her.

"We'll bring it out to your cave when it's ready," Kylar said.

Braen grunted and told Elene, "You ought to find yourself a real man."

"You know," Kylar said as Braen shuffled back toward the smithy, "I know a wetboy who'd like to pay that cretin a visit."

"Kylar," Elene said.

"I don't like the way he looks at you," Kylar said. "Has he tried anything with you?"

"Kylar, not tonight, all right?" Elene said, nodding toward Uly.

He was suddenly aware of the ring box in his pocket. He nodded. Putting a serious look on his face, he attacked Uly, who squealed, and flipped her upside down and draped her over his shoulder. He pretended not to realize she was there as he went back to cooking.

Uly yelped, kicking her legs and holding onto the back of his tunic with a death grip.

Aunt Mea came into the kitchen, clucking. "I can't believe it, we're all out of flour and honey."

"Oh, no," Kylar said. "How am I going to make the fifth mother sauce?" He set down his spatula and hunched over, extending his hands through his legs. On cue, Uly slid headfirst down his back and grabbed his hands in time for him to pull her through his legs. She landed on her feet, breathless and laughing.

"Isn't it someone's birthday?" Kylar asked.

"Mine! Mine!" Uly said.

He pulled silver out of each of Uly's ears while she giggled. Two silvers—it was a bonus the noble had given him. It left him and Elene with nothing again, but Uly was worth it. When he put them in Uly's hands, her eyes got big. "For me?" she asked like she couldn't believe it.

He winked. "Elene will help you find something good, all right?"

"Can we go right now?" Uly asked.

Kylar looked at Elene, who shrugged. "We can go with Aunt Mea," she said.

"I've got to peel the peas anyway," Kylar said. They snickered. He smiled at Elene and marveled again at how beautiful she was. He was so in love he thought his chest would burst.

Uly pranced to the door and showed Aunt Mea her coins. Elene touched Kylar's arm. "Are we going to be all right?" she asked.

"After tonight we are," he said.

"What do you mean?"

"You'll see." He didn't smile. He didn't want to give it away. If he smiled, he'd grin like a fool. He couldn't wait to see the look on her face. He couldn't wait for other things as well. He shook his head and went back to cooking. Contrary to what he'd said, the meal wasn't hard to prepare. It was just messy. He slipped off his ring and put it on the counter before he picked up the raw meat—there wasn't much romantic about smelling like dead cow.

Elene and Uly and Aunt Mea had only been gone for about thirty seconds when there was a knock on the door. Kylar put down the spatula again and walked to the door. "What'd you forget this time, Uly?" he said as he grabbed a hand towel and opened the door.

It was Jarl.

Kylar felt like the wind had been knocked out of him. He couldn't believe his eyes. But there he was, lean, athletic, impeccably dressed, as beautiful a man as you'd ever see, his dazzling white teeth showing an uncertain smile. "Hey-ho, Azo," he said.

Why that greeting? Was Jarl just being cute, or was he also throwing in an appeal to their history together? Definitely the latter. For a long moment, they just stood there, looking at one another. Jarl wasn't here for a visit. Jarl didn't visit. For the God's sake, the man was the Shinga. A true Shinga, the leader of the most feared Sa'kagé in Midcyru.

"How in the nine hells did you find me, Jarl?" Kylar said, being cute too. It was what Jarl had expected Kylar to say the last time Jarl had shown up unexpectedly.

"Aren't you going to invite me in?"

"Please," Kylar said. He put some ootai on and sat across from Jarl, who helped himself to a seat by the window. Silence.

"There's this job—" Jarl began.

"Not interested."

Jarl took that in stride. He pursed his lips and looked around the humble room quizzically. "So, uh... what is it about this that you like again?"

"Didn't Momma K teach tact?"

"I'm serious," Jarl said.

"So am I. You show up after I tell you I'm out of the business, and the first thing you do is insult the place I live?"

"Logan's alive. He's in the Hole."

Kylar just stared at him, uncomprehending. The words collided with each other and shattered on the floor, shards sparkling with the light of truth, but the whole nothing more than splinters and points too sharp to touch.

"All the wetboys are working for Khalidor. The resisting nobles have retreated to the Gyre estates. Several of the frontier garrisons are still manned, but we have no leader who can unite us. There's some trouble up in the Freeze that the Godking is worried about, so he hasn't done anything to consolidate his power yet. He thinks that the noble families will tear each other apart. And if we don't have Logan, he's right."

"Logan's alive?" Kylar asked stupidly.

"The Godking has our former wetboys looking for me. It's part of why I came here. I had to get out of Cenaria until we could get word out that Kagé himself is protecting me."

"No," Kylar said.

"Every day, the chances that Logan will be discovered get worse.

Apparently none of the prisoners in the Hole has recognized him, but they've started throwing a lot of people down there. It might please you to know that Duke Vargun is one of them. Look at it as a little bonus. When you rescue Logan, you can kill that twist, too."

"What?" Kylar said. Wheels were turning too fast for him to catch up. "Jarl," he said. "Tenser isn't Tenser Vargun. Don't you see? He got himself thrown in the Hole so he can do the hardest time there is. Then they produce the real baron—alive—and Tenser is released. He comes to the Sa'kagé a month later with a grudge for his false imprisonment and all the access of a duke and what happens?"

"We take him in," Jarl said quietly. "How could we resist?"

"And he destroys you, because he's not Tenser Vargun," Kylar said. "He's Tenser Ursuul."

Jarl sat back, stunned. After a minute, he said, "You see, Kylar? This is why I need you. Not just for your skills, for your mind. If Tenser's there right now, he's only going to wait long enough that his stay in the Hole is credible, and then he'll tell his father that Logan's in there. We have to go now. Now!"

The ring box was burning against Kylar leg. He looked through the open window as Jarl spoke, seeing the city he'd hoped would be his home for the rest of his life. He loved this city, loved the hope here, loved healing and helping, loved the simple pleasure of being praised for his potions. He loved Elene. She proved to him that he could do more good by healing than by killing. It all made sense . . . and yet . . . and yet. . . .

"I can't," Kylar said. "I'm sorry. Elene would never understand."

Jarl rocked back on two legs of the chair. "Don't get me wrong, Azo, because I grew up with Elene too, and I love the girl. But why do you give a shit what she thinks?"

"Fuck, Jarl."

"Hey, I'm just asking." Then he let the question sit, his eyes never leaving Kylar's face.

The bastard, he really had been studying under Momma K for all those years.

"I love her."

"Sure, that's part of it."

Again, that I'm-waiting stare.

"She's good, Jarl. I mean, like people aren't good where we came from. Not good because it will get her something. Not good because people are watching. Just good. At first I thought she was just made that way, you know, like your skin is black and I'm devastatingly handsome."

Jarl raised an eyebrow. He didn't laugh.

"But now I've seen that she has to work at it. She does work at it, and she's been working at it for as long as I've been working at learning to kill people."

"So she's a saint. Doesn't answer my question," Jarl said.

Kylar was silent for a full minute. He rubbed the grain of the wood table with a fingernail. "Momma K used to say that we become the masks we wear. What's under the mask for us, Jarl? Elene knows me in a way no one else does. I've changed my name, changed my identity, left everything and everyone I've ever known. I'm all lies, Jarl, but as long as Elene knows me, maybe there is a real me. Do you know what I mean?"

"You know," Jarl said. "I was wrong about you. When you got yourself killed saving Elene and Uly, I thought you were a hero. You're no hero. You just fucking hate yourself."

"Excuse me?"

"You're a coward. So you've done bad stuff. Join the club. You know what? I'm glad you did; it made you something better than a saint."

"A killer's better than the saint? What sort of fucked-up Sa'kagé thinking is—"

"It made you *useful*. Do you know what it's like in Cenaria right now? You wouldn't believe me. I didn't come here to find a killer. I came to find The Killer, the Night Angel, the man who's more than just a wetboy because the problems we have now are bigger than any wetboy could handle. There's only one man who can help us, Kylar, and that's you. Believe me, you weren't my first choice." He stopped abruptly.

"What's that supposed to mean?"

Jarl wouldn't meet his eye. "I didn't mean—"

"What were you about to say?" Kylar said in a dangerous tone.

"We had to be sure, Kylar. We were very respectful, I want you to know that. It was Momma K's idea. He used to be immortal, we had to make sure..."

"You dug up my master's corpse?" Kylar demanded.

"We put it—him—back just how you'd buried him." Jarl winced. "It was maybe a week after the invasion—"

"You dug him up while I was still in the city?"

"We couldn't tell you beforehand, and afterward there was no reason to. Momma K said the body would be there, that Durzo had given his immortality to you, but when she saw him....It was the scariest thing I've ever seen, Kylar. I mean, I was practically raised by the woman and I've never seen her like that. Hysterical, weeping and screaming—here we are, in the middle of the cloudy night, we'd paddled out to Vos Island with oars wrapped in wool, and she starts wailing, out of her mind. I was so sure a patrol would come that I wanted to get off the island immediately, but she wouldn't leave until he was just how you left him."

Like Kylar cared that Durzo be left on that damned rock. If they were going to dig him up, they could have at least brought him.... *Where? Home? What home did Durzo Blint ever have?*

"How'd he look?" Kylar asked quietly.

"Shit. He looked like he'd been in the ground a week, what do you think?"

Of course he did. *Dammit, Master Blint, why'd you give* me *your immortality? Were you just sick of living? Why didn't you tell me anything?* But then, maybe he had told him in the note he'd given Kylar: the note that had been soaked with blood, illegible. "You want me to break into the Hole and save Logan?"

"Do you know who the Godking keeps as his concubines? Young girls from noble families. Prefers virgins. He guesses how much humiliation and debasement each girl can take. Puts them in tower rooms with balconies where all the railings have been torn off so the jump beckons every day. It's a game for him."

Kylar kept his voice hard. "Get to the point."

"He took Serah and Mags Drake. Serah killed herself in the first week. Mags is still there."

Serah and Mags were practically Kylar's sisters. Mags had always been his pal. Always quick with a laugh, always smiling. He'd been so self-absorbed since the coup that he'd barely thought of them.

Jarl said, "I want you to rescue Logan, and then I want you to assassinate the Godking."

"Is that all?" Coldly amused. It was a tone Kylar had heard Durzo use a hundred times. "Let me guess, Logan first because my odds with the Godking aren't so great?"

"That's right," Jarl said angrily. "That's how I have to think, Kylar. I'm fighting a war, and people better than us are dying in it every day. And you're sitting around because of what some girl thinks?"

"Don't you talk about Elene."

"Or what? You'll breathe heavily on me? You're the dumbass who swore off violence. Yes, I know about that. Let me tell you something. Roth made a lot of people miserable. I'm glad you killed him, all right? He fucked me up bad. But he doesn't hold a candle to his father." Jarl swore. "Look at yourself! I know this hit is impossible. I'm sending you after a god. But if anyone in the world can do it, it's you. You were made for this, Kylar. Do you think you made it through all the shit you made it through so you can sell hangover potions? Some things are bigger than your happiness, Kylar. You can give hope to an entire nation."

"It'll only cost me everything," Kylar whispered. His face was gray.

"You're an immortal. There'll be other girls."

Kylar gave him a disgusted look.

Jarl's expression changed instantly. "I'm sorry. I guess there will be other Godkings and other Shingas too. I just... we need you. Logan will die if you don't come. So will Mags, and so will a lot of other people you'll never know."

It would have been easier if he disagreed with anything Jarl said. Kylar had asked Momma K, "Can a man change?" Here was his answer, and it sucked the life right out of him. "All right," Kylar said. "I'll take the contract."

Jarl smiled. "It's good to have you back, my friend."

"It's bad to be back."

"I didn't want to say it before, but have you done something to piss off the local Shinga?" Jarl asked. He took Kylar's expression to be an admission. "Because one of my sources told me the Shinga put out a contract on a Cenarian wetboy. He didn't know any details, but uh, I don't figure there's all that many Cenarians wetboys hanging around. The longer you're here, the more you put Elene and Uly in danger."

Durzo had taught Kylar that the best way to cancel a contract was to cancel the contract-giver. For Elene and Uly and Aunt Mea and even Braen to be safe, Barush Sniggle had to die.

Kylar stood woodenly and went upstairs. He returned a minute later with a visage as dark as the wetboy grays he wore once again.

Vi looked at the bow in her hands, trying to convince herself to pull back the red-and-black arrow. She was on a rooftop looking into the midwife's home. She'd been there for an hour. Her back was to a chimney, and she'd wrapped herself in shadows. She wasn't invisible by any means, but crouched low in the dying light, with the sun behind her, she was close enough.

She'd come to Caernarvon to escape this. She'd thought the only way to not kill Jarl and still escape the Godking's wrath was to kill Kylar. In the time she was away, Jarl would flee or be killed by another wetboy.

How could he have come here?

She wanted to shoot past him, shoot Kylar and pretend that Jarl wasn't here, pretend that she'd never gotten the note. But she didn't have the shot to take Kylar down, and lies would go nowhere with the Godking. Jarl sat right in front of the window. The window was even open. Vi was using a Talent-tension bow, a bow so powerful that only a person with the Talent could draw it, so the red-and-black traitor's arrow could have punched right through a window, through shutters for that matter. But she didn't even need it.

Jarl sat there, utterly exposed. He never would have made such a mistake in Cenaria, but here he felt safe. He'd fled straight into Death's arms.

Yet she waited. Damn Jarl for his stupidity. If Vi didn't kill him, the Godking would know. He would find her. *Damn you, Jarl. Damn you for your kindness.*

Finish the job. Hu Gibbet liked to torture his deaders first, but he only did it when he was sure he wouldn't be interrupted. Hu Gibbet always finished the job. The perfect shot never comes. Take any shot that kills.

Cursing under her breath to activate her Talent, Vi stood and drew the arrow to her cheek. It moved her out of the silhouette of the small chimney into the dying light. She was shaking, but it was barely thirty paces. "Damn you, Jarl, move!" she said.

She could run away. In Gandu or Ymmur the Godking would never find her. Would he? She couldn't believe it. She had told no one she was coming here, left no sign, and yet he knew. If she fled, the Godking would send her master after her, and Hu Gibbet never failed. For everything that Vi's beauty accomplished for her, the one thing it made nearly impossible was hiding. She'd never worried about disguises. She'd never thought of it as a weakness. Until now.

"Come on, Kylar," she whispered. "Just walk in front of the window. Just once." She was shaking violently now, and not just from the Talent burning in her, not just from the tension of holding the bow drawn for so long. Why did she want Kylar dead so badly?

She saw a leg, a leg dressed in wetboy grays, but no more appeared. Dammit. If Kylar was going out, she was in serious trouble. She'd heard that he could make himself invisible, but that was just the typical wetboy lies. They all bragged about their abilities so they could drive prices up. Everyone wanted to be another Durzo Blint.

But this was Durzo's apprentice, the man who'd killed Durzo. Fear gripped her.

Jarl's face was drawn with compassion, sorrow. At that look—that look she'd seen before when Jarl had taken care of her after Hu Gibbet came in to test the new skills Momma K had been teaching her and found her lacking and beat her senseless and violated her in every way he could imagine—at that look, Vi's vision went blurry. She blinked and blinked, refusing to believe it was tears. She hadn't cried since that night, since Jarl had held her, rocking her, helping her put the fractured pieces of herself back together.

Jarl stood and walked to the window. He lifted his eyes and saw Vi, her dark silhouette limned with sunlight. Surprise lit his eyes, and as it was followed by recognition—what other wetboy had a woman's silhouette?—she could swear she saw her name on his lips. Her fingers went limp and the bowstring slipped.

The red-and-black traitor's arrow leapt across that narrowest of chasms: the distance between a wetboy and her deader. It cut a red path through the air as if the night itself were bleeding.

26

"Elene, I'm sorry," Kylar wrote in a shaky hand. "I tried. I swear I tried. Some things are worth more than my happiness. Some things only I can do. Sell these to Master Bourary and move the family to a better part of town. I will always love you." Taking the ring box from his pocket, he placed it on top of the scrap of parchment.

"What's in the box?" Jarl asked.

Kylar couldn't look back at his friend. "My heart," he whispered and slowly uncurled his fingers from the box. "Just some earrings," he said, louder. He turned.

Jarl saw right through him. "You were going to marry her," he said.

A lump rose in Kylar's throat. There were no words. He had to look away from Jarl's eyes. "Have you ever heard of cruxing?" he asked finally.

Jarl shook his head.

"It's how Alitaerans execute rebels. They stretch them on a wood frame and pound nails through their wrists and feet. To breathe, the criminal has to lift his weight on the nails. It sometimes takes a man a day to die, asphyxiated by his own weight." He couldn't complete the metaphor, though he could feel himself being stretched out, a rebel against fate in a malevolent universe bent on crushing all things good, stretched between Logan and Elene, nailed to each with loyalty owed and gasping under the crushing weight of his own character. But it wasn't just Elene and Logan that stretched him here. It was two lives, two paths. The way of the shadows and the way of the light. The wolf and the wolfhound. Or was it wolfhound and lapdog?

Kylar had thought he could change. He'd thought he could have everything. He'd run headfirst into either/or and chosen both. That was what had driven him to the crux—not the machinations of a trickster god or the implacable roll of Fortune's wheel. Kylar's options had spread further and further apart, and he'd held on until he couldn't breathe. Only one question mattered now: What kind of man am I?

"Let's go," Kylar said, all wolfhound.

Jarl was standing at the window, pensive. "I was in love once," Jarl said. "Or something like it. With a beautiful girl nearly as fucked up as I am."

"Who was she?" Kylar asked.

"Her name was Viridiana, Vi. Beautiful, beautiful—" Jarl looked up and stiffened. "Vi?"

He went down in a spray of blood, an arrow passing fully through the center of his neck. His body dropped to the wood floor like a sack of flour. He blinked once. His eyes were neither afraid nor angry. His expression was wry.

Can you believe that? his eyes asked as Kylar drew him into his lap.

And then Jarl's eyes said nothing at all.

"Can I show Kylar?" Uly asked. She was clutching the very doll that Kylar had picked up a few days before. Elene smiled; Kylar was doing better at being a father than he knew.

"Yes," Elene said, "but you run right home. Promise?"

"Promise," Uly said, and ran.

Elene watched her go, feeling anxious, but she always felt anxious about little things. Caernarvon wasn't like the Warrens. Besides, the house was only two blocks away.

"We need to talk, don't we?" Aunt Mea said.

It was getting late. The sun's rays slanted down on merchants who were packing up their goods and heading home. Elene swallowed. "I promised Kylar. We agreed that we'd never tell anyone, but—"

"Then don't say another word." Aunt Mea smiled and took Elene's arm to guide her back to the house.

"I can't," Elene said, stopping her. "I can't do this anymore."

So she told Aunt Mea everything, from the lie of their marriage to their fights about sex to Kylar's being a wetboy and trying to leave it behind. Aunt Mea didn't even look surprised.

"Elene," she said, taking her hands. "Do you love Kylar or are you with him because Uly needs a mother?"

Elene paused to fully humble herself in the face of the question, to make sure what she would say was true. "I love him," Elene said. "Uly is a part of it, but I really love him."

"Then why are you protecting yourself?"

Elene looked up. "I'm not protecting—"

"You can't be honest with me until you're honest with yourself."

Elene looked at her hands. A farmer's cart loaded with the day's unsold produce rattled past them. The light was fading and the street was beginning to get dark. "We have to get back," Elene said. "Dinner must be getting cold."

"Child," Aunt Mea said. Elene stopped.

"He's a killer," Elene said. "I mean, he's killed people."

"No, you were right. He's a killer."

"No, he's a good man. He can change. I know it."

"Child, do you know why you're talking to me even though you promised Kylar you wouldn't? Because you agreed to something that isn't in your nature. You make a terrible liar, but you tried because you promised. Isn't that what he's done?"

"What do you mean?" Elene asked.

"If you can't love Kylar for the man he is—if you only love him for the man you think he could be—you'll cripple him."

Kylar had been so unhappy. When he'd started going out at night, she hadn't asked, hadn't wanted to know what he did. "What am I supposed to do?" she asked.

"Do you think you're the first woman who's been afraid to love?" Aunt Mea asked.

The words cut deep. It cast a different light on their nightly making out and fighting. She'd thought she was being holy by not making love with Kylar, but she was just terrified. She felt so far out of control already that surrender in the bedroom would have left her powerless. "Can I love him if I can't understand him? Can I love him if I hate what he does?"

"Child," Aunt Mea said. She gently laid a thick hand on Elene's shoulder. "Loving is an act of faith as much as believing in the God is."

"He isn't a believer. An ox and a wolf can't be yoked together," Elene said, knowing she was grasping at straws.

"You think a yoke only refers to wedding rings or lovemaking? You don't need to understand him, Elene, you need to love him until you do." Aunt Mea took Elene's arm. "Come on, let's go eat our dinner."

They walked back to the house together, Elene feeling lighter than she had in months—even if she was going to have to have a big talk with Kylar. She felt a new sense of hope.

Elene threw the door open, but the house was silent, empty. "Kylar?" she said. "Uly?"

There was no answer. The food was cold on the counter, the jelly Kylar had been making congealed and cracked. Her heart clogged her throat. Every breath was an effort. Aunt Mea looked horrified. Elene ran upstairs and clawed at the box of Kylar's wetboy clothes and his big sword. It was empty. There was no sign of anything.

She walked back downstairs, the truth coming to her as slowly as the setting sun.

"Are we going to be all right?" she had asked him.

"After tonight we are," he'd said, unsmiling.

Kylar's wedding ring sat next to the stove. There was no note, nothing else. Even Uly was gone. Kylar had finally given up on her. He was gone.

Vi slung the wiggling child off her shoulder as they came into the stable of the seedy inn where she'd put up her horse. The stable boy lay unconscious and bleeding by the door. He'd probably live. It didn't matter; he hadn't seen Vi before she'd clubbed him with the pommel of her short sword.

The girl squeaked through the rag Vi had tied over her mouth. Vi knelt and grabbed the girl's throat in one hand. She pulled out the gag.

"What's your name?" Vi asked.

"Go to hell!" The girl's eyes flashed, defiant. She couldn't be more than twelve.

Vi slapped her, hard. Then she slapped her again, and again, and again, impassively, the way Hu used to slap her when he was bored. When the girl tried to get away, she clamped her hand down on her throat, the threat explicit: the more you wiggle, the more you choke.

"Fine, Go To Hell, you want me to call you that, or something else?"

The little girl cursed her again. Vi spun her in to her body and clamped a hand over her mouth. With the other hand, she found a pain point in one of the girl's elbows and ground her fingers in.

The girl screamed into her hand.

Why haven't I killed her yet?

The job had gone flawlessly. Kylar had taken Jarl's body after arming himself for hunting. Vi had only seen brief glimpses of blades being sheathed and disappearing—surely it was a trick of the light and the distance, Kylar couldn't really be invisible. Regardless, after a while he'd taken Jarl's body and Vi had gone into the house.

She intended to set a few traps. There was a perfect contact poison that she could smear on the door latch of his bedroom and a needle trap that would fit perfectly in the little box he kept under the bed. But she couldn't do it. Still reeling from Jarl's murder, she walked around the house like a common prowler.

Vi found a note and a pair of earrings that looked expensive—the note said as much—even though they were oddly mismatched, one larger than the other. She pocketed both but didn't touch the thin gold wedding band by the stove. Let the happy little family keep its heirlooms. She wasn't sure what the note meant. Kylar had tried? Tried to protect Jarl?

The door opened, surprising Vi, and the little girl had walked in. Vi bound and gagged her, then stood looking at the mess she'd got herself into.

She was finished. She couldn't kill this child. She couldn't even kill Kylar. No, that wasn't true, she was sure she could still kill Kylar. The only way she could escape the Godking with her life was to please him. He would be more pleased if she delivered Kylar alive. If she delivered Kylar alive, the Godking would never know her weakness. She'd buy herself time to recover whatever it was that had cracked in her as she'd watched Jarl die in a spray of blood.

Galvanized, Vi went back to Kylar's bedroom. She carved the Cenarian Sa'kagé's glyph into the bedside table in a fine, light hand. Beneath it she traced, "I've got the girl." When Kylar came back, he'd find his daughter gone and he'd scour the entire house. He'd find it, and he'd follow Vi straight to the Godking.

So now all Vi had to do was figure out how to smuggle a wailing child out of the city.

"Let's try again," Vi said. "What's your name?"

"Uly," the little girl said, tears making her face blotchy.

"All right, Ugly, we're leaving. You can come with me alive or dead. It doesn't matter. You've served your purpose. I'm going to tie your hands to the saddle, so you can jump off the horse if you want, but you'll just get kicked and dragged to death. Your choice. Open your mouth."

Uly opened her mouth and Vi stuffed the gag in. "Be silent," she said. She scowled at the rag. "Say something."

"Mmm?" Uly said.

"Damn." Vi fixed her will on the rag. "Be silent!" she whispered. "Again."

Uly's mouth moved, but no sound came out. Vi pulled out the rag; it wasn't necessary now. It had been a little trick she'd discovered a few years ago by accident. It was spotty, but a merely silent child would be easier to get out of the city than a gagged one. Vi saddled her horse and the second-best horse in the stable.

In half an hour, Caernarvon was fading into the distance, but freedom was still a long way off.

27

Cold fury burned the world white. Kylar sprinted across the rooftop. He reached the edge and leapt, soaring through the night air. He cleared the twenty-foot gap easily and ran up the wall. He pushed off it, grabbed the extended roof beam, and flipped himself up onto it, not even wobbling.

He'd done it all while invisible, a fact that would have pleased him immensely a few days ago. Today, he had no ability to feel pleasure at all. His eyes scanned the dark streets.

Before he'd left, he'd cleaned Jarl's blood from the floor—he wasn't going to make Elene deal with that. He'd taken his friend's body to a cemetery. Jarl wouldn't rot in a sewer like some guttershite. Kylar didn't even have the money to pay a grave digger—*thanks, God*—so he left Jarl and swore to return.

Jarl was dead. Part of Kylar didn't believe it, the part that had thought the soft life of a Waeddryner healer might be his. How could he have believed that? There was nothing soft in a Night Angel's life. Nothing. He was a killer. Death rose in his passage like mud swirling behind a stick dragged across the bottom of a clear, still pond.

There. Two punks were hassling a drunk. Gods, was that the same drunk he'd left to his fate the other night? Kylar dropped from the roof, swung off the next level, and in ten seconds was on the street.

The drunk was already down, bleeding from his nose. One of the punks was tearing the man's purse from his belt while the other stood watch, a long knife in his hand.

Kylar let himself shimmer into partial visibility, muscles gleaming iridescent black, eyes black orbs, face a mask of fury. He only intended to scare the
knife-wielder, but as the hoodlum's eyes widened at the sight of him, Kylar
swore he saw something so dark in them that it compelled him to act.

Before he knew it, the punch sword was drinking heart's blood. The
hoodlum's knife dropped on the ground.

"What are you doing, Terr?" the mugger asked, turning.

A moment later, Kylar had the mugger pinned against the wall by his
throat. He had to suppress the urge to kill, kill, kill.

"Where's the Shinga?" he demanded.

Terrified, the man flailed and screamed. "What are you?"

Kylar caught one of the mugger's flailing hands in his own and squeezed.
A bone popped. The man screamed. Kylar waited, then squeezed harder.
Another bone popped.

The stream of curses was unimpressive. Kylar ground the mugger's
hand to pulp, then grabbed his other hand. The man started gibbering as he
looked at his mangled hand. "Oh shit oh shit oh shit, my hand."

"Where's the Shinga? I won't repeat myself again."

"You f—no! Stop! Third warehouse down from dock three! Oh, gods!
What are you?"

"I am retribution," Kylar said. He cut open the man's neck and dropped
him. The drunk gaped at him. He looked like he thought he'd gone crazy.

The warehouse was definitely the Shinga's place, but Barush Sniggle
wasn't there. Kylar supposed it was too much to expect. There were, however,
ten guards waiting inside the front door. Kylar stared down at them from the
ceiling beams, looking for one who might know more than the others.

The presence of the guards was evidence enough that Barush Sniggle
had sent the wetboy who killed Jarl. Kylar had no idea how they'd learned
that he was the one who'd made Sniggle wet himself the other night, but
killing the wrong man for it was exactly what this Shinga would do.

Kylar dropped behind a man who looked like the leader. He broke the
man's right arm and drew the man's sword.

Half of the thugs were down before they grasped the idea that they actually were supposed to fight the invisible man killing them. Those who
fought, fought poorly. Dress a thug in armor and give him a sword instead
of a cudgel and you don't get a soldier, you get a thug who swings a sword
like a piece of wood. They hurried to Death's embrace.

Kylar stood over the leader, the last man alive, and again allowed his
eyes and face to become visible. He put one foot on the man's broken arm
and touched the sword to his neck.

"You're the wetboy." The man cursed. He was sweating, his broad face pasty. His bushy black beard quivered as he trembled. "He said you were a girl."

"Wrong, tell me," Kylar said.

"The Shinga said he pissed off some Cenarian wetboy. We were supposed to kill you if you came here."

"Where is he?"

"If I tell you, will you let me live?"

Kylar looked into the man's eyes, and curiously didn't feel or imagine—or whatever it had been the other times—the darkness that demanded death. "Yes," he said, though the killing rage was still on him.

The man told him of a hideout, and another trap, an underground room with only one entrance, another ten guards.

With teeth gritted against the white-cold fury, Kylar said, "Tell them the Night Angel walks. Tell them Justice is come."

28

The grate squealed open and Gorkhy's face appeared in the dim light of his torch. He looked pleased. Logan hated the man with all his heart. "Fresh meat, kiddos," Gorkhy said. "Sweet, fresh meat."

Some of the prisoners behind Gorkhy started sobbing. It was a deliberate cruelty to bring them here at this time of day. It was noon; the howlers were shrieking for all they were worth, hot fetid air gusting up out of the Hole like a giant, endless fart. It made the torches dance and the figures of the Holers seem to leap and twist as their sweat gleamed.

Since Logan had jumped down the Hole eighty-two days ago, they had only thrown one prisoner in the Hole. Gorkhy had done it, and he had thrown the man into the Hole—straight into the Hole. The convict's face had smacked wetly against the lip of the Hole and his body had plunged into the abyss. So now the animals and the monsters crowded around the Hole as they did when Gorkhy threw in bread. It wasn't to save the prisoners' lives. It was to save their meat.

"All right, my lovelies," Gorkhy said. "Who's first?"

Keeping an eye on Fin, who was also eyeing him, Logan stayed back from the edge of the Hole. He had the longest reach, but catching a falling body was different from catching falling bread, and Fin had uncoiled his sinew rope from around his body.

There was a scuffle above and curses and a woman flung herself at the grate. Gorkhy tried to intercept her, but she dove under his arms. She dropped headfirst toward the floor, then jerked to a stop as Gorkhy caught her dress.

She screamed and kicked as she hung directly over Logan's head. He jumped and grabbed one of her flailing arms and yanked, but his hand slipped. She dropped a few more feet forward so that she was hanging upside down, ten feet from the stone floor.

"Fin!" Lilly cried. "Get him!" Gorkhy was on his knees, holding on to the girl's dress with one hand and onto the grate with the other. His head was exposed. For Fin, who practiced incessantly with his lasso, it was an easy target.

Gorkhy was cursing, but he was strong. Logan jumped and reached for the girl's hand again, but missed. Fin came running with the lasso in his hand. The rest of the Holers were howling and flinging feces at Gorkhy. Logan jumped again and caught the girl's hand.

Her dress tore and she fell on top of Logan. He was barely able to break her fall, only trying to angle her away from the abyss.

Logan staggered to his feet and saw Gorkhy's face livid in the torch-light, still exposed, just waiting for a noose to drop around his neck, just begging to be dragged into the Hole and torn apart. Turning, Logan saw Fin just feet away, but the man had dropped his lasso. Logan barely had time to see the glittering steel in Fin's hand before Fin stabbed him.

Flesh parted along Logan's ribs and his left arm as he twisted hard to avoid the blade. Fin's hand got caught between Logan's left arm and his body as Logan twisted and Logan heard the knife fall to the stone floor. Logan brought a fist toward Fin's head, but the man ducked, fell to the floor and scurried back. Logan started to go after him, determined to kill the man while he had the chance, but as he moved forward, behind him the Holers closed on the girl.

He couldn't leave her. He knew what they saw when they looked at a young, half-naked woman, dazed from her fall. He'd heard the rapists reminisce about it, tell how many sweets they'd banged. Some of them couldn't even bang Lilly: a willing woman left them limp.

Logan roared with pain and frustration. The animals collapsed backward.

The girl had picked up the knife and was standing now with her back to the wall. She braced herself to keep from falling. From the way she stood, she'd sprained her ankle in the fall.

"Stay back," she said, waving the knife around ineffectually. "Stay back!" Her eyes darted from Logan to the abyss and then to Gnasher.

The girl was shaking. She was pretty in a fragile sort of way, with long blond hair and fine features. She was barely dirty, though, so she couldn't have been in prison long. Long enough for Gorkhy, though, damn him to the ninth circle of hell. There was fresh blood staining her torn dress between her legs.

Logan held his hands up. "Easy," he said. "I'm not going to hurt you. But we need to move or they'll start falling on us."

Her eyes flashed up the grate and she began scooting along the circular wall.

Gorkhy had been pulled away from the grate by the other guards. The rest of the prisoners were herded to the grate. The first man didn't want to jump in, so they pushed him.

The fifteen-foot fall onto solid rock broke his legs, and the Holers were on him in seconds. To Logan's dismay, Gnasher joined them, flinging aside others and sinking filed teeth into living flesh.

The second man froze at the spectacle he could hear but barely see. The guards pushed him in and he, too, became meat. After that, most of the other prisoners were willing to hang from the grate and drop in themselves.

Logan had no time for it. On another day, he might have fought for meat himself. But he wouldn't feed today, not with this girl here. Her presence made him remember better things. He wanted to weep.

"Gods," he said. "Natassa Graesin." The words escaped his lips. He shouldn't have said anything, but the shock of seeing another noble was too great. At seventeen, Natassa was the second-eldest Graesin daughter. She was his cousin.

Natassa Graesin stared at him, her wide, frightened eyes taking in the tall, emaciated wreck of what had been a huge, athletic body. He was a shadow of what he had been, but though he had withered, he was still tall, unmistakably tall.

He held his hands up to silence her, but he was too late.

"Logan? Logan Gyre?" she said.

He felt his world ending. In all the time he'd been down here, he'd been only King or Thirteen. In the madness of hunger, he'd eventually joined the others who stood around the Hole to catch bread—with his long reach, he got more than most, at the cost of letting Gorkhy know that a tall blond man was in the Hole. But he'd never, never, never used his real name.

Shooting a glance over his shoulder, he saw that new prisoners were still dropping in the hole, sprawling as they hit the ground. In the near-total darkness, they were blind, terrified, whimpering and shrieking and cursing and weeping as they heard the Holers tearing into the fresh meat. The Holers were fighting and Gorkhy was laughing and cheering at the spectacle, taking bets on what would happen with each prisoner, and the howlers were howling. A lot of noise, a lot of confusion, a lot of distractions. Perhaps it had passed without notice.

But one of the new prisoners wasn't whimpering, wasn't confused, wasn't distracted. Tenser Vargun didn't appear frightened, despite the noise and the heat and the stink and the darkness and the violence. His head was tilted toward Logan and Natassa, his eyes squinting against the midnight dark. He looked thoughtful.

29

*E*lene couldn't breathe. Kylar hadn't only left her; he'd taken Uly. The rejection was complete. Things had seemed to be going so well.

No, things *had* been going so well. Elene couldn't believe it, wouldn't believe it. She scoured the kitchen for some sign. She found a stain on the floorboards, dark against dark wood, hastily cleaned up. Nothing looked like it had been spilled from the cooking, but she couldn't tell what it might be. Then she found a deep, thin gouge in the floor nearby.

She went upstairs. Kylar's wetboy grays were gone, as was Retribution. She was sliding the box back under the bed when she saw the Cenarian Sa'kagé symbol scrawled into the bedside table. "We have the girl," the script below it said, in a careful, neat hand. Elene's heart dropped again.

Someone had taken Uly, and Kylar had gone after them. The revelation brought fear and joy intermingled. Kylar hadn't abandoned her, but Uly had been kidnapped by someone who knew who he was. Someone was trying to trap Kylar. But where had Kylar been when Uly was taken? If someone had grabbed Uly on the street, they might have left a note on the front doorstep, but Elene didn't think they'd dare to break in with Kylar downstairs.

There was a shout from downstairs and pounding on the door. "Open the door. In the name of the Queen, open the door!"

When Elene saw Aunt Mea let the city watch in, her heart seized with fear again. In Cenaria, the guards were considered so corrupt that no one trusted them. But then Elene saw Aunt Mea's obvious relief.

It took almost an hour to sort things out. A neighbor had seen Kylar leave carrying a body over his shoulder, a handsome young man with dark skin, his hair in microbraids, capped with gold beads. Elene knew instantly it had to be Jarl. After Kylar left with the body, the neighbor had gone running for the guards. The guards were only halfway to the house when they were met by the neighbor's wife, who'd seen a woman with a bow enter the house about a minute before Uly returned home, and then leave with the girl. From the evidence, the watch thought the woman was the murderer, thank the God, but they still wanted to talk to Kylar.

Elene lay in bed late that night, mourning Jarl and trying to make sense of it. Why would Jarl come here? Because he was in danger? Because he wanted Kylar to do a job? Just to visit? Elene had to think it was to get Kylar to do a job. Jarl was too important to leave Cenaria on a whim, and if he had left because he was in danger, he'd have had bodyguards. So Jarl had been killed—by accident?—while trying to hire Kylar. Kylar had either agreed to do the job, or he was going out for vengeance. Either way, he'd left before Uly's kidnapping. He might not know about it.

By noon the next day, Kylar still hadn't returned. There was a knock on the door and Elene hurried to answer it. It was one of the guards from yesterday.

"I just thought you should know," the young man said, "we talked to the gate guards as soon as we could, but shifts change and it's hard to get word to everyone. A young woman matching the killer's description left yesterday, headed north. She had a little girl with her. We've already sent men after her, but she's got a good head start. I'm sorry."

After the guard left, Braen and Aunt Mea looked at Elene as if they expected her to burst into tears.

"I'm going after Uly," Elene said instead.

"But—" Aunt Mea began.

"I know, believe me, I know I'm the last person who should go. But what else am I going to do? If Kylar comes back here, tell him where I went. He'll catch up with me, I'm sure. If he's already gone after them, I'll meet him on his way back. But if he doesn't know Uly's been kidnapped, I might be her only chance."

Aunt Mea opened her mouth to protest once more, then closed it. "I understand."

Elene's things fit in a small pack, and by the time she got downstairs, Aunt Mea had packed her enough food for a week. "Is Braen going to say goodbye?" Elene asked.

Aunt Mea took Elene outside. "Braen says goodbye in his own way." There was a horse saddled in front of the shop. It was sturdy and gentle looking. Elene's eyes flooded with tears. She'd thought she was going to walk. "He says he's had some big orders recently," Aunt Mea said, obviously proud of her son. "Now go, child, and may the God go with you."

Kylar was standing over the grave he'd dug and doing his best to get drunk. It was still two hours before dawn. The cemetery was quiet. The only sounds were leaves rattling in the wind and the complaints of night insects. Kylar had chosen this cemetery because it was the richest one on his way out of the city. After killing the Shinga, he'd robbed the man so he had plenty of money, and Jarl deserved the best. If the grave keeper were true to his word, there would even be a headstone here in a week.

They made quite a pair. Jarl laid out on the ground next to the hole, the gore a darker black than his skin, limbs slowly stiffening. Kylar was more blood-spattered than his dead friend, cruor drying into hard ridges on his limbs, cracking as he worked, reconstituting as he perspired. It made him look like he was sweating blood.

The grave was finished. Now Kylar was supposed to say something significant.

He drank more wine. He'd brought four skins and already emptied two. A year ago, two would have flattened him. Now, he wasn't even tipsy. He finished the third skin then dutifully took deep draughts of the fourth until it was gone.

His eyes kept going back to Jarl's corpse. He tried to imagine the wounds closing as his own had so long ago. But they weren't closing. Jarl was dead. He'd been alive one second, and now he was simply not. Kylar finally understood the wry look in Jarl's eyes, too.

The Cenarian wetboy that Shinga Sniggle had ordered killed wasn't Kylar. It was Vi Sovari, and it was Vi Sovari who had killed Jarl with a red-and-black traitor's arrow.

It was just like Jarl to find humor in it. Jarl confessed his love for a woman as she released the arrow that killed him.

"Shit," Kylar said.

There were no words to express the magnitude of the ruin before him. Jarl was no more. This thing in front of Kylar was a slab of meat. Kylar wished he could believe in Elene's God. He wanted to think Jarl and Durzo were in a better place. But he was honest enough to know that was all he wanted—some half-assed good feeling. Even if Elene's God were real, Jarl and Durzo didn't follow him. That meant they got to burn in hell, right?

He climbed down into the grave and pulled Jarl's body in. Jarl's skin was cold, clammy; morning dew was condensing on it. It didn't feel right. Kylar laid him down as gently as he could and climbed back out. He still didn't feel drunk.

Sitting on the pile of soft dirt next to the grave, he realized it was the ka'kari's fault. His body treated alcohol like any poison, and healed him of it. It was so efficient that he'd have to drink massive quantities to get drunk. Just like Durzo had.

And I dismissed him as a drunk. It was yet another way Kylar had misunderstood his master, another way he'd blithely condemned the man. It made everything ache all over again.

"I'm sorry, brother," Kylar said, and realized as the words crossed his lips that Jarl had been exactly that to him: an older brother who looked out for him. Why was Kylar condemned to having revelations about what people meant to him only after they were dead? "I'll make it worth something, Jarl." Making Jarl's sacrifice mean something meant abandoning Elene and Uly and the life that might have been. He'd sworn to Uly that he wouldn't abandon her as every other adult in her life had. And now he was doing it.

Was it like this for you, master? Is this where that ocean of bitterness began? Is giving up my humanity the cost of my immortality?

There was nothing else to do, nothing more to say. Kylar couldn't even weep. As the first birds of morning began singing beauty to the waking sun, he filled the grave.

30

For two days, Uly didn't speak or eat or drink. Vi drove them at a grueling pace along the queen's road heading west and then north. The first night they passed the great estates of the Waeddryner nobility. By the time they stopped, a few hours after sunrise, they were in farmland. The fields were bare, the rolling hills covered with the irregular stubble of harvested spelt.

The first day, Uly waited until Vi had been breathing regularly for about ten minutes, then she bolted for her horse. She hadn't even untied the beast before Vi yanked her away. The second day, Uly waited for an hour. She got up quietly enough that Vi almost missed it. Uly got the tether undone that time, and nearly jumped out of her clothes when she turned to reach for the horse's head and saw Vi standing behind her, hands on hips.

Both times, Vi beat her. She was careful not to injure the girl. No broken bones or scars for this one. She wondered if she was being too easy on the girl, but she'd never beaten a child before. Vi was used to killing men, used to giving Talent-strength to her muscles and letting her victims deal with the consequences. If she did that with Uly, the child would die. That didn't fit Vi's plans.

By the third day, Uly wasn't doing well. She still hadn't taken a drink. She refused anything Vi offered, and she was losing strength. Her lips were cracked and parched, her eyes red. Vi couldn't help but feel a grudging admiration.

The girl was tough, no doubt about it. Vi could stand pain better than most people, but she hated not eating. When she was twelve Hu had routinely withheld her food, giving her only one meal a day "so she wouldn't get fat." He'd put her back on full meals when he decided it was all going to her tits. But worse than the starving were the times he'd withheld water because he thought she was being lazy.

The bastard never did grasp the concept of a woman's cramps.

She'd had to pretend the thirst didn't bother her, because she'd known if she let it show, it would have become his favorite punishment.

"Look, Ugly," she said as she made camp in a small valley as the sun began to rise. "I don't give a shit if you die. You are more useful to me alive than dead, but not by much. Kylar will follow me to Cenaria now either way. You, on the other hand, would probably like to see Kylar again, right?"

Uly stared back at her with sunken eyes full of hate.

"And I'd guess he'd kick your ass if you die for no reason. So, hey, if you want to keep starving, you'll die pretty soon. Tomorrow, I'll have to tie you to the saddle, and you might not make it through the night. That inconveniences me, but it hurts Kylar more. If you'd rather die like a kitten than stay alive and fight me, go ahead. But you're not impressing anyone."

Vi put a skin of water in front of Uly and set about securing the horses. She wasn't worried about Uly escaping now. The girl was too weak. But Vi Talent-locked the ropes anyway. She was going to sleep today, dammit.

The rolling hills here were covered with forests broken now and then by a small village in a group of farm fields. The road was still broad and well-traveled, though. They'd made excellent time. There was no way to tell how far ahead of Kylar they were, but Vi had avoided villages and she had no doubt that had given Kylar precious hours on them. Yesterday evening, she'd traded the horses. If Kylar had somehow divined which tracks were theirs among the many, he'd be thrown.

Still, at the rate they'd been traveling, they'd passed numerous other parties, and though she could swaddle herself in a formless cloak that disguised her sex and identity, there was no disguising that Uly was a child. Nor was there any practical way to pass unseen on the barren hills they'd already come through. Usually, they'd just barreled past the traders' wagons and farmers' carts. It was an uneasy balance. They made better time on the road, but they were more likely to be recognized.

Her only contact with Kylar had been when she'd tried to kill him at the Drake house. Ironically enough, King Gunder had hired Vi, who'd tried to assassinate his son, to kill Kylar, who'd tried to protect him.

She'd had Kylar under her hips and under her knife the very day she took the contract. She'd liked him. He'd been surprisingly calm for a man in his situation. Calm and a little charming, if you thought lame humor in the face of death was cute.

And she would have killed him, but she'd hesitated. No, not hesitated. It hadn't been lack of will that stayed her hand that day so much as pride that she'd accomplished such a difficult job so quickly. Hu never complimented her work. Though under duress, Kylar's compliments had seemed genuine, and there weren't that many people a wetboy could talk shop with. So Vi had given in to the temptation Kylar had laid out for her, stalling so obviously that she'd let it work.

Then the do-gooder count had broken into the room and Kylar landed a knife in her shoulder as she escaped. Months later her shoulder still throbbed at times. She'd lost a little flexibility, despite instantly heading to the wytch Hu used for his healing.

Next time, she wouldn't hesitate.

She knew she should feel elated that she'd killed Jarl. She was free now. A master wetboy. Hu would have no say over anything in her life, and if he tried, she could kill him without worrying about the repercussions in the Sa'kagé. That is, if the Sa'kagé survived whatever the Godking had planned.

I killed Jarl. The thought wouldn't go away. Hadn't gone away for two days. *I killed the man who was the closest thing I've ever had to a friend.*

There hadn't been much to the kill. Any child could climb up on a roof and shoot an arrow. She'd wanted to miss, hadn't she? She could have missed. She could have just not taken the shot. She could have gone inside and joined Kylar and Jarl and fought against the Godking. But she hadn't.

She'd killed, and now she was alone again, going somewhere she didn't want to go, taking a little girl against her will, forcing a man she respected to follow her into a trap.

You are a cruel god, Nysos. Could you not leave me with more than dust and ashes? I, who serve you so faithfully. From my knife and my loins flow rivers of blood and semen. Do I not deserve an honored place for that? Do I not deserve one friend?

She coughed and blinked rapidly. She bit her tongue until it threatened to bleed. *I will not cry. Nysos can have his blood and semen, but he will never have my tears. Curse you, Nysos.* But she didn't say it aloud. She had served her god too long to risk his wrath.

She had even made a pilgrimage of sorts—it had been on her way to a kill—to a small town in the Sethi wine country that was holy to Nysos. The harvest festival was dedicated to the god. Wine flowed freely. Women were expected to abandon themselves to whatever passion moved them. They even had an odd form of storytelling where men stood on a stage holding masks and enacting while the audience watched a three-part cycle full of the suffering of mortals and their need for gods to straighten it out, followed by a bawdy, vicious comedy that seemed to make fun of everyone in the village, even the writer of the enactment. The town loved it. They clapped and wailed and sang along drunkenly with the holy songs and fucked like rabbits. For a week, no one was allowed to turn down a sexual advance. For Vi, it turned into a long week. It was one time in her life that she'd felt justified in complaining about being beautiful. She'd taken to wearing baggy clothing in the hopes she would entice fewer men.

All that service, Nysos. For what? For life? Hu's nearing forty, and for all that he says he serves you, the only times a god's name passes his lips is in curses.

By the time Vi came back to where the bedrolls were laid out, Uly had finished the entire bag of water. She looked like she was about to be sick.

"If you throw up on those blankets, you'll sleep in them dirty," Vi said.

"Kylar's going to kill you," Uly said. "Even if you are a girl."

"I'm not a girl. I'm a bitch, and don't you forget it." Vi tossed the bag with their food at Uly, who dropped it. "Eat slow and not much, or you'll puke and die."

Uly took her advice and soon flopped down on her bedroll and was asleep in seconds. Vi stayed up. She was tired, achingly, grindingly tired. She only thought this much when she was exhausted. It did no good to think. It was worthless.

She busied herself making the camp invisible. It was a foggy morning. They weren't far from the road, but they were in a small hollow. The stream came burbling down from the Silver Bear Hills with enough volume that most of the noise the horses might make would be covered, and with the cold camp they'd made, the human presence was barely notable here. She'd done her best to hide the horses behind a thicket. She squatted with her back to a tree and tried to convince her mind how tired her body was.

In the distance, she heard a clatter. It was dampened by the fog, but it could only be one thing: horses. She drew a sword and a knife, and dipped the knife into her poison sheath. She looked at Uly and considered trying to magically silence the girl, but it would expose her and she didn't know if it would work anyway, so she just pressed her back to a tree and peered toward the sound.

Moments later, Kylar appeared, leading two horses. He passed twenty paces away. He must have been riding almost straight through, switching from horse to horse. He barely slowed as he approached the ford. Vi's horse stomped a foot and one of the horses Kylar was leading neighed.

Kylar cursed and jerked the reins. Uly rolled over as Kylar splashed through the stream. The horses climbed the other bank and clattered into the distance. Kylar never even turned his head.

Vi chuckled and lay down. She slept well.

When she woke that evening, Uly was still asleep. That was good. Vi didn't have time to chase the girl. In her place, another kidnapper would have just bound the girl and been done with it. But the strongest ropes weren't the kind that bound hands. Hopelessness was Vi's weapon, not hemp. Ropes of Uly's own devising would bind her forever.

Ropes of my own devising. I know all about that, don't I?

She kicked Uly to wake her, but not as hard as she meant to. The girl's salvation had been so close, and she'd never even known it.

31

The most valuable skill Dorian ever learned turned out to be a simple one: he figured out how to eat and drink without breaking his trance. Instead of having Solon watch him for the inevitable signs of dehydration and wake him, Dorian was able to maintain his trances for weeks.

Though he knew he appeared utterly disconnected from reality, the opposite was true. From his little room in the garrison at Screaming Winds, Dorian watched everything. The Cenarian garrison at Screaming Winds had been bypassed by Khalidor's invasion. Most of the Khalidoran army had simply used Quorig's Pass more than a week east. With the death of Logan's father, Duke Regnus Gyre, the garrison was being led by a young noble named Lehros Vass. He was well-meaning, but he didn't know what to do without a commanding officer.

Solon was giving advice that over the days sounded less like advice and more like orders. If Khalidor attacked Screaming Winds now, they would attack from the Cenarian side, so he shifted the defenses, moved the men and the supplies inside the walls. No one expected an attack, though. The truth was that Screaming Winds now protected nothing. Garoth Ursuul could let them grow old and die here, and all he would lose would be a trade route that hadn't been used for hundreds of years.

Far to the South, Feir was doing less well, though he was tracking Curoch admirably. Feir had a hard road in front of him, and Dorian could do nothing to make it easier. Sometimes it made Dorian sick. He'd watched Feir die a dozen ways, some of them so shameful he wept even through his trance. At best, Feir would have about two decades and a heroic death in front of him.

As always, Dorian strayed close to his own futures. He'd found a way to do it that didn't risk madness. He simply watched the futures of other people at the places they met him. It didn't work well, though. He would see half a dozen ways a person might interact with him, and how their choices might affect the meeting, but not his own. So he could see what, but not why. He couldn't follow a single line of his own choices to see where it would lead him. Once in a while, he could watch his own face through other people's eyes and guess what he was thinking, but those were rare flashes. It was taking too long, even with his trance stretching over a month, and while he pieced his own life together, everything else changed.

So he started touching his own life directly. He knew several things instantly. First, he was going to be a source of either hope or despair for tens of thousands within a year.

Second, a gaping hole stretched across his possible futures. He traced it back and realized the hole was because in some paths, he would choose to renounce his gift of prophecy. He was stunned. He'd thought of it before, of course. In all his training with the healers, disabling his gift was the only cure he'd been able to find for his growing madness. But Dorian's gift had seemed a gift for the whole world, and he'd gladly borne the consequences because he knew he'd be able to help others avert disaster.

Third, Khali herself was coming to Screaming Winds.

Dorian's heart dropped into his stomach. If she passed the garrison, she would go to Cenaria and take up residence in the hellish gaol they called the Maw. Garoth Ursuul would have two of his sons build ferali. He would use one against the rebel army. There would be a massacre.

Khali and her entourage were still two days away. Dorian had time. He looked back at his own life, trying to figure out how to avert disaster. In a moment, he was swept up in the current. Faces streamed past him, became a maelstrom, sucking him down. His young wife, crying. A girl, hanged. A little village in northern Waeddryn where he might live with Feir's family. A red-haired boy who was like a son to him, fifteen years from now. Killing his brothers. Betraying his wife. Telling his wife the truth and losing her. A gold mask of his own face, weeping golden tears. Marching with an army. Neph Dada. Walking away from an army. Solitude and madness and death, a dozen different ways. Down every path, he could see only suffering. Every time he chose any good for himself, those he loved suffered.

"You knew?" his wife asked. "You knew all along?"

"No!" Dorian shot upright in bed, waking.

Solon flinched in the chair across from Dorian. He gestured, and the lamps in the room lit. "Dorian? You're back! I hope whatever you were doing was important, because I wanted to wake you about a hundred times."

Dorian's head was aching. What day was it? How long had he been catatonic?

His answer was in the air itself. Khali was close. He could feel her.

"I need gold," Dorian said.

"What?" Solon asked. He rubbed his eyes. It was late.

"Gold, man! I need gold!"

Solon pointed to his purse on the table and pulled on boots.

Dorian spilled the gold coins into his hands. It barely even hit his palm before the coins melted into a glob, instantly cooled and wrapped around his wrist. "More. More! There's no time to lose, Solon."

"How much?"

"As much as you can carry. Meet me in the back courtyard, and rouse the soldiers. All of them. But don't ring the alarum bell."

"Dammit, what is it?" Solon demanded. He grabbed his sword belt and strapped it on.

"No time!" Dorian was already running out of the room.

In the courtyard, Dorian could swear he smelled Khali even more strongly, though the scent was purely magical. She was perhaps two miles distant. It was midnight now, and he suspected she'd strike an hour before dawn, the wytching hour, when men are most susceptible to the night's terrors and Khali's delusions.

Dorian tried to untangle what he'd seen. He couldn't imagine the garrison would hold, and if Khali caught him, the results would be as terrible for the world as for him. A prophet, delivered into her hands? Dorian thought of the futures he'd seen for himself. Was it so great a sacrifice to give up seeing those rush inexorably toward him? But if he gave up his visions, he would be blind, rudderless, and useless to anyone else. It also wasn't a simple procedure. He'd described it to Solon and Feir as being like smashing his own brain with a sharp rock in order to stop seizures. Ideally, he could sear one part of his own Talent in such a way that it would eventually heal, but not for years. If Khali captured him, she might think his gift was gone forever, and kill him.

He had begun preparing the weaves before he realized he'd made up his mind. The fact that it was dark and he couldn't replenish his glore vyrden was no problem because the amount of magic he needed was slight. He set up the weaves deftly, sharpening some and setting them aside, holding the prepared portions as if in one hand. As the magic came together, he realized that all his time in his visions, juggling different streams of time and holding place markers at decision points, had paid off in his magic. Not five years ago, he'd come this far with the weave, practicing it to see if he could hold seven strands simultaneously. It had been brutal, especially knowing that letting any one slip could make him an amnesiac, an idiot, or dead. Now, it was easy. Solon came into the yard and saw what he was doing, a look of horror on his face, and even that didn't distract Dorian.

He sliced, twisted, pulled, seared, and covered one section of his Talent.

The courtyard was curiously silent, strangely flat, oddly constricted. "My God," Dorian said.

"What?" Solon asked, his eyes full of concern. "What have you done?"

Dorian was disoriented, like a man trying to stand after losing a leg. "Solon, it's gone. My gift is gone."

32

Three days north of the Silver Bear Hills, Kylar came to the small town of Torras Bend. He'd been pushing hard for six days, barely stopping long enough to rest the horses, and his body ached everywhere from his stint in the saddle. Torras Bend was halfway to Cenaria, at the base of the Fasmeru Mountains and Forglin's Pass. The horses needed the rest, and so did he. South of town, he'd even had to submit to a Lae'knaught checkpoint looking for magi. Apparently, Waeddryn's queen didn't have the will or the power to expel the Lae'knaught either.

He asked a farmer for directions to the town's inn and soon found himself in a warm building filled with the smells of roasting meat pies and fresh ale. Most inns smelled of stale beer and sweat, but the people of northern Waeddryn were fastidious. Their gardens lacked weeds, their fences lacked rot, their children very nearly lacked dirt. They prided themselves on their industry, and the attention to detail of these simple folk was incredible. Even Durzo would have been impressed. All in all, it was a perfect place to rest.

Coming into the common room, Kylar ordered enough food to make the goodwife raise her eyebrows. He sat by himself. His legs were throbbing and his butt was sore. If he never saw another horse again, it would be too soon. He closed his eyes and sighed, only the heavenly odors coming from the kitchen keeping him from going to bed immediately.

In what was obviously a nightly ritual, probably half the men of the village pushed their way through the inn's great oak door to share a pint with their friends before going home. Kylar ignored the men and their inquisitive glances. He only opened his eyes when a stout, homely woman in her fifties set two enormous meat pies in front of him, along with an impressive tankard of ale.

"I think you'll find Mistress Zoralat's ale is as good as her pies," the woman said. "May I join you?"

Kylar yawned. "Ah, excuse me," he said. "Sure. I'm Kylar Stern."

"What do you do, Master Stern?" she said, sitting.

"I'm a, uh, soldier, as a matter of fact." He yawned again. He was getting too old for this. He'd considered saying "I'm a wetboy" just to see what the old goat's reaction would be.

"A soldier for whom?"

"Who are you?" he asked.

"Answer my question, and I'll answer yours," she said, as if he were a recalcitrant child.

Fair enough. "For Cenaria."

"I was under the impression that country no longer existed," she said.

"Were you?" he said.

"Khalidoran goons. Meisters. The Godking. Conquest. Rape. Pillage. Iron-fisted rule. Ring any bells?"

"I guess some people would be deterred by that," Kylar said. He smiled and shook his head at himself.

"You frighten a lot of people, don't you, Kylar Stern?"

"What was your name again?" he asked.

"Ariel Wyant Sa'fastae. You can call me Sister Ariel."

Any vestige of fatigue vanished instantly. Kylar touched the ka'kari within him to be sure it was ready to call up in an instant.

Sister Ariel blinked. Was it because she'd seen something, or had he just let his muscles tense?

"I thought this was a dangerous part of the world for people like you," Kylar said. He couldn't remember the stories, but he remembered something linking Torras Bend with mages' dying.

"Yes," she said. "One of our young and foolhardy sisters disappeared here. I've come to look for her."

"The Dark Hunter," he said, finally remembering.

At tables around them, conversations ceased. Dour faces turned toward Kylar. From their expressions, he could see that the topic wasn't so much taboo as it was gauche. "Sorry," he mumbled, and began attacking a meat pie.

Sister Ariel watched in silence as he ate. He felt a twinge of suspicion, wondering what Durzo would have said if he knew Kylar was eating food served to him by a maja, but he'd died twice already—maybe three times— and lived again, so what the hell? Besides, the pies were good, and the ale was better.

Not for the first time, he wondered if it had been the same for Durzo.

He'd lived for centuries, but had he been unkillable, too? He must have. But he had never risked his own life. Was that only because by the time Kylar knew him, the ka'kari had abandoned him? Kylar wondered sometimes if there were a downside to his power. He could live for hundreds of years. He couldn't be killed. But he didn't feel immortal. He didn't even feel the sense of power that, when he was a boy, he thought he would feel once he became a wetboy. He was a wetboy now, more than a wetboy, and he felt like he was still just Kylar. Still Azoth, the clueless, scared child.

"Have you seen a beautiful woman come riding through here, sister?" he asked. Vi had seen where Kylar lived. She would tell the Godking and he would destroy everything and everyone Kylar loved. That was how he worked.

"No. Why?"

"If you do," he said, "kill her."

"Why? Is she your wife?" Sister Ariel asked, smirking.

He gave her a flat look. "The God doesn't hate me that much. She's an assassin."

"So, you're not a soldier, but an assassin hunter."

"I'm not hunting her. I wish I had the time. But she may come through here."

"What's so important that you would abandon justice?"

"Nothing," he said without thinking. "But justice has been too long denied elsewhere."

"Where?" she asked.

"Suffice it to say that I'm on a mission for the king."

"There is no king of Cenaria except the Godking."

"Not yet."

She raised an eyebrow. "There's no man who can unite Cenaria, even against the Godking. Perhaps Terah Graesin can, but she's scarcely a man, is she?"

He smiled. "You Sisters like to think you've got it all figured out, don't you?"

"Do you know that you're an infuriating young ignoramus?"

"Only as much as you're a tired old bag."

"Do you truly think I'd kill some young woman for you?"

"I don't suppose you would. Forgive me, I'm tired. I forgot that the Seraph's hand only reaches beyond its ivory halls to take things for itself."

Her lips pressed into a thin line. "Young man, I don't take well to impudence."

"You've succumbed to the intoxication of power, Sister. You like watching people jump." He raised an insolent eyebrow, bemused. "So color me scared."

She was very still. "Another temptation of power," she said, "is to strike down those who vex you. You, Kylar Stern, are tempting me."

He picked that moment to yawn. It wasn't feigned, but he couldn't have found a better moment. She turned red. "They say the old age is a second childhood, Sister. Besides which, the moment you drew power, I'd kill you." *By the gods, I can't stop. Am I really going to get on the wrong side of half the world's mages because one old lady irritates me?*

Instead of getting angrier, Sister Ariel's face grew thoughtful. "You can tell the moment I draw magic?"

He wasn't going there. "One way to find out," he said. "But it would be a bother to dispose of your corpse and cover my tracks. Especially with all these witnesses."

"How would you cover your tracks?" she asked quietly.

"Come now. You're in Torras Bend. How many of the mages who have been 'killed by the Dark Hunter' here do you think were really killed by the Dark Hunter? Don't be naive. The thing probably doesn't even exist."

She scowled, and he could tell she'd never thought of it. Well, she was a mage. Of course she didn't think like a wetboy. "Well," she said. "You're wrong about one thing. It exists."

"If everyone who's ever gone into the woods has died, how do you know?"

"You know, young man. There's a way for you to prove that we're all crazy."

"Go into the woods?" he asked.

"You wouldn't be the first to try."

"I'd be the first to succeed."

"You're awfully full of braggadocio about the things you'd do if you only had the time."

"Fair enough, Sister Ariel. I accept your correction—until the day Cenaria has a king. Now if you'll excuse me?"

"One moment," she said as he stood. "I'm going to draw the power, but I swear by the White Seraph that I won't touch you with it. If you must kill me, I won't try to stop you."

She didn't wait for him to respond. He saw a pale iridescent nimbus surround her. It shifted quickly through every color in the rainbow in deliberate succession, though some colors seemed somehow thicker than others. Was that an indication of her strength in the various disciplines of magic? He readied the ka'kari to devour whatever magic she threw at him—hoping he remembered what he had done before, and not sure that he did—but he didn't strike.

The nimbus didn't move. Sister Ariel Wyant merely inhaled deeply through her nose. The nimbus disappeared. She nodded her head, as if satisfied. "Dogs find you very odd, don't they?"

"What?" he asked. It was true, but he'd never thought much of it.

"Maybe you can tell me," she said, "why, after days of hard riding, don't you smell of sweat and dirt and horse? Indeed, you have no scent whatsoever."

"You're imagining things," he said, backing away. "Goodbye, Sister."

"Until we meet again, Kylar Stern."

33

Momma K stood on a landing overlooking the warehouse floor. Agon's Dogs, as they'd taken to calling themselves, were training under his watchful eye. The force had shrunk to a hundred men, and Momma K was sure that by now its existence was well-known. "Do you think they're ready?" she asked as Agon labored up the stairs on a cane.

"More training would make them better. Battle will make them better faster. But it will cost lives," he said.

"And your wytch hunters?"

"They're no Ymmuri. Ymmuri can riddle a man with arrows from a hundred paces while galloping away from him. The best I can hope for is ten men who will get in range, stop, shoot, and move on before the fireballs get to them. My hunters aren't worthy of the bows they carry—but they're a damn sight better than anything else we have."

Momma K smiled. He was underplaying his men's capabilities. She'd seen those men shoot.

"What about your rent girls?" Agon asked. "This mission will cost lives. Are they ready for that?" He stood close beside her as they watched his men spar.

"You would have been amazed if you could have seen their faces, Brant. It was like I gave them their souls back. They'd been dying inside, and now they've come back to life, all at once."

"No word yet from Jarl?" Agon's voice was tense and Momma K could tell that, for all that he had clashed with the young man, Agon was worried for him.

"There wouldn't be. Not yet." She put her hands on the rail and accidentally brushed his fingers.

Brant looked at her hand and then in her eyes and quickly away.

She winced and pulled her hand away. Decades ago, Agon had been arrogant, not obnoxious with it but merely full of youthful confidence that he could do pretty much anything better than pretty much anyone else. That was gone now, replaced by a sober understanding of his own strengths and weaknesses. He was a man well tempered by the years. Gwinvere had known men ruined by their wives. Small women who felt so threatened they undercut their husbands for so many years that those men no longer trusted themselves. Such women had made Momma K wealthy. She knew men with perfectly good wives who were regulars, men addicted to the brothels as others were addicted to wine, but much of her business came from men desperate to be considered manly, strong, good lovers, noble.

It was one of the many ironies of the business that they came to a brothel for that.

Men, Momma K believed, were too simple to ever be truly safe from the temptations of a house of pleasure. It had been her business to make sure those temptations were multifaceted, and she'd been good at her business. Her establishments weren't just whorehouses. She had meeting rooms, smoking rooms, dignified parlors, lecturers on all the topics men love. The food and drink were always finer than her competitors' and priced lower. At her best establishments, she brought in chefs and wine masters from all over Midcyru. As a restaurateur, she would have been a dismal failure. The food side of her business operated at a loss every year. But at her houses, men who came for the food stayed to spend their coin other ways.

The few Brant Agons of the world didn't bang her girls for two reasons: they were happy at home, and they didn't walk through the doors in the first place. She was sure Agon had been derided for that. Men who didn't frequent the houses of pleasure were always mocked by those who did.

Brant had conviction, integrity. He reminded her of Durzo.

The thought sent a lance through her stomach. Durzo had been dead three months. Gods, how she missed him! She'd been helplessly in love with Durzo. Durzo was the only man in her life who would ever understand her. She'd been too terrified of that to let love grow. She'd been a coward. She'd starved their relationship of honesty, and like a plant potted in a shallow bowl, the relationship had been stunted. Durzo was the father of her child. He'd only found out a few days before he died.

Momma K was fifty now, almost fifty-one. The years had been kind to her, at least most days they seemed so. She usually looked fifteen years younger than she was. Well, at least ten If she tried, she thought she still had what it would take to seduce Brant.

Once a whore, always a whore, huh, Gwin? She used to despise old women who clung to their lost youth by their lacquered fingernails. Now she was one. Part of her wanted to seduce Brant just to prove to herself that she still could. But she didn't want to seduce Brant. It had been years since she'd taken a man to her bed. For all the thousands of times it had been work, there had been times she'd liked or admired her lover of the moment. And there had been Durzo. The night they conceived Uly, he'd been so blasted on mushrooms that he hadn't been much of a lover, but to have the man she loved share her bed had filled her to overflowing. She was so shot through with love and grief that she'd wept during their lovemaking. Even in his drugged state, Durzo had stopped and asked if he was hurting her. After that, it had taken all her skill to bring him to completion. Durzo had been a tender man when it came to taking his pleasure.

Now their child was being raised by Kylar and Elene. It was the only deception she didn't regret. With those two, Uly would do well.

But she was tired of deceit. Tired of taking and never giving. She didn't want to seduce Brant. She knew he wanted her, and his wife was probably dead. Probably, but he couldn't know. Wouldn't know. Ever. How long would a man like Brant Agon wait for the woman he loved?

Forever. That's the kind of man he is.

Thirty-some years ago, they'd met at a party, her first ever at a noble's home. He'd fallen instantly in love with her and she'd allowed him to court her, never telling him what she did, what she was. He'd been gallant, confident, determined to make his mark on the world, and so sweetly careful in his courting that he hadn't asked her for a kiss for a month.

She'd indulged in the fantasy. He would marry her, take her away from all the horrors she wanted so desperately to leave behind. She hadn't had that many noble clients, yet. It was possible, wasn't it?

The night of their first kiss, a noble had referred to her as the sweetest harlot he'd ever had. Brant overheard it, instantly challenged the man to a duel, and killed him. Gwinvere had fled. The next day, Brant had learned the truth. He enlisted and tried to get himself honorably killed fighting on the Ceuran border.

But Brant Agon had been too capable to die. Eventually, despite how he despised bootlicking and politicking, his merit had pulled him through the ranks. He married a plain woman from a merchant family. By all accounts, it was a happy marriage.

"How long will it take to get everything ready?" she asked. She would hope Brant's infatuation had died. She would help him dodge the truth. She was good at that, at least.

"Gwin."

She turned and looked him in the eye, her mask in place, eyes cool. "Yes?"

He blew out a great breath. "I loved you for years, Gwin, even after..."

"My betrayal?"

"Your indiscretion. You were what? Sixteen, seventeen? You deceived yourself first, and I think you suffered for it more than I did."

She snorted.

"Regardless," he said. "I bear you no ill will. You are a beautiful woman, Gwin. More beautiful than my Liza ever was. You are so brilliant that I feel I have to sprint just to keep up with you jogging. I felt quite the opposite with Liza. You...affect me profoundly."

"But," she said.

"Yes. But," he said. "I love Liza, and she has loved me through a thousand trials, and she deserves all that I have to give. Whether or not you have tender feelings for me, while I have hope that my Liza lives, I would ask— beg—that you would help me remain true to her."

"You've chosen a hard road," she said.

"Not a road, a battle. Sometimes life is our battlefield. We must do what we know to do, not what we want to do."

Gwinvere sighed, and yet somehow felt lighter. Dodging Brant's attraction could have so easily turned into dodging his presence, and she needed to work closely with him now. *Is honesty so easy? Could I have just said, "Durzo, I love you, but I fear you'll destroy me"?* Brant had just offered her his vulnerability, confessed her effect on him, and yet seemed not weaker but stronger for it. *How was that? Is truth so powerful?*

She swore then, in her own heart, that she would not tempt this man for her own vanity. Not in her voice, not in accidental touches, not in her dress, she would lay down every weapon in her arsenal. The resolution made her feel oddly...decent. "Thank you," she said. She smiled companionably. "How long till they're ready?"

"Three days," Brant said.

"Then let us make the night run red."

34

Solon dropped the two leather five-hundred-weight bags he carried and grabbed Dorian as the prophet tottered. At first, he didn't understand what Dorian had said.

"What are you talking about?"

Dorian pushed Solon's steadying arm away. He put on his cloak and sword belt and picked up two pairs of manacles. "This way," he said, grabbing one of the bags from Solon and heading down the open road away from the wall.

The land leading to the wall was rocky, barren ground. It had been cleared of trees out to a hundred and fifty yards, and though the road was broad enough for twenty men abreast, it was rutted and pitted from the wear of many feet and wagons over ground that alternated between soil and solid rock.

"Khali is coming," Dorian said before Solon could ask what was happening again. "I gave up my prophetic gift in case she captures me."

Solon couldn't even answer.

Dorian stopped beneath a black oak that grew on a rocky outcropping that hung over the road. "She's here. Not a half a league away." Dorian didn't even take his eyes off the tree. "It'll have to do. Make sure you only step on rock. If they see tracks, they'll find me."

Solon didn't move. Dorian had finally gone crazy. The other times it had been obvious: he'd simply been catatonic. But now, he seemed so rational. "Come on, Dorian," Solon said. "Let's go back to the wall. We can talk about this in the morning."

"The wall won't be there in the morning. Khali will strike at the wytching hour. That gives you five hours to get the men out of there." Dorian hoisted himself up on the ledge. "Throw the bags up to me."

"Khali, Dorian? She's a myth. You're trying to tell me that a goddess is half a league from here?"

"Not a goddess. Perhaps one of the rebel angels expelled from heaven and given leave to walk the earth until the end of days."

"Right. I suppose she's brought a dragon? We can talk about—"

"Dragons avoid angels," Dorian said. Disappointment etched his features. "Are you going to abandon me now when I need you? Have I ever lied to you? You thought Curoch was a myth too, before we found it. I need you. When Khali comes through the wall, I'll go out of my mind. You've seen me when I thought I could use the vir for good. That was like one part wine and ten parts water; this is pure liquor. I will be lost. Her very presence brings out the worst. The worst fears, the worst memories, the worst sins. My hubris will come out. I might try to fight her, and I'll lose. Or my lust for power will break me and I'll join her. She knows me. She will break me."

Solon couldn't take the look in Dorian's eyes. "What if you're wrong? What if it is the madness you've warned about for so long?"

"If the wall stands at dawn, you'll know."

Solon threw the bags up to Dorian and then climbed carefully up the rock, making sure he didn't leave so much as a footprint.

"What are you doing?" he asked as Dorian smiled at him and poured the gold onto the ground. Next Dorian pulled on the manacles and the iron chains holding them together tore apart as if they were made of paper. He dropped a manacle onto the pile of coins and it fell into the coins as if they were liquid. The other three manacles followed and the piles of coins shrank each time. Dorian reached through the gold and pulled out each of the manacles, now sheathed in gold, and placed one on each of his wrists. He stretched the iron of the second pair and locked those manacles around his thighs just above the knee.

It was amazing. Dorian had always said that his power with the vir had dwarfed his Talent, yet here he was, molding gold and iron artfully and effortlessly.

In another moment, Dorian had shaped the rest of the coins into four narrow spikes and what looked like a bowl. He stopped, and now he concentrated. Solon could feel the brush of spells flowing past him, sinking into the metal. After two minutes, Dorian stopped and spoke under his breath to the black oak.

"There will be a contingent with her, the Soulsworn," Dorian said. "They've given up much of what it is to be human to serve Khali. But they aren't the danger. She is. Solon, I don't think you can defeat her. I think you should take the men away from here. Take them somewhere where their deaths might accomplish something. But...if she makes it to Cenaria, Garoth Ursuul's sons will make two ferali. They will use them on the resistance. This I have seen."

"You didn't really do it, did you? You didn't really destroy your gift," Solon said.

"If I don't see you again, my friend, may the God go with you." Dorian said. He fused the gold spikes to the manacles and knelt behind the tree. He slid the spikes into the wood with unnatural ease. His hands were set high and far apart. As he knelt there, obviously ready to pray his way through whatever ordeal he thought was coming, Solon felt a stab of envy. This time, it wasn't for Dorian's power or Dorian's lineage or Dorian's simple, humble integrity. He envied Dorian's certainty. Dorian's world was very clear. To him, Khali wasn't a goddess or a figment of the Khalidorans' imagination or just an ancient monster who'd conned the Khalidoran people into worshipping her. She was an angel who'd been expelled from heaven.

In Dorian's world, everything had a place. There was a hierarchy. Things fit. Even a man with Dorian's vast powers could be humble, because he knew others were far above him, even if he never met one of them. Dorian could name evil without fear and without rancor. He could claim that some did evil or served it without hating them. Solon had never known anyone like that. Except perhaps Count Drake. Whatever happened to him? Did he die in the coup?

"What does all this do?" Solon asked, picking up what had been a gold bowl. Now, it was something between a helmet and a mask. It would fit completely over Dorian's head, with only two small holes in the nose for breathing. He turned it over. It was a perfect sculpture of Dorian's face, weeping tears of gold.

"It will keep me from seeing her, from hearing her, from shouting out to her, from moving from this place. It will keep me from indulging in the last temptation—believing myself strong enough to fight her. I hope it will also keep me from using the vir. But I can't bind myself magically. I need you to do it for me. After she's passed, I'll be able to escape when the sun rises and refills my Talent, so you needn't worry for me. If you need your gold, it will be here."

"You're leaving, no matter what."

Dorian smiled. "Don't ask where."

"Good luck," Solon said. There was a lump in his throat that reminded him of how good it had felt not to be alone again. Even fighting with Dorian and Feir had been better than peace without them.

"You've been a brother to me, Solon. I believe we'll meet again, before this is done," Dorian said. "Now hurry."

Solon fit the gold helmet over Dorian's head and bound it with the strongest magic he could, completely emptying his glore vyrden to do it. He'd do no more magic until sunrise. It wasn't a comforting thought. As he climbed down from the rock outcropping, he swore that he saw bark growing over Dorian's arms where they otherwise would have been exposed.

From the road, Dorian was invisible. "Goodbye, brother," Solon said. Then he turned and strode toward the wall. Now he just had to convince Lehros Vass that he wasn't stark raving mad.

35

The Godking perched on the fireglass throne he'd ordered cut from the rock of the Maw. To him, the sharp-edged blackness was a reminder, a goad, and a comfort at once.

His son stood before him. His first *son,* not just the seed of his loins. The Godking spread his seed far and wide. He never considered the weeds that took hold to be sons. They were just bastards, and he gave them no thought. The only ones who mattered were the boys who would be Vürdmeisters. The training, though, was more than most could survive. Only a few boys out of scores of wytchborn survived to become his aethelings, his throne-worthy sons. Each of those had been given an uurdthan, a Harrowing to prove his worth. So far, only Moburu had succeeded. Only Moburu would he acknowledge as his son. And still not yet his heir.

The truth was, Moburu pained him. Garoth remembered the boy's mother. An island princess of some sort, captured in the days before the Sethi Empire had destroyed Garoth's attempt at a navy. He'd been intrigued by her, and while an endless procession of other women born high and low, willing and not, made its way through his bedchamber, he'd actually tried to seduce her. She'd been as passionate as he was calculating, as hot as he was cold. She'd been exotic, enticing. He'd tried everything except magic. He'd been certain with a young man's certainty that no woman could long resist him.

After a year, she still held onto her haughty disdain. She despised him. One night he'd lost his patience and raped her. He'd meant to have her strangled afterward, but was oddly ashamed. Later, Neph had told him the woman was pregnant. He'd put the child out of his mind until Neph told him the boy had survived the trials and was ready for his uurdthan. Garoth had given Moburu an uurdthan he'd been sure would be the death of him. But the man had completed that task as easily as every other Garoth had put before him.

The worst part of all was that the heir presumptive to Khalidor's throne didn't even look Khalidoran. He had his mother's eyes, her throaty voice, and her skin—her Ladeshian skin.

It was a bitter gall. Why couldn't Dorian have made it? Garoth had held such high hopes for Dorian. He'd liked Dorian. Dorian had achieved his uurdthan and then had betrayed Garoth. Garoth had held lower hopes for the one who'd called himself Roth, but at least Roth looked Khalidoran.

Moburu wore the regalia of an Alitaeran cavalry officer, red brocade on gold with a dragon's head sigil. He was intelligent, quick-witted, utterly self-assured, roughly handsome despite his Ladeshian skin (Garoth grudgingly admitted), reputed to be one of the best riders in the cavalry, and ruthless. Of course. He stood as a son of the Godking should. He wore humility as naturally as a man wore a dress.

It irked Garoth, but it was his own fault. He had designed his seeds' lives so that those who survived would be exactly what Moburu was. His problem was that he'd designed all those tests to present him with candidates. He had hoped to have a number of sons. If he did, their attention would be fixed on each other. Brother would plot against brother for their father's favor. But now, with Dorian gone, Roth dead, and none of the others beyond their uurdthan, Moburu was alone. The man's ambition would force him to turn his eyes on the Godking himself soon. If he hadn't already.

"What news from the Freeze?" the Godking asked.

"Your Holiness, it is as bad as we thought. Maybe worse. The clans have already sent out the summons. They've agreed to truces so they can winter close enough to the border to join the war band at spring. They're spawning krul, and maybe zel and ferali. If they've learned to do that, they'll be increasing their numbers for the next nine months."

"How did they find a spawning place in the Freeze, for Khali's sake? Under the permafrost?" Garoth swore.

"My lord," his son said. "We can counteract that threat easily enough. I've taken the liberty of ordering Khali brought here. She'll come through Screaming Winds. It's faster."

"You did what?" The Godking's voice was icy, dangerous.

"She'll massacre one of the Cenaria's most formidable garrisons— saving you a headache. She'll arrive in a few days. Beneath this castle is perfect spawning ground. The locals call it the Maw. With Khali here, we can breed an army such as the world has never seen. This ground is steeped in misery. The caverns beneath Khaliras have been mined for seven hundred years. The krul our Vürdmeisters can produce there are nothing compared to what's possible here."

The Godking's muscles were rigid, but he allowed nothing to show on his face. "Son. Son. You have never spawned krul. You have never forged ferali or bred ferozi. You have no idea what it costs. There's a reason I used human armies to conquer the highlanders and the river clans and the Tlanglang and the Grosth. I've solidified our rule within and expanded our borders four times—and never once used krul. Do you know how people fight when they know that if they lose their entire families will be eaten? They fight to the last man. They arm the children with bows. Their women use kitchen knives and pokers. I saw it in my youth, and it gained my father nothing."

"Your father didn't have the vir you do."

"There's more to it than vir. This conversation is over." Moburu had never dared speak to him this way before—and ordering Khali brought here without asking!

But Garoth was distracted. He had lied. He had made krul, ferozi, and even ferali. Ferali had killed his last two brothers. He'd sworn then: never again. Never again with any of the monsters except for the few breeding pairs of ferozi he'd been working on to someday send into the Iaosian Forest for Ezra's treasures. But those he'd already paid for. They required nothing more of him.

But Moburu might be right. That was the worst of it. He had gotten used to treating Moburu as a partner, a son in the way other fathers treated their sons.

It had been a mistake. He'd shown indecision. Moburu was surely already plotting for his throne. Garoth could kill him, but Moburu was too valuable a tool to throw away carelessly. Curse him. Why hadn't his brothers turned out? Moburu needed a rival.

The Godking lifted a finger. "I've changed my mind. Think out loud for me, son. Make your case."

Moburu paused for a moment, then swelled with self-confidence. "I'd admit that our armies could probably counter the wild men from the Freeze. Even if the clans stay together, our Vürdmeisters would tip the balance in our favor. But to do that, we have to send every capable meister north. Quite honestly, there couldn't be a worse time. The Sisters grow suspicious and frightened. Some of them are saying they need to fight us now before we grow any stronger. We know the Ceurans will seize any weakness to come pouring over the border. They've wanted Cenaria for hundreds of years."

"The Ceurans are split."

"There's a brilliant young general named Lantano Garuwashi who's gathering a large following in northern Ceura. He's never lost a duel or a battle. If we send our armies and our meisters north, attacking us could be just what he needs to unify Ceura. Unlikely, but possible."

"Go on," the Godking said. He knew all about Lantano Garuwashi. Nor was he worried about the Sisters. He'd personally arranged for their present political crisis.

"It also seems the Sa'kagé is much better established and more capably led than we had believed. It's obviously the work of this new Shinga, Jarl. I think it shows that he's moved into a new phase of—"

"Jarl is dead," Garoth said.

"That can't be. I haven't found any sign—"

"Jarl has been dead for a week."

"But there haven't even been rumors of that, and with the level of organization we've found . . . I don't understand," Moburu said.

"You don't have to," the Godking said. "Go on."

Oh, Moburu looked less confident now. Good. He obviously wanted to ask more, but didn't dare. He floundered for a moment, then said, "There are rumors that Sho'cendi is sending a delegation to investigate what they call the alleged Khalidoran threat."

"Your sources call it a delegation?" Garoth asked, smiling thinly.

Moburu looked uncertain, then angry. "Y-yes, and if the mages decide we're a threat, they could return to Sho'cendi and come back with an army by spring—the same time all our other threats may materialize."

"Those delegates are battlemages. Six full battlemages. The Sa'seuran believe they've found and lost Jorsin Alkestes' sword, Curoch. They think it may be here in Cenaria."

"How do you know that?" Moburu asked, awed. "My source sits just outside the High Sa'seuran itself."

"Your brother told me," the Godking said, pleased with this turn of the conversation. He was back where he belonged. In control. Alive. Moving the world on the fulcrum of his desires. "He's one of the delegates."

"My brother?"

"Well, not a brother yet. Soon. I suppose you can guess his uurdthan. It is somewhat more difficult than your own."

Moburu absorbed the insult, and Garoth could see it sank deep. "He is to recover Curoch?" Moburu asked.

Garoth smiled his thin-lipped smile. He could see Moburu thinking. A son who recovered Curoch would be highly favored, highly powerful.

Indeed, one of Garoth's ulcers had Curoch's name on it. If any of his sons recovered Curoch, that son might not hand it over. Curoch would give him enough power to challenge Garoth himself. Moburu would think of that immediately. But Garoth already had plans for that. Many plans, from the most facile—bribes and blackmail—to the most desperate—a death spell that might throw his consciousness into the murderer's body. That was not a spell one could safely test, so the best thing was to keep the sword out of his sons' hands.

"But you have raised some excellent points, son. You have become valuable to me." Oh, how it grated to say that to this half-breed. Son! "I will grant your wish. You will build me a ferali."

Moburu's eyes widened. Oh, he had no idea. "Yes, Your Holiness."

"And Moburu?" Garoth let the silence sit until Moburu swallowed. "Impress me."

36

You want us to flee, and you won't say why? Is that supposed to impress me?" Lord Vass asked.

Three hundred soldiers had gathered in the dark courtyard, the moon a sliver in a night sky aflame with stars. Three hundred soldiers dressed for battle, bundled against the fierce cold that had already descended on these mountains, though summer's heat had barely lost its edge in Cenaria City. Three hundred soldiers and their commander—who wasn't Solon. Three hundred men who were watching the exchange between Solon and Lehros Vass.

"I admit," Solon said quietly, "that it sounds weak. But I only ask for a day. We leave for one day, and then we come back. If I'm wrong, it's not like there are any looters who will have taken anything. We're the only people in these godforsaken mountains aside from the highlanders, and they haven't raided the wall in three years."

"It's abandoning our post," the young lord said. "We're sworn to hold this wall."

"We have no post," Solon snapped. "We have no king, we have no lord.

We have three hundred men and an occupied country. Our oaths were to men now dead. Our duty is to keep these men alive so they can fight when we have a chance. This isn't the kind of war where we gloriously charge the enemy lines with our swords waving."

Lord Vass was young enough that he flushed with anger and embarrassment. Of course, that was exactly the kind of war he had in mind, and it had been a mistake to belittle it. How long had it been since Solon had lost those illusions of war?

The men weren't moving a muscle, but they all saw the anger on Lord Vass's face, the red made redder in the flickering torchlight.

"If you would have us leave, I demand to know why," Lord Vass said.

"A contingent of Khalidoran elites known as the Soulsworn is coming. They're bringing the Khalidoran goddess Khali to Cenaria. They'll attack the wall at the wytching hour."

"And you want to leave?" Vass asked, incredulous. "Do you know what it will mean when we capture the Khalidoran's goddess? It will destroy them. It will give our countrymen hope. We'll be heroes. This is the place to stop them. We have the walls, the traps, the men. This is our chance. This is just what we've been waiting for."

"Son, this goddess..." Solon gritted his teeth. "We're not talking about capturing a statue. I think she's real."

Lehros Vass looked at Solon, first incredulous, then indulgent. "If you need to run away, you go ahead. You know where the road is." He chuckled, giddy with his own grandeur. "Of course, I can't let you go until you give me my gold back."

If Solon told him where his gold was now, Vass would have his men go get it immediately. Dorian would be left helpless.

"To hell with you," Solon said. "And to hell with me too. We'll die together."

Sister Ariel Wyant sat five paces from the first magical boundary that separated the Iaosian Forest from the oak grove. For the past six days, she'd had her eye on what appeared to be a plaque twenty feet inside the forest. It didn't look like it had been there long: undergrowth hadn't covered it yet.

Her first hope in all her examinations of the ward had been that Ezra had made the ward hundreds of years ago. With another magus, she would have expected the weaves to disintegrate after so much time. Weaves always disintegrated. But with Ezra *always* didn't mean always. The proof shimmered just beyond mundane sight before her.

The second hope was that, given Ezra's power and the power of the other magi of his era, he would be defending himself against opponents far more powerful than any alive today. Sister Ariel didn't have the arrogance to think herself equal to those Ezra would have expected. She could only hope that her light touches against the weaves would be beneath notice. Termites were tiny, but they'd destroyed many a mighty house.

So for six days, she'd examined and reexamined the weaves that divided the Iaosian Forest from the oak grove. It was as beautiful as a black widow's web. There were traps both large and small. There were weaves that were meant to tear apart with the faintest touch, weaves that were meant to be unraveled, weaves that couldn't be broken with double Ariel's strength. And each had a trap.

Ariel could guess exactly what Sister Jessie had done. She'd probably tried to conceal her Talent. For the first day, it looked like a perfect strategy. It was a strategy that would have worked, had Ezra been simple. Sister Jessie was weak enough that she could compress her Talent and then shield it. That would make her Talent invisible to other Sisters or to male Seers—now there was a strange thought, how many times had Talented women used exactly that strategy to hide themselves or their talented daughers from Sisters who came to recruit for the Chantry? Ariel shook her head. It wasn't time to get distracted. The problem was that Ezra's weaves didn't just register Talent. As nearly as Ariel could tell—and she had to guess because of the complexity and delicacy of the weaves—Ezra's weaves detected mages' bodies.

Everyone knew that mages were different from regular people, but not even Healers today understood exactly how magic changed a mage's flesh. That it did so was undeniable. Mages aged differently, sometimes more slowly the more Talented they were, but sometimes not. Regardless, their very flesh was altered in subtle ways by their constant interactions with magic. Apparently Ezra knew exactly what those ways were. Sister Ariel should have guessed that. Among no few other achievements, he had been a Sa'salar, a Lord of Healing. He had created the Dark Hunter—created a living being!

Oh, Sister Jessie, did you walk right through this wall of magic? Did you really think yourself cleverer than Ezra himself? How many mages' bones litter this damned forest?

She was letting her mind get off the problem at hand. She was still alive. She had made it past the first barrier. Now she needed to do something with that accomplishment. She needed to get that damned gold plaque. It was stuck, twenty feet away, just at the top of a small hillock. It was so close, and yet she had no hope of getting it. Her examination of Ezra's traps had left her convinced of it. It would take her years to dismantle his traps. Years, if ever. Even if she had the time, she would never be sure that she hadn't missed something. She could never be sure how many other layers of protection were left. Ezra might have spun this ward in a few days. He might have intended that this layer be penetrated by weak mages. Sister Ariel could spend her whole life dismantling traps and never uncover Ezra's real secrets.

If she'd come here as a younger woman, she might have thought it a worthy use of her life. But as a younger woman, she'd been much more idealistic. She'd believed in the Chantry with the kind of foolish faith that most people reserve for their religion. If Ezra did possess devastatingly powerful artifacts, would Ariel really want to deliver those to the Speaker? Would she trust Istariel with something that would multiply her power ten times?

Stop it. Ariel, you're letting your mind wander again.

She looked at the plaque. Then she started laughing. It was so simple. She stood and started walking back to the village.

She returned an hour later with a full stomach and a rope. Master Zoralat had been kind enough to show her how to make and throw a lasso. For the last two days she'd wondered how to get the plaque—and for two days she'd thought of only magical means. Stupid stupid stupid.

The next several hours proved her clumsy as well. How many times in her life had she sneered at the men who worked the Chantry's stables? This was the kind of exercise every Sister should be exposed to—in front of all the stable hands in the Chantry.

The day ended and she still hadn't lassoed the plaque. She did her cursing in the forest and went home. The next day she returned, her arm and shoulder aching. It took her another three hours, during which she cursed herself, cursed the rope, cursed Ezra, cursed her lack of exercise, and just cursed—but all silently.

When the lasso finally dropped around the plaque, she could swear the gold glowed briefly. She wanted to extend her senses to see what had just happened, but it was too far away. She decided there was nothing to do but pull the damned thing in.

At first, the plaque wouldn't move. It was somehow stuck. Then, as Ariel pulled, part of the hillock shifted and rolled over, freeing the plaque. It wasn't a hillock; it was Sister Jessie's body. She'd been dead for weeks. Mold grew over her bright robes, obscuring the bloodstains. It looked like a claw had torn away half of her head in a single terrible swipe. Since her death, no animals had disturbed her body: there were no bears or coyotes or ravens or other carrion feeders in Ezra's Wood, but the worms were well into their work.

Sister Ariel looked away, allowing herself a moment to be a woman confronting an acquaintance's mutilated body. She breathed slowly, glad that Jessie's body was as far away as it was. She'd been this close for days, and she'd never even smelled decay. Was that a trick of the wind, or magic?

The plaque had been clutched in Sister Jessie's hands.

Sister Ariel carefully walled up all the emotions she felt and set them aside. She would examine them later, allow herself tears if tears must come. For now, she might be in danger. She looked at the plaque. It was too far away to tell what symbols if any were on its surface, but there was something about it that chilled her to the bone.

The square plaque had hooks embedded in the rope. They looked as if they had formed when the lasso had landed to help her pull it out.

She pulled the plaque close to the ward but kept it on the far side. There was no telling what pulling something that might be magical through the barrier would do. The script was Gamitic, but Ariel found she remembered it surprisingly well.

"If this is the fourth day, take your time. If it's the seventh, pull this through the ward now," the script said.

The runes went on, but Ariel stopped and scowled. It wasn't at all the sort of thing someone would usually write on a plaque. She wondered to whom the words could possibly have been addressed. Perhaps this plaque had been part of some ancient test? A rite of passage for mages? How had Sister Jessie interpreted it? Why had she thought it was so important?

She read on: "Days at the ward, Horse Face. You're a lousy throw, by the way."

Ariel dropped the rope from nerveless fingers. She'd been called Horse Face when she was a tyro. She tried to translate the words another way, but the Gamitic runes made it clear that it was a personal name, a specific insult, not generic.

Looking at the way the plaque had caught on the rope now, she was suddenly sure that it had *grabbed* the rope. As if it was sentient. The hooks weren't equally placed on opposite sides of the plaque. Instead, it was as if they had grown in response to the lasso's touch.

The plaque glowed and Sister Ariel stumbled backward in fright.

It was a mistake. Her foot caught in a loop of the rope and as she fell, she yanked the plaque through the ward.

She scrambled to her feet as quickly as her fat limbs would lift her. The plaque was no longer glowing. She picked it up.

"Prophecy," it said, the Gamitic runes dissolving into common as she touched the plaque. "Not sentience."

She swallowed, not sure she believed it. The script continued to appear before her, as if written by an invisible quill. "If this is the seventh day, look two stadia south."

Stadia? Perhaps units of measure didn't translate. How far was two stadia? Three hundred paces? Four hundred?

Fear paralyzed Sister Ariel. She'd never been the type for adventures. She was a scholar, and a damned good one. She was one of the more powerful sisters, but she didn't like charging into things she didn't understand. She turned the plaque over.

"Wards in trees," Jessie al'Gwaydin had written in a panicked hand. "Don't trust him."

Oh, perfect.

Sister Ariel was rooted to the ground. The words Sister Jessie had written could only have been written with magic. Surely Sister Jessie wouldn't have used magic inside the wood. It would have been suicide.

She *is* dead.

It could all be a trap. The plaque might have triggered something as it was pulled through the ward. There might be a trap in the trees to the south where the plaque was trying to get her to go. Maybe she should go write down everything, ignore the trap, play by her own rules.

But Sister Ariel didn't go back to Torras Bend to write in her journal. She'd studied the ward to the south. If there had been a trap, she'd already triggered it.

There was a time and a place for haste. Apparently, that was now and here.

37

So you're kind of a pain in the ass. Why'd Kylar take you in?" Vi asked.

They'd been on the trail for a week, and if Uly wasn't the best company, at least she was more interesting than the horses and the trees and the little villages they had to avoid. Vi wasn't making conversation, she was gathering much information. Kylar was coming to kill her.

"He did it because he loves me," Uly said, as defiant as usual. "Someday he's going to marry me."

She'd said such things before, and it had immediately aroused Vi's suspicions, but after asking a few questions that left Uly puzzled, Vi had realized her suspicions were wrong. Kylar wasn't a pedophile.

"Yes, yes, I know. But he couldn't have loved you before he knew you, could he? You said that when he took you out of the castle was the first time you saw him."

"I thought he was my real father at first," Uly said.

"Hmm," Vi said, as if she weren't very interested. "Who are your real parents?"

"My father's name was Durzo but he's dead now. Kylar won't talk about him. I think my mother is Momma K. She always looked at me funny when we stayed with her."

Vi had to grab the back of her saddle to steady herself. Nysos, that was it! She knew Uly looked familiar. Uly was Durzo and Momma K's daughter! No wonder they'd concealed her. It also explained why Kylar had taken her in.

Inexplicably, the thought made her ache. She couldn't imagine taking in one of Hu's bastards. For that matter, she couldn't imagine Hu caring about one of them. Suddenly Uly was twice as valuable to the Godking. Holding Uly would mean controlling Momma K.

Maybe it would be enough to free Vi from his clutches. But Vi knew better. The Godking rewarded his servants well. Any vice she had, she would be allowed to indulge to satiety. He'd give her gold, clothes, slaves, whatever she wanted. But he'd never give her freedom. She'd proven herself too valuable for that.

The more Vi learned about Kylar, the more she despaired. She needed Uly to talk, because she needed to know everything about her enemy she could. Everything she learned was from a twelve-year-old girl who had a crush on the man, but Vi was good at sifting truth from opinion. Still, Kylar was sounding more and more—fuck!

She wasn't going to think about that again. It just left her feeling worse. Damn this trail. Damn this long trip. One more week and she could wash her hands of this. Maybe she wouldn't even stick around for her payday, much as she deserved it. She'd drop off the girl with a note about what she'd done, and she'd disappear. She'd killed Jarl. She'd deliver Kylar and Momma K to the Godking. Surely he wouldn't waste his resources sending someone after her then. Even if he did, he wouldn't come after her with the fury he would have if she betrayed him. She could disappear. There were only a few people she feared, and all of them were too valuable to be sent after her.

One of them was Kylar, but he wouldn't survive long. Maybe he'd killed Roth Ursuul, thirty elite highlanders, and some wytches—Uly seemed to know a lot about that—but he'd never survive the Godking.

Vi would head to Seth or Ladesh or deep into the mountains of Ceura where her red hair wouldn't be so unusual. She'd never spread her legs for another man, and she'd never take another contract. She didn't know what a normal life looked like, but she'd give herself time to figure it out. After this.

She pulled the scrap of note she'd taken from Kylar's house and read it again. "Elene, I'm sorry. I tried. I swear I tried. Some things are worth more than my happiness. Some things only I can do. Sell these to Master Bourary and move the family to a better part of town. I will always love you."

"Hey, ugly." Vi said, "what did Elene and Kylar fight about?"

"I think it was about how the bed wasn't creaking."

Vi furrowed her brow. What? Then she burst out laughing. "Well, that's normal enough. Was that all?"

"Why, what's it mean?" Uly asked.

"Fucking. Men and women fight about it all the time."

"What's fucking?" Uly asked.

So Vi told her as explicitly as possible, and Uly looked more and more horrified.

"Does it hurt?" Uly asked.

"Sometimes."

"It sounds gross!"

"It is. It's messy and sticky and sweaty and smelly and gross. Sometimes it even makes you bleed."

"Why do girls let them do that?" Uly asked.

"Because men make them. That's why they fight about it."

"Kylar wouldn't do that," Uly said. "He wouldn't hurt Elene."

"Then why'd they fight about it?"

Uly looked sick. "He wouldn't do that," she said. "He wouldn't. I don't think they ever did it anyway 'cause the bed never creaked and Aunt Mea said it would. But Aunt Mea said it was fun."

The bed never creaked? "Whatever. Is that all they fought about?" Vi asked.

"She wanted him to sell his sword, the sword Durzo gave him. He didn't want to, but she said it proved he still wanted to be a wetboy. But he didn't. He really wanted to be with us. It made him really mad when she said that."

So he wanted out, too. That's what he meant in the note when he said he tried. He tried to leave.

Nysos! Kylar might not even know she'd taken Uly. She didn't know if that was a good thing or not. It did explain why he'd gone charging past them in the fog that morning, though. He would have been sure she'd return to Cenaria as quickly as possible.

Several hundred paces ahead, Vi saw the forest change. No, not change. It transformed as abruptly as if the earth had been split with an axe. On the near side, the forest was like what they'd been riding in for days. On the far side, enormous sequoys grew. They must be near Torras Bend. It didn't mean much to her, but it looked like the riding would be easier under those great trees. There was almost no undergrowth in a forest that old.

They were only fifty paces from the sequoys when an old woman stepped out from the trees in front and to one side of them. She looked as startled as Vi felt. She was holding a glowing sheet of gold in her hands.

Glowing gold could only mean magic. The woman was a mage.

"Stop!" the old woman yelled.

Vi snapped her body back in the saddle and yanked the reins of Uly's horse out of her hands. As she sat back up, she jabbed her heels in and looked toward the mage. The woman was running heavily, awkwardly—and not toward Vi and Uly. She was running away from the old forest and she had flung aside the glowing gold sheet.

What the hell? It was strange, but not so strange that Vi stopped. In all the world, the only people she had to fear were wetboys, wytches, and mages.

The horses charged for the forest, almost throwing Uly out of the saddle.

The mage was only thirty paces away now, almost even with them. She ran a few more steps, and Vi could have sworn that the woman was emerging from something like a vast, nearly invisible bubble covering the forest.

The woman brought up her hands and spoke. Something crackled and whipped forward. Vi dropped her body as far on the opposite side of her horse as she could. There was a concussion nearby and Uly flew off the horse.

Vi didn't stop to look. She grabbed a throwing knife from an ankle sheath and threw it as she brought herself back up into the saddle. It was a long throw—twenty paces at a target she couldn't see before the she released the knife—but it was really only meant as a distraction. Vi looked back.

Uly was lying on the ground, unconscious.

There was no hesitation. A wetboy doesn't hesitate. A wetboy acts, even if it's the wrong action. Vi couldn't stay still, it made her a target. She dug her heels into her horse's flanks again. The horse lunged forward—

And promptly crashed into the ground, its front legs cut out from under it.

Vi pulled her feet from the stirrups. She would land in a ball, roll free of the horse, draw throwing knives—except the horse fell faster than she expected. She slapped into the ground hard, her body flipping over as she skidded on her back. Her head kissed an iron-hard root and black spots swam before her eyes.

Up, damn you! Get up! She got on her hands and knees and tried to stand, eyes watering, head ringing.

"I'm sorry, I can't let you do that," the old woman said. She looked like she actually meant it.

No. It can't end like this.

The beefy old woman raised a hand and spoke. Vi tried to throw herself to one side, but she didn't make it.

38

*I*t was two small cuts. A line along the ribs, and a matching line across the inside of his arm. Neither was deep. The knife had cut skin but not muscle. Even together, they were nothing a clean bandage and some fresh air wouldn't have seen heal in a few days.

But in the Hole, nothing was clean. Fresh air was only a memory.

Logan recognized the signs, but there was nothing he could do. He was hot and cold already, shivering and sweating. The odds were, he wouldn't come out of the fever. After all the time he'd spent in the Hole, he was a shadow of his former self. Cheeks sunken, eyes bright, face skeletal, his tall frame now skin and bone.

If he survived, he could get worse yet, he knew. For all that he'd starved, Logan still didn't have the malnourished, emaciated look that those who had been in the Hole for years had. His body was clinging to its strength with a stubbornness that surprised him. But the fever cared nothing for that. It would take days, at the least, to fight off the fever. Days of total vulnerability.

"Natassa," he said. "Tell me again about the resistance."

The younger Graesin daughter had a hunted look in her eyes. She didn't respond. She was looking across the hole at Fin, who was gnawing on sinews to add to his rope.

"Natassa?"

She sat up. "They move around. There are a number of estates that welcome them in the east, especially—especially the Gyres'. Even the Lae'knaught have helped."

"Bastards."

"Bastards who are our enemy's enemy."

She said that like she'd said it before. Damn, she had said it before, hadn't she?

"And our numbers are growing?"

"Our numbers are growing. We've been conducting raids, small groups going and doing anything they can to hurt the Khalidorans, but my sister wouldn't let us try anything big yet. Count Drake has set up informants for us in every village in eastern Cenaria."

"Count Drake? Wait, I asked that before, didn't I?"

She didn't respond. Her eyes were still on Fin. Fin had killed four of the newcomers in the last three days. Three days? Or was it four now?

Count Drake was part of the resistance. That was great. Logan hadn't known if the man had made it out alive.

"I'm glad Kylar didn't kill him, too," Logan said.

"Who?" Natassa asked.

"Count Drake. He betrayed me. He's the reason I'm down here."

"Count Drake betrayed you?" Natassa asked.

"No, Kylar. Dressed all in black, called himself the Night Angel."

"Kylar Stern is the Night Angel?"

"He was working for Khalidor all along."

"No, he wasn't. The Night Angel's the only reason there's a resistance at all. I was there. We were all herded into the garden and he saved us. Terah offered him whatever he wanted to escort us out of the castle, but he only cared about you. He left us to try to save you, Logan."

"But he—he killed Prince Aleine. He was the one who started all of this."

"Lady Jadwin killed Aleine Gunder. She's been given a portion of his estates as her reward."

It didn't seem possible. After everything had been stripped away from him, Natassa was giving him back his best friend. He'd missed Kylar so much.

Logan laughed. Maybe it was the fever. Maybe he'd imagined that she said that because he wanted it so much. He was so sick that the entire world hurt. Everything was fuzzy, so fuzzy. He thought he was going to start blubbering like a little girl.

"And Serah Drake? Was she with you, too? She's part of the resistance? Kylar saved her?" Logan asked. He'd asked that before, hadn't he?

"She's dead."

"Did she...did she suffer?" He hadn't dared ask that before.

Natassa looked down.

Serah. His fiancée, not so long ago. She seemed part of another life. Another world. He had loved her once. Or thought he loved her. How could he have loved her when she'd barely crossed his mind in all the time he'd been down here?

She'd betrayed him. She'd slept with his friend, Prince Aleine Gunder, when she had never even slept with him—the man she said she loved. Had that been it? Had that betrayal extinguished his feelings for her? Or had he ever loved her at all?

He'd thought that he was finally understanding love on his wedding night.

Everyone who's infatuated thinks he understands love. But Logan couldn't help it. What he'd felt for Jenine Gunder—the fifteen-year-old girl he'd been so sure was too young and immature for him—had seemed like love. Maybe she'd been snatched away before he'd had time to see her flaws, but Jenine Gunder—Jenine Gyre, his wife, if only for a few tragic hours— was the woman who had haunted his thoughts. He'd dreamed of her in the moments before sleep yielded to the hard stone and cruel stink and howling and heat of the Hole—her full smile, her bright eyes, her golden curves in candlelight as he had seen her just once, so briefly, before the Khalidoran soldiers had broken into the room, before Roth had cut her throat.

"Oh, gods," Logan said, putting his face in his hands. Suddenly, the grief rose up in him. His face contorted and he couldn't stop the tears. He'd held her, her body so small and vulnerable against him, as she'd bled. Gods, how she bled! He told her everything would be all right. He'd spoken peace to her, and that was all the protection he could give her, because he could do nothing else.

Someone wrapped an arm around him. It was Lilly. Gods. Then Natassa hugged him, too. It made it worse. He was sobbing uncontrollably. Everything was fuzzy and getting fuzzier. He had held off grief for so long, but he couldn't do it anymore.

"I'll be with you soon," he'd told Jenine. It was true now. He was going to die here. He already was dying.

He looked at Natassa's face, and she was weeping with him. The poor girl; she'd been captured, betrayed by someone in the resistance and put down here with these monsters. Logan didn't know how much she wept for him and how much she wept for herself. He didn't blame her. She had to know that once he was gone, the Holers would take her.

Even Lilly was crying. He wouldn't have imagined she was capable of it. Why was she crying? Was she afraid that once the Holers had Natassa—who was younger and prettier—that she'd lose her power and her position? That she would be killed?

Looking at Lilly's face, Logan hated himself for the cynicism of that thought. He'd been down here too long. The look on her face wasn't fear. It was love. Lilly wasn't weeping for herself; she was weeping for him.

Who am I to deserve such devotion? I'm not worthy of this.

"Help me up," he said, his voice raw.

Lilly looked at Natassa, and her tears ceased. She nodded. "Up we go."

Everyone in the Hole was looking at Logan now. Some with curiosity, some with hunger. Fin looked positively jubilant.

"All right, you fucks!" Logan said. It was the first time he'd used profanity, and he could see that some of them noticed. Well, the crazier they thought he was, the better.

"Listen up. I've kept a little secret from you because I didn't know what fine upstanding felons you all are. I've kept a little secret that might make a big difference—"

"Yes, yes, we know," Fin said. "Our little King thinks he's Logan Gyre. He thinks he really is the king!"

"Fin," Logan said. "There's two good reasons for you to shut your shit hole. First, I'm dying. I've got nothing to lose. If you keep that tooth-filled anus of yours shut, I'll die and you won't have to do a damn thing. But if you keep talking, I'll come kill you. I might be weak, but I'm strong enough to drag your poxy asshole down the hole if I don't mind falling in myself. Believe me, if we start fighting, there's more than one person down here who'll make sure we both go in."

"And the second reason?" Fin practically hissed. He was uncoiling his rope, adjusting the noose on the end of it.

"If you don't shut up," Logan said, "It'll be your fault that I throw this down the hole." He reached inside his belt, and pulled out an iron key. "It's the key to the grate," Logan said.

Instant hunger filled every eye. "Give it here!" someone said. The Holers started pressing close, and Logan staggered toward the hole. He held the key out over the darkness and swayed back and forth, in not completely feigned dizziness.

The threat quieted the Holers.

"I'm feeling real sick, real dizzy," Logan said. "So if you all want this key to go to its little home up there, you'll listen real close."

"How could you have held onto it for all this time?" Nine-Finger Nick demanded. "We could have escaped months ago!"

"Shut up, Nick," someone said.

Logan looked around, trying to see where the greasy Khalidoran duke was, but the faces were a blur. "If we want to use the key, we have to work together. Do you all understand? If one person does the wrong thing, we all die. The worst thing is, we have to trust each other. It will take three of us to reach the lock." They started murmuring, some volunteering, others objecting.

"Shut up!" Logan said. "We do this my way, or I throw away the key! If we do this my way, we'll all get out. Understand? Even you, Fin. Once we get up into the Maw, I have a plan that will get at least half of us out. Maybe all of us. They've been doing construction at the other end of this level, and I think can use that as long as we kill Gorkhy before he raises an alarm. But you all have to do exactly what I say."

"He's crazy," Nick said.

"It's our only chance," Tatts said. "I'm in." Everyone looked at Tatts in wonder. It was the first time anyone had heard the tattooed Lodricari speak.

"Good," Logan said. "We need three people to make a tower to reach the grate. Gnasher will be the base, I'll be second, and Lilly will unlock the grate. From there, we've got two options—and which one we choose is up to Fin."

Fin looked even more suspicious.

"First option, all of you who are light enough and strong enough to climb up the three of us can get out, but I won't let Fin climb out. So me and Gnasher and Fin will die."

"If anyone's going, I'm going," Fin said. "You're not—"

"Shut up, Fin!" someone said, suddenly brave at the prospect of freedom.

"Second option, Fin gives Lilly his rope. She can tie it to something up there and we all climb out. Fin, it's your rope, so it's your choice. Oh, and if I don't get out, I'm not telling you my plan to get out of the Maw."

Everyone looked at Fin. Logan was suddenly sweating again. *Come on, body, just a little longer.*

"You can use the rope," Fin said. "But you want to use my rope, I'm going to be part of the tower. I'll open the grate."

"Forget it," Logan said. "No one here trusts you. If you get out, you'll leave us here."

There was mumbled agreement to that, even from some of the Holers on Fin's side.

"Well I'm not climbing up that toothy freak. You want my rope, I'm part of the tower, and that's final."

"Fine," Logan said. He'd figured it would be this way all along. He'd just needed to offer the first position so Fin could feel that he'd won something. "I'll be the base. You be second. Lilly opens the grate." Logan handed her the key. "Lilly," he said loudly enough for everyone to hear. "If Fin tries anything, you throw the key down the hole, got it?"

"If anyone tries anything, I throw the key down the hole," she said. "I swear by all the gods of hell and pain and the Hole."

"We do this one at a time," Logan said. "I'll tell you who goes next." He drew the knife and handed it to Natassa. "Natassa, anyone comes close before their turn, you stick them with this, all right?" Again, he said it loudly so everyone would know.

"Natassa will be the first out. She'll tie the rope to something up there so we can all climb out. Fin and me will be the last, but everyone's going to get out. We've paid for our crimes."

Fin walked around the hole, uncoiling the sinew rope from around his body. He rolled it into big loops with an almost frightening ease. He claimed to have strangled thirty people before he was caught, not counting islanders and women. Underneath the ropes, he looked like anyone who'd been in the Hole for a long time. Scrawny, skin deep brown with dirt, reeking, his mouth bloody sometimes from the scurvy that every long-time Holer suffered.

He smacked his lips as he stepped close to Logan and sucked blood through his teeth. "We'll settle us later," he said. He took the coiled rope and settled it around his neck.

Logan wiped the sweat off his brow. He wanted to kill the man now. If he grabbed the rope and shoved, maybe....Maybe. It wasn't worth the risk. He was too weak, too slow now. He should have tried this plan earlier, but earlier, Fin would never have come this close to him. Fin would have expected Logan to try to kill him any other time, and before Logan had regained the knife, trying it would have made him too vulnerable.

Bracing himself against the wall with his hands, Logan squatted. Fin edged close to him, sneering and swearing under his breath. He finally put a foot on Logan's thigh, stepped onto his back, and then up onto his shoulders, walking his own hands up the sheer wall.

Surprisingly, the weight wasn't that bad. Logan thought he could make it. He just had to lock his knees and lean on the wall, and he could make it.

There was no way he'd be able to climb up the rope on his own strength, but maybe his friends would pull him out. If he went out last, he'd tie the rope around himself and Lilly and Gnash and Natassa could pull him out. If only he'd stop shivering.

"Hurry," he said.

"You're too damn tall," Lilly said. "Can you squat down?"

He shook his head.

"Shit," she said. "Fine. Ask Gnasher to help. You're the only one he listens to."

"Ask him what?" It should be obvious, he knew, but he wasn't thinking clearly.

"To lift me," Lilly said.

"Oh. Gnash. Pick her up. No, Gnash, not like that." It took some coaching, but finally, Gnash understood, and squatted beside Logan while Lilly climbed up onto his back and then stood on his shoulders. Then she put the key in her teeth and started trying to transfer over.

Logan was much taller than Gnasher, so Lilly had to step up onto Logan's shoulder, where Fin was already standing. The uneven weight made Logan sway.

"Stay still," Fin hissed. He cursed Logan repeatedly as Natassa put a hand on Logan's shoulder, trying to brace him.

Logan felt cold wash over him. "Go," he said. "Just hurry."

Lilly's weight pressed down again on his left shoulder, then weight shifted back and forth above him as she and Fin tried to balance. Logan couldn't tell what they were doing. He squeezed his eyes shut and held onto the wall.

"You can do this," Natassa whispered. "You can do this."

The weight shifted suddenly, hard to the right, and the Holers gasped. Logan sagged and then fought, his right leg shaking with the exertion.

The burden suddenly lightened and there were little gasps around the Hole. Logan squinted up and saw that Lilly was on Fin's back, and she had grabbed the grate above her with one hand, stabilizing herself and taking some of her weight.

Then they heard the sound they dreaded. It was the sound of leather and chain mail clinking and protesting, curses floating freely, a sword tapping on the rocks. Gorkhy was coming.

39

The wytching hour had come. An icy wind scoured clouds through the mountains' teeth. It was cold, too cold for snow. The wind cut through cloaks and gloves, made swords stick in their scabbards, made the men shiver at their posts. The clouds looked like phantoms scurrying over the killing fields and rushing up and over the walls. Thick wide braziers of coal that were burning all along the walls did nothing to stave off the chill. The heat was carried off and swallowed into the night. Beards froze and muscles stiffened. Officers barked at the men to keep moving, shouting over the familiar scream of the wind.

Those high screams were usually the subject of endlessly retold jokes and comparisons to the men's last bedchamber conquests, sometimes done with imitations. Regnus Gyre had never disciplined the men for howling into those winds. It staved off fears, he said. Anywhere else, it would be a distraction, would make the men unable to hear invaders, but you couldn't hear a thing at Screaming Winds anyway.

No one howled tonight. Tonight those screams seemed ominous. And if the men's hearing was bad, their sight wasn't much better. The swirling, racing clouds were thick enough and obscured the moon and stars so fully that they'd be lucky to see fifty paces out. The archers would only be useful to about that distance anyway, with this wind. It had been Regnus's nemesis. No matter now much the archers trained, shooting into that damn inconstant wind, their accuracy never improved much. One or two had an uncanny sense of when the wind would gust and could hit a man-size target at sixty paces, but that wasn't nearly the advantage a garrison usually got from holding a wall.

Solon had taken a position on the opposite side of the first wall from Vass, hoping that if worst came to worst, he'd be able to help the men without Vass's interference.

He couldn't hate the boy. Armies were full of men like Lehros Vass, and he was a good enough man. Better than most. He was just a soldier who needed a commanding officer, and the times had conspired to make him one instead. It was a cruel trick of fate that would probably make Vass be remembered as a bold idiot who'd gotten his men slaughtered, rather than as a heroic soldier.

The waiting was the worst. Like every soldier, Solon hated the waiting. It was good to be an officer when it came time to wait. You could fill your time encouraging the men to stand strong. It kept you from having the time to worry yourself.

Solon thought he saw something through the swirling clouds and darkness. He stiffened, but it was nothing. "It's time. Remember, don't look directly at her," he told the men near him. He pulled out the beeswax plugs he'd been rolling in his fingers to warm, and jammed one in his ear, then paused.

He thought he saw something again, but it wasn't the outline of a man or a horse, but an enormous square—no, it was nothing. Around him, other men were leaning forward, squinting into the darkness.

Then his skin began prickling. Like most male mages, Solon had little talent as a Seer. The only magic he could usually see was his own. But he could feel magic, especially when it was close, and always when it was used against him. Now he felt as if he had walked outside on a humid day. The magic wasn't intense, but it was everywhere. It was so diffuse that if Dorian hadn't put him so much on edge, he would never have noticed it. "Do any of you know how to tie knots well?"

The soldiers exchanged puzzled looks. Finally, one of them said, "I practically grew up on a fishin' boat, sir. I reckon I know 'bout every knot there is."

Solon grabbed the coil of rope tied to a bucket that the soldiers used to refill the water cisterns at the top of the wall. He cut the bucket free. "Tie me up," he said.

"Sir?" The soldier looked at him like he was crazy.

Is that how I looked at Dorian? Sorry, friend.

The magic was thickening.

"Tie me to the wall. Tie me so I can't move. Take my weapons."

"I, sir, I—"

"I'm a mage, dammit, I'm more susceptible to what she's—dammit! She's coming!" Soldiers were turning, staring at him. "Don't look at her. Don't believe what you see. Damn it, man, now! The rest of you, shoot!"

That was an order more of them were comfortable with. Even if Lehros Vass was angry at them in the morning, the most they'd have to do is go fetch their arrows in the killing ground before the walls.

The former sailor looped the rope around Solon expertly. In moments, Solon's hands were tied behind his back, secured to his feet, and only after that was his cloak bound around him so he wouldn't freeze. Then the man bound him to the winch they used to raise the bucket.

"Now a blindfold and my other earplug," Solon said. The man had bound him facing over the wall. Solon should have told him to make sure he couldn't face her. "Hurry, man."

But the soldier didn't respond. He was looking over the wall into the darkness, as was everyone else.

"Elana?" the soldier said. "Elly, is that you?" His face flushed and his eyes dilated. He threw his cloak off. Then he jumped off the wall.

He was halfway to the ground before he flailed wildly, suddenly aware, trying to find something to save himself. The rocks broke his body cruelly and the wind swallowed the sound of his death scream.

There was a sudden flurry of arrows as men began obeying Solon's earlier command to start shooting as soon as anything strange happened. The fog billowed and he saw the vast wagon being drawn forward, surrounded by Khalidoran soldiers, pulled by six aurochs. Solon's heart leapt as he saw a dozen Khalidorans cut down by the first wave. The aurochs took several arrows and didn't even falter.

But the rain of arrows was slowing.

Across the wall, Solon saw men flinging themselves off the wall. Others were shaking their heads, each lost in a private vision, bows held in limp hands.

Don't look, Solon. Don't look.

I won't believe it. Just a quick—

The magic roared past him as he were flying at tremendous speed.

And then calm.

He blinked. He was standing in the Hall of Winds. The magnificent jade throne shone green like the waters of Hokkai Bay. Upon the throne sat a woman he barely recognized. Kaede Wariyamo had been sixteen when he'd left the Islands. Though he'd known from the times he'd played with her when they were both young that she would be beautiful, her transformation had made him awkward. She'd reproached him for avoiding her. But he'd had no choice. He knew he had to leave forever, but he'd never been prepared for what the sight of her would do to him.

Twelve years later, she had grown in grace and confidence. If he hadn't known her so well, he never would have seen the slight apprehension in her eyes—will he still think I'm beautiful?

He did. Her olive skin still glowed, her black hair poured around her shoulders like a waterfall, her eyes still gleamed with intelligence and wisdom and mischief. Perhaps there used to be less wisdom there and more mischief, but those lips looked like they still held three lifetimes of smiles. And if she had the faintest smile lines around her eyes and lips—what a tribute to a life well lived. To him, they were a mark of distinction.

His eyes swept over her body, clad in light blue silk nagika, cut to emphasize the perfection of each curve, bound at the waist by a narrow belt of gold, the silk looped up over one shoulder. Her stomach was still flat, athletic. There were no stretch marks. Kaede had never borne children. His eyes lingered on her exposed breast.

Perfect. She was perfect.

He was interrupted by her laugh. "Have you been on Midcyru so long you've forgotten what breasts look like, my prince?"

Solon blushed. After so many years of seeing women treat ordinary parts like they were erotic, and erotic parts like they were ordinary, he was thoroughly confused. "I apologize, Your Majesty." Remembering himself, he tried to kneel, but something was interfering with his motion.

It didn't matter. All that mattered was before him. He couldn't take his eyes off her.

"You've been a hard man to find, Solonariwan," Kaede said.

"It's just, just Solon now."

"The empire needs you, Solonariwan. I won't make any demands of you besides the—besides producing an heir, and if you require rooms for a mistress, it will be arranged. The empire needs you, Solon. Not just for your family. For you. I need you." She looked terrifically fragile, as if the wind would break her. "I want you, Solon. I want you as I wanted you twelve years ago and as I wanted you before that, but now I want your strength, your fortitude, your companionship, your..."

"My love," Solon said. "You have it, Kaede. I love you. I always have."

She lit up, exactly like she had when she was little and he'd given her a special present. "I've missed you," she said.

"I've missed you," he said, a lump rising in his throat. "I'm afraid I was never able to explain why I had to leave—"

She stepped close to him and put a finger on his lips. Her touch sent shockwaves through him. His heart thundered against his ribs. Her very scent suffused him. His eyes couldn't find a place to rest as he looked at her. Every beautiful line and curve and color and tone led to another and another.

Smiling, she put a hand on his cheek.

Oh gods. I'm lost. *She had that same uncertain, wavering look that she'd had that last day, when she kissed him and he'd nearly torn her clothes off. She kissed him and her lips were all the world. She started ten-*

tatively, just touching that exquisite softness against his lips, and then drawing him out. She was suddenly aggressive, just as she had been that day, as though her passion had only been building for all the time he was gone. Her body pressed up against him and he moaned.

She broke away from him, breathing hard, her eyes fiery. "Come to my chambers," she said. "This time, I swear my mother won't break in on us."

She climbed up a tall step and looked at him over her shoulder as she took a few steps away, her hips swaying. She grinned devilishly and brushed the nagika strap off her shoulder. He tried to step up after her, but he slipped back to his place on the floor.

Kaede slipped the gold belt off her waist and dropped it carelessly. Solon strained to climb up that damned step. Something was cutting off his breath.

"I'm coming," he said, wheezing.

She shimmied and the nagika dropped to the floor in a silk puddle. Her body was all bronze curves and shining waterfalls of black hair.

He coughed. He couldn't breathe. He'd thrown this away once, and he wasn't going to give it up now. He coughed again and again and dropped to his knees.

Kaede was just down the hall, smiling, the light playing over her lean body, her long long legs, her slim ankles. He climbed back to his feet and strained against the ropes again.

Why is she smiling? *Kaede wouldn't smile when he was choking to death.*

Kaede wouldn't be like this at all. *Her mannerisms weren't similar to the girl he had known, they were exactly the same, fitted to an older face.*

A woman who'd been a queen for ten years wouldn't let down all the barriers that fast. She was everything he'd hoped or imagined—the real Kaede would be furious with him.

The vision disappeared all at once, and Solon was back on the wall. He was staring over the edge, only the ropes keeping him from falling to his death.

Around him, men were dying horribly. One's stomach had swollen to three times its normal size and he was still reaching into the air, as if shoving food down his throat. Another was purple, screaming at someone who wasn't there, but he was no longer screaming words. His voice was a wreck and every once in a while, he coughed and blood flew out of his mouth, but he never stopped screaming. Another was shrieking, "Mine! It's mine!" and beating the stone wall with his hands as if they were attacking him. His hands were bloody stumps, ruined, but he never stopped. Others were lying down, dead, with no indication of what had killed them.

Many had killed themselves by one means or another, but some had been scorched with magic or exploded. The wall ran red with their already freezing blood. The gate had been blown apart while he'd been in his trance and dark figures were marching toward them now, driving the team of aurochs pulling the enormous wagon.

It was Khali. Solon had no doubt of that.

"Has Dorian gone mad yet?" a woman's voice asked. "That was my little gift, you know."

Solon looked, but couldn't see the source of the voice. He wasn't sure it wasn't coming from inside his own head. "He's completely cured, actually."

She laughed; it was a deep, throaty sound. "So he is alive."

Solon wanted to crumple. They'd thought Dorian was dead. Or at least they didn't know. "Let's get this over with," Solon said.

She chuckled. "You've been told many lies in your life, Solonariwan. They lied to you when you were growing up. They lied to you at Sho'cendi. They stole from you. I'm not going to offer you power, because the truth is, I can't give you power. The vir doesn't come from me. That's just another lie. I wish it did. The truth is, the vir is natural, and it's vastly more powerful than your pitiable Talent. The truth is, Dorian's Talent was weak before he used the vir, and you know how powerful his Talent is now."

"It's enslaving. Meisters are like drunks looking for their next glass of wine."

"Some of them, yes. The fact is, some people can't handle drink. But most people can. Maybe you'd be one of the people who can't, like Dorian, but I wouldn't bet on that. The truth is, Dorian always liked his special place in the sun, didn't he? He liked having you look up to him. Having everyone look up to him. And what would he be without his power, without his extra gifts? He'd be so much less than you, Solon. Without the vir, he'd have no gifts, and his Talent would be minuscule compared to yours. So where would that put you if you used the vir? Even if you just used it once, just to unlock the hidden Talents you don't even know you have? What could you do with that kind of power? Could you go back to Seth and make things right? Take your place with Kaede on the throne? Take your place in history?" She shrugged. "I don't know. I don't really care. But you're pathetic, you magi. You can't even use magic in the dark. Really."

"Lies. It's all lies."

"Is it? Well, then, you hold on to your weakness, your humility. But if you ever change your mind, Solonariwan, this is all you have to do. The power is there, and it's waiting for you." And then she showed him. It was simple. Instead of reaching toward a source of light, the sun or a fire, or instead of reaching into his glore vyrden, he just had to reach toward Khali. A little twist and it was there. An ocean of power, being constantly fed from tens of thousands of sources. Solon couldn't understand it all, but he could see the outlines. Every Khalidoran prayed morning and night. The prayer wasn't empty words: it was a spell. It emptied a portion of everyone's glore vyrden into this ocean. Then Khali gave it back to those she willed, when and as much as she wanted. At heart, it was simple: a magical tax.

Because so many people were born with a glore vyrden but lacked the capability or the teaching to express it, Khali's favorites would always have ample power—and the people would never even know they were being robbed of their very vitality. That didn't explain the vir, but it did explain why the Khalidorans had always used pain and torture in their worship. Khali didn't need the suffering, she needed her worshippers to feel intense emotions. Intense emotions were what allowed marginally Talented people to use their glore vyrden. Torture was simply the most reliable way to spark emotions of the right intensity. Whether the torturer and tortured and spectators felt disgust, loathing, fear, hatred, lust, or delight made no difference. Khali could use them all.

"My Soulsworn will find you now, and you'll die," Khali said. "You emptied your glore vyrden already, didn't you?"

"Begone," he said.

She laughed. "Oh, you're a good one. I think I'll keep you." Then her voice was gone, and Solon crumpled to the stones. Khali was in Cenaria. The Ursuuls would make ferali and the rebels would be massacred. All his service here had been for nothing. All he had just learned was for nothing. He should have gone home to Seth twelve years ago. He'd failed.

He opened his eyes and saw one of the Soulsworn, draped in heavy sable cloaks, their faces obscured behind blank black masks, picking through the dead along the wall. Now and then one would stop, draw a sword and dispatch someone. They wiped their swords afterward, so the blood wouldn't freeze their blades to the inside of their scabbards.

They were coming toward him. There was nothing he could do. He was bound and the horizon was barely gray. No weapons. No magic. The vir was his only way out. Even if it was suicide, at least he could take a lot of them with him.

Maybe he could outsmart her. If he could just survive—and how stupid to be killed by some thug in a costume—he could fight Khali. She wasn't invincible. She wasn't a goddess. He'd talked to her. He'd understood her. He could fight her. He just needed the power to do it.

Solon's heart thudded in his chest. It was exactly what Dorian had said he himself would be tempted to do. Solon had thought the temptations had stopped, but this was the last one. The hardest one. Dorian was right. He'd been right about everything.

O God... Sir, if you are there... I despise myself for praying now when I've got nothing to lose, but shit, if you just help me to live through—

Solon's prayer was interrupted as a heavy corpse fell on him. Solon opened his mouth and took a deep breath. He was just exhaling when warm blood from the corpse poured into his mouth. It was metallic and already thickening.

He almost threw up as the blood spilled over his chin, down his neck, through his beard, but he froze as he heard a foot scuff on stone nearby.

The Soulsworn pulled the body off him, but didn't walk away.

"Look at this one, Kaav," he said with a thick Khalidoran accent.

"Another screamer. Love it when they do that," a second voice said. "Must have pissed off the men, huh? Must have been one of the first to go if they tied him up like that."

The first Soulsworn stepped close and bent over Solon. Solon could hear the man's breath hissing through the mask over his face. The man stood and kicked Solon in the kidney.

Pain lanced through him, but he didn't make a sound. The man kicked him again and again. The third time, Solon's body betrayed him, and he tensed his muscles. It was just too hard to lie limp.

"He's still alive," the man said. "Kill him."

Solon's heart leapt into this throat. It was over. He had to grab the vir and die.

Wait. The thought was so calm, so simple and clear that it seemed to come from outside of him.

Solon held still.

The second I hear steel, I'll... He didn't know. He'd take the vir? Then Khali would have him.

The other man grunted. "Shit, my blade's froze. Coulda swore I got it cleaned off."

"Ah, forget it. Between the cold and the bleeding he'll be dead in five minutes. If he coulda gotten out of the ropes he would have when She came through."

And they walked away.

40

*W*hen Vi woke, bound tightly at wrists, ankles, elbows, and knees, the first thing she saw was a middle-aged woman with thin, graying brown hair, a thick slab of body, the stance of a woman who had never worn anything but practical shoes, a round, lined face, and piercing eyes. The maja was staring at her. A fire was burning behind Vi, and a small bundle near her that was probably Uly, bound and trussed like she was.

"Fock eww," Vi said. She was gagged. Not just some little gag of a handkerchief tied around her mouth, a serious gag. It felt like a rock had been wrapped in a handkerchief and stuffed in her mouth, then thin leather ties wrapped every which way around her face, guaranteeing she couldn't speak.

"Before we start, Vi," the woman said. "I want to tell you something very important. If you do escape from me—which you won't—do not run into the forest. Have you ever heard of the Dark Hunter?"

Vi scowled as well as she could with her mouth stuck partially open, then decided she had nothing to lose by letting the old woman talk. She shook her head.

"That would explain why you were rushing headlong into death, I suppose," the woman said. "I'm Sister Ariel Wyant Sa'fastae. The Dark Hunter was created some six hundred and maybe fifty years ago by a magus named Ezra, perhaps the most Talented magus who ever lived. Ezra was on the losing side of the War of Darkness. He was one of Jorsin Alkestes' most trusted generals, the kind of man who seemed to be able to do everything, and everything he did he did superlatively. I'm sorry, superlatively means he did everything excellently."

"I oh wha ih eenz, idj," Vi said, though it was a lie.

"What? Never mind. Ezra created a creature that sensed magic and certain kinds of creatures that are now extinct—krul, ferozi, ferali, blaemir, and what have you—for which you may thank whatever gods your superstitions support. He created his perfect hunter too well, and he couldn't control it. It began killing anyone with the Talent, escaping while Ezra slept. Finally, they battled—of course no one knows what happened because no one was there. But the Talented children of Torras Bend stopped dying and no one ever saw the Dark Hunter again, nor Ezra. However, whatever Ezra did, it didn't kill the Dark Hunter. He only walled it in. Here About ten paces north of where I regrettably had to kill your horse is the first ward. That ward marks you for death.

"Every magus or maja or meister to attempt Ezra's Wood in six hundred years has died. Powerful mages carrying potent artifacts died, those artifacts in turn lured other mages, and so forth. Whatever happens in the wood—even if the Dark Hunter is a myth—whatever happens there, no one comes back." Sister Ariel paused and then her voice became bright and cheery, "So, if you escape, don't go north." Ariel scowled. "You'll pardon me if I'm not doing this right. I've never kidnapped anyone before—unlike you."

Shit.

"Oh yes, Ulyssandra was rather eager to tell me all about you, wetboy."

Double shit.

"But about that. You're not a wetboy, Vi. You're not even a wetgirl. Oh, there have been such things, but what you are is a *maja uxtra kurrukulas,* a bush mage, a wild mage—"

"Ock ew! Ock ew!" Vi thrashed against her bonds. It was no use.

"Oh, you don't believe me? A wetboy, Vi, even of the female variety, can use her Talent without speaking. So if you are a wetboy, why don't you escape?"

There was nothing, nothing in all the world that Vi couldn't stand as much as feeling helpless. She'd rather have Hu paw her hair. She'd rather have the Godking mount her. She bucked on the ground, tearing her skin against the ropes. She tried to scream. It made part of the handkerchief go down her throat. She gagged and coughed and for a moment, she thought she was going to die. Then she regained her breath and lay limp.

Ariel scowled. "I really don't like this. I hope you'll realize that someday. I'm going to take off your gag, understand? You can't get away from me, even with your Talent, and you'll have to learn that sooner or later, so we might as well make it clear now to spare you as much pain as possible. But before you fight me, I do expect your first words to be curses or lies or an attempt to use magic, so before you do that, I'd like to ask you a question."

Vi's eyes burned holes in the woman. The bitch. Just let her take out that gag.

"Who is the extremely talented Vürdmeister that put this spell on you?"

Thoughts of escape evaporated. It was a bluff. It had to be a bluff. But how?

Nysos. What did the bastard do to me? It was just what the Godking would do, put some fucking spell on her. Hadn't she imagined something of the sort when she was in the throne room? What if it hadn't been her imagination?

"Because that spell is really something," Sister Ariel said. "I've been studying it for the past six hours while you've been unconscious, and I still can't tell what it does. One thing I do know is that it's trapped. And he's—it definitely bears the marks of being a man's magic—he's anchored it in some interesting ways. I'm considered strong among my sisters. One of the stronger magae to attain the colors in the last fifty years. And it's too strong for me to break, that's clear immediately. You see, there are weaves you can unravel and there are weaves you have to burst—Fordaean knots if you will—are you familiar with Fordaean knots? Never mind. This spell has both. The traps might be unraveled. But the core weave will have to be broken most carefully. Even if I could do it myself, it would probably leave you with some permanent mental damage."

"Nnn ga."

"What? Oh." Sister Ariel stayed seated cross-legged and murmured. The bonds fell from Vi's face. She spat out the handkerchief—it *had* been wrapped around a rock, the bitch!—and breathed. She didn't grab her Talent. Not yet.

"The rest?" she asked, gesturing to her other bonds.

"Mm. Sorry."

"It's a little hard to talk to you lying on my side."

"Fair enough. *Loovaeos.*"

Vi's body was pulled upright and scooted backward to a tree.

"So that's your bait? A bluff about some spell on me that we won't be able to take off until we get to the Chantry—where it just so happens it will be impossible for me to escape?"

"That's it."

Vi pursed her lips. Was it her imagination, or was there a slight glow around Ariel? "That's pretty good bait," she admitted.

"Better than we offer most girls."

"You always kidnap girls?"

"Like I already said, this is my first time. It doesn't usually come down to kidnapping. The sisters who do the recruiting have lots of ways to be persuasive. I was deemed too tactless for such work."

Big surprise. "What's the usual bait?" Vi asked.

"Just to be like the recruiters, who tend to be beautiful, charming, respected, and—not least—always get their own way."

"And the hook is?" Vi asked.

"Oh, we're continuing the fishing metaphor?"

"What?" Vi asked.

"Never mind The hook is servitude and tutelage. It's like an apprentice-ship, seven to ten years of service before you become a full Sister. Then you're free."

Vi had had enough of apprenticeship to last her for ten lives. She sneered. *Keep her talking. I might as well learn what I can.* "You said I'm not really a wetboy. I do all the wetboy stuff."

"Have trouble with the Embrace of Darkness, don't you?"

"What?"

"Invisibility. You can't do it, can you?"

How did she know that? "That's just a legend. It drives up prices. No one goes invisible."

"I can see you're going to spend a lot of time unlearning things you think you know. True wetboys can go invisible. But mages don't do invisi-bility. Your Talent has to practically live in your skin. Invisibility requires a total body awareness so profound that it extends to feeling how light is touching every part of your skin. What you are is something different—in fact, something forbidden by a treaty a hundred and thirty—umm—thirty-eight years old. The Alitaerans would be shall we say highly over-wrought if we'd trained you this way. You see, if you mastered a few more things, you'd be a warmage. Oh, you're going to cause the Speaker a few headaches, I can see that already."

"Fuck you," Vi said.

Sister Ariel leaned over and slapped her. "You will speak civilly."

"Fuck you," Vi said without intonation.

"Let's settle something now, then," Sister Ariel said, standing. *"Loovaeos uh braeos loovaeos graakos."* Vi was yanked to her feet. Her bonds dropped away. A dagger flew from her pack and dropped at her feet.

Vi didn't reach for the knife. She didn't stop to take the time. She cursed her Talent into a titanic punch into Sister Ariel's stomach.

The force of the blow blasted Sister Ariel off her feet. She flipped over the fire and skidded across the dirt on the other side, but Vi didn't move. She didn't even try to run. She was looking at her drooping hand.

It was like she'd punched steel. Bones were sticking out of her skin. Her knuckles were a mass of blood. Her wrist was broken. Both bones in her forearm had snapped. One of them was pressing against the skin from underneath, threatening to jut out.

Sister Ariel stood and shook her big, loose dress. Dust puffed out. She snorted as she looked at Vi, who was cradling her arm.

"You should really strengthen your bones before you strike with your Talent."

"I did," Vi said. She was going into shock. She sat—or maybe fell.

"Then you shouldn't punch an armored maja." Ariel tsked as she looked at Vi's destroyed hand. "It seems you've more Talent than sense. Not to worry, that's common enough. We know how to deal with it. The truth is, Vi, that your body magic is untrained, undefined, and no match for any schooled sister. You could be so much more. Do you even know how to heal yourself?"

Vi was shaking. She looked up dumbly.

"Well, if you ever want to use your hand again, I can heal it. But it hurts and I'm slow."

Vi offered up her arm, mute.

"Just a second, I need to ward Uly's ears. Otherwise your screams will wake her."

"I won't—I won't scream," Vi swore.

As it turned out, she lied.

Logan froze. Another time, he might have tried to get everyone down to build their tower again once Gorkhy was gone, but he knew he'd never summon the strength to try it again.

"What's going on down here?" Gorkhy demanded.

What? We've been silent. How did he hear anything?

Pressing in to the wall as much as he could, Logan looked up and saw that Fin was doing the same thing, and, sitting on his shoulders, Lilly was too.

Torchlight slanted through the grate as Gorkhy came the last few feet. From where he was standing now, Lilly was only a few feet from his shoes. With the sheer edges of the Hole below the grate, though, the torchlight wouldn't fall on Lilly unless he stepped closer.

They heard Gorkhy sniffing, and the torchlight shifted as he leaned forward. He cursed them. "Animals. You stink worse than usual." Gods, he was smelling Lilly. "Why don't you wash yourselves?"

This could go on for a while. If it was a bad day, he'd empty his bladder onto them. Logan shook with rage and weakness. There was no reason for a Gorkhy. There was no understanding it. Gorkhy gained nothing by tormenting them, but he did, and he loved it.

Go away. Just go away.

"What's going on down there?" Gorkhy said. "I heard some noise. Whatcha doin'?"

The torch shifted again and light dipped perilously close to Lilly. Gorkhy was walking around the grate, holding up the torch, staring as deeply into the Hole as he could. He was moving counterclockwise, away from them first.

The Holers were frozen. None of them were cursing or fighting or talking or anything. It was a dead giveaway. Only Natassa moved, away from Logan.

The light cut a path across the grate and lit up Lilly's entire head.

"GO TO HELL, GORKHY!" Natassa shouted.

The torch shifted away from Lilly suddenly. "Who's . . . ah, it's my little girl? Isn't it?"

"You see my face, Gorkhy?" Natassa asked. Clever girl. "This is the last thing you're ever going to see, because I'm going to kill you."

Gorkhy laughed. "You got a mouth on you, don't you? But then, you already showed me that before we sent you down there, didn't you?" He laughed again.

"Fuck you!"

"Did that too, ha ha. You were the hottest little thing I've had in years. You been letting the rest of them boys have a piece? I was your first, though. You never forget your first. You'll never forget me, will ya?" He laughed again.

Logan marveled at Natassa's courage. She was taunting the man who had raped her, just to give them a chance.

"How's Lilly takin' it? I'm sure all them boys would rather stick you than that old whore. How's it going, Lilly? Competition get fierce all the sudden? Where are you, Lilly?" He shifted again, searching the depths for Lilly.

"I threw that bitch down the hole," Natassa said.

Logan was shaking so hard he could barely stand.

"No shit? You are a little wildcat, aren't you? I bet you even tempt our virginal little King, don't you? You banged her yet, King? I know Lilly was a little scabby for you, but this is some fine meat, eh, King? Where are you?"

Across the Hole, Tatts said, "Fuck you," into his hands. Muffled, it sounded almost like Logan. At the quick thinking, Logan felt a rush of warm feeling for the Holers. Gods, they were all in this together, and they'd get out together, too.

Gorkhy laughed. "All right, well, it's been fun. You all let me know when you're hungry. I got extra steak tonight, and I'm so full I don't think I could force another bite down."

Logan had no strength left. He wanted to cry out, his body felt so weak. He couldn't even feel himself standing. He just knew that if he tried to move he'd collapse. His body was bathed in cold sweat. His vision was blurring.

Logan heard ragged breathing, breaths of relief, a moment later.

"He's gone," someone said. It was Natassa. She was standing next to Logan again, and her eyes were full of fierce tears. "Just hold on, Logan. We're close."

Something rattled loudly on the grate.

"What are you doing?" Fin hissed. "Lilly, what the hell—"

"I didn't even touch it! I swear!" she said.

"Get down!" Logan cried.

But it was too late. There was already the sound of running steps and a moment later Gorkhy was over the grate, Lilly and Fin and Logan fully lit by his torch. With savage speed, he smashed Lilly in the face with the butt of his spear. All of them collapsed.

Even as the bodies landed on him, crushing him to the sloping stone floor, Logan saw his treasure—the key he had saved for months—fly free of Lilly's hand. It rang as it bounced off the stone floor, gleaming in the cutting light of the torch—and fell into the hole.

Every one of his hopes, every dream, was tied to that key. As it disappeared into the hole, it dragged them along with it.

A second of fragile peace passed as every eye watched the key disappear. Then one by one, the Holers grasped the new reality—which was just like the old reality before they'd known the key existed. Fin was punching someone—it had to be Lilly because when he got to his knees, he was holding his rope. Then he punched Logan in the face.

Logan couldn't stop him. Fin was too strong; all of Logan's strength was exhausted. He fell limp.

There was an inhuman snarl and a solid form slammed into Fin, sending him flying, tumbling right to the edge of the hole.

It was Gnasher, and he crouched over Logan, baring his teeth.

On his hands and heels, Fin scrambled to get away from Gnasher. When Gnasher didn't follow, Fin stood slowly.

Logan tried to sit up, but his body refused to obey. He couldn't even move. The world swam before his eyes.

"I get the new bitch first," Fin said.

Gods be merciful.

"You'll be the first to die, you asshole!" Natassa screamed. She was trembling, holding the dagger like she had no idea what to do with it.

The Holers—the fucking animals!—surrounded her on three sides. She retreated to the edge of the hole, slashing at the air with the dagger.

Above them, Gorkhy was laughing. "Sweet meat, boys, sweet meat!"

"No," Logan said. "No. Gnash, save her. Save her, please."

Gnasher didn't move. He was still snarling, making everyone stay away from Logan.

Natassa saw it. If she could only get to Logan's side of the Hole, everyone's fear of Gnasher would keep them back. But Fin saw it too. He unlimbered a coil of rope into a lasso.

"You can make this easy, or you can make it hard," Fin said, smacking bloody lips.

Natassa looked at him, her eyes fixed on the lasso in his hands as if she'd forgotten the dagger in her own. She looked across the hole and met Logan's eyes.

"I'm sorry, Logan," she said. Then she stepped into the hole.

The Holers cried out as she fell out of sight.

"Shut up and listen!" Gorkhy screamed. "Sometimes you can hear 'em hit bottom."

And the bastards, the animals, the monsters, they did shut up and listen, hoping to hear a body smash against the rocks below. They were too late. The Holers grumbled the customary curses about lost meat, and looked over to Lilly. Logan's tears were as hot as his fever.

"Now who the fuck's Logan?" Gorkhy shouted. "King, was she talkin' to you?"

Logan closed his eyes. What did it matter anymore?

41

*I*t's time, Fatty," Ferl Khalius said. "He's not crazy enough to follow us across this."

They were fourteen hundred feet up Mount Hezeron, the tallest mountain on the Ceuran border. So far, the hike had been arduous, but the worst exposures had been of a dozen feet. From here, there were two ways over the mountain: through the notch to one side, or straight across the face. Ferl had nearly started a brawl at the last village by asking which way a brave man in a hurry would go.

Some of the villagers maintained that the face was never a good option, but that it would be especially bad this time of year. Even a light dusting of snow or freezing rain would make the path suicide. Others had maintained that going over the face was the only way to make it through the mountains before the snows hit. Getting stuck in the steeps and the deeps that made the devil's pass through the notch would be certain death if it snowed.

And snow was coming.

Baron Kirof wasn't doing well. He was so scared of heights he'd been crying. "If—if he'd be crazy to follow us, what does that make us?"

"Eager to live. I grew up in mountains tougher than this." Ferl shrugged. "Follow or fall."

"Can't you leave me?" Baron Kirof was pathetic. Ferl had brought him along because he didn't know what would happen when he fled, and he'd wanted a bargaining chip. But maybe it had been a mistake. The fat man had slowed him down.

"They want you alive. If you stay here, that Vürdmeister will blast me off the rock. If you're with me, he might not."

"Might not?"

"Move, Fatty!"

Ferl Khalius looked at the dark clouds grimly. His tribe, the Iktana, was a mountain tribe. He was one of the best climbers he knew, but he'd never liked climbing. Battle he liked. Battle made you feel alive. But climbing was arbitrary, the mountain gods capricious. He'd seen the most devout clansman plunge to his death when he'd put his weight on a stone that had held Ferl—who was heavier—only a moment before. In battle, a stray arrow might kill you, of course, but you could move, you could fight. Death might still come, but it wouldn't find you scared, clinging to a bit of rock with slick fingers, praying against the next blast of wind.

This traverse wasn't the worst he'd seen. It climbed perhaps a hundred feet and its entire length was narrow, maybe three feet wide. Three feet was pretty damn wide. It was the sheer drop that made that three feet seem ever so much smaller. Knowing that if you slipped you had absolutely no chance of catching yourself, that stumbling meant certain death, that did things to a man.

It was doing things to Fatty Kirof.

The baron, unfortunately, had no idea why he was important. Ferl hadn't been able to find out anything either. But Fatty was important enough that the Godking had sent a Vürdmeister after them.

"You're going first, Fatty. I'll take all the gear, but that's all the mercy you get."

It wasn't mercy. It was practicality. Fatty would go slower with a pack, and if he fell, Ferl didn't want to lose his supplies.

"I can't do it," Baron Kirof said. "Please." Sweat was coursing down his round face. His little red whiskers quivered like a rabbit's.

Ferl drew his sword, the sword he'd given so much to protect, the sword that would make him a clan warlord. It was everything a warlord could want, a perfect sword, down to the highland runes on the steel that Ferl recognized but couldn't read.

He gestured with the sword, a little shrug that said, "Take your chances with the path, or take your chances with the sword."

The baron started onto the path. He was muttering too low for Ferl to hear him, but it sounded like he was praying.

Surprisingly, Fatty made good time. Ferl had to slap him once with the flat of his blade when he froze up and started scooting. They didn't have time to scoot. If they weren't far enough away from the Vürdmeister when he made it out of the trees, Ferl was dead. He'd chosen to go behind Fatty because it was the only way to keep the man moving, but it meant that he was exposed to whatever magic the Vürdmeister threw at them. If they weren't far enough away to make the Vürdmeister worry that he would kill the baron, it would be all over.

The view was breathtaking. They were past the middle of the exposure, and they could see forever. Ferl thought he could see Cenaria City, far to the northwest. It made it seem that they'd hardly covered any ground at all. But Ferl wasn't interested in the cloudless expanses to the north. He was interested in the slight prick he'd just felt on his skin. Snow.

He looked up. The leading edge of the black wall of clouds was directly above them.

Fatty stopped. "The path is getting narrower."

"The Vürdmeister's out of the woods. We've got no choice."

The baron swallowed and started shuffling forward, his face pressed to the rock, his arms spread-eagled.

Behind them, the Vürdmeister was standing with his fists on his hips, furious.

Ferl looked ahead. Another thirty paces, and just one more hard section where the ledge narrowed to a foot and a half across. Fatty was sucking down the thin air, frozen.

"You can do this," Ferl told him. "I know you can."

Miraculously, Fatty started moving, shuffling, but with confidence, as if he'd found some well of courage in himself that he'd never known he had. "I'm doing it!" he said.

And he did. He made it past the narrowest part of the ledge and Ferl followed hard on his heels, kicking gravel out into space and trying not to follow it.

The ledge began to widen and Fatty turned to walk rather than shuffle—even though the ledge was still less than three feet wide. He was laughing.

Then there was a blur of green past them and the ledge exploded in front of them.

As the smoke blew away in the icy winds, the clouds opened up and it started snowing. Big, fat flakes were driven in circles and horizontal lines by the wind. Fatty and Ferl both stared at the gap in front of them.

It was barely three feet across, but there was no room to run for the approach. The far side didn't look stable, either.

"If you do this," Ferl said, "I'll never call you Fatty again."

"Go bugger yourself," Fatty said—and jumped.

He scrambled on the other side, but he made it.

Another missile hit the rock over Ferl's head and rock chips cut his face and rained down over him. He shook his head to clear his eyes, lost his balance, and then found it again, all in a moment. He took two steps and leapt.

The ledge crumbled under his feet faster than he could scramble up it. He threw out his arms, grabbing for anything.

A hand grabbed his. The baron yanked him to safety.

Gasping, Ferl bent over at the waist, hands on his thighs. After a moment, he said, "You saved me. Why'd you—why?"

The baron's answer was lost as the rock behind them exploded again.

Ferl surveyed the rest of the ledge. It was another thirty paces before they would disappear around a corner from the Vürdmeister. The ledge from here on was five feet wide or wider, too wide for one of the missiles to demolish, but they were still exposed, and Ferl sure as hell wasn't going to stay in the back anymore. He sheathed his sword and grabbed the baron, turning him around.

"This is the only way we get out of this," he said.

"It's fine," the baron said. "I'm not climbing back across that ledge, and I have no idea what to do in the wilderness anyway. I'm with you."

They started backing up together, Ferl looking at his feet and then at the Vürdmeister across the face from them. The young man had a glowing green missile circling slowly around his body. He knew his quarry was getting away from him. The missile started spinning faster and faster.

Ferl forced the baron closer to the edge in a silent threat.

The missile slowed and they could see the Vürdmeister's mouth moving in inaudible curses. Ferl extended his middle finger to the man in a silent salute. A moment later, laughing, the baron copied the gesture.

Then a stone shifted under Ferl's heel as he stepped backward. He was slipping, pulling Baron Kirof right on top of himself.

There was only one thing to do. He pushed the baron toward the edge as hard as he could, propelling his own body to safety.

He landed on his butt on the ledge. He could see the baron's fingers clinging to the edge. Ferl rolled close and saw the baron's eyes as round as saucers.

"Help!" the baron shouted.

Ferl didn't move.

In the end, Fatty was simply too fat. He held on for a moment longer, then his spindly arms couldn't hold him anymore. His fingers slipped off the rock.

The fall took a long time, but Fatty never screamed. Together, Ferl and the Vürdmeister watched him sail to the rocky shores of death.

On the other side of the mountain, the Vürdmeister's face seemed to fall as far as the baron's body. The Godking was not understanding of failure.

Ferl scooted back from the edge and around the bend. He congratulated himself on having the foresight to keep the pack.

42

The Gyre estate at Havermere had undergone huge changes since Kylar passed through with Elene and Uly on the way to Caernarvon. Then, it had been nearly empty. Without a lord to protect them, some of the farmers had moved away. The coming harvest and this year's fortunate lack of Ceuran or Lae'knaught raids were the only reasons the rest stayed.

Now, the estate was filled to overflowing, and it took Kylar only a moment to guess why. The resistance had moved its base to Havermere. They were a few days' hard ride outside Cenaria, which put them close enough to strike at patrols but far enough to flee if the Godking mustered a large force against them. The richness of the harvest and the resources of the Gyre household—which included hundreds of the best horses in the country, a substantial armory, and walls that would be defensible at least against anyone who wasn't using magic—made it a perfect base. Kylar wondered if they had seized it by force, or if the Gyre steward had welcomed the army in.

He paused as he first caught sight of the company in the early morning darkness. If he wanted to, he could probably avoid detection—or at least interference. They probably hadn't seen him yet, not in this light, though he had no idea how good their sentries were. Finally, he figured he might as well find out what was happening in Havermere. If Logan were still alive and Kylar managed to rescue him, this would be where they would come. If he could let Logan know what was waiting for him, all the better.

Still, before he rode on, he fixed his Durzo disguise to his face. It was much easier than the only other disguise he'd constructed—Baron Kirof— and probably less dangerous. The rebels who knew Baron Kirof would want to kill him. The rebels who knew Durzo would probably pretend they didn't—no one in their right mind would admit to knowing a wetboy. And it was better than going as himself.

A Kylar Stern who showed up in the rebel camp was a Kylar Stern who was committing himself to their cause. Besides, he didn't know yet if the Kylar persona was safe. Elene had told Lord General Agon, and Kylar didn't know if Agon had passed the word along.

So here he was, sitting on his horse, trying to fix Durzo's face to his. It wasn't easy, even though he'd spent days—weeks—perfecting the disguise. The problems were manifold.

First, you had to remember the face perfectly. Even after years of looking at Durzo Blint, that was harder than Kylar would have imagined. He'd spent weeks after initially starting the project remembering just how the little lines at the corners of Durzo's eyes turned down, placing the pocks that had pitted his cheeks, getting the shape of the eyebrows right, adjusting the wisps of his thin beard. Then, when he'd thought he had that perfect, he'd realized he was only beginning.

A static face wasn't a disguise. He needed to anchor every moving spot of that face to his, so that it moved almost the same way. Almost. The fact was, even after ten years of being raised by Durzo and years of picking up little mannerisms from him, Kylar's facial expressions weren't much like Durzo's. So, the Durzo face glowered when he frowned, smirked when he smiled, and sneered when he grimaced, plus a hundred other things that he'd added as they occurred to him during long hours spent making faces at himself in the mirror.

Even then, the disguise wasn't complete. Durzo had been tall. Kylar was just pushing average. So after making his disguise, he projected it upward a good six inches. When someone tried to stare Durzo in the eye, he was looking over Kylar's head. It took a lot of discipline to remember to stare at the person's neck so Durzo would be looking back into their eyes. That was one thing Kylar hadn't fixed yet: he'd tried to make it so he could look wherever he wanted and Durzo's eyes would follow from six inches higher, but he hadn't figured out how yet.

And of course, if anyone tried to touch the face or the shoulders he projected, the illusion was destroyed. Kylar had tried to make the illusion ethereal, so something that touched it would slip right through. It hadn't worked. The Talent mesh—or whatever it was—was physical. If anything thicker than rain hit it, it broke apart. Kylar had tried to take that the other way, too, and give it physical form, so that light touches against it might feel resistance like a real face or real shoulders would provide. That hadn't worked either.

All in all, it was a damned lot of work for what turned out to be a mediocre disguise. Now Kylar understood why Durzo had preferred makeup.

He nudged his horse's flanks with his heels, and they descended into Havermere.

The sentries didn't appear surprised to see him riding out of the dawn, so maybe their perimeter was better than he'd thought. "State your business," a tough-looking teenager said.

"I'm a native of Cenaria but I've lived in Caernarvon for the last few years. I heard things had settled down for the most part. I've got family in Cenaria and I'm going to see if they're all right." It was quick, and he'd probably explained too much, but a nervous trader would probably do the same.

"What's your trade?"

"I'm an herb merchant and apothecary. Normally, I'd take the opportunity to bring some herbs along with me, but my last cargo was destroyed by bandits. The bastards burned my wagon when they found it didn't have any gold in it. Tell me, who did that help? Anyway, I can make better time this way."

"Are you armed?" the young man asked. He seemed more relaxed, though, and Kylar could tell he believed him.

"Of course I'm armed. Do you think I'm mad?" Kylar asked.

"Fair enough. Go ahead."

Kylar rode into the camp that was spread out before Havermere's gates. It was well-organized, laid out in neat rows with toilets at regular intervals away from the cooking pits, numerous permanent or semi-permanent buildings, and clear lanes for foot and horse traffic. But it wasn't very military. Some of the structures looked like they were planning on staying through the winter, but the fortifications around the camp were laughable. From the looks of things, all the nobles and their personal guards had taken residence in the Gyre estate, while the soldiers and civilians who had thrown in their lot with the rebels were out here, trying their best to make do.

Kylar was looking at a wood building, trying to divine its purpose, when he almost rode down a man wearing a pince nez and limping on a cane. The man looked up and appeared as shocked as Kylar was.

"Durzo?" Count Drake asked. "I thought you were dead."

Kylar froze. It was so good to see Count Drake alive that his control of the disguise almost wavered. The count looked older now, careworn. He'd walked with a limp since Kylar had known him, but he'd never needed a cane before.

"Is there some place we can talk, Count Drake?" Kylar barely stopped himself from calling him "sir."

"Yes, yes of course. Why are you calling me that? You haven't called me Count Drake in years."

"Uh . . . it has been a while. How did you get out?"

Count Drake squinted at him, and Kylar stared at Count Drake's chest, hoping that Durzo's eyes were meeting Count Drake's. "Are you well?" Count Drake asked.

Dismounting, Kylar extended his hand and clasped Count Drake's wrist. The man clasping his wrist back felt real, solid, the way Count Drake had always felt. He was an anchor, and Kylar was overwhelmed between an urge to tell him everything and shame just as strong.

The danger in talking to Count Drake was that everything became clear as he listened. Decisions that had seemed so muddy became suddenly simple. Something in Kylar shied away from that. If Count Drake really knew him, he'd stop loving him. A wetboy doesn't have friends.

Count Drake led him to a tent near the center of the camp. He sat in a chair, his leg obviously stiff. "It's a little drafty, but if we're still here we'll shore it up before winter."

"We?" Kylar asked.

The joy leached out of the count's eyes. "My wife and Ilena and I. Serah and Magdalyn didn't—didn't make it out. Serah was a comfort woman. We heard . . . she hanged herself with her bed sheets. Magdalyn is either a comfort woman or one of the Godking's concubines, last we heard." He cleared his throat. "Most of them don't last very long."

So it was true. Kylar hadn't thought Jarl was lying, but he hadn't been able to believe it. "I'm so sorry," Kylar said. Words were totally inadequate. Comfort women. Bound into the cruelest, most dehumanizing form of slavery Kylar knew: magically sterilized and given a room in the Khalidoran barracks for the convenience of the soldiers—a convenience used dozens of times a day. His stomach churned.

"Yes. It's a, an open wound," Count Drake said, his face gray. "Our Khalidoran brethren have given themselves over to the worst appetites. Please, come inside. Let's talk about the war we have to win."

Kylar stepped inside, but the churning in his stomach didn't stop. It intensified. As he saw Ilena Drake, the count's youngest daughter, who was now fourteen, that guilt crushed in on him. God, what if they'd caught her, too?

"Could you heat up some ootai for us?" the count asked his daughter. "You remember my daughter?" he asked Kylar.

"Ilena, right?" Ilena had always been his favorite. She had her mother's cool complexion and white-blonde hair and her father's penchant for mischief, untempered by her father's years.

"Pleased to meet you," the girl said politely. Damn, she was becoming a lady. When had that happened?

Kylar looked back to the count. "So what's your title or your position here?"

"Titles? Position?" Count Drake smiled and spun his cane on its point. "Terah Graesin has been bargaining off titles, trying to tie families into the rebellion. But when it comes to actually getting things done, she's glad to have my help."

"You're joking."

"Afraid not. That's why we're still here—what is it? Three months since the coup? She's only allowed small raids against supply lines and poorly defended outposts. She's afraid that if we get handed a big loss the families will back out and swear their allegiance to the Godking."

"That's no way to win a war."

"No one knows how to win a war against Khalidor. Nobody's fought successfully against an army reinforced with wytches in decades," Count Drake said. "There are reports that the Khalidorans are having troubles along the Freeze. She's hoping that most of them will be sent home before the snows block Screaming Winds."

"I thought we held Screaming Winds," Kylar said.

"We did," Count Drake said. "I even got news from my friend Solon Tofusin to signal them when we were ready to march for war. The garrison there had the best Cenarian troops in the realm, veterans, every one."

"And?" Kylar asked.

"They're all dead. Killed themselves or lay down and let someone slit their throats. My spies say it was the work of the goddess Khali. That just adds to the duchess's caution."

"Terah Graesin," Ilena said, "does most of her campaigning on her back."

"Ilena!" her father said.

"It's true. I spend every day with her maids-in-waiting," Ilena said, scowling.

"Ilena."

"Sorry."

Kylar was shaken. It was impossible. Gods were superstition and madness. But what superstition would drive hundreds of veterans to suicide?

Ilena hadn't taken her eyes off Kylar since he came into the tent. She looked at him like he was going to try to steal something.

"So what's the plan?" Kylar asked, taking ootai from the frowning girl. Too late, he realized he wouldn't be able to drink it—Durzo's lips were in the wrong place.

"So far as I can tell," the count said, pained, "there isn't one. She's talked about a big offensive, but I'm afraid she doesn't know what to do. She's been trying to hire wetboys; there was even a Ymmuri stalker here a few weeks ago—scary sort—but I think she's trying to stack the deck but not play the game. She's gathering an army, but she doesn't know what to do with it. She's a political creature, not a martial one. She doesn't have any military men in her circle."

"It sounds like this is going to be the shortest-lived rebellion in history."

"Stop encouraging me." Count Drake sipped his ootai. "So what brings you here? Not work, I hope?"

"What kind of work do you do?" Ilena asked.

"Ilena, be silent or be gone," Count Drake said.

At her expression, which was at once wounded and peeved, Kylar coughed into his hand and looked away to keep from laughing.

When he looked up, Ilena's expression had changed altogether. Her eyes were bright and wide.

"It is you!" she said. "Kylar!"

She threw herself into his arms, knocking the delicate ootai cup from his hands and utterly smashing the illusion as she hugged him.

The count was shocked into silence. Kylar looked at him, aghast.

"You big oaf, hug me!" Ilena said.

Kylar laughed and hugged her. Gods, it felt good—really, really good—to be hugged. She squeezed as hard as she could, and he picked her up as he hugged her. He pretended to squeeze as hard as he could. She squeezed harder until he cried out for mercy. They laughed again—they'd always hugged like that—and he set her down.

"Oh, Kylar, that was so the slam," she said. "How did you do that? Can you teach me? Will you, please?"

"Ilena, let the man breathe," her father said, but he was grinning. "I should have recognized the voice."

"My voice! Oh, sh—darn!" Kylar said. Altering his voice would either require some great acting—which seemed to be beyond him—or more magic. That meant more hours working with a single disguise. When would he find the time to do that?

"Well," the count said, tucking away his pince nez and picking up the pieces of his shattered ootai cup, "it would seem we need to talk. Shall Ilena be excused?"

"Oh, don't make me go, father."

"Um, yes," Kylar said. "See ya, squirt."

"I don't want to go."

Count Drake gave her a look and she wilted. She stomped her foot and marched out.

Then they were alone. Count Drake said gently, "What happened to you, son?"

Kylar picked at a ragged fingernail, stared at a few splinters of the shattered ootai cup on the ground, looked anywhere but at those accepting eyes. "Sir, do you think a man can change?"

"Absolutely," Count Drake said. "Absolutely, but usually he just becomes more himself. Why don't you tell me everything?"

So Kylar did. Everything from the Jadwin estate to breaking his oaths to Elene and Uly, and the raw, gnawing sore that left in his stomach. Finally, he was finished. "I could have stopped it," he said. "I could have ended the war before it began. I'm so sorry. Mags and Serah would be safe if I'd killed Durzo before..."

The count was rubbing his temples as tears leaked down his cheeks. "No, son. Stop that."

"What would you have done, sir?"

"If I knew stabbing Durzo in the back would save Serah and Magdalyn? I'd have stabbed him, son. But it wouldn't have been the right thing to do. Unless you're a king or a general, the only life you have the right to sacrifice for the greater good is your own. You did the right thing. Now let's talk about this little jaunt to the Maw. Are you sure this rumor is true?"

"The Shinga came to tell me himself—and died for it."

"Jarl's dead?" Count Drake asked. It was a blow, Kylar could see.

"You knew about Jarl?" Kylar asked.

"He'd been talking with me. He was planning an uprising to give us a chance to split Ursuul's forces. The people believed in him. They loved him. Even the thieves and killers were beginning to believe they could have a new start."

"Sir, after I rescue Logan . . ."

"Don't say it."

"I'm gonna go after Mags."

Count Drake's face was gray once more, hopeless. "You save Logan Gyre and you do it fast. Ulana will be sorry she missed you, but you have to go now."

Kylar stood and replaced the Durzo mask. Count Drake watched and his face regained some life. "You know, you have tricks that are—well, the slam."

They laughed together. "One more question," Kylar said. "I've been thinking that it might be good for rumors to get out that Logan is alive before he shows up. I mean, it will give the people something to hope for and it will make it easier for him to consolidate power when he does appear. Should I tell Terah Graesin he's alive?"

"It's a little late for that," a voice said from the opening of the tent. It was Terah Graesin, in a lavish green dress and cloak lined with new mink. She was smiling a thin smile. "Why Durzo Blint, I haven't seen you in ages."

43

Usually Garoth summoned his concubines to his rooms, but sometimes he liked to surprise them. Magdalyn Drake had entertained him for a long time, but as always, his interest was beginning to wane.

Tonight, he'd woken, hours past midnight, with the infernal itch and a headache and an idea. He would enter silently and wake Magdalyn roughly. He loved Magdalyn's scream. He would beat her savagely and accuse her of plotting against him.

If she begged and swore it wasn't true like most frightened women would, he'd throw her off the balcony. If she cursed him, he would bang her, matching her defiance with an equal degree of brutality, and she would live another day. Before he left, he would hold her tenderly in his arms and whisper that he was sorry, that he loved her. Decent women always wanted to see something good in him. He shivered in anticipation.

He extended the vir through the closed door, hoping to detect the even sound of her breathing in sleep. Instead he felt something different. She was awake.

Garoth opened the door, but she didn't notice him. She was sitting on her bed, facing the open door to her rail-less balcony. She was dressed only in a thin nightgown, but she didn't seem to feel the cold air blowing in the open door. She was rocking back and forth.

He swore loudly. She didn't respond. He touched her skin and it, too, was cold. She must have been sitting like this for hours.

Other concubines had pretended madness in an attempt to escape his attentions. Maybe Magdalyn Drake was the same. Garoth slapped her and she fell off the bed. She didn't cry out. Grabbing a fistful of dark hair, Garoth dragged her onto the balcony.

Coming right to the edge, he pulled her to her feet. He grabbed her throat in one thick hand and pushed her back until her toes were barely on the edge. His fingers wrapped almost all the way around her throat. He took care to choke her as little as possible, but if he released her, she would fall.

Her eyes finally came into focus. The shadow of death tended to have that effect on people.

"Why?" Magdalyn asked sadly. "Why do you do this?"

He looked at her, confused. The answer was so obvious that he wasn't sure he'd understood the question. "It pleases me," he said.

And strangely—but Magdalyn Drake had always been a strange girl, it was part of why she appealed to him—Magdalyn smiled. She pulled toward him, but not like a woman dangling off a precipice would pull toward her only hope of life.

She kissed him. If it was an act, it was a damn convincing one. If her mind had broken, it had broken in an intriguing way. Magdalyn Drake kissed him, and Garoth swore it was with real desire. His arousal came back stronger than ever as she climbed him, her lean young legs wrapping around his waist.

He thought of taking her back inside, but it was impossible to stay fully in control, about to make love with a woman who might be trying to kill him. She kissed her way to his ears.

"I've been listening to you and Neph," she said, washing her hot breath back in his ear.

He usually didn't let his concubines talk while he fucked them, unless they were cursing him, but Garoth didn't want to destroy this fragile insanity.

Magdalyn kissed him again, then pulled away. She leaned back. Holding him with her legs, she let go of his neck and leaned back. He grabbed onto her hips to keep her from plunging to her death. Upside down, she waved her arms above her head, looking over the castle and the city below, laughing.

Garoth's pulse pounded loud in his ears. He didn't even care who might be watching. Whatever kind of madness this was, it was intoxicating.

She shimmied her hips and said something again.

"What?" he asked.

"Let go," she said.

She seemed to have a tight grip with her legs, so he let go, ready to catch her with the vir if need be. He wasn't going to let this end without taking his pleasure. Not now.

Magdalyn tugged her nightgown free from where it was trapped between their bodies and stripped it off. She dropped it over the edge, laughing again as the flimsy cloth spun toward the flagstones below.

Then she sat up and kissed Garoth again, pressing her young body against him. She stripped his robe back roughly. Then she burrowed into him, moaning as her skin touched his, warm against warm in the cold night air.

She nuzzled his neck. "I heard you talking about the Night Angel," she said. "Kylar Stern."

"Mmm."

"I want you to know something," she whispered into his ear, making him shiver. What the hell was she saying? "Kylar's my brother. He's coming for me, you dirty fucker, and if I don't kill you, he will."

She bit his carotid artery as hard as she could and tried to throw them both off the edge.

The vir reacted before Garoth could, exploding at his neck. The vir lashed from his limbs, flinging him inside even as Magdalyn Drake spun out into space.

He stood shakily and summoned Neph.

The Vürdmeister found him standing on the balcony, looking at the ruin of the young woman crushed in the courtyard below.

"Take care of her, Neph. Tell Trudana I expect the best," the Godking said, greatly moved. "Hers was a great spirit."

"Shall I..." The Lodricari coughed his fake cough and Garoth hated him anew. "Shall I send in another concubine?" He pointedly didn't look toward the evidence of Garoth's continued arousal.

"Yes," Garoth said tersely. *Curse you, Khali, yes.*

"If you'll excuse us, Count Drake," Terah Graesin said. "I have need of your quarters."

Count Drake limped out on his cane as several guards took up position outside the tent.

Kylar was still reeling. Terah Graesin knew Durzo. That meant he was supposed to know her, and he didn't. If she knew Durzo, that meant she knew Durzo through his work. That meant she had hired him.

"So," she said. "Logan's alive. That's...terrific." Terah Graesin had a silky, low voice. It was reputed to be sexy, but then, everything about Terah Graesin was supposed to be sexy. Kylar didn't see it. Oh, she was pretty. She had a wide mouth, full lips, and the kind of figure that was unattainable for the majority of noblewomen who spent their days doing nothing more strenuous than issuing orders to the servants. Maybe it was that she was a little too self-consciously good-looking. She wore lots of makeup—expertly applied and subtle, but lots—and had tweezed her eyebrows down to tiny lines. The truth was, she held herself like he ought to admire her, and it pissed him off.

What pissed him off more was that to look her in the eye with his disguise, he had to stare straight at her admittedly perky breasts. Dammit, why were breasts so intriguing?

"So who's paying you to save Logan Gyre?" she asked.

"You don't really expect me to answer that," Kylar said. The only card he had to play was that Blint tended to be blunt and secretive. If she knew him, she'd know that much.

"Master Blint," she said, seeming to come to a decision, but still speaking in that same consciously sexy voice, "you're the only man I know who's killed two kings. How much can I pay you to kill a third?"

"*What?!* You want me to kill the Godking?"

"No. Simply don't save Logan Gyre. I'll double whatever your employer is paying."

"What?" Kylar asked. "Why? You need all the allies you can get right now. Logan would bring thousands to your banners."

"The problem is...well, can you keep a secret, Durzo?" She smiled.

"Would you trust a murderer with your secrets?"

"I knew you'd say that!" she said triumphantly, almost giggling. "You said the same thing last time, remember?"

"It's been a while," Kylar said, his throat constricting.

"Well, I'm glad you remembered long enough to kill my father."

Kylar blinked.

"Tell me, did you do it before or after you killed King Gunder?"

"I'm paid to kill, not to talk about it." *Gods! Her own father?*

"And that's why I can trust you. Though I will remind you that I've already given you money for not killing me—so you can't do to me what I did to my father."

"Of course not." It took him a second to puzzle it out. She must have met Durzo when the wetboy had taken a job for her father, Duke Gordin Graesin. Perhaps Gordin had hired Durzo to kill King Davin? Duke Graesin must have thought Regnus Gyre would become king after King Davin died, thereby making Gordin's other daughter Catrinna a queen. Logan's mother, Catrinna Graesin, had been Terah's half-sister, though older than Terah by almost twenty years.

"So why let Logan die?" he asked.

"Because I don't give up things that belong to me easily, Durzo Blint. As you know."

"Don't you think you might want to worry about taking the throne from the Khalidorans before you worry about murdering your allies?"

"I don't need a civics lesson. Are you interested in making money for doing nothing, or do you wish to make me your enemy? I will be queen one day, and you'll find me an implacable foe."

"Seven thousand crowns," Kylar said. "How do I know you're good for it? If the Khalidorans wipe you out, I'm not getting stiffed."

She smiled. "Now there's the Durzo Blint I remember." She pulled a fat ring off her finger with an even fatter ruby in it. "Please don't pawn it. It belonged to my father, and it's not worth even half of the eight thousand I'll give you for it after I take the throne. There'll be a bonus if you bring me proof of Logan's death."

"Fair enough," Kylar said.

"I foresee some of my allies becoming…problematic in the future. I'll have other jobs for you. That is, if you haven't lost your edge."

"What's that supposed to mean?"

"When you didn't answer my summons a month ago, I had to go elsewhere."

"You'll never find anyone as good as me." That, at least, was classic Durzo Blint.

Terah Graesin licked her lips and her eyes filled with sudden hunger. Kylar didn't recognize the look, but he didn't like it, whatever it was. She smiled.

What is she waiting for? Me to make a pass at her? The moment passed.

"Well, then, good day," she said in a level tone that didn't tell Kylar whether he was right or wrong. She stepped close to him to kiss each of his cheeks. It put his real face right at level of her chest, but he was lucky. She didn't lean close enough to touch either his real lips with her breasts or his phantom cheek with her lips. The illusion stayed intact.

As soon as she was gone, he fled. He jumped on his horse and went north out of the camp, worried that Terah might have someone watching the western exit. He shifted his disguise so that Durzo's face was where his own was, rather than above it so that he could see the guards' expression. The guards let him out without question, however, and when he was a mile out, he began to let down his guard. His heart was still pounding as he thought about what this meant for Logan. Even if he got his friend out of the Maw, the road ahead wouldn't be easy. At least now he would know who his enemies were.

Kylar entered a thin stretch of trees when something whispered coolly in his mind: *~Duck.~*

"What?" he said aloud.

An arrow drove through Kylar's chest.

It rocked him back in the saddle, but his horse kept walking, oblivious. Kylar coughed blood. He'd made so many mistakes. Durzo would never have forgiven him for his carelessness. Letting down his guard, going back to the path when he'd worried someone might have been sent after him, taking his own horse rather than stealing someone else's. It only took one mistake to get you killed, and he'd made many.

Gods, his lungs burned.

~I told you to duck.~

A shadowy form stepped out from behind a tree and took his horse's reins in one hand, holding a sword in the other.

The wetboy let down his shadows—they weren't nearly as good as Durzo's, never mind Kylar's. It was Scarred Wrable. "Well, son of a bitch," the wetboy said. "Durzo Blint? Shit."

"Howdy, Ben," Kylar said. Son of a bitch was right. He'd kept the Durzo disguise—and if he'd kept it at Durzo's height, Ben Wrable would have shot his arrow right over Kylar's shoulder.

It was taking more and more effort to maintain the Durzo disguise, and Kylar was painfully aware that it was important he do so. If Terah thought she'd killed Durzo, Kylar could still come back. That had its own set of problems, but far fewer than revealing that he was both Durzo Blint and Kylar Stern and immortal.

"Shit, Durzo! I didn't even know it was you. That uppity Graesin bitch said 'special job, easy, pay ya double.' What the hell you riding on the path for, D?"

"Just . . ." Kylar coughed. "Made a mistake."

"It only takes one, I guess. Shit, buddy. I woulda fought ya at least."

"I would have killed you," Kylar said. He was stirred by a sudden panic. What if this was his last life? He had no guarantee that he would come back. The Wolf had never explained it. Gods, he'd been totally crazy when he'd let Baron Kirof kill him for money.

"Probably." Scarred Wrable swore again. He'd gained his nickname from the innumerable scars he had on his face. He'd come to Cenaria as a child from somewhere in Friaku and spent time as a slave. He was one of the few men who'd gained his freedom from the fighting pits. Kylar thought the scars were self-inflicted, but the man spoke without an accent. Whatever rituals he practiced he'd learned from rumors about the Friaki, not from observation. "How am I supposed to brag about this, Durzo? I just shot you with a goddam arrow. That's no way to kill the world's greatest wetboy."

"Seems to be working all right." Kylar coughed.

"Shit," Ben said, disgusted.

"Make something up," Kylar said. He sprayed more blood again as he coughed. He'd forgotten dying was so much fun.

"I can't do that," Wrable said. "It dishonors the dead. They haunt you if you do that."

"I feel really fucking sorry for you," Kylar said. He was slipping out of the saddle. He hit the ground with a thump and smacked the back of his head on the ground, but whatever he'd done, the disguise held.

Ben scowled. "Wait," he said, working it out. Scarred Wrable had never been the brightest torch on the wall. "You mean, you mean it would honor you more if people thought you'd been killed in heroic combat?" Scarred Wrable asked. He liked the idea. "You'd let me say that and not haunt me? I'd make you sound good, I swear."

"Depends," Kylar said. His vision was already beginning to white out. "Are you going to hack anything off my corpse?" That would be just his luck. He'd wake up without a head or something. How would that work? Would he die for real if someone took his head?

"The bitch did want proof."

"Take her the ring. Take my horse, my clothes, whatever you need, but leave my body alone, say you're superstitious or something and you can tell the story however you want. Just put my body..." Kylar lost the thought. His head was getting thick. He thought he could feel his heart laboring as blood spilled inside his chest.

"Fair enough. You ready, friend?" Ben asked.

Kylar nodded.

Ben Wrable stabbed him through the heart.

44

I've been working on the web," Sister Ariel said. "It's trapped in some really interesting ways. Who put it on you again?"

"How about if I tell you, you let me go?" Vi said. *Not very subtle, are you, Bitch Wytch?*

They were heading back to the trail after taking a huge detour around the rebel camp at Havermere. Vi could tell that Sister Ariel had wanted to go into the camp but thought that it would give Vi chances to escape.

"Why are we going west?" Vi asked. "I thought the Chantry was northeast."

"It is. But I still haven't finished what I was sent to do," Ariel said.

"What was that?" Uly asked. She was sitting on the cantle behind Vi right now, and both of them were leashed magically. Vi was glad that Uly asked the question. Sister Ariel answered Uly's questions. That probably had something to do with Vi's repeated escape attempts, which had left them both bruised and irritable.

"I'm looking to recruit someone special, and I'm hoping I can find a woman who fits the bill in the rebel camp. Unfortunately, I don't trust Vi as far as I can throw her."

"That's pretty far," Uly said.

Vi scowled. Not only had Ariel left her with the scratches from where she'd landed in brambles, but afterward she'd spanked her. Life in the saddle was a sore life.

"So I don't count as someone special?" Vi said. "You already said I'm vastly talented. Or whatever." She sneered as she said it, but she was curious—and, strangely, a little hurt that she didn't measure up.

"Oh, you're both very special. But neither of you qualifies for what I need," Ariel said. The bitch was enjoying being mysterious.

"What do you mean, both of us?" Vi asked.

"I'm taking you both to the Chantry, but neither of you can fulfill—"

"Why are you taking us both?"

Ariel looked at Vi, puzzled. Then she laughed. "Uly's Talented, Vi."

"What?" Vi was incredulous.

"Oh, it's rare to find Talented women, I don't deny it. But if only one woman in a thousand is Talented, that doesn't mean that you only find two Talented women together once in a million times. You see?"

"No," Uly said. Vi didn't either.

"People with the Talent tend to feel an affinity for each other, even if neither of them knows why. We frequently find them together, which is great for us...usually. Perhaps you're too young for this much truth, Ulyssandra, but that affinity is probably the only reason why an otherwise heartless murderer didn't add you to her already overburdened conscience."

"You mean she would have killed me? Would you, Vi?" Uly asked.

Vi was glad the girl was sitting behind her so she couldn't see the guilt written all over her face. Why did she care what Uly thought?

"You can look at it in a negative light or a positive one, Ulyssandra," Sister Ariel said. "Negative: she normally would have killed you. Positive: she didn't—and she's had many opportunities to change her mind since then and still hasn't. You might even say Vi likes you."

"Do you like me, Vi?" Uly asked.

"I'd like to kick you in the head," Vi said.

"Don't take it too hard," Sister Ariel said. "With the way she was raised, Vi's a—well, let's be charitable—let's call her an emotional cripple. She's probably only poorly able to differentiate between most of her emotions, feeling comfortable only with rage, anger, and condescension because they make her feel strong. Indeed, I'd guess her interactions with you may well be the first positive ones she's had in her entire life."

"Stop it," Vi said. Ariel was cutting her into pieces and scoffing at the bits.

"This is positive?" Uly said.

"She doesn't shy away from your touch, Uly. When you ride with her, she's at ease. For anyone else, she'd be constantly on guard."

"I'll kill the little wench the first chance I get," Vi said.

"Bluster," Ariel said.

"What's that mean?" Uly asked.

"It means horseshit," Vi said.

"So you just keep being nice to her, Uly," Ariel said, ignoring Vi, "because probably no one else in your tyro class will like her very much."

"In *our class*?" Vi asked. "You're putting me with the children?"

Sister Ariel looked surprised. "Why yes. And you should be nice to Ulyssandra, because she's got more Talent than you do. And none of your bad habits."

"You cruel, cruel bitch," Vi said. "I know what you're doing. You're trying to break me, but I'll tell you what. Nothing can break me. I've been through everything."

Sister Ariel turned her face to the setting sun that limned the treetops of a small copse in front of them. "That, my dear, is where you're wrong. You are already broken, Vi. You were broken years ago and you healed hunched. And now you're broken again and trying to heal even more hunched. I won't let that happen. I'll break you one more time if I have to so you don't have to be a cripple anymore. But I can't make the choice to be healthy for you. And I don't promise a lack of scars. But you can be a better woman than you are now."

"A woman who looks a lot like you?" Vi sneered.

"Oh no. You're more passionate than I ever was," Sister Ariel said. "I'm afraid I'm a bit of an emotional cripple myself. Too much brain, they say. Too comfortable in my own mind. I never had to come out. But I was born this way; you were made. And you're right; you'll not learn what you need to know from me."

"Were you ever in love?" Uly asked.

Vi wondered where the hell that came from, but the question must have been a good one because it hit Sister Ariel like shovel across the face.

"Huh. That's a—a very good question," Ariel said.

"He left you for someone who wasn't so cold and ugly, didn't he?" Vi asked, with a little twist of satisfaction.

Ariel said nothing for a moment. "I see you aren't without claws," Ariel said, quietly. "Not that I expected any less."

Uly jabbed her fingers into Vi's ribs to chastise her, but Vi ignored her. "So you never got around to your point. Why are we going west?"

"There's a sister who lives this way. She's going to nursemaid you two while I scout out the rebel camp for a suitable woman."

"What are you looking for?" Uly asked.

"We should start looking for a place to set up camp. It's getting dark. Looks like we're not going to make it to Carissa's tonight," Sister Ariel said.

"Aw, please?" Uly said. "It's not that dark and we don't have anything else to talk about."

Sister Ariel seemed to chew it over. She shrugged. "I'm looking for a highly Talented woman who is ambitious, charismatic, and obedient."

"Ambitious and obedient? Good luck," Vi said.

"If she were willing to be obedient to the Speaker, she'd have personal instruction, a rapid rise through the ranks, a lot of attention and power—but all those are easy. The problem is that she has to be new because we have to be sure of her loyalties, and she has to be married. A woman whose husband is Talented would be the real gem."

"So when you find this married woman, you're going to kidnap her?" Vi asked. "Isn't that a little risky?"

"Another person might have said immoral, but ... well, a truly kidnapped woman wouldn't cooperate. Ideally, we'd like to have the man on the premises. Just sticking a wedding ring on a woman's hand isn't going to cut it. The more permanent and steady the marriage appears, the better."

"Why not have Vi do it?" Uly asked. "She doesn't want to be stuck in classes with me and the other twelve-year-olds anyway."

Ariel shook her head. "Believe me, I thought of her first, but she's totally unsuited to the task."

"You mean as a student or a wife?" Vi asked.

"Both. No offense, but I've known men who married the wrong woman, and they were all miserable. I'm sure we could ask some man to marry you, and we'd get lots of takers. You're a beautiful woman and around beautiful women men tend to think with their—" she looked at Uly and cleared her throat—"irrational side. Even if we could bribe the right fool, and believe me, the Chantry would—they won't put some man's happiness ahead of the Chantry's welfare—even then it wouldn't happen. Vi isn't trustworthy. She isn't obedient. Nor is she intelligent enough—"

"You really are a bitch," Vi said, but Sister Ariel ignored her.

"—and besides, she'd probably try to run away, which would destroy her usefulness to us and waste all our effort. So, like I said, totally unsuitable."

Vi stared at her hatefully. She knew the whole discussion had just been a ploy to cut her down, tell her how unworthy she was, but the intelligence comment had cut deeper than anything. For all the times that she'd been complimented in her life—men did a lot of that when they were trying to get up your skirts—whether the compliments had been crass or poetic, they had always been about her body. She was smart, dammit.

Sister Ariel stared right back at her. Then she seemed to look deeper.

"Stop!" she said.

Vi stopped. "What?"

Sister Ariel nudged her horse awkwardly until after a few attempts she got it to move beside Vi. She reached out and grabbed Vi's face in both of her hands.

"That son of a bitch," Ariel said. "Don't let anyone heal this, do you understand? He's—wow—look at that. If anyone touches this with magic, there are weaves of fire that will be unleashed around all of the major blood vessels in your brain. And that looks suspiciously like . . . have you lost control of your body at any time you can remember?"

"What do you mean, like pissed myself?"

"You'd know what I mean if it had happened. I'm going to have to see if Sister Drissa Nile will come back. She's the only one I'd let touch this."

"Who's that?" Uly asked.

"She's a healer. The best with tiny weaves that I know. Has some little shop in Cenaria, last I heard."

"You're not going to tell me anything else about this weave that's supposed to kill me?" Vi said.

"Not unless you tell me who set it."

"You can go—"

"If you curse me one more time, you'll regret it," Sister Ariel said.

The last punishment had been bad enough and the satisfaction for cursing small enough that Vi choked back her words.

They had entered the copse of trees when Vi spotted something partly hidden under leaves off the side of the path, something like dark hair glowing in the dying sunlight.

Uly followed her gaze. "What's that?"

"I think it's a body," Vi said. And then, as they left the path to take a closer look, her heart soared. It was indeed a body—a death that meant life for her. It was freedom and a new start. The dead man was Kylar.

45

Elene's whole body was in pain. She'd been riding as hard as she could bear for six days, and she still hadn't made it to Torras Bend. Her knees hurt, her back hurt, her thighs were in agony, and she still wasn't gaining any time on Uly and Uly's kidnapper. She knew that because she asked everyone she passed on the road if they'd seen a woman and child riding hard to the north. Most of them hadn't, but those who had remembered. If anything, Elene had been falling behind. And it was all up to Elene now.

The guards of the city watch had passed her yesterday, going back to Caernarvon. They'd assured her that a woman, especially a woman encumbered with a child, couldn't have ridden faster than they had. They had given up and gone home. One look at their faces and she knew she would have no luck convincing them otherwise. They were tired and probably under orders not to cross the Lae'knaught who sometimes wandered this far east. Elene let them go. What mattered more than the city watch was Kylar. He'd come this way, too. At some point, he'd passed the kidnapper and Uly—because he hadn't been looking for them.

But she was almost to Torras Bend. Tonight she would sleep in a bed. Bathe. Then she would find out if the kidnapper had headed toward Cenaria, as Elene suspected. And have a hot meal. Elene was daydreaming when she saw the Lae'knaught.

They straddled the road in the middle of some of the largest wheat fields south of Torras Bend. If Elene had wanted to go around them, she'd have to go miles to the east and risk crossing into Ezra's Wood, which was supposed to be haunted. As it was, it was too late. They'd already seen her, and the knights had horses saddled and ready to give chase.

Elene approached them directly, suddenly acutely aware of being a woman traveling alone. There were six men, all armed, and as she neared, all of them stood to intercept her. Over chain hauberks, they wore black tabards emblazoned with a golden sun: the pure light of reason beating back the darkness of superstition. She'd never come across the Lae'knaught, but she knew Kylar didn't think much of them. They professed not to believe in magic, but hated it at the same time. Kylar said they were nothing more than bullies. If they really hated Khalidorans, he'd said, they would have come to Cenaria's aid when the Godking invaded. Instead, they'd hovered like vultures, picking up recruits among the fleeing Cenarians and scavenging off Cenarian lands.

One of the standing knights stepped forward. He held his twelve-foot ash lance carefully. It looked too long to use on foot, but Elene knew that once mounted, all of the knights' awkwardness would vanish. "Halt, in the name of the Bringers of the Freedom of the Light," he said. Elene guessed he couldn't be more than sixteen. As Elene stopped, he stepped forward and grabbed the reins. She wasn't sure what they were so nervous about, and then she realized what should have been immediately obvious. When they saw a woman traveling alone, they saw vulnerability. No normal woman would travel alone, therefore, she must not be a normal woman. She must be a wytch. Elene's stomach tightened.

"Thank goodness," Elene said, sighing as if with relief. She almost said thank the God, but she didn't think the Lae'knaught believed in gods, either. "Can you help me?"

"What is it? What are you doing alone on these roads?" one of the older ones asked.

"Have you seen a young woman, maybe with red hair, traveling with a young girl? Maybe two days ago? No?" Elene slumped, and the sudden pained look on her face was real, even slumping hurt after how much she'd ridden. "I guess she would certainly have avoided you, given what she is. You're certain you didn't see anyone, maybe trying to avoid you by traveling farther east?"

"What are you talking about, young lady? What's happened? How can we help?" the knight asked. From the change in his voice, Elene knew he no longer saw her as a threat. Acting weak and vulnerable had done the trick.

"I've come from Caernarvon," Elene said. "We were originally from Cenaria, but we left as soon as those awful men and their wytches invaded. We were making a new life, Uly and me—Uly's the little girl, my ward. Her parents were killed by the wytches....We thought we were safe in Caernarvon, but she was kidnapped, sirs. I just had to follow her. The city watch came a way, but then they turned back. I'm afraid I'll never catch up."

"It's just like those damn Sisters, kidnapping a child," the youngest knight said. "That letter said—"

The older knight barked, "Marcus!"

The men were all looking at each other, and Elene knew that her near-truths had not only worked, but that they knew something more. The knights withdrew, leaving the young Marcus standing and looking at her scars awkwardly. Then he realized he was staring, and coughed into his hand.

The older knights returned after a few minutes. The eldest spoke again, "Usually, we'd like to take you to the underlord to tell him all this yourself, but I can see that time is crucial. In fact, we'd love to go with you to help, but our orders are to stay south of Torras Bend. Politics. The thing is, there was a messenger this morning. We intercept all correspondence from Chantry wytches. Well, here. We've already made a copy." He handed her a letter.

"Elene," the letter read in a looping, flowing script, "Uly is safe now, I have taken her from the custody of the woman who took her from you, but I'm afraid I can't send her home. Uly is Talented, and she is on her way to the Chantry, where she will receive the best tutelage in the world and material advantages beyond what you could hope to provide. I understand that you have no reason to believe that this letter is from me. If you wish, you may go to the Chantry to see Uly yourself, or even take her home, should you both wish it. As soon as she arrives safely at the Chantry, she will write to you. I apologize, and if other events weren't so pressing, I would deliver this message myself. Sincerely, Sister Ariel Wyant Sa'fastae."

She had to read the letter two more times before she could grasp what it was saying. Someone had kidnapped Uly from her kidnapper? Uly was Talented?

In the end, the letter changed nothing. Elene still had to go to Torras Bend and find out what the villagers knew. If what it said was true, she would have to go north and on to the Chantry. If not, she'd have to head west, to Cenaria. Still, the kidnapper wouldn't have known that Elene was following her. It wasn't like she'd been closing in on them.

"Damn wytches," the young knight said. "Always kidnapping little girls, turning them away from the Light and into more like themselves."

"Marcus!"

Elene was suddenly relieved she'd told the truth to these men. If her story hadn't lined up with the letter, things would have gone very differently. "No, it's all right," she said. "I'll have to press on hard if I've hoping of finding Uly before she gets in their clutches."

"Be careful," the older knight said. "Not all of these villagers love the Light."

"Thank you for your help," Elene said. With that, she rode on toward Torras Bend, her mind awhirl.

46

*W*henever Ariel saw something she thought was fascinating or puzzling, she had a curious talent for memorizing it. It had been an enormous benefit when studying, of course, because she was able to picture whole sections of scrolls and find whatever she needed.

She was lucky enough now to not be looking at the corpse. She was looking at Vi's and Uly's faces—and each face's expression was locked in the vault of her memory. Vi's was all exhilaration, a thrill that might just have come from seeing death. Ariel hoped that wasn't it. She hoped there was more to it than that, that Vi had had some personal reason to want Kylar dead. If not, Vi might be less useful than she thought. For now, she disregarded Vi's expression. She put it away to examine another time. It was Uly's expression that truly intrigued her.

Kylar had been a father figure to the girl. Uly was a tenderhearted child. She hadn't grown up in the Warrens or any other place where she had to see death on a daily basis. The sight of her adoptive father stripped to his underclothes and lying dead by the side of the road should have left her shocked. She should look distant or in denial—not curious. Had she just not recognized him yet? Then Uly's expression shifted to something Ariel thought was elation. Elation? Surely that couldn't be right. Why would the girl be happy?

Ariel was interrupted as she realized she was having her own emotions about seeing Kylar dead. She tried to label them as quickly as possible so she could file them away and get back to the task at hand. Disappointment, yes. She'd been planning something clever for Kylar and it wasn't going to work now. A little bit of grief. Kylar had seemed like the kind of man she would like. Curiosity at how such a capable man had let himself be killed. Some sorrow for how it would affect Uly—*good enough, that will do.* Having labeled her emotions, she set them aside.

Uly looked up and saw Ariel staring at her. "He's not dead," Uly said. "He's just hurt."

"Girl," Vi said. "I've seen lots of dead people. He's dead."

"He'll get better."

It sounded like denial, and Vi obviously took it as such, but it wasn't.

Sister Ariel unrolled the mental scroll to examine the expression on Uly's face and watch it change. Curiosity to elation. Curiosity to elation. Uly saw that he was dead—it was obvious from how pale he was that he'd been here for quite some time, maybe a day—but Uly wasn't surprised and she wasn't worried. Why? Did she really believe he'd get better?

Sister Ariel reached out with her Talent and touched Kylar and realization whooshed over her—no, it crashed over her like a ten-foot wave, leaving her breathless and sputtering. Her magic was sucked from the air into Kylar's body, channeled a hundred different ways to join in the healing that was going on within him.

The magic would have baffled her. The magic combined with Uly's expression that said she'd seen this before and was elated, that told her everything.

Kylar was a creature out of legend. A legend no Sister believed. Until now.

"You're right, Uly," Sister Ariel said gently, meeting Vi's gaze as if to say "play along." "How about we set up camp and you can start on our dinner while Vi and I tend to his wounds? She and I know more about healing, and you can make sure there's dinner ready for him when he wakes up."

Ariel dismounted and helped Uly down.

"I don't want to go. I want to stay here," Uly said.

"Uly," Vi said. "The best way you can help is to get dinner ready. You'll get in the way here."

"Come on, child," Ariel said. She led Uly away as Vi got off her horse and began pulling leaves away from Kylar's body. Ariel turned and mouthed "start digging." Vi nodded.

If she'd had time to think, Ariel wouldn't have played such a desperate hand. A thousand factors were in play and playing too fast for her to calculate the odds.

She took Uly about twenty paces into the woods and bound her and gagged her with magic, setting her on the far side of a tree trunk. "I'm sorry, child. It's for the best."

"Mmm!" Uly said, her eyes wide, but the sound was barely a whisper.

Ariel came around the tree just in time to see Vi vault onto her horse's back and gallop off into the woods. Ariel shouted and threw a ball of light whizzing past her, but didn't put any heat into it. She wasn't going to light the forest on fire just to scare the girl. Besides, she might have accidentally hit her.

In moments, even the sound of hoofbeats faded. Sister Ariel shook her head and made no attempt to follow.

So much for the obvious part of the gamble. What Vi did now was the real trick. *Good luck, Vi. May you come back to us ready to heal.*

She hoped that someday she might sit with Vi in her chambers at the Chantry and laugh about what they'd done today, but she didn't think it would happen. Not after what she'd just done. Passionate women tended to hate women like Sister Ariel. Or at least they hated being coldly manipulated—but what choice did Ariel have?

"And now you," she said, turning. "My undying warrior. How do you work?"

"I didn't see you last time," Kylar told the Wolf. "I thought maybe I was done with you." The Wolf was sitting in his throne in the Antechamber of

Mystery, his lambent yellow eyes weighing Kylar. The indistinct ghosts who populated the indistinct chamber murmured beyond Kylar's hearing. The whole place still unnerved him.

He couldn't feel the floor beneath his feet. He couldn't see the ghosts when he looked directly at them. Couldn't tell if the chamber actually had walls. His skin prickled, but he couldn't have said if it was warm or cold here. He couldn't smell. Aside from his voice, he heard nothing. He had a sense of noise, voices, the scuff of feet beyond his hearing, but that was only an intuition. He was disembodied and somehow he'd carried along some of his senses but not all of them, and none of them reliably. Only a few things were clear here: the Wolf, and the two doors. One was plain wood with an iron latch, the other gold with light leaking around the edges.

"I was too furious to bear the sight of you," the Wolf said.

He didn't look much happier now. Kylar couldn't think of anything to say. Furious? Why?

"It took Acaelus fifty years to rack up three deaths. You've done it in less than six months. You took money for a death. Money. Wasn't the price for that blasphemy enough? Will you never learn?" the Wolf asked.

"What are you talking about?" Kylar could sense that the ghosts or whatever the insubstantial people were who crowded the chamber had gotten very quiet.

"You sicken me."

"I don't—"

The Wolf held up a burn-scarred finger and the weight of the small man's authority was such that Kylar stopped immediately.

"Acaelus took money once, too, after his first wife died. I think he didn't really believe in his immortality until then. He took money twice and did something worse once. After that, I showed him what it cost. It stopped him, as it should be stopping you. If you persist in throwing lives away, I will make you rue every day of your interminable life."

It was like a bad dream: the frowning tribunal holding him to a standard he didn't understand, declaring his guilt, the looming watchful figures, the doors of judgment, the threat of a truth he couldn't bear. He would have shaken himself, pinched himself—if he'd had a body to shake or pinch. If he didn't remember being killed.

"I don't know what you're talking about. What the hell am I supposed to do?" Kylar asked bitterly. "What am I for?"

Light flashed in those hard gold eyes and the world telescoped. Perspectives changed and Kylar felt suddenly awkward. Fat and uncoordinated, he was seated in a small chair. His fingers were short and pudgy and wailing filled his head. His head itself seemed almost unbearably heavy. He flailed and realized he was the one screaming.

He was back in a body, but it wasn't his. He was a baby. In front of him, the gray-haired man, now a giant, held a spoon full of gruel. "OPEN WI—IDE!" the Wolf crooned, pushing the gruel toward Kylar's face.

Kylar snapped his screaming mouth shut.

Light flashed once more and he was back in his own body.

The man smiled wolfishly at him. "You are nothing but a fat, awkward child in the land of giants. You close your mouth instead of eating. You speak when you should listen. What are you for? Any answer I gave you'd reject. So why should I waste my time? You're as arrogant as your master ever was, and you don't have a shred of his wisdom. I find you wanting."

"What am I supposed to do?"

"Better. Do better."

Part of Ariel wished she could slow whatever was happening in Kylar's body. As it was, he was almost recovered. As she watched, the arrow in his chest wobbled and began to shift. Then it quivered and began to rise out of his body as if being pushed from within.

With an audible plop, the arrowhead broke through skin that had already healed flush around the shaft. The arrow fell to the side and Ariel grabbed it and put it in her pack next to the gold tablet for later study.

The skin over Kylar's heart the arrow had just broken was knitting together so quickly she could see it. In moments, it was smooth once more, unscarred. Sister Ariel reached out with her magic, but as soon as it touched Kylar's body it was absorbed. A tremor passed through him and his heart started beating. A long moment later, his chest rose and he coughed violently, spitting half-congealed lumps of blood out of his lungs. Then the coughing passed. Sister Ariel tried to watch without touching, but the streams of magic were so fast she couldn't begin to understand them. She put a hand close to his body, and the air felt cold there. The grass beneath him was wilted and white.

It was like his whole body was sucking up energy in any form and using it to heal him. What would happen if he were put in a cold, dark room? Would the healing stop? How the hell was he translating all that energy into magic? How was he doing it at all, much less unconsciously?

Gods, studying such a man might even tell the sisters about the afterlife. That was something they'd given up on long ago, considering it outside the realm of experimentation. Kylar could change everything.

She pooled magic in a white ball in her hands and brought it close to his body to watch the way the magic was sucked in like water down a drain.

Amazing.

Now this, this was a puzzle she could devote her life to solving.

The last of the magic dissolved from her hands and Kylar's eyes flicked open.

Sister Ariel raised her hands. "I'm not here to hurt you, Kylar. Do you remember me?"

He nodded, his eyes darting around like a wild animal's. "What are you doing here? What's happened? What did you see?"

"I saw you dead. Now you live again. Who killed you?"

Kylar seemed to deflate, too tired or too rattled to bother with a denial. "It doesn't matter. A wetboy. Nothing personal."

"A wetboy like you and Vi?"

He stood, feigning stiffness. She knew he was feigning it because she could see that he was in absolutely perfect condition now. "Graakos," she whispered under her breath, armoring herself.

"What do you want, wytch?" he asked. Abruptly, the tendrils of magic she'd extended toward him vanished. Not just vanished; they blew apart like smoke in strong breeze. He'd done that—scattered her magic. His eyes glittered dangerously. Would her magical armor disappear just as easily? For the first time in decades, Sister Ariel was in danger from a man.

"I want to help you, if your cause is just," she said.

"You mean if I'll help you in return?"

She shrugged, willing herself to calmness. "What are the extents of your powers, young man? Do you even know?"

"Why would I tell you?"

"Because I already know you're Kylar indeed. You're the killer who is killed. The undying dier. What's your real name? How did you get this power? Were you born with it? What do you see when you're dead?"

"Shouldn't have told you my name, should I? You overeducated types will be the death of me. Or the ruin of me, at least."

Having seen how the healing worked, Ariel knew the shell of this man, his body, wouldn't change, wouldn't age in a thousand years. Kylar might be centuries old, but no matter how she looked at him, she saw a young man behind those cool blue eyes. A young man's bravado, a young man's invincibility. He'd certainly evinced a young man's foolishness in telling her so much already. "How old are you?" she asked.

He shrugged. "Twenty, twenty-one."

"So the Society's wrong?"

"The Society?" Kylar asked.

Drat. How can I be so subtle with Vi and so clumsy with this boy? She knew why, though. She wasn't used to dealing with men. She'd spent too much time cloistered in the company of women. She understood women. Even if they could be terrifically illogical, over the years she'd learned to gauge when illogic was about to strike. Men were a different matter entirely. It would have been, well, logical, that she would feel more at home in the company of men, but it wasn't the case. Still, every word Kylar said was teaching her volumes. He hadn't lied about his age. That felt true—but who didn't know their exact age? Was that because he couldn't remember how long he'd been in this incarnation? She felt that it was something different. Still, she shouldn't have said anything about the Society. Now she'd have to tell him more. If she refused to share, so would he.

" 'Lo, the long night passes and he is made new.' That Society," she said. Kylar was rubbing his eyes like they felt funny. He seemed overwhelmed, which was good, because she didn't want to explain how she knew about the Society. "They believe you come back from the dead and they hope to learn how. Apparently, their belief is justified. And what more could a man hope for but to conquer death?"

"Lots," Kylar snapped. "I'm immortal, not invincible. It's not always a blessing." He was still disoriented. He looked like he was regretting every word he said. He wasn't stupid, this one. Reckless, maybe, but not stupid. "So, Sister, what do you plan to do about me? Chain me and bring me to the Chantry?"

As he said it, it spun a fantasy out for Ariel. What temptation! Oh, she'd never try to chain him with magic. But she had something better than magic. She had Uly. A few lies about how Uly would die if she weren't taken to the Chantry immediately, a subtle weave to make Uly sick a few times, and Kylar would come with her of his own accord. Kylar's existence would be hidden from most of the sisterhood. Only Istariel would know. Ariel herself would study the man.

Oh, the challenge of it! The sheer intellectual puzzle. The depth of the magical complexity! It was intoxicating. She would be part of something great. Kylar wouldn't lead a bad life. They'd provide him with everything he asked for. The best food, the best apartments, training with the sword-masters, visits with Uly, whatever entertainments they could bring to him, and doubtless they'd be curious to breed him with Sisters to see what gifts his progeny had. For his sake, they would surely choose the most attractive women. Most men would find such duties quite pleasant. He would have whatever he wanted but freedom. He was immortal! What were a few decades for him? One single lifetime of pampered luxury and the knowledge that by resting in opulence he would change the course of history. He would have meaning and purpose, just by indulging.

What might happen if the sisterhood—if Ariel herself—unraveled his secrets? Perfect healing for anyone injured, without scars. Immortality! How powerful would the Chantry become if they could choose to whom to give a thousand years of youth?

What would that do to the world?

She, Ariel Wyant, had finally found a puzzle worthy of her gifts. No, not a puzzle, a mystery. She would take her place in history as the woman who gave humanity eternal life. It was breathtaking, and—she realized after far too long—terrifying.

She laughed under her breath. "I see now why the Society has gotten nowhere with you. The temptations are simply too great, aren't they?"

The young man didn't answer. He seemed to have determined that anything he said would tell her more. At the same time, it seemed to her that he thought she knew things that he wanted to know.

"You said in Torras Bend that you were a Cenarian soldier," Ariel said. "But it doesn't seem like you're with the rebels. From how long your body was lying here, I'd guess you didn't even stop at the camp for orders. So here's the deal. You tell me what you're really doing, and I'll help you. You do happen to be alone in the woods, in your undergarments, in the cold, without a horse, without money, and without weapons. I'm sure the being without weapons part isn't a problem, but the rest certainly are."

"Oh, so we're friends now?" Kylar asked, arching an eyebrow. "To me, the question seems to be why I don't kill you to keep the Chantry from finding out about me."

"You're immortal, not invincible," Ariel said, smirking. "If I needed to, I could kill you a dozen times as I dragged you to the Chantry. Neither of us knows if by killing you with magic I might disrupt the delicate balances that bring you back to life, so that's a risk for both of us, isn't it? Of course, after killing you with magic once, I could kill you manually thereafter. And of course, you might kill me. So it's a conundrum for me as well. I might end up with a bag of meat for all my troubles. You might end up dead. Permanently dead."

"If you tell the Chantry of my existence, I'll have every Sister in the world on the lookout for me. For the rest of a very long life. Maybe for me it's better to take the risk once, with one Sister, than to have to deal with every newly frocked tart looking to make a name for herself for all eternity."

"So you'd murder me in cold blood?" she asked.

"Call it preemptive self-defense."

She stepped closer to him and peered into the cool blue eyes. He was a killer, yes. A wetboy, yes. But was he a murderer? The saddest thing about all he'd said was that he was right. If he wanted freedom, if he prized secrecy as much as he or his predecessor or predecessors had, he should kill her. If the Chantry learned he existed, they would never rest until they had him. He was uniquely suited to elude them, but who wanted to live a hunted life? He could escape for five years or fifty, but not forever. The Chantry would never give up. Never. He would become every ambitious Sister's greatest ambition, the greatest test and greatest prize imaginable.

Ariel pictured Istariel interrogating this man. She was shocked to see how ugly the scene became. Istariel would want immortality—not for the Chantry, for herself. She wouldn't pursue a slow, studied method of experimentation. Istariel hated growing old, hated losing her beauty, hated stiff joints and the smell of growing old. To Istariel, Kylar would be an obstacle, defying her, condemning her to death by refusing to yield his secrets.

And what if they pried his secrets from him? What kind of stewards of immortality would the Sisters be?

The answer was disheartening. Who was pure enough and wise enough to know to whom to grant everlasting life? Who, having received the gift, could be trusted not to abuse it?

"You must be a good man, Kylar," she said quietly. "Don't let your gift corrupt you. I won't share your secret with the Chantry. At least not until I can speak with you again. I know you have no reason to trust me, so here." She drew a knife from her belt and handed it to him. "If you must kill me, do so." She turned her back.

Nothing happened.

After a long moment, she turned around. "Will you let me help you?" she asked.

He looked weary. "Logan Gyre is alive," he said. "He's in the Maw's deepest pit, a place called Hell's Asshole."

"You think he's still alive?"

"He was a month ago. If he made it through the first two months, he's made it through the hardest part. I'd guess he's still kicking."

"And you mean to bring him out?"

"He's my friend."

Ariel breathed slowly to get hold of herself. She wanted to berate this boy for his idiocy. How dare he endanger the ka'kari for a mere king? "Do you know what it will mean if Garoth Ursuul gets his hands on your ka'kari? What it will mean for the world?" Sister Ariel asked. It might be terrible for the world for the Chantry to unlock Kylar's secrets; it would be apocalyptic if the Khalidorans did.

"Logan's my friend."

Ariel bit her tongue, literally. If Istariel ever found out what she was about to do, expulsion from the Chantry would be the least of Ariel's punishments.

"Well, then. All right." She exhaled. "I'm going to help you. I think I can do something really special. I think, yes. Don't ask another Sister to do this. It will only be possible because of how much I've already seen of you. But hold on. I need you to take a note to someone."

"What are you doing?" Kylar asked as she found a scrap of parchment and scribbled on it, then magically sealed it.

"Either trust me or don't, Kylar. If you don't trust me, kill me. Since you've already decided not to do that, you might as well make yourself internally coherent and trust me." He blinked at the rush of words, but she continued anyway. "I can get you to the city by tomorrow night, maybe tomorrow afternoon."

"It's a three-day ride—"

"But you have to promise me two things. Promise you'll deliver this letter first, and promise you'll rescue Logan second. Swear it."

"What's in the letter?"

"It's to a healer named Drissa Nile, and it's not about you. Events you'll put into motion will require changes in the Chantry's position. Our people need to know how to react if you save Logan Gyre, you understand?" It wasn't the whole truth, of course, but she wasn't going to tell him the letter was mostly about her clever plan for Vi, which did concern Kylar. "When you get to the city, eat a huge meal and sleep for as long as your body needs. It'll still put you ahead by a day or two."

"Hold on, hold on," Kylar said. "I don't want Logan to rot in there any longer than I have to, but why do you care that I save a day or two?"

Ah, yes. Reckless, not dumb.

"Vi's ahead of you. She's heading for Cenaria."

"That bitch! Going to report her successful hit, no doubt. Wait, how do you know where she's heading?"

"She was traveling with me." Sister Ariel winced.

"What?!"

"You have to understand, Kylar. She's enormously Talented. I was taking her back to the Chantry. She escaped me just after we found your body. She thinks you're dead." Now the tricky part. "Jarl is the one who told you about Logan being alive?"

"Yes, why?"

"Did she . . . did she torture Jarl before she killed him?"

"No. She didn't talk to him at all."

And the hook—letting the lie sit in the water as if you had no interest in it, not fleshing it out so much that it looked too good: "Then I don't know how she knew, but she said something about the king and a hole. I think she knows about Logan."

Kylar's face paled. He'd bought it. Now he'd go after Logan immediately, rather than trying to kill Vi.

Light! Sister Ariel had thought that she loved studying. She'd always been comfortable in her cloistered life. Now she understood why Sisters left the Chantry to do work in The World. That's what they called it, The World, because the Chantry was another reality entirely. Ariel thought she didn't care what happened in The World, thought that books would always be more fascinating that some petty kingdom's petty politics. But right now, she felt so alive. Here she was, sixty-some years old, thinking on her feet, gambling futures—and loving it!

"She's only got a few minutes on me. I can catch her and kill her now! Let me have your horse!"

"It's dark, Kylar, you'll never—" Stupid! She'd been thinking like a Sister, not like an assassin. She'd just given him more reason to kill Vi.

"I can see in the dark! Give me your horse!"

"No!" she said. *He can see in the dark?*

A change came over Kylar in an instant. One moment, he was a furious young man, his intensity such that despite standing in his undergarments in the cold he still looked formidable. The next moment, his entire body flashed iridescent. The coruscation went beyond the visible spectrum into the magical, leaving Ariel's eyes watering. When she blinked them clear, Kylar was utterly changed.

In Kylar's place stood an apparition, a demon. Every curve and plane of Kylar's body was sleeked in black metal, his face a mask of fury, his muscles exaggerated but not his power. Ariel realized she was seeing the Angel of the Night in all its fury. She was denying the avatar of retribution his chance to mete out justice.

There was no dissembling, no clever deception in her fear. She stumbled backward and put a hand on her horse—as much to steady herself as to keep the frightened beast from bolting.

"Give. Me. The horse," Kylar said.

So Ariel did the only thing she could do. She drew a sliver of magic and killed the horse. *That's two innocent beasts I've killed for Vi.*

Kylar leapt some inhuman distance into the woods as soon as Ariel touched her magic. But as the horse crumpled to the earth, she released the magic and raised her hands.

She didn't even see him move, but a second later Kylar was standing in front of her, the point of her knife an inch from her eye. Light! Had she thought she enjoyed this? Gambling futures looked different when your own was on the table.

"Why protect a murderer?" the black-sleeked demon asked.

"I'm trying to redeem Vi. I won't let you kill her until I've tried."

"She doesn't deserve a second chance."

"And who are you to say that, immortal? You get as many second chances as you want."

"It's not the same thing," Kylar said.

"I'm only asking you to save Logan first. If you don't accept my help, you'll be lucky to get to Cenaria this week."

The glowering mask disappeared into his skin, but he still looked furious. "What do I have to do?"

She smiled, hoping he couldn't see how her knees were trembling.

"Hold onto your trousers," she said.

47

Applying the last touches of kohl around her eyes, Kaldrosa Wyn looked deep into the mirror. *I can do this. For Tomman.*

She couldn't have said why, but she wanted to look perfect tonight. Maybe it was just that tonight would be her last night. Her last night whoring or her last night, period.

The costume was pure fantasy, of course. A Sethi woman would never wear such a thing on deck, but for tonight it was perfect. The trousers were so tight that she hadn't even been able to get them on until Daydra had laughingly told her that she couldn't wear underclothes beneath them. ("But you can see right through them!" "And your point is...?" "Oh.") For some reason, they exposed not just her ankles but even her calves—horrifying!—while the blouse was just as tight and sheer, with a lacy flounce at the wrists—ridiculous!—and down the front an open V that reached to her navel. Buttons on the shirt suggested it could be closed, but even if Kaldrosa could have stretched the tiny piece of fabric over her slender frame—she'd tried—there were no buttonholes.

Momma K had been very pleased with Master Piccun's work. She insisted that being scantily clad was sexier than naked. Tonight, Kaldrosa didn't mind. If she had to run, she'd be harder to grab in this than in skirts.

She came into the foyer and soon the other girls came out of their rooms. Everyone was working tonight except for Bev, who was too scared. Bev was pretending to be sick and was staying in her room all night. Kaldrosa almost panicked when she saw them. All of them looked fantastic. Every one of them had spent extra time on makeup and hair and clothes. By Porus' spear. The Khalidorans would notice. They'd have to notice.

Her suitemate, Daydra, who'd saved her more than once by calling for bashers when she heard Kaldrosa scream her codeword, smiled at her. "Here goes nothing, huh?" Daydra said. Daydra looked like a new woman. Though barely seventeen, she'd been a successful prostitute before the invasion, and tonight wasn't the first time that Kaldrosa saw why she had done so well. The woman glowed. She didn't care if she died.

"You ready?" Kaldrosa asked, knowing it was a dumb question. Their floor was going to be opened to clients in just a few minutes.

"So ready I've told all my girlfriends at the other brothels."

Kaldrosa froze. "Are you insane? You'll get us all killed!"

"Didn't you hear?" Daydra asked quietly, her face somber.

"Hear what?"

"The palies killed Jarl."

The breath whooshed out of Kaldrosa. If she'd held onto any slim hope for the future, it had been because of Jarl. Jarl and his radiant face, his talk of expelling the Khalidorans and going legitimate, of building a hundred bridges across the Plith and eliminating all the laws that bound the Warren-born and the slaveborn and former slaves and the impoverished to the city's west side. Jarl had spoken of a new order, and when he spoke, it sounded possible. She'd felt powerful in a way she never had before. She'd hoped.

And now Jarl was dead?

"Don't cry," Daydra said. "You'll mess up your makeup. You'll get all of us crying."

"Are you sure?"

"The whole city's talking about it," Shel said.

"I saw Momma K's face. It's true," Daydra said. "So you really think any lightskirt's going to rat us out to them? After they killed Jarl?"

The last door on the landing opened and Bev came out wearing her bull dancer costume, ponytails wired up into twin horns, midriff bare, and short pants. The dancer's knife at her belt didn't look like the usual blunted blade. Bev was pale but resolute. "Jarl was always kind to me. And I'm not going to listen to that damned prayer of theirs one more time."

"He was good to me, too," another girl said, choking back tears.

"Don't start," Daydra said. "No tears! We're gonna do this."

"For Jarl," another girl said.

"For Jarl," the rest of the girls repeated.

A bell tinkled that told the girls their guests were coming.

"I told some other girls, too," Shel said. "I hope that's all right. As for me, I get Fat Ass. He killed my first suitemate."

"I get Kherrick," Jilean said. Under her makeup, her right eye was still a puffy yellow.

"Little Dick's mine."

"Neddard."

"I don't care who I get," Kaldrosa said. She clenched her jaw so hard it hurt. "But I'm taking two. The first one's for Tomman. The second's for Jarl."

The other girls looked at her.

"Two?" Daydra asked. "How are you gonna do two?"

"I'll do what I have to. I'm getting two."

"Fuck it," Shel said. "Me too, but I'm taking Fat Ass first. Just in case."

"I'm in," Jilean said. "Now shut up. We're on."

The first man up the stairs was Captain Burl Laghar. Kaldrosa's heart stopped beating. She hadn't seen him since she'd moved in to the Craven Dragon to escape him. She stood frozen until he came to stand in front of her.

"Well, if it isn't my little pirate bitch," Burl said.

She couldn't move. Her tongue was lead in her mouth.

Burl saw her fear and stuck his chest out. "See? I knew you were a whore before you did. I could tell you liked it the very first time I banged you in front of your husband. And here you are." He smiled and was obviously disappointed that none of his sycophants were with him to laugh. "So," he said finally. "You happy to see me?"

Inexplicably, the fear vanished. It was just gone. Kaldrosa smiled impishly.

"Happy?" she said, grabbing the front of his trousers. "Oh, you have no idea." And she led him to her room. For Tomman. For Jarl.

*　　*　　*

That night, a gray-haired cripple climbed to the roof of the manse that had briefly belonged to Roth Ursuul but was now infested with hundreds of Rabbits. He balanced on his crutch in the moonlight and screamed into the night, "Come, Jarl! Come and see! Come and listen!" As the Rabbits gathered to watch the madman, a wind kicked up off the Plith. Tears shining in his eyes like stars, the general began reciting a dithyramb of hatred and loss. He sang a threnody to Jarl, a dirge for the hope of a better life. The words swirled with the wind and not a few Rabbits felt that not only the winds but the spirits of the murdered were gathering to the general's voice, rising with the cadences of vengeance.

The humbled general screamed and shook his crutch at the heavens as if it were a symbol of every Rabbit's impotence and despair. He screamed at the very moment the winds fell still.

The Warrens answered. A scream rose. A man's scream.

As if released by that sound, the winds roared. Lightning cracked against the castle looming to the north, and the light painted the general black against the sky. Black clouds covered the moon and rain lashed down.

The Rabbits heard the general laughing, crying, defying the lightning, waving his crutch at the heavens as if conducting a wild chorus of rage.

Screams rose that night from the Craven Dragon as never before. Women who had refused to scream for their clients before now screamed loudly enough to make up for all their previous silence. Beneath those screams, the grunts and whimpers and soft cries and begging of dying men were never heard. Forty Khalidorans died at the Craven Dragon alone.

Momma K's plot had been for one brothel, after which she planned to smuggle the girls out of the city. It was supposed to make the Khalidorans think twice about brutalizing the working girls. But the plan, whipped up by the news of Jarl's death, spread like wildfire. One brothel owner invented a holiday as an excuse to serve lots of ale cheap to get his customers as drunk as possible. He called it Nocta Hemata. The Night of Passion, he claimed, smiling broadly at his guests. Another brothel owner who'd worked with Jarl for years confirmed that it was an old Cenarian tradition. The Night of Abandon, he said.

Across the city, fueled by drugged food and excessive drink, brothels celebrated an orgy unlike any ever seen. The air filled with shrieks and screams and wild ululations. Screams of terror, screams of vengeance, frenzied screams of blood lust and blood debts repaid. Men, and women, and even the small men and women in children's bodies who were the guild rats killed with savagery too terrible to comprehend. Bereaved men, women, and children stood over bloodied Khalidoran corpses and called upon the ghosts of their dead beloved to see what vengeance they had wrought, called upon Jarl to see what retribution they had exacted from the flesh of the enemy. Dogs howled and horses panicked at the feral smells of blood and sweat and fear and pain. Running men and women poured through the streets in every direction. There was too much blood for even the torrents of rain to wash away. The gutters ran red.

Soldiers arrived to find the doors of brothels adorned with dozens of small trophies, one cut from each rapist's body. But every brothel was empty of all but corpses. In the early hours of the morning, gangs of aggrieved husbands and boyfriends tore apart the drugged Khalidorans who had escaped the brothels and were wandering, trying to find their way out of the Warrens. Even the fully armed and lucid units sent to investigate wandered into ambushes. Rocks were thrown from rooftops in storms, archers picked off soldiers from a distance, and every time the soldiers charged, the Rabbits who had spent months learning to disappear did it again. It was like attacking ghosts, and every narrow twisting alley had a perfect place for an ambush. The Khalidorans who entered the Warrens didn't leave.

That night, the Godking lost 621 soldiers, 74 officers, three brothel owners who had acted as informants, and two wytches. The Rabbits didn't lose a soul.

Forever after, both sides would call it the Nocta Hemata, the Night of Blood.

Logan woke. He didn't move. He just let the fact wash over him until he was sure it was true. He was alive. Somehow, he had survived unconsciousness and delirium. Here.

He remembered snippets of Gnasher roaring, standing over him. Of Lilly putting a damp rag over his forehead. Between those fragments, like pus in a suppurating wound, were nightmares, garish beasts of his lost life, of dead women and gloating, ghoulish Khalidoran faces.

When he moved, he knew he wasn't out of the woods. He had a kitten's strength. Opening his eyes, he struggled to sit up. Around the Hole, he heard muttering. It sounded like everyone else was as surprised as he was. People who got sick down here never survived.

A meaty hand grabbed him and pulled him to a sitting position. It was Gnasher, grinning his fool's grin. A moment later he was kneeling, hugging Logan, crushing the wind out of him.

"Easy, Gnash," Lilly said. "Let him go." Logan was surprised when Gnasher actually let go of him immediately. Gnasher didn't listen to anyone but him.

Lilly smiled at him. "Good to see you're back."

"I see you made a new friend," Logan said, feeling jealous and guilty for it.

She dropped her voice. "You should have seen him, King. He was magnificent." She grinned her gap-toothed smile and rubbed Gnasher's knobby head. He closed his eyes, his filed teeth showing as he smiled broadly. "You did good, didn't you, Gnash?"

"Yehhss," he said, his voice rising oddly through the middle of the word.

Logan almost fell over. It was the first time he'd heard Gnasher speak.

"You can talk?" he asked.

Gnasher smiled.

"Hey, whore," Fin called from across the Hole. He had uncoiled most of his sinew rope and was adding a newly braided section to it. Logan saw that there were now only seven Holers left. "Time for you to get back to work."

"You'll wait'll I'm good and ready," Lilly said. "I haven't let any of 'em have a throw since you got sick," she told Logan.

"What's that sound?" Logan asked. He hadn't noticed it at first because it was so constant, but there was some sort of chipping sound and a low murmuring echoing down into the Hole from elsewhere in the Maw.

Before she could answer, Logan felt something shift in the air. The Holers looked at each other, but every face was blank. Something had changed, but no one could tell what.

Logan felt weaker, sicker. The air seemed thicker than it had been before, oppressive. He was once more aware of the stench and the foulness of the Hole—smelling it for the first time in months. He felt as if he were for the first time aware of the sludge covering the surface of life. He was being covered in filth and there was no escape. Every breath filled him with more toxins, every movement stroked more filth along his body, ground oil deeper into every pore. Just to exist was to let that scum be pressed into him, to let darkness pierce his skin so deeply that it tattooed him, making filth forever part of him, so anyone who ever saw him would see every evil he'd ever done, every unworthy thought he'd ever entertained.

He was barely even aware of the noise clattering through the Maw. Prisoners were screaming, begging for mercy. The screams spread and rose in pitch and desperation as the prisoners closer and closer to the Hole started joining the screaming. Beneath the high-pitched wails, Logan heard that clattering sound again, as of iron wheels grinding against rock.

Around the Hole, hardened murderers were curled into the fetal position, holding their hands over their ears, pressing up against the wall. Only Tenser and Fin didn't cower. Fin looked to be in raptures, his ropes lying limp on his lap, his face upturned. Tenser saw Logan staring.

"Khali has come," Tenser said.

"What is it?" Logan asked. He could barely move. He wanted to throw himself in the Hole to end the horror and the despair.

"She is god. The very stones here drip with a thousand years of pain and hatred and despair. The entire Maw is like a gem of evil and here is where Khali will make her home, in the blackest depths of unmined darkness." Then he began chanting, over and over, *"Khali vas, Khalivos ras en me, Khali mevirtu rapt, recu virtum defite."*

Tatts was next to Tenser and he seized the man. "What are you saying! Stop it!" He grabbed Tenser by the throat and dragged him to the edge of the Hole.

Instantly, black webs sprang up all over Tenser's arms and Tatt's eyes bulged. He choked. His mouth worked and his throat made little gasping sounds. He stumbled back from the Hole, releasing Tenser, and fell to his knees. Tatt's face was red, veins bulging in his neck and forehead and he gasped for no apparent reason.

Then he dropped to the ground, heaving great breaths.

Tenser smiled. "You great tattooed ass, no one lays a hand on a prince of the empire."

"What?" Nine-Finger Nick asked for all of them.

"I'm an Ursuul and my time with you is done. Khali has come, and I'm afraid she's going to be needing all of you. That is our prayer: *Khali vas, Khalivos ras en me, Khali mevirtu rapt, recu virtum defite.* 'Khali come. Khali live in me. Khali take this my offering, the strength of those who oppose you.' A prayer that is answered today. Khali is now a Holer. You will live in her holy presence. It is a great honor, though I confess, not one highly sought."

Above, Logan heard the sound of what could only be wagon wheels reach the third level of the Maw.

"Why are you here?" Nick asked.

"That doesn't concern you, though it is my doing that we're all still here." Tenser was smiling like this was the best thing that had ever happened to him.

"What?" Nick asked.

"You bastard," Lilly said. "You made the key not fit the lock. You knocked it out of my hand. You summoned Gorkhy, you fuck!"

"Yes, yes, yes!" Tenser laughed. He held a hand out and red light burst from it. The Holers shrank back, blinking eyes that hadn't seen light in months. The red light floated up through the bars high above.

Far down the hall, someone cried out, seeing the light.

Behind Tenser, Fin picked up a loop of his rope.

"Don't even think it," Tenser said. He grinned ghoulishly. "Besides, Khali's presence won't mean death for all of you. You, Fin, you may do very well in her service. The rest of you will do well to follow his example."

An old man shuffled into sight above the bars. The grate flipped open and Logan recognized Neph Dada. Before the Vürdmeister could see him, Logan scooted into his little niche.

Tenser rose through the air gently as the Vürdmeister's magic lifted him. He laughed all the way.

The grate slammed shut and Logan poked his head out. A spotlight of red light blinded him, pinned him in place. "Oh," Tenser Ursuul said, "And don't think I've forgotten you, King. I can't wait to tell my father that I found Logan Gyre hiding in the deepest depths of his own dungeon. He'll love it."

48

Garoth Ursuul was not pleased to see his aetheling. He hadn't summoned Tenser and despite all the precautions Neph Dada had taken—bringing Tenser to Garoth's private chambers and magically tearing out the tongues of any servant they passed so they couldn't speak of what they'd seen—this castle still had too many eyes. It was all too likely that someone had seen Tenser come. Certainly the prisoners in the Maw would have seen him leave.

In Garoth's estimation, there was an even chance that Tenser had just destroyed his usefulness. Garoth didn't like his aethelings to take liberties. No one made decisions for the Godking.

Tenser saw the displeasure on Garoth's face and hurried through the end of his story.

"I, I thought Logan might make a perfect sacrifice for Khali, may her name be revered forever, as she takes her new home," Tenser said, his voice quavering. "And I figured that by now Baron Kirof must have been captured "

"You did, did you?" Garoth asked.

"He hasn't?"

"Baron Kirof plunged to death from a mountain pass, trying to escape," Neph said. "His body was not recoverable."

Tenser's mouth moved like a fish's as he tried to absorb the news.

"Your guilty verdict will have to stick," Garoth said. "It doesn't matter. These Cenarians have not appreciated my mercy anyway. They will be a lesson for future conquests. Your usefulness, boy, is at an end. The Cenarians are not pacified. You have failed your uurdthan."

"Your Holiness," Tenser said, falling to his knees. "Please. I'll do anything. Use me however you like. I'll serve with my whole heart. I swear. I'll do anything."

"Yes," Garoth said. "You will."

On his own merits, Tenser was nothing special. He'd survived his training, barely. But he was not a son of Garoth's soul. He never would be. He would never be his heir. But Tenser didn't know that. More important, Moburu didn't either.

"Neph, where is the virgin queen?"

"Your Holiness," the wizened Vürdmeister said, "she awaits your pleasure in the north tower."

"Ah yes." Not that Garoth had forgotten, but he wouldn't have Neph know how much the girl intrigued him.

"I could send for her immediately if it pleases you to sacrifice her," Neph said.

"The pair of them would be a nice offering for Khali as she takes her new *ras,* wouldn't they?" Garoth asked. But he wouldn't surrender Jenine, and he needed Tenser to distract Moburu. "My seed, I have ... great hopes for you," Garoth said. "The death of Baron Kirof wasn't your fault, so it pleases me to give you a second chance. Go make yourself presentable so you look like my son, and then fetch this Logan Gyre. I won't have him escape from under my nose a second time. I will give you your new uurdthan anon."

As soon as the door closed behind Tenser, Garoth turned to Vürdmeister Dada. "Take him to the Maw and have him build a ferali beside his brother's. Help him and praise his work in front of Moburu. Do as much of it yourself as you must. Now send in Hu Gibbet."

*   *   *

"I'm not sure how this is going to work," Sister Ariel said. The woods were fully dark now, except for the light of her magic. "If I saw correctly, this form of magic should be especially easy for you to absorb. Just take in as much as you can."

"Then what?" Kylar said.

"Then you run."

"I run? That's the most ridiculous thing I've ever heard." *You speak when you should listen,* the Wolf's voice echoed in his head. He gritted his teeth. "Sorry. Tell me more."

"You won't get tired. . . . I think. You'll still pay a price for whatever of your own magic you use, but you won't pay nearly as much for what you take from me," Sister Ariel said. "I'm ready, are you?"

Kylar shrugged. The truth was, he felt more than ready. His eyes were tingling the same way they'd tingled when he'd first bonded the ka'kari. He rubbed them again.

I'm getting more powerful. The thought was a revelation. He'd been learning to control his Talent better during his training on the rooftops, but this was different. This was different, and he'd felt it before.

He'd felt it every time he'd died. Every time he died, his Talent expanded, and something was changing in his vision, too. The thought should have been exhilarating. Instead, he felt the cold fingertips of dread brush down his naked back.

There must be a cost. There must be. Of course, it had already cost Kylar Elene. The thought made him ache anew. Maybe the costs were merely human ones.

The Wolf had spoken of Durzo committing a blasphemy even worse than taking money to die. Had Durzo committed suicide? Yes. Kylar was sure of it. Had it been just for curiosity? A lust for power? Or had he felt trapped? Suicide was impossible.

To a man as unhappy, as lonely, as isolated as Durzo had been, being bound to life would surely be odious. *Oh, master, I'm so sorry. I didn't understand.* And just like that, the raw wound that was Durzo's death tore open again. Time had done little to heal Kylar. Even knowing he had released Durzo from an existence he didn't want was no consolation. Kylar had murdered a legend, murdered a man who had given him everything, and he had done it with hatred in his heart. Even if Durzo had intended it as a sacrifice, Kylar hadn't killed him for mercy. He'd murdered him for raw vengeance. Kylar remembered the sweet bile of fury, of hatred for every trial Durzo had put him through, that bile had saturated him, kept him strong as he clung wounded to the ceiling of that tunnel in the stacks.

Now Durzo was truly dead, released from the prison of his own flesh. But it felt lonely and raw and unjust. Durzo's reward for seven centuries of isolation and service to some goal that he didn't understand shouldn't have been death. It should have been an unveiling of the worth of that goal. It should have been reunion and communion commensurate with seven hundred years of isolation. Kylar was just coming to understand his master now, and now that he wanted to make things right, there was no Durzo to make it right with. He'd been clipped out of the tapestry of Kylar's life, leaving an ugly hole that nothing could fill.

"I can only hold the full measure of my Talent for so long, young man," Sister Ariel said, sweat beading on her forehead.

"Oh, right," Kylar said.

A pool of concentrated light burned in Sister Ariel's hands. Kylar put his hand in it, willing the power into himself.

Nothing happened.

He brought the ka'kari up to the skin of his palm. Still nothing happened.

It was strangely embarrassing to look so inept. "Just let it happen," Sister Ariel said.

Just let it happen. That pissed him off. It was that falsely wise crap that teachers pulled. Your body knows what to do. You're thinking too much. Right.

"Will you look away for a sec?" he asked.

"Absolutely not," Sister Ariel said.

He'd done this before while wearing the ka'kari as a second skin. He knew it could be done.

"I can't hold this for much longer," Sister Ariel said.

Kylar drew the ka'kari into a ball in his hand and palmed it, holding his hand palm down over the pool of magic in the sister's hands. He thought it was quick enough she didn't see it. *Come on, please work!*

~Since you ask so nicely . . . ~

Kylar blinked at that. Then the pooled magic winked out like a candle in a high wind. Kylar only had a moment to be unnerved before the thought was obliterated. Where the metallic sphere touched his palm, Kylar felt like he was holding lightning. He lost control of his body as it arced through him, freezing him in place, ignoring his desire to pull away—pullawaypullaway!—before he fried.

Sister Ariel was pulling back, but the ka'kari stretched between them, sucking magic like a lamprey sucking blood.

Kylar felt himself filling, gloriously filling with magic, with power, and light, and life. He could see the very veins in his hands, the veins in the few remaining leaves overhead. He could see life squirming and wriggling everywhere in the forest. He saw through the grasses to the fox's burrow, through the bark of the fir tree to the woodpecker's nest. He could feel the kiss of starlight on his skin. He could smell a hundred different men from the rebel camp, tell what they'd eaten, how much they'd worked, who was healthy and who sick. He could hear so much it was overwhelming, he could barely pull the strands apart. The wind made leaves clang against each other like cymbals, there was a roar that was the breathing of two— no, three large animals—himself, and Sister Ariel, and one other. The leaves themselves were breathing. He heard the heartbeat of an owl, the thunderous wallop of . . . a knee hitting the ground.

"Stop! Stop!" Sister Ariel said. She was slumped on the ground, and still magic flowed from her.

Kylar yanked the ka'kari back and took it into his body.

Sister Ariel fell, but he didn't even notice her. Light—magic—life— dazzled, bled, exploded from every pore on his body. It was too much. It hurt. Every beat of his heart scoured his veins with more power. His body was too small.

"GOOOOO," Sister Ariel said. It was ludicrously slow. He waited while her lips moved and the whisper thundered forth. "SAAVE . . ." Save? Save what? Why didn't she just say it? Why was everything so slow, so interminably, so damnably slow? He could barely hold himself still. He was bleeding light. His head throbbed. Another chamber of his heart compressed while he waited and waited. "THE . . ."

Save the king, his impatience supplied. He had to save the king. He had to save Logan.

Before Sister Ariel spoke again, Kylar was running.

Running? No, running was too pedestrian a term. He was moving twice the speed of the fastest man. Three times.

It was sheer joy. It was sheer moment, for there was nothing but the moment. He dodged and twisted, he looked ahead as far as his glowing eyes could see.

He was moving so fast that the air began to battle against him. His feet couldn't gain the traction they needed to push him faster. He threatened to leave the earth.

Then he saw a camp ahead, right in the middle of his path. He jumped and he did leave the earth. A hundred paces he flew. Two hundred. Straight at a tree.

He threw the ka'kari forward and jerked as he slammed through the three-foot-wide trunk. Wood exploded in every direction, but he kept going. Behind him, he heard the tree cracking and beginning to fall, but he was already too far away to hear it land.

So he ran. He extended the ka'kari before him so it cut the wind, extended it behind him so that it pressed his feet to the earth so he could run faster still.

The night faded, and he ran. The sun rose, and still he ran, a glutton devouring miles.

Sister Ariel crawled back to the tree where she'd bound Ulyssandra. It took a long time, but she had to. She wasn't sure if she slept that she would ever wake up. Finally, she reached Uly. The little girl was awake, her eyes red, tear tracks covering her cheeks. So she knew Kylar had awakened, and that Sister Ariel had concealed her, betrayed her.

There was nothing Sister Ariel could say. There was nothing either of them could do, anyway. Sister Ariel had loosed Vi and Kylar like twin hunting falcons. There was no calling them back now. If Uly were still here when Ariel woke, she'd take the girl to the Chantry. It would be a long trip, and it might give her some time to think about what she'd just experienced.

By all the gods, the boy had sucked her dry and still had room for more. Her! One of the most powerful women in the Chantry! He was so young, so blithe and terrifying.

It took all her willpower to unbind Uly. Touching magic now was like drinking liquor while hung over. But in a moment, it was done, and she collapsed.

49

Somehow, Logan had believed that there was something special about him. He'd had everything taken from him. His friends had been taken, his wife taken, his hopes taken, his freedom taken, his dignity taken, his naïveté taken. But his life had been spared.

Now that would be taken, too. The Godking wouldn't leave him down here. Logan had already died once and been resurrected. This time, Garoth Ursuul would want to see Logan die with his own eyes. There would doubtless be torture first, but Logan couldn't care.

If he'd been stronger, he would have tried one last desperate plan, but his fever had left him a shell. At the least, he could throw away his own life to kill Fin. He could have done it—before the fever. He'd just never been willing to make that sacrifice while he still had hope. He'd always wanted to preserve his own life, and so now he'd lost his life and gained nothing. Not even for his friends.

Logan brooded in the darkness. Mercifully, whatever Khali was, it had moved further away, and the smothering feel that had so suffused the Maw was now just a dull pressure. Everything that had seemed so unbearable about the Hole—the stink, the heat, the howling—was again familiar, if not comfortable.

"Bitch, come here," Fin said.

Lilly stood and patted Logan's shoulder. She whispered to Gnasher, probably telling him to watch over Logan, and then she left.

Of course she left. He didn't even blame her, though it made him feel even more empty and desolate. Lilly had to be practical. The sentimentality of all the books Logan had once loved died when it came within smelling distance of the Hole. Lilly was a survivor. Logan was going to be dead within an hour or two. Life went on. Logan's heart might blame her, but his mind couldn't. In any other circumstance, he would have condemned himself for eating human flesh.

Then Gnasher got up and walked away.

Do I reek so much of death? It wasn't fair to blame Gnasher and not blame Lilly, but Logan did. He suddenly hated the simple, misshapen man. How could he leave? After all he'd lost, Logan wanted to at least believe he had gained a friend or two.

Gnasher probably didn't even know Logan was going to die. He'd just gone to play with the end of Fin's sinew rope—Fin was too busy banging Lilly to pay him any mind. Logan looked at Gnash and tried to see him with pity. The simpleton was surely here for less reason than Logan was. He hadn't betrayed Logan, he just saw a chance to play with something new. Fin never let anyone touch his rope.

Logan smiled as he saw Gnasher sit down and grab the rope in both hands, squeezing it as hard as he could with all the concentration in the world, as if it were going to get away from him. The man truly lived in a different world.

Logan was aware of the other Holers staring at him. He could tell what they were thinking. King. He'd called himself King as a grim joke when he'd jumped down here—a stupid, insane joke, but the joke of a man who'd just watched his wife bleed to death. It was taking them some time to absorb the fact that it was all real.

Tatts stood and walked over. He squatted beside Logan. Beneath the grime that covered his skin, his dark tattoos looked like vir. He sucked at his gums and spat blood; the scurvy was getting to him, too.

"I would have liked it," Tatts said, speaking for only the third time Logan had ever heard. "If you'd been the king. You got balls like no royal I ever heard of."

"Balls!" Fin paused in his rutting and propped himself up on his hands and laughed. He was a gruesome sight, sweating and dirty, his mouth bloody, the sinew rope half undone, half still wrapped around his naked body. "Someone else is gonna have his balls soon enough."

Logan looked away, still embarrassed to see Lilly doing what she needed to do to survive, so he almost missed it. Lilly shoved and Fin cried out and Logan saw him at the edge of the Hole on his side, precariously balanced, arms scrambling.

Then Lilly kicked him in the groin with all her strength and he fell in the Hole.

Lilly flung herself away from the coils of rope that snapped taut beneath her. Tied to Fin, coil upon coil disappeared down the Hole.

Gnasher's arms jerked out and his entire body jumped forward. Then again and again as the sinew rope jerked Fin to a stop, dropped again, stopped again, and then began unwinding at great speed as gravity uncoiled the rope wrapped around Fin's body.

Finally, Fin's body must have hit bottom, because the weight on the rope eased.

Lilly cried out and hugged Gnasher and kissed him. "You did perfect! Just perfect!" She turned to Logan. "You, on the other hand, could have been a lot more helpful."

Logan was stunned. He'd tried to think of ways to kill Fin for—well, for however long he'd been in this hell. Now he was just gone. Gone, and Logan hadn't done a thing.

"Now listen to me," Lilly said. "All of you. We're fucked. We always have been. We all done what we done, and ain't one of us worth trusting. But King ain't one of us. We can trust him. We ain't got but half a chance, and to have even that, it needs all of us."

"What're you asking?" Nine-Finger Nick asked.

"We had a key. Now we've got Fin's rope. But we got no time. I say we lower King and Gnash into the Hole. King cuz we can trust him and he saw where the key fell, and Gnash because he's the only one strong enough to climb back up the rope if he needs to. They go down and take a look around, see if they can find a way out from down there or find the key. One way or the other, it might give us a chance to get out before the palies come back."

"Why don't we all climb down?" Nick asked.

"Cuz we all got to hold the rope, idjit. There's no place to tie it."

"We could tie it to the grate," Nick said.

"Fin's body's still tied to it. We'd have to make a tower three people high and then lift Fin's body weight—it's impossible. After King goes and unties Fin's body, we can do that. Then all of us can get out. Or if there's no way out down there, he might find the key and we'll be able to make a rush up here."

"We'd have to go past that…thing," Nick said, fearful.

"Nobody said it was a good chance," Lilly said. "You want to stay, you die for sure."

Tatts nodded. He was in.

"I still say we lower someone else," Nick said.

"I got us the rope," Lilly said. "We do it my way or not at all."

"Come on, Lill—"

"Would you trust us to hold the rope with you on it, Nick? We let it go and we'd get your cut of the food."

That shut Nick up.

"Can you trust us, King?" Tatts asked.

"I trust you." *I don't have anything to lose.*

It took them a few minutes to explain it to Gnasher, and even then Logan wasn't sure the man understood. They got the rest of the Holers arranged holding the rope. Lilly stood at the front. She told the Holers that even if they let go, she wouldn't. If they wanted to keep her sexual favors, they'd better not let go.

"I owe you everything," Logan told her. Lilly was anything but a beautiful woman, but right now, she looked radiant. She looked proud of herself for the first time Logan had ever seen.

"No, I owe you, King. When you came down here, I told you to hold onto something good, but you're the one who showed me how. I'm more than this, no matter what I done. If I die now, it don't matter. I ain't good, but you are, and I'm helping you. No one can take that away. You just promise me, King, when you get it all back and go to your fancy parties, you remember. You're the king of us criminals, too."

"I won't forget." He stepped up to the edge to the Hole. "Lilly, what's your real name?"

She hesitated as if she almost didn't remember, then said shyly. "Lilene. Lilene Rauzana."

He straightened his back and spoke, "By the powers vested in our person and in our royal office, be it known that Lilene Rauzana is absolved of all crimes committed heretofore and that all penalties thereof are commuted. Lilene Rauzana is innocent in our sight. Let the record of her wrongs be taken as far as the east is from the west. So let it be written, so let it be done."

It was a ridiculous thing for a man in rags to say to a prostitute. Somehow though, it was right. Logan had never had more power than at this moment, when he had the power to heal. The Holers didn't even mock.

Lilly's eyes spilled tears. "You don't know what I done," she said.

"I don't need to."

"I want to make it right. I don't want be like I been—"

"Then don't. As of now, you're innocent."

With that, Logan stepped into the Hole.

50

It turned out that Sister Ariel Wyant Sa'fastae had stayed in Torras Bend for several weeks, and the villagers knew her well. Though few people were comfortable having a Sister in their presence, she had struck them as scholarly, absent-minded, and kind. The description was an immense comfort to Elene. It meant the letter was probably legitimate.

That left her with a problem. Did she go north, toward the Chantry after Uly, or did she go west, after Kylar?

She'd decided she had to go after Uly. Cenaria wasn't safe for her. Her presence would make Kylar's work harder to accomplish, and she couldn't help him. The Chantry was safe, if intimidating, and Elene could at least make sure that Uly was safe—if not take her home.

So she'd continued north the next morning. Aside from nearly exhausting her small savings, a night in a bed had only seemed to remind her body of all its aches, so she wasn't making good time. She'd get to the Chantry faster if she made her horse go faster than a walk, but the very thought of a canter made Elene groan. The mare's ears flicked up, as if wondering what she was saying.

Then Elene saw the rider, forty paces away. He wore black armor, though no helmet, and he carried neither sword nor shield. He was hunched over in the saddle on a small, long-haired horse. The man's hand was pressed to his side, covering a wound, his pale face spotted with blood.

As Elene pulled her mare to an abrupt stop, he looked up and saw her. His lips worked but no words came. He tried again. "Help. Please," he said in a hoarse whisper.

She flicked her reins and came to his side. Despite the pain on his face, he was a handsome young man, barely older than she was. "Water," he begged.

Elene grabbed her water skin, then paused. The young warrior had a full wineskin dangling from his saddle. His pallor wasn't the paleness of blood loss; he was Khalidoran.

His eyes lit with triumph even as she dug in her heels. He snatched the rein nearest him. Elene's mare danced in a circle that the man's smaller horse quickly followed. Elene tried to jump out of the saddle, but her leg was trapped between the horses.

Then his mailed fist flashed. It caught her above the ear. She fell.

It was a descent into Hell. Logan was still too weak to do even half of the work in lowering himself, but Gnasher seemed content to do almost all of it, lowering them hand under hand. Logan just watched.

The first twenty feet was sheer black fireglass that made up the Hole, utterly smooth and featureless. Then the Hole opened up in an enormous chamber.

Iridescent green algae clung to the distant walls and gave off just enough light to see dimly, and it was as if they'd plunged into an alien world. The rotten-eggs smell was sharper down here, and puffs of heavy smoke rolled up toward them, obscuring Logan's view of thousands of stalagmites jutting unevenly from the invisible cavern floor. The howlers were quiet, and Logan prayed they would stay that way. Over the months, he'd lost his confidence that the sound was merely wind rising through the rocks.

Gnasher was beginning to breathe heavily, but he maintained the same pace, hand under hand. All around them except from directly beneath the Hole itself, stalactites glistened like icy knives and the sound of water dripping from their tips lay just beneath the rush of wind. The wind barely moaned as it rose from the depths.

They descended for two more minutes before Logan saw the first corpse. It was desiccated from the hot dry winds, but it must have been a Holer who had fallen, been pushed, or jumped decades or centuries ago. The body rested, impaled for so long on a stalagmite that the rock was growing over it, the stone slowly entombing the man.

Then there were others. Gnasher had to slow his descent several times to push off from stalagmites, and each time, they saw inmates who'd never had rope. Some were even older than the first, their bodies gashed from hitting several stalagmites on the way down. Some were missing body parts, having had them sheared off by the rock or fallen off through the years, but the slickness of the stalagmites had prevented rats from getting to them, and the sere wind had kept them from rotting. The only unrecognizable bodies were the few along the wetter areas by the wall that had become homes for the algae. These glowed green, like ghosts trying to pull out of the wall.

Finally, they began reaching ledges, most of them too far off to one side for Logan and Gnash to reach, but on one against a wall, he saw a corpse seated. His dried-out bones were intact. Somehow this man had lived through the descent, whether he'd used a rope or just fallen and been spared through some miracle. Then he'd died down here. His empty eye sockets stared a question at Logan, "Can you do better?"

Suddenly, the sinew rope shook. Logan looked up, but there was only blackness. His vision below was blocked by Gnasher.

"Let's hurry, Gnash."

The big man protested wordlessly.

"I know, you're doing great. You're doing fantastic, but I don't know how long Lilly can hold the rope. We don't want to end up like these guys, do we?"

Gnasher went faster.

They passed another ledge and Logan saw that the ground around the base of the stalagmites was thick with soil rather than bare rock. Soil? Here?

Not soil. Human waste. Generations of criminals had been kicking their feces into the Hole. Among the spires of rock, not all of it was dried, so the entire area smelled like an open sewer with rotten eggs mixed in.

Logan started to turn away when he saw something glint as they passed right next to another ledge. He looked again and couldn't see anything.

"Stop for a second, Gnasher."

Logan reached his hand into the six-inch deep layer of shit and groped around. Nothing. He pushed his arm in up past the elbow, ignoring the slime that oozed all over his skin. There.

He pulled out a lump of something and wiped it against his other arm. It was the key.

"Amazing," he said. "A miracle. We aren't going to die down here after all, Gnash. Now let's get to the bottom and untie Fin's body, then we can try to climb back up. They might even be able to pull us up."

As it turned out, they were close to the bottom, or at least another ledge. There was a steam vent nearby that billowed acrid smoke over them, obscuring everything below and killing the luminescent algae, so Logan couldn't see far enough to tell where they were. If, indeed, such a question had any meaning in hell.

Gnasher stopped and grunted. He stepped away from the rope, spreading his fingers out to ease the pain in them. Logan put his feet back on semisolid ground—the sewage here was only a few inches deep—with a sigh. He hadn't held nearly as much weight as Gnasher had, but he was still exhausted.

Then he saw the rope. It was loose.

"Gnasher," Logan called, his throat tight. "How long's there been slack in the rope?"

Gnasher blinked at him. The question didn't mean anything to the simpleton.

"Gnash, Fin's alive! He could be—AH!"

Something sharp stabbed into Logan's back and he fell.

Fin more fell than jumped on top of him. The convict moved like he'd dislocated his hip, and he was bleeding from his head, his mouth, both shoulders, and one leg. In his right hand, he held the broken, bloodied tip of a stalagmite. As he fell on Logan, he began slashing. He was injured and pitifully weak, but Logan was weaker.

Fin's sharp rock bit into his chest, gashed open his forearm as he tried to block, cut from his forehead past his ear. Logan tried to throw Fin off the ledge, but he was too weak.

There was a feral roar louder than the roar of a sudden eruption of the vent below them. Hot steam and fat drops of boiling water flew past them a moment before Gnasher hit.

He knocked Fin off of Logan and bit his nose, rising a moment later with a bloody chunk in his filed teeth. Fin screamed a bubbly scream. Before he could scream again, Gnasher grabbed Fin's dislocated leg, pulling him away from Logan.

The wounded man screamed again, louder, higher. He reached out, tried to grab anything to get away from Gnasher. Then Fin's body caught between two stalagmites. Gnasher either didn't see or didn't care. He had decided to pull Fin away from Logan, and that was what he was going to do. Logan saw the misshapen man's shoulders bunch, the muscles stringy knots of power. Gnasher braced his feet and roared as Fin screamed.

There was a rending sound as the dislocated leg gave way. Gnasher stumbled and fell as he ripped Fin's leg off and sent it sailing into the abyss.

Fin locked hateful eyes on Logan as he gasped his last breaths, his life's blood spurting from his torn hip, his face ghost-pale. "See you...in hell, King," he said.

"I've already done my time," Logan said. He held up the key. "I'm leaving."

Fin's eyes flared with hatred and disbelief, but he didn't have the strength to speak. The hate slowly left his open eyes. He was dead.

"Gnash, you are amazing. Thank you."

Gnash smiled. With his filed, bloody teeth, it was a gruesome sight, but he meant well.

Logan trembled. He was bleeding pretty badly. He didn't know if he'd make it, even if they ran into no problems getting out of the Hole and out of the Maw. But there was no reason for Gnash to die, too, or Lilly. And Gnash wouldn't climb the rope without him, he knew that.

"All right, Gnash, you're strong. Are you strong enough to climb out of here?"

Gnasher nodded and flexed. He liked being called strong.

"Then let's get out of this hell," Logan said, but even as he grabbed the rope, he felt a slackness in it. A moment later, the entire length of the sinew rope fell around them. There would be no climbing out. There would be no using the precious key. There would be no escape. The Holers had dropped the rope.

"Where the hell are they?" Tenser Ursuul demanded. The Holers barely recognized him in his fine tunic with his face shaved and his hair washed.

"Where do you think they are? They escaped," Lilly said.

"They escaped? Impossible!"

"No shit," Lilly said.

Tenser flushed, embarrassed in front of Neph Dada and the guards accompanying him.

A magical light bloomed in the Hole, illuminating everyone. It even dipped to the cutout where Logan had so frequently hidden. There was no one there.

"Logan, Fin, and Gnasher," Tenser said, naming those missing. "Logan and Fin hated each other. What happened?"

"King wanted—" Lilly started to say, but something cracked across her face and sent her sprawling.

"Shut up, bitch," Tenser said. "I don't trust you. You, Tatts, what happened?"

"Logan wanted to build another pyramid. He wanted to attract Gorkhy and see if we could grab his legs and get the key off of him. Fin wouldn't go for it. They fought. Fin threw Logan in the Hole, but then Gnasher attacked him and all of them fell in."

Tenser cursed. "Why didn't you stop them?"

"And fall in myself?" Tatts said. "Anyone who's tangled with Fin or Logan or Gnash gets killed, buddy—Your Highness. You were down here long enough to know that."

"Could they have survived the fall?" Neph Dada asked in his icy voice.

One of the newer inmates yelped and everyone looked at him. "No," he shouted. "Please!" A bright ball of magical light stuck to his chest and another to his back and lifted him over the Hole. Then he fell.

Everyone crowded around the hole, watching the light disappear into the darkness.

"Five . . . six . . . seven," Neph said. The light winked out right before eight. He looked at Tenser. "No, then. Well, I can't say your father will be pleased."

Tenser cursed. "Take them, Neph. Kill them. Do whatever you do, but make it painful."

51

*H*u Gibbet crouched on the roof of a warehouse deep in the Warrens. In a more prosperous time, it had been used to store textiles. Later, smugglers had used it. Now, it was a crumbling ruin that housed guild rats of the Burning Man guild.

None of that mattered to Hu, except for the inconvenience of having to kill the ten-year-old boy who was standing guard. Or maybe it had been a girl. Hard to tell. The only thing that mattered to Hu was a slab of stone on the floor by one crumbled wall. It looked like it weighed a thousand pounds and it was as weathered as all the other stones, but it opened on hinges that not even the guild rats knew about. It was the second exit for one of the largest safe houses in the city.

Right now, if Hu's source was correct, the safe house held approximately three hundred whores, enough food and water to keep them for a month, and the real prizes: Momma K and her lieutenant, Agon Brant. Hu didn't expect those two to be here, not really. But he could always hope.

He always had trouble with the big jobs. A big job required such balance. The pleasure in so much blood threatened his professionalism. It was so easy to get caught up in the sheer joy of it—watching blood spill or dribble or spurt, blood in all its glorious hues, the red red blood fresh from the lungs, the black blood from the liver, and every shade in between. He wanted to bleed every body dry to please Nysos, but on the big jobs he couldn't usually take the time. It made him feel like he was doing things halfway.

Plus it always left him depressed. After he'd killed and bled thirty or thirty-two at the Gyre estate, he hadn't been the same for weeks. Even all the killing during the coup couldn't satisfy him. It was all a letdown. The Gyre estate had been the best. He'd still been in the estate when the duke got home. He'd watched Regnus Gyre run from room to room, mad with grief, slipping in the Nysos-pools Hu had left in every hall. He'd been so excited by watching that he couldn't even kill the duke, though he knew the Godking wished it.

He'd finished that job the next night, of course, but that had been nothing. Not even close.

This job wouldn't be too hard. There would be some tight moments early on. First, he had to get in. He'd kill the children if he had to, but guild rats were slippery. They knew every hole in the Warrens the size a walnut and could fit into it with room to spare. It would be better not to give them the chance to warn anyone.

After he got in, there would be a guard or two on the back exit. It was an exit that had never been used, and there was only so long a man could stare at a wall before he got bored and tired, so the guards there might well be asleep.

Then Hu would need to kill the guards at the front exit without raising an alarm. Then he'd have to block or destroy the front exit. After that point, it wouldn't matter if the whores found out he was there or not. He could handle whores.

Then...well, the Godking had told him that he had twenty-four hours to do whatever he wanted. "Hu," the Godking had said, "make me a cataclysm."

The Godking planned to open up the place afterward and march every noble in the city through it. When the bodies were starting to get ripe, they'd start marching the rest of the city through it. The residents of the Warrens would go last. Then the Godking would have a public ceremony. People selected at random from among the Rabbits, the artisans, and the nobility would be sent into the massacre site. While they were inside, the Godking's wytches would seal the exits.

Garoth Ursuul expected it would provide a forceful deterrent to future rebellion.

But Hu felt uneasy. He was a professional. He was the best wetboy in the city, the best in the world, the best ever. He treasured that position, and there was only one thing that could threaten it: himself. He'd taken stupid risks at the Gyre estate. Idiotic risks. It had all worked out, but the fact remained that he'd been out of control.

There had just been too much blood. Too much thrill. He'd walked like a god through an orgy of worship that was death. He'd felt invulnerable during the hours he'd butchered the Gyres and their servants. He'd spent time displaying the bodies. He'd hung up several by their feet and cut their throats to bleed them to create that glorious lake of blood in the last hallway.

His job was to kill, and he'd gone dangerously beyond that. Durzo had been a killer. He took lives with the impersonal precision of a tailor. Durzo Blint would never have put himself at risk. It was why some people had considered him Hu's equal. Hu hated that. He was feared, but Blint was respected. His niggling worry was that the judgment was deserved.

That was why three hundred might be his undoing. The beast within would come out. Three hundred might be too much.

No. He was Hu Gibbet. Nothing was too much for Hu Gibbet. He was the best wetboy in the world. Tactically, this job wouldn't be nearly the challenge some other jobs had been, but when people whispered his name, this would be what they remembered. This would be his legacy. They would remember this all over the world.

The guild rats were all asleep, huddled together in clumps against the cold. Hu was about to drop through the hole in the roof when he saw something.

At first, he thought he was imagining it. It began as a whisper of wind, a puff of dust scattered in the moonlight. But the dust didn't settle, and there was no wind tonight. Still, the dust seemed to swirl in one place, gathering in one of the patches of moonlight in the warehouse near the children.

One of the children woke and gave a little cry, and in a second, every child in the guild was awake.

The whirlwind became a tiny tornado. Though there was still no wind, something was taking shape, black specks obscuring and spinning at a dizzying pace to a height of six feet. The tornado glowed an iridescent, scintillating blue. Sparks shot out and danced across the floor and the children cried out.

Taking shape through the tornado was a man, or something like a man. The figure flashed blue, spraying light in every direction, and not even Hu was fast enough to cover his eyes.

When he looked again, a figure unlike any he had ever seen stood before the children who were cowering wide-eyed on the floor. The man appeared to be carved from glossy black marble or shaped from liquid metal. His clothes weren't so much clothes as skin, though he appeared to wear shoes and was sexless, his whole body was unrelieved black and every contour was crisply defined. He was lean and every muscle was etched, from his shoulders to his V of a chest to his stomach to his legs. There was something funny about his skin, though. At first, the man or demon or statue made of flesh had reflected light like burnished steel. Now, only parts of him gleamed: the crescents of his biceps, the horizontal slashes of his abdominal muscles. The rest of him faded from glossy black to matte black.

Most frightening was the demon's face. It looked even less human than the rest of it. The mouth a small gash; cheekbones high; hair a disheveled, spiky black; brows prominent and disapproving above overlarge eyes out of a nightmare. The eyes were the palest blue of the coldest winter dawn. They spoke of judgment without pity, of punishment without remorse. As the figure studied the children, Hu became more and more certain that the eyes were actually glowing. Wisps of smoke curled out from them from whatever infernal fires burned within that hellish figure.

"Children," the figure said. "Be not afraid." There were gulps all around, and despite the words, every guild rat looked on the verge of bolting. "I will not harm you," the demon said. "But you are not safe here. You must go to Gwinvere Kirena, the one you know as Momma K. Go and stay with her. Tell her the Night Angel has returned."

Several children nodded, wide-eyed, but they all seemed frozen to the ground.

"Go!" the Night Angel said. He stepped forward through a shadow that cut the moonlight on the warehouse floor and an eerie thing happened. Where the shadow cut across the Night Angel, the demon disappeared. An arm, a diagonal slash of his body, and his head disappeared—except for two glowing spots that hung in space where his eyes should be. "Run!" the Night Angel yelled.

The children bolted like only guild rats can.

Hu knew that he should kill this Night Angel. Surely the Godking would reward him. Besides, the demon blocked Hu's entrance to his assignment. The Night Angel stood between him and more than three hundred succulent kills.

But it was hard to breathe. He wasn't afraid. It was simply that he didn't do jobs for free. He'd kill this angel, but he'd leave for now, make the Godking pay him for it. If the Night Angel knew about the underground chamber, it was already too late. If the Night Angel didn't know about the chamber, the whores would still be there tomorrow. He'd go get a contract on the Night Angel today and come back tomorrow and kill all the whores and the Night Angel too. It was completely logical. Fear had nothing to do with it.

The Night Angel turned his face up and as his eyes locked on Hu Gibbet's, they flashed from a smoldering blue to a fiercely burning red. In the next moment, the rest of the Night Angel vanished except for the burning red points of light.

"Dost thou desire thy judgment this night, Hubert Marion?" the Night Angel asked.

Cold dread paralyzed him. Hubert Marion. No one had called him that in fifteen years.

The Night Angel was moving toward him. Hu was on the verge of fleeing when the Night Angel stumbled. Hu stopped, puzzled.

The ruby eyes dimmed, flickered. The Night Angel sagged.

Hu dropped to the floor and drew his sword. The Night Angel drew itself up once more by an act of will, but Hu read exhaustion there. He attacked.

Their swords rang in the night, then Hu's kick blew through a block and connected with the Night Angel's chest. The creature flew back, its sword flying from its hand. It landed in a heap and began to shimmer.

In moments, the Night Angel was gone. In its place lay a man, naked, barely conscious.

It was Kylar Stern, Durzo's apprentice. Hu cursed him, his fear bleeding into outrage. It was all tricks? Illusions?

Hu stomped forward and slashed at Kylar's exposed neck. But his blade went completely through the man's head without resistance—shattering the illusion. Hu had barely stopped the slash when he felt a rope tighten around his ankles and yank him off his feet.

Fingers dug into his right elbow, hitting the pressure point and enervating his arm. A hand grabbed his hair and smacked his face against the floor again and again, breaking his nose with the first smack. On the third time, Hu's descending face came down on a rock. It ripped into his eye. Then he was rolling over and over.

He thrashed with all his Talent and hit nothing. Then his arms were behind his back and with a swift jerk upward, both shoulders were dislocated. Hu screamed. When he next thought to thrash, he found his arms and legs tied together.

From his remaining eye Hu caught sight of Kylar Stern, wobbling, clearly exhausted, but still pulling Hu across the floor by his cloak. Hu thrashed again, trying to kick something, anything, trying to stand. Kylar dropped him on his back and Hu screamed again as it put pressure on his bound, dislocated shoulders. Kylar stood over him.

Whatever the black skin had been, illusion or something else, Kylar obviously didn't have the power to hold it now. He stood naked, but his face was as much of a mask as the mask had been. Hu gathered his Talent to try another kick.

Kylar's foot streaked down first, breaking Hu's shin. Hu screamed against the exploding blackness of pain that threatened to make him fall unconscious, and when he looked again, Kylar was kicking a section of the floor. It came open on unseen hinges. Inside, a hidden water wheel turned, driven by the flowing waters of Plith River. Hu realized it must be the mechanism that opened the huge door of the safe house, its mighty gears currently disengaged, spinning slowly.

"Nysos is the god of waters, right?" Kylar asked.

"What are you doing?" Hu shouted, hysterical.

"Pray," Kylar said, his voice pitiless. "Maybe he'll save you." Kylar did something with Hu's cloak. For a moment, nothing happened. Then the cloak tightened around Hu's neck. It started dragging him across the floor.

"Nysos!" Hu screamed through the strangling tightness. "Nysos!"

The cloak pulled him into the water and for a long, blessed moment, the tension around his neck vanished. Hu kicked his good leg and found the surface. Then the cloak tightened and drew him into the gear. The disengaged gear pulled him out of the water by his throat and then flipped him over, dragging him back under the water again. He couldn't breathe. It dragged him out of the water again, flipped him again, and pulled him back under the water.

This time, he kicked as he came out of the water. It gave him enough slack to suck in a great breath, then he was flipped and plunged under the water once more. Hu tried to fight his bonds, but any pressure he put on his shoulders was agony. His arms were tied so tightly he couldn't pop his shoulders back into their joints and his good leg kicked against nothing but water.

He screamed again as he came out of the water, but the gear ground on. Up, down, up, down.

Kylar watched Hu Gibbet pulled from the water and then pulled under, over and over, sometimes begging, sometimes coughing up dirty river water. He felt no remorse. Hu deserved it. However Kylar knew what he knew, he knew that. And maybe it was as simple as that.

Swaying on his feet, Kylar looked for the switch to open the safe house. He hadn't been faking his exhaustion. He was just lucky that he'd had enough Talent left to fool Hu. In a fair fight, Hu would have taken him. Kylar had no illusions about that. But Durzo had taught him there was no such thing as a fair fight. Hu let himself be taken by surprise because he thought he was the best. Durzo had never considered himself the best; he just thought everyone else was worse than he was. It might seem like the same thing, but it wasn't.

Finally Kylar found what he was looking for. He grabbed a plank beside the rock and pulled it up.

The spinning gear slid sideways until its teeth met another gear's. They grated for a moment, then meshed together and turned. Hu was pulled inexorably out of the water one more time. He screamed. His head caught between the great teeth of the gears and his scream pitched abruptly higher. The gears stopped, straining.

Then Hu's head popped like bloody pimple. His legs jerked spastically and his whole body arched out of the water. Then his corpse flopped to the side and the gears turned on, blood staining the water.

The enormous rock lifted, revealing a tunnel into the earth. An alarm bell clanged in the depths.

In moments, a pair of guards thundered up the steps, spears in their hands.

"Have to...evacuate," Kylar said. He wobbled and neither man made a move to help him. "Godking knows you're here. Tell Momma K." Then he passed out.

52

Feir Cousat huddled as much of his bulk behind a tree as he could. It was two hours before dawn, and the figure lying beside the fire had been still for hours. In just a few moments, Feir would know whether all his gambles had paid off.

His search for Curoch had taken him to Cenaria, through the camps of the Khalidoran highlanders, and into the mountains on the Ceuran border. His hope and his despair for weeks had been that he hadn't even heard a whisper of a special sword. That meant if he was on the right track, Curoch might be held by a man who had no idea what it was. That scenario was vastly preferable to the idea of trying to take it from a Vürdmeister. Any Vürdmeister with the ability to use Curoch would have the ability to kill Feir a hundred ways.

What was more likely was that he was on the wrong track. He'd made a dozen guesses as he'd narrowed his list of possibilities. First, he'd taken a Khalidoran uniform and stitched messengers' insignia on it and sat at lots of campfires. When they'd been in school, Dorian had taught him Khalidoran, so even when the conversation lapsed into the old tongue—all young Khalidorans were bilingual; the Godking thought they could better rule if they knew the schemes of those they conquered—he knew what they were saying.

Because they hadn't immediately found Curoch, and Feir guessed rumors would have spread about that if they had, he figured someone must have taken the sword. He found the units that had done the cleanup detail on the bridge. Most of the men had been from units nearly destroyed in the fighting. Later they'd been lumped into a new unit and sent home guarding the wagons taking loot back to Khalidor—the very wagon train he and Dorian and Solon had been following.

Because Dorian had sent him south, Feir knew that the sword hadn't gone with the baggage train. So he'd asked after anyone from those units who hadn't gone home, and he'd found one.

Finding where Ferl Khalius had gone was an entirely different matter. In fact, Feir had never found the man. Instead, he'd followed a Vürdmeister who had been sent south. The Vürdmeister tracked Ferl Khalius and Feir tracked the Vürdmeister. He'd watched the Vürdmeister throw missiles at Ferl Khalius and the lord he'd kidnapped. The Vürdmeister lost interest as soon as the lord fell from the heights of Mount Hezeron.

While the Vürdmeister used his signal stick to tell the Godking of his failure, Feir had crept close. The falling snow and the concentration required to work magic had covered Feir's approach. As soon as the Vürdmeister was finished, Feir killed him.

Then he'd done something he would never do again. He'd crossed the broken ledge, in the snow. He'd jumped across a five-foot gap, from slick snow to slick snow. There had been places steep enough that his feet slid back as far as he climbed. He'd ended up using magic to melt some of the ice just long enough to take a few more steps. He'd made it, but it had been close.

Curoch was worth it.

He drew his sword and stepped forward in a modified *zshel posto,* a fighter's stance for keeping balance and agility on slick ground. In a few quick steps, he was over the man. His sword dipped and stabbed through the figure's chest—a chest made of snow wrapped in a cloak.

Feir cursed and whipped around as the real Ferl Khalius charged out of the woods, Curoch held high. Feir barely had time to move. The highlander's slash would have cut through Feir, except that he had thrown himself to one side. As it was, Curoch knocked the blade from his hand.

"Naw much honor in stobbin' a sleeping mon," Ferl said with a thick Khalidor accent.

"The stakes are too high for honor," Feir said. He had thought the man had no idea he was being followed. "Give me the sword," Feir said, "and I'll let you live."

Justifiably, Ferl looked at him like he was crazy: he was armed, Feir wasn't. "Me give it ta you? This is a warchief's sword."

"A warchief? That sword is worth more than your entire clan and every other clan for a hundred miles put together."

Ferl didn't believe him, but he didn't care, either. "It's mine."

Three points of white light, each smaller than Feir's thumbnail, appeared before him and whizzed at Ferl Khalius. The man wasn't half bad, but there was only so fast anyone could move a sword.

The two missiles that Ferl blocked with the sword blasted off into the night. The third missile went right below Ferl's hands into his belly. Feir reached out with difficulty—magic at a distance was never his strength— and yanked the missile up. It burned a path to Ferl's heart.

The highlander fixed his eyes on Feir and toppled sideways.

Feir picked up Curoch without elation. He'd been right. All his guesses and gambles had paid off. If anyone ever heard this story, the bards would make it a legend. He'd just recovered one of the most powerful magical artifacts ever created.

So why did he feel empty?

It had been so easy this time. Slow, but easy. Maybe Ferl had been right. It hadn't been honorable, but when one person had Curoch, the fight was never fair.

But that wasn't it, either. He'd recovered this damn sword three times—three! He could be declared the Official Finder of the Blasted Sword. He had it, but he could never use it. He was mediocre and he'd made the mistake of being friends with the great.

Solonariwan Tofusin Sa'fasti had been a prince of the Sethi empire. His Talent put him in the top ranks of all living mages. Dorian was another prince, a Vürdmeister and more. He was a magus of the kind that came along once a generation. Feir was a cordwainer's son with middling Talent and a good hand with a sword. He'd been an apprentice smith when his Talent had been discovered, and he'd later attended the Maker's school and then been hired as a smith and blades instructor at Sho'cendi, where he'd met Solon and Dorian.

Dorian had disavowed his birth, and neither he nor Solon had been officially granted any special treatment. But that, Feir knew, didn't mean they'd gotten no benefit from their noble birth. No matter what happened to Dorian or Solon, they knew that they were something special. They knew they mattered. Feir never had that. He was always second place, if not third.

The signal stick flashed and Feir pulled it out. The young Vürdmeister he'd killed had kept a translation key on him. Evidently it had been the first time he'd been entrusted with a signal stick, so Feir had been able to translate the flashes of light into letters, but they were still in code, and in Khalidoran. Breaking that code was simple. The first letter was its Khalidoran letter plus one, the second was the letter plus two, and so on. But the letters were spelled out rapidly, and Feir had nothing to write on, and his Khalidoran vocabulary was limited.

The Godking was using them exactly the way Feir would have. He was coordinating distant troops and meisters. It was simple and yet an enormous advantage. His commands were delivered instantly, while his opponents had to wait hours or days for messengers. In those days or hours, situations changed, plans changed.

No wonder he's devastated every army to come against him.

"Gather...north...of..." the signal stick flashed. Then it paused and the blue modified to red. What the hell did that mean? Feir spelled out the letters and on a hunch, transliterated them into Common. "P.A.V.V.I.L.S. G.R.O.V.E." Pavvil's Grove. It turned blue and went too rapidly for Feir to catch, but it repeated one section twice. "Two days. Two days." Then it went dark.

Feir let out a long breath. He'd passed through Pavvil's Grove on his way south. It was a small logging town that produced some of Cenaria's only oak. There was a plain north of the town suitable for a battle. Clearly, the Godking had a plan to wipe out the rebel army there.

Feir could get there in two days. But it was still two hours until dawn. Did the Khalidorans count a day from dawn or from midnight? Did two days mean two, or three?

Feir cursed. He could break an obscure cipher in another language, but he couldn't count to three. Great.

The signal stick turned yellow—something it had never done before. "Vürdmeister Lorus report..."

Oh, no.

The stick flashed, "Why...going...south?"

Feir blanched. So the signal sticks didn't just communicate, they transmitted his position. That wasn't good.

"Punishment will...when you return." My punishment will be decided when I return? "...Lantano...rumored to be near you. Any sign?"

Feir wanted to grab his own ignorance by the neck and shake the life out of it. What was rumored to be near him?

"Vürdmeister? Lorus? Failure to respond will..."

Feir threw the stick away and scurried backward. Nothing happened. A minute passed. Still nothing happened. He was beginning to feel silly when the signal stick exploded with such force that it shook snow from the trees for a hundred paces.

Well, that'll wake the neighbors.

The neighbors. That wasn't a pretty thought. And Lantano? The name sounded familiar.

Feir climbed a rock hill nearby to get a better view of his surroundings. He almost wished he hadn't. Four hundred paces to the south an army was camped, with perhaps six thousand men. The usual camp followers added perhaps four thousand to that: wives and farriers and smiths and prostitutes and cooks and servants.

The army's flags bore a stark black vertical sword on a white field: Lantano Garuwashi's sigil. That was the name, Feir remembered: a general who'd never been defeated, a commoner's son who had won sixty duels. If the stories were to be believed, sometimes he fought with wood practice swords against his opponents' steel to make things interesting.

The neighbors had definitely heard the noise, and a knot of ten horsemen was riding toward Feir right now. At least a hundred others followed.

53

Kylar opened his eyes in an unfamiliar room. It was getting to be an all-too-common occurrence. This rendition was small, dirty, cramped. The bed smelled as if the straw hadn't been changed in twenty years. His heart raced as he prepared himself for whatever might come next.

"Relax," Momma K said, coming to stand near his bed. It was a safe house doubtless, on the north side of the Warrens by the smell.

"How long?" Kylar asked, his voice a croak. "How long have I been out?"

"Nice to see you, too," Momma K said, but she smiled.

"A day and a half," a man's voice said.

Kylar sat up. The speaker was Lord General Agon. That was a surprise. "Well, looks like the huge new wall around the city isn't the only thing that's changed."

"Amazing what the bastards can do when they try something constructive, isn't it?" Agon said. He had a crutch and moved like his knee pained him.

"It's good to see you, Kylar," Momma K said. "The rumors have already started about how the Night Angel killed Hu Gibbet, but the only people who know that it was actually you are my guards. They've been with me a long time. They won't speak." So his identity was safe, but Kylar wasn't going to be distracted. He'd come too far, too fast, and given too much with only one thing in mind. "What do you know about Logan?"

Momma K and Agon looked at each other.

"He's dead," Momma K said.

"He's not dead," Kylar said.

"The best information we have—"

"He's not dead. Jarl came to tell me, all the way to Caernarvon."

"Kylar," Momma K said, "the Khalidorans found out who Logan was yesterday. As best we can tell, he either was killed by another inmate because of it, or he threw himself down the Hole to avoid what the Godking would do to him."

"I don't believe it." *Yesterday? While I was sleeping? I was this close?*

"I'm sorry," Momma K said.

Kylar stood and found a new set of wetboy grays piled on the foot of the bed. He began getting dressed.

"Kylar," Momma K said.

He ignored her.

"Son," Agon said, "it's time to open your eyes. No one likes that Logan's dead. He was like a son to me. You can't bring him back, but you can do some things that no one else can."

Kylar pulled on his tunic. "And let me guess," he said bitterly. "You two already have some ways you want to put my talents to use?"

"In a few days, Terah Graesin's army will meet the Godking's army just north of Pavvil's Grove. She'll get there first and have the advantage both of terrain and numbers," Momma K said.

"And the problem is?"

"That the Godking's going for it. After the Nocta Hemata, he should be twice as careful as he ever has been, but he's walking straight into this. Kylar, our spies have only caught hints, but I'm sure this is a trap. Terah Graesin won't listen. She wouldn't fight until the Godking presented her with a fight she couldn't lose. Now she has that, and nothing will stop her. All we know is that he's doing something magical, and it's big."

"Don't say it," Kylar said.

"We want to hire you for a hit, Kylar," Momma K said. "A hit worthy of the Night Angel. We want you to kill the Godking," Momma K said.

"You're insane."

"You'll be a legend," Agon said.

"I'd rather be alive." It was eerie. It was exactly what they'd wanted him to do before he left the city. It was exactly what Jarl had died to ask. Kill the Godking. Redeem all the pain and waste of his wetboy training. One kill, and he could hang up the sword, satisfied that he'd done more than his part. One kill that would save thousands. It had the feel of destiny.

"Even if Logan is still alive, it won't be any good to save his life if you let his only chance to have a kingdom be destroyed," Agon said. "If he's survived this long, he can make it for another day or two. Kill the Godking and save the kingdom, then go looking for our king."

Kylar selected weapons from the wide array Momma K had prepared for him, and secreted them about himself in silence.

"You'll doom us all," Agon said. "You have the kind of power I'd die for, and you won't use it to help us. Damn you." He turned on his heel and hobbled out of the room

Kylar looked at Momma K. She didn't leave, but she didn't understand, either.

"It's good to see you again, too, Momma," Kylar said. He took a deep breath. "I left Uly with Elene. They're both going to be all right. I left them with enough money that they'll be taken care of for the rest of their lives. And Elene will love her. I did the best I could....Jarl..." Suddenly, tears were hot in his eyes.

Momma K put a hand on Kylar's arm and he looked down.

"I know it doesn't make sense," he said. "But I swore to leave this behind me. I broke that vow for Logan. That cost me Elene's love and Uly's trust. I didn't abandon them so I could steal another life, but so I could save a life. Do you understand?"

"Do you know who you remind me of?" Momma K asked. "Durzo. When he was younger, before he lost his way. He would be proud of you, Kylar. I...I'm proud of you, too. I wish I could believe that the fates wouldn't be so cruel as to make you sacrifice everything just to find Logan dead, but I don't have that kind of faith. But I tell you what I do believe in. I believe in you." She hugged him.

"You're different," he said.

"It's all your fault," she said. "Next I'll go senile."

"I like it," he said.

She put her hands on his cheeks and kissed his forehead. "Go, Kylar. Go and please do come back."

Logan had fallen asleep twice now, each time expecting that he wouldn't wake up. He had stopped eating: he wouldn't touch Fin's body. He had stopped smelling the thick, corrosive air. He had stopped noticing Gnasher's little moues of concern. He had stopped bleeding, too, but it was too late. He had no strength.

After Gnasher had helped him sit up against a stalagmite, Logan saw another crushed body lying broken in the gloom not ten feet away. It was Natassa Graesin. The screams of the howlers didn't frighten her now. Her limbs were mangled but her face looked at peace. Her eyes held no accusation. They held nothing.

The most passion Logan could wake was simple regret. He was sorry for Natassa, who'd never even told him how she ended up down here. He was sorry for all the things he would never do. He had never truly desired the throne. He'd always suspected that being a king was far harder than it looked. In the Hole, he'd sometimes regretted that he wouldn't be remembered as someone who mattered.

Now, as he sat with his back propped against the stalagmite that would someday flow over his body and entomb him for eternity, he wished for simpler things. He missed sunlight. He missed the smell of grass, of fresh rain, of a woman. He missed Serah Drake and all her trivialities. He missed his wife. Jenine was so young, so smart, so pretty. She had been a diamond found and then lost forever. He missed Kylar, his best friend. Another diamond stripped away, found, and lost.

Logan wished for love and children and the running of his estates. A simple life, a big family, a few close friends. That would give him all the immortality he needed.

For a while, he prayed to the old gods. There was nothing else to do, and Gnasher wasn't much for conversation, but the old gods had nothing to say. He even prayed to Count Drake's One God. He wasn't sure how one was supposed to pray to the god of all things. Why would He care? Logan gave it up.

Mostly, he tried to ignore the pain.

He was about to close his eyes to try to die again—or sleep, whichever—when Gnasher started howling. It was a high, piercing, irritating sound unlike anything Logan had ever heard.

The vent belched acrid smoke, and the figure Logan glimpsed for an instant was devoured in the thick cloud and darkness. Then, as the cloud dissipated, a demon strode out of it.

For the first time Logan had ever seen, Gnasher showed fear. He retreated to Logan's side and crouched, whimpering, but that was as far as he would retreat. The simple man's loyalty knew no bounds.

The demon walked forward slowly, its glowing blue eyes fixed on Logan. Was this a howler? Or was this Death, finally come to claim him? Logan wasn't afraid.

"Well, shit, man," Death said with a familiar voice. "I thought I was going to have to climb all the way up the Hole to find you."

"What are you?" Logan croaked.

The demon's face shimmered and melted off of Kylar's face. Logan was sure he'd finally gone crazy.

"Sorry, I forgot about the face," Kylar said. He was half-grinning his crazy smirk to cover his concern. "You, ah, look like the south end of a northbound horse." It was one of Logan's old lines—gods!—from back when he barely knew a tenth of the curses he'd learned in the Hole. Kylar smirked again. "Is, ah, the big guy here going to be all right?"

Gnash was trembling all over, and even Logan couldn't tell if it was from anger or fear. "Gnash," Logan said, "he's a friend. He's here to help." Gnasher's expression didn't change, but he didn't move to attack. "It really is you, isn't it?" Logan asked.

"Here to save the day," Kylar said. When Logan failed to respond, he came over and checked Logan's body. The expression on his face was grim. "Well, what's one more miracle, huh? You're still kicking," he said to himself.

Logan felt himself drifting away from consciousness as Kylar helped him to his feet. Kylar was speaking, and part of Logan realized that he was just trying to keep Logan with him. He did his best to listen to Kylar's voice and ignore the voices of pain and death calling to him.

"...because it's damn near impossible to get into the Maw now. Not like the old days...they say someone or something has taken up residence. I mean, 'residence,' like the Maw's a palace or something."

"Khali," Logan whispered.

Kylar was taking them deeper into the Hole. Logan stumbled again, and when he opened his eyes, he found he was lashed to Kylar's back. That couldn't be right. Even with all the weight Logan had lost, Kylar shouldn't have been able to carry him this easily. But the sensation didn't fade. Kylar was picking his way farther and farther down. There was no path and no luminous moss down here, but Kylar moved surely, and kept talking, his voice itself warding off Logan's terror of the dark.

"...was in the Stacks once, and I remembered how the pipes seemed to go down into the very center of the earth. I figured that the Maw goes down and the stacks' pipes go down and they're right next to each other. I thought that if I went deep enough, the tunnels might connect.

"You ever seen the inside of those pipes in the Stacks, Logan? Sheer metal, going straight down just about forever. Big windmill blades spinning as they catch the rising air. I figured I could take the slow way down or the fast way. You know me, you can guess which I took. I grabbed a shield made myself a little sled with hand brakes so I could steer a little.... I tell ya, it was a helluva ride. I almost made it all the way down, too. Good thing I'd lost most of my speed before that last fan. I was sure it was turning faster. I pity the poor bastards who'll have to climb down to fix it."

Then Kylar stopped. He breathed deeply. "I'm not going to lie to you. This is the bad part. We have to go under water. This is the line, Logan. This is what separates the Hole from the Stacks. The water's hot, and it's tight, and it's going to feel like you've been buried. I promise you, if you can make it through this death, you'll come out into a new life. You just hold your breath, and I'll do all the work."

"Gnasher," Logan said.

"Gnasher? Oh, the big guy? Uh, he doesn't look like he likes water much, Logan."

Logan couldn't see Gnasher. It wasn't just dark down here. It was utterly black. There wasn't even lighter blackness. It was a single, unalleviated, embracing darkness. It was hot, wet, heavy, oppressive darkness that seeped into his very lungs. He had no idea how Kylar was seeing Gnasher, but Logan wouldn't leave him here.

"Will you . . . come back and get him?" Logan asked.

There was a long silence.

"Yes, my king," Kylar said finally.

"I'm . . . I'm ready."

"You just count. I got through in about a minute. It might take us a little longer together."

A minute?

"Before we go . . . I'm sorry, Logan. I'm sorry for all of this and for how much of it's my fault. I'm sorry I didn't tell you what I was. I'm sorry that I didn't kill Tenser when I had the chance. I'm . . . just sorry."

Logan said nothing. He couldn't find the words and the strength to give Kylar what he deserved.

Kylar didn't wait. He began taking great breaths and Logan followed his example. A moment later, they plunged into the water together. Logan leaned close to Kylar's body, trying not to get in the way of his arms, trying to make his body streamlined in the water.

The water was hot, stinging hot, and clearly Kylar didn't mean for this to be a leisurely swim. Logan felt them turn upside down, and then Kylar must have been grabbing on to rocks to pull them down, because they were moving fast. In fact, they were moving faster than Logan thought was possible underwater. He knew Kylar was strong: he'd wrestled and sparred with him, but the speed they were moving shouldn't have been possible with the mass Kylar was pulling through the water.

Ten. Eleven. The water was pressing on every side, tight and constricting. Some part of Logan marveled that Kylar had done this already, alone, without any sure idea that the tunnels did connect, or how long of a swim it would be. At fourteen seconds, Logan's lungs were already burning.

He held on, trying not to hold on too hard, trying to preserve his strength. The pain was nothing, he told himself.

It was twenty seconds before he felt them level off. His back scraped against rock. It felt different, though he couldn't have said what sense told him so. He thought they had entered a tunnel, and from how Kylar was moving, it was a narrow tunnel.

Forty. Forty-one. Now the pain was undeniable. The air was pressing its way up his throat, begging for release. It hammered at him. Just a little release, just a little.

At fifty, they got stuck. Abruptly, all forward motion ceased. The shock of it made Logan open his eyes. Hot, sour water attacked his eyes and he coughed. An enormous bubble of life-giving air rushed from his lungs.

Kylar pulled and pulled. Logan felt something tearing, whether it was his ragged tunic or his skin, he didn't know, but then they were moving again.

He had less than half a lungful of air. Kylar was moving at incredible speed again, but they still weren't heading upward.

Then Logan felt Kylar turn, but his friend didn't push upward. Instead, in a frenzied motion illuminated with blue magical light, he drew a short sword from his belt. Logan was thrown this way and that as Kylar slashed and stabbed at something flashing like silver lightning in the water.

There was no way he could take any more. Kylar started moving upward, but Logan couldn't make it for another twenty seconds. He couldn't hold on that long.

At sixty-seven seconds, he let the last of his air go.

They were moving up so fast he felt it play against his face as they shot up. They passed the bubble.

His lungs burned. He surrendered and breathed.

Scalding water poured into his lungs—followed by air. Logan coughed and coughed and the hot, acrid stuff shot from his nose and mouth. It seared his sinuses, but a moment later, sweet cool air replaced it.

Kylar untied him and lowered him gently to the ground. Logan lay on his back, just breathing. It was still dark, but high overhead, up the metal tubes up the stacks, he saw the twinkle of distant torches. After the black waters, it felt like stepping into a universe of light.

"My king," Kylar said. "There's something in the water. Some giant, terrible lizard. If I go back, I don't know if I'll return. You're in no shape to make it out alone. Without me, you'll die here. Do you still want me to retrieve the simpleton?"

Logan wanted to say no. He was more important to the kingdom than Gnasher. And he was afraid to be left alone. Life was suddenly so close, and he didn't want to die.

"I can't abandon him, Kylar. Forgive me."

"You'd only need forgiveness if you'd asked me to leave him," Kylar said, and then he dove into the water.

He was gone for five agonizing minutes. When he broke the surface of the water, he was swimming at such great speed that it carried him into the air. He landed on his feet. He'd made a harness of the rope and had pulled Gnasher behind him. Now he grabbed the rope and pulled it in rapidly.

Gnasher virtually flew clear of the water. He took a deep breath and smiled at Logan. "Hold breath good!" he said.

Kylar swept Logan into his arms as something huge broke through the water behind them. Something slapped into Kylar and sent all three of them sprawling.

Then the chamber was lit with iridescent blue light that came from Kylar himself. He was darting about, flipping from stalagmite to stalagmite, using them to change direction unpredictably. Fear clamped down on Logan's throat. Whatever Kylar was fighting, it was huge. Enormous webbed hands crashed through stalagmites like they were twigs. Rocks rained down everywhere as Logan curled into a ball. Great gusts of air burst from a maw visible only as the teeth and eyes reflected Kylar's blue fire. Silvery-green light blinked on and off.

The most terrifying thing was being unable to see. The battle raged mere paces away, and Logan could do nothing, not even observe it. He heard clanging and guessed it was Kylar's sword ringing off of the creature's hide, but had no idea. He had no idea how Kylar was fighting it at all in this pitch black, and no hope of fighting it for himself. He didn't even know how big it was, or what it looked like.

He lost sight of Kylar—or Kylar disappeared, because even the beast paused and snorted. It began sniffing the air, its huge head weaving back and forth.

Suddenly, it shot toward Logan and Gnasher. Logan threw his hands out and felt slimy hide rush past his fingers. Stalagmites crashed down everywhere. Then it pulled back and turned its head. A light as silvery cold as the moon bloomed in its green-marbled eyes and then the great snuffling head turned.

The slimy snout slid past Logan's cheek as the beast's head turned. It sniffed and sniffed. Logan's fingers brushed a broken chunk of stalagmite and he grabbed it. The motion attracted the creature. It pulled back and the light from its eye illumined Logan like torchlight. The great cat's eye turned to him and came into focus.

Logan buried the jagged rock into that great eye and ground it back and forth. Luminous green-silver light spilled on Logan with the creature's blood. The eye went out like a blown candle and a howl filled the chamber, echoing back from the great distances all around. A moment later, a dark figure blurred past Logan and attacked the blind eye.

The creature shrieked again and thrashed backward. An enormous splash sounded, and then all was quiet.

"Logan," Kylar said, his voice shaking with the aftereffects of adrenaline, "was that . . . was that Khali?"

"No. Khali's . . . different. Worse." Logan laughed uncertainly. "That was just a dragon." He laughed again like a man set free from his senses.

Then all light faded.

When he woke, the three of them had been fitted with harnesses, and Kylar was hoisting them all by a rope that must have been attached to a pulley high above. They were ascending the central shaft of the Stacks. It was a huge metal tube, thirty paces across, and all of the enormous fans had been stopped. How did Kylar manage that?

The trip took several more minutes, and the whole time, Logan was aware of his arm burning and tingling where the creature's eye blood had spilled on him. He didn't have the courage to look at it.

"We have a man inside who helped me," Kylar said. "The Sa'kagé is now one of your most important allies, my king. Maybe your only ally."

A few minutes later, they reached a section where the pipes turned horizontal. With great care, Kylar untied Logan and then Gnasher. He cut the ropes and let them fall into the abyss. The pulley followed. He led them down the narrowing horizontal section until they reached a door. Kylar tapped on it three times.

The door opened and Logan found himself face to face with Gorkhy.

"Logan, meet our inside guy," Kylar said. "Gorkhy, your money is—"

"You!" Gorkhy said. His face showed the same disgust Logan felt.

"Kill him," Logan croaked.

Gorkhy's eyes bulged. He grabbed at the guard's whistle he carried on a lanyard around his neck. Before it reached his lips, though, his head spun free of his body. The corpse dropped without a sound.

It was that fast, that easy. Kylar dragged the body down the tunnel to drop it into the shaft and returned a minute later. Logan had just ordered his first kill.

Kylar didn't ask for an explanation. It was an eerie, awesome, awful thing. It was power, and it felt disconcertingly . . . wonderful.

"Your Majesty?" Kylar said, opening the door out of the shaft, out of the nightmare. "Your kingdom awaits."

54

*W*hen Kaldrosa Wyn and ten of the other girls from the Craven Dragon emerged from Momma K's safe house, the Warrens were changed. There was a nervous excitement in the air. The Nocta Hemata had been a triumph, but repercussions were coming. Everyone knew it. Momma K had told the girls they needed to leave her subterranean safe house because the secret of its existence had leaked. Somehow, the Night Angel had saved them all from being slaughtered by Hu Gibbet.

Kaldrosa had heard rumors of the Night Angel before, right after the invasion, but she hadn't believed them. Now they all knew he was real. They'd seen Hu Gibbet's body.

Momma K had told them she would smuggle them out as quickly as possible, but moving three hundred women out of the city was going to take time. They had ways to get around or under the Godking's new walls, but it wasn't easy. Kaldrosa Wyn's group was supposed to go tonight. Momma K had told them that if they wanted to stay in the city, if they had husbands or boyfriends or family to go back to, all they had to do was not show up at the rendezvous tonight.

The Warrens were quiet, expectant, as the women made their way to the safe house. They were conspicuous, of course, all of them still dressed in their rich whoring clothes. Master Piccun's designs seemed obscene in the broad daylight, in the context of open streets. Worse, some of the girls' costumes were stained with brown-black smears of dried blood.

But the women passed no guards, and it was soon clear that the Khalidorans didn't go into the Warrens now. The residents who saw them looked at them strangely. One alley they tried to traverse was blocked by a building that must have been knocked down during the Nocta Hemata itself, and it forced Kaldrosa Wyn and the others to walk straight through the Durdun Market.

The market was busy, but as the former whores passed through it, a wave of silence preceded them. Every eye was on them. The girls set their jaws, ready for the derision their clothing would surely evoke, but nothing happened.

A stout fishwife leaned over her stall and said, "You done us proud, girls."

The women were caught off guard. The approval hit them like a slap in the face. Everywhere it was the same. People everywhere nodded in greeting and acceptance, even the women who a week ago would have sneered at rent girls even as they envied their good looks and easy lives. Even as the Rabbits waited for the Godking to crush them, as they knew he must, they shared a unity forged of persecution. The Rabbits had surprised themselves with their own bravery that night, and somehow, the whores bore their standard.

The gloriously solitary two-day ride to Cenaria had only one problem. There was no irritating child. No domineering hag. No verbal sparring. No humiliation. But the time gave Vi an opportunity to see how flimsy her plans were.

The first plan was to go to the Godking. It had seemed great for about five minutes. She'd tell him that Kylar was dead. She'd tell him Jarl was dead. She'd ask for her gold and she'd leave.

Right. Sister Ariel's musings about the spell on Vi were far too specific to be guesses. They were also far too plausible. Vi would either have a short leash or a long leash, but she'd have a leash. Garoth Ursuul had promised to break her. It wasn't the kind of promise he'd forget.

In truth, Vi felt broken already. She was losing her edge. It was one thing to feel bad for killing Jarl. Jarl had kept her alive. He'd been a friend and someone who would never demand the use of her body. He hadn't been a threat, physically or sexually.

Kylar was a different matter altogether, and yet even now, riding slowly through the streets of Cenaria, her hood close around her face, Vi couldn't stop thinking about him. She was actually sorry he was dead. Maybe even sad.

Kylar had been a damn good wetboy. One of the best. It was a shame he'd been killed with an arrow, probably from hiding. Not even a wetboy could stop that.

"That's it," Vi said aloud. "Could happen to anyone. Makes me realize my own mortality. It's just a shame."

It wasn't just a shame. That wasn't what she felt, and she knew it. Kylar had been kind of cute. If you could think "kind of cute" with a mental sneer. Kind of charming. Well, not that charming. But he did try.

Really, it was Uly's fault. Uly had talked and talked about how great he was. Fuck.

So maybe she'd entertained a whim that Kylar could be the kind of man who could understand her. He'd been a wetboy, and somehow he'd left it and become a decent person. If he could do it, maybe she could, too.

Yes, he was a wetboy, but he was never a whore. *You think he could understand that? Forgive it? Sure. You go ahead with your little crush, Vi. Bawl your eyes out like a little girl. Go ahead and pretend you could have been an Elene, making a little home and having a little life. I'm sure it would have been great fun to suckle brats and crochet baby blankets.*

The truth is, you didn't even have the courage to admit you had a crush on Kylar until you knew he was safely dead.

All the things Vi had always hated about women were suddenly showing up in herself. For Nysos' sake, she even missed Uly. Like some sort of fucking *mother*.

Well that was nice. Boo hoo. Do we feel better now? Because we still have a problem. She sat on her horse outside Drissa Nile's shop. The Bitch Wytch had said the weaves were dangerous, but Drissa might be able to free Vi from the Godking's magic. Looking at the modest shop, Vi thought the smart money was on the Godking.

The Godking would make her a slave. Drissa Nile would either free her or kill her.

Vi went inside. She had to wait half an hour while the two diminutive, bespectacled Niles took care of a boy who'd been splitting firewood and buried an axe in his foot, but after his parents took him home, Vi said that Sister Ariel had sent her. The Niles closed shop immediately.

Drissa seated her in one of the patient rooms while Tevor drew back a section of the roof to let sunlight in. They looked alike, baggy clothes over short, lumpy bodies, graying brown hair as straight as sheaves of wheat, spectacles, and single earrings. They moved with the easy familiarity of long partnership, but Tevor Nile clearly deferred to his wife. They both appeared to be in their forties, but scholarly Tevor seemed perpetually befuddled, while Drissa left no doubt that she was aware of all things at all times.

They sat on either side of her, holding each other's hand behind her back. Drissa rested her free hand on Vi's neck, and Tevor laid his fingers on the skin of her forearm. Vi felt a cool tingle in her skin.

"So, how do you know Ariel?" Drissa asked, her eyes sharp through her spectacles. Tevor seemed to have completely sunk into himself.

"She killed my horse to keep me from going into Ezra's Wood."

Drissa cleared her throat. "I see—"

"Gwaah!" Tevor yelled. He jerked backward and fell off his stool, smacking the back of his head against the stone of the fireplace.

"Don't touch anything!" As fast as he fell, he was on his feet again.

Vi and Drissa stared at him, baffled. He rubbed the back of his head. "By the hundred, I nearly incinerated all of us." He sat down. "Drissa, look at this."

"Oh," Vi said. "Ariel said it was trapped in some interesting ways."

"Now you tell me?" Tevor asked. "Interesting? She calls this interesting?"

"She said you were the best with small weaves."

"She did?" Tevor's demeanor changed in an instant.

"Well, she said Drissa."

He threw his hands up. "Of course she did. Damn Sisters can't admit a man might be good, not even for a second."

"Tevor," Drissa said.

He was abruptly calm. "Yes, dear?"

"I'm not seeing it. Can you lift it—"

She exhaled all at once. "Oh my. Oh my. Yes, don't lift it."

Tevor didn't say anything. Vi turned to see what his expression was.

"Please hold still, child," Drissa said.

For ten minutes, they worked in silence. Or at least Vi thought they worked. Aside from something like feather brushes on her spine, she felt nothing.

Finally, Tevor grunted as if satisfied.

"Are we done?" Vi asked.

"Done?" he said. "We haven't started. I was inspecting the damage. Interesting? I'll say it's interesting. There are three side spells protecting the primary spell. I can get them. Breaking the last one is going to hurt, a lot. The good news is that you came to us. The bad news is that by touching the weave, I've disrupted it. If I can't break it in perhaps an hour, it will blow your head off. You might have said it was a Vürdmeister who put the spell on you. Any other surprises?"

"What's the primary spell?" Vi asked Drissa.

"It's a compulsion spell, Vi. Go ahead, Tevor." The man sighed and sank back into himself. He didn't seem to be able to speak while he was working. Drissa, on the other hand, had no problem. Vi could see her hands beginning to glow faintly even as she spoke. "It's going to start hurting soon, Vi, and not just physically. We can't numb you to the pain because he's trapped that area of your brain. Numbing you is one of the first things a healer would do, usually, so he's made it lethal. Hold still now."

The world went white and stayed white. Vi was blind.

"Just listen to my voice, Vi," Drissa said. "Relax."

Vi was breathing quick, shallow breaths. Suddenly, the world returned. She could see.

"Four more times and we'll have the first spell," Drissa said. "It might be easier if you close your eyes."

Vi snapped her eyes shut. "So, uh, compulsion," she said.

"Right," Drissa said. "Compulsion magic is very limited. For the spell to hold, the caster must have authority over you. You have to feel you owe the caster your obedience. It would be worst with a parent or a mentor, or a general if you were in the army."

Or a king. Or a god. Holy hells.

"Regardless," Drissa said, "the good news is that you can throw off a compulsion if you can throw off that person's hold over you."

"Brilliant," Tevor said. "Bloody brilliant. Mad and sick, but genius. Did you see how he's anchored the traps in her own glore vyrden? He's making *her* sustain *his* spells. Horribly inefficient, but—"

"Tevor."

"Right. Back to work."

Vi's stomach muscles convulsed like she was throwing up. When it passed, Vi said, "Throw it off how?"

"Oh, the compulsion? Well, we should be able to break it this afternoon. It is a little tricky, though. If you try to untie it the wrong way, you just make it tighter. It won't be a problem for you."

"Why's—" Vi's convulsing stomach cut off the rest of her question.

"Magae are forbidden the use of compulsions, but we learn to protect ourselves from them. If you didn't have us, to throw off the compulsion requires an outward sign of an inward change, a symbol to show you've changed your loyalties. You'll have that covered too, as soon as you take the white dress and the pendant."

Vi looked at her blankly.

"When you enroll in the Chantry," Drissa said. "You do intend to enroll in the Chantry, don't you?"

"I guess," Vi said. She hadn't really thought about the future, but the Chantry would be safe from the Godking.

"Two. Ha," Tevor said triumphantly. "Tell her about Pulleta Vikrasin."

"You just like that story because it makes the Chantry look bad."

"Oh, go on, ruin the story," Tevor said.

Drissa rolled her eyes. "Long story short, two hundred years ago the head of one of the orders was using compulsion on her subordinates, and they didn't find out until one of the magae, Pulleta Vikrasin, married a magus. Her new loyalty to her husband broke the compulsion and led to several sisters being severely punished."

"That was the worst rendition of that story I've ever heard," Tevor said. He looked at Vi. "That marriage not only probably saved the Chantry, but in the twisted minds of those spinsters it also confirmed that a woman who married would never truly be loyal to the Chantry. I can't wait until the Chattel gather and—"

"Tevor. One more?" Drissa said. Again the little man went back to work. "Sorry, you'll get more than enough Chantry politics soon. Tevor's still bitter about how they treated me after we got ringed." She pulled at her earring.

"Is that what those mean?" Vi said. No wonder she'd seen so many earrings in Waeddryn. They were wedding earrings.

"Besides a few thousand queens out of your purse, yes. The ringsmiths tell women that the rings will make their husbands more submissive, and they tell men that they'll make their wives more, shall we say, amorous? It's said that in ancient times a ringed husband could be aroused by no woman but his wife. You can imagine how well they sold. But it's all lies. Maybe it was true once, but the rings now barely have enough magic to seal seamlessly and stay shiny."

Oh, Nysos. Kylar's note to Elene suddenly made a lot more sense. Vi hadn't stolen some expensive jewelry; she'd stolen a man's promise of his undying love. Vi had a sick feeling in her stomach again, but this time she didn't think it had anything to do with Tevor's magic.

"Are you ready, Vi? This one's really going to hurt, and not just physically. Lifting compulsion will make you relive your most significant experiences with authority. I'm guessing it won't be pleasant for you."

Good guess.

Drissa Nile was the only one who could help now. Logan was in bad shape. Getting him off of Vos Island had been easy enough, but it had taken time and Kylar wasn't sure how much of that Logan had left.

Logan had been stabbed in the back, and he had all kinds of cuts, including some along his ribs and arm that were red, inflamed, and filled with pus.

Few mages had made the city their home for the last couple of decades, but Kylar was starting to believe that the Chantry never abandoned any corner of the world. He knew of a woman in town who had a great reputation as a healer, and if anyone was a mage in the city, she was. It'd better be so; if anyone needed healing magic, it was Logan. Especially with that stuff on his arm.

Kylar wasn't even sure what it was, but it seemed to have burned its way into the flesh. The strangest thing was that it appeared not to have fallen randomly on Logan's arm, like he would have expected from gushing blood, but in a pattern. Kylar didn't even know if he should put water on, cover it, or what. Anything might make it worse.

And what the hell had that thing been? In repayment for the many cuts it had given him, Kylar had taken a fang from the beast, but his survival had been as much luck as skill. If there hadn't been so many stalagmites in the chamber, the creature's speed would have overmatched anything Kylar could do. Its skin was impregnable, even with all the strength of Kylar's Talent. He'd guessed that its eyes would be vulnerable, but it had already protected them from him three times before it got distracted by Logan and Gnasher. And the swim—that thing speeding after him under the water—had been sheer terror. He'd probably dream of it for the rest of his life.

Regardless, saving Logan was the best thing he'd ever done. Logan had needed to be saved, had deserved to be saved, and Kylar had been the only one who could save him. This was Kylar's purpose. This redeemed his sacrifices. This was why he was the Night Angel.

He crossed into the Warrens with his odd cargo and loaded them into a covered wagon. Then he drove to Drissa Nile's shop.

The place was in the wealthiest location in the Warrens, right off the Vanden Bridge, and it was fairly large, with a sign above it that read "Nile and Nile, Physickers," over a picture of the healing wand for the illiterate. Like Durzo before him, Kylar had avoided the place, fearing that a mage might recognize what he was. Now he had no choice. He pulled up in back of the shop, grabbed Logan from the bed of the wagon, and carried him to the back door with Gnasher following him.

The door was locked.

A small surge of Talent took care of that. The latch burst and wood splintered. Kylar carried Logan inside.

The shop had several rooms off a central waiting area. At the sound of the latch bursting through the frame, a man was emerging from one of the patient rooms where Kylar glimpsed two women talking before the physicker closed the door. A quick glance confirmed that the front door was barred, too.

"What are you doing?" the physicker asked. "You can't break in here."

"What the hell kind of physicker locks his doors in the middle of the day?" Kylar asked. As he looked into the physicker's eyes, he knew the man wasn't a criminal, but he did see something else, a warm green light like a forest after a storm when the sun comes out.

"You're a mage," Kylar said. He had thought that this man had simply been a front, a male physicker that Drissa Nile had used to take away the attention from her own too-miraculous cures. He was wrong.

The man went rigid. He wore spectacles, and the right lens was much stronger than the left, giving his suddenly widened eyes a disconcertingly lopsided appearance. He said, "I don't know what you're talking—" Kylar felt something brush him quickly, try to probe him, but the ka'kari didn't allow it. The mage never finished his sentence. "You're invisible to me. It's like—like you're dead."

Shit. "Are you a healer or not? My friend's dying," Kylar said.

For the first time, the man turned his bespectacled eyes to Logan. Kylar had thrown a blanket over the king to ward him from curious eyes. "Yes," the man said. "Tevor Nile at your service. Please, please put him on the table there."

They went into an empty room. Tevor Nile threw the blanket back and clucked. Kylar had laid Logan on the table face down. The physicker sliced open Logan's blood- and dirt- and sweat-encrusted rag of a tunic to look at the gash on Logan's back. He was already shaking his head.

"It's too much," he said. "I don't even know where to start."

"You're a mage, start with magic."

"I'm not a—"

"If you lie to me one more time, I swear I'll kill you," Kylar said. "Why else a hearth that size in a room this small? Why else the retractable section of roof? Because you need fire or sunlight for magic. I'm not going to tell anyone. You have to heal this man. Look at him. Do you know who he is?"

Kylar rolled Logan over, throwing away the rag of a tunic.

Tevor Nile gasped, but he wasn't looking at Logan's face. He was look-ing at the glowing imprint on his arm.

"Drissa!" he shouted.

From the next room, Kylar could hear the sound of the two women talking. "...you think? What do you mean you think? Is it gone or isn't it?"

"We're fairly certain that it's gone," a woman said.

"DRISSA!" Tevor yelled.

A door opened and closed and then their door opened and Drissa Nile's irritated face appeared. Like her husband, she had a wizened look, despite being maybe in her late forties. Both were small and scholarly, wearing spectacles and shapeless clothes. As with her husband, Kylar saw no taint of evil in her, but there was definitely that something extra there that he thought was magic.

Two mages married to each other. In Cenaria. It was an oddity, certainly, especially here. Kylar could only believe that it was the most fortunate oddity possible. If two mage healers couldn't fix Logan, no one could.

Drissa's irritation disappeared the second she saw Logan. Her eyes went wide. She came close and stared from his glowing arm to his face and back again in wonder.

"Where'd he get this?" she asked.

"Can you help him?" Kylar demanded.

Drissa looked at Tevor. He shook his head. "Not after what we just did. I don't think I've got enough power in me. Not for this."

"We'll try," Drissa said.

Tevor nodded, submissive, and Kylar noticed the rings in their ears for the first time. Gold, both of them, matching. They were Waeddryners. If it had been any other circumstance, he would have asked them if those damn rings really did hold spells.

Tevor drew back the section of roof to let the cloudy morning sunlight in. Drissa touched the wood already stacked in the hearth and it began blazing. They took up positions on either side of Logan and the air above him shimmered.

Kylar brought the ka'kari up within him to his eyes. It was like putting spectacles on a man nearly blind. The weaves over Logan that had been just barely visible to him were suddenly clear.

"Do you know herbs?" Drissa asked Kylar. At his nod, she said, "In the great room, get Tuntun leaf, grubel ointment, silverleaf, ragweed, and the white poultice on the top shelf."

Kylar came back a minute later with the ingredients, plus a few others he thought would be helpful. Tevor looked at them and nodded, but didn't seem capable of speech.

"Good, good," Drissa said.

Kylar began applying the herbs and poultices while Drissa and Tevor worked the weaves of magic. Over and over, he saw them dipping a weave as thick as a tapestry into Logan, adjusting it to fit his body, raising it above him, repairing it, and dipping it into his body again. What surprised him, though, was the way some of the herbs responded.

He'd never considered that normal plants might react to magic, but they obviously did. The silverleaf that Kylar had packed into the stab wound on Logan's back turned black in seconds—something he'd never seen it do.

For Kylar, it was like watching a dance. Tevor and Drissa worked together in perfect harmony, but Tevor was tiring. Within five minutes,

Tevor was flagging. His parts of the weaves were getting shaky and thin. His face was pale and sweaty. He kept blinking and pushing his spectacles back up his long nose. Kylar could see the mage's exhaustion, but could do nothing about it. Critiquing a dancer was different from being able to step in and do better. That was what he wished he could do. He wasn't sure how he knew, but it seemed that Drissa was attempting smaller and smaller changes in Logan each time, and he still had some things terribly wrong in him. Looking at him through the healing weave, his entire body seemed to be the wrong color. Kylar touched him, and he felt hot.

Kylar felt impotent. He had Talent here. Talent to spare, even after everything, he still had Talent. He willed the ka'kari back, willed himself to be unshielded, tried to will all that magic into Logan. Nothing happened.

Take it, damn you. Get better!

Logan didn't stir. Kylar couldn't use the magic; he didn't know how to form any weave, much less one as complex as what the Niles were doing.

Tevor looked at Kylar apologetically. He patted Kylar's hand.

At the contact, light blazed through the entire room. It burned beyond the magical spectrum into the visual, throwing their shadows on the walls. The weaves over Logan, which had been flagging, dimming, fading into nothing just a moment before, now burned incandescent. Heat flashed through Kylar's hand.

Tevor gaped like a fish.

"Tevor!" Drissa said. "Use it!"

As Kylar felt the Talent flood out of him, he felt his magic all the way through Tevor being pulled down into Logan's body. It was out of his control. Tevor was directing Kylar's Talent completely. Kylar realized that Tevor could turn that magic to kill him, and having submitted like this, Kylar wouldn't be able to stop him.

Sweat broke out on Drissa's face and Kylar could feel the two mages working feverishly. They ran magic through Logan's body like a comb through tangled hair. They touched the glowing scar on his arm—still glowing, hours later—but there was strangely nothing wrong. It wasn't something they could fix. The healing magic moved right past it.

Finally Drissa breathed and let the weave dissipate. Logan would live, in fact, he was probably healthier than when he'd gone into the Maw.

But Tevor didn't let go of Kylar. He turned and stared at him, eyes wide.

"Tevor," Drissa said, warning.

"What are you? Are you a Vürdmeister?" Tevor asked.

Kylar tried to draw the ka'kari up to sever the connection, but he couldn't. He tried to ready his muscles with Talent strength, but he couldn't.

"Tevor," Drissa said.

"Did you see? Do you see this? I've never—"

"Tevor, release him."

"Honey, he could incinerate us both with this much Talent. He—"

"So you'd use a man's own magic against him after he submitted it to you? How do the Brothers look on that? Is that the kind of man I married?"

Tevor dropped his head and his hold on Kylar's Talent simultaneously. "I'm sorry."

Kylar shivered, drained, empty, weak. It was almost as disconcerting to get control of his Talent back as it was to give it away. He felt like he'd gone two days without sleeping. He barely had the energy to be excited that Logan was going to make it.

"I think we'd better see to you and your simple friend. Your wounds can use more mundane treatments," Drissa said. She lowered her voice, "The, ahem, king should wake this evening. Why don't you come with me to another room?"

She opened the door and Kylar stepped into the waiting area. Gnasher had curled up in a corner and was sleeping. But directly in front of Kylar was a beautiful, shapely woman with long red hair. Vi. She was staring at him down the length of a bare sword. Its tip touched his throat.

Kylar reached for his Talent, but it slipped through his fingers. He was too tired. It was gone. There was nothing he could do to stop her.

Vi's eyes were red and puffy like she'd just gone through a wringer, though how or why Kylar had no idea.

She stared down the length of steel for a moment that seemed to stretch and stretch. He couldn't read the look in those green eyes, but it was something wild.

Vi stepped back three measured and balanced steps, Valdé Docci, the Swordsman Withdraws. She knelt in the center of the room, bowed her head, pulled her ponytail to one side, and laid the bare sword across her hands. She raised the sword in offering.

"My life is yours, Kylar. I surrender to your judgment."

55

Seven of the eleven rent girls had left the safe house to see if they had families they could go back to. Six had come back, weeping. Some were now widows. Others were simply rejected by fathers and boyfriends and husbands who could see only whores and disgrace.

Kaldrosa's courage failed her; she never left the safe house. For some reason, she'd been able to face death. She'd emasculated Burl Laghar and watched him bleed to death, tied to her bed, screaming into a gag. Then she'd moved the body, put fresh sheets on the bed and welcomed in another Khalidoran soldier. He was a young man who'd always had sex first and afterward was half-hearted in the beatings and the invocation. He always seemed disgusted with himself. She asked, "Why do you do it? You don't like hurting me. I know you don't."

He couldn't look her in the eye. "You don't know what it's like," he said. "They have spies everywhere. Your own family will turn you in if you make the wrong joke. He knows."

"But why beat up whores?"

"It's not just whores. It's everyone. It's the suffering we need. For the Strangers."

"What do you mean? What strangers?"

But he wouldn't say any more. A moment later, he stared at the bed sheets. Blood in the mattress was soaking through the fresh sheet. Kaldrosa stabbed him in the eye. The whole time, even when he came after her, bleeding, roaring, furious, she'd never been afraid.

Facing Tomman, though, that was too much. They'd fought bitterly before she left for Momma K's. He would have forcibly restrained her except that he'd been beaten so severely he couldn't get out of bed. Tomman had always been jealous. No, Kaldrosa couldn't face him. She'd leave with the others and go to the rebel camp. She didn't know what she'd do there. They were inland and nowhere near a river, so jobs as a captain would likely be scarce. In fact, if she couldn't obtain clothes that covered her up more, honest labor of any kind would be scarce. Still, after Khalidorans, being a rent girl for Cenarians might not be too bad.

There was a knock on the door and all the girls tensed. It wasn't the signal knock. No one moved. Daydra picked up a poker from the fireplace.

The knock sounded again. "Please," a man's voice said. "I mean no harm. I'm unarmed. Please, let me in."

Kaldrosa's heart leapt into her throat. She went to the door in a fog.

"What are you doing?" Daydra whispered.

Kaldrosa opened the peep window, and there he was. Tomman saw her and his face lit up. "You're alive! Oh gods, Kaldrosa, I thought you might be dead. What's wrong? Let me in."

The latch seemed to lift itself. Kaldrosa was helpless. The door burst open and Tomman swept her into his arms.

"Oh, Kally," he said, still delirious with joy. Tomman had always been a little slow. "I didn't know if—"

He only noticed the other women gathered around the room then, their expressions either joy or jealousy. Though he was hugging her and she couldn't see his face, Kaldrosa knew that he must be blinking stupidly at the sight of so many beautiful, exotic women all at the same time, and all of them scarcely wearing anything. Even Daydra's virginal dress breathed sensuality. His hug was slowly stiffening, and Kaldrosa was limp in his arms.

Tomman stepped back and looked at her. His hands flopped off of her shoulders like a fish onto the deck, spastically.

It really was a beautiful costume. Kaldrosa had always hated her skinny figure; she thought she looked like a boy. Wearing this, she didn't feel scrawny or boyish; she felt trim, nubile. The open-fronted shirt not only showed that she was tanned to the waist, but also conspired to give her cleavage and expose half of each breast. The scandalous trousers fit like a glove.

In short, it was exactly the kind of thing Tomman would have loved to see Kaldrosa wearing in their home—for the brief interludes that extended between when she surprised him with it and when he caught her after chasing her around the house.

But this wasn't their home, and these clothes weren't for Tomman. His eyes filled with grief. He looked away.

The girls went very quiet.

After an aching moment, he said, "You're beautiful." He choked and tears cascaded down his face.

"Tomman…" She was crying too, trying to cover herself with her arms. It was a bitter irony. She was trying to cover herself from her husband's eyes, when she had flaunted herself for strangers she despised.

"How many men have you been with?" he asked, his voice cracking.

"They would have killed you—"

"So now I'm not man enough?" he snapped. He wasn't crying now. He'd always been brave, fierce. It was one of the things she loved about him. He would have died to save her from this. He'd never realized he would have died and then she'd have had to do this anyway.

"They hurt me," she said.

"How many?" His voice was hard, brittle.

"I don't know." Part of her knew that he was like a dog crazed with pain, snapping at its master. But the disgust on his face was too much. She was disgusting. She surrendered to the deadness and despair. "A lot. Nine or ten a day."

His face twisted and he turned away.

"Tomman, don't leave me. Please."

He stopped, but he didn't turn. Then he walked out.

As the door swung gently shut, she began keening. The other girls went to her, their hearts broken anew as her grief mirrored theirs. Knowing she would not be comforted, they went to her because she had no one else who would, and neither did they.

56

Momma K stepped into the physickers' shop as Kylar swept the sword up into his hand, but she was too late to stop him.

Vi didn't move. She knelt motionless, her shiny red hair pulled out of the sword's path to her neck. The sword descended—and bounced off. The shock of the collision rang the sword like a bell. The sword whisked out of Kylar's nerveless grip.

"You will not do murder in my shop," Drissa Nile said. Her voice carried such power, and her eyes such fire, that her diminutive frame might as well have been a giant's. Even though Kylar had to look down to meet her eyes, he was intimidated. "We've accomplished an excellent piece of healing with this woman, and I'll not have you spoil it," Drissa said.

"You healed her?" Kylar asked.

Vi still hadn't moved. She faced the floor.

"From compulsion," Momma K said. "Am I right?"

"How did you know that?" Tevor asked.

"If it happens in my city, I know," Momma K said. She turned to Kylar. "The Godking bound her with a magic that forced her to obey direct orders."

"How convenient," Kylar said. His face contorted as he crushed the tears that were rising. "I don't care. She killed Jarl. I mopped up his blood. I buried him."

Momma K touched Kylar's arm. "Kylar, Vi and Jarl practically grew up together. Jarl protected her. They were friends, Kylar. The kind of friends that never forget. I don't believe anything less than magic could have compelled her to hurt him. Isn't that right, Vi?" Momma K put her hand under Vi's chin and brought her face up.

Tears streamed down Vi's face in mute testimony.

"What did Durzo teach you, Kylar?" Momma K asked. "A wetboy is a knife. Is the guilt the knife's or the hand's?"

"Both, and damn Durzo for his lies."

There was a knife on Kylar's belt, but he'd already tested its edge. Sister Drissa had blunted it, as he had guessed she might. But she didn't know about the blades up his sleeves. Nor could she stop the weapons that were his hands.

Vi saw the look in his eyes. She was a wetboy. She knew. He could get a knife out and across her throat in the time it took Drissa to blink. Let the healer try to cure death. Vi's eyes were black with guilt, a mishmash of dark images he couldn't comprehend. A short rush of black figures passed through his mind's eye. Her victims?

~She's murdered fewer people than you have.~

The thought hit him like a shot in the solar plexus. Some guilt. Some judge.

And the look on her face was all readiness above the tears. There was no self-pity, no avoidance of responsibility. Her eyes spoke for her: *I killed Jarl; I deserve to die. If you kill me, I won't blame you.*

"Before you decide, you have to know there's more," Vi said. "You were a secondary target. After.... After Jarl, I couldn't do it—"

"Well, that's commendable," Momma K said.

"—so I kidnapped Uly, to make sure you'd follow me."

"You what?" Kylar said.

"I figured you'd follow me back to Cenaria. The Godking wants you alive. But Sister Ariel captured me and Uly. When we found you, I thought you were dead. I thought I was free, so I escaped Sister Ariel and came here."

"Where's Uly?"

"On her way to the Chantry. Uly's Talented. She's going to be a maja."

It was horrifying and yet perfect.

Uly would be a Sister. She'd be taken care of, educated. Kylar had imposed Uly on Elene. Elene hadn't chosen to have a daughter who was more the age of a little sister. It wasn't a burden that had been fair for Kylar to ask her to assume. This way, and with the fortune that Kylar had left her, Elene would be free to have her own life again. It was all logical.

He had a niggling doubt that he wasn't thinking the way Elene would think, he could do nothing about that. Finding out that the damage had been minimized—hadn't it?—eased his mind.

A sudden fire lit in Momma K's eyes at the thought of her daughter being taken to the Chantry, but Kylar couldn't tell whether she was upset that her daughter had been taken or pleased that her daughter would certainly become a woman of consequence. Either way, Momma K quickly smothered it. She wasn't about to let strangers know Uly was her daughter.

If he got through this, Kylar would go to the Chantry and see Uly. He wasn't angry that they'd taken her from Vi. If anything, he owed them. And for a girl who was Talented, going to the Chantry wasn't really optional. It was supposed to be dangerous for a child to learn on her own. But if Uly didn't want to stay and they tried to keep her, Kylar would tear down the White Seraph around the Sisters' ears.

But just thinking about Uly made him think about Elene, and thinking about Elene threw his emotions into turmoil, so Kylar asked, "Why are you so eager to save Vi?" Momma K never worked on just one level.

"Because," Momma K said, "if you're going to kill the Godking, you'll need Vi's help."

Say one thing for Curoch: the mages are wrong. It wasn't in the form of a sword for purely symbolic reasons. The son of a bitch could cut.

It was a good thing, too. The sa'ceurai were implacable. They were called *sa'ceurai,* Old Jaeran for "sword lords," for good reason.

Nonetheless, Feir was a Blade Master of the Second Echelon. The first clash left three of the Ceuran warriors dead and gave Feir a short, tough pony.

Soon, Feir's height and weight proved a liability again. The pony tired and slowed. In the darkness, Feir let it go. Unfortunately, the little warhorse was trained too well. It stopped and waited for its rider the moment it was released. Feir solved that problem tying a small weave of magic under its saddle that randomly prickled. It would keep the beast running for hours. If he were lucky, the sa'ceurai would lose his trail and follow the horse.

He was lucky. It bought him a number of hours—hours on foot. It brought him to the crest of the mountain. He had cut a sapling before he'd hiked above the tree line, and now he was working on the wood with Curoch. The sword had an edge like he couldn't believe, but it wasn't a plane, or a chisel. Right now, he needed both and a few other tools besides.

Dorian once told him about a sport the more suicidal highland tribes practiced. They called it *schluss*. It consisted of strapping small sleds to one's feet and going downhill at incredible speeds. Standing. Dorian contended that they could steer, but Feir hadn't figured out how. All he knew was that he had to go faster than the Ceurans pursuing him, and there was no way he could build a full sled in the time he had.

What he couldn't accomplish with the blade, he accomplished with magic: he was a Maker, after all. Wood chips flew as the sun rose.

But he had skylined himself like a fool, standing right at the edge of the mountain so that his figure was clearly visible for miles. The sa'ceurai saw him before he saw them. They had dismounted and were walking on top of the snow with broad woven bamboo shoes strapped to their feet. The gait they had to assume to keep from tripping over the snowshoes was comical—until Feir realized how fast it let them travel. They would cover in a few minutes what had taken Feir half an hour lumbering through the snow.

He worked faster. He almost forgot to turn up the front tip of each long, narrow sled. He shook his head. He'd caught that mistake, what else had he missed? He didn't have time to fashion proper fasteners, so he wove a web of magic around his shoes and feet and bound them directly to the wood planks. He stood—

—and immediately caught an edge and fell.

Damn, why'd I square the edges? He should have left them curving like a boat's hull.

Standing was embarrassingly difficult. Feir cursed as the Ceurans came closer. He was a Second Echelon Blade Master—and he was this clumsy? This was madness. He should have just run downhill.

He rolled over onto his butt and finally used the length of the planks to lever himself into a squat. He stood and tried to step forward. The schlusses, which he had smoothed and polished, did exactly what they were supposed to do: they slid back and forth, and Feir barely moved.

Feir looked over his shoulder. The sa'ceurai were a bare hundred paces back now. If it came to a fight, the schlusses would doom him. He stumbled, caught an edge, and threw his foot to the side to catch himself. He staggered—and slid forward.

The joy was as great as he'd felt when he'd been named a Maker in the Brotherhood. He turned each schluss outward and pushed forward.

It worked until he got to the edge and started moving downhill faster than he could step. Each schluss went the way he had pointed it: out. His legs stretched until they could stretch no more and he pitched forward on his face.

The mountain was steep and the snow mercifully deep. Air was scarce as Feir flipped over and over through the powder. He was dimly aware that he needed to point the schlusses downhill. After six or seven rolls, it happened.

Suddenly Feir burst out of the omnipresent snow. The snow was at least three feet deep, but he was on top of it.

His heart was a thunder in his chest. He was headed straight downhill at incredible speed. In moments he was going faster than the fastest horse, and then faster and faster still. Controlling the two schlusses independently was almost impossible, so he quickly lashed them together with magic, both front and back, giving each a little leeway.

There were more crashes, and sometimes the snow wasn't as forgiving. Finally, Feir learned how to steer. He steered around a rocky death and looked downhill for the first time, squinting against the white. He blinked. *What is that line in the snow?*

He shot over the precipice. For two seconds, there was no schluss of sleds on snow. The world was silent except for the blast of wind in his ears.

Then he landed. He crashed through a world of white powder, flipping, arms and legs pulled every which way. Then the miracle happened again and he popped out of the snow to fly downhill once more. His heart hammered. He laughed.

He had Curoch. He was safe. The Ceurans wouldn't follow him down the mountain. Doing so would put them in Cenaria. He'd escaped!

"Incredible," Lantano Garuwashi said. He was a big man for a Ceuran. His red hair hung thick and long with dozens of narrow sections of differently colored hair bound in. In Ceura, it was said that you could read a man's life in his hair. At a boy's clan initiation, his head was shaved bald except for one forelock. When the forelock had grown the length of three fingers, it was bound with a tiny ring and the boy declared a man. When he killed his first warrior, the forelock was bound again at the scalp and he became sa'ceurai. The shorter the span between the two rings on their forelocks, the better. Thereafter, when the sa'ceurai killed an enemy, he bound the slain man's forelock to his own hair.

At first, a few warriors had thought Lantano only had one ring, because his first two were right on top of each other. He killed his first opponent at thirteen. In the seventeen years since, he'd added fifty-nine locks to his own hair. Had he been born a little higher, all of Ceura would have followed him. But a sa'ceurai's soul was his sword, and nothing could change that Lantano had been born with an iron sword, a peasant sword. Lantano was a warlord because Ceuran tradition allowed any man of excellence to lead armies, but for Lantano it had become a trap. As soon as he stopped fighting, his power ended. He'd begun fighting for Ceura's regent, Hideo Watanabe. Then, when the regent ordered him to disband, he became a mercenary instead. Desperate men flocked to his banners for one reason: he never lost.

The giant was becoming a speck in the distance.

"War Master, do you wish us follow?" a stump of a man with a score of locks tied in his balding hair asked.

"We'll try the caves," Lantano said.

"Into Cenaria?"

"Just a hundred sa'ceurai. It'll be a cold winter. Killing this giant will give us a tale to keep us warm."

57

Momma K wanted Agon and his army to take Logan to the rebel camp. If he were to be king, he needed an army. Kylar refused to leave his friend, at least until Logan was conscious. When Kylar fainted, Agon asked Momma K if they should load Logan into the wagon. Momma K cursed and railed but said no.

They never asked Vi's opinion. She was content. She wanted to atone for what she'd done, but she didn't want to think.

Even as she sat with Kylar and Momma K and Agon, a part of her urged her to kill them. The Godking rewarded those who served him well. She could wipe out all the greatest threats to the Godking's rule in one minute.

She didn't obey that thought. She'd been judged innocent. She'd come completely clean.

Almost. She'd realized only lately that perhaps the most damaging thing she'd done to Kylar was something that had seemed trivial at the time, a small gesture of contempt. She'd pocketed the note and pair of earrings Kylar had left for Elene.

It was only today that she'd learned they were wedding rings. Drissa and Tevor had explained the custom at length. Between taking those and the note, Vi had left Elene with nothing.

She hadn't been brave enough to tell Kylar about that, had she?

It was just too much truth. She could have accepted Kylar killing her, but she didn't know what to do if Kylar despised her. If he knew her, he would despise her. There was no way love could overcome so much.

Love? What am I thinking? Limit yourself to fighting and fucking, Vi. You're good at those.

The door to a patient room opened and Kylar came in. Logan stepped in from another.

For the first time, Vi saw Kylar smile. It did something strange inside her when he smiled like that—and he wasn't even looking at her. He bowed deeply. "Your Majesty," Kylar said.

"My friend," Logan said. He was achingly thin, his bones poking at his skin. Despite that, he had an unmistakable aura of rallying health. Dressed richly once more, he was handsome despite his ordeal. He crossed the distance quickly and hugged Kylar.

"I'm sorry," Kylar said. "I came too late that night. I found blood and I thought...I'm so sorry."

Logan squeezed Kylar silently, heaving great breaths until the emotions died down. Finally, he stepped back and held onto Kylar's shoulders.

"You've done so well, my friend. I'm the one who's sorry. I'm sorry I ever doubted you. Someday soon we will have to talk. You—you did some things down there that..." Logan looked around, aware of the others. "That I'm really curious about. And I seem to have some holes in my memory, like how I got this."

He pulled back his sleeve and Vi and Momma K gasped. Sunken into his arm was something like a glowing silvery-green tattoo. He didn't show the whole thing, but to Vi the lines looked stylized and abstract, not random.

"Your Majesty," Drissa Nile said. "I would be...very cautious about showing that."

"I'm sorry to press you," Momma K said, "but we have to make some decisions."

"You mean I have to make some decisions," Logan said, his tone whimsical.

"Yes, Your Majesty, pardon me."

Logan addressed Kylar first. "You have done us greater service than we could demand or hope for. I won't order you, but we deem it most mete for..." He got a faraway look and let the sentence trail off.

"Sire?" Kylar asked.

Logan snapped back into the present. "Odd. I've been cursing with the worst of the Holers for months, and now I'm back to 'deeming' and judging what is 'mete.' " He shook his head and smirked ruefully. "Kylar, it comes down to this. If you can kill the Godking before our armies close for battle, we might avert battle altogether. I ask you to do this, but I won't order it. You've already made enormous sacrifices to save me. And I know that you don't trust this woman, but if she can help, use her help. Her surrender when she could have killed us is proof enough of her good intentions for me. Vi is as much a weapon as you are, and I can let none of the weapons in my small arsenal lie idle."

"You think that's the right thing to do?" Kylar asked.

Logan gave him a measured look. "Yes."

"Then it's done," Kylar said. "What are you going to do?"

"I'm going to ask Terah Graesin for my army. Then I'm going to take back our country."

"It won't be that simple," Momma K said.

Logan smiled a wan, distant smile. "It never is."

58

Elene woke with a blinding headache. She couldn't move her arms or legs; when she tried, her feet and hands tingled. Opening her eyes, she saw three other captives, bound hand and foot as she was. Another rope bound them to each other. They lay in the darkness, their forms lit only by the flickering light of the Khalidorans' fire. Elene lay nearest to the six Khalidorans, who were laughing and drinking, slipping between words Elene understood and what she guessed must be Khalidoran.

She didn't dare move too much and alert them, so all she could see of them was the young man who'd captured her. From the conversation, she picked up that his name was Ghorran. The others mocked him for getting hurt by some woman.

For a moment, the gravity of Elene's situation threatened to overwhelm her. Kylar didn't know she was here. No one knew she was here. No one was going to come save her. These men could do anything they wanted to her, and there was nothing she could do to stop them. Her chest tightened with fear and she couldn't think, couldn't breathe.

Then she started praying, reminding herself that the God knew she was here. It was a small thing for the God to save her. Eventually, she calmed. By that time, several of the soldiers had gone to their blankets to sleep, leaving Ghorran and someone she couldn't see talking in hushed tones.

"I don't think Vürdmeister Dada has even told His Holiness what we're doing," Ghorran said. "There's a reason Black Barrow is forbidden ground. If His Holiness finds out, what happens to us?"

"Neph Dada is a great man, and most zealous in his service of Khali. If he serves her, and His Holiness does not, whose side would you rather be on?" the other asked.

"I heard he wants to raise a Titan, is that what you're saying?"

The other man laughed quietly. "The Vürdmeister wants to do a hundred things. Of course he wants a Titan, but that isn't why he needs untouched young women, is it?"

"Khalivos ras en me," Ghorran said, awed. "Khali come live in me."

"Indeed."

"Is it possible?"

"The Vürdmeister thinks so."

Ghorran breathed a curse. "Then what about the boy? What's he for?"

"Mm, not that important. They'll kill him and see what they can raise from his body. The meisters just want the corpse fresh."

Elene had heard of Black Barrow; it was an ancient, dead battlefield. It was said nothing grew there to this day. But she couldn't understand any of the rest of it, except that Vürdmeister Neph Dada had something planned for her that was worse than slavery. She lay her head back down and saw that the captive nearest her was awake. He was a young boy. He looked terrified.

59

$\mathcal{M}$omma K had saved Logan's life today.

His little army, consisting of Lord General Agon, Momma K, and Agon's Dogs, was riding into the rebel camp to cheers. It would have been much different if Momma K hadn't planted rumors that Logan was returning after triumphing over the worst horrors of the Maw. Without the rumors as forerunners, the band would have been greeted as an unknown army, and Terah Graesin could have had Logan killed. Doubtless, many tears would have been shed afterward about the terrible mistake.

The old, naive Logan wouldn't have believed that Terah Graesin would do such a thing. Logan the Holer knew differently. He was a changed man, quieter, sobered. He knew all too well what people would do when they were threatened.

And Terah Graesin had to see Logan as a threat. She'd rallied support for the last three months. She'd survived assassination attempts and lost family members. She'd assembled an army and had brought it to the eve of battle. All to be queen.

Logan's appearance threatened to make her ambition implode on the eve of her triumph. His legitimacy was unquestionable: he'd come from the nation's leading family, he'd been declared the Gunder's heir, and he'd married into the Gunder family. Numerous families had sworn fealty to Terah Graesin only because they had thought they were free of their earlier oaths to the Gyres.

Any other time, Logan would have gone to Havermere and sent missives to all the families in the realm, including the Graesins. He would have given Terah a chance to see her coalition falling apart, and then offered her a suitable position.

This wasn't any other time. The rebel army was assembled less than a mile from the Godking's. The Cenarians outnumbered the Khalidoran army two to one. The Khalidorans had meisters and Vürdmeisters, but it still looked like a sure victory.

To Logan, Agon, and Momma K, it looked like a Cenarian massacre in the offing. So here he was, riding at the head of his tiny army of a hundred into the heart of the rebel camp.

He was lucky it was an overcast day, because after three months in the Hole, his eyes couldn't handle full daylight. Squinting didn't lend itself to a particularly regal look.

They were nearing the cluster of the nobles' pavilions when a group of a dozen horsemen rode out to meet them. They were led by an officer carrying an unstrung Alitaeran longbow like a staff. Logan and his army came to a stop.

"Declare yourself," Sergeant Gamble said.

"This," Agon said loudly enough for the man and the bystanders to hear, "is King Logan Gyre, by law and tradition heir to the throne and now king of our great land. The king is dead, long live the king."

It was a declaration of war, and the word would blaze through the camp within minutes. Momma K had already sent word to Logan's steward, and the Gyre men-at-arms were already positioned nearest the noble pavilions. They cheered.

"The queen will see you now, my lord," Sergeant Gamble said.

Logan dismounted in front of Terah Graesin's pavilion. When Momma K and Agon Brant made to follow him, the guards stopped them. "Only you, sir," one of them said.

Logan stared at the man. He said nothing. For a moment, he let the beast rise within. He had not lived through hell to be stopped by a guard. The feeling flew past determination to rage. He felt his forearm tingle.

The guard stepped back and swallowed. "My lord," he said weakly, "only nobles are—"

Logan stared at him and the words dried up. Momma K and Agon followed him inside.

The queen's pavilion was huge. Tables and maps and nobles were scattered liberally around the interior. Some of the men looked positively comical, their fat squashed into armor they hadn't donned in twenty years. Black and white tiles sat in two bowls on one of the tables. *By the gods, they're voting on their battle plan.* Beside Momma K, Brant Agon made a strangled sound of outrage.

Momma K was looking around the room as quickly as she could, counting allies, potential allies, and sure enemies. She knew she could give Logan a crown if he gave her two weeks to work her special brand of truth. With only one day until a major battle against the one enemy everyone hated, the odds changed drastically. Her only hope was that someone disposable would attack her or Logan or Brant Agon first. Then she could ruin him, and making an implacable foe of him wouldn't hurt Logan too much.

"Why Logan Gyre, how the mighty have fallen," Terah Graesin said, emerging from behind several taller lords, sashaying across the luxurious rugs. "Who would have expected you to appear in the company of whores and has-beens? Or is it cripples and cunts?"

The nobles snickered.

"Looking to get into the business?" Momma K asked.

You could have heard a feather drop in the sudden silence. Momma K couldn't care less about their shock. Terah Graesin had greeted Logan with claws out. That wasn't good.

A young man pushed forward from the crowd. "If you speak like that again, I'll kill you myself," Luc Graesin said. He was Terah's brother, seventeen years old, handsome, and a damned fool.

Oh, Luc, you have no idea. I know your secret. I could end you right now.

Except that she couldn't. Here, now, wild truths delivered without prelude wouldn't be believed. Terah Graesin would only dig in her heels. "Pardon me," Momma K said, "Titles are switching hands so fast recently, I'd forgotten I was speaking to a duchess."

"Queen!" Luc said. "Your queen!"

Momma K lifted her eyebrows as if he were trying to put one over on her. A little reminder to everyone how far and how fast Terah Graesin was attempting to rise. "But here stands the rightful king," Momma K said. "Designated heir by King Gunder IX and received by common acclamation. The man to whom you've already pledged fealty." But she knew she'd already lost. She saw it in the defiance, the absolute hatred, in Terah Graesin's face.

"That's enough, Gwinvere," Logan said.

She smiled her acquiescence. She stepped back, her head down, abruptly meek.

"May I remind everyone," a voice near the maps said, "that tomorrow we face the Godking and his wytches?" It was Count Drake, ever the peacemaker.

"We need no reminders," Terah Graesin said. "We have our army, we have our battlefield, we have the advantage, and in a few more moments, we'll have our battle plan."

"No," Agon said.

"Excuse me?" Terah asked, indignant.

"You have His Majesty's army," Agon said. "My lords, many of you were there at the feast before the coup. Garret Urwer, your father died beside me in the north tower. As did your uncle, Bran Braeton. They died going to save our king, Logan Gyre. You were there—"

"Enough!" Terah Graesin cried. "We know what the mad king said."

So the king had been insane when he'd designated Logan his heir. It wasn't a perfect line of attack, but it was good enough. Given time, Momma K would have reminded everyone of the timing of the coup, of the irrelevance of the king's sanity to the legality of his decrees, and of Logan's marriage to Jenine. Given time, Momma K could have orchestrated pressure from all sides to get Terah to surrender her claim. Now all that was immaterial. She simply had to wait for the inevitable.

"My lady," Duke Havrin Wesseros said, "they say only what would be said in backrooms and great rooms throughout the kingdom if there were time. It seems to me that we all have decisions to make now, and little time in which to make them."

"I won't hear their lies," Terah hissed.

"Don't you see?" Duke Wesseros said. "If you won't hear them out, Logan will leave, and he won't leave alone. He'll take half of our army with him, maybe more. Does anyone fancy taking on the Khalidorans with half an army?"

Closer. But you're worried about the wrong person leaving.

Agon said, "As you say, the king was mad when he died. The Sa'kagé poisoned him at the feast."

"Poisoned? You murdered him, Brant!" Garret Urwer cried out.

"Yes, I killed him," Agon said. "I won't justify that deed now. What's important is that Khalidor wished to wipe out the royal family to cause exactly this. They wished to split any resistance before it could begin. King Gunder saw that coming, which is why—not the night of the coup, when he was poisoned, but earlier in the day—he married his daughter Jenine to Logan. Many of you have sworn oaths to Lady Graesin. But your fealty was already owed to Logan Gyre. Thus, you're released from your oaths to the duchess."

"I release none of you!" Terah Graesin shrilled.

Pandemonium broke out. Nobles were screaming at each other, gathering in clumps to talk with their advisers and the lords closest to them, some pressing toward Terah Graesin, others pressing toward Logan. Logan watched it all, impassive. He understood, too.

"Hold on," Duke Wesseros said. He looked a lot like his sister Nalia, the last queen. He'd been out of the city checking on lands the Lae'knaught had seized in eastern Cenaria when the coup had occurred. He raised his hands and gradually the nobles quieted. "The hour grows late, and an army waits for us," Duke Wesseros said. "Stand to the side of the man or the woman you would have rule us."

"Why don't you vote with the stones instead, that people may vote for who they truly wish to lead?" Momma K said. Inwardly, she cursed. She should have let one of the other lords suggest it, but Wesseros had brought up voting so quickly that Momma K hadn't had the chance. All the talk was worth nothing if they didn't have a blind vote.

"Tomorrow we must stand on the field of battle. I think today we have the courage to stand in a tent," Terah Graesin said. Clever bitch.

Silence fell again, and then people started moving.

Momma K had been depressingly accurate in her estimations of who would end up where. For the most part, the minor nobles looked like they would prefer to go to Logan but didn't dare defy their lords, which was why Momma K had wanted the blind vote. Terah had concentrated her bribes on the powerful.

As it was, they had a three-way split. Logan, Terah, and undecided.

"As I suspected," Duke Wesseros said. He led the undecided camp. "The rhetoric has done nothing. With the assassinations of the Gunders, only three great families are left in our country, and here we stand. It seems to me that there is a golden mean, a middle way. Logan Gyre, Terah Graesin, with the fate of all your countrymen at stake, will you put aside your own selfish ambitions?" The buffoon. The idiot. The pox-ridden windbag. He thought he was being smart. If the duke hadn't created a third camp, Logan at least would have had a majority. They would still have had a chance.

"What are you talking about?" Terah asked.

Logan already knew. Momma K could see it in his stony face.

"This night, on the eve of a battle that will determine the future of our land, will you split our forces, or will you join them? Logan, Terah, will you marry tonight?"

Terah looked around the room quickly, judging who stood with her. Her support was eroding. She looked at those who stood defiant on Logan's side, those who stood passive with Duke Wesseros. Then she looked at Logan. It wasn't the look a woman gives a suitor. It was a probe for weakness.

"For the country I love, yes," Terah Graesin said.

"Logan?"

"Yes," Logan said woodenly. Gods help him.

60

They had erected a platform so the entire army could see the wedding. Men had already gathered from their fires, and their officers were beginning to organize them into ranks for the ceremony as the moon rose. Besides the army, several thousand commoners and camp followers had crowded around the platform.

"Logan," Count Drake said, closing the flap of the little tent where Logan was getting ready, "You can't do this."

For a long moment, Logan didn't answer. When it emerged, his voice was low and stern, "What else can I do?"

"The One God says he will provide an escape from every temptation."

"I don't believe in your god, Drake."

"Truth doesn't depend on your belief in it."

Logan shook his head slowly, like a bear emerging emaciated after months of hibernation. "Marrying Terah is no temptation. My father married a beautiful, poisonous woman and I saw what it did to him."

"A lesson you would do well to heed. The difference being that your mother wasn't capable of nearly as much destruction."

Logan's eyes flashed, the bear slowly raising his head to tower above all others. "If there's a way out that doesn't destroy us, you tell me what it is! I don't want to marry—"

"I didn't say marriage was the temptation."

"Then what is?"

"Power," Count Drake said, thumping his cane.

"Damn it, man! It's marry her or doom us all. You think I haven't figured out a way to get the majority of these people to follow me? I have! I could take maybe two-thirds of them and leave. That would leave a third to die. You want me to ask thousands to die so I can avoid a bad marriage?

"No, Logan." Count Drake leaned on his cane. He looked like he needed its support. "My question is, can you be the king that you need to be with such a queen beside you? Terah Graesin was caught off guard today. You caught her in a moment of weakness. That won't happen again."

"Well, thank for you illustrating the bleakness of my future," Logan said. "But if you can't help me escape it, help me get dressed."

"My king," Count Drake said, "sometimes the way out of a hole isn't climbing."

"Get out," Logan said.

Count Drake bowed and left sadly.

Logan lifted the circlet and put it on his head. Momma K had seen to it that he looked a king. He had been shaved, his hair cut, his body anointed with oils and adorned with furs. He was dressed in a fine dark gray tunic and cloak trimmed with white samite. He'd reached the age of majority immediately before the coup, but he'd forgotten to choose his own sigil. Now he saw that Momma K had chosen one for him. It incorporated the Gyre's white gyrfalcon on a field sable, but his falcon wore broken chains on its feet, and the sable field was a black circle reminiscent of the Hole. The gyrfalcon's wings were spread. It was a worthy sigil. His father would have been proud.

What would you do, father? As a young man, his father had married to save the family. With the benefit of hindsight, would he have done it again?

The tent flap opened and Momma K stepped inside. She looked at him with a shallow but genuine compassion. She couldn't understand. She'd never loved as Logan had loved. To her, it must look like this was the obvious choice. Marry Terah, deal with the problems later. In his position, Momma K would scheme and manipulate and have Terah killed if it came it to it.

"It's time," she said.

"The sigil is perfect," Logan said. "Thank you."

"Did you notice the wings?" she asked. "The wingtips extend beyond the circle, Your Majesty. The gyrfalcon will always fly free."

Together, they walked up onto the platform. It was a circle almost the same size as the Hole. It was a circle to symbolize the perfect, eternal, unbreakable nature of marriage. As Logan climbed, with thousands of eyes turned on him, to take his place right at the center, where the fall to death had been, his heart lurched. He felt sick, claustrophobic. He remembered stretching over the Hole, stretching as far as he could. For what? For pissed-on bread he wouldn't give to an animal.

Music began playing and his pissed-on bread stepped up daintily onto the platform.

Part of Logan was ravenous for her, as he had been ravenous in the Hole. For the past three months, he'd been so weak, so starved, so preoccupied with surviving that he'd barely spared a thought for sex. Before the Hole, it seemed he'd barely spared a thought for anything else. Now that he was out and regaining his strength, that old Logan was coming back. Terah Graesin was tall and lithe, her curves almost boyish, but her smile was all woman. She moved like a woman who knew what men liked and knew that she had it. The starving, greedy part of Logan wanted to fuck her.

And pissed-on bread always looked so good, until you tasted it. But at least it filled you up, no matter how you felt about it afterward. At least he'd have sex. By all the gods; at twenty-one, he was still a fucking virgin!

The irony of the thought made him smile grimly. Terah saw the smile and smiled back. She did look fantastic. Her hair was teased up into—well, something fancy. Logan wondered how many tailors had been cursing at each other for the last two hours as they'd somehow altered one of her dresses into a wedding dress. It was the traditional green of fertility and new life, slim cut to Terah's slim body, with ornate groom ties up the back, and a long expanse of leg exposed that was certainly not traditional but welcome nonetheless. It was completed with a stylish veil symbolizing chastity that worked perfectly with the dress, if not so well with the woman in it.

Well, I'll have as much sex as I want, if her reputation is at all deserved. The thought sloshed in his stomach like warm piss. No, better not to think about her reputation.

Whatever he felt, Terah Graesin somehow pulled off what he had thought was impossible. She was sexy and regal at the same time—to her it was all power, whether it came from her status or her personality or her body. They were all tools to impose her will.

Power. Count Drake said the temptation was power.

Terah came to stand beside him and took his hand shyly. The people cheered. It was just like Jenine Gunder had taken his hand when her father had announced their marriage. Logan swallowed his rising gorge. For Jenine, it had been a spontaneous act. Terah had been at that dinner. She'd seen what Jenine had done and how people had approved. She was imitating Jenine deliberately.

"Relax," Terah said. "You're five minutes away from everything you ever wanted."

You're a fool if you believe that, Terah. Logan painted a smile on his face and willed his body to relax. No, it wasn't what he would have chosen, but he would be able to change everything. He could defeat King Ursuul. He could root out the Sa'kagé. He could abolish the poor laws. He could . . .

That was it. That was what Count Drake meant. That was the temptation of power. He'd turned his ambition in his own mind. *It isn't for me, he'd* told himself, it's for the people. But that wasn't altogether true, was it? He'd liked ordering Gorkhy's death; he'd liked dismissing the count: Logan spoke and things happened. People obeyed. He'd been so powerless for so long in the Hole that the idea of never being subject to anyone was honey on his tongue.

Fine, Count Drake, I understand. Now where's the way out?

It was too late. On one side stood a hecatonarch in his rich cloak—a hundred colors for the hundred gods. On the other stood a man in simple brown robes, a patr of the One God. Duke Wesseros took his place in the middle. Terah had made sure that their marriage would be performed in triplicate. The cheering crescendoed as fifteen thousand people shouted themselves hoarse for the couple they thought would save them.

"May I address the people?" Logan asked.

"Absolutely not," Terah said. "What kind of a ploy is this?"

"It's not a ploy. I just wish to speak to those who will bleed and die for us. I haven't had the chance to do that."

"You're going to set them against me," Terah said.

"How about," Duke Wesseros said, "how about Logan swears not to say anything negative about you? And if he does, I'll step in and stop him? Is that acceptable, my lord?"

"Yes."

"My lady?" Duke Wesseros said, "He is their king."

"Make it quick."

"Logan, five minutes," Duke Wesseros said. He stepped close and lowered his voice. "And may the spirit Timaeus Rindder inspire you."

It was a contingent declaration of support. Timaeus Rindder had been an orator of such skill he'd turned a chariot race loss into a coup, though he had been bound by exactly the restrictions that Duke Wesseros had put on Logan. In framing the rules the way he had, Duke Wesseros was saying, "If you can get the people on your side, I'll come, too."

"My friends, tomorrow we will stand together in the clash and roar of battle." Logan had barely spoken the first sentence when his words were doubled and redoubled in volume. He paused, then saw Master Nile standing near the front, smiling. Logan pretended that it wasn't important, and in a moment, everyone else did, too. "Tomorrow, we will face a foe whose face we know. You have seen his face darkening your doors. You have seen his boots muddying your floors. You have seen his torches setting fire to your fields. You've felt his fists and whips and scorn, but you refused to yield!"

Logan's nerves and self-criticism—*Could I have said that better? Is my voice steady? Why is it so hard to get a full breath?*—faded as he looked at the upturned faces of the people who would be his people. He'd had no idea just a few months ago who the Cenarian people were. He'd known and loved the Gyre's smallfolk, but had shared the noblemen's fashionable disdain for the unwashed masses. How easy it was to ask a nameless, faceless mob to die.

"My friends, I spent the last three months in the depths of Hell's Asshole. I was trapped with the shit and the stink of humanity. I spent my time fearing death and things worse than death. They took my clothes. They took my dignity. I saw the good suffer with the evil. I saw a woman violated and a woman kill herself so she wouldn't be violated again. I saw good men and bad make their deals with the darkness. And I made my own. To survive.

"My friends, I was imprisoned beneath the ground. You were imprisoned above it. You knew the fears I knew. You saw the horrors I saw, and worse. We had friends killed. We knew that to resist was to die...and my friends, my people, we looked at the odds against us and we saw no hope. We fled. We hid." Logan paused, and the people were silent.

"Were you there with me?" Logan asked. "Did you feel rage? Did you feel powerless? Did you watch evil and do nothing to oppose it? Were you ashamed?"

The men and women didn't look to the left or the right, afraid that their neighbors would see the tears in their eyes. Their heads nodded, yes, yes.

"I was ashamed," Logan said. "Let me tell you what I learned in the Hole. I learned that in suffering, we find the true measure of our strength. I learned that a man can be a coward one day and a hero the next. I learned that I'm not as good a man as I thought I was. But the most important thing is this: I learned that though it costs me dearly, I can change. I learned that what has been broken can be made new. Do you know who taught me that? A prostitute. In a bitter woman who made her living in shame, I found honor, courage, and loyalty. She inspired me and she saved me.

"Today, there are women here who taught you the same lessons. Many of you are ashamed of your mothers and your wives and your daughters who were raped, who were pressed into sexual slavery at the castle, who sold themselves in brothels so they might survive. You've shunned them, rejected them.

"But I say your wives, mothers, and daughters have shown us how to fight. They gave us the Nocta Hemata. They have given us courage. They have shown us the road from shame to honor. Let every woman who fought that night stand forth!"

A few women stepped forward immediately. Bolstered by their courage, others emerged. Men moved aside silently. In moments, a crowd of three hundred women gathered in front of the platform. Some let tears fall, but their backs were straight, their chins high. Men in the ranks were openly weeping now. Not just the men who must have known this small sample, but men from the countryside, men who must have known their own women to be shamed and dishonored, men who were now ashamed of themselves.

"Today," Logan said. "I declare you the inaugural members of the Order of the Garter. A garter, because you have taken shame and turned it to honor. Display it with pride and tell your grandchildren of your courage forever. And no man shall ever join your order unless he displays the highest levels of heroism and courage."

The people cheered. It was the best thing Logan had ever done.

"I'm afraid," Logan said, quieting the crowd, "that your garters aren't ready yet. It seems we don't have all the materials on hand. You see, we're going to make them out of the Khalidoran battle flags."

They cheered.

"What do you say, men? You think we can help them out?"

They cheered louder.

"Now brothers, please, welcome your beloved. They need you. And sisters, welcome these shamed and broken men. They need you.

"There are just a few more things for me to say." Logan breathed deeply. He'd gone longer than he intended already. He hadn't established the Order of the Garter to gain support. It was just something that needed to be fixed. But somehow, wherever he looked, he saw faces full of hope.

"A few months ago, I didn't want to be king," Logan said, "but something changed me in the Hole. Before the Hole, I could see you as a mob. Now, I see you as brothers and sisters. I can ask you to bleed with me, to die with me, and I do. Many of us will bleed tomorrow, and some of us will die." He looked down at the Hole on which he stood. *Is this your way out, Count Drake? Oh, father, would this make you proud?* "I can ask you to bleed to throw off your chains, but I cannot ask you to bleed for my ambition."

The crowd quieted.

"In the Hole, I learned that a man or woman may wield power over life and death, but there is no power over love. My friends, I love you and this nation and the freedom we will win. But I feel no love for this woman. I will not marry Terah Graesin, not this day, not ever."

"What?" Terah Graesin yelled. She stepped forward. "Stop him, Havrin!"

But Duke Wesseros held her back and Master Nile didn't amplify her voice. "Terah," the duke said, "if you try to stop him now, it'll be civil war right here."

A roar was going through the crowd and men were looking at their neighbors, unsheathing their weapons, and trying to see who would join which side.

"STOP!" Logan cried, and his voice boomed over the assembly. He held his hands up. "I won't have a single man die to make me king, much less a thousand." He turned. "Lady Graesin, will you swear fealty to me?"

Her eyes flashed and this time Master Nile did amplify her voice. "Not if it cost a thousand thousand lives!"

Logan held his hands up to forestall the furor. "My friends, we have no hope of defeating Khalidor if we are not united. So," he turned to Terah Graesin, who looked less than beautiful with a rage-splotchy face, "grant me that you will establish the Order of the Garter and that you will pardon my followers of all crimes up to this day... grant me that, and I will swear fealty to you."

Terah Graesin hesitated only a moment. Her eyes were wide with disbelief, but she recovered before any cry could go up. "Done," she said. "Swear it now."

Logan knelt and reached toward the center of the platform where Terah stood. In the perfect inverse of a gyrfalcon stretching its wings beyond the black circle of submission and imprisonment, he reached his hand back in. It made all the difference.

Sometimes the only way out of the Hole isn't climbing. He touched her foot in the oath of submission.

"In recognition of your valor," Queen Graesin said in a tone that dripped poison. "You will have the honor of leading the first charge. Your honeyed words will doubtless impress the Vürdmeisters."

61

Kaldrosa Wyn stood with hundreds of women at the front of the crowd, all of them in various states of shock, disbelief, and tears. There were too many emotions to hold them all in. Usually Kaldrosa Wyn hated crying. Now, her tears were a relief.

She felt as if her heart had just tripled in size. Duke Gyre amazed her. Here was a man who set aside the greatest ambition in the world for love. He'd cracked the hard shell of bitterness she'd been growing around her heart. He'd turned them from whores to heroes. He was a saint, and that bitch was going to send him to his death.

Then the throng was around her and the other women, men pushing into the lines, looking for their spurned beloved. Next to Kaldrosa, Daydra was sobbing. A bear of a man pushed through the mob to get to her, and as she saw him, her cries crescendoed. He was an older man, her father, and his eyes were streaming, snot dribbling into his great bushy moustache. Before he could say a word, Daydra fainted. He caught her as she fell and lifted her into his arms as easily as a baby. Another couple embraced next to Kaldrosa, just squeezing, squeezing.

Kaldrosa tried not to hate these women for their joy. She did feel new, different, the mountain of shame sliding off her shoulders. But Tomman was surely back in Cenaria. Would he be so quick to forgive? Would she ever again get to lie in his arms after lovemaking, in that time when all things were made new?

The crowd was beginning to thin, and the women who'd not found their lost loves were clumping together. They looked at each other and they knew each other, even women who'd never met. They were sisters. But even then, they were not alone. The goodwives who'd listened to the speech from the back and had known that there would be girls left over had finally pushed their way through the ranks of men and—strangers all—they embraced and wept together.

Off to one side, Kaldrosa Wyn saw Momma K, watching. There were no tears in the great woman's eyes, but though her back was as straight as a rod, she looked like she wished there had been a man who pushed through the crowd for her. Kaldrosa was starting to walk toward her, marveling at her own bravery—go to comfort Momma K!—when she saw him.

He was wearing the uniform of one of General Agon's wytch hunters: a strange short bow in one hand, a quiver on his back and boiled leather armor over a dark green tunic piped with yellow. But as he scanned the crowd, her fierce, fiery Tomman looked scared. Then their eyes met.

Like a puppet with its strings cut, Tomman dropped to his knees. The bow fell in the mud, forgotten. His face contorted. He put his arms out, eyes welling with tears. It was a more abject apology than he would ever have found in words.

Kaldrosa ran to him.

*   *   *

"I feel like I've been here more than some of the people who live here," Kylar said.

"Quiet," Vi said.

When he'd come to get Logan, Kylar had taken a skiff barely big enough to hold them. Though small, the vessel had been incredibly fast, and he'd been able to evade the single boat that had patrolled Vos Island. Now three boats were on patrol, so they were going to cross to Vos Island the same way he had when he'd come to rescue Elene.

Following her lead, Kylar looped a knee over the rope and climbed hand over hand across the line as it dangled beneath the bridge. Vi's shot had been perfect, so they were able to pull the line much tighter than he had on his previous trip. When she passed the remains of his bolt stuck in the wood from his horrible shot four months ago, she stopped. "Legend, my butt," she mumbled.

Which brought Kylar's attention to her butt. Again. While the first word that popped into his mind wasn't *legendary,* Vi's butt was quite pert. Nicely round. Worthy of the stretchy-tight garb she wore. Unlike many athletic women, Vi had curves. Nice hips and awe-inspiring breasts.

Why am I thinking about Vi's breasts?

Kylar kept pulling himself hand over hand, scowling. This was a distraction he didn't need. He looked at Vi's butt again. Shook his head. Looked again. *Why am I attracted to her butt? How weird is that? Why do men like butts anyway?*

Vi reached the castle wall and let down a rope. She whispered something and shadows obscured her. It wasn't great, not nearly what Durzo had been capable of, much less Kylar. Her shadows were merely black, and obscured the recognizable humanity of her shape. Still, it was less conspicuous than a half-naked tart whose entire body shouted, "Look at me!"

Following her, Kylar slid down the rope quickly. They huddled in the shadow of a rock as the patrol boat passed.

"So, you haven't said anything about my grays."

Kylar raised an eyebrow. "What? Do you want me tell you if your trousers make your butt look big? They do. Happy?"

"So you have been looking at my butt. What do you think of the rest?"

"Are we really talking about this? Now?" Kylar glanced at her breasts again—and got caught.

"The haughty disdain thing will work better for you if you don't blush," Vi said.

"They're great," Kylar said. He coughed. "Your grays, that is. Not that your breasts—I mean style is perfect for you. Just over the line between sexy and obscene."

She refused to take offense. "First I take their attention, then I take their life."

"It looks cold." This time, he didn't look at her breasts. Barely—despite the small attention-getters standing at attention on top of her large attention-getters.

"I'm a woman. I don't get to pick clothes for comfort."

"I can't believe I'm having a conversation this long about clothes."

"You call this a long conversation about clothes?" Vi asked. "Haven't had many lovers, have you?"

"Just one. And not for long, thanks to you," Kylar said.

That shut her up. Thank the God.

He got up and started moving. They had to hide every time the patrol boat passed, Vi so she wouldn't be seen, and Kylar so Vi wouldn't know he could go invisible. Kylar had worn fairly tight clothes himself, an old pair of grays that Momma K had had fetched for him. The more anyone knew about the extent of his powers, the more vulnerable he was.

They reached the sunken gate to the Maw an hour after midnight. There was no one guarding it.

Kylar tried the latch. It wasn't locked. He looked at Vi. Obviously, he liked that as much as she did. Still, how could the Godking know they were coming? He moved to open the door when Vi touched his arm. She pointed to the rusty hinges, motioning for him to wait.

She touched each of the hinges in turn, murmuring, then nodded to him.

He tried the rusty door. It opened silently.

"Well, I'll be damned," Vi said. "So it doesn't just work on little girls."

Kylar eased the door shut and stared at her. "Why don't you try it on yourself?" he asked.

"I already did," she said. "Anyone further than five feet away can't hear me."

"That's not what I meant. Anyway, how can you be sure it works?"

"You didn't hear what I just called you."

"Which was?"

"True, but not clever enough to repeat."

He hesitated. "Vi, before we go in, I need to ask you something."

"Shoot."

"I got into wet work because of a child named Rat. He was Garoth Ursul's son, and it was to please Garoth that Rat cut up Elene's face and raped Jarl and tried to rape me."

"I didn't know," Vi said. "I'm sorry."

"It's not important," Kylar said gruffly. "I got away."

"I didn't," Vi said quietly. She sank into herself, into those years of nightmare. "For me it was my mother's lovers. She knew what they did, but she never stopped them. She always hated me for what I cost her. As if I was the one who fucked some stranger and got pregnant and made her run away. I don't know if she wanted me at first or if she was just too much of a coward to take ergot or tansy tea."

Vi knew it was a reasonable fear. A sufficient dose to induce an abortion was a hairsbreadth from a lethal dose. Every year, Hu claimed, thousands of girls who "took sick and died" had actually taken too much poison. Others took too little and bore maimed children.

"After she ran away, my mother had nothing to survive on but her looks. She was too proud to be a whore outright, so she attached herself to one bastard after another. She could never do what had to be done."

"And that's how you're different from her?"

"Yes," she said softly. Then she came to herself. Why had she been talking so much? She'd never told anyone about that shit. She'd never had anyone who would have cared. "Sorry, you didn't need to hear that. You had a question?"

Kylar didn't answer. He was looking at her in a way no one had ever looked at her before. It was the look a mother gave her child when she fell and bloodied her knees. It was compassion, and it went right through her, past her sarcasm and her bravado. It knifed through the ice and dead flesh that were all she thought she had inside and found something small and alive and bathed it in warm light. He was seeing all the putrefying yuck that she'd walled up, and he wasn't recoiling from her the way he should have.

"Hu Gibbet made you kill her, didn't he?"

She looked down, unable to face the open warmth any more. She didn't trust her voice.

"Second kill? One of the boyfriends first?"

She nodded.

This was ridiculous. They were having this conversation outside the Maw? "What was your question?" she asked.

"When I quit wet work, I couldn't let it go, and it's only now that I know why. When Jarl showed up at my door, part of me was relieved. I had what I'd wanted for my whole life, but I still wasn't happy. Have you ever had someone look at you and understand you and totally accept you? And for some reason, you just couldn't accept that acceptance?"

Vi swallowed. Her heart filled with longing.

"That's what Elene was for me. I mean, is for me. I promised her that I'd never kill again, but I can't be happy if I don't finish this. When I left, I left her a pair of wedding rings so that she'd know I still love her and want to be with her forever, but I'm sure she's furious with me."

The weight in Vi's pocket burned. She told her tongue to move, to tell him, but it was lead in her mouth.

"If it were any hit but this, she'd never forgive me. If I do this, the Khalidorans will lose, Logan will be king, the Warrens will be different forever, and Jarl won't have died in vain. If there is a One God, like Elene always says there is, he made me for this kill."

Jarl? How can he talk so calmly about Jarl to me? "So what was your question?" She sounded a bit militant, even to her own ears—Jarl! Gods! Her emotions were so out of control she couldn't even identify them—but Kylar answered gently.

"I needed to know if you were in this with me. All the way to the Godking. All the way to death, if it takes that. But I think you've already answered me."

"I'm with you," Vi said. Her whole heart swore it.

"I know. I trust you." Looking in his eyes, Vi knew he was telling the truth. But the words made no sense. Trust? After what she'd done?

He turned back to the door.

"Kylar," she said. Her heart was pounding. She'd tell him about Jarl first, then the note and the earrings, everything. She'd throw herself at his feet and dare him to accept all of it. "I'm sorry. About Jarl. I never meant—"

"I know," he said. "I don't see his murder in you."

"Huh?"

"Vi..." he said softly. As he put a hand on her shoulder, tingles shot through her whole body. She looked at his lips and he was stepping close and her head was tilting of its own accord, her lips parting slightly, and he was so close she could feel his presence like a caress on her exposed skin, and her eyes closed, and his lips touched her—forehead.

Vi blinked.

Kylar dropped his hand as if her shoulder was on fire. Something black flitted across the surface of his eyes.

"What the fuck was that?" Vi demanded.

"Sorry. I almost—you mean my eyes? I was checking if you were using a glamour. I mean, I'm sorry. I was just— Uh, let's get this done, huh?"

Now she was totally confused. He'd thought she'd used her glamour? Did that mean he'd wanted to—he almost what?—no, surely not.

What were you thinking, Vi? "*Sorry I killed your best friend, Kylar, wanna fuck?*"

Kylar opened the door and Vi saw the gaping mouth for which the Maw was named for the first time. The Maw looked like a dragon opening its mouth to swallow her. Red glass eyes with torches behind them glowed with evil intent. Everything else was carved from black fireglass: the black tongue they walked on, the black fangs poised overhead. Once they stepped into the mouth, there was no light.

"This is wrong," Kylar said. He stopped. "This is totally different."

When Kylar had saved Elene and Uly, the ramp into the Maw had led down a short tunnel and then forked. The nobles' cells had been to the right, and the rest to the left. The ceilings had been about seven feet high everywhere, giving a claustrophobic feeling to the Maw.

"I thought you were in here a couple months ago," Vi said.

"Looks like the wytches have been busy."

They entered a vast subterranean chamber. The ramp that had once descended thirty feet now plunged more than a hundred. The nobles' cells and the cells from the first and second levels of the Maw were gone. The ramp was wide enough for four horses abreast and it spiraled around a great central pit. At the bottom, they could see a gold altar with a man tied to it and meisters around him.

"Shit," Vi breathed. "We have to go down there."

Kylar followed her eyes. She wasn't looking at the man on the gold table. She was looking at the south end of the pit, where a small tunnel led toward the castle.

The place felt wrong. It wasn't the altar or the darkness. The smell of the Hole was thick here now. Sulphuric smoke crawled along the floor. It reminded Kylar of his fight with Durzo.

Beneath the smoke, there were other smells. Old blood and the cloying stench of decaying flesh. Beneath the darkness and the queer chanting of the wytches and the reedy cries of pain from deep in the tunnel—mercifully toward the Hole, not the way he and Vi would go—there was something else.

It was a heaviness. Oppression. Kylar had made the night his home for too many years to be afraid of the dark—he thought. But here, in the very air he breathed, was something deeper, darker, more ancient and more vile than he could imagine. Just smelling the reek made him remember killing. He recalled the shameful glee he felt as the noose slipped around Rat's ankle. He remembered when he'd poisoned a saddlemaker's stew and the man hadn't been hungry and had let his son have it. He remembered the exact shade of purple the boy's face had turned as his throat had swollen shut and he'd suffocated. He remembered a hundred deeds he was ashamed of, a hundred other things he should have done and hadn't. He stood paralyzed, breathing the foul air.

"Come on," Vi said. Her eyes looked haunted, enormous, but she was moving. "Breathe through your mouth. Don't think, just do."

Kylar blinked stupidly and came back to himself and followed Vi. The presence was Khali. Just like Logan had warned.

They made their way down into the pit. Kylar walked near the edge, looking down. As he got nearer, he could see that the meisters weren't sacrificing the man, at least not in any conventional sense. Their victim was a Lodricari with tattoos covering his entire body. His skin hung thin and loose on his big, withered frame. He was bound with thick chains face down on the gold table and he was stripped to the waist.

Six meisters were seated at the points of the gold Lodricari star inlaid in the floor, cross-legged, their eyes closed, chanting. Two more stood on either side of the altar. One was holding a hammer and the other...

Kylar couldn't believe it until he moved to the very last spiral and the level of the floor. The first meister was holding a carpenter's hammer and gold nails while the second was holding a horse's spine in his hands, positioning it above the tattooed man's tailbone.

The meister set the spine in place and the other meister, gritting his teeth, set the six-inch-long golden nail above it. He slammed the hammer down. The tattooed man screamed and bucked. In two more heavy whacks, the nail sank all the way in. Then both meisters backed up and Kylar saw their victim well for the first time.

There was something wrong with his skin. At first, because of all the tattoos, Kylar couldn't tell what it was, but between the tattoos he could see that the man was flushed. His veins pressed against the surface of his skin as if he were lifting a great weight. That would have been understandable, given what he was enduring, but the veins weren't in the right places. Thick veins and arteries, blue and red, pushed up against his skin everywhere. And the skin itself seemed oddly dimpled, as if he had pockmarks over his entire body.

The meisters stepped back and called out an order. A prisoner was brought out of the north tunnel, where Kylar could see a holding cell with a dozen men in it. The man was shackled hand and foot and a rope was tied around his neck. A young, pretty meister took the rope and unstrung it, taking care not to let any part of her body enter the circle of magic. She stood on the far side of the circle from the prisoner, who was bleating with fear. Cold sweat poured from the man's face and urine coursed down his leg. His eyes were locked to the man on the altar.

The young meister began pulling on the rope around the man's neck, drawing him toward the circle. He took one hobbled step before he started fighting, and then it was too late. He lost his balance and came shambling forward to keep himself from falling. When he saw that his path would bring him straight to the tattooed man, he threw himself to the side.

With his hands shackled behind him, the victim had no way to catch himself. His face cracked against the fireglass floor.

The meisters who weren't seated or chanting cursed. The woman repositioned herself, flinging the rope over the altar. A meister joined her and they began pulling the semiconscious man toward the altar again.

Why don't they just use magic? But then Kylar looked through the ka'kari and thought he knew why.

This entire chamber was full of magic. It billowed from the meisters the way sulphuric smoke billowed up from the Hole. It seeped along the ground. The very air was thick with it—everywhere but around the altar. There, the air was dead. The meisters were creating something that would resist magic—even theirs. But as Kylar looked closely, he saw that the man wasn't untouched by their magic. All the meisters who were chanting were weaving something together in the air above the altar, and they were sinking it into him at two points. In the back of the man's neck, on either side of his spine, sat two diamonds, each the size of a man's thumb, nailed in. In the visible spectrum they were invisible, covered with blood and grime and the man's hair. In the magical spectrum, they blazed. Only through them could the meisters touch the man's body.

The meisters finally pulled the prisoner up, gagging and choking. Kylar felt Vi tug on his tunic, an urgent let's-get-the-hell-out-of-here, but he ignored her. The prisoner lurched forward and fell on top of the altar, across the tattooed man.

Though he landed at an angle and should have rolled off, he stuck. The meisters dropped the rope and stepped back fast, almost fleeing. The pitch of the chanting rose. The prisoner screamed, but Kylar couldn't see why. The tattooed man's muscles were bunched, his skin flushing even redder— and then blood washed over his back.

The prisoner was yanked off his feet and sucked onto the tattooed man's back. Then the prisoner's tunic was ripped away and Kylar saw the tattooed skin writhing. Each of those thousands of pockmarks was opening as a fanged little mouth. Everywhere, tattooed skin was chewing into the prisoner.

As the prisoner was consumed straight into that tattooed back, the man on the altar screamed in agony equal to his victim's. Through thc ka'kari, Kylar saw whole ribs ripped from the prisoner and pulled through the undulating back and attached to the new spine. Skin swelled and grew over the spine as well. The meister chanted and Kylar saw that they were directing the growth. Whatever this tattooed beast was, they weren't making it. It had already been made. They were just growing it into a shape fit for war.

In another ten seconds, the prisoner was gone. Sort of. Parts of him had been incorporated into the new creature. The monstrosity on the altar had gained perhaps half of the prisoner's mass. The prisoner's spine had reinforced its spine. Ribs had given the torso more length. Skin had been stretched over the new growth, though now it too was pockmarked with those little mouths. The prisoner's bones had been ground down and transported to the creature's skull, which had doubled in thickness.

The meister in charge barked something that sounded like approval, and then motioned for the next prisoner.

Vi jerked on his sleeve again. Kylar turned and looked into the shadows where her eyes would be.

"You go ahead," he whispered. "I'll catch up."

"You're about to do something stupid, aren't you?"

Kylar smiled grimly. She just shook her head.

62

Lantano Garuwashi led his bloodied, exultant men out of the caves that had let them pass through the mountains. Two hundred sleeping Khalidorans had filled the last chamber. Their four wytches had slept deepest in the cave, probably thinking it the safest place, and died before the alarm had even gone up. The rest of the Khalidorans, disoriented, managed to kill as many of themselves as Garuwashi's men had.

In the predawn light, the sa'ceurai emerged southeast of Pavvil's Grove. Two armies camped opposite each other on the plain. It surprised

Garuwashi that it was the Khalidorans who'd been in the caves. Fighting on their home territory, it should have been the Cenarians who had reserves hidden there. If this cave was a sample, the Godking could easily have another five thousand men tucked out of sight, deployable within ten minutes.

It was almost enough to make Garuwashi turn back. Unless the Cenarians had better tricks up their sleeves, it looked like Khalidor was going to be Ceura's northern neighbor permanently.

Still, this would be the last battle of the season. If he could see the outcome, Garuwashi would know if the rebels would be able to regroup or if they were wiped out. He would see Khalidoran tactics firsthand, which might save him in the future.

"Have the men fan out," he told his balding captain, Otaru Tomaki. He stepped to the entrance of the cave, binding in the four forelocks of black hair he'd taken with the quick precision of long practice.

"You won't believe our luck, War Master," Tomaki said.

Garuwashi cocked an eyebrow.

"Sir, he's right there." Tomaki pointed.

Barely three hundred paces away, through the trees, Garuwashi saw the giant running up a hill toward the battlefield. He was heading for the Cenarian camp. He looked over his shoulder. For a moment, Garuwashi couldn't see why because of the trees. Then four Khalidoran cavalrymen burst from the trees up the hill.

The giant saw that he wasn't going to make the crest of the hill before they caught up with him. He stopped and drew his sword.

"The gods have delivered him into my hand," Garuwashi said. "After he kills the horsemen, we'll see if this giant's a match for Lantano Garuwashi."

"You secure the tunnel to the castle," Kylar whispered. "When they come after me, we'll need to move fast."

"What are you going to do?" Vi whispered.

They were bringing out another prisoner. This one shuffled forward like a lamb.

"Just go," Kylar whispered.

"I'm not your fucking lackey," Vi said, raising her voice to a dangerous level.

"Well, then. You do what you have to," Kylar said.

Vi glared—and went.

Kylar waited while the meisters argued briefly and then cut the prisoner's clothes off him to make him easier to digest. Kylar had an idea of what to do, but everything had to be in place. That meant waiting so Vi could secure the tunnel. It meant letting the prisoner die.

He hated it. But he waited. *Dammit, man, fight. That will give me all I need.* But the naked prisoner did nothing. He stared at the writhing mass on the gold altar with horror.

Why don't you fight? All they can do is kill you.

At the last moment, the man let out a strangled sob and tried to stand, but the rope around his neck yanked him forward. He stuck to the creature and screamed. The chanting rose again and meisters who weren't chanting from the corners of the Lodricari star watched wide-eyed as the prisoner was devoured. This time it was even faster than before.

Kylar fully cloaked himself, the ka'kari whooshing over his skin like a well-worn tunic. He ran toward the altar, right past a chanting meister.

As he stepped into the circle circumscribing the Lodricari star, his skin burned with the potency of magic in the air. Khali's voice shrieked through him, a voice of despair, of suicide, of shame, of corruption.

Another step and he jumped, flipping his body into a no-handed cartwheel over the altar and the creature chained to it. It was like jumping through lightning. Needles jabbed every surface of his skin, injecting every vein with power. As he passed over the creature's misshapen gray head, he grabbed the diamonds.

They slid out as if the creature's skin were butter. He landed on the other side of the altar and flung the diamonds away like burning coals. In another second, he was out of the star and leaping for the wall, which was inscribed with runes and designs cut deep enough that he could cling to them. Whatever happened next, he was content to get the hell out of the way and watch invisibly.

Eyes flicked open around the star. The creature was still devouring the prisoner, but the meisters' magic hung in the air like the dangling tentacles of a jellyfish. It had nowhere to go.

The chanting meisters broke off, one by one. Every one turned toward Kylar and stared, mouth agape as if seeing the impossible.

They can see me! Kylar clung to the wall like a spider, facing out, his hands and feet wedged in cracks behind him, waiting for the first attack.

The silence was broken by the sound of a snapping chain and a throaty, almost-human roar. The creature, long-backed now like an enormous caterpillar, shook itself and the rest of the chains popped like roasting corn. Kylar was forgotten.

Standing on six human arms, the creature rushed a meister and trampled him. Six arms and hands tore the meister apart and stuck his limbs to its body. The little mouths worked better than any glue. A fireball caromed off the beast's hide. It wasn't so much blocked as redirected. The fireball lost no momentum, did no damage.

Three more fireballs followed in the next moment, each flying away and bursting against the walls or the floor. The meisters shrieked. One ran up the stairs that spiraled out of the depths. The creature ran after her, but instead of following her up the stairs, it cut across the circular hall. It tried to grab her. She fell back against the wall, as far away from the grasping hand as she could get.

It was far enough. At that height, the creature's arm couldn't reach her. She started scurrying back up the stairs on her hands and feet. Kylar thought she was going to get away, but then the creature slumped. Its arm-legs sagged. Under the surface of its skin, long arm bones slid, one after another, to the arm reaching for the woman. The hand detached and slid forward, each section locking with the sickly sucking sound of a joint being dislocated and relocated. In no time, the arm had added four more arm-lengths. The creature grabbed the woman and pulled her onto itself. Her screams became muffled burbles.

The creature rounded and crushed three more meisters against the wall. It paused as all its little mouths chewed through their clothing and flesh. A fourth wytch grabbed one of the three by the hand, trying to pull her free. He put a foot on the creature's hide to get leverage. But even though the creature didn't seem to notice, it was as if its very skin was possessed of intelligence or at least insatiable hunger. The meister hadn't pulled for a second when his eyes bulged. He threw himself backward, but his foot stuck to the creature's hide. He landed on his back, screaming. For a second, it looked like he might pull free, at the cost of all the meat on his foot.

One flank tremored, the way a horse's flank twitches to rid itself of flies, and in a wave, the toothy skin lapped up over the meister's foot up to his ankle. Another twitch and it reached up to mid-calf. Another, and the creature was digesting four meisters.

It was all the break Kylar needed. He launched himself off the wall and ran up the south tunnel toward the castle. He passed four bloody meisters that Vi had dispatched on the way. He found Vi rifling through the purse of a dead guard standing in front of a formidable oak door. He smiled recklessly. She looked at him, wide-eyed.

"Shit, Kylar, you're glowing."

"I was amazing back there," he said, forgetting that he should have been invisible.

"No, I mean, shit, Kylar, you're glowing."

Kylar looked down. He looked like he was on fire, all in purples and green in the magical spectrum and in a dull, forge-fire red in the visible spectrum. No wonder the meisters had been staring. He'd jumped through the heart of all their magic and it had been too much for the ka'kari to devour. It was bleeding excess magic as light.

Without thinking, he tried to suck the ka'kari back in. It was like taking a bellyful of hot lead into his glore vyrden. "Ow! Ow!"

"Did you kill it?" Vi asked.

Kylar looked at her like she was crazy. "Didn't you see what that—that thing did?"

"No. I obeyed my orders and secured the tunnel." Vi, Kylar realized, could be a real snot. "Not that it does a whole helluvalotta good, because there's no key. They must have been afraid of that—that thing," she mimicked. "Now we're going to have to go back. I'd recommend sneaking, but you seem to be on fire."

Kylar pushed past Vi and put his hands on the near edge of the oak door, one above the other.

"What are you doing?" she asked.

Gods, the door was thick. Still, if he couldn't take the magic in, why couldn't he channel it out? He felt the whoosh of magic leaving him. He looked down and saw tunnels the exact size and shape of his hands bored through the foot-thick oak and iron hinges.

Swallowing—*how the hell did I do that?*—Kylar pushed on the door. It didn't budge until he used Talent-strength, then it yawned open, twisting on its locks, then crashing to the floor.

Kylar stepped through. When Vi didn't follow, he turned. She had an expression on her face so stunned and puzzled and eloquent, he knew exactly what she was going to say.

"What the hell are you?" Vi asked. "Hu never taught me anything like that. Hu doesn't know anything like that."

"I'm just a wetboy."

"No, Kylar. I don't know what you are, but you're not just anything."

63

*W*hy have you denied me my royal garments?" the girl demanded. The princess was wearing a drab dress several sizes too big and had pulled her hair back in a simple ponytail. The Godking had denied her even combs.

"Do you believe in evil, Jenine?" Garoth sat on the edge of Jenine's bed in the north tower. It was before dawn on the day that he would finally massacre the Cenarian resistance. It would be a good day. He was in high spirits.

"How could I sit in your presence and not?" she spat. "Where are my things?"

"A beautiful woman does things to a man, young lady. It would not do for you to be ravished. It would displease me to have you broken so soon."

"Do you not have control of your men? Some god you are. Some king."

"I do not speak of my men," Garoth said quietly.

She blinked.

"You stir me. You have what we call *yushai*. It is life and fire and steel and joy-of-living. I have extinguished it in my wives before; that is why you're cloistered and forbidden comely clothes. It's why I sated myself with one of your ladies-in-waiting: to protect you. You will be my queen, and you will share my bed, but not yet."

"Not ever!"

"See? *Yushai*."

"Go to hell," Jenine said.

"You are a woman cursed, aren't you? Mine is the third royal family you've belonged to—and the first two didn't fare so well, did they? Your husband lasted—what?—an hour?"

"By the One and the Hundred," she said, "may your soul be cast in the pit. May every fruit within your grasp turn to worms and rot. May your children betray you—"

He slapped her. For a moment, she worked her jaw, blinking the tears out of her eyes.

Then she continued. "May—"

He slapped her again, harder, and felt a dangerous surge of pleasure down to his loins. Damn Khali.

She was about to spit on him when he gagged her with the vir.

"Never tempt a man beyond what he can endure. Do you understand?" he asked.

She nodded, eyes wide at the black vir raking his skin.

The vir released her. Garoth Ursuul sighed with disappointment, denying the Strangers. Jenine looked terrified.

Good. Perhaps it will teach her caution. After Neph had produced the princess as a gift and apology for what a mess Cenaria had become, Garoth had been instantly smitten. He had first sent Princess Gunder to Khaliras with the baggage train carrying all the best plunder, but he hadn't been able to get her out of his mind. He'd ordered her brought back. It was a crazy risk. If the Cenarians learned she was alive and saved her, they would have a legitimate ruler. And this girl would rule, given the chance and a little luck. She was fearless.

"Back to my question, Jenine. Do you believe in evil?" the Godking asked. Best to engage his mind, if this interview weren't to end in tears for her and sated disgust for himself. "Some people call it evil when my soldiers knock on a door in the night and ask a man where his brother is and the terrified man tells them. Or when a woman sees a full purse lying in the road and takes it. I'm not asking if you believe in weakness or in ignorance that harms others. I'm asking if you believe in an evil that glories in destruction, in perversion. An evil that would look on the face of goodness and spit on it.

"You see, when I kill one of my seed, it's not an act of evil. I know when I rip the beating heart from that young boy's chest that I'm not just killing him. I'm inspiring such fear in all the others that it makes me more than a man. It makes me unquestionable, unfathomable, a god. That secures my reign and my kingdom. When I want to take a city, I herd the inhabitants of nearby villages in front of my army. If the city wants to use war engines against my men, they have to kill their friends and neighbors first. Brutal, yes. But evil? One might say it saves lives because the cities usually surrender. Or they do when I start catapulting the living into the city. You'd be amazed at what the simple sound of a scream changing in pitch and ending with a thump will do to soldiers when it's repeated every thirteen minutes. They can't help but wait, can't help but wonder—do I recognize this voice? But I digress. You see, I don't call any of that evil. Our society rests on the foundation of the Godking's power. If the Godking doesn't have absolute power, everything crumbles. Then comes chaos, war, starvation, plagues that don't discriminate between the innocent and the guilty. Everything I do staves that off. A little brutality preserves us like a surgeon's knife preserves life. My question is, do you believe in an evil possessed of its own purity? Or does every act intend some good?"

"Why are you asking me?" Jenine asked. She had gone pasty pale. It would have made her look Khalidoran if it weren't tinged with green.

"I always talk to my wives," the Godking said. "First, because only madmen regularly speak to themselves. Second, there is the off chance a woman might have an insight."

He was baiting her, and was rewarded as she recovered some of her yushai. She reminded him of Dorian's mother, and Moburu's.

"I think evil has agents," Jenine said. "I think we allow evil to use us. It doesn't care if we know what we're doing is evil or not. After we've done its will, if we feel guilty, it can use that to condemn us in our own eyes. If we feel good, it can immediately use us for its next objective."

"You are an intriguing child," Garoth said. "I've never heard such an idea." Garoth didn't like it. It made less of him: a mere tool, ignorant or knowing, but always complicit. "You know, I almost left this throne. I almost rejected everything it is to be in the lineage of gods."

"Really?"

"Yes, twice. First when I was an aetheling, and then when I was a father. Strength brought me back, both times. *Non takuulam.* 'I shall not serve.' You see, I had a son named Dorian. He reminded me of me. I saw him turning away from the path of godhood, as I almost had." He paused. "Have you ever stood on a height and thought, I could jump?"

"Yes," Jenine said.

"Everyone does," Garoth said. "Have you stood with someone else and thought, I could push him?"

She shook her head, horrified.

"I don't believe you. Regardless, that is how it was with Dorian. I thought, I could push him. So I did. Not because it helped me, just because I could. I brought him into my confidence and he almost turned me away from godhood—so I betrayed him in the most profound way I could imagine. It was the moment closest to a purity of evil I have come.

"You see, to my eyes, the world holds only two mysteries. Evil is the first, and love is the second. I have seen love used, exaggerated into a mockery of itself, perverted, faked, betrayed. Love is a fragile, corruptible thing. And yet I have seen it evince a curious strength. It is beyond my comprehension. Love is weakness that once in a great while triumphs over strength. Baffling. What do you think, Jenine?"

Her face was stony. "I know nothing of love."

He snorted. "Don't feel bad. One interesting thought is more than I get out of most of my wives. Power is a whore. Once you finally hold her, you realize that she is courting every man in sight."

"What's the purpose of all your power?" Jenine said.

He furrowed his brow. "Whatever do you mean?"

"I'd say that's your problem, right there."

"Now you speak with the insight I'd expect from a woman. Which is to say none."

"Thanks for clarifying."

Ah, so she was as smart as they said. He'd wondered when he'd heard she was requesting books. Better not to let women read. "You're welcome. Now, where was I?"

She answered, but he didn't hear her. Something had just happened to Tenser's ferali. He could feel it through the webs of magic he'd anchored throughout the castle. Whatever had just done that, it was more powerful than he'd expected.

"I can tell you're not happy here, so I'm sending you to Khaliras," he said, walking to the door. "If you send any messages or attempt escape, I'll round up all your friends and a hundred innocents and kill them." He strode across the room and kissed her fiercely. Her lips were cold and utterly unresponsive.

"Goodbye, my princess," he said.

He paused outside the door until he heard her burst into tears, the rustle of covers as she threw herself on the bed, and what he thought was Logan's name. He'd have to give orders about that. If Jenine found out Logan was alive, she'd never bend to Garoth's will. That tug on the web pulled him, but still he paused. Usually, a woman's weeping meant nothing to him, but today.... He turned the feeling over like a strangely colored stone. Was this guilt? Remorse? Why did he have the insane desire to apologize?

Curious. He'd have to think about this later. When Jenine was at a safe distance.

He ordered six huge highlanders from the Godking's Guard to take her to Khalidor immediately, and then went down the stairs.

64

Feir searched the Cenarian army in the dusk, looking for Solon or Dorian. Neither man could be found. When he asked why the garrison at Screaming Winds wasn't here, a count named Rimbold Drake told him of the massacre and shared a worry: If Khali had slaughtered veterans, what would happen if they brought her here?

Desperate, Feir rode on. He was carrying the only possible salvation for the entire ignorant army. To make matters worse, he was no seer, at least not in any useful sense. He could see weaves of magic that were close as if through a Ladeshian enlarging glass, but if you put a man even as Talented as Solon fifty paces away, Feir couldn't see so much as a flicker.

After frenzied inquiries, he'd found two mages: a husband and wife, neither very Talented, but both healers. They said they'd seen no great Talents in the entire army. But then Tevor Nile had gazed around hopelessly—and stopped.

"Drissa," he said.

She came and took his hand. Both of them fixed their attention on a foothill a few hundred paces from the army.

"Lend us your power and we'll lend you our sight," Drissa told Feir. He'd done it, feeling queasy to surrender himself while carrying Curoch, and then the foothill was ablaze in light.

The men were too far away for Feir to recognize faces, and they'd taken care not to skyline themselves, but each man's Talent blazed, as individual as the patterns of his irises. Feir knew those men, had rubbed shoulders and locked horns with them. They were six of Sho'cendi's most powerful magi. Feir knew what they'd come for.

No doubt the bastards actually believed Curoch belonged to them. But they could wield the sword; he couldn't. If he took Curoch to them and swore to surrender it conditionally, any one of those men could incinerate the entire Khalidoran army. Feir didn't have Solon's silver tongue, but with Curoch in hand, his leaden tongue might do just fine.

So he rode pell-mell for the brothers on a horse he borrowed from the

Niles, praying that he could get to them before the armies closed ranks. If he reached them in time, Cenaria might win without losing a man.

The path took him into a ravine out of the sight of the magi, and there he'd promptly run into Khalidoran outriders. His horse had been killed by an archer, and then the lancers had come for him, disdaining arrows for the sport of killing a man on foot.

Now three of them were dead, and Feir had bigger problems. Beyond the Khalidorans, unbelievably, were sa'ceurai.

So as he fought the last horseman, he tried to move into the magi's line of sight. Gods! They were barely a hundred paces away. If they saw Feir, not even a thousand sa'ceurai would be able to stand between those six magi and Curoch.

The sa'ceurai wouldn't let Feir break their ranks. They were too disciplined. What they would do was judge him by how he fought, and sa'ceurai had very particular notions about how one should fight.

The Way of the Sword had peculiar notions about fighting. It entailed assuming every time you went into battle that you would die, and disdaining death so long as you died honorably. The ultimate way to strike an enemy was strike him in the fraction of a second before he landed a killing blow.

To Feir's way of thinking, that was fine and practical when the margins were slim, as they were between the best fighters. If you cared too much about getting hurt, you'd never brave the damage you'd need to take to kill the best. That would make you flinch. If you flinched, you'd die and— worse, to the Ceuran mind—you'd lose.

Killing three horsemen was no mean feat. A veteran horseman was worth ten footmen. But a mage on foot wasn't just a footman, and Feir had had no compunction about using magic to help slay the first three. He knew he could kill the last Khalidoran bearing down on him, but the how of it eluded him. What impression did he want to leave with these sword lords? To a Ceuran, combat was communication. A man might deceive with his words, but his body spoke true.

Feir sheathed Curoch—that was another problem he'd think about later—and ran toward the horseman on the lance side. In battle, the man would be content to let his mountain pony run Feir down, but now, Feir was sure the man would try to kill personally. And...there!

The man leaned out to the side and leveled his ten-foot ash pole. Feir leapt into the air. It was no great leap, but the Khalidoran was riding a twelve-hand mountain pony rather than some hulking eighteen-hand

Alitaeran destrier. Feir's flying sidekick took him over the lance and his foot caught the Khalidoran's face.

Feir realized two things at the point of impact: First, the Ceuran villagers who'd devised a kick to unseat horsemen probably didn't try it when the horse was galloping. Second, something popped, and it wasn't the Khalidoran's neck.

He crashed to the ground. When he stood, his ankle screamed and black spots swam in front of his eyes. But there was no revealing his weakness, not in front of sa'ceurai. Even as he stood, they closed the circle. One of them checked the Khalidoran, with a knife drawn to dispatch him, but he was already dead.

Feir stood in haughty silence, meat-slab arms folded, but his heart was cold. There was one more bend of solid rock between him and the magi on the hill. If he could move ten paces and draw in his Talent, they would see him despite the trees. But he couldn't move ten paces. He couldn't move five.

Outside the circle of drawn swords and nocked arrows, a man was checking each of the corpses. Everywhere through his hair were the bound forelocks of his dead opponents. Most were bound at both ends—sa'ceurai he'd killed—but others were bound only to his hair—foreigners. The circle of iron parted and Lantano Garuwashi looked up at Feir.

"You stand as tall and fight as well as a nephilim, yet you didn't even bloody your sword with these dogs. Who are you, giant?" Lantano Garuwashi asked.

A nephilim? Feir wracked his brain for everything he knew about Ceura. Thank the gods, it was a fair amount. Most sword masters learned a lot about Ceura, since not a few of their trainers were exiled Ceurans who had served on the wrong side of one or another of their incessant wars. But a nephilim? The Way of the Sword. The first men crafted from—iron? The soul of a man is his sword....

I can't fight! I'm lame! Lantano Garuwashi saw me fight and now he'll want to prove he's bigger than this "giant."

That was it! "These were the heroes and the great men of old." The nephilim were the children born of mortal women to the sons of the gods. Or was it the God? Ah, hell, he couldn't remember if Ceurans were polytheists. Well, he'd just have to be religiously obscure.

"Be not afraid," Feir said.

He saw consternation ripple across those iron faces. Who told Lantano Garuwashi not to be afraid? Feir figured that if he was going to bluff, he might as well play it to the hilt.

Speaking of hilts... now might be the time for Curoch to do its trick.

Part of Curoch's latent magic was that it would become any shape of sword its owner wished. Parts of it never changed, but enough of it could to help Feir take on his suddenly conceived role of Divine Messenger. He'd read descriptions of a Ceuran sword that ought to do nicely, so he willed Curoch to take the right shape—*is that all I have to do?*

He drew the sword slowly, and kept his eyes on Lantano Garuwashi's until the man looked down. Around the circle, eyes were widening, men were gasping, jaws were dropping—among these, Lantano Garuwashi's elite!

Feir followed their eyes. Curoch had not only understood the type of sword Feir wanted it to emulate, it had known the very sword itself. Feir had imagined that a sword "with the fires of heaven along the blade" meant either the patterns of exquisite steel or an engraving of fire. Another translation was "with the fire of heaven in the blade." Curoch had taken the latter approach.

Twin dragons, Feir didn't have to look to know that they would be twins, each subtly different, were engraved on either side of the blade, near the hilt. Each was breathing fire toward the tip of the blade. But it wasn't an etching of fire. It was fire, inside the sword. Where the fire burned, and for several inches past it, the sword blade became as transparent as glass. It was as if Feir were holding a bar of flame. The sword stayed a constant length, but fires within grew and shrank depending on—Feir didn't know what it depended on, but right now the dragons blazed out fire all the way to the tip of the sword, three and a half feet from the hilt, and then the fire died down.

Feir had been looking to impress, but the looks on the sa'ceurais' faces were closer to worship. He was barely able to wipe the amazement off his own face before eyes began turning back to him.

Lantano Garuwashi looked as if he'd just been stabbed with fear for the first time in his life. Then it was gone, and out of all the men, only he looked angry. "Why does a nephilim bear Ceur'caelestos?" The Blade of Heaven. Feir had a sudden suspicion that Curoch had become that particular blade too easily. It was like it had known what it should look like. *What if it isn't pretending to be Ceur'caelestos, what if it* is *it?*

I didn't make an impressive blade. I made the most holy artifact these people know. How do I go limping away now? It didn't matter. It was too late to stop.

"I am a mere servant. I bear a message for you, Lantano Garuwashi, should you be sa'ceurai enough to accept it." Feir laced his voice with magic, altered it, added resonance and depth befitting the voice of heaven.

"This path lies before you. Fight Khalidor and become a great king." Not the greatest message for a god, but short enough that Feir's lack of eloquence might not shine through. With the added tones and volume, he thought it respectably awe-inspiring.

But Garuwashi didn't look awed. He drew his sword slowly. It hung from his grip, limp and dull. Feir saw his mistake too late. Why had he held out that particular prize? He'd told Garuwashi he would be a king, but to a son of a commoner, it was an impossibility. Garuwashi's sword was plain iron, a battered, sad thing he held with fierce pride because it was such a deep shame to him.

An iron sword would never rule. There was no trading swords. A sa'ceurai's soul was his sword. To Ceurans, that wasn't an abstraction. It was fact.

That sharp, sad length of iron gave stark testament of Feir's lie. Garuwashi's grip tightened on his soul and the tip of the blade lifted in defiance. Around the circle, the sa'ceurai still held their weapons, but the bows were no longer drawn, and the swords had been forgotten. The sa'ceurai looked as if this moment were being etched forever into their minds. Their War Master, the greatest sa'ceurai of all time, facing a nephilim bearing a sword out of legends—and their Lantano Garuwashi showed not a shred of fear.

"If I am sa'ceurai enough?" Lantano Garuwashi asked. "I will die before I accept mockery, even the mockery of the gods. I am sa'ceurai enough to die by the sword of heaven or I will be sa'ceurai enough to kill the gods' messenger."

Then he attacked with the speed that had made Lantano Garuwashi legend.

Feir couldn't fight. Fighting this man with only one good leg was suicide. Feir blocked Garuwashi's first attack and then reached out with magic and yanked the man toward him.

The Ceuran flew into him and the men pressed against each other, swords crossed, faces inches apart. Curoch—or Ceur'caelestos, whichever it was—flared to life. The dragons breathed fire out to the tip of the blade.

Feir's only thought was that his arms had to be stronger than Garuwashi's. If the man stood at a distance, he'd murder Feir, but in close to Feir's massive arms, Feir had a chance. But before either of the men could do anything, light began to bloom in a second bar between the two men. It must have taken only a second, but for that second, it seemed both men's martial training abandoned them. They each stood merely straining to throw the other off-balance, each trying to ignore what each wanted so desperately to look at. Feir hadn't done anything—maybe Curoch was reacting to the magic he had used to pull Garuwashi to him. Garuwashi's sword went red and then white. It burned brighter than Curoch and then, as the men pushed against each other, Garuwashi's sword exploded.

As explosions go, it was gentle but implacable. No burning fragments of sword tore through Feir's flesh, but there was no stopping the force, either. He was flipped head over heels backward and landed face down, a good fifteen feet away. He tried to stand, but the pain in his ankle stabbed through him so fiercely that he knew he would black out if he did. He stayed on his knees. He stared up the hill and took in as much power as he could hold.

Look, damn you, Lucius! Look! He was still hidden by trees, but if one of the seers just looked they would see him.

Thirty feet away, Lantano Garuwashi rose to his feet. Impossibly, he was holding his sword—no, not his sword. His sword had vanished, disappeared. There weren't even smoldering fragments of it left. With a look of absolute wonder in his eyes, he held Ceur'caelestos and it looked perfect, as if Lantano Garuwashi had been born for that sword and the sword made a thousand years ago with Lantano Garuwashi in mind.

If the sa'ceurai had been astonished before, now they were stricken dumb. They dropped to their knees even as Feir was. One of them said, "The gods have given Lantano Garuwashi a new sword." He meant that the gods had given Lantano Garuwashi a new soul, a legend's soul, a king's soul. In every eye, Feir saw that the men approved. They had known it. They had served Lantano Garuwashi before he had become The Lantano Garuwashi, King Lantano, before he had defied and humbled a nephilim.

Now Feir was on his knees, unable to stand. Lantano Garuwashi's eyes were aflame with destiny as he looked down on the giant.

"Indeed, it is as the gods foresaw. Ceur'caelestos is yours," Feir said. What else could he say?

Lantano Garuwashi touched the blade to Feir's chin. "Nephilim, messenger and servant of the gods, you have the face of an Alitaeran, but you fight and speak as only sa'ceurai can. I would have you serve me." His eyes said, *or you can die.*

Feir needed no nephilim from the gods to tell him his destiny. He glanced up the hill, and no help came. He wasn't surprised; he already was what he would forever be: The Small Man Who Served Great Men. He would forever be The Man Who Lost Curoch. He lowered his head, defeated.

"I . . . I will serve."

65

ℱour hundred paces away, Agon heard the explosion and whipped his head around, trying to locate its source. The Khalidoran army was camped to the west, but none of those distant soldiers reacted as if the explosion had come from there. He looked at his captain.

"I'll send a runner to Lord Graesin," the captain said. The queen had placed her little brother Luc in charge of the scouts, seeming to think that she had to give the young cretin some responsibility, and thinking that it was one he couldn't possibility screw up. The seventeen-year-old had decided that all scouts would report only to him. Only after the scouts reported to him, sometimes waiting for an hour or more in line behind other scouts, were they able to go to the lords who needed to know.

Combined with everything else, it made for a lot of swearing from Agon's officers. None of them voiced their fears. There was no need. Every veteran knew that they were going into battle with a raw army. Calling it an army was, in fact, a stretch. The units hadn't trained together enough to act coherently. Different lords had different signals, and in the crush and cacophony of battle, voices frequently couldn't be distinguished. One officer wouldn't be able to give a hand signal to the officer down the line to relay the general's orders or even to react to a new situation. That, with the queen's positioning of units according to politics, made every veteran grit his teeth.

Agon was lucky to get even the thousand men he had. He only had them because Duke Logan Gyre had spent all his political capital asking it—and the men who had previously served under Agon threatened mutiny if he didn't lead them.

So Agon had a tenth of the Cenarian army. The queen had given him the center of the line, though she pretended that that honor had gone to the lord stationed next to Agon.

"Forget it," he said. "The battle will be over before we hear back from a scout. How are the men?"

"Ready, Lord Gen—my lord," the captain said.

Agon looked at the lightening sky. It was going to be the kind of day a man should spend beside a fire with ootai—or brandy. Dark clouds obscured the rising sun, extending the darkness into the day and delaying the inevitable battle. The flat field, which was really a dozen farms together, was bare. The wheat harvest had been taken in and the sheep moved to winter pastures. Low stone sheep fences crisscrossed the battlefield.

It would be a messy, slippery, awkward place to fight. That was a mixed blessing. Between the fences and the mud, the Khalidoran heavy cavalry would be cautious and slow. Making a heavily armored horse carrying a heavily armored man jump over a fence onto muddy ground was a good way to kill both. On the other hand, it would slow Agon's men, too, and that meant it would give the Khalidoran wytches more time to fling fire and lightning.

Agon drew his horse up before his foot soldiers and archers. He had no horsemen except for his Sa'kagé guards and wytch hunters.

Having heard Logan speak last night, Agon knew that if he were here now, Logan would have made these men see themselves as part of something vast and good. Logan would have given each of them a hero's heart. Under Logan, these men wouldn't hesitate a second to give their lives. Those who survived, even if they lived maimed for the balance of their lives, would count themselves blessed to have shared the field with the man. Agon wasn't like that.

"I am a simple man," Agon told the group lined up to face the horrors of magic and death. "And I have only simple words to give you. Most of you have fought with me before, and it…" Gods, were those tears? He blinked them away. "It honors me that you would have me lead you again. This will be no easy fight. You know that. But we fight an evil that cannot be allowed to win. It is up to us to stop this evil, and today is our only chance.

"Men, if we win, I will be stripped of command, so if you do what I'm about to ask you, you may be punished, but I ask you regardless. Duke Gyre has been given the…honor of leading the first charge." The men rumbled at that. They knew what the queen was hoping. Agon held up a hand. "If he survives the first charge, I ask that you guard him with your lives." Agon dared say no more. If they won, the queen would doubtless hear of everything he'd said.

His men were left sober and dutiful, ready. Agon wished he were the kind of leader who left them cheering and fiery-eyed, but this, with these men, would do.

He rode toward the conferring lords to get last-minute instructions, not that he intended to obey them. Agon had thought long and hard about how to charge a force that included wytches, and he thought he'd come up with a better strategy than any of these peacocks could. But it brought him close for the last time to Logan.

"My lord," Agon said.

Logan smiled. "General," he said. He looked dashing in his family armor, though it had taken some alterations to make sure it didn't hang loose on his bony frame.

Agon struggled to find words. "Sir," he said. "You will always be my king."

Logan put his hand on the general's shoulder and looked him in the eye. He said nothing, but his face told Agon everything.

Then a Sethi woman on horseback emerged from the line. Agon didn't recognize her. She was armored, wearing a sword and carrying a lance.

"My lord," she said, addressing Logan. "Captain Kaldrosa Wyn. We've arrived."

"What are you talking about?" Logan asked.

She raised a hand and the ranks of men parted in curiosity as thirty women armored as Kaldrosa was came through the ranks, each leading a horse. Not all of them were beautiful, and not all of them were young, but all them were members of the Order of the Garter.

"What do you think you're doing?" Logan asked.

"We're here to fight. Everyone wanted to come, but I limited it to women who have some experience fighting. We're pirates and merchant guards and pit fighters and archers, and we're yours. You have given us new lives, my lord. We won't let her throw yours away."

"Where did you get the arms?"

"The women who can't fight all helped," Captain Wyn said.

"And thirty horses?"

"Momma K," Agon guessed, scowling.

"Yes," Momma K's voice rang out behind them. Thank the gods, at least she wasn't armed. "Duke Gyre, your steward found a few fine warhorses that the queen's auditors somehow . . . overlooked. You'll find these ladies eager to accept any order that includes fighting."

"These women aren't—" Logan stopped. He wasn't about to insult them. He lowered his voice. "They'll be slaughtered."

"Momma K didn't ask us to do this," Kaldrosa Wyn said. "She told us we were fools. But we wouldn't be swayed. Sir, yesterday you took away our shame. You gave us honor. It's fragile yet. Please don't take it away."

"What's going on here? What are these whores doing in front of my army?" Terah Graesin shouted, reining her horse in viciously by Agon.

"They're fighting for you," Agon said. "And there's not a damn thing you can do about it."

"Oh, I can't, can I?" Terah asked.

"No, because of that." Agon pointed. In the first hazy light of dawn, the Khalidoran army was advancing.

As Kylar and Vi ascended from the Maw into Castle Cenaria, the hot stink in the air faded and even the taint of Khali seemed to hang less heavily. He'd walked these halls just four months ago, taken some of the same passageways on his way to kill Roth Ursuul. This time, however, he used a different strategy.

By now, Khalidorans would know all the castle's secrets: the back passages and false walls, the spy holes and hidden doors. This time, there would be no taking the tunnels right into the throne room. But this far from the throne room and the king's chambers, the tunnels were safer for Vi, who couldn't become invisible. So an hour before dawn, they entered the passages and moved silently over the heads and behind the backs of scores of soldiers.

Kylar didn't think they could have any idea he was coming, so he hoped their presence only meant that with a battle looming, Garoth Ursuul wanted more security. The sheer numbers of soldiers worried him. With a battle coming, an ordinary commander would leave a skeleton crew at the castle.

The king's chambers were in the west wing. Kylar and Vi left the tunnels in an empty servant's room at the base of the last flight of steps before the king's apartments. Kylar poked his head out into the hall.

The door to the king's bedchamber was at the end of a long, wide hallway. Two highlanders with spears stood guarding the door. Other than the numerous doors to servants' rooms that lined the halls, the hall offered no cover. Again, Kylar thought, not a problem for him, but a serious problem for Vi. Maybe he shouldn't have brought her along. Momma K thought he would need her, but it was starting to look like she'd just slow him down. He was going to have to take down both guards by himself. It was possible, but each man had a bell rope to sound an alarm. Kylar had no doubt he could kill them both, but killing both and getting them away from their ropes?

Stepping back into the room Kylar said, "Why don't you wait here until they're—"

Vi was topless, unfolding a dress she'd taken from her pack. Kylar gaped, frozen. When his eyes finally lifted, Vi's expression was perfectly casual. He turned his head, blushing. A pack hit him in the stomach. "Grab the bodice, would you?" Vi said.

He pulled the bodice out of the pack and handed it to her as she wriggled into a tight servingwoman's dress. She leaned over and pulled up the legs of her pants so they wouldn't show under the dress, again giving Kylar an eyeful. He coughed.

She grabbed the bodice from his nerveless fingers. "Seriously, Kylar, stop acting like such a virgin—" Virgin! How he absolutely loathed the word! "I'm sure it's not the first time you've seen a woman naked."

Actually, it was, but Kylar would have died—for real—before he admitted it to Vi. Elene had never let him see her breasts, though she hadn't always stopped his hands from straying into that golden territory. She'd always wanted to save everything she could for when they were really married. And if Kylar had eroded those boundaries somewhat—bastard—every step seemed huge, a precious gift. It had been vastly frustrating then, but as Vi laced the bodice rapidly and adjusted the amount of cleavage, it was different. For Vi, showing her breasts was nothing. She didn't even turn as she grabbed each breast within the bodice and pulled it this way and that to show it to best advantage. Kylar had thought that Elene's were the ultimate of all breasts, but Vi's breasts were fuller, larger. You couldn't look at her and not notice her breasts. It automatically made her sexual— and yet... and yet, to her, they were just tits. Tools.

Elene was less blatantly sexual, maybe less sexual, period. But there was something cheap about Vi's sexuality, something that told Kylar she took no joy from it. That had been taken from her, taken by her mother's lecherous lovers, by Hu Gibbet, by Momma K's clients and casual fucking. Kylar's emotions skittered from aroused to mournful.

Vi picked up a wicker laundry basket and stuffed it full of clothes, including her own tunic. Under the last tunic, she secreted a dagger.

"How do I look?"

The outfit did look oddly familiar. She'd shown substantially less cleavage that day, in keeping with the modesty of the Drake household, but they were exactly the same clothes Vi had worn when she tried to kill him. "Son of a bitch," he said.

She chuckled and turned, modeling for him. "Does it make my butt look big?"

"You get your big ass in the hall."

She laughed and put the basket on her hip. She was provocative, gorgeous, tempting, and now she had to add fun to the mix? Dammit, he'd almost kissed her outside! No doubt he'd be wearing a knife in his back if he'd done it, but for a second he'd even thought that she wanted him to. She sashayed down the hallway, and the Khalidorans' eyes locked onto her. One of them muttered an oath.

"Hello," Vi said, coming to stand in front of the guard on the left. "I'm new here and I was wondering if—" Her knife slashed so deeply across the man's neck it almost decapitated him.

Kylar broke the other man's neck with a sharp twist and a meaty crack.

Vi looked over where he was—or wasn't, since he was invisible.

"Un-fucking-believable," she said. She cleaned the dagger and put it back in the basket. "Fine, you come in after ten seconds or as soon as you hear my voice. If the Godking wakes up, I'll distract him and you kill him. If he stays asleep, I'll take him."

She opened the door slowly and silently and stepped inside.

A few moments later, she came out. Her face was green. "He's not there," she said.

"What's wrong?" Kylar tried to step past her, but she blocked him.

"You don't want to go in there."

He pushed past her.

The room was full of women. They stood frozen, like statues in various poses. One, on all fours, naked, supported a sheet of glass on her back, forming a table. Another, a tall noblewoman Kylar recognized but couldn't name, stood on tiptoe, stretching seductively, one arm and one leg wrapped around a post of the Godking's massive four-poster bed. Chellene lo-Gyre sat, legs crossed in her shift, in a wing-backed chair. Kylar didn't know anything about her except her reputation for a fiery temper. Her expression showed it, as did her disheveled hair and the tension in her lean muscles. Most of the women were naked, the rest wore little. Two, on their knees, held a washbasin. Two others held a mirror. One was manacled to the wall, a scarf around her neck. Kylar's breath stopped.

It was Serah Drake. Like all of them, she wasn't as still as a statue; she was a statue. With a little cry, Kylar touched her face, touched the lips he'd once kissed. They were as yielding as living flesh, but cool, and there was no life in her open, shining eyes. Her flesh—all of the women's flesh—had been frozen in place with some magic, then left here. As art.

Beneath the scarf, Kylar could see the bruises circling Serah's neck. He looked away. There were two ways to die when hanged: if you fell far enough, your neck would break and you'd die quickly, otherwise you stran-gled slowly. Serah had died the hard way.

He stepped away, but everywhere his eyes turned, he saw gruesome detail. The women wearing bracelets concealed gashed wrists; chemises concealed pierced hearts; those wearing more clothing did so to conceal the imperfections of their taxidermy: they were the ones who'd thrown them-selves from their balconies and now had bulges where no bulges belonged.

Kylar staggered like a man drunk. He needed air. He was going to throw up. He burst out onto the Godking's wide balcony.

She sat on the stone railing, feet hooked through the posts for balance, leaning far back, naked, a nightgown in her hand, fluttering in the wind like a flag. Mags.

Kylar screamed. Talent leaked through his fury and the scream reverberated over the castle, echoing back from the courtyard far below. All life in the castle stopped. Kylar didn't notice, nor did he notice the ka'kari rushing over his skin, the face of judgment covering his anguish.

He hammered a palm down on the stone railing and crushed it on one side of Mags, then again on her other side, then he lifted her and carried her back inside. The feeling of her skin, so like living skin, was obscene. But her limbs were locked in place. He laid her on the bed, then tore the bolts holding Serah Drake to the wall. He laid Serah beside her sister. As he covered them, he saw that each girl's left foot was signed in a bubbly script, as if their corpses were art: Trudana Jadwin.

Vi was staring saucer-eyed from him to the shattered six-inch stone railing. "Fucking fuck," she whispered. "Kylar, is that you?"

He nodded stiffly. He wanted to remove the mask of judgment, but he couldn't. He needed it right now.

"I checked the concubines' rooms," Vi said. "Nothing. He must already be in the throne room."

Kylar's stomach flipped. He jerked involuntarily.

"What?" Vi asked.

"Bad memories," Kylar said. "Fuck it. Let's go."

Dawn was coming. By killing the two guards, they'd tipped their own hourglass. Someone would check the men's post soon—probably at dawn. Worse, the Cenarian army's glass was already draining. The battle would begin soon and then the nasty surprises would start. If Logan were to have a chance to be king, Kylar needed to hand him a victory. Killing Garoth Ursuul would unman the Khalidorans.

They walked through the halls brazenly, Vi in her serving girl uniform, and Kylar invisible but flitting from doorway to doorway as if he weren't, in case any meisters were wandering the halls. As they came to the last hallway, they passed six of the largest highlanders Kylar had ever seen. Kylar dodged behind some statuary as he saw that the highlanders were accompanied by two Vürdmeisters. Most curious of all, the protection seemed to be for one woman—apparently one of the Godking's concubines or wives—all wrapped up in robes and veils so that not an inch of her skin showed.

When Kylar drew his knives to kill them, Vi laid a hand on his arm. He turned judgment's eye on her and she flinched, but she was right. A fight here was a distraction that might jeopardize the real mission, and there was nothing that was going to stop Kylar from killing Garoth Ursuul.

Kylar's stomach was a riot. It didn't quiet even when the group rounded a corner and disappeared. This was the same hallway he'd stood in with Elene and Uly, when he'd gone to his first death.

He calmed. Garoth Ursuul was far more powerful than Roth Ursuul, but Kylar was more powerful now, too. He was more confident. He'd been a boy trying to prove he was a man then, now he was a man making a choice, knowing what it might cost.

He smiled recklessly. "So, Vi, you ready to kill a god?"

66

The men perched on the crest of a hill south of the battlefield: six of the Sa'seurans' most powerful magi. Their clothing betrayed none of that. Each dressed in the plain clothes of a trader from his own homeland: four Alitaerans, a Waeddryner, and a Modaini. Their sturdy packhorses even bore a respectable amount of trade goods, and if their mounts were a little better than most traders would own, they weren't so fine as to attract comment. But if the men's clothes didn't betray them, their bearing did. These were men who strode the earth with the assurance of gods.

"This oughtn't be pretty," the Modaini said. Antoninus Wervel was a short butter-tub of a man with a bulbous, florid nose and a fringe of brown hair combed over his shiny pate. In the Modaini fashion, he wore kohl around his eyes and had darkened and lengthened his eyebrows. It gave him a sinister look. "How many meisters you figure they've got?" he asked one of the Alitaeran twins, Caedan.

The gangly youth twitched. Caedan was one of two Seers in the group, and he was supposed to be spotting. "Sorry, sorry. I was just—are that man's bodyguards all women?"

"Surely not."

"They are," Lord Lucius said. He was the leader of the expedition, and the other Seer. But he was more interested in the opposing side. "The

747

Khalidorans have at least ten meisters, probably twenty. They're standing close together."

"Lord Lucius," Caedan said timidly. "I think they've got six Vürdmeisters there, back farther, in the middle. It looks like they're gathered around something, but I can't tell what it is."

The butter-tub hmmphed. "How many of the Touched fight for Cenaria?" He said it to irritate the Alitaerans. In Modai, *touched* meant Talented, not *crazy* as it did in Alitaera.

Caedan was oblivious. "There's a man and woman in the Cenarian lines, both trained, standing together. Several others untrained."

"And among the Ceuran raiders?"

"I haven't seen the Ceurans since they went around the bend."

The other young Alitaeran, Jaedan, looked unhappy. He was the identical twin of the young Seer, with the same handsome features, same floppy black hair, and totally different gifts.

"Why are they being so stupid?" he asked. "We all saw the Lae'knaught army coming up from the south. Five thousand lancers who hate the Khalidorans more than anything. Why don't the Cenarians wait until they get here?"

"They might not know the Lae'knaught are coming," Lord Lucius said.

"Or they might not be coming. They might be waiting to pick off the victor. Or Terah Graesin might want all the glory for herself," Wervel suggested.

Jaedan couldn't believe it. "We aren't just going to sit here, are we? By the Light! The Cenarians will be destroyed. Twenty meisters. We can take them. I'm good for three or four, and I know the rest of you are as good or better."

"You forget our mission, Childe Jaedan," Lord Lucius said. "We haven't been sent to fight in anyone's war. The Khalidorans aren't a threat to us—"

"The Khalidorans are a threat to everyone!" Jaedan protested.

"SILENCE!"

Jaedan cut off, but the defiance on his face didn't alter a whit. The Cenarian line began moving at a slow jog, allowing the army, like an enormous beast, to gain momentum.

Caedan twitched. "Did—did any of you feel that?" he asked.

"What?" Wervel asked.

"I don't know. Just—I don't know. Like an explosion? May I go see what the Ceurans are doing, Lord Lucius?"

"We need your eyes on the battle. Watch and learn, childe. We have a rare opportunity to see how the Khalidorans fight. You, too, Jaedan."

The Khalidoran army was formed in loose ranks, with space beside every warrior for an archer. The archers readied themselves now, each putting arrows in the ground where they could be grabbed quickly. In the front of everyone, the two-man teams of meisters sat on horseback. To the Seers, they glowed.

"What will they do, Caedan?" Lord Lucius asked.

"Fire, sir? And lightning second?"

"And why?"

"Because it will scare the shit of the Cenarians? I mean, uh, the effects on morale, sir," Caedan said.

The Cenarian line was still jogging forward. They were four hundred paces away now. The group under General Agon had advanced to the fore and split. But they didn't just split into one or two or even three groups. His few horsemen, and his foot soldiers, formed a fragmented line as long as the Cenarian front.

"What the hell is he doing?" one of the Alitaerans asked.

For a long moment, no one answered. He couldn't hope to break the Khalidoran line with such a ragged line of his own. His move also left a gap in the Cenarian center. But even as the men watched, another of the Cenarian generals, Duke Wesseros, ordered his men into the gap.

"It's genius. He's minimizing his losses," Wervel said.

For a moment no one asked. If there was one thing magi hated more than not understanding something, it was not understanding something after someone had understood it first and had given them a hint.

"What?" Jaedan asked.

"Think like a meister, childe. You'd have enough vir for what, five? ten? fireballs before you're spent. Usually, you'll kill two to five men with each fireball. With the line this thin, you'll kill one. You might even miss completely. Agon knows he's gambling. If the main line comes to support his line too late, his first line will be slaughtered, but if they hit within five or ten seconds, he'll have saved hundreds and nullified the, uh, effects on morale. It looks like we've found a general who knows how to fight meisters. There might be hope for Cenaria after all."

At two hundred paces, the line picked up speed.

The archers in the Khalidoran lines loosed their first volley, and a flock of two thousand black-feathered arrows took flight. For a long second, they darkened an already bleak sky, casting the shadow of death across the dawn. When they dove back to earth, they buried their barbed beaks in earth and armor and the flesh of men and horses.

Again, the dispersed ranks saved hundreds, but up and down the Cenarian line, men flopped over onto the stubbly fields, going from a full sprint to the rest of death in an instant. Others fell, injured, legs or arms pierced, and were trampled by their friends and countrymen a moment later. Horses lost riders and continued the charge merely because the horses to their right and left still charged. Riders lost horses and pitched to the earth at great speed, sometimes flying free of the saddle and rising to run with their earthbound comrades, sometimes getting caught in the saddle and crushed beneath their horse's body.

The Khalidoran army performed as only veterans can. The archers loosed as many arrows as they could in a few seconds, then, as a flag went up, each grabbed his remaining arrows and retreated. There were perfect lines in the ranks to allow each archer to get to the back behind the spearmen and swordsmen who would protect them from the melee. As they retreated, without even a separate order being given, the rear lines filled in the gaps the archers had left. The maneuver was nothing special, but the speed at which the army carried it out with thousands of enemies sprinting toward it was.

The meisters loosed fire. Their original plan in shambles, some of the meisters hurled balls of fire at the charging horses while others, still hoping for the effect of running into a firestorm, swept gouts of fire across the stubbly fields. What would have ordinarily broken up and disoriented an entire line in the crucial seconds before impact didn't even slow the Cenarians.

The crash of the lines was distinctly audible to the magi, even as far away as they were. Men and horses impaled themselves on spears and their momentum carried them into the Khalidoran ranks. Others crashed full force into Khalidoran shields and sent men sprawling, but the Cenarians in that first rank must have been veterans. In most armies, no matter what their commanders told them, many of the men would slow before that last impact. The idea of crashing full force into a line bristling with swords and spears was too viscerally paralyzing for most men. These had no such doubts. They burst into the Khalidoran line with all their might. It was an awesome and fearful sight.

But they were almost swallowed up before the main body of the Cenarian line hit the Khalidorans. The shock of it rippled through the entire Khalidoran line, pushing them back a good ten feet.

On their horses, the meisters laid about themselves with fire and lightning, but far behind the Cenarian front lines, archers on horseback were hunting them, riding back and forth, stopping, shooting arrows from short bows and moving on. The shots seemed impossible—a short bow killing from two or three hundred paces? Caedan checked the archers again, but they weren't Talented, he was sure of it. To Caedan, it was like watching candles being snuffed one at a time as meisters toppled from their saddles.

The lines heaved back and forth and disintegrated into a thousand clumps of individual combat. Horses wheeled and stamped and kicked and bit. Meisters burned holes in men, set fire to others, laid about themselves with cudgels or swords of pure magic, and sometimes fell dead, pierced by arrows.

In five minutes, seventeen of the twenty meisters were riddled with arrows and the Khalidoran line was stretching at the middle. The giant Cenarian who'd led the first charge seemed to be a beacon of hope. Wherever he went, the Cenarians pushed to go there, too. And now, he was pushing to cut all the way through the Khalidoran line.

Caedan muttered an oath. "Where did *they* come from?" he asked. The magi followed his eyes. Rank upon rank of Khalidoran highlanders were forming up to each side of the battlefield.

"The caves," Wervel said. "What are they doing?"

The highlanders spread out and jogged toward the flanks and back of the battle. There were at least five hundred of them, but they didn't charge into the battle. They didn't seem at all disturbed that they were losing the advantage of surprise. They spread their line thinner and thinner, as if to cup the entire rear of the battle.

"Sir," Caedan said. "I thought you only tried to surround an enemy if you outnumbered him."

Lord Lucius looked disturbed. He was looking to the back of the Khalidoran line where the Vürdmeisters were gathered. "What is that chained between the Vürdmeisters?"

"That isn't a—" one magus said.

"Surely not. They're just legend and superstition."

"May the God have mercy," Wervel said. "It is."

No," Vi said. "I can't."

Kylar turned the face of judgment on her.

"You—you don't know what he's like. You've never looked into his eyes. When you see yourself in his eyes, you look in the face of your own wretchedness. Please, Kylar."

Kylar gnashed his teeth. He looked away. It seemed like it took conscious effort, but slowly that terrifying mask melted away and his own face emerged—his eyes still icy cold.

"You know, my master was wrong about you. He was there when Hu Gibbet presented you to the Sa'kagé. He told me how you trashed those other wetboys. He told me that if I didn't watch out, you'd be the best wetboy of our generation. He called you a prodigy. He said that there wouldn't be five men in the kingdom who could beat you. But they don't have to. You've beaten yourself. Durzo was wrong. You aren't even in the same class as me."

"Fuck you! You don't know—"

"Vi, this is what matters. If you're not with me now, it's all horseshit."

As his eyes bored into her, she felt herself changing. She was angry at herself, and at him, and at herself again. She couldn't let Kylar down. She had never let anything be more important than herself. And now, in the blind stupidity of infatuation, it was more important that she have this man's respect than that she live.

The infuriating thing was that it wasn't even a contest. And yet her weakness for Kylar was propelling her toward strength against the one she really should fear—Nysos! This was all too confusing.

"Fine!" she practically spat. "Turn your back!"

"Got a dagger?" Kylar asked as he turned.

"Shut up, you smug sonuvabitch." *Oh, brilliant, Vi. You realize you like him, so you insult him—for helping you find your guts.* She pulled off the dress and pulled on her wetboy tunic. She was being a real wench. AAAHHH! She'd just had eight emotions in the space of three seconds.

"Fine," she said. "You can turn back around. I'm sorry for...before. I was hoping to—" What had she been hoping? To impress him? Entice him? To see the heat of desire in those cool eyes? "—to shock you," she said.

"You, uh, succeeded."

"I know." She couldn't help but smile. "You're not like any man I've ever known, Kylar. You've got this, this, innocence about you."

He scowled.

"When you've been where I've been, it's really...cute. I mean, I didn't know guys could be like you." Why was she running off at the mouth all of the sudden?

"You barely know me," Kylar said.

"I...shit, it's not just like it's a list of facts that prove you're different, Kylar. You feel different." She was flustered. Was he being deliberately dense?

"Ah, fuck it," she said. "Do you think we could ever work out?"

"What?" Kylar asked. The tone of his voice should have shut her up.

"You know. You and me. Together."

Incredulity spread across his face, and the expression confirmed every damning thought she'd ever had about herself.

"No," Kylar said. "No, I don't think so."

No, she could tell he meant, you're damaged goods.

She shut down. "Right," she said. Once a whore, forever a whore. "Right. Well, we've got work to do. I've got a plan."

Kylar looked poised on the verge of saying something. She'd caught him totally off guard. Shit, what did she expect?

Nysos, so he looked at your tits. So he's nice to you. You're still the one who killed his best friend, kidnapped his daughter, and split up his family. Shit, Vi, what were you thinking?

"All right," she said before he could say anything. "If we go in the side here, they'll know it's an attack. We have no idea what their strength is or how many of them there are. But if I walk right in to report on your, well, your death, they won't suspect a thing. If you go in the side door, you can decide when to strike. As soon as I see palies go down—preferably starting with the king—I'll fight too, all right?"

"Sounds pretty weak," Kylar said. "But it also sounds better than anything I've got. But one thing..." He trailed off.

"What?" She was eager to go now, to stop talking, stop messing up.

"If he kills me, Vi...Get my body out of there. You can't let them have it."

"What do you care?"

"Just do it."

"Why!" Now she was taking her frustration out on him. Beautiful.

"Because I come back. I don't stay dead."

"You're mad."

He held up a black shiny ball. It melted and wrapped around his hand like a glove. His hand disappeared. A moment later, it was a ball again. "If Ursuul takes this, he takes my powers. All of them."

She scowled. "If we make it through this, you have a lot of questions to answer."

"Fair enough." Kylar paused. "Vi? It's been good working with you." Not waiting for her response, he squeezed the ball and disappeared.

Vi turned down the hall and started walking. Ironically, she ran into no patrols at all until she came to the four soldiers guarding the main doors of the throne room. The men eyed her with disbelief. They seemed to forget their weapons as their eyes lingered exactly where they were supposed to.

"Tell the Godking that Vi Sovari has come to receive her reward."

"The Godking isn't to be disturbed except in the case of—"

"This counts," Vi hissed at the man, first leaning forward until his eyes were pegged to her cleavage and then pushing his chin back up with the knife that had materialized in her hand. He swallowed.

"Yes, ma'am."

The guard eased the great double doors open. "God, our God of the High Realms, Your Holiness, Vi Sovari begs admittance."

The guard stepped aside and motioned to her. "Good luck," he whispered, smiling apologetically. *The bastard. How dare he be human?*

Standing in the last hall, Kylar brought the ka'kari to his eyes. He didn't see any magical alarms. Invisible, he moved to the door. The hinges were well-oiled.

"Come in, come in, Viridiana," he heard the Godking say. "It's been too long. I was afraid I was going to have to enjoy the death of ten thousand rebels all by myself."

Kylar cracked the door open as the Godking spoke, and as the man took in the admittedly impressive sight of Vi in her version of wetboy grays, Kylar stole into the throne room. He slipped behind one of the enormous pillars supporting the ceiling. The servants' entrance he'd used opened near the base of the fourteen steps to the dais. Ursuul sat at the top of the steps in his black fireglass throne.

In the center of the vast room was a rolling plain at the base of the mountains. There were tiny figures on each side of the plain, moving in concert. Kylar realized they were miniature armies, lining up in the dawn light. It wasn't a painting or embroidery of a battle; it was a battle. Fifteen thousand tiny, tiny figures strode across the plain. Kylar could even pick out flags of the noble houses. The Cenarian lines were forming up, following...Logan? Logan was leading the charge? Madness! How could Agon let the king lead a charge?

The great doors closed behind Vi as the Godking waved her in. Kylar had never seen the man, or even heard him described. He'd expected someone old and decrepit, swollen or sagging from a life of evil, but Garoth Ursuul was in excellent health. He was perhaps fifty, looked at least ten years younger, and though he had the thick body and cool skin of a Khalidoran highlander, he had a fighting man's arms, a lean face with an oiled black beard, and a head shaved bald and gleaming. He looked like the kind of man who not only would shake your hand but when he did, you'd find calluses and a firm grip.

"Don't mind the battle," the Godking said. "You can walk through it; it won't harm the magic, but be quick. The rebels are about to charge. It's my favorite part."

Through the ka'kari, however, Garoth Ursuul was a miasma. Twisted, screaming faces streamed behind him like a cloud. Murder lay so thick on him it blotted out his features. Betrayals and rapes and casual tortures wreathed his limbs. Threaded through it all, like noxious green smoke, was the vir. It somehow fed off and deepened all that darkness, and it was so powerful it seemed to fill the room.

As he stood behind the pillar, Kylar noticed a small group of the tiny men fighting three feet away from him. Off the battlefield proper, a big man was about to be ridden down by four Khalidoran lancers.

Except the man wasn't ridden down. In seconds, he killed three lancers. There was something familiar about him. *Feir Cousat!*

Kylar knew he should be trying to figure out a way to move without being seen, but he was rapt in the drama unfolding silently, inches away. The Ceurans' parted leader came forward. Feir drew a sword that looked like a bar of fire. It stunned the Ceurans. Feir and the leader fought for about half a second: the first time their swords crossed, there was a flash of light. The Ceuran came away with the sword.

"What was that?" the Godking said.

"What?" Vi asked.

"Out of the way, girl."

As Feir knelt before the Ceuran (knelt? Feir?), the image of the battle suddenly spun around, putting the Khalidoran lines at the base of the steps and the Cenarian lines close to the great doors.

Garoth hmmphed. "Just some raiders."

Kylar brought some of the ka'kari to his fingertips, sharpened it into a claw, and tested it against the pillar. His fingers sank in like it was butter. He eased back on the magic and tried again until he was able to sink his fingers in and get a grip. This is going to be fun.

He shook his head. It seemed the ka'kari had no limitations, and that was just making Kylar more aware of his own.

Kylar sent some of the ka'kari to his feet and climbed the pillar. There was a tiny hiss and a tinge of smoke at every step, but it was as effortless as climbing a ladder. Kylar reached the fifty-foot ceiling in seconds.

Figuring out how to adjust the claws to work on the ceiling took a few seconds, but then he was clinging to the throne room's high, vaulted ceiling like a spider. His heart was in his throat. He crept across the ceiling until he was directly above the throne, his body shielded from view by one of the arches, only his invisible head exposed.

The Godking gave a running commentary to Vi. "No," he was saying, "I don't know why the Cenarians are using that formation. Seems awfully open to me."

Kylar watched, upside down, as the Cenarian ranks slammed into the Khalidoran line. The first rank to hit them was thin—he wondered if they'd lost so many from the archers, but a few seconds later, the next line slammed into them.

The Godking cursed. "Damn them, brilliant. Brilliant."

"What is it?" Vi asked.

"Do you know why I made all this, Vi?"

Heart pounding, Kylar released the ceiling with his hands and slowly uncurled, upside down. He drew his daggers, hanging on the ceiling with his feet, bat-like. Garoth Ursuul stepped directly beneath him.

Then there was no fear, only calm certainty. Kylar dropped from the ceiling.

One of the dark faces twisting in the miasma around the Godking screamed. Green-black caltrops of vir burst in every direction from the Godking. Kylar hit one and they all exploded.

The concussion blasted Kylar off course. He sprawled sideways, missed his landing, and tumbled down the stairs. He rolled across the landing and down the second flight. When he came to rest at the bottom of the stairs, his head was ringing. He tried to stand and promptly fell.

"I made it because a god ought to have some fun. Don't you agree, Kylar?" Garoth smiled a predatory smile. He wasn't surprised. "So, Vi, you've done what you promised. You killed Jarl, and you brought Kylar to me."

Kylar had trusted her. How could he have been so foolish? It was the second time he'd walked into a trap in this room. Inexplicably, he felt calm. He felt lethal. He hadn't come this far to fail. This kill was his destiny.

"I didn't betray you, Kylar," Vi said in a small, desperate voice.

"Oh, he put a spell on you that made you do it? I gave you a chance, Vi. You could have been different."

"She didn't betray you," the Godking said. "You betrayed yourself." He pulled out two diamonds, each the size of his thumb. They were the ones that had held the monster downstairs together. "Who else would have the physical prowess to snatch these but a wetboy, and who else could survive the magic but the bearer of the black ka'kari? I've known you were here for an hour."

"So, why are you going to reward her?" Kylar asked.

"What, you want me to kill her, too?"

Kylar scowled. "I did until you said that."

The Godking laughed. "You're an orphan, aren't you, Kylar?"

"No," Kylar said. He stood. His head was slowly clearing, and he could swear he could feel his body healing his bruises.

"Oh right, the Drakes. Magdalyn told me all about that. She thought you'd save her. Sad. When you killed Hu Gibbet, you really upset me. So I killed her."

"Liar."

"Hu's dead?" Vi asked. She seemed absolutely thunderstruck.

"Do you ever wonder who your real father is, Kylar?"

"No," Kylar said. He tried to move and found thick bands of magic around his body. He examined them. They were simple, unvaried. The ka'kari would devour them easily. *Go on, keep smiling, you fiend.*

Garoth smiled. "There's a reason I knew you were coming, Kylar, a reason you're so extraordinarily talented. I'm your father."

"WHAT?"

"Ah, just joking." Garoth Ursuul laughed. "I'm not being much of a host, am I? You came in here all prepared to fight some big battle, didn't you?"

"I guess so."

Garoth was in high spirits. "I could use a bit of a warm-up myself. What do you say, Kylar? Want to fight a ferali?"

"I don't actually have a choice, do I?"

"No."

"Well, then, golly, I'd love to fight a ferali, Gare."

"Gare," the Godking said. "Haven't heard that in thirty years. Before we start…" He turned. "Vi, decision time. If you serve me willingly, I can reward you. I'd like that. But you'll serve regardless. You're chained to me. The compulsion won't allow you to hurt me. It won't allow you to let anyone else hurt me while you live, either."

"I'll never serve you!" she said.

"Fair enough, but you might want to leave the worst of the fighting to the boys."

"Fuck you," she said.

"A distinct possibility, child."

Garoth gestured and a door flew open behind him. "Tatts, why don't you come in?"

The ferali shuffled in. It now had the shape of an enormous man, tattoos still visible on its lumpy skin. Despite his height—at least nine feet—and the thickness of his limbs, Kylar saw that the ferali wasn't as big as it had been just an hour before. The monster's face was all too human, though, and it looked ashamed.

"It'll all be better in a moment. I promise," the Godking said. He slammed the diamonds into the ferali's spine. It cried out with a voice no longer human, and then was still. Garoth abruptly ignored it. "Do you know why you've never heard of a ferali? They're expensive. First, you need diamonds or you can't control the damn things. But you already figured that out, didn't you? Second, you have to take a man and torture him until there is nothing left but rage. It usually takes hundreds of tries to find the right kind of man. But even that isn't enough. The magic involved is beyond what even a Godking can do unaided. They require Khali's direct intervention. That has a cost."

"I don't understand," Kylar said. He was studying the ferali. It only had so much mass. It could only change shape so quickly. Fixing those things in mind would change everything.

"Neither did Moburu or Tenser. They do, now. This time I made them pay the price. You see, Khali feeds on suffering, so we dedicate every cruelty we can invent to her. In return, she gives us the vir. But for greater power, Khali asks more.

"When I was warring with my brothers, She offered to help me create a ferali if I would host a Stranger. You're not familiar with them? My first was named Pride. He was a small price to pay for godhood. Unfortunately, Khali didn't tell me that a ferali will devour itself if given no other meat. I didn't make another until my son Dorian betrayed me, and I've found Lust to be a more odious companion—as Vi shall discover, my appetites grow ever more exotic. Hold on, that line's not doing well, is it?" On the phantom battlefield, Logan was pushing the Khalidoran line out into a half moon.

"Hmm," the Godking said. "Much faster than I expected." He pulled out a stick. It started flashing in his hand. From the edges of battlefield, thousands more Khalidoran troops began closing on the Cenarian army's flanks. Other ranks moved to reinforce the arcing section of the line.

Garoth wasn't trying to win the battle. He merely wanted to fence in the Cenarians so he could unleash Moburu's ferali on them. Kylar felt sick. What would it do with an unlimited number of victims?

"It will take a few minutes before they get in position," Garoth said. "Where was I?"

"I think we were at the fight-to-the-death part," Kylar said.

"Oh, no, no. You see," Garoth went up to the carved fireglass throne and sat. Kylar could see him erecting magical wards around himself. "Left alone, a ferali is nearly mindless, but—and this is the beautiful thing— they can be ridden. Tell me, how much fun is that?"

"It's a lot more fun if I can move," Kylar said.

"Do you know why I've gone to so much trouble to bring you here, Kylar?"

"My excellent wit?"

"Your Devourer has another name. It is also called the Sustainer. It heals everything shy of death, doesn't it?"

"It won't help you," Kylar said.

"Oh but it will. I know how to break the bonding. There's an unnatural growth in my brain. It's killing me, and you've brought the only thing that can save me into my hands."

"Ah. The tumor it can help," Kylar said, "but your arrogance is terminal."

The Godking's eyes flashed. "How droll. Come. This 'Night Angel' business is finished."

"Finished?" Kylar said. "I'm just warmin' up."

The bonds dropped away and Vi started fighting. She swore constantly under her breath to use her Talent, but she wasn't angry. She'd always thought she was a cold, heartless bitch. She'd taken hold of that identity. It had made her strong against the nightly emptiness, the soul bankruptcy she'd carried for as long as she could remember. With the declaration that she would never serve the Godking—melodramatic or not—she felt that she'd made her first deposit in that bank ever.

Now she was fighting for something. No, for someone, and it was the first selfless thing she'd ever done.

The ferali hunched and its bones sped beneath its skin. In the time it took Vi to armor herself, it had become something like a centaur, except instead of a horse's body, it had a cougar's. It was shorter, more mobile on its four legs, but it had a human torso and arms. It grabbed a spear in its human hands and launched itself after Kylar, who dashed behind a pillar.

Vi sprinted up the steps three at time, to attack the Godking. He was about to find out how wrong he'd been about the compulsion. Let Kylar fight the beast; she'd cut it off at its source.

She was drawing back her sword when she hit the ward that extended ten feet around the Godking like a bubble. It was like sprinting into a wall.

She found herself sprawled on the stairs—she must have rolled partway down them without even noticing. Her nose was bleeding and her head was ringing. She blinked at Kylar.

The man was a virtuoso. As the ferali charged with spear leveled, Kylar waited until the last moment and then launched himself forward. Knives flashed as he passed over the beast and its spear passed inches under him, harmlessly. But he wasn't done. He threw out a hand and somehow hooked the marble pillar, scoring it with a smoking gouge. As the ferali spun to catch him, Kylar emerged from the other side of the pillar and flew over the ferali's back, blades flashing again.

Kylar landed in a crouch, one hand on the ground, the other on his sheathed sword. The ferali paused, bleeding profusely, the mouthy skin cut open over the back of one hand, one shoulder and across the cougar's haunches. The blood was red, all too human, but even as Vi watched, the gouges knit together in scars. The ferali threw its spear at him. Kylar deflected it with a hand, but the ferali was already moving.

As Kylar leapt toward the wall, the ferali slashed one arm at him, and in the space of the heartbeat that it took for its arm to move forward, the arm elongated, bones snapped into place and an enormous scythe-blade of a claw swept through the air. Kylar flipped off the wall directly into the path of the claw. It slammed him to the ground.

Vi thought he was surely dead, but even as Kylar hit the ground, the claw snapped off and skipped along the floor away from the ferali. Kylar had somehow managed to draw his sword and block the slash. The ferali, its left leg hanging limp and boneless, looked stunned. It sank into itself, becoming a great cat.

Before the beast could attack again, Vi finally gathered her wits and charged it, screaming. It wheeled. She danced just outside of the range of its claws, the sides of which it had armored into bone. Kylar got back to his feet, but was swaying from side to side, dazed. The ferali dashed away from Vi and touched its belly to the ground where its dead claw lay.

In a second, that flesh was part of the ferali again. Bones shifted and it stood as a tall man with bone-swords for arms. It seemed more comfortable in this guise, thickly muscled, quicker than any man, much of its skin reinforced with bone armor plates.

Together, Vi and Kylar fought. Kylar was capable of aerial moves Vi couldn't even comprehend, flipping off walls and the pillars, always landing on his feet like a cat, always leaving bloody furrows with his steel claws. Vi had less strength, even with her Talent, but she was quick. The ferali morphed again and again. It became a slight man with a living chain that it whipped around its head and flung around the pillars, hoping those mouthy links would catch either one of them. One of the links snagged Kylar's sleeve in midflight. It flipped him off balance and he crashed into the floor. The ferali pulled the chain in until Vi's sword passed in the inch between Kylar's skin and his sleeve and freed him. Kylar didn't even pause. He was just up and fighting.

Then the ferali was a giant with a war hammer. Marble exploded as it laid about itself with the huge weapon. Kylar and Vi ranged through the illusion of battle on the throne room floor, fighting as desperately as those men and women fought.

As they fought together, Kylar and Vi began to not just fight in unison, but with unity. As Vi understood Kylar's strengths, she could move, counting on him to react appropriately. They were warriors, they were wetboys, and they understood. For Vi, who had always had trouble with words, battle was truth.

She and Kylar fought together—leaping, meeting in mid-air, pushing off to go flying a new direction before the ferali could respond. They covered each other, saved each other's lives. Kylar clipped off the end of a bone mace Vi could have never avoided. Vi said, "Graakos"—and jaws closed on Kylar's arm and then bounced off.

It was, for her, a holy moment. She had never communed with another, never trusted another so implicitly, as she communed with and trusted Kylar. In this, through this, she understood the man in ways a thousand thousand words wouldn't have revealed. They were in total harmony, and the miracle was how natural it was.

At the same time, despair rose in her. They cut the ferali a hundred times. Two hundred. They attacked its eyes, its mouth. They cut off parts of its body. It bled, and its total mass decreased by a few pounds, but that was all. They cut it and it healed. But they could never make a mistake. Once that skin touched theirs, they would die.

~I also cut.~

Kylar alighted on the side of a pillar and stopped. Runes were glowing in ka'kari black edged in blue along his arm. He stared at them. "You what?" he asked.

"I didn't say anything," Vi said. Her eyes were on an enormous spider chittering on the floor in front of her.

"Stupid! How slow am I?" Kylar said, dropping to the floor.

~Is that a rhetorical question?~

The ka'kari poured a dark liquid from his hand onto his sword. But then the liquid solidified as a thin sword. Kylar cut left and right and spider legs went flying. It wasn't like hacking through bone, he was shearing them off like butter.

He dodged back, and the spider gathered its legs to itself, but this time, the stumps kept bleeding. They smoked and wouldn't allow new limbs to be grown there. It morphed back into the man with swords for arms, but now the wounds were on the man's chest, still flowing with blood and smoking. It roared and attacked Kylar.

Kylar slashed left and right and the sword-arms tumbled across the floor. He rammed the ka'kari into the ferali's chest. With a sharp motion, he pulled it down to the creature's groin. Smoke billowed, blood gushed. Kylar yanked the sword up, making another huge cut.

He saw it too late. The ferali's skin drew back from the sword, like a pond might crater when a stone falls into it, only to burst upward. The skin rushed up the sword all at once.

It engulfed Kylar's hand.

He threw himself back, but the ferali, limp now, fell forward with him, attached to his hand. Kylar jerked the sword back and forth and smoke gushed from the ferali as he gutted it, but it didn't lose its grip.

Kylar reached for a dagger, but he'd used them all in the battle. "Vi," he shouted. "Cut it off!"

She hesitated.

"Cut off my hand!"

She couldn't do it.

The skin twitched again and it rushed up his forearm.

Kylar screamed and twisted. A blade of ka'kari formed along the ridge of his left hand and he cut off his right arm. Released from the pull of the dying ferali, he collapsed backward.

He held the gushing stump in his left hand. A moment later, black metal shimmered in every exposed vein and the bleeding stopped. A black cap sheathed his stump. Kylar looked at Vi dumbly.

Ten feet away, the ferali's corpse was oozing. It began to break apart, weaves of magic unraveling. The mouthy skin rippled and evaporated and then all that was left was stinking ropes of meat and sinew and bone.

"That," the Godking's voice said, "was impressive, Kylar. You showed me some things that I wasn't aware the ka'kari could do. Most instructive. And Vi, you'll serve admirably, and not just in my bed."

*   *   *

Something in Vi snapped. In the last two days, she'd changed everything. A new Vi was fighting to be born—and the Godking was here, saying nothing had changed. The new Vi would be a stillbirth. She'd go back to being a whore. She'd go back to being the same cold, hard bitch.

She'd thought that life was the only one open to her, so she'd borne the unbearable. But having seen a way to be a woman she didn't hate, she couldn't go back.

"Get it through your fat head, Gare," she said, even as she felt magical bonds wrapping around her limbs and Kylar's again. "I won't serve you."

Garoth smiled godly benevolence. "The feisty ones always make me hard."

"Kylar," Vi said. "Snap out of it. You gotta help me kill this fucking twist."

The Godking laughed. "Compulsion doesn't hold on everyone, Vi. The Niles' magic would have freed most people. About nineteen years ago, there was some Ceuran slut that I seduced during a diplomatic trip. I sent men to collect her when I found out she was pregnant, but she ran away before they got there. When I found out she bore a girl, I dismissed the matter. I usually have my daughters drowned—it's good practice for my boys, it makes them tough—but it wasn't worth the effort. Compulsion, Vi, only works on family, and sometimes not on boys. You—"

"You're not my father," Vi said. "You're just a sick fuck who's about to die. Kylar!"

"Now Vi, let's not get all teary-eyed," Garoth Ursuul said. "You're nothing to me but five minutes of pleasure and a spoonful of seed. Well, that's not true. You see, Vi, you're a wetboy I can trust. You will never disobey me, never betray me."

Vi was gripped by terror tighter than the magic that bound her limbs. Possibilities were dying on every side.

Kylar stirred. His eyes came back into focus. He wiggled his eyebrows at her, trying to be charming. The outrageous cuteness of it cracked her paralysis. His pale blue eyes said, You with me?

Hers answered him with a fierce, desperate joy that needed no translation.

Under his breath, Kylar said, "You take his attention, I'll take his life." He smiled and the rest of Vi's fear blew away. It was a real smile, with no desperation. There was no doubt in Kylar's eyes. Any additional obstacle—whether magical bonds or the loss of an arm—would only sweeten his victory. Killing the Godking was Kylar's destiny.

"You leave me no choice," Garoth Ursuul said. He pursed his lips. "Daughter, kill Kylar."

The ka'kari opened and devoured the bonds holding Vi and Kylar. Vi was moving, beginning a flashy, eye-grabbing stunt.

Then...everything stopped.

There was a gap of volition. In her mind's eye, Vi was leaping through the air, flying toward the Godking, her blade descending, his face twisting into a rictus of fear as he saw that his shields were gone, as he realized she'd defeated his compulsion—

But that was only her imagination.

A shock of impact ran up Vi's arm. Her wrist flexed as if to complete a horizontal slash through a heart, but she saw nothing, knew nothing except that there was a blank.

The gap cleared, and Vi was aware once more. Her fingers were uncurling from the familiar grip of her favorite knife. Kylar—so slowly, so painfully slowly—was falling. He drifted toward the floor, his head arcing back in a slow whiplash from having her knife rammed into his back, his dark hair rippling from the shock. It wasn't until he hit the floor that Vi realized that Kylar was dead. She had killed him.

"That, my dear daughter," Garoth Ursuul said, "is compulsion."

69

Kylar pushed through the fog in a rush. In a moment that seemed out of joint, as if time didn't work the same way here, he was back in the indistinct room, once again facing the lupine, gray-haired man with his hair pure white on one temple.

"Two days isn't going to cut it," Kylar said. "I need to go back now."

"Impertinence last time, demands this time," the man said.

The man cocked his head, as if listening, and Kylar was again aware of the others. They were invisible when Kylar looked directly at them, but definitely there. Could he see them a little better this time? "Yes, yes," the Wolf said to a voice Kylar couldn't hear.

"Who are they?" Kylar asked.

"Immortality is lonely, Kylar. Madness need not be."

"Madness?"

"Say hello to the grand company of my imagination, gleaned from those profound souls I have known over the years. Not ghosts, just facsimiles, I'm afraid." The lupine man nodded his head again toward one of them and chuckled.

"If they're not real, why are you talking to them and not to me?" Kylar asked. He was still angry and this time, he wasn't going to take the man's chiding or his mysteries. "I need your help. Now."

"You'll find such urgency hard to hold onto as the centuries pass—"

"It'll be real hard if Garoth Ursuul takes my immortality."

The Wolf tented his fingers. "Poor Garoth. He believes himself a god. It will be his undoing, as it was mine."

"And another thing," Kylar said. "I want my arm back."

"I noticed you managed to lose that. You actually pulled the ka'kari out of every cell of the arm you lost. Was that intentional?"

"I didn't want the ferali to have it." Cell?

"A wise thought, but a poor choice. Do you remember what they call your ka'kari?"

"The Devourer," Kylar said. "So?"

The Wolf pursed his lips. Waited.

"You're joking," Kylar said. He felt sick.

"Afraid not. You didn't have to fight. What the ka'kari did while coating your sword it could have done while coating your body. You could have just walked through the ferali."

"Just like that?"

"Just like that. Because you cut your arm off instead—and pulled the ka'kari out of it first—your arm won't grow back. Sorry. I do hope you can fight with your left."

"To hell with you! Send me back or Ursuul wins."

The man gave him a toothy grin, as if being damned amused him. "Sending you back two days early will cost me," his eyes flicked up. "Three years and twenty-seven days of my life. Sort of like the rich stealing from the poor, wouldn't you say, immortal?" He held up his burn-knotted hand before Kylar could curse him. "I'll send you back if you make an oath to me. There's a sword. It's called Curoch, and I'd be lying if I didn't tell you that it's intensely desired by any number of powerful factions. You know the town of Torra's Bend?"

"Torras Bend?"

"That's the one. Get the sword and take it there. Go into the wood, past the oak grove, stop forty or fifty paces from the edge of the old forest, and throw Curoch in."

"Is that where you live?" Kylar asked.

"Oh no," the man said. "But something else does. Something that will guard Curoch from the world of man. If you do this, I will send you back now, and when you deliver the sword, I'll make your arm grow back."

"Who are you?" Kylar asked.

"I'm one of the good guys. At least as much as I can be." His golden eyes danced. "But I want you to understand something Acaelus never did: I'm not a man," he paused, grinning, and Kylar did indeed wonder how much humanity was behind those lupine eyes, "to cross lightly."

"I figured."

"Are you in?"

"That's odd," the Godking said, coming to stand over Kylar's corpse. "Where's the ka'kari? I sense . . . it's in his body?"

"Yes," Vi said, unable to stop herself.

"Fascinating. I don't suppose you know what all it does?"

To her horror, Vi found herself answering. It hadn't been a direct question, so she veered as hard as she could. "No. I know it makes him invisible." She'd tried to say "made," but she couldn't force the past tense into the sentence. She hoped he didn't notice.

"Well, regardless, your lover will have to wait. I have a massacre to attend."

Vi screamed and grabbed Kylar's sword. Garoth watched her curiously. The sword swung in an arc—and stopped. She stopped it herself. She couldn't do it.

"Amazing, isn't it?" he said. "Funny thing is, I learned compulsion from one of your southron mating rituals—ringing—but you people completely misunderstood its true power. Anyway, feel free to watch the battle—and stop grunting, dear. It's unbecoming."

Abruptly, his eyes went vacant. Vi tried to move the sword, but it was impossible. The compulsion was undeniable.

As the wytches released the ferali, Vi sat on the steps before the throne to watch. But even that terrible spectacle couldn't hold her attention.

She should have given up long ago. All her fighting was a farce. She'd done everything the Godking had wanted her to do. She'd killed Jarl and she'd killed Kylar. In the years to come, she'd doubtless kill hundreds more. Thousands. It wouldn't matter. No one else could ever mean what Jarl and Kylar had meant to her. Jarl, her only friend, dead by her hand. Kylar, a man who had somehow stirred... what? Passion? Maybe just warmth, in a cold dead heart. A man who could have been... more.

She hated every man she'd ever known. It was man's nature to kill, to destroy, to tear down. Woman was the giver of life, the nurturer. And yet... Kylar.

He stood athwart her suppositions like a colossus. Kylar, the legendary wetboy who should have been the very quintessence of destruction, had saved a little girl, adopted her, saved a woman, saved nobles who didn't deserve saving, and tried to leave the bitter business. *Would have left it, too, if not for me.*

If not for Vi, Kylar would be in Caernarvon, leading some sort of daylight life that Vi couldn't even imagine. And what was it with Elene? Kylar could have had any woman he wanted, and he'd chosen a girl covered with scars. In her experience, men went for the hottest bitch they could get their cock in. If the bitch was hot, they didn't care that she was a bitch. Kylar wasn't like that.

Vi had an awful flash of intuition. She saw Elene—a woman she'd never met—as her twin and opposite. Elene had scars an inch deep, but beneath that she was all beauty and grace and love. Vi was all ugliness except for the thin veil of her skin. Kylar's love was a mystery no more. The man who could see past Jarl's murder could easily see past a few scars. Of course he loved Elene. Or had, before Vi killed him.

Kylar had said he would come back. But he wouldn't come back. The Godking had won.

Vi pulled her knife out of Kylar's back and rolled him over. His eyes were open, blank, dead. She closed those accusing eyes, pulled his head into her lap and turned to watch the Godking massacre Cenaria's last hope.

70

*A*ll pretense of scholastic detachment was gone. At first, the magi had to strain to see the ferali. It entered the battle virtually unnoticed.

Within a minute, one of the mages said, "McHalkin was right. I thought he made it up."

"We all thought he made it up. What does this mean about all those other creatures in his writings?"

"Gods, it's just like he said. It's being ridden, possessed."

On the battlefield, the beast's presence was becoming known. It had become a great bull, plowing through the lines of Cenarians. Whatever gashes the soldiers managed to inflict were quickly filled, and the creature grew.

The clamor of battle, the shouts of rage and pain and ringing steel had been drifting up to the promontory since the battle began. Now, new sounds rose: screams of terror.

The enormous bull lumbered out the side of the Khalidoran line. Half a dozen men, some still alive, were stuck to the beast. It paused as it digested them and began rearranging itself. The ferali curled into a ball and sheets of plate metal bobbed to the surface of its skin. It unfolded itself and stood.

The ferali now wore the shape of a troll. It was three times the height of a man, its skin was armor and mail and gawping little mouths. It had even taken into itself the swords and spears of its dead opponents, which now bristled from its back and sides.

The Cenarians' first reaction was surprisingly heroic. They charged the beast.

It was futile. It beat its way through the lines, never moving so fast that the Khalidoran line couldn't close behind it, and everywhere it went, killing, it was careful to lift every man it had killed or maimed in one of its four arms and stick him to its skin, or impale him on the spears on its back. One would be devoured, and then the next, and the next, and the next.

If the soldiers even wounded the beast, the magi couldn't tell. Never slowing, it tore apart line after line.

In the face of that inexorable death, General Agon charged part of the Khalidoran line with everything he had, trying to escape. By luck or leadership, hundreds of his men joined him, all attacking one place, desperate. The Khalidoran line bowed and nearly broke, but the Khalidoran prince Moburu's cavalry reinforced the line until the ferali waded through the ranks to get there. Abruptly, the charge broke off, and the Cenarian generals tried to get their men to charge another way. But the din of battle, the confusion of being ringed by the Khalidorans, and the terror at the ever-enlarging beast was too much.

The Cenarians were fighting in a desperate frenzy. They were moments away from panic.

"We have to go help them," Jaedan said.

The magi looked at him like he was insane.

"What? We're some of the most powerful magi in the world! If we don't help them, they'll die. If we don't oppose Khalidor now, it'll be too late."

"Jaedan," Wervel said quietly. "The ferali is almost impervious to magic—and that was to the ancients. It's already too late."

Lord Lucius was in no mood to placate the youth. He said, "We were sent to find, or find word of, the great sword. If Curoch is here, believe me, Jaedan, we will know of it presently. If the Cenarians have it, they will use it now. The council—"

"The council isn't here!" Jaedan said. "I think—"

"What you think is irrelevant! We will not fight. That's final. Understood?"

Jaedan's jaw clenched with the effort of holding back words he would be made to regret. He turned his eyes back to the men dying because of Lord Lucius's apathy. "Understood, sir."

One thing the stories never mentioned about battles—the stories Logan had loved so much as a boy—was the smell. He thought that after the Hole, nothing could ever shock him again, but he was wrong. He'd lost count of the men he'd seen die in the Hole, but whatever the number was—twelve? fifteen?—it was nothing compared with the number dead here in the first charge alone. The smell had been excitement and fear and rain and mud, insignificant smells next to the sights of flashing steel and proud horses, the fierce faces of the women who rode with him.

The Khalidorans had hemmed them in. Without flags or hand signals to communicate with distant commanders, the Cenarians couldn't escape. If too few joined a charge, it went nowhere. If too many, they'd be massacred from the rear. The Cenarian army was paralyzed, and more and more Khalidorans emerged—from where? Why the hell hadn't they known they were there? Had Luc Graesin blown his assignment or had he betrayed them? It didn't matter now, only avoiding slaughter mattered, and the stench filled his nostrils.

It was the men packed tightly together, their heat and their sweat and their fear commingling with the terror of the panicky horses. It was a sewer, as the dead and the fearful lost control of their bowels. It was gastric juices from stomachs cut open, intestines slashed, dying beasts kicking at the earth and bawling. It was blood so thick it gathered in pools with the rain. It was the sweeter smell of women's sweat, their numbers dwindling but still fearless so long as Logan was fearless.

Wherever he went, the Cenarian lines rallied. It wasn't only his presence.

It was these magnificent women, streaked with blood and cursing like sailors. The very sight of them bewildered the Khalidorans.

If it weren't for the Order, Logan would have died in the first charge. They fought with nearly suicidal frenzy to be at his side, and they'd paid the price for it. Of the thirty women who'd ridden with him, only ten remained. With such a small bodyguard, Logan surely would have been overwhelmed had not more than a hundred men joined them in the minutes after the first charge—Agon's Dogs. He'd given them words, and now they gave him their lives.

Logan couldn't have said how long it was into the battle when a new smell cut through the ranks. It was something rancid, which made no sense. Tonight, the armies would leave plenty of meat on the field to rot, but nothing should be rotten yet. He heard and felt the Cenarians reacting long before he saw the source of their newest fear. Then, from the back of his horse, he saw what looked like a bull, a bull the height of a destrier, blasting through the lines and out of the battle, dragging men with it.

A different creature returned. It was a troll with four arms, four eyes, lumpy grayish skin, and blades sticking out of its back. Logan knew that he should have been afraid, and part of him marveled that he wasn't. Fear simply wasn't there.

Battle became simple, one understanding that led to one fact: that creature was killing his people. He had to stop it.

General Agon led another charge. His men smashed into the cavalry like a balsa hammer on an anvil. It was all Agon could do to break away from that damned cavalry officer with Ladeshian skin and Alitaeran clothes and horses.

Logan charged at the beast. It seemed to be even bigger now. One entire arm now was a scythe blade and the troll swept it across the field about three feet above the ground, reaping a full harvest. There was no way to dodge. Some men jumped, and others dove to the ground, but most were cut in half. The troll moved forward, arms lifting the dead and impaling them on the lances and swords that studded its body.

Logan rode into the space created as the Cenarians pushed back as far back from the troll as they could. His white charger danced nervously.

The troll stopped and regarded Logan. It made an indistinct roar that nearly took Logan's horse out of his control, then shook itself. A human head pushed out of the troll's belly.

"Logan," the head said in a perfectly human voice with only a touch of Khalidoran accent. The head pushed further out of the troll's stomach toward Logan.

"Ursuul," Logan snarled.

"There's something you should know about Jenine."

Logan hadn't been strong when the battle began. Months of privation had left him emaciated and weak. He'd survived today on luck and the ferocity of the Order of the Garter and Agon's Dogs, not his own strength or skill, but at the passage of Jenine's name across this beast's foul tongue, Logan felt the power of righteous rage.

"Your lovely, lovely wife is ali—"

Logan's sword flashed and he struck the head off. It burst apart the ground into clumps of rotting flesh.

For a moment, the beast froze. It didn't move a muscle, and as the moment stretched, the Cenarians suddenly cheered, thinking that Logan had somehow killed it.

Then the troll raised its arms to the skies and bellowed a roar that shook that very ground. Two of its eyes fixed on Logan, and the enormous bone scythe drew back.

Vi brushed back Kylar's hair with gentle fingers. Before them, the ferali had transformed into a troll and was wading through the Cenarian lines. She barely saw it. She was staring at Kylar's dead face. For the first time, she realized how young he looked. Kylar was serene, beatific. Vi had murdered him. She'd delivered immortality to the Godking.

Something splashed on his cheek. Vi blinked. *What the hell?* The drop slid down his cheek to his ear. She blinked again, more rapidly, refusing to believe she was crying. What had Sister Ariel said? Something about being an emotional cripple? Vi looked at her tear, glimmering on Kylar's ear, and wiped it away. *That bitch called me stupid.*

And so she was. Her finger froze.

It hit Vi like a warhorse at a full gallop. She hadn't escaped Sister Ariel at all.

Suddenly, Vi couldn't breathe. She saw the Sister's trap now, laid out for her in every word Ariel had spoken. She saw the bait and the consequences. It wasn't escape, but it was escape from the Godking.

It only required Vi to do something worse to Kylar than anything Hu Gibbet had ever done to her. She put an unsteady hand into a pouch and found the box right where she'd put it. She opened the box and looked at the Waeddryner wedding rings tucked inside.

If she did this, it would be like rape, and Vi knew rape.

Yet it was the only way. Sister Ariel had the Niles plant all the information Vi would need. They'd told her she needed to show "an outward sign of an inward change" to break the compulsion, a transfer of loyalties. They talked of the powerful magic in some of the old rings, how they held a type of compulsion spell. And the Bitch Wytch had dangled the carrot herself: quick advancement, private tutoring, being important.

Vi didn't care. She wouldn't do this for herself. She'd do it because if she didn't, the Godking would become immortal. Vi would become his pet assassin, a one-woman plague slaying any who dared defy him. She'd do this for those poor bastards getting eaten alive on the battlefield. She'd do this because if she didn't, Kylar would die, truly die.

But he would never forgive her.

She ran her fingers through Kylar's hair. His face looked cold and still, judgmental. She would escape; she would change, but Kylar and Elene would pay the price.

The earring pierced her left ear, and the hoop melded together seamlessly. The pain made her eyes water. Tears streaming down her face, she pierced the other ring through Kylar's ear.

A rush of warmth lit her from head to toe. She felt the compulsion shrivel and burst apart. That was nothing compared to the sudden longing she felt. She gasped. In her very skin, her stomach, her spine, she felt Kylar. He was healing, but he was hurt so badly it made her ache. Her fingers tingled where she was touching his face. He was more handsome than ever. She wanted him to know her. She wanted to confess the truth and be forgiven and have him love her back. She wanted him to hold her, to touch her cheek, to run his fingers through her hair and—

That thought exploded against everything she'd ever known. Vi pushed Kylar roughly out of her lap and staggered to her feet. The rush of emotion was too much, too intense, too vast to read, yet it didn't feel alien. It didn't feel counterfeit. It felt like her love was being purified, the coal blown on so that it flared up into fire. It left Vi gasping. She could hardly bear to look at Kylar. But she was free. The compulsion was gone.

Free! Free of the Godking. On the floor, a lone horseman stood in front of the massive troll. Vi took her dagger and staggered toward her father. She grabbed his body and made him stand. She shook him.

"Father! *Father!*" someone was screaming. Who the hell was screaming that on the battlefield? A moment later, Garoth realized what it must be and brought his consciousness back to the throne room. Logan could wait a few seconds. To hell with him if he didn't want to know Jenine was alive.

"Father," Vi said, "can you tell me one thing?" She had obviously come to terms with her compulsion, because she was touching him.

" 'Father?' I'm right in the middle of something, do you mind?"

"Did you make me kill Jarl? Was it compulsion?"

He smiled. The lie came easy to his lips. "No, moulina. You did that yourself."

"Oh." The single syllable popped like a little bubble from her lips.

Garoth grinned and slid back into the ferali. Garoth roared toward the heavens and brought his scythe-arm back. Logan rode straight at him until his horse shied. Logan kicked and sawed at the reins, but the horse refused to obey. It turned around in a desperate circle and stumbled on a body. As Garoth swung the enormous scythe at a level to cut Logan in half, one of the mounted wytch hunters burst into the clearing and leapt out of his saddle, tackling Logan. The scythe swept through both horses' necks and the beasts went crashing to the earth in twin sprays of blood.

Logan rolled away and got to his feet. Beside him, the archer was already drawing an arrow. He shot one of Garoth's eyes and then another. Garoth blinked and new eyes pushed out the old. It didn't matter. Logan was standing, defiant but defenseless. Garoth's next slash would tear the little man in half—

Something hot went into his back. Once, twice, three times. Again and again. He lifted the ferali's hands to its back, wondering what could pierce his thick hide, wondering why his other eyes hadn't seen the attack, but there were no arrows or spears in his back.

The ferali was fading, and as Logan charged at him to stick his sword in his belly, Garoth realized it wasn't the ferali that was bleeding.

He was.

He heard the sound of weeping and he was back in the throne room.

Vi was hugging him against her breast, and stabbing him, again and again, against herself, as if she wished the dagger would go all the way through him into her own heart.

Garoth told his limbs to move, but they were empty slabs of meat. His body was dying, dying! and his vision was going black, black—

He triggered the death spell. It was a terrible risk, trying to hurl his consciousness into another body. If Khali granted this, her price would be grievous, but he had nothing to lose.

The vir ripped from his arms and engulfed Vi in a forest of black fingers. They pulled her closer.

He was close! It was working! He could feel it!

And then every finger of vir was sheared off by an iridescent blade passing between Garoth and Vi. The vir, cut off from their source, froze, cracked, and evaporated into black smoke. Garoth turned and saw the impossible.

Kylar was alive. He stood with judgment writ on every feature and a blade of black ka'kari in his fist. Realization swept through Garoth like a tidal wave.

The Devourer devoured life itself. The Sustainer sustained life itself. It was not just extended life or healing. It was true immortality. Garoth had had a chance for real godhood, and he'd let it slip right through his fingers. Impotent rage washed through him.

Then Kylar's ka'kari-blade descended once more toward his head.

Logan rammed his sword into the troll's belly and the creature rocked back. It dropped to its knees as if it had suddenly lost all coordination. Logan jumped backward and narrowly avoided being crushed. He wasn't sure what had just happened, but it didn't seem that the troll's reaction was right. Logan had seen it take worse wounds and not even flinch.

Both armies' eyes were fixed on Logan and the beast. Logan stabbed it again, and a third time, but the wounds sealed as soon as the sword pulled out.

As it was still on its knees, the plates covering most of the beast's stomach slid out to its sides—gurgling and grinding like a breaking nose, but repeated a hundred times. From the gap between the plates, something pressed out against the skin, bulging and glooping. In another second, the form resolved itself. Pushed out from the troll's stomach, like a living bas-relief, was a woman. Her face worked and a mouth appeared.

"I can't fight it, King. So hungry. Just like in the Hole. I can't stop, King. Look at what they made me. It won't let me kill me, King. So hungry. Like the bread. So hungry."

"Lilly? I thought it was Garoth," Logan said.

"He's gone. Dead. Tell me what to do, King. I can't stop me. I'm so hungry it's eating myself."

Logan realized that even in the time since Garoth Ursuul's face had protruded from it, the troll had shrunk. It was devouring itself. He had to do something fast. They couldn't kill it. The beast healed its wounds without even conscious thought, and now the form of Lilly was becoming indistinct.

"Lilly," Logan said. "Lilly, listen to me."

She rallied, and her form protruded once more, though this time without a mouth.

"Lilly, eat the Khalidorans. Eat them all, and run up into the mountains. All right?"

But she was gone. The plates snapped back into place and the troll lumbered to its feet. It fixed its eyes on Logan and raised its scythe, all trace of Lilly gone.

Logan walked straight toward it. "You wanted to make things right, Lilly? You remember, Lilly?" Logan asked, hoping that he could draw her back with the sound of her name. "You want to earn your pardon, Lilly? Am I your king or not?" The ferali blinked, paused. Logan's voice pitched with an authority he'd never known he had, and pointing at the Khalidorans he shouted, "GO! KILL THEM! I COMMAND IT!"

The ferali blinked, blinked. Then in a movement faster than any Garoth had ever made in it, it slashed an arm through the Khalidorans behind it. Logan turned and saw thousands of pairs of eyes locked on him in disbelief.

Logan Gyre, the man who commanded a ferali to stop, and it did.

The battle had come to a standstill. Khalidorans and Cenarians stood within easy reach of each other and didn't fight. The ferali, easily thirty feet tall now, commanded all attention. It didn't turn. It merely went gelatinous for a moment, and then what had been its front was its back, and it was facing the Khalidorans.

A fireball arced up from a meister and ricocheted off its skin harmlessly. Ten more followed and did nothing. Lightning hit an instant later and barely left a black mark on its skin. The ferali crouched and flexed every muscle in its body. All the arms and armor that Garoth had incorporated in the beast exploded from its body in all directions, breastplates and mail shirts and spears and swords and war hammers and daggers and hundreds of arrows rattling to the ground in a great circle.

A glowing white homunculus streaked out of the Khalidoran lines and stuck to the ferali. In a line between the Vürdmeister and the homunculus, the air seemed to distort as if anything viewed through it were being seen in a bent mirror. The air bubbled in a streak toward the ferali.

Ten paces from the ferali, the distortion in the air ripped open with red fire. The pit wyrm struck. But its lamprey mouth closed on nothing. The ferali was unbelievably fast. The pit wyrm twisted, black and red fiery skin lurching further into reality, forty feet, sixty, with no sign of its body tapering.

Logan heard weapons rattle to the ground, dropped from nerveless fingers as the titans warred.

But the battle lasted only one strike more. The pit wyrm missed again, and the ferali didn't. An enormous fist crushed the wyrm's head and snapped its body like a whip onto the Khalidoran lines beneath it. It broke apart in bloodless black and red clumps that sizzled on the ground like water drops on a hot skillet, hissing into green smoke and disappearing.

The ferali turned to the Khalidoran lines and a dozen arms sprang from its body. It began snatching up soldiers like a greedy child snatching sweetmeats.

Then the men on both sides remembered the battle. The Cenarians remembered their weapons and the Khalidorans remembered their heels. They cast away weapons and shields to run faster.

A shout went up as the Khalidorans around the ferali broke. Logan couldn't believe it. The impossibility of it was too much to accept.

"Who do you want to go after them?" General Agon asked. He and a bloodied Duke Wesseros had appeared out of nowhere.

"No one," Logan said. "She can't tell friend from foe. Our fighting's done."

"She?" Duke Wesseros asked.

"Don't ask."

Agon rode off shouting orders, and Logan turned to the man who'd tackled him from his horse. He didn't recognize him. "You saved my life. Who are you?" Logan asked.

The Sethi woman who'd been stuck to his side for the entire battle, Kaldrosa Wyn, stepped up. "My lord, this is my husband Tomman," she said, fiercely proud.

"You're a brave man, Tomman, and no mean shot. What boon would you ask?"

Tomman looked up, and inexplicably, his eyes shone. "You already gave me back more than I deserve. You gave me back my love, my lord. What's more precious than that?" He extended his hand, and his wife took it.

The Cenarian ranks reformed in the tightest square the generals could manage and just watched as the Khalidorans were massacred. There was no retreat. It was a rout. The rest of the circle broke, men running in every direction. The ferali tore through them. It became a snake and rolled over whole sections of the line, men sticking to its body, screaming. Then it was a dragon. Always it had dozens of hands. Always it was quick and terrible. Piteous screams rose on every side and men tore at each other in their panic. Some crouched behind the sheep fences, some huddled in the lee of boulders, some climbed trees at the edges of the field, but the creature was meticulous in its savagery. It picked up men everywhere—whether alive or dead or wounded or feigning death or hiding or fighting—and devoured them.

Not all the Khalidorans fled. Some turned and fought. Some rallied their fellows and attacked with more courage than the Cenarians would have believed possible, perhaps more courage than they would have shown themselves. But in the face of that horror, courage was irrelevant. The brave and the cowardly, the high and the low, the good and the bad died alike. And the Cenarians watched open-mouthed, not one forgetting that the massacre should have been their own. The few times that a Cenarian here or there cheered, no one took up the cry. The ferali tore this way and that, not catching every group of Khalidorans, but getting most of them, and always, always veering far from the Cenarian ranks, as if it feared the temptation of going too near them.

Finally, having devoured the last group large enough to be worth its time, the ferali fled toward the mountains. Cenaria was either blessed or lucky or Lilly was in better control than Logan had hoped, because it headed in a direction where there were no villages for a hundred miles.

In the silence, someone let out a whoop. For a moment, it hung alone in the air. Logan had been given a new horse and, mounted, he turned and was again aware of thousands of eyes on him. Why were they all looking at him?

Then someone cheered again and the thought wormed its way into Logan's consciousness: They had won. Somehow, against everything, they had won.

For the first time in months, Logan felt his mouth curl into a grin. That let loose a flood and suddenly, no one could stop smiling, or stop yelling, or stop pounding each other on the back. Which noble's flag they had fought under no longer mattered. Agon's Dogs embraced Cenaria City levies: former thieves and former guards standing together as friends. Nobles stood arm in arm with peasants, shouting together. The shattered links binding the country together seemed to be reforming even as Logan looked over the tight-packed army. They had won. The costs had been grievous, but they had stood against the might of a monster and the magic of a god, and they had won.

A cry began to emerge over the sound of swords and spears pounding rhythmically against shields.

"What are they saying?" Logan shouted to Agon, but even as he asked, Logan made out the words, shouted in time with each crash of sword on shield: "KING GYRE! KING GYRE! KING GYRE!" It was audacious; it was treasonous; it was beautiful. Logan looked through the throng for Terah Graesin. She was nowhere to be found. And then he did smile.

The dead god fell like a sack of wheat. Vi was trembling, but she didn't seem to have been harmed by the vir that had wrapped around her. Kylar stared at Garoth Ursuul's corpse, disbelieving.

Kylar's destiny was dead on the floor and Kylar hadn't killed him.

The Wolf had kept his part of the deal: Kylar was alive. But something felt different. Vi was staring at him, still shaking with emotion, tears still wet and hot on her cheeks. He glanced up and read shock and fear in every line of her body—along with a tinge of hope?

What the hell? Since when can I see what a woman feels?

Vi was spattered with the Godking's blood. It was invisible against the background of her dark wetboy grays, but there was something terrible about seeing flecks of red wetness splattered in her cleavage.

As Kylar looked at her, she was so distraught he wanted to take her in his arms. She needed him to love her, to lead her out of the valley of death that was the way of shadows. He knew the way out, now. It was love. They'd go find Uly, and he and Vi would walk that path together—

Me and Vi?

Her eyes went wide with fear and remorse. She was weeping. For a split second he wanted to understand, but then his fingers went slowly up to his ear. There was an earring there, a perfect hoop with no opening, and it was swimming with magic so potent he could feel it in his fingertips.

"I'm so sorry," she said, backing away. "I'm so sorry. It was the only way." She turned and he saw his last gift to Elene—his pledge of love that he had sold his birthright for—sparkling in Vi's ear.

"What have you done?!" he bellowed, and he could see that his rage was amplified through the earring. As it buffeted her, he could feel her remorse and terror and confusion and desperation and self-loathing and . . . hells, her love? Love! How dare she love him?

Vi fled.

He didn't follow. What would he do if he caught her?

She burst through the main door of the throne room, and the guards looked after her, stunned.

They turned and saw Kylar standing over the body of the Godking.

Then it was whistles and alarms and charging highlanders and chanting meisters. Kylar was glad for the nepenthe of battle. It blotted out a future that would never hold Elene. It took all his attention. With only one hand, killing was actually a challenge.

Lantano Garuwashi couldn't stop touching the Blade of Heaven, though of course he kept it sheathed. Once a sa'ceurai drew his sword, he did not sheathe it without first letting it taste blood. As night descended, his men covered the mouth of the cave so their campfires wouldn't be seen by the celebrating Cenarians. After conferring with the spy who'd returned from the Cenarian camp, Garuwashi stood up on a ledge.

In the firelight, his men's eyes glowed with destiny. They had seen wonders denied to their fathers and grandfathers before them. The Blade of Heaven had returned.

Garuwashi began without preliminaries, as was his way. "The Cenarians did not win this battle. That creature won it for them. Tonight, they drink. Tomorrow, they will begin hunting down the scattered Khalidorans. Do you want to know what we will be doing while these buffoons swat at flies?" Men nodded. They held the Blade of Heaven. They followed the Garuwashi. They were invincible.

"Tonight, we will gather the uniforms of the Khalidoran dead. At dawn, we will attack and inflict enough losses to infuriate the Cenarians. We will draw their army east, always just slipping through their fingers. In three days, the rest of our army will arrive here. In five, they will take the undefended Cenaria City. In a month, this country will be ours. In the spring, we will return to Ceura and give them their new king. What do you say?"

Every man cheered but one. Feir Cousat sat silent, stoic. His face might as well have been carved of marble.

EPILOGUE

*H*orses' hooves clattered behind Dorian as he came over the last rise in the foothills and saw Khaliras. He stepped aside and waited patiently, enrapt by the view. The city was still two days' distant, but between the Faltier Mountains and Mount Thrall the plains spread broad and flat. The city and the castle rose with the mountain, one lonely spike in an ocean of grazing land. It had once been his home.

The party began passing Dorian, riding on magnificent horses. Dorian got down on his knees and gave a peasant's obeisance. It wasn't a normal scouting party. Nor were they regular soldiers, though their armor said they were. Their weapons and horses gave them away. The six huge soldiers were members of the Godking's Guard. And from their smell, despite the half-cloaks, the meisters accompanying them were actually Vürdmeisters. They could only be coming from Cenaria, probably bearing great riches in the few chests they carried.

Dorian was stealing brief glimpses when he saw the real treasure. A woman rode with meisters, wearing thick robes, her face veiled. Something seemed oddly familiar about the way she carried herself, and then he saw her eyes.

It was the woman he'd foreseen. His future wife. A shiver passed through his whole body and he remembered bits and pieces of his old prophecies—something about the process of searing his gift had blocked his memories of them.

When he came to himself, he was still kneeling. His muscles were cramped and the sun hung low in the sky. The party was miles ahead of him out on the grasslands. He'd been unconscious for half the day.

Solon, where are you? I need you here. But Dorian knew the answer. If Solon had survived Screaming Winds, he was probably already sailing home to Seth to face his lost love. That woman, now Empress Kaede Wari-yamo, would be furious. Because of Dorian's prophecies, Solon had abandoned his homeland in its hour of need. Dorian could only hope that Solon's path wasn't as lonely as his own.

Because even without prophecy, Dorian knew that whichever way he went, he would walk a path in darkness, alone, suffering so much that giving up his visions had seemed a good idea.

With fear and trembling, Dorian stood. He looked at the path before him and the path behind, the road to Khaliras and his future wife—Jenine, that was her name!—or the road back to his friends. Death and love, or life and loneliness. The God felt as distant as a summer in the Freeze.

Face set, back straight, Dorian continued his long walk to Khaliras.

Ghorran was always watching Elene, his gaze dark, intense. The first day, that hadn't been a problem, because she hadn't needed to relieve herself. The second day, it had. Elene had followed him a short distance into the woods, then stepped behind a bush for some privacy. He waited until she was squatting and lifting her skirts, and then followed her just to shame her. Of course, then she couldn't go.

That night, as they did each night and each morning, the Khalidorans prayed, *"Khali vas, Khalivos ras en me, Khali mevirtu rapt, recu virtum defite."* Ghorran threw Elene to the ground and straddled her. As he prayed, he ground his fingers into the pressure points behind her ears. She screamed and felt warm wetness soak her dress as she lost control of her bladder.

When the prayer was finished, Ghorran got up, clouted her ear, and said, "You stink, filthy bitch."

They didn't let her wash when they crossed a small mountain stream. When Ghorran took her aside that evening, Elene hiked up her skirts and relieved herself as he watched. He took no special delight in watching until she blushed and looked away. "Tomorrow," he said, "I make you wear shit on your face. Yours or someone else's. Your choice."

"Why do you do this?" Elene asked. "Isn't there anything decent in you?"

The next morning, however, they were awakened early. They set out immediately. The captives traveled in a line, tied together, walking behind the Khalidorans. Elene was sixth in line out of six captives with the young boy, Herrald, right in front of her. It took her a while to figure out why the Khalidorans were anxious because they beat the captives if they talked.

There were only five Khalidoran soldiers this morning.

That night, Ghorran seemed to have forgotten his threat. When he took

Elene aside to let her relieve herself, he kept the camp in easy sight. Elene squatted among the tamaracks, which were dropping their golden needles with the onset of autumn, and pretended his presence didn't bother her. "The meisters might meet up with us tomorrow," Ghorran said, keeping his eyes on the camp. "We'll hand all of you over then. That bastard Haavin probably run off, the coward."

Elene stood, and not ten paces from the oblivious Ghorran, she saw a man leaning against a tree. The stranger wore a multitude of cloaks, vests, pocketed shirts, and pouches of all sizes, all of them horsehide, all tanned the same deep brown and worn soft from long use. Twin, forward-curving gurkas were tucked into the back of his belt, an elaborately scrimshawed bow case was slung over his back, and hilts of various sizes hung among the garments. He had an affable face; wry, almond-shaped brown eyes; and loose straight black hair: a Ymmuri stalker. He touched a finger to his lips.

"You finished?" Ghorran asked, glancing toward her.

"Yes," Elene said. She glanced back to the stalker, but he was gone.

There were only four soldiers when they camped that night at the edge of the woods to take advantage of the shelter of the trees. The Khalidorans quarreled about whether they should press on in the darkness or if Haavin and the other missing man had really run away. The night was short, and Ghorran woke Elene in the dark of the morning.

He took her silently into the woods. She hiked up her skirts like it didn't bother her. "How did your chest get hurt?" Elene asked.

"That wild bitch stabbed me with a pitchfork after I killed her husband and gutted her brats." He shrugged, like letting her stab him was a moment of carelessness, embarrassing but not serious.

To Ghorran, eviscerating children held no special significance. He had hurt Elene and shamed her; she could forgive those. But that dismissive shrug blew on the small spark of fury in her heart. For the first time in her life since Rat, Elene hated.

Ghorran had brought a bow with him and now he strung it. "This day, we get to camp," he said, "Neph Dada will do terrible things to you." Ghorran licked his dry lips. "I can save you."

"Save me?"

"What he does should not be done. It is Lodricari foulness. If you run now, I will put an arrow in your back and spare you."

His mercy was so bizarre that Elene's hatred dissolved.

A flash of light burst from the camp fifty paces behind them, throwing shadows against the trees. A scream followed it. Then the sound of galloping horses.

Elene turned and saw a dozen unfamiliar Khalidoran horsemen charging into the camp from the north. They had come early to collect their slaves.

"Run!" a shout rang out, louder than a man should have been able to yell.

Through the trees, Elene saw the Ymmuri stalker fighting the Khalidorans. He cut through two of them in a single move. Fire leapt from one of the horsemen's hands, but he dodged it.

Ghorran nocked an arrow and drew it, but there were too many trees and Khalidorans between him and the Ymmuri. Then, only paces away, the young boy Herrald burst from the woods, running away.

Ghorran turned and aimed, leading his new target.

All Elene thought was *no*.

She grabbed Ghorran's dagger from his belt, brought it over his arm, and buried it in his throat. He spasmed and the arrow leapt from the bow, whistling harmlessly over Herrald's head.

The bow dropped from Ghorran's fingers, and he and Elene regarded each other, shock widening his eyes. The dagger was lodged squarely in the center of his throat, its wide blade blocking his windpipe. He exhaled, his chest straining, and air whistled. He put a hand to his throat and felt the blade, still unbelieving.

Then he tried to inhale. His diaphragm pumped like a bellows, but he couldn't get air. He fell to his knees. Elene couldn't move.

Ghorran ripped the dagger out of his throat and gasped, but the gasp turned to a gurgle. He coughed and blood sprayed over Elene.

He kept trying to breathe as his lungs filled with blood. In moments, he dropped to the forest floor.

Despite the blood on her face, her dress, and her hands, despite the piteous look on Ghorran's face and the horror of watching a man die, Elene didn't feel sorry. She had hated Ghorran only a minute before, but she hadn't killed him out of hatred. He simply had to be stopped. If she could have the moment back, she'd do the same thing. And just like that, she understood.

"My God, what a fool I've been," she said aloud. "Forgive me, Kylar."

With magic bursting in the woods behind her, setting the trees alight, Elene ran.

On the north side of Vos Island in the gloom of the rainy autumn day, Kylar stood staring at the unmarked cairn he'd built. Durzo's grave.

Kylar was spattered with blood, his wetboy grays scored and singed with magic. In a rage he'd fought for hours, killing every Khalidoran soldier and meister he laid eyes on. From the slowly diminishing magic on the throne room's floor, he'd seen Logan's stand, seen the ferali turn, and witnessed the destruction of the Khalidoran army. He'd seen how the men had looked at Logan. Though the figures were tiny, it was written in every line of their bodies.

Logan would march his army home, and in two days when they arrived, he would find his castle swept out and cleansed of the Khalidoran presence—except for Khali, but that was one creature Kylar was going to steer clear of. Let King Gyre invite some mages to take care of that.

"We won, I guess," he told Durzo's grave. Kylar knew there was no use railing against his life. He was the Night Angel, and he didn't get celebrations. As Durzo had told him long ago, he would always be separate, alone.

~It is just so hard to be immortal,~ the ka'kari said.

Kylar was too exhausted to be surprised or offended. The ka'kari had spoken before, he remembered now, trying to save his life. "So you can talk," he said.

The ka'kari puddled into his hand and formed a stylized face. It smiled and winked at him. Kylar sighed and sucked it back into his skin.

Kylar stared at his stump. He'd lost his arm for nothing. He'd made an oath to the Wolf for nothing. Everything Kylar had ever learned, everything he'd ever suffered, had been for one thing: killing Garoth Ursuul was Kylar's destiny. Garoth was the vile fount from which Kylar's and Jarl's and Elene's misery flowed. It was only fitting that the man who'd led Kylar to become a wetboy would be Kylar's last deader. Without Garoth, there would be no Roth. Without Roth, Elene would be unscarred, Jarl would be alive and whole, and Kylar would be—what?—well, not a wetboy.

Count Drake had once told Kylar, "There's a divinity that shapes beauty from our rough-hewn lives." It was a lie, as Kylar's destiny was a lie. Perhaps that was why this was so hard: he'd begun to believe in Elene's divine economy. So now he hadn't just lost Elene, who'd been part of him from the beginning, who'd made Kylar believe good things about himself; he'd also lost his destiny. If he had a destiny, he had a purpose: some pearl being built around the evil he'd suffered and inflicted. If he'd been shaped for a purpose, maybe there was a Shaper. If there was a Shaper, perhaps its name was the One God. And perhaps that One God was a bridge over the chasm between killer and saint that separated Kylar from Elene. But there was no bridge, no God, no Shaper, no purpose, no destiny, no beauty. There was no going back. He'd been cheated of justice and vengeance and love and purpose at once.

He'd thought he could change, that he could buy peace for the price of an old sword. But Retribution was only an instrument of justice. It was Kylar who thirsted to mete it out. He'd killed many men today, and he couldn't make himself feel sorry for it. This was what it was to be the Night Angel. Perhaps a better man could lay down the sword. Kylar could not, not even though it had cost him Elene.

Every time he thought of Elene, her face morphed into Vi's. Every time he thought of Vi, his fantasies morphed from meting out punishment to fantasies of another kind.

"Master," he said to the cairn. "I don't know what to do."

Finish the job. He knew exactly the intonation Durzo would have given the words, exasperated but firm.

It was true. The Wolf had fulfilled his part of the deal: Kylar had come back from death immediately. It turned out to be a lousy trade, but a deal was a deal, so Kylar would go steal Curoch and ride to Torras Bend and get his arm back. It sounded simple enough. After all, stealing wasn't hard when you could make yourself invisible. It wouldn't be a second too soon to get his arm back, either. His stump was aching, and he wouldn't have thought it, but losing a hand threw off his balance.

You're not here because you don't know what to do, boy. You always knew what to do.

That was true, too. Kylar would do this job and then go find Vi and kill her.

~*You won't kill her,*~ the ka'kari said.

"Chatty all of a sudden, aren't you?" Kylar asked.

The ka'kari didn't answer. It was right, though. Kylar wasn't here for direction. Not really. He just missed his master. It was the first time he'd been to the grave since Durzo had died.

Tears started flowing, and Kylar knew only that they were tears of loss. He'd lost his master; he'd lost the girl he betrayed his master to save; he'd lost his master's daughter. He'd lost his one chance at a peaceful life. Mild-mannered herbalist! It had been a sweet delusion, maybe, but it had been sweet. Kylar was lonely, and he was tired of being lonely.

A gopher had dug a hole near the foot of Durzo's cairn. Durzo would be pissed if he had to spend eternity with gophers pawing his corpse. Kylar looked at the hole, irritated. It was deep enough that to normal eyes, the hole would just appear black, but Kylar saw a distinct metallic glimmer at the bottom.

He got on his knees and his stump—oww—and shifted to his elbow—better—and reached in. He stood with a small, sealed metal box in hand. One word was etched on it: "Azoth." It sent a shiver through him. How many people knew that name? Kylar cracked it open awkwardly between his stump and one hand. There was a note inside.

"Hey," it said in Durzo's tight handwriting, "I thought it was my last one, too. He said I got one more for old time's sake..." Kylar eyes blurred. He couldn't believe it. The letter went on, but his eyes were drawn to the final words: "MAKE NO DEALS WITH THE WOLF." The letter was dated a month after Kylar had killed his master. Durzo was alive.

BOOK 3

Beyond the Shadows

For Kristi, for all the usual reasons
&
For my dad, for your excellence and your integrity,
and for raising kids who whisper, "Peep!"

1

$\mathcal{L}$ogan Gyre was sitting in the mud and blood of the battlefield of Pavvil's Grove when Terah Graesin came to him. It was barely an hour since they'd routed the Khalidorans, when the monstrous ferali forged to devour Cenaria's army had turned instead on its Khalidoran masters. Logan had issued the orders that seemed most pressing, then dismissed everyone to join the revelries that were sweeping the Cenarian camp.

Terah Graesin came to him alone. He was sitting on a low rock, heedless of the mud. His fine clothes were so spattered with blood and worse they were a total loss anyway. Terah's dress, by contrast, was clean except for the lower fringe. She wore high shoes, but even those couldn't keep her entirely free of the thick mud. She stopped before him. He didn't stand.

She pretended not to notice. He pretended not to notice that her bodyguards—unbloodied from battle—were hidden in the trees less than a hundred paces away. Terah Graesin could have only one reason to come to him: she was wondering if she was still the queen.

If Logan hadn't been so bone-weary, he would have been amused. Terah had come to him alone as a show of vulnerability or fearlessness. "You were a hero today," Terah said. "You stopped the Godking's beast. They're saying you killed him."

Logan shook his head. He'd stabbed the ferali, and then the Godking had left it, but other men had given it more grievous wounds than he had. Something else had stopped the Godking, not Logan.

"You commanded it to destroy our enemies, and it did. You saved Cenaria."

Logan shrugged. It already seemed long ago.

"I guess the question is," Terah Graesin said, "did you save Cenaria for yourself, or for all of us?"

Logan spat at her feet. "Don't give me that horseshit, Terah. You think you're going to manipulate me? You've got nothing to offer, nothing to threaten. You've got a question for me? Have a little respect and just fucking ask."

Terah's back stiffened, her chin lifted, and one hand twitched, but then she stopped.

It was the hand twitch that captured Logan's attention. If she had raised her hand, was that the sign for her men to attack? Logan looked past her into the woods at the edge of the field, but the first thing he saw wasn't her men. He saw his own. Agon's Dogs—including two of the astoundingly talented archers Agon had armed with Ymmuri bows and made wytch hunters—had stealthily circled behind Terah's bodyguards. Both wytch hunters had arrows nocked, but not drawn. Both men had obviously taken care to stand where Logan could see them clearly, because none of the other Dogs were clearly visible.

One archer was alternately looking at Logan and at a target in the woods. Logan followed his eyes and saw Terah's hidden archer, aiming at Logan, waiting for Terah's signal. The other wytch hunter was staring at Terah Graesin's back. They were waiting for Logan's signal. Logan should have known his streetwise followers wouldn't leave him alone when Terah Graesin was near.

He looked at Terah. She was slim, pretty, with imperious green eyes that reminded Logan of his mother's. Terah thought Logan didn't know about her men in the woods. She thought Logan didn't know that she had the stronger hand. "You swore fealty to me this morning under less than ideal circumstances," Terah said. "Do you intend to keep your troth, or do you intend to make yourself king?"

She couldn't ask the question straight, could she? It just wasn't in her, not even when she thought she had total control over Logan. She would not make a good queen.

Logan thought he'd already made his decision, but he hesitated. He remembered how it felt to be powerless in the Hole, how it felt to be powerless when Jenine, his just-wed wife, had been murdered. He remembered how disconcertingly wonderful it felt to tell Kylar to kill Gorkhy and see it done. He wondered if he would feel the same pleasure at seeing Terah Graesin die. With one nod toward those wytch hunters, he would find out. He would never feel powerless again.

His father had told him, "An oath is the measure of the man who gives it." Logan had seen what happened when he did what he knew was right, no matter how foolish it looked at the time. That was what rallied the Holers around him. That was what had saved his life when he was feverish and barely conscious. That was what had made Lilly—the woman the Khalidorans crafted into the ferali—turn on the Khalidorans. Ultimately, Logan's doing what was right had saved all of Cenaria. But his father Regnus Drake had lived by his oaths, through a miserable marriage and miserable service to a petty, wicked king. He gritted his teeth all day and slept well every night. Logan didn't know if he was as much of a man as his father. He couldn't do it.

So he hesitated. If she raised her hand to order her men to attack, she would be breaking the covenant between lord and vassal. If she broke it, he would be free.

"Our soldiers proclaimed me king." Logan said in a neutral tone. *Lose your temper, Terah. Order the attack. Order your own death.*

Terah's eyes lit, but her voice was steady and her hand didn't move. "Men say many things in the heat of battle. I am prepared to forgive this indiscretion."

Is this what Kylar saved me for?

No. But this is the man I am. I am my father's son.

Logan stood slowly so as not to alarm either side's archers, then, slowly, he knelt and touched Terah Graesin's feet in submission.

Late that night, a band of Khalidorans attacked the Cenarian camp, killing dozens of drunken revelers before fleeing into the darkness. In the morning, Terah Graesin sent Logan Gyre and a thousand of his men to hunt them down.

2

The sentry was a seasoned sa'ceurai, a sword lord who'd killed sixteen men and bound their forelocks into his fiery red hair. His eyes probed the darkness restlessly where the forest and the oak grove met, and when he turned, he shielded his eyes from his comrades' low fires to protect his night vision. Despite the cool wind that swept the camp and set the great oaks groaning, he wore no helmet that would muffle his hearing. But he had no chance of stopping the wetboy.

Former wetboy, Kylar thought, balancing one-handed on a broad oak limb. If he were still a killer for hire, he'd murder the sentry and be done with it. Kylar was something different now, the Night Angel—immortal, invisible, and nearly invincible—and he only served death to those who deserved it.

These swordsmen from the land whose very name meant "the sword," Ceura, were the best soldiers Kylar had ever seen. They had set up camp with efficiency that spoke of years of campaigning. They cleared brush that might conceal the approach of enemies, banked their small fires to reduce their visibility, and arranged their tents to protect their horses and their leaders. Each fire warmed ten men, each of whom clearly knew his responsibilities. They moved like ants in the forest, and once they finished their duties, each man would only wander as far as an adjacent fire. They gambled, but they didn't drink, and they kept their voices low. The only snag in all the Ceurans' efficiency seemed to come from their armor. With Ceuran bamboo-and-lacquer armor, a man could dress himself. But donning the Khalidoran armor they had stolen a week ago at Pavvil's Grove required assistance. Scale mail mixed with chain and even plate, and the Ceurans couldn't decide if they needed to sleep armored or if men should be assigned to each other as squires.

When each squad was allowed to decide for itself how to fix the problem and didn't waste time asking up the chain of command, Kylar knew his friend Logan Gyre was doomed. War Leader Lantano Garuwashi paired the Ceuran love of order with individual responsibility. It was emblematic of why Garuwashi had never lost a battle. It was why he had to die.

So Kylar moved through the trees like the breath of a vengeful god, only rustling the branches in time with the evening wind. The oaks grew in straight, widely spaced rows broken where younger trees had muscled between their elders' shoulders and grown ancient themselves. Kylar climbed out as far on a limb as he could and spied Lantano Garuwashi through the swaying branches, dimly illuminated in the light of his fire, touching the sword in his lap with the delight of recent acquisition. If Kylar could get to the next oak, he could climb down mere paces from his deader.

Can I still call my target a "deader," even though I'm not a wetboy anymore? Thinking of Garuwashi as a "target" was impossible. Kylar could still hear his master Durzo Blint's voice, *"Assassins,"* he sneered, *"have targets, because assassins sometimes miss."*

Kylar gauged the distance to the next limb that could bear his weight. Eight paces. It was no great leap. The daunting part was landing on a tree limb and arresting his momentum silently with only one arm. If Kylar didn't leap, he'd have to sneak between two fires where men were still passing intermittently, and the ground was strewn with dead leaves. He'd jump, he decided, when the next good breeze came.

"There's an odd light in your eyes," Lantano Garuwashi said. He was big for a Ceuran, tall and lean and as heavily muscled as a tiger. Stripes of his own hair, burning the same color as the flickering fire, were visible through the sixty locks of all colors he'd claimed from opponents he'd killed.

"I've always loved fire. I want to remember it as I die."

Kylar shifted to get a look at the speaker. It was Feir Cousat, a blond mountain of a man as wide as he was tall. Kylar had met him once. Feir was not only a capable hand with a sword, he was a mage. Kylar was lucky the man's back was to him.

A week ago, after the Khalidoran Godking Garoth Ursuul killed him, Kylar had made a bargain with the yellow-eyed being called the Wolf. In his weird lair in the lands between life and death, the Wolf promised to restore Kylar's right arm and bring him back to life quickly if Kylar stole Lantano Garuwashi's sword. What had seemed simple—who can stop an invisible man from stealing?—was getting more complicated by the second. Who can stop an invisible man? A mage who can see invisible men.

"So you really believe the Dark Hunter lives in those woods?" Garuwashi asked.

"Draw the blade a little, War Leader," Feir said. Garuwashi bared the sword a hand's breadth. Light poured from a blade that looked like a crystal filled with fire. "The blade burns to warn of danger or magic. The Dark Hunter is both."

So am I, Kylar thought.

"It's close?" Garuwashi asked. He rose to a crouch like a tiger ready to pounce.

"I told you luring the Cenarian army here might be our deaths, not theirs," Feir said. He stared back into the fire.

For the past week, since the battle of Pavvil's Grove, Garuwashi had led Logan and his men east. Because the Ceurans had disguised themselves in dead Khalidorans' armor, Logan thought he was chasing the remnants of the defeated Khalidoran army. Kylar still had no idea why Lantano Garuwashi had led Logan here.

But then, he had no idea why the black metal ball called a ka'kari had chosen to serve him, or why it brought him back from death, or why he saw the taint on men's souls that demanded death, or, for that matter, why the sun rose, or how it hung in the sky without falling.

"You said we were safe as long as we didn't go into the Hunter's wood," Garuwashi said.

"I said 'probably' safe," Feir said. "The Hunter senses and hates magic. That sword definitely counts."

Garuwashi waved a hand, dismissing the danger. "We didn't go into the Hunter's wood—and if the Cenarians want to fight us, they must," Garuwashi said.

As Kylar finally understood the plan, he could hardly breathe. The woods north, south, and west of the grove were thick and overgrown. The only way for Logan to use his numerical superiority would be to come through the east, where the giant sequoys of the Dark Hunter's Wood gave an army plenty of space to maneuver. But it was said a creature from ages past killed anything that entered that wood. Learned men scoffed at such superstition, but Kylar had met the peasants of Torras Bend. If they were superstitious, they were a people with only one superstition. Logan would march right into the trap.

The wind kicked up again, setting the branches groaning. Kylar snarled silently, and leapt. With his Talent he made the distance easily. But he'd jumped too hard, too far, and he slipped off the far side of the branch. Little black talons jabbed through his clothing along the sides of his knees, along his left forearm, and even from his ribs. For a moment, the talons were liquid metal, not so much tearing his clothes as absorbing them at each tiny point, and then they solidified and Kylar jerked to a stop.

After he pulled himself back onto the branch, the claws melted back into his skin. Kylar was left trembling, and not just because of how close he'd come to falling. *What am I becoming?* With every death reaped and every death suffered, he was growing stronger. It scared the hell out of him. *What does it cost? There's got to be a price.*

Gritting his teeth, Kylar climbed headfirst down the tree, letting the claws rise and sink from his skin, stabbing little holes in his clothes and in the tree bark. When he reached the ground, the black ka'kari bled from every pore to cover him like a second skin. It masked his face and body and clothes and sword, and began devouring light. Invisible, Kylar advanced.

"I dreamed of living in a small town like that Torras Bend," Feir said, his back as broad as an ox before Kylar. "Build a smithy on the river, design a water wheel to drive the bellows until my sons are old enough to help. A prophet told me it could happen."

"Enough of your dreams," Garuwashi cut him off, standing. "My main army should be almost through the mountains. You and I are going."

Main army? The last piece clicked. This was why the sa'ceurai had dressed as Khalidorans. Garuwashi had drawn the best of Cenaria's army far to the east while his main army was massing in the west. With the Khalidorans defeated at Pavvil's Grove, Cenaria's peasant levies were probably already hurrying back to their farms. In days, a couple hundred Cenarian castle guards were going to face the entire Ceuran army.

"Going? Tonight?" Feir asked, surprised.

"Now." Garuwashi smirked right at Kylar. Kylar froze, but he saw no flash of recognition in those green eyes. Instead, he saw something worse.

There were eighty-two kills in Garuwashi's eyes. *Eighty-two!* And not one of them a murder. Killing Lantano Garuwashi wouldn't be justice; it would be murder. Kylar cursed aloud.

Lantano Garuwashi jumped to his feet, the scabbard flying from a sword that looked like a bar of flame, his body already in a fighting stance. The mountain that was Feir was only a little slower. He was on his feet, turning with naked steel in his hand faster than Kylar would have believed from a man so big. His eyes went wide as he saw Kylar.

Kylar screamed in frustration and let blue flame whoosh over the ka'kari-skin and the great frowning mask he wore. He heard a footstep as one of Garuwashi's bodyguards attacked from behind. Kylar's Talent surged and he back-flipped, planting his feet on the man's shoulders and pushing off. The sa'ceurai smashed into the ground and Kylar flipped through the air, blue flames whipping and crackling from his body.

Before he caught the branch, he dropped the flames and went invisible. He flipped from branch to branch one-handed, with no attempt at stealth. If he didn't do something—tonight—Logan and all his men would die.

"Was that the Hunter?" Garuwashi asked.

"Worse," Feir said, pale. "That was the Night Angel, perhaps the only man in the world you need fear."

Lantano Garuwashi's eyes lit with a fire that told Feir he heard the words "man you need fear" as "worthy adversary."

"Which way did he go?" Garuwashi asked.

3

$\mathcal{A}$s Elene rode up to the little inn in Torras Bend, utterly exhausted, a gorgeous young woman with long red hair in a ponytail and an earring sparkling in her left ear, was mounting a roan stallion. The stable hand ogled her as she rode north.

Elene was almost on top of the stable hand before the man turned. He blinked at her stupidly. "Hey, your friend just left," he said, pointing to the disappearing redhead.

"What are you talking about?" Elene was so tired she could hardly think. She'd walked for two days before one of the horses had found her. And she'd never found out what had happened to the other captives or the Khalidorans or the Ymmuri who'd saved her.

"You could still catch her," the stable hand said.

Elene had seen the young woman well enough to know that they'd never met. She shook her head. She had to pick up supplies in Torras Bend before she headed to Cenaria. Besides, it was almost dark, and after her days on the trail with her Khalidoran captors, Elene needed a night in bed and desperately needed a chance to wash up. "I don't think so," she said.

She went inside, rented a room from the distracted innkeeper's wife with some of the generous amount of silver she'd found in her horse's saddlebags, washed herself and her filthy clothing, and immediately fell asleep.

Before dawn, she pulled on her still-damp dress distastefully and went downstairs.

The innkeeper, a slight young man, was carrying in a crate full of washed flagons from outside and setting them upside-down to dry before he finally went to bed for the night. He nodded at Elene in a friendly manner, barely glancing up. "The wife will have breakfast ready in half an hour. And if—oh hell." He looked at her again, obviously seeing her for the first time. "Maira didn't tell me...." He rubbed his hands on his apron in what was obviously a habitual gesture, because his hands weren't wet, and stalked over to a table piled high with knickknacks, notes, and account books.

He pulled out a note, and handed it to her apologetically. "I didn't see you last night, or I'd have given it to you straight away." Elene's name and description were written on the outside of the note. She unfolded it and a smaller, crumpled note fell out. The smaller note was in Kylar's hand. It was dated the day he'd left her in Caernarvon. Her throat tightened.

"Elene," she read, "I'm sorry. I tried. I swear I tried. Some things are worth more than my happiness. Some things only I can do. Sell these to Master Bourary and move the family to a better part of town. I will always love you."

Kylar still loved her. He loved her. She'd always believed it, but it was different to see it in his own messy writing. The tears flowed freely. She didn't even care about the disconcerted innkeeper, opening and shutting his mouth, unsure what to do with a woman crying in his inn.

Elene had refused to change and it had cost her everything, but the God was giving her a second chance. She'd show Kylar just how strong, deep, and wide a woman's love could be. It wasn't going to be easy, but he was the man she loved. He was the one. She loved him, and it was as simple as that.

It was several minutes before she read the other note, this one written in an unfamiliar woman's hand.

"My name's Vi," the note said, "I'm the wetboy who killed Jarl and kidnapped Uly. Kylar left you to save Logan and kill the Godking. The man you love saved Cenaria. I hope you're proud of him. If you go to Cenaria, I've given Momma K access to my accounts for you. Take whatever you want. Otherwise, Uly will be at the Chantry, as will I, and I think Kylar will go there soon. There's . . . more, but I can't bear to write it. I had to do something terrible so we could win. No words can erase what I've done to you. I'm so terribly sorry. I wish that I could make it right, but I can't. When you come, you can exact whatever vengeance you wish, even to my life. Vi Sovari"

The hairs on the back of Elene's neck were standing up. What kind of a person would claim to be such an enemy and such a friend? Where were Elene's wedding earrings? "There's more"? What did that mean? Vi had done something terrible?

The lead weight of intuition dropped into Elene's stomach. That woman outside yesterday had been wearing an earring. It probably wasn't—it surely wasn't—

"Oh my God," Elene said. She ran for her horse.

The dream was different every night. Logan stood on the platform, looking at pretty, petty Terah Graesin. She would walk over an army of corpses— or marry a man she despised—to seize her ambition. As it had that day,

Logan's heart failed him. His father had married a woman who poisoned all his happiness. Logan could not.

As he had that day, Logan asked for her fealty, the round platform reminding him of the Hole where he'd rotted during the Khalidoran occupation. Terah refused. But instead of submitting himself so the armies wouldn't be split on the eve of battle, in this dream Logan said, "Then I sentence you to death for treason."

His sword sang. Terah stumbled back, too slowly. The blade cut halfway through her neck.

Logan caught her, and abruptly, it was another woman, another place. Jenine's slashed throat gushed blood over her white nightgown and his bare chest. The Khalidorans who'd broken into their wedding chamber laughed.

Logan thrashed and woke. He lay in darkness. It took him time to reorient himself. His Jenine was dead. Terah Graesin was queen. Logan had sworn fealty. Logan Gyre had given his troth, a word that meant not just his oath but his truth. So if his queen ordered him to stamp out the last few Khalidorans, he complied. He would always be glad to kill Khalidorans.

Sitting up in the dark of the camp tent, Logan saw the captain of his bodyguards, Kaldrosa Wyn. During the occupation, Momma K's brothels had become the safest places in the city for women. Momma K had accepted only the most beautiful and exotic. They had drawn the first Khalidoran blood of the war during a city-wide ambush that had come to be called the Nocta Hemata, the Night of Blood. Logan had honored them publicly and they had become his. Those who could fight had fought and died—and saved him. After the Battle of Pavvil's Grove, Logan had dismissed the rest of the Order of the Garter except for Kaldrosa Wyn. Her husband was one of the ten wytch hunters, and they'd go nowhere without each other, so she'd said she might as well serve.

Kaldrosa wore her garter on her left arm. Sewn from enchanted Khalidoran battle flags, it glimmered even in the darkness. She was, of course, pretty, with olive Sethi skin, a throaty laugh, and a hundred stories, some of which she claimed were even true. Her chain mail was ill-fitting, and she wore a tabard with his white gyrfalcon, its wingtips breaking a black circle. "It's time," she said.

General Agon Brant poked his head in the tent, then entered. He still needed two canes to walk. "The scouts have returned. Our elite Khalidorans think they're setting an ambush. If we come from the north, south, or west, we have to go through dense forest. The only way is through the Hunter's Wood. If it really exists, it'll wipe us out. If I were facing fourteen hundred men with only one hundred, I don't think I could do any better."

If the situation had arisen a month ago, Logan wouldn't have hesitated. He would lead his army through the open spaces of the Hunter's Wood, legends be damned. But at Pavvil's Grove they'd seen a legend walk—and devour thousands. The ferali had shaken Logan's conviction that he knew the difference between superstition and reality. "They're Khalidoran. Why didn't they head north for Quorig's Pass?"

Agon shrugged. It was a week-old problem. This platoon wasn't nearly as sloppy as the Khalidorans they knew. Even as they fled from Logan's army, they'd raided. Cenaria had lost a hundred men. The Khalidorans hadn't lost one. The best guess Agon could make was that they were an elite unit from some Khalidoran tribe the Cenarians hadn't encountered before. Logan felt like he was staring at a puzzle. If he didn't solve it, his people would die. "You still want to hit them from all sides?" Agon asked.

The problem stared at Logan, mocking him. The answer didn't come. "Yes."

"Are you still insisting on leading the cavalry through the Wood yourself?"

Logan nodded. If he was going to ask men to brave death from some monster, he would do it himself, too.

"That's very...brave," Agon said. He'd served nobles long enough to make a compliment speak volumes of insult.

"Enough," Logan said, accepting his helmet from Kaldrosa. "Let's go kill some Khalidorans."

Vürdmeister Neph Dada hacked a deep, rasping, unhealthy cough. He cleared his throat noisily and spat the results into his hand. Then he tilted his hand and watched the phlegm drip to the dirt before turning his eyes to the other Vürdmeisters around his low fire. Aside from the young Borsini, who blinked incessantly, they gave no sign that he disgusted them. A man didn't survive long enough to become a Vürdmeister on magical strength alone.

Glowing faintly, figures were laid out in military formations on the ground. "This is only an estimation of the armies' positions," Neph said. "Logan Gyre's forces are in red, roughly fourteen hundred men, west of the Dark Hunter's Wood, in Cenarian lands. Maybe two hundred Ceurans pretending to be Khalidoran are the blue, right at the edge of the Wood. Further south, in white, are five thousand of our beloved enemies the Lae'knaught. We Khalidorans haven't fought the Lae'knaught directly since you were all still at the tit, so let me remind you that though they hate all magic, *we* are what they were created to destroy. Five thousand of them is more than enough to complete the job the Cenarians began at the Battle of Pavvil's Grove, so we must tread carefully."

In quick detail, Neph outlined what he knew of the deployment of all the forces, inventing details where it seemed appropriate, and always speaking over the Vürdmeisters' heads, as if expecting them to understand intricacies of generalship that they had never learned. Whenever a Godking died, the massacres began. First the heirs turned on each other. Then the survivors rallied meisters and Vürdmeisters around them and began anew until only one Ursuul remained. If no one established dominance quickly, the blood-letting would spread to the meisters. Neph didn't intend for that to happen.

So as soon as he was certain that Godking Garoth Ursuul was dead, Neph had found Tenser Ursuul, one of the Godking's heirs, and convinced the boy to carry Khali. Tenser thought carrying the goddess would mean power. It would—for Neph. For Tenser, it meant catatonia and insanity. Then Neph had sent a simple message to Vürdmeisters at every corner of the Khalidoran empire: "Help me bring Khali home."

By answering a religious call, every Vürdmeister who didn't want to throw away his life backing some vicious Ursuul child had a legitimate escape. And if Neph tamed these first Vürdmeisters who'd arrived from their postings in nearby lands, when Vürdmeisters arrived from the rest of the empire, they too would fall in line. If there was one thing Godkings were good at, it was inculcating submission.

"The Dark Hunter's Wood is between us," Neph motioned to encompass the Vürdmeisters, himself, and Khali's bodyguard, a bare fifty men in all, "and all these armies. I personally have seen over a hundred men—meisters and not—ordered into the Wood. None has emerged. Ever. If this were merely a matter of Khali's security, I would not bring this to your attention." Neph coughed again, his lungs afire, but the coughing was calculated, too. Those who wouldn't bend the knee to a young man might be content to bide their time serving a failing old one. He spat. "The Ceurans have the sword of power, Curoch. Right there," Neph gestured to where his phlegm had fallen, at the very edge of the Dark Hunter's Wood.

"Has the sword taken the form of Ceur'caelestos, the Ceurans' Blade of Heaven?" Vürdmeister Borsini asked. He was the young blinking one with a grotesquely large nose and big ears to match. He was staring into the distance. Neph didn't like it. Had Borsini been eavesdropping when the scout reported?

Borsini's vir, the measure of the goddess's favor and his magical power, filled his arms like a hundred thorny black rose stems. Only Neph's vir filled more of his skin, undulating like living tattoos in Lodricari whorls, blackening him from forehead to fingernails. But despite his intelligence and power, Borsini was only in the eleventh shu'ra. Neph, Tarus, Orad, and Raalst were all twelfth shu'ra, the highest rank anyone aside from the God-king could attain.

"Curoch takes any shape it pleases," Neph said. "The point is, if Curoch goes into the Hunter's Wood, it will never come out. We have a slim chance to seize a prize we've sought for ages."

"But there are three armies here," Vürdmeister Tarus pointed out. "All outnumber us, and each would happily kill us."

"Attempting to claim the sword will most likely end in death, but may I remind you," Neph said, "if we don't try, we will answer for it. Therefore, I will go. I am old. I have few years remaining to me, so my death will cost the empire less." Of course, if he had Curoch in hand, magnifying his magical power a hundredfold, everything would change, and all of them knew it.

Vürdmeister Tarus was the first to object. "Who's put you in charge—"

"Khali has," young Borsini interrupted before Neph could. *Dammit!* "Khali has sent me a vision," he said. "That's why I asked what the Ceurans call the sword. Khali told me that I am to fetch Ceur'caelestos. I am the youngest of us, the most dispensable, and the fastest. Vürdmeister Dada, she said she will speak to you this morning. You are to await her word by the prince's bedside. Alone."

The boy was a genius. Borsini wanted a chance at the sword, and he was buying off Neph in front of all of them. Neph would stay with Khali and the catatonic prince and when he emerged, it would be with "a word from the goddess." In truth, Neph hadn't wanted to go after the sword at all. But the only way he was certain the others would make him stay was if he'd tried to go. Borsini's eyes met Neph's. His look said, "If I get the sword, you serve me. Understood?"

"Blessed be her name," Neph said. The others echoed. They didn't fully understand what had just happened. They would, in time. Neph said, "You should take my horse; it's faster than yours." And he had woven a small cantrip into its mane. When the sun rose—at about the time a rider would get to the south side of the wood—the cantrip would begin pulsing with magic that would draw the Dark Hunter. Borsini wouldn't live to see noon.

"Thank you, but I'm an awkward hand at new horses. I'll take my own," Borsini said, his voice carefully neutral. His enormous ears wiggled, and he tugged at his enormous nose nervously. He suspected a trap and knew he'd avoided it, but he wanted Neph to think it was luck.

Neph blinked as if disappointed and then shrugged as if to cover and say it didn't matter.

It didn't. He'd tied that cantrip into the mane of every horse in the camp.

Kylar had never started a war.

Approaching the Lae'knaught camp required none of the stealth he'd used to approach the Ceurans. Invisible, he simply walked past the sentries in their black tabards emblazoned with a golden sun: the pure light of reason beating back the darkness of superstition. Kylar grinned. The Lae'knaught were going to love the Night Angel.

The camp was huge. It held an entire legion, five thousand soldiers, including a thousand of the famed Lae'knaught Lancers. As a purely ideological society, the Lae'knaught claimed they held no land. In practice, they'd occupied eastern Cenaria for eighteen years. Kylar suspected this legion had been sent here as a show of force to deter Khalidor from trying to push further east. Maybe they just happened to be here.

In truth, he didn't care. The Lae'knaught were bullies. If there had been a shred of integrity in their claim of fighting black magic, they would have come to Cenaria's defense when Khalidor invaded. Instead, they'd bided their time, burning local "wytches" and recruiting among the Cenarian refugees. They'd probably been hoping to come to the rescue after Cenaria's power was obliterated and take even better lands for their pains.

Without provoking anyone, Cenaria had been invaded from the east by the Lae'knaught, from the north by Khalidor, and now from the south by Ceura. It was about time some of those hungry swords met each other.

A smoking black blade slid from Kylar's left hand. He made it glow, wreathed in blue flames, but kept himself invisible. Two soldiers chatting instead of walking their patrol routes froze at the sight. The first one was a relative innocent. In the other's eyes, Kylar could see that the man had accused a miller of witchcraft because he wanted the man's wife.

"Murderer," Kylar said. He slashed with the ka'kari-sword. The blade didn't so much cut as devour. There was barely any resistance as the blade passed through noseguard, nose, chin, tabard, gambeson, and stomach. The man looked down, then touched his split face, where blood gushed. He screamed and his entrails spurted out.

The other sentry bolted, shrieking.

Kylar ran, pulling his illusions around him. As if through smoke, there were glimpses of gleaming iridescent black metal skin, the crescents of exaggerated muscles, a face like Judgment, with brows pronounced and frowning, high angular cheekbones, a tiny mouth, and glossy black eyes without pupils that leaked blue flames. He ran past a knot of gaunt Cenarian recruits, wide-eyed at the sight of him, weapons in hand but forgotten. There were no crimes in their eyes. These men had joined because they had no other way to feed themselves.

The next group had participated in a hundred burnings, and worse. *"Raper!"* Kylar yelled. He slid the ka'kari-sword through the man's loins. It would be a bad death. Three more died before anyone attacked him. He danced past a spear and lopped off its head, then kept running for the command tents at the center of the camp.

A trumpet shrilled an alarm, finally. Kylar continued down the lines of tents, sometimes slipping back into invisibility, always reappearing before he killed. He cut loose some of the horses to create confusion, but not many. He wanted this army to be able to react quickly.

In minutes, the entire camp was in pandemonium. A team of horses dragging their hitching post bolted, the post whipping back and forth, tangling in tents and dragging them away. Men screamed, shouting obscenities, gibbering about a ghost, a demon, a phantasm. Some attacked each other in the darkness and confusion. A tent went up in flames. Whenever an officer emerged, shouting, trying to bring order, Kylar killed. Finally, he found what he was looking for.

An older man burst out of the largest tent in the camp. He threw a great helm on his head, the symbol of a Lae'knaught underlord, a general. "Form up! Hedgehog!" he shouted. "You fools, you're being beguiled! Hedgehog formation, damn you!"

Between their terror and his voice being muted by the great helm, few men listened at first, but a trumpeter blew the signal again and again. Kylar saw men starting to form loose circles of ten with their backs to each other, spears out.

"You're only fighting yourselves. It's a delusion. Remember your armor!" The underlord meant the armor of unbelief. The Lae'knaught thought superstitions only had power if you believed in them.

Kylar leapt high into the air, and let himself become visible as he dropped in front of the underlord. He landed on one knee, his left hand to the ground, holding the sword, his head bowed. Though the cacophony continued in the distance, the men nearby were stunned to silence. "Underlord," the Night Angel said. "For you I bear a message." He stood.

"It is nothing but an apparition," the underlord announced. "Gather! Eagle three!" The trumpeter blew the orders and soldiers began jogging to take up positions.

Over a hundred men crowded the clearing in front of the underlord's tent, forming a huge circle around him, spears pointing in. The Night Angel roared, blue flames leaping from his mouth and eyes. Flames trickled back down the sword. He whipped the sword in circles so fast it blurred into long ribbons of light. Then he slapped it back into its sheath with a pulse of light, leaving the soldiers blinking away after-images.

"You Lae'knaught fools," the Night Angel said. "This land is Khalidoran now. Flee or be slaughtered. Flee or face judgment." By claiming to be Khalidoran, Kylar hoped to draw any backlash onto the Ceurans-disguised-as-Khalidorans who were trying to kill Logan and all his men.

The underlord blinked. Then he shouted, "Delusions have no power over us! Remember your armor, men!"

Kylar let the flames dim, as if the Night Angel were unable to sustain itself without the Lae'knaught's belief. He faded until the only thing visible was his sword, moving in slow forms: Morning Shadows to Haden's Glory, Dripping Water to Kevan's Blunder.

"It cannot touch us," the underlord announced to the hundreds of soldiers now crowding the edges of the clearing. "The Light is ours! We do not fear the darkness."

"I judge you!" the Night Angel said. "I find you wanting!" He faded completely and saw relief in every eye around the circle, some men and women openly grinning and shaking their heads, amazed but victorious.

The underlord's aide-de-camp led his horse to him and handed him the reins and his lance. He mounted, looking like he knew he needed to start giving orders, reasserting control, getting the men to act so they wouldn't think, so they wouldn't panic. Kylar waited until he opened his mouth, then bellowed so loudly he drowned out the man's voice.

"Murderer!" Crescents of biceps and knotted shoulder muscles and glowing eyes were all that appeared, followed by a whoosh of flame as the spinning sword came alight. A soldier toppled to the ground. By the time his hcad rolled free of his body, the Night Angel was gone.

No one moved. It wasn't possible. An apparition was the product of mass hysteria. It had no body.

"Slaver!" This time, the sword appeared only as it jutted out of the soldier's back. The man was lifted on the sword and flung headlong into the side of the iron cauldron. He jerked, his flesh sizzling on the coals, but he didn't roll away.

"Torturer!" The legion's gentler's stomach opened.

"Unclean! Unclean!" The Night Angel screamed, its whole figure glowing, burning blue. It killed left and right.

"Kill it!" the underlord screamed.

Wreathed in blue flames that whipped and crackled in long streams behind him, Kylar was already flipping clear of the circle. Staying visible and burning, he ran straight north, as if heading back to the "Khalidoran" camp. Men dove out of his path. Then Kylar extinguished the flames, went invisible, and came back to see if his trap had worked.

"Form up!" the underlord shouted, his face purple with rage. "We march to the forest! It's time to kill some wytches, men! Let's go! Now!"

6

Eunuchs to the left," Rugger said. The Khalidoran guard said. He was so muscular he looked like a sack full of nuts, but the most noticeable lump was the wen bulging grotesquely from his forehead. "Hey, Halfman! That means you!"

Dorian shuffled into the line on the left, tearing his eyes away from the guard. He knew the man: a bastard who'd been whelped on some slave girl by one of Dorian's older brothers. The aethelings, the throne-worthy sons, had tormented Rugger unrelentingly. Dorian's tutor, Neph Dada, encouraged it. There was just one rule: they couldn't do harm to any slave that would keep him from performing his duties. Rugger's wen had been little Dorian's work.

"You staring at something?" Rugger demanded, poking Dorian with his spear.

Dorian looked resolutely at the floor and shook his head. He'd altered his appearance as much as he dared before coming to the Citadel to ask for work, but he couldn't take any illusion too far. He would be beaten regularly. A guard or noble or aetheling would notice if a blow didn't hit the proper resistance or if Dorian didn't flinch appropriately. He'd experimented with altering the balance of his humors so that he might stop growing a man's hair, too, but the results had been horrifying. He touched his chest—now mercifully back to male proportions—just thinking about it.

Instead, he'd practiced until he could sweep his body with fire and air so as to be hairless. With the speed his beard came in, it would be a weave he would have to use twice a day. A slave's life included little privacy, so speed was essential. Mercifully, slaves were beneath notice—as long as they didn't draw attention to themselves by staring at guards as if they were freaks.

Slouch or die, Dorian. Rugger smacked him again, but Dorian didn't move, so Rugger moved down the line to harass others.

They were standing outside the Bridge Keep. Two hundred men and women were at the keep's west gate. Winter was coming, and even those who'd had good harvests had been beggared by the Godking's armies. For the smallfolk, it hardly mattered if the army passing through was enemy or friend. One looted, the other scavenged, but each took what it wanted and killed anyone who resisted. With the Godking emptying the Citadel to send armies both south into Cenaria and north into the Freeze, the coming winter would be brutal. All the people in the line were hoping to sell themselves into slavery before winter arrived and the lines quadrupled.

It was an icy clear autumn morning in the city of Khaliras, two hours before dawn. Dorian had forgotten the glory of the northern stars. In the city, few lamps burned—oil was too precious, so few terrestrial fires tried to compete with the ethereal flames burning like holes in the cloak of heaven.

Despite himself, Dorian couldn't help but feel a stirring of pride as he looked over the city that could have been his. Khaliras was laid out in an enormous ring around the chasm that surrounded Mount Thrall. Succeeding generations of Ursuul Godkings had walled in semicircles of the city to protect their slaves and artisans and merchants until all the semicircles of different stone had connected to shield the whole of the city.

There was only one hill, a narrow granite ridge up which the main road snaked in switchbacks designed to encumber siege weapons. At the top of the ridge the Gate Keep sat like a toad on a stump. And just on the other side of the rusty iron portcullis's teeth lay Dorian's first great challenge.

"You four, go," Rugger said.

Dorian was third of four eunuchs, and all shivered as they approached the precipice. Luxbridge was one of the wonders of the world, and in all his travels, Dorian had never seen magic to rival it. Without arches, without pillars, the bridge hung like a spider's anchor line for four hundred paces between the Gate Keep and the Citadel of Mount Thrall.

The last time he'd crossed Luxbridge, Dorian had only noticed the brilliance of the magic, sparkling, springy underfoot, coruscating in a thousand colors at every step. Now, he saw nothing but the building blocks to which the magic was anchored. Luxbridge's mundane materials were not stone, metal, or wood; it was paved with human skulls in a path wide enough for three horses to pass abreast. New heads had been added to whatever holes had formed over the years. Any Vürdmeister, as masters of the vir were called after they passed the tenth shu'ra, could dispel the entire bridge with a word. Dorian even knew the spell, for all the good it did him. What made his stomach knot was that the magic of Luxbridge had been crafted so that magi, who used the Talent rather than the foul vir that meisters and Vürdmeisters used, would automatically be dropped.

As perhaps the only person in Midcyru who had been trained as both meister and magus, Dorian thought he had a better chance of making the crossing than any other magus. He'd bought new shoes last night and fitted a lead plate inside each sole. He thought he'd eliminated all traces of southern magic that might cling to him. Unfortunately, there was only one way to find out.

Heart thudding, Dorian followed the eunuchs onto Luxbridge. At his first step, the bridge flared weirdly green and Dorian felt his feet tingling as vir reached up around his shoes. An instant later it stopped, and no one had seen it. Dorian had done it. Luxbridge felt that he was Talented, but Dorian's ancestors had been smart enough to know that not every Talented person was a mage. The rest of Dorian's steps, shuffling like the other nervous eunuchs', brought sparks out of the magic that made the embedded skulls seem to yawn and shift as they stared hatefully at those who passed overhead. But they didn't give way.

If Dorian felt some pride at the genius of Luxbridge, the sight of Mount Thrall brought only dread. He'd been born in the bowels of that damned rock, been starved in its dungeons, fought in its pits, and committed murder in its bedchambers and kitchens and halls.

Within that mountain, Dorian would find his *vürd,* his destiny, his doom, his completion. He would also find the woman who would become his wife. And, he feared, he would find out why he had cast aside his gift of prophecy. What was so terrible that he wanted to throw away his fore-knowledge of it?

Mount Thrall was unnatural: an enormous four-sided black pyramid twice as tall as it was wide and extending deep below the earth. From Lux-bridge, Dorian looked down and saw clouds obscuring whatever depths lay below. Thirty generations of slaves, both Khalidoran and captured in war, had been sent into those depths, mining until they gasped out their last breaths in the putrid fumes and added their own bones to the ore.

The pyramid of the mountain had been sheared straight down one edge and flattened, leaving a plateau in front of a great triangular dagger of mountain. The Citadel sat on that plateau. It was dwarfed by the mountain, but as one approached, it became clear that the Citadel was a city unto itself. It held barracks for ten thousand soldiers, great storerooms, vast cisterns, training places for men and horses and wolves, armories, a dozen smithies, kitchens, stables, barns, stockyards, lumberyards, and space for all the workers, tools, and raw materials needed for twenty thousand people to survive a year under siege. And even at that, the Citadel was dwarfed in comparison to the castle that was Mount Thrall, for the mountain was honeycombed with halls and great rooms and apartments and dungeons and passages long forgotten that bored into its very roots.

Neither the Citadel nor the mountain had been full in decades and with the armies sent north and south, the place was even quieter than usual. Khaliras was now home to only the smallfolk, a skeleton crew of an army, less than half of the kingdom's meisters, enough functionaries to keep the reduced business of the kingdom operating, the aethelings, and the God-king's wives and concubines and their keepers.

Head among those keepers was the Chief Eunuch, Yorbas Zurgah. Yorbas was an old, soft, perfectly hairless man, even shaving his head and plucking his eyebrows and eyelashes. He sat huddled in an ermine cloak to ward off the morning chill at the servants' gate. Before him was a desk with a parchment unrolled on it. His blue eyes studied Dorian dubiously.

"You're short," Chamberlain Zurgah said. He himself had a typical eunuch's height.

And you're fat. "Yes, my lord."

"'Sir' will suffice."

"Yes, sir."

Chamberlain Zurgah stroked his hairless chin with fingers like sausages encased in jeweled rings. "You have an odd look about you."

In his youth, Dorian had rarely seen Yorbas Zurgah. He didn't think the man would remember him, but anything that caused greater scrutiny was dangerous.

"Do you know the penalty for a man who attempts entry to the harem?" Zurgah asked.

Dorian shook his head and looked steadfastly at the ground. He clenched his jaw and, without raising his eyes, tucked his hair back behind his ears.

It was what he considered a stroke of genius; he'd given himself silver streaks in his hair, paired with slightly pointed ears and several webbed toes. They were features that only one tribe in Khalidor possessed. The Feyuri claimed to be descended from the Fey folk and were equally despised for that and their pacifism. Dorian appeared to be half Feyuri, which was exotic enough and from a group despised enough that he hoped no one would stop to think how his Khalidoran half made him look a lot like Garoth Ursuul. It also explained why he was short. "It's the...other reason they call me Halfman, sir."

Yorbas Zurgah clicked his tongue. "I see. Then here are the terms of your indenture: you will serve whatever hours are asked of you. Your first tasks will include emptying and cleaning the concubines' chamber pots. Your food will be cold and never as much as you'd like. You are forbidden to speak with the concubines and if you have trouble with this, your tongue will be torn out. You understand?"

Dorian nodded.

"Then only one thing remains, Halfman."

"Sir?"

"We have to make sure you're a halfman after all. Remove your trousers."

7

Lantano Garuwashi sat in Kylar's path, his sword naked across his lap. Mountainous Feir Cousat stood beside him, meat-slab arms folded. They blocked a narrow game trail that led along the southern edge of the Hunter's Wood. Feir muttered a warning as Kylar approached.

Garuwashi's sword was unmistakable. The hilt was long enough for one or two hands; pure mistarille inscribed with gold runes in Old Ceuran. The slightly curving blade was inscribed with a dragon's head, facing the tip of the blade. As Kylar came closer, the dragon breathed fire. The flames traveled within the blade, and before them, Ceur'caelestos turned clear as glass. The flames rolled out farther as Kylar approached. Kylar brought the ka'kari to his eyes and saw Ceur'caelestos in the hues of magic.

That was when he knew the sword was the product of another age. The magics themselves had been crafted to be beautiful—and Kylar couldn't understand the least of them. He sensed playfulness, grandeur, hauteur, and love. Kylar realized he had a tendency for getting into things that were way over his head. Not least of which was trying to steal such a sword from Lantano Garuwashi.

"Drop the shadows, Kylar, or I'll help you drop them," Feir said.

Fifteen paces away from them, Kylar dropped the shadows. "So, mages can see me when I'm invisible. Dammit." He'd suspected as much.

Feir smiled joylessly. "Only one in ten men. Nine in ten women. I can only see you within thirty paces. Dorian could've seen you half a mile away, through trees. But I forget myself. Baronet Kylar Stern of Cenaria, also known as the Night Angel, war son of wetboy Durzo Blint, this is War Leader Lantano Garuwashi the Undefeated, the Chosen of Ceur'caelestos, of the Aenu Heights Lantanos."

Kylar clasped his left hand to his stump and bowed in the Ceuran style. "War Leader, the many tales of your deeds attest to your prowess."

Garuwashi rose and slid Ceur'caelestos into its sheath. He bowed and his mouth twitched. "Night Angel, likewise the few tales of yours."

The horizon was brightening, but it was still dark in the forest. It smelled like rain and coming winter. Kylar wondered if they would be the last smells he would experience. He smiled on the rising tide of despair. "We seem to have a problem," Kylar said. *Several, actually.*

"What's that?" Garuwashi asked.

I can't fight you invisible without killing Feir first, and even if I did, neither of you merits death. "You have a sword I need," Kylar said instead.

"Are you out of your—" Feir asked, but cut off at Garuwashi's raised hand.

"Forgive me, Night Angel," Garuwashi said, "but you're not left-handed, and you move like the loss of your sword hand was recent. If you so desire death that you would challenge me, I will not deny you. But why would you?"

Because I made a deal with the Wolf. Mere hours afterward, Kylar had found Durzo's note that ended, "MAKE NO DEALS WITH THE WOLF." Maybe this was why. *I can't win.*

~Not unless I give you a hand,~ the ka'kari said in Kylar's mind. The black metal ball that lived within Kylar spoke rarely, and it wasn't always helpful when it did. *You're hilarious,* Kylar thought back at it.

Garuwashi's eyes flicked down to Kylar's wrist. Feir was agog.

Kylar glanced down and saw jet black metal writhing from his stump. It resolved itself slowly into a hand. He tried to make a fist, and it did. *Are you joking?*

~I'm not that cruel. By the way, Jorsin Alkestes didn't like the idea of his enemies coming back to life. If that sword kills you, you're really dead.~

Funny, the Wolf failed to mention that. Kylar wiggled the black fingers. He even had some sensation in them. At the same time, the hand was too light. It was hollow, the skin thinner than parchment. *Hey, while you're doing miracles . . .*

~No.~

You didn't even listen!

~Go ahead.~ It felt like the ka'kari was rolling its eyes. How did it do that? It didn't even have eyes.

Can you fix its weight?

~No.~

Why not?

The ka'kari sighed. *~I stay one size. I'm already covering all your skin and making a hand for you. Invisibility, blue flames, and an extra hand not enough for you?~*

So making a dagger of you and throwing it would be a bad idea?

The ka'kari went silent in a huff, and Kylar grinned. Then he realized he was grinning at Lantano Garuwashi, who had sixty-three deaths tied to his hair, and eighty-two in his eyes.

"You need a minute?" Garuwashi asked, lifting an eyebrow.

"Uh, I'm ready now," Kylar said. He drew his sword.

"Kylar," Feir said. "What are you going to do with the sword?"

"I'm going to put it somewhere safe."

Feir's eyes widened. "You're taking it into the Wood?"

"I was thinking I'd throw it in."

"Good idea," Feir said.

"Perhaps a nice idea. But not a good one," Garuwashi said. He closed the distance between them in an instant. The swords rang together in the staccato melody that would climax in death. Kylar decided to feign a tendency to overextend on his ripostes. With a swordsman as talented as

Lantano Garuwashi, he should only have to show the weakness twice and spring the trap the third time.

Except that the first time he overextended, Garuwashi's sword was into the gap, raking Kylar's ribs. He could have killed Kylar with that thrust, but he held back, wary of a trap.

Kylar staggered back, and Garuwashi let him regroup, his eyes showing disappointment. They'd barely crossed swords for five seconds. The man was too fast. Ridiculously fast. Kylar brought the ka'kari to his eyes and was even more stunned.

"You're not even Talented," Kylar said.

"Lantano Garuwashi needs no magic."

~*Kylar Stern surely does!*~

Kylar felt an old familiar shiver, an echo from his past. It was the fear of dying. With Alitaeran broadswords, Kylar could have crushed Garuwashi with the brute strength of his Talent. Against the elegant Ceuran sword, Kylar's Talent did almost nothing for him. "Let's get on with it," Kylar said.

They began again, Garuwashi feeling Kylar out, even giving ground, seeing what Kylar could do. But there was no holding back. Kylar had seen that. Soon Kylar would tire and try something desperate. Garuwashi would be waiting for it—how many desperate men had he seen in sixty-three duels? Surely every man who had survived the first clash of blades had the same sick feeling in his stomach that Kylar had now. There was no room for self-delusion once the blades began singing.

Something changed on Garuwashi's face. It wasn't enough to tell Kylar what he was going to do; but it was enough to tell him that Garuwashi thought he knew Kylar's strengths. Now he would end it.

There was a beat. Kylar waited for Garuwashi to advance, those damn long arms of his unbelievably quick, the stance fluid and sure.

"You feel it, don't you?" Garuwashi asked, withholding his attack. "The rhythm."

"Sometimes," Kylar grunted, his eyes not leaving Garuwashi's center, where he would see any movement begin. "Once, I heard it as music in truth."

"Many died that day?" Garuwashi asked.

Kylar shrugged.

"Thirty highlanders, four wytches, and a Khalidoran prince," Feir said.

Lantano Garuwashi smiled, not surprised at Feir's knowledge. "Yet today you fight woodenly. You are stiff, slower than usual. Do you know why? That day you faced death no less than you do today."

Wrong, but I didn't know that then.

"Today," Garuwashi continued, "you are afraid. It narrows your vision, tenses your muscles, makes you slow. It will make you dead. Fight to win, Kylar Stern, not to not lose." It was disconcerting to hear good advice from the man who was about to kill him.

"Here," Garuwashi said. He lifted Ceur'caelestos and Kylar saw the edges go blunt. "I'll know when you're ready."

Feir leaned up against a tree and whistled quietly.

Garuwashi attacked again and within seconds, the dull sword scraped Kylar's ribs. A few more seconds passed in furious ringing and the dull blade grazed his forearm, then jabbed his shoulder. But even as the blows rained down on him, Kylar began to remember his master Durzo's merciless sparring. His fear receded. This was the same, except now Kylar had more endurance, more strength, more speed, and more experience than a year ago. And he'd beaten Durzo. Once. Kylar's vision cleared and his pulse slowed from its frenzied hammering.

"That's it!" Garuwashi said. Ceur'caelestos went sharp once more and they began.

Kylar was aware of Feir. The second-echelon Blade Master was seated cross-legged on the ground now, jaw slack. The man was muttering to himself, "Gabel's Game to Many Waters to Three Mountain Castles—good, good—to Heron's Hunt to—was that Praavel's Defense? Goramond's Dive to—what the hell? I've never—Yrmi's Bout, good gods, some variation on Two Tigers? Harani Bulls to…"

The fight accelerated, but Kylar felt a calm. He was, he realized, *smiling*. Madness! Yet it was so, and Garuwashi's thin lips were drawn up in a little smirk of their own. There was beauty here, something precious and rare. Every man wished he could fight. Few could, and only one in a hundred years fought this well. Kylar had never thought to see another master on a par with Durzo Blint, but Lantano Garuwashi might even be better than Durzo, a little faster, his reach a little longer.

Kylar dove behind a sapling a second before Garuwashi sheared it in two. As Garuwashi pushed aside the falling tree, Kylar thought. He only had one thing Lantano Garuwashi didn't. Well, aside from invisibility.

~Oh, don't use that! It wouldn't be fair*!~*

What Lantano Garuwashi didn't have was years of fighting against someone better than he was. Kylar was studying Garuwashi's style in a way Garuwashi had never needed to study anyone's. It was straightforward. Garuwashi basically depended on his superior speed, strength, reach, technique, and flexibility to win. And—there!

Kylar went through half of Lord Umber's Glut and then modified it, twisting the last parry so Ceur'caelestos missed his cheek by a breath. His own sword gashed Garuwashi's shoulder—but Garuwashi's counter was already coming. Kylar threw up an arm and instinctively brought the ka'kari up along the ridge.

White light blazed and threw thousands of sparks, as if Kylar's arm were an enormous flint and Ceur'caelestos steel. Kylar's arm burned.

The warriors staggered back and Kylar knew that if Garuwashi had put any more force into that counter, it would have destroyed the ka'kari.

~Please...please don't ever do that again.~

"Who taught you that?" Garuwashi demanded, his face bright red.

"I..." Kylar stopped, confused. His left arm was throbbing, bleeding where Ceur'caelestos had scraped it.

"He means the combination, Kylar," Feir said, his eyes wide. "That move's called Garuwashi's Turn. No one else is fast enough to do it."

Kylar fell back into a ready stance, not in fear now, but futility. He'd thrown his best at Garuwashi and barely scratched him. "No one taught me," he said. "It just seemed right."

The anger dropped from Lantano Garuwashi's face in an instant. This was a man, Kylar saw, of sudden passions, unpredictable, intense, dangerous. Garuwashi drew a white handkerchief and reverently wiped Ceur'caelestos clean of Kylar's blood. He sheathed the Blade of Heaven.

"I will not kill you today, doen-Kylar, peace rest with your blade. In ten years, you will be full in your prime. Let us meet then in Aenu and fight before the royal court. Masters such as we deserve to fight with minstrels and maidens and lesser masters in attendance. Should you win, you may have all that is mine, including the holy blade. Should I win, at least you will have had ten years of life and glory, yes? It will be an event anticipated for a decade and retold for a thousand."

In ten years Kylar would indeed be in his prime, and what Garuwashi wasn't saying was that he would be past his own. Garuwashi would then be what, forty-five? Perhaps his speed and Kylar's would be equal then. He would still have his reach, and both would have a lot more experience, but that was the more precious coin to Kylar. Would the Wolf care if Kylar waited ten years? Hell, if Kylar didn't get himself killed, he wouldn't even see the Wolf for...well, probably ten years. Then again, if Kylar died on this sword, he wouldn't see the Wolf at all.

Grimacing, Kylar said, "You tell me, if I promised you that I was going to get something for you, would you want it now or in ten years?"

"If you try now, you'll die. In ten years, you'll have a chance."

A month ago, Kylar had one goal: to convince his girlfriend Elene that eighteen years as a virgin was quite enough. Then Jarl had been murdered while delivering the news that Logan Gyre was trapped in his own dungeon. Kylar's loyalties to the living and the dead had given him two new goals that had cost him the first. He'd abandoned Elene as he'd sworn he wouldn't in order to save Logan and avenge Jarl by killing the Godking. It had cost him an arm, a magical bond to the beautiful disaster named Vi Sovari, and an oath to steal Garuwashi's blade.

Now all Kylar wanted was to make sure his sacrifices hadn't been for nothing, and then to go make things right with Elene.

As if to punish him for his faithlessness, he now imagined her saying, "An oath you only keep when it's convenient isn't an oath at all."

"I can't put it off," Kylar said. "Sorry."

Garuwashi shrugged. "It is a matter of honor, yes? I understand. That is a—"

"Pit wyrm!" Feir shouted, leaping to his feet.

Kylar turned and all he could see was a hole tearing in space ten paces away, and through it, hell and rushing fire-cracked skin. In the forest, a big-nosed, big-eared Vürdmeister was laughing.

8

*P*iss. You're different, Halfman," Hopper said. He was a tall, lean, white-haired old eunuch who was training Dorian—*Halfman,* he reminded himself. Hopper handed him a pot.

"What do you mean?" Halfman asked.

"Two shits." Hopper handed Halfman two more chamber pots. Halfman emptied half of the piss into each, swished it around, and emptied the pots into an enormous clay jar set in a wicker frame. "A piss for every two shits. The rest of the pisses go last. They're easy. You get a puke or a slippery, you use two pisses on those. No one wants to smell that all day."

Halfman thought Hopper wasn't going to answer him, but after they finished emptying the pots into the enormous clay jars—six of them today, it meant one more trip for Halfman than usual—Hopper paused. "I dunno. Look at how you sit all straight."

Cursing inwardly, Halfman slouched. He'd been forgetting. Thirty-two years of sitting up straight like a king's son was dangerous. Of course, no one spent as much time with him as Hopper, but if the old eunuch had noticed, what would happen if Zurgah or an overseer or a meister or an aetheling did? His half-Feyuri appearance had already isolated him. He was regularly singled out for extra chores and beatings for imagined infractions. The nights he didn't go to bed aching were rare.

"Don't forget yourself. Puke—how the girls manage to nick wine is beyond me—if you do, well..." Hopper lifted his sandal-clad feet one at a time and wiggled his big toes. Those two toes were all he had left. He'd been caught teaching the bored women of the harem a dance, he said, and the only reason he'd been let off so easily was because Zurgah liked him, and the dance hadn't involved touching or speaking to the women. Other eunuchs, Hopper said, were killed for less. "Twenty-two years since my little dance. Twenty-two years I been with the chamber pots, and I'll stay with 'em till I die. Now help me with the empties. You remember the process?"

"One clean water rinses ten pisses or four shits."

"Bright one, you. Help me rinse the first forty, then you can take pots out."

They worked together in silence. Halfman had made no progress finding the woman who would be his wife. The Citadel held two separate harems, and several women were kept apart from either one. Halfman had been assigned to the common harem.

More than a hundred of Garoth Ursuul's wives and concubines lived here—wives were the women who had produced sons, concubines those who had produced either daughters or nothing, which were considered equivalent. Given that Garoth Ursuul had to be near sixty, all of the women were surprisingly young. No one ever said what happened to the old wives.

It was strange to be in his father's harem. He was seeing a different and oddly personal side of the man who had shaped him in a hundred ways. Like most Khalidorans, the Godking favored solid women with wide hips and full buttocks. There was a northern saying, *volaer ust vassuhr, vola uss vossahr.* Literally, "a man's horses and his brides should be big enough to ride." Most of the common women were Khalidoran, but the Godking's harems included all nationalities except the Feyuri. All were beautiful; all had large eyes and full lips; and he preferred taking them, Hopper said, as soon after their flowering as possible.

Life in the harem, though, bore little relation to the stories southrons told. If it was a life of luxury, it was also one of enforced boredom.

Each day, as he gathered the chamber pots from the concubines' rooms,

Halfman stole glances at the women. The first thing he noticed was that they were always fully clothed. Not only was the Godking out of the city, but winter was coming. With no possibility of being asked to serve any time soon, some of the women didn't even bother brushing their hair or changing out of their bedclothes, though there seemed to be a form of social censure that kept anyone from slipping too far.

"They used to sit there all winter, half-naked and made up like fertility whores, huddled around the fires and shivering like puppies in the snow," Hopper said. "Now we give 'em a signal when His Holiness is on his way. Just wait'll you see it. You've never seen anyone move so fast. Or if one of them's called for by name, every last one of the others will descend on her. Khali's blood, you can't even see her for a good five minutes. Then when she comes out of that circle, you'd swear they traded her for the goddess herself. Much as they hate each other and scheme and gossip, when the Godking calls, they help each other. It's one thing to gossip and lie about a woman," Hopper lowered his voice, "but none of them wants to be the reason a girl gets sent to the aethelings."

Dorian's stomach turned. So they knew. Of course they knew. Dorian's seed class had been taught flaying on a disrespectful concubine. Dorian, as the first of the class, had been assigned her face. He remembered his pride as he had presented it to his tutor Neph Dada whole, even the eyelids and eyelashes intact. The ten-year-old Dorian had worn that face to dinner as a mask, making japes with his seed class while Neph smiled encouragement. God help him, he had done even worse things.

What was he doing here? This place was sick. How could a people tolerate this? How could they worship a goddess that delighted in suffering? Dorian sometimes believed that countries had the kind of leaders they deserved. What did that say about Khalidor—with its tribalism and endemic corruption held in check only by its deep fear of the men who styled themselves Godkings? What did it say about Dorian? This was his people, his country, his culture—and once, his birthright. He, Dorian Ursuul, had survived. He'd demolished his seed class one at a time, pitting brother against brother until only he survived. He'd accomplished his uurdthan, his Harrowing, and shown himself worthy to be called the Godking's son and heir. This, all of this, could have been his—and he didn't miss it for a second.

He loved many things about Khalidor: the music, the dances, the hospitality of its poor, its men who laughed or cried freely, and its women who would wail and keen over their dead where southrons stood silent like they didn't care. Dorian loved their zoomorphic art, the wild woad tattoos of the lowland tribes, the cool blue-eyed maidens with their milk-white skin and fierce tempers. He loved a hundred things about his people, but sometimes he wondered if the world wouldn't be a better place if the sea swept in and drowned them all.

As sacrifices for abundant livestock, how many of those blue-eyed girls had laid their mewling firstborn sons on Khali pyres? For abundant crops, how many of those expressive men had caged their aged fathers in wicker coffins and watched them drown slowly in bogs? They wept as they did murder—but they did it. For honor, when a man died, if his wife wasn't claimed by the clan chief, she was expected to throw herself on her husband's pyre. Dorian had seen a girl fourteen years old whose courage failed her. She'd been married less than a month to an old man she'd never met before her wedding. Her father beat her bloody and threw her on the pyre himself, cursing her for embarrassing him.

"Hey," Hopper said, "you're thinking. Don't. It's no good here. You work hard, you don't have to think. Got it?" Halfman nodded. "Then let's strap this on and you can work."

Together, they strapped the wicker basket to Halfman's back. There were thongs that wrapped around each shoulder and his hips to help him bear the great weight of the clay pot full of sewage. Hopper promised to have another pot ready by the time Halfman got back.

Halfman trudged through the cold basalt hallways. It was always dark in the slaves' passages, with only enough torches burning so the slaves could avoid colliding.

"I'm tired of banging toothless slaves," a voice said around the next intersection of hallways. "I hear the new girl's in the Tygre Tower. They say she's beautiful."

"Tavi! You can't call it that." Bertold Ursuul was Dorian's great-grand-father, and the man had gone mad, believing he could ascend to heaven if he built a tower high enough and decorated it solely with Harani sword-tooth tygres. His madness embarrassed Garoth Ursuul, so he'd forbidden the tower to be called anything but Bertold's Tower.

Dorian stopped. There was a torch at the intersection and no way he could retreat without being noticed. The aethelings—for no one else spoke with such arrogance—were coming toward him. There was no escape.

Then he remembered. He was Halfman now, a eunuch slave. So he slouched and prayed that he was invisible.

"I talk how I please," Tavi said, coming into the intersection just as Halfman did. Halfman stopped, stepped aside, and averted his eyes. Tavi was a classic aetheling: good-looking if with a hawkish nose, well-groomed, well-dressed, an aura of command, and the stench of great power, despite being barely fifteen years old. Halfman couldn't help but size him up instantly—this one would be the first of his seed class. This would have been one Dorian would have tried to kill early. Too arrogant, though. Tavi was the kind who needed to brag. He would never make it through his uurdthan. "And I can fuck who I please, too," Tavi said, coming to a stop. He looked down each of the halls as if lost. His indecision froze Halfman in place. He couldn't move without possibly moving into the aethelings' path.

"Besides," Tavi said, "the harems are too closely guarded. But the Tygre Tower's just got two dreads at the bottom, and her deaf-mute eunuchs."

"He'll kill you," the other aetheling said. He didn't look pleased to be having this conversation in front of Halfman.

"Who's gonna tell him? The girl? So he'll kill her, too? Fuck! Where are we? We've been walking this way for ten minutes. All these halls look the same."

"I said we should have gone the other—" the other aetheling began.

"Shut up, Rivik. You," Tavi said, speaking to Halfman. Halfman flinched as a slave would. "Khali, you stink! Which way is it to the kitchens?"

Halfman reluctantly pointed back the way the aethelings had come.

Rivik laughed. Tavi cursed. "How far?" Tavi asked.

Halfman would have found some other way to answer, but Dorian couldn't help himself. "About ten minutes."

Rivik laughed again, louder.

Tavi backhanded Dorian. "What's your name, halfman?"

"Milord, this slave is called Halfman."

"Ooh hoo!" Rivik hooted. "We got a live one here!"

"Not for long," Tavi said.

"If you kill him, I'll tell," Rivik said.

"You'll tell?" The disdain and disbelief on Tavi's face told Halfman that Rivik's days as a sidekick were numbered.

"He made me laugh," Rivik said. "Come on. We're already late for lecture, you know how Draef will try to turn that on us."

"Fine, just a second." The vir rose to Tavi's skin and he began chanting.

"Tavi..."

"It won't kill him."

The magic was a slight concussion inches from Halfman's chest. It threw him back into the wall like a rag doll. The wicker splintered and the clay pot shattered, geysering human waste over Halfman and the wall behind him.

Rivik laughed louder. "We've gotta remember this next time we're bored. Khali's tits, it reeks! Imagine if we could break one of those pots in Draef's room."

The aethellngs left Haltman gasping on the floor, wiping ooze from his face. It was five minutes before he stood up, but when he did, it was with alacrity. In the fear and in the miming of fear, he had almost missed it. The newest concubine could only be one woman. His future wife was at the top of Bertold's Tower, and she was in danger.

The pit wyrm tore through the hole in reality and went for Kylar. The great wyrm was tubular, at least ten feet in diameter, its skin cracked and blackened, fire showing through the gaps. When it lunged, its great bulk heaved forward and its entire eyeless front opened as it vomited its cone-like mouth. Kylar leapt as each concentric ring snapped out. Each ring was circled with teeth, and when the third ring caught a tree, teeth the size of Kylar's forearm whipped around into the wood. The pit wyrm sucked itself forward, its lamprey-like mouth inverting as the rings bit into the wood in turn, shearing a ten-foot section out of the tree trunk before Kylar landed.

Instantly, the pit wyrm lunged again. It had no visible means of propelling so great a mass. It didn't gather itself to strike like a serpent, but moved instead as if this were but one head or arm attached to a much larger creature crouched on the other side of that hole. Again, it went for Kylar.

He flipped through the air as the tree the pit wyrm had cut fell, crashing to the ground, throwing up dust in the misty morning light. Kylar grabbed a tree and spun, the ka'kari giving him claws enough to sink into the bark and throw him back over the pit wyrm's back. His sword flashed as he flew over the pit wyrm, but the blade bounced off the armored skin.

There was something white in the corner of Kylar's eye. He dropped to the forest floor and saw it: a tiny white homunculus with wings and the Vürdmeister's face, grinning at Kylar under an enormous nose. It clawed at Kylar's face.

Kylar blocked. The homunculus's talons sank smoothly into Kylar's sword.

The pit wyrm lunged again even as Feir hammered its side, his sword ringing in the mists but doing no damage, not even slowing the wyrm. The pit wyrm couldn't be distracted, wouldn't stop until it reached its target.

Its target wasn't Kylar. It was the homunculus.

Kylar dropped the sword and flipped once more. He landed on the side of a tree, thirty feet up, fingers and toes sinking into the wood. The pit wyrm slammed into Kylar's sword on the ground, the cone of teeth slapping around the homunculus, digging deep into the soil as each ring of teeth slapped forward, devouring the white creature and everything around it. The pit wyrm pulled back, shaking dirt and roots and dead leaves through the air. Satisfied, it began to slide back into whatever hell it had been called from.

Then it shivered.

Feir was still striking the creature. For some reason, he wasn't using magic. The mountainous mage struck again, a mighty hammer blow—with no effect.

By the time Kylar's eyes found the real reason the pit wyrm had shivered, Lantano Garuwashi was halfway through its body. He was hacking at it near the hole in reality. But he wasn't *hacking*. Wherever Garuwashi cut with Ceur'caelestos, the pit wyrm's flesh sprang apart, smoking. The look on the sa'ceurai's face told Kylar that the man was enrapt—he was the world's best swordsman, wielding the world's best sword, facing a monster out of legend. Lantano Garuwashi was living his purpose.

Garuwashi's sword moved with Garuwashi's speed. In two seconds, he had cut through the entire pit wyrm. The thirty-foot section of wyrm crashed to the forest floor, thrashed once, and then broke apart in quivering red and black clumps, dissolving in putrid green smoke until nothing was left. The stump writhed bloodlessly until Garuwashi slashed it with six slices in blinding succession and whatever was controlling it yanked it back into hell.

Kylar sprang off the tree and landed ten paces from Lantano Garuwashi. Having never fought a pit wyrm, the sa'ceurai couldn't have known that they didn't just appear; they had to be called. He let down his guard.

The big-nosed Vürdmeister acted before Kylar could, stepping out from behind a tree and unleashing a ball of green flame. Garuwashi brought Ceur'caelestos up, but he wasn't prepared for what happened when that sword came into contact with that magic.

When Ceur'caelestos met the vir, a dull thump shook the gold needles off the tamaracks. The morning mists blew outward in a visible globe, the moss shriveled and smoked on the trees, and the concussion blasted Feir and Garuwashi and the Vürdmeister from their feet.

Only Kylar was still standing, shielded from the magical explosion by the ka'kari covering his skin. The men fell in all directions, but Ceur'caelestos stayed in the center of its own storm. It spun once in the air and stuck in the forest floor.

Kylar swept Ceur'caelestos into his hand. The fallen Vürdmeister didn't try to stand. He gathered power, the vir on his arms wriggling in slow motion, their undulations becoming a movement that Kylar could strangely read—the magic would be a gout of flame three feet wide and fifteen feet long.

Before the Vürdmeister could release the flame, Kylar ran him through.

The Vürdmeister's cool blue eyes widened in pain, and then widened again in sheer terror as every inky rose-thorn tracing of vir in his entire body filled with white light. Light exploded from his skin. The Vürdmeister's body bucked and thrashed, then went limp. The vir was gone without a trace, leaving the dead man's skin the normal pasty hue of a northerner. Even the air felt clean.

In the distance, to the northeast, a Lae'knaught trumpet blasted the command to charge. It was far away—within the Dark Hunter's Wood.

"The bloody fools," Kylar murmured. He'd lured them in, but it was still hard to believe they'd fallen for it. He looked at Curoch. *The things I do for my king.*

~You're not really going to throw it away, are you?~

I gave my word.

~You have the Talent and the lifetimes it would take to become that sword's master.~

I can't exactly go out in public with a black metal hand, can I?

~Wear gloves.~

"We need to leave—right now," Feir Cousat said. "Using magic this close to the wood is like begging the Dark Hunter to come. And there's some kind of magic beacon on the Vürdmeister's horse. I chased it away, but it's probably too late."

So that was why Feir hadn't used magic in fighting against the pit wyrm. Smart.

"You have taken my *ceuros*," Lantano Garuwashi said with a moral outrage that Kylar didn't understand. Then he remembered. A sa'ceurai's soul was his sword. They believed that literally. What sort of abomination would steal another man's soul?

"Did you not take it from someone else?" Kylar asked.

"The gods gave me the blade," Lantano Garuwashi said. He was quivering with rage and loathing, despair fighting to the fore in his eyes. "Your theft is not honorable."

"No," Kylar admitted. "Nor, I'm afraid, am I."

A plaintive howl unlike anything Kylar had ever heard ripped through the wood. It was high and mournful, inhuman.

"Too late," Feir said, his voice strangled. "The Hunter's coming."

The Wolf had told Kylar to stay back forty paces from the Hunter's Wood, so Kylar gave it fifty. He looked through the lesser trees of the natural forest to the preternatural height and bulk of the sequoys. He felt small, caught up in events vast beyond his comprehension. He heard the whistling of something speeding toward him. He hefted Curoch and threw it as far into the Wood as he could. It flew like an arrow. As it crossed into the air over the wood, it burned like a star falling to earth.

The entire forest began to glow golden.

The whistling stopped.

The three men stood side by side, staring into the wood. Feir thought that he was the only one who was properly terrified. Kylar had distracted the Hunter by throwing Curoch into the wood, but there was nothing to stop it from coming back.

Kylar calmly folded his legs and sat on the forest floor. The black skin retreated into the young man, leaving him in his underclothes. He studied the stump where his metallic right hand had been, barely noticing as the Wood's autumnal glow deepened to a bloody red and then began to lighten to green.

Lantano Garuwashi, now soulless, stared with disbelief. But he wasn't seeing anything except the disappearance of Ceur'caelestos. The man who would be king was suddenly *aceuran*—swordless, an outlaw, an exile, not even to be acknowledged. The cruel rain of implications was beating his future to dust.

In the last week, Feir had seen this man act publicly as if Ceur'caelestos had been destined for his hands. But in private moments, Feir had seen glimpses of the young hedge sa'ceurai with an iron sword, who knew that whatever excellence he attained, he would never be accepted among those born to greater blades. It was an enormous turnaround for a man who'd reconciled himself to hard realities—and now he was staring a new, much harder reality in the face.

Feir wondered how long it would be before Garuwashi decided to kill himself. Lantano Garuwashi wasn't a man who would easily give up his life. He believed in himself too much. But this disgrace would surely overwhelm that.

The thought left Feir oddly hollow. Why should he mourn Lantano Garuwashi's death? It would mean Cenaria would escape another brutal occupation and Feir would be released from his service to a hard and difficult man. But Feir didn't want Garuwashi to die. He respected him.

Magic flashed so intensely Feir's vision went white. It lasted only a fraction of a second. Kylar gasped.

Blinking away tears, Feir looked at him. Kylar appeared unchanged: still half-naked, still staring toward the wood. He stood slowly and stretched his arms.

"Much better," Kylar said, grinning.

He had both arms. He was whole. Kylar shook himself and his skin was cloaked in black again. He didn't cover his face with the grim mask of judgment; this time, he carried a slim black sword in his hand.

Lantano Garuwashi dropped to his knees and spoke to Feir, " 'This path lies before you. Fight Khalidor and become a great king.' This you told me, and I heard only my heart's desire: that I would show those effete nobles in Aenu what their mocking was good for, that I would be Ceura's king. I did not fight Khalidor, and now my ceuros is lost. Thus has Lantano Garuwashi reaped death for faithlessness." He turned. "Night Angel, will you be my second?"

A brief look of confusion passed over Kylar, then his eyes showed recognition. After Garuwashi made a lateral cut through his own stomach with a short sword, his second would strike his head from his shoulders to finish the suicide. It was an honor, if a grisly one, and Feir couldn't help but feel slighted.

"Feir, nephilim, messenger from the gods whom I ignored, I would have you serve another way," Garuwashi said. "Please, carry my story to my warriors and to my family."

A chill went down Feir's spine. Not only would every sa'ceurai in the world know that Lantano Garuwashi had died here, but they would know Ceur'caelestos had been thrown into the Wood. No matter how Feir told the story, it would be retold until it fit Ceuran beliefs. The best swordsman, the best sword, and the deadliest place would be tied together forever in Ceuran myth. Every new sixteen-year-old sa'ceurai who thought he was invincible—in other words, most of them—would head for the Dark Hunter's Wood, determined to recover Ceur'caelestos and be Lantano Garuwashi reborn.

It would mean the death of generations.

Kylar's face changed. It started as black tears pouring from his eyes. Then his eyes themselves were covered in black oil. Then in a whoosh, the mask of judgment was back. Black eyes leaked incandescent blue flame. Studying Lantano Garuwashi, he cocked his head to the side. Feir felt a chill at the sight of that visage. Any shred of childhood that had been left in the young man Feir had met six months ago was gone. Feir didn't know what had replaced it.

"No," the Night Angel pronounced. "There is no taint in you that demands death. Another ceuros will come to you, Lantano Garuwashi. In five years, I will meet you at dawn on Midsummer's Day in the High Hall of the Aenu. We shall show the world a duel such as it has never seen. This I swear."

The Night Angel slapped the thin blade to his back, where it dissolved into his skin. He bowed to Garuwashi and then to Feir, and then he disappeared.

"You don't understand," Garuwashi said, still on his knees, but the Night Angel was gone. Garuwashi turned wretched eyes to Feir. "Will you be my second?"

"No," Feir said.

"Very well, faithless servant. I don't need you."

Garuwashi drew his short sword, but for once in his life, Feir was quicker than the sa'ceurai. His sword smacked the blade from Garuwashi's hand and he scooped it up.

"Give me a few hours," Feir said. "The Hunter is distracted. With five thousand flies in its web, one more may go unnoticed."

"What are you going to do?" Garuwashi asked.

I'm going to save you. I'm going to save all your damned stiff-necked, infuriating, magnificent people. I'm probably going to get my damn fool self killed. "I'm going to get your sword back," Feir said, and then he walked into the Wood.

$\mathcal{A}$ high, tortured howl woke Vi Sovari from a dream of Kylar fighting gods and monsters. She sat up instantly, ignoring the aches from another night on rocky ground. The howl was miles away. She shouldn't have been able to hear it through the giant sequoys and the deadening morning mists, but it continued, filled with madness and rage, changing pitch as it flew with incredible speed from the Wood's center.

Only then did Vi become aware of Kylar through the ancient mistarille-and-gold earring. She'd bonded Kylar as he lay unconscious at the God-king's mercy. It had saved Cenaria and Kylar's life, and now Vi and Kylar could sense each other. Kylar was two miles distant, and Vi could feel that he held something of incredible power. She could feel him reaching a decision. The power departed from him, and he felt an odd sense of victory.

Suddenly, it was as if the sun were rising in the south. Vi stood on shaky knees. A hundred paces away, at the enormous sequoys of the Dark Hunter's Wood, the air itself turned a brilliant gold, radiating magic. Even to Vi, untrained as she was, it felt like the kiss of a midsummer's sunset on her skin.

Then the color deepened to reddish gold. Every dust mote floating in the air, every water droplet in the mists was a flaming autumnal glory.

When Vi was fifteen, her master, the wetboy Hu Gibbet, had taken her to a country estate for a job. The deader was some lord's bastard who'd made himself a successful spice merchant and decided not to repay his underworld Sa'kagé investors. The estate was covered with maples. That autumn morning Vi moved through a world of gold, carpeted with red-gold leaves, the very air awash in color. As she stood over the corpse, she had mentally retreated to a place where glorious crimson leaves weren't paired with pulsing arterial blood. Hu beat her for it, of course, and to those beatings Vi had mentally acquiesced. A distracted wetboy is a dead wetboy. A wetboy knows no beauty.

The howl ripped through the wood again, freezing her bones. Moving fast, terribly fast, it changed pitch higher and then lower and then higher, all in the space of two seconds, as if it were flying to and fro faster than anything could possibly move. Everywhere it went, it was followed by the faint, tinny sound of rending metal. Then came a man's scream. More followed.

There was a battle in the wood. No, a massacre.

All the while, the wood pulsed with magic. The flaming red was fading to yellow green and then to the deep green of vitality, the scent of new grass, fresh flowers.

"Kylar has given it new life," Vi said aloud. She didn't know how she knew, but she knew Kylar had put something into the Wood—and that something was rejuvenating the entire forest. Kylar himself felt invigorated, well in a way he hadn't felt in the week she'd shared the bond with him. Whole.

Vi felt something wrong behind her. Her hands flashed to the daggers at her belt. Then she was on her back. Even as air whooshed from her lungs, a crackling ball of blue energy hissed and spat through the air where she'd been standing a moment before.

The most Vi could do was gasp, trying to catch her wind. It was several blind seconds before she could sit up.

Before her, a man wrapped in dark brown leather put his foot on a corpse's face and wrenched a dagger from its eye. The corpse was wearing the robes of a Khalidoran Vürdmeister, and black, tattoo-like vir were still twitching under the surface of his skin. Vi's savior cleaned his dagger and turned. His feet made no sound. A multitude of cloaks, vests, pocketed shirts, and pouches of all sizes covered the man, all of them horsehide, all tanned the same deep brown and worn soft from long use. Twin forward-curving gurkas were tucked into the back of his belt, an unstrung scrim-shawed short bow was slung over his back, and Vi could see numerous hilts protruding from his garments. He unlaced a brown mask that concealed all but his eyes and pulled it back around his shoulders. He had an affable face; wry, almond-shaped brown eyes; loose black hair; and broad, flat features with high cheekbones. He could only be a Ymmuri stalker.

Stalkers were reputed to be the greatest hunters of all the Ymmuri horse lords. They were said to be invisible in the forests or on the grassy steppes in the east where the Ymmuri lived. They never shot prey that wasn't running or on the wing. And they were all Talented. In other words, they were grassland wetboys. Unlike wetboys, they didn't kill for pay but for honor.

And fuck me if there isn't more truth to the stories about them than there is to the ones about us.

The stalker folded his hands behind his back and bowed. "I am Dehvira-haman ko Bruhmaeziwakazari," he said with an odd cadence that came from growing up speaking a tonal language. "You may...hearken?...call, yes, *call* me Dehvi." He smiled. "You are Vi, yes?"

Vi rose, swallowing. This man had snuck up on her—a wetboy—and thrown her to the ground easily, and now he stood smiling and friendly. It was as unnerving as having a blue ball of death pass inches from her face.

"Come," Dehvi said. "This place is safe no more. I will escort you."

"What are you talking about?" Vi asked.

"Magic…calls to? asks to? hearkens to? the demon of the Wood." Dehvi wrinkled his nose. Vi knew what he meant, but she wasn't sure what word he was looking for.

"Beckons!" he said, finding it. "That beckon means death."

"That call," Vi said, putting his words together slowly. Magic called the Hunter. The Vürdmeister had used magic, and Vi was Talented. The Hunter might be coming.

The stalker frowned. "These word give me difficults. Too many meanings."

"Where are you taking me?" Vi asked. *And do I have any choice?* Her body relaxed to Alathea's Waking and her fingers dipped casually to check her daggers on their way to brush the dirt from her pants—except the daggers were gone.

The stalker regarded her coolly. Clearly she hadn't checked casually enough. "To Chantry."

He turned and knelt beside the corpse, muttering under his breath in a language Vi didn't recognize. He spat on the man three times, cursing him not with foul words as Vi cursed, but actually commending the man's soul to some Ymmuri hell.

"You wish to go?" Dehvi asked, offering her the daggers.

"Yes," Vi said, taking them gingerly. "Please."

"Then come. The demon hunts. Is best to leave."

12

*W*hen Dorian had first been studying to become a Hoth'salar, a Brother of Healing, he'd invented a little weave to mimic the symptoms of influenza by killing the life that inhabited the stomach, with devastating results that cleared up within a day or two. Several times, to Solon's and Feir's vast amusement, Dorian had used it for other than scholarly reasons. Now "influenza" swept through the eunuchs, and Halfman was pressed into double shifts and unfamiliar tasks. He'd even made himself sick first to eliminate suspicion.

Today, two of the most trusted eunuchs were sick. Halfman climbed the stairs to the Tygre Tower, an unheated basalt obscenity that looked on the verge of toppling in a high wind. He moved past thousands of the great marsupial cats. They looked like wolves with exaggerated maws, sword-like canines, and orange and black stripes. Everywhere one looked, the tygres looked back. There were tapestries, etchings, tiny statues, ancient mangy stuffed specimens, necklaces of teeth, paintings of tygres tearing apart children. The styles were a hodgepodge, unimportant. All that had mattered to Bertold Ursuul was that they featured sword-tooth tygres.

Dorian reached the top of the tower breathless, shivering from the cold, sorry that the food he'd carried had long lost its warmth, and apprehensive about who would be up here. If she were one of the Talented wives or concubines, she might smell the magic on him. The depth of the women's ensnarement was such that any who found a traitor would report him immediately.

Dorian knocked on the door. When it opened, his breath whooshed out.

She had long dark hair, large dark eyes, a slender but shapely figure under a shapeless dress. No cosmetics heightened her eyes and none rouged her lips. She wore no jewelry. She smiled and his heart stopped. He'd never met her, but he knew that smile. He had seen that dimple on the left side, a little deeper than the one on the right. She was the one.

"My lady," Dorian said.

She smiled. She was a small young woman with sad, kind eyes. So young!

"You can speak," she said, and her voice was light and pure and strong, the kind of voice that begged to sing. "They've only sent deaf-mutes before. What's your name?"

"It is death for me to speak, milady, and yet.... How afraid of them are you?" Halfman asked. Giving his real name was the ultimate commitment. He wanted to throw it down at her feet and abandon himself to her whim, but that was madness on a par with the madness he'd escaped by throwing away his gift of prophecy.

Jenine paused, biting her lip. Her lips were full, pink despite the coolness of this high tower. Dorian—for Halfman would never have dared—couldn't help but imagine kissing those soft, full lips. He blinked, forcing things carnal from his mind, impressed that this young woman was actually devoting thought to his question. In Khalidor, fear was wisdom.

"I'm always afraid here," she said. "I don't believe I will betray you, but if they torture me?" She scowled. "That isn't much to give, is it? I will keep your confidence to the last extremity I can endure. It is a poor and lame vow, but I have been stripped of riches outside and in." She smiled then, the same beautiful, sad smile.

And he loved her. May the God who saved him have mercy, he couldn't believe it was happening so fast. He'd never believed in instant love. Such a thing could surely be only infatuation or lust, and he couldn't deny that he felt both. But at seeing her, he had an odd feeling of meeting an old friend. His Modaini friend Antoninus Wervel said such things happened when those who had known each other in past lives met. Dorian didn't believe that. Perhaps, instead, it was his visions. At Screaming Winds, he'd been in trances for weeks. Though his memory had been mostly scoured of those images, he knew he'd lived lifetimes with this woman in those visions. Perhaps that had primed him for love. For he believed that this was real love, that here was the woman to whom he would yield body and mind and soul and future and hopes, unflinching. He would marry her, or no one. She would bear his son, or no one would.

It was either that—or the insanity Dorian had feared for so long had finally caught up with him.

"They call me Halfman," he said. "But I am Dorian Ursuul, first acknowledged son and heir to Garoth Ursuul, and long since stricken from the Citadel's records for my betrayal of the Godking and his ways."

"I don't understand," she said. Her forehead wrinkled. He'd seen that wrinkle, in his visions, when it had become a worry line, permanent on her brow. He had to stop himself from reaching a hand up to smooth it away. It would be too familiar. By the God, he thought he'd left all the confusions of being a prophet behind! "Why are you here?"

"For you, Jeni."

She stiffened. "You may call me Your Highness, or—as you have evidently come at great risk—you may call me Jenine."

"Yes, of course, Your Highness." Dorian's head swirled. Here he was, a prince himself, being granted permission to address a young girl by her full name. That grated. And it disappointed. Love at first sight was bad enough, but finding out that it wasn't mutual . . . well, he would have thought her a flighty girl if she'd thrown herself at him, wouldn't he?

"I think you'd better explain yourself," she said.

Stupid, Dorian. Stupid. She's far from home. She's seen her land laid waste by your people. She's isolated. She's scared—and you're not exactly at your best for romance, are you?

Ah hell, she thinks I'm a eunuch! There was a nice dilemma. How does one interject into a polite conversation, "By the way, in case you're ever interested, I do have a penis."?

"I know it seems implausible, Your Highness," he said. "But I've come to res... help you escape."

She put her hands on her hips—damn she was cute!—and said, "Oh, I see. You're a prince. I'm a princess trapped in a tall tower. You're here to rescue me. How droll. You can go tell Garoth I got teary-eyed and breathless—and then you can go to hell!"

Dorian rubbed his forehead. If only the snippets he remembered of his visions had given him good ways to deal with Jeni's—Jenine's—anger.

"All I need to know, Your Highness, is if you want to leave and risk death or if you'd rather stay in your comfortable tower until my father—who's old enough to be your grandfather—comes to take your dignity, your maidenhead, and your sanity. You're a little old for my father's preferences, but since you're a princess, I'm sure he'd give you a chance. If you produce a Talented son, you'll be allowed to live. You will watch him grow up only from a distance, so that your 'womanly weakness' doesn't cripple him. When he's thirteen years old, the two of you will be reunited and allowed to spend the next two months together. Then my father will surprise both of you by visiting personally and asking what you've taught his seed in the time he's given you. It doesn't matter. What matters is it will be the first time your son will have had a god's undivided attention. At the end of the interview, your son will be asked to kill you. It's a test few fail."

Her big eyes had gotten huge. "You didn't fail it, did you?"

"The north is a brutal mistress, Your Highness. No one leaves her without scars," Dorian said. "I've got a plan, but it won't be ready for five days, and everything depends on getting through the pass to Cenaria before the snow flies and the passes close. All I need to know is, if I risk my life to come again, will you leave with me?"

He could count the heartbeats while she thought. She surveyed her prison with clenched teeth. She pulled her high collar aside and Dorian saw a scar so wide he knew she must have been healed with magic almost immediately. A cut throat like that would have left her dead in a minute or two. "Back home in Cenaria, I was secretly in love. Logan was a good man, a true friend to my brother, intelligent, and half the women in the city were after him because he was so handsome—the other half were after him because he was heir to a duchy. Logan Gyre would have been a good match for me and for our families, but there was bad blood between our fathers, so I never dared hope my dream might come true. Then an assassin murdered my brother, and my father was left without an heir. He thought that if he made Logan his heir, it would forestall attempts on his own life. So Logan and I married. Two hours later, Khalidorans murdered my entire family to eliminate the heirs to the throne. But a wytch named Neph Dada thought I was too pretty to throw away, so he cut my throat in front of my husband and Healed me afterward. Logan they killed later, after subjecting him to gods know what tortures. These people have taken everything I love." She turned, and her eyes were molten steel. "I'll be ready."

Dorian picked up her bread knife. With his Talent, he elongated it and gave it two edges, while she watched. "There's an aetheling named Tavi," he said. "He's fearless while the Godking's still in Cenaria. He may come to...dishonor you. If he does...my advice is to only use this if you have the perfect opportunity. Otherwise, don't throw away your life."

The look in her eyes told him if Tavi came, Jenine would try to kill him. Failing that, she'd turn the knife on herself. And yet Dorian gave her the knife, knowing she deserved the choice.

"Now," he said, "perhaps we can speak of lighter things. Sorry that your food is cold. The hike up the damsel-in-distress's tower is a long one."

She smiled at that, a little, shy smile that reminded him of her age, and made him feel like a degenerate old predator. She fingered the dagger he'd shaped for her. "You really are a wytch, aren't you?"

"Not now. That magic is evil. I left it long ago and trained with the magi."

"Could you use your magic to bring me warm food?" Her eyes sparkled with mischief and as they laughed together, he fell in love with her all over again.

"If I could manage a disguise that convinced Yorbas Zurgah I'm a eunuch, I think I can warm your food. Here." And he warmed her gruel right then, hoping his I-do-have-a-penis was subtle enough.

She cocked an eyebrow at him. "Here I was thinking that if I'd been in an enchanted sleep and my prince needed to awaken me I'd have been out of luck."

"Uh, in the books I've read, he wakes her with a kiss," Dorian said.

"You've been reading the wrong books."

Dorian coughed and blushed, and Jenine giggled wickedly.

They spoke for hours. For the next four days, Dorian warmed the princess's meals, and the princess warmed to him. She was still devastated by the loss of her family and her kingdom and her husband, but his presence gave her hope. He saw the beautiful, sunny girl she had been emerge, and he saw evidence of the decisive, shrewd, charismatic woman she would become.

Dorian's respect and love and desire for her grew. They were the happiest days of his life.

Kylar's new right arm was still tingling. It looked just like the hand and forearm he'd lost a week ago except that it bore no scars and was the pallid shade of skin that had never seen the sun. The Wolf had thoughtfully given him a swordsman's calluses, but the rest of his skin was highly sensitive. The slightest breath of wind sent waves of sensation. The skin was hairless, but the nails were grown in and perfectly trimmed. The little finger that Kylar had broken as guild rat and that would never fully straighten before was now flawless.

The Wolf takes pride in his work. It's better than the hand I lost.

Kylar found his destrier waiting in the woods where he'd left it. Tribe carried him like he weighed nothing and it ate leagues for breakfast, but though he hated to admit it, the destrier intimidated him. Kylar was no horseman, and they both knew it. This morning, Tribe didn't give any trouble as Kylar approached him carefully, absorbing the ka'kari back into his skin before he came within sight. As usual, Kylar had only worn underclothes beneath the ka'kari skin. The ka'kari could go over his clothes, but then the Night Angel looked lumpy—not exactly fear-inspiring. Tribe stared at him, making Kylar feel strangely self-conscious.

"Ah, son of a—" Kylar said. His underclothes had a huge hole right over the crotch. No wonder it was breezy. "Why do you do that?"

Tribe stared at him like he was crazy.

~Do what?~ the ka'kari asked.

"Eat my clothes!"

~I am the Devourer.~

"You could leave my clothes alone. And my swords."

~Some people like short swords.~

"People like swords with edges!"

~*Good point.*~

"Stop devouring my stuff. Understood?"

~*No. Especially not when you ignore my puns.*~

"It wasn't a request."

~*I understand. I won't obey.*~

Kylar was stricken silent. He grabbed worsted trousers, tunic, and his spare underclothes from the saddlebags and started to dress. He was stuck with this ka'kari for how long? Oh, right. Forever.

~*You really don't understand this? You?*~ the ka'kari asked. ~*You, a man of flesh and blood and spirit, could not remain a mild-mannered herbalist for two months. But you expect me, a blend of metals and magic artificially infused with some small measure of intelligence and personality, to change* my *nature? As for the dull swords, I wasn't the one who sold Retribution, was I?*~

Kylar hadn't thought of that. Retribution's blade stayed perfect, despite having been covered with the ka'kari for years. And he'd sold it for nothing.

No, he'd sold it to show Elene how much she meant to him. The thought of her made him ache all over again. Now he'd fulfilled his vow to the Wolf. Now, finally, he could find Elene and make things right.

Or at least more right. He reached up and touched the seamless earring in his left ear that chained him to Vi Sovari, who now was only miles away, heading east and north toward Forglin's Pass. Why was Vi going to the Chantry? Kylar pushed it out of his mind. That bitch was the last thing he wanted to think about.

Kylar suddenly grinned. "A small measure of intelligence and personality, huh?"

The ka'kari swore at him. Kylar laughed.

"Besides," Kylar said quietly, "I have changed."

"I believe you," a man said behind him.

In an instant, Kylar's sword was out. He spun, slashing. The man was tall like a hero of legend, his armor enameled white plate, with a polished mail coif that flowed around his shoulders in a cascade of steel. His helmet was tucked under his arm, and his face was gaunt, blue eyes bright. Kylar stopped the blade mere inches from Logan Gyre's neck.

Logan smiled. Kylar faltered. Abruptly, he sheathed his sword and dropped to a knee. "Your Majesty," he said.

"Stand up and hug me, you little puke."

Kylar hugged him and saw Logan's bodyguards, half a dozen of Agon's scruffy Dogs led by a beautiful woman with—of all things—a shiny garter on her arm. They were all staring at him suspiciously. Kylar upbraided himself for letting no less than eight people get so close before he noticed them. He was slipping. But then Kylar let his self-recriminations go as he felt his friend's embrace. Logan's months in the Hole had left too many sharp planes on his face and body for him to be handsome again yet, and feeling his slimness as he hugged Kylar was alarming, but there was an aura of rallying strength about him. Logan still had the same broad shoulders, the same noble carriage, and the same ridiculous height. "You're calling me little?" Kylar asked. "I probably outweigh you now. Smallest Ogre I've ever seen."

Logan laughed, releasing him. "You look good too. Except—" he turned Kylar's pale new arm over in his hand "—have you been sunning with one glove on?" He waved a hand absently. The bodyguards withdrew.

"I hacked the old arm off," Kylar said. "Had to get a new one."

Logan chuckled. "Another story you're not going to tell me?"

"You wouldn't believe me if I did," Kylar said.

"Try me."

"I just did."

"What is it with you and the lies?" Logan asked, incredulous, like Kylar was a kid with frosting and crumbs on his face claiming he'd never even seen a cake.

Kylar went cold. When he spoke again, his voice was as harsh and remote as Durzo Blint's. "You want to know why I lied to you for ten years."

"You were spying on me. I thought you were my friend."

"You pampered little fuck. When you were worrying about being embarrassed by the nude statue in the entry of your mansion, I was sleeping in sewers—literally—because that's the only way a guild rat can stay warm enough on a freezing night to stay alive. When you were worrying about acne, I was worrying about the rapist who ran my guild and wanted to kill me. So yes, I apprenticed to a wetboy to get out. Yes, I lied to you. Yes, if you'd ever done anything wrong, I'd have told the Sa'kagé. I didn't like it, but I did it. But let me ask you this, you self-righteous bastard: when you were in the Hole and it was kill or be killed, what did you do? I lived in a Hole my whole fucking life. And you tell me who's more responsible for what Cenaria has become: my father, who was too weak to raise a child, or yours, who was too weak to become king?"

Logan's face drained. With his gauntness, it made his face look like a gray skull with burning eyes. His voice was flat. "To take the throne, my father would've had to murder the children of the woman he loved."

"And how many children died because he didn't? That's the burden of leadership, Logan: making the choice when none of the choices are good. When you nobles won't pay, others have to, people like me, kids with nothing."

Logan was silent for a long moment. "This isn't about my father, is it?"

"Where the fuck is your crown?!" Kylar demanded. Through the ear-ring bond, Kylar could feel Vi's concern over the jumble of his emotions. She was feeling—dammit—Kylar tried to wall her out, push the feelings off to one side.

The big man looked haggard. "Did you ever meet Jenine Gunder?"

"When would I meet a princess?" It took Kylar a second to remember that Logan had been married to Jenine—albeit only for a few hours. Khalidor's coup had come the very night of Logan's wedding. She'd bled to death in Logan's arms.

"You'd think I'd be over it," Logan said. "Honestly, I'd always assumed that a girl as beautiful and as happy as she was had to be stupid. What an asshole I was. Kylar, have you ever looked into a woman's eyes and found that she made you want to be strong, and good, and true? Protective, fierce, noble? Finding Jenine was finding something better than I ever dared to dream." Kylar didn't want to hear it. It reminded him of Elene. And if he thought about Elene, his anger would die. "I was supposed to go from that to Terah Graesin?" Logan asked. "I couldn't. Not for a crown. Not for anything."

"But I saw everyone on the battlefield, bowing to you."

"I'd given my troth . . ." Logan trailed off.

Kylar threw his hands up, despairing.

Logan's eyes filled with dim sorrow. "I did what I thought was right."

~Imagine a king who does that.~

Kylar looked at Logan as he hadn't looked at him even when he'd rescued him from the Hole. Then, he had only been able to see the physical wounds. Now he saw more. There was the gravitas of pain deep in Logan's eyes. "You'd do it again," Kylar said.

Logan forced a weak laugh. "Hey, I'm already having my doubts."

"No you're not."

The laughter died. "Yes, I am," Logan said quietly, his eyes never leaving Kylar's, his gaze never wavering. "But yes, I'd do it again. This is who I am." He had never been more royal.

Let me see him. Kylar put his hand on his friend's arm and saw Logan, through his own eyes, less handsome, but fierce, primal in the filth of the Hole, tearing raw flesh from a human leg with his teeth, weeping. There he was hating the Holers, sinking into the filth, becoming a Holer in his own eyes. There he was deciding over the hard knot of hunger that gnawed him day and night that he would share his next meal lest he abandon being human altogether. There he was, handing out food and hating those who accepted, but doing it. That small core of nobility became the most important possession Logan had, and he would pay any price for it.

That lesson was bound up with Serah Drake, who had been Logan's fiancée before King Gunder forced him to marry Princess Jenine. Logan had loved Serah once, but that love had withered over the years, finally propped up only by false kindness. He'd been planning to marry the wrong woman because he didn't want to hurt her feelings. Breaking his engagement had been the right thing to do, but it had seemed too cruel. But if they hadn't been engaged, Serah wouldn't have been at the castle the night of the coup. She'd still be alive. In the Hole, sharing food had been the right thing to do. It had seemed stupid, but in the end, the Holers helped Logan because he helped them first. Logan's failure and his success had driven home the same lesson: Do what you know is right, and you'll get the best consequences in the end.

It was, Kylar thought, why Logan might be great. You could count on him. He was loyal, he was honest, and he would fight to the death to do the right thing. Always.

"We've both come pretty far," Kylar said. "You think we can be friends?"

"No." Grimly, Logan shook his head. "Not friends. Best friends." Then he grinned, and the last year seemed to roll off Kylar's back. They were the kind of friends who would stand and be counted. For Kylar, who had always kept dirty secrets that threatened everything, the feeling was precious beyond words.

"What happens now?" Kylar asked.

"One more errand and then, well...I'm going to write a book."

Kylar tented his eyebrows. "No offense, Your Ogrishness, but what are you going to write a book about?"

"You know how I've always loved words. I'm going to write a book of words."

"I was under the impression that that's what most books are."

"Not composed of words. I'm going to write a book defining all the words in our language. I'm calling it a dictionary."

"You're writing in Jaeran?"

"Yes."

"Defining Jaeran words?"

"Right."

"So you'll have to already know Jaeran to read it?"

"You make it sound stupid," Logan said, scowling.

"Hmm." Kylar gave an I-wonder-why-that-is? shrug. The idea of Logan's commanding form sequestered in a candlelit study, squinting at manuscripts, was funny—except that Logan thought he was serious. Logan was scholarly, but he was no scholar. He was born to lead. This book idea was a pretense to shield him from seeing Terah's mistakes and from his own impulses to do something about them.

Minutes ago, Kylar had thought he was done. He'd kept his oath to the Wolf. He thought that now he'd be free to go make things right with Elene. But now Terah Graesin was queen. She probably had a contract out on Logan already. The best way to cancel a contract was to cancel the contract-taker. And Terah Graesin deserved canceling. *One more kill, and I can change a country. With Logan as king, things can be different. There won't have to be guilds or guild rats anymore.* Elene was still safe in Waeddryn. He could do this in a week and be on his way.

"Look, we have to talk more, but first," Logan said, "I need to piss, and then I need to figure out what to do about the Khalidorans and this Lae'knaught army."

"What army?" Kylar asked.

"I just—what do you mean, what army? You have that look in your eye."

"Those Khalidorans aren't Khalidorans; the Lae'knaught've been wiped out, and we need to get to Cenaria before the Ceuran army does."

"The Ceuran—what? What?"

Kylar just laughed.

14

Dorian sat in the chute room, balancing the crap pot strapped to his back on the edge of one of the chutes. This was the last pot of the day, and Dorian was sore, exhausted, and grumpy—and he got to spend most of every day in the company of beautiful women. The chute room slave spent every day in this foul room, directing the slaves who brought in all of the Citadel's human waste and maintaining the sewage chutes, and he was the happiest slave Dorian had ever met. Dorian still gagged every time he opened the door. How the hell could Tobby be chipper?

Aching, Dorian stretched his back as he waited for Tobby to finish with the slave from the guards' quarters. Tobby pulled two levers, waited for a few moments, and then pulled a chain to the sound of distant clanking, then the man untied the top rope on his pack and Tobby tipped the pot over, sloshing the contents down the chute. A rope attached to the bottom kept the pot from following the sewage down the chute.

After he finished, Tobby walked over to Dorian. "This your last run?"

Dorian yawned and stretched. "Yes, I—" he lost his balance and the weight of the crap pot yanked him backward toward the open maw of a chute. He screamed—and jerked to a stop as Tobby threw himself against Dorian's knees.

For several moments, it was agony as the weight of the pot pulled against the sinews of his legs and stomach, trying to pull him into oblivion or rip him in half, but as the open-topped pot released its contents down the chute, the pain faded.

Once the pot was empty, Tobby was able to help Dorian out of the chute. "Trying to follow your predecessor, huh?" Tobby asked.

"What?"

Tobby chuckled. "Why'd you figure they needed another eunuch? Last harem carrier did what you just did . . . only I wasn't so fast that day."

"Shit," Dorian said.

Tobby laughed loudly like a braying donkey. Surely the man couldn't be amused by feces. Dorian began shaking from his brush with death. Good God, it hadn't even occurred to him to use his Talent.

"Funny thing is," Tobby said, "he didn't die from the ride. *They* killed him."

"What do you mean? Where does this chute go anyway?"

"Where does this shit go anyway?" Tobby echoed, then laughed again. "Down to the mines. Nearly drops on the heads a them sorry bastards. Soon as Arry fell in the chute, I routed him to one of the safe ones. Would have saved his life, if he had sense."

"Safe ones?" Dorian asked.

"You don't know shit, do you?" He punched Dorian in the arm. "Good one, eh? Eh?"

"Funny," Dorian said, forcing himself to smile ruefully.

"Didn't see that one coming, did ya?"

"Nope, didn't see that coming."

"I got a million of 'em," Tobby said.

"I bet." *If ever there was a man who deserved his slavery, I've met him.* "Why are some chutes safe?" Dorian asked.

"These chutes been here hunerds of years. First there was only one chute. At first it was a couple hunerd foot drop, from the bottom of the chute to the bottom of the chasm—well, after a couple hunerd years with twenty thousand folks shooting shit down it, there was no drop at all. Good ol' Batty Bertold got real nervous, thought an army or the pit slaves themselves might climb up the chute and attack the Citadel from within. So he built this. Now, when the shit gets within fifty feet of the bottom of the chute, we switch to a new chute. We let that first one sit until it's all soil. Then the pit slaves cart it up and the guards sell it for fertilizer. Course, I got to use all the chutes at least once a day so they don't rust up and so the pit slaves can't tell where the soil is firm under a few inches of crap and where the soup is deep enough to drown in. When Arry went down, I switched up the chutes so he'd have a chance."

"How fast can you do that?" Dorian asked.

Tobby tsked and pulled the third and the eighth lever and pulled the last chain. It took him about three seconds.

Dorian whistled, fixing the positions in his mind. "What happened to him?"

"He gave some shit to one of the meisters down there. Can't say I blame him, after what he'd been through."

"Sounds like he had a shitty day." Dorian felt dirty for the pun.

"Uh huh," Tobby said, not catching it. "Two meisters guard the pit slaves. It don't make 'em happy. They don't take no shit. They turned Arry inside out." He shook his head, somber. A moment later he grinned. "They don't take no shit, huh? Huh?" He punched Dorian's arm.

Dutifully, Dorian laughed. *I could take two meisters.*

When Dorian returned from emptying the crap pots, the concubines were keening. Dorian had never heard anything like it. He set the crap pot down and stared at Hopper.

"It's the Godking," the old man whispered, frozen by the sound from the next room. "We just got news. He's dead."

Dorian's heart stopped. *My father's dead.*

He wandered into the great room of the harem in a daze. Nearly two hundred women were gathered in the cold marble luxury of the place. They were tearing their clothes, ripping out their hair, beating their naked breasts, scratching bloody furrows in alabaster skin. Black tears rolled from kohled eyes. Some had flung themselves on the floor, weeping uncontrollably. Others had fainted.

In grief as in love and in drink, Dorian's people were extravagant, but these women's tears were not for show. They had all lived in awe and terror of the Godking, and few of them would have dared love him. None of his favorite concubines were here. No one would report who had wept and who had not. But His Holiness had been the center around which their lives revolved. Without that center, everything collapsed.

They would be compelled to throw themselves on Garoth's pyre to accompany him into the afterlife and be his slaves forever. And Garoth had always liked his women young.

Dorian saw one beautiful girl, Pricia. She was barely fourteen and just past her flowering, sitting alone, staring into space. She was still a virgin. Yorbas Zurgah had intended her as a present to the Godking when He arrived home.

"You have a chance," Dorian told her woodenly. "The next Godking might claim you."

"All my friends are going to die," Pricia said, not even looking at him.

Her answer shamed him. She hadn't been thinking of herself. This place was starting to make him think cynically, like the old Dorian.

The other implications of Garoth's death pounded Dorian a moment later. The Godking had left no clear heir, and whichever aetheling succeeded him would certainly kill off the others. If the concubines knew of Garoth's death, the aethelings would soon, if they didn't already.

Jenine!

Dorian burst into the eunuchs' room where he'd left Hopper.

"Get them all out of here," he ordered the old man. "Start with the virgins."

"What?"

"Hide them in my room. At least one of the aethelings will try to seize the Godking's harem as a declaration that he should be the next Godking. Or the guards may go crazy. You can't hide all of them, but at least the virgins will have a chance to be claimed by the next Godking. If they get raped, they'll die with the others."

Hopper nodded at once. "Done," he said.

Dorian ran up the Tygre Tower. The dreads guarding at the base of the tower were gone, and his heart dropped. He sprinted up the steps three at a time. He heard raised voices as he came up the last twenty steps. "...come, or I hurt you and then you come."

"All right," Jenine said, defeated.

The latch had been melted off the door. The fucker. It was Tavi, come to violate Jenine. Dorian kicked open the door just in time to see Jenine pull out the dagger he'd given her and bury it in a young man's chest. He screamed and his vir rose to the surface of his skin instantaneously. A white ball the size of a fist slammed into Jenine's chest and threw her across the chamber.

He turned at the sound of the door bursting open, but he didn't have time to move before Dorian's flame missiles hit him. Six burrowed through his chest and out his back before he fell facedown, dead. It wasn't Tavi. It was Rivik, Tavi's sidekick. Dorian went to Jenine.

She was whimpering, struggling to breathe, her chest concave with six broken ribs. Dorian put his hand on her chest, Seeing the damage. She relaxed as he washed away her pain. Bone after bone snapped into place seamlessly, and in moments, Dorian was done.

Jenine stared at him, wide-eyed. "You came."

"I'll always come for you."

She inhaled experimentally. "I feel ... perfect."

Dorian smiled shyly and then started grabbing candelabra, tygre statuary, anything he could find made of gold.

"We can't carry all that," Jenine said.

Dorian dropped the unwieldy pile on the table. He winked at her and put his hands on each object in turn. One by one, they melted. The gold puddled onto the table, separating and connecting into lumps like quicksilver. The lumps began congealing, thinning, hardening, until each was flat disk bearing the likeness of Garoth Ursuul.

"What ... how ...?" Jenine stuttered.

"The coins are only worth a fraction of what the art was, but they are a more *liquid* asset." He smiled as she giggled in wonder.

He allowed himself that smile, but things were not going according to plan. Dammit, everything was ready for tomorrow. The worst of it wasn't the wasted preparations, the lack of horses, the lack of warm clothing for the perilous crossing through Screaming Winds, the lack of dried food. It was that Dorian had used southern magic. Any meister who smelled him would sense it. Luxbridge might drop him into the chasm.

The chaos in the castle might not help them. More soldiers and meisters would surely be running about, and more aethelings definitely would. It meant that all Dorian's meticulous memorization of guards' watch routes and personal habits was for nothing.

Still, he was here, the armies of the Godking were not, nor were any of the Godking's older sons; Jenine was alive and safe, and the passes south were still open. In his wrath, he had vented far too much magic on Rivik, but he still had some left, enough to take care of a meister or even a Vürdmeister if caught unawares.

"What are you doing?" he asked as Jenine turned Rivik's body over. He didn't want her to have to look at that.

"I can't go like this. I'm taking his clothes," she said.

Together, they stripped Rivik. There was blood on the front of the tunic where Jenine had stabbed his chest, and six small burn holes on both front and back, but otherwise the tunic was fine. Rivik had been a slight youth, so the tunic was only a little big.

Jenine threw off her blouse and pulled on the dead youth's tunic, not asking Dorian to look away or turn his back. He stared at her slack-jawed, frozen, then looked away, embarrassed, then wondered why he was embarrassed and she was not, and looked again and looked away. He was twice her age! She was beautiful. She was brazen. She was being perfectly sensible; they didn't have time to be coy. Her head emerged from the tunic and she saw the look on his face. "Hand me the trousers, would you?" she asked nonchalantly.

The color in her cheeks told him it was a bluff, so he matched brazenness for brazenness and watched her as she pulled off her skirt. She snatched the trousers from his hands. "If you don't watch it, Halfman, you're going to be considerably more than half a—" she said with a significant glance at his trousers, but then her eyes went past Dorian to the body behind him. Her jest died and her high color drained away. "Let's get out of here," she said. "I hate this place. I hate this whole country."

She finished dressing in silence and pulled on the floppy hat Dorian had frequently worn to cover his own face as much as possible, piling her long hair on top of her head in a bundle. In the end, it was a poor disguise, not because of the clothes, but because Jenine didn't walk like a man, and couldn't learn in the few moments Dorian was willing to spare trying to teach her. But if she didn't look like a man, she didn't look like a princess either. They'd just have to hope everyone was distracted.

15

Feir had asked for two hours to get Lantano Garuwashi's sword out of Ezra's Wood. He had no idea how much of that time had passed. In fact, he couldn't remember how he'd come here. He looked up at the towering sequoys stretching to the sky.

Well, at least, he knew where here was. He was definitely in Ezra's

Wood. He looked at his hands. Both of them were scraped and his knees hurt, as if he'd fallen. He touched his nose and could tell it had been broken and then set properly. There was still crusty, dried blood on his upper lip.

Dorian had told him stories about men who'd taken a blow to the head and forgot themselves, either forgetting everything before the blow, or more commonly completely losing the ability to remember anything at all after the blow. They could meet a person, the person would walk out of the room, and five minutes later return and be greeted as a stranger once more. For several moments Feir felt a panic rising inside him at the very thought, but aside from his nose, his head didn't feel as if he'd taken a blow. He could remember leaving Lantano Garuwashi, he could remember approaching the vast bubble of magics that surrounded Ezra's Wood, and he could remember the turmoil within those magics as—miles to the east—the Lae'knaught had entered the Wood and been trapped within it. Feir had used that turmoil as a distraction for his own attempt. But from that point, he could remember nothing.

He was facing the bubble now, as if he was leaving. He took a few more steps, disoriented and came around the trunk of another giant sequoy. Before him, not fifty paces away, just outside the magic, were Lantano Garuwashi and, oddly, Antoninus Wervel.

Maybe I have gone mad. Antoninus Wervel was a red mage, one of the most powerful and most intelligent men to walk the halls of Sho'cendi in decades. He was a fat Modaini man, and he'd been a casual friend for years. To see him sitting awkwardly cross-legged beside Lantano Garuwashi, who sat as gracefully as he did everything, was surreal.

Then the men saw Feir and both rose. Antoninus called something out, but though he was only forty paces away now, Feir couldn't hear him.

Feir walked straight to the wall of magic. Whatever clever magic he'd used to get into the Wood, it obviously hadn't been clever enough. He was alive only by the forbearance of whatever it was that lived here. So Feir walked straight through the magic. It slid around him, and for a moment, he could swear something in the Wood felt amused.

Then he was out.

"What are you doing here?" he asked Antoninus Wervel.

Antoninus laughed. "You escape the Wood, something no mage has done in seven centuries, and you ask what *I'm* doing?"

"Do you have my sword?" Garuwashi demanded.

Feir was carrying a pack strapped to his back that he hadn't been carrying when he entered the Wood. "Him first," he said.

Antoninus lifted his kohled eyebrows, but said, "I came with a delegation from Sho'cendi to recover Curoch. After the Battle of Pavvil's Grove, the delegation turned back. They were sure that if Curoch had been present in such a desperate battle with so many magi and meisters present, that someone would have tried to use it. No one did, so they decided to backtrack and follow other leads. The truth is, I don't think Lord Lucius trusts everyone in our delegation. He and I don't care for each other, but he knows where my loyalties lie, so he released me. So now it's your turn, Feir. Did you recover Ceur'caelestos?"

The Modaini was too damn smart. Feir could tell that the man had put together Feir, who'd held one nearly mythical sword, with the appearance of another nearly mythical sword and found no coincidence.

Feir opened the pack. There was a note inside with directions and instructions, written awkwardly, as if the hand writing it had been writing in an unfamiliar language. Feir read it quickly and remembered bits and pieces of what had happened in the Wood. Setting the note aside, he pulled a hilt out of his pack—a hilt only, with no sword. It was a perfect replica of the one on Ceur'caelestos, and it would fit Lantano Garuwashi's sheath perfectly. As long as the sa'ceurai didn't draw his sword, no one would ever know.

"What is this?" Lantano Garuwashi demanded.

"It's three months," Feir said.

"What?" Garuwashi asked.

"That's the time I need," Feir said. "I'm a Maker, Garuwashi, and I received instructions in the Wood—a prophecy left by Ezra himself, centuries ago. If you prefer death, I will be your second, but if you want to live, take this hilt. Antoninus and I will go to Black Barrow and do things no one has done since Ezra's time. I will make Ceur'caelestos for you by spring." Or at least a damn good fake. "You can be the king you've always wished to be."

Lantano Garuwashi stood for a long moment, eyes hot and then cold, trapped between his desires and his honor. He swallowed. "You swear you will bring me my ceuros?"

"I swear it."

Lantano Garuwashi took the hilt.

Logan and Kylar rode at the head of Logan's five hundred horse and nine hundred foot. Logan's bodyguards rode ten paces back, giving them privacy. The sharpened-tooth simpleton Gnasher rode in his usual spot beside Logan, but he didn't care what they might say; he just liked to be close. Kylar unrolled a worn letter.

"Whatcha got?" Logan asked.

Kylar gave him an inscrutable look, shrugged, and handed it to him. In small, tight handwriting, it said, "Hey, I thought it was my last one, too. He said I got one more for old time's sake. He might even have been telling the truth. Be careful who you love. Don't follow prophecies. Don't let them use you to bring the High King. Your secret is your most important possession. You're more important than I ever was, kid. Maybe for all those years I was just holding it for you. MAKE NO DEALS WITH THE WOLF."

"I assume this all means something to you," Logan said.

"Not all of it," Kylar said.

"Who's the Wolf?" Logan asked.

"Someone I made a deal with right before I found that letter."

"Ouch. And the High King?"

Kylar grimaced. "That was part I was hoping you could help me with."

Logan thought. "There was a High King who held Cenaria and several other countries maybe four hundred years ago, but Cenaria's been held by lots of different countries in the last thousand years. Sounds like an Ursuul thing. They're the only ones in Midcyru in a position to rule over other kings. I'd guess they're dredging up a prophecy to give themselves legitimacy. Is the secret what I think it is?" Logan asked.

"Here we are," Kylar said. They had circled Ezra's Wood, looking for signs of the Lae'knaught. Kylar said it was something Logan needed to see for himself.

Fifty paces away, Logan saw a wall of dead men. Hundreds of them pressed against an invisible barrier, trying to escape the forest. In places, bodies were piled twenty feet deep as men had clambered over the dead, hoping to reach the top of the invisible wall. There was no movement. No one was merely injured. Every body had been mangled, torn with sharp claws that must have had godlike strength. Helmets had been crushed flat. Heads were simply missing. Swords had been snapped like twigs. Even the horses were dead, heads torn off, sinews ripped through the skin, some muscles snapped instead of torn.

For as far as the eye could see into the sequoys, there was only devastation, and as far as the eye could see west and east, Lae'knaught were pressed against an invisible wall. They'd tested every place they could before dying, and found it everywhere impregnable. Gore still drained from the bodies, sliding against the wall like glass, but strangely, there was no smell. The magic sealed in even the air.

Logan heard vomiting from his bodyguards.

"The villagers of Torras Bend say someone tries to go into the Wood every generation. It happens so much that their term for suicide is 'walking into the Wood,'" Kylar said. Logan turned. Kylar's eyes were hollow, stricken. "I did this," Kylar said. "I lured them here so they'd fall into the Ceurans' trap instead of you. These souls are on my tab."

"Our scouts heard the fighting. That's why we held back. What you did here saved fourteen hundred lives—"

"At the cost of five thousand."

"—and maybe saved Cenaria." Logan stopped. It wasn't making a dent. "Captain," he said. "Bring the men forward in groups. I want everyone to see this. I don't want any Cenarian to ever make the mistake we almost did."

Kaldrosa Wyn saluted, obviously glad to be given a duty to take her away from the massacre.

Logan changed tack. "Kylar, I know you think you're a bad man, but I've never seen anyone who will go to the lengths you will to do what you've decided is right. You are an amazingly moral man, and I trust you, and you're my best friend." Logan looked steadily at Kylar to let him read the truth.

Kylar gave a sarcastic, you-can't-be-serious grimace that slowly melted. The tension left his face as the truth sank in. Logan meant every word. Kylar blinked suddenly. Once, twice, and then looked away.

Oh, my friend, what have you gone through that being called moral nearly makes you weep? Or was it being called friend? Logan thought. He had been isolated for months in the Hole and found it hell. Kylar had been isolated for his entire life.

"But?" Kylar asked.

Logan heaved a deep sigh. "Not stupid either, are you?" Kylar flashed that old mischievous grin, and Logan loved him fiercely. "But you were a wetboy, Kylar, and now you're something even more dangerous. I can't claim that I don't know what you might do to Terah—"

"Do you really trust me?" Kylar interrupted.

Logan paused, maybe for too long. "Yes," he said finally.

"Then this conversation is finished."

"Dorian," Jenine said, "I think you should come look at this."

He stepped to the window and looked out over Khaliras. Marching into the city were twenty thousand soldiers, two thousand horses, and two hundred meisters. Dorian's little brother Paerik had returned from the Freeze. Serfs were piling out of the way of a group of horsemen who had advanced before the army. Dorian didn't have to see the banners to know it had to be Paerik himself.

Dorian and Jenine ran down the stairs two at a time, winding down and down to the base of the Tygre Tower. The grim cats favored him with their fanged smiles, mocking him. There was still time. If they could get to the front gate, they could cross Luxbridge a few minutes before Paerik arrived.

As always, the slaves' tunnels were dark. In the distance, figures clashed with sword and spell, but Dorian was able to take them around the worst of the fray. He could See his half-brothers from a great distance.

The path they were forced to take took them down a rough hewn stone tunnel past the Khalirium, where the goddess resided. The very stone down here stank of vir. Dorian rounded a corner a mere hundred paces from the castle's front gate and found himself staring at the back of an aetheling. Usually, he would have Seen the young man, but the proximity of the Khalirium confused him. He froze. Jenine yanked him back into the rough tunnel.

"Khali's not here!" the aetheling said.

Someone else cursed. "Moburu really took her to Cenaria? Damn him. He really does think he's the High King."

"So much for seizing Khali. What do we do now?" the first asked.

Khali was still in Cenaria? No wonder it didn't feel quite as oppressive down here as Dorian remembered.

"We gotta join Draef. If we help him stop Paerik at the bridge, he might let us live. Paerik or Tavi will kill us no matter what."

Dorian and Jenine scooted back into the tunnel as quickly and as quietly as they could, but it was almost fifty paces before it intersected with another hallway. No way they could run that far without the aethelings hearing or seeing them. As soon as they found a large cavity in the rough wall, Dorian pushed Jenine into it and then pressed himself as close as he could, but his thin sleeve caught on the stone and tore.

One of the aethelings stepped into the tunnel and raised his staff. A flame blazed up on it, illuminating the hall and his face. He was perhaps fourteen, as was the youth beside him. Both were short and slender and homely, bearing little of their father's robust good looks, and only a small portion of his power.

I can take them. Even with southern magic, Dorian was stronger than they were. But he didn't want it to come to that. *Come on, turn. Turn.*

If they turned, Dorian could take a shortcut and beat them to Luxbridge. With the advantage of surprise and with Khali hundreds of miles away, he could surely take this Draef and cross Luxbridge. Everything was so close he could taste it. Had not the God favored him already by holding off the snows?

Lord, please...

"I swear I heard something," one of the boys said.

"We don't have time for this, Vic," the other said.

But Vic strode forward, his staff held high. He came within ten paces and paused. Dorian readied himself.

Hold, a quiet voice said, cutting through the jumble of Dorian's thoughts. *Take the chutes.*

For a moment, Dorian believed it was the voice of the God. He could remember the exact positions the levers required. Dorian could easily overcome two meisters who weren't expecting him. From there, he and Jenine could climb out—there had to be a stair out for the meisters. Of course, he'd already thought about it for himself, but not for Jenine. The thought of riding a sewage chute down the God-only-knew how many feet in the close darkness with the stench all around was horrible enough for him, and he'd been working human waste.

Jenine would think he was a coward, running away from fourteen-year-old boys. Maybe she wouldn't come with him at all. Maybe she would come, but despise him afterward. What kind of man makes the woman he loves crawl through shit?

Vic stepped closer. Five paces away now. Dorian was frozen, one eye exposed. Surely Vic would see them. He had to! And if Dorian didn't raise some defense, Vic would murder them where they stood. But if he did raise a defense, Vic would sense it. Either way was a decision.

It wasn't the voice of the God. It was the voice of fear. I can take them.

Dorian stepped out of the crevice and lashed out at Vic with fire missiles.

He recognized his mistake the moment the missiles diverted and flew down the tunnel toward Vic's brother. The boys were twins. Fraternal twins or Dorian would have recognized it at once. Twins could make a weave to protect each other at the expense of protecting themselves. That defense, if given fully, was far stronger than a meister could give himself.

The counterstrike came from Vic, much stronger than he should have been capable of. It was a hammerfist, a spinning blue cone that in his youthful enthusiasm Vic had actually embellished to look like a flaming fist. Rather than dodge it, Dorian had to stop it completely to make sure it didn't kill Jenine behind him. Another fist came a second later from Vic's twin, rattling stones down from the low ceiling of the tunnel. Dorian blocked it, too, suddenly aware of how much magic he'd used today. He was getting exhausted.

With fingers of magic, he reached beneath Vic's shield and twisted it onto himself. It surprised the boy so much that he abandoned his next attack. Down the hall, his twin did not. His next hammerfist was whipped in a tight circle by the shield that was now protecting Dorian, and arced into Vic instead. It crushed his body flat against the tunnel wall.

Dorian flung a single fire missile down the hall. With Vic dead, the twin was now unshielded, and the fire missile pierced his chest. He grunted and fell.

Picking up Vic's staff—the damn thing was an *amplifiae,* it was what had made the aetheling's blows more powerful than they ought to have been—Dorian pulled Jenine down the hall. They could still make it to the bridge. It was close now. The last hallway was clear, and though the mighty gate was closed, the sally port opened from the inside.

Almost there!

With a boom, the mighty double gates were flung open. The rancid stench of vir washed over Dorian and Jenine. Four young men stood before them, their skin awash with the knotted dark tattoo-like vir. They were ready; they'd sensed Dorian coming.

Dorian threw up a hurried shield, as thick as he could manage with the rest of his Talent, and turned to flee. The damned amplifiae didn't help at all; it was attuned to vir. In rapid succession, the shield absorbed a hammerfist, eight fire missiles, the staccato jabs of a needler, and the diffuse flame called a dragon tongue, meant to finish an opponent after his shields were down. But Dorian's shields weren't down, he could survive another wave so long as none of them dared a pit wyrm.

"Draef!" a young man called out triumphantly from behind Dorian. It was Tavi, with three of his own aethelings, blocking the hall's other exit. The first group stopped attacking Dorian instantly.

Dorian looked from one camp to the other, and they looked at him. He and Jenine were trapped between them. "Hold!" Dorian shouted. "I am Dorian Ursuul, the Son-That-Was. I know they expunged my name from the records, but I'm sure you've heard the rumors. I'm real, and you can't afford to attack me."

Tavi spat. "You're not even a meister."

"Why?" Draef asked at the same time.

"Even if I were only a magus, I won't go down easily. If either of you attack me, you'll leave yourselves open to be attacked by the other. But I am an Ursuul of the twelfth shu'ra." *Just a touch, just a touch.* He could manage that much and still not surrender to the vir.

Dorian reached down, and the vir rushed from the depths like a leviathan and rode the surface of his skin in great knots that obscured almost all of his skin. Quickly, he pushed it back.

The aethelings, all of them sixteen or seventeen years old at most, looked at him with awe. Several of the boys standing with Tavi looked on the verge of bolting.

"An illusion!" Tavi shouted, hysteria edging his voice.

"An illusion that smells?" Draef asked contemptuously. *Yes, Draef is the first of this seed class. Tavi's the pretender.* "What do you want?" Draef asked.

"Just to leave. I'll go, and then you can slaughter each other to your heart's content." As he addressed Draef, Dorian let his eyes go to the staff amplifiae he carried. He hadn't used the aetheling's hand speech in years, but with his body blocking Tavi's view, he moved his hands to signal over the amplifiae—*for you.*

Draef's eyes glittered. The amplifiae would be enough to turn the battle.

"Dorian," Jenine whispered. She was still slouched unassumingly by his side, trying to look like a body servant, and Dorian wasn't about to draw attention to her.

"Fair enough, get out," Draef said. His fingers signaled *when?*

Through clenched teeth, Jenine whispered, "Tavi's looking at me funny."

Dorian was trying to remember the finger speech vocabulary he hadn't used for so many years to answer Draef's question. There it was, he remembered. *When we get to the bridge.*

Draef looked satisfied, though tension still stood stark on every feature, and Dorian and Jenine started walking. Only now did Dorian risk a look back to Tavi. He was afraid that the young man's quick hatred might be roused even by meeting his eyes. Dorian had won, but with the overween ing arrogance this aetheling possessed, it was best not to appear to take any joy in the victory.

The eight aethelings all had their eyes jumping from Dorian to their opponents on the opposite side of the hall. For them, any move Dorian made might be the distraction they or their enemy might take advantage of. And whether he made out of the hall alive or not, they would fight. Soon.

Out of the side of his mouth, Dorian said, "Remember to walk like a—" It was too late; Jenine had been drilled on proper comportment for far too long.

"She stays!" Tavi shouted suddenly and reached out with vir to grab Jenine.

The move set one of Draef's boys off. He threw up a crackling shield reflexively.

That unleashed a magical firestorm. Dorian threw a shield around himself and Jenine. A fire missile made it through before the shield formed and scored his ribs. He hunched and almost lost the shield. Jenine grabbed him and held him upright.

The hall filled with magic, stroke and counterstroke, gouts of fire, lightning bolts that smote the rocks as shields diverted them, the rocks cascading from the ceiling turned into missiles themselves and hurled down the hall. Most of the attacks weren't directed at Dorian and Jenine, but they were in the line of fire.

Dorian's shield thinned, layer after layer snapping, melting, withering. The aethelings were all fresh. This battle would last long after Dorian's shields finally gave way. He was going to die, and worse, he was going to let Jenine die. He had failed her.

No, not while I have breath. God, forgive me for what I'm about to do. It was no true prayer to beg forgiveness while choosing to sin—but he meant it fervently all the same.

Dorian reached to the vir. It came, joyfully.

Someone was screaming, a terrible scream compounded a hundred times by the vir to shake every hall and tunnel of the Citadel. Dorian stood and flung his arms out. As they passed in front of him, he saw that his skin had totally disappeared beneath the all-absorbing, wriggling blackness. Nor did the vir stop at the bounds of his body. They lashed out from his arms—out farther and farther, like great wings—and came down on either side, barely registering the aethelings' last desperate attacks.

He felt the boys crunch beneath those mighty wings like beetles popping under his boot. Their shields broke like shells and the softness within was ground to gory smears on the rock.

The vir sang power and hatred and strength. *It is vile, and I love it.*

He stopped screaming, and it was long seconds before the sound stopped echoing back from the Citadel's halls. Dorian quieted the vir from his skin with effort. "Are you all right?"

Jenine's big, beautiful eyes were wider than he'd ever seen them. She tried to speak, couldn't, and nodded instead.

"I'm sorry," Dorian said. "It was that or die. We're almost there."

But as they stepped through the now-smoking gate, Dorian saw that he was wrong. Halfway across the glowing spans of Luxbridge was a man in a majestic white ermine cloak like Garoth Ursuul had worn. He wore the gold chains of a Godking around his neck and vir swam on his skin.

Dorian's brother Paerik Ursuul had come to claim his throne, and blocking the bridge with him stood six full Vürdmeisters.

On the third night, after they made it through Forglin's Pass and set up camp, Dehvi finally spoke to Vi. "Let us train together, wetboy."

"I'm not a wetboy," Vi said quickly.

"You were Hu Gibbet's apprentice."

Vi's mouth dried up. "Yes." The very name brought back ugly memories.

Dehvi drew a pair of sais. "The Night Angel did kill him."

"I know. I couldn't be happier." Vi wished she'd had the guts to do it herself.

The smile faded into puzzlement. "You seek no vengeance?"

"I've fucked men for smaller favors. I wanted to kill Hu since I was thirteen."

Dehvi scowled. "Too much talk." He bent over Vi's bedroll where she had put her sword. He poked the point of one sai at the juncture of blade and hilt and flicked her sword to her. She caught it and tested the edge. It was blunted with a thin shield of magic, but a strong blow would still cut. Dehvi checked all six points of his sais. Vi had never fought against sais. A sai looked like a short sword with a narrow blade, except that the hilts swept in a broad U for catching blades. Each tine was sharpened.

Holding the sais in one hand, Dehvi removed his horsehide cloak and draped it over a rock. Vi followed suit reluctantly. Then Dehvi turned, bowed, said something incomprehensible in Ymmuri, spun the sais in his hands, and took an impossibly low ready stance.

Vi's doubts about such a low stance were broken at the first clash. She lunged toward his face. He nearly leapt forward, catching her sword with one sai and then the other and twisting as he sprang like a snake. Vi's sword spun from her grasp and she found a sai touching her throat while the other jabbed the small of her back. Dehvi's face was impassive. He stepped back wordlessly and flicked her blade back to her.

She lasted fifteen seconds the second time, and didn't lose her blade, though Dehvi twisted it far out of the way and touched her ribs with the other sai. After a few minutes, she was beginning to understand. Then Dehvi changed stances. He sidestepped her first cut, not even using the sais, and swept her feet out from under her.

She pulled herself out of the mud and found him grinning. Hu Gibbet had leered at her sometimes, and mocked her often, but Dehvi's grin was innocent. It suggested that if she could see herself, she'd laugh too.

Suddenly, she was crying, hot tears spilling down her cheeks. Dehvi gave her the look she deserved: utter bewilderment. She laughed at the ridiculousness of it, rubbing her tears away. "Hu shit on everything, Dehvi. Every time he trained me, it was all mockery and bruises and humiliation. For fuck's sake, this is actually *fun*. And I'm learning so much more from you. You're better than he ever was. No wonder you kick ass."

"Asses I have kicked," Dehvi said. "Though finding them less sensitive than other places."

Vi laughed and blinked her eyes to keep that bizarre flood down.

"You did marry in Waeddryner way," Dehvi said. He tugged his own ear to indicate her earring. "But are not Waeddryner. Who is husband?"

Well, that helped with the crying. She cleared her throat. "Kylar Stern. Sort of."

Dehvi's eyebrows raised.

"It's, uh, complicated."

He shrugged and drew a sword. He touched the edge to make sure it was shielded, and they began sparring again. Vi sank into it, releasing her worries about the life she was fleeing from and the life she was fleeing to. Even as she lost, time and again feeling the dull poke of Dehvi's sword, for the first time she had the sense that fighting was something she was really good at. When she countered a move that had caught her before, Dehvi might barely nod, but it was as good as effusive praise.

Dehvi shifted fighting styles no less than six times, and Vi sensed that he knew quite a few more, but the last one felt familiar. Vi was sunk so deep into her own body that she barely noticed that she'd spoken until she saw Dehvi miss a step. Her riposte brushed his stomach. She'd said two words: "You're Durzo." Her eyes told her it was impossible. Her knowledge of illusory masks told her it was impossible. But she knew, and his reaction confirmed it. "What are you doing here?" she asked.

"It was the accent, wasn't it? Always takes me a while to get it back. You got some Ymmuri uncle or something?" Dehvi said, his voice abruptly Cenarian.

"You fight like Kylar. What are you doing here?"

"You bonded Kylar with the most powerful surviving set of compulsive wedding rings in the world. Was that your own idea?"

"The Godking put a compulsion on me. Sister Ariel said ringing was the way to break it."

"I thought Kylar was in love with that Elene girl. Why'd he marry you?"

Vi swallowed. "I sort of ringed him when he was unconscious."

Dehvi's expression went blank, and Vi had a sudden intuition that Durzo's blank look was as indicative of pending violence as Hu Gibbet's rages. Dehvi said softly, "I'm here to decide if I should kill you to free Kylar from the bond. You're not making much of a case for yourself."

She tossed her sword into the mud and shrugged. *Fuck it. Kill me.*

Dehvi-Durzo looked at her strangely, weighing her. "Have you ever felt that you were part of a grand design, Vi? That some benevolence was shaping your fate?"

"No," Vi said.

Dehvi laughed. "Me neither. Goodbye, Vi. Watch out for that husband of yours; he'll change you." Then he left.

Solonariwan Tofusin stood on deck as the Modaini merchant ship lumbered toward Hokkai Harbor. It had been twelve years since he'd been to the Sethi capital, the city he had once called home. The sight of the two great chain towers guarding the entrance to the harbor, shining white in the autumn sun, filled his heart to bursting.

As they passed between the towers, as always, his appreciation of the seemingly delicate towers became awe. Built during the height of the Sethi Empire, the chain towers stood on narrow peninsulas. The base of each tower abutted the ocean so the chain couldn't be attacked without taking the tower. The chains themselves lay under water except during maintenance and war. Then, the great teams of royal aurochs would winch the chains apart until they were at or barely below the water line at high tide and five to eight feet above it at low tide. During a battle, the aurochs would turn the chains. A single blade shaped like a shark tooth was attached to each link. Because of the half twist in the chain at each axle, a ship pressing against the mighty chains would find half the teeth chewing through his hull in each direction. It made the entire chain a saw that had destroyed more than one fleet, and deterred many more.

Above the sparkling blue waters—gods, Solon thought, the bay was a color to shame sapphires—Hokkai rose on its three hills. Above the ubiquitous docks already filling with wintering ships, the great city rose in thousands of whitewashed walls with red tile roofs. After the ugly hodgepodge of Cenarian architecture, it was a relief.

But the most beautiful sight of all, magnificent Whitecliff Castle reigning over the highest hill, filled Solon not only with awe but something akin to terror. *Kaede, my love, do you hate me still?*

After Khali and her Soulsworn had massacred everyone at Screaming Winds, Solon had had nothing to do. His friend Feir had left days before they knew of the danger. When the garrison commander ignored Dorian's warnings that Khali was coming, Dorian disappeared. Solon had been the only man to escape. He'd found himself suddenly without ties to anything. It had been Dorian's prophecy that had kept him from going home more than a decade ago. Solon had served Regnus Gyre as prophecy dictated— and failed. Regnus was dead. Solon had served for a decade, only to be dismissed the day before Regnus was murdered. Kaede was the Sethi empress now. She wasn't likely to be happy to see Solon, but if she killed him, so much the better.

He labored with the sailors. He could have paid for his passage, but no Sethi worth his salt would sit in a cabin while others were hoisting sails, not even on a wide-bellied Modaini merchant ship. The Sethi preferred small, light ships. It meant their merchants had to make twice as many trips, but they made them twice as fast. A Sethi ship also had to ride a storm rather than plow through it, but the Sethi accepted the ocean's whims and loved her and feared her equally.

As the ship came to rest in the bay, the Modaini merchant captain emerged from his cabin, his eyes and eyebrows freshly kohled. Solon always thought it gave the dark-haired Modaini a sinister aspect, but the captain was an affable man. He tossed Solon his pay and welcomed him to sail with him any time before going to speak with the harbormaster, who had rowed out to collect the harborage tax and inspect the cargo.

The harbormaster clambered up the webbing onto the deck with the ease of a man who did it a dozen times a day. Like most Sethi, he wore no tunic until winter, and the sun had darkened his skin to a deep olive. He had a prominent nose, brown eyes, the figure-eight earring of Clan Hobashi, two silver rings on his right cheekbone, and two silver chains strung between the earring and cheek rings—an assistant to the harbormaster, then.

The man had barely spoken two words when he saw Solon and broke off in mid-sentence. Solon, still bare-chested as he had been for the whole trip, wasn't as tanned as most Sethi. But despite his light tan and the white hair growing in to replace the black, he was unmistakably Sethi—and he wore no clan rings. The harbormaster's long knife came out in a heartbeat. There were only two groups in Seth that wore no rings.

"What's your name, clanless?"

The Modaini captain looked aghast. He had never made a trip to Seth and didn't know their customs, which was why Solon had chosen his ship.

"Solon," Solon said, not giving his clan name, as an exile wouldn't.

The harbormaster grabbed Solon's chin and looked closely at his cheeks and ears, first on one side, and then, frustrated, on the other. His eyebrows tightened in confusion. Not only were there no scars where the clan rings had been torn out, but there were no scars from where the rings had been put in.

"Raesh kodir Sethi?" he demanded. *Are you not Sethi?*

"Sethi kodi," Solon acknowledged, his Old Sethi diction perfect.

The harbormaster released Solon's face as if burned. "What *was* your name?"

"Solonariwan Tofusin."

One of the Modaini sailors cursed. The harbormaster's tanned face turned green. He noticed that his long knife was still out and tucked it away as if it were scalding. "I think you'd better come with me . . . uh, your lordship."

"What's going on?" the captain asked.

Neither Solon nor the harbormaster answered. Solon clambered into the rowboat with the harbormaster. The sailor who'd cursed said, "The Tofusins reigned for five hundred years."

Not exactly. It was four hundred seventy-seven.

"Reigned? They don't anymore?" the captain asked, his voice strangled. Hopping into the rowboat, Solon couldn't help but smile.

"No, cap'n. The last one died ten years ago. If this one really is a Tofusin, there'll be all sorts of hell to pay."

That, on the other hand, is dead on.

$\mathcal{K}$hali's blood," Paerik swore, striding confidently across Luxbridge toward Dorian. "That was rather impressive. Who are you?" His eyes took in Jenine but dismissed her.

"It's all right," Dorian told Jenine, though it wasn't. He'd destroyed a few teenage boys who had underestimated him. Paerik Ursuul was a man in the prime of his powers. And he was fresh. And he had six battle-hardened Vürdmeisters backing him.

One of the Vürdmeisters whispered in Paerik's ear. Paerik straightened. "No, surely not. Dorian?" He stepped forward and Dorian stepped forward as well, not willing to let Paerik reach the end of Luxbridge unchallenged. Paerik smirked. Seeing that smirk, Dorian hated him, despised him, wanted to crush him.

"I am Dorian," Dorian said defiantly. Six Vürdmeisters and Paerik. Damn it, he only wanted to leave. The dark clouds overhead rushed past, coldly impartial.

"We thought you long dead, *brother*," Paerik said. "A mistake we shall soon remedy."

Dorian lashed out with vir and Talent both, splitting the weaves to sweep the Vürdmeisters off the bridge and at the same time yanking at the magical underpinnings to drop the bridge into the abyss.

They rebuffed the attacks with ease. Even with the amplifiae, Dorian was no match for seven Vürdmeisters together.

"Brother, brother," Paerik admonished. "This bridge will not drop a true-born Ursuul." He laughed and skulls embedded in Luxbridge seemed to laugh with him, their eyes glowing with magical fire. "Indeed, if any of Garoth's sons were in danger, it would be you, Dorian: the mage-trained."

"That's what I'm counting on," Dorian said. He stepped forward, out of the shoe he had cut free with his Talent, and put one bare foot on the bridge.

There was a flash as the last quarter of the bridge sensed a magus and unraveled.

Paerik screamed, falling with a shower of skulls that laughed no longer. He and the Vürdmeisters plummeted down and down. They flung vir at the distant walls, hoping to catch themselves, but the walls themselves were bespelled to deny magic purchase. The Vürdmeisters passed out of sight into the thick foul clouds of the abyss. Dorian could sense their magic for several more seconds, trying anything, everything, desperately. Then they winked out, all at the same time.

Before them, Luxbridge reformed itself. Dorian stepped back into his lead-lined shoe and tested it on the bridge. It flared green and began to turn transparent. He had simply used too much Talent too recently for the thin defense of the lead plating to be adequate, so he stretched the vir forth once more and reached under the bridge to steady it.

"We must go quickly," he told Jenine. "Stay close."

She nodded, biting her lip. By the God, she was beautiful. She was worth it.

Dorian stepped onto Luxbridge, and it held. It was even more eerie, he thought, to walk across the span without the skulls. Looking at the harmless skulls of the dead scared him less than looking at clouds far beneath his feet.

In moments, they made the crossing. The guards standing at the Gate Keep gaped and dropped to their knees. Dorian recognized Rugger.

"I'm sorry," he said. Rugger looked up, sure he was about to die. Dorian Healed the man's wen with a touch. Without the ugly protuberance, Rugger wasn't half bad-looking. Rugger's hands went to his forehead, disbelieving.

Hand in hand, Dorian and Jenine stepped through the iron portcullis and looked over the city from their perch.

Paerik's army wound through the city and out onto the plain. The front of it was just beginning the climb up the ridge where Dorian and Jenine stood. The men and women on the leading edge weren't soldiers; they were meisters and Vürdmeisters, two hundred strong. And they were already halfway to Dorian. They couldn't help but have been aware of the magical firestorm he just been part of. Every one of them had their eyes fixed on him.

"Are we going to die?" Jenine asked.

"No," Dorian said. "These people have lived under tyranny so long, they have no idea what to do after you've killed their leader. One more bluff, and we're on our way home." *What home is that, Dorian?*

"You really think you can bluff *that*?" Jenine asked, pointing to the entire army.

Dorian smiled, and he realized how long it had been since he'd thought about the future. He was no prophet now, but yes, he was sure. He was about to gamble it all for one last time. A few orders, a few curses, maybe a few deaths, and he and Jenine would be on their way to Cenaria. It would work. It could, anyway.

Something cold touched his cheek. Dorian blinked.

"What?" Jenine asked, seeing the hope die in his face. "What's wrong?" She followed his eyes up.

"It's snowing," he said softly. "The passes will be closed. We're trapped."

In the distance, barely audible beneath the hiss of falling snow, Dorian thought he heard Khali laughing.

Snow made the worst weather for invisibility. In Cenaria, snow usually melted as soon as it hit the ground, but tonight it was sticking long enough to show footprints. The sleet itself gave shape to Kylar's body as it ran down his limbs. Kylar had to move as slowly toward the Ceuran camp as if he were an assassin. At least he still remembered how to sneak. And at least the clouds blocked the moon. Still, it was cold. As usual, Kylar was only wearing underclothes beneath the ka'kari, and it wasn't enough.

He tugged at his earring, pushing down the distant awareness of Vi. Shivering, Kylar climbed a rocky knoll to get a better view. The Ceurans had four men camped on the windy hill, huddled around a banked fire, with oil-soaked torches nearby so they could give signals to the army below. Kylar sat five paces from a weary sentry. The man was a peasant foot soldier rather than a sa'ceurai. His armor was made of plates sewn onto fabric. Rather than being fastened with leather, which was durable but would harden and shrink if it got wet too often, Ceurans always fastened their armor with ruinously expensive Lodricari silk laces.

After the Battle of Pavvil's Grove, Garuwashi's plan had been to pull the Cenarian army east after his "Khalidoran" raiders while the main strength of his own army swept behind them and took the capital. It would have worked, but for something he never could have foreseen: walls.

Most of Cenaria's old walls had been cannibalized for their stones. By the time Kylar was a child, generations of Rabbits too poor to pay for masonry had finally left the Warrens without walls. The richer east side had seen a similar if slower erosion. But in the last few months while Kylar was gone, walls had appeared around the entire city. It was breathtaking. With Cenaria's endemic corruption, it would have taken five generations of kings and millions of crowns to equal what Garoth Ursuul's cruelty and magic had done in two months. Of course, he'd also had a ready supply of stone from all the houses Terah Graesin's followers had abandoned. And when those ran out, they simply demolished more homes and took what they needed.

Now, the Ceuran army was laid out in a crescent hugging the south and east of the city. On finding walls, Garuwashi's generals had prepared a siege until their leader could join them—which he had, by now. The west side of the city was an alternately boggy and rocky peninsula that held the Warrens. West of that was the ocean. North of the city were mountains and only one crossing of the Plith River. Garuwashi had contented himself with burning that bridge so he could concentrate his forces on the east side of the Plith and the two gates he would probably assault.

Garuwashi's army camped like the raiders Kylar had seen at the edge of Ezra's Wood. Tents made up a grid pattern, with small streets separating the tents and wider streets between platoons, commanders' tents at regular intervals, couriers' tents next to those, and latrines and fires laid out with precision.

What they didn't have were wagons. Whatever tunnels the Ceurans had taken were evidently not big enough, or too steep, or too claustrophobic for horses. Garuwashi had sacrificed everything for speed. The war leader himself had probably only caught up to his army in time to see the horror of the walls for himself. And now it was snowing.

This was not going to be a protracted siege. When Terah Graesin had left Cenaria, those who had followed her had put their possessions to the torch to keep them from falling into Khalidoran hands. How many granaries had gone up in those fires? Perhaps a better question was, how many bakeries and mills and warehouses were left? For their part, Lantano Garuwashi's men had the freedom of movement, but all the crops had been taken into the city long ago. Lantano's men could raid villages a few days out—but without horses, they couldn't bring the food back quickly, and they could only bring what they could carry. Even if they stole horses and built a few wagons, that would take time—and they had an entire army to feed.

Each side was going to be absolutely desperate within days.

Logan's force outside the walls wasn't likely to do much to sway the balance, not without communication with Terah Graesin. If they could tell the queen to hold on and not do anything stupid, Logan could use his cavalry to destroy any attempts Garuwashi made at foraging. In a standoff involving thirteen thousand foot soldiers, a few hundred horses could make all the difference. If Terah didn't do anything stupid.

Which meant someone needed to talk to her.

~Someone? Let me guess.~

Kylar had six hours until dawn. It was going to be a busy night. Before he left, just for fun, he tied the silk laces of the sentry's leggings together.

19

I'm sorry, Jenine," Dorian said. "I'm sorry we didn't leave earlier." With snow falling now, they would have had to leave a week ago to make it through the passes. A week ago, he hadn't even found Jenine yet. There was nothing he could have done differently. Still.

"You did everything you could. You were magnificent," Jenine said. The way she said it, with such bravery and unguarded admiration, told him she expected to die. Of course she did. Twenty thousand good reasons for that were marching through the city. She was so brave it made Dorian ache.

"I love you," he said. It just slipped out. He opened his mouth to apologize, but she put a finger on his lips.

"Thank you," she said. She reached up and kissed him gently.

It shouldn't have meant so much, those words, that kiss, coming from a girl who thought she was about to die, but they were liquid fire and hope and life to Dorian.

"We do have one chance," he said.

"We do?"

He shook himself and Halfman—at least the Feyuri ears and eyebrows and the less comfortable portions of his eunuch disguise—burst apart and disintegrated.

Rugger gasped. "Dorian?" he blurted out.

Dorian glared at him. Rugger dropped to his face. "Your Holiness," he said.

It was that simple. Garoth Ursuul had ruled absolutely, and if one disregarded the moral dimensions, he'd ruled efficiently and well. His death left a vacuum, and a people that expected to be ruled as they had been. They were a people accustomed to obeying orders instantly. Dorian and Jenine ran across Luxbridge and into the castle.

From somewhere deep in his mind, Dorian dredged up the correct sequences and shifted the halls so that the front gate led to the Lesser Hall, which then led to the Greater Hall, and finally to the throne room. The stones ground and shook, and obeyed him.

Before going to the throne room, Dorian ran to his old barracks. Hopper refused to open the door, so Dorian had to break it open. He quickly apologized to the terrified concubines, who all looked at him like they should know him, but didn't. Hopper recognized him faster and dropped to his face.

"Hopper, dammit, I don't have the time. Go to the Godking's chambers and get me the finest clothes you can as fast as you can. I need you girls to dress Jenine appropriately, and then I need two or three of you to be throne ornaments—but it's dangerous. Only volunteers, and only if you can be ready in five minutes."

"I don't want to leave you," Jenine said as he moved to go.

"If this is going to work, you must," Dorian said.

She started to protest, then nodded. He ran from the room.

He didn't go to the throne room. He went to his brothers' dormitories. They were littered with bodies. The aethelings had grasped what the Godking's death meant immediately. Several times in his search, Dorian saw younger children hiding beneath beds or in closets. He left them unharmed. All he was looking for were amplifiae, and in several of the rooms, he found many. The older aethelings had collected or created as many amplifiae as they could, knowing that one day they might be the difference between life and death. Dorian scooped as many as he could carry and ran to the throne room.

The throne room itself had been the site of one of the worst battles. Twenty dead aethelings and two Vürdmeisters sprawled in the shit and stench of death. Two young men were still alive, though too badly hurt to use the vir. Dorian stilled their hearts and took his throne amid the stench of burnt flesh and hair and the coppery smell of blood. All the amplifiae he had gathered were useless to him. He had some power left, but it would kill him to use what he would need to overmatch the number of Vürdmeisters marching toward the throne room right now.

Jenine and Hopper and two young concubines jogged into the hall, Hopper as awkward as his namesake.

"You look stunning," Dorian told Jenine. She was wearing green silks and emeralds. "Ladies," he told the concubines, "your bravery will not be forgotten."

"They're across the bridge," Hopper said. He produced some of Garoth's magnificent clothing, and the women stripped Dorian and dressed him as quickly as they could.

Dorian thought of the meisters hurrying here even now. Would they go slowly enough to try to read the residue of the battles they passed? What would they make of the gap in Luxbridge? He draped the heavy gold chains of office around his neck.

"You, there. And you, over there," he told the concubines. "Jenine, on the floor beside the throne. Sorry there's no chair. Hopper, over by the door in case I need you."

He sat then in the great onyx throne and as he put his hands on the sinuous arms of the chair, he felt connected to the whole Citadel, but most especially to its heart—its empty heart now, where Khali should have been. Dorian thanked the God that she wasn't there. He didn't know if he could survive that. He could feel the meisters approaching the great doors, so through the throne that made the Citadel like part of his body, he threw the doors open with a crash.

The meisters and Vürdmeisters hesitated. There were hundreds of them, and they took in the carnage of the dead aethelings and the easy majesty of the man on the throne at once. Most of them had obviously expected to see Paerik. Their jaws dropped. Others had known, had been able to read the vir to know he died—and, as usual, hadn't shared their knowledge with their fellows, hoping it would give them an edge.

"Enter," Dorian commanded, amplifying his voice enough that all could hear, but not booming as an amateur would. Vürdmeisters would not be cowed by a simple weave, and using it too forcefully would make them suspect him.

He let those who were able to read the battle read it. Then he waited. He let them look around the room, stare at the women, stare at the magic, even glance at Hopper. He let them look at him, let those who remembered him gasp and mutter about who he was. Dorian the heir, returned from the dead. Dorian, the rebel. Dorian, the defiant. Dorian, the erased. He waited, and it made him remember when his father had been grooming him to rule. They had walked one day together in a wheat field.

"How do you keep such ambitious people in your grip?" Dorian had asked.

Garoth Ursuul had said nothing. He simply pointed to a stalk of wheat that grew above its fellows and lopped its head off.

These men were the ones who had survived generations of that process. None of them spoke for ten seconds, twenty, a minute. Dorian waited until he was sure one young Vürdmeister was about to speak. Then with his vir, he flung a staff at the man.

Two hundred shields sprang up in the throne room. The amplifiae hit the young wytch's shield and fell to the ground. Dorian favored them with a condescending look and slowly the meisters lowered their shields. The young man who'd been about to speak scooted forward and picked up the staff, looking abashed. Then Dorian threw another amplifiae to the meister on his right. She caught it. Then he threw another and another until he'd dispensed all of the dozens he had, even his own.

There weren't enough for every meister, of course, but there were enough to make Dorian's point. A king didn't arm his enemies.

Dorian raised his vir to the surface of his skin, and brought them not only into his arms, but up around his face. He allowed them to break through his scalp and form a living crown. There was pain there, pain as they broke his skin and as they broke through channels of power that he had blocked long ago. He was powerful again now. Powerful and dread.

"Some of you recognize me as Dorian, first seed, first aetheling, first survivor of training, first to accomplish his uurdthan, first son of Garoth Ursuul."

"But Dorian is dead," one of the younger meisters said, deep in the crowd.

"Yes, dead," Dorian said. "You have read the chronicles. Dorian is dead these twelve years. As now Paerik is dead. And Draef is dead. And Tavi. And Jurik. And Rivik. And Duron, and Hesdel, and Roqwin, and Porrik, and Gvessie, and Wheriss, and Julamon, and Vic. Dead, all of those who questioned my resolve. So now each of you has a choice. Will you question my resolve and try to take this throne, or will you gather my enemies and bring them to me?"

Dorian's face was perfectly impassive. It had to be. He had no Talent left, and no vir left if he wanted to live. The throne had some interesting powers, but not enough to destroy two hundred meisters.

He wondered suddenly if any of them realized how fragile he was. It wouldn't take an attack to destroy Dorian. It would only take a single sneer.

But these were men schooled not to sneer at authority, no matter how much they despised it. The moment stretched unbearably, and then one young man hit his knees before his Godking. Then another. Then it was a rush not to be the last.

This, at least, I owe you, father. You cruel, brutal, amazing man. They called you a god and you made them believe it.

The new Godking affected not to be surprised. He started issuing orders, and they obeyed, running to secure the safety of the concubines, running to capture the living aethelings, running to take care of the armies, to summon the leaders of the city and the highland and lowland chiefs, to gather the meisters who had gone into hiding during the fighting.

"What have I done?" Dorian asked Jenine quietly when it was done.

She didn't answer. There were still men and meisters in the throne room. It should have felt good to assume so much power, so much power to change everything he'd hated about his homeland. Instead, he felt trapped.

"Your Holiness," the young red-haired Vürdmeister who had been the closest to opposing him said. "If...if Dorian is dead, Your Holiness, what may we call you?"

Godking Dorian was impossible, of course. Not only because his father had wanted him dead. Dorian didn't want Solon or Feir or any magus to ever hear of this. Better they think him dead. *Looks like I had to go through the shit one way or the other, huh, God?* But the God didn't answer. The God was far away, and Dorian's challenges were here, immediate and deadly.

"I am...Godking Wanhope." Wanhope was an archaic word that meant despair. When he looked at Jenine, she looked frightened but resolute. He squeezed her hand. *She's worth it. We'll make it through this. Somehow.*

20

As Vi descended from the pass in the afternoon, the snows became sleet and finally rain. Forests yielded to farms, though she met no one on the road. Anyone with sense was inside. Vi rounded a corner and found herself staring at Sister Ariel, sitting on a mare with all the grace of a sack of potatoes. In contrast to how miserably drenched Vi was, the Bitch Wytch wasn't even wet. An inch above her skin and clothing, the rain sheared away, ran in rivulets over an invisible shell, and dropped to the ground. She smiled beatifically. "Hello, Vi. It's good to see you're alive. I received a very odd message this morning telling me to expect you."

"From Dehvi?" Vi asked.

"Who?"

"Dehvira-something Bruhmaezi-something," Vi said.

"Dehvirahaman ko Bruhmaeziwakazari?" Sister Ariel asked, getting both the cadence and the tone perfect. Bitch!

"That was it."

Sister Ariel smirked. "You are a very impressive young woman, Vi, but the Ghost of the Steppes—if not only a legend—is two hundred years dead. Someone was having fun with you."

"The what?" Vi asked.

"Why are you here, Vi?" Sister Ariel asked. "No lies. Please."

Instantly, Vi felt herself caught between rage and tears again, out of control. She'd never been like this before. Since murdering Jarl, she'd been a disaster. Ringing Kylar had only made it worse. Even the things that should have been good, like learning Hu was dead, and helping kill the man who claimed to be her father, Godking Garoth Ursuul, had instead only thrown her further off balance. "I'm here to become you, you bitch. To manipulate rather than be manipulated. To become the best." She tugged at her earring. "And to get this fucking thing off."

Sister Ariel's face stilled, her lips going white. "For your sake, I strongly suggest you come up with other reasons when the Gatekeeper interviews you. So how about you shut your mouth, and I'll pretend you're a normal young woman looking to join our sisterhood?"

It took a long time for Vi's rage to subside enough for her to nod.

They rode together through the rain and soon the city emerged from the low-lying cloud. "It's called Laketown," Sister Ariel said, "for the obvious reasons."

The city and the Chantry rested at the confluence of two rivers, which made a reservoir above Vestacchi Lake. All the buildings of the city and the Chantry rested on islands in the reservoir, the nearest of which was fifty paces from the shore. Arching bridges connected every island to its neighbors and several to the shore, but streets themselves were absent. Instead, low, flat punts navigated the waterways. Some of them were covered against the rain, others exposed. Regardless, the punts moved far faster than they should have.

Vi and Ariel entered the part of Laketown that had grown on the shores by the bridges, but all the merchants seemed to be huddled in their daub-and-wattle homes, with their chimneys or chimney holes smoking.

"By some ancient magic we still can't duplicate, the islands are actually floating," Sister Ariel said. "The entire dam can be opened and the islands flushed out into the lake in times of war. Of course, we haven't had to do that for centuries. And a good thing, too. I understand towing all the islands back up here is a lot of work."

"It's beautiful," Vi said, forgetting herself. "The water's so clean."

"This city was built at a time when magic was used to benefit farmers and fishermen. There were special streams in every city that would take the stains out of your clothing. There were plows that could be pulled by a single ox that would break six furrows in a single pass. There were free public baths with water as hot or cold as you wanted. Charms that kept meat from spoiling. People thought of magic as a tool, not only as a weapon. In Laketown, the slops and nightsoil are supposed to be thrown into these pipes that—see, no smell?—that take them directly to the dam. Of course, you can never get everyone to obey even a sensible law—like not throwing nightsoil in the water you drink—so the lake itself has spells that cleanse it."

Sister Ariel led them to a white punt on the far end of the dock. A boy dodged out into the rain to take their horses and Vi took her bags and stepped onto the punt. She took some comfort in Sister Ariel's obvious terror that the boat was going to capsize. As soon as they were settled on the low, wet seats, the punt began moving by itself.

Vi grabbed the side of the boat in a white-knuckled grip.

Sister Ariel smiled. "This magic, on the other hand," she said, "we can do. It's just too much trouble, these days." They skimmed quickly into the wide water streets and the little boat turned on its own.

"There are currents that shift on the turning of the glass. If you know what you're doing, you can get from one side of the city to the other going downstream all the way."

After a few minutes, they emerged into an enormous opening with no islands except the biggest one of them all. "Behold the White Lady. The Alabaster Seraph. The Chantry. The Seraph of Nerev. And for you now, Vi, home."

The Chantry had looked big before, but only now as they approached it did it become apparent how massive it was. The entire building was carved in the likeness of a winged, angelic woman. She was too solid to actually be alabaster, too perfectly white to be marble. The stone shone, even in the dim light of this dreary day. Vi imagined it would be blinding in the sunlight. As they came closer, Vi saw that what looked from a distance like erosion or pitting from age in the statue-building's surface were actually windows and decks for the myriad of rooms inside, each nearly invisible because the surrounding stone was the same dazzling white.

The Seraph's wings were half-unfurled, and she bore a sword in her left hand, point down, and a cool look on her face. As the punt circled around the back of the island, Vi saw that the Seraph's right hand held a set of scales behind her back, with a feather on one side and a heart on the other.

Hundreds of docks crowded the back side of the island, and despite the rain, dozens of boats were loading and unloading all manner of supplies and people. Their white punt skimmed straight to the nearest set of docks, passing beneath an arch of living wisteria, impossibly still in bloom with a riot of purple flowers. The punt came to rest, and two sisters in black robes greeted them.

"Vi, go with them," Sister Ariel said. She paused, then added, "No threat they make is idle. It has been years since anyone died during initiation, but it is a possible. May whatever god you believe go with you. And if you believe in none, good luck."

The worst part wasn't that the last god Vi wanted with her now was Nysos, to whom she had offered her body and soul and the blood of so many innocents. The worst part was that Sister Ariel's good wishes sounded absolutely sincere.

The first step was breaking into the city. Kylar knew there had to be dozens of smugglers' routes, but that wasn't the kind of information smugglers handed out at Sa'kagé parties. He did know what he was looking for, though. It would be hidden within a few hundred paces of the walls, and it would emerge somewhere onto rock so as not to take hoofprints and wagon tracks, and it would be somewhere close to one of the main roads.

On the low hills surrounding the city, a month ago buildings had lined every road: taverns, farmhouses, hostelries, and any of the innumerable trade houses that catered to travelers who hadn't the coin for accommodations or services in the city. Now, there were no buildings.

The Ceurans had taken everything. They had dismantled every building and brought the materials into their camp. Kylar could only imagine the frenzy the Sa'kagé must have been in, trying to decide which tunnels to collapse and which to salvage, hoping to preserve their own way out of the city if all else failed.

He moved through the Ceuran camp slowly, dodging from shadow to shadow. He had eschewed invisibility for a hazy black, hoping it would be harder to see than the odd distortions of sleet hitting something that wasn't there.

His eyes should have given him a distinct advantage in searching for a smugglers' entrance. He finally found a large, low rock sitting feet from the main road with trees on either side of it. It was perfect. If the rock swung open, smugglers could pull their wagon onto the main road unseen and leave no tracks. Kylar brushed the sleet away from the rock and saw tell-tale scrapes from the iron-bound wagon wheels grinding against the rock. This was it.

Ten minutes later, he still hadn't made any progress. Every two minutes, he had to hide as a sentry made his rounds, and every five minutes a different sentry overlapped from the opposite side. Kylar couldn't blame the interruptions, though. He just couldn't find the catch that opened the door. Maybe it was the sleet, making his fingers clumsy with the cold. Or maybe he just wasn't as good as he thought.

Immortal, not invincible. Why'd Durzo have to be right all the time? Come to think of it, where the hell is Durzo?

The thought affected Kylar more profoundly than he expected. He'd lived for months thinking his master was dead. In all those months, Durzo hadn't bothered to come see Kylar. Kylar had thought himself his master's best friend. Even when Aristarchos ban Ebron had told him all of the heroes his master had been, Kylar had still thought that his relationship with Durzo was special. In a way, learning all the great men his master had been made Kylar feel better about himself. But time had moved on, and apparently so too had Durzo. Whatever brief importance Kylar had had in that man's seven-century-long life, it was finished.

Kylar sat down on rock. The sleet soaked through to his underclothes in seconds. It made him feel even worse.

~Don't tell me you're going to cry.~

You mind?

~Wake me when the self-pity's done, would you?~

Damn you, you sound just like Durzo.

~So I stay with the man night and day for seven centuries and he rubs off on me. You only spent ten years with him, and look how much like him you are.~

That caught Kylar off guard. *I'm not like him.*

~No, you're just out here trying to save the world by yourself—again—by coincidence.~

He did this kind of thing a lot?

~Ever hear of the Miletian Regression? The Death of Six Kings? The Vendazian Uprising? The Escape of the Grasq Twins?~

Kylar hesitated. *Um, actually…no.*

The ka'kari sighed. Kylar wondered how it did that.

"I'm an idiot," Kylar said. He stood up. His butt was numb.

~*An epiphany! Long overdue, too. But then, I've come to expect small things.*~

Kylar walked to the wall. The last few hundred paces were empty of Ceuran soldiers—none of them were foolish enough to stray within bow-shot. The only place the Ceurans had moved closer was along the shores of the Plith, where they were moving great quantities of rock to fill in part of the river. All along the shore and the approach to it, they'd built a corridor to protect the workers from arrows. The wytches had protected every approach to the city except the river. Kylar supposed that they'd figured a couple of meisters standing on either bank could keep any ships or swim-mers from making it through the narrow passage. The Cenarians didn't have that luxury. This was where Garuwashi would attack. Once one bank was filled in enough, he could start sending skirmishers in.

If the sa'ceurai came and fought one-on-one with Cenarian soldiers, Kylar had no doubt who would have the larger pile of corpses at the end of the day.

Kylar walked to the wall. The great stones had been hardened with spells, and fitted more tightly to their neighbors than weight and mortar could accomplish. Kylar brought the ka'kari to his hands and feet.

~*I should make you swim.*~

Kylar smirked and felt the stone dimple under his fingers and toes. He began climbing.

Any hopes he had that Terah Graesin wasn't going to do something stu-pid died as he reached the top of the wall. With four hours until dawn, men were already preparing to attack the sa'ceurai. Most of the soldiers were still asleep, and the horses still in their stables, but a huge area had been cleared inside the south gate. Flags had been planted so that the regiments could find their positions first thing in the morning, and squires were scur-rying around, making sure armor and weapons were in top condition. From the size of the area cleared, Kylar guessed that the queen was preparing an all-out attack at dawn, committing perhaps fifteen thousand men for the attack.

He squinted at the flags, doing the math. He wouldn't have said she had so many men.

The answer was in the flags nearest the gate. More than one flag bore a rabbit. The queen had conscripted Rabbits—and put totally untrained peasants at the spearhead of the attack on the most highly trained sa'ceurai in the world? Genius. It was one thing to throw your peasants against the other side's peasants when you had space to try to bring in cavalry from the

873

side or something, but when the Cenarians came pouring out the gate, Garuwashi's sa'ceurai would meet them immediately. The battle would be confined to one front—the peasants would find themselves all alone, getting slaughtered, unable to move forward because of the sa'ceurai, unable to move back because the rest of the army was trying to get out of the south gate.

It would probably only be minutes before they panicked, and then it was only a matter of how many people would be slaughtered before Luc Graesin called off the attack and tried to shut the gates before the sa'ceurai got into the city.

Kylar dropped into the great yard and stole a leather gambeson from a pile, along with trousers and a tunic. A minute later, he stepped out from behind a smithy as a boy hurried past pushing a cart filled with cheap swords and pole arms.

"So the Rabbits get to lead the attack? Hit 'em at dawn?" Kylar said, waving at the battle flags. "How'd that happen?"

The kid lit up. "We volunteered."

"I know a man who volunteered to snort guri pepper sauce. It didn't make it a good idea."

"What are you saying?" the kid asked, offended.

"Why's the queen letting them go first?"

"It's not the queen. It's her brother Luc. He's Lord General now."

"And?"

The kid scowled. "He said the uh, the casualties would be highest among the first ones out. You know, till we took out their archers. The Rabbits ain't scared of nothing."

So the new Lord General manages to cull his bravest citizens and ensure a crushing defeat, all at once. Brilliant.

"You mind? I got work to do," the kid said.

Kylar stole a horse. He didn't have the time to walk to the castle. As he mounted, a groom came toward him. "Hey, who are you? That horse belongs to—"

Kylar brought the mask of judgment to his face in a rush and whipped his head toward the man, snarling, blue flame leaping up in his eyes and mouth.

The groom leapt backward and tripped into a horse trough with a yell.

Kylar rode as fast as he could. He left the horse and the stolen clothes before he got to East Kingsbridge and went invisible. He ran the rest of the way, leaving guards with their heads swiveling, trying to find where the patter of running feet had come from. Rather than run through the twisting, illogical halls of the castle, he climbed the wall. In minutes, he dropped onto the queen's balcony, which was still missing part of the railing where Kylar had freed Mags Drake's corpse. He looked inside.

The queen wasn't alone.

22

"Before I sent you after Sister Jessie, you said you'd been studying something for two years," Istariel Wyant, the Speaker of the Chantry, said. They were sitting in her office, high in the Seraph, sharing ootai and strategy. "What was it?"

"The *ka'karifer*," Ariel said.

"The what? My Hyrillic isn't what it used to be."

A doubtful look crossed Ariel's face. "Your Hyrillic was never what it used to be. If I recall correctly, your marks in all your language classes—"

"The question, Ariel," Istariel snapped, with more vigor than she intended. Only perhaps a dozen Sisters in the Chantry would recall how poorly she had performed in a few of her classes, and none of them would dare correct the Speaker. None except Ariel, who was not correcting her because she thought being Istariel's sister gave her license: Ariel would correct anyone.

"The bearers of the stones of stones," Ariel said. "Colloquially that would have meant stones of greatest power. The original bearers were Jorsin's Champions of Light: Trace Arvagulania—fascinating, I think you would have liked her. She was one of the foremost minds of the age in an age famous for great minds. Probably not matched even to the present day, though I know Rosserti argues that Milovian Period is as important, I personally find his contentions regarding the Alitaeran succession to be weak: I think there were complete breaks with Miletian traditions during the Interregnum. But I'm getting side-tracked. Trace, this brilliant but horribly ugly woman—in some accounts the ugliest woman of the age, though I think those legends are as greatly exaggerated as most of the others—was given a stone that conferred all beauty upon her. The poets couldn't even agree what she looked like. I believe, in keeping with Hrambower's paper

Sententia—damn all Lodricari scholars and their clotted syntax but there you have it—that the confusion was because the ka'kari's power was not that it shifted Trace's appearance, but that it directly affected viewers' perceptions of her, in each case making her what would be most attractive to them. Imagine the fortune Ezra could have made in cosmetics!" She waited for Istariel to laugh. She didn't.

"Fascinating," Istariel said, her tone flat.

"Of course that ka'kari disappeared and has never resurfaced. I imagine it would have, if it were anything but a legend. There is much stronger evidence in support of the red ka'kari's existence. Originally, it was given to Corvaer Blackwell—ironically enough, Lord Blackwell would henceforth be known as Corvaer the Red—and after he died during the Battle of Jaeran Flats, it was taken by a man named Malak Mok'mazi, Malak Firehands in our tongue, though obviously that translation doesn't preserve the alliteration. Accounts from both sides claimed that he fought from *within* the conflagration that swept the plain and broke the Gurvani army. Again, after his death—apparently fire isn't much good against poison—" Ariel barked a laugh, which Istariel didn't share. "Uh hmm, well, it seems to have reappeared in various hands throughout history. Some of those had credible witnesses. Herddios, whom we trust for all sorts of other stories that have checked out, claims to have personally—"

"Did you learn anything *new?*" Istariel said, doing to her best to feign interest. Limited interest.

Ariel licked her lips, her eyes flicking up to the ceiling as she thought. "I concluded that a review of all the currently available literature on the subject still left the most pertinent questions open. And most of the less pertinent ones as well."

"So it took you two years to figure out that you weren't going to figure anything out." It was a graceless way to put it, but then, with Ariel, it paid to be blunt.

Ariel grimaced. "That's why I was willing to go see about Jessie al'Gwaydin."

And not because your Speaker asked you to. For a moment, Istariel was jealous of her oblivious older sister. Ariel was a rock and the waves of politics passed her with sound and fury and she didn't even notice. She was a bore, but a useful one. Whenever Istariel had needed an expert opinion on the magical sides of dilemmas, Ariel could be loosed on the problem like a hound to scent. And she wouldn't share her findings with anyone except the books she wrote and Istariel. All in all, Ariel was worth far more than the trouble she caused. But did she have to be so boring?

If Ariel had turned her brilliant mind to politics.... Well, Istariel had thought of that before, in her more paranoid moments. If Ariel had the inclination for such things, Ariel would be the Speaker and Istariel would probably be some farmer's brood mare. The key to handling Ariel was understanding that she was a believer; not a believer in some god, but a believer in the Chantry. There was something endearingly naive in women who believed all that "Seraph's handmaiden" tripe. It made them far easier to handle than the magae who believed only in themselves. Point in a direction, say "good of the Chantry," and Ariel would do anything.

"Ariel, I've got a problem I need your help with. I know you've never accepted a tyro—"

"I'll do it."

"—but I want you to think about the good of the—What?"

"You want me to teach Viridiana Sovari so she's protected until she can destroy Eris Buel and the Chattel. I'll do it."

Istariel's heart jumped into her throat. So nakedly laid out, it was a plot whose discovery would bring down a Speaker. "Never say that!" she hissed. "Not ever. Not even here."

Ariel cocked an eyebrow at her.

Istariel smoothed her dress. "She's being initiated this evening?"

"As we speak. Apparently there are some difficulties. It's been hours."

Istariel frowned. "How Talented is this girl? Is she Eris Buel's equal?"

"No," Ariel said. "Not even close."

Istariel cursed.

"You misunderstand. She surpasses Eris Buel in every way. Vi Sovari is more Talented than I am."

Istariel's eyes widened. Like most Sisters, she was loath to admit when others were stronger. She would have thought Ariel, being so accustomed to being stronger than everyone, would chafe at the idea at least a little.

"Ulyssandra will be more Talented still, given five years," Ariel said.

"That's great news. But I don't have five years. I don't have one. I need you to turn this Vi Sovari into something special by spring. The Chattel are arriving then as a show of strength to make their demands heard." *And maybe to bring down a speaker.*

"You will make concessions," Ariel said, not quite a question.

"They wish us to start a men's school. Did I say wish? They demand. They demand recognition of their new 'order' and the attendant seats on the council, which would make them by far the most powerful order in the Chantry. By themselves they would have a majority in any vote that came to the floor. They demand a repeal of the marriage bans so they may marry magi. They demand a repeal of the Alitaeran Accords. The nations of Mid-cyru will have reason to fear that we wish to return to the Alkootian mago-cracy. These Chattel will unite the nations against us. We're a bastion of light in a dark world, Ariel. Concessions I can countenance. Destruction I cannot."

"What is it you want me to teach Vi?" Ariel asked. That was it; Istariel had her.

Istariel paused, stuck between discretion and wanting to make sure her dense sister did what needed to be done. "Like we do with every Sister, help Vi figure out what her strengths are, and train them."

Ariel's eyes widened and narrowed in a heartbeat. The girl was nearly a battle maja, and they both knew it. In fact, Ariel's response was so swift, Istariel thought she might have suspected the order. Or maybe Ariel was just that smart.

Well, there it was, as much discretion and direction as Istariel could afford to give and still hope to retain her seat if any word of this came out. Istariel would have to keep her distance from Ariel and Vi, of course. Even Ariel would understand that... if she noticed. Now, to smooth things, to maintain the illusion.

"You are to be commended for bringing such great Talents into our fold, Sister Ariel. I don't believe two recruits with such potential have been brought to the Chantry for perhaps fifty years." She smiled. It was fifty years since she and Ariel had arrived.

"Longer, surely."

"You deserve to be rewarded," Istariel said, her smile freezing. "Is there anything I can get for your studies?" Ariel, of course, would say service was enough.

"Absolutely," Ariel said.

By the time she left, Ariel had muscled Istariel into consenting to every item. Ariel hadn't even had the grace to offer something she didn't really want so Istariel could say no and claim some small victory for her pride.

Istariel sat back and looked at her hair in her mirror, wanting it to be perfect for her meeting with the Alitaeran emissary. At least her blonde hair was still beautiful. She had the other Sisters swearing it was magic that she could have a mane so glossy and thick and perfect. It wasn't, but it always pleased her to hear the allegation.

Her mind cast back to Ariel's statement that she should be fascinated by ugly Trace Arvag-whatever-her-name-was. Istariel frowned, the face in the mirror showing any number of unattractive lines on a dignified but quite plain face. If Ariel had a sense of humor, Istariel would suspect she were the butt of a very subtle joke.

She snorted. Ariel, a sense of humor. Now there was a joke.

23

$\mathcal{K}$ylar peered through the glass inset in the balcony door. In the darkness of the queen's bedchamber, a couple was writhing on the queen's bed. From their frenetic pace, they were either very close to completion or very energetic. From habit, Kylar looked at the hinges of the balcony door, then realized they could squeal like a herd of pigs and never be noticed. He looked back through the window, suddenly shy. Still going.

A gentleman would wait. A wetboy would use the distraction. Kylar slipped inside.

The young man grunted and froze. Hands smacked loudly as the woman grabbed his buttocks and urged him to keep going. He thrust twice more, then wilted.

"Fuck!" Terah Graesin said, pushing him off her. "I thought I was going to make it this time."

"Sorry, Sis," Luc Graesin said.

Kylar felt suddenly lightheaded. The ka'kari whistled softly. *~I haven't seen royal incest for a couple centuries, and that was in Ymmur, where it's expected.~*

Luc snuggled into Terah's side and laid his head on her chest. Considering that he was substantially taller and bigger than his sister, it was oddly submissive. Kylar was struck by the difference in their ages. Luc was perhaps seventeen and looked younger; Terah was twenty-five and looked older. How long had this been going on?

Durzo had taught Kylar that when something surprised you on a job, only one question mattered: does this change what I have to do? The answer now was no, unless Luc stayed all night. Kylar put aside all the speculations about what this meant and refocused. There was nothing to do but wait, so Kylar moved behind a pillar in a quiet corner of the room.

Luc propped himself up on an elbow. "Sis, I wanted to talk to you about tomorrow morning. This morning, whatever."

"You're going to lead your first battle," Terah said, pushing a lock of hair back behind his ear. "You're going to be safe. I've given the Guard commands to keep you back from—"

"That's just it, Ter." Luc got out of bed and began dressing. "I didn't fight at Pavvil's Grove. I didn't go on any raids. I didn't fight highlanders at Screaming Winds—"

"Do not bring up Logan Gyre."

"I'm the Lord Commander of the Royal Armies of Cenaria, and my experience of battle is limited to the fistfight I had with the pig keeper's boy. I was ten. He was eight. I lost and you had him thrashed."

"Generals fight with their brains. Your scouts were instrumental to our victory at Pavvil's Grove," Terah said.

"How do you do that?" Luc asked, pausing in the act of lacing his tunic. "You fit two lies in one sentence. It wasn't our victory. It was Logan's. Why we rule now rather than having our heads on pikes, I don't know. And I completely botched handling the scouts. Men wondered if I was trying to screw up. I was so bad they thought I was a traitor."

"Who said that?" Terah asked, her eyes alight.

"It doesn't matter."

"What do you want, Luc? I've given you everything."

Luc threw his hands up. "That's what I'm trying to say! You've given me everything that a man might earn after a lifetime of—"

"What do you want?" she interrupted.

"I think we should stop."

"Stop?"

"You and me, Ter. Us. This." He wouldn't meet her gaze.

"Do you still love me?"

"Sis..."

"It's a simple question."

"Insanely," Luc said. "But if people find out, they'll install Logan in a second."

"Logan won't threaten us forever."

"Sis, he's a good man. A hero. You're not going to kill him."

She smiled dangerously. "Don't tell me how to rule, Luc."

"Terah," he said.

"You listen to me. You'll bitch and moan and fret, like always. And I'll take care of it, like always. I take the risks, you take the rewards. So why don't you and your conscience go fuck all the maids, while *I* get called a slut."

"You expect me to believe you didn't sleep with all those lords?" Luc asked.

She slapped him. "You bastard. They never laid a hand on me."

"So much can be accomplished without hands."

She slapped him again.

"Don't, don't do that again," Luc said.

She slapped him again. He did nothing.

"I let them call me a slut," Terah said. "I let you fuck other women. I wake up two hours before dawn on the nights you visit so a maid can change my sheets so that when my laundress—who's a Sa'kagé spy—washes them there's no evidence of us. Why? Because I love you. So I think I deserve a little gratitude."

Luc held her stare for a few moments, then deflated. "I'm sorry, Ter. I'm just scared."

"Go get some sleep. And come to me after your victory." Her smile held a promise.

Luc's eyes lit with boyish mischief. "How about I come to you now?"

"No," she said. "Good night, Luc."

"Please?"

"Good night, Luc."

After Luc left and the queen had been asleep for half an hour, Kylar drew his bollock dagger. It was pitted and blunted from the corrosive powers of the Devourer.

~Sorry.~

He reached out to prod Terah. Stopped. There were things more menacing than a pitted dagger.

Kylar studied Terah Graesin as he'd learned to study his deaders. She was a woman whose bearing and reputation were a greater part of her appeal than nature's gifts. In this unguarded, unrouged moment, she looked more like a skinny farm girl than a queen: her lips thin, cracked, colorless. Her eyebrows tiny lines. Her eyelashes short. Her nose slightly hooked. Her milky skin marred by several pimples. Her face obscured by strands of loose hair.

In that moment, he couldn't help but respect Terah Graesin. She'd been born into one of the great families of Cenaria, but her spirit was indomitable. She had risen past men who despised her for her youth, her sex, her reputation. Terah Graesin hadn't become queen by accident. But here, Terah Graesin was just a woman alone, about to be woken by a nightmare.

Sometimes, Kylar couldn't help but pity the bastards. Durzo had taught Kylar that the best wetboy understood his deader better than the deader understood himself. Kylar believed it, but every time he did something calculated to inspire terror, he wondered if he was trading away his humanity. It was one thing to terrify goons. Was it different to terrify a young woman in the intimacy of her bedchamber?

But Terah Graesin wasn't merely a woman. She was a queen. Her idiocy would kill thousands—and she planned to kill Logan, the rightful king. *Act now. Doubt later.*

Kylar went to the other side of Terah's bed and pulled back the covers to give himself space to sit. With the patience of a wetboy, he eased his weight onto the mattress by degrees. Finally, he sat, legs folded, hands draped on his knees, back straight, the face of judgment angry.

The young queen was sleeping on her side, with her hands tucked under her pillow, so it was easy to grab the thick down blanket and pull it down. Caught between the necessity for patience—any rapid change would wake her—and the coldness of the room which would have Terah reaching for blankets even in sleep, Kylar pulled back the sheet to uncover her nakedness.

Kylar didn't look. If anything, he was disgusted. He wanted her off-balance, vulnerable. She stirred. He schooled himself to stillness, sitting upright once more, and began to glow a cool blue, gradually brightening.

This was the shaky part: a deader's startle response was involuntary. Scaring a screamer and telling them not to scream was futile. He could wake her with a hand across her mouth, but that wouldn't give the flavor of terror he was looking for.

Terah Graesin woke slowly, as he hoped. Squinted, then opened her eyes slowly. Blinked, once, twice as if against the dawn light that usually came in her windows. Focused closer, closer. Then, all in a rush, the Night Angel came into focus, eyes burning with blue flame, puffs of fire escaping his lips with every breath, body alternately invisible, wispy as black smoke, and gleaming hard iridescent black metal muscle. Her breath caught, and a squeak came out. Not loud, thank the God.

Her legs spasmed and kicked and she grabbed for the covers. Flailing, she scooted toward the edge of the bed. Kylar sat motionless as a god and reached out only with his Talent. He was still clumsy with this, but he made a lucky grab and caught Terah's throat with his first try. The hand of Talent pinned her to the bed.

Drawing up a rigid hand in a striking position called a knife hand, Kylar made it literal by forming the ka'kari into a leaf-shaped blade over his hand. He whispered, "A scream would be a mistake, Terah. Understood?"

He used her name to make it more familiar, more creepy when she remembered it.

Eyes wide, she nodded.

"Cover yourself, whore. You reek of your brother's seed," he said. He released her throat and drew the ka'kari back from his hand. With jerky motions, she pulled up the sheets and held them in white-knuckled fists, drawing her knees up, trembling.

The Night Angel said. "While you rule my city, I demand you rule well."

"Who are you?" she asked, voice tight, still off balance.

"You will call off this attack. Garuwashi has no food. He can not hold this siege."

"You're here to help me save Cenaria?" she asked, incredulous.

"I will save Cenaria, with you or from you. Give me two days. Garuwashi doesn't know how bad it is in the city. He will negotiate."

Terah Graesin was already recovering. "He's refused me. He swore never to negotiate with a woman." That was news to Kylar. Why wouldn't Garuwashi negotiate?

"Not with you then," Kylar said. "With Gyre."

Her eyes lit with fury. "Gyre? You're Logan's creature? You were the one who saved us in the garden during the coup! All you cared about was him. You saved him, didn't you? You saved him and now you want him to get the glory. After all I've done to get here, you expect me to let Logan win? I'd rather die!" She stood haughtily and grabbed her robe from a chair. "Now I suggest—"

Kylar was on her. Before she could even think to scream, he slammed her onto the bed, straddled her, punched her solar plexus to knock the wind from her and clamped a hand over her face. He grabbed a hairpin from her bedside table and drove it through the meat of her arm. He let her gasp in a breath and then filled her mouth with the ka'kari to keep her from screaming.

Unable to expel her scream from her mouth, air gushed from her nose and blew snot all over his hand. He ground the hairpin back and forth, then grabbed another.

She bucked and kicked and tried to scream through her nose, so he blocked her nose with the ka'kari too.

Her eyes bulged and the veins on her neck stood out as she struggled in vain to breathe. She tried to flail, but Kylar had her arms pinned with his knees. He brought the hairpin into her view and touched the point to her forehead.

Though her throat was still working convulsively, Terah Graesin stilled. Kylar traced the point of the hairpin down her forehead, between her eyes, then across the delicate skin of one eyelid.

For a moment, he couldn't help but wonder what Elene would think if she saw him here, doing this. The queen's terror sickened him, and yet he held the cruel smile on his face. He lifted the hairpin away from her eye so she could see Judgment. "You'd rather die?" the Night Angel asked. "Really?"

The sight of the Alabaster Seraph growing larger as the punt approached did nothing to calm Elene. If Elene had read Vi's letter correctly—it seemed like so long ago now—Vi had ringed Kylar without his permission, with the very wedding earrings Kylar had intended for Elene and himself. Elene had never been so furious for so long.

She knew it was destructive. She knew it would eat her alive. Only weeks ago, she'd killed a man, and she hadn't felt the wash of hatred she felt now.

Elene knew she was being disobedient, holding onto her resentment, her righteous wrath. But it made her feel powerful to hate the woman who'd done her wrong. Vi deserved hatred.

The punt docked in a small slip magically shielded from the rain and the boatman pointed her to a line. Elene joined two dozen other people, mostly women, who had come to petition the Chantry. An hour later, when she gave her name and asked to see Vi, the Sister found a note about her and sent a tyro running.

Several minutes later, an older maja with the loose skin and ill-fitting clothes of a woman who's lost too much weight too fast came out. "Hello, Elene. My name is Sister Ariel. Come with me."

"Where are you taking me?"

"To see Uly and Vi. That's what you want, isn't it?" Sister Ariel turned and walked away without waiting for a response.

Many steps later, they stopped at a hospital floor with hundreds of beds, lining the circumference of the Seraph. Most of the beds were empty, but Sisters with green sashes moved among those that were occupied, sometimes touching the walls, which immediately turned transparent, letting in the diffuse morning sun.

"Is Uly ill?" Elene asked.

Sister Ariel said nothing. She led Elene past dozens of beds. Some of the girls on them had arms or legs wrapped in gauze, and here and there, ancient-looking magae slept, but most of the injured had no obvious wounds. Magical wounds, Elene supposed, didn't always leave evidence on the body.

Finally, they stopped at a bed, but the woman on it wasn't Uly, it was Vi. It took Elene's breath away. She had thought from the glimpse of the redhead on the trail that she'd never seen Vi before, but she had. Vi had been at the fateful last party at the Jadwin estate. That night, Vi had come as a blonde, wearing a dress that was a scandal in red. Elene remembered the swirl of emotions she'd felt that night clearly: shock that someone would wear such revealing attire, judgment, fascination. Elene—and every other man and woman—hadn't been able to take her eyes off the woman. Immediately after those first emotions, without ever losing her outrage, she'd felt jealousy, longing, the sick-stomach sensation of not measuring up to such beauty, wishing that she could attract such stares, and knowing she never would—and would never wear such clothes even if she could—but wishing all the same that she might, just for a few moments. Vi was that woman, and if anything, with her glossy flaming red hair rather than what must have been a blonde wig, Vi was even more striking.

Then, as Elene stepped closer to the bed, she saw Vi's other ear. She wore a single earring, mistarille and gold, sparkling in the morning light coming through the walls. It was half of the exact pair of beautiful wedding earrings Elene had pointed out to Kylar. The wash of emotions Elene had already been feeling suddenly had a boulder dropped in it. This was her competition? This...creature had ringed Kylar? No wonder he'd chosen her. What man wouldn't?

Unnoticed, Sister Ariel had come to stand beside Elene, and now she spoke, her voice barely a whisper. "When she's asleep, I see what a beautiful woman Viridiana would have been."

Elene shot a look at the Sister. *Like she could be* more *beautiful?*

"She is brittle and sick and hard and abused. Her character is as base as her body is beautiful. You'll see, when she wakes. She is a walking tragedy. The trade she was taught would wreck anyone with a soul. You know that from Kylar's experience. But Vi didn't just learn a sick trade, she learned under Hu Gibbet—all too often literally under him, from the time she was a child. Whenever I—old and fat as I am—see her asleep, I still get jealous I still forget that Vi's beauty has been no friend to her." Sister Ariel paused, as if captured by a thought. "In fact, the only friend she ever had—male or female—was Jarl, and the Godking compelled her to kill him."

Elene didn't want to hear it. "What's wrong with her? I mean, why is she here?"

Sister Ariel sighed. "Our initiation doesn't only require aptitude, it requires focus. Vi has aptitude to an almost appalling degree. She is as Talented as she is beautiful. I was and am worried that learning that may spoil her. Learning our art properly takes patience and humility, and women with enormous Talent tend to lack both. So I pushed her into the initiation immediately. With what she's done and been through in the last weeks, she had no focus at all, almost no will even to live. It was nearly a death sentence." She shrugged. "Elene, I know Vi has done you great wrong. These marriage rings are ancient. I'm studying the rings now to see if it's even possible to break the bond. I don't have high hopes. And I know—she confessed—that she ringed Kylar when he was unconscious. The other Sisters don't know that. It is considered one of the greatest crimes among us. Even if she did do it to save a country, and to save Kylar himself, Vi surely deserves whatever vengeance you would give her. If you choose, you should be able to wake her. If you wish to stay here at the Chantry, rooms will be provided for you. If you wish to speak with Uly, she should be finishing her morning classes in two hours. I will be in my room if you need me. Ask any tyro—any of the young women dressed in white—and they will take you wherever you wish to go."

With that, Sister Ariel left Elene alone with Vi.

Elene looked around as the Sister disappeared. There was suddenly no one else in sight. She touched the knife at her belt. She could kill Vi and simply leave. She'd killed now. She knew how.

She squeezed her eyes tight shut. *God, I can't do this.*

After a long moment, she breathed, unclenched her jaw, willed herself to relax, opened her eyes.

Vi lay as before, beautiful, peaceful, graceful. But instead of imagining her again at the Jadwin estate, attracting lust and jealousy like a lodestone, Elene imagined her as a child. Vi had been a beautiful child in the Warrens as Elene had been a beautiful child in the Warrens. Neither had emerged unscathed. Elene looked at Vi and chose to fix that child-Vi in her mind's eye, the beautiful, carefree little girl with flame-red hair before the Warrens had sullied her.

She's never had a friend. Elene didn't know if it was her own thought or the One God's voice, but she knew instantly what He was calling her to do.

Elene breathed deeply, frozen to the spot. *It's too hard, God. There's no way. Not after what she's done. I want to hate her. I want to be strong. I want to make her pay.* She spoke, and raged, and complained about the justice of making Vi suffer, and through it all, the God said nothing. Yet through it, she felt His presence. And when she was finished, He was still there, and Elene knew her choice was simple: obey or disobey.

She breathed deeply one more time, then sat in the chair beside Vi's bed and waited for her to wake.

From the stairs, staring through a crack in the door, Sister Ariel breathed for the first time in what seemed like many minutes. She released her Talent and eased the door shut. Another gamble, another win. She hoped her luck didn't run out any time soon.

25

After a two-hour wait with the nervous master of the docks, the Mikaidon came to collect Solon. The Mikaidon was the keeper of civil order in Hokkai, an office that not only put him in charge of law enforcement but also gave him considerable political clout, as he was the only person who could investigate and search noble persons and properties. Solon recognized him. "Oshobi," he said. "You've risen in the world."

Oshobi Takeda grunted. "So it is you." He wore the regalia of his office like a man who used it as armor, not ornamentation. Oshobi was perhaps thirty, muscular, and imposing. He wore his plumed helm open, of course, showing the electrum rings of Clan Takeda framing his right eye, with six steel chains connecting behind his head to his left ear. The fishes on his helm were gilded, as was his galerus, the leather and plate armor covering his left arm. His trident was as tall as he was. The type of net that dangled over his back, draping cloak-like from spikes on his shoulders, was usually edged with lead weights to help it spread out when thrown. Oshobi's net was weighted with small daggers. It could be used not only as a net, but as a shield or even a flail by a skilled warrior. Given the numerous scars and rippling muscles on Oshobi's bare chest, Solon guessed that a skilled warrior was exactly what Oshobi Takeda had become. He had grown into his name. Oshobi meant the great cat, or tiger, but Solon remembered the older boys calling him Oshibi: little pussy. Solon couldn't imagine anyone calling him that anymore.

"I request the honor of an audience with Empress Wariyamo," Solon said. It was a calculated statement, not asserting his own status, and recognizing hers.

"You're under arrest," Oshobi told him. In a blink, he lifted the net from the spikes on his shoulders. He looked like he wanted an excuse to use it.

The man was a cretin. Solon was a mage and Oshobi should remember it. Of course, Solon didn't look like one. After his decade serving Duke Regnus Gyre, he looked as hard and scarred as a warrior himself, albeit one with unnaturally white hair growing in. "On what charge? I do have certain rights, Mikaidon. If not as a prince," he brushed his unpierced cheek, "then certainly as a nobleman." His heart fell. So Kaede was furious. Should he be surprised?

"Your brother gave up all the Tofusins' rights. You can walk, or I can drag you."

What did my brother do? Solon had been at various schools learning magic for his brother's entire reign and Dorian's prophecies had sent Solon to Cenaria at the time of Sijuron Tofusin's death. They hadn't been close; Sij was a decade older than he was, but Solon's memories of him were pleasant. Apparently, Oshobi's weren't.

Solon said, "That's a tough one, Oshibi."

Oshobi flicked the butt of his trident at Solon's head. Solon caught the haft squarely in his hand and looked at the Mikaidon contemptuously.

"I'll walk," Solon said. His heart was turning to lead. During Sijuron's reign, Solon had been crisscrossing Midcyru with Dorian and Feir, searching for Curoch, so he hadn't been surprised that he hadn't heard much from home. And then, when he'd concealed his own identity and headed to Cenaria to serve one of Dorian's prophecies, he hadn't told anyone back home where he was going. But now, the silence seemed ominous. And in the years since, he hadn't been able to dispel his ignorance. From the necessity of keeping his identity secret, Solon had avoided all Sethi he saw, and those who saw him spotted the lack of clan rings and avoided him as an exile. But even the usual news one might hear from foreigners had mostly been lacking, as though the Sethi people hadn't wanted to share anything with outsiders.

But as they made their way to the castle, Solon soaked in the scents and sights of his old home and some of his tension eased. This land was balm to him. He'd forgotten how much he'd missed the red hills of Agrigolay. As the Mikaidon's stout, four-wheeled chariot rolled up the cobblestone road to the imperial palace, Solon's eyes were drawn to the west. As in most cities, the approach to the palace was jammed with buildings, homes, and shops as densely as possible. But in Seth, only the eastern side of the Imperial Way had buildings. The west side was centuries-old vineyards, rolling over the hills in perfect rows as far as the eye could see. The grapes hung heavy on the vine, and there were men checking their ripeness. The harvest would be any day.

Most kingdoms required their lords to offer a certain number of men for war every summer. In Seth, the levies were needed in fall, for the grapes. Already, Solon saw, enormous broad baskets had been stacked at the ends of the rows. There was no need for walls to protect the vineyards. The wines of Seth were its pride and its life's blood. No Sethi citizen would harm the vines, nor suffer a stranger to do so, and the theft of cuttings from these vines had precipitated war between Seth and Ladesh. The loss of half a dozen ships had been counted a small price when they successfully sank the Ladeshian merchantman that was carrying the cuttings back to Ladesh to begin rival vineyards, along with its escort. Ladesh had its silk monopoly, but anyone who wanted great wine bought it from Seth.

To Solon, like most Sethi, the vineyards were rich not only with beauty but also with meaning. The cycle of planting and grafting and pruning and nurturing and waiting—all resonated with meaning for every citizen.

They came over the last rise and Solon saw Whitecliff Castle for the first time in twelve years. It was white marble, a testament to the vast wealth the empire had enjoyed at its height: no white marble was quarried on the islands, and shipping it across an ocean was so expensive that every time Solon saw the castle he was awed and almost ashamed of his ancestors' wastefulness. Outbuildings, smithies, barracks, servants' housing, barns, kennels, granaries, and storehouses ringed the hill cheek by jowl within the granite walls, but the crown of the hill was all castle. Steps broad enough for horses led up the first tier into the outer hall. The outer hall had a roof but no walls, leaving it oddly open to the elements. Enormous grooved marble pillars held a majestic roof of marble, onyx, and stained glass.

At the base of the steps, Oshobi drew his team to a halt. "Are you going to make this easy or hard?" he asked.

"I'm here to solve problems, not cause them," Solon said.

"Too late for that," Oshobi said. "There's a room for you on the first floor."

Solon nodded. A visiting noble would be put on the second floor, and he should have rated the third floor, but it was better than the dungeon, and it would give Kaede time to decide what to do about him.

They climbed the steps together, drawing only a few looks. Oshobi was obviously a familiar sight, and Solon's clothing was Cenarian, not Sethi, so from a distance, he supposed the lack of rings wasn't remarkable. Besides, it was almost harvest time, and everyone had too many things to do.

Sky watchers had aided the construction of the outer hall, so the stained glass panels provided art appropriate to the season. Currently, the sun lit the whole outer hall purple with scenes of harvest and grape crushing, women dancing in vats with their skirts held up higher above their ankles than absolutely necessary and men clapping and cheering them on. Elsewhere there were scenes of war, of sailing, of fishing, of grand balls, of festivals to Nysos. Some of the panels were brighter than others, reminding Solon of when he was a boy and a rare hailstorm had broken dozens of the panels. He remembered his father cursing their ancestors. Who would use glass for a ceiling? Of course there was no choice but to replace the broken panes, though the price was ruinous. One couldn't let one's entryway fall into a shambles.

Oshobi and Solon walked through the great black oak doors into the inner entry. Here, white staircases framed each side of the room, a great imperial purple carpet led further into the palace, and gold and marble statuary lined the hall. As they headed past the stairs to a side door, however, one of the smallest, oldest men Solon had ever seen came to Oshobi. The man stopped before he said anything, however, and gaped at Solon. He was the old Wariyamo chamberlain, a slave who had chosen to stay with the family permanently rather than take his freedom on the seventh year, and he obviously recognized Solon. After a moment, he recovered and whispered to Oshobi, who promptly reversed direction and gestured for Solon to follow him into the great hall.

They walked through the great hall, past decorative geometric patterns and starbursts—all designed with swords and spears. It was another wasteful display meant to send a message to visiting emissaries: we have so many armaments, we decorate with them. It was, Solon thought, a more reasonable waste than the stained glass. The great hall was empty except for the guards at the far door, and both of them were too young to recognize Solon. They opened the doors to the inner court promptly, so Oshobi wouldn't even have to slow. Oshobi led Solon past the great throne from which Solon's father and brother had ruled, and headed into the inner court.

The doors opened at the base of stairs, braced by lions. They ascended twenty-one steps, and Solon felt his throat tightening. Then he saw her.

Kaede Wariyamo had black hair and perfect olive skin. Her eyes were deep brown, nose stately, mouth wide and full, neck slender. In keeping with the impending harvest, her hair was bound in a single tail and her nagika was simple cotton. A nagika was a dress that looped over one shoulder, the cloth gathered to the opposite hip and falling long to the floor, fully covering the ankles, leaving one breast bare. It wasn't, as Solon had explained to Midcyri on numerous occasions, that Sethi men didn't find breasts pleasing or innately feminine. They simply weren't erotic in the same way. In Seth, a man would comment on a woman's breasts as a Midcyran commented on a woman's eyes. But after ten years in Midcyru, Solon's pulse quickened to see the woman he loved and who'd once loved him so exposed. Kaede was twenty-eight years old now, and most of the innocent girl he had known had receded from her face. The intelligence had come more to the fore, and a steel that had once been buried deep now lay close to the surface. The holes of the clan piercings on her right cheek had long closed, but the dimples remained, showing the world she had not been born an empress.

Solon thought she was more beautiful than ever. He remembered the day he had left to train with the magi. He had kissed that slender neck, caressed those breasts. He could still remember the smell of her hair. It had been in this very room, where they'd thought no one would find them. He had wondered often when she would have made him stop, or if. But they'd never found out. Her mother, Daune Wariyamo, had found them and berated them both, calling him such foul names that had he been a little older he would have thrown her from the palace. Nor had she spared her daughter the vitriol. Solon had failed Kaede there. He had allowed his own shame to keep him from protecting Kaede, who was even younger and more vulnerable. It was only the first of his regrets with her.

"Oh, Kaede," he said, "your beauty would shame the very stars. Why did you never write?"

The sudden softness in her eyes steeled. She slapped him, hard.

"Guards! Take this bastard to the dungeon."

26

$\mathcal{M}$en were gathering in the great yard before the city's south gate when Kylar arrived. The queen's messengers canceling the attack wouldn't arrive for a few more minutes. Kylar was almost certain that they would. However, Durzo had taught him that when you deal with human beings, never count on logic or consistency. Either way, Kylar's work wasn't finished.

The sa'ceurai were still sleeping. Kylar didn't make the mistake of thinking that this meant the morning's attack would take them off guard. They simply could sleep in and still slaughter Cenarians without missing breakfast.

The sleet had stopped, so Kylar was able to make good time to Lantano Garuwashi's tent. The war leader was asleep on a simple mat on one side of the room.

Kylar stopped at a table full of maps. He'd never seen such detailed maps. There were maps of the city with three different colors of blocks put on different objectives. Kylar wasn't even sure what the colors signified. There were maps of the city's surroundings, with elevation marked, the conditions of roads labeled, and a remarkably accurate chart of the Smugglers' Archipelago. Blocks with regimental flags stuck in them represented the various forces arrayed within and without the city, even the new Rabbit regiments, which meant they already had spies in the city who were managing to pass messages out. There were broader national maps, with both knowns and unknowns marked. They didn't know who held Screaming Winds in the north. They weren't sure of the Lae'knaught's strength in the southeast. But on the last map were blocks representing Cenaria's death.

Blocks on that national map represented Logan's force, guessed to be slightly larger than it was, and behind them, Ceuran reinforcements.

I'm not a general, I'm only a killer. And a fool. Kylar had glanced at what was in front of his eyes and thought he had a more accurate view of the situation than the city's generals. Lantano Garuwashi had rushed to the city without horses or baggage, but that didn't mean he hadn't told them to follow.

He had. They were just a few days out, behind Logan's army, and Logan had never seen them. In the meantime, Garuwashi had already dispatched a contingent of sa'ceurai to skirt Logan's force and go back to guard the supply train.

Among the papers were plans to hire pirates to cut off smugglers' routes into the city and others to encourage insurrection in the Warrens. They were already in negotiations with the Sa'kagé, which the generals knew had smuggling routes into the city. Currently, the Sa'kagé wasn't offering good terms, but the generals were confident that the Sa'kagé's offers would get sweeter as soon as the supply train arrived and the hungry Cenarians watched them feast.

Kylar felt sicker the more he read. Of course the Sa'kagé would treat with the Ceurans. It was one thing to refuse to collaborate with Khalidorans who wanted to wipe out all of Cenaria, quite another to betray a disliked queen to a reasonable man who wouldn't interfere with the Sa'kagé's business. As soon as that supply train arrived, Momma K would see the end. She would try to minimize the bloodshed, but which was better: For thousands to starve in the Warrens, or for a hundred noble heads to roll? The smuggling tunnels would soon fill with sa'ceurai.

"Night Angel," Lantano Garuwashi said in greeting, rising from his mat.

Checking, Kylar was sure he was still invisible. He looked at the papers in his hand, apparently hanging in midair. He dropped the invisibility. "Good morning, warleader."

Lantano Garuwashi was one of the rare men who looked more daunting half-naked than he did in full armor. There was no fat on his body, and where most quick swordsmen were built with lean muscles like Kylar, Garuwashi had the upper body of a blacksmith, each muscle sharply defined— and big. He had a smattering of scars on arms and chest and stomach, but not one of them was deep enough to have cut muscle and thereby impede his motion. They were the wounds of a man whose mistakes had been infrequent and small.

He shook his head as if to shake off sleep, but Kylar thought it was more calculated to rattle the bound ends of those sixty-odd locks in his own hair like a bowl full of marbles. Lantano Garuwashi grinned joylessly at Kylar. "I've been expecting you," he said.

Kylar couldn't believe it, but how else would he sleep so lightly that he woke at the sound of papers being turned fifty feet away? "If you expected me, there'd be fifty sa'ceurai ringing this tent."

"I knew you were coming as soon as my sentry reported that someone tied his leggings together."

Kylar's jaw dropped. "He reported himself?"

Garuwashi smiled, self-satisfied. Kylar wanted to think of him as smug, but it was an infectious kind of smile. "I punished him lightly and rewarded him well—as he expected."

"Son of a—" Every time Kylar took something for granted, he got hit in the face with it.

~Is there a lesson here?~

Kylar ignored the ka'kari. "So, if you expected me.... All this is gutter-shite." He dropped the papers on the table. "There's no supply train."

Garuwashi's grin faded. "It's coming," he said. "If you don't believe me, wait two days. You tell me, do you think all those reports could have been written between the time you were playing with my sentry and now? That would be a massive effort, wouldn't it? And it would be stupid of me to throw it away by telling you I expected you."

Kylar blinked. "So what's the game?"

Garuwashi began pulling on his clothes. "Oh, are we being honest with each other?"

"Might be quicker than lying."

Garuwashi hesitated. "Fair enough. I'm preparing to be a king, Night Angel."

"A High King?" Kylar asked.

Garuwashi looked puzzled. "You say this like it means something to you."

Kylar cursed his ineptitude. "A rumor I heard."

"Why would I wish to be a high king? Cenaria and Ceura are neither large nor distant from each other. Naming under-kings would simply give me rivals." He waved it away and tied the thin silk robe around his waist. "In a year, I will be king of Ceura. I have a reputation now and most of it serves my purposes. But in our capital Aenu, the effete nobles call me a barbarian. 'Skilled at war, yes, but can a butcher be king?' This is how they attack a man who is too excellent. So I have a small interest in capturing this city without killing. We both know that I can take Cenaria. I let you read long enough to see that, yes?"

"So what do you want?" Kylar asked.

"Surrender. Unconditionally. I will give you my word to be merciful. We will leave in the spring to claim my throne, and once I take it, I will grant this realm once more to your queen."

Kylar couldn't stop a twitch of annoyance.

Garuwashi caught it. "You prefer Duke Gyre be made king? Done. I will even restore half of the royal treasury. Beyond this, my men will spend the winter wiping out the Sa'kagé. Tell me, is not that alone worth the price of feeding and housing us? Is it not worth more than half the treasury?"

~Especially considering that the treasury's empty?~

Then Kylar realized Lantano Garuwashi knew that the Khalidorans had taken everything. Garuwashi was merely offering the queen a victory for her pride: You want half the treasury? Here's half of nothing! And letting his Ceurans talk of Garuwashi remitting half of the Cenarian treasury would help his reputation for magnanimity, no matter how little half was.

"You would have Cenaria trust you? You're saying this to a people who recently suffered under the most brutal tyrant imaginable?"

"It is a difficulty." Garuwashi shrugged. "We can do this however you please. But if my men must pay for this city with their blood, they will take blood in return. Take those papers to the queen. Take a few days to see if I'm bluffing. And by the way, this attack this morning, it's not a good idea. Send these rabbits after sword lords, and this siege will end today."

Kylar waved it off. "It's canceled already. Stupid idea."

"So, you do have the power to change things. I'd wondered."

It was a throwaway comment, but it struck Kylar. *How did I get here?* He was blithely negotiating for tens of thousands of lives and the fate of a country.

How would Logan take it? Kylar could obey the letter of his oath and everyone except Terah would win. He wouldn't kill Terah: Lantano Garuwashi would do it for him.

Garuwashi was an honorable man, but that wasn't the same as a good man. The Ceuran culture didn't require him to be apologetic about craving power. He would be true to his oaths. He would be merciful—by his own definition of mercy, and Kylar had no chance to get to know him well enough to know what that was. The Ceuran nobles called him a barbarian? What if they were right?

But Cenaria had more than lives at stake. Kylar hadn't stayed in the city long after killing Godking Ursuul, but everyone had been brimming with stories and pride about the Nocta Hemata.

Cenaria had been burnt to the ground, and something good was trying to grow in the ashes. Was Cenaria a land where the small became great despite overwhelming odds—as they had in the Nocta Hemata and the Battle of Pavvil's Grove? Or were they Midcyru's whipping boy—doomed to be overrun by their neighbors, fending off aggression only through the threat of such deep corruption that no one would want to rule them?

There were great souls in Cenaria. Momma K and Logan and Count Drake and Durzo were giants. Could they not be heroes as they might be in another country? Couldn't a Scarred Wrable have been a lauded soldier instead of a hired killer? Kylar thought so, but two things stood in the way: this man's invasion and Terah Graesin.

"I'm afraid I can't let you do this," Kylar said.

Fully dressed now, Lantano Garuwashi tucked his thumbs into his sash, which would normally hold his swords. It must have been habit, a not-so-subtle hint to whoever challenged him of Garuwashi's prowess. He removed his thumbs nonchalantly. "Are you going to kill me?" he asked. "I should find it difficult to fight an invisible man, but I thought we'd covered this ground already."

Kylar ignored him. He was looking past the Ceuran to the man's bed mat. There, for all the world looking like Ceur'caelestos, was a sword in its scabbard. A sword that Lantano Garuwashi hadn't tucked into his sash. A sword that Kylar had thrown into Ezra's Wood.

"Nice sword," Kylar said.

Lantano Garuwashi flushed. Though he smiled to cover it immediately, with his fair skin it couldn't be hidden.

"Whatever will your men say when they find out it's a fake? You have a vested interest in not spilling blood? How about a vested interest in not drawing your sword?"

Given the circumstances, Kylar thought Lantano Garuwashi mastered his rage rather well. His eyes went dead and his muscles relaxed. It wasn't the relaxation of a sluggard, but a swordsman's relaxation. Kylar had heard that Garuwashi once ripped out an opponent's throat before the man could draw his sword. He hadn't believed that an un-Talented man could do such a thing. Now he reconsidered.

Lantano Garuwashi didn't attack, though. Instead, he merely picked up his false Ceur'caelestos and tucked it into his belt. He forced a marginally pleasant expression to his face. "I have a secret of yours, Night Angel. You have an entire identity built as Kylar Stern. You wouldn't wish to lose that, would you? All your friends, all your access to the kinds of things the Night Angel couldn't find out on his own."

"Remind me to thank Feir for that." Kylar paused. Did this Ceuran never run out of tricks? "It would hurt me in any number of ways to lose Kylar Stern. But Kylar Stern isn't all I have or all I am. I can change my name."

"Changing a name is no great thing," Garuwashi admitted. "In Ceura we know this. We sometimes do it to commemorate great events in our lives, but a face—" he cut off as Kylar rubbed a hand over his face and put on Durzo's visage. "—ah, that is something else entirely, isn't it?"

"Losing my identity will cost me years of effort," Kylar said. "On the other hand, if you can't draw your sword, you can't lead your men at all, no matter how overwhelming your strength is. I know Ceura well enough to know that a king can't rule with an iron sword, and there's no such thing as an aceuran sa'ceurai."

Lantano Garuwashi raised an eyebrow. He glanced at the sheathed sword on his hip. "If you wish to reprise our duel in the wood, I will oblige. Feir Cousat went into the Wood that day after my sword. As none ever has before, he returned, on my word as a sa'ceurai. I still bear Ceur'caelestos. If you force me to draw it, I will sate its spirit with your blood."

It was a serious oath, but the words of his vow didn't mean what he wanted Kylar to infer. "You bear nothing but a scabbard and a hilt. Say that I lie, Garuwashi, and I'll stand before your tent and challenge you before your army. Your sa'ceurai will tear you apart with their bare hands when they find you've lost Ceur'caelestos."

The muscles on Garuwashi's jaw stood out. He said nothing for a long time. "Curse you," he said finally. The iron in him seemed to melt. "Curse you for taking my sword, and curse Feir for making me live. He did come out of the Wood. He said he'd been chosen to make another Ceur'caelestos for me. He knew the sa'ceurai would never understand, so he gave me this hilt and swore to return by spring. I believed him." Garuwashi breathed deeply. "And now you come again to destroy me. I don't know whether to hate you or admire you, Night Angel. I almost had you. I saw it in your face. Do you never run out of tricks?"

Kylar didn't let his guard down. "You don't even want Cenaria, do you? You just thought it would be another quick victory that would make your legend grow."

"What is a warleader without war, Night Angel? I was invincible before I took Ceur'caelestos, and now you wish me to lose—against Cenaria? You don't know what it is to lead men."

"I know what it is to kill them. I know what it is to ask others to pay for my mistakes."

"Do you know what it is to refuse to be satisfied with the meager portion life hands you? I think you do. Can you imagine me squatting in a field next to my one servant with my trousers rolled up, picking rice? These hands were not made for a hoe. You took this name Kylar Stern. Why? Because you were born with an iron sword, too.

"My men need food, but they need victory more. With me or without me, they are here for the winter," Lantano Garuwashi said. "The tunnels we widened to get through the mountains are rivers and ice now. If you expose me, the sa'ceurai will kill me, but then what? They will vent their fury on your people. For everyone's sake, Night Angel, let that go. Go instead and tell this queen to surrender. I give you my word that if she does this, not a single Cenarian will die. We will take nothing more than food and a place to winter. She will be granted her throne once more when we leave in the spring."

And you won't ask for anything else once you have Cenaria and Ceur'caelestos both, right?

Kylar shook his head. "You'll surrender."

"I can't," Garuwashi said through gritted teeth. "In surrender, even Cenarians lay down their swords at the victor's feet."

Kylar hadn't thought of that. It wasn't the thought of surrender that was impossible for Lantano Garuwashi, it was the physical act.

"Maybe," Kylar said, "maybe there's a third way."

When Dorian's half-brother Paerik had brought his army to Khaliras to seize the throne, he had abandoned a vital post. The general who had served under him, General Talwin Naga, stood in front of the throne, explaining how the wild men would invade in the spring.

"Sixty thousand of them?" Dorian asked. "How could they raise so many?"

"Raise may be exactly the word, Your Holiness," the tiny Lodricari man who had accompanied General Naga said.

"Who are you?" Dorian asked.

"This is Ashaiah Vul," the general said. "He was your father's *Raptus Morgi,* Keeper of the Dead. I think you need to hear what he can tell you."

"I've never heard of such an office," Dorian said. And "raptus" didn't primarily mean keeper, either. It meant taker, stealer. Dorian's stomach turned.

"By your father's order and his father's before him, it was a quiet office, Your Holiness," Ashaiah Vul said. He was utterly bald, with a knobby skull and a pinched face with nearsighted eyes, though he looked barely forty years old. "I was known only as the Keeper. Your father's Hands discouraged questions."

The Hands. There was another problem. Whoever led the informers, torturers, spies, and guards who served as the Godking's thousand hands had yet to show himself. Regardless, Dorian doubted Ashaiah Vul would dare lie about them.

"Go on," Dorian said.

"I think you may want to come with me, Your Holiness. I suggest you leave your guard here."

Is this the first attempt on my life? If so, it was rather clumsy. That made it all the more impossible to refuse. When the attempts on Dorian's life began, he had to defeat them ruthlessly. Then they would end. "Very well." Dorian signaled the guards to stay and dismissed the general.

In the hall, they immediately ran into Jenine. "My lord, I'm so glad to see you," she said, giving him a version of a Khalidoran bow mixed with a Cenarian curtsey, chin up, eyes closing demurely only for a moment, right hand sweeping into the Khalidoran courtiers' flourish while the left hand flared her skirt as she curtsied. She made the mixed curtsey look graceful, too. Obviously she'd practiced it. It occurred to him then that there was no Khalidoran form of a woman's salute to an equal male. Khalidoran women who were equals would nod to each other, but were always inferior to men in the same social rank, and invisible to men of lower rank. And all women prostrated themselves before a Godking. This was Jenine's offering of a middle ground. He smiled, pleased with her solution.

Dorian nodded more deeply than any Godking before him would have. "My lady, the pleasure is mine. How may I serve you?"

"I was hoping to spend the day with you. I don't want to be in your way. I just want to learn."

Dorian glanced at Ashaiah Vul. The man, of course, had his eyes averted. He wouldn't dare to disapprove of a Godking's decisions, or to even look at a Godking's woman. "I'm afraid I'm going to go see something remarkably unpleasant. You don't want to see it. I don't want to see it. You should probably wait in the throne room. I'll be back shortly." Dorian turned.

"I do want to see it," Jenine interjected. Ashaiah Vul gasped at her audacity, then studied the floor once more as both of them looked at him, his face going red.

"A thousand pardons, my lord, I spoke hastily. Forgive my rudeness," Jenine said. She chewed her lip. "I—My father never looked at things he didn't want to see, and it got him and my whole family killed, our country laid waste. Dealing with things we don't like is part of ruling. My father refused to do it because he was weak and venal. How else am I to learn if not from you?"

"What I'm going to see is beyond anything your father had to deal with, real or imagined," Dorian said.

"Even so." Jenine was unmoved, and Dorian couldn't help but smile. He loved her strength, even as it surprised him.

"Very well," he said. "Ashaiah, show us what you were going to show me alone. All of it."

Ashaiah Vul said nothing, pretended to have no opinion—and maybe, in fact, had no opinion. A Godking's unwelcome order was like a day of unwelcome weather. You might not like it, but you didn't have any illusions that you could change it, either. So Ashaiah took them deep into the bowels of the Citadel, and then into the tunnels of the mountain itself. Dorian could smell vir on the man, though not much. He was at best a meister of the third shu'ra.

Finally, Ashaiah Vul stopped in front of a door that looked like any of the hundreds of others this deep in the Citadel. The dust in this hall was so thick it was more like soil, and it was plain that this room hadn't been visited any more recently than any of the others. He unlocked the door and opened it.

Dorian held his vir as he followed the Lodricari into the darkness. His first sensation was that this room was huge, cavernous. The air was musty, thick, fetid.

Ashaiah mumbled an incantation and Dorian snapped three shields into place around both himself and Jenine. A moment later, light coursed up the arch where Ashaiah held his hand against the wall. It spread from arch to arch, across a painted ceiling over a hundred feet above. In a few seconds, light bathed the chamber.

This had been a library once, a place of beauty and light. The walls and pillars were the color of ivory and lace. The mural was like something out of a forgotten legend, light coming out of darkness, creation. It gave a sense of divinity and purpose. Long cherry shelves had once held both scrolls and books and tables had been arranged with space for scholars to study.

Now, it held clean, white bones. The chamber was hundreds of paces long, and half as wide, and everywhere, the books and scrolls had been removed. In their place, on every shelf, on every table, were bones. Old, old bones. Some shelves held entire skeletons, labeled with tags tied to their wrists. Some held skeletons of human bones but arranged in inhuman shapes. But mostly, the shelves held matching bones, with boxes for the small ones. An entire shelf of femurs. Boxes of finger bones. Pelvises stacked. Spines whole and in boxes for each vertebra. And skulls in a large central area: mountains of skulls.

Dorian dropped the shields. This was no attack. At least not on his body. "What is this?"

Ashaiah glanced at Jenine, then, obviously deciding he must speak the truth, said, "Should the wild men invade, this is your salvation, Your Holiness. It is your corpusarium. When General Naga speaks of the clans raising an army, this is what he means. Two years ago, a barbarian chieftain found an ancient mass grave and discovered a secret we had long thought was ours alone."

"Raising the dead?"

"Sort of, Your Holiness."

"Sort of?"

"The souls of men are inviolate," Ashaiah Vul said.

"I always liked purple."

Ashaiah blinked, not daring to chuckle. Jenine was too busy staring around in wonder. He didn't think she even heard him. "We don't have the power to bind men's souls to their bodies. Your predecessors tried to make themselves immortal doing that, but it never worked well. This is different. We call it raising because we use the bones of the dead and unite them with a kind of spirit we call the Strangers. The result is the krul. They were originally called the Fallen because whenever they fall in battle, they can be raised again if a Vürdmeister is present."

"Take me one step at a time," Dorian ordered, his queasiness increasing.

"It starts in the pits. It always has. The Godkings have always said that the ore beneath Khaliras was powerful, and that that's why the slaves and criminals and captured enemies are forced to work there. It's a lie. We don't need their service; we don't need the ore. We need the prisoners' bones and their agony. Their bones give us a frame. Their agony draws the Strangers."

"What are these Strangers?" Dorian asked.

"We don't know. Some of them have been here for millennia, but despite the length of their experiences, we are a puzzle to them. They don't have physical bodies—though my master said that once they walked the earth, took lovers, and had children who were the heroes of old, the nephilim. The southrons claim the name was because the Strangers were once children of their One God who were thrown out of heaven." He smiled weakly, clearly regretting saying anything about a southron religion.

"What happened?"

"We don't know. But the Strangers long to wear flesh again. So we take the bones of our dead and sanctify them for the Strangers' use. Incidentally, this is why Godkings have themselves cremated; they wish to avoid our use of their bones."

"And then?"

"Real bones are necessary but not sufficient to give the fallen a sense of embodiment, and it is for embodiment that they trade their service. We give them flesh. It doesn't have to look human. Some Godkings believed that any shape is possible, putting human bones into a horse's or a dog's shape. It makes binding the fallen more difficult as they wish to be men, not horses, but it makes a fine horse."

"And the musculature, the skin and so forth, does it need to be crafted as painstakingly as the skeletons?" Dorian asked. He'd trained as a Healer, and he couldn't imagine the intricate magic necessary to create a whole living body.

"Given the correct skeleton and enough clay and water, the Strangers help the magic form muscles and ligaments and skin. They're never as sturdy as man. Godking Roygaris was able to craft krul that lived for a decade or more, but he was a brilliant anatomist. He was able to make krul horses, and wolves, and tigers, and mammoths and other creatures we no longer have names for."

"They function like living beings?"

"They are living beings, Your Holiness. They breathe, they eat, they..."—he looked at Jenine again—"defecate. They just don't feel as men do. Pain that would incapacitate a man will do nothing to them. They won't complain about hunger. They will mention it if it's gone long enough that they are about to stop functioning."

"They speak?"

"Poorly. But they can see better in the dark than a man, though not as far. Eyes are difficult to make correctly. They make poor archers. They have emotions, but the palette is different from men's. Fear is incredibly rare. They know that as long as the line of Godkings survives, if their body is destroyed, they will most likely be put into another sooner or later."

"Are they obedient?"

"Perfectly, in most circumstances, but they have an incredible hatred toward the living. They won't help build anything, not even engines of war. They only destroy. Experiments have been tried where a krul was put in a room with a prisoner and told that if he killed the prisoner, he would be killed in turn. Every time, the krul killed the prisoner. It was tried with women, with old men, with children: it didn't matter, except they killed children more quickly. You couldn't ask them to take a city and not kill those who surrendered. They also hunger for human flesh. Eating it seems to make them stronger. We don't know why."

"My father gathered these bones, but never used them." That was odd. Dorian turned it over in his mind. Perhaps Garoth Ursuul was too decent.

"Your pardon, Your Holiness. Your esteemed father did use them, once. When Clan Hil rebelled. Afterward, he noted that the Hil fought to the last man when they knew they would be eaten and profaned. Your father said he wished to have men left alive to rule; the krul wished only for ashes. He held them off for a great emergency. The emergency never came, so there's quite a stockpile."

"How many do we have?"

"About eighty-five thousand. When we organize them, we have to preserve their hierarchy. Their number system is different than ours."

"What do you mean?"

"Even our words for numbers are predicated on multiples of ten: ten, a hundred, a thousand, ten thousand, a hundred thousand, a million. Their number system is based on thirteen—my master said that was where our superstitions about thirteen come from. They're rigidly bound to those numbers. A meister can lead twelve krul himself, but if he wishes to lead thirteen or more, he must master a thirteenth, which is different—a white krul called a daemon. The white krul are faster, over six feet tall, and take more magic to raise. Platoons are thirteen squads—a hundred sixty-nine krul. So after you raise thirteen squads, if you wish to add a single krul, you must raise a bone lord. Bone lords speak well, they're smarter, tough, and they can use magic."

"Vir?"

"No. It's either the Talent or very similar. Thirteen bone lords make a legion. If you don't lead it yourself, a legion needs a fiend. Thirteen fiends make an army, twenty-eight thousand five hundred sixty-one krul. Your Holiness has enough for three armies, if you can master two arcanghuls to lead the other two armies. All told, that gives you a force of more than eighty-five thousand."

"What would happen if I had thirteen arcanghuls? What is that? Close to four hundred thousand krul?"

"I don't know, Your Holiness." The man looked fearful, however, and Dorian thought he was lying.

"Has it ever been tried? I won't have you lie to me."

The man blinked furiously. "The only rumors I've heard about that are blasphemous, Your Holiness."

"As Godking, I pardon your blasphemy."

The man blinked again, but after a few moments seemed to master his fear. "My predecessor, Keeper Yrrgin, said that the first of your line, God-king Roygaris, tried. He needed hundreds of thousands of skeletons for the attempt, so he invaded what is now the Freeze. Keeper Yrrgin said it was once a great civilization, filled with mighty cities. Roygaris took it with little difficulty, for they thought him their ally. And then he put them in camps and killed them all—an entire civilization. Keeper Yrrgin said that above the thirteen arcanghuls, Godking Roygaris found a rank he called night lords. With one night lord, Roygaris conquered the rest of the Freeze, and his armies only grew. He couldn't be content. He thought he was closing in on the mysteries of the universe. He thought if he could master thirteen night lords, he would master God. I can't imagine that there were ever so many people in all the world, but my master told me that he succeeded in capturing and putting to death almost five million people, and that there, above the night lords, he found..." the man face was pasty and sweating, his voice low and hoarse. "There he found Khali. She destroyed him and became our goddess. She gave us the vir to bind us to her and to make us destroyers. This is why agony is worship to her, because like all the Strangers, she hates life."

"What happened, Ashaiah?"

The man's voice was a whisper, "Jorsin Alkestes."

Dorian's heart went cold. He'd heard this history, but only from the southern perspective. The Mad Emperor and the Mad Mage. The conqueror and his dog. Now, Ashaiah was saying that Jorsin and Ezra had stopped a goddess and her army of five million krul.

"Elsewhere our armies would suffer losses in the day and be remade in the night. That alone made us almost invincible. But Alkestes somehow warded all of the great city of Trayethell and leagues around it so that the krul couldn't be raised there."

"Black Barrow?" Dorian asked. The city was in southeast Khalidor, but it had never been inhabited. It was cursed. No one lived within leagues of the place. Indeed, all of eastern Khalidor was sparsely populated. "Who else knows about these bones and about the krul?"

"I have a number of deaf-mutes who assist me. We take all the castle's and the city's dead. I never allow anyone in the larger chambers. Paerik and Moburu were the only aethelings who knew. General Naga learned it from Paerik. No one else."

No one else.

"So Paerik wasn't a fool," Jenine said, speaking for the first time since they'd entered the vast room. "With twenty thousand men, he was facing sixty thousand. Paerik didn't come here for the throne—or at least not only for the throne—he came for the krul. What does it mean, my lord?"

Dorian felt sick. She seized on exactly the crux of it. "My father suffered a huge setback by being stalled in Cenaria. It was a distraction, a mistake. He thought he could grab it and send home riches and food, but the supplies he hoped to send home were put to the torch instead by the fleeing Cenarians." Dorian rubbed his face. "So when the barbarians come down from the Freeze, Khaliras will be indefensible. Its citizens would want to cross Luxbridge and live here in the Citadel. As they wait out the siege, they'll have to be fed—and we have no food. Our military's good at following orders, but no good at taking initiative. If I throw them into a battle facing three-to-one odds, they'll get massacred. There's no way to win."

Jenine said nothing for a moment, then glanced around at the stacks and stacks of bones. "You mean there's no way to win except..."

He looked at the bones of men and thought of all the stories of krul he'd ever heard, and he thought of dipping so deeply into the vir, and he thought of men dying no matter what he did. "Yes," he said. "There's no way to win except to raise these monsters. It will be an orgy of death."

"Whose deaths? The invaders' or your innocent people's?"

"The invaders'," Dorian said. So long as he did everything right.

"Then let us raise monsters," Jenine said.

28

After dressing appropriately, Kylar walked to Logan's tent. Logan's bodyguards nodded and pulled back the flap for him. The sun was poised on the horizon, but the tent was still dark enough that lanterns were needed to illuminate the maps that the officers, Agon, and Logan were studying.

Kylar joined the group silently. The maps were accurate, aside from missing the supply train.

"They outnumber us six to one," Agon said, "but they don't have any cavalry. So we ride out, the wytch hunters pick off a few officers and we melt back into the hills. We start gathering food so we can make it through the winter, and send out more scouts so we find any supply train they might have coming. It's the only way. They didn't expect walls. They'll starve before we do."

"The supply train is right here," Kylar said, pointing on the map. "It's accompanied by a thousand horse."

There was silence at the table.

"We have lost a scout in that direction," an officer said.

"Are you certain?" Agon asked. "How big is it?"

Kylar dropped a sheaf of notes on the table.

There was silence as the men picked up the rice paper sheets and read. Only Logan didn't read as the officers shared the notes back and forth. He stared at Kylar quizzically, obviously wondering what he was trying to accomplish.

"How did you get these, Wolfhound?" an officer asked, using the nickname the soldiers had given Kylar.

"I fetched." Kylar gave him a toothy smile.

"Enough," Agon said, throwing his papers down on the table. "It's worse than we feared."

"Worse?" the officer said. "It's a disaster."

"General," Kylar said to Logan, "can I have a word with you? Alone?"

Logan nodded and other men filed from the tent, carrying the notes for further study. "What are you playing at, Kylar?"

"Just making you look good."

"An impending slaughter makes me look good?"

"A disaster diverted makes you look good."

"And you have a plan."

"Garuwashi wants food and a victory. I propose we give them to him."

"Why hadn't I thought of that?" Logan said, uncharacteristically sarcastic. He was really worried, then. Good.

"It doesn't have to be a victory over *us*," Kylar said. Then he explained.

When he finished, Logan didn't look surprised. He looked profoundly sad. "That would make me look good, wouldn't it?"

"And save thousands of lives and the city," Kylar said.

"Kylar, it's time for us to finish that conversation."

"What conversation?"

"The one about king-making and queen unmaking."

"I don't have any more to say."

"Good, then you can listen," Logan said. He rubbed his unshaven face and his sleeve fell to show the edge of the dully glowing green tattoo etched in his forearm. "People commonly misquote the old Sacrinomicon and say that money is the root of all evil, which is moronic if you think about it. The real quote is that the love of money is the root of all sorts of evil. Not as pithy, but a lot truer. In the same way, what I am capable of doing in the pursuit of power and sex, the man I choose for Logan Gyre to be will not allow. My hunger for food couldn't make me a monster in my own eyes. Not even when I ate human flesh. I was driven to that by necessity, not perversion. I suppose the same could be said for you, for killing. I saw it on your face when you killed my gaoler Gorkhy. You do it, but you don't love it. If you loved it, you'd turn into Hu Gibbet."

"There is a foul pleasure in it," Kylar said quietly.

"There's pleasure in having a full belly too, but for some it's dangerous pleasure. When I ordered you to kill Gorkhy, you didn't feel that." Logan saw his tattoo was uncovered and covered it. "I did. I gave an order and he died. I killed with a word. And I loved it. And I wanted more."

"So now what? You going to become a hermit, move to a cottage in the woods?"

"I'm not that selfish." Logan scrubbed a hand through his hair. "If I asked you, would you kill Terah Graesin?"

"Absolutely."

Logan closed his eyes. He'd obviously expected it. "If I didn't ask you, would you do it anyway?"

"Yes."

"Have you been planning it?"

"Yes."

"Dammit, Kylar! Now I know."

"So why'd you ask?" Kylar asked.

"To remove the excuse. Can you rule justly after you take the throne unjustly?"

"Good question to ask the woman who stole yours."

"How, Kylar?"

"Schedule a meeting with her and drink a lot before-hand."

"Dammit, man, how were you going to kill her?"

"A botched abortion. I'd poison whatever abortifacient she uses. Many of those potions are dangerous. If it appeared she'd taken double what her apothecary recommended, it would look like a tragic and shameful accident for a single, wanton young queen. If the nobles tried to cover up the details, the rumors would swirl around what a whore Terah was, rather than speculations that she was assassinated. And it would make the virtuous new king look even better."

"Gods," Logan breathed. "How long did it take you to come up with that?"

Kylar shrugged. "Couple minutes."

There was pain in Logan's eyes, as if he had to struggle to speak. "It's brilliant, Kylar. It's brilliant—and I forbid it."

"You forbid it?"

"Yes."

"And how do you propose to forbid me anything?" Kylar asked.

Logan looked astonished.

"Despite all my efforts, you're not my king. You can't forbid me a damn thing."

Logan's face darkened and all his usual conviviality drained away. It made Kylar conscious of just how tall Logan was. His lean seven-foot height made him a looming, merciless skeleton. "Know this," Logan said. "If I'm crowned because of Terah Graesin's murder, I'll have you executed."

"You'd kill me for Terah Graesin?"

"I'd execute you for treason. An attack on Cenaria's sovereign is an attack on Cenaria."

"She shouldn't be queen."

"But she is."

"You had no right to swear fealty."

"I did what I had to do to save the people, Kylar. Now I must abide by my word. Politics is ethics writ large."

"Politics is the art of the possible, and you know it," Kylar said. "On the eve of battle, the tides changed so you couldn't be king, so you changed course. The tides are changing again."

Logan folded his arms. His voice was granite. "My word stands."

"Can you love an idea more than you love a man and not become a monster? How many friends will you sacrifice on the altar of Justice, Logan?"

"If you force my hand, at least one."

They were standing on a precipice. Socially, Logan had always been Kylar's superior. Morally, Kylar had always felt inferior, too. But they'd never been placed in a direct hierarchical relation. Now Logan was giving an order. He would not be moved.

Kylar could only accept his order and accept all his orders henceforth, or reject it and them forever. There was part of him that yearned to obey. He was convinced that killing Terah was the right thing, but Logan's moral compass was a more accurate instrument than Kylar's. What was it about submission that was so hard? Kylar wasn't being asked for blind servility. He was being asked to obey a man he knew and loved and respected, who in turn respected him.

The wolfhound is pampered by the fire. The wolf is hunted in the cold.

"Do you know how much I love you, Logan?" Kylar asked. Logan opened his mouth, but before he could say a word, Kylar said, "This much." And left.

29

$\mathcal{K}$ylar was back in the city on his way to the one safe house he was confident hadn't been discovered during the Godking's reign when the ka'kari spoke.

~Would you be excited about Logan being king if he told you politics is the art of the possible and asked you to murder his rivals?~

I'm already damned. My crimes might as well accomplish something.

~So you'll serve clean water out of a filthy cup? You must have better tricks than I do.~

The safe house was on the east side, far enough from the fashionable areas that it had been on the city's outskirts. Now the building was gone. The entrance itself, a flagstone set flush with the ground, was only paces from the Godking's new wall. The neighborhood, once unfashionable, was buzzing with activity. After the Godking's death, thousands of people had fled the Warrens, either hoping to reclaim their lives or hoping to claim someone else's better life. The fires that the displaced had started on their way out of the city had left great swathes of it bare and black. Too few buildings remained to shelter everyone, even without the thousands who had left the city with Terah Graesin. Now they all were back, and there were no building materials to be found. With an army besieging the city and cold rains starting, people were desperate.

Kylar sat with his back to the wall to listen to the tones of the city. There was no way he was going to get into the safe house before nightfall. Even invisible, he couldn't lift a flagstone in the middle of what was now a de facto street without dozens of people noticing. The safe house had another entrance, of course. Unfortunately, a new wall was sitting on it.

The gossip was angry. Terah Graesin had stopped the free flow of traffic across the Vanden Bridge this morning, and it had nearly caused a riot. Kylar listened to a proclamation that promised a return to the way things had been before the invasion. The squatters would be driven back into the Warrens, and those legitimate merchants and petty nobility who had been uprooted would be granted their old homes and lands as soon as they could prove their claims. The herald was greeted with hisses and jeers.

"And how in the nine hells am I supposed to prove that I owned a smithy, when the queen burned it and my deeds to the ground?" one man yelled. Kylar would have been more sympathetic if he didn't recognize the man as a beggar. Others, however, joined a chorus of agreement.

"I'm not going back!" a young man yelled. "I lived in the Warrens long enough."

"I killed six palies in the Nocta Hemata," another shouted. "I deserve better!"

Before the crowd's fury gained more momentum, the herald beat a hasty retreat.

Within an hour, scribes were openly hawking badly forged deeds. An hour after that, a Sa'kagé representative showed up. His deeds were not only higher quality and much more expensive, he said the Sa'kagé guaranteed that no duplicate deeds would be forged. He could only sell deeds for this neighborhood, and he had an allotment of what kind of shops could be represented. Thus, unless the owner still possessed the original deed, Sa'kagé deeds were as good as gold. Within minutes, the non-Sa'kagé scribes had been chased off or coerced to join.

Meanwhile, food prices were skyrocketing. Tough loaves of bread that wouldn't sell for six coppers in the morning were selling for ten after a full day hardening in the sun. As the sun set, people improvised wood frames with cloaks or blankets stretched over them to make lean-tos against the wall. Others wrapped themselves tight in their cloaks, tucked their purses inside their tunics, and slept where they lay, alone or in groups for warmth.

Not everyone slept, of course. Darkness brought out the guild rats looking for easy bags. One even bent over Kylar, who hadn't moved in so long she thought him asleep. Kylar waited until the urchin—he couldn't even tell for sure under the grime but he thought it was a girl—had a hand on his purse. Then he struck, spinning the child into his arms, with both hands twisted behind her back and Kylar's other hand locked around her throat.

"Please, sir, I was up for a piss, and now I can't find my da."

"Kids who have parents don't say 'piss' when they talk to adults. What guild are you?"

"Guild, sir?"

Kylar clouted her ear, but not as hard as Durzo would have.

"Black Dragon."

"Black Dragon?" Kylar laughed softly. "That was my old guild. How much are dues these days?"

"Two coppers."

"Two? We had to pay four." Kylar felt like an old fart, talking about how much harder things were when he was growing up. He let her go. "What's your name, kid?"

"Blue."

"Well, Blue, tell the tall kid not to try that fat man's purse. He's not asleep. If you all get out of here for an hour, I'll leave enough to pay your dues for a week. If you don't, I'll yell that I've caught a thief and tell everyone to watch out for guild rats, and you'll have to move on anyway—and you'll all be lucky to escape a beating."

He let her go, and while she was gathering her crew, he went invisible and lifted the flagstone. Hidden doors set into the ground were never as secure as those set into walls. No matter how expertly constructed, once you opened a door in the ground, you displaced the dirt on the door as well as the dirt that inevitably got packed into the seams. It would be the last time Kylar could use this safe house. A safe house you were afraid to use wasn't a safe house at all, but Kylar needed a noble's clothing, gold, and—thanks to the ka'kari—new weapons.

Instead of climbing down the ladder, he jumped, and quickly pulled the flagstone shut. He checked his traps—one on the ladder and two on the door. All were intact. Then he opened the wood door slowly. The hinges protested and he made a mental note to oil them.

The tiny safe house was pristine, if stale. Kylar checked the top of one of the small chests. Across the latch was balanced a piece of his own hair. The hair, of course, wasn't a foolproof indicator of tampering. Even in a sealed safe house, your own entry could disturb the air enough to displace a hair, but if the hair was in place, it was unlikely that anyone else had entered.

Kylar shook his head. He wasn't even planning to stay here more than a few minutes, but Durzo's habit of checking traps and examining every corner for threats had sunk deep.

And where was Durzo? What had he been doing? Had he simply moved on to another life? Was it so easy for him to leave everything behind? The idea soured Kylar's mood. Durzo was the central figure in Kylar's life, and he'd abandoned him. Durzo had given him the ka'kari, a treasure of untold worth, but he hadn't given Kylar his trust—or his time.

A dusty glass case sat next to the dusty desk. Kylar opened the case. Inside, labeled in Durzo's neat hand, were dozens of jars of herbs, potions, elixirs, and tinctures. Durzo had told Kylar that some wetboys mislabeled their herbs deliberately, so as to confuse or kill anyone who stole from them. Durzo said anyone who had the resources and guts to steal from him could identify an herb or hire someone to do it for him. Kylar suspected the real reason was that Durzo couldn't bear to mislabel anything.

That he wouldn't mislabel his supplies, however, didn't mean that Durzo did label all of them. Durzo believed that safe houses had a one-in-four chance of being discovered in any given year, so he spread the most valuable items of his collection out among them to minimize losses. Managing such an inventory was probably half the reason Kylar's master had been so paranoid. For in this now-worthless safe house, in an unmarked vial smaller than Kylar's thumb, was a substance that looked like liquid gold. It had cost Durzo half a year and as much as a manse on Sidlin Way. Its proper name was philodunamos. Durzo called it bottled fire.

Whereas almost every other tool of the trade was mundane, if rarely known, bottled fire was magic. The only people who could make it were the Harani aborigines, whose magic was tied to emotion and song. After being driven from their lowland homes two centuries ago, they hadn't had access to the materials they needed to make philodunamos. How Durzo had known what those were, how he had gathered them, and how he had coached a Harani mage into making such a lethal substance, Kylar had no idea.

Sitting at the desk, Kylar rooted around until he found the gold-plated tweezers, a wad of cotton, and a candle. Then he couldn't find a tinderbox. Since he could see in the dark, he never carried one anymore. Without a tinder-box, he couldn't light the candle, without the candle, he couldn't clean the tweezers, without clean tweezers, he couldn't pull off a wisp of cotton to dip into the bottled fire, without the cotton, he couldn't test an appropriately tiny measure of the bottled fire. He swore under his breath.

~Why do you make things so hard? Use me. I'm sterile.~

You telling me there's no little ka'kari gravel out there?

There was a pause, then, unimpressed, ~And I thought Durzo's humor was lacking.~

Nonetheless, in a moment, the ka'kari puddled in Kylar's palm and formed an instrument with a flexible bulb on one side that tapered down to almost a needle-point on the other. Kylar had never seen anything like it before. ~Squeeze me and put me in the philodunamos.~

"You're amazing," Kylar said.

~I know.~

"Humble, too."

Kylar opened the vial and sucked out a single drop. He dripped it on a rag, closed the vial, and pushed his seat back. The ka'kari dissolved back into his skin. Kylar put the vial of bottled fire on the other side of the room and closed the herb cases, only drawing out one vial of water. The gold drop of philodunamos dried in moments, becoming hard and flaky. Kylar dropped the rag on the ground and dripped some water on it. The water wicked outward until it touched the philodunamos.

There was a whoosh of flame as high as Kylar's knee. The fire consumed the rag instantly and still burned for another ten seconds, then guttered out.

"It's tricky," Durzo had said. "Water, wine, blood, sweat, most anything wet should trigger it. But it can get unstable. So by the Night Angels, don't even open it if it's muggy."

Kylar smiled as he tucked the vial away. Sweat. He'd pour the bottle on Terah Graesin's incestuous bed if only such a death were public enough. He collected his clothing and gold and turned to grab a sword from the weapons wall, then something stopped him.

"You bastard," he said.

Hanging on the wall, impossibly, as if Kylar hadn't sold it for a fortune in a city two weeks' ride away, was a big, beautiful sword with the word Mercy etched on the blade. There was no explanation, no message of any kind— except for the smirk implicit in resetting Kylar's traps and replacing his single strand of hair. Durzo had redeemed Kylar's birthright. For a second time, Durzo was giving him Retribution.

30

$\mathcal{K}$ylar stood in a hazy corridor decorated with brightly colored animals, facing a door. There were no sharp edges to anything. It was as if he were looking at the world through sleep-blurry eyes. The door opened without his touch, and as soon as he saw her, his heart lurched. Vi was lying on a narrow bed, weeping. She was the only thing in the world utterly clear, sharp, and present.

She raised a hand in supplication, and he went to her. She seemed as unsurprised by his presence as he was. For a moment, he wondered at that. Where was he? How had he come?

The thoughts disappeared the moment he touched her hand. This was real. Her hand was small in his, delicate and finely shaped, the skin as callused as his own. Unlike Elene's, Vi's third finger was slightly longer than her forefinger. He'd never noticed that before.

It was the most natural thing to sit on the bed and pull her into his arms. She lay across his lap and clung to him, suddenly weeping harder and grasping him convulsively. He held her tight, willing his strength into her. He could feel her need for it. She was confused, lost, scared of this new life, scared of being known, scared of never being known. He didn't have to read her face, he felt it within himself.

She turned tear-swollen eyes to his face and he looked into her deep, green eyes. He was a mirror to her and he reflected back truth against every fear.

The tears slowed and her grip relaxed. She closed her eyes as if the intimacy was too much. She put her head in his lap, sighing, her body finally relaxing. Her long, fiery red hair was unbound. Though it was messy and tangled and crimped from where she had worn it in a ponytail all day, he was amazed. It was glossy, silky, mesmerizing, a color that only one in a thousand women had. His eyes followed a strand of her hair past tear-wet eyelashes to a nose with faint freckles he'd never noticed before to her slender neck.

Vi wore an ill-fitting plain nightdress. It was too short for her and the knot had come loose, leaving it gaping open. Her nipple was dark pink, small on her full breast, lightly puckered in the room's coolness. The first time Kylar had seen Vi's breasts, she'd exposed herself to shock him. This time, he could feel that she was unaware of it.

The unexpected innocence of Vi's exposure roused something protective in him. He swallowed and moved the cloth to cover her. Despite that Vi could feel him as clearly as he could feel her, she didn't notice. Was she merely that exhausted, or was she so divorced from her body that she didn't attach any significance to her breast being covered? Kylar didn't know, but either way, the wave of compassion he felt overpowered his desire. He barely glanced at her shapely legs, naked to mid-thigh, as he covered them with a blanket.

She burrowed into him, so vulnerable and so damn gorgeous he couldn't think straight.

He ran his fingers through her hair to call back the more protective feelings. Instead, Vi melted instantly, yielded completely, a wave of tingles coursing from head to loins. His heart lurched. The only thing he'd ever felt close to this was when he'd kissed Elene for half an hour and then spooned behind her, tracing kisses across her ears and neck and skimming his fingertips across her breasts—and it was always then that she stopped him, afraid of losing control completely. Vi sailed right over that brink. She was his, utterly, completely.

He was drunk on her ecstasy. The bond between them burned like fire. He couldn't stop himself. He slowly combed his fingers through her hair, rubbed her scalp, combed his fingers through her hair again. She shifted her hips, making tiny sounds. She rolled over in his lap so he could reach the other side of her head. It put her facing his stomach, inches from the undeniable evidence of his own arousal.

He froze. She felt it and her eyes flew open. Her pupils were pools of desire. "Please, don't stop," she said. "I'll take care of you. Promise." She gave the bulge of his trousers a peck.

Her casualness threw Kylar. There was a disconnect here, in what was supposed to be a connection. It wasn't *let's share this,* it was *let's trade.* It wasn't love—it was commerce.

"I'm sorry," she said, picking up on his confusion. "I was being selfish." She threw back the blanket and in the illogic of a dream, her ugly night-dress was simply gone. In its place, a fitted red nightgown clung to her curves. She stretched like a cat, displaying herself to marvelous advantage. "You first. It's all yours."

"It's all yours," not "I'm all yours." She was offering herself like a sweet-meat. It was nothing to her.

The door opened abruptly and Elene stood there. Her eyes took in Vi, half-naked, draped over Kylar, her hand on his crotch and Kylar stupidly enjoying it.

Kylar scrambled out of bed. "No!" he cried.

"What?" Vi asked. "What are you seeing?"

"Elene! Wait!"

Kylar woke and found himself alone in the safe house.

Dorian was in his chambers with Jenine, poring over maps of the Freeze and the Vürdmeisters' estimations of the clans' strength, when the Keeper of the Dead entered. Dorian and Jenine followed the man into one of the cheerier rooms where a body lay wrapped in sheets. Two huge highlanders in nondescript southron clothes but with the bearing of soldiers stood after making their obeisance.

Ashaiah Vul opened the cloth around the corpse's head. The stench was magnified tenfold. The bald head had been split in half, but not cracked. Nothing had been broken or torn. There was simply a slice missing from his crown to his neck.

In that instant, Dorian knew not only the victim, but also the killer. Only the black ka'kari could make such a cut. Kylar had done this. The rotting sack of meat was Dorian's father Garoth. His knees felt suddenly weak. Jenine came to stand close beside him, but she didn't touch him, didn't take his hand. Any show of comforting him would make him look weak to his men.

"How did you do this?" Dorian asked.

"Your Holiness," the highlander who had a birthmark over the left half of his face said, "we thought you'd want His Holiness's body for the pyre. There was a demon in the castle. It did this. The lieutenant went with our ten best men to kill it. He ordered us to take the body, sire. They were supposed to meet us, but they never came."

"How was your journey? Really."

The man stared at the floor. "It was real hard, Holiness. We got jumped three times. Sa'kagé twice and once some damn traitors in Quorig's Pass who went bandit after we lost at Pavvil's Grove. They thought we were carrying treasure. Red's not breathing right since I pulled the arrows out." He nodded at the other highlander, who didn't have red hair. "We hoped the Vürdmeisters might take a look once you're finished with us, sire."

"They weren't bandits. They were rebels." Dorian stepped forward and put his hand on the highlander's head. Red tensed, uncertain. He had blood clots and infections all through his lungs. It was amazing he'd lived as long as he had. "This is beyond the Vürdmeisters," Dorian said. "What about you?"

"I'm fine, Your Holiness."

"What happened to your knee?"

The man blanched. "My horse got killed. Fell on it."

"Come here. Kneel." The men knelt and Dorian was infuriated at the waste of their bravery. If Dorian weren't such a skilled Healer, one would die and the other live a cripple, and for what? To deliver bones. These heroes had made great sacrifices for nothing. "You have served with great honor and courage," Dorian told them. "In the coming days I will reward you appropriately." He Healed them both, though it was oddly difficult to use his Talent.

There was a low spate of awed cursing from the men as the magic swept them clean. Red coughed once and then inhaled deeply. They looked at Dorian with awe and fear and confusion, as if they couldn't believe that saving their lives was worth the Godking's own effort.

Dorian dismissed them and turned back to his father. "You sick bastard, you don't deserve a pyre. I should—" Dorian broke off, frowning. "Keeper, the Godkings always leave orders that their bodies be burned so that they may not be used for krul, yes?"

"Yes, Your Holiness," Ashaiah said, but he looked gray.

"How many times have those orders been obeyed?"

"Twice," Ashaiah whispered.

"You have the bones of every Godking for the last seven centuries except two?" Dorian was incredulous.

"Sixteen of your blood were used to raise arcanghuls and subsequently destroyed. We have the rest. Do you wish me to prepare a substitute corpse for Garoth's pyre, Your Holiness?"

Garoth Ursuul deserved no less for all the evil he'd done, but refusing his father a decent burial would say more about Dorian than it would about the dead man. "My father was monster enough in life," Dorian said. "I'll not make him one in death."

Only after the little man left did Jenine come hold his hand.

We're not going back, are we?" Jenine asked, coming before the God-king's throne. Dorian waved the guards away. He stood and walked to her, taking her hands in his.

"The passes are snowed in," he said gently.

"I mean we're not ever going back, are we?"

She said we. It made him tingle, that unconscious admission of unity. Dorian waved a hand at the gold chains of office he wore. "They would kill me for my father's crimes."

"Will you let me go?"

"Let you?" That hurt. "You're not my prisoner, Jenine. You can go whenever you wish." *Jenine.* Not Jeni. That formality had stuck. Maybe she feared she had merely traded gaolers. "But I have to tell you, I've just received news that Cenaria is under siege. The last warriors to make it through Screaming Winds saw an army surrounding the city."

"Who?"

"Some Ceuran general named Garuwashi and thousands of sa'ceurai. It may be that come spring—"

"We've got to go help them!" Jenine said.

He paused, letting her think. Sometimes she did act sixteen. "I could order my army to attempt the pass," Dorian said. "If they were lucky and the weather cooperated and the rebel highland tribes didn't attack while my army was spread out, we might only lose a few thousand. By the time we got there, the siege would probably be finished. And if we arrived in time and seized the city ourselves, do you think Cenaria would welcome us? The Khalidoran *saviors?* They will not have forgotten what my men did a few months ago. And my soldiers who lose brothers and fathers and sons in the passage, or who lost friends in the Nocta Hemata, will want the spoils of war.

"If I forbade rapine and murder, they might obey me, but it would plant doubts about me. Two hundred of my Vürdmeisters—that's more than half—have disappeared. I don't yet control the Godking's Hands, who are the only people who will tell me where those Vürdmeisters have gone, or who is leading them. Garoth Ursuul had other aethelings I haven't accounted for. I may be facing civil war in the spring. So if it came to it, who do you think the Vürdmeisters will follow, Khali, who gives them their power, or the once-treasonous aetheling?" The line between her eyebrows was deep with anguish now, helplessness, but Dorian wasn't finished. "And if they do follow me, and we are successful, what will your people say? They've installed a new queen, Terah Graesin."

"Terah?" Jenine was incredulous.

"Will the people welcome back young Jenine with a Khalidoran army? Or will they say you're a puppet, so young that I'm manipulating you, perhaps without your knowing it? Will Queen Graesin surrender her power?"

Jenine looked ill. "I thought...I thought it was going to be easy after we won. I mean, we won, right?"

It was a good question. Perhaps it was the only question that mattered.

"We won," Dorian said after a long moment. "But the victory cost us. I can never go south again. All of my friends besides you are in the south. They'll see my reign as a betrayal." That made him think of Solon. Had Solon even made it out of Screaming Winds alive? The thought made him ache. "If you want to assert your right to Cenaria's throne, I can deliver it, but that would cost you too.

"The price will be that everyone sees that a Godking has given you the throne. Do you think you're ready to rule? Without help? At sixteen, do you know how to pick advisers, how to tell when the chancellor of your exchequer is embezzling, how to deal with generals who see you as a child? Do you have a plan to deal with the Sa'kagé? Do you know why the last two Ceuran wars ended and what obligations you have to your neighbors? A plan to deal with the Lae'knaught who occupy your eastern lands? If you don't have all those covered, you'll need help. If you accept help, you'll be seen to be accepting help. If you don't accept help, you'll make mistakes. If you trust the wrong people, you'll be betrayed. If you don't trust the right people, you'll have no one to protect you from your enemies. Assassination has as long of a history in your kingdom as slaughter does in mine. Do you have an idea of whom you will marry and when? Do you plan to concede rule to your new husband, share it, or keep it?"

"I have answers to some of those questions, and I know some people I can trust—"

"—I don't doubt it—"

"—but I hadn't considered all of those." She got very quiet. "I'm not ready."

"I do have . . . an alternative," Dorian said. His heart pounded. He wanted to use the vir. In his old life, before the One God found him, he'd learned a glamour to seduce women. Now he could use it, just a little, just to help Jenine get over her fear and disappointment and to see Dorian as a man. He wouldn't make her do anything she didn't want to do.

He quashed the impulse. *Not that way.* If Jenine didn't choose him freely, it was all for nothing.

"Stay," Dorian said. "Be my queen. I love you, Jenine. You are the reason I came to Khalidor. This throne means nothing to me without you. I do and will always love you. A queen is what you are, what you are meant to be, and there is work for you here. My fathers haven't had queens; they had chattels, harems, playthings. Khalidor's people are no worse than any other, but this culture is sick. I thought once that I could run away. I see now that that's not enough. I've found my life's work: changing reverence for power to reverence for life. You have no idea what your mere presence will do. Our marriage will redefine marriage for this entire country. That's no small feat, and it will bring no small amount of happiness to the women *and* the men here."

"You want me to marry you because I'll help you in your work?"

"Jenine," he said quietly. "Lovers always want to make a private world. Just you and me and nothing else matters. The truth is, everything else does matter. Your family, my family, the different ways we were raised, the obligations we have, the work we do—it all matters. A marriage can be a refuge, but I'd be a fool to ignore what and who I am now, and what and who you are. But the answer is no, I don't want to marry you because I want you to help me. I want *you*. You're worth more than all the rest of it combined. I'd rather serve in a hut with you than rule all the world without you."

She averted her eyes. "You honor me, my lord."

"I love you."

She met his eyes now, but uncertainty still painted her features. "You are a good man, Dorian Ursuul, and a great man May I think about it for a few days?"

"Of course," he said. His heart died a little. "Let me think about it" isn't the answer a man wants to his proposal. Of course, most men managed a little romance before asking.

In one way, he was horribly disappointed in himself. In another, he was content. He wanted Jenine's mind to consent to this match, not just her heart. Romantic feelings would come and go. He didn't want her to choose in haste and regret at leisure.

She excused herself and the guards let in Dorian's next appointment. It was Hopper. The man limped in quickly and prostrated himself. Jenine hesitated halfway out the door. She had told Dorian that there was something about Hopper that she wanted to share with him, but they hadn't gotten around to it.

"Your Holiness," Hopper said, "the women have been in an uproar. They begged me to ask if you'll be accepting any of them into your harem."

Jenine turned away, as if embarrassed to be eavesdropping, but she didn't hasten to leave, either.

"Of course not," Dorian said. "Not one of them."

32

Terah Graesin had moved the coronation up. No matter that an army was encamped around the city, and that with their scant supplies already dwindling it was wildly inappropriate to have a party, Terah had decided she couldn't wait two months. Her coronation would be in three days. So Momma K had to come to the castle to meet the new court bard. She knocked on his door.

He opened, squinting, and looked about as pleased as Momma K expected. She'd commissioned a piece from him on their last meeting—for the queen's birthday. She hadn't mentioned the coronation was the same day. In retaliation, he'd gotten himself hired as the court bard, meaning she was paying for a piece he'd have to compose anyway.

"Do you know who I am, Quoglee Mars?" Momma K asked. As she stepped past him into his small apartment, he sniffed to smell her perfume. Quoglee's sense of smell was as good as his eyesight was bad. Her spies said he'd even spent time with Alitaera's royal perfumer.

He hesitated. Then, "You are Madame Kirena, a woman of great power and wealth." Quoglee's voice was a tenor so clear it was a pleasure even to hear him speak.

It was a pity nothing else about the man was beautiful. Quoglee Mars resembled nothing so much as a squashed frog. He had a wide, fleshy mouth that turned down at the edges, no neck, a perpetual squint, and a small round gut like a ball. Rather than trousers, he wore baggy yellow tights on his skinny legs, and he had a tiny tricorn hat with a feather in it. He was one of the ugliest men Momma K had ever seen, save for a few lepers far gone in their disease. "I heard your new tale, "The Fall of the House of Gunder." It was fearless. Beautiful. You should write more," she said.

Quoglee bowed, accepting the praise as his due. "I usually prefer the honesty of instrumentals. The pipe and lyre never lie, nor by their tones do good men die."

"An odd sentiment from a minstrel who's been chased from half the capitals of Midcyru because he can't stop himself from telling the truth." Which was why she'd asked if he knew who she was. At least he was capable of discretion. She smiled.

"May I ask why you're here?" Quoglee asked, squinting at her.

Damn all artists. Their bribes had to come as introductions to the influential, in gifts of clothing or instruments, in arranging special concerts and making sure they were well received. Of course, a bard rarely minded when some beautiful young music aficionado offered to polish his flute, either. But it all had to be discreet. The only punishment they could think to face for Momma K's displeasure was indifference. Years ago, Momma K had sent a gorgeous little flute case to a newly popular bard called Rowan the Red. The girl had given him some grossly ignorant compliment which she wouldn't have if she were the educated young noblewoman she was pretending to be. Instead of taking her to his room and giving her better things to do with her mouth, Rowan had quizzed her and publicly made her look a fool. It didn't take him long to guess who might have sent her. When Momma K's most gifted wetboy Durzo Blint had arrived a few hours later, the bard was already writing a song mocking her and making wild allegations, some of them true. No one ever heard that catchy tune, or any other tune from Rowan the Red, but it had been a near thing, and since then, Momma K avoided bards when she could.

But bards were too good a resource to abandon. They plied Momma K with every tidbit they knew and lapped up every morsel she dropped. Indeed, they often gave her new information, for bards were always present at parties even if her other spies were not. But Quoglee was different. Quoglee's stories were rare, and the nobles regarded them as absolute truth; other bards often repeated them. He was hard to interest, but once that interest was piqued, he was a bulldog.

"Do you know who I am, Quoglee Mars?" she asked again.

Again, he hesitated. "You're the owner of half the brothels in the city. You're a woman who crawled out of the gutter to climb higher than anyone would have believed. My guess is you're the Sa'kagé Mistress of Pleasures."

"One of my girls has a small Talent of foretelling," Momma K said. "She doesn't dream often, but when she does, she's never been wrong. Two years ago she dreamed of you, maestro, though she'd never seen or heard of you and indeed, you hadn't yet come to Cenaria. She described you perfectly. She said a song burst from your mouth like a river. The river was the purest, clearest water she'd ever seen. She said I tried to stop it, but the waters overwhelmed me and I drowned. The next night she dreamed the same dream, but this time I tried to strike you down before you could sing, but the song was unstoppable, and again I drowned. On the third night, I swam. I think the name of your river is Truth, Quoglee Mars, so I ask again: do you know who I am?"

"You're the Shinga of the Sa'kagé," he said quietly.

Though she'd been prepared for it, hearing the truth spoken aloud frightened her. But this was why she'd hired Quoglee Mars in the first place. She'd paid him for a flute piece, then had her informants drop hints to him of a much bigger story, the kind of tale Quoglee couldn't resist telling. But the man was incredibly bright, and that made him dangerous. "How'd you learn?" she asked.

"Everyone knew you were Jarl's right hand. When he disappeared, none of the Sa'kagé's work was interrupted. Agon's Dogs continued training, the Nocta Hemata happened, and there was no rush of thugs' bodies floating in the Plith. The Sa'kagé isn't an organization to put off a struggle for succession just because there's a war. You've been Shinga for more than a month, haven't you?"

Momma K let out a long, slow breath. "Fifteen years," she said. "Always behind puppet Shingas. Shingas don't tend to die of natural causes."

"So what are you buying? I'm guessing you want more than a flute piece."

"I want you to sing a song of Terah Graesin's secrets."

"Do you know what those are?" Quoglee asked.

"Yes."

"Are you going to tell me?"

"No."

"Why not?"

"Because I've made my living telling lies and you know it. Because the truth is damning enough. Because you're renowned for winkling out the truth on your own."

"So if you can't dam the river, you wish to channel it. How do you propose to buy me off?"

"You want more than coin?" she asked, knowing the answer.

"Oh yes."

"Then I'll give you what you wish," she said.

"I want your story. You will answer every question I ask, and if you lie in any particular, I will use your tale to cast you in a devastating light."

"Now you tempt me to take my chances with prophecy and signal the wetboy I have waiting behind that curtain to kill you. A whore's truth has too many sharp edges. I will tell my story and not spare myself, but I will not share the secrets of the men I could destroy with what I know. It would be my death, and some few of them deserve better. I will give you more of my story, and more about the Sa'kagé, than you could ever learn alone, but that is all. And you will not tell it for at least a year. I have work to do first."

Quoglee's skin had turned green, making the impression of a frog complete. "You don't really have a wetboy behind that curtain, do you?" he asked.

"Of course not." Quoglee was a coward? Odd. "Do we have a deal?"

He inhaled deeply, as if trying to smell the wetboy, and slowly he regained his balance. "If you tell me why you're doing this. I don't believe it's because of some whore's dream."

She nodded. "If Logan Gyre were king, Jarl's dream of a new Cenaria might come to pass. Things wouldn't have to be how they were for my sister and me growing up, or how they are for the guild rats now."

"Sounds awfully…altruistic," Quoglee said.

Momma K didn't let his tone anger her. "I have a daughter."

"Now that I didn't know."

"I'm the richest, most powerful person in this country, maestro. But a Shinga's power dies with her, and my wealth will be taken by whoever finally murders me. Having a daughter has cost me the man I love and quite nearly my life. But as much as she endangers me, I endanger her much more. I need Logan Gyre to become king because that's the only way I can go legitimate, and going legitimate is the only way I can pass anything on to my daughter except death."

Quoglee's eyes were wide. "You don't just mean to be a merchant or even a merchant queen, do you? You mean to establish a new noble house. How would you buy such a thing?"

"That's a tale I'll tell after the coronation. Do we have a deal?"

"You want me to learn a queen's darkest secrets and make a song of it...in three days? That's ridiculous. Impossible. There isn't a bard in Midcyru who could do such a thing. But." He paused theatrically, and Momma K had to restrain herself from rolling her eyes. "But I am no mere bard. I am a genius. I'll do it."

"Sing fearlessly, maestro. I will make sure your song isn't interrupted."

Quoglee blinked rapidly and he sniffed again. "That's it. Head notes of bergamot and galbanum with a third I can't recall. The heart notes are jasmine and daffodil over base notes of vanilla, iris, amber, and forest. Nuec vin Broemar, the royal Alitaeran perfumer himself showed me that perfume. He said it was his queen's own perfume. No one else ever..." he trailed off, his eyes widening.

Momma K smiled, glad the gesture hadn't been wasted.

A small tongue wet his wide, fleshy lips. "May I just say, Madame Kirena, you frighten and intrigue me in almost equal measures."

She chuckled. "I promise you, maestro, the feeling is mutual."

Scarred Wrable was on time. He always was. This time their meeting was in the castle's statue gardens. Scarred Wrable wore the hundred-colored robe of a hecatonarch, the long sleeves covering his ritually scarred arms and hands, the chasuble covering the lattice of scars across his chest and neck. He smirked at her. "Yes, my child? Do you have sins to confess, or sins to contract?"

Terah Graesin favored him with a contemptuous stare. "You blaspheme, coming as a priest."

"Out of a hundred gods, there's got to be one with a sense of humor. What's the job, Your Highness? If people see you talking to me too long, they might think you really are confessing. They might wonder why."

"I want you to kill Logan Gyre. Sooner is better." She itched her bandaged arm. It was healing from where that damned shadow had stabbed her, but slowly.

Scarred Wrable spat on the brushed white gravel, forgetting he was supposed to be a priest. "Yah, right."

"I'll pay you twice what I paid you to kill Durzo Blint."

"Funny how you didn't tell me I was killing Blint until afterward."

"It turned out all right, didn't it?"

"Only 'cause I caught him unawares," Wrable said.

"I thought you said you fought him man to man," she said coolly.

He flushed. "I, I did, but it was a near thing. And you didn't pay me half enough."

"Oh, so that's it. Bargaining. How tiresome. Name your price, assassin."

"I'm a wetboy, as you should damn well know. I killed Durzo Blint. As to bargaining," he shook his head. "This ain't bargaining."

"How much?" Dammit, she'd worn high, thick sleeves to conceal the bandage on her arm, but it hurt, and she didn't dare touch it—not in front of Wrable, who'd tell the Sa'kagé.

"It would be a hell of a job, wouldn't it? They say Duke Gyre killed an ogre fifty feet tall at Pavvil's Grove. They say he's served by a madman with filed teeth who's ripped men clean in half and a two-legged wolf-hound and a thousand sword whores. I even heard tell of a demon that came looking to save Logan, back during the coup. That's a fearful lot of fearful friends that man has, and a fearful lot of fearful enemies a wetboy would make by killing him."

"I'll give you ten times the usual, and I'll make you a baronet, with lands." It was a princely sum, and she could tell Scarred Wrable was stunned at the amount.

"Tempting. But no. The only wetboy who'd take this job would be Hu Gibbet."

"Then send him to me!" Terah snarled.

"Can't. He's feeding the fish for taking jobs Mother Sa'kagé didn't approve. And Mother Sa'kagé has told all her little chicks, no jobs on Gyre."

"What?" Terah asked. "Don't you know who I am?"

"I will tell the Nine you tried."

Fury washed Terah to her toes. "If the Sa'kagé stands against me, so help me, I will destroy you all."

"By the High King's beard, woman!" Scarred Wrable said. "We said no to one job. There's a big difference between turning down a job and being your enemy."

"You will do this, or I will stamp you out," Terah said.

"That is a damn fool thing to say to a wetboy. But then you're a damn fool woman all round, aren't ya? Do you have any idea what Logan is doing this morning? No? While you're here trying to murder your allies, Logan is saving his."

"What are you talking about?"

"The Nine says that you have a week to take back your threats against them, and to give you a hint of what kind of a war you'd be starting, they've arranged for a small diplomatic disaster this morning. They ask that you keep in mind that future disasters need neither be small—nor diplomatic."

Ice shot down Terah's spine. They'd arranged a disaster already? Before she'd even threatened them? "How did you know?" she asked.

"We know everything," Scarred Wrable said.

"Your Majesty!" a servant came running into the statue garden. "The ambassadors from the Chantry and the Lae'knaught were both brought to your breakfast, as ordered. The stewards tried to seat both of them in the place of honor. They're furious."

"I didn't invite—" Terah turned to snarl at Scarred Wrable, but the man was gone.

33

Solon," Kaede asked, standing in the darkness outside his cell, "why does my mother hate you?"

Solon sat up, brushing filthy straw from his hair. "What has she done?" It was early morning and chilly, and Kaede wore a purple samite wrap over her shoulders. Solon was relieved he wouldn't have to spend the interview trying not to gape at her breast like a mainlander—relieved and disappointed.

"Do you know why or not?" Kaede demanded. The steel in her voice reminded him of his visions when Khali came to Screaming Winds, trying to tempt him to his death. He'd known those visions were false because Kaede wasn't furious with him. Being right had never felt worse.

Standing, Solon walked to the bars. "It will not be easy to tell or hear."

"Humor me."

Solon closed his eyes. "After I completed my training with the blue mages twelve years ago, I came home, you remember? I was nineteen. I asked my father for permission to seek your hand. He told me your family would never consent."

"My mother never stopped at anything to advance my family. That's why I never understood her hating you. She should have been pushing me to marry a prince."

Solon lowered his voice. "Your mother feared that you were my sister."

In rapid succession, emotions flitted over Kaede's face: bewilderment, incredulity, understanding, surprise, revulsion, incredulity again.

"Kaede, I don't wish to slander either of our parents. The liaison was brief—only as long as my mother's last ill-fated pregnancy. When she and the baby both died, my father took it to be the gods' judgment on him. By then your mother was pregnant. Years later when my father noticed my interest in you, he requested a green mage come to tell him whether you were his daughter. In return for determining your patrimony and keeping their silence, I was to take my schooling with the green mages. Neither they nor my father expected me to show any Talent. They merely hoped to have a Sethi prince as a friend. As it turned out, I wasn't that Talented at Healing." Though he had met Dorian there, which had changed his life, and not only in good ways. "Regardless, they told my father that you were definitely not my sister, but your mother never trusted magi. Her fears told her that you looked more like my father than yours."

Kaede's eyes were cool. "How do I know any of this is true?"

"I wouldn't lie about my father. He was a great man. It wounded me when he told me he'd been faithless to my mother. It wounded him, too. He was different after she died. Can you think of anything else that makes sense of your mother's actions? Why don't you ask her?"

"Why didn't you come back?"

Solon's face was haggard. "I was nineteen when I learned. You were barely sixteen. I tried to reassure your mother that the mages were telling the truth. She thought I was threatening her. You were young and I didn't want to poison you against her by telling you. I had an offer for more training at Sho'cendi, so I took it. I wrote to you every week, and when you never responded, I sent a friend to deliver a letter personally. He was thrown out of your family's estate and told you were betrothed and you never wanted to hear from me again."

"I was never betrothed," Kaede said.

"Which I didn't find out until later. I was going to come home then, but a prophet told me I had two paths before me: 'Storm-riving, storm-riding, by your word—or silence—a brother king lies dead,' if I came home, I would kill my brother; if, on the other hand, I went to Cenaria, I might save the south from Khalidor."

"So did you?" Kaede asked.

"What?"

"Did you save the world?" Her tone had an edge of deep anger.

"No," Solon said. He swallowed. "I hid that I was a mage from a man who was like a brother to me, a man who would have become king. When he found out, he dismissed me. The next day, he was killed by an assassin I could have stopped had I been there."

"So you come home like a whipped dog looking for scraps."

Solon gave Kaede a gentle look, seeing pain under her anger. "I came home to make things right. I have no idea what happened here. No Sethi on the mainland will talk about it."

"You took the wrong fork of the prophecy," Kaede said. "You should have killed him."

"What?"

She pulled the samite wrap tight and looked out Solon's window. "Your brother was a horror. He squandered all the goodwill the people felt for your family within a year. His invasion of Ladesh cost us three of our four fleets, and the Ladeshian counterstroke cost us the last of our colonies. He forced my brother Jarris to lead a hopeless attack, and when it failed, he threw him in the dungeon. Where he was strangled. Sijuron claimed Jarris hanged himself. He forced the great families to sponsor week-long parties that they had no way of paying for. He raised taxes on rich and poor alike but gave dispensations to his friends. He built a menagerie that housed over a thousand animals. While people begged at the gates, he ordered silk beds made for his lions, and soon began throwing those who displeased him to those beasts. He liked to train with the military, but would order men killed for not really trying when they sparred with him—or for daring to bruise the imperial flesh when they did try. He took to carrying knuckle bones which he made anyone he encountered roll—the sides ranged from winning a purse of gold to death.

"I came across him one day and he made me roll, though usually the high families were exempt. I won. He made me roll again. I won four more times, until he had no more money. He was furious, so he ordered his retainers to pay me. I realized that he was going to make me roll until I rolled my death. So I challenged him to one last roll: I said let three sides be death, and the other three be marriage. My audacity intrigued him. He said that if I was going to beggar him, I might as well be his wife." Her eyes were cold with hatred. "Sijuron was quite the wit. He only gave me two of the six sides.

"I won. He kept his word and threw a huge wedding party at my family's expense. After he fell asleep, I cut his throat. I walked back to the great hall in my bare feet and my shift, my arms covered in blood to the elbows. The party was still going. It was barely midnight and those parties always had a curious frenzy: everyone knew they might die at the king's least whim.

"Everything stopped when I walked in. I sat in the king's seat and told them what I'd done. They cheered, Solon. Someone pulled his body into the great hall and the gentle nobles of this empire ripped him apart with their bare hands. I've been undoing the damage he inflicted on this kingdom ever since. In nine years, I haven't been able to fix half of what he destroyed in three."

Solon was aghast. "And you never married."

"Never remarried."

"Oh."

"I've been too busy. Besides, they call me the Black Widow, those who hate me. I don't mind. It's good that they fear me. For all that I'm a hundred times the monarch your brother was, I made missteps early and alienated some who might have been friends. I have learned since, but some men will never forgive a slight. My hold on this throne is a daily struggle—one that you could easily upset."

"I have no desire for a crown. I will swear that in front of all the court."

"Then what is it you want, Solon?"

His eyes never wavered. "Just you," he said.

"There is no just me," she snapped. "I am queen, but look at my face and you will see the holes where my clan rings were. Your cheek has never been pierced. Do you think that doesn't matter? If I am queen, what would you be?"

"Is a queen not a woman?"

"Not first."

"Is there any room beneath that crown for love?"

He saw glacial sorrow beneath the regal calm, and then it was gone. "I loved you once, Solon. When you left again, I was devastated. People prayed for your return, hoping you could restrain your brother, or later, hoping you'd replace him. I prayed for your return too, for other reasons. But you never came. I prayed even on the night of my wedding that you would come set things right. I prayed as your brother pulled me to his bed that you would burst through the doors. You didn't." Her voice was low, but cold. "Besides," she said. "I married your brother."

"But you said you—" he stopped, cursing his tactless stupidity.

She closed her eyes. "Afterward," she said. "I meant to get him so drunk that he'd pass out, but for once he wasn't in the mood to drink, and I—I was too frightened. I waited until it was over and he was asleep. Even after what he'd just done, I was barely able to cut his throat. In his sleep, he looked so much like you."

"I'm so sorry," Solon said.

She slapped him. Hard. "Don't you dare pity me. Don't you dare."

"It's not pity. It's love, Kaede. I hurt you, and I allowed you to be hurt, and I'm sorry."

"In two days, I marry Oshobi Takeda."

"You don't love him."

"Don't be stupid." Of course she didn't.

"Kaede, give me a chance. I'll do anything."

"You can watch the festivities from your cell. Goodbye, Solon."

Terah sat impatiently on the black monstrosity of a throne Garoth Ursuul had built. It had taken her half the morning to soothe the Lae'knaught and Chantry ambassadors. Her attempts to figure out who'd arranged her diplomatic disaster had been futile. Fingers pointed this way and that, and there was no telling who was lying.

Finally, Luc came in, resplendent in his cloth-of-gold Lord General's cloak, calfskin boots, and trim white tunic and breeches. "The rumors are true," he said, kneeling on the top step in front of her throne. "Logan has arrived with fourteen hundred men."

"They didn't lose anyone breaking through the Ceuran army?" Terah asked. The first report merely said that Logan had made it to the gates. Her orders not to open the gates for him had been diverted or ignored. She'd hoped the Ceurans might kill him for her.

Luc looked confused. "They didn't break through. They signed a treaty." Seeing the look on his sister's face, Luc hurried on. "When I demanded to know by what right they'd negotiated a treaty, they said by yours. They were surprised I didn't know."

Terah sagged into the throne. This had the Sa'kagé's grubby fingerprints all over it. "What are the details of the treaty?"

"I didn't ask."

"Idiot!"

He swallowed. "There are Ceuran wagons full of rice and grain going to every corner of the city. They're giving the Ceurans' food to our people."

"They let the Ceuran army inside the walls?"

"Just Lantano Garuwashi and the wagons. But the gates are still open. People are going out to the Ceuran camp and celebrating with them."

In minutes, Terah was on a balcony, looking over the city. It was a crisp autumn day, the sun bright but barely warm. Vanden Bridge was aglitter with sunlight reflected off hundreds of men in armor. "Logan's parading through the Warrens?" Terah asked. Why would he do such a thing? Who would feel safe there?

"The Rabbits worship him," Luc said.

The procession filed back to the east side and turned toward the castle. The streets had been crowded when Terah's army had paraded, but as Logan came, the city seemed to have emptied itself. The cheering itself sounded different. It scared the hell out of her.

"Summon my advisers," she said. "I need to know everything about this treaty before Garuwashi reaches the castle. Is he my ally, my vassal, or my overlord? Gods forbid, is he my husband? Go, Luc, go!"

After applying the appropriate makeup, Kylar secured Retribution to his back, dressed in loose rags so stinking and filthy he was loath to wear them, and donned a satchel full of nobleman's clothes. He reset the door's traps with poisons that would sicken but not kill and then perched on the ladder. It was early morning now and the exit was blind. He'd been waiting a quarter of an hour, attuning himself to the sounds of the street.

He heard the loud clop of a horse's hoof strike his flagstone. That was it. He waited one more second as he drew the ka'kari over his clothing and went invisible. He threw open the flagstone as a wagon passed overhead, crawled out, spun on his stomach, dropped the hidden door closed, and flung dust over the clean flagstone. The wagon's back axle caught on Retribution. It spun Kylar back around and dragged him for several feet before he twisted free. The driver cursed and looked back, but saw nothing.

Kylar stood, invisible, and made his way into an alley. He dropped the shadows and examined his rags to see what damage the ka'kari had inflicted on them this time. It wasn't bad, except for a few new holes in the back that might show Retribution. He twisted the satchel to lie across his back, affected a limp, and headed for the Heron's Rest. It was at the crossroads of Sidlin and Vanden, and thus one of the few inns in the city where he could enter in rags and leave in silks without attracting attention.

He hadn't gone two blocks when he saw the ambush. Guild kids were hiding amid the ashes and rubble that clotted the alley. Most of them held rocks, but he caught glimpses of one or two clutching Khalidoran swords, relics, no doubt, of the Nocta Hemata. There was time to turn aside, but Kylar didn't for one reason: he saw Blue. He'd forgotten to hide the money he'd promised her. She might have even lived up to her side of the bargain and moved her crew, though he doubted it.

The biggest kid in the guild was the first to stand up. He was short for sixteen, and gaunt like all of them, though he didn't have the distended belly of malnourishment that some of the littles had. He held a Khalidoran sword and his eyes darted around to the other kids for support. "Give us your coin and that bag and you can go," he said. He licked his lips.

Kylar looked around the circle. Seventeen of them, all scared witless, most of them littles. Blue was squinting at him suspiciously. He grinned at her. "I forgot to give you this," he said, fishing in a pocket for a gold coin. It was far more than he'd promised, but these kids could use it. He tossed it to her.

One of the bigs mistook the move and whipped his rock at Kylar's head. Kylar dodged and the missile nearly brained another big on the other side. That big flung his rock and in a moment, the circle exploded in flying rocks and slashing steel.

With a surge of Talent, Kylar leapt ten feet in the air, flipped, drew Retribution, coated it with the ka'kari. As he landed, he spun in a circle, Silver Bear Falls to Garran's Zephyr, hacking the blades from the hilts of three swords. From Retribution, the ka'kari released a pulse of magic that rushed over Kylar's skin.

What was that?

~Impressive. Look.~

The guild had frozen, and even those bigs who were suddenly holding broken swords were staring at Kylar, not their swords. He glanced at himself and saw that somehow he'd lost his tunic and his skin was shining as if lit from within, as if he were bursting with barely restrained power. *I didn't tell you to do that.*

~You wanted to stop them without killing them, didn't you?~

"I told you it was him," Blue said.

Kylar had an awful feeling of déjà vu. They thought he was Durzo. Had the ka'kari put that face on him, too? He was standing as Durzo had stood over a decade ago when Azoth's guild had tried to mug him. But now he was standing on Durzo's side. It looked different from here.

"It's Kylar," Blue whispered.

"Kylar," two kids echoed. The awe in their voices made it clear that they thought they were mugging a legend. Around the circle, rocks rattled to the ground. The circle drew back, the guild caught between flight and curiosity. Only now did the bigs turn wide eyes to their faintly smoking swords, a few absently rubbing limbs or ribs bruised from flying rocks.

"How do you know that name?" Kylar demanded, feeling a sudden shiver of fear.

"I heard Jarl talking at Momma K's once," Blue said. "He said you were his best friend, he said you used to be Black Dragons. And Momma K told us once that the best Black Dragon ever apprenticed with Durzo Blint. I put it together."

Kylar couldn't move. Durzo had said it long ago, the truth always comes out. If these kids knew that Kylar was a wetboy and Durzo's apprentice, there was no telling how long before an enemy knew it. It might have spilled already, or his enemies might never think to ask a bunch of guild rats. There was no way to know.

It wasn't Kylar's fault, but "Kylar" had to disappear. His time was finished. If he ever came back to Cenaria, it would have to be as a different man with a different name and different friends or none. Kylar would have to abandon everything, as Durzo had abandoned everything every ten or twenty years. It was the price of immortality.

"Please, sir," the scared big who'd first confronted him said, licking his lips again. "Apprentice Blue. She's the smartest. She deserves to get out."

"You think this is out?" Kylar snarled. "I'll be dead inside a week!" He pulled the ka'kari to his skin and sent a jolt of blue fire through it. The kids threw up their hands to shield their eyes, and when they looked again, Kylar was gone.

35

Followed by generals, bodyguards, Lord Agon, and a bluff Ceuran named Otaru Tomaki, Logan and Lantano Garuwashi strode into the throne room. Logan knelt before the throne, as did the other Cenarians; the Ceurans bowed low; Lantano Garuwashi inclined his head, rings clacking in his long red hair.

"Arise," Queen Graesin said. She was warmly regal in a soft red gown with emerald piping, and matching jewels at her ears and throat. She descended the seven steps to where Garuwashi and Logan stood. "Duke Gyre," she said, smiling, "you have served us excellently. We shall reward you as richly as you deserve." She turned to Lantano Garuwashi. "Your Highness, it is an honor. Be welcome in our court."

Logan barely kept from breathing a sigh of relief. So she had gotten his letters after all. There had been something odd in her replies, a lack of the expected sneer. Perhaps she had decided that with her rule secure, she should start acting more like a queen.

"Please, call me Garuwashi. I am no king, yet," Lantano Garuwashi said, with a little smirk and something more besides. The traditional Ceuran doubled silk half robes over loose trousers tended to hide a man's build, but Garuwashi could have dressed in a pile of old sheets and still oozed masculinity. His hair shone like red gold, pulled back in a pony tail and interwoven with dozens of other strands, like a tiger's stripes. His jaw was pronounced, his face lean and clean shaven, shoulders broad, waist small, sleeves cut shorter than usual either for freedom of movement or to show thickly muscled arms. Terah Graesin, Logan saw, appreciated them; Garuwashi returned her glances boldly.

"Nor am I a queen, yet," she said. "Though it would please me greatly if you would be my guest at my coronation."

"I would be honored. And perhaps by this time next year, you can be my guest at mine."

"May I show you around my castle?" Terah asked, extending her hand to Garuwashi and dismissing the rest of them.

From the looks in their eyes, Logan expected Lantano Garuwashi would be mounting the ramparts in no time.

36

Her name was Pricia. She was the fourteen-year-old concubine who had wept for her friends and not for herself when Garoth died. She'd hanged herself with a silk belt. She was naked, her clothing folded neatly in a pile to one side, all her beauty gone. Her face was discolored, eyes open and bulging, tongue protruding, shit running down her fair legs. Dorian touched her and found her body only slightly cooled. From his touch, her body swung slightly. It was obscene. Dorian rubbed his face.

He should have known. The concubines had probably learned that Garoth's body had been recovered even before Dorian had. For the Godking's bodyguards, the recovery meant a small reclamation of honor. To the concubines, it meant death.

The former Godking's wives would be expected to join him on his pyre. Only the virgins and the concubines the next Godking desired would be spared. Dorian had said he was claiming no one. The women thought they would all be burned.

"When did you figure it out, Hopper?"

"Your Holiness?" Hopper asked. "I'm not sure I understand the question."

"Try again."

Hopper cleared his throat, fearful. "I was with the rest of the concubines. Pricia came into this room to fetch something. I had no idea—"

"Try. Again," Dorian said coldly.

Hopper searched Dorian's face, his eyes wide, panicky. He must have seen something that satisfied him, because he said, "Ah." The mask of fear dissolved and he bowed. "I knew you were an Ursuul after I told you that you seemed different. An eccentric slave would continue as before. A pretender would redouble his efforts to appear servile."

"What is your position within the Godking's Hands?" Dorian asked.

"I am their chief," Hopper said, inclining his head.

So it was as Jenine had suspected. Who better to keep an eye on the Godking's people and secrets than a eunuch whose awkward gait made him seem a buffoon? Hopper was at the confluence of the Godking's eunuchs, concubines and wives, and servants. Through them, he had eyes on every important Vürdmeister, atheling, and general in the realm. "How did you really lose your toes?" Dorian asked.

"When His Holiness your father offered me the position, he said that would be part of the price. I welcomed the chance to make such a sacrifice." He smiled ruefully. "Being gelded, on the other hand, wasn't so welcome."

"He offered? Did you have the option to refuse?"

"Yes. His Holiness was always fair with us."

It was a new side to Garoth Ursuul, a kinder side than Dorian had known. It was unsettling. "Why didn't you expose me?"

"Because I didn't have anyone to report to, and I didn't know what you were trying to accomplish. By the time I did, you had accomplished it. It was, if you will pardon my presumption, one of my few failures as Chief of the Hands."

No wonder he didn't know what I intended. I didn't intend it.

Hopper swallowed. "Your Holiness, I suspect some of the aethelings and Vürdmeisters know what I am. I guard against mundane spying, but I have not the means to stop their vir."

It was astonishing how Dorian had blundered into success. He'd kept Hopper in the throne room the day he had seized power. The Vürdmeisters had come into the room and had seen not only a fearless Dorian, but Hopper off to one side, tacitly endorsing him. How much weight had that carried?

Dorian suddenly felt sick to his stomach. He suspected it was a lot.

He looked again at Pricia's body dangling in the room. Death was so common here that life wasn't considered sacred. Or did the cause and effect run the other way?

"What is your name, Hopper? Your real name."

"I was ordered to forget—I'm sorry, sire, my name was Vondeas Hil."

"I thought Clan Hil was annihilated." Garoth had used the krul to wipe them out.

"The Godking saved me from..." he hesitated. "From the fleshpots. He thought I had potential. I did my best to prove him right."

The fleshpots. So the krul and their feeding habits were no great secret.

"Vondeas Hil, I will remember your name and the sacrifices you have made. Will you serve me as the Chief of my Hands?"

Vondeas bowed low.

"I have questions for you. Where are my two hundred missing Vürd-meisters?"

"Vürdmeister Neph Dada sounded a religious summons when His Holiness your father died. He called all Vürdmeisters to help him bring Khali home. Currently, your Hands believe them to be in your eastern lands."

Eastern Khalidor was sparsely populated. There were no major cities there, and hadn't been since Jorsin Alkestes had turned Trayethell into Black Barrow. "They're at Black Barrow?" Dorian asked.

"In its vicinity, at least. We don't know the exact location. Spies who've attempted to infiltrate the camp haven't returned."

Well, that at least was one problem that could wait. Meisters and magi, Vürdmeisters and archmagi had been smashing themselves against Black Barrow for centuries. Neph Dada at the head of two hundred Vürdmeisters was a serious problem, but at least Dorian would have until spring to consolidate his forces—and Neph wouldn't bother putting together an army.

All Dorian's former tutor cared about was magic. Still, it was a problem that bore looking into.

"Redouble your efforts. I want to know what they're trying, and what—if anything—they've accomplished."

"Yes, Your Holiness."

"How many aethelings are completing their uurdthans?"

"Seventeen that I know of."

"How many of those are in a position to form a credible threat to me in the next six months?" Dorian asked.

"You must understand, Your Holiness, your father kept secrets even from me, so anything I tell you is complete to the best of my knowledge, and I did know more than he knew I did, but I cannot have full confidence that I knew all of his aethelings. I know that Moburu Ander lives and is attempting to subvert the wild men. I have reports that he believes himself to be some kind of prophesied High King. Your father cared little about that. He cared more that there appeared to be some evidence of collusion between Neph Dada and Moburu, though he and I believed any association between the two to be tenuous at best."

"Yes, I can't imagine Neph letting anyone live after they'd served his purpose. Nor would one of my brothers."

"The only other aetheling I know about was one I was not supposed to know, and I never learned his name. He was part of a delegation of war magi that Sho'cendi sent to recover Curoch. The magi made it as far as Cenaria, and witnessed the Battle of Pavvil's Grove, then returned to Sho'cendi, satisfied that Curoch was not present."

Dorian scowled. He had been certain that some of his brothers must be attempting to infiltrate the school of fire as he had been sent to the school of healing, but learning that one had been successful left the sick taste of betrayal in his mouth. He knew most of the magi that might have been sent on such a mission. Had he been friends with one of his own traitorous brothers? He shook his head. That was a distraction. Moburu and Neph were the real problem, and surviving until he could consolidate his men against them.

"Very well, Hopper. Thank you."

Hopper bowed once more, and when he straightened, he wore the slightly befuddled expression of Hopper once more.

"Dorian? Dorian, I've been looking all over for you," Jenine said, coming into the room.

Dorian was shocked to realize that he was still standing in a room with a hanged child. For all the good things he'd gained from learning to focus, he didn't think being able to ignore the ruin of a young girl was among them. By the God, it was a travesty, and he'd sat here, blithely contemplating politics. What was he becoming? His stomach threatened to rebel.

Jenine wore a shy smile. From where she stood, she couldn't see Pricia's hanged body. She was dressed in a simple gown of green silk that was gathered under her breasts. "I've made my decision," she said, walking forward. "I will marry you, Dorian, and I will learn to love you as you love me."

"Jenine, you shouldn't—" But he was too late. Jenine saw the hanged naked body and the first expression on the face of the woman he loved upon their betrothal was horror.

"Oh gods!" Jenine said, putting a hand to her mouth.

"I killed her," Dorian said and threw up.

"What?" Jenine asked. She didn't come to him.

"She killed herself rather than be forced to burn on Garoth's pyre," Hopper said quietly.

Dorian was on his knees. He blinked his eyes and grabbed a rag off the floor to wipe the vomit from his mouth. It was only after he wiped his beard clean that he looked at the cloth in his hand. It was Pricia's underclothes. They still smelled of her perfume.

He vomited again and staggered to his feet. This time he wiped his mouth on his cloak and turned so he couldn't see Pricia's body. "Hopper," he said. "Please take care of her. And double the watches on the concubines. Jenine, I need you to help me make a hard decision. It may have... consequences for our engagement."

37

$\mathcal{V}$i poured cold water into the basin from a copper pitcher and splashed her face. On the narrow desk by the door, she saw a note addressed to "Viridiana." Vi didn't touch it. She'd get ready when she was good and ready. The room was terrible. More like a broom closet. The unfinished stone walls were barely far apart enough to fit the narrow bed with its thin straw mattress. At the foot of the bed was a chest for her belongings and the washbasin. The chest was empty. They'd even taken Vi's hair ties. Tyros possessed only what the Chantry gave them. In Vi's case, that meant one ill-fitting white tyro's dress. The infuriating thing was that she knew that they had a dress that fit perfectly, as if Master Piccun had a fit of genius as he worked with what should have been terminally uninspiring wool and had somehow conquered the cloth to make Vi look beautiful.

That, obviously, was not the intended effect. That dress had been spirited away, and this white sack put in its place. They hadn't bothered tailoring a shift for her. The one she'd woken in was obviously used, if—she hoped—clean, and the previous owner had been fatter than she was tall. The shift didn't even come down to Vi's knees.

Vi brushed her hair back irritably. They'd taken her damn hair ties. She wasn't going to her lectures. She wasn't leaving the room. They'd taken enough. She looked around the room for something she could use. Her eyes fell on the copper pitcher. "To hell with them," she said to activate her Talent as she ripped off the handle. In a minute, her hair was pulled back into a fiercely tight braid. "To hell with them," she said again, and squeezed the copper into a tight circle binding her hair.

She picked up the note and unfolded it. "Viridiana, after your classes this morning, please come to the private dining hall. Elene wishes to meet you. Sister Ariel"

Vi couldn't breathe. Elene? Oh, fuck. She'd known Elene would show up eventually, but so soon?

The door burst open and a wild-eyed, frumpy teenager stared around the room suspiciously, her arms raised as if she were summoning vast powers. "What's going on here?" the girl demanded. "You were using magic! Twice! Don't deny it."

Vi laughed, first nervously, then openly, glad for the distraction. The girl was practically wheezing from running. Her cheeks were flushed, sweat beading on her pale forehead under dark hair. She was fat enough and short enough that Vi wondered if this lard barrel had been the prior owner of her shift. She was perhaps fifteen, her white cotton dress edged with blue, and a brooch of gold scales prominent on her chest. "You got me," Vi said.

"You admit it!"

Vi raised an eyebrow. "Of course. Now get out. And knock next time."

"It's forbidden!"

"Knocking's forbidden?" Vi asked.

"No."

"Then try it next time, Chunky."

"My name is Xandra, and I'm the Floor Monitor. You used magic, twice. That's two days in the scullery for your first offense. And you disrespected me. That's a week!"

"You little shit."

"Swearing! Another day! They told me you'd be trouble." Xandra was shaking. It made her fat jiggle.

"You've got to be fucking joking," Vi said.

"Disrespect, swearing again! That's it! You'll report to the Mistress Jonisseh for a switching immediately."

"You call that disrespect, you squealing sow?" Vi stepped forward. Xandra opened her mouth and raised her arms. Vi said, "Graakos."

The shield snapped in place instantly, and whatever Xandra threw at her grazed right off it. Vi grabbed the girl's arm, twisted and heaved her out of the room. Xandra slid a good ten paces across the hallway's polished floor. As Vi stepped into the hall, she saw at least thirty little girls staring at her, wide-eyed, most of them under twelve.

"Please knock next time," Vi said. She turned on her heel and slammed the door.

From the hall, she heard Xandra quaver, "Slamming a door, that's—"

Vi opened the door and stared daggers at the girl, who was still lying in a heap against the far wall. The words dried up in Xandra's mouth. Vi slammed the door again, and sat on her bed, picked up the note, tried not to cry—and failed.

38

*I*n all his life, Kylar had never seen the people of the Warrens so happy. Agon's Dogs had stayed with the wagons full of grain and rice to manage the distribution. All the Dogs were members of the Sa'kagé, and they had taken it into their minds to make sure that the food was fairly distributed. "We got our bit coming," Kylar heard a Dog tell a scowling Sa'kagé basher. "I've heard it from high up. Now make sure those guild rats share!"

The Rabbits joined long queues that moved slowly but steadily forward, and a hard-bitten old coot broke out a tin whistle, sat on his new sack of rice, and began to play. In moments, the Rabbits were dancing. A woman soon had several pots boiling and anyone who dropped a measure of their rice or grain into one pot immediately could take a full, seasoned measure from another. She served bread and rice and soon wine. Someone offered herbs, someone else butter, another meat. In no time, it was a feast.

In a break between songs, one of Agon's Dogs stood up and yelled. "Ya might recognize me. I'm Conner Hook, and I grew up in this neighborhood. I seen ya and I know ya and I'm tellin' ya now, by the High King's bollocks, if any of ya come tru' the line twice, I'm callin' out yer name, and we're gonna fookin' add yer ass to the meat pot, got it?"

A cheer went up—and the line thinned considerably. For the Rabbits, to whom corruption was the unquestioned norm, it was a gift as unexpected as the free food itself. Kylar listened, and heard many a toast to Logan Gyre and many variations of the tale of him slaying an ogre and teary, drunken renditions of his speech establishing the Order of the Garter, and the word "king" muttered a dozen times. He smiled darkly, then froze.

He glimpsed a lean woman with long blonde hair on the far side of the square. In contrast to the Rabbits, she was so clean she was radiant, and he caught a flash of white teeth as she smiled. His heart stopped. "Elene?" he whispered.

The woman disappeared around a corner. Kylar went after her, pushing and dodging his way through the jubilant, dancing crowd. When he got to the corner, she was already fifty paces down the twisting alley, turning onto yet another. He ran after her with the speed of his Talent.

"Elene!" He grabbed her shoulder and she jumped, startled.

"Hi...Kylar, right?" Daydra asked. She had been one of Momma K's girls. Playing the virgin was her specialty. From a distance, she looked like Elene.

Kylar's heart lurched, and he wasn't sure if it was more from disappointment or relief. He didn't want Elene here. He didn't want her in this pit of a city or anywhere nearby when he murdered the queen, but at the same time, he wanted to see her so badly it ached.

She smiled at him awkwardly. "Um, I don't work the sheets anymore, Kylar."

He flushed. "No, I wasn't—I'm sorry. I..." He turned and made his way to the castle.

39

Feir Cousat and Antoninus Wervel emerged from Quorig's Pass after noon. As they approached Black Barrow, the evergreen forest that carpeted the foothills ended. Feir hunkered down in his coat against the deep autumn chill and climbed a low rise. The sight took his breath away. No one had lived in Black Barrow for seven hundred years. The land should have been long overgrown with grass, trees, undergrowth. It wasn't. The grass, at the least, should have been an autumnal brown. It wasn't. Seven centuries ago, the decisive battle of the War of Shadow had been fought in the early summer, and the grass at Feir's feet was still short and green. He saw the raw depression where a farmer's stone fence had been pulled from the earth, the stones taken into the city so that they might not be used as missiles by the enemy's siege engines. Nothing had grown in the bare depressions that marked where this fence had stood—seemingly only days before. Time had stopped here.

Lifting his eyes, Feir saw more: ruts from the passage of wagons, grass beaten flat by marching feet, holes for the firepits and latrine pits of an abandoned military camp. But no tents or tools. Anything that could be looted had been taken long ago, but everything that remained stayed unchanged.

That didn't only apply to the land. Two hundred paces away, the bodies began. First, a few marking the edge of the battle, and then hundreds, and then thousands, until in the distance the ground lay under a black blanket of the dead. The epicenter of death was a perfectly round dome of black rock the size of a small mountain covering the city and the hill where the castle had once been. At the base of the dome, siege engines on broken wheels, half-consumed by fires, tottered but hadn't fallen despite the centuries.

The dome was surrounded by a larger circle of magic in the land itself, miles across, called the Dead Demesne. Outside the circle, time continued, wind blew, rain fell. Inside the Dead Demesne...they didn't.

Feir rolled his great shoulders, readying himself. He cupped his hands close to his face and conjured a fire with his Talent. Then he stepped across the boundary into the circle of death. Nothing happened. He let the fire die.

"That's odd," he said aloud. Antoninus grunted in assent. Feir squinted at the air.

The Dead Demesne—like Black Barrow itself—was Emperor Jorsin Alkestes' work. He had made it lethal to use the vir within the circle, but because vir had similarities to the Talent, there was always some dissonance in the circle when anyone tried using the Talent. Little things would be different, like mage fire being red instead of orange. But Alkestes' weave was gone.

Feir rubbed his scruffy beard. It was good for him. He wouldn't have to factor it into the work he'd come here to do. But someone had broken what Jorsin made. That was not good.

Examining the air over the circle in the same way he had examined the circle in Ezra's Wood, Feir studied the magic. He could feel an emptiness in the weaves—the great magics Jorsin had woven didn't break without leaving a trace. Unfortunately, he couldn't tell much except that that the weaves had been broken recently. But to break a spell Jorsin Alkestes had made using Curoch would have required someone incredibly powerful here wielding some artifact, or a couple of hundred magi or Vürdmeisters working together. Feir couldn't imagine anyone with a shred of sense or decency participating in such a scheme. So that meant Vürdmeisters.

Jorsin's other weaves, the ones sealing the ground and sealing the dead, were perfectly intact. Feir didn't think they would be so easily broken, either. He hoped not.

Feir scanned the distant trees, suddenly queasy that unfriendly eyes might be hiding within them. He walked across the plain quickly, the air curiously odorless even as he approached the first body.

The creature was the black of a bloated corpse and man-shaped but ill-proportioned. Its arms were too long, its face too long, lower jaw jutting forward, ragged hooks of teeth stabbing up into the air from its lower jaw, mismatched black and blue eyes staring. It was massively muscled. Its skin was hairy, bordering on fur, and it had neither clothes, nor weapon. It was a krul. The meisters could not make life, but they could mimic and mock it. There were, Dorian had once told Feir, dark mirrors of almost every natural creation.

Feir and Antoninus walked on. It was going to get worse. A lot worse.

Soon, dead krul lay everywhere. Thousands had been killed bloodlessly by Jorsin's magic, but thousands more bore the marks of their deaths. Ugly faces had been crushed by war hammers or flailing hooves. Chests were caved in from being trampled. Throats were cut, torsos disemboweled, eyes hung by optic nerves from broken sockets, and blood glistened freshly in the wounds, never drying, never congealing.

Paths had been cleared through the bodies, and they followed them mutely. It wasn't long before Feir saw a human arm amid the krul, then a leg that appeared to have been half eaten. The bodies were piled knee deep on either side of them. Then they began passing krul who'd been killed by magic. There were great craters in the battlefield empty of all but pulverized scraps of meat. Others had been burned or cut in half or shocked. Some had torn their faces to ribbons with their own claws.

The krul began to vary, too. Pure white krul with spiraling rams' horns led every unit of twelve, and larger ones seven feet tall appeared more rarely still. They walked past an entire platoon of four-legged feline krul the size of horses, with jet-black skin, sparse hair like a rat's tail, and exaggerated maws like a wolf. Rarer still were those like bears, easily twelve feet tall and with thick fur the color of new blood. As they trekked through the vast battlefield, it seemed every natural animal had found a dark mockery here. Bats, ravens, eagles, fanged horses, horned horses, even dark, red-eyed elephants carrying archers lay in ignominious death.

"The monsters," Antoninus said quietly. "Was nothing holy to them?"

Feir followed Antoninus's gaze and saw the krul children. They were most beautiful of all the krul, with balanced features, big child's eyes, pale skin close to a human shade, and long claws for fingers. These still wore their human clothes. Even the looters hadn't touched them. Feir almost gagged. They moved on, ever closer to the great black dome.

After a while, Feir felt inured to the horror. There were a thousand thousand permutations of death, krul of every shape and size and sometimes men and often horses, but the magical fixedness of it, the lack of smell, the stillness of the air, lent it a certain unreality, as if the dead were figures carved of wax.

If Jorsin was to be believed, one million one hundred thirteen thousand eight hundred and seventy-nine krul lay dead here. Various magi scholars had guessed that between five hundred thousand and a million krul would face them. Against fifty thousand men. The rest of Jorsin's armies had been drawn away by his own treacherous generals.

Then Jorsin had done all this, with Curoch—the very blade Feir had gone into the Wood to retrieve. Of course, he had only retrieved instructions. Curoch was safe in Ezra's Wood forever, and thank the gods for that.

"Well, here we are," Antoninus said as they finally touched the dome of Black Barrow. "Now we can forge our counterfeit Ceur'caelestos and save Lantano Garuwashi and all his men. Indeed, maybe all the south."

Feir said, "All we have to do is find Ezra's secret entrance to Black Barrow, find Ezra's workshop and his gold tools, find seven broken mistarille swords, rediscover a forging technique every present-day Maker says is a myth, find one giant ruby, and avoid detection by a couple of hundred Vürdmeisters plotting gods know what."

"Oh," Antoninus said, waggling his great, single kohled eyebrow, "here I thought it was going to take all winter."

A knock sounded on Vi's door hours later. "It's Sister Ariel. May I come in?"

"I can't stop you. There's no lock on the door," Vi said.

Sister Ariel came in. She said nothing for a time, staring around the bare room with apparent nostalgia.

"What do you want?" Vi asked.

"A bit nervous about going to the lecture, huh? Or was it your meeting with Elene that's got you acting more like a tyrant than a tyro?" Sister Ariel said.

"I fucked up," Vi said, sulking, knowing it, hating it, and sulking anyway. "Now they hate me, like always."

"They're twelve years old. They don't dare hate you."

"Is that supposed to make me feel better?"

"I'm not terribly concerned about your feelings, Vi. However, given the difficulties of your case and that I discovered you, and most of all because I couldn't come up with an excuse quickly enough, I've been put in charge of your tutelage."

Vi groaned.

"My feelings exactly. First of all, this room is entirely inappropriate for you."

"I get a better room?"

"You get to share a room. You were given a single in deference to your age. That was a mistake. You're isolated enough as is. As of this afternoon, you'll have a roommate. In case you're curious, the room will be only slightly larger than this one." Vi pitched back onto the bed. "Now, since you are my responsibility, you'll go to lecture. Now. Elene will have to wait until later."

Vi didn't move.

"Do we need to repeat certain lessons we learned on the trail?" Ariel asked.

Vi stood quickly.

"And by the by, lest you being put under my care be seen as a reward, all the punishments that your unfortunate floor monitor imposed will be carried out, as well as a few of my own. Follow." Ariel left, and Vi had no choice but to follow her like a whipped dog.

The Chantry had been constructed with beauty and practicality as its first considerations. Cost had obviously been no object. Even here, in the tyros' area, the arched ceilings were ten feet high, incised with a different pattern in every quarter. The tyros occupied the lowest level of the Chantry, though storerooms, archives, and the like lay beneath the water line. Because it was housed entirely within the giant statue of the Seraph, the interior of the Chantry was arranged in circles: living quarters arrayed along the quadrasecting halls, and lecture halls around the outside to take advantage of the sunlight necessary for magic.

Though white marble predominated, the tyros' floor didn't feel austere. A castle with so much stone would be cold and dark, but here the floors were warmed to welcome bare feet, and the ceiling itself was luminous. The walls were filled with bright, cheery scenes to comfort girls away from home for the first time: rabbits, unicorns, cats, dogs, horses, and animals Vi had never seen played together. They were drawn fancifully, but exquisitely.

Vi touched a painted pink puppy curled in sleep next to an impossibly friendly lion. Its eyes opened and it licked toward her fingers, its pink tongue pressing against the wall as if it were just on the other side of a glass. Vi yelped and jumped backward, clawing at her belt for a dagger that wasn't there.

"His name's Paet," Sister Ariel said. "He was one of my favorites. He doesn't wake until noon."

"What?"

"It's a timepiece. Watch this," Sister Ariel said, stopping outside one of the classrooms.

Gently, the ceilings pulsed violet, red, yellow, green, and blue in succession as a bell tolled. Seconds later, several hundred girls between ten and fourteen poured into the halls in a flood of noise and motion. Vi saw more curious glances than frightened ones. Apparently the rumors hadn't spread to the entire school yet. She folded her arms and scowled.

"Class starts in five minutes. Can you read and write?"

"Of course," Vi said. Her worthless mother had done that much.

"Good. I'll collect you at noon. Oh, and Vi? If you have a question during class, raise your hand. Sister Gizadin is a stickler. When called on, stand with your hands behind your back. If you don't, they'll think you're being disrespectful. Oh, and no magic. And remember everything. Lectures are arranged in triads to help with that."

"Triads?" Vi asked, but Sister Ariel was already gone.

Five minutes later, Vi was seated in a too-small chair at a too-small desk in the front row of a lecture hall. Three walls were unadorned white stone. The east wall, however, was as transparent as glass. The late morning sun poured down, bathing Lake Vestacchi and the snow-capped mountains beyond in light. The lake was the deepest blue Vi had ever seen, and dozens of fishing boats dotted the surface.

Vi barely noticed when her whispering classmates suddenly quieted. A squat Sister tut-tutted and the wall shimmered, becoming opaque white like the others in seconds. Without preliminaries, Sister Gizadin began: "There are three reasons glamours should be used sparingly. Anyone?" Not a girl made a move. "First, glamours are unpredictable. Second, glamours are unnatural. Third, glamours are unappreciated.

"*Unpredictable*. First, a glamour may affect only men or only women or only children. Second, a glamour may affect some people much more strongly than others. Third, a glamour will attract people according to their own predispositions. It may impart, particularly in men, an overwhelming sexual desire for the caster. Or it may impart a slavish servitude, where the person finds in you every good thing they could imagine. Or it may impart a simple attractiveness and persuasiveness.

"*Unnatural*. First, a glamour can operate by exaggerating a quality you already have. That could be exaggerating your inherent attractiveness, or it could exaggerate people's perception of your courage or honor or strength, or it could exaggerate a bond such as friendship that you share with the glamour's target. Second, a glamour may feign the attractive features of another person. Third and most powerfully, a glamour may tap the subject's mind for what he finds most attractive. One man might say the caster was blonde and blue-eyed whilst the man beside him would swear she was buxom and green-eyed. But this type of glamour is unusual and challenging to use. And obviously, if the two men talk after that maja leaves, they will notice the discrepancy.

"That leads us to the third reason glamours should be used sparingly: Glamours are unappreciated. First—" she stopped, irritated. "Viridiana, stop fidgeting. You have a question?"

"What if you can control all that?" Vi asked, standing up and putting her arms behind her back, feeling like a child. "It's not that hard."

All the girls in the class looked at Vi as if they couldn't believe she'd dared speak.

"Do you really wish me to believe that you have natural mastery of one of the more difficult relational spells?"

"I didn't say mastery," Vi said defensively. The truth was, she was still off-kilter, the thought of having to go talk to Elene hanging over her like a death sentence—which, she realized, it might actually be.

"Unless you've actually cast this spell, sit and be silent."

Vi paused, then scowled. "I have."

"Oh? Pray tell." Sister Gizadin gave a condescending smirk.

Fine, bitch. "I was fucking this guy and he was having trouble waking the snake," Vi said. Sister Gizadin's eyes went huge. "So I kicked in a sex glamour. That usually does it in about five seconds. I mean, it's embarrassing. If you use too much, they're done before they get naked. With this one, the glamour did nothing. In your terms, I guess I was exaggerating my natural attractiveness. So I played around with it until I felt something give. His eyes glazed over and he started talking about my boyish figure—while holding two hands full of tit."

Sister Gizadin's mouth was open, but no words came out.

"Anyway," Vi said, "it wasn't hard. I mean, I'm most experienced with glamours for sex, but I figured those out with a pointer or two from a courtesan, so with Sisters teaching me, how hard can the other glamours be?"

For a long time, no one said anything. Vi noticed belatedly that everyone was gaping at her. Sister Gizadin's mouth closed. She began to speak, and then stopped. Finally she looked past Vi to a buck-toothed twelve-year-old who raised her hand. "Yes, Hana?" Sister Gizadin asked.

Hana stood with her hands behind her back. "Please, Sister, what kind of mage is a courtesan?"

Vi laughed.

That snapped Sister Gizadin out of it. "Sit, both of you!"

They sat.

"Unappreciated," Sister Gizadin said. "Even if people's perceptions of the caster are not altered, there is still a feeling of wrongness after a glamour. During the spell, they won't notice they're being manipulated, but afterward, especially if they were wildly manipulated, they'll realize that their reactions were out of proportion. The irresponsible use of glamours is one reason why magae have historically been distrusted. No one wants to

be manipulated, and in essence, glamours are all about manipulation. That's all. Class dismissed."

It was as if Vi had never spoken. Sister Gizadin didn't answer Vi's question, or Hana's. Indeed, she didn't seem affected in the slightest, except, Vi realized later, that she'd forgotten to teach the last portion of her lecture in triads.

Momma K adjusted the topazes hanging in her long hair, examining herself critically in Master Piccun's mirror. She'd found a note on her bedside table when she woke. It was written in Durzo's cramped hand, "I live. I will come for you." That was all. Bothersome man. She'd gotten up and dyed her hair one last time: a natural gray. No, silver, she decided.

Then she'd come here. It hadn't been easy to order Master Piccun to make her blue dress for the coronation more muted and higher cut than any she'd ever worn, but at least his hands had strayed when he took her measurements—as they always did. When his hands stopped wandering, she would know she was old.

"You are extraordinary," he said. "I have this meeting with every one of my beautiful clients. Normal women make new compromises with age daily, so it's less of a shock to them. Beauties seem to run into it all at once, and it happens here. They ignore my advice and order the latest fashion one more time, and then they see themselves. Some accuse me of making them look bad on purpose. Others stare at the old stranger in the mirror, shocked. Always there are tears."

"I'm not much for crying."

"You know when I'm only flattering, Gwinvere. The body is my canvas, and I tell you, your body is years from that day of tears. You have something ineffable. You walk through life like a dancer, all strength and beauty and grace. I have this client, stunning girl, a bit muscular to be fashionable—I told her to start sitting on her ass and eating chocolates—but saved from being boyish by these hips and tits that would make a goddess green. By Priapus, the girl can wear anything—and will. I'd make her clothes for free, just to see her wear them."

"Now you're going to make me jealous," Gwinvere said. He knew she was kidding, though a small part of her wasn't. Aemil Piccun was talking about Vi Sovari.

"What I mean to say is that if I put up portraits of her and you at her age, a man would be hard-pressed to choose between you, but in person, it's no contest. Her beauty is wasted on her. She is divorced from her flesh, joyless. You, on the other hand, have this ability to enjoy a man enjoying you on any of a dozen levels. If I could imbue a dress with what you have, I would not be a tailor, I would be a god. Of all my clients, you will always be my favorite, Gwinvere."

She smiled, oddly moved. With Master Piccun, you always expected lechery, but you never expected him to mean anything by it. Now, he meant every word he said. "Thank you, Aemil. You warm my heart."

He grinned. "I don't suppose I've warmed any other parts of you, hmm?"

She laughed. "I'm tempted, but there are so many women who will be needing discounts on their dresses for the coronation. They'd be so disappointed if I exhausted you."

"It's cruel to ruin a man by showing him what an artist of the bedchamber can do, and then denying him your talents for fourteen years straight."

"Fourteen?" she asked.

"Fourteen long, long years."

"Mmm," she said, relaxing almost imperceptibly. "It has been a long time."

He stepped close.

Momma K slipped away, opened the door, and beckoned the lissome noblewoman waiting in the front room. "Careful, sweetie, I think he'll want to start with the discount."

The noblewoman gasped. Master Piccun coughed. "Cruel, Gwinvere. Cruel."

41

Jenine had been spending her days trying to decide if Garoth Ursuul's wives and concubines would die. Dorian waited for her in the black rock halls that she usually lightened with her presence. But today, and for the days since he'd laid the question before her, that sunny presence had been clouded.

"My love," he said gently, "we have to decide today."

"Part of me hates you for making me decide, but this is what it is to be a queen, isn't it? You are wise, milord. If you decided for me, I would doubt you either way."

He breathed. When she'd said "part of me hates you," his heart stopped beating. Every Godking for centuries had been cremated with his wives and concubines, save for a few concubines that the next Godking wished for himself. If Dorian kept his first promise to Jenine, every woman in the harems would be obliged to throw themselves—or be thrown—onto Garoth Ursuul's pyre, with only the dubious reward of getting to spend all eternity as his slaves. The alternative was to claim all of them, which the Khalidorans would see as selfish and dishonoring to the dead, but a God-king was not expected to be selfless.

There was a third alternative, of course. Dorian could outright ban the practice of throwing the living on funeral pyres. In a few years, he intended to do exactly that. But he was already being painted as a soft southerner. The Vürdmeisters were sharks, and mercy would hatch a dozen plots against his life. What would Solon have told him to do? Dorian pushed the question aside: Solon would have told him to get the hell out of Khalidor.

"In some ways," he said, "if we are to change what marriage is to mean in these lands, it makes sense to let them die. From there we have a blank slate."

"So we throw away eighty-six women's lives to prove that women have value?"

Dorian said nothing. He offered his hand and she took it. They began walking toward his apartments. "I don't know how to take the cruelty out of the choice."

"I don't know if it will work, milord." Jenine always called him milord. She couldn't call him Dorian, of course. "Your Majesty" was too distant. "Your Holiness" was out of the question, and she knew what *Wanhope* meant: she refused to call her bridegroom "Despair." "There's something wrong with these girls. Did you know they're taken from their families when they're nine years old? They're trained to be exactly and only what the Godking wants. The only currency they know is the Godking's favor. They're not allowed to learn to read. They never go anywhere. They never meet anyone but each other and the eunuchs. It twists them. Yet they're not innocents. They gossip and backstab as much as anyone. Perhaps more, because they've nothing useful to occupy them. All the same, they're not animals either, though they've been treated as such. And most of them are just girls. I can't ask them to all die for me. You must claim them, milord, but I ask this: that you give each the choice. These women have never chosen anything for themselves. Let them choose now."

"You...you think some of them will choose death?"

"I heard women describe nights with Garoth that left them literally with scars—and they were proud of them. They really believe that your father was a god. Some do want to serve him forever."

Dorian felt like a stranger in his own land. He said nothing as they walked past a knot of aethelings who'd stopped in the hall, prostrating themselves until he passed. At the door of his apartments, he stopped and said, "Jenine, I swear to you that those women will be my concubines in name only. They will not share my bed."

She put a finger on his lips. "Shh, my love. Don't swear about what you can't control." He had a sudden sense that he'd done this before. He'd dreamed it, just last night, and had forgotten the dream until this moment. But in the dream, there had been a smell, harsh stench of . . . what? "If nothing else, I can control myself, my queen."

She smiled a sad smile too wise for her years. "Thank you, but I won't hold you to it."

"I'll hold myself to it."

She squeezed his hand, and then the sharp tang of vir hit his nostrils. He turned to the prostrate aethelings too late. Two boys without a mustache between them were standing, twin balls of green fire streaking toward Dorian and Jenine. They were barely five paces away.

Dorian watched, expecting the green missiles to pierce his flesh. He was reaching for the vir, but it was too late to pull a shield together—but then the vir was there, already forming, already acting to protect him, pushing hard from below, only asking his assent.

Yes.

The green missiles were within a hand's breadth when the vir leapt up. The green fires twisted away, looped behind him and Jenine as Dorian threw his arms around her, and sped back toward the youths. There was a sound like eggs breaking and then sizzling meat as the missiles took each aetheling in the forehead, cracking their heads and scorching their brains, smoke puffing from perfectly round holes before they dropped to the ground, dead.

Dorian's shields sprang up around him and Jenine only then, though he'd acted as fast as he could. There was no other sound in the hall.

The dead children gaped at him, brains smoking. The living ones didn't dare look up. Fury rushed through Dorian. They hadn't just tried to kill him; they'd tried to kill Jenine. He looked at the Vürdmeister who was in charge of these aethelings. The man was cowering, prostrate, at the back of the line. Dorian couldn't think. The vir lashed out from his hand, yanked the man to his feet by his throat. He gave a strangled yelp, waving his hands in denial, before a huge fist of Dorian's vir smashed his chest against the rock wall.

Blood exploded over the wall and the aethelings at the back of the line, but no one moved. With effort, Dorian dropped the shields, pushed the vir down. His head was throbbing.

The aethelings had moved against him. It was a stupid, childish attempt, and it had almost succeeded because he hadn't thought to guard himself against boys who were eight years old. There'd been no follow-up to take advantage of the distraction, so Dorian couldn't know if the children had been directed by a Vürdmeister, unless it was simply to test Dorian's strength or to see if the vir would save him. In some ways, it wasn't important.

What was important was that something had to be done about the aethelings. They were vipers. If eight- and nine-year-olds had already acted, there was no doubt that the older boys were plotting, and a wedding would give them all sorts of opportunities. Delay looked like weakness, and weakness put not only himself but also Jenine in peril. That, he wouldn't tolerate.

Jenine started crying, and Dorian banished the aethelings and comforted her, but his mind was far away, and every thought was bloody.

42

Kylar was dressed in servant's garb, and there were many new servants in the castle as Tcrah's retinue meshed with the remnants of Garoth's which had meshed with the remnants of King Gunder IX's, so getting into the servants' entrance was no problem. Once inside, he headed to the scullery and grabbed a tray of freshly polished silver goblets, balanced it in one hand, and walked toward the Great Hall. In the bustle and hum of activity and shouted orders and snarls of men and women under pressure working together for the first time, no one paid any attention to him. He was invisible not because of the ka'kari, but because of the practiced anonymity Durzo had spent so many hours teaching him.

For the moment, all of the tables were stored in the servants' room adjacent to the Great Hall. After the coronation, the tables would be carried in fully set. The goblets went onto one of the high tables adjacent to the queen's table. Unfortunately, her table was still empty: it wouldn't be set until immediately before the banquet, and then only under the watchful eyes of the Queen's Guard would her cupbearer lay out the castle's finest goldware for the high table with his own hand.

These were not insurmountable difficulties. However, Terah Graesin didn't have a reputation as a drinker, so if Kylar used a poison mild enough that her cupbearer wouldn't be affected when he tested her wine, she might not drink a lethal dose. The same was true of her eating utensils. She was a dainty eater.

So after setting down the goblets, Kylar grabbed a pile of rags dirtied in polishing the tables and headed down a back hallway. He walked purposefully, though he had no idea where the castle's laundry was. He scanned the ceilings and walls for the spy holes and crawlspaces that honeycombed the castle. When he saw a crawlspace, he leapt, grabbed the edge with his fingertips, and pulled himself up.

Inches from his face, a decaying web of vir crisscrossed the opening. Kylar's fingers were almost touching it. Hanging on by one hand, Kylar rolled the ka'kari through the web. The web popped harmlessly like a soap bubble.

From the secret passages, it was only a matter of finding his way. Kylar crawled or walked as the passages required and kept the ka'kari over his eyes so he could see every magical trap. In an hour, he'd found the royal treasury. The opening here was covered by stout iron bars.

The ka'kari made short work of that.

You know, before you came along, assassinating a queen would have been hard.

~Is that a complaint?~

As the sheered bars came off in Kylar's hands, he stopped. *I'm like a god.* The thought jolted him. For some reason, it was the look on Blue's face that did it. Perhaps children didn't bother to cover their awe, or perhaps it was that he had been a Blue himself not so long ago. But as he thought about the awe in the guild rats' faces, he remembered the other faces: Caernarvon's Shinga's, Hu Gibbet's, even the Godking's face had held a note of awe. For the guild rats, it was a dream, for the others, a nightmare. But the incredulity was the same. He was the impossible.

For some reason, it had never sunk in. He was still Kylar, maybe still Azoth underneath it all. But now. . . . This was so easy. Kylar had longed to be more than guild rat. He'd longed to be more than wetboy. Now, he was more than a man. The rules didn't apply to him. He was stronger than a man, faster, a hundred times more powerful. Immortal. Death was temporary. If the most basic mortal concern—dying—didn't apply to him, what else didn't?

It was an intoxicating thought, but a lonely one. If he was more than a man, what communion could he have with men? Or women? The thought brought Elene sharply to the fore. His chest felt hollow. He would give his other arm if he could be with her again, his head in her lap, her fingers running through his hair, accepting him.

Odd, that. He could think of Elene with love, but as soon as his thoughts wandered near the hazy line of appreciation and desire—there, there was Vi with her red hair nearly glowing, the curve of her neck begging to be nuzzled, her eyes a challenge, nubile figure tempting him. He could sense her, somewhere far to the east. She was sleeping. Sleeping? At almost dinner time? Life at the Chantry must not be so bad.

He imagined slipping into bed behind her. Her hair was unbound, spilling over her pillow like a copper waterfall. Her hair was glorious, like some god had captured the last rays of the dying sun and given them to her. Kylar leaned close and inhaled deeply. Vi sighed in her sleep. She burrowed into him, her body conforming to his. His breath caught.

For a moment, he swore he wasn't wearing any clothes. Then they were back. Vi let out a moue of disappointment. *What the hell am I doing?* Certain now that he was indeed clothed, Kylar relaxed fractionally. Vi's breathing was slow and even. Kylar brushed a lock of hair behind her ear to see her face. She looked somehow smaller, more fragile, but no less beautiful. Without the customary tension, her face looked younger. She looked her age. Unlike Terah Graesin, whom sleep paled, sleep lent Vi's features grace.

Terah Graesin. The castle. *Where the hell am I?*

Seeing gooseflesh rising on Vi's arm, Kylar pulled the blanket up over both of them. He ran a hand gently from her shoulder down her arm. His hand continued down her hip to her leg. She was wearing a loose short shift and he stopped when his hand touched her warm, smooth skin. Then his hand came back up her leg, under her shift. He was a man out of control, his pulse pounding in his ears, the room indistinct, thoughts indistinct, only his nerves alive.

Her leg was lean, tight even in sleep. He trailed his hand over her hip. His fingertips glided over the depression between hip and navel, and then over her dancer's stomach, the perfect blend of warmth and soft over hard. He traced her lowest ribs as she breathed, still evenly though perhaps not so deeply as before, glorying in her. Kylar wasn't tall or thickly built, but Vi's slender form against him made him feel strong and tender and manly.

He leaned close, breathing her in, and then he kissed her neck. Goose-flesh rose, and this time he knew it wasn't the cold. He kissed her again, tracing her hairline. His fingers brushed the underside of her breast Her back arched, grinding her buttocks against his groin. He was naked once more and her shift had ridden up. She was hot against him. "Yes," her whole body whispered, "yes."

A key grated in a lock. The sound was out of place. Then the other key grated, popping open a second lock.

~Kylar!~

I'm back. Sorry, I was... elsewhere.

~I'm in your body, Kylar. Some things you can't hide from me. Tumescence is one of them.~

Tumescence? What? Oh, God. I didn't want to know that.

Below, through the screen, Kylar saw the door to the treasury open. An officious little man clucked as he gazed around the barren room. There were only three chests. He opened the smallest and Kylar caught a glimpse of the crown, but the man sighed. "Where the hell is that pillow?" he muttered. He went out, closed the door, and began locking the locks.

Kylar pulled back the screen and dropped into the room, landing silently almost on top of the chests. He pulled the stopper out of the vial, formed the ka'kari into its bulb shape and drew out a generous dose of philodunamos. He stopped the vial and tucked it back into a pouch and grabbed the crown. It was a simple, elegant piece with only a few emeralds and diamonds on it. From the paucity of precious stones and gold in the other chests, Kylar guessed the simplicity had not been a stylistic choice. He modified the ka'kari even as he pressed the bulb, giving it a narrow brush as its tip, rather than a needle. As quickly as he dared, he drew a narrow band around the inside of the crown, with a glob at the back. As soon as Terah Graesin began to sweat under the gold band on her forehead, the bottled fire would wreathe her head in flames, and the glob would cause a small explosion into the back of her head. He didn't want Terah Graesin to be publicly burned; he wanted her dead. If she lived, the people's pity might offset their negative feelings for a time. If she lived, she would accuse Logan of the deed and execute him.

The philodunamos went on evenly, and dried quickly. The first lines Kylar had painted took on a flat gold sheen close to the color of the crown itself, although Kylar could see some ridges in it. He hoped the damn stuff didn't flake off. Still, he didn't guess that anyone was going to be putting it on before the coronation. It should be fine.

He heard a key in the lock at the same time he noticed that the glob of paint at the back of the crown was still wet. Unthinking, Kylar blew on it. He cut his breath off instantly, but saw one hard edge crack open and turn red. It glowed like a coal for a moment, then dimmed, even as a key rattled in the second lock. Kylar set the crown down gingerly in the chest and widened the ka'kari into a fan. He fanned the crown furiously as the key clicked open the third lock. He drew the ka'kari over himself, disappeared, and tried not to breathe.

The officious little man held a purple velvet pillow with long gold tassels off the corners. He closed and locked the other two chests, then lifted the crown reverently with two hands—keeping his fingers on the outside, thank God—and placed it on the pillow.

He walked out of the room. Kylar jumped back up to the open screen, pulled himself into the crawlspace, and headed for a place to change into his nobleman's clothing.

Terah Graesin was dead. She just didn't know it yet.

43

$\mathcal{V}$i woke in the darkness in a cold sweat. Sister Ariel had muttered darkly about some ineptitude or other that kept Vi from getting a new room and roommate immediately, but after the dream Vi had just had, she was glad to be alone.

She got out of bed, and the moment her feet touched the warm floor, dim light bloomed in the ceiling. Vi barely noticed. She pulled on the frumpy tyro's dress and headed out the door. Her stomach felt tight and sore. As she stepped into the hall, light bloomed like a star against the wall. Then, as if an unseen hand were drawing in big, bold lines, the light became a star suspended in a spider web, which was draped between an elk's antlers. The beast regarded Vi tiredly but stood to accompany her, the star illuminating her section of the hall with warm light.

Vi forgot herself and touched the beast. The light remained, but all else faded. The web around the star was replaced by an old iron lantern. The elk disappeared and in quick strokes was replaced with a bearded, fatherly woodsman. He nodded to Vi and lifted the lamp high. She touched the figure and it faded to be replaced with a grinning dog, balancing the star on its nose. She began walking, and it walked beside her. It was amazing. This entire floor was made to be a safe place for children.

In sudden fury, she punched the wall. The dog faded and a jester replaced it. Vi choked back a sob and hurried to the stairs at the center of the building. When she arrived at Sister Ariel's room, the door swung open before Vi knocked. "Come in," Sister Ariel said. She handed Vi a steaming cup of ootai. Her eyes looked bleary.

Vi was speechless. She stepped inside and took the cup in her left hand.

"Sit," Sister Ariel said. Her room wasn't large, and most of it was covered in piles of books and scrolls, but there were two chairs.

Vi sat.

"Pay attention and hold still," Sister Ariel said. She took Vi's swollen right hand and tsked. "*Savaltus.*" Pain shot through Vi's hand, then passed and her bruises faded. "You have an unfortunate habit of hitting things that are harder than your fist. The next time your recalcitrance evinces itself in self-mutilation, I won't heal you."

Vi had no idea what the words meant, but she got the gist. "I want you to make it stop," Vi said.

"Excuse me?"

"You tricked me into ringing Kylar. I want this damn thing off."

Sister Ariel cocked her head to one side, doglike. Her eyes gleamed. "Had a lucid dream, did you?"

"Fuck! Stop using words I don't understand!"

Something smacked Vi's butt so hard she screamed. "The tongue is a flame, child," Sister Ariel said, her eyes cold. "We who speak to use magic learn to control it, else it burns us. Do you know what I was doing while you were studying today?"

"I don't give a shit."

Sister Ariel shook her head. "I have no moral qualm with your cursing, you fecal-mouthed cretin. When a guttershite curses, the world can't even hear it, Vi. When a maja curses, the world trembles. So I've come up with some punishments. I expect that you will exhaust them before I exhaust your defiance. But we're committed now. Your defiance makes only the path longer. *Sa troca excepio dazii.*"

Though she'd briefly seen the aura of magic surround Sister Ariel, Vi felt nothing. "What have you done?" she asked, eyes narrowing.

"That, my dear, is half the fun. With each new punishment, you get to guess. Now, you came because you had a particularly vivid dream, did you not?"

Vi stared into the bottom of her cup. Why was she suddenly squeamish to talk about sex? "It was him. He came to my bed. It was real."

"And?"

Vi looked up. "What do you mean and?"

"You dreamed of bedding a man. So what? Are you afraid you'll get pregnant?"

Vi's eyes locked back on the ootai. "We didn't, um, actually...you know."

"Then why are you here?"

"Is it because of the earrings?"

"Your dream? Definitely. They allow husbands and wives who can't be together to still communicate. Or conjugate. Only a few even of the oldest rings could do that, by the way. As I recall, not a few Sisters wasted decades studying it to find a way to pass messages instantly over great distances. It never worked. I can't recall why. But after the Third Alitaeran Accord banning magae from marrying Talented men, no one's studied it."

"So what I dreamed, Kylar dreamed?" Vi paled.

Sister Ariel looked at her quizzically. "That's what I said, isn't it?" It made Vi feel stupid all over again. "So it frightened you?"

"Not exactly," Vi admitted.

"Sometimes talking with you is like trying to master the Vengarizian Weave."

"Ah fuck this," Vi said. Suddenly, her mouth seemed to be on fire. She jumped to her feet, but Sister Ariel spoke and something hit the backs of her knees and she fell into her chair. "What the fuck was—"

Her mouth filled with fire again, and seeing the not-quite-suppressed smirk on Sister Ariel's face, Vi understood. After another five seconds, the pain stopped, leaving Vi gaping with pain and outrage. She touched her tongue, expecting it to be burned, but it felt normal.

"My mother used soap," Sister Ariel said, "but I couldn't figure out a weave for that. Now, you woke me for a reason. After you tell me what it was, you can go back to bed."

After thirty seconds, Vi realized Sister Ariel was serious. "Have you ever even fu—had sex?" Vi asked.

Sister Ariel said, "Actually, I lost my maidenhead riding a horse."

"I had no idea you were so coordinated." Vi had tried that once. It hadn't ended well.

Sister Ariel burst out laughing. "I didn't know you had such a wit," Ariel said. "I like you more and more, Vi."

Oh, *from* riding a horse, not *while* riding a horse. Vi laughed. She couldn't help it. She'd sooner die than squander even such a small bit of

Ariel's regard. It was also an artful dodge of Vi's question. Hell, it was no use. Vi was tired and her stomach still felt as if she needed to shit. "I've— I've bedded dozens of men," she said.

"Good job," Sister Ariel said. "The correction, I mean, not the promiscuity."

"I never felt anything, with any of them, not since I was a kid. But with Kylar..."

"I'm no authority, but I think it's supposed to be different with someone you love."

That word set Vi off. "Not 'I didn't feel anything *for* them'! I didn't *feel* them! I'm totally numb down there. But tonight—" her mouth snapped shut. Since she was a child, fucking had been something Vi observed, something men did to her. Gradually her powerlessness had become her power. Men were slaves to their meat. Vi's body was simply currency, with the advantage that she could spend it again and again.

When she'd first thought of fucking Kylar, it had only been to think that after what she'd done to him, she owed him. Tonight had been horribly different. Different even from her earlier dream of Kylar. She had wanted Kylar in more ways than she could have imagined. Her body ached for him. It was like something lying so deeply asleep in her that she'd thought it dead was waking. Fucking Kylar wouldn't be a casual gift of the use of her body. It would be surrender.

"You have to get this earring off," Vi said. She was shaking, cold sweat beaded on her forehead. "Please, before I go see Elene. She's still here, isn't she?"

"I'm sorry, child. Yes, she's here. You'll speak with her tomorrow." Sister Ariel sighed. "Viridiana, I've read everything I could find on those rings. The bond is unbreakable. It seemed like a good idea when they made them, I suppose. First they were used to bond a magus and maja who knew what they were getting into. Then others began to use the rings in political marriages. Kings and queens alike began to demand that the ringsmiths exaggerate the compulsion properties toward one side or the other, like yours are exaggerated to give you control. I don't know if we can understand the depth of human misery those magi wrought. But seeing what they had done, the Vy'sana, the Makers, took an oath to make such rings no more. They gathered those they could find and destroyed them and every text on their making. That ring in your ear is at least four hundred years old. That it survived to the present age is nothing less than a miracle."

"A miracle? You call this a miracle?"

Sister Ariel spread her hands helplessly.

*   *   *

Her carriage was waiting for her, but when Momma K got in, she wasn't alone. The dark blob in the opposite seat resolved itself into Scarred Wrable as soon as she sat. "Good evening, Momma K," he said. "Headed to the coronation?"

"As a matter of fact, I am. You need a ride?"

"I don't think so. It seems I've fallen out of favor with the queen."

"It seems?"

"I wake up from a good long drunk and go to get some hair of the dog and I got five guys telling me stories about what I did to the queen. Somehow, it's the wrong day. I was drunk, but I shouldn't have slept for a day and a half!"

Durzo. Her stomach twisted.

Ben Wrable's face was as pale as his scars. "It's Durzo, isn't it?"

"Don't be ridiculous. Durzo's dead."

"I know. I killed him, remember?" Oh, yes. Wrable had killed Kylar when Kylar had been disguised as Durzo. "He swore he wouldn't haunt me, but now my best client wants me dead."

"You still killed him. That had to be upsetting."

"You're not playing with me, are you? You didn't send some other wet-boy to talk with Queen Graesin?"

"I didn't send anyone. I didn't arrange for the ambassadors to be insulted. I haven't moved against Terah Graesin." Yet. "Get out of the city for a while, Ben. Durzo probably just wanted to make sure you didn't take any more jobs for the woman who ordered his death."

Ben Wrable nodded, unthinking, and that unthinking nod confirmed what Momma K had suspected: it was indeed Terah Graesin who'd ordered Durzo killed. The bitch. Well, she'd get hers. Soon.

The Great Hall was filled with the cream of the realm, though given the hardships of the last year, that cream was more like watered milk. Many of the lords and ladies of the realm wore garments they wouldn't have had their servants wear a year ago. The number of nobles was also considerably reduced. Some had been killed in the coup or at Pavvil's Grove. Others had sided early with the Godking and had since fled. The chamberlain had done his best to fill in the ranks and bedeck the Great Hall appropriately, but the pageantry seemed thin. For once, however, there was no criticism. It was too hard to critique the royal guards' threadbare uniforms hastily patched with the colors of House Graesin while wearing a stained dress and borrowed jewels.

Kylar stepped in through a servants' entrance. He had no wish to be announced; he just wanted to see the effects of his handiwork. There was, however, one problem with the servants' entrance: it was full of servants.

"Milord? Milord?" a cheerful man asked.

"Uh, that will be all," Kylar said. *If I use you to cover these clothes, are you going to eat a hole in the crotch?*

~Hard to say.~ The ka'kari seemed to smirk.

"Ah, milord? Is milord lost?" The cheerful servant didn't wait for an answer. "Milord may follow me." He turned and began walking, and Kylar had no choice but to follow. Some servants, he thought, were too smart for their own good.

The servant marched him to the main entrance and handed him off to the chamberlain, a humorless man who looked him up and down, cocking his head like a bird. "You're out of order, marquess, you were to enter after your lord."

Kylar swallowed. "I'm sorry, you've mistaken me. I'm Baronet Stern. You needn't announce—"

The chamberlain double-checked his list. "Duke Gyre informed me pointedly that I was to announce you." He promptly turned and struck the ground with his staff. "Marquess Kylar Drake, Lord of Havermere, Lockley, Vennas, and Procin."

Feeling like he wasn't in control of his own body, Kylar walked forward. Eyes turned toward him, and more than once he heard "Wolfhound." Logan hadn't only legitimized Kylar by giving him a real title, unlike the baronetcy of Lae'knaught-held lands, he'd promoted him to dizzy heights. A marquess was beneath only the dukes of Cenaria. Kylar's chest tightened. It was a real title, with real lands and real responsibilities. Worse, Logan must have worked with Count Drake to have Kylar formally adopted. Kylar's bogus pedigree had been wiped clean. Logan was putting his own integrity behind Kylar. It was his last attempt to save Kylar from himself.

Kylar took his place to Logan's left in the front row. Logan smiled, and the bastard was so charismatic Kylar felt himself smiling along with him, too astonished to be pissed off.

"Well well, my friend," Logan said. "I half expected you to be slinking around up in the rafters. So glad you decided to join us mortals on the ground."

"Uhm, rafters, right. So overdone." Kylar cleared his throat, flabbergasted. "You're causing quite the scandal."

Still facing the front, Logan said, "I won't give up my best friend without a fight."

Silence. "You honor me," Kylar said.

"Yes, I do." Logan smiled, clearly proud of himself, but charmingly so.

"Did Momma K...?"

"I came up with this all by myself, thank you, though Count Drake augmented it."

"The adoption?"

"The adoption," Logan confirmed. "Six rows back. Left side."

Kylar looked, and the blood drained from his face. In a section of poorer barons, a middle-aged blond lord and lady in even more modest clothing than most stood under the Stern banner. Beside them was a young man, as dark as they were light: their son, Baronet Stern.

"That might have been...awkward," Kylar said.

"We all need friends, Kylar," Logan said. "Me most of all. I've lost almost everyone I can trust. I need you."

Kylar said nothing. He noticed Logan's clothing for the first time. The duke was wearing a somber tunic and trousers, finely cut, but unrelievedly black. They were mourning clothes. Logan was still mourning Jenine, his whole family, many of his retainers, and perhaps Serah Drake as well. That old sick feeling rose in Kylar's stomach once more. Logan and Count Drake both were gambling their honor, which to each of them was his most sacred possession, on Kylar. Terah Graesin's assassination now would be more than a tragic difference of opinion. To Logan, it would be betrayal.

There was nothing to do. Marquess Kylar Drake sat in the front row, with eyes constantly on him. Perhaps the Night Angel could invisibly drop from the rafters and scoop up the deadly crown, but Marquess Drake could only watch the consequences of his choices unfurl. Kylar stood as Terah Graesin was announced, as she strode regally to the front, as the patr and the priest lifted prayers and blessed her coronation. Finally, the two divines and Duke Wesseros together lifted the crown from its purple pillow.

Not yet. Dear God, not yet. Kylar hadn't even thought of what would happen to those crowning Terah if she was already sweating. Symbolizing all the gods and the land itself, the three men placed the crown on Queen Graesin's brow.

Nothing happened. She accepted a scepter from Duke Wesseros and a sword from Lord General Graesin, held each for a long moment, then handed each back. The men bowed low, then she bade them rise as she sat. The men retreated, and Kylar's heart edged back out of his throat. Trumpets pealed and Kylar jumped. Everyone stood and applause thundered through the Great Hall.

The queen smiled as everyone cheered. She stood and gestured generously with her hands. Doors banged open on every side and a procession of servants streamed in, bearing tables and food. Musicians and jugglers mingled with the crowds as the servants rearranged the room for a feast. Kylar barely saw it. His eyes were latched on Terah Graesin.

Logan clapped him on the shoulder. "Well, that's that, huh?" Kylar didn't turn. "Come, Marquess Drake, tonight you sit at the high table."

Kylar allowed Logan to usher him to a seat between a nattering forty-year-old third cousin of the Gunders, who was hoping to press a claim to the Gunder duchy, and Momma K, who was seated at Logan's right. She smiled at Kylar's open wonder.

"Don't tell me he got you a title, too," Kylar said.

"You forget, Kylar, I've been to more court functions than you have—although I admit, not many in the last decade. To the abiding fury of every eligible woman in the room, Duke Gyre chose to escort me this evening."

"Really?" Kylar asked, incredulous. Belatedly, Kylar remembered that Gwinvere Kirena had been the courtesan of an age, though she'd retired by the time Kylar knew her. She had doubtless escorted many of the lords in this very room to similar functions. He knew there had been a convenient fiction early in her career that Gwinvere was a visiting Alitaeran countess, but after a time, even that had been unnecessary. A woman as beautiful, as charming, as graceful a dancer, as skilled a singer, as adept a conversation-alist, and as discreet as Gwinvere Kirena was the exception to many rules.

Momma K raised an eyebrow.

"Uh, sorry, I didn't mean..."

Logan came to his rescue, he said, "I asked her before anyone else could. I find there are so few beautiful women in this realm intelligent enough to form complete sentences."

"Yawp," Momma K said, in a perfect coastal Ceuran drawl. "Where's thet spittoon?"

Kylar laughed out loud. The truth was more likely that wearing mourning clothes and showing up with an older woman were the best ways Logan could fend off unwanted advances. If Logan had shown up with a young woman as his escort—or none at all—the matchmakers would have started in on him, mourning clothes or no mourning clothes. Kylar was still chuckling when he saw Terah Graesin, a few places beyond Logan, and his laughter died.

"Kylar?" Momma K asked. "Is something wrong?"

He shook himself. "I keep waiting for her head to explode." To his right, the nattering grasper gasped. He ignored her. He couldn't take his eyes off the queen. She drank. She leaned close to Lantano Garuwashi on her right and shared private observations. She jested with a lord at one of the lower tables who'd spilled his wine over his wife. She chatted with her brother who sat at her left. All the while, her death was waiting.

Kylar had expected it to explode soon after the crown was placed on her head, while she was still standing alone before the lords. Now, if he'd put too much philodunamos under her crown, he might kill others, too. Luc Graesin, though a relative innocent, wouldn't be much of a loss. But Lantano Garuwashi? Killing the legendary Ceuran would be disastrous.

"What I don't understand," Logan was saying to Momma K, "is why, out of all people, you are pushing Jarl's proposals." The name made Kylar pay attention.

"If I said it was because Jarl gave me hope, would you believe me?" Momma K asked.

A troubled look crossed Logan's face, and Kylar saw the old naive Logan briefly at battle with the Logan who'd spent months in the Hole. "I'd believe that was part of it," he said.

She smiled. "The fact is, Jarl's plans are not just good for the Rabbits—they're good for everyone. Do you know how much the average Rabbit spends when he visits a whorehouse?" She laughed at the look that crossed Logan's face. "I was being rhetorical, Your Grace. Three silver pieces. One on drink, two for the girl. I make one silver in profit. The average merchant buys wine, a meal, sometimes tobacco, sometimes riot weed, then a girl. I keep more than a crown in profit. And when nobles visit? Desserts, dancers, bards, jugglers, aperitifs, fine wines, plus other services you'd probably prefer I not mention. I take seven crowns in profit. So, if you were a cutthroat merchant queen, which would you choose?"

Logan's cheeks were pink, but he nodded. "Point taken." Kylar could barely believe his eyes. Logan, talking calmly about the economics of prostitution?

"The problem with how the people have looked at the Rabbits is that they see them as grubby, uncultured, and dangerous. I see them as potential customers."

"But you're not hurting for money. You own, what? half of the, uh, houses of pleasure in this city?" Logan said. Momma K gave a feline smirk, and at that expression, Kylar realized that she didn't own half the city's brothels. She owned them all. "And I've heard you don't pay taxes, ever. Even if we were able to figure out exactly which magistrates in this city take bribes and which don't—" as Logan said it, Kylar realized Logan was speaking with the one woman in the city who *could* tell him—"if we removed them, you would suddenly have a raft of expenses you never had before. I can't imagine you'd come out ahead. If you were the city's most astute merchant, would you choose taxes or no taxes?"

"In the past twenty years, I've had nobles seize entire brothels no less than fifteen times. Banks I had an interest in have been seized ten times. I've lost sixty bouncers to nobles who resented being thrown out. In a particularly bad year, a certain high noble took a taste to killing whores, and I lost forty-three girls. When someone finally killed him, his father retaliated by burning six of my brothels to the ground, one of them with all of my employees locked inside." The coldness in Momma K's eyes was frightening. "So, while we can debate how many months without taxes pays for a seized brothel, ledger sheets can't explain what it is to find your young protégé has been kidnapped. They can't tell you what it is to live wondering how long it will be before the twist tires of her, and whether he will then kill her or release her. Your Grace, I have learned to use this city's corruption, but I shall not weep to see it destroyed."

Momma K's face was turned toward Logan, so Kylar couldn't read it, but her voice carried the ring of truth, and he heard depths to the stories that Logan couldn't know. Momma K had been Shinga during all those atrocities. With all the Sa'kagé's resources, she could have brought her own justice to every case through men like Durzo Blint. But with every prostitute's death or ill-treatment, she had to decide if justice was worth the possible retaliation. After that nobleman had burned her brothels, Momma K could have sent a wetboy after him—but she'd have risked splitting apart the city in civil war. No wonder she'd turned into such a hard woman.

"I had no idea such things took place," Logan said.

Beyond him, Queen Graesin put a hand on her crown and adjusted it on her forehead. A bolt of lightning arced through Kylar, but nothing happened. He willed his muscles to relax and stabbed the untouched filet on his plate.

"The question is, is it possible?" Logan was saying. "I mean, building a few bridges over the Plith isn't going to change things. We'd be fighting against established interests."

"We ended slavery, and we did it without a war. The time is ripe. People have seen so much tumult in the last year that one more upheaval—if it gives them hope—could change everything. The Nocta Hemata showed the city that the Rabbits can be brave. Pavvil's Grove showed that they're willing to bleed for this country. Things can be made new."

Yes, as soon as the queen's head explodes.

There was something about the way she said "we ended slavery." She didn't mean we as in we, Cenaria. If she had become Shinga around the time Count Drake left the Sa'kagé, that meant she'd either been part of abolition movement, or she had decided not to oppose it despite the enormous profits it made for the Sa'kagé. She had to be part of the reason Count Drake's enemies hadn't killed him. Kylar wondered at her, this woman who had taught him to read, who had championed him to Durzo, who had helped end slavery and gave the guild rats a safe place to stay in the winter. At the same time, she had ordered dozens or even hundreds of kills. She had bribed magistrates, established dens of gambling and prostitution and riot weed, extorted honest shop keepers, sprung crooks from gaol, crushed her competitors by every means, and enriched herself every step of the way. She was a fearsome woman indeed. Kylar was glad that she'd always liked him.

But none of these ideas would leave the ground while Terah Graesin reigned. Yesterday she had sealed the Warrens. Tomorrow she was going to build new bridges?

Logan and Momma K continued their discussion, but Kylar stopped listening and merely watched. Logan asked piercing questions about the city's trades and economics, who moved what, where merchants bought which goods, what the tariffs were with different countries, how merchants avoided the more egregious taxes. That moved into history and seamlessly into what they thought of the current state of the country, from who had been hurt worst by the wars to who had cooperated with Khalidor and how much of that would be held against them, to which lands no longer had lords and who was pressing claims to them. As Kylar watched, he realized that this must be what it was like for a neophyte soldier to watch him fight. Logan and Momma wove names and histories and connections among nobles licit and illicit and business dealings and rumors through their speech like masters of the loom. Though Logan was clearly less experienced and had access to only the licit half of the city's information, he still surprised Momma K from time to time with his analyses. And even as they were obviously engrossed in their own conversation, Logan took time to exchange pleasantries with Lantano Garuwashi at his left, who seemed intent on the queen anyway, and to make eye contact with the nobles at the lower tables who sought his glance, and thank the servers and even applaud the beaming new court bard who was terrifically talented even if he did look like a frog.

Beyond Logan, Terah Graesin was focused on her triumph, and enjoying it, accepting congratulations, drinking—dammit, poison would have worked—and flirting openly with both Lantano Garuwashi and her brother. There Kylar saw a microcosm of two reigns. Logan intent on bettering a country, Terah intent on herself.

And as the evening progressed, he realized that someone had cleaned the crown before the queen donned it. It put a decision Kylar had thought he'd already made back in his lap.

It was good to be with his friends. Here, at the high table, Kylar was suddenly legitimate, and no longer alone. He could stay here with the people he admired and loved. Momma K and Count Drake and Logan could be his companions for the rest of his life. He could find Elene and bring her back and give her this life. A life beyond the shadows. Maybe he didn't have to be the wolf in the cold.

Gods! He was immortal! Would it be so bad to let himself have one lifetime of happiness? Drake and Momma K had ended slavery while a corrupt king reigned. Surely between Logan and Count Drake and Kylar and Momma K they could mitigate whatever damage a foolish queen did.

From the middle of the table, Queen Graesin caught Kylar staring at her. She winked.

As the feast ended, Queen Graesin stood and headed for one of the adjoining rooms arm in arm with Lantano Garuwashi. Lantano Garuwashi was graceful and intimidating in his broad, loose pants that draped like a skirt, and a silk shirt with starched tabs over his wide shoulders, leaving his heavily muscled arms bare. The rest of the high table stood next and Kylar moved to follow her. Logan put a hand on his arm and pulled a fat ring engraved with horses off a finger. "This is a symbol of your new office, Marquess." From a pocket, he produced another, much smaller signet ring shaped with what looked like tiny dragon. Kylar recognized it. "This is the ring of House Drake. Take them. There's life beyond the shadows."

Kylar had given his life before. He'd died to save the woman he loved. He'd died to get money to get out of Cenaria. He'd died for refusing Terah Graesin's contract on Logan. He'd died opposing the Godking. It had never been fun, but he'd begun to trust that he would come back. Every other death had cost him only the pain of dying. This death would cost him his life. He would have to leave forever. Start over completely in a far land. It would be like every one of his friends had died at the same time.

"You'll make a great king," Kylar said.

"How many men are you willing to kill for that idea?"

"It's not an idea. It's a dream. Now if you'll excuse me, Your Grace, the longer people see you talking with me, the more I will sully your reputation." Kylar turned and followed Terah Graesin into the next room.

"Your Grace," Momma K said, returning from mingling. "I think we should stay. I hear the new bard has composed a wonderful new song."

46

Quoglee Mars hadn't eaten. He would eat later, if at all, with the servants. But tonight, it didn't bother him. He wandered the tables and played whatever asinine music the threadbare nobles requested. He accepted their applause and moved on, eager to please the next batch of up-jumped plebeians.

After dinner, the castle was opened up and the tables spirited away so the nobles could mingle and have a chance to pay their respects and exchange a few words with the new queen. Entertainments had been spread through numerous rooms with desserts and liqueurs. Quoglee waited until the party had been going for a while before he mounted the platform where the high table had been. The guards who wandered the party had all wandered out, and several of the kingdom's more important nobles were in the room—and, most important, Queen Graesin wasn't.

Leaning his head down as if oblivious to them all, he began playing as only Quoglee Mars could play. For years, he knew, students of music would test their hand against this. Could they manage this overture in the time their tutors told them Quoglee Mars had played it? And some of them doubtless would crash through it with Quoglee's speed, and afterward, their tutors would tell them the difference between hitting notes and milking them.

Quoglee played impetuosity and youth, fervor and passion, sudden flares of anger, tempestuous, never slowing. Around that driving center, he wrapped sweetness, and love, and sorrow, pride against love, scaling higher and higher, with tragedy following a step behind.

Then, before the resolution, he stopped abruptly.

There was a moment of silence. The cretins were all looking at him, silent, expectant, not knowing if they could clap yet. He dipped his head, not even this perturbing him.

The applause was thunderous, but Quoglee held up a hand quickly, silencing it. The room held perhaps two hundred nobles, at least a hundred hangers-on, and dozens of servants. Miraculously, there were still no guards, and what speaking Quoglee had to do, he had to do without interference. "Today," he said in his stage voice, which carried better than a shout, "I wish to play something new that I've written for you, and all I ask is that you allow me to finish. This song was commissioned by someone you know, but someone who is more special than you know. It was, in fact, commissioned by the Shinga of your Sa'kagé. I swear every word of this song is true. I call it the Song of Secrets, and your Shinga wishes me to dedicate it to Queen Graesin."

"That's plenty far, Sergeant Gamble," Scarred Wrable said, stepping out of the shadows in a doorway that connected one of the side rooms with the Great Hall. With a practiced hand, he slid an arm between the sergeant's rich cloak and his back and cut through leather to bring the point of a dagger to rest against the man's spine. "There's nothing in there that interests you."

"What are you bastards doing in the Great Hall?"

"No theft, nor murder, and that's all you need to know, Sergeant."

"It's Commander Gamble now."

"It'll be the late Commander Gamble if you move that hand another inch."

"Ah. Point taken."

"In case you're thinking of raising an alarm, you might want to take a careful look around the room and tell me what you see."

Commander Gamble looked. Eight royal guards were in the room. Six of them were conversing individually with young male noblemen that the commander didn't recognize. The two others were stationed on either side of Queen Graesin and not talking to anyone, as they were commanded not to while guarding the queen. However, another group of three nobles near them did seem especially vigilant now that Commander Gamble studied them. He cursed aloud. He'd had no idea the Sa'kagé even had so many wetboys. "Let me guess that if anyone raises the alarm, you have orders."

"If you cooperate, not only will you and all these men live, but no one will blame you afterward. You might even keep your job."

"Why should I believe you?" Commander Gamble asked.

"Because I don't need to lie. I've got two dozen friends and a knife in your back."

Two dozen? Commander Gamble chewed on that for a moment. "Well then," he said. "Why don't we get a drink? I've got a special bottle—down in the kitchens."

Food paused, poised inches from open mouths, forgotten. Servants froze in the act of collecting glasses. For a moment, no one even breathed.

In a city of fatal secrets, Quoglee Mars had told everyone that he knew the greatest secret of them all. If that was the prequel to his song, what would his song hold?

Quoglee presided over the silence like the maestro he was, a smug smirk tugging at his lips. He judged the silence as if it were music, each beat of rest landing in perfect order. Then, a moment before the revelation could spark a firestorm of comment, he lifted one finger.

From the crowd, a woman's voice broke in a single high, clear note she held for impossibly long, and then, never pausing for a breath, it devolved into a plaintive run and finally words, decrying loneliness. All eyes turned to a barrel-chested soprano in ivory that no one recognized. As she sang, she strode through the crowd until she joined Quoglee on his platform. His voice joined hers, crossing and interweaving melodies, even as the words clashed, lovers singing of love and love denied.

From the corners of the room, the instruments, light viol and muscular bass and harp, played against the voices, but by the magic of music, each stood clear. The repetition of the vocal pleas against the instrumental injunctions allowed the ear to follow one and then the next and the next. Had it been speech, it would have been unintelligible. But in music, every line was pellucid, individuated, stark in its call. A sister's passion, a brother's confusion, youth in turmoil, society frowning condemnation, secrets born in the bedchambers of an exalted house. A woman defiant, passionate, letting nothing stand in her way.

Though he didn't name them, Quoglee had taken no pains to conceal the objects of his song, but as always, some nobles caught on earlier than others. Those who understood couldn't believe what they were hearing. They searched the room for guards, sure that someone must stop this beautiful outrage. But no guard was at his post. The Sa'kagé had chosen this night to unveil its power. There was no way this could be an accident. This room, which held two hundred of the kingdom's elite, now swelling ever more as the curious came to see what held everyone transfixed, was normally protected by at least a dozen of the Queen's Guard. Quoglee sang treason, and no one stopped him. The beauty of the music and the seduction of a rumor held the nobles in a spell. It was Quoglee's masterpiece. No one had ever heard such music. The strings warred with each other, and the forbidden love warred with itself, the music claiming this twisted love was love indeed, even as the boy twisted against his conscience and the woman demanded her rights as a beloved.

Then, as they sang, finally in harmony, having declared an armistice, surrendering to a forbidden love which must remain secret, a new voice joined the fray. A young soprano, lean, in a simple white dress joined Quoglee and the mezzo soprano, singing notes of such purity they tore the heart. In her innocence, she stumbled upon a secret that would wreck a royal house.

The brother never knew. The elder sister saw all she had, all she desired, threatened by her own sister, and in her conflicted heart, she hatched a desperate plan.

Unnoticed by the rapt nobles, a young man had entered the chamber only moments after the first notes sounded. Luc Graesin made no move to silence Quoglee Mars. From the back of the room, he only listened.

The voice of Natassa Graesin spiraled into the Hole, betrayed by her own blood, murdered. She wailed, her voice discordant, fading into oblivion, her life a sacrifice to a perversion. The music played the matching leitmotifs of fatal secrets and Cenaria once again.

"Nooo!" Luc Graesin screamed.

The musicians cut off the last, lingering notes in shock. Luc burst through the doors, fleeing. No one followed.

*S*eeing Count Drake, Kylar slipped through Queen Graesin's entourage, but for once the casual invisibility of ordinariness failed him. A woman's hand touched his elbow. He turned and found himself staring into Terah Graesin's eyes. Those deep green Graesin eyes were breathtaking, especially as Kylar involuntarily stared deeper.

In another place, another time, born to different parents, Terah Graesin's evils would have been meaningless, for she was merely obliviously selfish. She had desires, and others existed to fulfill them. Her betrayals were casual because she barely gave them a thought. Had she been born a miller's daughter, the damage she did would have been confined to jilted lovers and cheated customers.

"I thought Logan and Rimbold had told me everything about you, Kylar Drake, but they could have warned me how handsome you are," Terah said, flashing white teeth that somehow reminded Kylar of a shark.

For some reason, the comment flustered Kylar. He'd always considered himself very average-looking, but looking into her eyes, he knew—knew—that she meant what she said, even if she was saying it aloud to flatter him. He blinked and began blushing and whatever it was that made him see into Terah faltered and disappeared. She chuckled, and it was a low, acquisitive sound.

"And such beautiful eyes," she said. "You've got eyes that make a girl think you can see right through her."

"I can," he said.

"Is that why you're blushing?"

That, of course, made him blush harder. He glanced back to Terah's ladies-in-waiting. They had dropped back. Apparently they knew that when Terah approached a man she wished to do so alone, but they were laughing prettily, no doubt at his expense. He caught a glimpse of one of them who didn't seem to be enjoying the comments, but then he lost her.

"Tell me, Marquess, what do you see when you look in my eyes?" Terah asked.

"It would be highly indiscreet for me to say, Your Highness," Kylar said.

For an instant, her eyes filled with hunger. "Marquess," she said gravely, "a man risks his tongue for speaking indiscreetly to a queen."

"Tongues should be used to commit indiscretions, not to discuss them."

Terah Graesin gasped. "Marquess! You'll have me blushing."

"I'd be content with having you."

Her eyes dilated, then she pretended to cool. "Marquess Drake, I consider it my duty to know the nobles who serve me. You will attend me in my chambers."

"Yes, Your Highness."

Her voice softened. "Wait ten minutes. The guards will allow you through the door. I expect your...discretion." He nodded, smirking, and she paused. "Have we met? There's something about you that seems so familiar."

"Actually, we did meet once." During the coup. "I'm sorry I didn't make more of an impression on you." Six inches into your heart would have been about right.

"Well, we'll remedy that."

"Indeed."

She slipped away and Kylar saw Lantano Garuwashi fifteen paces away, staring at him. Kylar's throat constricted, but though he didn't look pleased, Garuwashi made no move toward him. Kylar looked around the room blankly, forgetting why he'd come in here in the first place. A girl broke away from Terah Graesin's circle and whispered to the guards at one of the doors. She turned. His eyes took in the large eyes, perfectly coifed hair, clear skin, full lips, narrow waist, and lean, firm curves. It was Ilena Drake. She was one of the queen's handmaidens. Kylar had the sense of dislocation. He'd looked away from a little girl for a moment and found a woman in her place. Ilena Drake was stunning. As she pointed him out to the guards to tell them to let him through to see the queen, her eyes suddenly met his. Her face was a mask of disappointment and disgust.

She thought she was being used to help her big brother cheat on her friend, Elene. She thought he'd become a marquess and was so enrapt by the idea of bedding a queen that he'd left everything else behind. Worse than the anger was the monumental disappointment in her eyes. Until now, Kylar could do no wrong in Ilena's eyes. He had been the slam. Until now.

Queen Graesin, having made her excuses, left the room. Kylar turned away.

Rimbold Drake disengaged from a conversation and was limping toward Kylar, leaning on his cane. His eyes went from Kylar's face to his hands, and the rings that weren't there.

"She's beautiful," Kylar said.

"She looks like her mother Ulana did twenty years ago. Albeit with more fire," the Count said, proud despite his grief. Ulana Drake had been as much of a mother to Kylar as he had allowed. She had been a woman unfailingly graceful. She had seemed to grow only more beautiful as the years had passed. Kylar told the Drake as much.

The Count's jaw tightened, and he closed his eyes, mastering himself. A few moments later, he said, "It's enough to tempt a man to curse God." His eyes were stony.

Kylar opened his mouth to ask a question, then closed it. In the next room, through the crowd listening to the bard, he saw a gorgeous blond in a blue silk dress cut so low in back it barely covered her butt. Kylar's breath caught. For a mad moment, he thought it was Elene. Damn guilty conscience. Daydra and her perfect ass moved deeper into the crowd as if looking for someone. *And you told me you gave up working the sheets.*

Drake seemed to come back to himself. He cocked an eyebrow at Kylar. "Yes?"

Coming back to himself, Kylar realized another good reason to keep his mouth shut. "Nothing."

"Kylar, you're my son—or can be, if you say the word. I give you permission to be tactless."

Kylar wrestled with that. "I wondered if it's harder for you when this shit happens. Sorry. I mean, I think what happened with Serah and Mags and Ulana is awful and senseless, but I don't expect the world to make sense. I wondered if it was harder for you, since you think there's a God out there who could have stopped it but didn't."

Count Drake frowned, pensive. "Kylar, in the crucible of tragedy, explanations fail. When you stand before a tragedy and tell yourself that there is no sense to it, doesn't your heart break? I think that must be as hard for you as it is for me when I scream at God and demand to know why—and he says nothing. We will both survive this, Kylar. The difference is, on the other side I will have hope."

"A naive hope."

"Show me the happy man who dares not hope," Drake said.

"Show me the brave man who dares not face the truth."

"You think I'm a coward?"

Kylar was horrified, "I didn't mean—"

"I'm sorry," the Count said. "That wasn't fair. But come, if she's following the usual routine, Her Highness will be expecting you soon."

Kylar gulped. Drake knew? "Actually, I uh, did kind of want to ask.... How much do you know about my gifts?"

"Is this the place to speak about that?" Drake asked.

"It's the time," Kylar said. There were three men, six women, and two servants eyeing him. Of those, only one servant—certainly a spy, though whose was anyone's guess—was within earshot, and he couldn't remain within it for long without rousing suspicions. Kylar caught the man's eye and the force of his stare sent the servant scurrying for another plate of canapés. "I see guilt," he said quietly. "Not always, but sometimes. Sometimes I can even tell what a man did."

Count Drake blanched. "The Sa'kagé would kill for such a power." He raised a hand to forestall Kylar's protest. "But given that you're not interested in blackmail, to me it sounds like a terrible burden."

Kylar hadn't thought of it that way. "What I want to know is what it means. Why would I have such a power, or gift, or curse? Why would the God do such a thing?"

"Ah, I see. You're hoping I can give you some kind of justification for regicide."

Kylar glared bloody daggers at the spy returning with a full platter of hors d'oeuvres. The man abruptly changed course, nearly dropping the platter. "The existence of such an ability suggests something about my purpose, doesn't it?"

Drake looked pensive again. "That depends on what you see. Do you see crime, or sin, or simply feelings of guilt? If crime, do you see all crimes from murder to setting up a market stand without permission? If you're in another country where an action that's illegal here isn't illegal, will a man crossing the border look different? If you see sin, you'll have to figure out whose definitions of sin apply, because I guarantee that my God and the hundred gods don't agree, or even Astara with Ishara. If what you see is feelings of guilt, does the madman without a conscience appear cleaner than the girl who believes that her parents died in an accident because she lied about finishing her chores?"

"Shit," Kylar said. "How come everyone I know is smarter than me? Whatever it is, I see the unclean. I want to know if that implies that I have a duty to do something about what I see."

"Trying to derive ought from is, are you?" Drake asked, smirking.

"What?"

"She may deserve to die, Kylar, but you shouldn't kill her."

"Everyone will be better off if I do."

"Except you, and me, and my daughter, and Logan, and Momma K, and everyone who loves you."

"What do you mean?" Kylar was caught off guard.

"Logan will put you to death, and losing you will hurt us deeply."

Kylar snorted. Some loss. "Sir, thank you for everything you've done for me, and everything you tried to do. I'm sorry I cost you so much."

Count Drake bowed his head and closed his eyes, leaning heavily on his cane. "Kylar, I've lost my wife and two daughters this year. I don't know if I can bear to lose a son."

Kylar squeezed the man's shoulder, marveling how fragile it felt. He looked into the count's eyes. "Just so you know," Kylar said, "you pass."

"I what?"

Kylar gave the man who'd once single-handedly introduced and abolished slavery in Cenaria a lopsided grin. "Whatever I see—guilt or whatever—you don't have it. You're clean."

A look of stunned disbelief shot across Drake's face, followed by something akin to awe. He stood transfixed.

"May your God bless you, sir. You certainly deserve it."

48

Dorian and Jenine were sitting together in the garden. He had dismissed his retainers, and for a time, they had sat without speaking. "I'm sorry I killed that Vürdmeister," Dorian said.

Jenine looked up, surprised. "Why? Because it upset me, or because it was the wrong?"

After a moment, Dorian said, "I could have dealt with him in a manner less...brutal."

"He was responsible for those aethelings, wasn't he?"

"Yes," Dorian said.

Jenine plucked a red flower with six petals, each bearing a purple starburst. Khalidorans considered a blooming starflower an omen of great good luck, because they bloomed only once every seven years. Conversely, a dead starflower was the worst luck. In this garden, they bloomed constantly, but each bloom would die within hours of being plucked. The vir was not good at sustaining life.

After regarding the flower in her fingers for a long minute, Jenine said quietly, "Milord, I'm sure you know that my father was a fool. What most people don't know is that my mother was brilliant. My father feared her, and he tried to marginalize her so she wouldn't grow more powerful than he was. She knew it, and she let him because she didn't care to turn her mind to politics. It was too rough, too dirty, too *brutal* for her. My father made a thousand mistakes in ruling, but my mother's might have been bigger because she chose not to rule. I lost the man I love, a man who would have been a great king, because of that. So I'm not going to turn away because ruling is messy. My people will deserve better of me. Nor will I settle for the soft hypocrisy of criticizing you as you face threats I can barely imagine."

"I don't want to rule simply because I enjoy power. If it's for that, then it's for nothing. I want to undo everything that my father and his fathers have made of this country. I don't know if I can do it. I don't know if it can be done."

A quick scowl passed across her face, but she didn't speak for a few seconds. Dorian waited. Finally, she said, "Milord, I see you usually being so decisive, so strong, and then the next moment, you're in here, apologizing to me for something you had to do. Maybe you could have done it differently, but so what? There was an immediate threat and you dealt with it. I'm trying to tell you that you don't need to be weak for me. I've seen enough weak men in my life. I guess my question is—and it's probably the same question your people have—are you going to be king, or are you just trying to stay alive until you can run away?"

Her words caught him. He hadn't once thought of himself growing old as Godking. Had that been because he couldn't remember even a fragment of prophecy with himself as an old Godking, or because he'd been afraid to throw in his lot wholeheartedly with this land? He hadn't thought about how things would be even a year from now. In thinking for such a short term, he'd ignored problems. He hadn't done anything to seal the highland tribes to him. He hadn't moved against Neph. He hadn't moved against the aethelings. If Jenine saw his hesitation as weakness, how many others did, too?

"I am king," Dorian said. "And I will be until the end of my life, however long that may be."

"Then rule as you must to be king."

"Do you have any idea what that means? Here, with these people?" Dorian asked.

"No," she admitted. "But I trust you."

Dorian had thought of Jenine as naive. But he'd been wrong. Jenine was inexperienced. There was a difference. And she might well yet be horrified by what experience taught, but her eyes were open. Nor did she have an overflow of sympathy for the people who had killed her husband and her entire family. But a monarch had to be hard, didn't he?

Nodding as Jenine rose to go make more preparations for their wedding, distracted by his own thoughts, Dorian reached out with his Talent to lay a small weave on the starflower to preserve it. It was a simple weave and could make even the most delicate flower last a month. But Dorian had forgotten how much vir had been used in growing the flower. Vir and Talent touched and warred and the flower turned black and limp in Jenine's hands.

Dorian cursed. "I'm sorry, milady. You've given me much to consider. You are wise beyond your years. Thank you." He plucked another starflower and wrapped it in vir for Jenine. It would last a few days, but then he'd simply pick another.

The royal guards let Kylar pass without comment. Ilena Drake stood near the door, arms folded under her breasts. "I'm sorry," Kylar told her.

"How could you do this to Elene?" she asked.

He walked past her and strode through quiet corridors, up the stairs to the queen's apartments in a fog. The ka'kari flicked out of his hand into the form of a dagger, then sucked back in. Out, in, out, in. Was it always this simple for Vi? Some flirtation, a little innuendo, and your deader isolated herself, arranged your entry, and helped keep your presence secret? After the lengths to which Kylar had gone for some kills, walking in an unlocked door seemed like cheating. The guards hadn't even taken the dagger from his belt.

Leaning against the door frame, he breathed deeply. He'd seen so much death in this place. Terah Graesin's room was Garoth Ursuul's old room. There had been statues of dead girls in the room bare weeks ago. What had they done with those statues of flesh made stony? If he ever found Trudana Jadwin, he would make Hu Gibbet look kind.

Such bloody, bloody thoughts. Kylar knocked.

There was the scuffing of bare feet on marble, and then Terah Graesin opened the door. Kylar was surprised she was still fully clothed. She stepped close and kissed him softly, luxuriously, their only contact in their lips. She moved slowly backward, sucking on his lower lip. He followed, letting her take the lead. She closed the door and stepped into his embrace.

"We'll have to be quick," she said, in between kisses on his neck. "I can't miss my own party, but if your tongue is half as talented as you suggest, I guarantee to reciprocate very soon." She giggled wickedly.

What surprised Kylar was how easy it was. Terah was taller than Elene, and her lips not as full, but teasing her was the same. He traced fingertips down the backs of her arms, then, feigning growing passion, slid one hand to the back of her neck and the other to soft curve of her buttock. From the interplay of starched stiffness and yielding flesh, he could tell she'd removed her undergarments.

He lifted an eyebrow and she giggled again. "Like I said, quick and clean. Later we can do long and dirty."

You poor bitch, you don't even know what this is. What was he doing? Why didn't he end this sad farce? *Finish the job, Kylar.*

Kylar closed his eyes as Terah pushed him onto the bed, but as soon as he did, he imagined Vi standing beside the bed. She looked pissed. Kylar's eyes flew open as Terah crawled over him. She tugged her neckline down. "Kiss me," she said.

Vi seemed to be standing right there, her eyes flaming, daring Kylar to do it and feel her wrath. The image made no sense, but that didn't make it any less powerful.

Terah made a pouting sound and tugged her dress lower, brushing her bare breast against Kylar's face. His ear felt suddenly hot. Sickness and revulsion washed through him. His stomach cramped.

There was a wordless scream of animal rage from the doorway. Kylar blinked his eyes furiously, trying to clear away the black spots swimming in front of them. Terah barely sat up before a body collided with her, knocking her off of Kylar.

Kylar fell off the bed and staggered to his feet. As his vision cleared, he saw Luc Graesin on top of his sister, pummeling her with his fists and screaming obscenities. Finally, his chest heaving, Luc pulled himself off of her. "You killed Natassa," he said, drawing a short dagger from his belt. "You killed our sister."

"No," Terah said. "I swear." Blood was pouring from a gash across her eyebrow and her lips were fat and bloodied from Luc's fist.

The last piece of darkness Kylar had seen in Terah's eyes fell into place. "She sent a messenger to the Godking," Kylar said, "telling him Natassa was traveling to Havermere, and she arranged for there to only be two guards with her."

Terah gaped, but Luc's eyes never left her face. The guilt written there was plain. "I did it for us. She was going to betray us! For the gods' sake, help me, Kylar," Terah begged.

It was a mistake. She could have faced Luc down. The last thing she should have done was remind him of the other man she'd been about to fuck. Luc screamed again and stabbed her in the stomach. She shrieked and Luc cowered back, then attacked again, gashing her arm as she lurched to her feet. He stabbed at her back as she ran to a wall, caught the ribbing of her dress and dropped the dagger.

Terah found a bellrope and yanked on it over and over.

Luc picked up the bloody dagger and walked toward her, his face a mask of grief and rage, weeping and cursing. He stood in front of his sister as she collapsed on the floor. Kylar wondered if Luc saw what he saw. Terah Graesin without power, without the hauteur, was a pitiful shadow. She hunched into the corner, blubbering. "Please, Luc, please. I love you. I'm sorry. I'm so sorry."

Perhaps Luc did see the same thing as Kylar, because he stopped, paralyzed. He still held the dagger, but Kylar knew that he wouldn't use it now.

Terah's wounds weren't fatal, Kylar was certain of that, especially not with a green maja in the castle. Terah would recover, and she would owe the Chantry an enormous debt. She would put her brother to death and she would capitalize on people's sympathy for her to move against her enemies real or imagined. Poor Luc Graesin. The weak bastard wasn't even eighteen yet.

Kylar slapped the young man, hard, and plucked the dagger from his hands. Luc fell. "Look at me," Kylar told him.

The Royal Guards were on their way. They might arrive any moment. Kylar could cut Terah's throat, knock Luc senseless, climb out the window, and rejoin the party. Luc would be beheaded for treason and murder and Logan would be made king. Doubtless, whoever had told Luc about Natassa's betrayal intended exactly that.

Luc met his eyes and Kylar weighed the young man's soul.

Kylar cursed loudly. "You're no killer, Luc Graesin. You marched right up here, didn't you? Walked past a dozen witnesses? I thought so."

"What are you doing?" Terah demanded. "Help me."

Kylar looked into Luc's eyes again and saw a young man bound in chains not of his own making. Luc was no saint, nor purely a victim, but he didn't deserve death.

"Tell me one thing," Kylar said. "If you could take the throne, would you?"

"Hell no," Luc said.

He was telling the truth. "Then I give you these, Luc: first, knowledge: you're no killer. These wounds won't kill your sister. Second, your life. Make something of it. Third, I spare you a sight that would never leave you."

"What?" Luc asked.

Kylar punched him in the forehead. Luc dropped like a stone. Kylar rubbed Luc's bloody hands against his own. He cut Luc's tunic in two places with the dagger and finally stabbed him in the meat of his shoulder, shallowly.

Terah was aghast. "What are you doing?"

Kylar drew the mask of judgment over his face. "I've come for you, Terah." He let the ka'kari sink back into his skin.

She screamed. He grabbed a fistful of hair and pulled her to her feet. He planted the dagger in her shoulder, and with his right hand free, pressed it against her wounded stomach to get it bloody. He wiped the blood on both sides of his face and pulled the dagger out of her shoulder. He stood behind her, using her body as a shield between him and the door. She was begging, screaming, cursing, weeping, but Kylar barely heard her. He sighed and when he inhaled, he smelled her hair. It smelled of youth and promise.

There was the sound of jingling armor and heavy footsteps pounding up the hall. A dozen Royal Guards burst into the room, bristling with weaponry. Behind them Logan Gyre and Duke Wesseros and their guards pushed into the room. In seconds, they'd formed a half circle around Kylar and the queen. Dozens of weapons were leveled at Kylar.

"Put it down!" a royal guard yelled. "Put it down now!"

"Help me. Please," Terah begged.

"By the gods, Kylar," Logan shouted. "Don't do this. Please!"

For the job, it was perfect. Now dozens of witnesses had seen Logan command Kylar to stop. There remained only one thing. Kylar painted a desperate expression on his face. "Luc tried to stop me, and he couldn't," Kylar raved. "And you can't either!"

Kylar slashed the dagger through Terah Graesin's throat, and all the world screamed.

49

"Mother," Kaede said, coming into the study, "how are the wedding preparations coming?"

Daune Wariyamo raised her eyes from the papers spread all over her desk. She loved lists. "Our responsibilities are well in hand. Everyone has been informed of their precedence and the expected protocols. I only worry about Oshobi's mother. I'd say she has the brain of a hummingbird, except hummingbirds can hover for a moment or two. I expect the Takedas' half of the ceremony to be an unmitigated disaster." She pulled off her pince nez. "I heard some lunatic arrived, claiming to be a Tofusin."

A Tofusin, she said. As if there were more than one.

"He's nothing. Some white-haired freak," Kaede said, waving it away. "Mother, I want your opinion. An insult's been done to our family honor that may be on some people's minds as we go into this wedding, so I think I have to deal with it now. One of the cousins cuckolded her husband. She swears it was long ago and brief, but its effects continue. What should I do?"

Daune Wariyamo scrunched her eyebrows, as if the answer were so obvious that Kaede was stupid for asking. "A slut can not be tolerated, Kaede. A whore dishonors us all."

"Very well. I'll see it taken care of."

"Who is it?"

"Mother," Kaede said quietly, "I'm going to ask you a question, and if you lie to me, the consequences will be harsher than you can believe."

"Kaede! Is this how you to speak to your mother—"

"None of that, mother. What—"

"Your tone is so disrespectful, I—"

"Silence!" Kaede shouted.

Daune Wariyamo was too stunned for the moment to begin the usual tactics.

"Did you or did you not intercept letters that Solon sent to me?" Kaede asked.

Daune Wariyamo blinked rapidly, then said, "Of course I did."

"For how long?" Kaede asked.

"I don't remember."

"How long?" Kaede asked, her voice dangerous.

The empress's mother said nothing for a long moment. Then she said, "Years. Letters came every month, sometimes more often."

"Every week?"

"I suppose."

"What did you do with them, mother?"

"That Solon was worse than his brother."

"Don't you ever speak to me of that monster. Where are the letters?"

"They were a tissue of lies. I burned them."

"When did he stop sending them?" Kaede asked.

Her mother's expression went blank for a moment, then she said, "I don't know, ten years ago?"

"He didn't stop, did he? Don't you dare lie to me, by the gods, don't you dare."

"It's only a few times a year now. For all I knew, it was some impostor, hoping to break your heart again, Kae. Don't let this stranger ruin everything. Even if it is Solon, you don't know him. If you postpone this wedding, it could mean the end of you. Harvest is the only time for a queen to marry, and if you delay, the seas will be impassable. The lords from the other isles won't be able to attend. You need this. We can't offend the Takedas again."

Clan Takeda had been a thorn in Kaede's side since she'd taken the throne. They had angled and manipulated for years for this wedding, and if as a younger woman she had sworn she would never marry Oshobi, now she knew there was no other way. "Mother, is there anything else you haven't told me? Anything you want to confess?"

"Of course not—"

Kaede held up a finger. "I want you to think very carefully. You're not as good a liar as you believe."

Her mother hesitated, but the look on her face was that of a woman aggrieved that she could be suspect. "There's nothing."

Kaede had been wrong. Her mother was an excellent liar. Kaede turned to a guard. "Summon my secretary and the chamberlain."

"Kae, what are you doing?" Daune asked.

The officials stepped into the room in moments. Kaede had had them waiting outside. "Mother, the woman you called a slut and a whore is you. You betrayed my father and dishonored us."

"No! I never—"

"Did you expect to get away with it? You fornicated with an emperor—a man surrounded by bodyguards and slaves at all hours, and you the lady of a high house, with bodyguards and slaves of your own. Did you think no one would notice?"

There was real fear in Daune Wariyamo's face for the first time Kaede had ever seen. "It didn't mean anything, Kae."

"Until you got pregnant and didn't know who the father was."

Daune Wariyamo stood transfixed, as if she couldn't believe all of her secrets had yielded their rotten fruit on the same day. Around the room, officials and guards stood with mouths agape, barely daring to breathe.

"I wondered for years, Mother, why a woman so ambitious wouldn't want me to have anything to do with Prince Solon. It's because you were afraid he was my brother. You were afraid that your whoring would lead me, innocently, to an incestuous bed. Apparently your sense of honor is only diseased rather than nonexistent."

Tears were rolling down Daune's cheeks. "Kaede, I was young. He said he loved me."

"Did you believe the green mages when they examined me? I had no idea why at the time, I was only nine years old—too young to be showing Talent yet. They found out that I was a Wariyamo, didn't they? Weren't you relieved?"

"For a while. When Solon came home, a full blue mage at nineteen, he asked to see me secretly. That's when I knew. He tried to be so subtle, swearing how he would never hurt you, but under it all, there were threats, Kaede. What would happen when he got tired of you? What if I ever vexed him? He could destroy me with a word. I would be his slave for the rest of my life. What if you opposed him? He could lie, say the mages proved you were illegitimate. He was a mage himself; everyone would believe it. We'd lose everything. Our only hope was to keep him away from us. It wasn't like I was hurting him. I even got him an offer for more schooling at Sho'cendi, which was a high honor."

Kaede's face relaxed despite her fury. The decision had been made. The truth was out. Now there was room for sorrow. "So you ruined my chances of happiness because you couldn't believe that the man I loved would keep his word?"

"I was protecting us. No one's as good as they pretend to be," Daune said.

"True in your case," Kaede said. She turned. "Secretary Tayabusa, please record that the queen mother is henceforth stripped of all privileges and titles. She is banished from all the isles and territories of Seth, and if found on them after tomorrow, the penalty will be death. At dawn, Chamberlain Inyouye, you will have her accompanied to the harbor. You will pay her passage to whatever port she chooses. You will give her ten thousand yass, and make sure that she leaves. She may be accompanied by one servant if one can be found who volunteers to accompany her."

Everyone was stunned.

"Mother," Kaede said, "if this were the first time you'd lied to me, I wouldn't do this. It is, however, the last time. Guards, I wish two of you to stay with her at all times. I doubt she will attempt to harm herself, but she has shown herself to be an adulteress and a liar. I don't expect theft is below her."

"You can't do this," Daune said, breathing so rapidly Kaede expected her to pass out.

"I already have."

"I'm your mother!"

Kaede stepped forward and put her hands on each side of her mother's face. She kissed her forehead. She took hold of the six platinum chains strung between her mother's cheek and ear and tore them out. Daune screamed, her ear torn to ribbons, her cheek dribbling blood.

Kaede said, "No, you are Queen Mother no more. You are Daune Wariyamo no more. Henceforth, you are Daune Outcast. Guards?"

The captain of the guard and his second stepped forward and took the outcast by each arm to lead her from the room.

"Kae! Kaede, please!"

"Captain," Kaede said as the guards neared the door, almost dragging their prisoner. "About what happened here . . ."

The captain looked quickly at each of his men. "You can be assured of my men's complete discretion, Your Majesty."

Secretary Tayabusa cleared his throat. "And I have written down the names of everyone in this room. If anyone speaks of this, they will be discovered and punished accordingly." He leveled a heavy gaze at each of the various servants and functionaries in turn.

"On the contrary," Kaede said, "no one will be punished for speaking of what happened here. My dead mother shamed my family, and I will not grant her the mercy of covering her deeds in silence. Most of all, my betrothed and his family deserve to know the truth before they wed their honor to mine."

If the Takedas went ahead with the marriage obviously knowing the truth, they would have a harder time destroying her than if she married and then they "found out" about her shameful secret. Other than that, there were few things the Takedas could do. A coup was doubtful, despite Oshobi's popularity among the city guard. The Takedas' postponing the marriage until spring was most likely, and that would give her time. Time might give her opportunities. Best for her personally and worst for Seth, the Takedas might cancel the wedding and withdraw to their home island. That would mean they would come back in the spring for war.

At sunrise, Vi swung her feet over the side of her bed in her little room. She'd barely slept after leaving Sister Ariel, and she'd had horrible dreams about Kylar and oceans of blood. Maybe it was an omen. She was supposed to meet Elene this morning, first thing. She touched the water basin. "Cold," she said. When ice crystals began to spider across the surface, she broke the ice and washed her face, gasping despite herself. In minutes she finished her ablutions and pulled the ill-fitting tyro's robe over her ill-fitting shift. Vi tied back her hair with the white ribbons Sister Ariel had given her.

She heard the familiar scuff of Sister Ariel's steps before the Sister knocked on her door and came in without waiting for permission.

"You're up," Sister Ariel said, surprised. "You're going to see her?"

"She's up in the pommel of the Seraph's sword?" Vi asked.

"Praying still, Uly says. Vi," Sister Ariel paused. "You're one of us now. The Seraph will pay your debts. If you need to, you can offer her whatever it takes."

"I don't think she's looking for a bribe," Vi said.

"Nor do I." Sister Ariel paused again. "I expected I'd have to force you to go to her, Vi. The girl you used to be would never have done this. Well done."

Perfect, now it was impossible to back down.

Vi found the central staircase and began climbing. She was only a few floors up when the stones pulsed gently as they did every dawn. She paused on a landing as nearly invisible trickles of dust joined together into rivulets. They rushed past her feet as a small hole opened in the wall. The single day's accumulation of dust slipped through and the hole closed. Everywhere in the Seraph, the scene was repeated. Powered by the first rays of sunlight, all natural dirt was whisked away. Outside, the Seraph would appear to be briefly surrounded by a corona as magic repulsed dirt, grime, rain, or snow. The debris would cascade into the lake and there be dispersed by magic that kept the waters around the Seraph even cleaner than the rest of Lake Vestacchi.

There were, of course, still plenty of chores for the tyros. The magic was disengaged in any room where it might interfere with a Sister's experiments or sensitive artifacts, and it disregarded scraps of parchment, clothes, or anything else someone might leave on the floor. But without the magic, the tyros could have worked constantly and never been able to keep the Chantry clean. It was simply too big.

Vi reached one of the upper floors where full Sisters had their apartments. There was some pecking order to who had what floor and which Sisters got the treasured southern exposures, but Vi had no idea how it worked. Mercifully, no one was in the hall. Vi followed the unflickering lamps to the southwest corner. The Seraph held a sword in her left hand, its point at her feet, the hilt coming above her waist, held slightly to one side. The pommel of that giant sword was capped with a round jewel. The room was a globe from which Sisters could see sunrise and sunset. The walls were always transparent. It was a sanctuary for those who needed to meditate or, as in Elene's case, pray.

Taking a deep breath, Vi opened the door. Elene was seated, looking toward the eastern mountains. The view was breathtaking. Vi had never been so high in her life. The punts in the lake below looked the size of her thumb. The mountains glowed. The sun was a jagged half-circle barely peeking over them. But Vi's eyes sought out Elene's face. Her skin glowed in the gentle light, her eyes deep brown, her scars softened. She gestured for Vi to come stand with her, not glancing away from the horizon.

Tentatively, Vi stepped up beside her. Together, they watched the sun rise.

Not daring to turn and look Elene in the face, but not able to wait another moment, Vi said, "I'm sorry if I interrupted your prayers." She drew her knife and rested it across her palms. "I made you a promise. I've done you and Kylar a great wrong. If you wish...I deserve no less."

Elene took the knife. After a minute, she said, "His mercies are new every morning."

Vi blinked. She glanced over at Elene and saw a tear tracking down her cheek. "Uh, whose?"

"The One God's. If he forgives you, how dare I not?"

What?

Elene took Vi's right hand with her left. Then she stood, shoulder to shoulder with her, looking at the newborn sun. She held Vi's hand firmly, but with nothing vindictive or tense in her grip. There was an aura about her of tremendous peace, peace so thick it slowly calmed Vi's taut nerves.

After a few minutes, Elene turned to her. Vi was surprised to find herself brave enough to meet the woman's eyes.

"I believe the God has a purpose for me, Vi. I don't know what it is, but I know it isn't murdering you." Elene threw the knife aside. "We're in a big mess, but we're in it together. All right?"

50

Vürdmeister Neph Dada sat beneath an oak at the mouth of Quorig's Pass, awaiting his spy. He hadn't brought any of the two hundred Vürdmeisters he'd gathered to the meeting. If his spy was caught, he didn't want her to be able to tell the Chantry anything useful. Of course, the catatonic Tenser

Ursuul and Khali had traveled with him, and he kept them close—but hidden.

Eris Buel arrived at moonrise. She was not an attractive woman. Her eyes were close-set, her nose long, and her chin weak. She looked rather like a rat in makeup. Too much makeup at that. And she had moles. Everywhere. Garoth Ursuul had long let it be known that his female progeny were worthless to him except as killing practice for the aethelings. It was half true. Most of the girls served to weed out boys too weak to murder their own sisters, but Garoth sent wytchborn girls away at birth.

Few became as valuable as Eris Buel. Years ago, Garoth learned that Eris had roused the Speaker's suspicions. Rather than lose her, Garoth had shipped her off to Alitaera and arranged her marriage to a nobleman. Eris had then caught the crest of a rising tide of resentment among the Chattel, the former magae who'd left the Chantry to marry. She was now poised to head that movement back to the Chantry, demanding recognition. Eris might even overthrow the Speaker.

"Eris," Neph said, dipping his head.

"Vürdmeister." Eris liked to think too highly of herself, but she could obviously feel the nearness of Khali. That was enough to put anyone off-balance.

"I have a task for you," Neph said. "One of our spies tells me a woman named Viridiana Sovari has bonded a man with a set of compulsive earrings. Given the bond, we expect he will come to the Chantry soon."

"I know the girl. She's the talk of the Chantry," Eris said.

"She doesn't matter. Let me be blunt. This man, Kylar, may hold Curoch. We've hired an extremely skilled thief to take it from him. We have reasons to trust our thief, but Kylar is very resourceful. He may track our man down. So as soon as our man steals the sword, he'll signal you by raising two black flags on a fishing boat visible from your room in the Chantry. Check three times a day. When you see it, collect the sword and leave the city immediately. The thief is not to see your face or know anything about you, just as you know nothing about him. You'll pay him. He knows how much to expect." Neph handed her a purse full of Alitaeran gold. She looked startled at the weight.

Neph was lying to her, of course. He did believe that Kylar had briefly held Curoch, but he'd also seen how Ezra's Wood changed on the day that Vürdmeister Borsini had gone to his death, trying to take Curoch from Kylar. The Sword of Power was gone; once something went into the Wood, it stayed there.

What Neph's thief was trying to steal was a normal sword, with one difference: it had been reported to Neph that Kylar's sword had a black blade. Kylar was hiding his ka'kari—the black ka'kari, the Devourer of magic—on his sword. Neph was certain of it. If he was wrong, he would likely be dead by spring. He was running out of options. The things he'd thought would be easy had turned out to be viciously difficult.

With two hundred Vürdmeisters, Neph had attacked the weaves Jorsin Alkestes had laid on Black Barrow hundreds of years ago. Even together, they'd only broken the first spell: now it was possible to use the vir within the Dead Demesne, the unchanging circle of land around the dome of Black Barrow. Before, anyone using the vir there would die instantly. It was better progress than anyone before Neph had made, but in itself, it accomplished nothing. All the millions of krul around Black Barrow were still magically sealed. No one could raise them. No one could raise the Titan Neph had found beneath the mighty dome of Black Barrow itself. With Curoch, Jorsin Alkestes had been more powerful alone than Neph was with two hundred Vürdmeisters.

Neph's few successes seemed like nothing. He'd stirred up the wild men in the Freeze. He'd taught their shamans to raise krul, though he'd deliberately taught them imperfectly, in case he ever had to face them himself. He'd sown rumors about the weakness of the new Godking among the highland tribes.

It would be enough to distract the new Godking, but not enough for Neph to take the chains of office for himself. The Ursuuls had long claimed that only an Ursuul could take the vir from a meister. That claim had meant the meisters and Vürdmeisters had never been a threat to a true Ursuul— any magical fight would end instantly. Neph had been certain it was a lie. He had staked everything on the belief that once he held Khali, it would be a simple matter to learn to remove the vir from whomever he wished. But so far, he hadn't even come close.

If Neph didn't figure something out soon, any of the aethelings could show up any day and remove the vir from Neph himself.

There were ways out, but none was likely. If Neph actually recovered Curoch, of course, he could shatter Jorsin's work and anyone who rose against him even without the krul or the Strangers or Khali. If he could steal the black ka'kari, he could make it devour Jorsin's magics, raise the krul, and the krul would crush anyone who rose against him. He could use the black ka'kari to walk into Ezra's Wood and steal Curoch and everything else there. His last hope was to raise Khali herself. It had been Khali's wish for as long as she had been worshiped. It was enshrined in every Khalidoran's prayer: *Khalivos ras en me*. Khali, make your home in me. If

Neph could give Khali a body, she would give him everything. Neph was preparing the magic and trying to find a proper host for Khali in case he needed to do it, but it was a last resort. Khali would surely teach him how to deny the vir to the Godking if Neph gave her true embodiment. But if Khali had a body, if she could give him everything, could she not also take everything from him?

Neph turned pensive eyes toward Eris. He needed, as always with these arrogant children, to seal the lie. "If it is Curoch, Eris, I'll give you whatever you ask. But there are two things you should know. You have not the power to wield it even for an instant. It will kill you if you try. Second, I will kill you if you try." His vir squirmed up and down his arms as he laid a tiny weave on her. "I know you can untie that weave, but one of my other spies at the Chantry will be checking on you. If you tamper with it, she has instructions to kill you. Don't worry, the weave is small enough to escape any but the closest magical examination."

Eris's face paled. It would, of course, be her death if any loyal Sister found that weave. But Neph had also revealed that he had another spy close enough to her that the spy could check on the weave regularly. "How likely is it that Kylar has Curoch?" she asked.

"Not likely. But the prize is worth the possibility of losing you."

A green hue entered her skin. "I want Alitaera," she said defiantly. "That's my price. If it's Curoch, you'll take all Midcyru. I want to be queen of Alitaera. I have debts to repay."

Neph pretended to think about it. "Done," he said.

51

Kylar opened his eyes in darkness. His whole body ached, but he knew where he was instantly. Nothing else had the sewage-and-rotten-eggs smell of the Maw. They'd put him in one of the nobles' cells. He wouldn't have been surprised to find himself in the Hole, or dead. He was glad they hadn't killed him. It would be better for Logan if there was a trial first.

"I must have been twice your age when I killed my first queen," a familiar voice said. "'Course, I didn't make such a damn mess of it."

"Durzo?" Kylar sat up, but the man squatting on his heels across from him was unfamiliar. The laugh wasn't.

"I'm going by Dehvi now." The voice took on a tonal accent, "Dehvíra-haman ko Bruhmaeziwakazari I have the honor to be." Durzo's voice came back as he said, "They used to call me the Ghost of the Steppes, or A Breath in the Typhoon."

"Durzo? Is that an illusion?"

"Call it advanced body magic. It was one of the things I was going to teach you if you hadn't developed your Talent so damn slow. We've only got a few minutes. All the guards down here are honest, if you can believe it. And your trial's going on as we speak."

"Already?"

"Your pal the king seems to have high esteem for your powers. Almost accurately high. They drugged you. You've been unconscious for a week."

"Logan's the king?"

"Without opposition. He and Duke Wesseros are presiding over the trial. It's too bad you're missing it. You'd be amazed at what Gwinvere can get witnesses to say."

"Momma K's on trial?" Kylar asked. He was still off-balance. He couldn't place things. It was unreal to be talking with Durzo.

"No, no, no. But what she's doing is making sure the witnesses bring up Terah's indiscretions as many times as possible. The honorable judges are trying to quell the rumors, but Momma K's already won. No one thinks you killed a saint. That helps Logan, but you still killed a queen in plain sight of eighteen people. Logan wants to give you a nobleman's death, but they've already heard testimony that you're not a Stern—the Sterns were pretty adamant about that, go figure—and some lady who sat next to you at the coronation says you turned down the Drake's adoption. He gave you the rings and you refused to put them on. So you're looking at the wheel. I did that once. It's a real shitty way to die, especially for someone who heals as fast as we do."

"You came back," Kylar said. "You gave me Retribution. Again."

Durzo shrugged, as if it were nothing. He reached for a pouch, then stopped himself. "You put philodunamos on the crown?"

Kylar nodded.

"You wonder why it didn't work? Someone cleaned it off. The laundress swears she dumped some cleaning rags into the water and boom! There was a fire. No one believes her. She lost an arm and her job."

Kylar's stomach turned. He'd nearly killed an innocent. Again. What could a one-armed laundress do?

"So," Durzo said. "Time's wasting. You want to live or die?"

"I'll take any way out that doesn't make Logan look complicit or weak." At Durzo's grimace, he said, "And don't tell me you wouldn't give your life for a friend. I know better."

Durzo grimaced again and stood. "You're the damnedest kid I ever met. Good luck."

"Master, wait. Am I...am I doing the right thing?" Kylar asked.

Durzo stopped and when he turned, there was a smile on his face. It was a rare sight. "It's a gamble, kid. You always put your money on your friends. It's something I admire about you."

Then he was gone. Kylar shook his head. How had he got himself into this?

Six royal guards arrived soon thereafter. None of them looked happy, but while two of them had the cautious air of professionals, the other four seemed either nervous or angry or both. One of the angry ones pulled Kylar to his feet. Kylar was, he noticed now, manacled to the wall, and still wearing the clothing he'd worn the night of the coronation. They'd been nice clothes a week ago. His and Terah's dried blood made the front stiff and reeking.

"So you're the big wetboy," the gap-toothed guard sneered. "You don't look so tough when you don't have a helpless woman shielding you."

"Sorry I made you look bad," Kylar said.

Gap-tooth hit him in the stomach.

"Please don't hit me again," Kylar said.

"You didn't make us look bad, you murdering bastard."

The captain said, "Don't be an asshole, Lew. Of course he did."

"Upstairs they're making him sound like a god. Wetboy-this, wetboy-that. Look at 'im. He ain't nothing." Lew casually backhanded Kylar.

"Lew, I—" the captain cut off as Kylar disappeared.

One by one the guards realized Kylar had vanished. There was dead silence for a moment. Then it was broken by the clang of manacles hitting the stone floor.

"Where the hell—"

"Sir! He's gone!"

"Block the door! Block the—"

The cell door slammed closed with all the guards inside. The lock clicked. Kylar reappeared outside. Grinning, he waved the captain's keys at them.

"That didn't just happen," one of them said. "Tell me that didn't just happen." Another cursed under his breath. The rest still looked like they couldn't believe it.

"Captain," Kylar said, "will you please ask Lew not to strike me?"

The captain wet his lips. "Lew?"

"Yes, sir. Right, sir." Lew met Kylar's gaze and quickly looked away.

Kylar opened the cell door and the men shuffled out sheepishly.

"Should I, uh?" Lew asked, holding up the broken manacles.

The captain swallowed. "Uh, if you don't mind, Master...um, Kagé?"

Kylar put his wrists together. They put the manacles on him and walked out of the dungeons. No one said a word. No one laid a hand on him, either.

52

The courtroom was a large, rectangular hall that could hold hundreds of people. It was overflowing, and the doors had been thrown open so more people could stand at the back and watch. At the raised table at one end of the room, Logan Gyre and Duke Wesseros sat side by side. There were supposed to be three judges, but Logan hadn't wanted to impose the duty on the last surviving duke, Luc Graesin.

Facing the table was a small desk and chair inside an iron cage. The captain led Kylar to the cage and removed his manacles. The crowd watched, silently but with great anticipation, as though the wetboy was a monster on display who might gnaw the bars. Kylar stepped into the cage silently, glancing briefly at the gallery. Logan wondered if he was looking for friends. He wondered how many Kylar found.

The front two rows were made up of nobles. Lantano Garuwashi, silent but obviously wondering what Kylar was trying to accomplish, sat near Count Drake, whose jaw was set and eyes were grieved. Logan wondered how much Count Drake had known about his ward. Drake had been a model of integrity for as long as Logan had known him, and a Gyre banner man besides. The Stern family was in the second row, looking furious. The testimony had already established that they'd never known or seen Kylar, but they still felt their honor impugned. Aside from the usual nobles, there was a vast array of Cenarian humanity. The cream of the Warrens was here, men and women in fine clothes yet without titles. Logan wondered if all of those were Sa'kagé. He wondered how many were glad Kylar was here, and how many were grieved, or terrified for themselves that he might speak. Then there were a smattering of those drawn simply by the spectacle: a few Ladeshians, some Alitaeran merchants, and even a Ymmuri.

To Logan's right hand sat the witnesses. There were eighteen guards, as well as the grasping woman who'd sat next to Kylar at the coronation. Kylar sat.

"State your name for this tribunal," Duke Wesseros said.

"Kylar Stern."

"Sit down, Baron Stern!" Duke Wesseros barked as the unhappy nobleman jumped to his feet. The nobleman scowled and sat. "This court has accepted testimony from nobles who said you saved them during the Khalidoran coup. They called you the Night Angel. We have heard, sometimes despite our best attempts, about how you saved King Gyre from the Hole. We have heard you called Kagé, the Shadow. We even heard one man who claimed your name was Azoth. But one certainty we've established is that you are not, nor ever were, a Stern. What is your real name?"

Kylar looked amused. "I am the Night Angel, but if you'd choke on that, you can call me Kagé."

Duke Wesseros looked over to Logan. Logan had asked him to lead the proceedings. Logan nodded. "Kagé," Duke Wesseros said, "you stand accused of high treason and murder. How do you answer these charges?"

"Of murder, guilty. Of treason, not guilty. Terah Graesin was not a lawful queen. By marriage and adoption, Logan Gyre has been king since the death of King Aleine Gunder IX."

The courtroom erupted in whispers until Duke Wesseros raised his hands. He had threatened to clear the courtroom several times during the last week of testimony, and the crowd quieted quickly. "It is not your place to lecture your betters on Cenarian law."

"Then you tell me, Your Grace, was or was not Duke Gyre formally made King Gunder's heir and was or was not he married to Jenine Gunder, and did or did not that confer on him the right of succession?"

Duke Wesseros purpled, but said nothing. If he agreed, he would concede that Terah should never have been made queen and that he should have never sworn fealty to her. If he explained his decision was based on practicalities, he would sound like a weasel or a coward.

"I wouldn't have killed Terah Graesin if my betters had followed the law rather than their cocks and their coin purses," Kylar said.

This time, the whispers were forestalled by Logan's raised hand. He wore a thin gold band around his brow, but otherwise little to denote his kingship. "There is some truth in what you say. On the eve of Pavvil's

Grove, some of us made regrettable compromises. In the end, however, Cenaria's nobility delivered into Duchess Graesin's hands the scepter and the sword, and we placed the crown upon her brow. It is not the prerogative of a commoner to shed blood to correct what he sees as the nobility's errors. Therefore, Kagé, you stand convicted of murder and treason."

A hush fell.

"This tribunal has further questions, which we ask you to answer for both your own sake and Cenaria's. If you answer fully and forthrightly, you will be granted a merciful death. If not, you will be bound to the wheel." Logan held his face impassive, but his stomach turned. The wheel was a cruel death, as bad as Alitaeran cruxing or Modaini drawing and quartering. It was the established punishment for treason. Only treasonous nobles were beheaded, and it had been established that Kylar was no noble. A merciful death for testimony was the most Logan could do for his friend.

"I will answer all I can without compromising my honor," Kylar said.

"Are you a member of the Sa'kagé?" Logan asked.

"Yes."

"Are you an assassin?"

Kylar sneered. "Assassins have targets. Wetboys have deaders. I was a wetboy."

There was a sudden electricity in the room, like thunderheads were rolling by. The crowd had become an audience, and they were pleased with the show. They were getting a chance to peek behind the veil at the Sa'kagé, and they wouldn't miss it for the world.

"'Was'?" Duke Wesseros interjected.

"I split with the Sa'kagé during the coup. I don't kill for money now."

"So you claim no one ordered you to kill the queen?" Logan asked.

"The Night Angel is the spirit of retribution. No one orders me to do anything, Your Highness, not even you." A thrill ran through the crowd at the show of defiance.

"Strike him," Duke Wesseros said.

One of the guards stepped up to the cage but hesitated.

"Strike him!" Duke Wesseros demanded.

The man hit Kylar across the jaw, not hard. Logan could swear the man looked scared.

"Who hired you to kill Terah Graesin?" Logan asked.

"I planned and carried it out alone."

"Why?" Duke Wesseros asked. "A wetboy might have escaped."

"If I wanted to, I could escape right now," Kylar said.

There were titters in the courtroom.

"Well, I don't know if you're a wetboy, but you're certainly an accomplished liar," Duke Wesseros said.

Kylar glanced at the guards who'd accompanied him up from the Maw. The men looked positively ill. Logan felt a tingling on his right arm and for a moment, could swear he saw something moving from Kylar's fingers like the shadow of a shadow. He looked around, but no one else seemed to notice anything. Then Kylar's expression changed like he was deciding against an impulse. Logan had seen the expression enough to know it. "I am an accomplished liar," Kylar admitted. "I guess it doesn't matter. You've already established that I'm not a Stern, and that I killed the queen, so let's finish this."

"You deny the Sa'kagé had any part in the queen's death?" Duke Wesseros asked.

"Are you a moron or a stooge?" Kylar shot back. "I've given Cenaria a king who can neither be bribed or blackmailed. The Sa'kagé is furious with me. The question you're too afraid to ask is whether the king ordered me to kill Terah Graesin."

Duke Wesseros jumped to his feet. "How dare you impugn our king's honor! Strike him!" The court was in an uproar.

Logan stood. "No! Sit!" It took half a minute for everyone to obey, but finally they did. "It's a fair question. A fair question for us to drag into the light, because everyone's going to be asking it quietly in the days to come." Then Logan sat.

"Many of you were at Pavvil's Grove. You saw Logan kill the ferali," Kylar said. Logan almost goggled. He and Kylar both knew he hadn't killed the ferali. It had been Kylar's assassinating the Godking that had defeated the beast. "Many of you hailed Logan as your king, but he wouldn't accept the crown then, would he? Do you think he was afraid of Terah Graesin then? How many of her banner men do you think would have stood by her on that day if Logan had taken the crown? He held his honor that day as he has every day of his life. Do you think that if he had ordered me to murder her on the night of her coronation that he would have welcomed me to sit by him at the high table? Do you think he is such a fool that, knowing what I was going to do an hour later, he would remind everyone what good friends he was with a wetboy? I've been a Sa'kagé spy on Logan Gyre for ten years. In that time, Logan came to trust me as his best friend. So it turns out that the question isn't whether he had me assassinate Terah Graesin, because he didn't. The duke who was once betrothed to a mere count's daughter has always had too much honor for that. The real question is if our new king will pardon his friend for the murder that put him on the throne." Kylar turned and met Logan's eyes for the first time. "Well, Logan, how about it?"

Whatever else Kylar's time straddling Cenaria's worlds had done to him, Logan saw that his friend had learned the way of rumors among both the peasants and the nobility. He'd fingered exactly the questions people would ask. Indeed, he'd set up everything so the questions could have only one answer. Logan had wondered why Kylar had allowed himself to be caught. He had no illusions that it had been because Kylar couldn't escape. Now he saw all the connections that Kylar had known other people would make. The first question when someone was assassinated was always, who benefits? When Terah Graesin died, the answer was clearly Logan. That wasn't why Kylar had killed her, though. He'd killed her for all of Cenaria's people, because she would have been a disaster as a queen. So Kylar had needed to kill her in a way that freed Logan of suspicion.

In a way, Logan had forced Kylar's hand with the seating arrangements at the coronation. The Sterns had been there. If Kylar hadn't been placed so prominently, he might have escaped attention, but with too much scrutiny, Kylar's disguise would collapse. When it collapsed, everyone would have known that Logan's best friend was in the Sa'kagé—that would be damning enough. After all, how could Logan be a reformer when he came to the throne smeared with charges of corruption himself? This was Kylar's answer: to shine a glaring light on everything and force Logan to show decisively where his loyalties lay.

Kylar had no doubt what Logan would do, Logan saw that. It was the right thing to do. It was the only thing to do. But Logan had recently lost his father, his mother, his fiancée, and his wife. How was he supposed to condemn his best friend to death?

Logan remembered the sick pleasure he'd felt at ordering Gorkhy's death. It was the pleasure of power, and he'd felt it again when men had bowed before him. But suddenly, he hated his power. Kylar was giving his life so Logan could have power. He trusted Logan that much, and Logan knew he had it in him to be a monster. But there was nothing to do.

His face stony, Logan said, "A pardon is out of the question. You were our friend, but our justice will not be swayed. Whatever your intentions, even if it was to make us king, you have done murder in this realm. Justice demands your death. Justice will be satisfied. As king, I demand you answer one more question. If you answer, we will grant you a merciful death. If not, it will be the wheel. Kagé, what are the names and positions of everyone you know in the Sa'kagé?"

Kylar sighed and shook his head.

53

Kylar sat in the darkness and stench of his cell deep into the night.

He threw the ka'kari into the corner of the room. It bounced eerily noiselessly. He extended a hand and willed it back. It flew through the air as if on invisible strings and slapped into his palm. He threw it again and this time willed it to mold itself into a spike. He sucked it back through the air and when it hit his palm it squished and went back into his body.

He could escape. After he died this time, everything would be different.

He heard the sound of someone speaking in a distant hallway. A door opened, and soon Kylar heard the sound of a big man's footsteps. The face that eventually appeared, however, wasn't the one he expected.

"Lantano Garuwashi," Kylar said, standing and bowing.

"Night Angel." Garuwashi bowed equally low. "May I come in?"

Kylar smirked at how the man was treating this like a social visit. "Please."

Garuwashi unlocked the door and came in.

"How'd you get here?" Kylar asked.

"I asked permission."

"Ah."

"You rob me, Night Angel."

"How so?" Kylar asked.

"Our duel. It was to have been the height of our glory. A duel for the ages."

Kylar didn't know why, but that Lantano Garuwashi was peeved not to get to fight him five years hence somehow warmed Kylar. Perhaps it was the only way Garuwashi had to say that he would have liked to be Kylar's friend. "The Night Angels keep their word," Kylar said. "A Night Angel will be there, I promise."

"He will be your equal?"

"He may even be yours," Kylar said, grinning.

Garuwashi cracked a smile. He sat on the stone shelf opposite Kylar and folded his legs beneath himself. Kylar sat similarly on his bunk. "I don't understand Cenarian honor," Lantano Garuwashi said. "King Gyre will rule whether you do this or not. Why will you die for a people unworthy of you?"

"I don't know. I only know it felt like the right thing to do."

"Do you have a lover? Does she approve of this?"

Kylar hadn't even thought of it. The look on his face must have betrayed him, because Garuwashi shook his head, chuckling.

"You tell me, Night Angel, would you give *her* life to accomplish this?"

Kylar was as shocked that Lantano Garuwashi was asking the question as he was by the question itself. "I wouldn't ask anyone to die for my ideals."

"Yet you ask Logan to kill for them."

Kylar had no answer.

"Since you've never sent men to their deaths, let me make the question easier. Would your lover give her life to change this land?"

"Yes, gladly."

"Then perhaps she will forgive you one day."

Well, I plan to come back to life before she finds out. Instead, Kylar said, "I wouldn't have expected a sa'ceurai to care what a woman thinks."

Garuwashi burst into laughter. "No sa'ceurai wishes to marry a shadow. A woman should be as fiery as her hair. Ceuran women whisper on the streets and shout in the home. Young sa'ceurai think that means only in the bedroom." Garuwashi grinned. "They learn." Kylar couldn't help but smile too.

After a few more minutes, Garuwashi stood. "I must go," he said. "I will expect your successor at Midsummer's in five years. May your sword-soul shine ever brighter, Night Angel."

Lantano Garuwashi left, and to his surprise, Kylar slept.

He woke at the sound of a lock pick's scraping. He was alert instantly and stood stealthily. The door opened moments later, telling him that whoever was breaking into his cell was a professional. The locks on the nobles' cells were tight.

The door cracked open and Scarred Wrable's face appeared. He grinned to see Kylar awake and in a ready position. "You're Blint's apprentice after all, arn'tcha? Morning, lad."

"What are you doing here?" Kylar asked.

"There are two contracts out on you. One from inside. To kill ya." He meant inside the Sa'kagé. "The other one's from some nobles."

Kylar's eyes never left Scarred Wrable, though the man didn't have a weapon drawn. "Terah Graesin's folk?"

"Actually, some shadow saved a buncha lords during the coup. They think they owe you. You want to guess which contract I took?"

"Depends on who in the Sa'kagé took out the other one," Kylar said.

Scarred Wrable spat. "The one from inside wasn't from one of my usual clients, and Momma K likes you. I don't plan on betting against her. I took the nobles' contract." He drew a knife and extended it hilt first.

Kylar waved it off. "Tell them thanks, but I'm not here 'cause I can't escape."

"I told them you'd say that. They said I'd get half for trying. I don't know what you're trying to accomplish, but you're crazy brave."

"More one than the other, I think."

Scarred Wrable laughed. "How 'bout this, then. I lied when I said there's two contracts. There's three. Third one's same as the second: to free you. You got more friends than a wetboy oughta. You wanna guess who took it out?"

"Pray tell."

The wetboy grinned. "The king his own self. Iff'n I was king, I'd just let ya go. Guess nobles don't think like the rest of us. You coming?"

Damn you, Logan. Damn you for flinching. Kylar swallowed. "Staying."

Scarred Wrable's eyebrows lifted. Then he shrugged. "You oughta be a noble your own self. You're a man in love with death, Night Angel. See you on the other side."

They marched Kylar out of the Maw before dawn. His escort was fifty men. They bound his wrists with manacles behind his back, tied his elbows with hemp, and hobbled his feet. He was surprised when, instead of heading through the castle, the guards led him out the great double doors, up the black carven tongue, and out the throat of the Maw onto the rocky west side of Vos Island.

There was a barge waiting for them, and as soon as they chained Kylar to a post in the middle of it, they cast off, the men alert for threats from him or from any who might rescue him.

They had barely passed under West Kingsbridge when Kylar saw new construction on the Plith. Deep pilings had been sunk into the river bed south of Vos Island to support a central platform, which rested on the surface of the river. The pilings extended high above the platform and three spokes radiated from the center, supporting temporary spans to Vos Island, the Warrens, and the east side. The three-way bridge was temporary now, and low to the water, but the size and placement of the pilings told Kylar of the project's ambition. It would be a symbol of Logan's reign, a bridge that bound the city's sides and its government together. As they came closer, Kylar saw that what he had thought was merely the thickness of the temporary bridge's surface was something else.

Every one of the temporary spans—west to the Warrens, north to the castle, and east—was filled with people. The sun was barely lighting the sky, and there were thousands gathered. Everyone in the city had come. Even Lantano Garuwashi's soldiers had come.

As the barge came within sight, a cry went up, and it wasn't kind. These people loved Logan, Kylar knew instantly, and any traitor must be vile. From the safety of the mob, any fear they might have had for the Sa'kagé's avatar had vanished. Indeed, that probably made him more hated still. His disavowals in the courtroom made no difference; only the verdict mattered. The barge came closer and the yells were deafening. Looking on faces filled with hatred, Kylar supposed he was lucky the city had been starving—there was no rotten produce for people to throw.

Something splashed in the water twenty feet short of the barge.

"Shields up!" an officer barked.

The men crouched and raised their shields over their heads. Chained to the post in the middle, Kylar couldn't move. Rocks rattled off the shields and splashed in the water, then Kylar watched one arc perfectly. He turned his head. The rock gouged a furrow in his scalp and he staggered against the post, blood spilling over his ear. Another rock glanced off his shoulder and a third hit him in the crotch. The crowd cheered as he slumped.

He stood again, though spots swam before his eyes, blinding him. As they got closer, the hail thickened. Most of the throws missed, but rocks hammered his sides, his legs. A stone a handspan across landed on his foot, shattering bones. He screamed.

It was bad timing. A rock that would have been too high caught him in the mouth, snapping teeth and driving others through his lip. Another cheer went up.

Finally, the barge bumped against the platform. "Enough!" a woman shouted. Kylar lifted his head and saw a young woman in full armor standing in the center of the platform with her hands raised, trying to still the crowd. Then a stone hit him in the eye.

"Enough!" the woman shouted, but Kylar lost her voice under the shrieking voice of pain. His face was hot, his chained hands couldn't reach up to protect himself or feel the damage. Soldiers were jostling him, half carrying, half dragging him forward.

Kylar opened his eyes but could only see from his right. His first sight was of his bare foot, bleeding, ruined. It made him light-headed. He looked up, blinking, but blinking sent forks of lightning through his left eye. Blood was filling his mouth from his smashed lips. He didn't know if he'd swallowed or spit out the teeth, but jagged edges were all that remained.

When Kylar could finally try to make out the details, he saw that the platform was filled with Logan's retinue, including at least a hundred of Logan's bodyguards. Numerous other soldiers were scattered throughout the crowd, including along all three bridges, keeping a lane clear. On the far side of the platform, facing the castle, was the wheel. To one side, Logan sat in a gilded chair.

They dragged Kylar before him and a herald read out the charges. Kylar paid no attention to them. He looked only at Logan. Logan's eyes trailed over Kylar's wounds and he swallowed, but he didn't avert his gaze. His eyes met Kylar's and Kylar saw suffering as great as his own, but no wavering.

The herald finished with the charges with a question. "Yes," Kylar said loudly. "I killed Terah Graesin, and I'd do it again."

Logan stood and the muttering that had begun ceased instantly. "Kagé, Shadowed One, whom I knew as Kylar Stern, I owe you my life. You are a hero and I call you my friend, but you have betrayed this country and murdered her queen. I will not be a king who gives different justice to his friends. Kylar, my friend, I sentence you to hang by the wheel until you are dead."

Kylar said nothing. He merely bowed his head to Logan. Logan sat and made no attempt to quiet the crowd that now buzzed with the confirmation of the rumors they'd heard.

The soldiers dragged Kylar to the wheel. It was slightly taller than a man and open, with only four spokes radiating from the axle, which would be behind Kylar's back so he could face the crowds. There were blocks for his feet which adjusted at the ankle so his feet wouldn't slip free, a thick leather belt for his waist, and two sharply-ridged bars for handholds. The rest of the wheel bristled with iron spikes: all pointed inward.

The royal guards who'd brought him from the Maw began strapping him in place.

"Are you really the Night Angel?" Kaldrosa asked quietly, fitting the leather belt around his waist.

"Yes," Kylar said.

Kaldrosa leaned close as she strapped his wrist to the wheel and whispered, "There are two hundred fifty women here who'd be dead if you hadn't saved us from Hu Gibbet. It'll kill us to betray Logan, but if you—"

"Do your duty," Kylar said. He squeezed his eyes tight shut.

"Thank you," Kaldrosa said.

Once he was strapped in, the guards adjusted the spikes. If Kylar held himself in place, none of them would touch his body. However, as the wheel turned, he would have to support his weight by his ankles and by his hands, gripping knife-edged bars that would cut his fingers and palms to mincemeat. Once he weakened, the spikes would stab his sides, his legs, and his arms, enough to spur him to redouble his efforts, but never so deeply that they would kill. He would eventually die of blood loss, or his heart would burst.

As they finished, he lifted his gaze once more and scanned the crowd. He saw Momma K, and Count Drake. He saw the Chantry's ambassador faintly glowing in his sight, obviously hoping that this "Night Angel" would do something magical for her to report, and the Lae'knaught ambassador, dispassionate, more studying Logan's reaction than Kylar's suffering. He saw the women of the Order, horrified, one crying silently. He saw faces he had known from the Warrens, tavern keepers and whores and thieves and an herbalist. He saw nobles Kylar Stern had rubbed shoulders with and been ignored by.

Then Logan gave a signal, and the wheel rattled backward and settled down, water lapping over Kylar's feet.

Oh, yes, now Kylar remembered, there were more than two ways to die on the wheel. The wheel itself was perpendicular to the flow of the Plith; it used the river's current to turn it. When Kylar was turned upside down, his head would dip into the water low enough to cover his mouth. It would only be enough to drown him if he was unconscious and close to death anyway, but the coughing fit would make him stab himself in dozens of places.

Logan nodded. The wheel began to turn.

55

"Thank you for receiving me," Momma K said. She came out onto the castle balcony where Logan stood, his dinner untouched. He didn't lift his eyes from the river. It had been twelve hours since the wheel began turning. Behind him, Gnasher ate noisily and, with a total lack of stealth, stole Logan's biscuits.

"How could I deny you? When the Shinga plays, kings dance," Logan said flatly. He didn't turn. A wetboy had delivered her letter—her admission that she was the Shinga—just this morning. But the shock of it was muted by Logan's grief.

Momma K came to stand beside him at the railing. From this distance, all they could see was that there were still a few dozen people on the platform, half of them guards, and that the wheel was still turning. The signal flag to let Logan know when Kylar died still hadn't been raised.

"This changes everything," Momma K said.

"What hand did you have in Terah Graesin death?" Logan asked.

"None," Momma K said, "though not for lack of trying. I put Quoglee Mars on the right track, hoping he would discover that Terah betrayed her little sister Natassa. I even arranged for him to sing the night of the coronation. I made sure that no guards would stop him once he began, and I arranged for Luc Graesin to be there to hear it. I hoped Luc would kill Terah. Once you were king, I planned to have this talk with you regardless, though I was planning on waiting a month."

"In which time..." Logan led.

"The Ceuran food supplies and our own would run out," Momma K said.

"And?"

"I would come to you with enough food to feed the city through the winter."

Logan stared at her, not asking how she'd get it. "In return for what?"

"The thing is, Your Majesty, with this—" she gestured to the wheel— "you've proven that you have integrity. Integrity is rare here, but it won't change this city alone. You need allies for that, and if you want allies in this city, you will be seeking allies who have objectionable histories."

"Like you?"

"And like Count Drake, whom you conveniently forget was also once in Sa'kagé leadership."

Logan blinked.

"The point is, if you try to hold to account every official in the city who's ever taken a bribe or violated a trust or broken a law, you will have no officials."

"What do you propose?" Logan asked.

"The question is what you propose. What will the reign of King Gyre the First mean?"

Logan looked at his friend dying on the wheel in the distance. "I mean to make this mean something. I mean to destroy you Sa'kagé."

"That's a means, not an end."

"I mean to make Cenaria a great center of trade and learning, a place our people are proud to claim. We will be able to defend ourselves. We will live in peace, not in fear and corruption. The Warrens may never equal the east side, but I mean to make it possible for a man to be born in the Warrens and die in an eastside palace."

"How about a woman?" she asked lightly.

"Of course," he said.

She wore a small smile. "Sounds good. I'll take it."

A flash of anger passed over his face. "You could already buy a palace."

"I want you to appoint me duchess and grant me the Graesin lands, Your Majesty."

"There's not enough rice in the world to buy that."

It was his anger speaking. His best friend was dying. Momma K ignored it. "The Sa'kagé is a parasite latched onto Cenaria's face. Fully uprooting them is impossible, but their power can be broken. It may take years, and it will cost much of your treasure and perhaps your popularity. Success is not certain. Are you a king who can stay a course through a river of blood?"

Logan watched the wheel turn for a full minute. Then he said quietly, "While there is breath in my body, I will fight to make Kylar's death mean something. What will you do if I give you what you ask?"

"I will give you my complete loyalty. I'll be your spymaster. Last but certainly not least, I'll destroy the Sa'kagé."

"Why should I believe that you would so casually betray an organization that must include every friend you ever had?" Logan asked.

"Friends? The Sa'kagé relieves us of the burden of friendship. The truth is, in all my years I had only three friends in the Sa'kagé. One was a wetboy named Durzo; Kylar had to kill him because of something I did. One was Jarl, who died trying what I'm proposing. The last is dying for it as we speak. What I propose is a betrayal, that's true, but it's not a casual betrayal. If we do this, we'll need to keep my appointment secret for a time. Once the Sa'kagé learns of my new loyalties, they'll go underground, and I need to speak with as many of them as possible before that."

"Can they be broken?" Logan asked.

"Not with swords alone."

"What can go wrong?" Logan asked.

"You want the short version or the long one?"

"The long one."

So she told him. Then she told him the plans she had in place to counter every one of those possibilities. It took an hour. She spoke succinctly and asked him questions as well: was he willing to use wetboys to do work the guards could not? How much amnesty was he willing to extend? Would thieves walk free? Bashers? Extortionists? Rapists? Murderers? What would be the penalty for those who took bribes in the new Cenaria?

"Our first strike will have to be sharp. Seizure of funds, arrests, making legitimate employment available. Large carrots, large sticks. And most of our plans will probably only last until the first sword is drawn."

Logan said nothing for a long time. Then he said, "If we do this, I won't put you in charge of uprooting the Sa'kagé."

"What?"

"I won't put that much power in your hands. You could destroy anyone with a word, and I'd have no idea if you were telling the truth. Rimbold Drake will be in charge. You will work for him. Fair enough?"

Momma K's eyes were cold for a long moment. Then they cleared. "I can see that taking orders is going to take some getting used to. Yes, it's fair. Perhaps you are the king who can do this after all. Your Majesty, I swear my fealty to you." She knelt gracefully and touched his foot.

"Gwinvere Kirena, I hereby establish House Kirena, peers among the great houses of the realm. I grant to you and your house in perpetuity the lands stretching from the Smugglers' Archipelago in the west to the Wy River in the east, and from the boundaries of Havermere in the north to Ceuran border in the south. Rise, Duchess Kirena."

She stood. "Your Majesty, there is one more thing. Yesterday I received confirmation of an earlier report that I hadn't believed. In each case, my sources had nothing to gain by lying. Both have been trustworthy in the past. I don't know how this is possible, but I believe it is true. I didn't want to tell you before we concluded our own negotiations because I didn't want you to think I was trying to influence them."

"That's a lot of hedging. What is it?" Logan asked.

"Your wife didn't die in the coup, Your Majesty. Jenine's in Khalidor. She's alive."

Some time after dark, the wheel stopped turning. Kylar jerked his head up. He blinked through the river water coursing from his hair and looked around. Blinking still hurt, but he could make out shapes now with the eye that had been blinded in the morning.

A young man in armor stood before him. Obviously, he was one of Logan's bodyguards. "I was given a message, Sir Kagé," he said. "Aristarchos is healthy and safe at home now with his wife and children. The Society wishes to thank you and hopes that stopping the wheel for a few hours is a small repayment." He glanced up one of the bridges.

Through the darkness, Kylar saw a Ladeshian man he'd never met. The man raised his hand in greeting, though in the darkness, no one but Kylar could have seen him. Then the Ladeshian walked away. So Aristarchos ban Ebron had survived his addiction. Kylar hadn't known he had a family. He wondered what Aristarchos's wife thought when her beautiful husband came back with blackened and missing teeth, his looks and pride sacrificed to a cause she couldn't understand. The Society thanked Kylar?

"We can only stop the wheel until dawn, Sir Kagé. I'm sorry."

But Kylar barely heard him. He unclenched his bloody hands from the knife-edged grips and let the belt and the ankle straps hold his weight. His head sunk to his chest.

"Kylar?" Vi asked. They were in a little room with two beds, a basin, and a small chest at the foot of each bed. A small figure was asleep on one bed, and Vi was propped up on one hand in the other. She looked worse than Kylar had ever seen her. Her eyes were red and puffy, her face blotchy, nose runny, and handkerchiefs wadded in her hands. "Gods, what have they done to you?"

He looked at the sleeping figure on the other bed and shuffled over to her. "Uly," he said. "God, she's getting big. Uly?"

"She can't hear us," Vi said. "We're not really here. Come, sit down."

Kylar sat with difficulty. He smiled wanly. "Uly's your roommate?"

Vi nodded. "Thirteen years old and she's better than me at everything."

"Tell her I'm sorry. I abandoned her like everyone else. I made a lousy father."

"Quiet. Lie down."

"Get blood...sheets," he said, but he didn't resist. He put his head in her lap and closed his eyes.

"Kylar, I think I can help you," Vi said, brushing his hair back. "But I need you to tell me what happened. Who did this to you?"

Her fingers were warm and gentle. It was an effort to speak. "Doing," he said.

"Doing?"

"I'm being executed for murdering Queen Graesin. Logan's the king. I did that, Elene. That's worth my life, isn't it?"

"Elene's not here, Kylar. It's me, Vi."

Kylar winced as a muscle in his back spasmed. He drew quick little breaths.

Vi laid both of her hands on him and the cramps released. He heard her gasp and then warmth flooded through his body and a blessed absence of pain.

There was a long silence and Kylar began fading. Finally, Vi said, "But you'll come back, right? After you die?"

"No one ever explained it. Live every life like it's your last, huh?" He chuckled. He couldn't help it. He felt warm all over. When he opened his eyes to look up at Vi, she wasn't smiling. Her face was rigid with concentration and pain.

"Sleep," she said. "I'll help you all I can."

Logan rose before dawn. He hadn't slept. Sensing his mood, his guards hadn't slept either, but if they felt as wretched as he did, they concealed it. "I'm going to see Kylar," he told Kaldrosa. She nodded, having expected it. One of the things Logan was learning to hate about being king was that he couldn't go anywhere without a retinue. Given that the last two Cenarian monarchs—or six, if he believed Duchess Kirena—had been assassinated, it was reasonable. Still, though Logan hated dragging along twelve people with him wherever he went, it wasn't their fault, and it was beneath him to make their lives more difficult. So he simply had to act with more consideration.

Hot water arrived for his bath so promptly that Logan knew Kaldrosa must have told the kitchens hours ago that the king would require his bath early. It was a simple act, but illustrative. Many nobles ignored their servants as they ignored the ground beneath their feet. Logan's father had pointed out that a noble interacted with his servants more than he did with even his own family. It paid to treat them well, but it was a still rare servant who so actively anticipated her master's needs.

Logan stripped and bathed himself. As he scrubbed, he thought of how his apartments, though high above the Hole he'd lived in, had seen as much misery. Logan had seen the statues—hidden in a storeroom in the castle's bowels—of the Godking's women. They had all been young Cenarian noblewomen. Logan had known each by face and name and title. Every one of those women who had been so cruelly used, broken, murdered, and put on display. One of his first acts as king had been to return those girls to their families for burial. For some, there was no family left to return them to, so Logan had seen to those burials himself. He wished he could kill the dead Godking with his own hands, and the wheel would be too good for

Trudana Jadwin, who had signed each statue as if they were pieces of her art. The room got brighter as Logan stood, dripping, naked, oblivious to the towel one of his bodyguards offered.

Jenine was, most likely, one of those women now. Even if he could get her back, she might well be bereft of reason. Regardless, she wouldn't be the woman he had lost. He had to be prepared for that, had to be ready to love someone broken, wounded beyond healing. The fucking monsters. The room brightened with a white-green incandescence as Logan's rage crested. He closed his eyes and exhaled. He mastered his outrage, his fury at his own ignorance, his impatience, and his hatred. He cooled them and fit them to his purpose. What would it profit to yell and smash things in his own castle while Jenine languished in Khalidor?

Logan opened his eyes and became aware of Kaldrosa and Pturin, his short Ymmuri guard, gawking. The white-green lines etched in his forearm dimmed. Logan took the towel.

"The, uh, long-sleeved tunic?" Kaldrosa asked.

"Always. Thank you."

The sun was rising as Logan and his retinue arrived at the platform where Kylar was dying. The slow grind of the gears and the hiss of the flowing waters of the Plith, and the shifting strains of Kylar's weight on the straps holding him were the only sounds. Blood dripped from his sides where blades pierced his arms, his armpits, his ribs, missed his waist because the belt held him in place, but stabbed again into the sides of his thighs and calves. Blood dribbled from fists clenched around spiked handholds. Blood flowed freely from his scalp and each of his temples, refusing to clot because every revolution dipped his head underwater. He was a man limned in blood. And still he breathed.

There was another man who had been regarding Kylar in the dawn light, too. It was Lantano Garuwashi. He didn't turn as Logan approached.

The wheel turned Kylar sideways. Lacking the strength anymore to hold his body in place, he slid onto the points on the down side. As he inhaled, that motion made the spikes tear the holes in his chest larger. Blood welled up on the opposite side, and as he turned upside down, he made a feeble effort to hold himself up, but slid down. His head jabbed against three spikes and dozens more stabbed into his shoulders and arms. He took a deeper breath before his head went under water.

Logan's stomach clenched. It was with difficulty that he didn't throw up. He'd come to take his friend's body away, not to watch him suffer, not to watch him die.

Kylar's strength must have given way only minutes ago. It was impossible for a man to bleed so freely for long without dying. So Logan stood with Lantano Garuwashi and looked at what he had done for a minute, five minutes. Five minutes stretched to an unbearable ten, and still Kylar showed no signs of weakening further. It was unbelievable, impossible.

"Look at his feet," Garuwashi whispered.

For a moment, Logan had no idea what Garuwashi was talking about. There was nothing remarkable about Kylar's feet. They, at least, were spared injury. Then Logan remembered. When Kylar had been strapped to the wheel, they'd dragged him because a stone had crushed one of his feet. Another had blinded one eye. Now both feet and both eyes were whole. Logan's fleeting disbelief became wonder and then horror.

The wheel was intended as an excruciating death for traitors. It usually took hours. Kylar, however, was healing at an incredible rate. The wheel would kill him eventually, but after a day, he seemed like a man who had been on the wheel less than an hour. Logan had never intended such cruelty. This made the Hole look humane.

"You did right," Kylar said, startling Logan. His eyes were open, clear. "Go, my king. I'll be hanging around." He attempted a grin.

Logan abruptly began weeping. "How do I end this?"

Agon Brant cleared his throat. "Your Majesty, in times past when men were put on the wheel before a religious festival and a ruler wished to avoid defiling the city by having a man die during the festival, they would break the condemned's arms or legs so they'd be impaled more deeply on the spikes and die faster." He cleared his throat once more, never looking at Kylar. "I must also inform Your Majesty that the Lae'knaught ambassador is on his way. He refused to be put off any longer."

Logan closed his eyes and breathed deeply, slowly. He wiped his eyes and blinked. Looking up the makeshift bridge to the castle, he saw the Lae'knaught ambassador approaching. "Very well," Logan said. "Let him approach. Set up my chair and desk here." He'd deliberately leaked to the ambassador that he would be here, assuming the man would follow. Logan had meant to meet with the man in front of the wheel as a reminder of how hard Logan could be. But in his wildest nightmares he hadn't thought Kylar would still be dying while they met.

The wheel turned and Logan stood, facing it, watching Kylar until Agon Brant, acting as his impromptu chamberlain, announced the ambassador. "Your Majesty, Tertulus Martus, Questor of the Twelfth Army of the Lae'knaught, attaché to Overlord Julus Rotans."

Logan turned and sat at the field desk. Tertulus Martus's eyes flicked past him to Kylar. Standing, Logan's body obscured the visage of death. Sitting, it framed him. The ambassador couldn't look at him without being aware of the man dying behind him on the wheel.

"Your Majesty," Tertulus said. "Thank you for welcoming me, and congratulations on your recent ascension to the throne and your most glorious victories. If half the tales are true, your name shall live forever." He went on for some time. The Lae'knaught's Twelfth Army was their diplomatic corps. There hadn't been twelve Lae'knaught armies since before the Alitaeran Accords. Today, there were perhaps three—and maybe only two, given the massacre of the five thousand in Ezra's Wood. But Tertulus Martus had set the rudder before he began speaking, and he didn't even have to think as he spoke. His body was similarly controlled, betraying nothing. He stood with his feet fairly close together, so as not to appear combative. His hands were kept loose, so as to neither point nor clench into fists. His gestures were small. Logan watched his eyes instead.

The man was weighing him. This ambassador wasn't here to offer any deals, though he would surely soon offer something small. His anxiety to see Logan as quickly as possible came only from pressure from his superiors. They wanted to know if Logan was a threat. They had recently lost five thousand men, and they needed to know if this new king of an insignificant, corrupt kingdom could be trusted to do as Cenarian kings had done for twenty years: nothing.

Still saying nothing, Logan rose in the middle of the diplomat's sentence. With perfect calm, he knocked over the field desk, sending blank parchment, inkpot, and quill flying with a crash. He stepped on the desk and ripped off a leg.

With two mighty slashes, he broke Kylar's legs at the shins.

Kylar screamed. Deprived of support, his body sagged against a dozen blades under his arms. Jagged bones stabbed through the skin of his legs, gleaming wetly in the rising sun. He screamed again as the wheel turned sideways and the sides of his legs were pierced much more deeply. His head dunked under water in the middle of a scream and he came up coughing and retching.

His arms slid onto the blades again as he came fully upright and his screams trailed off into whimpers. Logan looked at the depth of the cuts and looked Kylar in the eye. There was great suffering, but there was no fear.

With two more heavy blows, Logan broke Kylar's forearms.

Kylar screamed again. Without the rigidity of those bones, his body sank unnaturally far, gravity stretching his arms like clay, his body sinking too far at every turn. He coughed blood with every breath, and blood streamed from him in rivers.

Logan heard several of his attendants throwing up, but he never turned away.

After seven revolutions, Kylar stopped coughing. The flow of blood slowed, and the tension in the distorted muscles relaxed. Logan gestured to a pair of the King's Guard. The wheel stopped. They checked for a pulse. There was none. They began removing the body.

Logan turned to Tertulus Martus, who for all his diplomatic training still hadn't managed to close his gaping mouth or narrow his wide eyes.

"Five hundred and forty-three years ago," Logan said, "a man was captured by a Khalidoran Vürdmeister and tortured for three months. This man kept his sanity, and his courage, and at the end of those three months, he escaped. He founded an order devoted to resisting and destroying black magic—Khalidoran magic. In time, this mission expanded to encompass the destruction of all magic and all who wield it. However, his order, the Laetunariverissiknaught, the Bringers of the Freedom of the Light, still harbor an especial hatred of those who wield the vir."

"Your Majesty displays a remarkable knowledge of—"

"Silence!" Logan roared, pointing the bloody table leg an inch from Tertulus's nose. The man stopped. "For the last eighteen years, you Lae'knaught have been squatting on Cenarian lands. This will end. Here are your choices. First, you can pack up and leave immediately. Second, you can fight us. You recently lost five thousand men, and I have a battle-seasoned army that's getting bored—and a Ceuran army to whom I've sworn a battle that will live in history. We will crush you. Or third, you can marshal your armies and march to Khalidor beside us. That way you can fight those you say you truly hate, and have a chance to defeat them. If you fight beside us, I will give you a fifteen-year grant to the lands you now occupy. But, and I can't stress this enough, after that time, you will leave Cenarian lands forever. Regardless of your choice, my armies will march in the spring. We will head east first. If you don't join with us, we will wipe you out, and we won't stop at our own borders. We will notify every kingdom on whose lands you might hide that we are coming. Perhaps one of them might join you to fight against us. But then again, they might choose to join us. It depends on how much goodwill you've built up with your neighbors."

Tertulus Martus laughed nervously. "Those terms are clearly not acceptable, but I'm sure our negotiators will be able to find something mutually—"

"If you don't choose to fight beside Cenaria, you will be choosing to fight against Cenaria. I win wars in such a way that I don't have to fight them twice."

"You can't come after us, not with your full strength, not with Khalidor to your north."

"Khalidor has suffered a great defeat and there are defensible passes between our borders. Khalidor doesn't hold any of my land. You do. I have made an oath to Lantano Garuwashi that he will have a great battle come spring. Together he and I can wipe you out. Such a victory, I dare say, would endear him greatly to the Ceurans back home. What we cannot do without you is destroy Khalidor. No matter what, the sa'ceurai will go home next summer. I have one year to destroy one or both of the greatest threats to my realm, so I've no reason to hold anything back, do I?"

"You're mad," Tertulus said, throwing away a lifetime of diplomatic training.

"I'm desperate. There's a difference. I have no intention of giving you a good deal, ambassador. You're overextended, weakened, surrounded by enemies, and quite frankly, you piss me off. I don't intend to negotiate. We've written up a treaty in full, with details on how your forces will be integrated with ours for the length of the war with Khalidor and details of how we will be sure that you leave Cenaria after your fifteen-year grant has expired. I will give you only enough time to take this to your Overlord, give him three days to discuss it with his advisers, and get back here. Any modifications he proposes will be considered a rejection of the treaty. That's all there is to it. On the other hand, if you truly hate Khalidor, if you hate black magic and how it has enslaved an entire country and seeks to destroy Midcyru, this is the opportunity of a lifetime. We could destroy Khalidor once and for all." Logan gestured and a scroll in an ornate case was brought forward. "Now I advise you to get your horse. Your answer is due three weeks from today. Delinquency will be considered a declaration of war."

57

Elene looked at the woman on the bed in the Chantry's hospital floor. Vi's eyes were swollen, her light freckles almost green against her pale skin. Two days ago, Vi had fallen unconscious with a cry as they'd been walking together. Elene had been surprised how well they'd been getting along, then this had happened. "Have you figured anything out?"

"It's definitely the bond," Sister Ariel said. That was good and bad. The only other guess they'd had was that Vi's rapid progress with her Talent had been hiding some flaw, and all her power had rebounded on her. From her talks with Sister Ariel, Elene had learned that Vi was terrifically Talented, but completely uneven in what she learned. Her wetboy training had enabled her to use her Talent easily, but she'd missed certain basics—and the Sisters had no idea which ones, so it seemed Vi mastered some difficult things as easily as breathing, and some easy things she couldn't get at all. When she'd collapsed, everyone had been frightened.

Of course, if it was the bond, that meant something had gone really wrong with Kylar. Elene looked at Sister Ariel.

"We've had pigeons from Cenaria that a treason trial was being concluded," Sister Ariel said. "I deduce from Vi's state that the sentence is being carried out even now. The wheel, I would imagine." She looked up and down the corridor. "With Kylar's special…gifts, it's taking longer than it should. And Vi has been helping him heal by taking some of his suffering onto herself. It's only making the inevitable last longer, so it's a cruel kindness, but it is well meant."

Kylar was dying, right now? Elene should have felt it, she should have known as Vi did. In fact, she would have, if Vi hadn't stolen her ring. Jealousy flashed through her, and she suppressed it only with difficulty. Dammit, why couldn't you forgive someone once and be done with it? "Why would she help him like that?" Elene asked.

"One can only guess. But then I don't claim to know much about love."

The word was a blow. Vi loved Kylar? This much?

Vi sat bolt upright and shrieked. Her eyes met Elene's. She grabbed her own shins. "No, I can't—I can't do it. I'm not strong enough. It hurts too much." She fell back on the bed, babbling, then shrieked again, holding her arms. "No, Kylar, no!" Then she lost consciousness, and Elene knew Kylar was dead.

Sister Ariel stepped forward immediately and grabbed Vi's earring. She tried to pry it off, but it wouldn't budge. "Dammit. The bond's not broken. Not even by his…" she trailed off, realizing that this place was too public to admit Kylar's immortality. "I was hoping—well, not hoping that he would…you know what, but that if he did, that the bond would break." Sister Ariel grimaced and looked away. "It was my last hope for you. The bond really is forever. I'm sorry, Elene. I'm sorry."

The walk through the golden halls of death was familiar now. Kylar glided forward, not really touching the ground. It was as if the mind constructed movement as walking, having to impose some order on a realm that existed without human analogues.

The Antechamber of the Mystery was exactly as he remembered it. The Wolf sat on his throne, yellow eyes lambent, hostility etched into his burn-scarred face. Two doors sat opposite him: the plain wood door through which Kylar would walk back to life, and the gold door leaking warm light around its edges, barred to him forever. The ghostly presence of others filled the room. They moved unseen, staring, talking about him.

"Congratulations, Nameless," the Wolf said. "You've proved you can sacrifice yourself like you don't care if you die. Like you don't give a damn about the living. How like the young." The wolfish smile was cruel.

Kylar was too tired to play games. The Wolf didn't intimidate him anymore. "Why do you hate me?" he asked.

The Wolf cocked his head, taken off guard. "Because you're a waste, Nameless. People love you more than you have any right to, and you treat them like they're shit to be scraped off your boots."

It was so unfair after what Kylar had gone through that he threw his hands up. "You know what, to hell with you. You can make your little cryptic comments and hate me if you want to, but at least call me by my fucking name."

"And what name is that?" the Wolf asked.

"Kylar. Kylar Stern."

"Kylar Stern? The stern, undying dier? That's not a name; it's a title. It's a judge."

"Azoth, then."

"You are many leagues from that shitless, witless rat, but even were you he, do you know what azoth is?"

"What do you mean?"

The Wolf laughed unkindly. "Azoth is an old word for quicksilver. Random, formless, unpredictable, literally mercurial. You, Nameless, can be anyone and thus are no one. You're smoke, a shadow that melts away in the light of day. Kagé they call you. A shadow of what you could be and a shadow of your master, who was a titan."

"My master was a coward! He never even told me who he was!" Kylar shouted. He blinked. The depth of his rage left him shaken. Where had that come from?

The Wolf was pensive. The ghosts in the room fell silent. Then, in a murmur unintelligible to Kylar's ears, one of them spoke to the Wolf. The Wolf folded his hands over his stomach. He nodded, acquiescing. "Prince Acaelus Thorne of Trayethell was a warrior and not much else. Neither introspective nor wise, he was one of the rare good men who love war. He didn't hate himself or life. He wasn't cruel. He simply gloried in a contest with the highest possible stakes. He was good at it, too, and he became one of Jorsin Alkestes' best friends.

"That nettled one of Jorsin's other best friends, an easily nettled archmagus named Ezra, who thought Acaelus a charismatic fool who happened to be good at swinging a sword. In return, Acaelus thought Ezra a coward who took Jorsin away from where he belonged in the front lines. When the Champions were chosen—the men and women who were Jorsin's final hope of victory—Ezra intended to bond the Devourer himself. It was by far the most powerful ka'kari and he had sweat and bled for it. The only man to whom he would willingly surrender it was Jorsin. But the Devourer didn't choose Ezra. Or Jorsin. It chose the sword-swinger.

"Perhaps you can appreciate why it seemed odd that an artifact which by its nature was concerned with concealment would go to a man completely lacking subtlety."

It did seem odd, though the choice had obviously proved wise.

"The Devourer didn't choose your master simply because he was an obscure choice. It chose Acaelus because it understood his heart. Acaelus loved the clash of arms, but most men who love battle love it because it proves their mastery over others. If the Devourer had given itself to a man who loved power as Ezra did, it would have spawned a tyrant of terrible proportions. Think of a Godking made truly a god and you have a bit of it. What your master loved, at his core, was the brotherhood of war. He thirsted for the camaraderie of men risking all to come through for each other.

"The Devourer is nothing if not talented at setting up tensions. For your master to take the black ka'kari, he had to leave that brotherhood. He had to give up what he loved most and become known as a traitor. That tension forced Acaelus to become a deeper, wiser, and sadder man. Then of course, there was the Devourer's greater tension and greater power. Your master was a man of war, but the vagaries of war are such that even the mighty might be clipped by a stray arrow or a falling horse or the mistake of a friend. So your master lived with the tension of his calling pulling against his fear for any he loved.

"Acaelus sought to live in peace. He had a few lifetimes as a farmer, a hunter, an apothecary, a perfumer, a blacksmith—can you imagine? Yet though they were full lives—sometimes married, even with children— they were not fulfilled lives, for a man who denies what is essential to his being is a man who drills holes in the cup of his own happiness. How could he help but resent those he loved as they kept him from his calling? Here was a man who could lead armies, who could defeat invasions almost single-handedly. This man was compelled to farm? By his own love? Time and again, he returned to the battlefield because the evil was too great to be ignored. And sometimes he was victorious and there was no price to pay. And sometimes his wife died, but it was worse when his children died; his marriages never survived his children's deaths. He was a man who never learned to forgive himself."

Kylar was missing some essential piece that the Wolf thought he understood, but the man kept speaking, and Kylar was so hungry to hear more about his master that he didn't dare interrupt.

"So in the end, he sought to defeat the power of the ka'kari by defeating love," the Wolf said. "He thought that if he refused to love, death could take nothing from him. He deafened himself to love's voice with killing and whoring and drinking. He became a wetboy because wetboys cannot love. He was ultimately successful, and the ka'kari abandoned him because he finally knew love's antithesis."

"Hatred?"

"Indifference. When Vonda's life was threatened, Durzo was relieved. The path he took was a reasonable one—he kept the ka'kari out of young Garoth Ursuul's hands—but the truth was that he didn't really care if Vonda died. That was what broke the ka'kari's bond."

"But he came back. Even after I bonded the ka'kari."

"Because he loved you, Kylar. He chose to die for you, to give up everything he still had—his sword, his ka'kari, his power, his life—for you. There is no greater love. Such a death was rewarded with new life."

"By who? You?" Kylar asked. The Wolf said nothing. "The ka'kari? The God?"

"Perhaps it is just the way greatest magic works: justice and mercy entwined. It's a mystery, Kylar. A mystery on a par with the question of why is there life at all? If you wish to answer the mystery by positing a God, you can, or you can say that it just is—and either way, be glad for it, for it is a gift. Or a most fortunate accident."

Kylar felt suddenly small in the workings of a universe vast beyond comprehension, vast and yet perhaps not ambivalent even to Durzo's suffering. One last life—a sheer gift. The ka'kari was even more strange and marvelous than he'd imagined.

"I thought..." Kylar shook his head. "I thought it was just amazing magic."

The Wolf laughed, and even the ghosts in the room seemed startled. "It is amazing magic, it just isn't *just* amazing magic. The most potent magics are tied to human truths: beauty and passion and yearning and fortitude and valor and empathy. It is from these that the ka'kari draw their strength as much as it is from the magic they are imbued with."

"And the darker truths?" Kylar asked.

"All human truths. Vengeance and hatred and glorying in destruction and ambition and greed and all the rest have power. The trick to being truly powerful is that your character be in line with the magic you attempt. Meisters make terrible healers. By the same token, most green mages have too much empathy to make war. The more fully human you are, the greater the diversity of your talents. The more deeply you feel, the more potent your gifts. That, Kylar, is why you called the ka'kari. You ached for love. Not only did you want be loved, as do we all, but you wanted to lavish love on your beloved. You wanted it with your whole being and you thought it had been denied you forever."

The way he said it embarrassed Kylar.

"Don't be embarrassed," the Wolf said. "What is more human than to love and be loved? Between loving and thinking that love was denied you, that tension amplified your power."

"That tension's with me still, isn't it?" Kylar asked. "For my love will always be dangerous to those I love."

"Clever, isn't it? Your power is tied to your capacity for love. The creator of the ka'kari gave you a gift and built into it the means to keep it forever powerful. No mean trick, that."

"A mean trick is exactly what it is," Kylar snarled. "What the hell am I supposed to do?"

"It's a problem," the Wolf said, shrugging.

But Kylar wasn't listening. He could feel the blood draining out of his face. "Oh my God," he said. His heart was a thunder in his ears, a rock in his chest. He'd meant he was dangerous to those he loved because his enemies could always threaten them. That wasn't what the Wolf meant. He'd been telling Kylar for five minutes and Kylar hadn't understood. Breathless, Kylar asked, "You mean every time I've died someone I love has died for me?"

"Of course. That's the price of immortality."

Kylar's throat constricted. He was suffocating. "Who...?"

"Serah Drake died when Roth killed you. Mags Drake died for Scarred Wrable's arrow on the trail. Ulana Drake died when the Godking killed you."

Kylar's knees buckled. He wanted to throw up. He wanted to faint. Anything, anything to not be. But the moment stretched on and in the midst of the gale, he found himself thinking, thank the God it wasn't Uly or Elene, and then he cursed himself for the thought. Who was he to weigh one life against another and be thankful that one should die, simply because he loved her less? He'd killed them. Count Drake had taken in a foul-mouthed, amoral guttershite and made him part of his family. And Kylar had murdered the Drakes through his carelessness, his arrogance. For every gift Count Drake had given Kylar, he'd repaid him with grief.

"And for my blasphemy? When I took money to be killed?"

"Jarl."

Kylar screamed. He tore his cloak. He pounded the ground with his fists, but there was no pain here, no body to mortify. The tears rolled down his cheeks and there was no comfort. "I didn't know. I didn't know. Oh, God."

The Wolf was astounded. "But of course you knew. Durzo left you a letter on his body. He explained everything. He told me he put it in his breast pocket."

"I couldn't read it! It was soaked with blood! I couldn't read a damned thing!" Then the last revelation hit him. "Who is it this time?" he asked, desperately. "Who dies for me this time?"

The Wolf was aghast. His lambent eyes and scarred face softened, and he looked fully human for the first time. "Kylar. I'm sorry. I thought you knew. I thought you knew all along."

"Please. I'll trade back! Let me trade back."

"It doesn't work like that. There's nothing either of us can do. This time it's Elene."

Kylar woke on a cold stone slab in a cold room. He didn't open his eyes. If he could have willed himself never to wake again, he would have. He was still except for his breath and the currents of his life's blood rushing through his veins. As always when he came back from the dead, his body felt wonderful. Absolutely whole, powerful, bursting with energy. He'd stolen a life and it came to him abundantly. He was overfull, spilling life in every direction. His health was a mockery.

Tears welled in his eyes and spilled down his cheeks to his ears. No wonder the Wolf had thought him a monster. He'd thought Kylar was throwing away the lives of those he loved and who loved him.

He lay on his back, but it only got worse, so he opened his eyes. The air was stale, dank. The ceiling was ornate, cool white marble. He was in a crypt. Only feet away, on slabs like his, were a man's body and a woman's. The man was big, holding a big sword. The woman's throat had been cut, and from how she'd decomposed, Kylar guessed she'd been bled dry. The man had died around the same time, surely during the coup. They were Logan's parents. Around them, the walls were filled with row upon row of Gyre corpses, stretching back centuries. Logan had put Kylar in his own family's crypt.

Kylar stood, not even feeling stiffness from having slept on marble. He'd been dressed in a cloth-of-gold tunic and white breeches, and fine fawnskin shoes. It was, of course, pitch black in the crypt. There was no way of telling what time of day it was, and the mouth of the crypt was sealed with a massive rock cut into the shape of a wheel taller than a man. If Kylar remembered correctly, the crypt was located outside the city and sunk beneath the ground. If so, he had a good chance of getting out without anyone knowing. Regardless, he had to get out, so he grabbed the wheel and heaved with his Talent.

Slowly, the massive stone rolled a half turn and settled into another rest. Kylar went invisible and stepped outside.

It was night, but the harvest moon was bright and high overhead. In the narrow stairwell that led to the crypt stood a young girl, her eyes wide with fear. It was Blue, the little guttershite from Black Dragon guild.

Kylar stopped, still invisible, and rubbed his face. Blue didn't move. He could tell she wanted to run but refused to. Brave little shite. "Kylar?" she whispered.

What was he supposed to do? Kill her? Avoid her and let her blab stories about the crypt opening? It was unlikely, but someone might open the crypt to check it out. And what would they do when they saw Kylar was gone?

"Kylar, I know you're there. Take me with you."

Staying invisible, Kylar asked, "Have you ever killed anyone, Blue?"

She gasped and swallowed, looking for the source of the voice. "No," she whispered.

"Do you want to kill people?"

"I'd kill Dag Tarkus. He kicked Piggy in the stomach for stealing and the next day he died."

"What if I told you that to be my apprentice you'd have to kill a dozen kids like Piggy? What if I told you you had to kill your whole guild?"

Blue started crying.

"You just want out, don't you?"

She nodded her head.

"Then I need you to do two things, Blue. First, never—*ever*—speak about this. If you tell anyone, bad people will find out, and they'll kill lots of good people. You understand? You can't even tell your best friend."

Blue nodded. "I got no friends, not after Piggy died."

"Go to the corner of Verdun and Gar. I'll meet you in an hour."

"Promise?"

"I promise."

Blue left and Kylar closed the crypt. He found a safe house and loaded up everything he needed, including Retribution, which he had left before he killed the queen, knowing his weapons would be confiscated. He wrote a note to Rimbold Drake, first explaining about the laundress he'd maimed and asking Drake to pay restitution, and then explaining what the Wolf told Kylar he'd cost the Drakes. He grabbed several bags of gold and a few poisons and changes of clothing, took a cloak and pulled the hood over his face.

He found Blue sitting at the intersection. She scrambled to her feet.

"Inside that house lives a good man, Blue. He was poisoned and nearly died during the coup, and the Khalidorans killed his wife and two of his daughters. He's the best man I know, and I think he might need you as much as you need him. In my note, I've asked him to raise you. He'll give you the only chance you'll ever have to make something of yourself. But it won't be easy. If you go in this house, you stay until you walk out a lady. Is that what you want?"

"A lady?" Blue asked, her face lit with impossible yearning.

"Say it."

"I want to be somebody. I want to be a lady."

"I believe you." Kylar put his hand to a crack in the door, sent the ka'kari through, and opened the latch. He opened the door and they walked past the porter's hut to the front door. Kylar handed a bag full of gold crowns to Blue. It was so heavy she could barely hold it. Then he put the note in her hand and threw back his hood, so she would never doubt that it was him. "Blue, I'm trusting you. I see souls. I weigh them. From yours, I know you're worth it. Be good to Count Drake. I wasn't as good to him as he deserved."

With that, Kylar pounded on the door and went invisible. He waited until the bleary-eyed count opened the door. Rimbold Drake looked at Blue, confused. She was too terrified to speak. After a moment, he took the note from her hand. After he read it, he wept.

Kylar turned to go.

"You were better than you know," Drake said to the night. "I forgive you any wrong you think you have done me. You will always be welcome here, my son."

Kylar disappeared into the night. It was where he belonged.

After two days, they moved Solon to another room. It was still locked, the windows covered with bars, the cedar door banded with iron, but this room had a view of Whitecliff Castle's courtyard. The courtyard was decorated in a style fit for the wedding, greens the color of the vines and the seas, and the purples of wine and royalty dominating.

"I don't know who you are, Pretender," one of Solon's guards said. He was a paunchy man with heavy jowls and haphazardly polished armor. "But enjoy the wedding, because it's the last thing you'll ever see."

"Why's that?" Solon asked.

"Because the Mikaidon wanted his first order as emperor to be your death."

The other guard, a rail-thin man with a single eyebrow, looked nervous and guilty. "Shut it, Ori. Nysos' blood, it's gonna be a bad enough day as it is." To Solon, he said, "We'll make it quick, I promise." He exited, watching Solon for any sudden movement, and locked the door behind himself.

Solon was surprised to find a tub full of water and fresh clothes in the room. He scrubbed himself and donned the clean garments, thinking. Oshobi was already giving orders to Kaede's guards. That couldn't be good, but it didn't necessarily mean what Solon suspected. Solon had never learned how much power Kaede intended to share once she married. When she talked with him two days ago she hadn't seemed desperate enough to grant Oshobi total power.

It made him feel sick. For the last two days, he'd thought through every option he had, and he couldn't find anything that would assert his own rights without undermining Kaede's. He didn't know what any of the political undercurrents were, so anything he did could have the opposite of the intended effect. But the clean clothes laid out for him, clothing fit for a noble, if not quite royalty, told him that Kaede most likely hadn't intended him to die today. Was this his chance? Or was she punishing him by forcing him to watch a wedding that she saw as his fault?

Outside, the nobles were gathering in order of precedence, standing as Sethi always stood to witness a wedding. Soon, at least four hundred of them surrounded the platform where the Empress and Emperor-to-be would be wed. Solon could pick out many faces he recognized, and saw a frightening number of absences, too. Had his brother killed so many? How had Sijuron become such a monster without Solon knowing?

The ring of the singing swords announced the beginning of the ceremony. On the platform, the dancers faced each other. Each wore a mask, the man the suitor's mask, which today was deadly serious. A pubescent boy wore the woman's mask, today lovely but austere in keeping with the empress's dignity. Each held a specially shaped hollow sword that would sing in the dance, tones varied by the dancers' grip and where each struck the other. The swords were pitched at octaves, and the duel—symbolic of the couple's courtship—was always partly choreographed and partly extemporaneous. It was a perennial favorite, and skilled dancers were the most expensive part of a wedding. The dances, proclaimed sacred to Nysos, ranged from the erotic to the comedic. It was also usually the most anxiety-provoking time of a wedding for the couple. Dancers being the artists they were, there was no guaranteeing they wouldn't make the man or woman or both look like fools, and the sword dance was often the only thing remembered about the wedding.

The dancers bowed low, but kept their eyes up, as if suspicious of each other, and then they began. For a time as they danced, Solon forgot that he was in a prison. They gave the boy a quick hand for Kaede's quick tongue, and a wide range. A woman known as a scold might be given a single note for an entire dance, while an excitable man might be given only notes at the extremes of the singing sword. The man playing Oshobi was a huge presence, forceful and manly and, if slower, also stronger than Kaede. Whoever they were, these dancers were incorruptible, unafraid of even a man who would be emperor. In their dance, Solon read the courtship perfectly.

Oshobi had always pursued with a single-minded determination. Kaede weakened early, then rallied for years. Always, Oshobi pursued, and the dancer gave a lightly mocking tone to it that only a skilled eye would have seen. There was the suggestion that Oshobi wanted not Kaede, but that which was behind her—missing opportunities at the woman as he aimed at the throne.

Kaede slowly tired, but the dancers underplayed it, not suggesting that Oshobi beat her into submission, but simply allowing her to slow to his level and make him look more brilliant as he matched and overmatched her, cadences singing together until Oshobi took up Kaede's line. As the dance wound to a close, Kaede bowed to her knees and spread her arms to take the ceremonial touch over the heart. In apparent haste, the dancer playing

Oshobi stepped forward too quickly and slipped, his sword tapped her throat for the barest instant before he righted himself and touched it to her heart.

It was so well done that even Solon believed for a moment that the dancer really had slipped. Everyone took it as that, or decided to take it as that: a slight error in an otherwise flawless performance. They cheered wildly and once the cheering stopped, the betrothed entered.

Solon's heart leapt to his throat as Kaede strode forward. She wore a purple samite cape with a long train, edged in lace. A crown of vines with ripe purple grapes was woven through her long black hair. It being her wedding, both of her breasts were bare, the nipples rouged, and beneath her navel her bare stomach was adorned with ancient fertility runes. A cloth-of-gold skirt hung low on her hips, trailing slightly behind her, her wine-stained bare feet barely winking out. Most women exposed more of their ankles, saying the juice of the grape is clothing enough for a wedding. Apparently Kaede really did believe that a queen was a queen first and a woman sometime later. But after a decade and a half in Midcyru, the modesty was lost on Solon. The sight of her here, like this, filled him with every sort of longing. The skirt had neither buttons nor clasps nor ties, nor underclothes beneath it. It was finished the morning of the wedding with the woman inside it. It was to be torn off by the groom in his passion. Revelers outside the wedding chamber would call loudly until the groom threw it out the window. In ancient times and in some rural areas still, the skirt was always white, and ripped open but not removed until the wedding was consummated. Then the revelers would parade with the "proof" of the woman's virginity, which as often as not was sheep's blood. Most mothers provided their daughters with a vial of it, in case she had broken her hymen licitly or illicitly. It was a tradition Solon was glad had mostly disappeared, not only because he thought it was gross, but also because he found it hard to imagine enjoying consummating his marriage with drunken screaming assholes pounding on the walls.

In the courtyard, Oshobi Takeda walked forward. Solon felt a stab of hatred. *He* should be walking forward now. *He* should be the one who tore Kaede's skirt tonight. Oshobi Takeda came into the circle bare-chested as well, runes of vigor and potency painted on the surface of a stomach so muscular and devoid of fat that it wasn't flat but ridged. He too wore vines through his hair and a simple green cape, paired with cloth-of-gold trousers that ended just below the knee.

Oshobi mounted the platform, barely looking at Kaede. Solon thought he must be either blind or homosexual to disregard such beauty. He turned and addressed the assembled nobles. "I came here today to marry our empress. It was in my heart to unite this land as it hasn't been united for more than a decade. I know all of us were dismayed when we heard of Daune Wariyamo's infidelities, and though it strained my family's honor, I came here determined to wed."

From his position, Solon could see what the nobles below could not. At every exit, armored city guards had lined up, and with them in irregular ranks stood many of the royal guards. The strength was, so far, hidden, but they could move in on the assembled nobles in moments. What Solon couldn't see was how Kaede was taking this prologue to treason.

He didn't have to wait long.

Kaede strode up onto the platform directly to Oshobi and slapped his face. "If you speak treason, Oshobi Takeda, I will have your head," Kaede said in a clear, fearless voice.

An older noble Solon recognized as Nori Oshibatu, long a friend of the Wariyamos, shot a look at Oshobi and stepped forward. "My dear, Kaede, our beloved empress, you sound hysterical. This is not befitting. Please, he only speaks." Nori pulled Kaede back into the crowd, where several other family "friends" closed around her.

Oshobi smiled like the big cat he was. "I came here to serve Seth, but this very morning, I discovered something my honor could not countenance. Daune Wariyamo had on her person letters from the late emperor's brother Solon to Kaede. In these letters, he spoke of his trysts with her in the castle and of a secret marriage."

"You lie!" Kaede shrieked.

Solon's heart sank. The trysts in the castle had only been attempted trysts, culminating in the disaster of her mother coming in on them naked and beating Solon with a shoe. It would have been worth it if she'd come in ten minutes later or—well, he'd been a young man—maybe two minutes later. The marriage, of course, was a total fiction.

But Oshobi was quick. "I have the letters here!" he said, brandishing a sheaf. "And this woman was with Lady Wariyamo when she came upon you fornicating in the castle." A slave woman was thrust forward. "I do so swear," she said in a tiny voice.

"Louder," Oshobi demanded.

"I swear it's true!"

The nobles were in the predictable uproar, but Oshobi was wise enough that he didn't call his men forward. Kaede was screaming, but someone put a hand over her mouth, and numerous men were restraining her.

"So you see, even if we believe that Kaede wasn't incestuous in her sluttish trysts in our nation's very heart, we know that she married Sijuron

Tofusin. A marriage null and void because she was already married—to the emperor's brother!"

Oshobi painted a sad look on his face. "I woke this morning, willing to dishonor my family because I wanted to do what was right for our country—"

Behind Solon, the door creaked open. He turned away from the courtyard to see his two guards enter. "All right," the paunchy one said, "we already let you see more of the show than we was supposed to. You can figure how it turns out from here. You ready?"

"Yes," Solon said. He drew in his Talent. "Which of you would like to die first?"

"Huh?" they asked in unison.

"Together then," he said, and stilled their hearts with his Talent.

The guards collapsed, one crumpling, the other falling full on his face. Solon took a sword and faced the barred window.

With a concussion that rocked the castle, Solon blew out the entire wall. Stones rained on the crowd fifty paces away. Everyone ducked and turned to see what had happened. *And Dorian always said I wasn't subtle.*

Solon jumped down lightly and strode toward the crowd. A guard stepped in his path, wide-eyed and gulping. Solon gestured as if shooing a fly and a wall of air flipped the guard aside.

"I am Solonariwan Tofusin, son of Emperor Cresus Tofusin, Light of the West, Protector of the Isles, and High Admiral of the Royal Fleets of Seth." It was a deliberately ambiguous construction, whether he was listing his father's titles, or claiming them for himself. "I have come home, and I call you a traitor and a liar, Oshibi. And even if your despicable lies were true, you have no claim to this throne while I live."

"We can remedy that," Oshobi snarled.

Solon advanced quickly onto the platform, not giving Oshobi time to think. "You would duel me?" Solon asked. He laughed scornfully. "A Tofusin does not dirty his hands with the blood of a dog."

Oshobi roared, drew his sword and hacked at Solon with all his considerable strength. Solon deflected it. His counterstroke cut halfway into Oshobi's neck. Oshobi's eyes went big, but he tried to complete one more slash while Solon's sword was stuck. A sliver of magic enervated Oshobi's fingers. The sword dropped.

"However," Solon said, "I'll make an exception for a Little Cat." He ripped the sword out of Oshobi's neck and blood sprayed over the platform as the big man dropped onto his face. Solon put his foot on the neck of his dying foe and pointed the sword at the nobles holding Kaede. "That's your empress," Solon said. "I'd advise you to take your hands off her."

60

After riding most of the night, Kylar camped a short distance off the road, merely unsaddling Tribe and throwing a blanket on the ground. A few hours later, Tribe's snort woke him. Kylar blinked and rolled to his feet.

"So you haven't forgotten everything I taught you," a brown-clad figure said, leading his horse to tie it next to Tribe.

"Master?" Kylar asked.

Dehvirahaman ko Bruhmaeziwakazari snorted. It was odd to hear the sound, so characteristically Durzo, coming out of the Ymmuri's mouth. He glanced at Retribution in Kylar's hand. "Good, I see you haven't managed to lose it again, yet. See that you don't, would you? You ready to ride?"

Kylar felt an odd excitement. He did feel ready to ride. The overflow of energy from his invocation of immortality hadn't worn off yet. "I'm not dreaming this, am I?" he asked.

Dehvi lifted an eyebrow. "There's one way to find out for sure," he said.

"What's that?"

"Go piss in the woods. If you feel wet and warm afterward, wake up."

Laughing, Kylar went and relieved himself. When he came back, Dehvi was seated cross-legged and had laid out a huge, albeit cold, breakfast.

Kylar tore into the food with gusto that surprised himself, though apparently not Dehvi. The scene still had an air of unreality, though, and Kylar kept glancing at him. Finally, the Ymmuri said, "If you're looking for Durzo's mannerisms, you're going to see fewer and fewer of them. I don't chew garlic anymore, for one. And I'm getting rid of the rest as fast as I can. A new face isn't much good if you still do everything else the same. I have done this a few times. So if you need me to prove who I am, let's get it over with."

"There is one thing Durzo told me that he never told anyone else. You've had all these names, and you always picked something with meaning: Ferric Fireheart, Gaelan Starfire, Hrothan Steelbender. Even the other wetboys had names that meant something: Hu Gibbet, Scarred Wrable. Why Durzo Blint? Is that another Old Jaeran pun?"

Dehvi laughed. "Trick question. I never told you why I chose it. But to answer, it was supposed to be Durzo Flint. I was drunk. Someone repeated it Blint, and I didn't care enough to correct them. Next?"

"Flint makes a lot more sense, you old bastard."

"Only by nature, not by birth. Anything else?"

Kylar got grim. "What does immortality cost?"

"Right to the gut, huh?" Durzo said. He cleared his throat and looked away. "Every new life costs the life of someone you love."

There it was, as simple as anything. If Durzo had told him that before the coup, everything would be different. Of course, Durzo had tried to tell him, in the letter.

"Is there any way to stop it?" Kylar asked.

"You mean stop your immortality or stop it from killing someone else?"

"Either. Both."

"The Wolf never told me the limits—maybe he didn't know himself. I avoided anything that would fully destroy my body like burning or being drawn and quartered."

"And Curoch?"

Durzo shot Kylar a sharp look. "A fatal blow from Curoch would blow apart the immortality magic. Jorsin feared the Devourer. He made sure there was at least one way to kill an immortal."

Kylar had a sudden feeling of dislocation. He was talking with someone who had known Jorsin Alkestes. Jorsin Alkestes! And Jorsin had feared the magic Kylar possessed. "What about stopping it from costing someone else's life?" Kylar asked.

Durzo sighed. "You think in seven centuries I didn't try? It's deep magic, kid. A life for a life. The Wolf can delay it, but not stop it, and it's not easy even for him."

Kylar cleared his throat. "What if, um, what if I were killed by Curoch during the time between me dying and the person who is going to die for me dying?"

The look on Durzo's face made it clear that Kylar's question was far too specific for him to dismiss as theoretical. "Boy, you have no idea what Curoch is like—"

"Yes I do, I threw it into Ezra's Wood."

"You what?!"

"I made a deal with the Wolf. I didn't get your note until afterward."

Durzo rubbed his temples. "And what did he give you in return for the most powerful artifact in the world?"

"He brought me back to life faster—and gave me my arm back, which I kind of cut off."

Durzo's flat stare was all too familiar, despite that it was coming through almond-shaped eyes. It suggested he was seeing previously undredged depths of stupidity. "And between assassinating a Godking and a Cenarian queen and rescuing a man from the Hole and making a king of him, when did you squeeze in the time to find and lose the world's most coveted magical sword?" Durzo asked.

"It only took me a week. Lantano Garuwashi had it. I dueled him for it."

"Is he as good as they say?"

"Better. And he's not even Talented."

"Then how'd you win?" Durzo asked.

"Hey!" Kylar protested.

"Kylar, I trained you. You're not the best. Someday, maybe. So either he's not as good as they say, or you got lucky, or you cheated."

"I got lucky," Kylar admitted. "Is it so bad though? I mean throwing Curoch in the Wood?"

"Do you know who the Wolf is?" Durzo asked.

"That was the next question."

"The better question is who the Wolf was. No one knows what he is now."

"I'll bite. Who was the Wolf?" Kylar asked.

"In Jorsin Alkestes' court, there was a mage with golden eyes. He was slightly less Talented than Jorsin himself in terms of raw power, but whereas Jorsin had to learn the arts of war and leadership and diplomacy in addition to magecraft, the golden-eyed mage had only magecraft to study, and he was the kind of genius of magic born once in a thousand years. He had few graces and fewer friends, but Jorsin meant the world to him. In the war, he lost everything: Jorsin, all his tomes of magic, his only other friend, Oren Razin, and his fiancée. He lost his sanity, too, and no one knows if he ever really regained it. He hid in a forest where he could work out his hatred. The forest, of course, took his name."

"Ezra's Wood," Kylar whispered. "The Wolf is Ezra?"

"Jorsin had a close friend who betrayed him, a man named Roygaris Ursuul."

"Oh God."

"During the war, Roygaris Made something—out of himself. We called it the Reaver. It was impervious to magic, faster than thought. It killed thousands of us." Durzo touched his cheek. "I was the first person to even wound it. My pockmarks are from where its blood sprayed me. Magic couldn't heal me. After the last battle, the Reaver was badly wounded. Instead of killing it, Ezra took it to the Wood. Fifty years later, there was a power struggle of some sort, and every living thing in that wood died—and dies to this day, whether animal, krul, mage, or the purest virgin. Armies from both north and south have perished there. Whatever it is, the Wolf has been collecting artifacts for seven centuries, and he gets the best of every deal."

Kylar felt suddenly cold. "What did you give him?"

"A couple of the ka'kari. He wants them all—and Curoch and Iures."

"Iures?"

"The companion to Curoch. The Sword of Power and the Staff of Law. Jorsin died the day Iures was finished, before he could use it. No one knows what happened to it."

"But what's the Wolf trying to accomplish?"

"I don't know. Kylar, we've held one ka'kari, and its power is awesome. Imagine what an archmagus could do with seven ka'kari *and* Curoch *and* Iures. Even if the Wolf is Ezra, would you trust a madman with that much power? Would you even trust yourself? What if the Wolf isn't Ezra, what if it's Roygaris?"

"So you've opposed him," Kylar said.

"After I gave him the brown ka'kari, I thought better of it. Since then, I've scattered ka'kari to the ends of the earth. This is no short-term ambition. It has taken the Wolf seven hundred years to get a few ka'kari and now Curoch, and perhaps Iures. He doesn't care if it takes another hundred years to get the rest. This is part of your burden. Make sure he doesn't get them all."

"But he might be on our side," Kylar said.

"You tell that to all the innocents he's murdered."

"What do I tell all the innocents you've murdered?"

Durzo blinked. He chewed on his lip. "The problem with the black ka'kari is that it doesn't work in a mirror. I could never see the state of my own soul, and you can't see yours either. But if you wish, bring it to your eyes now. Judge me."

Kylar didn't dare. Durzo had poisoned dozens during the coup alone. There were surely hundreds—thousands—more deaths on his soul. If Kylar saw profound guilt, he might not be able to stop himself from killing Durzo. Or at least trying. It wasn't a fight he wanted to win, and now that he knew the cost of losing, that was even worse. "What should I do about the Wolf?" Kylar asked.

"Nothing now. But if you hear that Mount Tenji isn't spitting fire for the first time in two centuries, or you hear that the Tlaxini Maelstrom has stilled, you need to move fast. Like I said, this is not a short-term threat."

"When does it end?"

Durzo snorted. His hand moved to his belt where he used to carry a small pouch of garlic cloves. He noticed and gritted his teeth. "It could be hundreds of years. It could be twenty. Giving him Curoch was a big mistake."

Thanks. "Can we win?"

"We? I'm mortal now, kid. At best I have thirty, forty years left? I'm not terribly interested in tangling with the Wolf. Can you win? It's possible. He can't live forever. His magic's only an imitation of ours. Yours."

"He made one black ka'kari, why not make another one for himself?" Kylar asked.

"Made it? No. Ezra found it. He studied it to make the others, but they were all inferior copies."

"It told me—"

"Let me guess, something about being crafted with 'limited intelligence'? The black ka'kari was ancient when I was born, Kylar. It told you that so it wouldn't scare the shit out of you. You're sharing your head with a being whose power dwarfs yours."

~I wouldn't say my power exactly dwarfs *yours.~*

"Give the fucker my regards," Durzo said.

~I loved you better than you loved yourself, Acaelus.~

"I have to say, though, if he tells you to move, do it," Durzo said.

Right. Thanks. The first time the ka'kari had spoken to Kylar, it told him to duck. He hadn't—and had taken an arrow through the chest moments later. "Wait," Kylar said. "You never answered my question about dying by Curoch before the ka'kari kills someone in my place."

"Don't," Durzo said. "It's not the ka'kari that kills anyone. It's us. You're twenty years old and you've died five, six times? That's not the ka'kari's fault."

"Fine, it's my fault. Curoch?"

Irritation passed over Durzo's face, but he let it go. "Dying by Curoch might leave the person you love alive. Equally possible is that it will kill *everyone* you love. It's a feral magic. Curoch means the Sunderer. It was not intended for gentle things. It's a bad gamble, kid."

Kylar exhaled heavily. "This is all kind of a lot to absorb at once."

"Then absorb while we ride. We're burning daylight."

They rode until dark, and ate together, speaking only of inconsequential things. Kylar told Durzo everything that had happened in his absence. Durzo laughed, sometimes in the wrong places, as if laughing at similarities to his own memories, but more frequently than Kylar remembered him ever laughing before.

Then Durzo began telling stories. Kylar was surprised to find him an excellent raconteur. "I was a bard one life," Durzo said. "I took it up to train my memory. I wasn't very good."

Some of the stories he told were familiar from bards' tales Kylar had heard, though the details were very different. He told of a young Alexan the Blessed caught with dysentery in the mountains during his first campaign taking off his plate cuisses and dropping his mail trousers to squat in the bushes and then getting ambushed. His descriptions of Alexan fighting with a sword in one hand and trying to hike up his armor with the other had Kylar howling. Then Alexan tumbled down the mountain and fell a hundred feet. They found him at the bottom without a scratch—or his trousers, which had caught in a tree ten feet from the bottom of the ravine, slowing his fall and saving his life. "The Tomii used *shitting* as an intensifier, like we might say someone was damn lucky, they said he was shitting lucky. That's why they called him Alexan the Shitting Lucky. Later some prude translated it Alexan the Blessed. He was a good kid." Durzo laughed. Then his smile faded. "Broke my heart to kill him. But he needed killing by the end."

Kylar looked at his master intently. He said, "You're different now."

Durzo said nothing for a long time. He was like a caterpillar half-metamorphosed. One minute he was the old, hard-as-nails Durzo. The next he was this laughing, reminiscing stranger.

"The Wolf has worked with me for almost seven hundred years. Ezra and Roygaris were the best Healers ever. Whichever the Wolf is, he's seen me die and come back dozens of times. He knows the magic and how exactly the ka'kari worked with my body. But he isn't a prophet. At least not a natural-born one, unlike Dorian. So even with all his magic, he can only get bits and pieces. When I died, I think he spent a long time trying to figure out if my being alive one more time would help him or hurt him. Then he decided to raise me."

Kylar wondered about that. The Wolf had said Durzo's resurrection was a mystery, a gift. Was he simply being modest, or did he really not know how Durzo had come back?

"Anyway, by the time the Wolf started working on me, my body had pretty much rotted away. So I feel like a new man." He grinned, then stirred their little fire, watching the sparks.

"So this life is different, isn't it?" Kylar asked.

"Sometimes to love is easy, but to accept love is hard. I used to always be the man who led the charge. The Devourer steals that. Tell me, what kind of man would put his eight-year-old daughter at the spear tip of a cavalry charge? A monster. But what kind of man would refuse to fight when his enemies threaten all he holds dear? That's why I trained relentlessly. That's why I became the perfect killer. Because every time I wasn't good enough,

I murdered someone I loved. I thought I finally defeated love when the ka'kari abandoned me, but then there you were in the tower, standing athwart fate and crying, No! I realized three things as your crazy ass dove into the river. First, you . . . cared about me."

Kylar nodded silently. To hear Durzo say it without scoffing was alien, and the man seemed to marvel at it himself.

Durzo plowed ahead. "I knew your regard wasn't easily won, and I knew you'd seen darker sides of me than I'd let even most of my wives see." He chuckled. "You know, I can ignore it when Count Drake loves me. He's a saint. He cares about everybody. No offense, but you're no saint."

Kylar smiled.

Durzo studied the fire. "Second, I . . ." He cleared his throat. "I'd tried to root out feeling anything at all with drinking and whoring and killing and isolation, and I'd made myself into a monster, but I'd still failed. I still cared about you more than I cared about myself. That tells me something about myself." He grew quiet.

"And third?" Kylar prompted.

"Third, ah hell, I don't remember. Oh, wait. I spent years beating into your skull how hard and unfair life is. And I wasn't wrong. There's no guarantee that justice will win out or that a noble sacrifice will make any difference. But when it does, there's something that still swells my chest. There's magic in that. Deep magic. It tells me that's the way things are supposed to be. Why? How? Hell, I don't know. This spring I'll turn seven hundred, and I still don't have it figured out. Most poor bastards only get a few decades. Speaking of which . . ." Durzo cleared his throat. "I've got bad news."

"Speaking of which which?" Kylar asked, chest tightening.

"Life being unfair and all that."

"Oh, great. What is it?"

"Luc Graesin? Kid you died on the wheel to save?"

"It was more for Logan than for Luc, but what about him?"

"Hanged himself," Durzo said.

"What? Who killed him? Scarred Wrable?" Kylar could see Momma K deciding that even a remote threat to Logan would have to be eliminated.

"No, he really hanged himself."

"Are you joking? After what I did for him? That asshole!"

Durzo grabbed his blanket and lay down, resting his head on his saddle. "Letting someone die for you can be tough. If anyone should understand that, it's you."

61

...get up in three seconds, I'm gonna nail you with a biscuit." Kylar struggled to open his eyes, and the voice went on without even slowing. "One, two, three." Kylar's eyes shot open, and he snatched the hard biscuit out of the air with such force that it exploded into crumb shrapnel.

"Dammit," he said, combing biscuit pieces out of his hair. "What'd you do that for?"

Durzo was grinning from ear to ear. "Fun," he said.

Kylar scowled. There was something different about his master. His eyes seemed a little more round, his skin a little lighter, the shirt he was wearing tighter across the chest and shoulders. "What are you doing?" he asked.

"Eating breakfast," Durzo said, chomping into another biscuit.

"I mean your face!"

"What? Pimple?" Durzo asked, patting his forehead, the word coming out "pimpuh?" around the biscuit.

"Durzo! You went to bed Ymmuri, and you woke up halfbreed."

"Oh, that. What, you want to hear more? I talked last night more than I've talked in a hundred years." Kylar thought he might not be exaggerating. "You need to learn everything at once?"

"You're mortal now. And you're *old*. You could keel over at any moment."

"Hm, you have a point," Durzo said. "You saddle the horses, I'll talk."

Kylar rolled his eyes—and began tending to the horses.

"You've tried illusory masks. I've seen your whole little scary-black-mask thing that the Sa'kagé found so impressive."

"Thanks," Kylar griped. It had been impressive, dammit. "Wait, when did you see that?"

"In Caernarvon."

"You came to Caernarvon? When did you—"

"Too late to save Jarl, but early enough to save Elene. Now stop interrupting," Durzo said. "You might have noticed there are some drawbacks to making masks of real faces, especially with disguises of people of different height from yours. I made some good masks in my time, but it was horrible work, and if someone touched you or it even started raining, the illusion would break. Then one time I died. Got a leg hacked off and bled to death. When I came back, as always, my body was whole. Look at yourself dead six times and not a scar. How can that be? How could I regrow an arm?"

"I thought you said it was a leg," Kylar said, throwing a saddle over Tribe's back. For once, the brute didn't try to bite him. "And what's that about Elene?"

"It was an arm. Just remembered. I'll tell you about Elene later. What I figured out is that somehow our bodies know what shape we're supposed to be. I mean, when you cut any man's arm, arm skin grows back there, not a nose or another head. Why? Because the body knows what's supposed to be where. I figured that if that was the case, all I had to do to make a perfect disguise was change the instructions. Hah, if only it were that simple. I figured out a few things along the way. Like Ladeshians aren't just really tanned. And if you change your height dramatically, expect to be uncoordinated for a year. And don't mess with your eyesight. And don't change things about your body that you merely don't like. Pretty soon you'll be so damn beautiful people will stop on the streets to watch you—it makes for a lousy disguise. Anyway, it took me—I don't know—a hundred years? I have about twenty bodies I do now. That is, bodies I've spent enough time in that I know how they work, understand their stride, their movement, their quirks. Twenty is probably too many, but I got nervous once when I found two different paintings of me made two hundred years apart from different sides of Midcyru and obviously me in both of them. Some Alitae-ran collector had the two hanging side-by-side in his study. I'd moved to Alitaera to start a new life and I was using that same damn body."

"Wait, you're telling me you could have chosen any face? And you chose the nasty ugly Durzo Blint face?"

"That's my real face," Durzo said, offended.

Blood rushed to Kylar's cheeks. "Oh, by the God, I'm so sorry. I mean, I'm sorry I said that, not that your face is..."

"Gotcha," Durzo said.

Kylar pursed his lips. "Bastard."

"Anyway, it takes time to make the transition, especially when you start, and doing it halfway can be rather horrifying. We're on the trail, so we may meet people. If the skin on the upper half of my body is blackest Ladeshian, but my legs are white, or if half my face is young and half old, folks don't take it too well. I can actually do it much faster now, but I figured I'd show you body magic that's merely intensely difficult before I show you the damn-near impossible stuff."

"Wait, does that mean you can make yourself look like anything? So you could be a girl?"

"I don't want to hear your twisted fantasies," Durzo said.

"Hey!"

"I've never been a girl or an animal. I have a small fear of getting stuck: once I made a disguise that I was a man without a trace of Talent. What was supposed to be a quick, one-month disguise while I infiltrated the Chantry instead took me a decade to undo and cost me my chance to recover the silver ka'kari," Durzo said. "Being stuck as a fat Modaini, bad. Being stuck as a woman, unthinkable."

"So why are you changing now? And what into?"

"I'll look like a fifty-year-old, rather affable Waeddryner count, who appears to have a small Talent that he's never tapped. Because the reason I'm leaving the woman I love behind and going with you to the Chantry— not my favorite place—is that I want to meet my daughter. In fact, I'd appreciate your help getting the disguise right. I'd like her to look at me and say, 'oh, I have his eyes.' "

But Kylar wasn't interested in that yet. He paused. "Master? What does it mean? The Wolf called me Nameless. If I learn to do what you do, I'll be faceless, too. If we can be anyone, who are we?"

Durzo smirked, and even in another face, that bemused smirk was Durzo Blint through and through. "The Wolf doesn't know what the hell he's talking about. I had a delusion once that every new life I started was new. Our gift doesn't give us so much freedom—or terror. What we are is Night Angels, of an order ancient when I joined it. What it means to be a Night Angel is a harder question. Why do we see the *coranti?*" At Kylar's questioning look, Durzo said, "The unclean. And seeing them isn't a compulsion, it's a sensitivity. There was a time when I could see a lie, but in the year before the black abandoned me, I could barely see a murderer. What does it mean? Why was I chosen?

"Jorsin sometimes had the gift of prophecy. He told me I needed to take the black. 'All history rests in your hands, my friend,' he told me. I believed him. I would have walked through a wall of flame for that man. But a hundred years later, all my friends were dead, the world descended into a dark age, and no one was even pursuing me. Maybe my grand place in history, my whole purpose, was to keep the ka'kari safe for seven hundred years until I could give it to you. You'll forgive me if that doesn't seem entirely satisfying. Imagine rallying an army: 'Come on, men! Let's get together and...wait!' But then again if reality is hard and flat and unjust, then it's better to adjust to what really *is* than to complain that it isn't what you wish. That was what made me lose faith in prophecies, in purpose, even in life, I guess. But having lost it, soon I doubted my lack of faith. There were niggling hints of meaning everywhere. At the end of the day, you choose what you believe and you live with the consequences."

"So that's it?"

"That's what?"

" 'Choose what you believe and live with the consequences' is all you've learned after seven hundred years? We're fucking immortal, and that's all you're going to tell me of why?"

Faster than Kylar remembered his master could move, Durzo's hand lashed out. His backhand cracked across Kylar's cheek and jaw. It stunned Kylar. A backhand hurt the person who delivered it nearly as much as the person who received it, so the only reason Durzo would choose a backhand was for the contempt implicit in it.

They stood looking at each other, silent. Mixed with Durzo's frustration, Kylar could see regret, but Durzo didn't apologize. Apologizing was one skill Acaelus Thorne hadn't mastered in seven centuries.

"Kid, every place I've turned left, you've turned right, and now you want me to tell you your destiny? Would it mean anything to you if I told you?"

Kylar said, "It would tell me where to turn right."

Despite himself, Durzo grinned. But it wasn't enough to bridge the sudden gap. Kylar could see now that his rejection of the lessons Durzo had tried to pass on had cut Durzo deeply—even if Durzo now agreed some of those lessons had been wrong. At the same time, Durzo was saying the same thing that the Wolf had told Kylar long ago. Kylar had never accepted other people's answers: not Durzo's bitter practicality, not Momma K's cynicism, not Count Drake's piety, and not Elene's idealism. Durzo was right about choosing what you believe and living with the consequences.

"I just…" Kylar trailed off. "We're immortal. We're Night Angels. I don't know what it means. I don't know why we're this way, or what we're supposed to do with it. Sometimes I feel like a god, and other times I don't feel like I change anything. If I'm going to live forever, I want it to be *for* something. I mean, you can't tell me that your destiny has been to hold the ka'kari for seven hundred years until I came along. That's ridiculous. Terrible. It's not good enough. You're a great man, not a lockbox." Kylar scowled. Gods, he'd just given Durzo a backhanded compliment—exactly how Durzo gave compliments to him.

Durzo's little grin told him he'd noticed, but he could also tell that the compliment meant a lot to the man. In all the times Kylar had been irritated that his master never properly appreciated how well Kylar did, he'd never really thought that Durzo might want to be appreciated too. Kylar hadn't bothered to tell Durzo how excellent he thought he was; he figured it was obvious. Maybe that was another knife that cut both ways.

"Being a lockbox wasn't the destiny I chose," Durzo said. "Right or wrong—or right or left—I've chosen to seek the ka'kari, take them, and scatter them so those who would use them for evil can't. I don't know if that's what Jorsin foresaw, but it's what I've chosen. Has it been meaningful and satisfying? Sometimes. I've had some good lives and some that were just damn awful. Now that you bear the black, I can lay my burden and my destiny down. Now I get different choices. So I'll train you until spring and see my daughter as much as I can. Then there's a woman I have to ask to love a man who doesn't deserve it. Your choices? Well, that's your shit." He smirked, acknowledging he was being a bastard.

Kylar sighed. He loved Durzo, but the man sure was a pain in the ass.

62

From an older brother, the compulsion weave is weak, Your Holiness," Hopper said. "It won't hold a determined aetheling for long."

"I know. I was the son who was able to break it when my father used it on me," Dorian said. He'd had another dream last night, and again couldn't remember it, but it had left him with a headache again. His Talent for prophecy was healing faster than he'd expected, but for the time being, it was useless to him. He couldn't remember his dreams, and the only thing that banished the pain was using the vir. It put him in a foul mood.

"I'm sorry, Your Holiness. I'd forgotten."

The plan had come together with frightening ease. Dorian was his father's son. He'd spent days thinking about what he might have missed, and had found no flaw. "The oath is a distraction. You tell them that their reward for swearing loyalty will be choosing a concubine to marry. That will sound like a very southron thing to do, very weak. It will give the aethelings hope. Hope—and lust—will keep them from organizing a defense. After each chooses, I want him led out by that concubine past his brothers, who will be waiting in line. The women should be dressed beautifully—and of course, they should know nothing except that they are to lead the aetheling to one of the empty upper apartments. Each aetheling should be very lightly guarded, but heavily watched. You understand? These are my brothers; they're not stupid. On the way, kill them. If you have a handful of soldiers and three or four Vürdmeisters you know we can trust, that should be enough to take care of all of them—at least with the compulsion spell in place. Their faces are not to be destroyed. I will require a precise accounting and viewing of the bodies. When you're done, isolate any of the Godking's seed who are too young to show whether they are wytchborn. Kill them. Induce abortions on the pregnant concubines. Letting any grow up to see who's wytchborn will give my enemies chances to smuggle them out."

"Very prudent, Your Holiness," Hopper said. His only expression was appreciation for a solid plan.

It was brutal, but it wasn't cruel. Dorian took no joy in this. He would strike once to the root, and rip out much of what made this kingdom a hell for its people. This way was kinder than waiting for dozens of aethelings to coerce hundreds of others into their plots. Dorian could wait, and have executions every month for years, and his people would live in terror as dark as his father had encouraged, or he could be as brutal as the north itself, and his people would live in peace, unafraid. It would be a clean slate, a new start. Dorian would be Wanhope not for his own despair, but because those who opposed him must despair.

"Yes," Dorian said. "Monstrous, but prudent."

Hopper didn't know how to respond. He bowed low. The Godking dismissed him.

It was a horror to be a god. On his wedding day, Godking Wanhope waded in blood. He'd known that his father had one hundred forty-six children, but seeing them dead and oozing and stinking, expressions frozen in death, bodies still warm, not all the blood congealed, was something else entirely. With vir, he blotted out his sense of smell as he examined the boys.

He'd run out of suitable concubines before he'd run out of aethelings to slaughter. That meant that some of the women—each of whom had witnessed the murder of an aetheling she had expected to be her new master— had to make two trips. Only those who'd been splattered with blood were excused. It had worked though, because the aethelings who'd come later were the youngest, and the least likely to pick up on a concubine's anxiety.

They'd got them all. Three of the older boys—three!—had broken the compulsion and fought, killing one Vürdmeister and two soldiers. In a perverse way, Dorian was proud of the boys.

Godking Wanhope took his time, steeled against the sight of dead children. Vipers, all of them. He was the fluke; he had always been the only one of his brothers with any moral sense. Vipers couldn't be tamed. He couldn't flinch now. He had to know if the job was done, or if he needed to be looking over his shoulder for the rest of his reign for a Vürdmeister who could hide his vir and betray the Godking himself—as he had in his own youth. He paid special attention to those whose faces had been damaged. But in each case, he could still smell the faint residue of his compulsion spell on their flesh, and he'd tied it in an unusual way so that he would recognize his own work. That was why he had to examine the bodies immediately.

If a Vürdmeister had betrayed him and hidden an aetheling, the traitor would have to find a boy of the correct age, kill him and destroy his face, change his clothing, examine the Godking's weave—and notice that it had been altered and how it had been altered—and lay it on the dead boy himself. It was all possible but barely, and by the time he was finished inspecting the boys, the Godking was sure it hadn't been done.

The next room was worse, though there was no blood in it except what came in on the Godking's white robes. Hopper had gathered all the wives and concubines. The fifteen women who had been pregnant were lined up against one wall. The Godking walked past them, touching swollen bellies and feeling no life within. Then he moved past the rest, feeling to see if any were pregnant.

He took his time. A weave to hide a pregnancy was easier magically than disguising the dead, but a bigger risk for a Vürdmeister. There was no guarantee that the hidden child would be wytchborn, much less suitable for an ambitious Vürdmeister to ride to the Khalidoran throne.

As he moved from woman to woman, he noticed something disquieting. There was no hatred in their eyes. He had made them help him murder one hundred forty-six children. He had killed their unborn, but few wept. More looked at him with adoration, worship. He had done something beyond their comprehension, and it had worked perfectly. In short, he had acted like the god they expected him to be—powerful, terrifying, inscrutable.

"This afternoon," he said, "each of you will have a choice. As you know, the tradition is for wives and concubines to join the late Godking on his pyre, except for those whom the new Godking wishes to save for himself. You have served me well. I would give all of you a place in my harem. Garoth's aethelings will join him in the fire. Let them serve him in the afterlife. But if it is your wish, I will not forbid you to join them."

Now, the women reacted as he would have expected. Some broke down and wept; others stood taller and prouder. Some were still uncomprehending. But in moments, all dropped prostrate, hands stretched out for his feet. *I am walking blasphemy.*

"Is there anything else?" he asked them.

One of the women, a curvaceous teen from the upper harem, raised two fingers.

"Yes, Olanna?"

She cleared her throat three times before she could speak. "Sia, Your Holiness. She wasn't counted among the pregnant girls. She got real sick and went to the meisters so she wouldn't lose her baby. She never came back."

Dorian's stomach twisted. It was like hearing his own death sentence, twenty years before the fact. He wondered if he'd dreamed of this and was only now remembering the dream, or if his dread was purely natural. He looked at Hopper, who'd paled. Hopper served the lower harem, so the detail had escaped him, but he still looked aghast to have missed it. Dorian gestured and the man shuffled out of the room as quickly as his stilted gait would allow. Wanhope would send men to hunt this woman and whatever Vürdmeister had taken her, but they wouldn't find her. Wanhope had forgotten the first rule of massacring innocents: one always gets away.

63

$\mathcal{A}$s Kylar and Durzo approached the Chantry, the Alabaster Seraph gleamed, presiding over a city freshly dusted with snow that made it match its mistress. The waters of Lake Vestacchi glowed light blue tinged with red in the early morning light.

They stabled their horses on the outskirts of town, and after speaking with an old woman who ran the tavern and seemed to recognize him, Durzo took a key from her. Eschewing the punts, Durzo led them across narrow, crowded sidewalks. Kylar gaped at the enormous Seraph and at the crisscrossing currents that made the city's streets, bumping into strangers. A few cursed him and shoved back, but stopped as soon as he leveled his cool blue eyes on them. Beneath his awe at the Seraph, though, was a growing dread. He could feel Vi. He adjusted his sword belt and blew out a breath uneasily. She was in there, up two or three stories. Her feelings were a mirror of his own.

Durzo took them into a small, dusty house with a thick door. Kylar noticed that his eyes and his master's checked all the same things: doors, narrow windows, rugs, plank flooring. Durzo was satisfied. He opened the bureau and lifted out the bottom drawer to reveal a false bottom. Kylar pooled the ka'kari in his hand. *I'm really going to miss your wit.*

~If I wanted sarcasm...~ it began, but Kylar willed it to cover Retribution. *~Wait!~* He dropped the sword into the space beneath the bureau. Both Retribution and the ka'kari were magical. He couldn't bring either to the Chantry. They would stay here until Kylar left.

Durzo replaced the bottom drawer, locked it into place, and took a few minutes to place a trap on it. In the meantime, Kylar worked on his disguise as Durzo had taught him. After he'd finished with the trap, Durzo studied him. "Not too bad," he admitted.

Minutes later, their little punt had scarcely docked next to a fishing boat flying two black flags when a familiar face turned up.

"Sister?" Kylar asked.

"There's a king in Cenaria!" Sister Ariel said, making it an accusation.

"Is this a password?" Durzo asked.

"Glory to his name," Kylar said. "Can we get out of the boat?"

"In Torras Bend, I called you arrogant. You said we'd discuss your arrogance when there was a king in Cenaria," Sister Ariel said, unamused. "Was that your doing?"

"Me? Who am I to meddle with kings?" Kylar said, smirking a yes.

"What's your name, young man? I seem to have forgotten. And who's this?"

"Kyle Blackson. Nice to make your acquaintance again, Sister Airy Belle, right?" She gave him a glare that could curdle milk. "This is Dannic Bilsin, Uly's dad."

"Seven hells," Sister Ariel said.

"Nice to meet you, too," Durzo said.

Kylar got out of the boat and Sister Ariel stepped close to him and sniffed. She stepped back, confusion rising sharply in her eyes. She looked around the docks to see how far away the other Sisters were. "What have you done to yourself?"

With Durzo's instruction, Kylar now appeared to be a man with a vast and untapped Talent. Otherwise, he smelled and looked like any man. As long as he didn't use the ka'kari or his Talent, his guise would remain in place.

"I'm here to see my wife," Kylar said.

"Vi's studying, but I can have her brought to you after lunch."

"I meant the wife I chose, not the one you did." Kylar smiled thinly. Sister Ariel's face drained.

"You have no idea what you're doing, do you?" she said.

"Maybe I'm not the only one."

"And you?" Sister Ariel asked Durzo. "Do you have demands that will cost lives, too?"

"I'm just here to see my daughter," Durzo said.

The funeral came before the wedding. Dorian didn't want the first thing he saw with his new bride to be insane women throwing themselves into a fire, shrieking as they burned to death. Nor did he want her to see the dozens of tiny bodies his men would throw on the fires first. He'd told Jenine that he'd purged the aethelings who'd been plotting against him, but he'd told her that he'd merely sent the younger ones away.

Well, hell counted as away, he supposed. Heaven certainly did.

Dorian, of course, had never seen the cremation of a Godking, but some of the older meisters had. There was a ritual to be observed, despite the fraud at the center of it: rarely had the body being cremated actually belonged to a Godking. But Garoth Ursuul's pyre wouldn't hold a substitute. Garoth had been a man deeply committed to evil, but he had been a great soul, too, a horror who could have been a wonder, and he was Dorian's father.

Only meisters were allowed to attend the divine funeral, but that restriction meant little, for nearly every ranking official in the Khalidoran government was a meister. Generals, bureaucrats, the masters of the treasury, and even the chiefs of the kitchens stood in attendance. Tax collectors and soldiers watched according to their rank. Dorian uttered the meaningless words of praise to Khali, and they uttered their meaningless refrains of devotion. The fires were started and Dorian could read the vir of every meister making a weave to block the acrid stench of human fat burning. When the fires roared hottest, Dorian had the harem brought before him and claimed almost all of them. There were raised eyebrows, but nothing more. A Godking was expected to be voracious. The eight wives and concubines who'd chosen death were brought forward, and that was regarded as a small, but adequate nod to tradition. The women had been provided with wine laced liberally with poppy, and six of them had indulged freely. Two were sober. All seemed content with their madness, not shrinking back even as the eunuchs lifted them to heave them into the fire.

The shrieking was awful, but mercifully brief. It was considered a greater sacrifice to Khali if their suffering were extended, but Dorian was already giving Khali more than her due. He should have forbidden the women to join Garoth. But if he had forced them to live and they truly had loved Garoth, such women might have become a poison.

Or they might have transferred their slavish devotion to me, the way a good dog finds a new master after its old master dies. Dorian watched their bodies sizzle, and pushed the thought away.

He nodded to the Vürdmeisters tending the fire and the blaze leapt higher, consuming the flesh and even the bones to ash. In minutes, it was done.

Dorian lifted his hand to gesture that the wedding was to begin. It would be a simple affair, though lavish by Khalidoran standards. Godkings never wed. When commoners did, a man simply said, "I take this woman to wife." From the woman, only a lack of explicit protest was required. Dorian planned something grander for Jenine but not too foreign for his meisters to stomach. But with his hand still raised, he paused. The moment had taken the ecrie lines of prophecy. Dorian felt a sick chill and readied the vir in case there was another assassination attempt. Hopper was whispering to a page, who strode respectfully to Dorian's side. Dorian was looking at his grand white robes, at the assembled faces. He'd seen this moment in a prophecy, why couldn't he remember?

He inclined his head to the page.

"Your Holiness, Hopper wishes you to be informed that a spy has returned from Cenaria. He reports that a man named Logan Gyre has been named king."

The world stopped. Jenine's husband was alive. Dorian felt as if he were outside his body, re-entering the madness he thought he'd left behind with his prophetic gift.

How dare you, God? What do you want from me? To tell her that he lives? I've given my soul for this! For You. I am become a monster so I can redeem these people. Don't You care about me? Don't You care about this damned country?

If You did, You would have saved these wretches Yourself. I did not seek these chains of office. I did not seek the Talent You gave me. I only asked for one thing: this woman. You made me with this yearning too deep for words, and You would have me sacrifice it at the moment the honey touches my lips?

I have not forgotten you. I know the plans I have for you.

Remembering me means nothing if You won't act for me. I have not betrayed You, You betray me. Non takuulam. *I shall not serve. You and I are finished.*

Godking Wanhope became aware of the stares of his meisters. He smiled and completed the gesture to Hopper. "Let our wedding commence," the god said.

65

$\mathcal{A}$ simple lunch was delivered to Durzo's room and Kylar and Durzo ate together in silence. "Guess you should head to your room, huh?" Durzo said. "They should be here any time." He cleared his throat, reaching for a garlic pouch he no longer carried.

"I'd give anything to see you meet your girl," Kylar said.

"I'd give anything to see you meet yours," Durzo said.

Kylar swallowed, realizing he was pacing.

"You can feel her?" Durzo asked.

"Three floors up, heading down. Almost as nervous as I am."

"I knew there was a reason I was never stupid enough to get ringed," Durzo said.

"Do you have any idea how Uly's going to react when she sees you?" Kylar asked.

Durzo shook his head.

"Then maybe you should shut your face."

"Ah, wook, wittle Kylie is all gwowed up. He mad at his massah."

In a flash, Kylar was on the verge of punching Durzo's face. Then he laughed. "Unbelievable, huh? Guess I'll go over to my room. Good luck."

Durzo patted his back as he walked out of the room. It was an oddly intimate gesture, but Kylar said nothing to draw Durzo's attention to it.

His room was even smaller than Durzo's, which barely had room for two chairs. Kylar's had only one chair and a bed. Kylar sat in the chair. Then he moved to sit on the bed. Then he stood so he could open the door before she even knocked. Then he changed his mind and sat again.

He cursed. She was just down the hall now, and she'd stopped—dropping Uly off at Durzo's room? Uly and Vi were together? Vi didn't seem to feel upset or guilty, which was weird, considering she'd kidnapped Uly, beaten her, and starved her only a few months ago. Then Vi was moving again, as tense as he was.

Kylar stood to open the door. There was a quick, firm rap, and then she opened the door, but Vi wasn't alone. Sister Ariel and another woman of a similar age but with long blonde hair stepped into the room, and Vi followed.

For the tiny room, it was too many people, even if three of them hadn't been magae. Kylar backed up to the wall.

"Kyle Blackson, this is Speaker Istariel Wyant. She's in charge here," Sister Ariel said.

"Nice to meet you," Kylar said. "Here the guest quarters or here here?"

"I'm the Speaker of the Chantry," Istariel said, annoyed.

"Then why aren't you the Chanter?" Kylar asked. What was with him? That had Durzo written all over it, and Vi's eyes went wide.

Istariel's lips thinned. "We have problems, young man, they may even be bigger than your ego."

"Why are we meeting here rather than your office?" Kylar asked.

She blinked. "What was it you said, Ariel, reckless but not stupid? Kyle, the Chantry and all of the south is entering a perilous time. We need Vi's help if we are to survive."

"You do?" Vi asked.

"Silence, child," Sister Ariel said.

"All of this was supposed to happen much more slowly," Istariel told Vi. "We meant to give you some semblance of a normal tutelage, because the service we require of you entails serious risks for you and the Chantry. The bare fact is that you may be—"

Sister Ariel cleared her throat.

"You *are* the most Talented woman to come to the Chantry in a century, Vi. You were married before you arrived, so your marriage is not in violation of the Third Alitaeran Accord. A woman's Talent isn't enough to guarantee her advancement, but a highly Talented woman is always conspicuous. Thus, you're highly visible, highly Talented, and married—to a man who's also highly Talented—and your marriage is not in breach of any treaty."

"Huh," Vi said. "What are the odds of that happening by chance?" She stared pointedly at Ariel, who had the decency to blush.

Istariel cleared her throat. "Yes, about that. Kyle, we never expected you to actually come here. In fact, Sister Ariel was adamant that you wouldn't."

"I wasn't aware how susceptible you would be to Vi's...charms," Ariel said blandly.

Kylar blushed. "That's not why I'm here."

"But here you are," Istariel said. "So you could destroy Vi—or at the very least destroy her usefulness to the Chantry."

"Which is why I get some truth. Right. Still doesn't answer why you have to sneak around to meet me," Kylar said.

Istariel's eyes flashed. "The Chantry has had a number of incidents involving Vy'sana wedding rings. A century ago, someone ringed a Speaker against her will."

"It's called ring rape," Ariel said.

Istariel turned a cold gaze on her sister. "Stop helping." She turned back to Kylar. "It was an attempt to subvert the entire Chantry in one stroke, and it came disastrously close to succeeding. That was only the most recent incident. There is enormous antipathy to forcible ringing."

"So if I tattle, Vi's finished. Why do you care?" Kylar asked.

"There's no reason for us to be enemies," Istariel said.

"I can think of one," he said, tugging his earring.

She averted her gaze. "Magae have been forbidden to marry magi for two hundred years, Kyle. The Alitaeran Emperor Dicola Raiis feared we had established a breeding program to make archmages so we could become the dominant force in world politics we once were. At the time, we were closely allied with the men's blue school, and the treaty required all the married magi to divorce. The men wanted to go to war, but the decision was the Speaker's, who was herself married to a Blue. She knew that they had no chance against the might of Alitaera, and she signed the accord. The split with the men was acrimonious. Relations have been strained since then. To protect ourselves, and perhaps for many other reasons including to stop the humiliating inspections of compliance, the Chantry has spread the prohibition of marriage to all men. Women who do marry are effectively finished. They are allowed no advancement within the Orders; they are sometimes denied further schooling, and they are often the objects of ridicule. Nonetheless, for their own reasons I suppose, many women choose this path."

"How many?" Kylar asked.

"Half."

"You lose half?"

"The only thing worse than losing them is getting them back the wrong way. There is a woman named Eris Buel who has become the de facto leader of a large number of these women. They want to come back. They want to reject the Alitaeran Accords—maybe all of them—and they want to establish a men's school here. At heart, though, they just want to be Sisters again. Our reports suggest that we may have more ex-magae here this spring than magae."

"How many are you talking?" Kylar asked.

"Eight to ten thousand. While we have that many active Sisters, ours are spread out throughout the world. If these Chattel—ummm, these married Sisters—arrive and demand to be readmitted and form their own order, we won't be able to deny them."

"What happens if they do form an order?" Kylar asked.

"Most likely? They immediately hold a vote of no confidence and oust me and put their leader in my place. At best, Eris Buel is angry, naive, and dangerous."

"You want Vi to kill her?"

"Light blind me, no!" Sister Istariel said. "We want Vi to replace her."

"What?!" Vi asked.

"You're more Talented than she is. You're prettier, and you're not as angry."

"Oh, you haven't seen Vi when she gets angry," Kylar said.

"Neither have you!" she snapped.

"The point is," Sister Ariel said, "Eris Buel doesn't lead the Chattel yet. These women come from all over Midcyru. Most of them don't know each other. They'll look for a leader once they're here. There's more. Istariel, tell them about the Khalidorans."

"Even though Khalidor doesn't occupy much of its eastern lands, they are still our neighbors," Istariel said. "After Garoth died, an unknown named Wanhope took the throne. We have reasons to doubt his rule will last. In the north, one of Garoth's other sons, Moburu, has joined up with the barbarians in the Freeze. They're rumored to have rediscovered how to raise armies of creatures that are less than human. Moburu is heading east either to fight or to join another group which we think has about fifty Vürd-meisters, led by a Lodricari named Neph Dada, at Black Barrow. The word is that he plans to raise a Titan."

"What's a Titan?"

"It's a myth. We hope. But as the mistress of a floating island, I can only think of one compelling reason a Khalidoran army would need a giant."

"You think they want to attack the Chantry?" Vi asked.

"I think they're fools," Istariel said. "But we only have a mercenary army of five hundred men and not a single battle maja. If the Khalidorans came through the pass with twenty thousand soldiers and a hundred Vürd-meisters, even without krul or a Titan, they could destroy us. Worse, the

Lae'knaught plan to march north at the same time. While there's a small and tempting prospect that our two enemies would converge and destroy each other before our eyes, if either attacked us first, even if we won, we would be so weakened that the other would annihilate us."

"So you want to turn the ten thousand Chattel into an army so they can die saving women who reject them," Kylar said.

There was an icy silence.

"I'm responsible for the lives of the women in my care, and the caretaker of the legacy of a thousand years of learning and freedom," Istariel said. "So if it costs Vi's life and her honor and your life and your freedom and my life and my reputation and a war with Alitaera to save them, I will gladly pay that and more. Kyle, you can destroy my plans and your wife simply by telling the first maja you see that you were ringed forcibly. I can't stop you. But neither can I free you. In the centuries when these rings were Made, they were studied by magae greater than any now alive, and *they* found the bond unbreakable. You can ask anything for your silence, but you can't ask the impossible. So what's your price?"

"Tell me exactly what you're buying," Kylar said.

"In the coming weeks, I've arranged to have very ugly and very public debate with some of my key councilors about the Chattel. Ariel will be one of those who splits with me. I'm going to take a strong stance that the Chantry will never allow the Chattel to rejoin. A few days later, some of the threats to our safety I've just told you about will be leaked. I will send to Alitaera asking for protection as per the Accords. My request will be impossibly large, so that even if Alitaera sends soldiers, the small number will be taken as an insult. Vi will begin training whoever wishes to join her and Sister Ariel in the arts of war. I will ban this training, but no action will be taken against those who 'defy' me. If Vi plays her part appropriately, she'll have a good chance to become the leader of these rebels. Come spring, Vi will negotiate with me on behalf of the Chattel. I will break down, the Chattel will be readmitted with certain conditions—mostly that they reside here for at least a year before they are given full voting privileges."

"Which," Ariel interjected, "will make sure that few of them actually do it. Most of these women have farms and shops and families to get back to."

"Yes, *thank you*, Ariel," Istariel said. "But those who truly wish to rejoin will be allowed to do so and still stay married. After we make it through the summer, we will renegotiate the Alitaeran Accords."

"What's to say you won't sacrifice Vi to the Alitaerans then?" Kylar said.

"Whatever goodwill she's built up with the Chattel will probably make her untouchable. If I betray her, it could be enough to make enough Chattel stick around to become full voting members and oust me. Regardless, the Alitaerans are next year's problem."

"So what's my part?" Kylar asked.

"You share a house with your wife. I don't care if you share a bed, but to all appearances, it must be a model marriage. You will spend enough social time together to maintain this fiction. Nothing elaborate, eat at an inn together once in a while, take walks, hold hands."

"Do you have any idea what it's like for me to be in the same room with her?" Kylar asked. "I'm in love with another woman, a woman I planned to marry. If I get aroused by a woman other than Vi, I nearly throw up. I can't control my dreams. I feel what she feels. I—"

"We can't fix it!" Istariel said. "Get rid of your old lover. Start sharing Vi's bed. After a while, you might even like each other."

"You cruel, cruel bitch," the thought was Kylar's, but it was Vi who spoke.

He was stunned, as were Ariel and Istariel.

"You want to pretend things are different, go ahead," Istariel said. "You ringed him. Are you going to make thousands die so you can feel properly guilty? Kyle, are you going to make thousands die so you can punish me or Sister Ariel? Is that going to make it better? Because you'll still be ringed next year, no matter what happens to the Chantry. Kyle, I'll give you whatever you want. Vi, you'll have more power and a better position than you could ever dream of. In time, you could become Speaker. It's your choice. You two figure it out and tell Sister Ariel. I can never be seen with you. Should we ever meet, I expect you to act as if you dislike me intensely. I suspect that won't be difficult."

She opened the door, glanced both ways, and left. Sister Ariel said, "Elene will come to your new house in a few hours. The story will be that she's your servant."

"I haven't said yes," Kylar said.

Sister Ariel looked at him gently for a long moment, then opened the door and went out.

"So what do we do?" Vi asked.

This close to her, Kylar was picking up flashes of images directly from her mind. There was Elene, throwing a knife aside. Kylar saw himself, flashing a grin, his handsomeness exaggerated. He saw himself reaching to touch her face gently. He saw himself holding her. He saw himself in the throne room, fierce and wild, slashing into Garoth Ursuul's head and saving Vi's life. He saw himself looking at her with horror as he discovered the earring. He saw himself above her, chest bare, muscles taut, his eyes locked on hers, pupils flaring. Then, again, horror and loathing.

Kylar looked at Vi, glad that she was wearing a shapeless sack of a white wool dress. But she was close enough that he could smell her. She wore no perfume. Perhaps her soap was lavender, but mostly, he smelled her, and she smelled incredible.

He saw Jarl go down in a sudden spray of blood and then he saw the shot from her perspective, her tears almost blinding her as she released the arrow. He felt her self-hatred, her guilt—and whether the compulsion had been magical or mundane, he forgave her.

It didn't need words. She felt it directly. Her eyes brimmed with tears.

Kylar cleared his throat, glanced at her breasts involuntarily, and blushed as she noticed. The image of holding her naked came back again, and he wasn't sure which of them it came from. "Holy shit," he said.

She glanced at the narrow pallet against the wall and quickly away, but the image couldn't be hidden: Kylar on her, handsome, muscular, his touch setting her skin afire, her legs wrapping around his, pulling him to her, his weight anchoring her to something deep and real and better than she deserved. "Gods," Vi said, "this takes foreplay to a new level." He could feel the warmth rising in her body.

"No," he said. "I've betrayed Elene in every way but that. Please, we can't do that, not ever. All right?"

Her arousal was gone instantly, replaced with confusion and guilt. She stepped forward and reached out to him.

He recoiled. "I don't think we should even, you know, touch."

She averted her eyes, her feelings of rejection and unworthiness seeping through the air. He wanted to reassure her, but he didn't.

"Right," she said quietly.

66

Sister Ariel stared at Kylar in a way that made it obvious she was using her Talent, trying to figure him out again. "Elene will be here any minute. Is everything to your satisfaction?" she asked.

He met her gaze. He wished he had the ka'kari to bring to his eyes, but Durzo had told him that for his disguise as a highly Talented man who had only tapped his latent Talent a few times in his life to hold, he couldn't use either ka'kari or Talent at all. So Kylar had left the ka'kari covering Retribution in Durzo's safe house. Of course, he could reform the disguise afterward, but it was always a question of whether he wanted to spend eight hours fixing the disguise for a momentary use of the Talent.

Kylar was starting to appreciate why Durzo had taught him so many mundane skills that had seemed like they were obsolete after he'd learned to tap his Talent.

"It's fine," he said. The Chantry had given him an enormous sum of money to purchase this small manse on the shores of the lake. He and Vi were moving in today, and the house had room for Elene and Durzo as well, though Uly would continue to live in the Chantry. For the most part, Kylar wouldn't see Vi. She would rise early, go to the Chantry, and not return home until late. Later, when her "rebellion" began, she and the Sisters who accompanied her would train in the manse's large walled yard. The manse, of course, had been selected for exactly that purpose.

"When did you learn this disguise?" Ariel asked. "It's remarkable. I wouldn't have believed such a thing was possible."

"Maybe you were just mistaken before."

"Oh, I've made mistakes, *Kyle,* and you figure prominently in them, but I have a perfect memory." She cleared her throat. "I want to apologize. Your predicament is more my fault than anyone's. I didn't know exactly what I was imposing on you, but I did manipulate Vi into doing it."

"And would you do anything differently if you could do it again?" Kylar asked.

She paused. "No."

"Then it's not really an apology, is it?"

Sister Ariel turned and left, leaving Kylar rubbing his temples.

"Hi," a voice said from the doorway.

Kylar looked up and saw Elene. She was smiling shyly. A thrill ran through him. He was frozen, taking her in. First he was surprised again at her beauty, the fine balance of her features, the glow of her skin. Then his eyes were drawn to the uncertainty of her smile, the wide and fragile hope in her eyes, waiting to see how he would react to her. Even when she was scared, she lightened a room. A huge lump rose in his throat. Before he could think more, he crossed the room and pulled her into his arms.

She hugged him fiercely and didn't let go. He held her tight and all the world was well. He smelled her hair, her skin, and that forgotten scent was the scent of home.

He didn't know how long it lasted, but all too soon he came to himself.

Elene felt the change instantly. She pulled back and took his face in her hands. She stared him straight in the eye, and when he averted his gaze, she pulled him back. "Kylar, there's something you have to know," she said.

"Something *I* have to know?"

"Yes," she said. "I know about everything, and I love you." Her grip on his face relaxed, and she trailed her fingers down his cheeks. "I love you."

"Elene," Kylar said. He wondered what made her name sound different from all other names as it crossed his lips, "it's more than just Vi."

"Both things," Elene said.

Kylar stopped. "Both things" as in the both things he was thinking about, or was she forgiving him for something else he didn't even know he'd done? During their brief time as a happy family in Caernarvon, Kylar would have let it go, afraid of being hammered with something he hadn't seen coming. Now, he shook his head. "Honey, this is too important not to put into words."

Elene cocked her head fractionally, and he saw that she noticed the change in him, and respected him more for it. It was one of the things that made being with Elene so intense: she was so open, he knew immediately what she felt, and it was often overwhelming. "I know about the ringing. Vi and I have had a number of long and uncomfortable talks. I know that you sold your sword for those rings, and that one of them was supposed to be for me. I know about Jarl." Tears came to her eyes but she blinked them away. "I know that you've shared some...intimate dreams with Vi because of the rings, and I know about the Chantry's deal and why they want you to act like Vi's husband. I don't like it, but it's the right thing to do. Some things have happened that have changed me, Kylar." She grimaced. "Kyle now, I guess, but let me just call you Kylar for another hour. Is that all right?"

He nodded, that damn lump in his throat getting bigger. "I like it when you say my name."

She smiled and suddenly tears welled up in her eyes. She fanned herself. "I told myself I wouldn't cry."

"You'll let yourself cry later?" he suggested.

She laughed suddenly, and it was better than music. "How do you know me so well?" She took a deep breath. "Kylar, in Caernarvon, I had some very firm ideas about what sort of man you were supposed to be. There is something in you that is fierce and wild and strong, and it fascinated me and frightened me. And when I got frightened, I tried to change you, and I didn't listen to you, and I didn't respect you the way you deserved, and I didn't trust you."

You had this crazy notion that I was going to take you to a far country and then leave you with nothing.

"So I cloaked my fears in some really righteous-sounding horseshit."

Kylar's eyebrows shot up. Elene, swearing?

She smirked, liking that she could shock him. But then her expression grew serious. "All of our fights about that stupid sword.... You couldn't sell Retribution because you are Retribution. That girl in Caernarvon, that shopkeeper's girl Capricia? You changed her life, and that was giving her what she deserved as much as it is when you kill bad men. The fact is, Kylar, I made my God look a lot like me instead of the other way around. I'm sorry. When I first found out that you'd sold that sword for me, I cried for myself, because I'd lost you. But later, I cried for you, because I'd told you that you weren't good enough for me.

"Kylar, what you do scares me. I can understand it in my head, but it's still hard to fit my heart around. It's, well, it's horrifying and terrifying for me."

"It's horrifying and terrifying for me, too."

She looked him in the eye still. "When I was escaping from the slavers, there was a Khalidoran who was going to kill a boy. I killed him. I killed the guilty so the innocent might live, and that's what you did with the queen, Kylar. I hope I never have to kill again, but I won't think that I'm better than you because you have to."

"What? Slavers? Wait, you got kidnapped?"

"There's a story more important than that, Kylar. When you died, I had a dream. A very short man appeared to me. He was handsome, with amazing white hair and yellow eyes and burn scars."

Kylar froze again. It could only be the Wolf.

"He told me what immortality costs. Every time you die, someone you love dies in your place. He told me that this time it's me. He said that the most he could do was hold off my death until spring."

"I didn't know," Kylar whispered.

"Kylar, I think the hardest thing for me in Caernarvon was that I realized you were important and I wasn't. Now instead of envying you or fighting against you, I'll fight with you. All the good you do for a lifetime will be possible because of me. I guess this is a kind of heroism that no one sees, but maybe that makes it better, not worse."

"I love you, Elene. I'm sorry I've been such a fool. I'm sorry I left."

"Kylar, you love a girl with scars; I love a man with a purpose. Love comes at a price, but you're worth it."

"How can you say that? I've killed you. I've stolen your life." Kylar swallowed, but that damn lump wouldn't go away.

"You can't steal what I freely give. I can live with eternity in mind because I know I'm going to be facing it soon, and I'm not going to waste a second of what I have left. Being here, with you, is exactly what I choose."

And then Kylar was crying. Out in the yard, he felt Vi fumble a weave in shock, then go back to it, trying to distract herself, trying to give Kylar privacy. Elene hugged him and in her arms he found such boundless warmth and unqualified acceptance that his tears redoubled. All his doubts and self-recriminations, his self-loathing and fear washed away. And when his tears stopped flowing, she cried. The tears were an ablution and, holding her, Kylar felt clean for the first time in years.

When the tears had passed, they looked at each other, tear-smudged face to tear-smudged face, and laughed and held each other more. Then, slowly, they spun out their stories. Elene told him of her trip to Cenaria and her capture by the slavers. Kylar told her of Aristarchos's attempt at killing him, about Jarl's death, about fighting the Godking and being ringed, of his work to enthrone Logan, and his death on the wheel, his discovery of the cost of immortality, and his reunion with Durzo.

Then she asked him about wet work, about his first kill, about his training, about the Talent and what he saw when he looked at people through the ka'kari. He told her the unvarnished truth, and she listened. She couldn't understand all of it, she said, but she listened without judgment, and she didn't draw back after hearing it.

As he spoke, Kylar slowly relaxed. He felt the tension of secrecy and guilt, the fear of discovery and condemnation—all the tension that he had carried for so much of his life that it was simply part and parcel of how he experienced life—begin to unwind. In Elene, he found rest. For the first time, peace.

He looked at her with new eyes, and her beauty was warm blankets on a cold winter morning. It was home after a long journey. It wasn't a beauty to covet, like Vi's; it was a beauty to share. If Vi's body was art shaped to stoke desire, Elene's whole being was shaped to share love. Elene had scars, her figure was attractive but not such as left men incapable of speech—and yet her beauty surpassed Vi's. The intuition that had kept Kylar from Vi even from the first time she'd tried to seduce him at the Drake estate suddenly crystallized: You don't share your life with a woman's body, you share your life with a woman.

"Marry me," Kylar said, surprising himself. Then, realizing that his mouth had only uttered what his whole heart longed for, he said, "Please, Elene, will you marry me?"

"Kylar…"

"I know it'll have to be secret, but it'll be real, and I want you."

"Kylar…"

"I know, this damn ring will probably keep us from making love, but we'll figure something out, and even if we don't, I love you. I want to be with you. I want to be with you more than I want sex. I know it'll be really hard, but I mean it. We can—"

"Kylar, shut up," Elene said. She smiled at the look on his face, smoothed her dress, and said, "I would be honored to be your wife."

For a moment, he couldn't believe it. Then, at her spreading smile and her delight in taking him off guard, light burst over a thousand hills. Somehow, she was in his arms, and they were holding each other and laughing and Elene was crying, and they were good tears, and then he kissed her and his whole body dissolved into that point where their lips met, and her lips were soft, full, warm, inviting, moist, responsive, eager. It was beautiful. It was amazing. It was the best feeling of his whole life, right until he threw up.

Their lovemaking was completely one-sided. Again. Jenine had been a virgin only a month ago, so Dorian told himself it was a lack of practice, that her awkwardness was an awkwardness of how. But Jenine was coordinated and Dorian was ravenous, so that justification was getting strained. She averted her gaze as he lay atop her, unable to match the intensity in his eyes. He buried his head in her hair, trying to ignore her body's lack of arousal. He finished alone.

He held her, inhaling the scent of her, trying not to feel lonely.

She never denied him, even when he came to her a second time in a day or a third, and that made it worse. She didn't pretend to climax, at least not yet. But even when she did climax, afterwards, the gap still wasn't bridged. In everything she didn't say, he saw a woman trying desperately to love him, and give love every chance to grow.

Even now as he held her, she held him. He'd tried everything short of vir to make her love him as he loved her. He had a kingdom to defend and administer, men to train, plots to unravel, reforms to institute, magic to practice, but every day, he carved out hours simply to spend with her, to talk with her, to listen, to dance, to recite poetry, to tend the garden together, to tell stories, to listen to bards, to laugh, and only to make love after all that. The hell of it was that it seemed to be working. Jenine seemed more comfortable with him, more delighted with his presence and humor, more in love—everywhere but in the bedchamber. Was that because she was sixteen and lovemaking was new, or was their love as much a lie as Logan's death? Or was everything fine except that it was poisoned in his own mind? What if she did love him, and he was simply going mad?

"What are you thinking about?" Jenine asked.

Dorian propped himself on his elbows and kissed her breast to give himself time to think. "How much I love you" would have been a partial truth. "How much I love you and you don't love me" would be too brutal. But love needed truth to grow. He rubbed his aching head. "I was thinking of how hard you're trying, and how much I appreciate it."

She burst into tears, and there was truth in how she clung to him.

Logan sat in his new throne. He had given the artisans three weeks to deliver it, and the men had barely met the deadline. He had wanted it simple, sturdy wood with no ornamentation, but Duchess Kirena had prevailed upon him that the Cenarian throne couldn't look like a dinner chair, so he had relented. This throne was sandalwood, almost glowing with a high polish, solid, elegantly shaped, and with a few fat rubies in each wing and in the front of the arms. By some magic, it was comfortable for Logan's enormous frame. He almost pitied the rulers who would succeed him. Sitting in Logan's throne, they would feel like dwarfs.

He lifted an eyebrow at Lantano Garuwashi, who knelt on a plain woven mat on the floor at Logan's right hand. It looked uncomfortable, but Garuwashi appeared at ease. He nodded and Logan gestured.

The Lae'knaught in Wirtu, their semi-permanent camp that was functionally their capital city, had sent a new emissary. The man had arrived on time, though not an hour early.

"Greetings, Your Majesty," the diplomat began. He went on for some time, listing Logan's titles and then his own, and then those of his master, Overlord Julus Rotans. Logan kept his face impassive. Going to Khalidor without the Lae'knaught would be suicide. By spring, Logan would have an army of fifteen thousand if he was lucky. Garuwashi's sa'ceurai added six thousand. Between them, they had less than a thousand horse. Cenaria's nobility were the only people in the realm who had the time and coin to become horsemen, and most of them hadn't bothered. Of those who had, many had been killed in futile resistance to Garoth Ursuul. Similarly, Lantano Garuwashi had attracted mostly peasants and hedge sa'ceurai and the masterless. His army was the best in Ceura, but not the richest by a long shot. Duchess Kirena's spies said the Khalidorans had at least twenty thousand soldiers and thousands of wytches.

Garuwashi's men were in charge of training all of Logan's forces, and they would train them for at least three more months, four if the winter was hard, which was an eternity for a peasant army to train, but Logan didn't relish the idea of facing greater numbers and wytches on Khalidor's own land. However it worked, what they called the Armor of Unbelief did seem to make the Lae'knaught less susceptible to magic, and if they could neutralize the meisters, that would demoralize the normal Khalidoran soldiers, who were used to their wytches crushing the opposition before they even raised their swords. It came down to one brutal fact: if Logan wanted Jeninc back, he needed the Lae'knaught.

". . . after detailed discussion of your proposals," the diplomat said. "The High Command has come to a decision."

Logan stood abruptly. "Throw him out," he told his guards. They seized the diplomat by both arms instantly.

"You haven't even heard me out!" the man yelled as they dragged him backward, his feet barely touching the ground.

"Oh," Logan said, scratching his jaw as if that hadn't occurred to him. "Very well then, go ahead. But make it fast. You're boring me." The truth was, he knew their response as soon as the man said "proposals," plural.

"We agree with everything in the first and second articles, there are just a few minor details in the third that you may not be aware violate some very important Lae'knaught principles of honor. I'm sure quite unintentionally, you ask us to blaspheme against our most closely held beliefs."

"Oh," Logan said. "Let him go. I'm sorry, sir, I didn't mean to offend. What articles in particular were troublesome?"

"As I said, uh, we agree that Khalidor is our mutual enemy and that the time to act is now. We agree that—"

Logan waved his hand petulantly. "You're boring me."

"We simply had some logistical problems with the distribution of our forces."

"Oh?" Logan said. He thought they'd have some problems with that. Lord General Agon had a low opinion of Lae'knaught loyalty, so he'd asked for a provision that specified that the Lae'knaught forces would be split and serve under Cenarian and Ceuran commanders. It was a trade-off militarily. The Cenarian commanders wouldn't use the lancers as efficiently as the Lae'knaught commanders could. The Cenarians simply hadn't commanded such forces before, so they didn't know their strengths and weaknesses. On the other hand, it would make treachery much harder to organize, especially with how active Duchess Kirena planned to keep her spies.

"If I may be blunt, Your Majesty, this idea of having lancers serve under your commanders is suicidal."

"Fair enough," Logan said.

The man was professional enough that he didn't show his surprise at Logan's sudden acquiescence. "There were also a few other small details, much less substantial, I assure you. But now that we're agreed in principle, I could meet with Your Majesty's officials to arrange—"

"Why would that be necessary?" Logan asked.

The diplomat paused awkwardly. "Uh, to work out the details of our alliance?" He asked, as if trying not to treat Logan like an idiot.

"Alliance?" Logan asked.

The diplomat opened his mouth, but no words came out.

"No, no, sir," Logan said. "This is no alliance. This is war. You rejected my terms. This summer, after Garuwashi's sa'ceurai are finished looting Wirtu and slaughtering all of your officers, I will propose the same terms again—with one small additional detail. Namely, the lancers will stay under Cenarian command permanently. And if you say no then, I will kill you all. Guards?"

The men grabbed the little diplomat again.

"Your Majesty, wait!"

Logan lifted a finger and the guards stopped. "The only words I need to hear from you are, 'Your Majesty, we accept your proposal.' If you have anything else to say, you can say it to Underlord Dynos Rotans, who accompanied you, oddly in servant's garb, though he outranks you and is known to have his brother's ear. Tell him he should have had the balls to come see me himself. It's an insult that he thought if things went really wrong, he could step in himself. I'm sick of Lae'knaught sycophants. Tell him he's forbidden to come to my court. I'll give you half an hour. Either come in that door with the words I told you, or find your horses." Logan nodded and the guards heaved the diplomat out the door.

When the doors closed, Garuwashi said, "You seemed to enjoy that."

"On the contrary, I'm within an inch of vomiting."

"Really? Because you just tried to provoke war over a senseless provision?"

"I knew this kid, small kid, nothing to look at. Someone picked on him once, and he flew at the guy like he'd lost his mind."

"Did the little kid win?"

"He got destroyed. But no one picked on that little kid again, because he approached every harassment as if his life depended on winning. There were no rules in a fight with him. He didn't care how badly he got hurt. He would win. I was always bigger and stronger than other kids, but I would fight fair and stop when someone conceded victory. I had to fight a lot more than he did."

"So you're basing your handling of the Lae'knaught on a metaphor from your childhood?" Garuwashi asked.

"Which is why I feel sick." But there was no way around it. Without the Lae'knaught, he couldn't get his wife back.

Lantano Garuwashi cleared his throat. "While we're on the subject of things that make us sick, I've had word that some members of the High Council are proposing that the Regent send an emissary to see if I am Ceura's lost king."

"You say that like it's a bad thing." Cenaria had enemies north, east, and inside, the last thing Logan needed was problems from the south.

"They will most likely send an army with the emissary." Garuwashi lowered his voice. "He will demand to see Ceur'caelestos."

"And?" Logan asked.

"Kylar didn't tell you?"

"Tell me what?"

"I am sorry you had to put such a man to death, Your Majesty. It is not many men who will guard another's honor when he owes him nothing." Garuwashi cleared his throat, and Logan could swear that the big redhead was flushed. "I, ahem, I no longer hold the Blade of Heaven. Kylar threw it into Ezra's Wood. A magus went into the Wood after it and said he'd received a prophecy from the mad mage himself that told him how to make a second sword for me, but the mage has not returned."

"But you carry—"

"A scabbard with a hilt. If I have to show my sword, I'm dead. Should this become known, they won't even allow me to slay myself to expiate the dishonor."

And I'll lose the best part of my army.

"I see," Logan said. "We will do all we must to give your mage the time he needs. I'm sure he will return. No man swears idly to Lantano Garuwashi."

They sat in silence, each tense for his own reasons.

"How is your campaign against the Sa'kagé?" Garuwashi asked finally.

"Impossible to tell. Well, except that I'm still alive, as are all of my advisers. This war may actually help us. It gives us something to offer to men whose only trade has been violence. We call it an earned amnesty. A different number of years of service for different crimes. How we'll pay for a standing army for the next five years, I don't know, but these people have to do something, and I'd rather have them kill my enemies than my people."

"And you fill your military with the untrustworthy."

"Yes. But are not many of your own men the masterless? In Ceura, are not such said to have no honor? All I can do is give men who want to change the chance to try, and help them feed their families in the meantime. No one who was in the Sa'kagé will be allowed in the city guard, and taking bribes is a hanging offense for guards. We'll have a lot of problems, but for the moment, a lot of people hate Khalidor enough that they'll fight with me to defeat them before they start fighting against me again."

"You think you'll win," Garuwashi said.

"As long as Duchess Kirena and Count Drake stay alive, I'd rather be me than the Sa'kagé." Logan shrugged.

Garuwashi grunted, a sound that could have been assent or interest or neither, and they waited silently once more.

The massive doors of the throne room opened, and the diplomat came in. It had only been fifteen minutes. The man's eyes were filled with hatred. "Your Majesty," he said, biting off every word, "we accept your proposal."

68

*W*ithin a month of their first secret meeting with Vi, the Chattel had dreamt up two dozen new spells. A gap-toothed farmwife with tobacco-stained teeth knew a spell that made food more filling. An Alitaeran widow had developed a weave to keep food fresh for months. Others added their knowledge and soon, they'd created biscuits half the size of a man's hand that would give him energy for the whole day, made him feel satisfied, and came in a dozen flavors. A village blacksmith's wife had crafted a spell that kept plows sharp, and it was easily applied to swords, but it had to be reapplied every day. Almost all the women had some experience as Healers, so they crafted bandages that stayed cleaner longer, packable spider webs to help blood clot instantly, potent salves for burns, poultices that could suck poison out of wounds. One could bond a simple repelling spell to fabric, making light tents or tunics stay dry even in a storm. A cowherd taught them a spell to firm treacherous, muddy roads. It would dissipate almost instantly, but if the magae spaced themselves along a column, an entire army could march safely through a bog.

Few of them could throw a fireball, but when a soft-spoken woman told Vi that she had crafted a spell-containing spell, they had something better. One woman would cast a spell-container, another would cast a simple fire spell, and a third would bind it to an arrow. The spell was smaller than a woman's fist, but the arrows wouldn't fly well until someone figured out how to smooth the spell over the entire length of the shaft. Then, the arrow flew true, struck the practice dummy's shield, and the spell-container burst, splashing fire over the shield and the dummy. The dummy was engulfed in fire in seconds. Magae around the yard stopped what they were doing and turned to watch.

Several of the herders knew spells that would temporarily sharpen sight, hearing, or smell. Working together, they made one spell that was more efficient than any of the three alone that would last the duration of a watch. It could be applied to sentries or scouts.

Then they took to reversing their spells. An enemy's food could be spoiled in a day. Making roads muddy was harder than making them dry, however, as a maja had to soften many layers of earth, rather than harden a few. Likewise, dulling the enemies' weapons during a battle was deemed impossible. Magically locating hundreds or thousands of moving swords and differentiating friends' from foes' was too difficult. They could make wounds fester and suppurate and attract flies, but most of the women were too sickened for such work. Those who had trained as Healers, who would have been best suited to it, said their vows precluded it.

The two fronts where they made no progress at all were the signal sticks and magically representing a battle. Garoth Ursuul had been able to see a battlefield and communicate instantly with his generals or men across his kingdom. In war, signal banners could be missed or captured or out of the line of sight. Trumpets' calls could be lost in the cacophony, and with either of those, the messages passed were both necessarily simple—withdraw, advance, come now—and public. Developing signal sticks would mean giving commanders the ability to hear scouts report from behind enemy lines, rather than hoping that they could cross back over and report hours or days later. It would mean ordering cavalry to reinforce a wavering line and having them move instantly, rather than minutes later. It would mean a general could split his armies and still coordinate their movements, or change their strategy as the situation changed, rather than being committed to meet on a specified day at a certain area and hope nothing kept the other half of your army from getting there.

The failure put Vi in an evil mood, which wasn't helped when Sister Ariel laughed at her. "Vi," she said, joining her on the field, "don't you see what you've accomplished?"

Vi grunted. "I've made war easier."

"Well, yes, you have, but you've done something more remarkable. Remarkable for any maja, but perhaps doubly so for you."

"What's that?" Vi asked, suspicious of any praise from Sister Ariel.

"You're teaching these women to wage war without trying to be men. The simple fact is, most women aren't really good at throwing fire or calling down lightning. If you'd insisted on these women becoming war magae as the Chantry thought of war magae, they'd have made little progress before spring. Instead, you've let them be who they are."

"It's common sense."

"By the Seraph's tits, Vi, a magus's fireball isn't any good if he can't cross a bog to get to the battle; his lightning bolt can't hurt anyone if he starves. We were right about you. It might be common sense, but the weaves you've encouraged these women to develop would never have been encouraged by anyone else. You want to know why? Because we all have blind spots, Vi, even you. The good thing is that yours are different from ours. Your commonsense answer violates one of our institutional creeds in place since the Third Alitaeran Accord, which is that the Sisterhood is complete. By abandoning certain areas of study, many would say you imply that men are better at those types of magic. That statement would be enough to paralyze most Sisters from doing the work you're doing. Even if they agreed it was true, they would spend a lot of energy trying to conceal the fact that they weren't studying fire and lightning and earthquakes."

"I'm not making any statements," Vi said. "I bet I can throw a better fireball than most magi, and I haven't even worked on it. I'm just trying to save our asses."

"Oh, just because a crisis threatens to wipe us out, you think we should stop infighting?"

Vi scrunched her eyebrows together. "Is that a real question?"

Sister Ariel laughed. "How are things, ahem, on the conjugal front?"

"What?" Right when Vi thought Sister Ariel was being kind, the woman had to pull out her big words to make Vi feel stupid.

"How are things with your husband?" Sister Ariel asked, after making sure no one was close enough to overhear.

At even the mention of him, Vi felt Kylar, only fifty paces away, training in the basement of their manse with Durzo. He seemed happy despite his many bruises. Vi Healed them secretly from time to time when Kylar was asleep in the mornings.

The last month had been awkward, but not nearly as bad as Vi had feared. Vi had expected to feel malice leaking through the bond at all times, and if Kylar had hated her, there was no way she could be anything but miserable. Mostly, though, he didn't think about her. She was training and studying as many hours a day as her body could stand and so was he. When she got home, she went to bed immediately.

Meanwhile, Kylar and Elene had found a patr to marry them in secret. Durzo, Uly, Sister Ariel, and Vi were the only witnesses. Kylar had moved into Elene's room, though consummating their marriage was impossible, and any time cuddling even flirted with the erotic, Kylar began to get sick. Oddly, they still had that newlywed glow. Maybe it was all intensified because they knew Elene didn't have much time left, so they touched whenever they could—though carefully—and spent hours talking.

Vi knew Kylar felt the absence of sex acutely. Some nights she'd lie awake on the opposite side of the wall from where he lay awake, Elene snuggled into his chest. She could feel the ache of desire, but as soon as he entertained the desire, his thoughts veered to Vi and with an iron self-control, he stopped those thoughts and began admiring everything he loved about Elene. Sometimes, Vi knew, that iron self-control was rusted all the way through, but still he closed the door.

They'd met twice in their dreams.

"You don't hate me," Vi said in the first dream. She marveled at it.

"I hate the price we have to pay."

"Can you ever forgive me?" she asked.

"I'm trying. You did what had to be done. You're not a bad woman, Vi. I know that you've been giving me and Elene space and time, and I know it's hard for you, too. Thank you." He glanced down at her night dress; this one actually fit, and his gaze was admiring, but deliberately brief. "I just wish you weren't so damn beautiful. Good night."

The second dream had been harder. It had been one of those nights where Kylar lay on the opposite side of the wall so tormented he thought he would burst. In the dream, Kylar stood at the foot of Vi's bed, naked. His eyes were closed and Vi drank in the sight of him, his hard lean limbs, flat stomach etched with hard muscles. She was wearing one of Master Piccun's night-dresses, which she'd left behind in Cenaria. It was white silk and short with sheer panels, but more pretty than provocative: a make-love-to-me, not a fuck-me. It was one of the first things she'd ever bought from Master Piccun, and in four years she'd never worn it. Men made love to their wives or girl-friends. Vi got fucked. Her hair was unbound and combed out glossy.

Vi had a revelation at the very moment Kylar opened his eyes. Kylar had never seen this dress. This wasn't his dream. It was hers. She froze, feeling more exposed than she had when she'd stood naked in front of the God-king. Garoth Ursuul had judged her not knowing her. Kylar had far more power. He was here because she desired him. Vi had long been the object of desire, and she'd mocked men for it.

Now, the numbness that had sat between her legs since the first time one of her mother's lovers raped her was thawing. The ache there was so foreign that Vi hadn't been able to name it. For all the fucking she'd done, Vi had not once taken a man to bed for pleasure, much less love. The receding numbness, though, not only allowed her to feel desire for the first time, it also threatened her. Through the ice, Vi could see the outlines of a mystery: she could imagine bringing her desire—of which fucking was a part, but not the center—to Kylar and experiencing union, wholeness in a fragmented world. She'd made fucking a simple physical exertion, as monotonous but as necessary to her work as exercising. If she ever wanted to experience what was beneath the ice, she'd have to feel the pain and violation frozen inside it. If Kylar were to speak while they had sex, she'd remember all the bastards who couldn't shut up. If he were to remain silent, she'd remember the brutes who fucked silently. If Kylar were to twine his fingers through her hair, she'd remember all the assholes who pawed her hair like she was an animal. If Kylar ripped her clothes off in his passion, she would remember when Hu Gibbet did it and spat on her face. If Vi were ever to enjoy Kylar's desire and allow herself to reciprocate, she'd have to trust him with her brokenness, and she'd have to wade through all the hells her numbness had spared her.

She understood all of that in the very moment Kylar's opening eyes met hers. She tensed and immediately her hair was back up in its ponytail, tight enough to hurt. Two waves of feeling raced through Kylar, the second chas-ing the first, and even with her emotional stupidity or however Sister Ariel had said it, Vi could name his feelings through the very air. The first was desire, and though it was physical, it wasn't only physical. A month of cud-dling the woman he loved had been a month of foreplay. But right after that, he withdrew.

"Vi," Kylar choked out. "I can't even be here." He ignored his own nudity, and her near-nudity, looking into her eyes and letting her read his.

Her rapists had shattered the bond between sex and intimacy, leaving her only with fucking. In ring raping Kylar, she'd left him with only intimacy. The difference was, the only person who could damage Kylar as she had been damaged long ago was Kylar himself. The integrity between what Kylar's body did and what his heart felt was still intact. He was sorely tempted, but so far unbroken. If he cheated on Elene, he would be a cheater in his own eyes—for the rest of a very long life.

He'd turned and walked out of her dream.

Vi cleared her throat and met Sister Ariel's gaze. "Things with Kylar are fine."

Dorian knew he was in trouble as soon as the dancing girl entered the throne room. He'd been meeting with the Graavar chieftain, a hulking highlander whose raven hair hung in great mats to his waist. The Graavar were a powerful highland tribe, and Grakaat Kruhn was highly regarded by all the tribes. He had come to test Dorian. It was a harmless bit of highlander play, mostly—the highlanders hadn't made a serious attempt at independence for more than a century—and Grakaat had found Dorian satisfactory in all ways. Until this.

"Your Holiness," Grakaat Kruhn said, his half-lidded eyes too self-satisfied by far, "I would like to present you with a gift to seal our treaty." He gestured and two girls came forward. The dancer was about sixteen, the other, who held a highland flute, was perhaps thirteen, and though they were both pretty, Dorian had no doubt they were the chieftain's daughters.

As the dancer began a sensuous *rondaa,* most of Dorian's guards and all of his courtiers averted their eyes. The highland version of the dance was different from what Dorian had seen as a youth. The girl wore a wide garment with exaggerated wide shoulders from which were suspended strips of cloth. Around the hips, the cloth had bells sown in. As her sister played, each gyration of the dancer's hips made the bells tinkle and revealed glimpses of her nakedness beneath. As in the lowland dance, the girl appeared to float, chest and head immobile while her body tantalized, but the lowland dance was more focused on the stomach, which this girl had fully covered. Nonetheless, in moments Dorian was drawn in. The chieftain's daughter was talented.

The *rondaa* gave way to a *beraa,* and removed the last doubts from Dorian's mind about what that chieftain intended. The *beraa* was faster, more erotic. The girl clapped her hands in time over her head, exposing the sides of her breasts, her hips snapping side to side, but now also undulating front to back in a motion that would torment any man with a pulse.

Dorian was trapped. He wasn't sure if he was glad that Jenine was sequestered for her moon blood or if he wished she were here. Perhaps her presence would have changed things. Grakaat Kruhn wouldn't have his daughter dance a *beraa* for the Godking unless he planned to give her to him. A marriage to seal a treaty had far less weight in the north than it did in the southron realms, but the smile that had been on the chieftain's face told Dorian something else.

Dorian thought that taking many wives would have quelled the rumors he'd begun by entering the castle as a eunuch, but if anyone found out that he wasn't using his harem, the Halfman jokes would begin again. A highland warrior like Grakaat Kruhn achieved his place through the force of his *virtu,* which meant not only virtue, but also strength and manliness. To the highlanders, the three concepts were one. What manliness could a eunuch have? How could a war chief submit to half a man?

Dorian made a small gesture and the throne room cleared quietly of everyone except his guards and several Vürdmeisters. Grakaat Kruhn looked disturbed, but his daughter didn't miss a step, and Dorian kept his attention full on her, not giving the chieftain any clues. Inside, Dorian's stomach roiled. *God, give me strength for what I'm about to do.* But he'd rejected the One God, and the thought of what the God would think of this cooled whatever arousal Dorian still had left. Would Jenine understand?

Maybe. If she didn't have to see it.

Damn the highlander. Dorian's Hands had given him news that Moburu was making a bid to take over the barbarian tribes of the Freeze. Moburu was calling himself the prophesied High King, and the hell of it was that he had been born on the right day—or missed it by three, depending on which scholar's calendar you believed. But even if Moburu died before spring and especially if he didn't, Dorian needed this highlander to bring all the other highlanders to him to face Neph Dada and his Vürdmeisters.

If Dorian faltered now, the story would get out instantly: the new Godking was either impotent or a eunuch. A southron, then. No true Godking at all. Grakaat Kruhn would have killed him with a teenage girl. *If I'm to be Godking, I've got to rule like a Godking.*

The dancer finished with an exuberance and intensity in her smoky eyes that surprised Dorian. Had she convinced herself to love him, a stranger? Or was there fear somewhere beneath, a terror she concealed, taking only its energy to fuel her dance?

Dorian wrapped his knuckles on his throne appreciatively, the Khalidoran equivalent of applause. He smiled and stood. "By Khali, Grakaat, they're amazing. They're stunning. Gorgeous. The younger one dances too?"

Grakaat looked confused. "I—yes, Your Holiness, but I meant—"

"I accept them. I've never had a more handsome gift. Child, what's your name?" he asked, turning to the flutist.

Her sudden fear confirmed what Dorian expected. Grakaat had intended to bait him with the dancer. The last thing he'd expected was that a eunuch would want both of his daughters. Between the young girl's fear and the older girl's incredulity, Dorian wanted to say, "I didn't want this. Your father used you as pawns against a god. A god can't let him win." But he said nothing.

"I'm Eesa," the girl said. She was barely flowered, pretty in an awkward girlish way. Dorian's stomach threatened to rebel. *Khali, give me strength.*

He remembered a spell to ease the girl's fright and accomplish his purposes. He'd used it often as a lecherous young man. "The Graavar seal marriage pacts publicly, don't they?" Dorian asked.

Fear shot through the chieftain's eyes and Dorian knew that the younger daughter was Grakaat's favorite. "It's a tradition we've not practiced in many—"

"A good tradition," Dorian said, "especially when there are...*doubts* about the groom's *virtu*." *Khali, give me strength.*

"I, I...Your Holiness." Grakaat was turning green. His men-at-arms averted their eyes.

Eesa still didn't know what they were talking about. Before she could figure it out, Dorian laid a tracery of vir on her. She visibly relaxed. Her pupils dilated, and she couldn't seem to look anywhere but Dorian's face. He continued the spell, delicately coaxing her body into deceiving her mind. Whatever he did to her now, she would enjoy. Later, if she were as horrified as she ought to be, they would tell her that he was a god, that there was no shaming in serving him however he desired, that she should feel honored to have attracted his attention.

"I don't know all the intricacies of your quaint barbarian customs, so a few pillows on the floor will have to do. That is, unless you object?" Dorian stood and shrugged out of his ermine over-robe. With the vir, he devoured the rest of his clothing with tongues of black flame. Naked, his flesh writhing with layer on layer of vir, thorns of it clawing out of his skin, a black crown of it springing through the skin of his head, Dorian glowered at the chieftain. The huge man trembled. He tried to turn his head, and found it locked in place. He tried to close his eyes, and found he couldn't blink.

The vir swept Dorian's courtiers' pillows into a pile three paces from Grakaat's feet.

Dorian let his glory fade and turned to the girl. He smiled at her. "Come, love." *Khali, give me strength,* Dorian prayed, and found he had it. God forgive him, his strength didn't flag for an instant.

Afterward, Dorian stood, his body gleaming with sweat. Eesa lay panting, oblivious, obscene. For the first time, Graakat Kruhn was staring at Wanhope with the fear a Godking deserved. The Godking said, "I'll be expecting you come spring. If your warhost numbers seven thousand, I will put you over the Quarl, Churaq, Hraagl, and Iktana clans. On spring's first new moon, we march to Black Barrow. The girls stay with me."

70

$\mathcal{V}$i woke to Sister Ariel shaking her. The windows were still dark, and the only light in the room was from a single candle. Vi sat up and gazed blearily at the maja, who was red-eyed and wearing the same tent-like dress she'd worn the day before.

"What are you doing?" Vi asked.

"I found it. I can help you."

"Help me with what?" Vi asked.

"Get up, I'll tell you on the way."

Vi dressed and followed Sister Ariel. Sister Ariel said nothing until they were on one of the punts that would convey them to the Chantry. Even then, she spoke quietly, leery of how voices traveled over the water, even in the pre-dawn fog that wreathed the lake.

"Long ago, there was an Alitaeran emperor named Jorald Hurdazin. By all accounts, he was a skilled and wise leader. In his younger years, he solidified Alitaeran control from what is now Ymmur in the east to the west coast of Midcyru. What is now Waeddryn and Modai were his last conquests, and with his marriage to Layinisa Guralt, the Seeress of Gyle—essentially its princess—the lands that are now Ceura came under his control as well, and there he stopped, mostly because of her influence. He spent the next twenty years consolidating his empire and for the most part bringing justice and prosperity to the lands he had conquered. He was, however, magically poisoned by one of his many enemies. The poisoning was caught early, but the magi could only delay its effects. They treated him every day, but soon determined that Emperor Hurdazin would die within two years. Obviously, this was a closely held secret, and obviously, they called as many green magi and magae as they could. To make matters worse, there was no heir, and in agreeing to bring Gyle into the Empire, Gyle's king had insisted that Jorald and Layinisa be married with rings like yours. For a man of his power, finding such rings was no problem, and though their marriage was first political and magical, all the histories I've read agree that Jorald and Layinisa deeply loved each other. The green magi found nothing to heal Jorald, and they soon found that Layinisa was infertile. Women with great Talents sometimes injure themselves with their magic, and infertility is common in those who use too much magic, or too much too soon.

"The emperor put as many magi as he dared trust to work on both magical problems. He believed that Layinisa might hold his empire after his death, but if she were infertile, that would only delay the collapse, and he didn't want to be yet another emperor whose empire died with him. In the end, it was Layinisa herself who discovered a way around the rings' bond."

"She did?" Vi asked.

"Don't get excited. Now we're here, say nothing until we reach the library."

They walked silently through the dark halls of the Chantry. Vi wondered for a moment that the building was beginning to feel like home. The dim magical torches that illumined the walls and followed them seemed normal now, the austere marble arches comforting in their strength rather than menacing. In a few minutes, they were deep in the Chantry's storerooms, far below the waterline, a place Vi had never been allowed to go. It was neither dark nor dirty, but it did have an air of abandonment. Numbered oak boxes lined the room to the ceiling. The one small desk had an oak box already upon it.

Instead of opening the box, however, Sister Ariel closed it and put it back on a numbered shelf and grabbed a different box two rows down. Vi understood that she had left out the wrong box in case some spy checked what she was studying. At first Vi wondered why the boxes were oaken, but then she looked again and saw the spell sunk into the wood. Each oak box had one spell to strengthen the box and make it watertight, one to make it fire resistant, and one to suck air from the box as it closed to preserve whatever was kept inside.

"Magically reactive materials are kept in special rooms on the next floor; these archives are for mundane records only. Because of how they're preserved, they only have to be copied by industrious tyros such as yourself every few hundred years—if they're not frequently opened," Sister Ariel said. The box opened with a hiss, and she gently lifted out sheets of bound parchment that to Vi's eyes looked scarcely ten years old.

"At the time of Jorald and Layinisa's marriage, binding rings had been forbidden for almost fifty years. They were still common among royal families, of course, who were rarely willing to surrender them. The rings continued to cause misery wherever they were used and all magi became more and more convinced that banning them had been one of the best decisions the Chantry and the brotherhoods had ever made. Every group eliminated knowledge of them and how to make them to the best of its ability. This did lead to bloodshed a number of times, especially among the Vy'sana, the Makers, who to this day are a small brotherhood. When Layinisa figured out how to circumvent the magic, there was a great debate among us. Some wanted to follow her research to find a way to fully break the bonding. The majority, however, feared that any dabbling in those arts again would lead to a full rediscovery of how to bond. The suffering of those few who were presently bonded was weighed against the possibility of vast suffering if bonding were rediscovered by the unscrupulous. I don't know if you've experimented with your bond, Vi, but it does have an element of compulsion. That's what made it break the Godking's compulsion on you. The order of the ringing makes the compulsion in your rings flow from you to Kylar."

"What?" Vi asked. "You mean..."

"I mean if you told Kylar to walk on his hands to Cenaria, you'd find his body somewhere in a mountain pass with stumps where his hands had been. It's a compulsion stronger by far than what the Godking used on you."

"But there's a way out?" Vi said, her throat tight.

"Not out, child. Because you're the mistress of the bond, however, you can do what Layinisa did."

"Which is?"

"She used the compulsion of the bond to force Jorald to divorce her and marry a princess. She was then able to suspend the bond to allow him to produce an heir."

"What happened?"

"He died but the empire lived, minus the country of Gyle, which was deeply insulted by Jorald divorcing their Seeress. Layinisa served Jorald's new wife and supported her regency for five years, until the new empress marched against Gyle, at which point Layinisa committed suicide. The enmity between Alitaera and Ceura didn't cool for centuries and would probably be raging right now if the countries still bordered each other. The point is, if you wish it, you can suspend the bond—partially. A maja named Jessa worked with Layinisa on the rings. Jessa was in the camp that wished to learn about breaking them, and when the Chantry forbade it, I suspected that she tried to defy them. Jessa was a Healer, but she was also interested in gardening, so I've been looking through her books. They're not terribly enlightening; others did far better, and she wasn't an important maja, so I think no one ever studied her books. If they did, they would have found what I have. She's hidden it in plain sight, and not well. She was no cryptographer. After I read the books, I began applying ciphers, then I worked on her marginalia. If you could read Old Ceuran you'd see how ridiculous this is—she'd capitalize a strange word in her margin notes and everything from that capital to the next capital was part of her secret message. If you look at all the marginalia from the last to the first, the message unfolds. I don't even understand everything Jessa wrote, but I think you will. Oh, one more thing: Vi, I haven't told Kylar or Elene about this, and I won't. This is your burden. It is yours to decide if the price is worth it."

Twelve hours later, with dark circles under her eyes, Vi found a cheerful Elene making breakfast.

"What is it?" Elene asked. "Are you well?"

"I know it's a month late, but Elene . . ." A timid smile broke through Vi's fatigue. "I have a wedding present for you."

71

They were calling him Solon Stormrider. They said that his hair was growing in white because of the snow-laden seas through which his longboats had plunged. Or they said it had turned white after the winter sea had chewed on him and found him too tough and spat him back out. His boat had capsized once, and even his magic had barely saved him as he swam a mile through storm-whipped seas. Of course, his hair had been growing in white since he'd used Curoch—long before this mad winter—and he'd explained that to the soldiers and sailors who'd begun to follow him, but they preferred their own versions.

Now it was spring, and Solon was heading back to Queen Wariyamo, having destroyed her enemies. He had bowed before her after saving her life, and she had told him, fury edging her voice, that the price for her hand was cleansing the isles of the rebellion he had started by killing Oshobi Takeda. Kaede didn't like being weak, didn't like needing anyone, but her temper always cooled in time. At least, it used to.

Everyone had expected Solon to wait for spring and take an army to each of the Takeda isles. Instead, he'd begun at once, alone. In a canoe, he'd paddled the eighteen miles to Durai. There, he'd given the ultimatum he would give a dozen times through the winter. Surrender, swear fealty to the queen, and give me all your weapons, or I shall slay every man who fights and take those who surrender as slaves.

Gulon Takeda had laughed at him, and died, along with eighteen of his soldiers. Solon had returned with twenty-four awed soldiers in a longboat. He had delivered them to the new Mikaidon and slept in a dockside tavern, not seeking so much as a word with Kaede. By the time he'd woken and gone out to his canoe, a score of the craziest sailors he'd ever met and a captain with a vendetta against the Takedas volunteered to join him.

Soon, storms battered them every time they left port, and Solon's command of weather magic grew by necessity. But Sethi winter storms were tamed by no mage, and it was a fight every day. Several times, the Takedas who had faced them were so stunned that anyone should be able to make the crossing they had surrendered on the spot. And when Solon returned to Hokkai yet again, victorious yet again, he found the Takeda soldiers he'd conscripted were a fully trusted part of the Sethi army, oddly proud to have been defeated by the Stormrider.

Now it was done. The Takedas' home island, Horai, hadn't expected an army for at least another six weeks. The leaders were totally unprepared, and having almost three thousand men to Solon's four hundred did them no good. Before the Takeda army could be rallied, its commanders were dead, and Solon's magic-enhanced voice had offered generous terms to the living. The rebellion was crushed and nearly all the dead were Takedas.

With the first day of spring, the first day clear enough that the merchants would be on their boats preparing for the first spring runs, checking for damage, repairing sails and nets, shouting orders at men rusty from months spent ashore, Solon's little fleet sailed into Hokkai harbor.

They were greeted as heroes, and the crazy sailors who had joined Solon first were now soldiers in truth. Sailors dropped their gear to greet them, captains forgot their shouting, and the shorebound traders and vintners streamed through the streets to greet them. The flood carried them to the castle, and Solon's heart thudded with fear and expectation. *Kaede, please, my love, don't take my glory as an insult. Without you, it all means nothing.*

The crowd brought him to Whitecliff Castle, shining in the spring sun. Kaede stood on the dais where months before she had almost been deposed. She wore an ocean blue nagika and a platinum tiara with sapphires. She raised her hands and the men and women quieted. "How fare the isles, Stormrider?"

"The isles are at peace, Your Majesty."

The people cheered, but Kaede's face was still somber. She let the people cheer, then raised her hands once more. "They say you are a mage, Stormrider."

"I am," he said.

The crowd grew quieter, noting the queen's solemnity. That solemnity brought to not a few minds the questions people had asked when Solon had first been sent to school with the Midcyri magi: where would his loyalties lie?

"They say you are a god, Stormrider, to have defied the winter seas alone."

"Neither a god, nor alone, Your Majesty. A loyal son of Seth who tracked the seas with men and women fearless as tygres, fiercer than storms, and hungrier than the seas. Not even winter seas could stop such from serving you."

The crowd stirred with hope, and Solon's Stormriders swelled with pride that he should share the glory so liberally, but Kaede cut it off quickly. "They say you were our prince, Stormrider. They say I've stolen your throne."

Silence.

"A prince I was, of an ancient house that my elder brother debased and dishonored. He broke the holy covenant between king and country, and I stand a prince no more. Should you command, I will sail to the sunset or to death's rocky shores. I am but a man." He lowered his voice, but still it carried across the silent crowd. "A man who loves you, my queen."

She stood silent and the crowd held its breath, but Solon could see her eyes shining. "Then Solon Stormrider, Solon Tofusin, come forward and receive your rewards as a mage, and a loyal son of Seth, and a man."

He was in a haze as the crowd pulled him forward, laughing and cheering and shouting. Kaede first presented him with a pendant with a glowing ruby lit from within, burning with ancient magics. He'd never seen it before, never heard of such an artifact, but before he could consider it, she put a crown on his brow. It was his father's crown, a circlet of seven golden grape leaves mingled with seven golden waves. "A ruby fit for a mage, a crown fit for Seth's most loyal son, and—if you will have me—a proud and troublesome woman ill-fit for any man."

"Except one," Solon said, and he swept her into his arms and kissed her.

*V*i didn't know how Elene had explained it to Kylar, though she had known when by Kylar's sudden burst of confusion and hope and longing through the bond. Tonight was the night. She'd gone over the magic a number of times with Sister Ariel. As Ariel had warned her, Vi wasn't severing the bond, only partially suspending it.

First, it was only suspended while Vi was actively using magic against it. If there was any good news, Vi thought, it was that Kylar was a virgin. That embarrassed him, but Vi thought it was extraordinary and kind of cute, which embarrassed him further. Now, though, she simply hoped it meant his lovemaking with Elene would be brief. Vi had told Elene—and Elene had decided not to tell Kylar—that the suspension of the bond worked only one way: Kylar wouldn't feel Vi, but Vi would still feel him.

Vi had her materials: an itchy wool robe that she hoped would distract her from whatever physical sensation bled through the bond, and a pitcher of wine for afterward to obliterate her thinking. Sister Ariel didn't exactly approve, but she didn't forbid it, either. Vi could only hope that Kylar was one of those men who promptly fell asleep after sex, because once she released the magic, he would feel her once more. If Kylar knew Vi was basically magically eavesdropping on his lovemaking, he would worry about it. Elene fully believed she would die by spring, and she deserved as much of Kylar's attention as she could get.

Kylar was coming up the steps. He and Elene had finished a romantic dinner in the kitchen—of course they couldn't go out where people might see them—and Elene was leading him by the hand. Vi felt his anticipation and disbelief. He probed toward Vi, but she made herself a stone wall and began chanting.

According to Sister Ariel, the weaves themselves weren't that challenging;

it was using them at the strength required for the time required that was difficult. Plus, Sister Ariel allowed, it was probably emotionally taxing. Ariel thought Vi could probably maintain them for twenty minutes.

Sister Ariel could probably withstand the emotional tax forever. The words Bitch Wytch made their way into Vi's chanting, but they didn't have the force they used to. After all, it was Sister Ariel who had done all the research to make this possible. Was that her way of saying sorry?

Layer upon layer of magic surrounded the bond, wreathing it like fog, and in moments Vi knew she was doing it right for two reasons. First, Kylar stopped, bewildered, as he was leaning forward to kiss Elene as they sat on the edge of their bed. Second, Vi could tell that he stopped leaning forward as he sat on the edge of his bed. Whatever Vi was doing to mute Kylar's side of the bond, it seemed to be amplifying her own.

Panic hit her, making it hard to breathe, but Kylar didn't feel it. She could tell he didn't feel her. He wondered at the absence and then joy spread through him like a fire. He pulled Elene into his arms and kissed her passionately.

It was hard to breathe. Vi could only choke out a series of curses to keep the magic going. She'd kissed men, of course, and had dozens more kiss her. She'd avoided it when she could, wishing she could be as numb there as below, but it was part of her work to kiss convincingly. Feeling Kylar kiss Elene was something different. It was fresh and innocent and full of rejoicing. Then it deepened, and Vi felt Kylar's surprise at the ferocity of Elene's passion. He fell—was pushed?—back onto the bed, and she settled on his hips. Then he was kissing her again, fumbling with the ties of her dress.

Vi cursed desperately, locking her eyes open, rubbing the wool across her forearm. It helped, a little, but Kylar's joy and free desire still lived in her head. Elene must have said something, because Kylar laughed. Vi could hear it through the wall, but as she felt it, she knew she'd never heard Kylar laugh like that. Maybe Kylar had never laughed like that in his whole life. It was playful and free and accepted and accepting, a joy wild and strong and content. This was the Kylar Elene had always seen, and with a pang, Vi knew Elene deserved him.

There was a tenderness so deep emanating through the bond that it ached, and Vi realized that of all things, Kylar was talking to Elene.

"Put him in a bed chamber with a naked woman and he *talks?*" Vi said aloud, still working her Talent. "No wonder he's still a virgin." It was too bad the weaves weren't harder, because she needed the distraction. Elene was scared, Vi realized, and embarrassed because she knew exactly what Vi was doing here in this room. Either way, Kylar was soothing her, lying by her side, his left arm under her head and his right arm embracing her, caressing her while he spoke soft assurances and slowly awakened her passion.

Vi had fucked so many times, with so many men, in so many ways, she thought she knew pretty much everything about sex. But Kylar and Elene, in their mutual ignorance, were experiencing something she never had. Their lovemaking fit into a pattern bigger than itself. There was no awkwardness even in their fumbling, because there was no fear of judgment.

"Oh, fuck me, oh—" Vi's voice squeaked and she lost the thought. Whatever Elene was doing, she was either naturally gifted or Kylar was extremely sensitive. Either way, the wave of pleasure through the bond was overwhelming. Vi's cheeks felt like they were on fire.

Then Vi felt Kylar's mischievous grin—dammit, it felt exactly the same way it looked—and his own pleasure faded into the pleasure of pleasuring.

"You bastard," Vi said. "I hate you. I hate you I hate you I hate you." When Vi fucked, she put on a persona like a mask, always. Kylar was making love as a whole man. Every aspect of himself was present—and Vi knew then that she loved him.

She'd been attracted to things about Kylar from the first time she saw that damned mischievous grin in Count Drake's house. She'd admired how he tried to leave the way of shadows, how he treated Elene and Uly. She appreciated his excellence in fighting. She'd felt a twinge of infatuation long ago—but then, she'd once been infatuated with Jarl, who was homosexual. In the past month, she'd even come to accept that she desired Kylar. But all those things weren't love. Perhaps she never would have known what love was if she hadn't talked so much with Elene, and if she hadn't felt it daily in Kylar's feelings for Elene.

Something banged into the wall inches from Vi, and she gasped. Her eyes widened. The magic almost escaped her, and only her fear of what would happen if it did helped her regain control. She scrubbed the wool against her arm—fuck she hated wool! "Dead babies. Bearded women. Back hair so long you can braid it. Moon blood. The smell of the Warrens on a hot summer day. Unwashed whores. Vomit. Dead babies. Bearded women. Back hair so—oh shit!" Vi bit the wool and held onto the magic for dear life.

A few moments later, Vi could breathe again. She checked the magic as a deep sense of ease and restfulness and well-being and intimacy and peace with the entire world rolled over Kylar. The magic was still intact. Vi grabbed the pitcher of wine and drank from it directly. "It's a good thing you're a virgin, Kylar. Were a virgin. I don't think I could've handled that for much—"

Vi realized something at apparently the same time Elene did: Kylar was still aroused. He asked a question, and Elene's answer was unmistakably and passionately affirmative. Vi set the pitcher down with shaking hands. Pleasure arced through Kylar again.

Oh gods, it was going to be a long winter.

As winter slowly faded in Khaliras, Dorian arrayed his army on the plain north of the city to face the invaders from the Freeze. The ground was still covered in melting snow that their feet churned into freezing slush. Every breath steamed a protest against battle in such conditions.

The wild men who inhabited the Freeze always fought bravely, but their only tactic was to overwhelm a foe by throwing a larger army at it. Once engaged, they fought man to man, never as a unit. Since its founding, Khaliras had never been taken by the brutes, though a few times it had been a near thing. Garoth had always said that the wild men had proportionally more Talented men and women than any people in the world.

The armies faced each other as the sky turned from inky blue to ice blue with the rising sun. Godking Wanhope's lines were only three deep, arrayed over as much of the plain as twenty thousand men would stretch. The wild men's army dwarfed his, and stretched much further and more thickly. There was no way Wanhope could keep them from flanking his army. In the middle of the wild men's line there was one huge block that the men shunned. If Dorian's reports were correct, he faced twenty-eight thousand krul, and even more wild men.

Three-to-one odds. Dorian smiled, fearless. The current of prophecy was streaming past him, and he saw a thousand deaths. Ten thousand.

"Milord, are you feeling well?" Jenine asked. Dorian hadn't wanted her to have to see this, but he'd been counting on Jenine more and more, not only for her advice, either.

He blinked and focused on her. Her futures were splitting off so sharply that he could barely see her as she was now, pretty, lips pale from the cold, bundled in furs. Flickering in front of her was a woman hugely pregnant with twins, and a woman with a crushed skull, features unrecognizable under the gore. "No, not well at all," Dorian said. "But well enough that I won't let my men die."

From this distance, the grotesque features of the krul weren't visible, though their plainly naked gray flesh was. That nakedness gave Dorian hope. The krul were created with magic, but they were creatures of flesh. The cold would cripple and kill them eventually. It wasn't easy to force the krul to wear clothing, as it wasn't easy to rein them in from slaughter, but each could be done. That the wild men's shamans hadn't meant their control was tenuous.

Dorian gave an order, and the slaves lowered his palanquin to the ground. Godking Wanhope stepped out and advanced onto the plain alone. Palming an obsidian knife, he shrugged off the priceless ermine cloak and let it fall to the mud. It was a gesture that would have infuriated him had he seen his father do it. Now, he understood. To protect what he loved, he had to keep control. To keep control, Wanhope had to be a god. A god was above ordinary concerns like ruining a cloak that cost more than fifty slaves.

The currents of prophecy were rising at the pressure of seventy thousand futures that Wanhope held in his hands. On his choices, tens of thousands would live and die. He looked at the army opposing him and saw ten thousand ravens swirling over them, waiting to feed. He blinked, and the ravens were gone, then blinked again, and they were back. But they weren't ravens. Nor did they only swirl over the wild men.

Dorian turned, eyes wide. Wispy, dark figures swarmed over his entire army, clotted the air above his men, darting this way and that. Here six perched on a single man, their claws sunk deep into his flesh. There only a single dark figure spun around another warrior, stabbing in one place and then another, as if trying his defenses. But those were the exception. Almost every man in Dorian's army had at least one figure clinging to him. And there were ranks among them; some were far more terrible. Dorian looked at General Naga nearby. A trio of the monsters clung to the man, two perched on his shoulders, one licking ephemeral blood from the general's fingers.

This close, Dorian could see their features. One had a cancer that swelled one eye grotesquely. Open, suppurating ulcers dotted their golden-skinned faces, dribbling black blood onto robes so black with that blood that Dorian could barely tell that they had once been white. It was those shredded robes, dripping ephemeral blood that made them all look like ravens. The cancered one dipped his claws into General Naga's skull and drew them out again and licked its claws greedily. But they weren't claws, they were finger bones, denuded of their golden flesh. It turned its good eye to Dorian. "What is he looking at?" it asked.

The other cocked its head and it met Dorian's gaze. "Us," it hissed in wonder.

"Odniar, ruy'eo getnirfhign em. Dirlom?" Dorian heard the voice. It was Jenine, but he couldn't understand what she was saying. Why couldn't he understand her, but he could understand these things? What were they, anyway?

He looked back to the army across the plain. He saw the krul, but this time, he saw through their flesh. Each of them held one of these creatures. *My God, these are the Strangers.* Dorian saw them, and he understood. The Strangers carried hell with them wherever they went. They fed on human suffering not because it sustained them, but because it was a distraction from their own suffering; it was entertainment. Wearing flesh was no escape. Rather it was simply the best distraction of all, a chance to feel, if only for a time, to experience the pleasures of food and drink, if only in a muted way, and to kill. That was the pinnacle, to take away that which men had and which they had no more.

"Odniar!" the voice was in his ear. Dorian turned and for a moment, he could see with his natural vision once more. Every one of his men was staring at him, fearful. Then his vision bifurcated and he could see fear rise like a fragrance from his men—to the delight of the swirling Strangers. He felt the fingers on his shoulders, bony fingers, but before he could turn to face what he knew must cling even to him, he felt natural fingers grab his bicep and squeeze hard.

Jenine swam into his vision, which was natural once more, then it split. She was pregnant, right now, but not with twins. A Stranger spun in tight circles around her, but hadn't yet found a place to rest. It wanted—by the God, it wanted their baby!

Dorian cried out and saw a fresh wave of fear rise from his men. A mob of the Strangers, now aware of his awareness of them, had congregated around him. They were walling him in.

"ODNIAR! Rodnia! Adimmt! Dornia. Dorian!" Jenine was whispering fiercely in his ear, her body pressed against him, turning him away from his men. He blinked, and saw only ground, and soldiers, and krul, and his wife. She'd called him back from madness, maybe using the thing which best anchored him to reality: his own name.

"I'm back," he said. "I'm here. Thank you." He shook himself, willed himself not to see beyond the veil again. He looked over his shoulder, nodded to General Naga to let the frightened man see that Dorian was well, and then strode forward.

Beneath the cloak, Dorian—Wanhope—had decided to go bare-chested.

A god felt not the cold. He strode forward, decisive to cover for his earlier hesitation, great knots of vir rising in his skin. He gestured and a young man was brought forward. Dammit, Wanhope hadn't wanted Jenine to see this. But it was too late, and there was no way she would go where she couldn't see him after he'd almost doomed them all by standing around looking lost.

The young man's name was Udrik Ursuul. All of the aethelings in Khali-ras had been killed, but seventeen who'd already left for their Harrowings still lived. Udrik had impregnated the wrong Modaini oligarch's daughter and had to flee, thus failing his uurdthan. He'd come home to beg mercy.

"Do you know, Udrik, if you raise thirteen legions of krul, you can command them yourself, but if you raise just one more, you have to master an arcanghul?"

"A what?" Udrik's brows were still heavily kohled, menacing despite his fright.

"It's a creature that these wild men didn't dare try to master," Wanhope said. "Tell me, brother, is it better for one man to die, or the whole people?"

Udrik's eyes widened, and then widened again as Wanhope cut his throat with the obsidian knife. He dropped to his knees, throat spurting, then tumbled awkwardly on his back. Dorian felt—or imagined—the jubilation of a thousand Strangers. He blinked. *Control, Dorian. Control it.* He didn't dare to watch what this next part looked like from that other reality.

Wanhope extended his arms and his wings toward the host before him. *"Arcanghulus!* Come! Be known to me!" The weaves spun out from him easily as if the vir itself was helping him, as if he'd done this a thousand times. Green lightning danced around him. A train of blue fire looped around him. Then the ground began to boil around Udrik's corpse. Clumps of dirt burst and stuck to the body. Flares danced over Udrik and the corpse's muscles tore, skin ripped.

The shamans saw their mistake. They hadn't dared raise an arcanghulus, and Dorian had. An aurochs-horn bugle called the wild men to charge. But only half did.

A bolt of lightning cracked the earth before Wanhope, blinding him, and thunder ripped over him and over both armies, dropping men to the ground on both sides.

When Wanhope's vision returned, the wild men's charge had faltered and broken. There was a man standing where Udrik had been and every eye was on him. He was easily seven feet tall, with hair of molten gold falling to the nape of his neck. Though his skin was the color of polished silver, it wasn't shiny or artificial. His eyes were an arresting emerald of a shade barely within human possibility. Perhaps one man in a million had such eyes.

Perhaps mimicking Wanhope, he too was bare-chested, though his body was lean and angular. He was the most beautiful man Wanhope had ever seen.

The arcanghulus laughed, and even his laughter was beautiful. "We're Strangers, Godking, not monsters."

"What is your name?" Wanhope asked.

"I am Ba'elzebaen, the Lord of Serpents."

"Awfully cold in the Freeze for a snake."

"I'm not in the Freeze any more, am I?"

"I would have you serve me, Ba'elzebaen," Wanhope said. He desperately wanted to look at Ba'elzebaen as he was, but he didn't dare. If he lost himself to madness now, Ba'elzebaen might take Dorian's body instead of Udrik's.

The Stranger chuckled. "And I would have the sun and moon bow down to me."

"But one of these things will happen."

Ba'elzebaen laughed as if at a precocious child. "I am stronger than you."

"It is only the will and the call that matters. I have called you, and my will is implacable." The stunning green eyes locked onto his, and Dorian had only to think of how Jenine would be taken if he didn't compel this snake. He felt the arcanghulus's will rise against him, higher and higher. Ba'elzebaen was ever so much more than this body before Dorian. He was immortal, omnipotent, there was nothing Dorian could do to stop him. It was hopeless. He should bow and beg for mercy.

Dorian knew that this was the arcanghulus's attack, and he held onto what he knew. The arcanghulus would obey, would bow, would serve. *I am Godking. I am implacable. I will destroy those who challenge me. I will not serve. I am a god.*

Ba'elzebaen relaxed and the attacks stopped. "Very well, Godking, I will serve you."

"Where is my half-brother Moburu?"

"He attempted to take over the ten tribes. He failed. Only one tribe joined him, but he did take enough bones to raise a legion of krul. He's heading for Black Barrow." A legion was about two thousand krul. It wasn't good, but it was far better than facing Moburu at the head of this army. "But it isn't Moburu you have to worry about."

"Neph," Dorian said, his suspicions confirmed.

"Yes. Neph is the one who taught the wild men to raise krul. All this was nothing more than a diversion to keep any Ursuul away from Black Barrow."

"What's he trying?"

"To make himself Godking, whether by raising a Titan or by giving Khali flesh."

Surely Neph Dada didn't mean to raise Khali herself. It would be madness. If what Dorian had seen of the Strangers' nature was true, giving their leader flesh would be inviting the devastation of all Midcyru. The good news was that no one since Roygaris Ursuul had been powerful enough to raise Khali. A Titan, on the other hand, was far more probable, and plenty frightening enough. Where in the Strangers' hierarchy did a Titan fall? Two ranks above Ba'elzebaen? Three? By the God.

But all that was a conversation for another time. "To claim the wild men's krul, we must strike down the shaman who controls them, correct?" Wanhope asked. "Who is it?"

Ba'elzebaen pointed to a wild man covered completely in woad tattoos. The man had dozens of shields surrounding him, both his own, and other magi's, but as Ba'elzebaen gestured, the shields simply melted away. Wanhope threw a single green fiery missile at the man. The mage watched it contemptuously, secure in his shields—and it burned a hole in his chest. He died with a shocked look on his face.

Ba'elzebaen smiled and Dorian noticed something strange in how the skin crinkled at the corners of his eyes: the arcanghul's skin was made of thousands of tiny scales. "Master," Ba'elzebaen said, "what would you have the Fallen do?"

"Kill the wild men. No feeding until nightfall, and then load the bones onto the wagons. We may need them to make more krul at Black Barrow."

"As you desire." Ba'elzebaen bowed. By the time he straightened, panicked cries were already rising from the wild men's army as the krul in their own ranks turned on them.

74

Spring is upon us," Elene said.

Vi joined her on the balcony, still sweating from her exertions with the hundreds of magae practicing in the yard below. Kylar was outside the city, training with his master again, and Elene had asked to meet. Vi tried to swallow away the lump in her throat as Elene turned and smiled at her.

"You've been avoiding me," Elene said.

Vi wanted to say that she'd been busy. She had. The Chattel were gathering; women were joining Vi's Shield Sisters every day; messages had to be passed secretly to the Speaker; and always tactics and magic had to be practiced. But all those weren't why she hadn't met with Elene. The past two months had seen them grow strangely closer, but the coming of spring was a naked sword.

"I need your advice, Vi. You know how Kylar's gift works, and you also know how his mind works. I'm afraid he'll try to do something stupid to save me, if..." She laid a hand on her stomach.

"If what?" Vi asked. Then it hit her. "Ah shit, you're pregnant!"

Elene blushed, and said quietly. "A Healer confirmed it for me this morning. I'm one month along. Haven't even had a touch of morning sickness. Lucky, I guess."

Lucky. That was one way to put it. If Kylar found out.... Actually, Vi had no idea what he'd do, but stupid heroism was likely. Unfortunately, she had no idea how stupid heroism would show itself.

"It complicates things," Elene said. Vi could see from her face that she didn't mean only for Kylar.

"I can make you tansy tea," Vi said.

Elene was incredulous. "If I wanted it to die, I'd wait a month! God, that's the most stupidly callous thing anyone's ever said to me."

Vi stood transfixed. *I'm stupid and callous. This is why you never let anyone in. If you do, they shit all over you.*

Elene closed her eyes and when she opened them, the anger was gone. "I'm sorry. I'm feeling really emotional and upset, but that doesn't make it right to take it out on you. You're not stupid. I'm sorry."

"But I am callous."

Elene paused. "You've been through hell, Vi. You are callous, but less and less every day, and I'm sorry I said that. Can you forgive me?"

The thing about Elene that made her a good friend and a pain in the ass was that she didn't lie, not even when apologizing. If she were less tenderhearted, the lack of guile would be infuriating. Hu Gibbet had "always told the truth" and used it to hammer everyone. Elene's gentleness made it hard to stay mad. "Yes," Vi said. "What do you need?"

Elene smiled slowly and it was like the sun breaking through dark clouds. When she smiled unself-consciously, she was beatific. It wasn't a courtesan's beauty—though the gods and Vi knew that Elene had spent a lot of time in the last two months exploring the courtesan's skills and pleasures—yet it was feminine and utterly alluring. When Elene felt joy, it was always joy shared. Her naïveté in expecting the best from others somehow drew out the best in them. "I'm glad you're my friend, Vi. I've been meaning to have this talk with you for a while."

She scowled, uncertain how to begin. Vi felt the lump rise again in her throat, but there was no leaving, no escape.

"I'm going to die," Elene said. "I'm scared, especially with this." She put her hand on her stomach protectively. "I've complained to the God a lot about it, to tell you the truth. I know you think I'm either totally holy or totally deluded, but I've asked God every way I know how to let me live without it disrupting His plan. I want to live, and I want Kylar to live, and I want our baby to live, and I want Kylar to do all the big things God created him to do."

"And what's your God say?" Vi asked. The way Elene related to her God wasn't at all how Vi had related to Nysos, but whether or not He was real, He was real in Elene's mind, and you don't mock the beliefs of someone so near death.

"He says He's with me."

"That's helpful," Vi said.

"Yes," Elene said, missing or deciding to miss the sarcasm. "Kylar thinks... Kylar fears that he's a man born to be forever alone. He thinks the last couple of months has been him cheating fate. He's not a man born to be alone, Vi, but some lies take a long time to heal. I don't have time. When I'm gone, I want you to take care of Kylar. In every way. He is the most precious thing in all this world to me, and I trust you with him. He'll need you. You'll know when he's ready, and when you are."

Vi had thought of it, of course. As she sat in her room with the newlyweds canoodling on the other side of a not-thick-enough wall, she'd thought of it a hundred times: this torture wouldn't last forever; Elene would die come spring. Worse, she'd thought that once Elene was dead, she might have Kylar herself.

"I've been selfish," Elene said, "I knew we only had a couple of months, so I've been selfish for myself and for Kylar. I know you've paid the price for that. I've seen your face some of the mornings after—" Elene cleared her throat, "after Kylar and I stayed up late. I know you love him, Vi, and I can't imagine how I would have felt if our places were reversed. If I were in your place, I'd look forward to... this ending. It's all right."

"It's not all right to wish your friend was dead," Vi said stiffly. Her eyes felt hot.

"For that and anything else you may have thought or done, I forgive you, Vi. Everything really is going to be all right. God has a purpose in this, even if we don't see it."

"You're leaving," Vi said.

"Yes."

"And you haven't told him."

"I've tried. Kylar's not ready to hear it. Vi, help him know that loving again is no betrayal. He's immortal, and living forever without love is hell."

"When are you leaving?" Vi asked.

"Now."

"Where?"

"King Gyre's marching into Khalidor in a few weeks. There are women in his army. I'll join them. At least that's my plan. God might have something different for me."

"Why join them?"

"To force Kylar to be there. He's sworn he wouldn't leave me again for Logan, but that's where he needs to be. If nothing else, I'll die fighting for something."

"You're not a warrior, Elene."

"No. But I am a fighter."

"Do you have any idea what Kylar will do when he finds out?" Vi said.

"I've left a letter for him on the table telling him that I'm staying at the Chantry overnight. I hope I lie better in writing than in person because I'll need the head start. But here's another letter that tells the truth." She paused. "Well, not the whole truth. I didn't tell him I'm pregnant. He's going to hurt enough. Please make sure he gets it." She handed the note to Vi.

"You're putting me in the middle of this?"

"He'd feel your complicity through your bond. You might want to stay at the Chantry for a couple days."

Elene hugged her. At first awkwardly and then fiercely, Vi hugged her back. Her eyes teared up faster than she could blink away, and through her bond, she felt Kylar's sudden alarm from a mile away. It wasn't in words, but she could feel his wonder: *are you* crying*?!* She sent a wave of reassurance to him, which left him even more befuddled.

"I don't want you to go," Vi said.

Elene pulled back and searched Vi's eyes. "You mean that. I can tell. Even with how hard this has been, you mean it."

"I've never had a friend," Vi said. "I don't want to lose you."

"You're a better woman than you know, Vi. God bless you."

75

"The passes are clear," Durzo said. "The magae are going to march tomorrow."

Kylar had known there was something different in his master's attitude as they'd sparred today. They sat together on a table in the practice room of Durzo's house, each holding a towel and blotting the sweat from their faces. Durzo didn't make eye contact. "You're leaving," Kylar said.

"If you can believe it, Uly's kicking me out the door," Durzo said ruefully.

"I thought you were getting along great."

"She's worried about her mom. Says I should have gone to her first."

"I think Uly's smarter than both of us put together," Kylar said lightly, though his heart was lead. Durzo was leaving him again, and if for the first time Durzo was letting him know about it beforehand, it didn't make it much easier.

"Watch out for women smarter than you, kid. By which—"

"You mean all of them, I know." Kylar shared a grin with his master.

"Guess I need to give you your gear," Durzo said. "You going with the magae?"

"If I go, Elene will go, and she'll die. I'm steering clear of this fight."

Durzo examined his fingernails. "I told you that's not how it works. She can fall in a puddle and drown as easily as take a sword in the guts. Death won't be cheated, not in this."

Kylar took it like a shot in stomach. He said quietly, "I won't let her die. I won't let anyone take her away. Not Death, not the Wolf, not God himself."

"Kid, remember your first time in the Antechamber of the Mystery? Was there one door or two? It wasn't Death or the Wolf or the boogeyman that made you immortal. This was your own damn choice."

"I became immortal so I could save Elene, not so I could kill her."

"You want her to live forever? Go ahead. See if you can make another deal with the Wolf so someone else will die in her place. Maybe you can choose which one of the other people you care about dies. Won't that be fun? Maybe then you can get a ka'kari for Elene, so she won't age. But be glad that the other ka'karis' immortality isn't like our own. She won't age, but she can still be killed. And be glad for that too. Because when she becomes a monster, corrupted by the very gift you sold your soul to give her, you'll be the one who has to do something about it."

Durzo's anger was too focused, his description too detailed. "You did that?" Kylar asked.

His master didn't answer him, wouldn't even look at him. He opened the bureau, released the bottom drawer and pulled it out. He lifted Retribution, skinned black with the ka'kari, from the false bottom.

"I can't let Elene die for me," Kylar said.

"You haven't got any goddam choice. You've had a few months to get used to the idea. That's more than the Wolf ever gave me. Be grateful. Now take your shit and get out." Durzo tossed the big black sword to Kylar.

As soon as the ka'kari touched his skin, it began shrilling. *~Why didn't you listen! I tried to tell you! It's gone. Three months gone. Stolen!~*

Dumbfounded, Kylar stared at the sword. Frustrated at his stupidity, the ka'kari sought to sink into his skin of his hand and he let it, forgetting that it would destroy his disguise. As the black metal rushed into him, it revealed a pitted, half-devoured sword blade. Retribution was gone, replaced with a counterfeit that Kylar hadn't noticed when they'd hidden the blade. It was impossible, but someone had stolen his sword before he hid it here, probably when he'd first been gawking like an idiot on the crowded sidewalks of Vestacchi.

Durzo was aghast. "Kid, you have no idea what that sword is. You have to get it back."

Then Kylar felt Vi through his bond. She'd been nervous since yesterday, and now he could feel her starting guiltily as she felt his emotions. Vi knew, and she was hiding in the Chantry, certain he wouldn't go there. For all his help, the Sisters had stabbed him in the back. They'd stolen Retribution.

"I know where it is," Kylar said.

The closer Kylar got to the Chantry, the more his anger grew. He became more and more certain from Vi's guilt that Elene was somehow involved too, and that lit a fire in him. He thought he could read her. Yesterday afternoon he'd gotten her note that said she had some things she needed to work on in the Chantry, and she still wasn't back. The timing seemed strange, but there was no doubting Vi's guilt as he came closer. Having the vastness of the Chantry against him blew his rage to a flame. They wanted him passive, tame, emasculated, obedient. He was sick and tired of it. Sick of being worked on by vast, remote powers he couldn't understand or counter. The Chantry was like fate, like the Wolf, like Death itself, working inexorably on the world, on Kylar, and turning a deaf ear to his pleas.

When he stepped out of the punt onto one of the Chantry's docks, two dozen pairs of eyes turned to him, scandalized. Some he recognized from Vi's training sessions; others were more hostile. A Sister was lecturing a class of teens on the workings of the punts. Others were doing maintenance magic on the little bay itself, reworking the rain shield overhead. He ignored them and strode toward the double doors that led inside.

A white robed woman stepped forward, "Sir, no men are allowed here."

He walked past her.

Before he could touch the double doors, magic bonds latched onto him arm and leg. "Please, sir, we don't wish to harm you—"

Kylar shrugged the bonds off as easily as he might shoo a fly. He turned and looked at the faces of the two Sisters tasked with guarding the door. They were stunned. One of them was readying a lash of magic.

"Don't," Kylar said, staring her in the eye. As he held her gaze, something in his eyes turned her resolve to water. The weaves slipped away. He threw the doors open.

Vi was in a panic upstairs. *Good.*

Kylar walked straight down a long hall to a set of huge double doors three times a man's height. Doors along the length of the hall opened and Kylar heard cries of alarm. The smaller door inset in the double doors slammed shut by magic and a young maja yelped. The scraping of metal on wood told him that the double doors had been barred. Kylar didn't slow; he didn't turn to the right or to the left. He gathered power to his hands.

~I've seen stupider things, but it's been centuries.~

The voice was the buzzing of a gnat. There was something beautiful in this simplicity. Someone had stolen Kylar's birthright. He was getting it back. This door was in his way.

Kylar's open hands shot into the doors. They bowed and then crashed open. One half of the timber that had barred the door shot across the floor toward dozens of tables. Perhaps two hundred magae were seated in the great hall, enjoying lunch. The splintered timber skimmed down one aisle at great speed, shooting between a Sister's legs and finally crashing against the first step of a great curving staircase.

As Kylar stepped through in a shower of kindling, the other great door sagged on its remaining hinge. Every eye turned to him.

Sisters began standing all around the room and shields blossomed everywhere, but the first woman on her feet was Sister Ariel. She moved faster than Kylar had ever seen her move, coming straight at him. "What do you think you're doing?" she shouted.

"Where's the Speaker? She's stolen from me," Kylar said.

"You will go no further!" Sister Ariel shouted. She was purple.

"Stop me," Kylar said. He could see that his smirk infuriated her.

Faster than he thought possible, she did. Giant chains of magic lashed his arms to his body, clamped his legs together. Magae around her openly gaped at her sheer power.

~*You deserved that. Take it, apologize, and come back later.*~

Kylar had had enough of taking it, apologizing, and coming back when it was convenient for someone else. He was sick of being trapped. He felt something mighty rising within him.

Fear flickered over Sister Ariel's face at whatever she saw. Kylar sucked in a great breath and flexed, tensing every muscle in his body, physical and magical. He felt suddenly gigantic, his body a tiny vessel for a giant soul. As he strained, a groan deeper than Kylar's voice came from his lips.

His chains shattered, blew apart with a magical concussion that swept through the room. The tables didn't move, the air didn't stir, but everything magical was flattened. Every nimbus in the room winked out. Only a few held for an instant before popping and blowing away.

A dozen of the standing magae simply folded and dropped to sit on their benches or the floor. No one else moved, not even Sister Ariel. "What are you?" she whispered. The question was mirrored in every eye.

"Out of my way," Kylar said. He strode forward. They got out of his way.

76

*I*stariel Wyant eyed the Alitaeran ambassador's untouched ootai. Marcus Guerin was bordering on fifty, bald with a fringe of blond hair, a small paunch, no bottom, and a restless intelligence in his blue eyes.

"There are some troubling rumors we've been hearing that I think we need to discuss," Ambassador Guerin said.

Istariel took the opportunity of taking a sip of ootai to cover her sudden rage. Someone had leaked this to the Alitaerans? If he'd learned about Vi's practices, that was one thing, but Istariel had only told three Sisters about her plan to withdraw from the Accords. If he knew about that, it was treason. She simply arched an eyebrow.

"What do you know about this 'High King'?" he asked.

Oh, those *rumors. Thank the Seraph.* "Little," she said. There was a twinkle in his eye that made her wonder if he had done that on purpose. Bastard. "What we've heard has only told us that you ought to know more than we do. He's Alitaeran, or at least raised in your glorious country. His name is Moburu Ander, though he claims Ursuul blood. We know he's half Lodricari, he led a company of lancers, and he's found a position of some importance among the savages of the Freeze." She knew more, but there was no point telling Ambassador Guerin.

"He's the adopted son of Aurelius Ander, of a once-powerful family that has fallen far in the last two generations. Moburu was adopted at fifteen, before that, we can't find any record or recollection of him anywhere, so we give some credence to his claim of Ursuul patrimony."

"I doubt that an absence of records was enough to make you believe he's an Ursuul," Istariel said.

The ambassador stroked his moustache. "The captain is both intelligent and charismatic. Nothing was ever found to link him to the scandals and disappearances that seem to swirl in his wake. Last autumn, the king's sister bore a daughter, Yva Lucrece Corazhi. The child and her wet nurse disappeared. At the same time, Moburu led his company—all of them—to a place called Pavvil's Grove, where they fought beside the Khalidorans. There are wild tales surrounding that, but most of Moburu's company escaped and headed north."

"You believe he kidnapped the child?"

"What I believe has no relevance. Some very powerful people in Skon insist that he did not. They are having a harder time explaining why he has taken an entire company out of our country without leave, though some whisper it's a secret mission for the king. There are generals who don't wish to appear fools who have not discouraged such whispers. There are even those who claim that Moburu's company itself is trying to recover Yva Lucrece."

"It appears to me that this man must be declared a traitor," Istariel said. "Otherwise, if he joins Khalidor again, this time to attack us, Alitaera will be making war on the Chantry."

The slight wince that passed the ambassador's face told Istariel she had voiced an argument he had presented to his superiors himself. "Our response to Captain Ander will be determined soon, and I promise you will be among the first to know." Ambassador Guerin's face looked like he was chewing lemons. "Now speaking of sharing intelligence," he said, "you never did turn over that intelligence you told us about a few months ago," he said. "But let's return to that in a moment. First, we were hoping this house of learning might tell us some more about who this High King is supposed to be, and how one identifies him."

Ariel leaned back in her chair. "Meaning you won't move against Moburu until you know if he's the real thing."

"Meaning it is wise to know all one can about one's enemies—and friends."

Istariel took another slow sip of ootai, considering. "The High King is a legend mostly confined to the rural areas of Khalidor, Lodricar, Cenaria, and Ceura. His coming is not spoken of by any of the prophets recognized by the Chantry. We keep track of prophecies spoken by those who have the perishingly rare Talent of prophecy. We think of that one as simply a hope kept alive in Lodricar and Khalidor as a longed-for end to oppression. In Cenaria and Ceura, it's probably more a wish to be consequential, something Cenaria hasn't been for centuries."

"Your pardon, Speaker, but I'm not terribly interested in why they believe as I am in *what* they believe. Does this have anything to do with the Ceuran Regency?"

"It could. The Battle of Mount Tenji was as crushing for the Ceurans as it was for Alitaera. King Usasi and his son and seven daughters were all killed; that was so devastating to the country that after that time Ceuran women were no longer taught the sword. The regency was established both because of the profound respect for tradition engrained in Ceuran culture, and the fact that the first Regent had no blood claim to the throne. The other contenders realized a regency meant that they themselves could hold power without needing a blood claim, if only they were powerful enough to take it. It suited everyone, and the myth of the coming High King gave them a hope of future glory. Our scholars' best guess is that there was a High King who ruled those lands for a single generation in the dark centuries that followed Jorsin Alkestes' fall."

"Wasn't Alkestes himself called the High King?"

"Rarely. In the early years of his reign, he ruled over seven kings and styled himself the High King. Three of the seven—Rygel the Blue, Einarus Silvereyes, and Itarra Lachess—rebelled. After that, Jorsin was Emperor Alkestes. We don't know if the latter High King claimed descent from Jorsin or not—almost all records of him were lost in the dark ages—but he only claimed the lands now encompassing Ceura, Cenaria, Khalidor, and Lodricar, not all of Jorsin's kingdoms."

The ambassador looked unimpressed. "So that's it? A long-dead legend?"

Istariel said, "Well, the magi give some credence to a prophet or two whom we don't recognize."

"And they know more?"

"They don't know more. They believe more."

"By the God's beard! I don't care what's true—I care what people believe! What are these prophecies?"

Istariel gave him a look that let him know he was treading on thin ice and didn't answer until he looked on the brink of apologizing. "They say he will be a dragon—the accepted interpretation is that he'll be Talented, though any conqueror brings fire. They say he will raise a standard of death—I hope that's clear enough, things aren't going to be all prancing ponies and cuddly kittens. Then the prophecies get strange. They say he'll bring peace—peace everlasting is a pretty normal staple of prophecies, right? Well, these prophecies say he'll bring peace for two years or eighteen. They say his coming will open the way for the return of Jorsin Alkestes, who will both be taken under his wing, and test the mettle or taste the metal—it's unclear which—of his sword."

"When was this prophecy given?" the ambassador asked.

"Five years ago. A magus named Dorian, who claimed to be a rogue Ursuul. Not exactly a reliable source."

"It sounds like a nightmare."

"Yes, and these things tend to spread with a religious fervor once they get started. Even if Moburu is the High King, I'd strongly advise King Alidosius to make sure he never sits in any throne—not unless you want to invite civil unrest or even civil war to Alitaera. Jorsin Alkestes still stirs all sorts of emotions. A High King would itself be bad enough, considering the sheer area such a man would rule, but in the Alkestian prophecies, he is a harbinger. Think what may happen in each of our lands if people really believe that the Lord of Hell is coming in bodily form, that creatures from their nightmares will walk again, that kingdoms are doomed to fall."

Ambassador Guerin looked moderately ill. "Yes, I'll convey all this to the king. Is that all?"

"No, I need to know if your lancers are on their way."

"You ask me this now, after you've only just given me the information which might make the king amenable to such a request?"

"I gave you the information when we got it. We need those soldiers now."

"I told you months ago that without access to whatever intelligence you had about an invasion we would be unable to grant your request. If you'll pardon an old military man speaking bluntly, we can't send five thousand lancers every time an old ally gets nervous. That's not what the Accords oblige."

An old military man? You haven't lifted a lance in thirty years. "The Accords oblige a robust defense of the Chantry, which seems even more pressing now that Moburu Ander's company—an Alitaeran company— fought for Khalidor at the Battle of Pavvil's Grove. We're facing two enemies here even without Moburu Ander's men, and each alone may be capable of annihilating us. The fact is, even the two thousand lancers you have across the border—yes, of course I know about them—probably won't be enough to defend us. The best I can expect is that they will hold our flank against the Lae'knaught while we go to Black Barrow."

"You're going to Black Barrow?" Marcus Guerin asked.

"The Khalidorans have learned to raise krul."

"Krul? A legend!" Marcus Guerin scoffed. "This is completely—"

"Have you been to Black Barrow, ambassador?"

His blue eyes looked troubled.

"Black Barrow is the only place where, once killed, the krul can't be Raised again. It's the only place we can fight them with any hope of winning."

"So you want us to help you invade your neighbor? That's an awfully bold interpretation of accords intended to curtail the Chantry's imperial ambitions."

Suddenly, from many stories below, the Speaker felt an unfamiliar magic. Though she'd only met a half dozen magi, and had never seen them use their Talents, she knew instantly that this was a magus—in her Chantry.

"Speaker, is something wrong?"

Istariel had only moments to decide how to react. Could she turn the presence of a hostile mage to her advantage? Would interrupting the meeting be to her advantage? Perhaps it could have been, if the Chantry's objective in this talk were anything positive. As it was, she wished only to back out of a centuries-old treaty without declaring war. "Yes, you slap us in the face with old, unfounded allegations, sir. We wish only to survive as a house of learning." A rush of magic much more familiar to her snapped in response to the intruder, whoever he was. Istariel was surprised at the force of it. It was a chaining magic, and the only maja she could imagine powerful enough to use it was Ariel, blessed oblivious Ariel. Or, perhaps, Vi.

"A house of learning?" the ambassador asked. "Does that include learning battle magic?"

So he knew. Dammit. "If our allies abandon us in the face of a massacre? Yes."

His lips thinned to a tiny line. "This is most precipitous."

Istariel opened her mouth to deliver a historical reminder when a magical concussion ripped through the Chantry. The constant buzz of magae's Talent ceased and, for the first time in centuries, perhaps the first time since it was built, the Chantry was utterly silent. The magic ripped through everything, though it destroyed nothing except whatever the Sisters were actively weaving. It had character, a distinct flavor: free and fierce, not hostile, but rather a strength unaware of itself. The impossible image that leapt to Istariel's mind was of a teenage archmage, and it shook her to her core. Ariel had tried to chain him, and he refused to be chained.

Magically, Istariel felt like a little girl trapped between screaming parents.

"Wh-what was that?" the ambassador asked.

By the Seraph, it was powerful enough even this un-Talented toad could feel it.

"We hereby withdraw from the Accords, ambassador. If Alitaera wishes to expel the magae from its dominions, they will leave peacefully. I do request, however, that you give us six months to show our good faith. This is no declaration of war with you. Please let the emperor know that we fight only to live."

The ambassador sat silently. He sipped his ootai, which Istariel was certain was cold by now, but he didn't seem aware of it. "The king always thought you were one of the Chantry's more moderate voices, Istariel. Surely the discussion needn't end on this. You wouldn't throw away hundreds of years of cooperation and progress."

The archmage was climbing the Chantry, getting ever closer. He'd used so much magic that he still burned with it. Istariel could almost see him through the floor. She didn't want to have this conversation now, but she couldn't exactly throw the ambassador out. "No," she said, "I don't wish to throw away anything, least of all our lives. Perhaps this fall I can come to Skon and meet with the emperor personally."

It wasn't some random archmage, Istariel realized. It was Vi's damned husband. What the hell was he doing? Was Vi attempting a coup? No, that made no sense, leading a coup with a man? Even Sisters with dual loyalties would automatically side against him. So it was something else entirely. That scared the hell out of her.

"Perhaps we could conclude this conversation later this afternoon," Istariel said.

"Your pardon, Speaker, but I can't imagine there's really anything more important than the dissolution or defense of an alliance three hundred years old. I must insist we finish."

Speaker Istariel sat back down at her desk and gathered her Talent to her, facing the door. He was almost here.

The door exploded inward, the hinges and latch ripping through the wood, the door slapping to the ground. A young man with his face set fiercely stepped in. Istariel unleashed a massive fist of air.

It turned aside in midair and smashed her collection of thousand-year-old Hyrillic vases. She lashed out again and punched a hole in the ceiling. Impervious, almost oblivious to her attempts to kill him, Kyle strode to her desk, put his hands on it, and leaned forward. She gathered her full strength; he blew in her face.

Her Talent scattered as if that puff had been a hurricane. He said nothing. He looked into her eyes and deep within his eyes was something that made her want to gibber like a madwoman. It was like staring at the night sky after learning for the first time that the stars were not pinpricks in the raiment of heaven, but each its own sun, billions of leagues distant. To stare into this man's eyes was to realize how small one was.

Kyle sighed, not finding what he wanted.

The Alitaeran ambassador, either finding his courage, or seeing no magic springing from the young man, stood. "I dare say, you young lout, I'm not going to let you disrespect any woman while I stand by! Stand and deliver, sir!"

Istariel saw an alien magic stir deep in Kylar's eyes, then Kylar said, "We'll talk about respecting women when you stop fucking your wife's best friend."

The ambassador's hauteur shattered. Kyle turned on his heel and walked out.

Istariel and the ambassador said nothing for a full minute. She cleared her throat. "Perhaps," she said, "we can agree that nothing of this leaves the room."

He swallowed and nodded.

Vi was up here somewhere. Kylar's encounter with the Speaker had left him shaken. He'd been sure that she'd stolen Retribution. One look in her eyes told him otherwise. Now, what had looked like an unexpected move that would bring him to the center of the deceiver's web and deliver his sword back into his hand was looking like a colossal blunder. Nonetheless, Kylar bulled forward. He was committed now.

The floors this high in the Chantry weren't large. The Seraph's head held the Speaker's office, a waiting room, some storerooms, the stairs, and a classroom. In that classroom was Vi. Kylar opened the door to the last room before the classroom. He'd kicked down enough doors.

This room was at the Seraph's eyes. It was a broad, open room, but despite the light pouring in from the glass-clear eyes, it had a distinctly unused feeling, as if no one had set foot here in decades. In the center of the room stood a woman wreathed in light. Her arms were crossed over her chest, chin pointed at the floor, eyes closed. She wore a short gossamer robe that ended at her knees. Halfway down her shins, her skin changed from a shade too golden to be merely sun-kissed to the purest white alabaster. As Kylar stood, stunned by this unexpected beauty, he saw the alabaster recede to her ankles, to her toes.

The woman took a gentle first breath. Her chin lifted. She opened her eyes. The irises were pure platinum.

"You're the Seraph," Kylar said dumbly.

"Indeed, and you are a man and you have awakened me, but you are not the One."

"Uh, sorry?" Kylar said. The Seraph stared at him and as he met those platinum eyes, all he could see was magic, oceanic and mercifully at rest. "Are you going to do something bad to me now?"

The Seraph laughed. "Should I? You've frightened my little sisters badly." She glanced at the door. "Except for the one who holds your bond. I'll leave you to her tender mercies, Nameless."

"I like that dress better than the one your statue wears. You've got great legs."

Her eyes widened, but he saw that she wasn't displeased. "Me too," she said, "but when one is three hundred feet tall, it behooves one to err on the side of modesty."

"I can't believe I said that."

She arched an eyebrow at him.

"Um, Lady? Ma'am? Sorry, what should I call you?"

"Impertinence suits you better, Nameless. Ask your question."

"I lost a sword. I thought the Speaker stole it, but I was wrong. Can you tell me if one of the other Sisters stole it?"

She tilted her head, weighing him. "You assume friendship quickly. I can't decide if that's a function of youth or naïveté or goodness or your singular powers. Not everyone can weigh a soul in a glance, Nameless."

"Sorry for the presumption, my Lady."

"Give me your sword hand."

He extended his hand and she studied the palm. He saw magic swirling over it. He said, "It's been three months since I—"

The magic died suddenly. The Seraph's eyes snapped up from his palm to his eyes, and in her platinum eyes, Kylar saw fear. "You fool," she whispered. "Do you have any idea what you've done?"

Between the intensity of her tone and her fear, Kylar felt a snake of terror twisting in his guts. What could make the Seraph afraid? "I lost my sword Retribution. It was my birthright—"

"Retribution? Was that Acaelus' attempt at a joke?"

Kylar said nothing. What had he revealed here? She'd told him he was naive to trust her. How much did she know now? "I don't know what you're talking about," he said woodenly. "It's a simple sword, inscribed with a word, either Justice or Mercy."

"And it depends on you to dispense whichever is deserved."

"Well, yeah."

"I don't suppose that reminds you of anything."

"Uh…"

"You see the state of souls. You mete out justice or mercy, giving people what they deserve. What does that make you?"

Kylar remembered the Wolf's words, laughing at his name, telling him Kylar Stern was a title. "A judge," Kylar said quietly.

"And a judge decides the application of what?" the Seraph asked, equally quiet.

"The law?" *Together, Jorsin Alkestes and Ezra created two artifacts: Curoch, the sword of power, and Iures, the scepter of law.* "But it's supposed to be a…" his voice trailed off. He'd seen Curoch shift into any shape it needed to be. He'd seen Retribution raise the words Mercy or Justice in different languages. Why not hide Iures as a sword? Where better to hide Iures than with Durzo, whose ka'kari concealed him? What better place to keep the ka'kari of concealment than concealing one of the greatest artifacts in history? Kylar should have known Durzo wouldn't have retrieved Retribution simply to spare Kylar of the inconvenience of having his swords blunted. How many times had Durzo told him the blade was priceless?

"Do you know where it is?" Kylar asked.

Holding his hand, the Seraph closed her eyes and glowed golden. The light started in her forehead and expanded until it filled the room, then it whooshed. For an instant, Kylar swore the entire Seraph—the big one— was aglow. Then the woman opened her eyes.

"It is in Trayethell."

"Trayethell?" Kylar remembered the name dimly. Acaelus Thorne had been the Prince of Trayethell. "It's in Black Barrow."

The Seraph hadn't released his hand. "Nameless, the Scepter...Iures gives a mage no additional power, but it gives a thousand times the control. A mage with Iures in hand could unravel anything given time."

So what was Neph doing? With Iures, he could take apart the shield around Ezra's Wood and take Curoch. What would he do once he had both? What would he not do? Even Jorsin Alkestes hadn't wielded both together.

There was no choice. Kylar was the judge. If Neph was invulnerable to magic, Kylar was the only one who could stop him. Kylar might be the only one who knew the full extent of the danger. He had to stop him. *God, how am I going to tell Elene?*

At the thought of Elene, Kylar felt Vi flinch through the bond. There was a deep guilt there, and fear.

Kylar turned from the Seraph, anger stirring once again. He opened the door to the classroom and strode in, slamming the door behind him. There were fifty senior students in the room, every one of them surrounded with a nimbus of magic. Vi stood in the center of them. She alone didn't hold her Talent. "What have you done?" Kylar demanded.

"She made me swear not to tell you," Vi said.

"What the fuck have you—"

"What have I done?" Vi shouted. "What have you done? Breaking in here and treating my Sisters like this? How dare you!" Kylar opened his mouth, but Vi cut him off. "No! Sit down and shut up!"

The words hit him like a whip through their earrings' bond. The compulsion made Kylar's mouth snap closed, and he sat instantly. There was no chair: he sat on the ground.

Vi was as stunned as he was. He tried to open his mouth, but it wouldn't budge. He couldn't move. Vi had told him that the rings broke her compulsion to Garoth because its bond superseded Garoth's magic, but Kylar hadn't appreciated what that meant until now. The earrings' bond was compulsive—one way. Vi could make him do anything she wanted, and she had known all along, Kylar saw from her expression. She simply hadn't invoked her power before.

The Sisters stared round-eyed at Vi. A moment before, they all had been terrified of this man who had violated the Chantry and broken the chains their most powerful Sister had laid on him. In the next, Vi had defended her Sisters, and he obeyed her command as if he had no choice. Whatever other repercussions Kylar's foolishness was going to have, he had certainly increased Vi's cachet with her Sisters.

A riot of emotions flooded through the bond, but Vi mastered herself quickly. "She went to join Logan's army," she said. "She was afraid you wouldn't fight otherwise." Aware of the other women listening to her conversation with her "husband," Vi said nothing more. She handed him a note. "You can stand now, and speak."

Kylar stood and took the note, but he had no words.

The door on the far side of the classroom banged open, and dozens of Sisters began pouring in, with Sister Ariel at their head. Almost all of them, Kylar realized, were magae who'd trained with Vi.

One of them threw something like a spear of coruscating red and silver light. It flew straight at Kylar's chest—then dissolved in midair.

Around the room, Sisters began kneeling, mouths dropping open once more. Kylar turned to see who had saved him. The Seraph walked into the room, glowing gold. "I'm sorry if my friend frightened you," the Seraph said. "Forgive him. We needed to speak about a threat that faces us all. If he fails, all our fighting will be for naught." The awed Sisters parted. With one last glance at Vi, Kylar left.

78

I won't watch you kill yourself," Durzo said. For the last three days, Kylar and Durzo had been traveling west. Durzo was traveling to Cenaria, to see Momma K at last, so he'd joined Kylar. The pass had been muddy and snowy, so they were setting up camp only a few hours from Torras Bend and a few hundred paces from Ezra's Wood.

Kylar spread his heavy saddle blanket on a fallen log next to the fire and sat. "I don't plan to die," he said.

"Oh, so there is a plan? I thought you were making it up as you went. It's getting dark. Our little stalker will be along within the hour." They'd been followed, clumsily, since they left the Chantry. Today they'd ridden hard, trying to make it to Torras Bend, and their pursuer hadn't been able to keep up.

"I don't think Khali exists," Kylar said.

"I didn't realize you were in the habit of having religious epiphanies."

"I mean, it exists, but I don't think she's a goddess."

"Oh?" Durzo asked.

"She—it—is a repository of magic. The Wolf said magic is strongest when it's attached to emotions. Khali is filled by the Khalidorans' worship. As they hurt people for her, they chant a prayer. But it's not a prayer. It's a spell. It empties their glore vyrden into the repository. And it's from that repository that the meisters and Vürdmeisters and Godkings draw their power. Because the talents for drawing in magic from the world and using magic are different, that means they can often use far more magic than mages. It means they can use it at night. Don't you see? The entire nation chants this spell twice a day. The repository is the key to Khalidor's power."

"And this has something to do with why you're committing suicide?"

"Curoch is anathema to that power. I saw that when I killed a meister with it. Curoch makes the vir explode. It bursts it from within."

"A few months ago, you assassinated a man who called himself a god; now you're going after a goddess in truth. Unless you can figure out a way to kill continents, after this you're going to have to retire."

"You know it's not like that," Kylar said, flushing.

"So you're hoping to find Khali and put Curoch in her and what? Just see what happens?"

Kylar scowled. "You make it sound stupid."

"Hmm."

"It's a way to win, really win, once and for all. Come on, how many times have you fought Khalidorans?"

"More than I like to remember," Durzo admitted.

"Look, I lost Iures. That's a disaster. I know it. It's also a disaster you helped cause when you never told me what the damn thing was. With Iures in Neph's hands, we're going to have a hard time killing him."

"We?"

"But if we destroy the vir, Neph won't even be able to use Iures. If he survives the vir's destruction, even if he has Talent, it will take him a while to think to use it. He'll be vulnerable. Master, he's been spending the last three months figuring out how to break into Ezra's Wood and take Curoch for himself. If one man holds both Curoch and Iures..."

"It wouldn't be good."

"It would be a cataclysm!" Kylar said.

"You realize that if you put Curoch into the center of all the vir in the world, it might make a qualitative rather than a quantitative difference?"

"Huh?"

Durzo shot him an exasperated look. "Curoch blew the vir out of one wytch and nothing happened. If it blows up all the vir in the world, something might."

"If it blew up every wytch in the world, I wouldn't complain," Kylar said.

"And if it blows you up with them?"

"At that point, I won't be able to."

"It might not obliterate you. It might just kill you and invoke your immortality. You know what that costs now. Are you willing to risk a friend's life for this? Hell, it might be *my* life. I don't know if *I'm* willing for you to risk it."

"We were given this power for a reason, master. I don't want to lose anyone. I don't want to die, but if my death can change a nation, if I can save thousands, how could I not risk it?"

Durzo grinned ruefully. "You damn fool. You realize, even if all your assumptions are correct—even then, you still have to steal the world's most coveted sword from the world's safest place then be pursued by the ultimate hunter until you reach the heart of an enemy country in the middle of a war in which any side will happily kill you as a traitor, a spy, a wytch, or all three?"

"I thought you'd like it," Kylar said, eyes sparkling.

Durzo laughed. "The Wolf is gonna have puppies."

"Well, I'm hoping not to see him any time soon. But I figured if I could convince you, then there wouldn't be much he could do about it."

"Convince me of what?" Durzo asked.

"To help," Kylar said.

"Oh no," Durzo said. "Count me out."

"You can't!"

"I can. Kid, you took away my immortality. That gave me back my life. I—"

"You owe me!" Kylar said.

"Not like this, I don't. I have one life left. One. Because of you, I can do with it whatever I want. I can love."

And Kylar couldn't. "But we can change the world!"

"Kid, do you know how many times I've changed the world? The Tlaxini Maelstrom used to be a shipping lane. The Alitaeran Empire stretched from coast to coast. Godkings have threatened the southlands and nearly gained ka'kari half a dozen times. Ladesh used to—look. The fact is, I've done my piece. Adventures are for the young, and I'm young by no measure. There's a woman I love in Cenaria, and neither of us is getting younger. I need to go."

"I need you," Kylar said. "Alone, trying to steal the world's most coveted sword from the world's safest place and being pursued by the perfect hunter into a war—"

"Yes, yes," Durzo said. "I've showed you most of my tricks—"

"Most of them?"

"—and you've developed a few of your own. You're not an apprentice anymore, Kylar—"

"Fine, but I'm hardly—"

"—you *are* a master. Your tutelage is finished."

"Don't cut me loose," Kylar said. His heart was in his throat.

"I'm cutting you free," Durzo said.

"But you're still better than me!"

"And I always will be," Durzo said. He grinned, and despite himself, Kylar couldn't help thinking that it was nice to see this once hard and bitter man smile. "In your memories. I'm smart enough to stop fighting you before you start winning. I reached the top of my game, and I had a good run. From here, I'll only get worse."

"But you still have so much to teach me."

"You think this isn't going to teach you something?"

"What if I fail?" It came out in a whisper.

"What if you do? It won't change how I feel about you."

"But I could doom the world! Don't you care?"

"If I spend my last hours in Gwin's arms, frankly, not much. Growing old with the woman I love would be my first choice, but dying reconciled with her isn't a bad second."

"So I'm alone."

"I told you that was the cost when you demanded to be my apprentice."

"I didn't know I was agreeing to eternity!"

"Cry me a river. You're pathetic. What's your plan for getting into the Wood?"

Stung, Kylar shrugged. "The ka'kari."

"The ka'kari." Durzo stated the question like Momma K would have. The old man really had spent too long with her.

"It absorbs magic, eludes magic, makes me invisible. I'll figure something out." Now he was sounding defensive.

"Whose Wood is this again?" Durzo asked. "Oh yeah, Ezra's. And who made the ka'kari? Oh, don't tell me. Ezra."

"Ezra didn't make the black."

"He understood it well enough to make six others. So tell me, fifty years after making six ka'kari he comes here—and at this point he and I aren't on such good terms—and he makes himself a fortress. You think it never occurred to him that I might try to come in?"

"Uh..."

"Kid, you can scare a few Sisters with raw power and bravado, but you're playing on a different plane here. If you live through Ezra's defenses—which by the way, you strengthened tenfold by throwing Curoch into the wood—you still have to get around a creature so powerful and so cunning that it may have killed Ezra himself, unless it is Ezra gone utterly mad. Either way, the Hunter isn't going to be impressed by raw magic. Your newfound confidence is inspiringly suicidal."

Kylar was silent. Then he said, "I won't be stopped."

"Shut up, she comes."

Kylar rolled the ka'kari into the center of the fire. The flames collapsed into the ball, dying instantly, plunging the clearing into darkness. Kylar jumped left and Durzo rolled right even as purple magic blazed through the clearing in jagged hands. Kylar extended a hand and the ka'kari leapt into it, flooding him with the energy it had absorbed from the fire.

He leapt from tree to tree, sinking black claws into the sides of each, and saw a maja flailing about herself, suddenly blind. Fires flared around her. She flipped them back and forth wildly like great scythes in her fear. The magic slapped against the trees, singeing bark, sending up gouts of steam, but the recent rains and snows prevented any fires from bursting forth. Durzo, on the ground, was beneath the swipes, and Kylar was above them.

In moments, the maja had exhausted her Talent and with no sunlight and no fire to draw from, her magic guttered out.

In the sudden darkness, both men moved. Kylar was on her almost before she could scream. He flew straight over her head, grabbed fistfuls of cloak and robe as he passed, and used her body weight like a beam to flip himself over and stop, which transferred his momentum to her. She flew backward half a dozen paces and crashed into a tree trunk, the breath whooshing from her lungs. Kylar landed on one knee on the forest floor and stood, blue flame trickling over his features.

By the time she'd taken two breaths, something was rising from deep beneath her skin. It was vir, and it rose as rapidly as a shark striking from the deep, starting at her fingertips, over her hands, and wrists, disappearing in a wriggle that made her sleeves tremble, up to her neck like a black blush, and then—it stopped. Durzo stood behind the tree trunk, his arms wrapped around it, fingers poking into two points in the side of the maja's neck. She shrieked as the vir bulged against the blockage like a river at flood assailing a levee. Her cries crested and then fell as the vir receded, faded and sank beneath her skin once more.

Durzo stepped from behind the tree and grabbed her by the scruff of her neck. Holding her before him, he buried his fingers in those points on her neck again.

"A trick you didn't teach me?" Kylar asked.

"You expect me to teach you all I know in a couple months? The vir needs a physical expression. Block the physical expression and you block the magical. It's a weakness of the Ursuul family's hidden vir."

"She's an Ursuul?"

"What better use for Garoth's Talented daughters?" Durzo asked.

"I thought he had them killed."

"Garoth wasn't a man to throw away tools, no matter how blunt. What's your name, sweetie?"

She didn't answer, so Kylar did for her. "It's Eris Buel. You little bitch. We had our suspicions about you."

"Not enough to save your precious wife," she snapped. In her eyes rose such hatred that Kylar felt his gift unfolding, saw the murders littering Eris's path to power, but there was no dead Elene, nor Vi. He saw betrayals, broken vows, and, far down on the list, receiving Kylar's sword from a thief and then delivering the blade to Neph's spies.

All the darkness demanded an answer. "Justice has been denied you too long," Kylar said. His dagger punched through Eris's solar plexus, driving the breath from her lungs once more, and her guilty eyes flared wide, the light in them dimming.

A hand cracked hard against Kylar's cheek. Kylar staggered from the force of the blow. "Dammit, we need to question her, you fool!" Durzo shouted. Durzo grabbed Eris by her hair, holding her upright. "The ka'kari, Kylar, give me the ka'kari, quick!"

Kylar handed it to his master. The bastard had nearly torn off his jaw. Kylar put a hand to his face and took it off, sticky. Kylar looked at his fingers. It wasn't blood.

Durzo dropped Eris's body.

Kylar rubbed the golden liquid between his fingers. "Peri peri and xanthos?" Kylar asked. It was a contact poison, and though it would only leave him unconscious, the tincture still left permanent scarring. "On my face?"

"You deserve a permanent slap-print, but you heal too well."

"Why?" Kylar's legs were getting shaky.

"I needed this," Durzo said, lifting the ka'kari. "Sweet dreams."

Kylar crumpled to the ground and his lips smashed on a root. His mouth filled with blood. *The bastard could have at least caught me.*

79

$\mathcal{N}$eph Dada strode through the dark streets of Trayethell. It was nearly noon, but he was inside the dome of Black Barrow, and the solid black rock dome above him cast the hidden city in perpetual darkness. He could only see his way by the bobbing yellow light hovering over his head and by the thousands of torches his Vürdmeisters had burning around the monolith at the covered city's heart.

Despite the darkness, Trayethell was an almost cheerful place. It had the air of a city whose inhabitants had stepped out and would be back momentarily. There was no dust, and the siege that had seen the city's death hadn't lasted long enough to destroy its beauty. Sections of the city were scorched and blackened or even leveled by magic, but many were pristine. Perhaps, though, the cheerfulness was all Neph's.

His fortunes had changed radically since winter began. He'd sent his thief to steal Kylar's sword, expecting to find that it was covered with the black ka'kari. As soon as he'd touched it with magic, he'd known it wasn't the ka'kari—it was something better. The sword was Iures, the Staff of Law. Like Curoch, Iures had been made by Ezra or perhaps by Ezra and Jorsin together. Unlike Curoch, Iures didn't amplify power, but it made vastly complicated weaves a hundred times easier to make—or unmake.

The cylindrical monolith was halfway up the hill to Trayethell Castle, extending up to the dome like a glass pillar. In the light of the torches, the monolith looked like a jar of churning smoke. The smoke betrayed only hints of the Titan imprisoned within. Here, a claw pressed against the glass, there, the side of a gigantic, disturbingly human-looking foot. It irritated Neph that he still felt a tremor at sight of the frozen monster. With Iures, he could destroy the monolith in an instant—after all, Ezra the Mad had used Iures to create the monolith, trapping the Titan until Jorsin Alkestes had killed it.

The glassy prison of frozen air was broken only by the Titan's death wound. Jorsin had unleashed a bar of fire from the top of Trayethell castle. It had burned through the prison and the Titan's chest in a perfect circle ten feet in diameter. The raw amount of magic necessary for such a thing made Neph hope Jorsin had been using Curoch.

Neph approached the monolith with small steps, coughing more from habit than necessity. Iures was doing wonders for Neph's health. The Vürd-meisters nearby made their obeisance and then returned to their work at his wave. Standing on scaffolding, they were lifting buckets of earth and packing it into the hole Jorsin had burned in the Titan. Soon, that earth would be made into flesh, and the Titan would rise. It would break open the great dome of Black Barrow, and then it would break any army that faced Neph.

Neph's tent was undisturbed. The fifty Soulsworn guards and his spells guaranteed that. Neph paused inside before entering Khali's room. Hiking up his robe, he touched his silver staff—the form he had chosen for Iures—and touched it to his ankle. It dissolved from his hand and wrapped smoothly around his ankle and calf. He willed it to be hidden, to remain inert even if touched with Khali's magic, to simply record all the magic that occurred around it. Khali didn't know about Iures, and Neph didn't intend for her to find out until it was too late. Iures changed everything.

Composing himself, Neph pulled back the flap. Tenser was sprawled on as fine a bed as they'd been able to make, his limbs loose, features slack, breath slow, eyes open but unfocused and rarely blinking. Neph pretended difficulty kneeling at Tenser's feet and extended the magic as Khali had taught him. "Holy One," he called. "I am here to serve."

Tenser's eyes closed then opened again, and She was present. Her presence filled the little tent like a sooty cloud, making it hard to breathe. "You have been neglecting your duties," Khali said. Her voice was Tenser's but the intonations were wrong, the accent unfamiliar. "This host has bedsores."

Neph's throat relaxed. "I will attend to it personally. Immediately. I've been about your business, collecting specimens for you." He cleared his throat but didn't cough. His coughing irritated Khali. "I was hoping we could talk about my reward."

Her laughter was amused, Neph thought. It was hard to tell because though Khali controlled Tenser's voice and eyes, She didn't control his facial expressions. They remained blank, slack except when tongue and jaw worked to make words.

Khali wanted to be truly embodied, not the rude parody of it She had in Tenser. She needed three things: Ezra's weaves on Black Barrow to be broken, a willing host, and a spell that would require the blood of an Ursuul and the combined might of Neph's two hundred Vürdmeisters. Godkings in the past had delivered two of the three, but none could dismantle Ezra's work, because Ezra had used Iures to deny Khali embodiment. But Neph could undo Ezra's spells—because Iures remembered every weave it had ever helped make.

"I want two things," Neph said. "Godking Wanhope will arrive soon to kill me. I want to deny him the use of the vir. Second, I want to live another hundred years."

"Impossible," Khali said.

"Fifty then. Forty."

"Once embodied, I can give you a hundred years. But I can't deny Dorian the vir."

Neph's heart sank. *Dorian* was Godking Wanhope? Of all Garoth Ursuul's sons, the last one Neph wished to face was his old pupil. "I thought You controlled—"

"I do," Khali said, cutting him off. "The vir are magical parasites. Most of them were wiped out in antiquity, but Roygaris Ursuul captured several. What he liked about vir was that in the early part of an infestation, they broke open new channels in their host's Talent, adding to the host's power. Of course, they slowly devour their host's Talent itself, but Roygaris hoped to keep the vir in that first stage indefinitely. He failed, until I helped him. We slowed the progress of an infestation, but they can't be stopped. Try to use your Talent; you'll see it's a shadow of what it was when you were young. But I taught Roygaris something far more important. The vir is a like a grove of aspens. Each looks like a separate tree, but they're one organism. Control the right part, and you control the vir of everyone who's been infected with that strain. Your vir, Dorian's, Garoth's, every Khalidoran's— they are all one. Roygaris and I made a grand bargain: his blood line would control the vir, and I would control the reservoir of magic. The vow was made in a way that breaking it will destroy the vir and the reservoir."

Neph had expected Her to lie. He hadn't known the details, but just holding Iures had made much of Khali's magic plain to him. "If I can't stop him from taking the vir from me, Dorian will kill me," Neph said.

"When I am embodied, I shall protect you. Your service will not be forgotten. This I swear."

Neph wondered about that. Did Khali really need to be embodied to protect him from a mere man? Was she not a goddess? Or was it simply that she *wouldn't* protect him because if he wouldn't help her she had no reason to help him? He wondered what Khali would do to the world if she were embodied. Would she wreak havoc on everything, simply because she hated life as all the Strangers did? Or was her thirst for power more nuanced? Neph's interactions with her had been as infrequent as he could afford, but he hadn't sensed the same all-encompassing rage from her that he had seen in the other Strangers.

It was vital to judge correctly—Neph wanted to be Godking, but he wanted to rule over more than ashes and the dead. Still, he might not have much choice. If by not raising her, he would certainly die, but by raising her, all the world might die, he would risk the world.

"I am an old man," Neph said, defeated. "I have not the strength for this task."

Tenser Ursuul's arm flopped up as if lifted on strings, his hand limp. Neph touched the extended hand, and Khali's magic flowed into him, invigorating him, setting cool fire to his lungs. When it faded, he felt stronger than he had in years, and Iures had recorded every detail both of the Healing, and of how Khali herself drew from the reservoir of magic. It might be enough.

"Thank you, Holy One." Neph had only days to figure out the magic necessary, but with Iures in hand, he might depose more than Dorian.

"The latest ones approach," Khali said. "Bring them in."

Neph went outside and gestured to the Soulsworn. There were six young women chained together standing with them, and they all looked terrified. Khali's potential hosts were all peasant girls. Neph's men hadn't had much to choose from in this wilderness. Neph led them inside. They were surprised that the goddess was a drooling young man. Perhaps they'd expected claws and fangs. Neph studied the girls as they studied Khali. Four were either ugly or plain. Khali hated ugliness. Two were pretty, but Neph could See that one had been raped—against Neph's explicit orders. He would kill someone for that. Khali wanted any violation of Her host to come at Her own hands. The other girl was even prettier, with big brown eyes and radiant skin, but she was disfigured with scars.

"What's your name, child?" Khali asked the scarred one.

"Elene Cromwyll...uh, Mistress."

"Would you like to live forever, Elene?"

The girl's big eyes filled with such longing that even Neph couldn't help but pity her. "More than anything," Elene said.

80

*F*eir was standing at a table in Ezra's secret workroom under Black Barrow with a polishing cloth in his hand. He wasn't polishing the blade. He'd polished it a dozen times already, and it didn't need polishing in the first place.

"It's finished," he said aloud. "Except for one thing." Feir unveiled the sword. His fraud was nearly Ceur'caelestos' twin. He had held Ceur'caelestos, had marveled at it, had studied every whorl in the patterns of the mistarille. The heads of twin dragons were etched in either side of his blade, facing the tip, dragons of sun and moon, in accordance with Ceuran mythology. The blade had a single edge, curving slightly to give it more cutting surface. The thicker spine of the blade was to give it strength, the flexible iron core compensating for the sharp, hard fragility of the steel edge. This blade's form was pure show. It was mistarille, and it wouldn't break even if a man stood on the side of the blade and the wielder lifted it. Despite its incredible strength, Ceur'caelestos was lighter than it should have been. The mistarille, folded and refolded like steel, had the same steel patterns Ceur'caelestos' blade had borne. The difference between the original and Feir's fraud was that the original held the "fires of heaven." In response to danger or magic or its wielder's mood, the dragons could breathe what looked like fire out to the tip of the blade.

Feir knew the weaves to duplicate that, now. What he didn't have was a heartstone to hold the weaves. Certain stones resonated with different frequencies of magic. A ruby resonated with fire magics, specifically those having to do with red and orange light. If a stone was pure enough and exactly the right size, which varied by weave, a resonance could be built that sustained itself. This was nearly always imperfect, which was one reason magic imbued in items failed after a time. Feir needed as perfect a ruby as possible to be the dragon's heart.

"This part was supposed to be simple," Feir said. Even his own voice was depressing. "The prophecy was 'The greatest red gives dragon's heart and head.'" The greatest red had to be a big ruby, a heartstone, but placed at the dragon's head on the sword.

Feir had done a dozen impossible things over the course of the winter. With the barest of clues he'd been given in his time in Ezra's Wood, he'd come to Black Barrow and found the secret tunnel to this room. He'd found the magically hardened gold tools. He'd avoided the hundreds of Vürd-meisters who shared the shadowed city with him and found seven broken mistarille swords. He'd discovered Ezra's notes—a treasure any Maker would give his right arm to read. By all the gods, Feir had learned to reforge mistarille! He'd made the most beautiful fraud in history.

But he couldn't find a red rock.

"Could any other smith now living make this?" Antoninus Wervel asked, his voice low.

Feir shrugged. Antoninus waited. Feir gave in. "No."

Antoninus picked up the blade reverently, and in spite of himself, Feir was warmed. Antoninus wasn't a Maker himself, but he appreciated the mastery required for what Feir had done. He turned the blade over, examining it. "I thought you put your crossed war hammers on it."

In a moment of vanity—well, two hours of vanity—Feir had etched his smithmark near the hilt. As a boy, he'd loved the stories about Oren Razin, one of Jorsin's champions. Feir had been the only person he knew who could even think of wielding two war hammers as Oren had. Later, he'd mostly given it up. It was a lot easier to find someone to train you with swords. "It's not much of a forgery if you put your name on it. It's still there, but you have to know how to uncover it."

"You should be proud, Feir. You've made a thing of beauty."

"Without the dragon's heart, I've made nothing."

81

"What troubles you, my king? You've been fondling that rock for two days," Kaede said.

Solon pulled her into his lap and cupped her breast. "Only when you don't let me fondle better things."

"You beast!" she said, but she didn't pull away. "I'm serious."

The first days of their marriage had been bliss, except for the rock.

Kaede's repentance at ordering him to subdue the Takedas by himself had led her to make all the wedding preparations. The very night Solon had arrived they had been married. Kaede refused to wait until later in the spring when the outlying nobles could attend. She said if they were offended, she would threaten to send her Stormrider to "visit" their isles.

But there were only so many hours a day that could be absorbed with lovemaking—though Solon and Kaede were doing their best—and that left Solon with time to consider the rock.

"I told you a little about my friend Dorian," Solon said. "And his prophecy over me."

"Something about killing your brother and a kingdom falling, right?"

Solon pulled back his white and black hair. "There's nothing quite as infuriating as having a man in a trance lay out your future in a sing-song: 'Storm-riving, storm-riding, by your word—or silence—a brother king lies dead. Two fears deriding, hope and death colliding, of the sword's man, regal third, true lies in your dragon's heart—or head. The north broken and remade on your single word.'"

Kaede looked puzzled. "Well, you got the storm-riding part."

"And before you ask, no, I didn't name myself that. I used to have no idea about the rest of it, except the brother king part. If I came home, I would have rallied the nobles to stop my brother Sijuron, thus my words would have left him dead. As it was, I served a man named Regnus Gyre, a man who would have been king and was like a brother to me. I didn't tell him I was a mage, and on learning it, he barred me from his company and was slain. The last part never made any sense to me, I only saw one king in the first part of the prophecy, my brother, so I thought Dorian was raving."

"But something has changed."

"This ruby, Kaede. I never heard of it. My father never spoke of it. Nothing is written about it in the royal records except to record its being in the treasury for at least two hundred years. It's listed as the dragon's heart. I think a third king, the regal third, the sword's man, depends on me bringing this ruby to him."

"What if you're the third king? What if you're the sword's man? You said it was a sword that turned your hair white. Perhaps a threat approaches here, and you need the ruby to withstand it. Solon, you can't leave. Not on some madman's word." Though she still sat in his lap, she was rigid, fear and anger rising in her.

Two fears deriding. The words were suddenly crystal. Damned prophecies could always be interpreted at least two ways, and usually both were correct.

"Kaede," Solon said, "there's a garrison called Screaming Winds that guards the pass between Cenaria and Khalidor. Dorian and I were there last fall. Dorian was unconscious most of the time, waking and scrawling fragments of prophecy and lapsing into trances again. One day he woke screaming. He demanded as much gold as I could get my hands on. I got it for him and we walked up into the hills to a stunted black oak. Dorian told me that Khali was coming and that she would tempt him. He said she would massacre everyone. He melted the gold and used it to cover his eyes and ears and made fetters for his arms and legs and asked me to drive stakes pinning him to the black oak. I wrapped him in blankets and left. The commander didn't believe my warnings. I wanted to leave, but I took too long, so I had the men bind me in ropes and I emptied my glore vyrden, but before the men could blindfold me or block my ears, She came."

"Khali?"

He stared into the distance. "I saw men throwing themselves off the wall. I saw a man tear his eyes out. And then, in a vision I thought was real, I saw you. I tried to go to you, but the ropes saved me. No one else survived. In fact, the Soulsworn came through and made sure everyone was dead. If a body hadn't fallen on me and covered me in blood while I was praying, they would have killed me too."

"So to what god should I offer sacrifices for saving your life?"

"None. It was a coincidence. A lazy soldier who didn't clean the blood from his sword in freezing weather and couldn't draw his sword."

"While you just so happened to be praying," she said. "That's quite some coincidence."

"Yes," Solon said, more roughly than he meant to. "That's what a coincidence *is*. Anyway, sorry, when I went to Dorian's black oak, he was gone. His tracks lead north, toward Khalidor, but I couldn't follow. I had to see you. Nothing else mattered. I signed on with a captain whose last run of the year was to Hokkai."

"So this is why you believe Dorian's prophecies," she said.

"This is the dragon's heart, Kaede. I'm the second king. A third king lives or dies by what I do with this."

"What are the two fears?" she asked quietly.

"My fear of Khali and my fear of speaking the truth. The latter was the fear that cost Regnus his life. I feel like I've been given a second chance, first to speak honestly with you, and second to face Khali again. 'Broken north, broken you, remade if you speak one word.' I've still got something broken inside, Kaede. I thought marrying you would fix it, and I can't tell you how happy I've been, and how much I want to stay here forever, but there's a part of me that still whispers 'coward.'"

"Coward? You're Solon Stormrider! You braved the winter seas. You put down a rebellion single-handedly. You resisted a goddess. How are you a coward?"

"Dorian needed me when he went into Khalidor. He's probably dead because I didn't go. Regnus is dead because I wouldn't risk telling him who I was. If the prophecy is true, there's a word I have to speak, a life I can save, and I can be remade."

Kaede's eyes were troubled. "Will it be enough? Will there not be ever one more thing you need to do to prove that voice wrong? Will you chase valor until it kills you?"

He kissed her forehead. "I've already done the hardest part: I've told you the truth. I won't go unless you give me your blessing. My loyalty is all to you, Kaede."

Her eyes filled with a weight of grief. "My love, I won't give your death my blessing."

Solon held her gaze for a long time, then he tossed the Heart of the Dragon aside. "Then I stay," he said.

Kaede pivoted, sitting astride him. She put her hands on both sides of his face and looked deep into his eyes. "Please don't ask again. Please."

"I won't."

Her lovemaking was so fierce it left him breathless. She rode him to a silent climax, and even as her pupils flared and her breath caught and her fingers clawed into his shoulders, her eyes never left his. Then she clung to him, shaking, tears and sweat mingling on his chest, but she didn't say a word.

82

I don't know if I should have married you," Jenine said. "I think I made a mistake."

They were sitting together in the enormous Godking's carriage, slowly rumbling toward Black Barrow. Despite the dangers of bringing her to a battle, Dorian hadn't been able to leave her behind. Some plot might unfold in Khaliras that would take her from him. And if he had another episode, she was the only person he trusted to cover for him.

"But you love me," he said. "I know you do."

"I do," she admitted. "I respect you and I enjoy your company and I think you're brilliant and honorable. You're a great man...."

"But?" he asked woodenly.

It came out in a rush. "But it's not like it was with Logan. I know it's not fair to compare you to a man who's dead—maybe I just remember all the good things about him now that he's gone, and I know—maybe it isn't fair to expect love to be the same every time. Maybe with Logan I fell in love the way a girl falls in love and a woman's love grows slowly and protects itself. I don't know what it's supposed to be like, Dorian, but sometimes I feel so empty. Maybe I should have waited."

I'm a fraud. But what could he do? Tell her the truth? Send her back to Cenaria and her infatuation for some petty princeling she didn't even know? Together they were changing a kingdom, bringing light to a dark land. What could Logan give her compared to that? Why should Logan's love be more deserving than his?

Jenine's love was growing. Dorian knew it. It would grow more still when she realized she was pregnant with their child, he knew it. He'd seen that in his moments of madness on the battlefield, and hadn't trusted it or anything else he'd seen there, but in the days since then, he'd looked at her again, and he was sure it was true. Not twins, as he'd first foreseen, but a child, a son. Maybe the twins were to be their next children. He'd been waiting for the right time to tell her the news, but no time had seemed right.

He still spent as much of his days with her as he could. Their lovemaking was less frequent now that he was using his harem, but whatever jealousy she might feel seemed outweighed by the sudden reversal of the concubines' feeling toward her. Dorian had given her the credit for preserving their lives. That generosity cracked their envy and hatred. Instead of defeated rivals, Jenine suddenly had sisters, and her isolation melted with the spring snow.

This was real. It wasn't perfect, but it was the best they could do. This was what it was to be Godking. Besides, if he and Jenine simply ran away, one of the Vürdmeisters would rule with even more brutality than Dorian's father had. Every relationship, every marriage, had its little lies. He was king. A king made choices for other people based on information they didn't have. That was the burden of rule. Dorian had weighed Jenine's choices, and he'd chosen.

"I'm sorry for laying this at your feet when you've got so many other concerns, but I promised myself when we married that I'd never lie to you, and silence was starting to feel like a lie. I'm sorry. I made my decision. I did marry you. I do love you. I just—it's just hard to be an adult all the time. You've trusted me to be your queen, and I still keep acting like a little girl. I'm sorry for being such a disappointment."

"A disappointment?" Dorian asked. "You've done better than I could have imagined. I didn't even begin acting like an adult until I was much older than you are. I'm so proud of you, Jenine. I love you more than anything. I understand you're confused. This is a confusing place. I understand you have doubts. We've been married for two months, and you've realized that you're committed to something for the rest of your life, and that's scary. Yes, it hurts me a little, but our love is big enough to take a few scratches. Thanks for telling me the truth. Come here." They hugged, and he felt her unreserved relief. He wished she would feel his hesitation, wished she would ask him what was wrong. If she asked, he would tell her about Logan. He would tell her everything.

After a few more seconds, she released him. He let her go, and the moment passed. "I love you, Dorian," she said, looking him in the eye and not seeing him.

"I love you too, Jenine." *I still don't call her Jeni. Why is that?*

Kylar opened his eyes slowly. His mouth felt like it was stuffed full of cotton. His whole body was a chorus of complaints from sleeping propped against a tree. Working his jaw to clear the cotton feeling, he sat up. He touched his cheek where Durzo had smeared the poison. The new skin was tender, but there would be no scarring: Durzo was right. The bastard was always right.

It was dawn in the woods. Kylar was about to curse aloud when he became aware of a presence in the wood. He filled his lungs with a deep, slow breath, willing his senses to come alive. There were no animals in the forest this morning, but whether all the birds had migrated and the squirrels were hibernating or if the reason was more sinister, Kylar didn't know. He slowly flexed the muscles in his legs and back, judging whether they would cramp if he tried sudden movement. He scanned the forest, turning his head slowly. The sound of his fresh beard grinding against the collar of his tunic was the barest whisper. The length of his beard confirmed that he'd only been unconscious overnight.

There was nothing in the forest. No sounds out of place. He thought he could trust his body to respond. Wind sighed through the big oaks, the few remaining leaves whispering secrets against him. But something had woken him. Kylar was sure of it. Instinctively, he reached for the ka'kari to cloak himself in invisibility, but the ka'kari was gone. Kylar reached instead into his sleeves, loosening the daggers there. He scanned the trees.

A puff of air hit the top of his head.

Kylar threw himself to the side as he buried a knife in the tree above his head. He rolled once, threw himself to his feet and jumped backward a good ten paces, daggers in his hands.

Durzo laughed softly. "I always did like watching you jump." He was clinging like a spider to the tree Kylar had slept against.

"You bastard, where's the ka'kari? What have you done?"

Durzo kept laughing.

"Give me the ka'kari," Kylar said.

"All in good time."

"Wait, why am I asking? I can—" Kylar extended his hand to call the ka'kari to him.

"Don't!" Durzo barked.

Kylar stopped.

"The Hunter's nocturnal," Durzo said. "Its sense of smell is better than any tracking dog, its hearing is acute, and its vision rivals an eagle's, even when it's running full speed. If I timed things right, you'll have until dark before it starts hunting you."

"What—"

Releasing one hand from where it gripped the oak, Durzo unlimbered a black sword from his back. He tossed it to Kylar.

"Whatever you do, don't take the ka'kari off Curoch. Everything magical that goes into the Wood is marked. It's given a scent, so if it's taken out of the Wood, the Hunter can find it. The ka'kari can mask that scent, but I couldn't figure out how to erase it with the time I had. So the second you take the ka'kari off Curoch, the Hunter will come. I don't know exactly how fast the Hunter is, but if you really need to use Curoch, take the ka'kari off, use it, and then get the hell away from it. It might be minutes, it might be hours, but the Hunter will come. It will risk everything to get this sword."

Durzo had saved Kylar's life again. Kylar had known that his chances of making it into Ezra's Wood were dismal, and his odds of stealing Curoch and making it back out were even worse. Durzo had known it, too. In his typical way, Durzo wouldn't say anything to tell Kylar what he meant to him, but he'd do anything to show it.

"You old bastard," Kylar said, but his tone said, *thank you, master.*

"I can give you magic for the run. If you don't push too hard, you should get there in time and still have energy to fight. I'm going to Cenaria. This way, the Hunter has to follow us in opposite directions. It should be enough. Don't run flat out like you did when Sister Ariel gave you power, got it?"

"Got it," Kylar said. That was why Durzo was clinging to the tree. It made him harder to track. Plus, Kylar suspected the ground had all sorts of traps.

Durzo wasn't done. He spoke quietly. "Kylar, the fact Curoch was in the Wood tells me Neph's using Iures to break Jorsin's and Ezra's spells on Black Barrow. It makes Elene's talk of a Titan plausible. It also means that you're taking the thing he wants most straight to him. If he takes Curoch from you, he could break the world. I don't mean that metaphorically. For seven centuries I've done all I could to keep artifacts of such power out of the hands of men and women who will use them unscrupulously. If you fail, he'll undo everything I've spent seven centuries doing."

"You trust me this much?" Kylar asked.

Durzo grimaced. "Come here, you're wasting daylight."

Kylar stepped close.

"When Jorsin Alkestes commissioned me for this task, Kylar, he bound me with an oath he claimed was as old as the Night Angels themselves. If you so desire, here it is." Durzo's back straightened, his voice deepened, and Kylar knew Durzo was remembering his friend and king Jorsin Alkestes. "I am Sa'kagé, a lord of shadows. I claim the shadows that the Shadow may not. I am the strong arm of deliverance. I am Shadowstrider. I am the Scales of Justice. I am He-Who-Guards-Unseen. I am Shadowslayer. I am Nameless. The *coranti* shall not go unpunished. My way is hard, but I serve unbroken. In ignobility, nobility. In shame, honor. In darkness, light. I will do justice and love mercy. Until the king returns, I shall not lay my burden down."

"Who's the king?" Kylar asked.

"Vows are a bitch, huh?" Durzo grinned.

"This is what the Sa'kagé is supposed to be, isn't it?"

"The Sa'kagé's always been made of thugs and murderers, but there have been moments, like diamonds studding a pile of shit, when they've been crooks with a purpose."

"Thanks for the image."

"You gonna say the words?" Durzo asked.

"You'd make me commit to something I don't fully understand."

"Kid, we're always committing to things we don't fully understand."

"I thought you'd lost your faith in this and everything else," Kylar said.

"This isn't about my faith; it's about yours."

It was standard Durzo evasion. You don't ask someone you care about to swear their life to horseshit. Durzo was continuing the conversation they'd started months ago about Kylar's destiny. In choosing a life in the shadows, in choosing obscurity, Kylar would avoid one of the greatest temptations of the black ka'kari—the temptation to rule. Its power made him almost a god already, and the danger was always that he could become what he sought to destroy. Durzo hadn't even trusted himself with so much power. Did Kylar think he was that much better a man than his master?

A man serving the shadows also saw things that no king could see. A man serving in ignobility saw wrongs that were hidden from those in power. No one bothered to hide anything from Durzo Blint—except their fear of him.

The oath of a Night Angel wasn't enough to make a destiny, but it was a start. *What am I for?*

Whatever else he didn't know, Kylar knew he longed for justice. By serving in darkness with eyes that saw through the darkness, by being welcomed into the shadows, he could give justice to those who'd escaped justice. Those overlooked, too unimportant for mercy would find better than they'd hoped for. Those who should be stopped would be stopped. The faces of the Night Angels were already Kylar's faces. I will do justice and love mercy.

"I'll say it," Kylar said.

Durzo grimaced, but beckoned him closer and laid a hand on Kylar's forehead. Kylar recited the vow from memory—Durzo smirking at him, as if asking, how well did I teach you? But as Kylar finished, Durzo's hand grew strangely warm, his face somber. He said, *"Ch'torathi sigwye h'e banath so sikamon to vathari. Vennadosh chi tomethigara. Horgathal mu tolethara. Veni, soli, fali, deachi. Vol lessara dei."* Durzo withdrew his hand, his deep eyes limpid and, for perhaps the first time Kylar had ever seen, at peace.

"What was that?" Kylar asked. Whatever else the words had done, Kylar felt power suffusing him, more gently than when Sister Ariel had given him power, but also more solidly.

"That was my blessing." Durzo smirked, acknowledging he was a bastard for blessing Kylar in a language he didn't understand. With the way he'd trained Kylar's memory, he surely knew Kylar would remember the words until he was able to track down the outlandish language they'd been spoken in. But it wasn't in Durzo to just tell him. "Now get the hell out of here," Durzo said. "I've got trees to climb."

83

$\mathcal{L}$ogan and Lantano Garuwashi stood with their retainers on top of a still-pristine tower that guarded the mouth of the pass, surveying what would be the battlefield to the north. The great dome of Black Barrow and the dark stain of devastation around it were miles away on the opposite side of the Guvari River. Logan saw wonders to every side. Before Jorsin Alkestes had buried Trayethell beneath Black Barrow, it had been one of the great cities of the world in a world where wonders were common. To the east was Lake Ruel, which had been dammed in ages lost. The dam still stood, feeding the Guvari River not through the sluice gates on its front, which had been closed for centuries, but over the top of the dam itself. A series of locks, long since broken, had once made it possible for cargo ships to reach the city from the ocean. Half a dozen bridges or more had once spanned the river, but all had fallen except two, the wider Ox Bridge and Black Bridge near the dam.

The tower in which they stood guarded the entrance to Ox Bridge. It commanded views of the pass behind them, the terraced slopes of Mount Terzhin to the southwest, and everything except whatever lurked on the far side of Black Barrow. Looking at the terraced hillside and the empty expanse at its base that they called the great market, Logan had a revelation. He'd always thought Black Barrow had enclosed the city of Trayethell. It hadn't. Jorsin had only enclosed the city's heart. Trayethell had spanned leagues. If what Logan was looking on was correct, the city had been bigger and more populous than any city now in the world.

"We'll have to move our men over Ox Bridge tonight," Garuwashi said. "It'll take maybe four hours for thirty thousand to cross. The camp followers will have to cross in the dark."

"Cross?" Logan said. "Do you see Wanhope's army? We have twenty-six thousand men, half of whom have never seen battle. Wanhope has twenty thousand, ten thousand more highlanders, and two thousand meisters—each of whom is worth a dozen men. You want us to fight with our backs against a river? No. We guard the bridges and put our men in the great market in case Wanhope tries to ford the river there. We'll see how well his men fight waist-deep in water. If necessary, we can retreat slowly into the passes."

"You're planning for defeat?" Lantano Garuwashi asked, incredulous. "This is lunacy. We cross the bridge, and we destroy it behind us. Desperate men fight best. If you leave them an out, they'll flee, especially your battle virgins. Give them no choice but to win or die, and they will fight almost like sa'ceurai."

"They outnumber us, and we have four magi. Four!"

"Numbers mean nothing. Each sa'ceurai is as a hundred men. We came here for victory." Behind them, several of Garuwashi's men voiced muffled agreement.

"I'll give you victory," Logan said.

"You'll *give* us nothing."

"That's not what I meant. Tonight under the cover of darkness, I'm sending ten thousand men west down the river. My Feyuri scouts say there's a crossing a few miles down. Ten miles downriver is Reigukhas. It's not a big city, but all Wanhope's supplies flow through there, and it's very defensible. We send our magi with my ten thousand, and they can take Reigukhas before dawn. If we can starve Wanhope's army, it will be his men who melt away in the night."

"They'll see our men heading west, unless you mean to march ten thousand without any light."

"The torches will only be visible for the first half a mile, then there's a forest between them and the Khalidorans. It'll look like men moving around among our campfires."

Garuwashi was quiet for a long time. Finally, he spat. "So be it, Cenarian. But I'm sending a thousand of my sa'ceurai with your men to take the city. None shall have glory greater than the sa'ceurai."

Thus it begins.

84

Dorian was meeting with his generals in the afternoon when he felt the first twinges of madness rising.

"Enough," he said, interrupting General Naga's report. "Here's what I want. Make sure our defensive positions are impregnable. I don't want them to even try us. Let them see our strength. In the meantime, I need better intelligence on Moburu's numbers. We know he has two thousand krul. How many men does he have? And where the hell is—" A vision flashed before Dorian's eyes of Khali herself, rising from the ground, perfect, whole, beautiful, embodied and smiling victoriously. The room had disappeared, and only she remained, potent, a black ocean of krul rising around her.

"And where the hell is Neph Dada?" he heard a voice say. Though he couldn't see the speaker, he knew it must be Jenine. "His Holiness demands you find out. He'll expect your report this evening. For now, begone."

Dorian blinked and the vision was gone. General Naga turned back as he reached the flap of the tent. He seemed reassured to find Dorian meeting his eye. "The queen speaks with my voice," Dorian said. "Is that a problem, general?"

"Of course not, Your Holiness. I will report when we get word." He bowed deeply, and left.

When the last of them was gone, Dorian let out a long breath. Jenine took his hand and he sat. "I need to use it," Dorian said.

"Every time you do, it's harder to stop," Jenine said.

She was right, but with so many armies in close proximity, Dorian needed to use his gift to make sure he didn't trigger a cataclysm. He'd done everything he knew to do militarily to discourage the Cenarians from attacking, but with Neph's men and Moburu's nearby, there were too many factors at play for him to not try to see the futures down the roads before him.

He'd studied his gift with a Healer's eyes, and he thought he understood why prophecy seemed easier to begin and harder to stop now. The vir had broken open new channels everywhere throughout his Talent, and it had penetrated his prophetic gift, too. All his magic, and now all his prophecies, passed through the tentacles of vir rather than their natural channels. Because the vir was thicker, everything passed more freely. It was quite possible that the vir, tainted itself, was tainting Dorian's gift with bizarre visions like those he'd had of the Strangers and his wife pregnant with twins, but there was no help for it now. He would stop using the vir and only use the Talent—after this.

"I love you," he said.

"I love you too," she answered. She had a quill and parchment to write down anything he said, in case he couldn't remember it afterward.

Then he dove in. He tried to hold onto enough of himself to speak what he saw, but the current was too strong. He saw a Titan rise from Black Barrow, and then he pulled downstream fifteen years to Torras Bend. There was Feir, standing at a smithy, ordering his young apprentice to gather wood. Then Dorian was a hundred years downstream, in Trayethell, somehow magically rebuilt, celebrating something, a vast parade working through the street. Dorian fought it, tried to throw himself back to a time where his visions would help him. He found himself standing in the guts of Khaliras, deciding whether to take Jenine out through the sewage chutes or try to fight their way out, everything would turn from this one choice—no, that was the past, dammit.

"Rodnia? Nidora?" He heard the voice calling for him, but it was too distant, and he hadn't found anything yet. There was a whisper as it called again, and then it was lost.

Jenine drew the curtain that separated Dorian's throne, where he was quietly mumbling, from the rest of his tent. "Dorian!" she whispered one more time, but the king didn't stir. She shut the curtain and said, "Come in, General Naga." The man had been knocking for more than a minute.

"Your Highness," he said, coming in and looking conspicuously at the drawn curtain. "My apologies, but we've just had a report from a spy. His Holiness must hear it."

"His Holiness is not to be disturbed right now."

"I'm afraid this requires immediate action."

Jenine lifted her brows as if the general were perilously close to being rude. "Then deliver your report."

General Naga hesitated, open-mouthed, as he struggled with the idea of reporting to a woman, much less a woman young enough to be his daughter, then wisely closed his mouth. When he opened it again, it was to say, "Your Highness, our spy reports that the Cenarians and Ceurans are planning to attack our supply lines at the city of Reigukhas. They plan to have ten thousand men sneak away tonight under cover of darkness. The Cenarian king said—"

"The Cenarian king?" Jenine interrupted.

For an instant, General Naga seemed stricken. "Sorry, I meant, the *Ceuran* king said that we would think any torches we saw tonight were merely men moving between their campfires. In truth, such movement would only be visible to us for a short section. The Cenarian queen—your pardons, Highness, I obviously am having a slight problem adjusting to so many queens—the Cenarian queen concurred." He swallowed nervously.

"Do you trust this spy?" Jenine asked. She didn't know whether she more wanted Dorian to wake up instantly and make the decision for her, or if she feared that he might wake up with a scream as he had the last few times.

"Absolutely, Your Highness."

"If we wait until we see the movement of torches tonight, will our men be able to get to Reigukhas in time to defend it?" Jenine asked.

"It will be a near thing."

"Then send fifteen thousand men now. If we don't see the torches moving tonight, we can send riders to get them to turn back."

"Fifteen thousand? From a defensive position, five should be more than adequate to defend Reigukhas, and would still preserve our superiority of numbers here."

He was probably right, and Jenine would have conceded to his experience if this had been a war, but it wasn't a war. Those were her people on the other side, too. Fifteen thousand men would be such an overwhelming defensive force that the Cenarians would call off an attack on the town as hopeless. Jenine was saving lives on both sides, and tomorrow, they'd be able to send emissaries to the Cenarians before blood was spilled. "Fifteen thousand, general. That is, unless you're still having a problem adjusting to this queen."

General Naga barely hesitated before he bobbed his head and withdrew. For an odd moment, Jenine thought he looked relieved.

As night fell, Logan and Garuwashi met once more at the top of the tower, this time alone, though each had bodyguards stationed out of earshot on the stairs. They watched the line of sa'ceurai, every one bearing a torch, heading down river. Then the kings turned, scanning the thousands of campfires dotting the plain around Black Barrow. The Khalidoran army and the highlanders stayed outside the circle around Black Barrow that was carpeted with those oddly non-decomposing bodies. They called it the Dead Demesne.

"Do you think it worked?" Logan asked.

"Wanhope's a wytch, not a warrior," Garuwashi said. "I think he'll believe everything his spy told him we said earlier."

In truth, Logan had sent ten thousand men west, but only until they were blocked from the Khalidorans' sight by the forest. Then the men were told to extinguish their torches and make their way back to camp. Logan was sure no small amount of grumbling was going on right now: the men had no idea why they'd been sent marching in circles, and he couldn't tell them in case more spies lurked in their ranks. Meanwhile, Garuwashi's thousand were continuing west. They would ford the river and come back on the opposite side as stealthily as possible. Dressed in muddied garb, they would crawl through the Dead Demesne. When the sun rose, they would lie in the shadows and huddle next to the corpses as if dead themselves. They would circle the long way around Black Barrow. Garuwashi figured it would take them two nights to get into place, but then, either on his signal or when they saw the opportunity, the men would don their armor, rise from among the dead, and attack the command tents. If Momma K's spies were right, Jenine was there. If not, they still might kill some of Wanhope's generals or even the Godking himself.

It was likely a suicide mission, but there had been no lack of volunteers. But the only Cenarians going were a hundred of Agon's Dogs, former sneak thieves and burglars and his wytch hunters with their Ymmuri bows.

Of course, as Agon and Garuwashi kept telling Logan, timing was everything. Those thousand men were among the armies' best. If Wanhope did split his forces and tomorrow went as planned, Logan and Garuwashi might be close to victory. Those extra thousand veterans could turn a Khalidoran retreat into a rout.

"The Feyuri scouts say that the Ceuran force following us is led by the Regent himself," Garuwashi said quietly. "I will be obliged to kill myself when he discovers I have no sword. My men will be invited to join me in suicide or return to Ceura immediately."

"How far back is he?" Logan asked, his throat constricting. Now he understood why Garuwashi had been so adamant that the thousand who snuck through the Dead Demesne be sa'ceurai. It was a service to Logan. Separated from command, they wouldn't know that their leader had been disgraced, so they would keep fighting.

"They will arrive tomorrow night."

"We can stop them in the passes," Logan said. "There are narrow—"

"He has twenty thousand sa'ceurai. My men would wonder why we were fighting the Regent, who only wants to see the Blade of Heaven. Even without him, they will expect me to lead them into battle. This is my last night."

They turned as a man cleared his throat at the stairs. The man was nearly as big as Logan, not quite as tall, but wide as an ox. He carried some flab, but it was only a thin layer over rock hard muscle. "Maybe not, my lord," Feir said, dipping his head. "I don't suppose either of you has a big ruby?"

They looked at each other, and Logan saw a thin, desperate hope in Lantano Garuwashi's eyes. He knew then that this man would kill himself in a heartbeat if he needed to, but there was nothing in Lantano Garuwashi that desired death.

"No?" Feir asked. "Damn. Well, I hope we can find someone who's good with illusions." The big man stepped forward and unwrapped a bundle to produce a sword. "My lord, I present you with Ceur'caelestos."

$\mathcal{V}$i and three hundred of the fittest war magae made it through the eastern fork of the pass an hour before dawn. Sadly, fittest wasn't the same as most Talented. The journey had taken longer than anyone had expected. Ushering eight thousand women—most of them middle-aged and every single one more than willing to share her opinion—through the mountains had been a nightmare. Most of the rest would arrive sometime during the day, but a sizable number wouldn't arrive until the next day, or the day after that. Even with bodies that appeared decades younger than their years, eighty- and ninety-year-olds were simply not going to hurry. Vi thought that if she never saw another woman in her life, she'd count herself lucky.

After some bickering with sentries that had ended when Vi lifted both men off the ground with her Talent and shook them, Vi was brought directly to King Gyre. He was among his men, reassuring them with his presence, and as Vi approached, he was cinching the leathers of a young horseman's pauldrons. Vi cleared her throat and Logan turned.

Vi had heard of Logan Gyre, of course, but seeing him was altogether different. He was perhaps the tallest man she'd ever seen, and perfectly proportioned. In his white enameled plate armor, gilded with a gyrfalcon with wingtips breaking a circle, he was the perfect picture of an energetic young king at war. He was muscular, his carriage erect, and though he walked with the knowledge that eyes were on him, he didn't seem to revel in it. There was also something odd about his right forearm. It seemed brighter than the other, somehow. "My lady," he said, nodding. "Is there something I can do for you?"

She stopped staring. "I'm Vi Sovari of the Chantry. I bring three hundred magae, and seven thousand more by tomorrow. We have come to help you."

"Thank you, I dare say we will have need of healers, but so many . . ."

"Your Majesty, we're war magae."

"War magae." The king's eyes widened.

"We have withdrawn from the Accords, that we may help you."

He scrubbed a hand through his blond hair. "This changes things. . . . They may have two thousand meisters, two hundred Vürdmeisters among them. We have ten magi. How can you help me?"

"Two thousand?" Vi despaired. "If they bring two thousand meisters against us before the rest of my Sisters arrive, we'll be worm food in an hour."

"I may have drawn off half of them. How long could you and your three hundred hold out against a thousand?"

"We might make it, and some of the Sisters should arrive during the day. My war magae are mostly good at defensive magic, Your Majesty."

"Good, then I want half of you to hold Black Bridge and the dam. Spread the others out through the lines." A messenger trotted up and Logan held up a finger, forestalling the man. "Oh, and thank you, Sister. Your aid is desperately needed and greatly appreciated. I hope to speak more with you this evening."

"You're welcome, and... Your Majesty, I know you were a friend of Kylar's. He'll be here."

Logan got a strange look on his face. "Yes," he said, "I'm sure he shall."

Vi was stationed with a hundred and fifty of her Sisters at Black Bridge, almost in the shadow of the great dam, when she realized what that look meant. Logan thought Vi meant Kylar would be here in spirit. Logan still thought Kylar was dead. *Stupid, Vi, stupid.*

Logan and Garuwashi were astride their mounts in the Great Market as the first rays of dawn revealed the God-king's armies arrayed across from their own. "They fell for it," he said. "They must have sent fifteen thousand men to Reigukhas. Last night, they had six thousand more men than we did. Now they have ten thousand less."

Lantano Garuwashi grinned. "Only two things can undo us now."

"Magic?"

"And young men so drunk on glory they forget their discipline," Garuwashi said.

"So when do we attack?" Logan asked.

"Right now."

It was still dark in the royal tent. Dorian ran a hand over Jenine's bare shoulder, down her back, and over her hip. Her beauty made him ache. He shouldn't have brought her here. It was too dangerous in too many ways. She wasn't asleep, but she feigned it for him. She knew how he enjoyed her. He inhaled the scent of her hair once more and sat up. He began dressing.

"That army is Cenarian," Jenine said in the darkness. "Those are my people."

"Yes," Dorian said.

"How do I find myself in my enemy's camp, my lord?"

"Have you ever wondered what would happen if someone threw a war and nobody came?"

"What do you mean?"

"I have no intention of killing any Cenarians," Dorian said, "though I understand why they won't believe that. We're here only to destroy Neph and Moburu. At dawn our emissaries will let the Cenarians know that we will not attack, but I don't think we have to worry about them. They've already taken a defensive position, as have we. They'll stay until they see us withdraw, and then they'll go home."

Jenine stood, and Dorian couldn't help but glory in her beauty. The familiar panic-edged desire swept over him. He wanted to grab her and make love frantically, right now, as if he might never have a chance to again. But it was almost dawn, there were things he needed to do.

"My people are aggrieved at your father's predations, and that savage Lantano Garuwashi is with them. They say he bathes in blood. What will we do if they attack? I will be our emissary," Jenine said. "They will believe me."

"No!" Dorian said.

"Why not?"

"It's dangerous."

"They will not attack a woman approaching under flag of parley. Besides, better a hazard to me than to forty thousand lives."

"It's not that," Dorian said, thinking furiously. "Your presence might precipitate war, my love. What will Terah Graesin do—even under a flag of parley, if she sees you alive? Your life would be the death of all her power. People will do horrible things to keep what they love, Jenine." The fact was, if he sent Jenine to Logan, the threat of Cenarian attack would end in one second—and so would his marriage.

Unless... what if Jenine chose him? She'd barely known Logan. What Dorian had built with her was... *real? It's built on a lie. Oh, Solon, what would you say if you could see me now?*

"You're right, my lord husband. I just wish there were something I could do."

Dorian kissed her. "Don't worry. It's going to be fine." He stepped through the tent flap and saw a young man sweating, obviously bearing a message for him, and obviously too afraid to wake a Godking. "What is it?" Wanhope demanded.

"Your Holiness. The warchief wishes me to tell you that the attack on Reigukhas was a ruse. Our spies were wrong. The Cenarians outnumber us by more than ten thousand now, and   Your Holiness, they're attacking."

Fighting in these damn robes was going to be a chore, but Vi was glad she hadn't worn her scandalous wetboy grays. Well, she'd worn them, but under the robes. Going into battle without her grays would be like going into battle with her hair unbound.

A blond man wider than he was tall brought his horse into the line next to her. A mage, she could tell. "Feir Cousat," he said. "You Vi?"

She nodded. They were positioned ten ranks back, behind pikemen and shield bearers who were guarding the bridge in front of the dam. From their elevated position, they could see the whole valley.

A flag went up among Garuwashi's men down in the market. The third time it waved, the Ceurans began marching toward the river. Lantano Garuwashi himself rode beside the front lines, and when he drew his sword, it glowed in the low light. A cheer went up.

Vi squinted at the sword. There was something wrong with it.

"What's wrong?" Feir asked.

"The glow . . . did you make that?"

"What?! You can see that from here?"

"It just looks like you. Like your work, I mean. I don't know."

The highlanders who made up the center of the Khalidoran line were slow to react. They did nothing until half of Garuwashi's five thousand had made the opposite bank. "What are they doing?" Feir asked. "The Khalidorans didn't shoot any arrows." Then the highlanders began trotting forward.

Garuwashi's flag dropped when the highlanders were thirty paces away and a shrill keening shriek sounded from every Ceuran throat. Shrieking, they charged. To a man, the sa'ceurai ran with their long swords trailing behind them, the other hand extended forward. Charge was too inelegant a term.

Then the lines crashed together. The average highlander was taller and thicker than the average sa'ceurai, but as the clash of arms and rattle of armor resounded to where Vi watched, it was highlanders who fell ten to one. The sa'ceurai whipped their swords under and up, or over and down, or feinted and threw their shoulders into the highlanders instead.

"Best solo fighters in the world," Feir said. "There are twice as many highlanders out there—and look."

Within minutes, the rest of the sa'ceurai had made the crossing. As Feir had said, both sides fought man-to-man, breaking into a thousand duels, though neither side was above hamstringing an enemy whose back was turned. Despite the bulkiness that made the sa'ceurai's lacquer armor look heavy, the men danced.

Lantano Garuwashi presided over it all, dealing death every time highlanders pushed through the lines to get to him, but mostly watching. The air around him winked and sparkled, and Vi figured those were arrows or magic the Khalidorans where shooting at him. A terrified-looking magus sat on a horse directly behind Garuwashi, making constant gestures as he protected the war leader.

Vi saw the effect of the meisters before she could see the meisters themselves. The sa'ceurai lines seemed to ripple back as if all of them had been struck at once. Then she saw green fireballs arcing over the highlanders to splatter among the sa'ceurai, the flame turning blue where it hit flesh and sizzling, black smoke rising from a hundred bodies on fire.

In that instant, the sa'ceurai advance faltered. Lantano Garuwashi waved his hand forward frantically, and his standard bearer was waving a flag furiously, but his men sank back. A dozen green fireballs splattered against Garuwashi's shields and they nearly collapsed. He swung his horse's head back toward the river and joined his men's retreat, waving his hands and cursing them all the way.

A cry went up from the highlanders and they surged forward. They'd routed the Ceurans.

But from the rear, where the Khalidorans couldn't see, it looked all wrong. While those in the front made big, panicky gestures, none threw down their weapons as they fled. The sa'ceurai closest to the river sheathed their blades and calmly carried the wounded between them in twos. Lantano Garuwashi's frenzied waving, the whipping flag—it hadn't been the same flag he'd used for the advance, had it?—it was all a setup.

"Palies comin'!" someone shouted.

Across the bridge in front of Vi, hundreds of Khalidoran soldiers were running to their places. Their archers loosed a flight of arrows. Feir threw his hands up and a shimmering transparent blue sheet of magic unrolled above the Cenarians, covering those at the foot of the bridge. The first arrows hit the shield and, to Vi's surprise, didn't burst into flame. Rather, they hit the shield like it was a pincushion, poked through it, and robbed of all speed, simply dropped the last five feet onto the Cenarians.

"Archers, shoot from outside the umbrella!" Feir shouted, but not before several of them had loosed shots into it. The outgoing arrows stabbed through the umbrella, flew half a dozen feet, then came to rest back on top of the umbrella again, lacking even the energy to make it back to the ground.

"Meisters!" someone screamed.

Before Vi found the dark figure across the bridge, something blasted her from her saddle. She met the rocky ground with far less speed than she had any right to expect.

"Make that 'vürdmeisters,' " Feir said, helping her up. "The bastards."

"You saved me," Vi said, noticing the unfamiliar shield around her as she stood.

"You owe me. Now do something. I'm tapped out."

A dozen green fireballs of various sizes arced across the bridge. Vi fumbled for her Talent, but her ears were still ringing. She was too slow.

Nonetheless, every one of the Khalidorans' falling fireballs was lifted like an arrow catching a sudden updraft, then curved in the air and smashed back into the Khalidoran lines. A woman whooped, and Vi recognized Sister Rhoga's voice. Vi's battle magae had practiced that weave for four days straight, but seeing it actually work took Vi's breath away.

Vi couldn't find her horse, though she had no idea how it could have gone anywhere through the massed ranks of pikemen, archers, and shield bearers who were holding the foot of Black Bridge. She pushed her way to the front.

The men maintaining the shield wall at the front line looked at her. Their shields were studded with dozens of arrows each. The Khalidoran archers had figured out that if they shot at a low enough trajectory, they could find targets here. "How much cover you want, Sister?" a skinny officer at least twenty years her senior asked. The first row of soldiers were on one knee, their shields covering them completely; the second row held their shields at an angle and a third held theirs overhead despite the umbrella. They were packed as tightly as possible.

"You, rest," Vi told a man in the second row. She pushed her way into place and poked her head through the shields.

She found the Vürdmeister by the swirling black vir-shield spinning in front of him. A moment later, half a dozen darts of mage fire plunged into his shield, magic breaking and spitting and sizzling in chunks on the bridge at his feet, but the Vürdmeister barely seemed to notice. He was looking down the river toward the ford at the Great Market.

The Khalidoran highlanders had pursued the sa'ceurai across the river, and thousands had now gained the Cenarian side. Vi's heart jumped into her throat.

A blue flare streaked into the sky over the Great Market. To Vi's right, a magus struggled out onto the narrow stone walkway that ran across the face of the dam. Because the waters poured over the top of the dam rather than through its centuries-closed sluices, the magus made his way through a deluge as water poured from fifty feet overhead. He held the handrail and climbed forward, hand over hand, struggling to keep his feet anchored to the stone. At the center of the walkway were two enormous pulleys, the chains wrapped around them still pristine. The chains themselves disappeared into the face of the dam where they would open the sluice gates. The magus threw thick blue ropes of magic at each of the pulleys, straining.

He had barely started when half a dozen Vürdmeisters who'd been hiding in the Khalidoran ranks burst forward. Fire, hammers of air, gales, and missiles engulfed the lone magus from every direction. The magus's shields held until a gleaming white homunculus winged its way to him. The magus screamed as the air ripped open and a pit wyrm struck.

The wyrm's jaws crunched through shield and man and one of the huge pulleys, then it pulled back into whatever hell it had come from and disappeared.

A moment later, half a dozen green fire missiles ripped into the other pulley, cracking it and snapping the chains.

Only as they destroyed the second pulley did Vi realize that she'd just seen Garuwashi's trap defanged. Garuwashi had feigned the rout to draw the Khalidorans into the river where he meant to drown them. But the Khalidorans had known. Why else would they have concealed the presence of six Vürdmeisters? Now Garuwashi had just had his trap turned back on himself.

"Feir!" Vi shouted. She turned and was surprised to see he was right behind her, the dread in his eyes telling her he understood. "Can you protect me?"

His eyes flicked to the Vürdmeisters, who to Vi's eyes looked all the same. "Three seconds, two thirds, and a sixth shu'ra. Shit. Maybe?"

One of the younger Vürdmeisters laughed, turning his head over his shoulder to say something. Vi lashed out, grabbed the hem of his robe, and yanked. If Vi had thought about it, she wouldn't have tried. She couldn't reach that far. She never had.

The man was halfway down the gorge before he screamed.

Feir's eyes were huge. "Nice grab."

"This is the stupidest thing I've ever done," Vi said. With her Talent, she pushed men aside right and left. The dam's walkway was a good thirty feet out and twenty down. She ripped off her robes.

"Distract them. Now!" she shouted.

The battle magae complied, flinging dozens of fireballs.

Vi ran through the space she'd cleared, a few quick steps taking her to a full sprint. She leapt into the void, barely remembering to shield herself. The jump was perfect. She landed with both feet on the middle of the walkway, splashing water every direction, then her momentum carried her into the wall of the dam. Her shield helped, it was still a twenty-foot fall. Vi crunched into the wall and then rebounded. She clawed blindly and felt stone under her fingertips for a brief instant, then she was flying into space.

Stupid, Vi, stupid.

She imagined she could hear Nysos laughing. She hadn't thought of the god of potent liquids in months, and here she was, killed by water.

She tensed for impact, but it never came. Vi opened her eyes and couldn't see anything through the torrent. Then she was clear of it. She saw a thick rope of Talent knotted around her and extending all the way back to Sister Ariel, who was grimacing with the effort. In another moment, Vi was next to one of the chains. She grabbed it and Sister Ariel released her.

Vi was instantly swept off her feet and spun by the force of the water, but with effort she regained her feet. Above her she saw the Vürdmeisters— there were only three now—throwing fiery death toward her, but nothing came even close. On the Cenarian shore two hundred women glowed like torches with Talent: her Sisters. They were protecting her, and nothing could stop them. Vi's heart swelled to bursting. These women would die for her. For the first time in her life, she belonged.

She was crying and laughing even as she found the other chain. She stood with one chain in each hand, each link as long as her forearm. She heaved, but without the pulleys it was just too heavy.

She moved back a step, out of the dam's shadow into the sun. It wasn't quite noon. She felt sunlight drenching her skin and she opened herself to it, opened herself until it burned, until it filled every pore with heat.

Then she heaved again. At first, nothing moved, and then she felt as if deep within the dam mechanisms were threatening to give way, protesting deep in their iron throats, and finally...turning. Her Talent extended beyond her arms, gripping the chains like half a dozen hands, grabbing, pulling, and grabbing again. Hissing filled her ears, and she opened her eyes. Something was glowing, blindingly bright. It was her. She was luminous. Vi glowed like the Seraph herself. Steam rose in great hissing billows where the water washed over her limbs.

The sluice gates cracked open, three on the left and three on the right. Vi pulled, feeling her strength waning. She had to finish. She pulled one more time and felt the gates lock open. The water pouring over the top of the dam onto her slowed, stopped. She could see again.

The six open gates below her jetted water into the valley with incredible force. The water blasted into the thousands of highlanders crossing into the Great Market. Men clambered for higher ground, stampeding toward shore, crushing their fellows underfoot.

Only Garuwashi's men were unfazed by the flood. Whether or not they had seen how near their trap had come to collapsing, the sa'ceurai were ready for it to work. Through all the high ground surrounding the Great Market, they closed ranks and shut down choke points expertly. Then they surged back, pushing Khalidorans to a watery death. In places, men clawed their way over the sa'ceurai's shields, but they were quickly cut down.

Vi became aware that everyone on the bridge was staring at her. They were all shouting, cheering. She was still holding the chains. They were suddenly unbearably heavy. She dropped them and staggered. Hands grabbed her, steadied her. A dozen Sisters had ventured out onto the slick walkway to come to her.

Sisters. My sisters. Vi started crying, and no one looked at her like she was stupid.

Lantano Garuwashi was the first to understand the implications of what occurred at the dam. The trap he and Agon and Logan had worked up had always assumed that they would be able to close the sluice gates after they opened them. With the destruction of the pulleys, it was a miracle they'd been opened in the first place. After flooding out the highlanders, he and Logan had planned to throw everything at the shaken Khalidoran army. Caught between the Ceurans and the Cenarians and the cursed ground of the Dead Demesne, the Khalidoran army would have broken in minutes. Instead, the allies' armies could only advance across the narrow bridges.

Garuwashi ordered the crossing and ordered magae to protect the bridges. If he'd been the Khalidorans, that's what he would try to destroy.

He was right. The counterattack was almost solely magical. Hundreds of meisters had hit each of the bridges, but then, suddenly, they'd been called off. The magae told him they could see a magical conflagration on the far side of Black Barrow itself, Khalidorans fighting barbarians, but they couldn't tell him anything else. Had he been able to ford the river, he could have taken advantage of the Godking's splitting his army. But that was water literally under the bridge. He established beachheads and put engineers to work widening the bridges by whatever means they could, but the situation looked grim.

As soon as the Khalidorans saw that his men were establishing fortifications and not attacking, they withdrew to high points hundreds of paces away and began working on their own.

In the early afternoon, Garuwashi found King Gyre in their command tent, which had been moved to the foot of Ox Bridge.

"Today was a great victory," Logan said. "They lost more than nine thousand highlanders. I lost ninety men holding the market. How many sa'ceurai?"

"One hundred fifteen in baiting the trap. Eight in springing it."

"Two hundred men, to kill nine thousand," Logan said. He didn't elaborate. It was a victory, but it was a victory that was a prelude to defeat.

"Tomorrow their fifteen thousand come back from Reigukhas, and you lose my sa'ceurai," Garuwashi said.

"How long until the Regent arrives?" Logan asked.

"An hour. His messengers have asked that he see me immediately." It wasn't right. After such a great victory, he should be looking on the morrow with relish. Instead, this night he would kill himself. Many of his sa'ceurai would join him. The twenty thousand sa'ceurai who accompanied the Regent would simply turn and go home.

"Can't you just use the illusion you used today?" Logan asked.

Garuwashi sighed. "Feir said there's something about the magic of the blade that interferes with illusions. The glow looked good from ten or twenty paces while the sword was cutting back and forth, but from up close? It wouldn't withstand a child's scrutiny."

"Your Majesties, if I may?" Feir asked. Garuwashi hadn't seen him arrive, despite his huge bulk. It was a measure of how exhausted he was. Logan gestured Feir to continue. "I made that sword. If we can find a ruby to hold the spells, I dare say I'm the only person in the world who could tell the difference between the new Ceur'caelestos and the real thing. We don't even need a special ruby. It just needs to be big. King Gyre, I'm sure your treasury has something that will work. It seems ridiculous that we'd give up this close."

"It's not giving up," Garuwashi snapped. "It's having our fraud discovered."

"What if they didn't discover it?" Feir asked.

"The Regents have been waiting centuries for this," Logan said. "I'm sure they have some kind of test to determine if the blade is real."

"So what if they do?" Feir asked. "The Regent's not Talented and you have magae at your disposal. With a little preparation, we can—"

"Get out," Garuwashi breathed. "I listened to you once and dishonored myself. No more. You know nothing of sa'ceurai. Begone, snake."

Feir's face drained of color. He stood slowly. Garuwashi turned his back to him. He almost hoped Feir would strike him down. Let Garuwashi die betrayed. Then any flaw found with the sword would be assumed to be the work of the betrayer. Something would be left of Garuwashi's name.

"If you would save this army and all these thousands of souls, the magae and I will be near," Feir said quietly. "If you would save only your precious honor, you can go to hell."

When Garuwashi turned, the big man was gone. King Gyre looked at him silently.

"What is a king without honor?" Garuwashi asked. "These men mean everything to me. They have followed me from villages and cities to foreign lands. Where I have gone, they have gone. When I have told a hundred to take a hill, knowing it would cost ninety their lives, they have obeyed. They are lions. If they are to die, they should die in battle, not dishonored by their lord. Tomorrow, you will face twenty thousand Khalidorans and two thousand meisters, who barely fought today. Without the sa'ceurai, your men will be shaken."

"Seeing six thousand men and their unbeatable general kill themselves may do that," Logan said dryly. "As will looking at the backs of twenty thousand sa'ceurai who could have been allies."

"You are a king. What would you do?" Garuwashi asked.

"You ask me that when I have such an interest in your answer?"

"I saw you put your closest friend to death for honor."

Logan looked at his hands. He said nothing for a long time. "The night before Kylar went to the wheel, I sent a man to break him out of my own gaol. Kylar refused to leave because it would hurt my reign. He believed in me that much. To be king means to accept that others will pay the price of your failures—and even your successes. Part of me died on that wheel. Whatever you decide, doen-Lantano, it has been an honor to fight beside you."

"King Gyre, if I choose expiation, will you be my second?"

Logan Gyre bowed low, his face rigid. "Doen-Lantano, I would be honored."

He'd been mad. Feir had followed the instructions of an insane archmagus who was seven centuries dead. Feir had made a sword that even he didn't fully understand. He had bent even Lantano Garuwashi to his will. He had believed, and now fraud would build on fraud unless Lantano Garuwashi chose to end it all.

Having sworn himself to the warleader, Feir would be expected to suicide along with Garuwashi, but he wouldn't. He knew that. Of course, the warleader might slay him. But Feir didn't think he'd allow that, either. So he would cheat again, and defend himself with magic. Every sa'ceurai in Midcyru would despise him. Perhaps one would hunt him down. That was Feir's future. Either that, or serving forever as Lantano Garuwashi's illusionist-in-chief, threading pretend flames onto his beautiful sword for the rest of his life.

That deception would destroy Lantano Garuwashi. If he ruled, he would rule badly, knowing himself to be dishonored. Garuwashi was not so young that honor was the only important thing in his life, but he was sa'ceurai to the roots of his soul. The best thing for Garuwashi would be to bury a blade in his own guts.

The sun sat low in the sky as Feir ducked to step into the council tent. Inside the tent sat King Gyre, Lord General Agon Brant, a wan Vi Sovari, and an older maja Feir didn't recognize. Feir took an empty seat. King Gyre sat with folded hands to Feir's right. His face was emotionless, but that in itself told Feir that the king was worried. As Feir pulled his chair in, something about Logan's right arm drew his attention. There was some magic there, woven small and tight into Logan's vambrace or his arm.

Logan noticed his attention and folded his hands in his lap, under the table. Feir dismissed it and continued looking around the table. Vi Sovari had covered herself with a modest maja's dress, but at the wrists and neck her gray-black skin-tight wetboy's garb was still visible. She had dark circles under her eyes and her skin was pale from her magical exertions at the dam. She was four places down the table, almost at the end of Feir's magical vision, but he could see she hadn't overextended her Talent. After Solon had used Curoch, he'd looked broken. His hair had grown in white, and he'd only escaped permanent injuries because Dorian was such a gifted Healer. With her escapades at the dam, Vi hadn't hurt herself at all. She'd come near the limit of her gifts, but hadn't exceeded it. Feir suspected that with a good night's sleep, she'd be ready to do as much tomorrow. She was easily the most powerful mage here. She might even equal Solon. And, sitting up straight now at a word from the old maja at her right hand, Vi felt huge. As a man's muscles looked most impressive after hard labor, so now did Vi's Talent feel enormous. It made Feir feel small, and he didn't like it.

The tent flap opened suddenly, and every eye turned to it, but the man who stepped in wasn't Lantano Garuwashi. It was a dark-haired, dark-eyed Alitaeran with a waxed mustache and an eagle sigil on his cloak pin. A Marcus then, from one of Alitaera's most important families, and certainly the leader of the two thousand Alitaeran lancers who'd arrived with the last of the magae this afternoon.

"I didn't realize this council had anything to do with the Alitaeran military," Lord General Agon Brant said. Clearly there was some bad blood there.

"This council decides if we've got an extra twenty thousand sa'ceurai or if we lose the six thousand we've got. I'd say that makes it a council of war. I'm Tiberius Antonius Marcus, Praetor, Fourth Army, Second Maniple. We're to defend the Chantry. Sisters, Your Majesty." He nodded to them.

"An honor, Praetor, please join us," Logan said.

Before the man sat, the flap opened again and Lantano Garuwashi strode in. He rested his hand over the pommel of his sword and walked to his seat and sat before acknowledging anyone.

"Well, everyone's here now except the Ceuran Regent himself, and of course, the dear Lae'knaught Overlord, who I suppose will walk in half an hour late and ask that we repeat everything," Lord General Brant said.

"I suppose he will," Logan said. "Since I told him this council wouldn't meet for another half an hour."

There were some snickers, but Feir breathed easier. A Lae'knaught overlord would likely have all sorts of magic-dampening paraphernalia that would spoil a perfectly good illusion.

What little chatter had been going around the room soon died as the sound of thousands of marching feet approached the tent. All twenty thousand sa'ceurai were coming.

This could get ugly

The tent flap opened and a teenage boy and a middle-aged man with a fringe of auburn hair around an oiled pate stepped in. The middle-aged man had four locks of hair bound to his, all of them Ceuran, all of them old. He stood aside to make way for the boy, who couldn't have been more than fifteen. The boy had fiery orange hair, cropped close to his skull, and a single, very long lock bound into his hair. He wore ornately embroidered blue silk robes and a ruby-encrusted sword.

Feir had the insane thought of breaking off the biggest ruby and using it for his fraud.

"Sisters, Lords, Praetor, Your Majesty," the middle-aged Ceuran said, "may I introduce Sa'sa'ceurai Hideo Mitsurugi, sixth Regent Hideo, Lord of Mount Tenji, Protector of the Holy Honor, Keeper of the High Seat, Lord General of the Held Armies of Ceura."

People around the table greeted the boy. Logan stood and clasped his forearm. The boy was a little overwhelmed, but even as he followed protocol to the best of his ability, he could barely take his eyes off Lantano Garuwashi. He must be the boy's hero, Feir thought. Of course, Lantano Garuwashi was probably every young sa'ceurai's hero.

Garuwashi eyed the middle-aged man more than the boy. Was he the real power? The boy a figurehead? As the boy and his minister got closer and took their seats, Feir's heart dropped. The middle-aged man was a court mage of some kind, his Talent formidable. Garuwashi caught Feir's eye and shook his head slightly. It was the signal to abandon the fraud.

It was over. Only death would follow.

Hideo Mitsurugi cleared his throat. "I guess, uh, we might as well do what we're here for, shall we?" His eyes flicked upward as he tried to remember his lines. "It has been brought to our attention that claims have been brought forward by you or by your followers, doen-Lantano Garuwashi. We understand you have claimed to wield the Blade of Heaven, Ceur'caelestos."

"I have made such claims, doen-Hideo," Garuwashi said. There was something almost cheerful in Garuwashi's face. He'd been doing something wrong that he hadn't liked, and now it was finished.

"By ancient law and prophecy, the holder of Ceur'caelestos is to be Ceura's king, a man to usher in the return of the High King, whose reign will announce the birth of the Champion of the Light." Mitsurugi paused. He'd lost his place. A panicked look came into his blue eyes.

The middle-aged mage whispered a prompt in the boy's ear. It seemed to embarrass Hideo almost to tears. "Do you claim the High Seat of Ceura, Lantano Garuwashi?"

"I do."

What was he doing? Feir shot a look over at Garuwashi's sword. The dragon of the pommel grinned emptily like a boy who'd lost both front teeth.

"Hold on," Lord General Agon said. "It was my understanding that Ceura's Regent is doen-Hideo Watanabe. How do we even know that—pardon me—this boy has the authority to test Lantano Garuwashi?"

"You dare!" the middle-aged sa'ceurai said, putting a hand to his sword.

"Yes, I dare," Agon said. "And if you draw that sword, I'll dare feed it to you."

"Ha. You're an old cripple."

"Which will make your death all the more embarrassing," Agon said.

"Stop!" Mitsurugi said. "Hideo Watanabe is my father." He looked down. "Was. He gathered this army. But before he marched, I learned that he didn't intend to test you, doen-Lantano. He intended to kill you—whether or not you held the real Ceur'caelestos. I confronted him for dishonoring the regency." Tears came to Mitsurugi's eyes. "We dueled, and I slew him."

Feir couldn't believe it. The boy killed his father for the *idea* of Lantano Garuwashi.

"I am Regent now, and by my father's blood that stains my hands, I have the right to test the man who would be our king," Hideo Mitsurugi said. "Please, doen-Lantano, show us Ceur'caelestos."

There was the sound of something tearing and everyone stopped and looked to the back of the tent, where a knife was cutting a vertical slash all the way to the ground. Instantly, every maja and magus embraced their Talent and a dozen hands went to the hilts of swords. An assassin would have a hard time with this crowd.

A hand poked in and waved. "Pardon me," a man's deep voice said outside the tent. "If I step inside, am I going to be skewered?" Not waiting for an answer, he stepped inside.

He had pure white hair with black tips, deeply tanned olive skin, and a muscular bare chest beneath a rich cloak. He wore loose white pants and a thick gold crown sat snug against his brow.

"Solon?" Feir asked, astonished.

Solon smiled. "Only to you, my dear friend. As for the rest of you, pardon my unconventional entrance, but you have twenty thousand surly sa'ceurai blocking the front of the tent. I am Solonariwan Tofusin, King of Seth. I would say emperor, but as of ten years ago we have no more colonies, so 'Emperor' is a tad pretentious. Your Majesty, King Gyre, I bring a thousand men to your efforts. I did also bring five ships, but someone flooded the river this morning and now I have only two and I'm lucky not to have lost any men. Sisters, should we emerge from this conflict alive, I will be asking the Chantry for reimbursement. Feir, it seems you travel in exalted company these days. Ah, this must be Sister Ariel Wyant, a legend in your own time, and Vi Sovari, both buxom and brilliant—I've heard so much about you."

"Eat shit," Vi said.

Gasps arose around the table, and Sister Ariel put her hands on her temples.

"Apparently all I've heard is true," Solon said.

He wasn't acting like himself. Solon never prattled, but now he was speaking so quickly that even if anyone had known what to say they couldn't have fit a word in.

"I have to tell you, on my way here, I saw a very dour Lae'knaught gentlemen speaking some rather choice words at being denied entry by the selfsame sa'ceurai who barred yours truly from said engagement. But here I stand, at considerable cost to my kingdom, and most especially my marriage—it took me weeks of moping about Whitecliff to secure my wife's permission to come. Oh, you married men can pretend to be the masters of your castles and keeps and so forth, but the mistress of the bedchamber is the mistress of the master, eh? Regardless, here I stand, and I must say, the crowning jewel of my visit is this: Lantano Garuwashi, it is a great honor to meet you." Solon strode over to the sa'ceurai and extended his hand.

"I don't clasp hands with fish," Lantano Garuwashi said.

Hideo Mitsurugi snorted, but no one else said a word.

Suddenly, Solon's rushed and—to Feir's eyes—panicky demeanor shifted. Solon had tripped over his tongue to get to Lantano Garuwashi, but now that he had the man's attention, he was utterly patient. "It seems to me," Solon said, "that a man born to an iron blade should not scorn the friendship of kings."

Dead silence settled on the room. No one spoke like that to Lantano Garuwashi.

Solon continued, "You have no peer when it comes to the spilling of blood, Lantano Garuwashi. If you died today, your only legacy would be blood. Wouldn't you rather your legacy was that of a man who spilled blood to quench the fires of war? Can butcher's hands become carpenter's hands? As a brother king, I ask you once more, and once only, will you take the hand of friendship?" Solon stood with hand extended.

It was an odd thing to ask a doomed man. Feir expected Garuwashi to spit in Solon's face. But Garuwashi stood. "Let there be peace between us," he said, and took Solon's hand.

Standing right next to them, his own bulk blocking most of the table from seeing what transpired, Feir saw sudden confusion in Lantano Garuwashi's eyes. He withdrew his hand from Solon's clasp with one finger still pressed against his palm, concealing something. Then he rested that hand on Ceur'caelestos's pommel. With a tiny sound, something clicked home, and Feir understood. Gods! "The greatest red gives dragon's heart and head." Feir had thought it meant the greatest red ruby, and it did, but it also meant the greatest red mage: Solon.

Garuwashi whipped the sword out of its scabbard and slammed it on the table.

A perfect ruby redder than ruby-red burned in the pommel, and it swam with deep magic, though Feir hadn't imbued it with any weaves. The mistarille blade had patterns like a folded steel blade, but its patterns glittered like diamonds, sparkling and then transparent, letting a man see all the way through the blade into the heart of its magic. As they watched, every diamond-like ripple faded to a purer translucence like a slow shockwave as the twin dragons breathed fire. The fire blossomed in a thick bar from hilt all the way to the point of the sword. The heat of it warmed Feir's face.

Feir had created something beyond himself. He was a great smith, but he wasn't this good. Awed, Feir turned to Solon. The new King Tofusin grinned at him.

"Call me fraud or call me king," Lantano Garuwashi said, and if there was a trembling of wonder in his voice, no one noticed it through their own.

Hideo Mitsurugi's jaw was slack. "Lantano Garuwashi, I declare you—"

"My lord!" the court mage interrupted.

Mitsurugi acquiesced. "My ancestors have looked forward to this day for centuries. We've wanted it and feared it. Perhaps the regents most of all. Frauds have been attempted, so the Regent's sword carries a test. I beg your pardon, doen-Lantano, but it is my duty." He drew his ruby-encrusted blade and gave the pommel a sharp twist. It clicked and he pulled half of the hilt off. Inside was a thin scroll woven with preservation magics. Mitsurugi read it, his lips moving as he puzzled out the old language.

"Lantano Garuwashi, banish the fires from the blade."

Garuwashi took the blade and the fires died. How did he know how to do that?

"I need a candle," Mitsurugi said, and someone slid one down the table to him. He picked it up and brought it toward the blade.

Terror seized Feir's breath. Mitsurugi brought the candle to the very spot Feir had hidden his vanity, his own smithmark. The crossed war hammers practically leapt out of the metal.

Mitsurugi sighed.

Feir's heart stopped.

Mitsurugi said, "Down to Oren Razin's crossed war hammers, it's real. This blade is Ceur'caelestos. Lantano Garuwashi, you are the lost King of Ceura. The sa'ceurai stand at your word."

Real. Not a forgery. The very things that made it different from Curoch were what convinced the Regent that Feir's blade was real. Feir's limbs felt weak. He had a single moment to think, *how embarrassing, I can't possibly pass—*

Then he passed out.

89

After Feir collapsed—and what was that about? Ariel wondered—the odious Overlord of the Lae'knaught, Julus Rotans, finally won his way through the waiting sa'ceurai and made it into the tent. Hideo Mitsurugi wanted to go immediately and announce that Ceura had found its king, but Logan had asked him to wait. Ariel still didn't know why.

Julus Rotans was in his late forties, his figure still trim and military and his features pure Alitaeran. He wore a white tabard emblazoned with a sun and a white cloak with twelve gold chevrons. Sister Ariel couldn't make out any other details: the man emanated such a deep aura of ill health she almost gagged. He didn't remove his gauntlets as he sat, and mercifully there were no open sores on his face, but Julus Rotans was a leper. Worse, his strain of leprosy was the simplest kind to Heal. Even Sister Ariel could do it—but it would take magic.

"So, everyone's here already," Julus Rotans said. "I see. No need to include the Lae'knaught in the planning, huh? Just throw us at the thickest part of the enemy, and whether we live or die, you win."

Logan Gyre didn't look perturbed. "Overlord, I have wronged you," he said. "Your representatives told me it was unfair and unwise—actually, I think the word was 'stupid'—for me to assume direct control over your men. Forgive me. I was worried they would betray me. That was unworthy of me, and it was indeed stupid."

The overlord's eyes narrowed, wary. Everyone else watched carefully.

"Today, due to the terrain, your men didn't fight, but tomorrow, we will rely on you. Your losses may be significant. You have our only heavy cavalry, and you will indeed hold the center. There have been . . . ugly rumors that your men wish to withdraw and let 'all these wytches' kill each other." Logan sighed. "I know you feel compelled to be here, Overlord Rotans, so I wish to drop the compulsion now. And I do so hereby: Overlord, I freely grant you the fifteen-year lease to the Cenarian lands for your use. I hereby release you from fielding an army and putting them at my service."

"What?" the overlord asked. He wasn't the only one incredulous at the table. Without the Lae'knaught's five thousand, the armies would be seriously weakened.

Logan held up one finger, and the overlord sat up, sure this was the teeth of the trap. "I only ask that if you wish to withdraw from this fight, that you declare your intentions immediately so that we may know how much of an army we will have."

Overlord Rotans licked his lips. "That's all?" It was too fair a request for him to protest. Logan didn't want the Lae'knaught fielding the army and then melting away at the first Khalidoran charge. He still looked puzzled, so he hadn't seen the teeth of Logan's offer yet, and the damn fool was about to speak. He was going to accept the offer if Ariel didn't do something.

"I'm only a woman," Sister Ariel said, "but it seems to me that such cowardice will make recruitment a challenge in a few countries. Let's see. Cenaria, of course, will feel betrayed. Ceura too. Oh, and I doubt the praetor would be impressed, so definitely Alitaera—that's a tough one to lose. Waeddryn and Modai may still send recruits; pity they're so small."

"And their people so historically reluctant to die for the light of reason," Praetor Marcus said with some satisfaction.

"And this is such a bad time to have trouble with recruitment," Sister Ariel said.

"Why's that?" Marcus asked, playing along.

"Some superstition in Ezra's Wood recently slew five thousand Lae'knaught."

Marcus whistled. "That's some superstition."

"You're vile, all of you. You're the friends of darkness," Overlord Rotans said.

"There's the crux," King Solonariwan Tofusin said. "You see, friends, the Lae'knaught have no country; they have only ideas. If they abandon us, they can survive the allegations of betrayal and cowardice; what will cut them is *hypocrisy*. They can betray us, what they can't betray is their principles. Today we faced perhaps a hundred meisters, but this Godking Wanhope brought two thousand. Where were the rest?"

"Do you actually know the answer to that question?" Lantano Garuwashi asked.

"We passed a town called Reigukhas on our way up the river," Solon said. "It was dead. From the magic still in the air, hundreds—perhaps thousands—of meisters worked for at least twelve hours raising krul. Those krul then devoured the city's inhabitants. Tomorrow we will face actual, real creatures of darkness, Overlord. I'd estimate their numbers to be in excess of twenty thousand."

"Shit, there goes our twenty thousand sa'ceurai advantage," Vi said.

"One sa'ceurai is not offset by one krul," Hideo Mitsurugi said, offended.

"Do you even know what a krul is?" Vi asked.

"The point is," Sister Ariel broke in, "when they have a chance to fight the spawn of darkness, the world will see that the Lae'knaught are hypocrites who prefer to turn tail."

Julus Rotans was actually shaking with rage. "Go to hell, wytch. Go to hell, all of you. Tomorrow you will see how the Laetunariverissiknaught fight. We will take the center of any charge. I will lead it myself."

"A generous offer. We accept," Logan Gyre said immediately, "with the caveat that I ask that you not lead any charge yourself. I'm afraid, Overlord Rotans, that there are simply too many who would wish to see you fall in this battle."

The obvious target of the comment was the magae, but Sister Ariel saw that what Logan feared was the Lae'knaught's own men, who were doubtless chafing at having to fight beside wytches. If Julus Rotans fell, the Lae'knaught would retreat. In offering an honorable exit from rash words— or had the Overlord actually hoped to die and thereby allow his men to retreat and the Cenarians and everyone else to be betrayed and slaughtered?—Logan Gyre not only kept the Overlord alive and his army at Logan's disposal, he also might have gained some goodwill from the man, who if nothing else had shown that he was willing to talk. Sometimes the devil you knew was better than the one you didn't.

Sister Ariel looked at Logan Gyre with newfound respect. In this meeting of kings and magi, praetors and overlords, he had taken command without the least effort. He must have had some intelligence of a Lae'knaught betrayal or he wouldn't have brought the matter up. Now he had effectively defanged the threat, and managed to look magnanimous doing it.

"Now, before we discuss specifics of our disposition on the battlefield, does anyone else have anything to add? Sister Viridiana?" Logan asked.

He looked at Vi, who looked like she'd been on the verge of offering something for a while.

Vi bit her lip. "There was an explosion of magic earlier this afternoon on the other side of Black Barrow. Our source said there was a fight between the Godking's meisters and a bunch following one of his rivals, a man named Moburu Ursuul."

"May the God see fit to send that traitor's soul to hell on the edge of my sword," the praetor whispered.

"Moburu is claiming to be some prophesied High King," Vi said. "Apparently, he seems to fulfill the conditions. I didn't think anything of it until the Regent said that making Lantano a king would clear the way for a High King."

Sister Ariel wondered if her own face was as pale as everyone else's around the table. She probably knew more about the High King than any of them, but it had never occurred to her that it might be a Khalidoran who fulfilled the prophecy.

"You said Moburu fought the Godking. Who won?" Logan asked.

"Moburu was driven to Black Barrow."

"In our prophecies," Lantano Garuwashi said, standing, "When Ceura has a king once more, that king will fight beside the High King. I will never fight beside this Moburu. This I swear on my soul." He put his hand on Ceur'caelestos and it flared to life in answer. Then he sheathed the blade and sat.

"That's good enough for me," Praetor Marcus said. "In Alitaera the prophecies of a High King speak of days of turmoil and woe, so I don't envy you the troubles the next decades may visit on you. But I think that's one problem we may safely dismiss for now."

"Sister Viridiana, you said you had two things?" Logan asked.

Vi glanced at Sister Ariel, "I'm not actually a full Sister yet. Anyway, I'm sorry to bring a personal matter before this council, but does anyone know where Elene Cromwyll is?"

No one showed any sign of recognition. "The name sounds familiar," King Gyre said. "Who is she?"

"She's Kylar's wife," Vi said. "And he's going to come for her."

Logan's face lost all color. Everyone else looked curious but unknowing, except for Solon and Feir, who both looked afraid. Afraid of Kylar? Regardless, they knew him. Sister Ariel's fear was for Vi. The damn fool girl had casually spilled a truth that could spell her own destruction. "Oh, by the way, I'm not married to Kylar." If Logan had proved how excellent he was at this kind of council, Vi had shown herself to stand at the antipodes.

"You're right, that's more of a personal matter. I'll speak with you about that later," Logan said. He thought Vi was crazy. Thank the gods. "Are there any other questions?"

"I have some," Praetor Marcus said. "What if Black Barrow isn't meant to keep things out? What if it's meant to keep something in? What if Moburu wasn't driven there? What if he went to get something?"

"Oh, gods," someone said.

The armies formed up while it was still dark. Stomach knotted with tension, Logan tended to his horse, checking the straps a third time. The allied armies were stretched left and right, extending further and deeper than anything he'd ever seen. The Lae'knaught's five thousand would lead the charge. Behind them, twenty thousand Cenarian infantry would take the center, flanked by twenty thousand sa'ceurai. Lantano Garuwashi's original five thousand sa'ceurai would secure the forest to the west to make sure the Khalidorans didn't have any nasty surprises hiding there, and if possible sweep from the forest into the Godking's camp. A thousand of Vi's Shield Sisters would hold the dam and the bridges from magical attacks. The other seven thousand had spread out among the armies according to a logic they didn't deign to share with Logan. The two thousand Alitaeran light cavalry and one thousand Sethi light infantry would be their reserves.

Much would depend on the first Lae'knaught charge. With twenty thousand krul added to their ranks, the Khalidorans would have forty-five thousand to stand against the allies' fifty-three thousand—or sixty thousand if one counted the Shield Sisters. The Khalidorans would have their backs to the Dead Demesne. If the first Lae'knaught charge could shatter them against it, the army could be halved and separated from command.

Of course, no one really knew how krul fought. The magi had offered centuries-old accounts of brutes with great strength, poor eyesight, and an inability to feel pain. That last was the most worrying. "What kind of a monster can't feel pain?" Garuwashi asked. Overlord Rotans jerked in his chair. "They'll die like anything else," he said, angry at the curious glances.

Odd man, never took off his heavy gauntlets in six hours of deliberations. And through it all, Solon had offered excellent suggestions that reminded Logan of how much time Solon had spent on tactics with Regnus Gyre. Solon, Logan's tutor, was now a king. It was all Logan could do to keep from demanding an explanation from the man right in front of everyone.

"Your Majesty," his guard Aurella said, "do you remember last month, when you went down to the Hole again?"

Logan made it a habit to go every month. He was sorry to inflict it on his bodyguards, but he hadn't stopped. Logan looked at Aurella, sitting ahorse, holding her sword like she knew what to do with it now. She was one of the few women of the Order of the Garter who'd chosen to join Logan's bodyguard rather than go back to their lives after Pavvil's Grove. Logan hadn't been surprised when Garuwashi had singled her out as a natural talent with the sword. Not as strong as a man, he'd said pointedly, but damn good for a woman. Aurella had wisely chosen not to take offense. Logan said, "You asked me what kind of idiot I was to keep going down to that hell, when it gives me nightmares every time." She had, of course, been more diplomatic.

"You told me it was to prove nightmares had no power over you," Aurella said.

"You're making me nervous."

"I think you should mount, sire."

Logan mounted. The gloom of night was lifting by slow degrees, revealing nothing more than the deeper blackness of the Dead Demesne advancing toward them. It took Logan far too long to understand what he was seeing. It was krul, bodies dark gray or mottled black or even white, loping forward in a massive wave. There had to be eighty thousand krul alone. The Khalidoran army was at least a hundred thousand strong, and every one of them stood between Logan and his wife. His right arm tingled as rage washed over him.

"Vi," Logan barked. "Give me light!"

"Look away!" the maja shouted. The order was an exercise in futility. The Sisters had given Vi a new dress, deeming both the scandalous wetboy grays and the plain robes of an Adept ill suited to the woman they were now calling Battle Mistress. The new dress was red, with skirts divided for riding. Logan suspected it might be woven entirely of magic. It shimmered despite the low light, and—as Vi's figure did in any garb—it demanded attention. "Luxe exeat!" she yelled.

Logan barely looked away in time, and despite his closed eyes, the light was blinding. There was a rush and when he looked, a white fireball was arcing out over the plain, then it froze in midair. Moments later, a dozen more followed from points all along the line, illuminating the charging krul, who'd already closed half the distance.

"Signal ready!"

Another maja in Vi's cadre gestured and a magical version of the signal flag flew into the air over Logan's head, glowing and big enough for the entire army to see.

The rattling of armor and stirrups, low curses and prayers, the creaking of leather, the popping of knuckles, and the synchronized clash of the Lae'knaught lances on shields yielded to the sudden ululations of the sa'ceurai battle chant.

"Advance!"

The magical signal winked out and was replaced with a waving red banner. The sa'ceurai ululations pitched higher, and the army rumbled forward.

Kylar came through the pass as the armies on the plains below sprinted the last paces toward each other. He was too far away to hear the crash, but he could see the shock of it passing through the ranks. He continued running, not slowing as he passed the camp followers who had gathered to watch the battle, many of them carrying all their possessions in case the battle turned out badly.

He lost sight of the battle as he sprinted down the valley. Those few armed men he encountered he passed before they could raise a challenge, until he got to Black Bridge. There, half a dozen men with pikes and short swords at their belts turned from the battle to watch his approach.

"Hold!" a young man shouted.

As Kylar stopped in front of them, a crack like thunder shook the earth. Kylar was the only one who kept his feet. He turned his eyes to Black Barrow. The slight rises and dips of the plain between him and the great dome were covered with warriors, both human and krul, but the battle slowed as those not in the front line looked to the great shining black sphere. Another thunder crack shook the plain, and this time, jagged cracks raced from the highest point of the dome down its sides. Men cursed in fear and wonder.

The third crack shattered the dome from inside. Huge chunks of black rock three feet thick exploded into the air and rained onto the Dead Demesne and the battlefield, crushing krul and men alike. Most of the dome still stood, quivering, edges sharp around the hole in its crown.

More sharp blows followed and the rest of the dome fell in, raising a huge cloud of black dust like a stain of night across the morning. Something huge moved inside it.

"What is that?" the young man guarding the bridge asked.

Kylar was already running.

Most of the fighting men had noticed nothing. The grim business of war took all their attention. The allies' armies were doing extremely well if what Kylar had seen of their relative numbers was accurate. He saw one of Agon's archers fit an odd arrow to his Ymmuri bow and shoot. Two hundred paces away, one of the Khalidoran signal flags went up in flames. It was obviously on purpose, because only one or two Khalidoran signal flags remained on the entire plain. Kylar wondered briefly whose good idea that had been.

Curoch was still strapped to his back and the black ka'kari concealed it. Kylar drew neither as he closed with the rear of the Cenarian line. His battle senses seemed to explode, obliterating conscious thought, blotting out everything but the sharp outlines of the figures in his path. This group was spearmen, packed tightly and surging forward. There would be no slipping through these men. They pushed against the backs of the men in front of them with oblong shields, holding their elbows up so their spears wouldn't become entangled in the press.

Kylar leapt lightly and pushed off one man's shoulder, twisted, pushed off another's spear hand, then planted both feet on the shoulders of a man in the second row and jumped as hard as he could. He was over the Cenarians so fast he didn't even hear their cries of surprise.

His leap took him over the first six lines of krul. Kylar read the bodies of those among which he would land. Five black creatures and one a diseased flaky white that seemed their leader. Two saw him. Kylar tucked his knees to his chest, flipped, then threw his feet forward at the last second. His feet connected with a big black krul over its eyes. Its head snapped back and its neck cracked. Kylar rolled to his feet.

He'd never seen krul before. They were shaped like men with grotesquely bulging muscles, their eyes small and piggish, brows prominent, shoulders heavy, necks almost nonexistent, but beyond that, each was different, as if they were the products of many different hands. The one closest to Kylar's left was covered with fur, two others were hairless. The one directly in front of him had a nose smashed upward into a snout. It also had thin curling horns. Three had an extra knuckle's worth of finger on their hands, sharpened into claws. Their skin or fur was the black of a bloated corpse, and they smelled of rot. None wore armor or clothes except the white one, and few had weapons other than their claws or horns. The white was taller than the others, more than six feet, and recovered first, swinging a huge dull blade at Kylar.

Kylar dodged it and crushed the white's throat with a kick. Kylar darted behind another, grabbed its horns, and broke its neck before he realized that perhaps a dozen black krul weren't moving at all; they simply stared at their dying white leader. It was hissing, trying to breathe. Unnerved by their sudden listlessness, Kylar paused for a moment—a pause that in a normal battle could have been lethal. He pulled a tanto from his belt and jammed it into the white krul's heart. Krul apparently kept their hearts where men did, because it died as he withdrew the blade.

What little light had been in the piggish eyes around him guttered out. The ten krul looked lost. For three impossible seconds, they didn't move. Kylar could sense them searching for something. Then, as if each had been yanked on a leash toward a new master, the krul bolted in ten different directions.

A jolt of fear more intense than any he'd ever felt lashed through Kylar's bond with Vi. She was two hundred paces to his left.

Kylar ran through the Dead Demesne, over corpses that looked oddly fresh but didn't stink. He was behind the main line of krul, but there were still hundreds that saw him. His Talent filled him like a fire. He was a blur.

As always, he could feel Vi more intensely the closer he got. She was in the middle of a thick knot of fighting. The sheer volume of magic was astounding. Magae flanked Vi and they faced a dozen Vürdmeisters with vir clawing through every inch of exposed skin. On a white charger in white enameled armor, Logan and a score of his bodyguards faced dozens of monsters. A great sword-tooth cat leapt for the king. Logan slashed his sword into the top of its head. Its claws scored his horse's armor as it fell dead.

A wash of fire spurted from a Vürdmeister toward the king and lapped against a shimmering shield one of the magae had put around him. A squat red krul, a head shorter than most of its kin but three times as wide, with skin that looked like it was entirely made of bone, grabbed a horse's leg. The horse whinnied as its leg cracked. It fell, spilling one of Logan's bodyguards to the ground. He jumped up and slashed at the creature, but his thin blade rang off its skin. He stabbed it; his blade bowed but then pierced the creature's skin. It ignored it and grabbed his arm, then his face. Gnasher grabbed the man's other arm and tried to pull him up onto his horse. His scream was muffled against the krul's palm until it crushed helmet and head together. Gnasher kept pulling, not understanding the guard was already dead.

Greenish krul with splayed legs like frogs leapt at Logan, trying to knock him from his saddle. Vi blasted them aside with Talent and body-guards opened their throats.

As Logan's knot of warriors ground slowly toward the Dead Demesne, a Vürdmeister beyond the fighting chanted calmly. Kylar saw the sword-tooth cat's split head mend, and moments later it stood. Everywhere, the scene was repeated. The Vürdmeisters were instantly replacing the most powerful krul they lost.

Kylar unlimbered Curoch and decapitated that Vürdmeister, and then another before it could raise the red-skinned ogre, and cut a third in half. Through the press of bodies, he saw Vi. A krul claw slapped into her arm, but bounced off as her blood-red dress hardened like armor. She sliced off the krul's arm and met Kylar's eyes. She pointed behind him.

It was the Titan, looming huge. It had cracked open Black Barrow and now it was coming to war. The sheer size of it was hard to believe. It was shaped almost like a man, its skin a coolly luminous blue under scale armor, its hair gold and short and spiky like an unruly boy's, its eyes black with silver vertical irises like a cat's, its muscles smooth and beautiful. But if it was a god from the front, it was a demon from behind. Huge spikes extended from its spine, reptilian wings draped from its shoulders, and a rat-like hairy tail dragged behind it. It wielded a spiked pole as a cudgel.

"Kylar!" Vi shouted. "Kill it!"

He could feel her intimately enough to know she hadn't meant to invoke the bond, but she'd done it anyway. Like he'd been lashed with a cat o'nine tails, his attention focused instantly, irrevocably on the Titan. He had no choice.

92

Kaldrosa Wyn was lying in the shadow of a huge krul corpse. This one was shaped like a bear with scabby pale skin devoid of fur. She was near the crest of a hill in the Dead Demesne, north of Black Barrow—or north of where Black Barrow had been. The dome had come down minutes earlier, scaring the hell out of her. From her position, she could see several hundred of the other soldiers. Most of them were sa'ceurai, the rest were Agon's Dogs. She'd come because her husband Tomman had, and if he was going to take a mission this dangerous, she was going with him.

A low whistle trilled in the distance, and seconds later, was repeated by someone closer. It was time. Kaldrosa pulled the muddy bag at her feet up and opened it. She dressed slowly, carefully, trying to work blood into her stiff arms and legs. They'd been crawling and lying in muck for two days, and it was a wonder she could move at all. They'd blackened their armor and weapons so they wouldn't reflect sunlight, but she was still as quiet as possible. They didn't want to spoil their gambit this close to its fruition.

The Ymmuri bows were the biggest problem. To string them, the Ymmuri warmed them by a fire for at least half an hour. That wasn't an option. Someone had foreseen it, though, and the archers gathered around an odd, kohled Modaini magus named Antoninus Wervel.

Otaru Tomaki, one of Lantano Garuwashi's advisers, was in command. Kaldrosa didn't know what he'd seen to make him decide they should attack now—or if he had seen anything. Tightening the last stubborn leather strap between Tomman's shoulder blades with numb fingers, she poked her head over the bear, not shrinking from its touch. Her horror at the monsters had peaked the first night. She might have gone mad if Tomman hadn't lain next to her, his fingers interlaced with hers. Now, the monsters were just meat, and oddly unstinking meat at that.

The Khalidoran command tents seemed almost abandoned. There were a score of rich pavilions in a rough circle, but only a half dozen guards patrolled the area, and they focused on a pavilion beside the largest one. Four female meisters stood around it. That confirmed it for Kaldrosa. It was the concubines' pavilion.

The Dead Demesne ended a hundred paces from the pavilions. Tomman and the other archers were creeping as close as they could. She knew Tomman could make the shot from two hundred paces, but they didn't want to take chances; everything depended on being quick and lethal.

Turning to sit against the bear, she stretched her arms and rolled her head. South of her hill, the black dust from the dome was settling in the city that had been hidden beneath Black Barrow. In the center was an expansive white castle. The city itself was at the highest point of the plain, so Kaldrosa could see nothing of the battle beyond it. She pulled on her helmet and turned in time to see every guard and meister in sight tumble to the ground with arrows stuck in them.

There was another whistle and a thousand men jumped to their feet and ran toward the pavilions. The sa'ceurai usually shouted war cries, but now they were silent. A few stumbled and fell with muscles cramping from their nights of exposure, but most reached the pavilions in seconds.

Otaru Tomaki held up a hand with four fingers extended, gave a tempo, and cut. A hundred sa'ceurai ringed the pavilion that had been guarded while the others fanned out. On the count Tomaki had given, they cut through the walls of the pavilion on four sides simultaneously and stormed in.

By the time Kaldrosa arrived, maybe five seconds later, the six eunuchs inside the tent were dead, and the lone woman was ringed by wary sa'ceurai. The woman was dark-haired, of a slender build, maybe sixteen. She was dressed richly and held a sword, waving it wildly. "Get away! Stay back!" she shouted.

It struck Kaldrosa that a hundred sa'ceurai were probably not the kind of rescuers a Cenarian princess would expect. "Your Highness," Kaldrosa said, "be calm. We're here to save you. We've come from your husband."

"My husband? What madness is this? Stay back!"

"You're Jenine Gyre, aren't you?" Kaldrosa asked. The girl fit the description, but she'd never seen her.

"Time!" Otaru Tomaki said. "We've got to go!"

"Jenine *Gyre?*" the girl laughed, twisting the name. "That's been one of my names."

"King Logan sent us. He's missed you terribly, Your Highness. You're the reason we're here," Kaldrosa said.

"Logan? Logan's dead." Their puzzled looks must have convinced her it was no trap. She went white. "Logan's alive? 'The Cenarian king.' Oh gods." The sword tumbled from her fingers. She passed out.

Otaru Tomaki caught her before she hit the floor. He hoisted her over a shoulder. "Good work, easier this way."

"I've never seen someone actually swoon," Antoninus Wervel said. The kohl connecting his eyebrows had smudged and run from his days in the Dead Demesne, making him look more freakish than menacing. "Very well, are we ready?"

"Thirty seconds," Tomaki barked.

The sa'ceurai, who'd held perfect order to that moment, bolted, looting every pavilion they could in a frenzy. Kaldrosa counted, and every last warrior was back by twenty-eight. At thirty, Antoninus Wervel extended his hands to the sky and a blue flame whooshed out, turning green at its apex.

Then they waited. A tense minute later, an answering green flare arced into the sky from the opposite side of Black Barrow.

"We go east, through the Dead Demesne," Tomaki said. "Go!"

93

*I*n the tumult of clashing arms, grunts, curses, clashing sword on sword or sword on shield, the thump of cudgels hitting flesh, the muted crack of breaking limbs or shattering skulls, the whistle of air escaping from a throat instead of a mouth, the familiar stench of blood and bile and death-loosened bowels and the sweat of exertion and the sweat of fear, Kylar was suddenly serene. He kicked low into a white krul's shin, snapping it. He slid past the falling beast, lunged to slide Curoch into another krul's throat, reversed his grip on the sword, and stabbed it through the white krul's skull before it hit the earth.

Its death and the sudden slackness in the krul nearest him gave Kylar a moment to look at the Titan. It had reached the thick of the fight, a hundred paces away. It swept its spiked club in a savage swathe. Krul and men alike were lofted into the air, pierced by spikes longer than swords and then flung free on its next slash.

Kylar plunged back into the maelstrom like a diver into a cool lake on a blistering day. Vi's command to kill gave the world a beautiful focus. There was no fear about protecting others less capable. No worry about advancing at a slow enough rate that the rest of a line of plodding sword-swingers could keep pace. No thought of concealing how good he was. Not even the muted horror of killing men. A dark facsimile of a Harani bull reared up before Kylar, lashing stump-like feet, slashing mighty tusks. Kylar dodged backward, hesitated until it was about to land on all fours, then dove beneath it. Curoch passed through the bull's abdomen like a comb passing through a princess's hair on the hundredth stroke. It was beautiful. The creature trumpeted in pain and its bowels squirted onto the ground. Kylar was already killing something else.

He'd acquired a stabbing spear somewhere, and now he spun into another knot of krul. None had time to swing weapon or claw at him. The spear spun and Curoch darted like a hummingbird, and eight beasts died. He wasn't fighting, or killing, or butchering. It was a dance. He didn't decapitate a krul unless he needed to change the direction of its falling body; it was faster to clip a single artery. Faster to cut a hamstring. Faster to cut across a face to take both eyes. He stopped killing the black krul half the time, focusing on the white, the bears, the aurochs, and the Harani bulls—anything that was in his path to the Titan.

He blinded a Harani bull in one eye, made it spin, slashing at him with its tusks, then speared its other eye. Blinded and mad with rage, it charged, plowing through line upon line of krul, trampling and killing. Kylar found himself laughing.

When the Titan was less than thirty paces away, for the first time, Kylar had a cut parried. This krul was different from any he'd yet seen. Where most krul seemed to be crafted on the idea that stronger-is-better, bigger-is-best, this creature was man-shaped and as lean as Kylar. Instead of skin, it had a blood-red chitin exoskeleton. Its face was a featureless chitin oval. It held two swords of the same material and stood in a perfect ready stance. It countered Three Daisies with Garon's Stand. Kiriae's Crouch with Boulders Falling. But when it tried to stop the Knot Loosed with Sydie's Wrath, Curoch punched through its chitinous chest. Kylar decapitated it to be sure and saw that the exoskeletoned red warriors were the only krul around the Titan. As the Titan swung its club, they easily rolled out of the path of every swipe. There were thirteen thirteens of them, swarming like fire ants.

Between the fire ants and the Titan, the Cenarian center was close to collapsing. The Lae'knaught, the Cenarians, the Ceuran reserves, and the Alitaeran reserves had all come here, but the center could not hold. The Titan was as tall as seven or eight men, and neither stupid nor slow. Where the cavalry bunched, it killed half a dozen horses and men in a single swipe. Where they spread out, the fire ants darted into the gaps and killed men at every turn.

The Titan lifted a foot to stomp on a horseman charging him, and the ants scattered. Kylar leapt through the gap. The Titan's foot came down, crushing man and horse to jelly and shaking the ground. Kylar jumped and grabbed its calf. The Titan wore scale armor made of scales so big that Kylar didn't dare imagine what they had come from, but the straps holding the armor together were thick leather and enormous hemp ropes. With Curoch sheathed, Kylar clambered up to the Titan's belt.

The Titan noticed him and spun so fast Kylar's feet lost their grip and swung out horizontal. Kylar saw chitin warriors crushed by the unexpected move. The Titan swatted at him and Kylar was batted into the folds of its furled wings.

Cocooned in soft, stinking leather, Kylar slipped toward the ground. He grabbed a wing bone as thick around as his thigh. He climbed as quickly as he could and Curoch came to hand as the Titan noticed that he was still hanging on. Kylar slashed once, twice, three times, and the soft, hand-thick membrane parted. He slapped Curoch onto his back and slipped through the hole as the Titan unfurled its enormous wings with a snap. Caught halfway through the wing, Kylar was almost knocked unconscious by the whiplash. The Titan furled its wings to try to shake him loose again and Kylar pushed through and jumped.

He caught himself on one of the huge spines protruding from the Titan's back. The Titan spun again, but didn't see him, and then was distracted by some attack Kylar couldn't see. Kylar's feet found purchase on a lower spine, and timing the movements of the Titan's body, Kylar clambered from spine to spine.

There was nowhere to brace himself for a blow to cut into the Titan's spine, so Kylar kept climbing until he reached the broad gorget that protected the Titan's neck. A fringe of metallic hair protruded over it, and Kylar grabbed a handful, bracing himself to ram Curoch into the back of the Titan's head.

Magic arced through the metallic hairs and blasted him off his feet. Kylar spun, hanging on by one hand.

He lost his grip and caught the gorget itself, his hand between the metal and the Titan's skin. Kylar swung around and hacked blindly into the Titan's neck. Magic burst from the Titan in a shockwave. The world went black and Kylar felt himself spinning into space. There was nothing to grab, no possible way to stop his fall—and from this height, falling would surely be lethal. It was like a dream: the rush of air, the sick emptiness in his stomach, the twist as he braced for the inevitable impact—but he didn't wake up. He crushed something, and heard as much as felt his bones snapping. His collarbone, right arm, every rib on the right side and his pelvis crunched and crackled.

When he blinked his eyes clear, he was flat on his back, a fire ant crushed beneath him. Kylar tried to move, but there was no way. Pain arced through him, so intense that black spots swam in front of his eyes. If he tried again, he'd black out. He was dead. Just like that, Kylar's battle was finished.

The Titan had staggered back several huge steps. Its neck was fountaining blood from the right side. Kylar had caught its carotid artery. It screamed. Then it caught sight of Kylar. If Kylar could read emotion in those silver and black cat's eyes, he would have thought he read satisfaction. The Titan stepped forward. It was dying, and it knew it, and it was going to fall on top of Kylar to crush him.

Kylar extended one finger to the Titan and lay back and looked at the sky. A speck floated in front of his eyes and he blinked, but it didn't go away. In the sky, diving from mountainous heights was a bird of prey, diving at great speed. Even in a dive, it was clear it must have had a thirty foot wingspan, and it was diving straight at Kylar.

Great, crushed by a Titan or by some huge bird. Beautiful.

There was no question of moving. So many bones were broken that breathing was excruciating. Kylar looked back at the Titan. The blood-fountain from its neck still gushed. It was rocking forward, its perfect white teeth bared at Kylar.

The bird snapped its wings open at the last second and swooped into the Titan's face with bone-shattering force. The Titan's head whipped back with a crack and it dropped like a stone—backward, onto the lines of krul.

Kylar lay back. He'd hoped to do more. He might have even been tempted to think his destiny would have been to do more, but he knew better. Anyway, at least he'd killed the Titan. That was surely worth something.

There was a ululating cry from the Ceuran lines, and the allies surged forward. Kylar saw men and horses leaping over him.

`   He'd barely closed his eyes when he felt magic sliding into him. With a sure and brutal hand, his bones were wrenched into place and reconstructed in rapid order. When the magic receded, Kylar lurched over and threw up. He hadn't even known he could be Healed so quickly. Who else would have tried?

"One of these times, you're really going to have to save my life. This is really getting old. By the way, I thought I told you to hold onto this."

Kylar gaped up at Durzo. His master was extending Curoch to him. Durzo was wearing a huge pack on his back that extended several feet above his shoulders—except it wasn't a pack. "Oh, hell no," Kylar said. "You cannot fly. Tell me you can't fly."

Durzo shrugged. "Hollow bones, changes to the heart and eyes if you want to see while you dive, careful re-apportionment of body mass—it's a real bitch. Helps if you study dragons."

"Dragons? No, don't tell me." Kylar stood, shaky from the vast amount of magic that had coursed through him. "I didn't think I could heal that fast—" he cut off as Durzo's wings melted into his back and his form subtly changed proportions. Durzo had taught him that shifting his features, even the relatively minor shifts from one human face to another, took eight to twelve hours. Now his master had lost thirty-foot wings in a matter of seconds. "Unbelievable," Kylar said.

"It's too hard for you," Durzo said, a note of apology sneaking into his voice.

"Do you know where Elene is?" Kylar demanded.

"Not for sure, but I know where the party is." Durzo looked like he was about to say more, but he stopped. His face drained of humor.

A moment later, Kylar caught what dismayed his master. By degrees, the ground beneath them seemed to sigh. The stench of the newly dead was magnified tenfold. Jorsin's spell locking the ground had been broken. The Dead Demesne shook off its chains and breathed.

Godking Wanhope saw the Cenarian flare arc high over his command tents and his heart stopped.

Jenine. They were taking Jenine.

He stood on the last flight of steps before a great dome of the ancient castle. It was the tallest building he'd ever seen, with towering arches and flying buttresses that scraped the very heavens. Inside, he could feel Khali—and Neph Dada. Dorian was surrounded by a dozen highlanders and two hundred Vürdmeisters: more than enough. The real battle would be between himself and Neph, his old tutor. Neph, who was making his play at usurpation. Neph, who had raised a Titan and the red *buulgari*—the fire ants, the bugs—which had been imprisoned near the Titan.

Nor was Neph Dada the only one making a play. Wanhope's brother Moburu had spent almost all his strength in cutting through Wanhope's forces yesterday to get to Black Barrow. Now he was emerging from one of the tunnels under the city. He had a ferali.

From the stairs, the Godking had a vantage of everything north and east of the castle. To the north, he could see the small Cenarian force cutting through the Dead Demesne to the east, where they would meet Logan Gyre's troops, led by the king himself. Moburu's force looked to be only a few hundred, and it would meet Logan's troops before the Cenarians who'd taken Jenine got there. Without the ferali, the Cenarians would obliterate Moburu's force. With it—well, it depended on how good Logan's magae were.

All in all, the resulting clash should give him plenty of time to go inside, take Khali and cut off Neph from the vir. Without vir, Neph and Moburu would be helpless, and the entire army of krul would finally be united. Wanhope had made mistakes, but the day was far from lost. He was turning to go inside when he saw Moburu's men turn and head for the Cenarians holding Jenine.

His heart pounded. He'd seen this scene as his gift came back. Moburu's ferali would demolish the kidnappers, and he would seize Jenine. Wanhope saw the picture vividly. Moburu held Jenine, his eyes wild, a spell wrapped around her head that would crush it like a melon if he released it.

It was too late for Jenine. Wanhope could see her head popping, brains squirting out of the narrow holes in the spell. He blinked. Even if he saved her, his marriage was finished. The Cenarians had taken her. She must know now that Logan was alive. If he rescued her within sight of Logan, would she thank him for it? Inside, at least, was power. With Khali, Wanhope had magic, wealth, every pleasure of the flesh, comfort. There was the study of things lost, of magics no one could teach but a goddess. There was everything but friendship, companionship, love—but what were those things if he was going to go mad and couldn't enjoy them anyway? This was his birthright, and people had been trying to take his birthright for as long as he'd lived. He'd given everything to be here. What would happen to his harem if he left? He'd given those girls a decent life, a better life than they could have imagined. He couldn't live without the vir. He'd quit it once, and quitting had nearly killed him. He couldn't do it again. Jenine was dead to him anyway. Besides, he wanted to crush Neph, to teach him finally who was the master and who the student, to avenge all the cruelties Neph had inflicted on him growing up.

Wanhope turned to go inside.

"Dorian?" a man shouted from halfway down the hill. "Dorian?!" In the cobblestone street, a hundred paces away, Solon emerged around a corner, riding a chestnut destrier. He gestured with one hand to what must have been soldiers in the street behind him, telling them to stop. "Dorian! My God, Dorian, it's good to see you! I thought you were dead!"

Godking Wanhope was wearing his white robes and heavy gold chains of office. The vir were darkening his skin, and Solon pretended not to see any of it.

Solon rode toward him, not touching his Talent, not holding any weapon, not making any move that might seem threatening, as if he were approaching a wild animal. "It is you. *Dorian*."

He said the word like it had power, like he was calling a dead man back to life. And it was life. Even with all the luxury and the fulfillment of every whim, Dorian had lived these last months hunted. There had been no rest, only stupor. There had never been communion, not even with Jenine.

The two hundred Vürdmeisters were getting nervous at Solon's approach. They could smell the potency of his Talent, and even to Wanhope's nostrils it reeked. He hated it. It smelled of light, scouring, revealing, shaming light. But the Vürdmeisters wouldn't attack Solon, not without the Godking's word. Solon ignored them. The man always did have brass balls. "Dorian," he said. "*Dorian.*"

Dorian had spoken a prophecy over Solon once. Ten, twelve years ago? It ended: "Broken north, broken you, remade if you speak one word." The cheeky bastard was asserting that the word was "Dorian"? He was turning Dorian's own prophecy back on himself? Solon had a little grin twisting his lips in the way Dorian knew so well. A laugh burst out of Wanhope and then was strangled in a sob. It sounded insane to his own ears.

He looked down the hill. Moburu had closed with the Cenarians holding Jenine, and the ferali was plowing through them in a cloud of black dust, tearing them apart, sticking their bodies to its flesh—growing.

Inside, Neph was working to give Khali flesh. The goddess would enslave all Midcyru, maybe all the world. Enslave and destroy. Without a body, she had turned Khalidor into a cauldron of filth, a culture of fear and hatred. What could she do with a body? The best thing Dorian could do was stop him. Godking Wanhope could stop Neph. He knew Neph. He knew how Neph would fight. The girl was a tangent, a distraction in the big picture. Dorian was too important, his skills too valuable to go after a girl when the real battle—the battle that would determine the fate of nations, perhaps of all Midcyru—was only paces away. Dorian would go inside as Godking Wanhope one last time. He would take the vir one last time, and destroy all Neph had wrought. He would destroy Khali's works—and he would die. His fighting would be done at last. Unable to live well, he would at least die well.

Besides, Jenine was dead to him.

"Dorian," Solon said. "Dorian, come back."

Jenine was dead to Godking Wanhope, she was dead even to Dorian—but she wasn't dead. This delusion was the same temptation that had snared him a hundred times: allow this present evil for some grand, future good. To change an entire nation, to undo the evil his father had wrought, he had taken a harem, raised krul, slaughtered children, raped girls, and started a war. In fact, he'd accomplished most of the things for which he hated his father, and in far less time. The truth was, Dorian had always been more interested in being known as good than in simply being good. And he was about to do it again. No wonder he'd been so willing to throw away his prophetic gift at Screaming Winds: he'd seen then what he was going to become.

"Go inside, kill the usurper," Godking Wanhope ordered his Vürdmeisters. "I'll follow momentarily." They went inside instantly. They might even obey. It didn't matter. He couldn't keep them here. They might try to stop him. "You too," he told his bodyguards, and they, too, obeyed instantly.

With his stomach revolting at even touching his Talent, weak and frail as it was, Dorian readied the weaves, not giving himself time to think. He knew these weaves; he'd used them once as a young man. It was probably too little, too late. There was no way he could pay for what he'd done. He should just smash Neph and die.

No, that was the same old voice he'd obeyed too many times. Every time he decided to think about the temptation, he fell into the temptation. Now was the time to act. To simply do good, whether or not anyone ever knew, whether or not it was enough.

With a deep breath and as much Talent as he could hold, he ripped the vir out of himself. Parts of his Talent ripped away with it, as he cut deep, deep. It ripped so many parts open that he knew he would never again control when his prophetic gift came or went. The madness he had feared and fought for so long would come, and it would stay, forever.

Finally, sickened, Dorian threw off the gold chains and the white cloak of his office. "Solon. Friend," he said, heaving a deep breath, "ride with me. Quickly. The madness comes."

95

Logan had no idea how the battle was going. Shortly after the signal had gone up that Jenine had been recovered and he'd committed himself to meeting those soldiers on the east side of the hill below the castle, flares had gone up behind them, calling for all of the reinforcements. But for the moment, none of it mattered.

At the base of the hill beneath the huge castle, the expedition Logan had sent to recover Jenine was caught in a battle with a few hundred Khalidorans. The ground here was covered with the black dust that was all that remained of Black Barrow. It had settled quickly, but as the forces fought and as Logan's men rode forward, they kicked it up once more, obscuring the battle.

With six inches of dust on the ground, Logan didn't dare a full charge. If that black snow concealed pitfalls, horses would fall. The riders behind, blinded by thick black dust, would ride right over their companions.

Logan and his foremost riders were within thirty paces when he saw something looming through the black dust. It was vaguely bear-shaped, but men were stuck to its skin, screaming. "Break! Break!" Logan shouted. "Ferali!"

He veered left. A crowd of Khalidorans appeared out of the dust before him, all pressing to get away from the ferali. The Khalidorans were panicked, totally unprepared for the sudden appearance of cavalry, and Logan's line plowed through them. His destrier trampled half a dozen before the press of bodies became so thick it stopped them.

A vast arm, its skin writhing with gaping little mouths, passed over Logan's head, brushing his helmet with a scraping sound as little teeth tried to chew through metal. Logan couldn't see the rest of the creature except as a shadow against the lesser blackness of the dust.

He lurched as a horse collided into the back of his destrier. It jarred him forward and the men before him slowly yielded, either crushed, or faces laid open from his destrier's teeth.

A crackling ball of mage fire whizzed through the air and exploded against the ferali's hide, doing nothing. The magae didn't know what they were facing.

More screams rose as the force of Logan's charge pushed his men directly into the ferali. Logan found horses wedged to either side of him. Gnasher on one side, Vi on the other, her red dress glowing from within as she hurled a flurry of fist-sized fire balls, some into the Khalidorans packed before them, and some at the ferali. "It's not doing anything!" she shouted.

The ferali suddenly disappeared, hunkering down into the earth.

"Ah, shit," Logan said. He'd seen this before. The ferali wasn't leaving or hiding, it was rearranging itself to use all its new meat. The press of the lines pushed men toward it.

The ferali exploded upward, and men and horses were flung into the air in every direction. They fell and crushed their fellows.

"Spread out! Spread!" Logan shouted. Vi threw up a flare, but Logan bet no more than a hundred men saw it.

Suddenly, he saw magic rippling through the air over his head, diffuse as a cloud.

With a sound like a slamming door, the magic plunged to the ground. Within a square a hundred paces on each side, the black dust dropped to the earth and was held there. The air was clear.

Logan looked up the hill and saw the source of the magic: Solon Tofusin, the man he'd thought he'd known for a decade. He stood with a dark-haired man on a promontory. The other mage was crackling with light, weaving a dozen strands of magic. Logan barely registered their presence before looking back to the battle.

He saw that they were caught in what had been an estate's garden. There were walls on two sides, and it was toward those walls that Logan had been trying to retreat. The ferali sat in the middle. It had forgone legs to simply squat with half a dozen arms, plucking men and horses from the ground indiscriminately, and if the clear air helped Logan and his forces, it helped the ferali too.

"Second, Third, Fourth battalions, circle behind!" Logan shouted. Vi threw up the signal, but getting an army to change direction wasn't a quick process. The Fourth Battalion might arrive in time to stop the Khalidoran force from retreating, but nothing could save the thousand men trapped with Logan in this garden.

Vi began attacking the ferali again, but now she was throwing a stream of balls of light toward the ferali's eyes. She wasn't trying to hurt it now, merely blind it, distract it, slow its killing. In moments, a dozen other magae followed her lead and dazzling streams of light flowed toward the great armed blob in the garden's center.

For moments it was paralyzed, then it picked up a horse from the Khalidoran side of the garden, where it could still see. It hurled the horse toward one of the magae, crushing her and half a dozen others. It extended an arm, and dozens of swords and spears bubbled to the surface and floated into its hand. It hurled all of them at the next maja.

Logan craned his neck to see how much the press had eased. Not enough.

"Jenine!" someone yelled. It was the man on the promontory with Solon, and it was a cry of utter despair. His arms were spread out, each hand swimming with intricate weaves—Logan wondered for a brief moment how he saw them; he'd never been able to see magic weaves before—then the man brought his hands together, squeezing the weaves into one ball. Magic leapt from his hands like an arrow and hit the ferali, and unbelievably, stuck. Magic never stuck to ferali.

The ferali was lifting another horse from the Khalidoran side of the circle. There was a woman in the saddle, clambering back, trying to throw herself off the back of the horse, but the ferali's hand was clamped over her dress. It was Jenine. Logan's heart jumped into his throat, but there was nothing he could do.

The man on the promontory screamed, and the magic in his hands went taut, like a rope tied to the ferali. Shrieking, he yanked.

The horse dropped from the ferali's hand and Logan lost sight of his wife.

The ferali's gray skin was shimmering. In a wave of black smoke, the skin evaporated. With a hiss of escaping gases, the ferali slumped, died, and burst apart, the maze of magic that held it together clipped like a Fordaean knot.

Logan's heels were into his destrier before the ferali's last arm hit the earth. He rode over mounds of stinking entrails and crashed into the first Khalidorans he saw between him and where Jenine had fallen. Logan caught a glimpse of the Fourth Battalion coming into place and sealing the northern exit from the garden.

A Ladeshian and two dozen men had dismounted and climbed onto a raised stone balcony. The mansion the balcony had been attached to was a ruin, but the balcony itself was pristine, commanding views of the whole garden. The Ladeshian raised his arms and threw fire into the sky. It faded slowly until it burned around him, forming the outline of a dragon.

"Behold!" Moburu shouted. "The High King is come! King Gyre, come make your obeisance!"

Moburu had no more than thirty men left, all of them stuck on the balcony with him. Logan ran up the steps. When he reached the top, he saw Jenine. Her rich velvet clothing was torn and dirty, smeared with black dust like soot, but she appeared uninjured. Her arms were bound to her sides and a spell sat around her neck and head, with vicious teeth dimpling her skin. The jaws were held open only by a thin weave Moburu held. If Moburu were killed, the jaws would snap shut and crush her skull. Logan didn't question how he knew it, but he did.

Seeing Jenine, Logan's heart surged with a mix of feelings too powerful for words. To see her alive after giving up hope took his breath away. No one would take Jenine away from him again. No one would hurt her. Logan held up his hand, forestalling those following him from attacking Moburu.

Moburu was raving, "It is written:

> " 'He passeth through Hell and waters below and rises,
> marked with death,
> " 'Marked with the moon dragon's gaze,
> " 'In the shadow of the death of the barrow of man's
> last hope he rises
> " 'And fire attends his birth.'

"I tell you," Moburu shouted, "this prophecy is fulfilled this day in your sight. I, Moburu Ursuul, son of the north, rightful Godking, rise this day to take my throne. Pretender, I challenge you. Your crown against mine," he lowered his voice, "and her life."

"Done," Logan said instantly. "Hand over the death spell to one of your wytches."

"What?" Vi asked. "Your Majesty, we have him! He's got nowhere to go!"

"No interference!" Moburu said.

"Done!" Logan shouted.

"And done!" Moburu turned and handed over the weave to a Vürdmeister at his left.

Logan tore off his helmet and pulled the crown from it. He tossed it to the same man. "Jenine," he said, meeting her wide eyes, "I love you. I won't let them have you."

The battle had ended. There were no Khalidorans left to kill here.

"I was born on the day foretold, twenty and two years ago. I bear the signs," Moburu shouted, his eyes shining. He raised his right arm, and displayed a glittering green tattoo reminiscent of a dragon. "Be prepared to greet your High King!"

"This is madness, Logan," Vi said. "The man's a Vürdmeister! You can't face him!"

Logan's eyes finally left Jenine. "Nice tattoo," he told Moburu. He drew his sword.

Logan's right arm felt burning heat. Logan looked down. The incandescent green pattern etched into his arm had melted through the chain mail of his sleeve. It burned as bright as the moon dragon's eyes. Logan caught one glimpse of fear in Moburu's face before Moburu's skin was overwhelmed with black knots of vir.

Moburu threw out a hand and a gout of magic leapt for Logan. Something burst from Logan's arm to meet it. All Logan saw was rushing scales and the burning green of the moon dragon's eyes, as if the entire creature had taken up residence in his arm and was now springing free, full-sized. Its mouth snapped shut on Moburu. Then it disappeared.

Moburu stood immobile. At first, Logan thought the moon dragon had been illusory or his imagination. It appeared to have done nothing at all to his opponent. Then, every tracery of vir within Moburu's skin shattered.

With a dragon's strength, Logan swung his sword down on the pretender. It caught Moburu at the crown of his head and sheared through him. Before the halves of Moburu's body hit the ground, Vi was on top of the Vürdmeister holding the death spell on Jenine.

He and every other Khalidoran and Lodricari and wild man on the balcony raised their hands slowly. The death spell dissolved. The Khalidorans dropped to their knees and looked at Logan with something in their eyes uncomfortably close to worship.

"Battle Mistress!" a voice called out in the sudden silence. It was the odd mage who'd killed the ferali. His eyes were unfocused. He smelled strange to Logan's sensitive nose. He laughed suddenly, then stopped and said somberly, "Battle Mistress, you're needed in the Hall of Winds! Come, quickly, or Midcyru is dead!" He turned to Logan. "High King, summon every man you'd have live to see the night!"

Jenine was staring at the madman with horror.

"Who is this man?" Logan demanded. *High King?*

The mage had made it onto the balcony. He held a thick gold chain in his hands, but abruptly seemed lost.

"Dorian," Jenine said. "Gods, what have you done?"

"Dead to me. Not dead but dead to me," Dorian mumbled.

"He's a prophet," Solon said, following in Dorian's wake. "What he speaks is true. There's no time, Your Majesty. We must go!"

Jenine was crying. Logan pulled her into his arms, not knowing exactly what her tears were for.

The ground trembled and sound rolled over the whole land, like the earth itself was sighing.

Solon swore a string of curses. "Neph's done it. Damn him. He's broken Jorsin's spell." Solon was staring at the black dust that covered everything within miles. It suddenly congealed, forming a thin sludge everywhere.

Logan turned to the Sethi king. "You're sure of this man? You'd bet sixty thousand souls on his word?"

"That and more," Solon said.

Dorian wept. Solon took the great gold chain from his hands and draped it over Logan's shoulders.

Logan turned to Vi. "Send up flares. All our armies to the castle, immediately. And then get yourself there. Fast."

96

Kylar and Durzo approached the Hall of Winds together, unlimbering their swords as one. Both men were liberally spattered with blood. They paused outside a rosewood side door. "You ready?" Kylar asked.

"I hate this part," Durzo said.

"Relax, I killed four Vürdmeisters once, didn't I?" Kylar asked, grinning evilly.

"There are two hundred Vürdmeisters in there."

"There is that," Kylar admitted.

"All right, we do the highlanders guarding the door in no more than five seconds. Then you draw the Vürdmeisters' attention, and I go for Neph Dada," Durzo said. He shrugged. "It might work."

"Not likely." Kylar patted Durzo's back.

Muted light flared to the tip of Curoch. Kylar threw open the door and Durzo dashed inside.

The four highlanders guarding the side door had their backs to them. In less than two seconds, all four were dying. Only after killing his two did Durzo allow himself to take in what everyone else was staring at.

The Hall of Winds was a vast circle topped by a high dome without any interior supports. The entire panorama of the ceiling and the walls themselves was imbued with magic. Looking east, it was as if the walls weren't there: he could see Logan's men battling a ferali. The presentation of what was happening outside continued as he looked south, but ended abruptly at a crack that had slivered down from the top of the dome. From south to west, the scene portrayed was of sunrise over the bustling city this once had been. It was a summer day; ships crowded the river. The terraced hills were a tapestry of gardens, bearing a thousand different kinds of flowers, and the city was vast beyond comprehension. Beyond the next crack was the night sky, half a moon shining brightly enough to cast shadows. Beyond that one was a narrow panel of a thunderstorm, with lightning flashing and rain falling in torrents. Other panels were dark, the magic gone, leaving plain stone.

But none of these wonders were what held the highlanders' and Vürdmeisters' attention.

In the middle of the domed room, the Vürdmeisters stood in concentric circles around Neph Dada, who held a thick scepter. At his feet, clutching a wrinkled leather fetish, was a slobbering Tenser Ursuul. Every one of the Vürdmeisters held the vir, and every one of them was linked to Neph Dada, who stood at the center of a vast web of magic. Thick bands of every color disappeared into the floor and the earth itself, and he was manipulating the weight of two hundred Vürdmeisters' vir, expanding that web. Iures was shifting in his hands, morphing faster than the eye could follow, twisting the web, expanding parts of it, pulling parts together.

Neither swordsman hesitated. Kylar dashed along the outside of the circle, his sword at neck level like a kid running a stick along a slat fence, except this stick cut throats, leaving twenty men dead. Then, even as the first yells went up, he leapt ten feet in the air and light exploded from him.

Durzo ran straight for Neph Dada, up one of the aisles, passing between dozens of chanting Vürdmeisters. He was within five paces of the wytch when Neph raised a hand. Durzo stopped instantly. He couldn't even bounce backward. Magic wrapped him every way.

Neph extended his hand again and air gelled in a wall, cutting off Kylar and another score of Vürdmeisters from the rest of the hall. Kylar plowed into them, and they—their vir still connected to Neph—could do nothing. In seconds, they were all dead. Neph reached with magic to grab Kylar, but the wetboy moved too fast. After a few seconds, Neph gave up. He threw up three more walls to make a wide cage, and then ignored him.

Returning his attention to Iures in his left hand, Neph began chanting once more. Iures morphed again into Retribution. Neph wrapped liver-spotted fingers through Tenser's hair and cut his throat open. Blood spilled all over the leather fetish Tenser held, hissing and spitting as if it were white hot. Tenser pitched over, dying as the magic released.

There was a second sigh through the land.

"It is finished," Neph Dada declared. "All Jorsin's works are broken. Khali comes." He released the vir back to the two hundred Vürdmeisters in the room. He slipped into a coughing fit, and when it stopped, he turned to Durzo. With a gesture, the bonds holding Durzo fell away. "You must be Durzo Blint. Or should I say Prince Acaelus Thorne? Oh, surprised? The Society of the Second Dawn has let its standards for membership slip, I'm afraid. I know all about you, Durzo Blint—even that you gave up the black ka'kari. Poor choice."

"Seemed good at the time," Durzo said, never shifting from his ready stance. "We gonna do this or not?"

"No," Neph said. He turned to Kylar and gave a little mocking bow. "Well met, Kylar Stern, Godslayer, ka'karifer. You're not using the black ka'kari. Why?"

"Lost it in a card game," Kylar said.

"Not a very good liar, are you? When a ka'kari is surrendered willingly, it must serve its new master. They can be broken, but it takes time. I'm an old man. I'd like to bond the black as soon as possible, but I can take it from your corpse if need be. If you don't give it to me, I'll kill your master. If the Society's right, this time he won't come back."

Kylar's face twisted. "My master understands about necessary sacrifices."

Neph turned to Durzo. "There you have it," he said. A sliver of magic jutted out of Durzo's chest. Neph had stabbed him from behind. The magic faded and Durzo stood, weaving.

"Dishonorable," Durzo said. His legs folded.

"What's honor? A ninety-year-old man fighting you with a sword?"

But Durzo made no reply. He was already dead. Kylar made a wordless sound of protest, staring at the corpse with disbelief. It was like seeing the sun set at noon. He'd known that Durzo would die someday, but not now, not so easily. Not without a fight.

Neph turned back to Kylar. "One more chance. Give me the black ka'kari. That's all I want. I'll leave you to Khali. You may even escape."

Kylar drew himself to his full height, and rolled his shoulders, loosening his muscles for action. "That sounds like a great deal, but there's three problems," Kylar said. He smiled. "First, I'm not Kylar." He laughed, and his face morphed into one leaner, pock-marked, with a wispy blond beard. He was Durzo Blint. "Second, that corpse isn't Durzo."

"What?"

"Third," he continued, "if someone would move his ass...." He cleared his throat.

Neph turned belatedly. In a smooth motion, the corpse stood—and was Kylar. Shields flew up around the Vürdmeister.

Skin sheathed in black metal, face covered by the mask of Judgment, Curoch sliding out of his fists as white-hot claws, Kylar punched. The Vürdmeister's shields popped like soap bubbles. Claws of Curoch crossed on either side of the Vürdmeister's spine, eight bloody points poking out of his back. "Third, I'm not dead," Kylar said, lifting Neph off the ground. "And this is Curoch."

"Shit, that's four things, isn't it?" Durzo said.

Neph Dada screamed. He threw his arms out spastically. The vir leapt to the surface of every inch of his skin. Neph shrieked and shrieked as white light blasted through every vein of vir. Kylar roared and ripped the claws in opposite directions, shearing the Vürdmeister in half.

The walls surrounding Durzo evaporated into nothing and there was silence in the Hall of Winds. Kylar sheathed Curoch on his back and gingerly picked up Iures. He tossed it to Durzo. "You could have given me a few more seconds," Kylar said. "You just taught me rapid healing ten minutes ago. What if I hadn't got it right on the first try?"

Durzo grinned. Bastard.

An earthquake rocked the ground.

Kylar looked at the dome, hundreds of feet overhead, swaying out of time with the ground. At Kylar's feet, he saw the focus through which Neph had been pulling all the power he'd worked on with Iures. It was a leather bundle, ancient, cracked, and yellowing, with gems sewn to it and a horrid, desiccated, hairless, boneless skull grinning formlessly from the front. It could only be one thing. This horror was Khali.

He hefted Curoch and jammed its point through the fetish.

A dozen Vürdmeisters cried out, but nothing happened. There was a hiss of escaping air, and the section of the floor beneath the fetish and Curoch sank.

Kylar stepped back and the floor opened like a coffin lid. There was a woman inside. Her hair was long and blonde, carefully arrayed in small braids and curls. Her long-lashed eyes were closed, her cheeks flushed, full lips pink, skin flawless alabaster. For some reason, to Kylar's eyes, the girl was a collection of details that refused to coalesce into a woman: a familiar dimple here, the sweep of her neck. Her dress was white silk, slim cut to her figure, backless, more daring or more scandalous than anything Elene would have worn. Elene. Kylar staggered back. "Elene!"

Her lips curved into a smile. She drew a breath. Lovely brown eyes opened. Kylar's knees went weak. She reached out a regal hand, and when he took it, she rose almost magically to her feet. Every move spoke perfect grace.

"You—you don't have any scars," Kylar said.

"I can't stand ugliness. I want to be beautiful for you," Elene said, and she smiled, and every part of her was beauty. "Kylar," she said gently, "I need Curoch."

He looked into her smiling face and was lost. Through the ka'kari, Elene looked like an archmage. Magic swirled thickly around her. Elene wasn't Talented, but this *was* Elene.

His heart froze.

Distantly, he heard the main doors of the hall bang open. His knees hit the floor.

"Kylar! No!" Vi shouted. Numbly, Kylar watched the doors open wide. Following Vi was Logan, one arm glowing green; Solon, Logan's old adviser, wearing a crown; the mountainous Feir Cousat; four magae, all greatly Talented; Dorian the prophet; Lord General Agon Brant; and Captain Kaldrosa Wyn with fifty of Agon's Dogs.

The scent of Elene filled Kylar's nostrils as she stepped close. What had she done?

His eyes snapped open as Elene snatched Curoch from his limp fingers. The look in Elene's eyes was foreign. She looked intoxicated as she gazed at the blade. She laughed and twirled.

"Trace, that's enough," Durzo said suddenly.

She stopped abruptly and stared at Durzo, disbelieving. "Acaelus? No, it can't be."

"Hand it over, Trace. And the white ka'kari, too. Release that girl's body."

Elene's eyes narrowed. "It is you."

"What happened to you, Trace? You were one of the Champions. Jorsin trusted you. We all did. What have you become?" Durzo asked.

"I am Khali." At the word, the Vürdmeisters dropped to their faces. She laughed again. "Look at my pets, so humble, and every one of them scheming even now." She looked around the Hall of Winds. She gestured with Curoch, and every crack in the dome was sealed, the scene unified: a spring day, mountains purple in the distance, flowers everywhere. "Do you remember this, Acaelus? We were supposed to be married here." Her white dress shifted like liquid metal, shimmering into a high-necked full green gown with thousands of crystals sewn into it.

"You were beautiful."

"I was a hag!" she shot back. "Bad teeth, bad skin, crooked back. Then Ezra gave me the white ka'kari. I heard you quarreling with him. You betrayed me first, Acaelus. You left me here in my wedding gown, shamed me in front of everyone. I waited hours. I was finally beautiful, and all you were was jealous."

Durzo's face was gray, and bits and pieces that Kylar had heard over the years fell into place. To save the black ka'kari and keep its incredible power secret, Jorsin had given it to "The Betrayer" Acaelus. Acaelus hadn't even been able to tell his fiancée that he had it, and knowing that he would soon have to act the betrayer, Acaelus had fled rather than marry. All without a word of explanation. Kylar remembered Durzo snarling at him when he was a child: "I will not allow you to ruin yourself *over a girl*." Momma K had said women had always been Durzo's downfall. The Wolf had said Durzo had once done something worse than take money for a death. Kylar had guessed it was suicide, but it was worse than that. Knowing the price of immortality was that someone he loved died in his place, Durzo had killed himself, hoping to kill Trace.

But Trace, an archmage in her own right and the smartest of the Champions, had figured out a way around the black ka'kari's death sentence. *~Acaelus and I always knew there was something strange about that death. We knew she fought the magic for months, but then her body died. We tried never to think of her again.~*

"Jealous?" Durzo said. "I had the black ka'kari, the most powerful of them all. Ezra and I quarreled because he gave you a ka'kari that confirmed a lie you believed. You weren't ugly then, Trace; you're ugly now. Look what you've done. For seven centuries the north has labored under your darkness. This is what Trace Arvagulania turned her mind to? This is what you created? Why?"

~*For immortality*,~ the ka'kari breathed to Kylar. Kylar could tell it was understanding for the first time. ~*The white ka'kari can create a glamour so powerful it can be used for compulsion. She tried to turn her ka'kari into a dark imitation of me, using it to compel worship, and then trying to steal life from her "willing" worshipers. But it didn't work because the soul of my magic is love—and love cannot be compelled. Trace has been disembodied until she could find someone who loves in a way that is totally foreign to what she has become. Someone willing—without compulsion— to let Trace have her body.*~

Now she'd found that person at long last: Elene.

"Why? I do it because I wish it. I am Khali. I am goddess. Someone has to pay the price for immortality. Tell me, Acaelus, who's paid for yours?"

Durzo paled. "Too many people. Come, Trace. Our time is done."

"My time has just begun." Curoch became a slender staff in her hand, and she raised it. A black cloud exploded in every direction, then disappeared. The walls of the Hall of Winds became clear as glass, showing the dark battlefield to every side. "Do you remember when Jorsin faced the grand armies of the Fallen?" Khali asked. "He could have stopped them, if he'd listened to me. He didn't have to fight them. He could have controlled them. He was a greater mage than Roygaris. These armies could have been Jorsin's, he could have simply taken them from Roygaris. We could have won."

As she spoke, it slowly became clear that the sudden darkness on the battlefield was moving, standing up. The black blanket was countless thousands of krul corpses rising from seven centuries of death, standing, healing, and moving into ranks. Earlier in the day, even with a hundred and fifty thousand men and krul fighting, all the armies together had occupied only a wedge of the plain south of the Hall of Winds. At Khali's gesture with Curoch, krul rose in a writhing black ocean north, south, east, and west as far as the eye could see. Kylar saw the Titan he'd killed get back to its feet. Dozens more like it stood around the battlefield. Beasts that dwarfed even Harani bulls rose. Birds great and small rose in clouds. Fire ants by the thousands. Flying beasts. Beautiful, fanged children. Brute wolves. Great cats. Horses with bone-scythes extending from each shoulder. Ferali by the hundreds. Kylar's mind couldn't take it all in. Jorsin had faced *this?*

The allied armies had reached the Hall, and now they turned outward, back to back, guarding the hilltop in a circle dwarfed by the numbers of krul they were about to face.

"I can banish them," Khali said. "All of them. But I need Iures to banish the Strangers. What do you say, Acaelus? Will you watch everyone you love die a second time?"

"You'll not have Iures from my hand," Durzo said.

"So be it," Khali said. "Kylar, kill him. Kill all of them." Her words washed over him with the whipcrack of authority. He recognized it as a compulsion spell even as he rose to obey. The spell was the full-grown older sister to the spell Garoth had laid on Vi, akin to the glamour Vi had used on him the first time they'd met, when she'd tried to kill him. But where that glamour had been anchored only by Vi's attractiveness, this compulsion hit every note from lust to awe at standing in front of another immortal, a goddess. It pulled on his adoration for Elene, his loyalty and trust for her as his wife. She was princess, goddess, immortal, lover, companion, wife—and all those bonds were amplified a hundredfold through Curoch. There was no question of disobedience.

Kylar stood. The black ka'kari formed twin swords in his hands. It was trying to speak to him, tell him how to combat the magic she was bombarding him with. But to use the ka'kari, he had to want to use it, and the compulsion stole his very willpower. He looked into Elene's big eyes and nothing mattered but pleasing her. Even as his heart despaired and he wanted nothing more than to throw himself on his own swords, he wanted to please her more.

"Kylar! Stop! I command you!" Vi shouted, advancing alone from among the magae. The command flashed like lightning through Kylar's compulsive wedding earring to the core of his being. It felt like he'd been falling from a great height only to have a rope tied around his wrists suddenly stop his fall. Kylar gasped with pain—and stopped.

Khali paused, surprised. She looked at Vi. "Dear girl," she said, "don't you know what happens when a woman contends with a goddess?" She turned to Kylar and put a hand on her stomach. "My love, you wouldn't betray the mother of your child, would you?"

He couldn't breathe. Elene's stomach was indeed slightly swollen. His child. The sudden delight on Khali's face told him it was true. Elene was pregnant. She'd known. She hadn't told him. The new claim to his loyalty added another layer to the power of the compulsion spell.

"Darling, kill them. Starting with that slut," Khali said. The command snapped tight like a rope around his ankles. He felt himself being torn between compulsions like a man on the rack.

One of the mages chose that moment to loose a fireball. It fizzled before it went an arm's length. Khali made a little snatching motion and Kylar saw every glore vyrden in the room emptied in an instant. The magi were left gasping.

"Kylar, help me," Vi cried. She fell to her knees, concentrating on him, sending strength to him. She reached for the nearest elements of their bond: His guilt at what he'd put her through, how he owed her better, and his desire for her.

Khali matched those and overmatched them. Khali tugged on what he owed Elene, on his desire for her, on the moments they'd shared making love. The compulsion spell worked by magnifying whatever hold a person had, whether authority, or love, or lust, or obedience. Fueled with the might of Curoch, it almost obliterated Kylar's mind.

Kylar raised his swords and started walking toward Vi. He could feel Khali's triumph, her pleasure at her mastery of him.

Vi's eyes held his as he walked closer. She reached up and pulled out the band that held her braid. Her hair spilled down like a copper waterfall. For the first time in her life, Vi made no attempt to protect herself, no attempt to cover this one thing that she had kept private as she had lost all else.

She spread her open hands and dropped the threads of lust and guilt in their bond. Kylar saw her then as he'd never seen her before. He saw the nights of agony with which she had paid for his nights of pleasure with Elene. He saw how gladly she'd done that for him, and at what cost. Vi loved him. Vi loved him fiercely. Kylar missed a step as she clung to that single cord—love—with all her might.

She looked up at him as he drew the twin swords back. "Kylar," she said quietly, at complete peace, "I trust you." Then, impossibly, she released the bond. Every claim she had to him, she dropped. She let him owe her nothing—not friendship, not honor, not dignity, not friendship, not her life—nothing at all.

With no claim to magnify, their wedding earrings failed.

It shook him like a bell had been rung from his ear through his whole body. It shook him from his suddenly freed wrists down to his bound ankles—and there, Khali had no answer to this kind of love. She knew only taking. It was like two people had been playing tug-of-war and one released the rope. All the magic held in tension by the wedding ring rushed outward—toward Khali. Kylar felt the huge wave of power passing through him as the vast pressures of the bond released into her, their force doubled and redoubled by her own pull on them.

There was a giant crack that rattled Kylar's teeth. Something tinged on the marble floor. It was Kylar's earring. The earrings were broken. The bond was broken. The compulsion had vanished. Kylar couldn't feel Vi—or Khali. He was free of both of them.

Ten paces away, Khali was rocking on her heels, stunned.

"I'm so sorry, Kylar," Khali said, but the tone was Elene's.

Kylar was at her side in an instant. "Elene?"

She pushed Curoch into his hands. "Quickly, quickly. I can't stop her. She's recovering."

"What are you talking about?" Kylar asked. "Honey?"

Tears were rolling down Elene's face. "Wasn't Vi magnificent? I'm so proud of her. I knew she could do it. You take care of her, all right?"

"I'm not letting you go."

Her eyes filled with sudden pain and her jaw tightened as a convulsion passed through her. "You know how I used to think I'd never be important like you are? I found it, Kylar. I found something I can do that no one else can. The God told me. Khali could only possess someone who let her, but she didn't know I can hold her in. You can kill her once and for all. You can kill the vir."

"But I can't kill them without killing you," he said.

She took his hand and smiled gently, acknowledging it. She was more beautiful than anything he'd ever imagined.

"No!" he shouted.

The ground shook. Kylar looked through the clear walls and saw one of the Titans pick up an entire building and hurl it at the allies. It crushed hundreds. There was no time. He looked back to Elene just as another spasm passed through her frame.

"But... Curoch," he said. "It can kill me. If it does, the spell that makes people die for me will be broken. I can still save you."

Kylar heard Durzo curse behind him, but he ignored him.

"Kylar," Elene said, "when Roth Ursuul killed you, that first time before we knew you were immortal, I prayed that I could trade my life to save yours. I thought the God said yes. I was so sure of it that I dragged you out of that castle. Later, I told myself that it was just a coincidence, but God *did* say yes. Yes in his time, not mine. My death then would have accomplished nothing. Now I can do something no one else can. Please, Kylar, don't be too proud to accept my sacrifice."

He clutched her hand convulsively. He was crying. He couldn't stop. "You're pregnant."

Tears coursed down her cheeks. "Kylar... there are so many people we love here. I'd give our son for them. Won't you?"

"No! No."

Elene held his face in her hands and kissed him gently. "I love you. I'm not afraid. Quickly now."

The ground shook again, and outside, choruses of magic rose into the sky. Whatever krul had been raised, some of the newer ones had Talent. But inside, no one moved, they all knew that their fates and the fates off all Midcyru's nations were balanced on Curoch's edge.

Kylar pulled Elene into his arms and hugged her fiercely. Sobs burst from him. He drew back Curoch, and slid it into her side. She gasped, squeezing him.

As Curoch pierced Khali, light exploded, engulfing him in fire. It was clean and hot and purifying. Kylar thought he might be dead. He hoped he was.

A voice in the darkness: "I thought it was finished. He killed Khali. Why are they still coming?"

"She lied," another voice said, Dorian's voice. "She wasn't the queen of the Strangers, only an ally. Our work isn't done yet. Not by half. We need Curoch."

Kylar opened his eyes as someone touched him. Sister Ariel stood over him, and he was curled on the floor with Elene. "We need the sword, child." Her voice was gentle, but firm. "Now. Khali's dead, Kylar, but Elene's not, not yet, but her wound can't be Healed. Nothing can mend what Curoch cuts," Sister Ariel said. "We need you. Both of you. Or we'll never stop the krul."

Curoch was buried almost to the hilt in Elene's side. Her eyelids fluttered briefly but didn't stay open. "I can't," Kylar said.

Sister Ariel put a thick hand on the hilt and drew it out swiftly. Elene grunted weakly and a wash of blood poured from her ribs.

"Open the doors!" Dorian shouted. "Both sides!"

"Do it!" Logan shouted. "Do everything he says."

The two hundred Vürdmeisters lay in concentric rings, all dead, all bleached white. The vir itself was dead.

But the krul hadn't been affected. They still surrounded the Hall of Winds in a vast, churning black ocean. And even now, some of the most frightful of them were winning their way to the front of their lines. Shoulder to shoulder, Ceurans and Lae'knaught and Cenarians and Sethi and Khalidoran soldiers fought the horde. Kylar had somehow thought that killing Khali would mean a total victory, but the krul on every side—tens of thousands, hundreds of thousands, millions of them—told another story. The army of men in the center was like a lonely rock in the face of the incoming tide.

God, there was no way they could stand up to so many.

Someone squeezed Kylar's shoulder. It was Logan. His cheeks glistened with tears of mingled joy and sorrow. "Kylar, brother, come. We have a chair for her." Logan squeezed his shoulder again, and that touch was worth a thousand words.

The earth shook again, but Kylar didn't turn from Elene, who was breathing lightly now. The flow of blood had slowed. The open doors had magnified the cacophony of the battle. Kylar barely heard it. He allowed himself to be prodded into place in a tight circle between the open doors. Sister Ariel laid Curoch unsheathed across a dozen palms.

Pushed by Durzo, Kylar put his hand on the blade. Durzo took Kylar's other hand in both of his. It was an uncharacteristically tender gesture, and Durzo held it until Kylar looked up at him. As ever, Durzo didn't have words, but there was a respect in his eyes, and shared heartache, and pride. It was the look of a father whose son has done something great, and that look from Durzo, told Kylar he was an orphan no more. Then, with Kylar's hand still in his, Durzo cupped his hand, a request in his eyes.

Kylar understood, and let the ka'kari flow out into his hand, and gave it to Durzo. Durzo nodded and released his hand. Then Vi put her hand next to his on Curoch, just touching him. Conscious once more, Elene put hers on the other side of Kylar's. Several powerful magi of both genders knelt, each reverently resting two fingers on the blade. Solon and Sister Ariel did the same. Durzo had Retribution—Iures—in hand. It was black-bladed but its grip was uncovered, and Durzo spoke quietly to Dorian as he handed the prophet the Staff of Law.

As he touched Curoch, Kylar became aware of everyone else touching the blade. They sounded like an orchestra warming up, each on his own instrument and pitch. Then, beneath them, Curoch began humming. As Dorian laid his right hand on the blade, his left still holding Iures, a gust of wind blew through the Hall.

Solon found his pitch first, a bass as deep as his speaking voice, wide and strong, oceanic. Sister Ariel matched him, a powerful mezzo, broad but sharper. Then the magi joined in a chorus of baritones and basses, pure and simple and masculine, laying the foundation. The magae settled over them, fine and feminine, adding depth and complexity. Vi joined, her Talent like a high note with a rapid vibrato, higher than any of the others could possibly go. Then a startling new voice joined, richer than any of the others, layered in mystery, a baritone with such depth and range it dwarfed all the others put together. Kylar's eyes shot open, and he and everyone else stared at Durzo, who had laid a single insolent finger precisely on Curoch's point.

Then Kylar felt his place. He sang a tenor, soaring over the other men, interweaving with Vi. He himself was startled at the power of his voice and noticed that all eyes had turned to him, as awed as they had been when Durzo joined. Fierce pride filled Durzo's eyes.

Through the euphony, Kylar noticed something else, suffusing the whole. It was hope. And that voice, if voice it could be called, was all Elene. Her hope—even as she was dying—drew forth hope from each of them. And with that revelation, Kylar saw that Curoch wasn't a simple tool of magic. It wasn't an amplifier of Talent. Curoch amplified the whole man.

Elene's beacon of hope, Durzo's titanic determination, Dorian's penitence and astounding focus, Ariel's intelligence, Logan's courage, Vi's longing for a new beginning, Kylar's love of justice, the bonds of brotherhood and sisterhood, sacrifice, hatred of evil, feelings martial and impulses nurturing. Through it all, the glue that made the magic was love, and love sounded each instrument from its top to its bottom notes—and each man and each woman performed beautifully, heroically, some capable of only a few notes, some with huge range but little depth, and some of them true masters, but each giving all.

The Hall of Winds itself reacted to the perfection of magic building inside its walls. Tapestries of colored light danced through the walls, magic made visible even to the non-Talented, and wove together as the magic wove together. Radiance bathed them, and the magic growing inside was echoed to the world. The warriors outside, battling incredible odds, felt a sudden assurance, as if they were children fighting a bully and the bully had just caught sight of their father coming.

As the music climbed, directed by Dorian, Kylar could see the score laid out before them. His vision widened and he saw not just his own part—climbing, climbing—another voice was needed. One beyond any of the people in the Hall. Their Talents built to a crescendo, and every one blazed like the sun. There was so much magic in Kylar's blood and in the air it was almost intolerable. He was standing in a furnace. Everything Kylar had was sinking into Curoch, and still the magic Dorian was attempting demanded more.

A distant whistling sounded, high over the roar of battle.

Kylar's eyes flicked open. He looked at Dorian.

The mage shifted his grip on Curoch, leaving the hilt free, shifting their holds so that the hilt pointed toward heaven.

The man was more audacious than Kylar could believe. Even with all these mages working together, they didn't have the power needed to end this. So Dorian had set a trap to join their will to the one beast that had the power to impose that will on the world. Kylar was aghast. He couldn't even understand everything Dorian was trying to do. Dorian grinned at him, and Kylar wasn't sure if what he saw in the man's eyes was sane or mad.

Through the southern door, Kylar could see all the way to the pass to Torras Bend, and as he watched, a streak of fire appeared.

It crossed the river, not bothering with a bridge, and plunged through the lines of krul without slowing. It moved too fast to see. Kylar could only judge its progress by the cloud of dust and smoke and blood that trailed it; the shockwave rippling through bodies crashing back to the earth long after it was gone. In seconds, it had gone from the distant pass to the old line where Black Barrow had stood. Kylar realized why Dorian had opened the doors: if he hadn't, the damn thing would have blasted right through the walls.

The whistling and the magic crescendoed as one. Through Curoch, for a split second, Kylar felt the Hunter as it seized the offered hilt of Jorsin Alkestes' mighty blade to snatch it away from them. And Kylar knew him.

A crack of thunder leveled everyone in the room. Magic obliterated everything.

When Kylar became aware, he was standing on the roof of the Hall of Winds. The Wolf stood next to him, and the world had the indistinct sheen Kylar had come to associate with the Antechamber of the Mystery. "So I'm dead," he said. He had no passion left in him.

"No," the Wolf said. "I can come into your dreams, it just takes a lot of magic. I have some to spare now."

"You're Ezra."

He inclined his head.

"Then what's the Hunter? I felt you in it."

"It's my hubris."

Kylar glanced at him. This was not an explanation.

"I tried to undermine the Dark Lord's own work by twisting the twisted back on the twister."

"The Dark Lord? You mean that metaphorically, right?" Kylar asked.

He chuckled. "You are still Kylar, aren't you? But not to worry, the Hands of Hell are still bound for another fifteen or twenty years. Until then, the Hunter and I will battle for control every day. I can only be here while it sleeps."

"What?"

"Do you see this, Kylar?" The Wolf—it was still hard to think of him as Ezra—gestured to the city. Kylar gave it a cursory glance.

"This is how it was when you lived here?" It was beautiful, but Kylar didn't care.

"This is real. This is what you and your friends have done."

Kylar looked with new eyes, stunned. The city was completely restored, and it was a marvel. The streets were straight, perfectly paved. The houses were immaculate, from the largest manse to the tightly packed row houses in the artisans' quarter. Fountains pumped sparkling clean water in squares throughout the city. Hanging gardens flowed over white marble walls. The dome of the Hall of Winds was covered with beaten gold. Nearby, the castle shone white and red. The fields below the city were carpeted with the green shoots of growing crops. The docks on the lake and the locks on the river were restored. The dam was closed and the water level rising. Every sign of war and death was gone.

"The krul's very bodies were turned into vegetation," Ezra said. "It's a better trick than anything Jorsin or I ever managed."

Flowers were budding everywhere, at every corner, bordering every field, rows of beautiful red flowers bursting from bulbs. Kylar had never seen their like, or known any flower to bloom so early in spring.

"How did Elene trap Khali?" Kylar asked. "I'm certain that she isn't Talented." Kylar paused. "Wasn't, I guess."

"There's more to magic than the Talent, Kylar. You've seen that yourself. When have you been most powerful? When you've acted in harmony with the deepest parts of your own spirit. Elene trapped Khali through love. It was a love that said *I love you too much to let you do more evil—not for the sake of your victims only, but for your own sake.* If it had been a rejection, Khali could have escaped and become disembodied once more. It was only Elene's love that made your justice possible. If I hadn't seen it, I wouldn't have thought such a thing could be done. Obviously, Khali didn't either."

Kylar had felt rejected when Elene had left him without telling him where she was going or that she was pregnant. This cast her in a different light. It hadn't been a rejection. She had simply seen that he wasn't mature enough or selfless enough to let her do what she needed to do. Elene had taken Khali not out of a rejection of Kylar, but out of a profound acceptance for who he was not only as a man, but as the Night Angel. Her only purpose in trapping Khali was so that Kylar could kill her. Elene had believed Kylar would do the right thing in the end so much that she had bet her very soul on it. For if he'd faltered, unable to give Elene up, Khali would have taken her over completely.

"What happens now?" Kylar asked, tears coursing down his cheeks.

"Your friend Logan will be crowned High King of Ceura, Cenaria, Khalidor, and Lodricar. He'll establish his capital here and rename it Elenea—not for you, but because he is a man who believes in honoring sacrifice. Within a few years, it will be one of the great cities of the world again. I suspect he will reign well." Ezra shook his head. "Feir Cousat will go to Torras Bend and set up a forge and start a family as he's always wanted. He'll take care of Dorian.

"Dorian was the architect of all this magic, but he's now completely mad. I don't know if it was the vir infecting his prophetic talent, or him ripping the vir completely out of himself, or the death of the vir that caused the madness. I don't suppose it much matters. But that he rooted out his own vir did save him. Indeed, he is probably the only Vürdmeister in Midcyru who didn't die along with the vir. Godking Wanhope will be declared dead. Durzo will be reunited with Gwinvere Kirena, who will eventually rule Cenaria, and rule more capably than any king or queen has ruled there for four centuries. Vi will return to the Chantry to finish her schooling. There will be calls to make her Speaker, which will scare the hell out of the current Speaker, Istariel Wyant. Vi will decline, but not before using her influence to make the Speaker swear that no Sister pursue you. To a surprising extent, they will actually obey."

"And what happens to me?" Kylar asked.

"You will be welcomed wherever you go in this guise. Sooner or later, the world will have need of you again. You are not a man to fade into oblivion, Kylar Stern. Secrecy, perhaps, intentional obscurity certainly, but never oblivion." He cocked his head to the side in his wolfish way. "I have a question."

"Yes?"

"You were four days away from the Wood when you unveiled Curoch. You knew that it would draw the Hunter?"

"Yes."

"How did you know that the Hunter would make it here in time to make a difference in the battle? Indeed, as it happened, *all* the difference. Without it, you didn't have nearly the power those spells required."

Kylar remembered removing the black ka'kari from Curoch before going to face Neph Dada. It had barely been a conscious act. He'd known that the Hunter hated krul and that it would be drawn to reclaim its stolen sword. Maybe he'd thought it would come earlier and kill a lot of krul. But more than a plan, it had simply been something that felt right. It felt like he was moving in consonance with the universe, with his own deepest character. If the Wolf was right, that was its own kind of magic. "I didn't know," Kylar admitted. "I believed."

The Wolf got pensive. "In this world of shadows, you believe? Despite all you've seen?"

Kylar took a breath, looking over the city in all its splendor and remembering what it had looked like not so long ago. "We live on a great battlefield, and you and I fight behind enemy lines," he said. "Like it or not, my lupine friend, you are one of the lights that helps me believe."

Ezra hmmed. "I will consider what you've said. The creature stirs. The day's battle begins."

"May the light shine on you, my friend," Kylar said.

"That's twice you've called me friend." Ezra seemed to taste the word as if it were a flavor long lost. Then he smiled, accepting it. "Thank you."

Ezra turned away, then hesitated. He turned back. "There is . . . one other thing. The red flowers? They're a modified tulip not native to Midcyru. They're known as the Heralds of Spring. They're the first flowers to bloom every year. They're a symbol of hope. I studied the magic, and . . . Elene made them, Kylar, all of them. She made them for you," Ezra's voice cracked. "I couldn't save her. I owed you that much, but I couldn't save her." Ezra pursed his lips, and his jaw clenched as he crushed his own emotions. He touched Kylar's shoulder. "I must go. May I not see you in the Antechamber of the Mystery for many, many years."

Tears flowed down Kylar's face. There were tens of thousands of red tulips. Every intersection, every field, every house was adorned with them. They were Elene's sign to him of her presence, her joy, her acceptance, her love. Only Elene would put such beauty in the middle of his pain. How was he ever going to live without her?

99

Logan dispatched perhaps the fortieth messenger of the day. Not being Talented seemed to have saved him from the brunt of the cost the magi who'd used Curoch had borne. Half of them were still unconscious, including Kylar. Vi had a white streak in her fiery red hair now, and Dorian's hair was gone utterly white like Solon's, though Solon retained his sanity, while Dorian had completely lost his. It was, perhaps, the better part of why

Logan had spared the man. Dorian had turned at the end, and he'd certainly saved Logan's life and the lives of everyone else—but they wouldn't have been in jeopardy if Dorian hadn't stolen Logan's wife in the first place. Or not in jeopardy today, at any rate.

Scrubbing his hands through his hair, Logan almost knocked his new crown off. A soldier had found it waiting in the castle and had presented it to Logan, who'd lost his Cenarian crown in the fighting. They'd wanted to start the coronation celebrations to crown him High King immediately, but Logan insisted on taking care of his men first, and with Lantano Garuwashi and Hideo Mitsurugi reporting to him, as well as one of the magi telling him about the conditions of Khalidor's human soldiers, the number of men Logan regarded as his own had exploded. Mercifully, he also had the services of eight thousand Sisters, most of whom had some ability with Healing. With more than one in ten of his people a Healer, far fewer died than would have otherwise. And Curoch's magic had left them in a paradise where they'd expected a wasteland.

Still, he'd had more than enough work to keep him busy until long after dark. Part of him was glad for it. It was one thing to raise an army to rescue your stolen bride; it was quite another to figure out how to repair a marriage when your wife had thought you dead, had remarried, and had been sharing another man's rule and his bed.

Logan rubbed his temples again and set the crown down on a desk. He looked around the room and realized he had no idea where he was. He'd left an immense throne room and walked at random. Kaldrosa Wyn and Gnasher and several other bodyguards had followed him, but they'd said nothing as they took up their positions outside the door. He guessed they knew he needed nothing so much as a quiet place. He sat.

There was a gentle knock and the door opened. It was Jenine. She looked small, fragile. Her face was gray. "Your Majesty," she said formally. "I'm pregnant."

"I know," Logan said flatly. "Solon told me you bear Dorian's child."

"I've just met with a Healer. It's twins. Boys." Her voice was wooden.

It was a disaster. Sons. Nor would they be simple bastards who could be put aside: they were the offspring of a Godking and a Cenarian queen, with ample claim to the High King's throne on the basis of their blood alone. Their very existence would be destabilizing. If Logan had sons of his own, it would only be inviting civil war.

"I found a Healer who said . . . she said this early it would be safe to abort them." Jenine's eyes were dead.

"That isn't what you want," Logan said.

"There's more you have to know, Your Majesty," Jenine said. "I—I loved Dorian. Not the way I loved you, but even as I watched him descend into the madness and evil, I cared for him. You can scrub his sons from my body, but I will not come clean so easily. I'm sorry. You waited for me, and I didn't wait for you. If you wish to put me aside, Your Majesty, I will make no trouble for you. And if you wish me to purge my womb, I will. My duty to my lord husband and my country is greater than my own—"

"I've always wanted to be a dad," Logan said.

"What?"

"Can you love me, Jeni?"

She blinked up at him. "I love you so much it hurts."

Logan took her right hand in his left. "You are my wife, my lady, my queen." He put his right hand on her stomach. "Let these boys be my sons."

She jumped into his arms and squeezed him so hard he coughed. Then they laughed together and cried together and sat talking together for hours until Logan asked a question and Jeni didn't answer. She was staring at his lips.

"What?" he asked. He brushed his lips, but there was nothing on them.

Then her mouth was on his and there was roaring in his ears and the room faded and her softness and warmth was better than anything Logan had ever imagined. Somehow she was on his lap straddling him and her hands were on his back, in his hair, on his face, always pulling him closer, and he was pulling her in to him, crushing her against him, begging, demanding to be closer than clothes would allow.

When he surfaced from that kiss, her eyes were warm, dark pools of desire, reflecting only him. Somehow her hair had become disheveled, but it had never been more perfect. He'd surfaced for a reason, but he had to kiss the curve of her neck, so he did—and then her throaty murmur demanded more kisses and he gave them gladly. Following the curving of her neck to his lips, her back arched and her hand was behind his head, pulling him down toward her breasts.

Damn, the girl knows what she wants. Guess Dorian taught her a thing or three. What if Logan the Virgin doesn't measure up?

It was like catching a lake of cold water on his lap. He must have tensed because she pulled back.

She looked in his eyes. She knew.

Now I've spoiled everything. It wasn't just one moment he had destroyed; he could have just destroyed the easy, unfettered spirit of her sensuality. Every time they made love she would have to be conscious of Logan thinking, "Did she learn this from Dorian? Was Dorian better?"

"I'm sorry," she said. She swallowed, and he could see her wilting inside.

He breathed. "I forgive you." She moved to get off his lap, but he caught her and held her against him. It wasn't an emotion, it was a decision. He forgave her, even of the things that weren't her fault. This was too precious to let the past destroy it.

"Jeni," he said as he had said the night of their wedding. "Jeni, will you kiss me?"

She smiled and laughed and almost cried—and kissed him, still laughing. She pulled away and beat her fists on his chest.

"What?" Logan asked, alarmed.

"You can't do this to me. I can't feel all this at once!"

He grinned, and felt that he was himself once again. The idealistic, noble Logan and the wry, carefree Logan and the fierce, primal Logan were being reunited, reintroduced to each other—and Logan would need all of them to be the man and husband and king that he wanted to be. "Then just feel this," he said.

He kissed her again softly, slowly drawing her in, and in the pleasant blur of minutes that followed, they rebuilt their passion.

The thoughts came again like buzzing flies, but Logan ignored them. *No, you won't have this. This is precious. This is ours.*

As their kisses became more heated, those thoughts—and all thoughts—dimmed into the background and disappeared altogether beneath the scents of lavender and faint sweat and her breath, and the feel of her weight on his lap and her hands on his body and her skin beneath his lips and—finally!—his hands won through all the layers of skirts and he felt slim, stockinged calves and his fingers traced that silk up to silkier skin. Jeni moved her hips against him.

Logan jumped to his feet and set Jenine on hers. Eyes wide, he cleared his throat, "The royal apartments can't be far," he said. "If you can wait five minutes—"

Jenine grabbed him. They didn't wait.

When Kylar opened his eyes, he was lying in a soft bed. High overhead, the ceiling was covered with an elaborate mosaic of a warrior hanging onto a Titan's neck, a huge black sword drawn back in his hand for a killing blow. It was Kylar, but the mosaic was centuries old. Kylar turned.

At first, he didn't recognize Vi. For the first time he'd ever seen, she wore her luxurious, wavy red hair unbound. A single streak of it was stark white. She was seated beside his bed, holding his hand, her green eyes closed in sleep. There were red tulips on the bedside table.

EPILOGUE

*E*lene's funeral was simple and small, despite being held in the Hall of Winds. The high king and queen joined Vi and Kylar and Durzo and Sister Ariel. Dorian sat cross-legged on the ground near the back, oblivious. Thankfully, he was silent. Feir stood near him, mostly watching Dorian to make sure he didn't do anything offensive. Amazingly, Elene's old patr from Cenaria had accompanied Logan's army to help with the wounded, and he preached with a simple eloquence that bespoke his long friendship with her. The walls and dome of the Hall of Winds showed the beautiful spring day outside, ripe and bright with promise.

Vi caught herself glancing at Kylar again and again. After being bonded to him, it was strange to have to read his emotions from his face. He wept freely, and there was something clean and healing in those tears. The patr finished the final prayer, and one by one, they made their way to the open coffin.

Kylar and Vi went last. Elene was absolutely stunning. Sister Ariel and Vi had made her gown. It was white silk, like the one she'd died in, but in line with Elene's modesty and taste. Her face was radiant. Unscarred, it was the face God had intended for Elene, but without her gentleness to animate it, it looked too austere. Here was the face of a queen, but Elene's beauty had always been warm and comforting, never intimidating. As Vi tried to sketch in the details that this husk couldn't capture, the vastness of the loss overwhelmed her. She had to brace herself against the coffin.

Finally, Vi drew a little weave Sister Ariel had taught her around the splay of red tulips Elene held against her chest. It would preserve the flowers for all time. Then Vi touched her friend's cold cheek and kissed her forehead. As she touched Elene's body while still holding her Talent, Vi was struck by something.

Elene wasn't pregnant. Vi straightened, her tears forgotten. Had Elene simply been mistaken? Elene had never been pregnant before, so she wouldn't know exactly how it felt. Vi joined the departing line of mourners. Her eyes fell on the High Queen, pregnant with twins, and then on Dorian, sitting by the door. The mad mage grinned at her, and that grin reminded Vi that Dorian the Mad had held both of the world's most powerful magical artifacts at the same time. Dorian had been responsible for guiding the magic that had wiped out all the krul and restored this entire city. Dorian had been magically linkcd to all of them. Dorian had been the most Talented Healer in living memory.

Vi's mouth dropped open. Then the insanity of voicing her wild suspicions made it snap shut. What was she going to do? Challenge a madman, tell a king his wife was carrying two different men's sons, and throw an insane hope at Kylar as if it would make up for Elene's death?

No, she would say nothing, not until she knew, maybe not for a long time. But if Elene and Kylar's child somehow lived, Vi swore—swore!—that no one would hurt him.

As the ceremony ended, Vi looked surreptitiously at Kylar. He stood tall. Even as tears coursed down his face, he seemed unburdened, more at ease, more confident, more...himself, than Vi had ever seen. She came and stood beside him as the mourners walked into the glorious spring sunshine to look out over their clean white city. Ten thousand red tulips were a reminder of the blood that had purchased it. Kylar took Vi's hand and squeezed.

Laerin, still not acceptable, but closer than your dreadful first draft. See my marginalia. ALL revisions required before re-submission. This is not debatable.

—Jor Baaden, Chamberlain

~~GLOSS~~

GLOSSARY

Compiled for King Arelun Braag in the
year 12 Anno Braag (1742 Anno Jorsini)

**by D. Laerin Votagsmere the Gold,
Chief Scholar, D.Kn., J.Sc.**

A Brief Note on the Languages of Midcyru and this Gloss

(16, 18, 22, and 24 thousand words, actually. And yes, I counted.)

~~As Your Majesty has astutely observed, the brief notes I have written for other compendia have numbered between ten and fifteen thousand words, so I will be brief.~~ This gloss will be approached as a reference to the preceding pages, rather than as a self-contained work of scholarship. Thus, your humble servant D. Laerin Votagsmere the Gold, D.Kn., J.Sc. will define the words and concepts herein by what the contemporaries (circa 670–680 A.J.) knew, rather than what we know now more than a thousand years later.

(I don't suppose this has anything to do with the king's order that you have to pay for the preface?)

Please note, Your Majesty, that there are a number of serious textual inconsistencies within the work that should keep us from reading it as history as the term is now understood. (For example, Kylar meets the Wolf in a mysterious otherworld. If neither of them was the scribe of this narrative, who wrote these sections? If either *was* the scribe, how did they read other people's thoughts in other parts of the narrative?) Rather, this narrative should be approached as a blend of history, mythology, and adolescent wish-fulfillment. ~~(Must all female assassins have large breasts? I rest my case.)~~

His Majesty likes large breasts. As you might have noticed from his choice of mistresses. Unless you wish this to be seen as an attack on Lady Versetti?

Despite our diligence, this gloss is incomplete because our limited funding has not allowed full exploration of all previous research. Though space doesn't permit tracing the historical movements of peoples here, Your Majesty may refer to the groundbreaking work, *Ethnic, Linguistic, and Racial Moves and Mutations: Midcyru 1 A.J. to 704 A.J.* The first twelve volumes should be particularly instructive.

Ground-breaking! Beautiful! I wonder who wrote...Oh. Look at that. D. Laerin Votagsmere. Hmmph.

AETHELING (ay THELL ing): "Throne-worthy son," a Khalidoran prince. Khalidoran succession is determined not by birth order, but by magical and political aptitude. Each aetheling is given an *uurdthan* to prove his worthiness.

AMPLIFIAE (am PLIF ee AY): As one might intuit, an amplifier of magic. ~~Given that these worked with both the vir and the Talent, some scholars at the time speculated that magic, though evincing itself through particular cultures differently, is a unified, singular force.~~

ALITAERA/ALITAERAN (AL eh TAIR ah): ~~(though the pronunciation should be AL eh TIE rah, as the word is Old Jaeran. For notes on the ways Old Jaeran mixed with Hyrillic languages and morphed into our current argot, see the seminal work On the Nature and Transmission of Linguistic Anomalies From 1 Anno Jorsini to 682 Anno Jorsini)~~ The most powerful kingdom of the south, ruled by a council of dukes and a weaker king. It has two capital cities, one in the west, one in the east.

ALITAERAN ACCORDS: A set of agreements between Alitaera and the Chantry instrumental in shifting the Chantry from a temporal power to an educational, religious, magical one. Primary among the restrictions (and most frequently broken) was that male and female magi couldn't marry, and that the Chantry would not train their magae in specifically martial magics. Individual maja frequently ignored the latter injunction or studied magics that could plausibly be used for other tasks—tiny fireballs to light cooking fires, etc. But as the Chantry was careful not to flout the rules too openly, magae who married Talented men ended their own chances of advancement. Later, the prohibition spread socially to marrying men at all.

ALKESTIA/THE ALKESTIA CYCLE (al KEST ee A): The story cycle of Emperor Jorsin Alkestes. Yearly festivals are held in several cities throughout Midcyru in his honor. The telling of the stories takes between five and ten days.

ARUTAYRO (Ah roo TAY row): "Bloodless." A meeting at which both parties swear to avoid violence.

BABY FARMS: Akin to orphanages, except that labor was expected of the children. Frequently, this practice turned abusive. In some infamous (possibly apocryphal) cases, those labors included prostitution and volunteering for vivisection.

BASHERS: Men used by the Sa'kagé whenever muscle is needed (extortion, punishment, etc). The Basher guild takes their name from these, though they have no special connection with them.

BATTLE OF JAERAN FLATS: For the purposes of this narrative, a nearly mythical conflict where one of the original Champions of Light Corvaer the Red died, and from which his ka'kari was taken by Malak Mok'mazi (Malak Firehands).

BERAA (bear AHH): The most erotic of Khalidoran dances. This style gave Khalidoran women such a reputation for loose morals that it was later claimed to be an invention of southerners. A staple of stories appealing to the exotic fascination about this northern clime, the beraa was a more frenetic dance than a rondaa. Here, the dancer would clap her hands and undulate her hips and toss her hair, all while maintaining the elaborate foot- and hipwork of the rondaa. Said to have caused two wars and innumerable duels. It is claimed that Marian Dayshar saved her expedition across the Freeze by dancing a beraa for her frostbitten men—who then marched twelve days across the wastes warmed by what they'd seen. When they arrived home, they were executed by her lover for it! See also RONDAA.

This! This! This is exactly the sort of thing the king will enjoy!

BIGS: Older children in a street guild, not dependent so much on age as on size or, sometimes, position. For instance, Jarl, though small, is recognized as a big at roughly ten years of age.

BLACK BARROW: A great, leagues-wide black dome, under which was buried the ancient capital city Trayethell. Believed to have been the site of Jorsin Alkestes' last stand. Unclear whether the following was also known contemporaneously: The only (?) place where, once killed, a krul cannot be raised again.

BLADEMASTERS: Pretty much what one would guess. Governed as a loose confederation. Though much has been lost over the centuries about them, one story which I believe (from Vol Trulen) says that Blademasters had a quirk that kept them from being impersonated too often: any Blademaster whose status as a Blademaster was challenged could not refuse a duel. Thus, when counterfeits sprang up, as they inevitably did as young men sought to trade-in on the Blademasters' high standing without going to all the bother of training, real Blademasters would be dispatched and challenge them. This lesson in blood apparently needed frequent repetition, however, as His Majesty is no doubt aware from the popular ballad, "The Sting of the Rose," ~~which to the best of my knowledge is otherwise completely false.~~

He loves that song. Don't ruin it for him.

CAERNARVON (care NAR vin): A city, the capital of Waeddryn, it sits on confluence of the Wy, the Red, and the Blackberry rivers. At the time, a prosperous and peaceful place, not yet subject to the turmoil for which it is now infamous.

CALCINATOR (KAL sin ate or): An alchemical apparatus for the reduction of liquids to powder.

CALLAE (KAL ay— ~~again a violation of its own Old Jaeran pro-~~ ~~nunciation, which should be KAL IE—such frequent exceptions~~ ~~to grammatical and pronunciative rules are probably part of the~~ ~~cause of this generation's sad indifference to the study of Old~~ ~~Jaeran, and their subsequent ignorance, folly, social ineptitude,~~ ~~and cultural barrenness.)~~

Never got around to a definition here, did you?

CENARIA (SIN are EE ah): 1) A small country on the Great Sea, poor despite its excellent harbors due to a series of wars of succession and an entrenched Sa'kagé. Borders Khalidor to its north, Ceura to the south, and Lae'knaught-controlled territory (of what is nominally Ceura and Modai) to the southeast. 2) The capital city of Cenaria. Cenaria (the city) is divided sharply into economic lines by the Plith River. The Warrens on the west side are built mostly over a swamp, and the socially undesirable are not allowed to leave—though with corrupt guards, etc, they often do so. The east side is home to merchants, exporters, former slavers (slavery had recently been abolished by the time of this narrative), the nobility, and more prosperous traders.

CEURA/CEURAN (COO RA/CUR in): Literally, The Sword. Country south of Cenaria and sometimes at war with them, though internal problems have kept Ceura from pursuing conquest on a large scale for a century. Starkly different culturally, Ceura has managed to influence Cenaria's architecture, arts, and understanding of warfare, while not being heavily influenced in turn. Home to a warrior culture, Ceura had not yet romanticized its history into the system of *ooshito* that is now associated with them. Ceurans at the time were brutally experienced with the horrors of war and were most interested in winning. This interest reached its zenith in the character ~~(now believed to be purely~~ ~~apocryphal)~~, Lantano Garuwashi.

Like boobs, the king likes his invincible warriors. Leave it if you like, but I ask you, does it really matter?

CEUR'CAELESTOS: The Blade of Heaven/ Blade of Power of the Ceurans. A big magical sword. ~~Supposedly~~ made of diamond— ~~but somehow it wouldn't break? Haha.~~ It supposedly had a fire that burned within it that would warn of danger, flaring out longer toward the point the nearer the danger was. ~~If this doesn't~~ ~~make His Majesty chuckle, I'm not sure what will.~~

There are other scholars in this land. Scholars who don't laugh up their sleeves at men-kings—who like magic swords. Be aware that most of said scholars would happily take your place, your lands, your titles, and your daughter's doubtful remaining virtues.

CHANTRY, THE (CHANT tree): A school of magic which was to become the premier school of magic by 300 A.J., administered by women since 217 A.J. and only open to women since 428 A.J, at which time the Alitaeran Accords were signed by Jezrill Godan and Queen Faelan Couzon. The Chantry was housed in what was contemporaneously Ossein, though their governance was left completely to the sisters. The Chantry was housed in, ~~if you can believe this,~~ a floating island in the middle of Lake Vestacci crafted into the likeness of a seraph(?). The translations are unclear, but perhaps an angel? Or a 'radiant woman'. An entire island, crafted in sculpture, that could be moved throughout a lake on magical currents. It was also called the Alabaster Seraph, the White Lady, and the Seraph of Nerev. There is no known scholarship on 'Nerev.'

CHATTEL, THE: Led by Eris Buel, married magae. As an order of primarily unmarried women, there were often more or less subtle judgments made about those women who chose to marry. (Marriage to Talented men was forbidden, and never or rarely actually practiced at the Chantry.) Those who married generally found that their opportunities for promotion to higher ranks were stymied. The belief was that a woman could have only one spouse— and that should be the Chantry. Those who chose to submit to a husband (regardless of the actual arrangement of the marriage, it was pejoratively alleged thus) were believed to be those who voluntarily submitted to a lesser person, i.e., becoming chattel, or slaves, to non-drafters. This was viewed as a perversion of the natural order (in which magic-users, naturally, were greater than non-magic-users).

CORANTI (CORE ahn tee): A later text related to this tells us that this means, "the unclean." That translation of the Hyrillic (?) cannot be verified from secondary sources. "Durzo" and "Kylar" can see the sins that stain men's and women's souls. Though apparently their sensitivity to such was variable. Also, whose definition of "sin" is never clarified. Murder and the like clearly counted. "Durzo" claimed to have been able to see lies at one point, but if one thing is clear from this entire account, it is that Durzo Blint lies.

CORPUSARIUM (CORE pus are EE um): A Khalidoran warehouse for bodies and bones. Not apparently for their veneration, but for their use in unspeakable rites.

CRUXING: ~~How Alitaerans at the time executed rebels and, sometimes, murderers. The condemned would hang suspended tied to~~

His Majesty's great-grandfather was cruxed. Not necessary.

~~beams in an X until asphyxia set in. An agonizing, humiliating way to die.~~

CUROCH (cure ROCK/coo ROCK): Legendary sword of Jorsin Alkestes, created by Ezra Sa'sogol, the finest Maker ever. Recovered by the Prophet and Feir Cousat, and subsequently taken 'for safe keeping' by the Sa'seuran. The Sword of Power. There is some connection hinted at with the Ceuran blade: Ceur'caelestos.

Thanks for the pronunciation guide on that one. Here I thought it was deh-DUR. You are a prince among men, Laerin!

DEADER (DEAD ur): A wetboy's target, thus called because the target was said to be dead as soon as the contract was accepted. The actual killing could be assumed accomplished at that time. Hyperbole, but in contemporary accounts, it is clear that many people believed this.

You think you need inform a monarch with four thousand war horses what a destrier is? Please, leave it in. You are paying for the parchment. I'll order more gold illuminations for the margins.

DEATH GAMES: Created by Count Drake, with an arena, food, wine, gambling; became a national obsession, entrenched the Sa'kagé. How the Sa'kagé allowed the practice to be ended is an enduring mystery.

DESTRIER: Large war horse, bred not merely to carry armored soldiers, but also to fight.

DIASPORA THAUMATURGICA (DEE asp OR a THOU ma TURG ick A): "Scattering of Mages"; The century after the collapse of the Shining Lands, when mages were persecuted across Midcyru. Multiple new schools were created throughout the realms, but each was crushed in turn. It is estimated that two thirds of the mages were killed.

DRAGON TONGUE: Idiomatic—a magical diffuse flame, Khalidoran (?)

DUST: A drug used by Khalidorans, induced euphoria, feelings of invulnerability, and sudden death.

THE ESCAPE OF THE GRASQ TWINS: A popular ballad contemporaneously, believed to be mythical. Unknown if the twins referred to are the same twins in *The Grasq Twins' Doom*. It is known that twins had a peculiar cultural resonance.

FALTIER MOUNTAINS: Mountains along northern border of Cenaria, southern border of Khalidor; Screaming Winds is primary pass between them. The cursed Black Barrow is at the mouth of the other pass, which is farther away from Cenaria City: Quorig's Pass.

FASMERU MOUNTAINS: Mountains at base of which is Torras Bend; on southern border of Ossein, eastern border of Cenaria

FEYURI (fay UR ee): Claim to be descended from Fey folk, despised for that and their pacifism. Rare by the time of this narrative.

FLETCHER: ~~A maker of arrows, one who fletches.~~

FORGLIN'S PASS: The passage between Ossein and Waeddryn.

FRIAKU (FREE ah COO): Far eastern country, famous for its horse lords.

FURIED: Unclear, perhaps Talented? Historical references are numerous usually to 'furied warriors' of Friaku, but those assume knowledge of the meaning of the word.

GALERUS: A retiarius: literally a "net-man" or "net-fighter." Sethi.

GANDU/GANDIAN (GAND oo): Island nation south of Waeddryn. A reclusive nation, which housed the men's school of healing magic. The nation and its peoples are almost absent from histories and tales both, except for its mages, who became a staple of romances for their near-mythical powers. Hero dying nobly at the end of your tale? A Gandian Hoth'salar will save the day!

GAOL (JAIL): A jail in Cenaria, the Maw served as the sole gaol. It is mostly underneath the castle. This position led several kings to divert the Plith into the Maw, sometimes 'accidentally,' to rid themselves of prisoners permanently. ~~That an underground prison could exist practically beneath a river is one of the key considerations that led current scholars to believe this entire history is myth. That and the busty magical assassins with god-like powers.~~

GODKING: One of the titles of Garoth Ursuul. Direct, unbroken descent from Khalidor's founder, Roygaris Ursuul, is claimed. Most scholars view such claims as more political than historical.

GORATHI (GORE ah TEE): Revered, almost worshipped warriors of Ymmur and Friaku. The 'furied gorathi' are referred to, always as something to fear, never with more explanation. Evidently they were a staple bogeyman at one time, and no more explanation of their purported powers was needed.

GRAAKOS: A Khalidoran invocation that summons a shield. Why this knowledge survives while other more useful knowledge perished is one of the frustrations of the way of scholars.

GRAAVAR HIGHLANDERS: A tribe of Khalidorans; tall, barrel-chested blue-eyed savages with black hair, short mustaches, a powerful tribe.

GRASQ TWINS' DOOM: As stated before. A song. Unknown if related to The Escape of the Grasq Twins.

GUILD: After the baby farms were shut down when slavery was outlawed in Cenaria, vast numbers of orphans were forced onto

The king is illiterate, not an idiot. The converse might be said of certain scholars.

The Way of Scholars? Catchy. You need to get out more.

the streets. Guards swept them out of the east side and confined them to the Warrens. Guilds were in the domain of the Sa'kagé, and though frequently exploited by the Sa'kagé, often it appears that the leaders of the Sa'kagé did not care for their welfare (despite having come from the guilds themselves). Generally, the guilds served as makeshift families for orphans and training grounds in their eventual trades, which were almost always criminal.

GUNDER: The gold coin of the realm, named for picture of Aleine IX they bear.

GURKA: A heavy, forward curving knife or short sword.

HAMMERFIST: Blue cone of magic, of the kind any magus taught at Sho'fasti would know.

HARAN (HAIR in): ~~Country either east of Ymmur—which is impossible, because we know the ancient country of Ymmur borders the sea—or set in a small enclave of Ladesh, far to west and south. Chalcus theorizes that Haran fell into the sea and that a remnant sailed halfway across the world to establish a colony in Ladesh. I find Hevort more compelling: that "Haran" simply signified a people far away and exotic or barbaric or strange. I point to their tales claiming it was~~ Home to the Haranese bull—an animal forty hands tall with iron for skin and teeth longer than spears! ~~How would such a beast chew its food? These tales tell us less about the purported savages they depict than they do about those who believe them.~~

There, fixed it for you.

The king loves horses. Add more here. I don't care if you have to make it up.

I suppose that having all your priests in one place made them much easier to massacre had nothing to do with it. Or was this an attempt at humor?

HAVERMERE: Ancestral estate of the Gyres in central Cenaria. Famous for breeding horses.

HECATONARCHS (heck KAT on arks): Priests of the hundred gods, they wore cloak of a hundred colors. An intriguing, short-lived phenomenon during the growth of the worship of the One God wherein it was believed a priest for any of the hundred gods could be a priest for all of them. Apparently the gods got jealous and wanted to each have their own priests.

HERBIARY: ~~A place devoted to the growing, and often selling, of herbs.~~

HERBS:

ARIAMU (AIR ee AH moo): A poisonous root?

HENBANE: Not fatal, but in combination with Kinderperil, can make a person ill for days if injected/pricked with it

JACINTH SPOOR: In combination with ariamu, a slow poison

GURI PEPPER: Used to spice food?

KINDERPERIL: A poison. From "dangerous to children"? Though apparently it could be concocted in lethal concentrations for adults, too.

NORANTON SEED (NOR ant un): Unknown.

PERI PERI (PAIR ee PAIR ee): In combination with Xanthos, a contact poison; in small doses, just leaves victim unconscious.

PRONWI (PRAWN wee): A seed. Now lost or referred to by some other name.

RAGWEED: Used for healing?

SILVERLEAF: The roots are poisonous, though the leaves are often used by physickers for healing.

TUNTUN SEED: Ground to powder, and breathed, will cause lungs to hemorrhage.

UBDAL (OOB dull): A root. Properties unknown.

XANTHOS (ZAN those): A contact poison?

YARROW ROOT: Unknown.

THE HOLE: Sometimes referred to more vulgarly herein. A Cenarian prison for the worst of the worst. In a pit, and then arranged around a pit with a floor sloping toward the hole, from which rose foul gases. *The king is no wilting flower, you can call it Hell's Asshole.*

HORAI: An island of Seth, the Takedas' home island.

HOTH'SALAR (HOATH sall ARE): Old Jaeran, "brother of healing." Also referred to as Green mages. Their school, Hoth'salarium is in the city of Horachi.

HOUSES: A slippery concept in Cenarian history, as the noble houses of Cenaria saw great tumult for centuries—new houses added, old houses destroyed. The Makells had been a noble house for three hundred years, and were destroyed shortly before this narrative, and of course, several new houses were created by the end of this narrative, which I had redacted at your Chamberlain's direction.

HYRIL (HERE ill): Ancient capital city of the Shining Lands. Believed mythical.

HYRILLIC (HERE ill ick): Having to do with Hyril, but usually used to refer to the language, though the people of Hyril didn't speak it. In Jorsin Alkestes' era, Old Jaeran was the vulgar tongue. It is believed Hyrillic was a scholarly language, or a thaumaturgical one. Few people in the world, if any, now speak or read Hyrillic. Apparently it was rare but not forgotten at the time of this narrative. Fragments remain in vocabulary, but the grammar has disappeared

IAOSIAN FOREST (eye O shun): Also known as Ezra's Wood, near the town of Torras Bend, nominally part of Waeddryn. Where the Archmage Ezra the Mad disappeared roughly fifty years after the fall of Jorsin Alkestes. Reputed to be the home of monsters. Many attempts to go into the wood, first to investigate, and later to recover magical artifacts the earlier efforts had carried in all failed. Everyone who went in simply vanished. Home of supposed Dark Hunter.

IURES (YOUR ace): Old Jaeran meaning, "the scepter or staff of law." A magical artifact created by Ezra the Maker. Lost. (There is some debate about whether Ezra the Maker was the same person as Archmage Ezra the Mad, with this scholar believing there were two men, possibly related, possibly the latter merely wished to evoke a kinship with the former. Otherwise Ezra would have had an incredible lifespan. Although it is also possible that the histories referring to meeting Ezra long after the Alkestes era were themselves fanciful. I hope Your Majesty may fund further exploration of this exciting area of study!)

Write now. Beg later.

JAERA: Either a hero or a dragon. Ancient even to those we consider the ancients. Details lost.

JAERAN, OLD (JAIR ran): Used in reference either to the Jaeran Plain east of Ceura or to the Old Jaeran language. Less commonly refers to the present day common language of almost all Midcyru. (Note: Though this is the second time in this gloss wherein the Old Jaeran 'ae' followed by an 'r' gives the 'air' sound, this is not, despite the claims of some scholars, because 'Jaeran' and 'Alitaeran' are actually Hyrillic words. Instead, as my own studies have proven, these are merely Old Jaeran used so commonly that the masses have changed the pronunciation through sheer repetition of their mistakes—as the verb 'to be' often has the most irregular forms. Cf. "Glottal and Epochal Revolutions through the Hyrillic/Alitaeran/Khalidoran Founding with Special Reference to Migrations following the Diaspora Thaumaturgica" by D. Laerin Votagsmere, D.Kn., J.Sc.)

This is exactly the kind of drivel you filled the first 'brief note' with. King Braag wants a story, not a cure for insomnia.

KARIAMU LODOC (CARE ee AM oo la doke): A Hyrillic phrase accompanying obeisance without exact translation, a formal apology and acceptance of consequences. (How an undereducated

~~wetboy in Cenaria learned it is the kind of thing that keeps lin-guists up at night.~~ *And chamberlains laughing. Erase.*

KA'KARI (ka CAR ee): A Hyrillic word, either singular or plural. Translation unclear. Highest orb(s) of _____? Magical artifacts possibly created or discovered through the use of both Curoch and Iures together? Or those artifacts were made through the use of the ka'kari? Ezra was reputed to be involved with both, as was Jorsin Alkestes. This scholar finds it impossible to choose between the conflicting reports, all of which seem equally unlikely.

> **BLUE:** Gaelan Starfire threw into the sea, creating the Tlax-ini Maelstrom.

> **WHITE:** Lost for 6 centuries (Garoth Ursuul's grandmother disproved that it was held in the Chantry).

> **GREEN:** Taken to Ladesh by Hrothan Steelbender and lost, 220 years before this narrative.

> **RED:** Cast into the heart of Ashwind Mountain (referred to as Mount Tenji in Ceura) by Ferric Fireheart, or by Gaelan Starfire.

> **SILVER:** Lost during the Hundred Years' War, could be any-where from Alitaera to Ceura, unless Garric Shadowbane destroyed it.

> **BROWN:** Rumored to be at the Maker's school in Ossein.

(Many additional details redacted from this list by request of the Chamberlain. Over my objections.) *Do you know what we call those who spoil stories for His Majesty? Homeless.*

KA'KARIFER (ka CAR ee FUR): A bearer of a ka'kari. Perhaps also one who is capable of bearing a ka'kari.

KHALIDOR/KHALIDORAN (KAL eh DOOR, KAL eh DOOR an): Country north of Cenaria and south of the Frozen Lands. Founded by Roygaris Ursuul after he betrayed Jorsin Alkestes. The Godkings claim direct descent from Roygaris himself, which is dubious. Khalidor had reduced Lodricar to a client state, and gradually absorbed it. None but the official records survive, and even those have been purged repeatedly, giving scholars precious few glimpses into Khalidoran history. It was apparently once much more prosperous than at the time of this narrative, with ancient mentions of rich farmland rather than tun-dra, and no mention of the ice sheets of the north. When Hiziki-rin made his dogsled explorations, he claimed to have found port cities far north of even the Ghostgate Ruins—ports now com-pletely encased in ice. As best we can guess, Khalidor was made of a blend of the ruling class who came after the fall of Jorsin Alkestes, the Lodricari, the mountain and lowlands clans, the Feyuri, and the River People—about whom nothing is known. Clans we know about:

CHURAQ

HRAAGL: Guarded the Khalidoran baggage train.

IKTANA: A mountain tribe of climbers.

QUARL

KHALI: A goddess of Khalidor. The rather more extensive description has been redacted by order of the Chamberlain.

KHALIRAS: The capital city of Khalidor; with extensive caverns deep beneath and around the city that have been mined for 700 years; the ore is said to be magical.

KHALIRIUM: The very room in which Khali resides.

KHALIVOS RAS EN ME(KAL ee vos ROSS on may): Khalidoran prayer: "Khali, come and make your home in me."

KRUL: ~~Entirely mythical. However, Your Majesty should understand that the people in this story DID believe in their literal existence. At least some people did. At least by the end of the narrative.~~ Monsters created by Khalidorans, perhaps by Khalidoran Vürdmeisters. Depending on the skill of the creator, could be made into the shape of horses, wolves, tigers, mammoths, fire ants (? I confess, this last makes no sense to me whatever), large frogs – they each hold a *Stranger*; originally called the Fallen, apparently because they can be raised again when they die.

> **KRUL:** A meister can lead twelve krul himself, but needs a white krul, that is a daemon, to lead more (13 krul equals a squad).

> **DAEMONS:** One daemon allows a Meister to control more than 13 individual krul. 13 Daemons equals a platoon.

> **BONE LORDS:** Smarter, capable of speech, and can use a dark representation of talent or something like it. If raised, they allow a meister to control more than 13 squads, or 1 PLATOON.

> **FIENDS:** The raising of 13 platoons requires a Fiend; 13 fiends makes 1 LEGION.

> **ARCANGHUL:** Allows the use of 13 legions to create 1 ARMY; one of which was used by Godking Roygaris to conquer what remained of the Freeze.

NIGHT LORD: Necessary for the creation of more than 13 Arcanghuls.

KHALI: The deity above the Arcanghuls, who killed Roygaris Ursuul and became deity of the Khalidorans, giving them the Vir.

Other legendary creatures which may or may not be krul per se—a taxonomy of creatures that don't exist being exceedingly difficult! Zel, ferali, ferozi, buulgari, blaemir, titans.

LADESH/LADESHIAN (la DESH, la DEESH an): A continent country across the Great Sea. Thus far, only Sethi vessels are known to have the skill to make the voyage. They do not allow any Midcyri to make the voyage west, though Ladeshians frequently make the opposite journey and have a sizeable minority presence in several Midcyri port cities. Fantastically rich, not only through the silk monopoly, but also through efficient governance unrivaled through the modern era.

LAE'KNAUGHT/LAETUNARIVERISSIKNAUGHT (LIE K'GNAW' HT/LIE tune ARE ee VEAR iss see K'GNAW'HT [like ka-knocked, but aspirated]): Militant anti-religious sect that effectively controls parts of Ceura and Modai, though it claims no interest in temporal power. (The word contains a dipthong that no longer exists in our language. The final syllable is aspirated. (Analogous to 'knight,' in which originally one pronounced both the k and the g.)

Fancy this—an interesting linguistic note. This one can stay.

LITTLES: The younger, and/or smaller children in a street guild.

LODRICAR/LODRICARI (LOW dreh CAR ee): A country east of Khalidor, a client state, since subsumed.

MAGIC: Super-normal power. Mages rely on sunlight or firelight for their power, though they can hold a small reserve beyond this. Wytches apparently have no such limitation. From whence their powers come—daemons as some claim, or elsewhere—is beyond the purview of this scholar.

MAGE: User of the Talent. Technically:

    MAJA/MAGAE (MAH ja/MAJ eye)for a woman/women.

    MAGUS/MAGI (MAJE us/MAJ eye)for a man/men.

    MAGI is also used for groups containing both men and women, or where it is unknown. An artifact of the inflected Old Jaeran language which rarely caused problems because it only surfaces when the discussions are written.

LOOP, RECURSIVE: See RECURSIVE LOOP.

MAGEFIRE: Fire, used by mages.

MAJA UXTRA KURRUKULAS (MA ja UX tra coo ROO kah lass): A bush mage, a wild mage (female).

THE MAW: Cenarian gaol on Vos Island, nearly underneath the castle itself. The front gate is a ramp leading down into a demonic visage carved in jagged black rock. The worst part of this gaol was called the Hole. ~~By all accounts The Maw was a miserable place.~~

Unlike other dungeons?

MEISTER (MY stir): Khalidoran, "Master [of Magic]," polite term of address for a wytch.

MIDCYRU: 1) All of the known world, 2) The continent.

THE MIKAIDON: Keeper of Civil order in Hokkai, akin to a shire reeve more recently.

MISTARILLE (MIST are ill): A light, unbreakable metal, mythical.

MODAI/MODAINI (mow DIE, mow DIE EEN ee): A fragmented country southeast of Cenaria practicing a form of anarchical pre-dictatorship wherin the leader is the person who can convince the majority of ignoranami that he or she will give them the most of what they want while only costing other people. Then, to keep the leader from ever becoming wise and eventually ruling for the good of the country rather than for the good of his backers, they switch leaders, almost always to one from the opposite faction, every five years. In this way, present leaders can always dodge responsibility and the perpetually discontented populace can always believe new lies.

The king will be glad to hear that you aren't one of these new-fangled demophiles. Here you seem such a man of the people.

MOULINA: An old Khalidoran term of affection. Or possibly contempt.

Very helpful.

MOUNT HEZERON: ~~The tallest mountain on Ceuran border, at least 1400 feet tall.~~

More details, please. Cut? Materials? Lady Versetti is planning a surprise for the king.

NAGIKA(NAH gee kah): A traditional dress worn by women of Seth; drapes over one shoulder, leaving one breast exposed. Less common by the time of this narrative as the Sethi interacted more with mainland cultures who apparently reacted poorly to this "immodesty."

That's it? That's the best you can do? The king will definitely ask about this. Make something up!

THE NAMELESS: Another term for the Night Angel.

NEPHILIM: From antiquity, mythical, the children of angels and men.

NIGHT ANGEL: ~~Upon Your Majesty's Chamberlain's insistence, I have reluctantly redacted this entry.~~

What's this, Laerin? Are you developing a spine? It doesn't fit you. May I suggest, "The topic of this narrative."?

NINE, THE: The leaders of the different areas a city's Sa'kagé controls. In Cenaria, they are the Trematir (The Master of Coin), the Urdt "The Gamesman" (gambling), the Fjidt "The Thief," the Duergust "First Striker" (bashers), the Garjudt "The Scourge" (slaves/extortion), the Mattir "The Mother" or "The Mistress of Pleasures," (prostitution), the Kuhluhk "Lord of Whispers" (spies), the Sahrasliss "The Master of Smuggling" and the Braavok "The Piper," (Younglings). Note: The names are Varagoli, a pre-Alkestian language spoken by the pygmy Rock People who were native to Cenaria in antiquity. The language and the people now extinct. ~~Proposals have been put forward that would allow greater research into these fascinating peoples.~~

NINER: Derisive nickname for Aleine Gunder IX.

NOCTA HEMATA: THE NIGHT OF PASSION/ABANDON/ Blood: Popular nickname for the night of the Cenaria uprising. Additional details redacted at the Chamberlain's direction.

NYSOS: God of blood, wine, and semen. The great dramatic festivals of Seth in his honor are the foundations of modern drama. Tellel suggests that these festivals were literal week-long orgies, drawing people from all over the world, at least at the height of the Sethi Empire.

OLD JAERAN: See JAERAN, OLD.

OOTAI (oo TIE): A popular, hot drink among the people of Midcyru. Bitter, and a stimulant. Now known as tea. Not legally available to us since Your Majesty's great-grandfather's trade war with the Kumare.

PATR: A priest of the One God.

PAVVIL'S GROVE: A small logging town near the Ceuran border. Site of the final battle between the Cenarian rebels and Khalidoran invaders.

PHILODUNAMOS: A poison, an explosive?

PHYSICKER: Archaic term for a physician.

PIT WYRMS: A type of krul (?), allegedly called forth by Vurdmeisters from hell itself.

PLANGA (PLANG gah): Tiny island nation off the southwest coast of Ceura, remarkable only for the number of sheep and the quality of its plate-glass. They discovered and kept secret the formulas for dyeing molten glass for several hundred years, but lacking the enlightened governance of Ladesh, and with a populace given to drink and poetry, they never translated wealth into power.

I see you've noticed the king doesn't like Plangans, lick-spittle.

PLITH: The river that separates the two halves of the city of Cenaria. (Or make that the one have, since the other half is the have-nots.) *My apologies for the pun. Were parchment cheaper, I would grab a clean sheet—as I fear that if I rub this one clean once more it shall rip.*

POTENTIATION: When two drugs interact to heighten the effects of one or both of them. The chemists I spoke with don't believe this effect was known in Midcyru at the time of this narrative.

QUORIG'S PASS: A week's travel east of Screaming Winds, a pass along the Khalidoran and Osseini border; Black Barrow lies at the mouth of the pass.

RAPTUS MORGI (RAP toose MORGUE ee): Keeper of the Dead; official Khalidoran title for the overseer of the Godking's krul at Khaliras.

RECURSIVE LOOP: See LOOP, RECURSIVE.

REIGUKHAS: A Khalidoran town, not far from Black Barrow. Site of a ruse by southern forces and the scene of a massacre for raising krul.

RONDAA (ron DAHH): A sensuous Khalidoran dance performed by women, usually for the enjoyment of their husbands, or suitors, or by prostitutes. The dancer wore a wide garment with exaggerated shoulder pieces, from which were suspended cut pieces of cloth. Under this, she wore suggestive underclothes, paint, or nothing at all. The cloth was sewn with bells which tinkled with each suggestive move of the dancers hips. The dance was otherwise typified by the contrast of the dancer's head floating still while her hips gyrated slowly. See also BERAA.

RURSTAHK SLAAGEN(RUR stock SLOG in): "The Devil of the Walls," Khalidoran highland clans' name for Duke Regnus Gyre.

SA'CEURAI: Old Jaeran for "Sword Lords." Title earned by young Ceuran swordsmen for killing another sa'ceurai. Though most scholars believe there must have been other ways to earn the title as well, else the sa'ceurai would have ceased to exist very quickly.

SA'FASTI (SA fast ee): Old Jaeran for "Lords of Movement," or "Lords of Music" (?). Male blue or energy mages, their school Sho'fasti is in the Alitaeran city of Jer'mai.

SAI: Short sword with a narrow blade, hilts swept up in broad U for catching blade, each tine sharpened.

SA'KAGÉ (SA COG ay): "Lords of the Shadows." [But not gender exclusive.] An underworld guild, varying forms of it were present in most Midcyri cities, but it is most organized and powerful in Cenaria. Usually governed by the Nine, whose functions differ in different cities, and a Shinga.

SA'SALAR: A Lord of Healing. A title eschewed by the time of this narrative either through humility or simple recognition that the Hoth'salar's gifts were much inferior to the Sa'salar's. It is believed that both the first Godking Roygaris Ursuul and Ezra the Maker were Sa'salari.

SA'SEURAN (SA SEWER an/SA SIR an): "Lord of Light", 1) A fire mage. 2) All the Sa'seuri together (the grammatically correct plural 'Sa'seuri' had already fallen out of use). 3) The leaders of Sho'cendi, the school of fire. ~~Apologies to His Majesty for the needless complexity!~~

SCHLUSS: Consists of strapping small sleds to the feet and going downhill on snow while standing, at incredible speeds. Either mythical or simply insane.

SCREAMING WINDS: A Cenarian garrison in the Faltier mountains along the Khalidoran border; also a pass through the mountains, by the same name.

I swear if you define one more common term, I'll burn this and you'll rewrite it from the tower.

SELLSWORD: ~~A mercenary.~~

SEQUOY: A giant tree that grows in the Iaosian Forest. Believed to be the most ancient growing things in the world.

SESCH (sesh): The 'game of kings,' played on a board of alternating squares with various stone or wood pieces. Interestingly, despite that it is believed that women most often had tightly circumscribed roles in their society, the piece representing a woman is the most powerful in the game.

SETH/SETHI (SETH/SETH ee): Seafaring people famous for sailing and red wines. Usually olive-skinned and brown-eyed.

Didn't the women go topless or something? I strongly suggest you add this.

SETH (SETH): The Island Empire of Seth had mostly crumbled by this time, losing the last of its colonies in the recent past due to the disastrous leadership of Emperor Sijuron Tofusin. The country would be revived, but it never again could be called an empire.

SHADOWCLOAKED/SHADOWSTRIDER: More names for the Night Angel.

SHALAKROI: A position of great authority in Ladesh, said in the text to be roughly equivalent to a duke, earned by scoring among the top tier in the Ladeshian Civil Service examinations. A remarkable system that led to the most efficient governance of the ancient world.

SHINGA (SHING gah): Not Old Jaeran, but said elsewhere to mean, "The Judge." The head of the Sa'kagé.

SHIV: A sharpened piece of metal, a makeshift knife.

SHO'CENDI (show KEND ee): "The School of Fire." Home of the Sa'seuri or Sa'seuran, the Lords of Fire, the fire mages. Also a term for the mage pyramid in Modai.

SHU'RA (SURE ah): A rank or differentiation of either Khalidoran magic or Khalidoran society or both. Vürdmeisters are always above the seventh (?), but no consensus exists on how many shu'ra there are. One former wytch claimed to have been of the fourteenth shu'ra. Many mages find this claim dubious, believing that the highest rank attainable is the 12th—except for the God-king, who is the sole member of the 13th.

SIDLIN MARKET: The primary market in Cenaria City.

SIDLIN WAY: A major arterial on the east side of Cenaria City.

SKONE: The eastern capital of Alitaera.

SLAVEBORN: Children either born to slave parents, or raised in the 'baby farms' and thus slaves themselves.

SLEKKED: Khalidoran, an obscene form of sodomized, i.e., in a bad position.

So delicately put for one so intimately familiar with it.

THE SNAKE OF HARAN/LADESH: Snake with seven heads, legendary.

SWORD FORMS:

    ALATHEA'S WAKING
    BOULDERS FALLING
    DRIPPING WATER
    GABEL'S GAME
    GARON'S STAND
    GORAMOND'S DIVE
    HADEN'S GLORY
    HARANI BULLS
    HERON'S HUNT
    KEVAN'S BLUNDER
    KIRIAE'S CROUCH
    KNOT LOOSED
    MANY WATERS
    MORNING SHADOWs
    PRAAVEL'S DEFENSE
    SYDIE'S WRATH

THREE DAISIES

THREE MOUNTAIN CASTLE

TWO TIGERS

VALDÉ DOCCI: The Swordsman Withdraws

YRMI'S BOUT

ZHEL POSTO: A fighter's stance for keeping balance and agility on slick ground.

Huh? With your burly physique and natural grace, somehow I expected you to know a lot about this, Laerin.

SYMBELINE WEAVE: A magical construction with 84 variations; requires perfect timing, structure, and vocal intonation. It became slang for something incredibly difficult.

TANTO: A short, straight blade for punching through armor.

TLAXINI MAELSTROM: Said to have been created when Gaelan Starfire threw the blue ka'kari into the sea.

More. The sea sucking in ships and then exploding water out? Exciting. EX-CIT-ING, Laerin. More death, more explosions, more magic, more breasts. This is not challenging.

TORRAS BEND: A small town ~~in northwest Waeddryn; three days horse ride north of the Silver Hills~~. A few hundred paces from Ezra's wood. Six hundred years before this narrative, Ezra created/captured the Dark Hunter and brought it to the wood that would be named after him. He began experiments. Soon thereafter, the Talented children of Torras Bend began disappearing, sometimes with blood left behind, the bodies apparently devoured. No one knows what happened, but eventually the Talented children stopped dying. At the time of this narrative, going into the wood was still believed to result in death for anyone, Talented or not.

TRAYETHELL (TRAY ah thell): 1) One of the Seven Kingdoms that eventually became part of the Shining Lands, 2) the capital of that kingdom, 3) the king of that kingdom, 4) a sword representative of the rule of Traythell. Became the site of Black Barrow, and the fall of Jorsin Alkestes.

TREMATIR (TRA mot ter): The Sa'kagé's Master of Coin. See NINE, THE.

TYGRE TOWER/BERTOLD'S TOWER: A tower of the Khalidoran capital/castle/cave complex ~~(say that five times fast!)~~, an unheated basalt obscenity that looks on the verge of toppling in a high wind.

UNDERLORD: A LAE'KNAUGHT rank, a general. No more is known about this.

The king is not familiar with the phrase "girding up one's loins." Attempts at humor don't fit you. Please stop.

UNGERT (UNG urt/un GIRT): The family prefers the former, but the latter pronunciation persists, accompanied by the same three or four puns those with unfortunate names must always suffer.

UURDTHAN (oo URD thawn): "Winnowing, or Harrowing" a mission given to a Khalidoran prince in contention for the throne. ~~Those who failed were killed.~~

VANDEN: The bridge separating the impoverished Warrens of Cenaria from the richer east side of the city.

VESTACCHI LAKE: ~~A lake in Ossein on which the statue-school of the Chantry floated. At the confluence of two rivers.~~

VIR (VEER): 1) The black markings on a wytch's arms, 2) The force or spirit that gives a wytch power. (More information redacted at the insistence of the Chamberlain.)

VOS ISLAND: ~~an island in Cenaria City formed by the natural barrier of the Plith River. Cenaria Castle, the Stacks, and the Maw are all located on this small piece of rock.~~

Yawn.

VÜRDMEISTER (VOO URD my STIR): A wytch above the tenth (the cursed) shu'ra. ~~(In Khalidoran, the umlauted u is a dipthong pronounced as one syllable. VOO URD should be pronounced together, even as the word 'fire' is FIE ER, but is fit into one syllable.)~~

VY'SANA (VEE ZAHN ah): "Shaper of the Earth," a Maker. A brown mage. The Vy'sani school is in Ossein, on the far side of Lake Vestacchi from the Chantry.

WAEDDRYN (WAYTH rin): A country east of Ceura and south east of Cenaria. Its ruler is a queen and has been for twenty-one generations. Its capital was the prosperous Caernarvon. No longer a military power as the queens had been unable to expel the Lae'knaught from their nominal borders.

WAKIZASHI (WALK eh ZAHSH ee): A short, curving sword, similar in shape to a longer katana, and often paired with one.

THE WARRENS: The poor half (geographically, it housed far more than half in terms of population) of Cenaria City, on the western side of the Plith. So named because there were main streets, and it was almost impossible for outsiders to traverse.

How about you spice this one up a bit? "The first wetboy was..." It needn't be strictly historical, Laerin.

WETBOY: A professional assassin with magical abilities, so named for blood they spill. Tools of Sa'kagé.

WHITECLIFF CASTLE: The home of the Sethi royalty. A jewel of the ancient world, crafted at unbelievable expense from white marble—all of which would have had to be shipped from distant ports. Still standing and now maintained by the Sivalti Order, who are in a century-long effort to raise the money to restore the stained glass ceiling. Now a library.

WYRMS: Not dragons, which are of course mythical, but a magical manifestation of some sort called (created?) by Vürdmeisters.

The king likes dragons. Just something to consider.

WYTCH: Indistinguishable in our language from ~~the word~~ 'witch', ~~though a native Khalidoran speaker could tell whether one were a foreigner or native speaker by one's pronunciation of it.~~ Little is ~~known definitively, as southern scholars have not fared well when traveling to lands occupied by wytches, namely Lodricar and the greater empire of Khalidor. What is known is~~ that wytches wield magic that mages grudgingly admit is more powerful than mages' magic—some mages say many times more powerful. ~~The magic has something to do with the ki, black, intricate markings all wytches grow (paint? tattoo?) on their arms. Because wytches didn't suffer the diaspora thaumaturgica, they have maintained a line to the knowledge of the ancients. The schools of mages have mounted many missions over the centuries to try to recover books or artifacts. None have returned. Indeed, some such expeditions seem to have been commanded in order to rid schools of certain trouble makers.~~

A pity we have no such recourse.

YMMUR (eem MOO ER): ~~Though those latter two are a dipthong~~ Far eastern country north of Friaku, more mountainous than Friaku, though plains comprise half of the country.

YUSHAI (YOU shy): Khalidoran term: life and fire, and steel and joy of living. Believed to be applied mainly or solely to young women.

Erase all geographical references. The king doesn't care about them except that the pronunciations are standardized so that when his bards read him the story they all say it the same way, otherwise he gets confused. We'll include a map for him.

Don't know much about seeds and roots, do you?

The proper plural for ignoramus is "ignoramuses," not ignorami. It's derived from ignoro, the perfect passive participle of which is ignoratus, one who has been ignored. As you obviously can't tell the difference between a noun in the nominative and a first conjugation verb in the first person, plural, indicative, I suppose that makes you an ignoramus. And from henceforth, an ignoratus.

As a third draft of this glossary is now necessary (no one calls them glosses anymore, Laerin, no one), the price of this copy will be deducted from your wages. If my calculations are correct, that leaves you owing the king 400 tol.

I noticed at least one glaring factual error. I would have thought a scholar of your caliber would be more fastidious. Enjoy looking for it.

Can I expect the final, corrected draft tomorrow?

—Tor Baaden, the King's Chamberlain

CHARACTERS

Characters of the Night Angel Cycle, Listed

To the King's maladroit monkey of minstrelsy Javar Nussio,
From D. Laerin Votagsmere the Gold, Chief Scholar , D.Kn., J.Sc.

Javar,

    The following is a reference for you as you read the king the tale. Please note that the average tenure for a court bard here is somewhat less than the time it takes to read the entire cycle aloud. Do your successors a favor and please use the pronunciations herein, lest you infuriate the king. If you do so, your inevitable upcoming retirement will be abruptly terminated by something less pleasant than employment. Having noted your butchery of terms with clear phonetic notation, I exchanged the lexically correct pronunciation aids and instead used small words and capitalization to make pronunciations obvious—even to you. And for the green god's sake, stop rolling your R's when you read Ceuran names.

    After your last disastrous gaffe where you read aloud the entry which was supposed to be a prompt for your memory alone, thereby revealing the true nature of the black ka'kari to the king long before book six, I have edited this entire folio. Now you will find the character list safe to read to the king at any point in the story, giving only what is known about that character at the time they are introduced. This means, of course, that some definitions are unforgivably bland: "Gwinvere Kirena, a courtesan" doesn't do the inimitable woman justice and doesn't begin to match the beauty of my previous entry, but your idiocy nearly lost me my job. Because certain entries are impossible without risk of you getting eggshells in the cake again, they have been omitted: "Wanhope", etcetera.

    Enjoy the king's favor while it lasts. Just yesterday I heard him asking Lady Versetti if you don't sometimes throttle the high notes a bit. (She answered in the affirmative.)

    Fret on that, you melodious macaque,

Laerin Votagsmere the Gold,
Chief Scholar, D.Kn., J.Sc.

AALYEP, GOODMAN: An herbalist whose shop is frequented by rich merchants and controlled by the Sa'kagé.

ABINAZAE, KING: Ruler of Cenaria 400 years prior to this tale; built the castle when Cenaria was a major power.

ACAELUS THORNE OF TRAYETHELL, PRINCE (uh KAY luss): A friend and warrior of Emperor Jorsin, he had no subtlety, hated lies, politics, and magic.

AENU HEIGHTS LANTANOS (EYE new): Lantano Garuwashi's family. Despite later attempts to claim lineage from Cortano Ryu Masato, the connection is either tenuous or specious.

AEMIL PICCUN, MASTER: Tailor to the Sa'kagé.

AEVAN, LORD: Noble whom Kylar helps by giving him an herbal remedy while working for Aunt Mea.

ALEXAN THE BLESSED: A prince who set out to war as a teenager after his father was assassinated. His early victories were likely due to the brilliance of his close advisors and some sheer incredible luck. His recklessness, genius, and charisma combined to make him nearly invincible. He later came to believe that he was a god, purged his advisors who'd served him so loyally, and was killed by a child while drunk. A rumor that the child was in fact a Feyuri spy (due to their slight stature) led the massacres of Feyuri communities throughout much of Alexan's crumbling empire. An alternate explanation for Alexan's demise offered in this text is believed inaccurate as is the provenance of another, fouler translation of 'the Blessed,' though some early manuscripts have that as well.

AGON'S DOGS: A small army of Sa'kagé trained by Lord Brant Agon.

AGRIGOLAY: The region surrounding White Cliff Castle; usually the Emperor's personal lands, the red hills of Agrigolay are home to Midcyru's finest vineyards.

ANDERS GURKA: A wetboy of Cenaria. No other records exist.

ANTONINUS WERVEL: One of the 6 Sa'seuran magi; Modaini. One of the most powerful magi of his era.

ARCHMAGI OF GANDU: Wielders of some of the most destructive magic in history; it was said that these men and women left much of Gandu uninhabitable for five hundred years. The Wastelands were only beginning to grow crops again at the time of the narrative. No evidence now exists whether this was true.

ARIEL WYANT SA'FASTAE: Tamriel's elder half-sister; looks like peasant but far more Talented than Tamriel. Ariel Wyant was one of the great minds of her generation, but horribly impatient with nonsense— this barred her from advance in the Chantry for much of her life.

ARISTARCHOS (ban Ebron, shalakroi of Benyurien in the Silk province of Ladesh): a handsome Ladeshian bard, a member of the Society of the Second Dawn. Not believed to be the same Aristarchos ban Ebron who seized the pirate hideout town of Edross.

ASHAIAH VUL: A tiny Lodricari man who was Garoth Ursuul's Raptus Morgi, Keeper of the Dead.

AUNT MEA: A midwife and healer, widowed, based in Caernarvon, a relation of Elene Cromwyll's. Mother of Braen Smith.

AZOTH/AZO (AY zoth/AY zo): A street orphan, colloquially a 'guild rat,' member of the Black Dragon street guild. The name was, at the time, an archaism for quicksilver. Given that most slaveborn picked names for themselves, or had names picked for them, either this name was picked because someone merely liked the sound of it, or it is a later invention grafted onto the tale. The great minstrel Paelos Groff wasn't above changing names to hit a rhyme.

BA'ELZEBAEN (BAY ELL zah BANE): Mythical. The Lord of Serpents, an Arcanghul.

BAMRAN GAMBLE, SERGEANT: A skilled archer with an Alitaeran longbow, a sergeant in the Cenarian army who kills a deserter to prevent his other soldiers from deserting a battle.

BARUSH SNIGGLE (BAR oosh SNIG ul): A Shinga of Caernarvon.

BERNERD (BURN-erd): Guard of the Nine in Cenaria. This tale has the only mentions of him in history.

BIM/WEESE/POD: Littles in the Black Dragon street guild of Cenaria.

BLUE: A member of the Black Dragon street guild, long after Azoth had left.

BOURARY, MASTER: Ring maker in Caernarvon.

BRAEN SMITH: Aunt Mea's hulking 20-yr-old son, a smith.

BRANT AGON, GENERAL: An experienced Cenarian general, who finds much of his power stripped from him by a jealous and fearful king.

BRAN/TALLAN: Gyre guards.

BORSINI, VÜRDMEISTER: A Vürdmeister of the 11th Shu'ra.

BURL LAGHAR, CAPTAIN: A Khalidoran captain, later emasculated and killed by Kaldrosa Wynn during the Nocta Hemata.

CAEDAN: One of the Six Sa'seuran magi. A twin of Jaedan, a Seer.

CAPRICIA: The proprietor of a shop that sells compulsion wedding rings.

CHELLENE LO-GYRE (SHA leen low GHIRE): One of the victims of Godking Ursuul; frozen magically by Trudana Jadwin as a statue.

CORBIN FISHILL: One of the Sa'kagé Nine, the BRAAVOK, master of the younglings, lisps. Killed by Durzo.

CRESUS TOFUSIN, EMPEROR: The ancient founder of the Tofusin Clan, also the name and title of the father of Solonariwan and Sijuron Tofusin.

DABIN VOSIIA: One of the Nine, the man in charge of the Sa'kagé's smuggling, also known as the SAHRASLISS.

DAG TARKUS: Someone who kicked Piggy in the stomach for stealing and the next day he died; Blue references him.

DARK HUNTER, The: See ROYGARIS URSUUL, EZRA

DAUNE WARIYAMO: The Queen mother to Empress Kaede Wariyamo.

DAVI: One of Rat's co-assailants on Jarl.

DAYDRA: A courtesan who looks like Elene Cromwyll.

DEHVI/DEHVIRAHAMAN KO BRUHMAEZIWAKAZARI: An Ymmuri stalker, a magically Talented hunter. A legend in Ymmur. Also known as The Ghost of the Steppes.

DICOLA RAIIS, EMPEROR (dee COAL ah RAY ees): Alitaeran Emperor, possible instigator of the Alitaeran Accords, who feared the Chantry had established a breeding program to make archmages. Insane, but also, apparently correct on this point.

DOLL GIRL: See ELENE CROMWYLL.

DORG GAMET: King Gunder's stable master, from the isle of Planga.

DRAKE:

> **RIMBOLD DRAKE, COUNT**: Regnus's solicitor and Durzo's associate; as the Trematir, Sa'kagé Master of Coin (one of the Nine), reintroduced slavery and the Death Games but eventually swore off and retired.

> **ULANA DRAKE, COUNT**: Count Drake's wife. A kind woman and no fool.

> **SERAH DRAKE**: The wild eldest daughter of Rimbold and Ulana Drake, longtime special friend of Logan Gyre, but not considered marriage material as her position is so far below his.

> **MAGS DRAKE**: Count Drake's middle daughter.

> **ILENA DRAKE**: Count Drake's youngest daughter.

DRISSA NILE, SISTER: A maja at a tournament, works as healer in Cenaria.

DUNNEL: A Gyre servant, murdered on the night Cenaria was invaded by Khalidor.

DURZO BLINT: [Note to bard: The first time His Majesty listens to this tale, please use the following definition ONLY: "A legendary wetboy of Cenaria, a master of poisons and numerous weapons with a compulsive personality. Famous for his refusal to take apprentices, despite the Sa'kagé's repeated attempts to convince him otherwise."

[On subsequent readings, or if the king demands you open the oven before the cake has had time to rise, you can add the following at your discretion.] Durzo Blint was—unless, like those ninnyhammers the Miluvians you believe he still lives!—an incarnation/identity (? highly contested) of the man first (? minorly contested) known as Prince Acaelus Thorne, born 17-20 years before 1 Anno Jorsini. Virtually no serious scholar disputes that Prince Acaelus Thorne did exist. Whether the following personae belonged to Acaelus as well is hotly contested, with Lucanus et al. accepting the first five, but only Rebus Nimble and Mir Graggor of the last six. The supposed annals of the Society of the Second Dawn accept all of the below, except Ferric Fireheart and Zak Eurthkin (spelled Earth Kin in their records, a later mistranslation?). Note that the "X!" is a click. Apparently, there were numerous kinds of these, some of which non-native speakers can't differentiate between. Do your best. On to the list, with all known details about each:

(missing page here)

DYNOS ROTANS, UNDERLORD (DIE nos ROW tanes): Brother to Overlord Julus Rotans.

ERIS BUEL: A woman who left the Chantry abruptly some years ago and married an Alitaeran nobleman. Leader of the married Sisters, who were (offensively) nicknamed the Chattel.

EZRA (the Mad/the Mage/the Archmage/the Maker): Friend and mage of Jorsin Alkestes, a *sa'sogol*—a Lord of Magic. One of the most skilled mages ever born. An orphan discovered and befriended by Jorsin (Ginvurin's assertion that Jorsin adopted Ezra has little support), Ezra served him loyally for his entire life. Ezra is either the creator or discoverer of Iures, Curoch, the ka'kari, the Shield of Eraclos, the Horn of Cataclym, the Warhammers of Oren Razin, the poisoner's the Water Weaver's Distaff, the rings of ruin, and over one hundred unbreakable, never-dulling swords said to be practice pieces for the later Great Swords. It should be noted that though he was the principle architect of these pieces, no few of them were made during the Siege of Trayethell, and other archmagi are known to have lent their advice, magic, materials, and skills, notably Oren Razin, Kren, and Jorsin Alkestes himself.

FERL KHALIUS: A highlander who appropriates something marvelously important after it's lost on a bridge.

FEY FOLK: Mythical race said to be possessed of unearthly beauty, large eyes, great intelligence, skin in earthen and metallic tones, and an affinity for magic. The Stones of Keeping are said to be their work, as was the Black Forest, before it was burned in your grandfather's time.

FEYURI: A minority group mostly in Khalidor, though some communities survived in rural areas of Ossein and Alitaera. Frequently bearers of pointed ears and odd skin tones. Alleged to be descended from Fey folk, despised for that and their pacifism.

FEIR COUSAT: Associate of Solon and Dorian at the great pyramid of Sho'cendi; born a peasant; looked fat and unwieldy, but was a Blademaster of the Second Echelon; also a Vy'sana (a brown mage or Maker).

FERGUND SA'FASTI: King Aleine Gunder's court mage, weak Talent.

GARAZUL, HIGH LORD: Kylar pretends he is the steward for this noble.

GARE CROMWYLL: Adoptive father of Elene Cromwyll.

GHORRAN: Khalidoran who guards Elene during her captivity.

GORKHY: Khalidoran guard of the Hole.

GRAAVAR HIGHLANDERS: Ursuul's shock troops, tall, barrel-chested, blue-eyed savages who wore their black hair short and their mustaches long.

GRAKAAT KRUHN: A Khalidoran highlander chieftain.

GRAESIN:

> **CATRINNA GRAESIN**: See CATRINNA GYRE.
>
> **GORDIN GRAESIN, DUKE**: 7th in line to the throne.
>
> **LUC GRAESIN**: Lord General for, and younger brother of, Terah Graesin.
>
> **NATASSA GRAESIN**: Younger sister of Terah Graesin.
>
> **TERAH GRAESIN**: Daughter of Gordin Graesin, eighth in line for the throne, younger half-sister of Catrinna Gyre.

GRAEBLAN, UNDERLORD: A Lae'knaught commander whose lancers once fought General Brant Agon.

GRASQ TWINS: Led 6 battles against each other; statue in the Gyre hall; the subject of two story cycles.

GULON TAKEDA: One of Solon's opponents.

GUNDER:

> **ALEINE GUNDER IX, KING**: A king of Cenaria, successor to King Davin Gunder.
>
> **DAVIN GUNDER, KING**: Father of Aleine Gunder IX.
>
> **PRINCE ALEINE GUNDER**: Eldest son of King Aleine Gunder IX and Queen Nalia Gunder.
>
> **NALIA GUNDER, QUEEN (NÉE WESSEROS)**: Aleine Gunder's wife, formerly betrothed to Regnus Gyre.

JENINE GUNDER: Oldest daughter of King Aleine Gunder and Nalia Gunder.

ALAYNA GUNDER: Younger sister to Jenine Gunder.

ELISE GUNDER: Younger sister to Jenine Gunder.

GWINVERE KIRENA/ MOMMA K: One of the Nine, Mistress of Pleasures.

GYLE, KINGDOM: Layinisa Guralt was the Seeress of Gyle (princess), joined Alitaeran Empire through marriage to Emperor Jorald but left after Jorald died.

GYRE (GHIRE/GUY err):

    REGNUS GYRE, DUKE: Called by the young men of Khalidor the Rurstahk Slaagen, the Devil of the Walls.

    CATRINNA GYRE (NEE GRAESIN): Older half-sister of Terah Graesin by 20 years; wife of Duke Regnus Gyre.

    LOGAN GYRE: The scion of House Gyre. An idealistic young man, handsome, intelligent, naïve.

HANA: A student at Chantry.

THE HOLE/HOLERS:

    FIN: Leads the "animals"; nastiest resident, always working on sinew rope

    LILLY: The only woman in the Hole.

    JAKE: Tossed into the Hole in first fight.

    SNIFFLES: One of the "animals"; killed and eaten.

    SCAB: One of the "animals".

    LONG TOM: Killed by Logan for meat.

    NINE-FINGER NICK: Another occupant of the Hole.

    YIMBO: One of the "monsters"; a big-boned red-haired Ceuran whose tongue had been cut out; killed by Fin.

    TATTS: One of the "monsters"; a pale Lodricari covered in tattoos who could speak but never did.

    GNASHER: One of the "monsters"; a misshapen simpleton with massive shoulders and a twisted spine and teeth filed to sharp points.

HAYLIN, GRAND MASTER: An armorer.

HIDEO WATANABE (Heh DAY oh WAT ah GNAW bay): Ceura's regent; his son is Mitsurugi. They dueled and Mitsurugi slew him when he found out Watanabe intended to kill Lantano Garuwashi.

HOPPER/VONDEAS HIL: A toeless old eunuch of the Khalidorans.

HU GIBBET: The second-best wetboy in Cenaria. The son of Saron and Jade Marion. Famous for his sadism.

HURIN GHER (HER in GHER): Commander Gher, originally a lieutenant; promoted by Godking Ursuul.

HURLAK, KING: Had honeycombed his expansion of Castle Cenaria with secret rooms and spy holes.

HUROL II, KING: Cenarian king, during whose reign an amendment to the common law provided that dukes could only be arrested with habeas corpus, two witnesses, and a motive; incarceration required two of those three.

HYRILLIC: The language Curoch is inscribed with. See Gloss.

ISTARIEL WYANT (IST are ee ul WHY ent): Speaker of the Chantry, sister of Ariel Wyant Sa'fastae.

JADWIN:

> **TRUDANA JADWIN, DUCHESS** (TRUDE AHN uh): sexually voracious and middle-aged, the king's mistress, and an artist of note.

> **JADWIN, DUKE:** Trudana Jadwin's serially cuckolded husband. A diplomat kept travelling by the king to make his affairs easier to conduct.

JAEDAN: Alitaeran, identical twin brother of Caedan on the Sho'cendi mages' expedition.

JA'LALIEL (JA LAY lee ul): The head of the Black Dragon Guild.

JARL: Childhood friend of Kylar; Ladeshian, assistant to Momma K.

JESSIE AL'GWAYDIN: Godking's spy in Chantry; later goes to Torras Bend.

JONISSEH, MISTRESS: In charge of discipline at the Chantry.

JONUS SEVERING: A wetboy with fifty kills to his name.

JORALD HURDAZIN, EMPEROR: Early Alitaeran emperor; a skilled and wise leader, in his younger years he solidified Alitaeran control from what is now Ymmur in the east to the west coast of Midcyru (Waeddryn and Modai) at the time of this narrative.

JORSIN ALKESTES, EMPEROR: The last great emperor of Midcyru. An archmagus of unrivalled power. His list of attributes reads like a god's: handsome, charming, a brilliant tactician, a warrior of unparalleled skill on all levels, a peerless magician, et cetera. Even if one casts a jaundiced eye on such lists, Alkestes' list of actual accomplishments makes many of them at least plausible. Early in reign, ruled seven kings and styled himself the High King. Three of seven kings rebelled: Rygel the Blue, Einarus Silvereyes, and Itarra Lachess, and when he conquered their lands again, he became "Emperor" Jorsin Alkestes.

JULUS ROTANS, OVERLORD (JOO luss row TANES): In his late forties, leader of the Lae'knaught and brother to Dynos Rotans.

KAAV: a Khalidoran soldier/torturer

KAEDE WARIYAMO (KAY dee wear EE AH mo): Last empress of Seth.

KAGÉ (COG ay): another name for Kylar

KA'KARIFERS/JORSIN'S SIX CHAMPIONS:

> **ARIKUS DAADRUL:** (ARE ick us DAY ah DRULL) Daadrul gets a skin of silver liquid metal that makes him impervious to blades.
>
> **IRENAEA BLOCHWEI** (EYE rin AY ah BLOCK way): Receives the power of everything green and growing.
>
> **TRACE ARVAGULANIA** (ARE vag YOU LANE ee ah): Went from grossly ugly to the most beautiful woman of the era; one of the original Champions, possessor of the White ka'kari.
>
> **CORVAER BLACKWELL/CORVAER THE RED** (CORE vair): The master of fire.
>
> **SHRAD MARDEN:** Controls water and can suck the very liquid from a man's blood.
>
> **OREN RAZIN** (OR in RAY zin): Ezra's only friend besides Jorsin; fought with twin war hammers, the master of earth; weighed a thousand pounds and could turn skin to stone.

KALDROSA WYN (KALL dro suh WIN): Sethi pirate captain marooned in Cenaria without a ship or crew. Married to Tomman.

KHALI (CAUL ee/ KA lee): The goddess of Khalidor.

KIROF, BARON: Former vassal of the Gyres; one of the first Cenarian nobles to bend the knee to Garoth Ursuul.

KYLAR STERN/KYLAR BLACKSON/KYLAR DRAKE: The name a young orphan boy Azoth takes after apprenticing with Durzo Blint. Later, Marquess, Lord of Havermere, Lockley, Vennas, and Procin, Wolfhound. (Also known as Marati, Cwellar, Spex, Kagé, The Night Angel, Shadow-strider, The Scales of Justice, Shadowslayer, He-Who-Guards-Unseen, Nameless.)

LANTANO GARUWASHI (LAN tan o gare oo WASH ee): The most famed sa'ceurai in the world. Born to an iron sword (id est, nearly a peasant), he is a warrior who has never lost a duel or a battle.

LAYINISA GURALT: The Seeress of Gyle, Jorald's empress, essentially the princess of Gyle.

LEFTY: Guard of the Nine.

LEHROS VASS: Young replacement leader at Screaming Winds.

LILLIAN ROSSY: A young woman convicted of murder when her abusive husband found her with another man.

LOGAN VERDROEKAN, KING: one of the earliest kings of Cenaria

LUCIUS, LORD: Leader of the Six Sa'seuran magi expedition; A Seer.

MAKELL: (House wiped out in 8 Years War)

 DARVIN MAKELL: a friend of Count Drake's father (who inherited a large fortune) and mingled with Gordin Graesin and Brand Wesseros.

MALAK MOK'MAZI/MALAK FIREHANDS: Allegedly took Corvaer the Red's ka'kari after the Battle of Jaeran Flats.

MARAHK ANSOZI: The object of a famed panegyric.

MARCUS GUERIN, AMBASSADOR: Alitaeran ambassador to the Chantry.

THE MIKAIDON: Keeper of Civil order in Hokkai.

NAMELESS, THE: Another name for The Night Angels.

NEPH DADA: Counselor and seer to Garoth Ursuul, a Vürdmeister and former tutor to Dorian, current supervisor of Roth, and a Vürdmeister of the 12th shu'ra.

NINER: A dismissive name for King Aleine Gunder IX.

NORTHMEN: Another term for the Khalidorans, particularly the Highlanders.

NUEC VIN BROEMAR: Royal Alitaeran perfumer.

OSHOBI TAKEDA: The Mikaidon of Hokkai.

OTARU TOMAKI: Lantano's captain and advisors.

PHINEAS SERATSIN: The Sa'kagé's Master of Coin.

POL: A young man in love with Elene Cromwyll.

PON DRADIN: The Shinga of the Cenarian Sa'kagé, master of the Nine.

PRICIA: A member of Garoth Ursuul's harem.

PROCL, MASTER: The best locksmith in Cenaria City.

PTURIN: Login's short Ymmuri guard.

PULLETA VIKRASIN: Maja who married a magus and broke compulsion from head of one of orders. Instigated a political crisis.

QUOGLEE MARS: A talented bard at the Cenarian court with Luc Graesin and Natassa Graesin.

RAT: At age 16, the Fist of The Black Dragon Guild – fat(nicknamed Ratty Fatty by Azoth).

REAVER, THE: See DARK HUNTER, THE.

REN VORDEN, MASTER: Regnus's guards master.

RINGSMITHS: Makers of the compulsion rings that are commonly used in weddings/marriages.

ROTH GRIMSON: One of the Sa'kagé's rising stars, guild head of the Red Bashers, owner of an opulent estate built in the middle of the Warrens.

RUEL, LORD: Among the first to die from poisoning during the Khalidoran invasion.

RURSTAHK SLAAGEN (RER schtock SLAY ah gen): A Khalidoran term for Regnus Gyre meaning devil of the walls.

SA'SACEURAI HIDEO MITSURUGI: Son of Hideo Watanabe. He killed his father in a duel. His full title is Sixth Regent Hideo, Lord of Mount Tenji, Protector of the Holy Honor, Keeper of the High Seat, Lord General of the Held Armies of Ceura.

SCARRED WRABLE: A wetboy, a friend or acquaintance of Durzo Blint.

SHADOWCLOAKED: Another term for the Night Angel.

SHADOWSTRIDER: Another term for the Night Angel.

SHEL: A prostitute at the Craven Dragon

SHINGA: SHING gah—Leader of the Sa'kagé

SIA (SEE ah): Pregnant member of Garoth Ursuul's harem.

SIJURON TOFUSIN, EMPEROR: Deceased at the time of this narrative; brother of Solon, former Sethi emperor, son of Emperor Cresus Tofusin.

SMILEY: Grand Master Haylin's fifth son.

SOLONARIWAN TOFUSIN (SOL on ar ee wan to FOO sin): Son of Emperor Cresus Tofusin, companion of Dorian and Feir, mentor of Logan Gyre. A version of his titles under which he spends most of his time in Midcyru: Lord Solon Tofusin, of House Tofusin, Windseekers of Royal House Bra'aden of the Island Empire of Seth. In truth, he is the son of Emperor Cresus Tofusin, Light of the West, Protector of the Isles, and High Admiral of the Royal Fleets of Seth. Later known as Solon Stormrider. Earned his blue robes at the Sho'fasti school; also studied at the Sho'cendi school.

SOULSWORN: A contingent of Khalidoran elite soldiers who give up much of what is human to serve Khali (mages).

SPEX: Another term for Kylar.

STIGLOR, CHANCELLOR: The first of the nobles to die of poisoning during the Khalidoran attack on Cenaria.

TALWIN NAGA, GENERAL: Paerik's general.

TAYABUSA, SECRETARY: A secretary at the Sethi court.

TERTULUS MARTUS: Questor of the Twelfth Army of the Lae'knaught, attaché to Overlord Julus Rotans.

TEVOR NILE: Husband of Drissa; also healer and magus.

THADDEUS BLAT: An officer who is drowned by Regnus in a brothel.

TITAN, THE: A creature believed killed by Jorsin, buried at Black Barrow, has claws, is the height of 13 men.

TOBBY: Khalidoran crap room slave.

TOM GRAY: A thug whom Kylar and Elene encounter at a toll and who later pursues them.

TOMMII (TOE my, TOE mee): A tribe/people who used "shitting" as an intensifier, like we say "damn lucky," they might say a person was "shitting lucky." Nothing else is known about them

TOMMAN: Kaldrosa Wynn's husband.

ULY/ULYSSANDRA: Supposedly Vonda Kirena's daughter.

USASI, KING: King of Ceura whose son and seven daughters were killed.

URSUUL (Ur soo OOL):

> **DORIAN URSUUL:** A prophet; Sa'seuran and Hoth'salar, and once a Vürdmeister of the twelfth shu'ra; first acknowledged son of Garoth Ursuul.

> **DRAEF URSUUL:** Another aetheling.

> **GAROTH URSUUL, GODKING** (GARE-oth): Godking of Khalidor, father of dozens of children, only the Talented or 'wytchborn,' and only the boys, are recognized as aethelings (throne-worthy sons).

> **TAVI URSUUL:** 15-yr-old aetheling.

> **MOBURU URSUUL** (MOE boo roo): For a time, Garoth's only acknowledged son after Dorian left. Also known as the adopted son of Aurelius Ander, Moburu Ander.

> **ROYGARIS URSUUL, GODKING:** Long-past Khalidoran ruler, founder of Khalidor, rival and friend and later bitter enemy of Jorsin Alkestes. An archmage, a Lord of Healing.

> **PAERIK URSUUL:** Dorian's younger brother.

> **UDRIK URSUUL:** Came home from exile to beg for mercy from Dorian, was killed by him.

> **TENSER VARGUN, DUKE:** One of Garoth's aethelings.

> **RUGGER:** A bastard son of Dorian's older brother, a guard at Khaliras.

> **RIVIK URSUUL:** Another aetheling, Tavi's sidekick; killed.

> **DURON URSUUL:** Deceased brother of Dorian.

> **GVESSIE URSUUL:** Deceased brother of Dorian.

> **HESDEL URSUUL:** Deceased brother of Dorian.

> **JULAMON URSUUL:** Deceased brother of Dorian.

> **JURIK URSUUL:** Deceased brother of Dorian.

> **PORRIK URSUUL:** Deceased brother of Dorian.

> **ROQWIN URSUUL:** Deceased brother of Dorian.

> **VIC URSUUL:** Deceased brother of Dorian.

> **WHERISS URSUUL:** Deceased brother of Dorian.

URWER, LORD: One of the Cenarian nobles caught in the castle when Khalidor invaded Cenaria.

VIN ARTURIAN, CAPTAIN: A guard captain.

VI/VIRIDIANA SOVARI: Hu Gibbet's young female apprentice, Talented, red-haired, buxom.

VONDA KIRENA: Momma K's sister, dead, former lover of Durzo Blint.

WENDEL NORTH: Regnus Gyre's steward.

WESSEROS:

> **BRAND WESSEROS, DUKE:** Queen Nalia Gunder's father.

> **NALIA WESSEROS:** See NALIA GUNDER

> **HAVRIN WESSEROS, DUKE:** Son of Brand Wesseros, brother to Nalia, a supporter of Terah Graesin.

WOLF, THE: A yellow-eyed being encountered in Antechamber of the Mystery.

XANDRA: Floor Monitor at the Chantry.

YORBAS ZURGAH: Chief Eunuch at the Citadel in Khaliras.

YOSAR GLIN, COUNT: A client who betrayed Durzo Blint.

YRRGIN, KEEPER: Predecessor to Dorian's keeper of the dead; had apparently done some research on the origins of the krul, as he told Ashaiah Vul about Roygaris Ursuul and the krul.

YVA LUCRECE CORAZHI: Rumored to Moburu Ursuul's daughter, she was born to the Alitaeran king's sister; she and her wetnurse were kidnapped/disappeared.

ZORALAT, MASTER & MISTRESS: Innkeepers at Torras Bend.

Javar,

That should be everything. If you have any other questions, please do ask me. Also, do you happen to know anything about seeds and roots? The king's herbalist and apothecary both are being unhelpful due to perceived slights long in the past. I could be convinced to put in a good word for you if you do.

Laerin

extras

orbit

meet the author

Travis Johnson Photography

BRENT WEEKS was born and raised in Montana. After getting his paper keys from Hillsdale College, Brent had brief stints walking the earth like Caine from *Kung Fu*, tending bar, and corrupting the youth. (Not at the same time.) He started writing on bar napkins, then on lesson plans, then full-time. Eventually, someone paid him for it. Brent lives in Oregon with his wife, Kristi. He doesn't own cats or wear a ponytail.

bonus chapters

Dear Readers,

The trouble of writing an epic story is the middle. Epic fantasy writers are good at middles. We write them well, or we wouldn't get published; we enjoy writing them, or our books would be short. But middles are treacherous things. (See middle age, mid-list, mid-section.) Have an idea for a new character halfway into your series? Voila! An elvish vampire prostitute with a lisp. Hilarious! Another! A cross-eyed genius obsessed with crickets who's actually a genie trapped in a mortal body until he can answer why crickets chirp but will be trapped forever if he tells anyone? Brilliant! Another!

And then reality hits in the form of the two heaviest words in Middle Earth: The End. You've made this mess, and now you have to clean it up.

I had the luxury of not getting published for a long time. (If you aspire to write, may you not be similarly blessed!) I wrote almost the entire Night Angel trilogy before it got picked up for publication. Though I didn't know it for all those years in my apartment with its turquoise door next to the projects, this was a mercy. The mercy was that I could go back and trim things that ballooned the text without advancing the plot. *Beyond the Shadows* wanted to be truly massive—or perhaps it wanted to become *Beyond the Shadows*, and *Even Farther Past Those Shadows*, and *We're Really Leaving Those Shadows Behind Now*.

extras

Writing more books in a series is great, but I want a narrative to have a certain shape, and I want each book to have turning points and enough of a climax to justify being its own novel. I wanted each book to tell a complete story, and I didn't see how splitting *Beyond the Shadows* would leave two whole novels, even if I could have gotten seven hundred pages out of each half.

So I cut. Deeply. In most places, this strengthened the novel. In some, it changed the novel, and I stitched the events together in new ways. If I shared those cut chapters, they wouldn't make sense, because I changed the rest of the novel to accommodate the new way.

But one cut in particular I've regretted. In *Beyond the Shadows*, Feir Cousat goes into Ezra's Wood and, somehow, impossibly, comes out again.

This is that story.

Brent Weeks

BONUS CHAPTER

Is this insanity what men call courage?

Feir's heart was a thunder in his ears as he walked toward the Hunter's Wood. He knew the history, and it wasn't comforting.

Seven hundred years ago Ezra the Mighty, the brightest star in the magical firmament of Jorsin Alkestes' short-lived Kingdom of Summer, had come to this wood. He came here defeated, bereaved, embittered. He created a monster, a perfect hunter to wreak his revenge. In the end, it escaped his control, turned on him, and killed him. Ezra's only victory over the creature was confining it to the wood.

The first mages and meisters had probably come to study that Hunter. They had never returned. Others had entered armed with their mightiest artifacts. They had never returned. Soon, ignoring the bans of their elders, young magi were flocking to the wood and dying in droves. Within that first century, the goal changed from studying the Hunter to eluding it. The prize became the hundreds of artifacts the previous magi had brought to the wood.

No one came back.

After the purges and the Alitaeran conquests and the Finaean campaign and the Alliance of Brothers, the magi knew they were a shadow of their former glory. A magus here and there would disappear in times of war or upheaval, sure that his great need would somehow overcome his greater inadequacies.

No one came back. No one.

Now Feir was trying. There were only three credits on his side of the ledger. First, Feir was probably the first magus to attempt to infiltrate the wood while the Hunter was being distracted by five thousand other intruders, which should be an excellent mundane distraction. Even the Hunter couldn't be everywhere at once. Surely. Second, probably no one else had entered after throwing an artifact of Curoch's magnitude into the Wood, which should be an excellent magical distraction. Third, Feir's Talent was small. A raging fire of a Talent like Solon or Dorian could never have done this, but Feir's Talent was diminutive, his specialty tiny weaves, and knowing that he would be so close to the wood, he had already compressed his Talent within the tightest shell he could, and he thought that work was the equal of anything any magus in the world could do—these days.

Doubtless the other dead magi and meisters had been confident, too.

The wood was glowing a deep red now and as Feir approached, he saw that the glow stretched to the east and west, curving slowly to the north. It was contained, an enormous globe of light that emanated from the wood's center. It was magic made visible. Feir had never thought himself arrogant in his abilities; the constant company of Dorian and Solon had prevented that, but looking at this miles-wide globe of magic was humbling. Feir knew how to make simple wards such as you might stretch over a door to warn yourself of intruders, but every ward he had known was stretched like a net. The actual magic always—always—took up only a thin fraction of the physical space it was warding. This ward, or these wards, weren't webs; they were walls. Miles of solid magic that had lasted seven hundred years and the assaults of untold thousands of magi.

He came within a foot of the wall. The vegetation changed abruptly on the other side, the oaks and tamaracks of the mundane forest ceasing and the enormous sequoys beginning. Wherever the mundane trees' branches encroached on that wall, even hundreds of feet in the air, they ended. Feir could hear the cries of men through the dead spaces between those sequoys and something howling, sometimes near, sometimes far away in such quick succession it made him wonder if all the stories were wrong and there wasn't one Hunter but many. Surely nothing could move so fast.

Feir stared at the wall as he would stare at a blade he was forging as he wove matrices into the steel to harden the edge, and looking like that, as a Maker himself, the secrets unfolded like a flower. The wall wasn't solid after all, it was thousands of webs laid together in hundreds of varieties. Webs that detected the smell of men, webs that detected heat, webs that detected the stench of wytches' magic, webs that detected women's magic and men's magic, webs that detected latent Talent that had never been tapped, webs that detected any animal and would snap only for those of man size or larger, webs that detected a hundred different spells. There were webs like locks, so thick they could only be broken, and webs like minuscule knots that would have to be untied. There were microscopic filaments attached to the knots that would have been invisible to ninety-nine out of a hundred magi.

The webs, all of them, were jangling, rattling, vibrating at the violation of five thousand Lae'knaught, some of whom—Feir could see from the webs—were Talented. Webs were snapping and reforming an instant later.

Defeating some of them was easy. As a Maker, he'd mastered weaves to seal himself away from whatever he was making. Those were tiny, laborious weaves; at first, they felt like trying to tie fishing line with a thumb and one finger, but Feir had perfected them long ago, and the magic required was minimal. In fact, many mages couldn't do them because they weren't able to draw such small amounts of power. That had never been Feir's problem. Today, his weakness was his strength.

A light flashed white through the wood, a magical concussion of some minor artifact being destroyed—a Lae'knaught great helm, Feir guessed—and several thick webs snapped right in front of Feir. Before he realized what he was doing, he stepped forward, pushing just the edge of the ball into which he'd compressed his Talent into the gap. The webs reappeared, reconnecting above and below the ball. Feir held as still as he could, barely breathing, hoping that movement wasn't tearing filaments he hadn't seen, hoping that in all the jangling of those thousands that this slight perturbation would go unnoticed.

The webs slowly morphed from red to green. They were, Feir realized, healing, growing. When they had first burned visible, they had been thin and cracked and dying, but since Kylar had thrown Curoch into the forest, it had been changing.

Gods, it feeds on the magic. The entire forest fuels itself, feeds itself, heals itself with the magic used against it.

But as the magic was growing and green with new life, it was also flexible. Looking down, looking through his own body to see the magic penetrating him, Feir used extra space his very breathing created around the ball to move forward. His Talent was small enough to slip through the mightiest bands of webbing, and he slowly, slowly pushed the filaments to the side, not interrupting them but instead directing their growth.

In minutes, as the glow burned fully, vibrantly green, it was done. The glow faded from the air and, though still jangling and snapping and reforming instantaneously, the webs no longer bit into Feir's ball of Talent.

He stepped into the wood. Turning, he looked at the empty air behind him. With his Sight, he could see a tiny hole in the wall, less than a handspan across. He had made it.

The wood was alive, redolent with the perfume of eucalyptus and sequoy and power. Feir felt as if he were part of the whole forest. To the east, he could feel the bodies of thousands of Lae'knaught. A quarter of their number lay dead, in pieces. The rest were screaming. They'd run back to the edge of the forest, fleeing—and were now pressing against air that had become an invisible, solid wall. They were trampling each other, suffocating each other, pushing pushing pushing against a barrier that their beliefs told them couldn't affect them. They were being slain by what they'd called superstition. Others were fleeing through the wood in every direction, screaming, throwing down weapons and armor that slowed them, hoping against hope that some other part of the wall would be permeable.

Then Feir felt the Hunter. It was as fast as thought, flying back and forth like an enraged animal, pausing here to savage a single body for ten seconds, ripping it to shreds, flinging the pieces about, then it was on the other side of the wood, a whistling sound as it cut through the air the only evidence of its passage. Everywhere, it killed. It gloried in the slaughter.

As yet, it hadn't detected Feir. If it worked its way methodically through the Lae'knaught army, it could be finished with the killing in mere minutes, but the creature seemed to have no method, only rage. None of the Lae'knaught had come as far as Feir yet, but as they fled and spread out, the Hunter's path might cross Feir's at any time.

But he had done it. He was here, undetected, unknown. He, the lowly worm, had triumphed where mighty dragons had fallen.

Feir took three victorious steps into the wood, a tremendous sense of glory and victory coursing through his blood. Then the ground beneath his feet gave way. He plunged into darkness.

BONUS CHAPTER

Feir could see nothing. Worse, he could feel nothing at all. He couldn't feel his lungs expand as he breathed. He couldn't feel ground beneath him, or even which direction *beneath* might be. He told himself to get up to his knees. Was he lying down? He couldn't tell.

He thought he might be shivering from pure terror, but there was no sensation of his skin. His magical senses were similarly blind. The forest that had felt like a second body was amputated. There was no sense of his own Talent. He'd fallen into a dead space.

Or maybe he *was* dead. He tried to scream—nothing. Gods, what if his sense of time was similarly deadened? Was he stuck like this forever? Was this the fate that every other mage and meister for nearly a millennium had found in Ezra's Wood?

He had no idea how long he existed in that bubble, that torture, when slowly, sensation returned to a single hand. His left hand. He was left-handed. He was touching bare stone, smooth and cold. He touched his face, pressed hard against the floor, and it felt like touching a corpse, because he didn't feel it in his face, only in those fingertips.

Soft, warm breaths gusted onto his fingertips. So he was alive. There was something slick there. His fingers rubbed together. Blood? He manipulated that face, feeling for a wound. It was the nose, broken, and bleeding freely and making the floor sticky. Without thinking, Feir the Maker—who'd mended broken bones along with broken plowshares and broken weapons—set his own nose. There was no sickening crunch, no gasp, no curse, no flinching. He touched that dead face to make sure he'd done it right. Yes, perfectly. He'd always been good with his hands.

He groped around his body, finding he could move his arm though he couldn't tell how. If he wanted his hand to explore the left side of his left leg, it would be there, with no sensation of the arm moving into position. He was lying on his stomach, so it was hard to get much of a sense of what else might be damaged.

But before he flipped his body over, Feir stretched his hand around the dead space. He didn't want to roll himself into a chasm or a fire or some other trap. His hand hadn't moved far when he found a groove. Next to it was another, and another, four in a row with a fifth set lower.

A handprint.

He hesitated, afraid. A handprint? Like someone had planned this. Like it was waiting for him. What fresh horrors might await him if he put his hand into that trap?

Then he realized that there was nothing else to do. How long could he wait here? How long had he been here already? Did he want to stay forever? He might have other injuries. He might be dying. Besides, whoever had made this place could clearly have killed him already. He put his hand in the handprint.

Sensation returned. Pain had never been so welcome. He must have dropped ten feet. The palms of his hands and his elbows and knees throbbed from the fall. His nose burned; he was glad he'd already set it.

Light trickled through the walls as if in little waterfalls through the stone, gradually brightening, but still wavering like rolling water the whole time.

The dead space was a stone chamber ten feet across and forty feet long. The first thing Feir saw was a solid gold sheet like parchment on the floor directly in front of him. Unthinking, he picked it up. Hyrillic runes on its surface slowly bent, shifting into something Feir could read.

In moments, the gold parchment said, "Hail and be hale, little brother. Drat, punning is horrific in your language, don't you think? Translation magics aren't worth a chipped *dwymor*—ach, see? Yes, my latter-day Maker, this missive is for you, Feir the Lesser of the lineage Cousat. Unless of course *you* have stumbled into this sanctuary, Grozel Verzarek, in which case, I give you this warning— Feir can touch what he wants, I've crafted this chamber for him, but if *you* touch anything in this chamber or this forest aside from the climbing stones behind you, it will be your death."

Grozel Verzarek? Feir had heard of the magus, but he couldn't place him. Then he saw a desiccated corpse lying in front of an ornate ironwood chest filigreed with gold at the far end of the chamber.

Well, perhaps I can place him.

Feir drew a slow breath. The gold sheet he held wasn't then the words of a living man, but a prophecy—or at least a letter from a man who'd prophesied that Feir would come. That could only mean Ezra, for who else would Ezra allow to work such magics in his own wood?

And that meant that Ezra had intended for Feir to get this far. He'd left the way open for him, knowing that would mean this other mage might get in, too. Feir felt sick. He wasn't as clever as he thought. He hadn't sneaked into the woods, Ezra had propped the door open for him.

Having been surrounded by great mages for his whole life, Feir shouldn't have let it get to him, but it did. There was something infuriating about finding out that someone that everyone else admired and said was the greatest really was worthy of admiration, and really was the greatest. Legends should fade the closer you walk to them.

He continued reading, "If you are here, Cousat, it means Curoch has come. And it never would have without you. You have served me unwittingly but well. Now, little brother, I would have you serve me again. You have held a great sword. Would you like to Make one?"

Feir's heart expanded until it seemed he wouldn't be able to contain it. The ironwood chest popped open. It was full of tools.

introducing

If you enjoyed
NIGHT ANGEL,
look out for

THE BLACK PRISM

by Brent Weeks

Two years after his untimely death, Matthew Swift finds himself breathing once again, lying in bed in his London home.
Except that it's no longer his bed, or his home. And the last time this sorcerer was seen alive, an unknown assailant had gouged a hole so deep in his chest that his death was irrefutable...despite his body never being found.
He doesn't have long to mull over his resurrection, though, or the changes that have been wrought upon him. His only concern now is vengeance. Vengeance upon his monstrous killer and vengeance upon the one who brought him back.

Kip crawled toward the battlefield in the darkness, the mist pressing down, blotting out sound, scattering starlight. Though the adults shunned it and the children were forbidden to come here, he'd played on the open field a hundred times—during the day. Tonight, his purpose was grimmer.

Reaching the top of the hill, Kip stood and hiked up his pants. The river behind him was hissing, or maybe that was the warriors beneath its surface, dead these sixteen years. He squared his shoulders, ignoring his imagination. The mists made him seem suspended, outside of time. But even if there was no evidence of it, the sun was coming. By the time it did, he had to get to the far side of the battlefield. Farther than he'd ever gone searching.

Even Ramir wouldn't come out here at night. Everyone knew Sundered Rock was haunted. But Ram didn't have to feed his family; *his* mother didn't smoke her wages.

Gripping his little belt knife tightly, Kip started walking. It wasn't just the unquiet dead that might pull him down to the evernight. A pack of giant javelinas had been seen roaming the night, tusks cruel, hooves sharp. They were good eating if you had a matchlock, iron nerves, and good aim, but since the Prisms' War had wiped out all the town's men, there weren't many people who braved death for a little bacon. Rekton was already a shell of what it had once been. The *alcaldesa* wasn't eager for any of her townspeople to throw their lives away. Besides, Kip didn't have a matchlock.

Nor were javelinas the only creatures that roamed the night. A mountain lion or a golden bear would also probably enjoy a well-marbled Kip.

A low howl cut the mist and the darkness hundreds of paces deeper into the battlefield. Kip froze. Oh, there were wolves too. How'd he forget wolves?

Another wolf answered, farther out. A haunting sound, the very voice of the wilderness. You couldn't help but freeze when you heard it. It was the kind of beauty that made you shit your pants.

Wetting his lips, Kip got moving. He had the distinct sensation of being followed. Stalked. He looked over his shoulder. There was nothing there. Of course. His mother always said he had too much imagination. Just walk, Kip. Places to be. Animals are more scared of you and all that. Besides, that was one of the tricks about a howl, it always sounded much closer than it really was. Those wolves were probably leagues away.

Before the Prisms' War, this had been excellent farmland. Right next to the Umber River, suitable for figs, grapes, pears, dewberries, asparagus—*everything* grew here. And it had been sixteen years since the final battle—a year before Kip was even born. But the plain was still torn and scarred. A few burnt timbers of old homes and barns poked out of the dirt. Deep furrows and craters remained from cannon shells. Filled now with swirling mist, those craters looked like lakes, tunnels, traps. Bottomless. Unfathomable.

Most of the magic used in the battle had dissolved sooner or later in the years of sun exposure, but here and there broken green luxin spears still glittered. Shards of solid yellow underfoot would cut through the toughest shoe leather.

Scavengers had long since taken all the valuable arms, mail, and luxin from the battlefield, but as the seasons passed and rains fell, more mysteries surfaced each year. That was what Kip was hoping for—and what he was seeking was most visible in the first rays of dawn.

The wolves stopped howling. Nothing was worse than hearing that chilling sound, but at least with the sound he knew where they were. Now . . . Kip swallowed on the hard knot in his throat.

As he walked in the valley of the shadow of two great unnatural hills—the remnant of two of the great funeral pyres where tens of thousands had burned—Kip saw something in the mist. His heart leapt into his throat. The curve of a mail cowl. A glint of eyes searching the darkness.

Then it was swallowed up in the roiling mists.

A ghost. Dear Orholam. Some spirit keeping watch at its grave.

Look on the bright side. Maybe wolves are scared of ghosts.

Kip realized he'd stopped walking, peering into the darkness. Move, fathead.

He moved, keeping low. He might be big, but he prided himself on being light on his feet. He tore his eyes away from the hill—still no sign of the ghost or man or whatever it was. He had that feeling again that he was being stalked. He looked back. Nothing.

A quick click, like someone dropping a small stone. And something at the corner of his eye. Kip shot a look up the hill. A click, a spark, the striking of flint against steel.

The mists illuminated for that briefest moment, Kip saw few details. Not a ghost—a soldier striking a flint, trying to light a slow-match. It caught fire, casting a red glow on the soldier's face, making his eyes seem to glow. He affixed the slow-match to the match-holder of his matchlock and spun, looking for targets in the darkness.

His night vision must have been ruined by staring at the brief flame on his match, now a smoldering red ember, because his eyes passed right over Kip.

The soldier turned again, sharply, paranoid. "The hell am I supposed to see out here, anyway? Swivin' wolves."

Very, very carefully, Kip started walking away. He had to get deeper into the mist and darkness before the soldier's night vision recovered, but if he made noise, the man might fire blindly. Kip walked on his toes, silently, his back itching, sure that a lead ball was going to tear through him at any moment.

But he made it. A hundred paces, more, and no one yelled. No shot cracked the night. Farther. Two hundred paces more, and he saw light off to his left, a campfire. It had burned so low it was barely more than coals now. Kip tried not to look directly at it to save his vision. There was no tent, no bedrolls nearby, just the fire.

Kip tried Master Danavis's trick for seeing in darkness. He let his focus relax and tried to view things from the periphery of his vision. Nothing but an irregularity, perhaps. He moved closer.

Two men lay on the cold ground. One was a soldier. Kip had seen his mother unconscious plenty of times; he knew instantly this man wasn't passed out. He was sprawled unnaturally, there were no blankets, and his mouth hung open, slack-jawed, eyes staring unblinking at the night. Next to the dead soldier lay another man, bound in chains but alive. He lay on his side, hands manacled behind his back, a black bag over his head and cinched tight around his neck.

The prisoner was alive, trembling. No, weeping. Kip looked around; there was no one else in sight.

"Why don't you just finish it, damn you?" the prisoner said.

Kip froze. He thought he'd approached silently.

"Coward," the prisoner said. "Just following your orders, I suppose? Orholam will smite you for what you're about to do to that little town."

Kip had no idea what the man was talking about.

Apparently his silence spoke for him.

"You're not one of them." A note of hope entered the prisoner's voice. "Please, help me!"

Kip stepped forward. The man was suffering. Then he stopped. Looked at the dead soldier. The front of the soldier's shirt was soaked with blood. Had this prisoner killed him? How?

"Please, leave me chained if you must. But please, I don't want to die in darkness."

Kip stayed back, though it felt cruel. "You killed him?"

"I'm supposed to be executed at first light. I got away. He chased me down and got the bag over my head before he died. If dawn's close, his replacement is coming anytime now."

Kip still wasn't putting it together. No one in Rekton trusted the soldiers who came through, and the alcaldesa had told the town's young people to give any soldiers a wide berth for a while—apparently the new satrap Garadul had declared himself free of the Chromeria's control. Now he was King Garadul, he said, but he wanted the usual levies from the town's young people. The alcaldesa had told his representative that if he wasn't the satrap anymore, he didn't have the right to raise levies. King or satrap, Garadul couldn't be happy with that, but Rekton was too small to bother with. Still, it would be wise to avoid his soldiers until this all blew over.

On the other hand, just because Rekton wasn't getting along with the satrap right now didn't make this man Kip's friend.

"So you *are* a criminal?" Kip asked.

"Of six shades to Sun Day," the man said. The hope leaked out of his voice. "Look, boy—you are a child, aren't you? You sound like one. I'm going to die today. I can't get away. Truth to tell, I don't want to. I've run enough. This time, I fight."

"I don't understand."

"You will. Take off my hood."

Though some vague doubt nagged Kip, he untied the half-knot around the man's neck and pulled off the hood.

At first, Kip had no idea what the prisoner was talking about. The man sat up, arms still bound behind his back. He was perhaps thirty years old, Tyrean like Kip but with a lighter complexion, his hair wavy rather than kinky, his limbs thin and muscular. Then Kip saw his eyes.

Men and women who could harness light and make luxin—drafters—always had unusual eyes. A little residue of whatever color they drafted ended up in their eyes. Over the course of their life, it would stain the entire iris red, or blue, or whatever their color was. The prisoner was a green drafter—or had been. Instead of the green being bound in a halo within the iris, it was shattered like crockery smashed to the floor. Little green fragments glowed even in the whites of his eyes. Kip gasped and shrank back.

"Please!" the man said. "Please, the madness isn't on me. I won't hurt you."

"You're a color wight."

"And now you know why I ran away from the Chromeria," the man said.

Because the Chromeria put down color wights like a farmer put down a beloved, rabid dog.

Kip was on the verge of bolting, but the man wasn't making any threatening moves. And besides, it was still dark. Even color wights needed light to draft. The mist did seem lighter, though, gray beginning to touch the horizon. It was crazy to talk to a madman, but maybe it wasn't too crazy. At least until dawn.

The color wight was looking at Kip oddly. "Blue eyes." He laughed.

Kip scowled. He hated his blue eyes. It was one thing when a foreigner like Master Danavis had blue eyes. They looked fine on him. Kip looked freakish.

"What's your name?" the color wight asked.

Kip swallowed, thinking he should probably run away.

"Oh, for Orholam's sake, you think I'm going to hex you with your name? How ignorant is this backwater? That isn't how chromaturgy works—"

"Kip."

The color wight grinned. "Kip. Well, Kip, have you ever wondered why you were stuck in such a small life? Have you ever gotten the feeling, Kip, that you're special?"

Kip said nothing. Yes, and yes.

"Do you know *why* you feel destined for something greater?"

"Why?" Kip asked, quiet, hopeful.

"Because you're an arrogant little shit." The color wight laughed.

Kip shouldn't have been taken off guard. His mother had said worse. Still, it took him a moment. A small failure. "Burn in hell, coward," he said. "You're not even good at running away. Caught by ironfoot soldiers."

The color wight laughed louder. "Oh, they didn't *catch* me. They recruited me."

Who would recruit madmen to join them? "They didn't know you were a—"

"Oh, they knew."

Dread like a weight dropped into Kip's stomach. "You said something about my town. Before. What are they planning to do?"

"You know, Orholam's got a sense of humor. Never realized that till now. Orphan, aren't you?"

"No. I've got a mother," Kip said. He instantly regretted giving the color wight even that much.

"Would you believe me if I told you there's a prophecy about you?"

"It wasn't funny the first time," Kip said. "What's going to happen to my town?" Dawn was coming, and Kip wasn't going to stick around. Not only would the guard's replacement come then, but Kip had no idea what the wight would do once he had light.

"You know," the wight said, "you're the reason I'm here. Not here here. Not like 'Why do I exist?' Not in Tyrea. In chains, I mean."

"What?" Kip asked.

"There's power in madness, Kip. Of course..." He trailed off, laughed at a private thought. Recovered. "Look, that soldier has a key in his breast pocket. I couldn't get it out, not with—" He shook his hands, bound and manacled behind his back.

"And I would help you why?" Kip asked.

"For a few straight answers before dawn."

Crazy, and cunning. *Perfect.* "Give me one first," Kip said.

"Shoot."

"What's the plan for Rekton?"

"Fire."

"What?" Kip asked.

"Sorry, you said one answer."

"That was no answer!"

"They're going to wipe out your village. Make an example so no one else defies King Garadul. Other villages defied the king too, of course. His rebellion against the Chromeria isn't popular everywhere. For every town burning to take vengeance on the Prism, there's another that wants nothing to do with war. Your village was chosen specially. Anyway, I had a little spasm of conscience and objected. Words were exchanged. I punched my superior. Not totally my fault. They know us greens don't do rules and hierarchy. Especially not once we've broken the halo." The color wight shrugged. "There, straight. I think that deserves the key, don't you?"

It was too much information to soak up at once—broken the halo?—but it *was* a straight answer. Kip walked over to the dead man. His skin was pallid in the rising light. Pull it together, Kip. Ask whatever you need to ask.

Kip could tell that dawn was coming. Eerie shapes were emerging from the night. The great twin looming masses of Sundered Rock itself were visible mostly as a place where stars were blotted out of the sky.

What do I need to ask?

He was hesitating, not wanting to touch the dead man. He knelt. "Why my town?" He poked through the dead man's pocket, careful not to touch skin. It was there, two keys.

"They think you have something that belongs to the king. I don't know what. I only picked up that much by eavesdropping."

"What would Rekton have that the king wants?" Kip asked.

"Not Rekton you. You you."

It took Kip a second. He touched his own chest. "Me? Me personally? I don't even own anything!"

The color wight gave a crazy grin, but Kip thought it was a pretense. "Tragic mistake, then. Their mistake, your tragedy."

"What, you think I'm lying?!" Kip asked. "You think I'd be out here scavenging luxin if I had any other choice?"

"I don't really care one way or the other. You going to bring that key over here, or do I need to ask real nice?"

It was a mistake to bring the keys over. Kip knew it. The color wight wasn't stable. He was dangerous. He'd admitted as much. But he had kept his word. How could Kip do less?

Kip unlocked the man's manacles, and then the padlock on the chains. He backed away carefully, as one would from a wild animal. The color wight pretended not to notice, simply rubbing his arms and stretching back and forth. He moved over to the guard and poked through his pockets again. His hand emerged with a pair of green spectacles with one cracked lens.

"You could come with me," Kip said. "If what you said is true—"

"How close do you think I'd get to your town before someone came running with a musket? Besides, once the sun comes up... I'm ready for it to be done." The color wight took a deep breath, staring at the horizon. "Tell me, Kip, if you've done bad things your whole life, but you die doing something good, do you think that makes up for all the bad?"

"No," Kip said, honestly, before he could stop himself.

"Me neither."

"But it's better than nothing," Kip said. "Orholam is merciful."

"Wonder if you'll say that after they're done with your village."

There were other questions Kip wanted to ask, but everything had happened in such a rush that he couldn't put his thoughts together.

In the rising light Kip saw what had been hidden in the fog and the darkness. Hundreds of tents were laid out in military precision. Soldiers. Lots of soldiers. And even as Kip stood, not two hundred paces from the nearest tent, the plain began winking. Glimmers sparkled as broken luxin gleamed, like stars scattered on the ground, answering their brethren in the sky.

It was what Kip had come for. Usually when a drafter released luxin, it simply dissolved, no matter what color it was. But in battle, there had been so much chaos, so many drafters, some sealed magic had been buried and protected from the sunlight that would break it down. The recent rain had uncovered more.

But Kip's eyes were pulled from the winking luxin by four soldiers and a man with a stark red cloak and red spectacles walking toward them from the camp.

"My name is Gaspar, by the by. Gaspar Elos." The color wight didn't look at Kip.

"What?"

"I'm not just some drafter. My father loved me. I had plans. A girl. A life."

"I don't—"

"You will." The color wight put the green spectacles on; they fit perfectly, tight to his face, lenses sweeping to either side so that wherever he looked, he would be looking through a green filter. "Now get out of here."

As the sun touched the horizon, Gaspar sighed. It was as if Kip had ceased to exist. It was like watching his mother take that first deep breath of haze. Between the sparkling spars of darker green, the whites of Gaspar's eyes swirled like droplets of green blood hitting water, first dispersing, then staining the whole. The emerald green of luxin ballooned through his eyes, thickened until it was solid, and then spread. Through his cheeks, up to his hairline, then down his neck, standing out starkly when it finally filled his lighter fingernails as if they'd been painted in radiant jade.

Gaspar started laughing. It was a low, unreasoning cackle, unrelenting. Mad. Not a pretense this time.

Kip ran.

He reached the funerary hill where the sentry had been, taking care to stay on the far side from the army. He had to get to Master Danavis. Master Danavis always knew what to do.

There was no sentry on the hill now. Kip turned around in time to see Gaspar change, transform. Green luxin spilled out of his hands onto his body, covering every part of him like a shell, like an enormous suit of armor. Kip couldn't see the soldiers or the red drafter approaching Gaspar, but he did see a fireball the size of his head streak toward the color wight, hit his chest, and burst apart, throwing flames everywhere.

Gaspar rammed through it, flaming red luxin sticking to his green armor. He was magnificent, terrible, powerful. He ran toward the soldiers, screaming defiance, and disappeared from Kip's view.

Kip fled, the vermilion sun setting fire to the mists.